ACE
No.1

A FLEETWAY LIBRARY

PICTURE
AIR ● ACE
LIBRARY

No.1

ACES
HIGH

The publishers would like to thank the team at IPC Media Ltd and DC Comics for their help
in compiling this book, particularly David Abbottt, Marc Hirsch and Sandy Resnick.

Published in 2009 by Prion
An imprint of the Carlton Publishing Group
20 Mortimer Street
London W1T 3JW

Copyright © IPC Media 2009

Published under licence from DC Comics

A catalogue record for this book is available from the British Library.

ISBN 978-1-85375-703-7

Printed and bound in Thailand

10 9 8 7 6 5 4 3 2 1

ACES HIGH

10 OF THE BEST AIR ACE LIBRARY COMIC BOOKS EVER!

GENERAL EDITOR:
STEVE HOLLAND

PRION

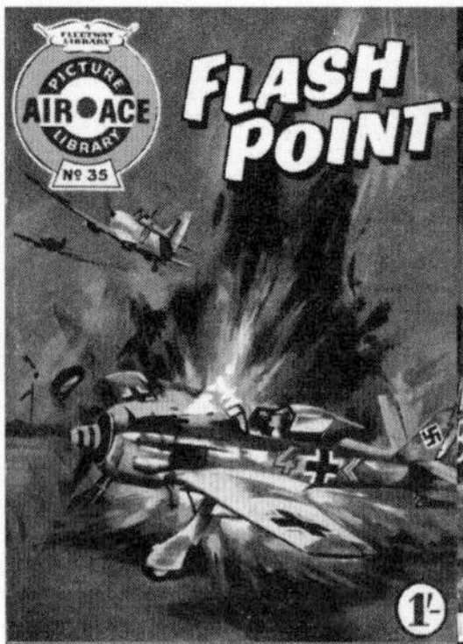
PICTURE AIR ACE LIBRARY
Nº 35
FLASH POINT
1/-
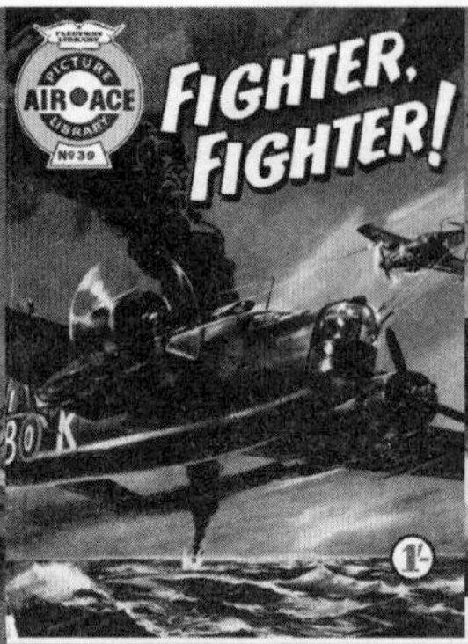
PICTURE AIR ACE LIBRARY
Nº 39
FIGHTER, FIGHTER!
1/-
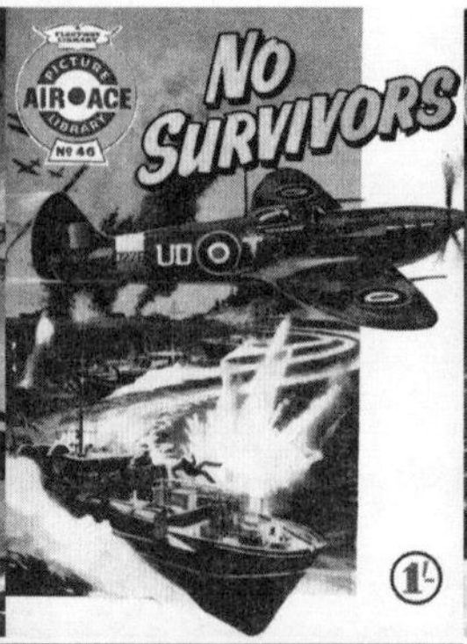
PICTURE AIR ACE LIBRARY
Nº 46
NO SURVIVORS
1/-
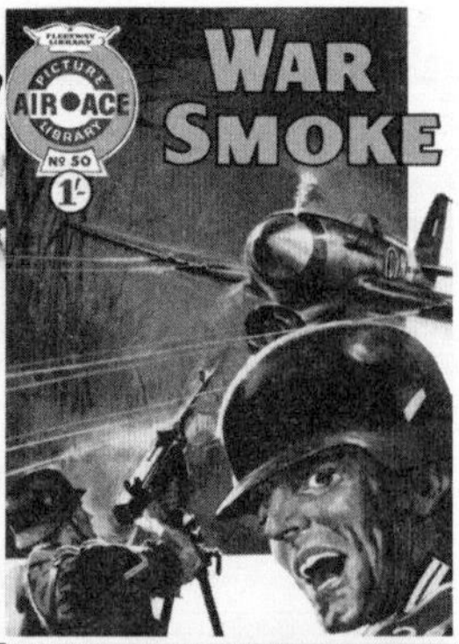
PICTURE AIR ACE LIBRARY
Nº 50
1/-
WAR SMOKE
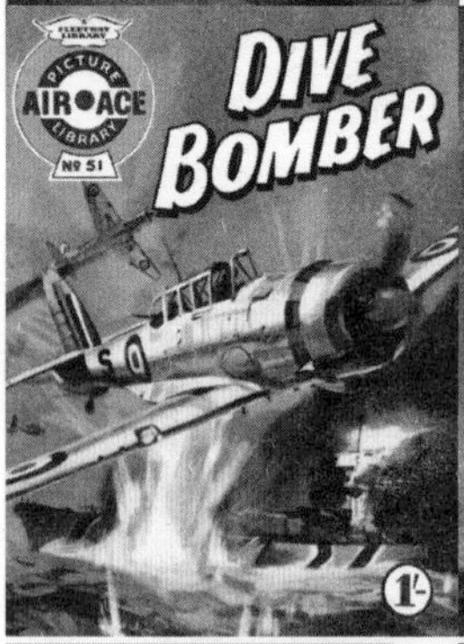
PICTURE AIR ACE LIBRARY
Nº 51
DIVE BOMBER
1/-
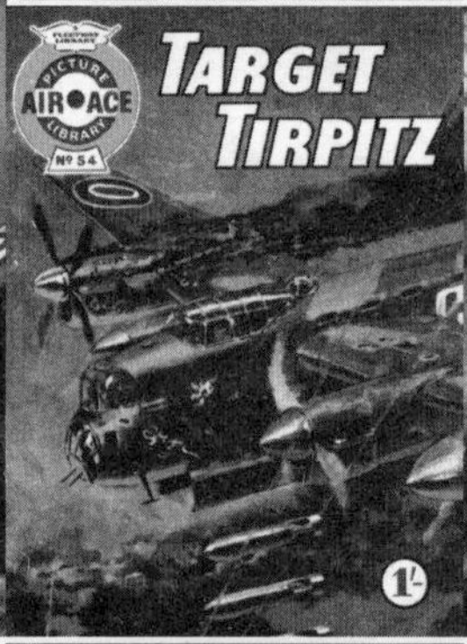
PICTURE AIR ACE LIBRARY
Nº 54
TARGET TIRPITZ
1/-
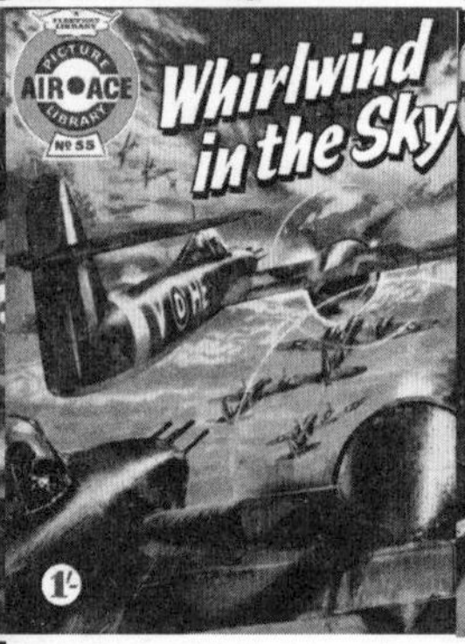
PICTURE AIR ACE LIBRARY
Nº 55
Whirlwind in the Sky
1/-
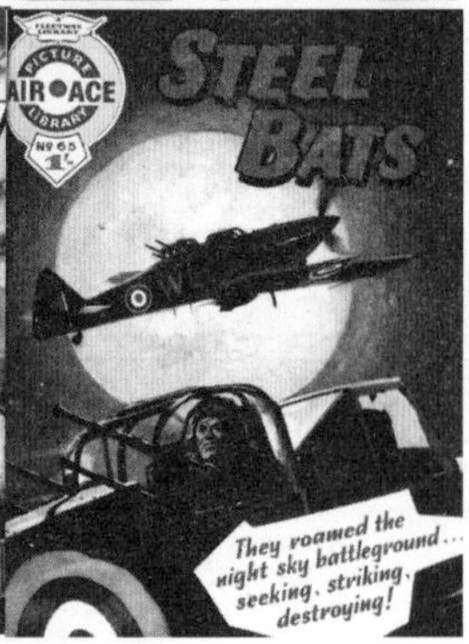
PICTURE AIR ACE LIBRARY
Nº 65
1/-
STEEL BATS
They roamed the night sky battleground... seeking, striking, destroying!
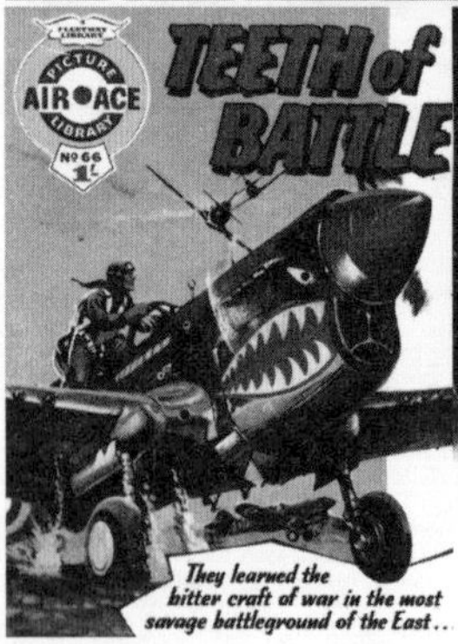
PICTURE AIR ACE LIBRARY
Nº 66
1/-
TEETH of BATTLE
They learned the bitter craft of war in the most savage battleground of the East...
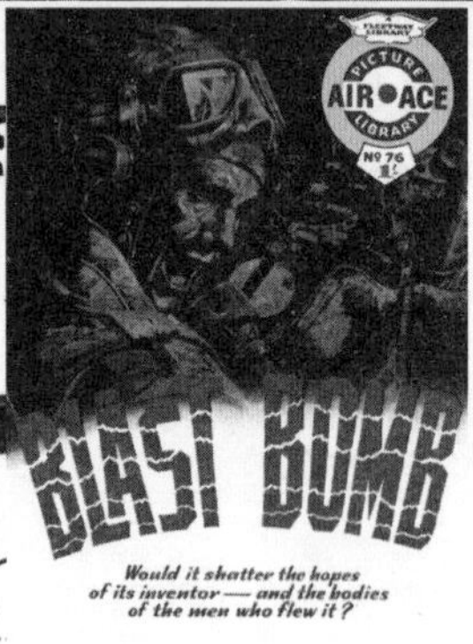
PICTURE AIR ACE LIBRARY
Nº 76
1/-
BLAST BOMB
Would it shatter the hopes of its inventor — and the bodies of the men who flew it?

CONTENTS

INTRODUCTION

The glamour of flying had been at the heart of many boys' adventure stories since the days of the Great War when the Royal Flying Corps was formed. Founded in 1912, with a Royal Naval Air Service following in 1914, the R.F.C. really earned its wings—as far as boys were concerned—in the pages of *Boy's Own Paper* where George E. Rochester penned stories of an airborne adventurer known as the 'Flying Beetle' and, of course, every boy loved Captain W.E. Johns' 'Biggles' adventures.

Countless flying tales appeared in the 1930s; flying records were still being broken and commercial travel by aeroplane was still uncommon, making flying the skyways an exciting new field for writers to set their stories. The thirties launched dozens of flying heroes—often combining skills in the air with skills at sport, like boxing air ace 'Rockfist Rogan'—and most air travellers could expect to have their flights interrupted by masked sky pirates or crash landings on isolated islands full of dinosaurs. Flying was often little more than an exotic way of re-telling the kind of stories that had been around for years.

It was with the coming of World War II that a new breed of flying story was born out of the true life heroics of 'The Few' who defended Britain from the German Luftwaffe during the summer and autumn of 1940. Winston Churchill gave the action its name in his famous speech on 18 June 1940 when he claimed that 'The Battle of France is over. I expect the Battle of Britain is about to begin...'

Air Ace Picture Library, launched in January 1960 following the success of *War Picture Library*, drew its inspiration from the wartime exploits of the R.A.F.'s Fighter Command, Bomber Command, Coastal Command and the Navy's Fleet Air Arm as well as various specialist units and the Americans' Army, Navy and Marines flyers. Squadrons were posted in every theatre of war, keeping the output of four new titles a month fresh, and with dozens of aircraft from Gladiators to Mustangs to choose from, authors had no problem serving up something new in each story.

Like its companion, *War Picture Library*, many of the stories were penned by authors who had lived through the action, giving them an authenticity that some earlier tales of aerial adventure lacked. These were real situations experienced by the fathers and uncles of young readers in the 1960s, their heroism boosted all the more by hugely popular movies *The Dam Busters*, *Reach For The Sky*, *633 Squadron* and others.

Fans who have become collectors of the war libraries hold *Air Ace* in high esteem for its stunning artwork by the likes of Ian Kennedy, F. Solano Lopez, Ferdinando Tacconi, Kurt Caesar, Mike Western and Luis Bermejo. The strips was drawn by the best artistic talents from Britain, Italy and South America. In the case of Kurt Caesar, a German born in France and domiciled in Italy, who had fought with the Afrikakorps and the Resistance, they had a truly international artist who had seen the war from almost every conceivable angle!

Steve Holland

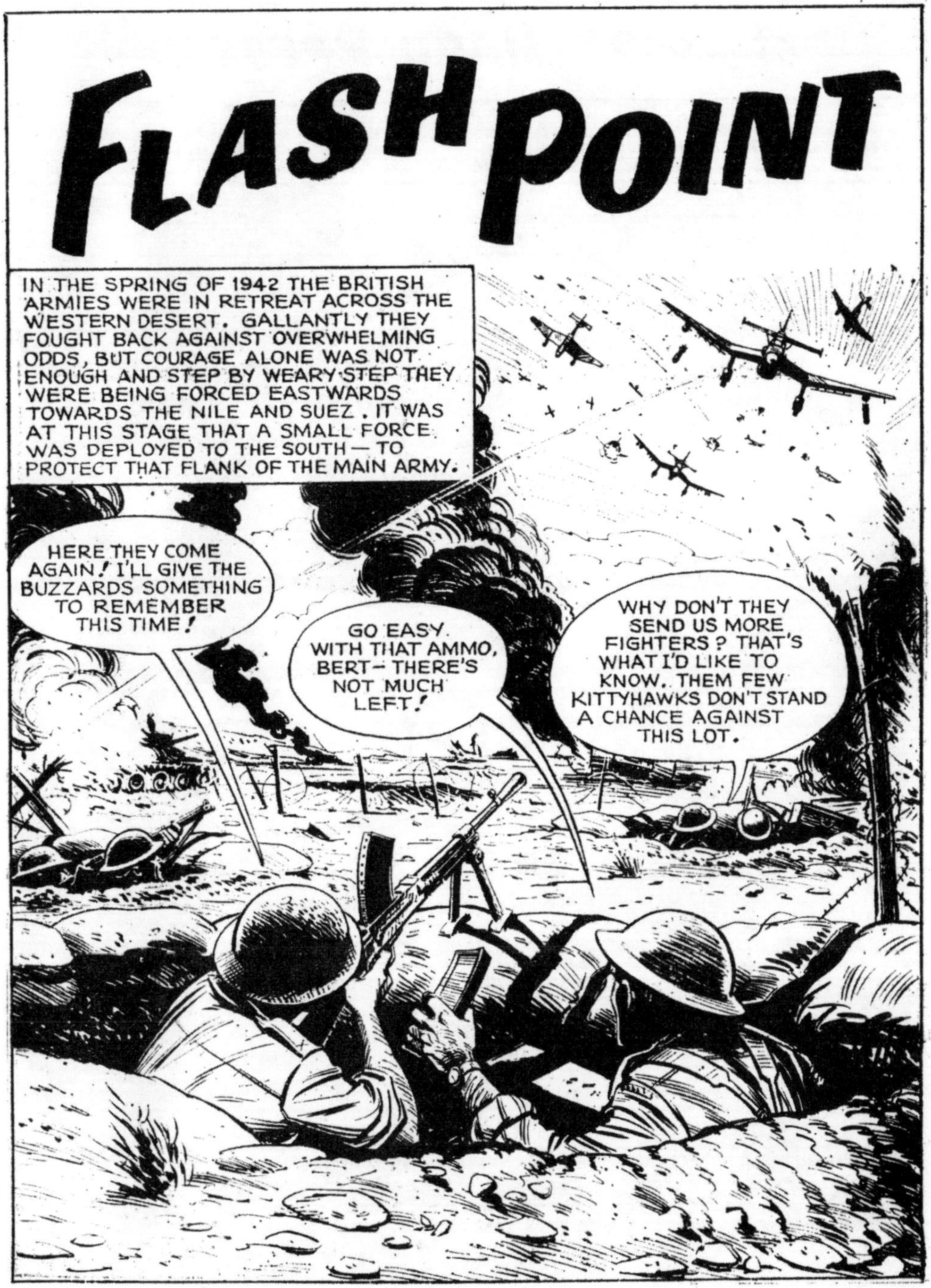
FLASH POINT
IN THE SPRING OF 1942 THE BRITISH ARMIES WERE IN RETREAT ACROSS THE WESTERN DESERT. GALLANTLY THEY FOUGHT BACK AGAINST OVERWHELMING ODDS, BUT COURAGE ALONE WAS NOT ENOUGH AND STEP BY WEARY STEP THEY WERE BEING FORCED EASTWARDS TOWARDS THE NILE AND SUEZ. IT WAS AT THIS STAGE THAT A SMALL FORCE WAS DEPLOYED TO THE SOUTH — TO PROTECT THAT FLANK OF THE MAIN ARMY.
HERE THEY COME AGAIN! I'LL GIVE THE BUZZARDS SOMETHING TO REMEMBER THIS TIME!
GO EASY WITH THAT AMMO, BERT— THERE'S NOT MUCH LEFT!
WHY DON'T THEY SEND US MORE FIGHTERS? THAT'S WHAT I'D LIKE TO KNOW. THEM FEW KITTYHAWKS DON'T STAND A CHANCE AGAINST THIS LOT.

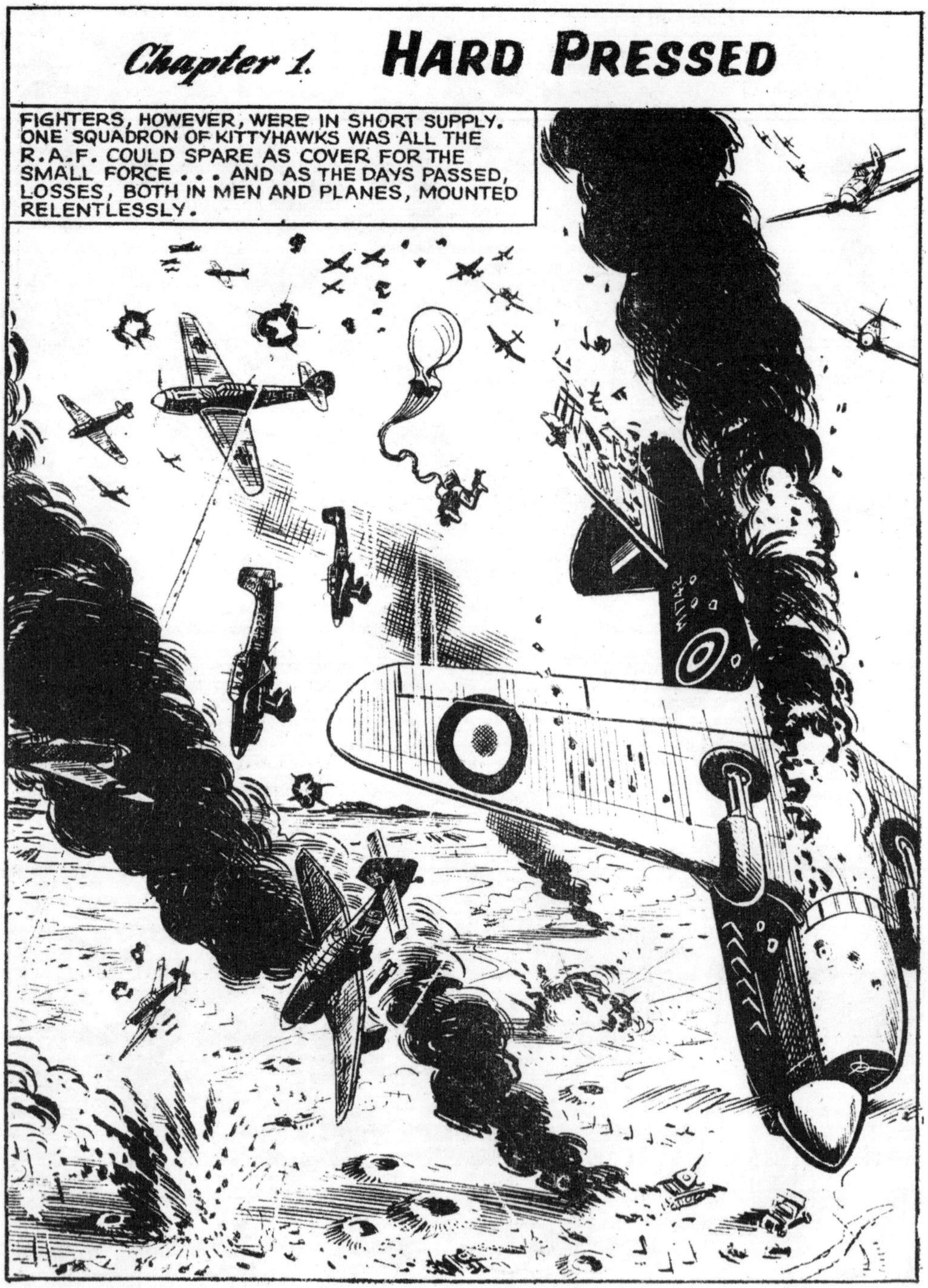
Chapter 1. HARD PRESSED
FIGHTERS, HOWEVER, WERE IN SHORT SUPPLY. ONE SQUADRON OF KITTYHAWKS WAS ALL THE R.A.F. COULD SPARE AS COVER FOR THE SMALL FORCE . . . AND AS THE DAYS PASSED, LOSSES, BOTH IN MEN AND PLANES, MOUNTED RELENTLESSLY.

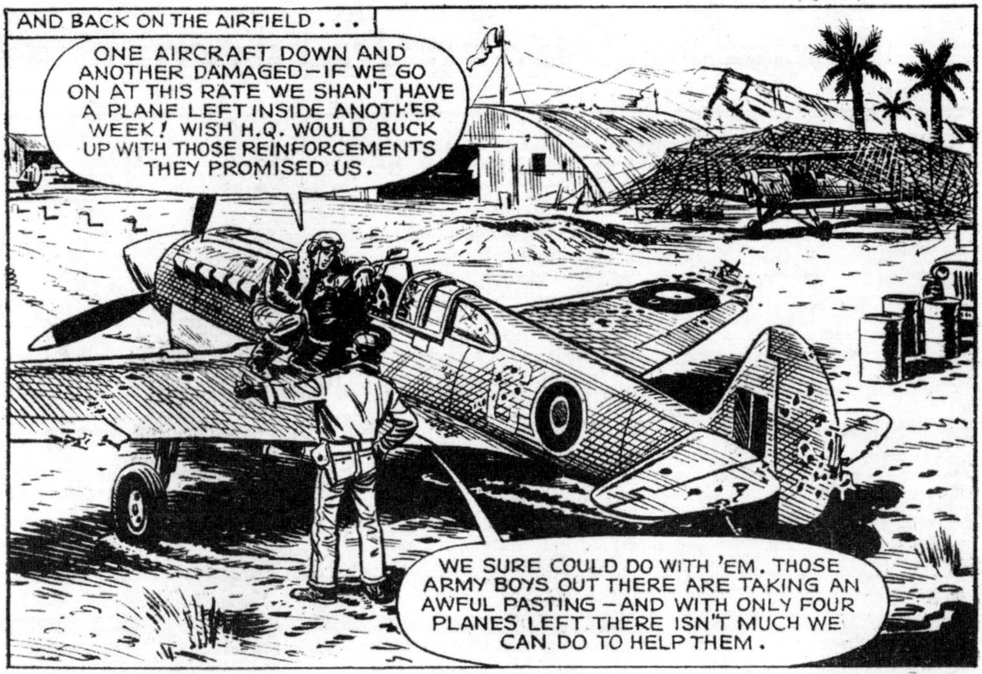
AND BACK ON THE AIRFIELD . . .
ONE AIRCRAFT DOWN AND ANOTHER DAMAGED—IF WE GO ON AT THIS RATE WE SHAN'T HAVE A PLANE LEFT INSIDE ANOTHER WEEK! WISH H.Q. WOULD BUCK UP WITH THOSE REINFORCEMENTS THEY PROMISED US.
WE SURE COULD DO WITH 'EM. THOSE ARMY BOYS OUT THERE ARE TAKING AN AWFUL PASTING—AND WITH ONLY FOUR PLANES LEFT THERE ISN'T MUCH WE CAN DO TO HELP THEM.

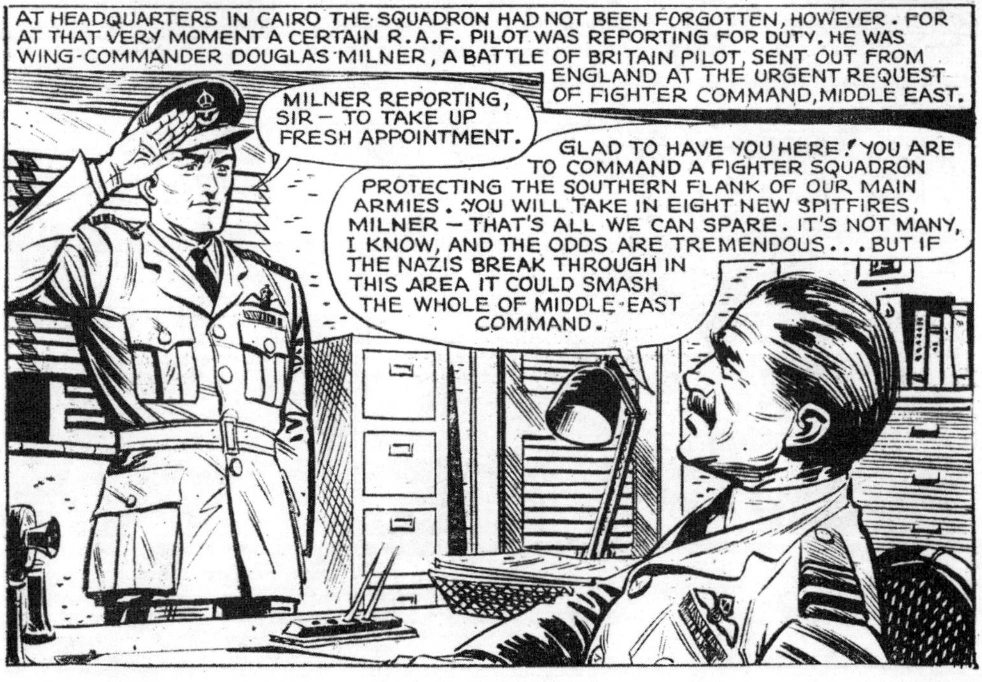
AT HEADQUARTERS IN CAIRO THE SQUADRON HAD NOT BEEN FORGOTTEN, HOWEVER. FOR AT THAT VERY MOMENT A CERTAIN R.A.F. PILOT WAS REPORTING FOR DUTY. HE WAS WING-COMMANDER DOUGLAS MILNER, A BATTLE OF BRITAIN PILOT, SENT OUT FROM ENGLAND AT THE URGENT REQUEST OF FIGHTER COMMAND, MIDDLE EAST.
MILNER REPORTING, SIR—TO TAKE UP FRESH APPOINTMENT.
GLAD TO HAVE YOU HERE! YOU ARE TO COMMAND A FIGHTER SQUADRON PROTECTING THE SOUTHERN FLANK OF OUR MAIN ARMIES. YOU WILL TAKE IN EIGHT NEW SPITFIRES, MILNER—THAT'S ALL WE CAN SPARE. IT'S NOT MANY, I KNOW, AND THE ODDS ARE TREMENDOUS . . . BUT IF THE NAZIS BREAK THROUGH IN THIS AREA IT COULD SMASH THE WHOLE OF MIDDLE-EAST COMMAND.

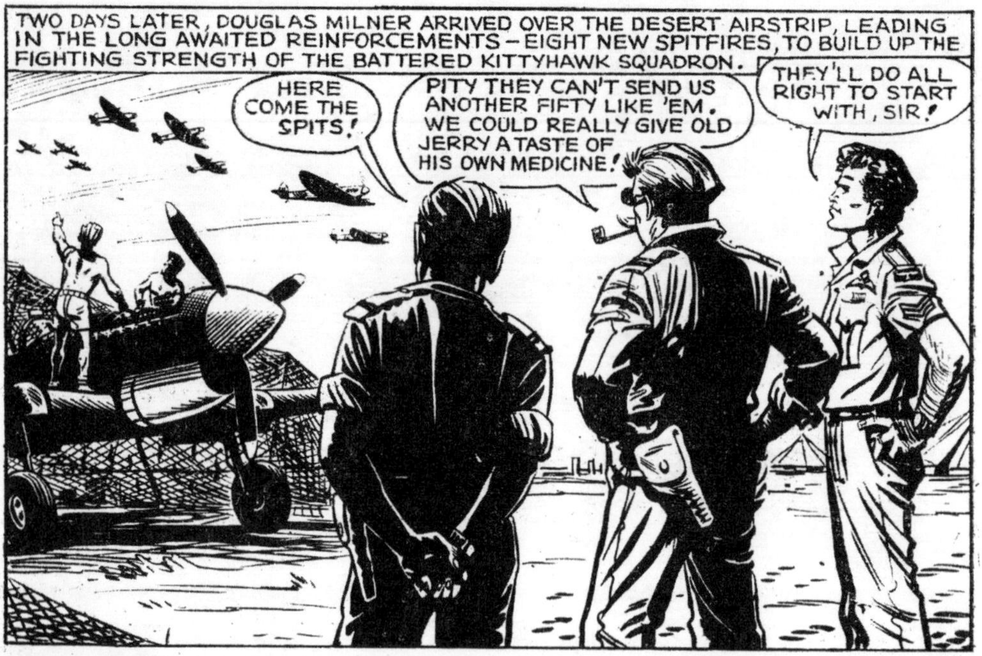
TWO DAYS LATER, DOUGLAS MILNER ARRIVED OVER THE DESERT AIRSTRIP, LEADING IN THE LONG AWAITED REINFORCEMENTS – EIGHT NEW SPITFIRES, TO BUILD UP THE FIGHTING STRENGTH OF THE BATTERED KITTYHAWK SQUADRON.
HERE COME THE SPITS!
PITY THEY CAN'T SEND US ANOTHER FIFTY LIKE 'EM. WE COULD REALLY GIVE OLD JERRY A TASTE OF HIS OWN MEDICINE!
THEY'LL DO ALL RIGHT TO START WITH, SIR!

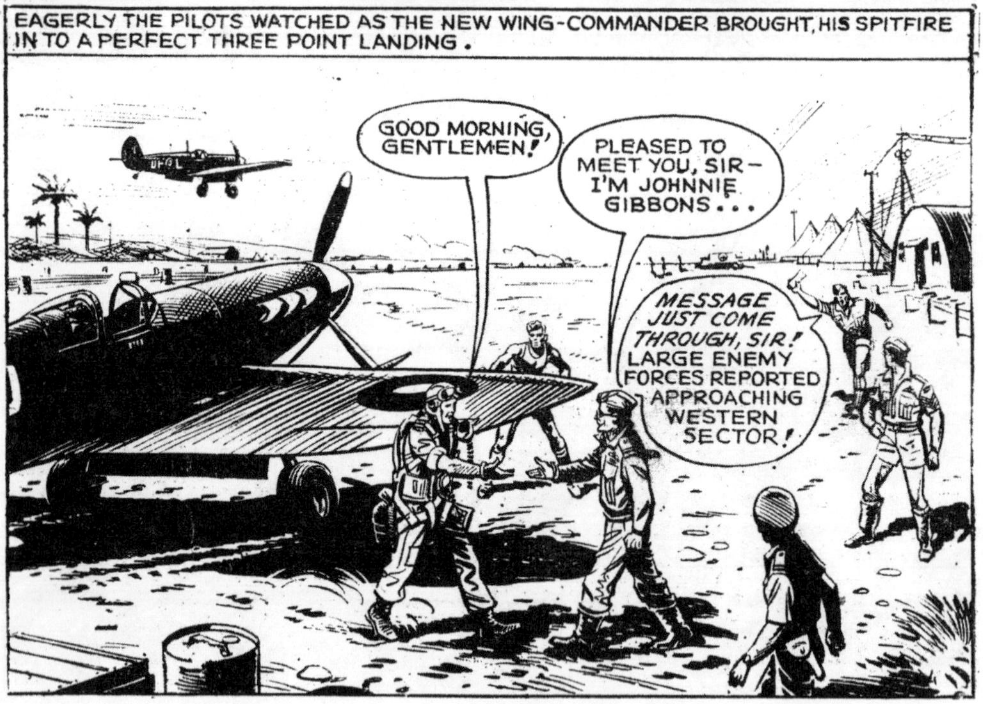
EAGERLY THE PILOTS WATCHED AS THE NEW WING-COMMANDER BROUGHT HIS SPITFIRE IN TO A PERFECT THREE POINT LANDING.
GOOD MORNING, GENTLEMEN!
PLEASED TO MEET YOU, SIR – I'M JOHNNIE GIBBONS...
MESSAGE JUST COME THROUGH, SIR! LARGE ENEMY FORCES REPORTED APPROACHING WESTERN SECTOR!

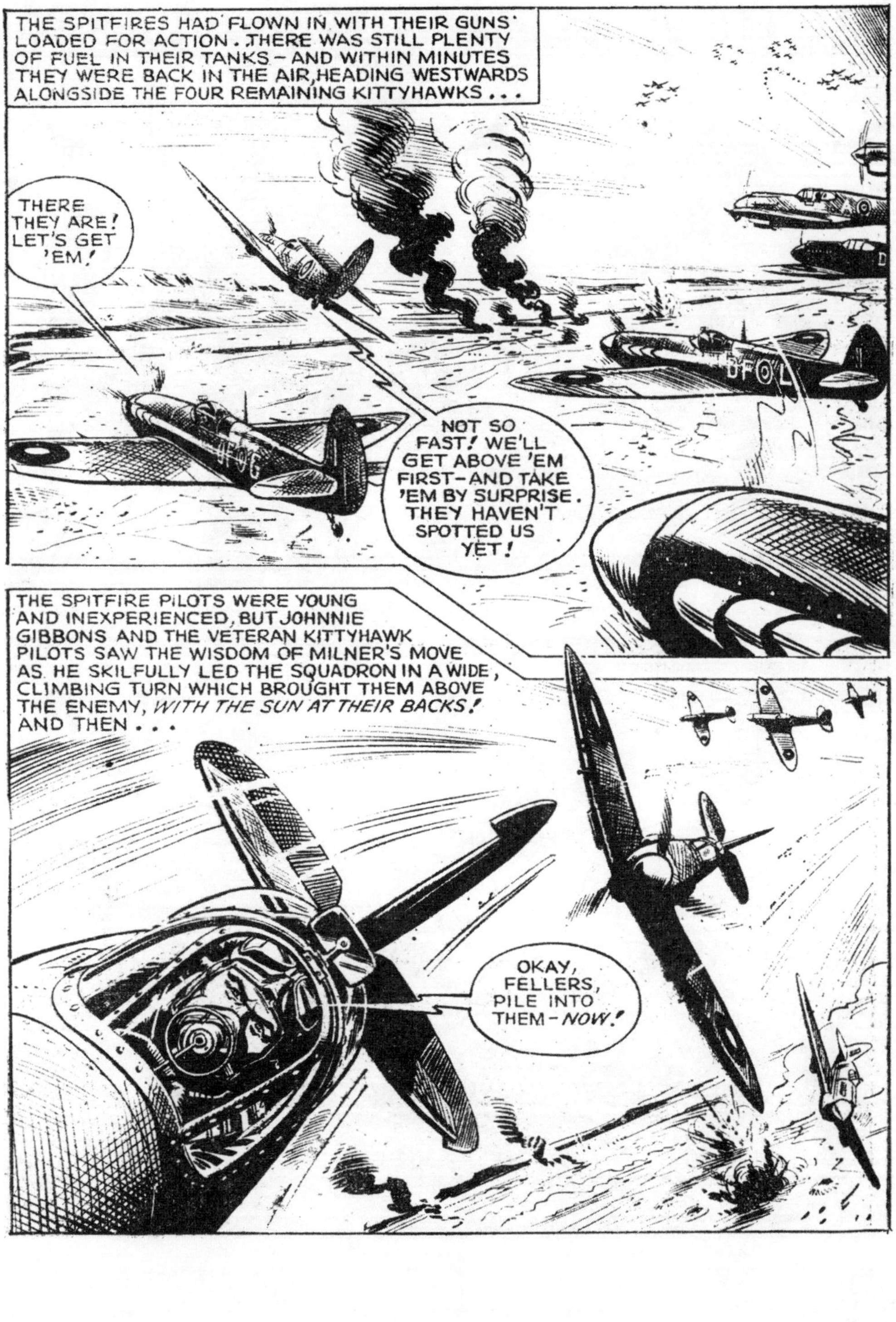
THE SPITFIRES HAD FLOWN IN WITH THEIR GUNS LOADED FOR ACTION. THERE WAS STILL PLENTY OF FUEL IN THEIR TANKS – AND WITHIN MINUTES THEY WERE BACK IN THE AIR, HEADING WESTWARDS ALONGSIDE THE FOUR REMAINING KITTYHAWKS . . .
THERE THEY ARE! LET'S GET 'EM!
NOT SO FAST! WE'LL GET ABOVE 'EM FIRST – AND TAKE 'EM BY SURPRISE. THEY HAVEN'T SPOTTED US YET!
THE SPITFIRE PILOTS WERE YOUNG AND INEXPERIENCED, BUT JOHNNIE GIBBONS AND THE VETERAN KITTYHAWK PILOTS SAW THE WISDOM OF MILNER'S MOVE AS HE SKILFULLY LED THE SQUADRON IN A WIDE, CLIMBING TURN WHICH BROUGHT THEM ABOVE THE ENEMY, *WITH THE SUN AT THEIR BACKS!* AND THEN . . .
OKAY, FELLERS, PILE INTO THEM – *NOW!*

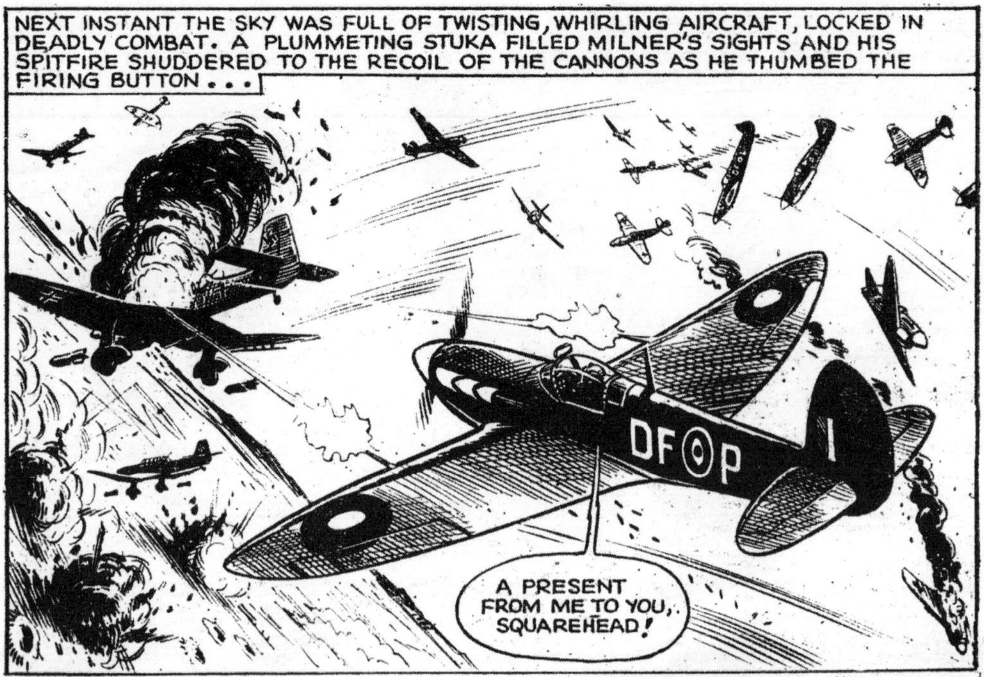
NEXT INSTANT THE SKY WAS FULL OF TWISTING, WHIRLING AIRCRAFT, LOCKED IN DEADLY COMBAT. A PLUMMETING STUKA FILLED MILNER'S SIGHTS AND HIS SPITFIRE SHUDDERED TO THE RECOIL OF THE CANNONS AS HE THUMBED THE FIRING BUTTON . . .
DF P
A PRESENT FROM ME TO YOU, SQUAREHEAD!

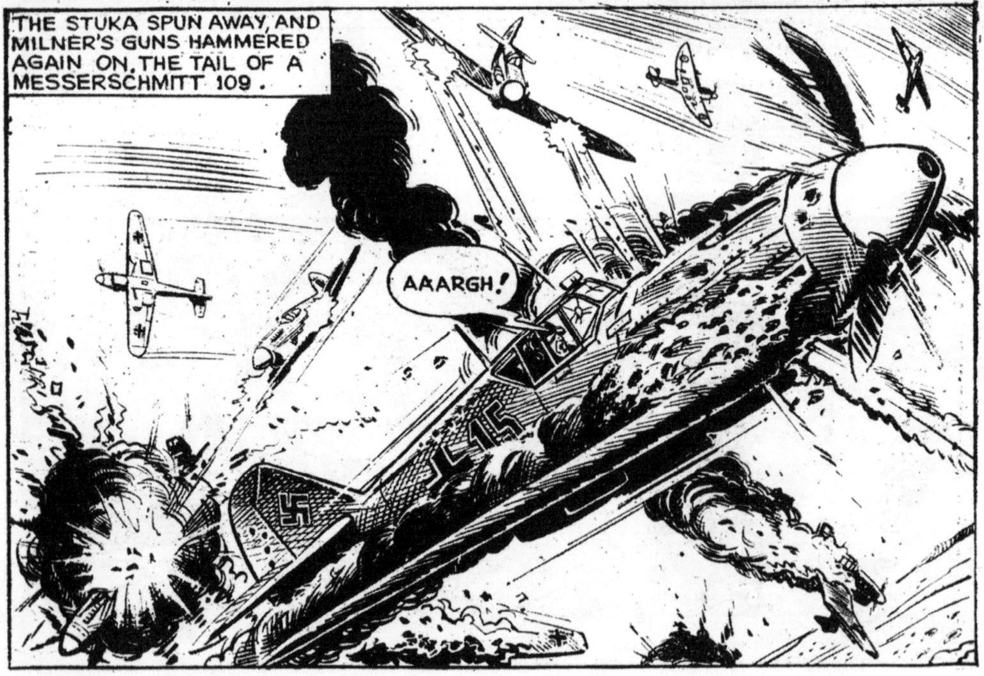
THE STUKA SPUN AWAY, AND MILNER'S GUNS HAMMERED AGAIN ON THE TAIL OF A MESSERSCHMITT 109 .
AAARGH!

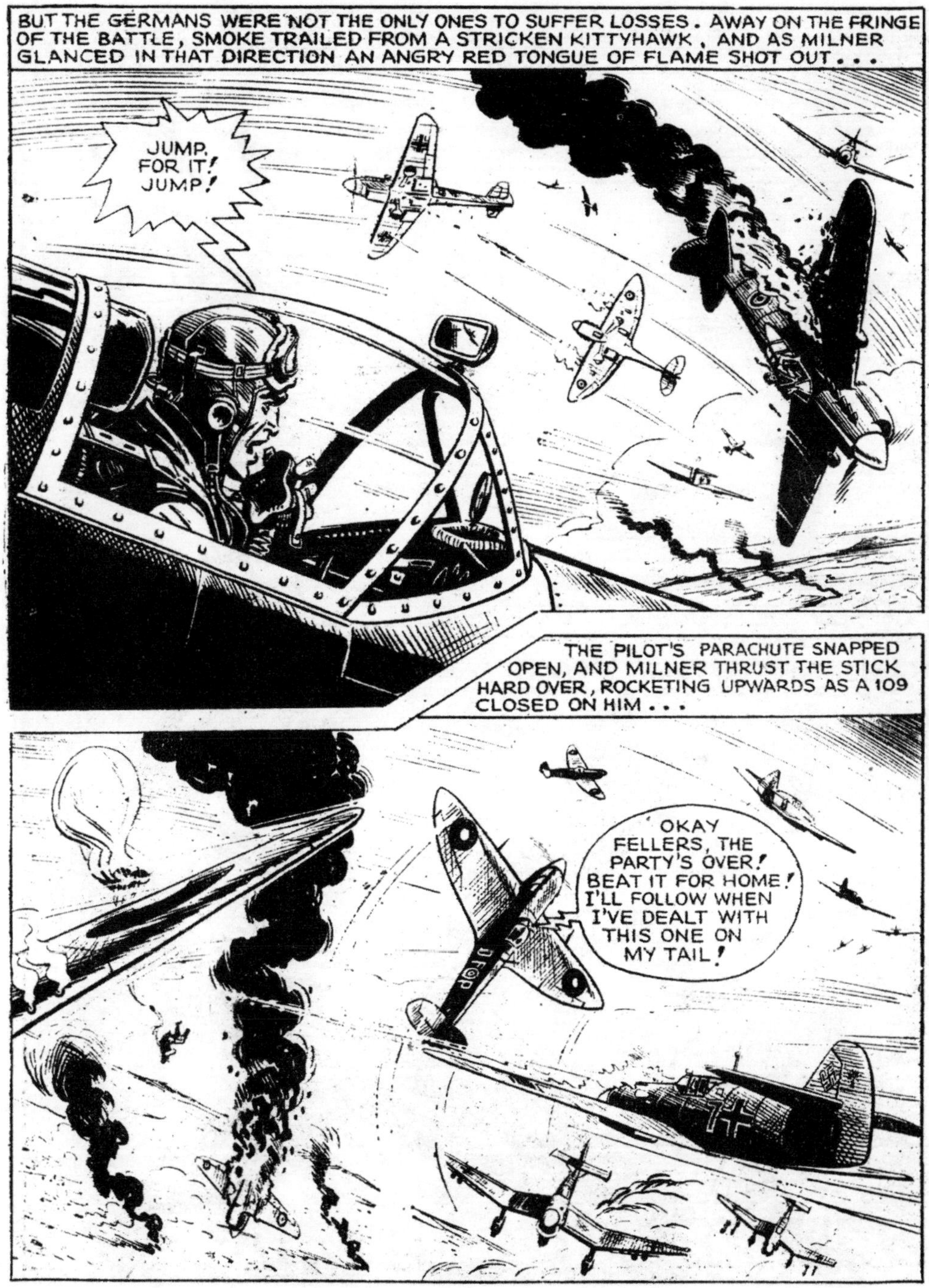
BUT THE GERMANS WERE NOT THE ONLY ONES TO SUFFER LOSSES. AWAY ON THE FRINGE OF THE BATTLE, SMOKE TRAILED FROM A STRICKEN KITTYHAWK, AND AS MILNER GLANCED IN THAT DIRECTION AN ANGRY RED TONGUE OF FLAME SHOT OUT...
JUMP, FOR IT! JUMP!
THE PILOT'S PARACHUTE SNAPPED OPEN, AND MILNER THRUST THE STICK HARD OVER, ROCKETING UPWARDS AS A 109 CLOSED ON HIM...
OKAY FELLERS, THE PARTY'S OVER! BEAT IT FOR HOME! I'LL FOLLOW WHEN I'VE DEALT WITH THIS ONE ON MY TAIL!

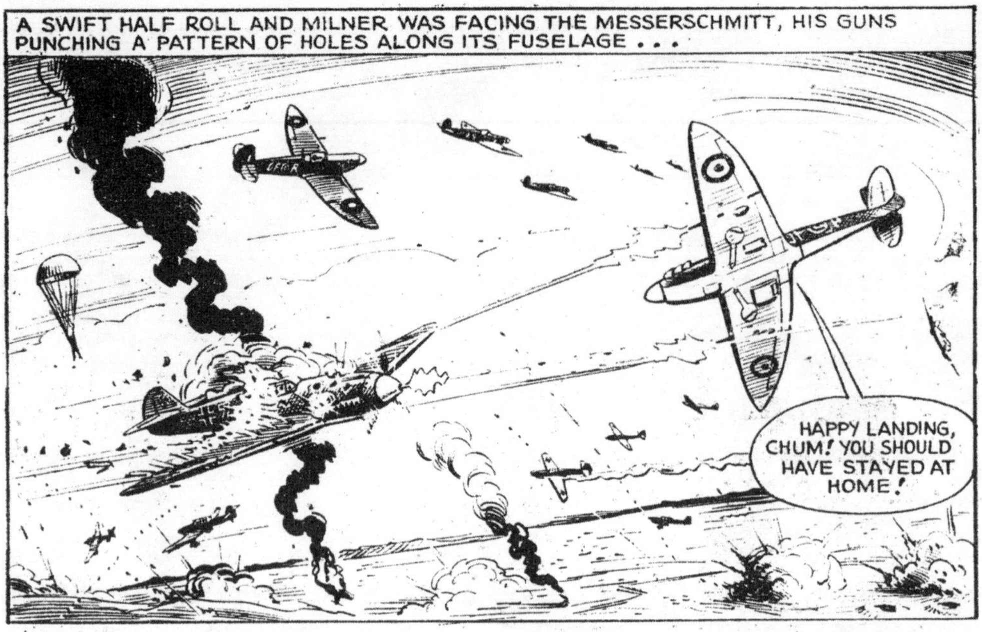
A SWIFT HALF ROLL AND MILNER WAS FACING THE MESSERSCHMITT, HIS GUNS PUNCHING A PATTERN OF HOLES ALONG ITS FUSELAGE . . .
HAPPY LANDING, CHUM! YOU SHOULD HAVE STAYED AT HOME!

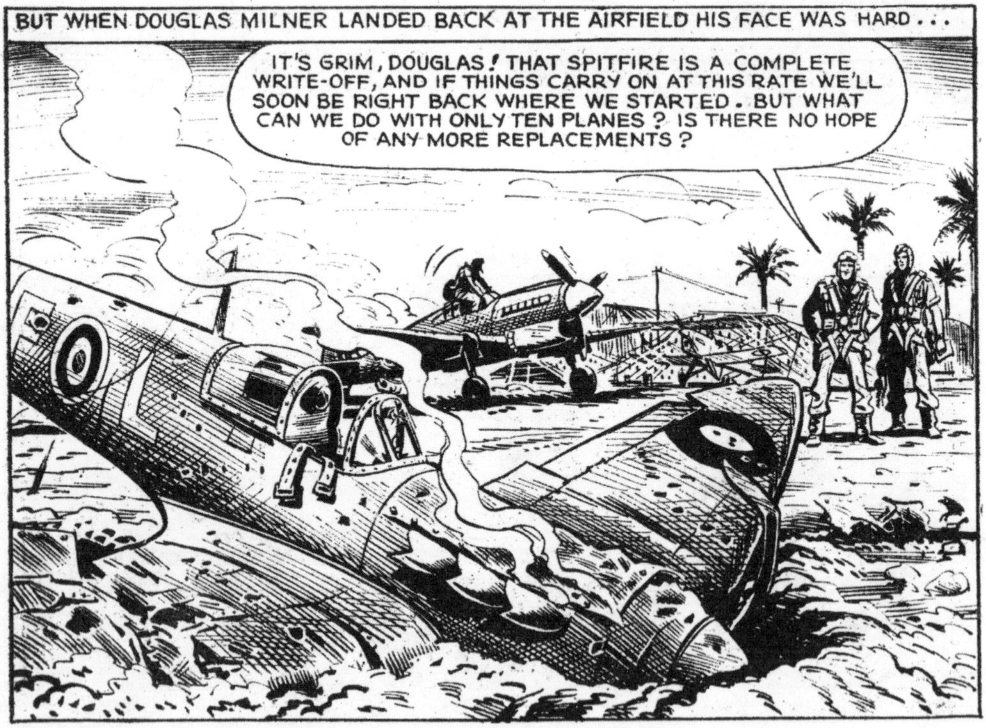
BUT WHEN DOUGLAS MILNER LANDED BACK AT THE AIRFIELD HIS FACE WAS HARD . . .
IT'S GRIM, DOUGLAS! THAT SPITFIRE IS A COMPLETE WRITE-OFF, AND IF THINGS CARRY ON AT THIS RATE WE'LL SOON BE RIGHT BACK WHERE WE STARTED. BUT WHAT CAN WE DO WITH ONLY TEN PLANES? IS THERE NO HOPE OF ANY MORE REPLACEMENTS?

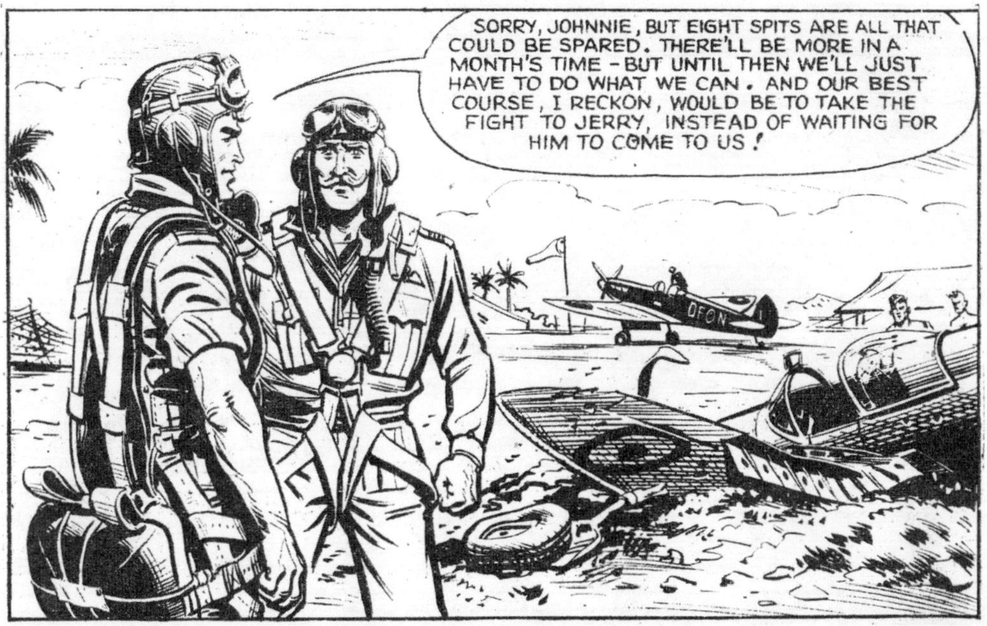
SORRY, JOHNNIE, BUT EIGHT SPITS ARE ALL THAT COULD BE SPARED. THERE'LL BE MORE IN A MONTH'S TIME - BUT UNTIL THEN WE'LL JUST HAVE TO DO WHAT WE CAN. AND OUR BEST COURSE, I RECKON, WOULD BE TO TAKE THE FIGHT TO JERRY, INSTEAD OF WAITING FOR HIM TO COME TO US!

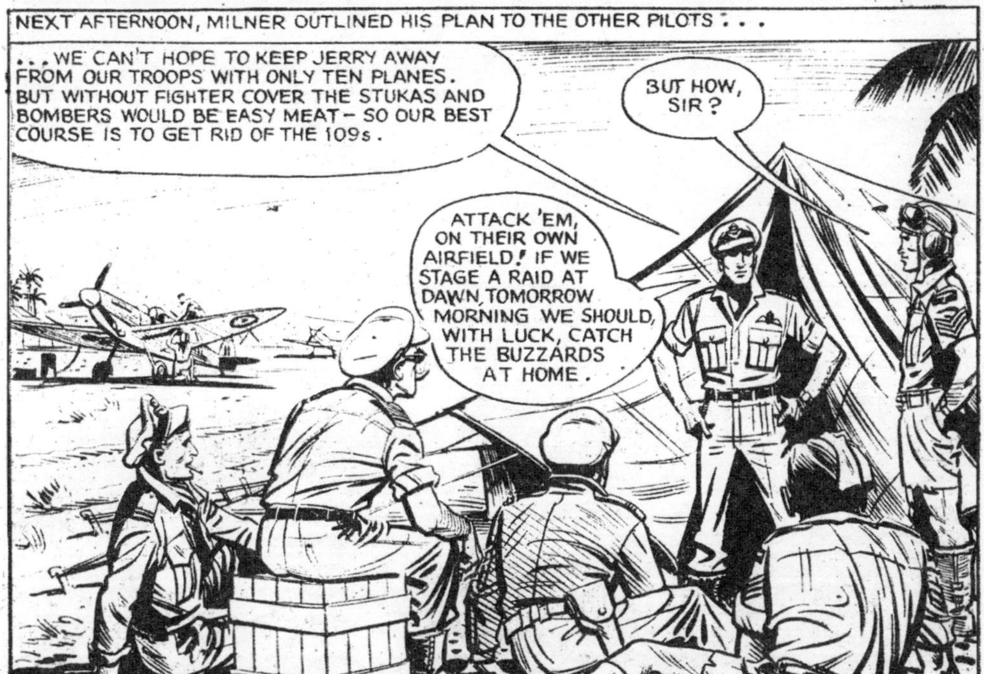
NEXT AFTERNOON, MILNER OUTLINED HIS PLAN TO THE OTHER PILOTS . . .
. . . WE CAN'T HOPE TO KEEP JERRY AWAY FROM OUR TROOPS WITH ONLY TEN PLANES. BUT WITHOUT FIGHTER COVER THE STUKAS AND BOMBERS WOULD BE EASY MEAT - SO OUR BEST COURSE IS TO GET RID OF THE 109s.
BUT HOW, SIR?
ATTACK 'EM, ON THEIR OWN AIRFIELD! IF WE STAGE A RAID AT DAWN, TOMORROW MORNING WE SHOULD, WITH LUCK, CATCH THE BUZZARDS AT HOME.

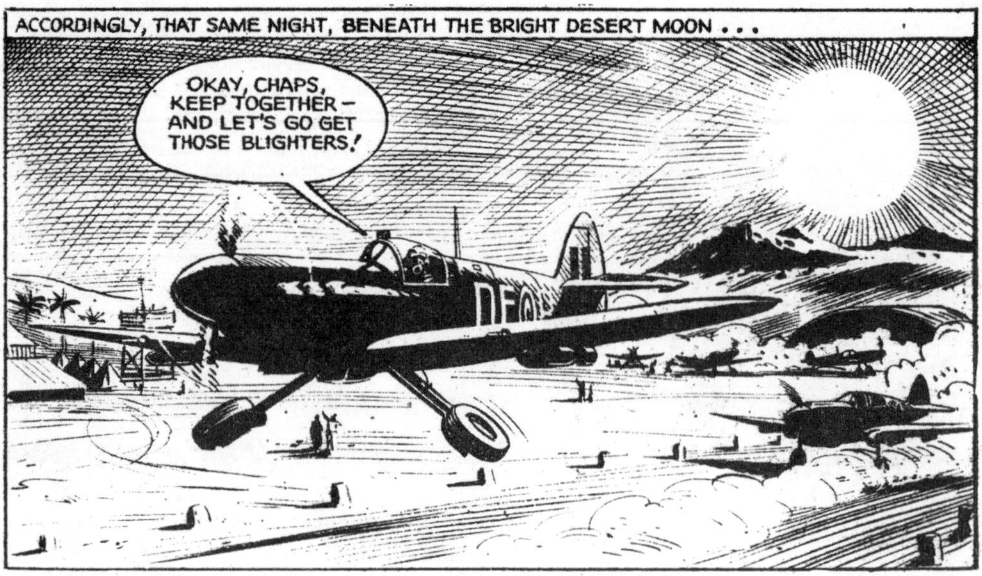
ACCORDINGLY, THAT SAME NIGHT, BENEATH THE BRIGHT DESERT MOON . . .
OKAY, CHAPS, KEEP TOGETHER — AND LET'S GO GET THOSE BLIGHTERS!

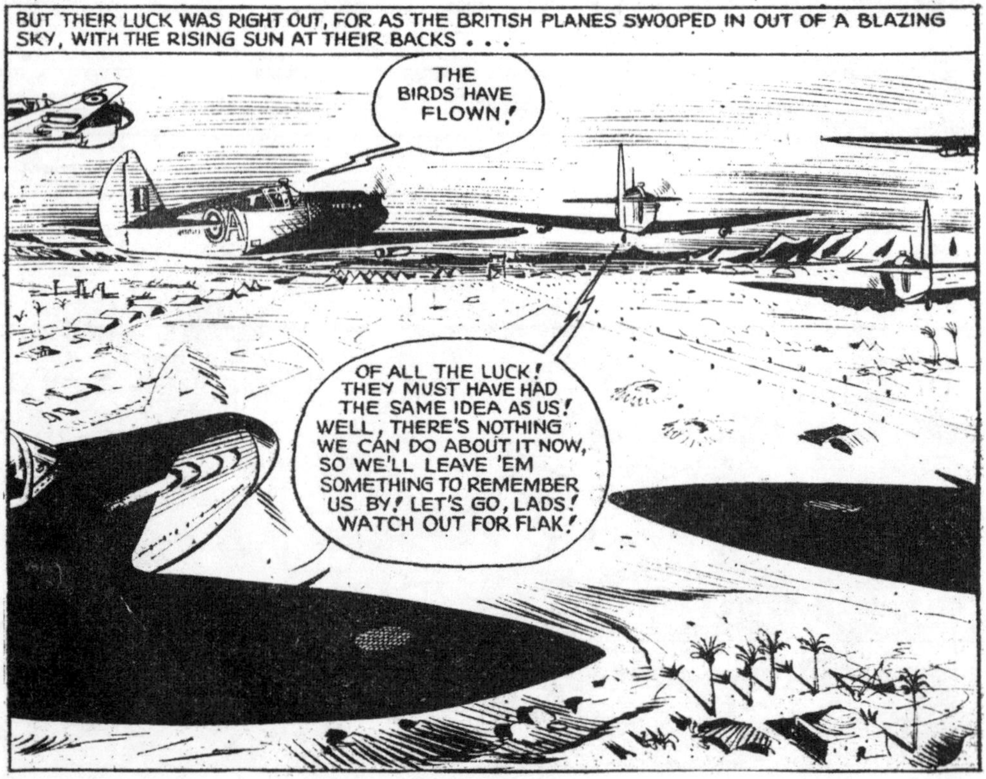
BUT THEIR LUCK WAS RIGHT OUT, FOR AS THE BRITISH PLANES SWOOPED IN OUT OF A BLAZING SKY, WITH THE RISING SUN AT THEIR BACKS . . .
THE BIRDS HAVE FLOWN!
OF ALL THE LUCK! THEY MUST HAVE HAD THE SAME IDEA AS US! WELL, THERE'S NOTHING WE CAN DO ABOUT IT NOW, SO WE'LL LEAVE 'EM SOMETHING TO REMEMBER US BY! LET'S GO, LADS! WATCH OUT FOR FLAK!

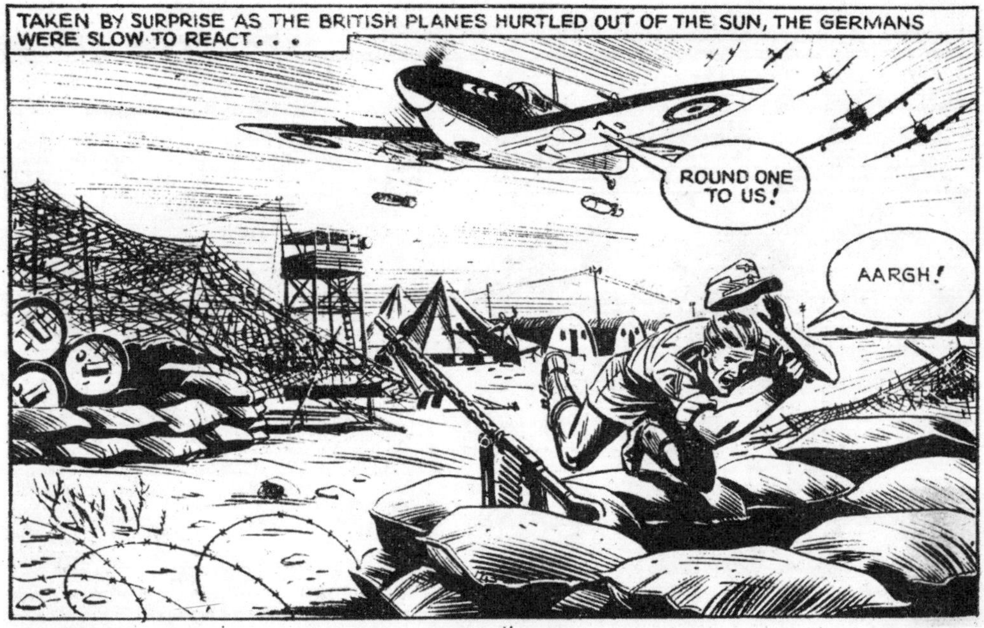
TAKEN BY SURPRISE AS THE BRITISH PLANES HURTLED OUT OF THE SUN, THE GERMANS WERE SLOW TO REACT . . .
ROUND ONE TO US!
AARGH!

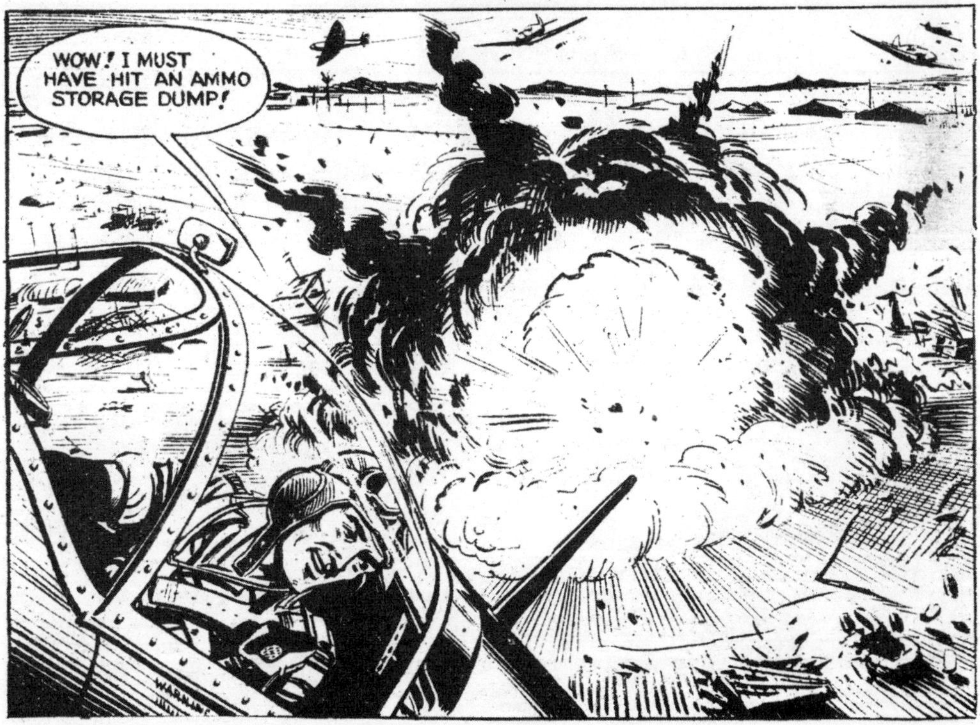
WOW! I MUST HAVE HIT AN AMMO STORAGE DUMP!

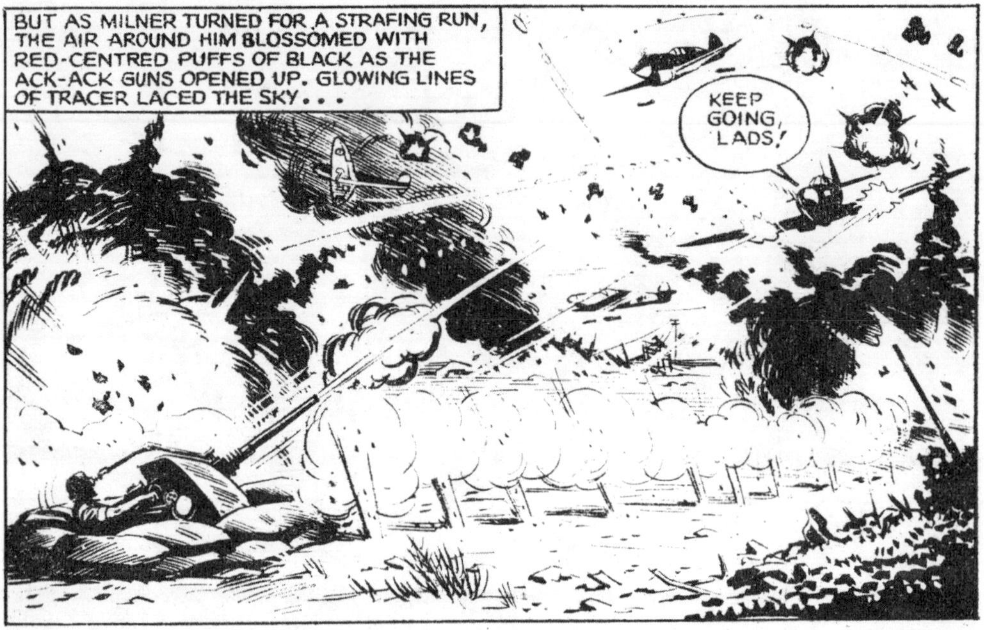
BUT AS MILNER TURNED FOR A STRAFING RUN, THE AIR AROUND HIM BLOSSOMED WITH RED-CENTRED PUFFS OF BLACK AS THE ACK-ACK GUNS OPENED UP. GLOWING LINES OF TRACER LACED THE SKY . . .
KEEP GOING, LADS!

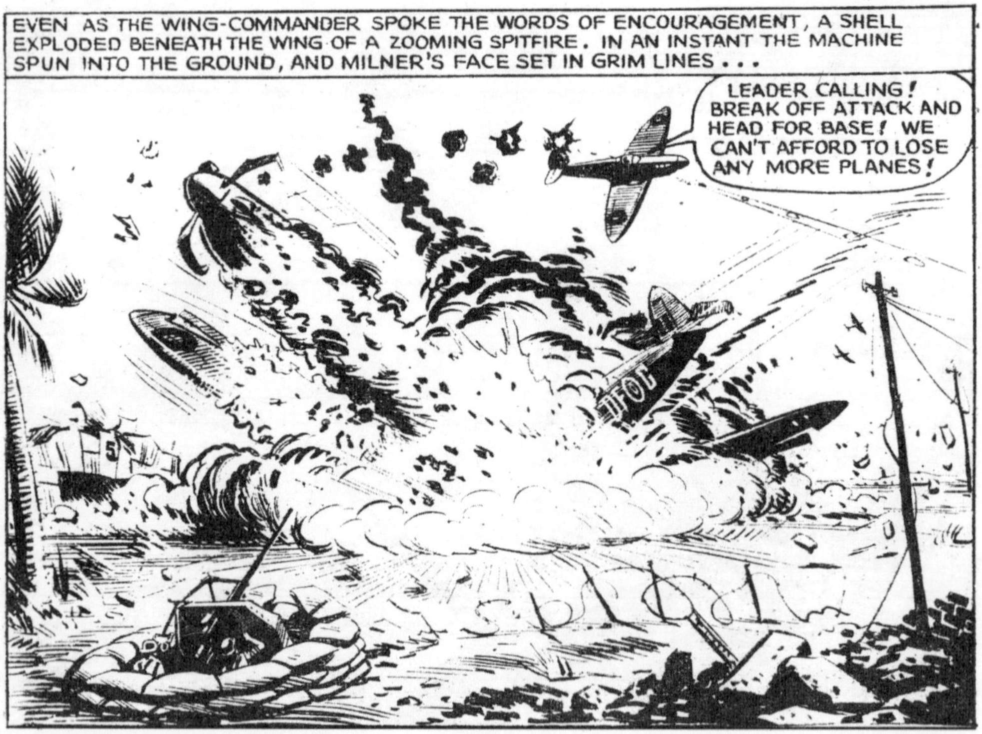
EVEN AS THE WING-COMMANDER SPOKE THE WORDS OF ENCOURAGEMENT, A SHELL EXPLODED BENEATH THE WING OF A ZOOMING SPITFIRE. IN AN INSTANT THE MACHINE SPUN INTO THE GROUND, AND MILNER'S FACE SET IN GRIM LINES . . .
LEADER CALLING! BREAK OFF ATTACK AND HEAD FOR BASE! WE CAN'T AFFORD TO LOSE ANY MORE PLANES!

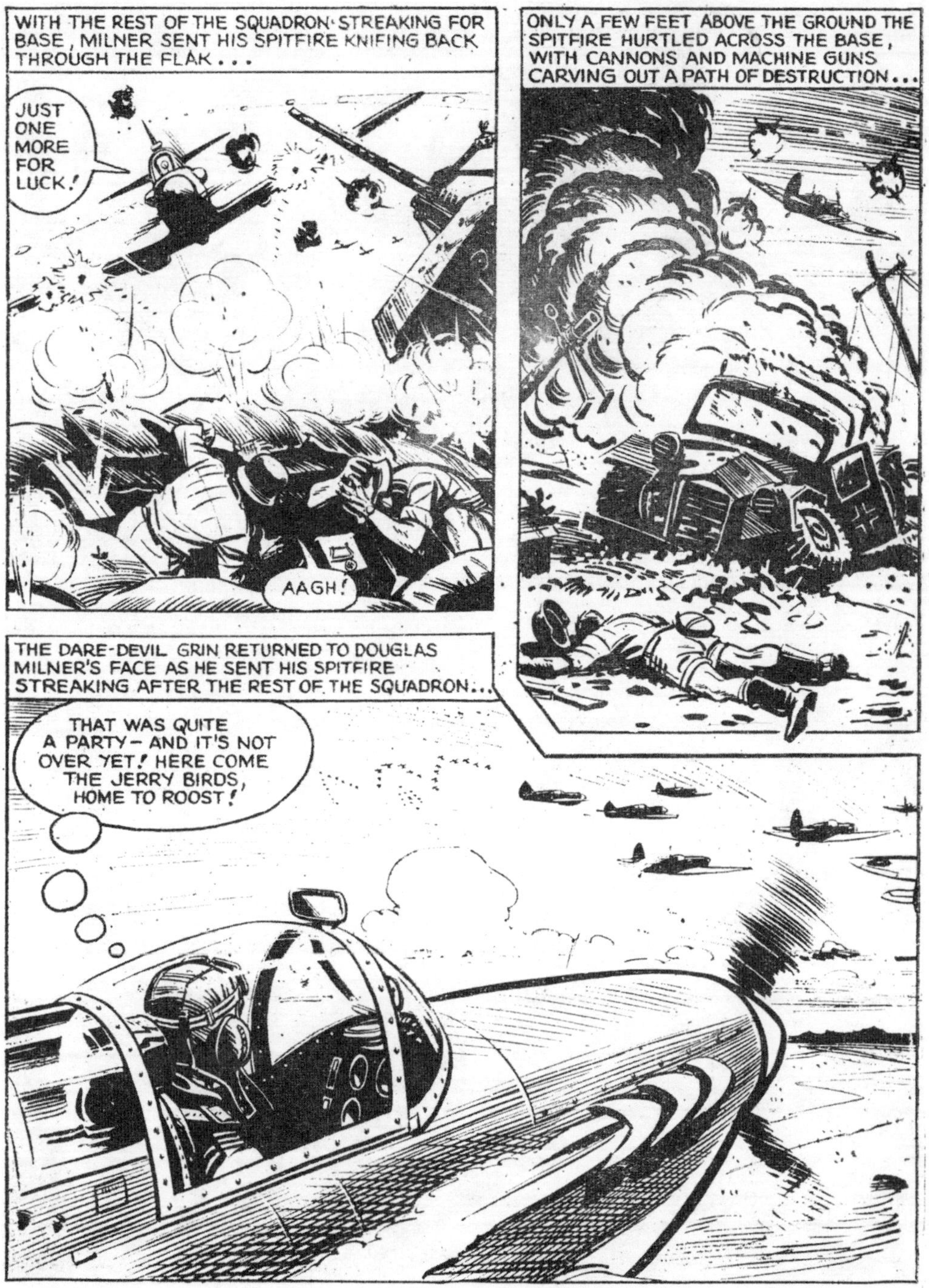
WITH THE REST OF THE SQUADRON STREAKING FOR BASE, MILNER SENT HIS SPITFIRE KNIFING BACK THROUGH THE FLAK...
JUST ONE MORE FOR LUCK!
AAGH!
ONLY A FEW FEET ABOVE THE GROUND THE SPITFIRE HURTLED ACROSS THE BASE, WITH CANNONS AND MACHINE GUNS CARVING OUT A PATH OF DESTRUCTION...
THE DARE-DEVIL GRIN RETURNED TO DOUGLAS MILNER'S FACE AS HE SENT HIS SPITFIRE STREAKING AFTER THE REST OF THE SQUADRON...
THAT WAS QUITE A PARTY – AND IT'S NOT OVER YET! HERE COME THE JERRY BIRDS, HOME TO ROOST!

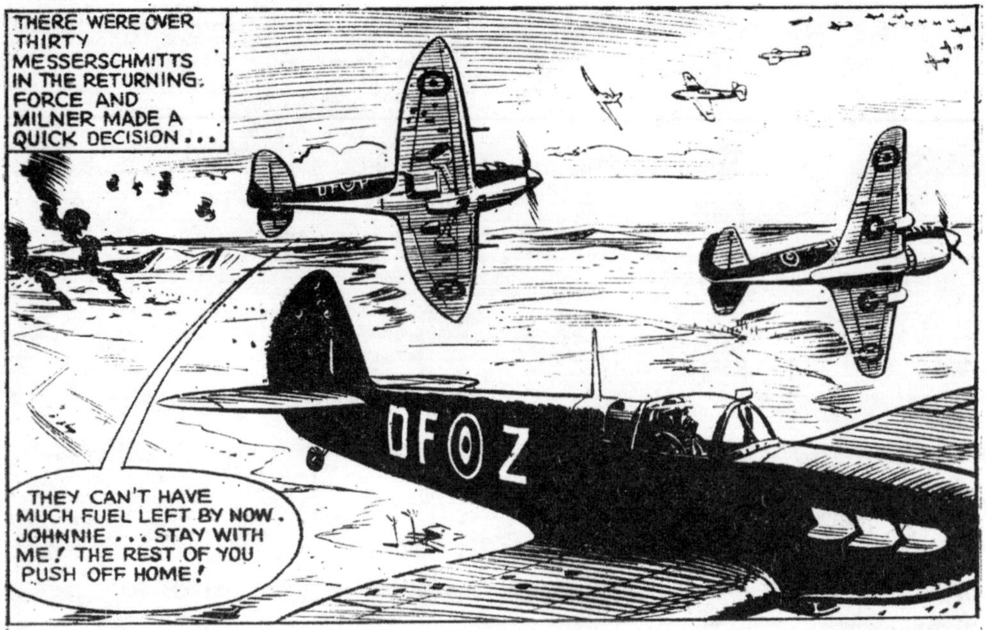
THERE WERE OVER THIRTY MESSERSCHMITTS IN THE RETURNING FORCE AND MILNER MADE A QUICK DECISION . . .
THEY CAN'T HAVE MUCH FUEL LEFT BY NOW. JOHNNIE . . . STAY WITH ME! THE REST OF YOU PUSH OFF HOME!
DF Z

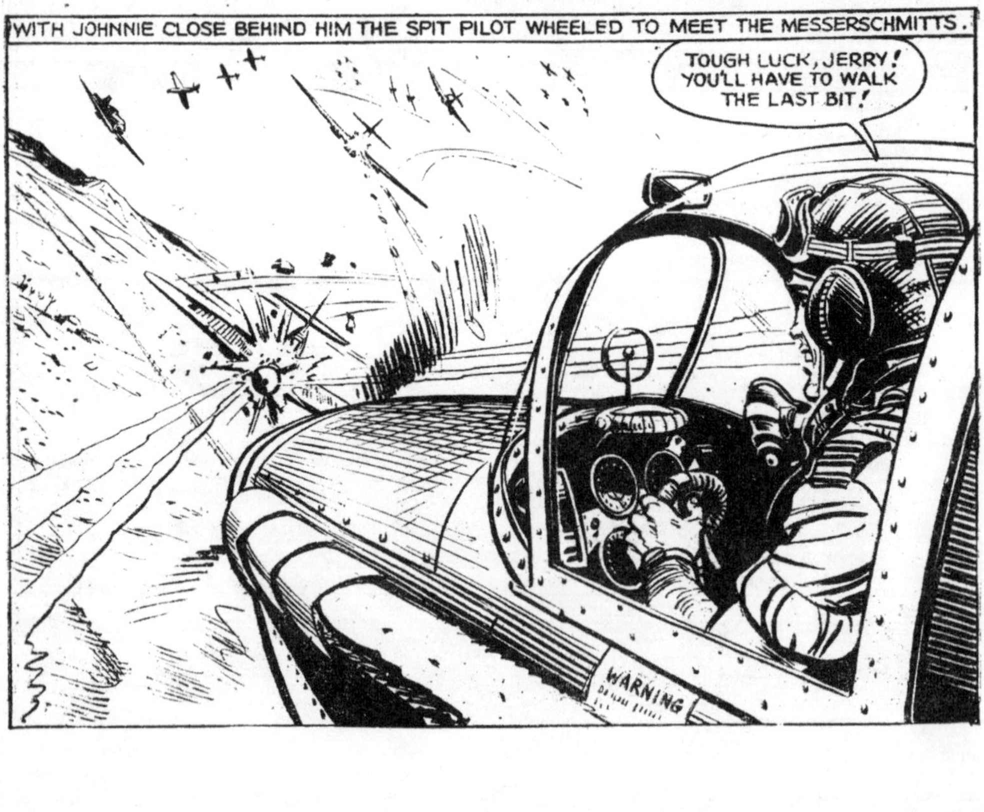
WITH JOHNNIE CLOSE BEHIND HIM THE SPIT PILOT WHEELED TO MEET THE MESSERSCHMITTS.
TOUGH LUCK, JERRY! YOU'LL HAVE TO WALK THE LAST BIT!
WARNING

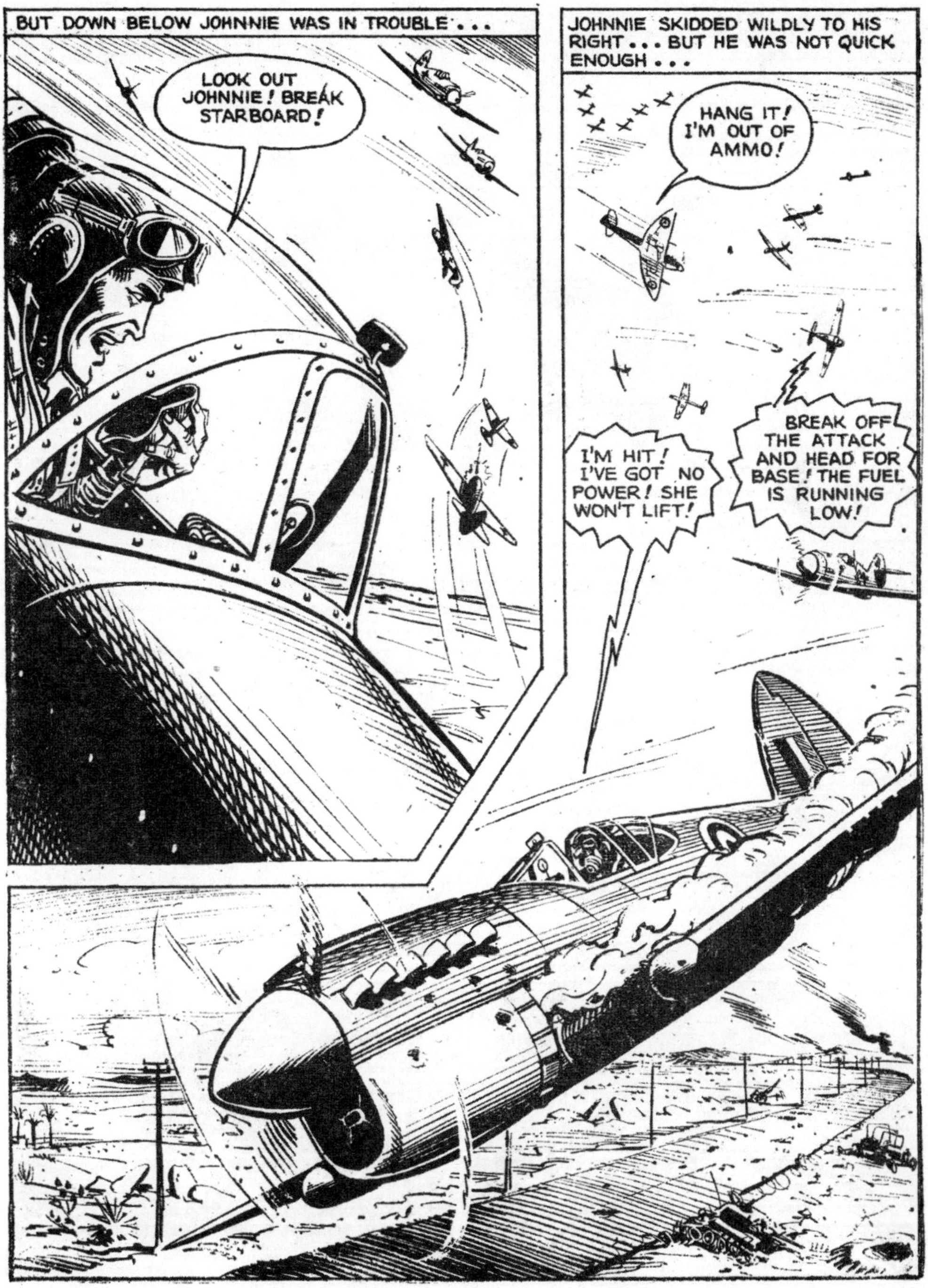
BUT DOWN BELOW JOHNNIE WAS IN TROUBLE . . .
LOOK OUT JOHNNIE! BREAK STARBOARD!
JOHNNIE SKIDDED WILDLY TO HIS RIGHT . . . BUT HE WAS NOT QUICK ENOUGH . . .
HANG IT! I'M OUT OF AMMO!
BREAK OFF THE ATTACK AND HEAD FOR BASE! THE FUEL IS RUNNING LOW!
I'M HIT! I'VE GOT NO POWER! SHE WON'T LIFT!

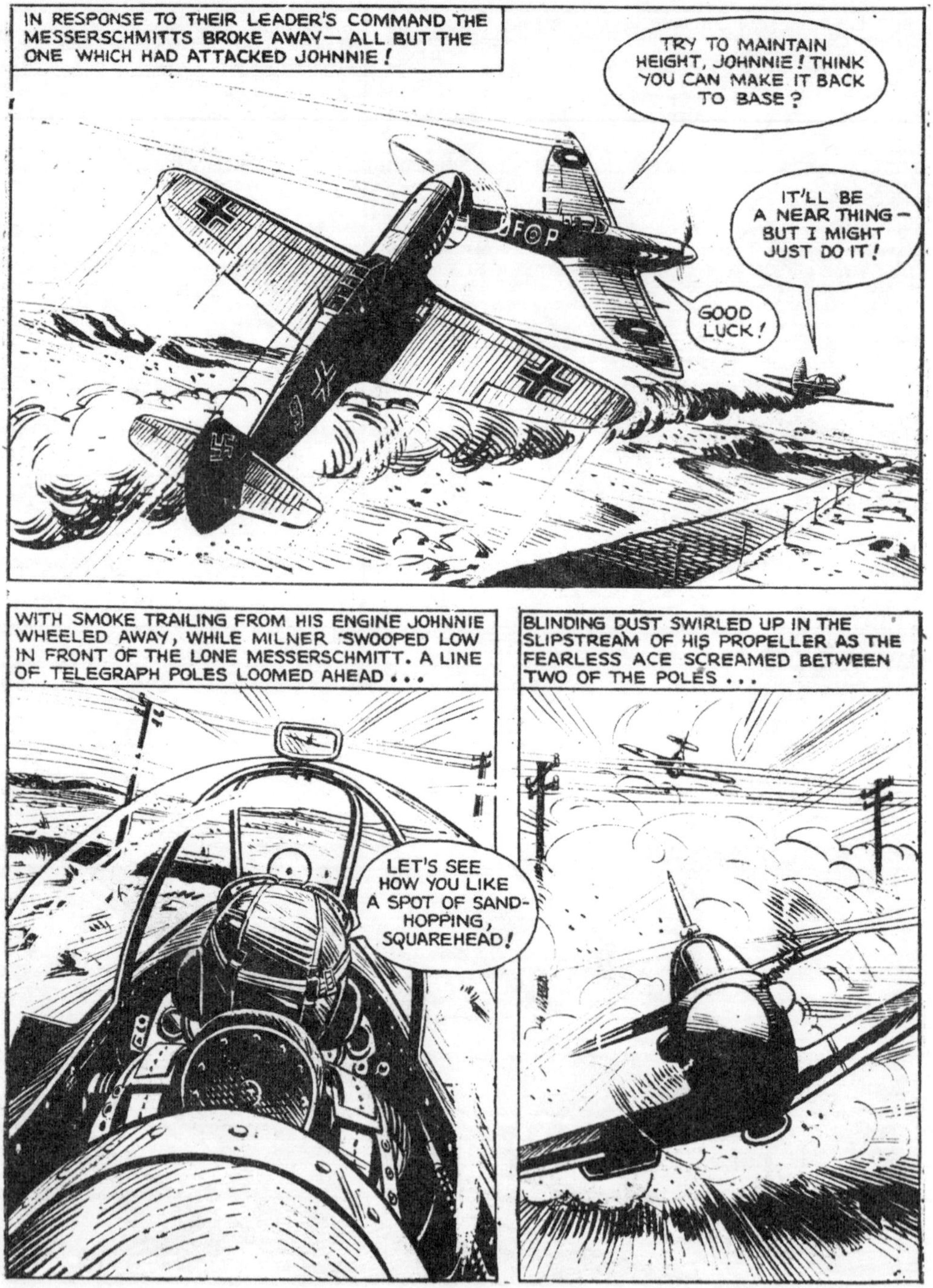
IN RESPONSE TO THEIR LEADER'S COMMAND THE MESSERSCHMITTS BROKE AWAY— ALL BUT THE ONE WHICH HAD ATTACKED JOHNNIE!
TRY TO MAINTAIN HEIGHT, JOHNNIE! THINK YOU CAN MAKE IT BACK TO BASE?
IT'LL BE A NEAR THING— BUT I MIGHT JUST DO IT!
GOOD LUCK!
F⊙P
WITH SMOKE TRAILING FROM HIS ENGINE JOHNNIE WHEELED AWAY, WHILE MILNER SWOOPED LOW IN FRONT OF THE LONE MESSERSCHMITT. A LINE OF TELEGRAPH POLES LOOMED AHEAD...
LET'S SEE HOW YOU LIKE A SPOT OF SAND-HOPPING, SQUAREHEAD!
BLINDING DUST SWIRLED UP IN THE SLIPSTREAM OF HIS PROPELLER AS THE FEARLESS ACE SCREAMED BETWEEN TWO OF THE POLES...

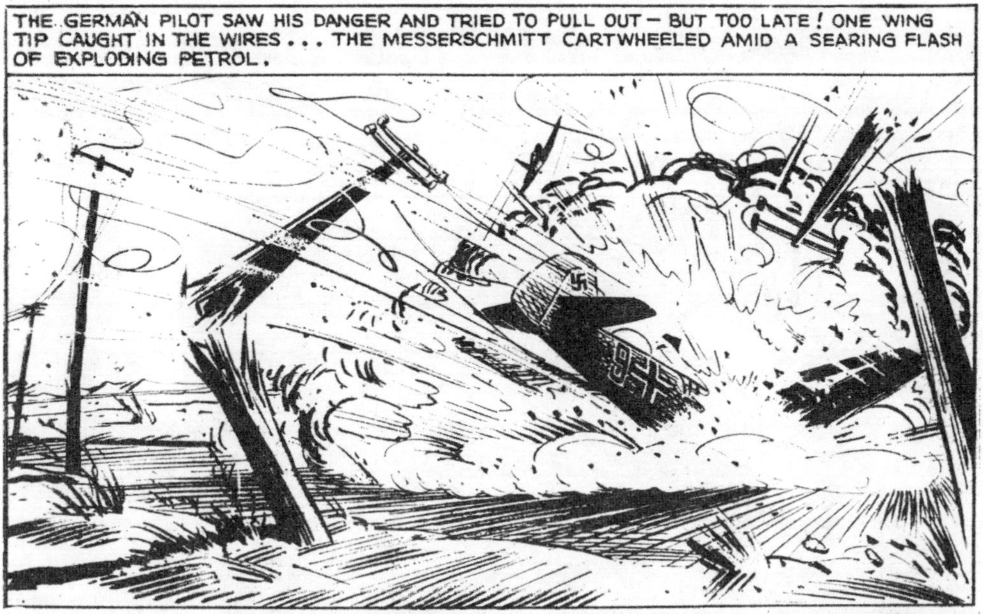
THE GERMAN PILOT SAW HIS DANGER AND TRIED TO PULL OUT – BUT TOO LATE! ONE WING TIP CAUGHT IN THE WIRES . . . THE MESSERSCHMITT CARTWHEELED AMID A SEARING FLASH OF EXPLODING PETROL.

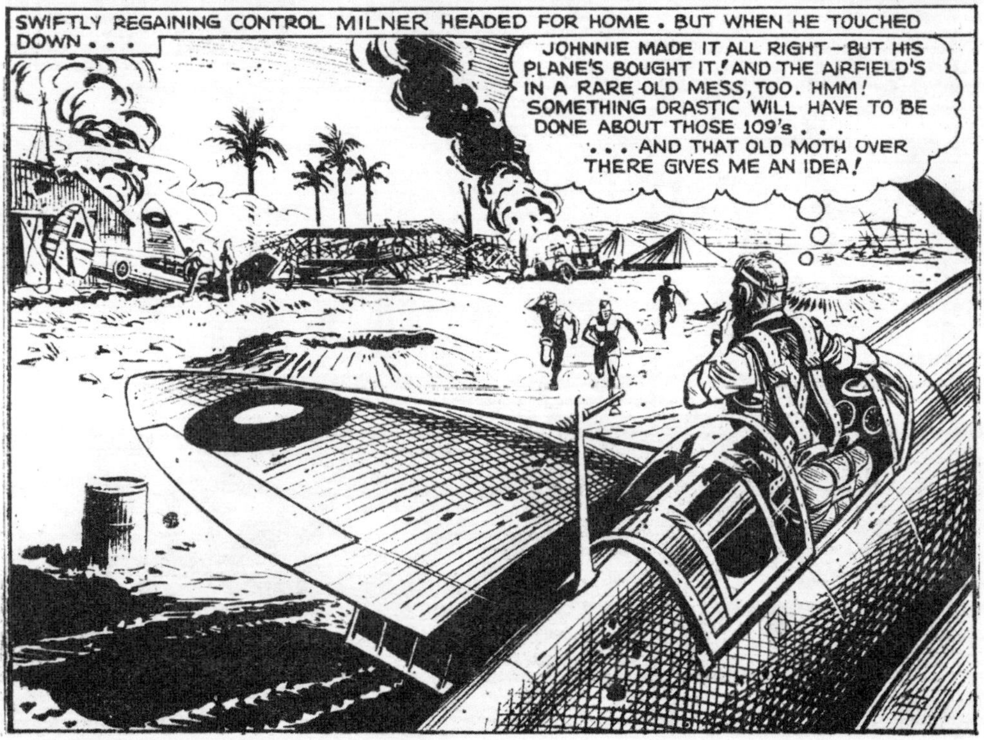
SWIFTLY REGAINING CONTROL MILNER HEADED FOR HOME. BUT WHEN HE TOUCHED DOWN . . .
JOHNNIE MADE IT ALL RIGHT – BUT HIS PLANE'S BOUGHT IT! AND THE AIRFIELD'S IN A RARE OLD MESS, TOO. HMM! SOMETHING DRASTIC WILL HAVE TO BE DONE ABOUT THOSE 109's . . .
. . . AND THAT OLD MOTH OVER THERE GIVES ME AN IDEA!

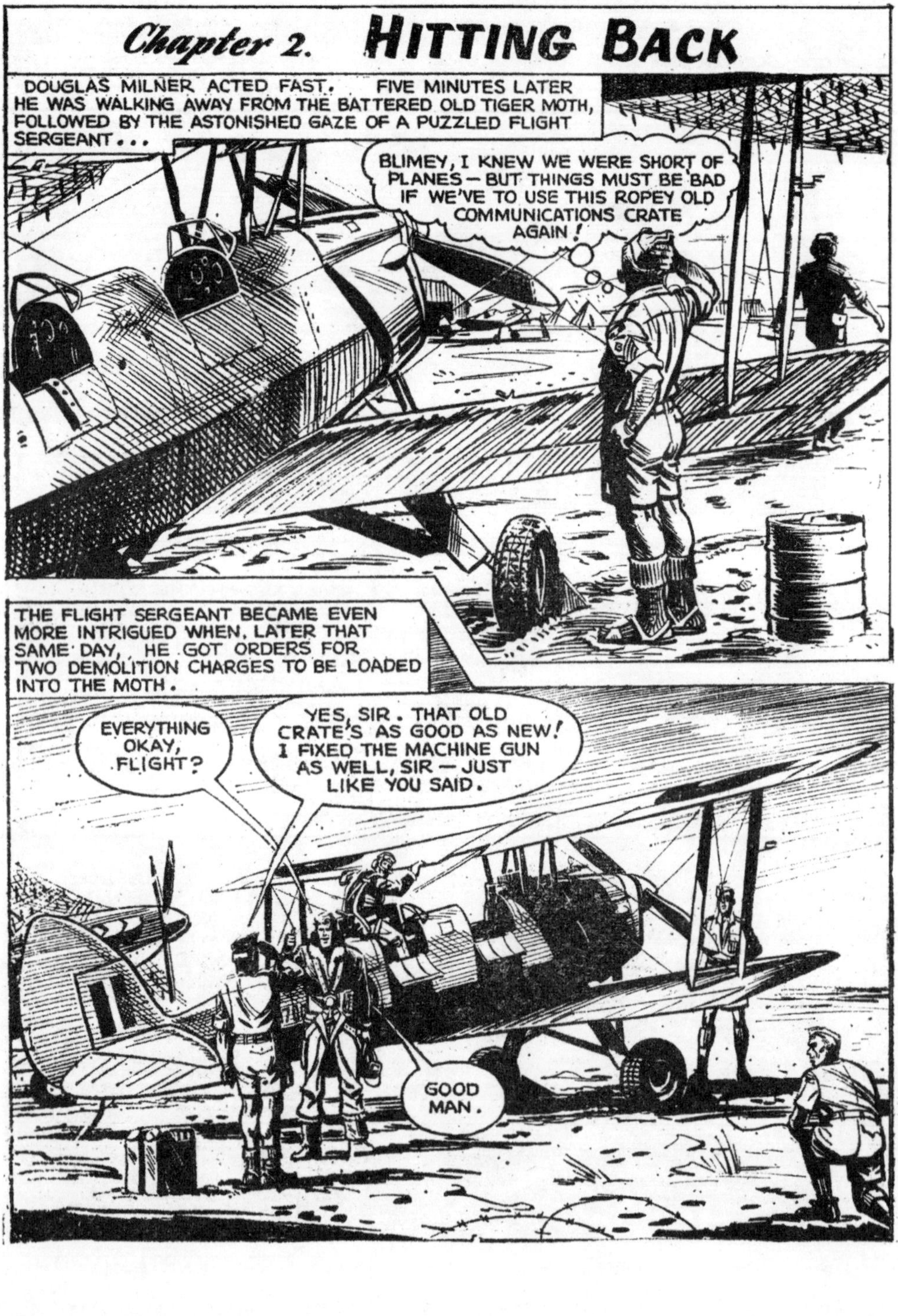
Chapter 2. HITTING BACK
DOUGLAS MILNER ACTED FAST. FIVE MINUTES LATER HE WAS WALKING AWAY FROM THE BATTERED OLD TIGER MOTH, FOLLOWED BY THE ASTONISHED GAZE OF A PUZZLED FLIGHT SERGEANT...
BLIMEY, I KNEW WE WERE SHORT OF PLANES — BUT THINGS MUST BE BAD IF WE'VE TO USE THIS ROPEY OLD COMMUNICATIONS CRATE AGAIN!
THE FLIGHT SERGEANT BECAME EVEN MORE INTRIGUED WHEN, LATER THAT SAME DAY, HE GOT ORDERS FOR TWO DEMOLITION CHARGES TO BE LOADED INTO THE MOTH.
EVERYTHING OKAY, FLIGHT?
YES, SIR. THAT OLD CRATE'S AS GOOD AS NEW! I FIXED THE MACHINE GUN AS WELL, SIR — JUST LIKE YOU SAID.
GOOD MAN.

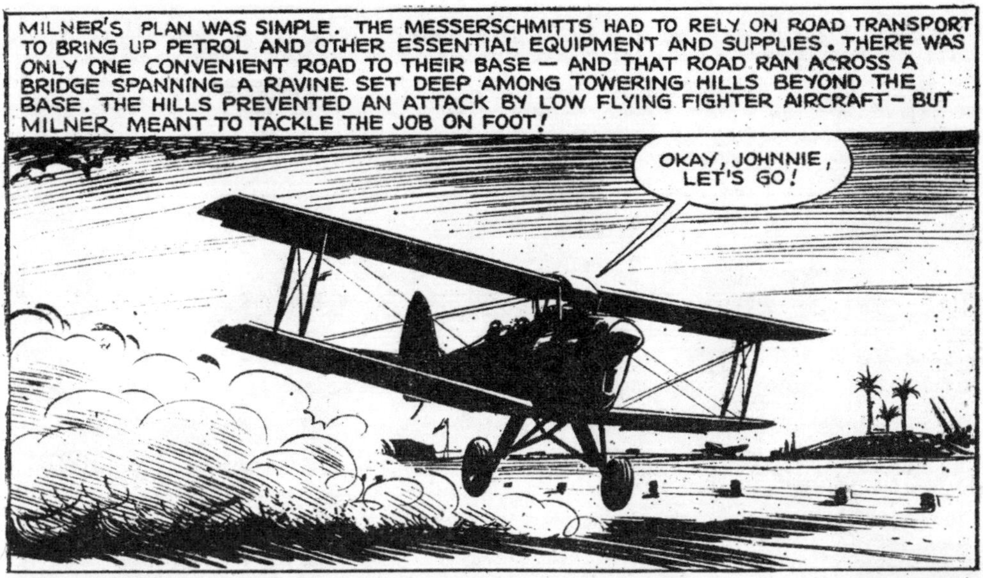
MILNER'S PLAN WAS SIMPLE. THE MESSERSCHMITTS HAD TO RELY ON ROAD TRANSPORT TO BRING UP PETROL AND OTHER ESSENTIAL EQUIPMENT AND SUPPLIES. THERE WAS ONLY ONE CONVENIENT ROAD TO THEIR BASE — AND THAT ROAD RAN ACROSS A BRIDGE SPANNING A RAVINE SET DEEP AMONG TOWERING HILLS BEYOND THE BASE. THE HILLS PREVENTED AN ATTACK BY LOW FLYING FIGHTER AIRCRAFT — BUT MILNER MEANT TO TACKLE THE JOB ON FOOT!
OKAY, JOHNNIE, LET'S GO!

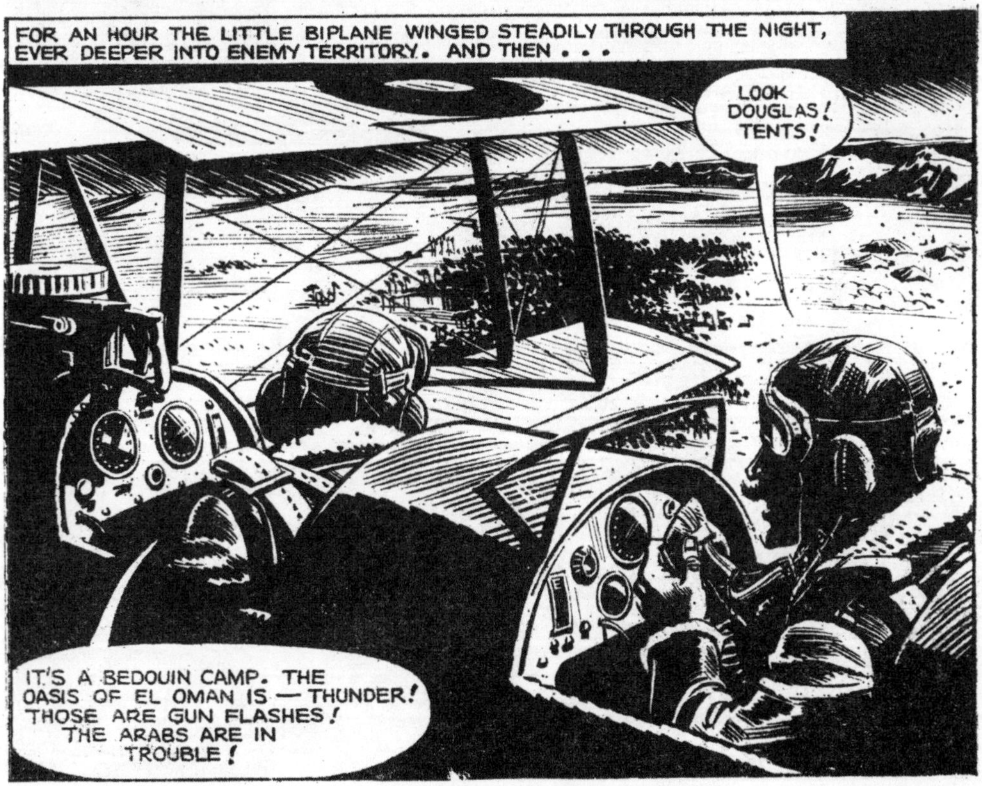
FOR AN HOUR THE LITTLE BIPLANE WINGED STEADILY THROUGH THE NIGHT, EVER DEEPER INTO ENEMY TERRITORY. AND THEN . . .
LOOK DOUGLAS! TENTS!
IT'S A BEDOUIN CAMP. THE OASIS OF EL OMAN IS — THUNDER! THOSE ARE GUN FLASHES! THE ARABS ARE IN TROUBLE!

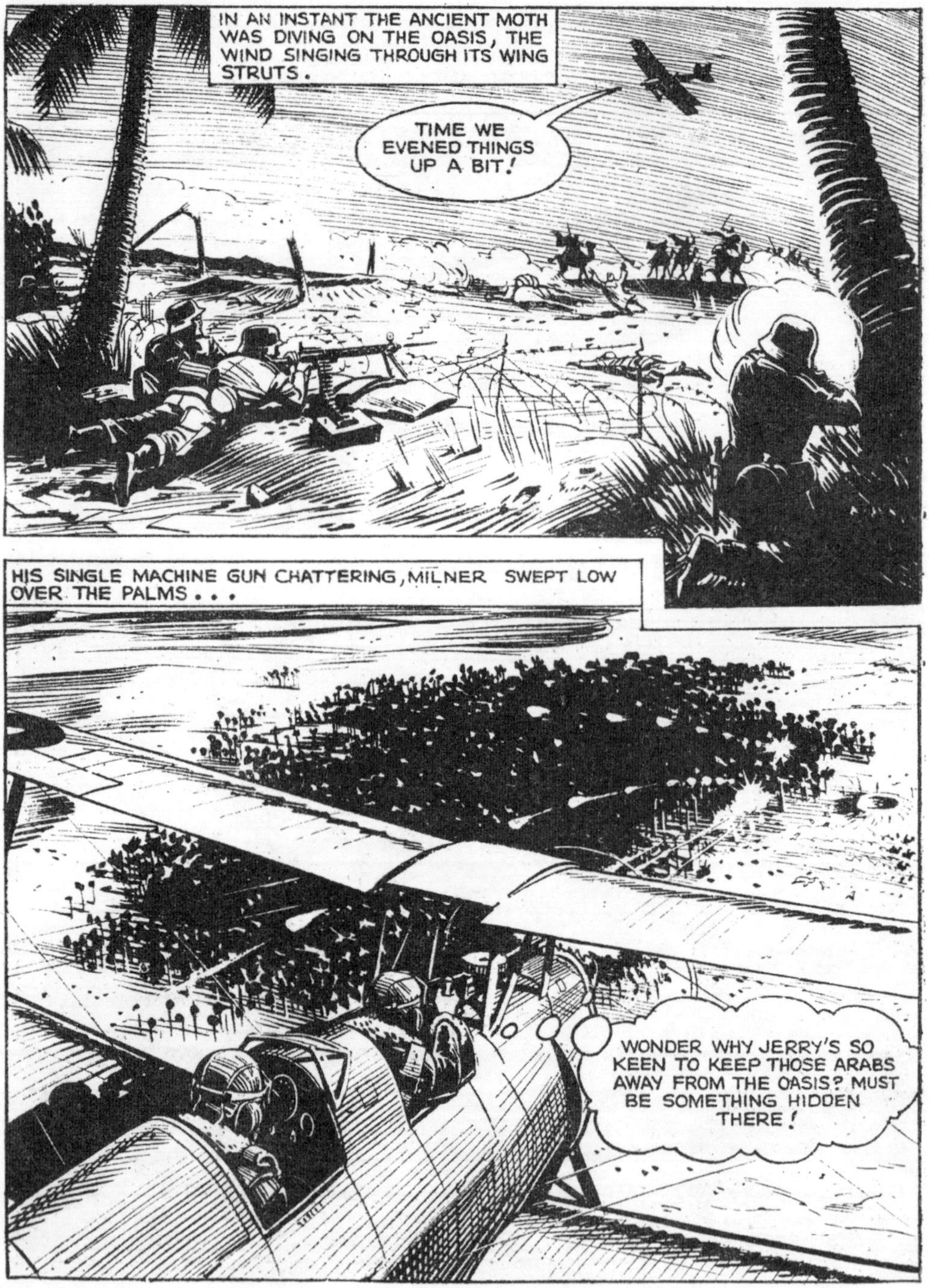
IN AN INSTANT THE ANCIENT MOTH WAS DIVING ON THE OASIS, THE WIND SINGING THROUGH ITS WING STRUTS.
TIME WE EVENED THINGS UP A BIT!
HIS SINGLE MACHINE GUN CHATTERING, MILNER SWEPT LOW OVER THE PALMS . . .
WONDER WHY JERRY'S SO KEEN TO KEEP THOSE ARABS AWAY FROM THE OASIS? MUST BE SOMETHING HIDDEN THERE!

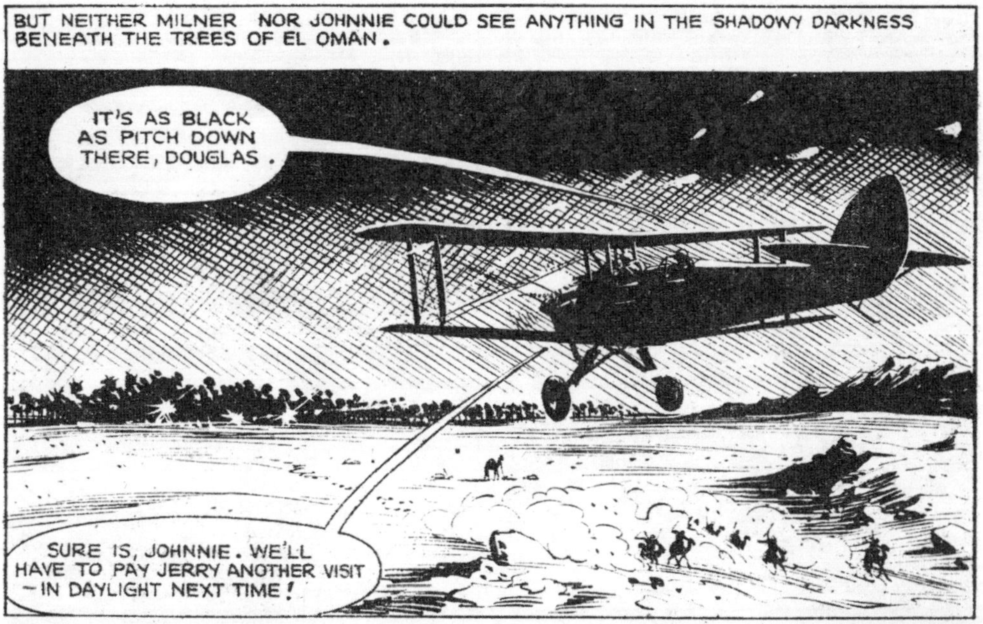
BUT NEITHER MILNER NOR JOHNNIE COULD SEE ANYTHING IN THE SHADOWY DARKNESS BENEATH THE TREES OF EL OMAN.
IT'S AS BLACK AS PITCH DOWN THERE, DOUGLAS.
SURE IS, JOHNNIE. WE'LL HAVE TO PAY JERRY ANOTHER VISIT —IN DAYLIGHT NEXT TIME!

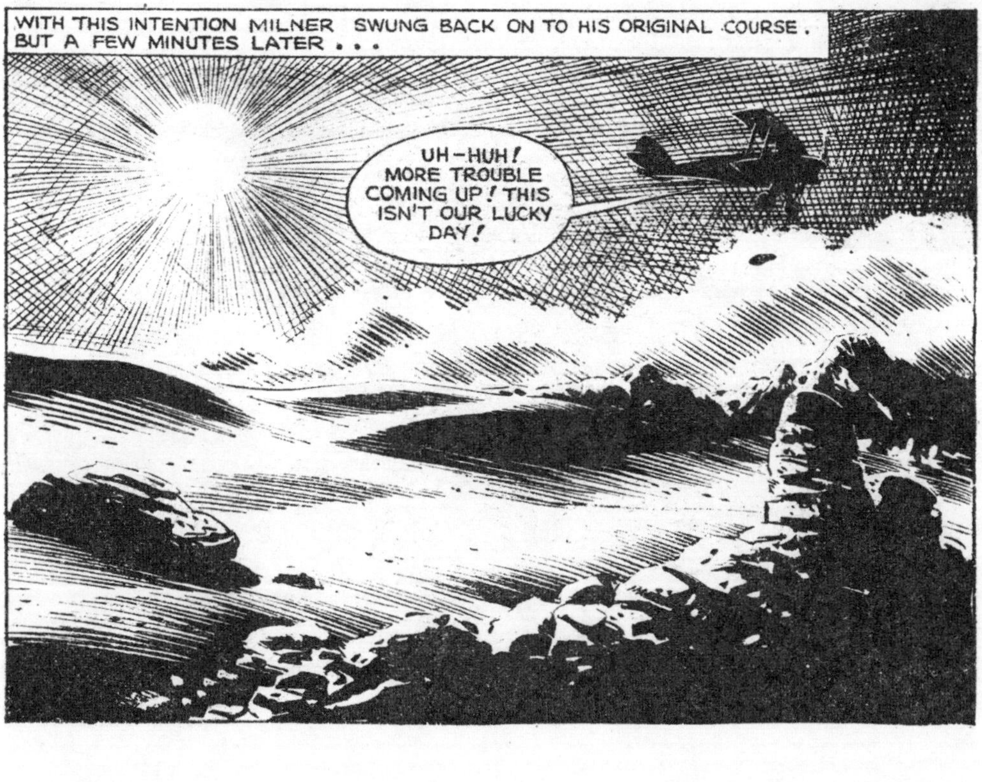
WITH THIS INTENTION MILNER SWUNG BACK ON TO HIS ORIGINAL COURSE. BUT A FEW MINUTES LATER...
UH-HUH! MORE TROUBLE COMING UP! THIS ISN'T OUR LUCKY DAY!

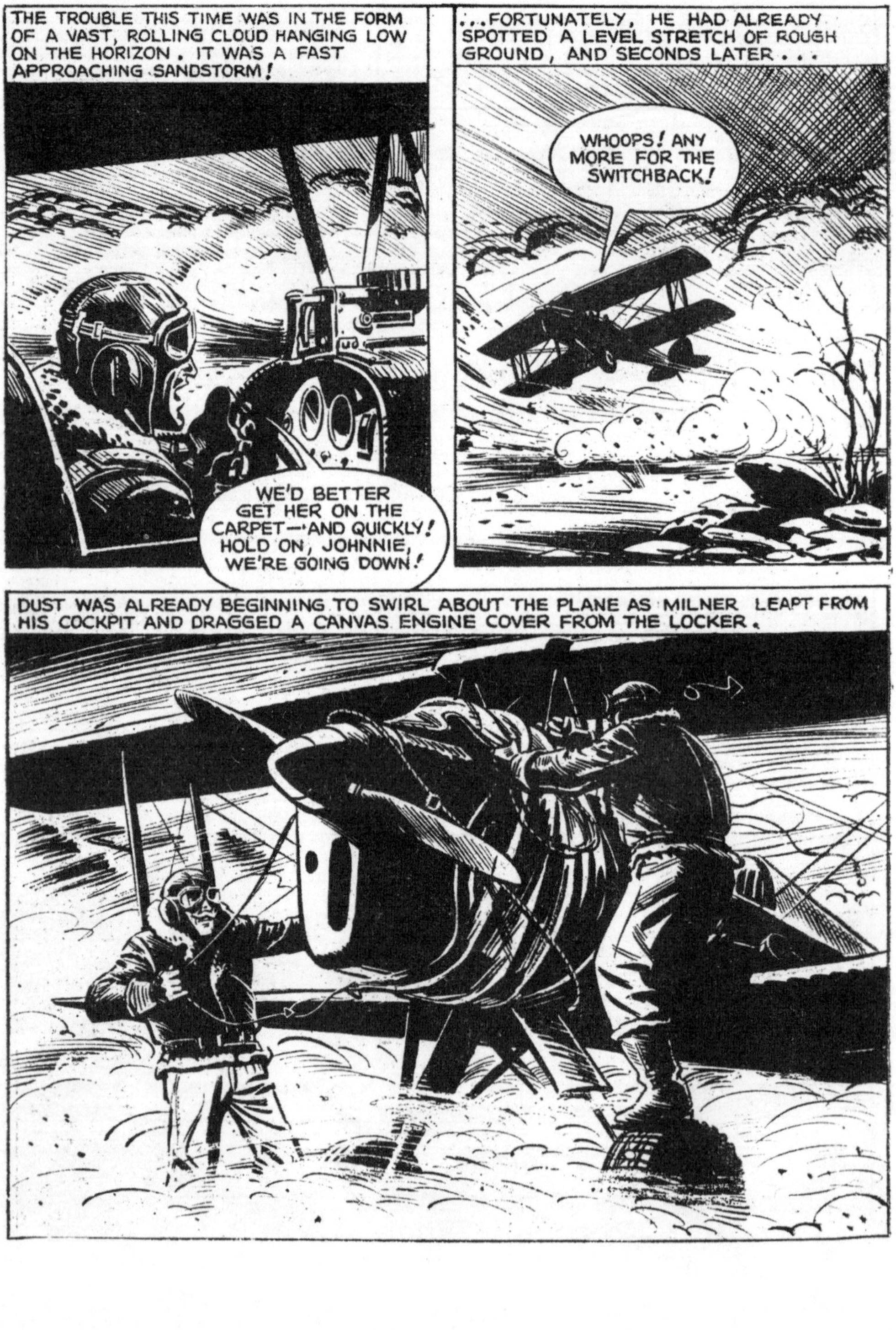
THE TROUBLE THIS TIME WAS IN THE FORM OF A VAST, ROLLING CLOUD HANGING LOW ON THE HORIZON. IT WAS A FAST APPROACHING SANDSTORM!
WE'D BETTER GET HER ON THE CARPET—AND QUICKLY! HOLD ON, JOHNNIE, WE'RE GOING DOWN!
...FORTUNATELY, HE HAD ALREADY SPOTTED A LEVEL STRETCH OF ROUGH GROUND, AND SECONDS LATER...
WHOOPS! ANY MORE FOR THE SWITCHBACK!
DUST WAS ALREADY BEGINNING TO SWIRL ABOUT THE PLANE AS MILNER LEAPT FROM HIS COCKPIT AND DRAGGED A CANVAS ENGINE COVER FROM THE LOCKER.

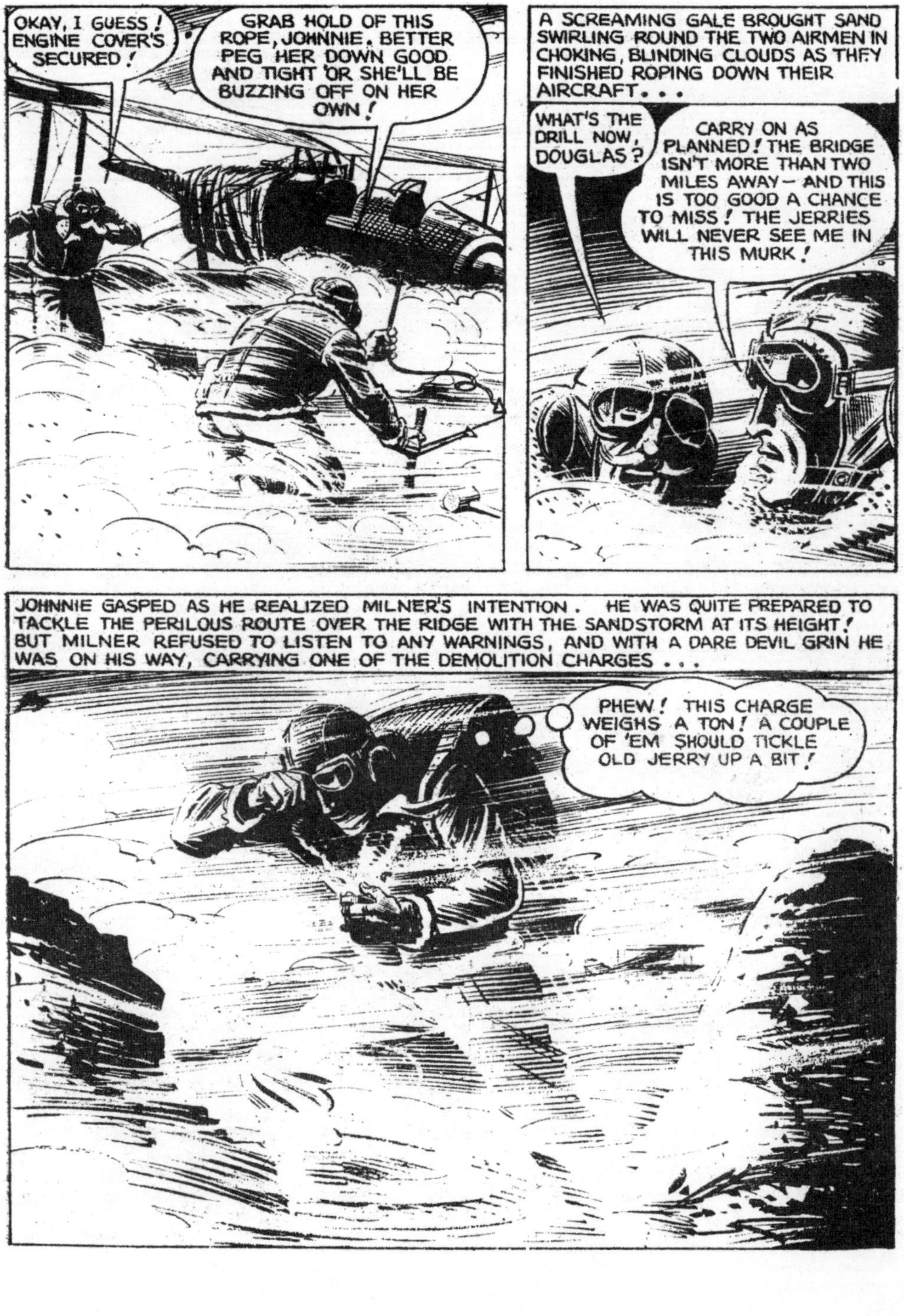
OKAY, I GUESS! ENGINE COVER'S SECURED!
GRAB HOLD OF THIS ROPE, JOHNNIE. BETTER PEG HER DOWN GOOD AND TIGHT OR SHE'LL BE BUZZING OFF ON HER OWN!
A SCREAMING GALE BROUGHT SAND SWIRLING ROUND THE TWO AIRMEN IN CHOKING, BLINDING CLOUDS AS THEY FINISHED ROPING DOWN THEIR AIRCRAFT...
WHAT'S THE DRILL NOW, DOUGLAS?
CARRY ON AS PLANNED! THE BRIDGE ISN'T MORE THAN TWO MILES AWAY— AND THIS IS TOO GOOD A CHANCE TO MISS! THE JERRIES WILL NEVER SEE ME IN THIS MURK!
JOHNNIE GASPED AS HE REALIZED MILNER'S INTENTION. HE WAS QUITE PREPARED TO TACKLE THE PERILOUS ROUTE OVER THE RIDGE WITH THE SANDSTORM AT ITS HEIGHT! BUT MILNER REFUSED TO LISTEN TO ANY WARNINGS, AND WITH A DARE DEVIL GRIN HE WAS ON HIS WAY, CARRYING ONE OF THE DEMOLITION CHARGES...
PHEW! THIS CHARGE WEIGHS A TON! A COUPLE OF 'EM SHOULD TICKLE OLD JERRY UP A BIT!

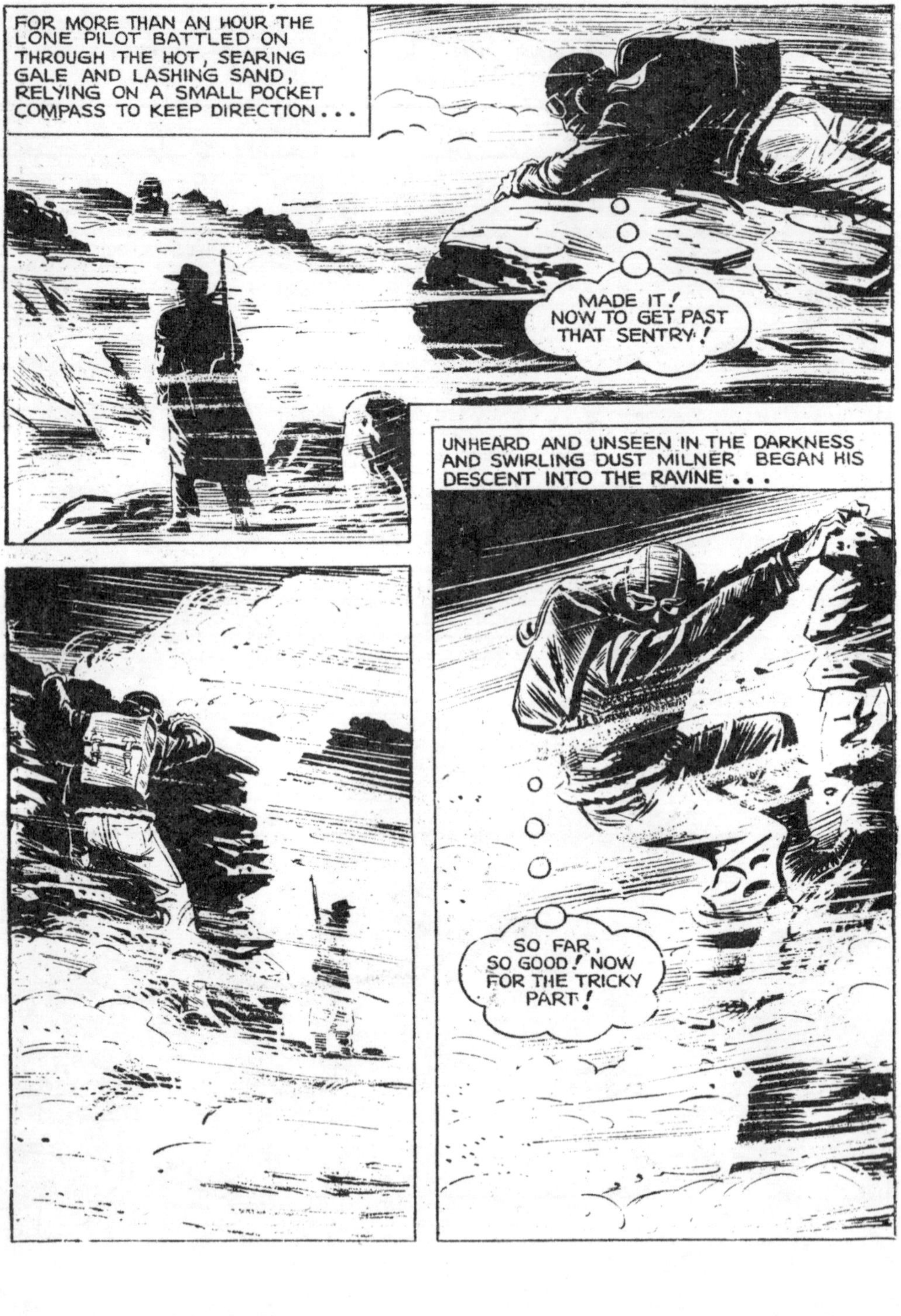
FOR MORE THAN AN HOUR THE LONE PILOT BATTLED ON THROUGH THE HOT, SEARING GALE AND LASHING SAND, RELYING ON A SMALL POCKET COMPASS TO KEEP DIRECTION...
MADE IT! NOW TO GET PAST THAT SENTRY!
UNHEARD AND UNSEEN IN THE DARKNESS AND SWIRLING DUST MILNER BEGAN HIS DESCENT INTO THE RAVINE...
SO FAR, SO GOOD! NOW FOR THE TRICKY PART!

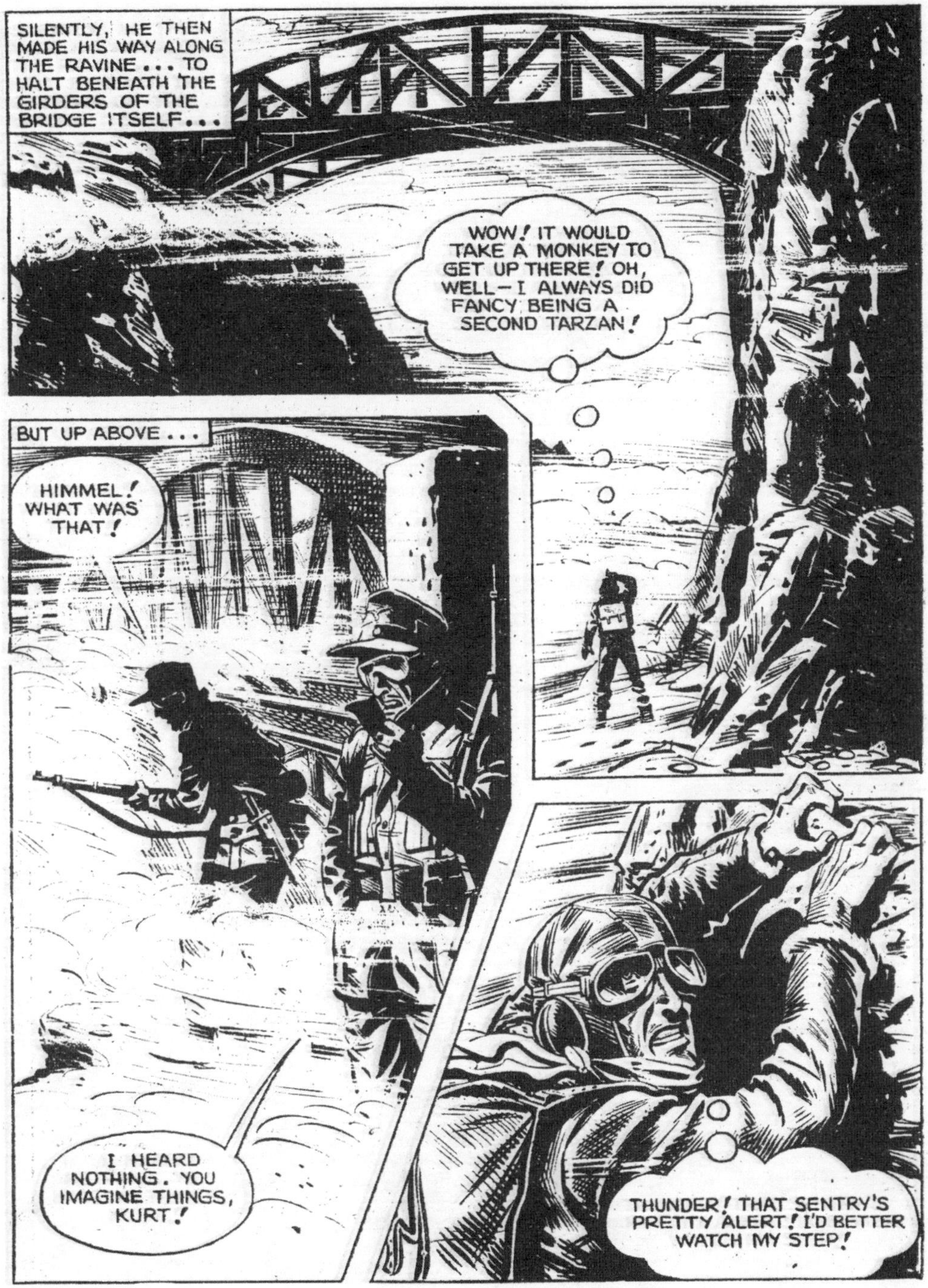
SILENTLY, HE THEN MADE HIS WAY ALONG THE RAVINE ... TO HALT BENEATH THE GIRDERS OF THE BRIDGE ITSELF...
WOW! IT WOULD TAKE A MONKEY TO GET UP THERE! OH, WELL—I ALWAYS DID FANCY BEING A SECOND TARZAN!
BUT UP ABOVE ...
HIMMEL! WHAT WAS THAT!
I HEARD NOTHING. YOU IMAGINE THINGS, KURT!
THUNDER! THAT SENTRY'S PRETTY ALERT! I'D BETTER WATCH MY STEP!

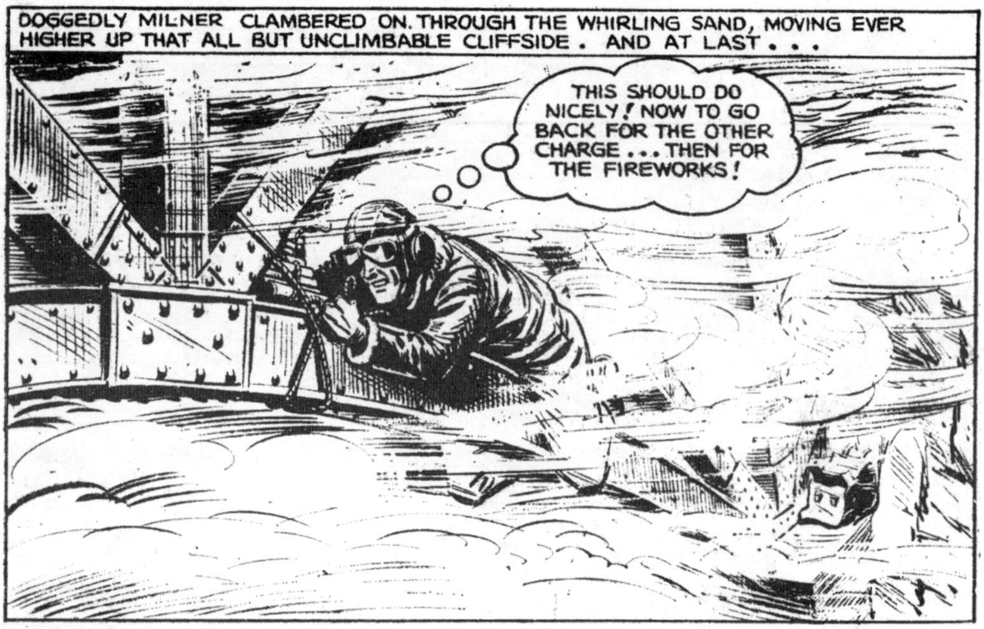
DOGGEDLY MILNER CLAMBERED ON. THROUGH THE WHIRLING SAND, MOVING EVER HIGHER UP THAT ALL BUT UNCLIMBABLE CLIFFSIDE . AND AT LAST . . .
THIS SHOULD DO NICELY! NOW TO GO BACK FOR THE OTHER CHARGE . . . THEN FOR THE FIREWORKS!

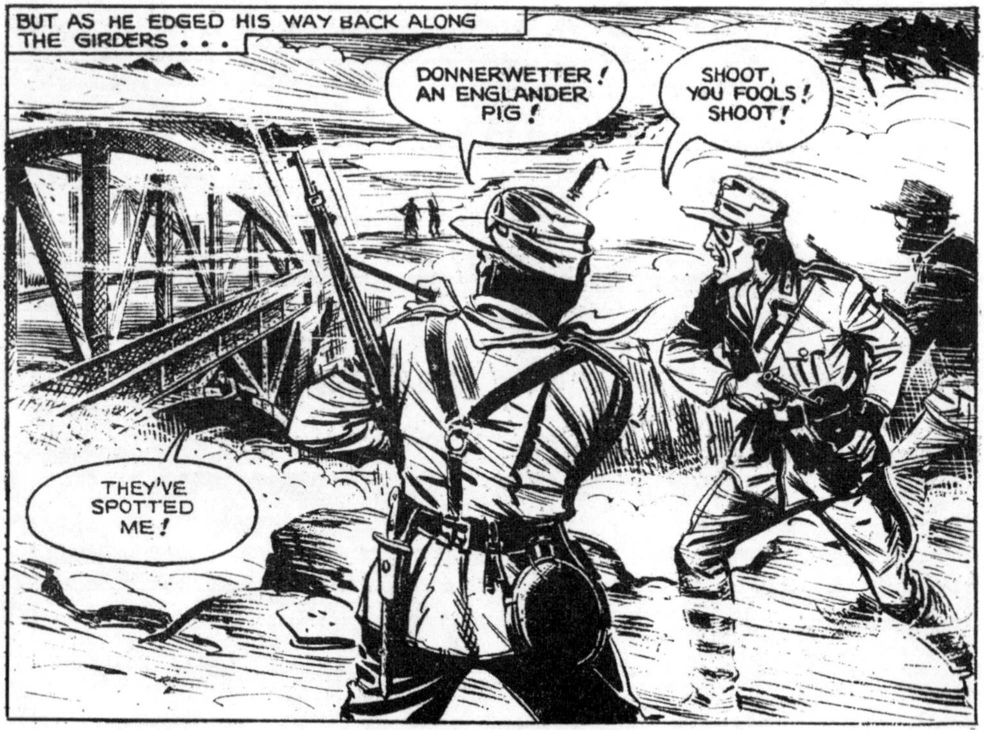
BUT AS HE EDGED HIS WAY BACK ALONG THE GIRDERS . . .
DONNERWETTER! AN ENGLANDER PIG!
SHOOT, YOU FOOLS! SHOOT!
THEY'VE SPOTTED ME!

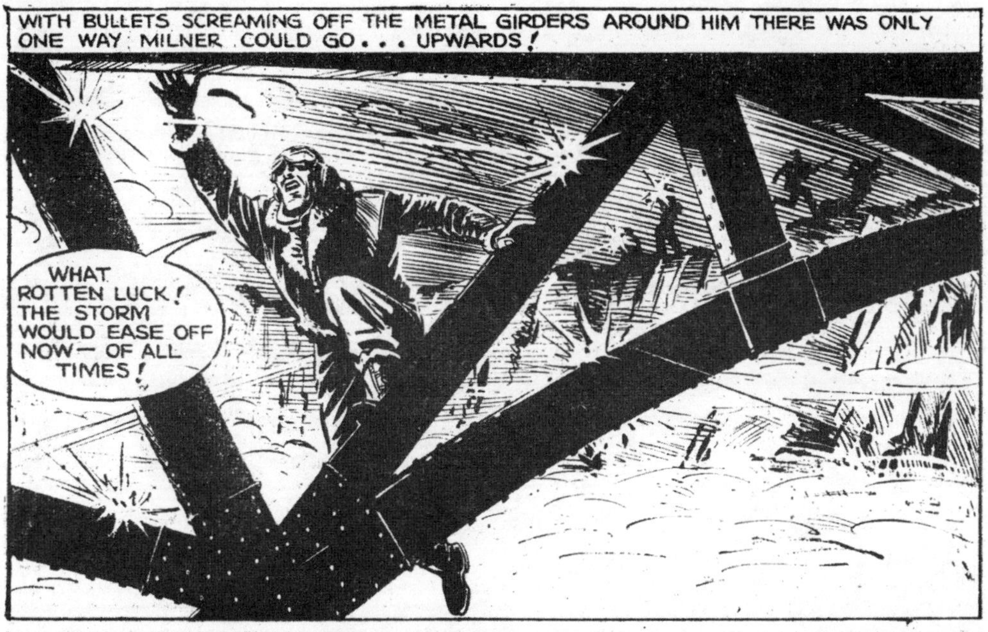
WITH BULLETS SCREAMING OFF THE METAL GIRDERS AROUND HIM THERE WAS ONLY ONE WAY MILNER COULD GO . . . UPWARDS!
WHAT ROTTEN LUCK! THE STORM WOULD EASE OFF NOW— OF ALL TIMES!

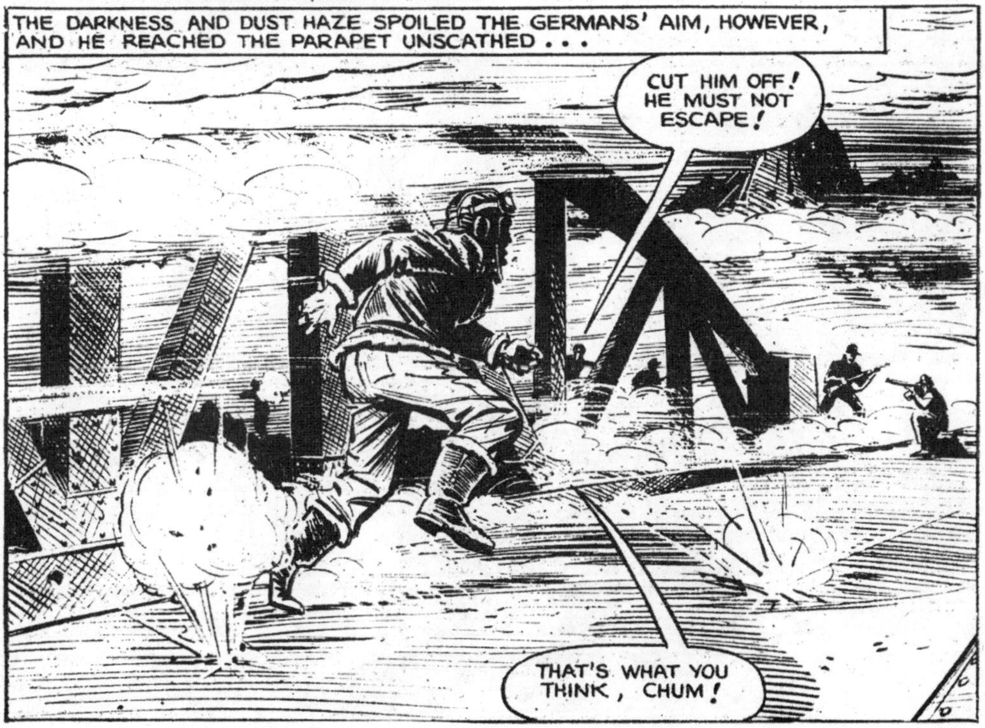
THE DARKNESS AND DUST HAZE SPOILED THE GERMANS' AIM, HOWEVER, AND HE REACHED THE PARAPET UNSCATHED . . .
CUT HIM OFF! HE MUST NOT ESCAPE!
THAT'S WHAT YOU THINK, CHUM!

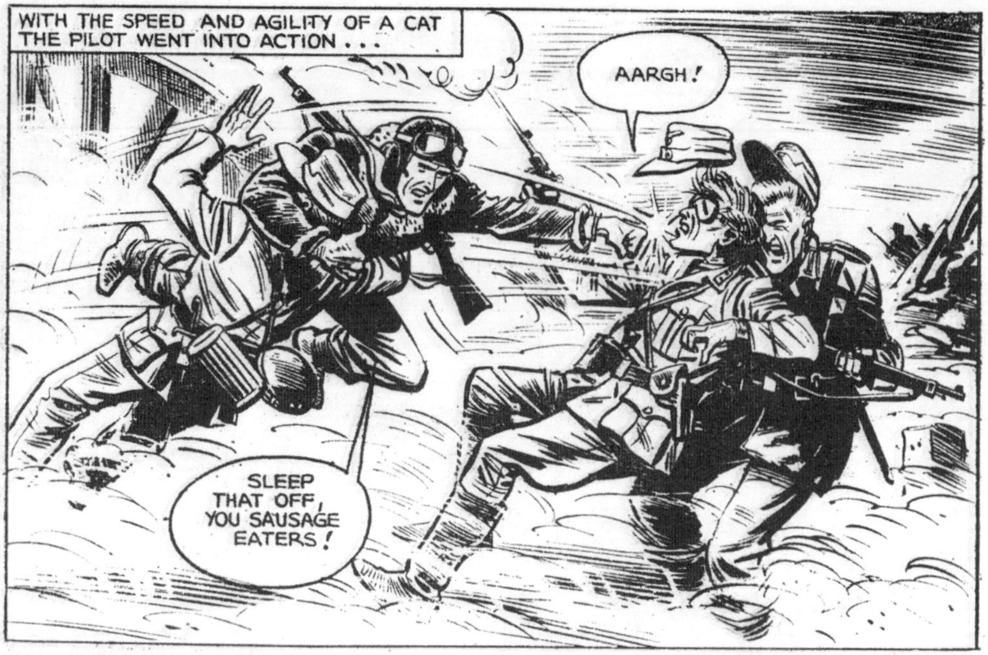
WITH THE SPEED AND AGILITY OF A CAT THE PILOT WENT INTO ACTION . . .
AARGH!
SLEEP THAT OFF, YOU SAUSAGE EATERS!

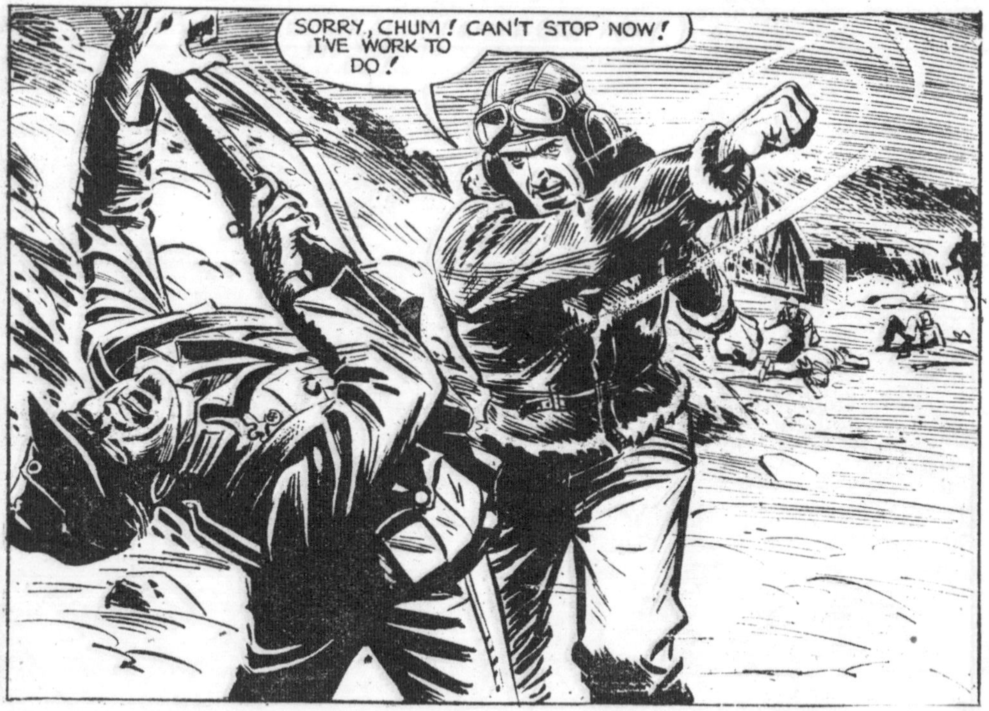
SORRY, CHUM! CAN'T STOP NOW! I'VE WORK TO DO!

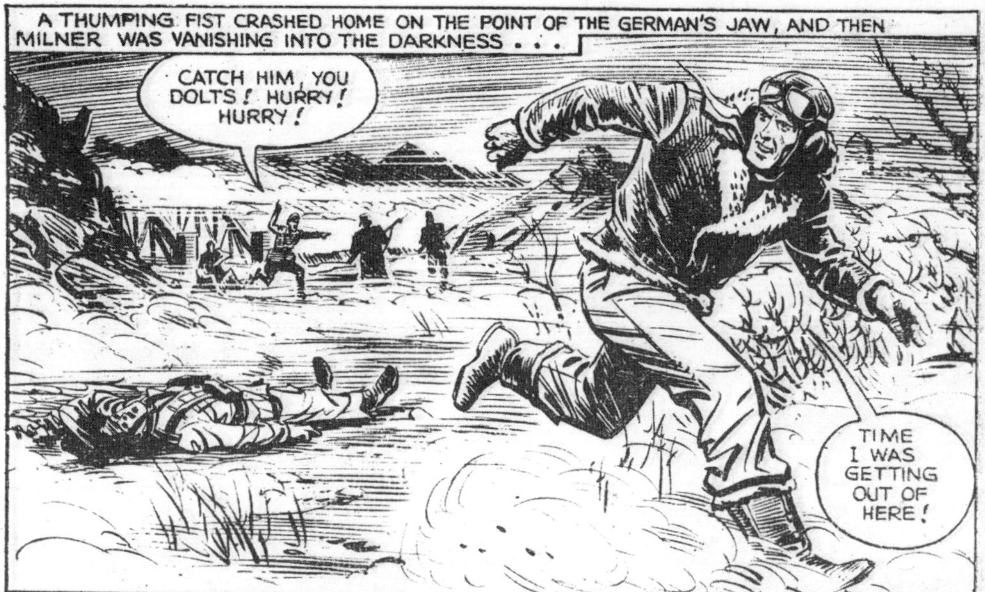
A THUMPING FIST CRASHED HOME ON THE POINT OF THE GERMAN'S JAW, AND THEN MILNER WAS VANISHING INTO THE DARKNESS . . .
CATCH HIM, YOU DOLTS! HURRY! HURRY!
TIME I WAS GETTING OUT OF HERE!

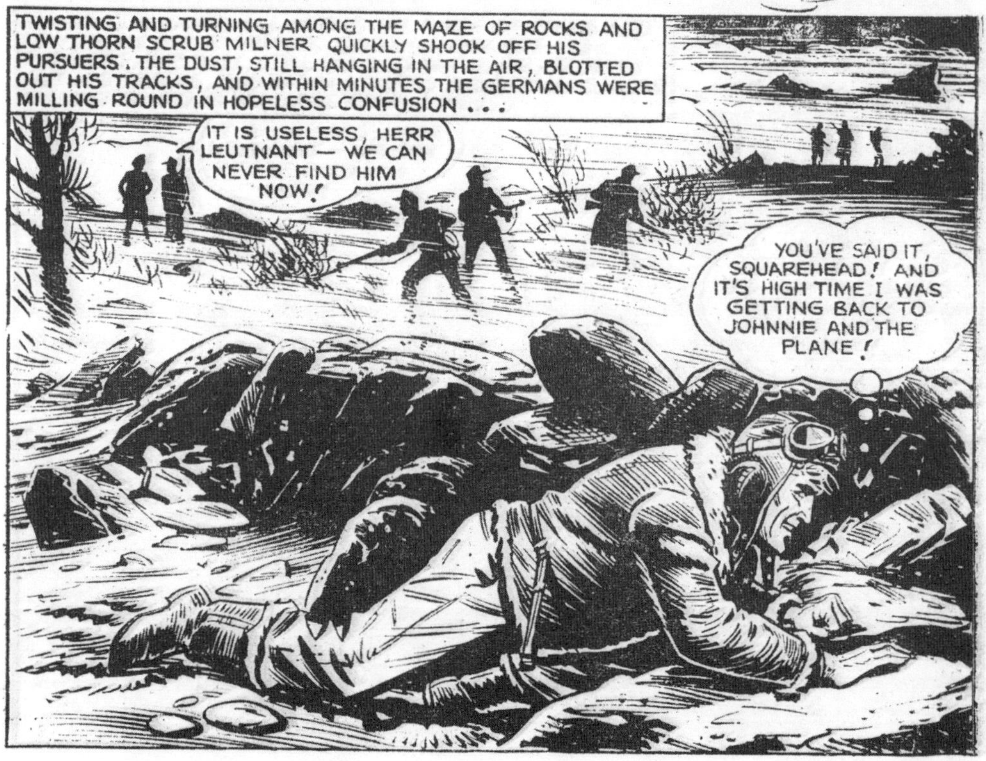
TWISTING AND TURNING AMONG THE MAZE OF ROCKS AND LOW THORN SCRUB MILNER QUICKLY SHOOK OFF HIS PURSUERS. THE DUST, STILL HANGING IN THE AIR, BLOTTED OUT HIS TRACKS, AND WITHIN MINUTES THE GERMANS WERE MILLING ROUND IN HOPELESS CONFUSION . . .
IT IS USELESS, HERR LEUTNANT — WE CAN NEVER FIND HIM NOW!
YOU'VE SAID IT, SQUAREHEAD! AND IT'S HIGH TIME I WAS GETTING BACK TO JOHNNIE AND THE PLANE!

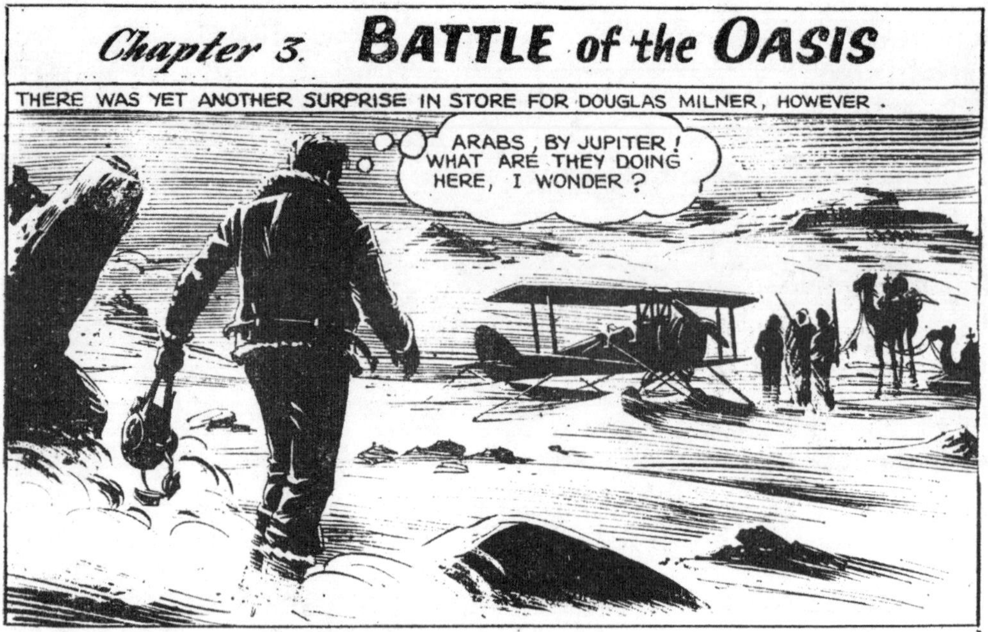
Chapter 3. BATTLE of the OASIS
THERE WAS YET ANOTHER SURPRISE IN STORE FOR DOUGLAS MILNER, HOWEVER.
ARABS, BY JUPITER! WHAT ARE THEY DOING HERE, I WONDER?

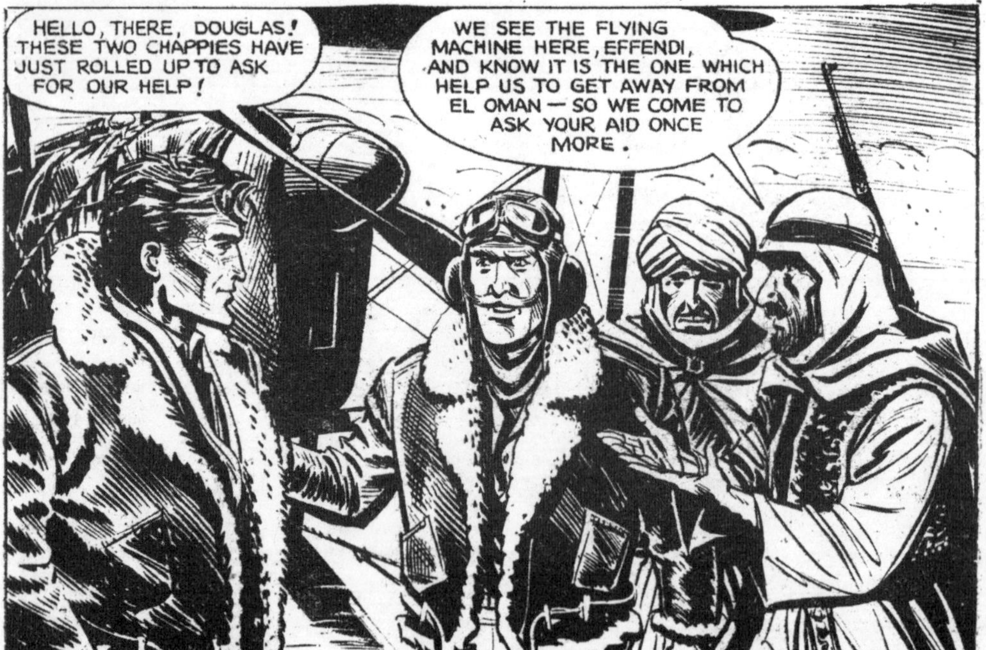
HELLO, THERE, DOUGLAS! THESE TWO CHAPPIES HAVE JUST ROLLED UP TO ASK FOR OUR HELP!
WE SEE THE FLYING MACHINE HERE, EFFENDI, AND KNOW IT IS THE ONE WHICH HELP US TO GET AWAY FROM EL OMAN — SO WE COME TO ASK YOUR AID ONCE MORE.

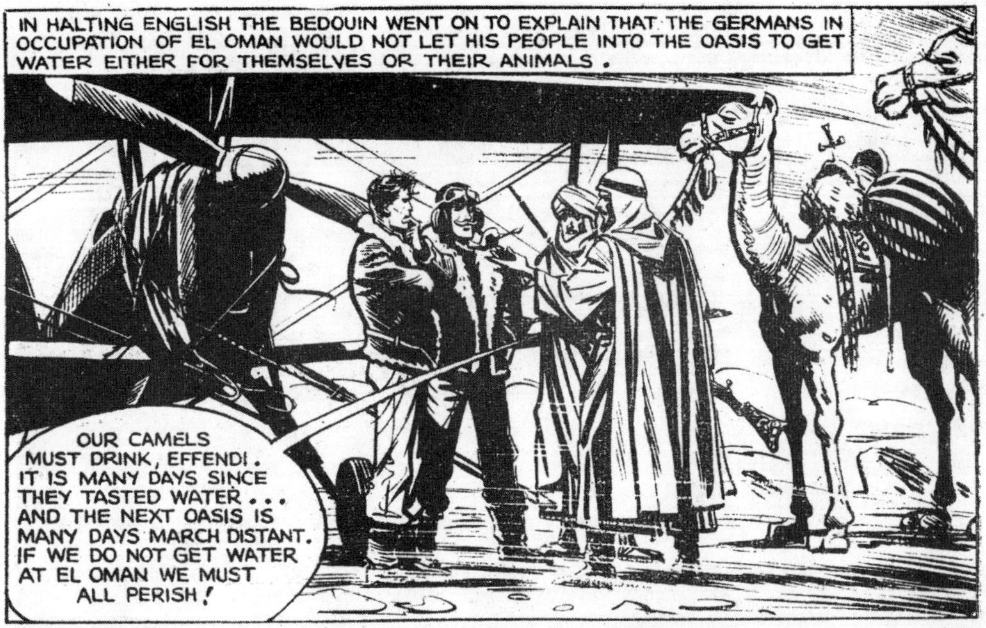
IN HALTING ENGLISH THE BEDOUIN WENT ON TO EXPLAIN THAT THE GERMANS IN OCCUPATION OF EL OMAN WOULD NOT LET HIS PEOPLE INTO THE OASIS TO GET WATER EITHER FOR THEMSELVES OR THEIR ANIMALS.
OUR CAMELS MUST DRINK, EFFENDI. IT IS MANY DAYS SINCE THEY TASTED WATER... AND THE NEXT OASIS IS MANY DAYS MARCH DISTANT. IF WE DO NOT GET WATER AT EL OMAN WE MUST ALL PERISH!

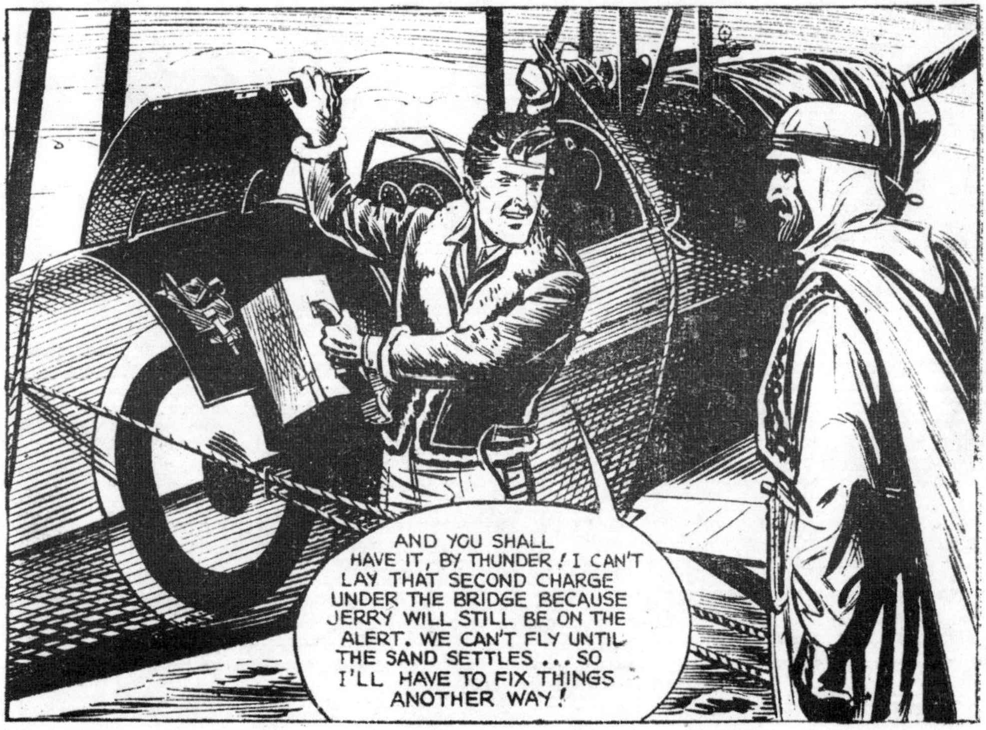
AND YOU SHALL HAVE IT, BY THUNDER! I CAN'T LAY THAT SECOND CHARGE UNDER THE BRIDGE BECAUSE JERRY WILL STILL BE ON THE ALERT. WE CAN'T FLY UNTIL THE SAND SETTLES ... SO I'LL HAVE TO FIX THINGS ANOTHER WAY!

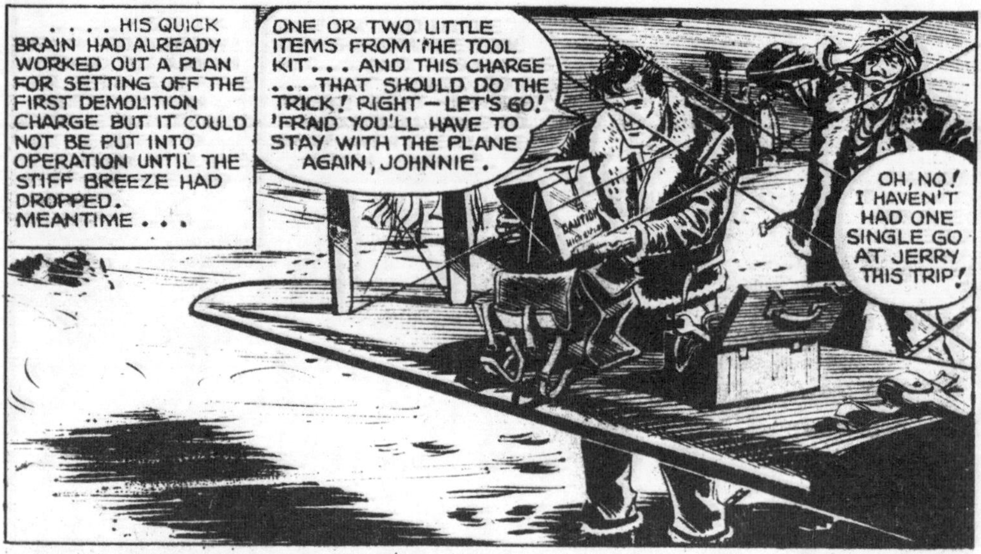
. . . . HIS QUICK BRAIN HAD ALREADY WORKED OUT A PLAN FOR SETTING OFF THE FIRST DEMOLITION CHARGE BUT IT COULD NOT BE PUT INTO OPERATION UNTIL THE STIFF BREEZE HAD DROPPED. MEANTIME . . .
ONE OR TWO LITTLE ITEMS FROM THE TOOL KIT . . . AND THIS CHARGE . . . THAT SHOULD DO THE TRICK! RIGHT — LET'S GO! 'FRAID YOU'LL HAVE TO STAY WITH THE PLANE AGAIN, JOHNNIE.
OH, NO! I HAVEN'T HAD ONE SINGLE GO AT JERRY THIS TRIP!

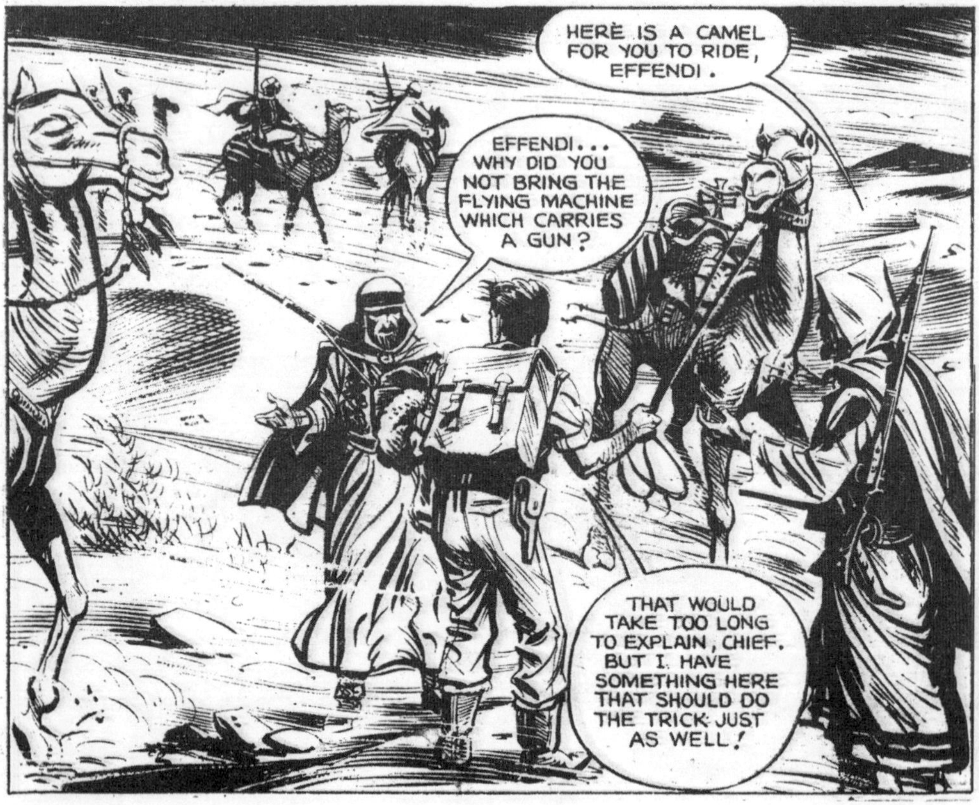
HERE IS A CAMEL FOR YOU TO RIDE, EFFENDI.
EFFENDI . . . WHY DID YOU NOT BRING THE FLYING MACHINE WHICH CARRIES A GUN?
THAT WOULD TAKE TOO LONG TO EXPLAIN, CHIEF. BUT I HAVE SOMETHING HERE THAT SHOULD DO THE TRICK JUST AS WELL!

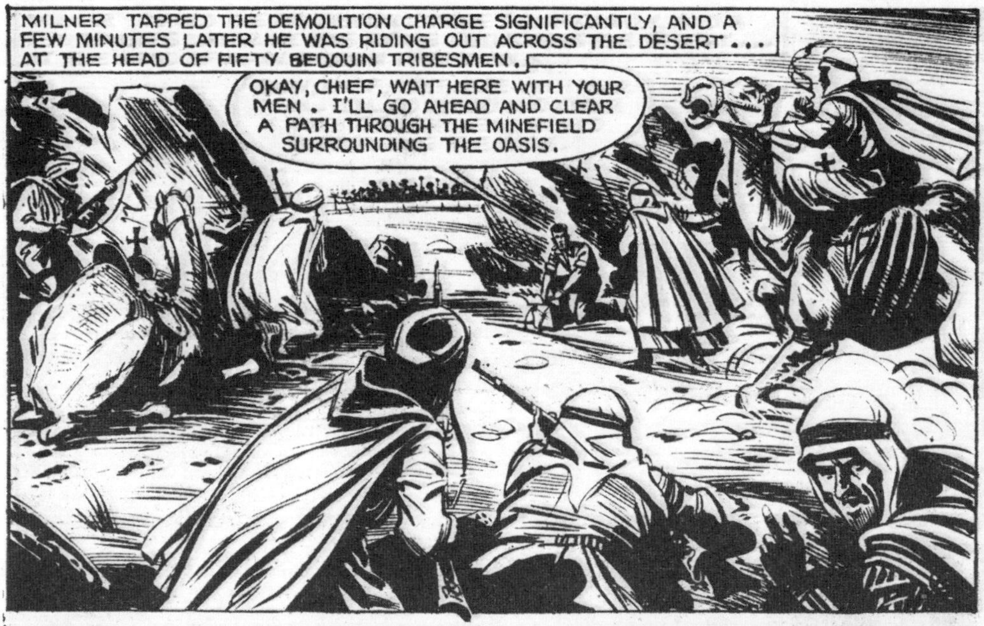
MILNER TAPPED THE DEMOLITION CHARGE SIGNIFICANTLY, AND A FEW MINUTES LATER HE WAS RIDING OUT ACROSS THE DESERT ... AT THE HEAD OF FIFTY BEDOUIN TRIBESMEN.
OKAY, CHIEF, WAIT HERE WITH YOUR MEN. I'LL GO AHEAD AND CLEAR A PATH THROUGH THE MINEFIELD SURROUNDING THE OASIS.

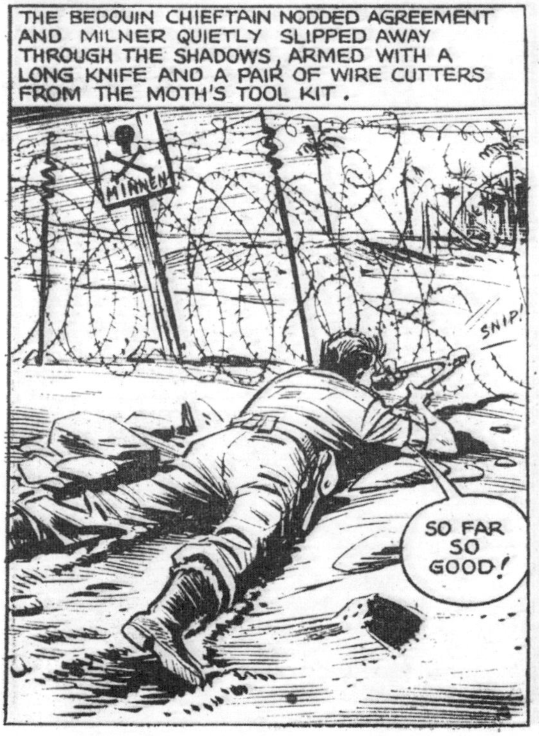
THE BEDOUIN CHIEFTAIN NODDED AGREEMENT AND MILNER QUIETLY SLIPPED AWAY THROUGH THE SHADOWS, ARMED WITH A LONG KNIFE AND A PAIR OF WIRE CUTTERS FROM THE MOTH'S TOOL KIT.
MINNEN
SNIP!
SO FAR SO GOOD!

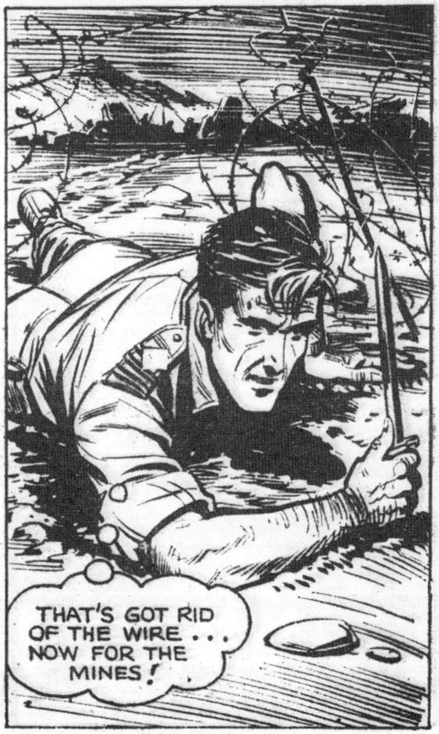
THAT'S GOT RID OF THE WIRE ... NOW FOR THE MINES!

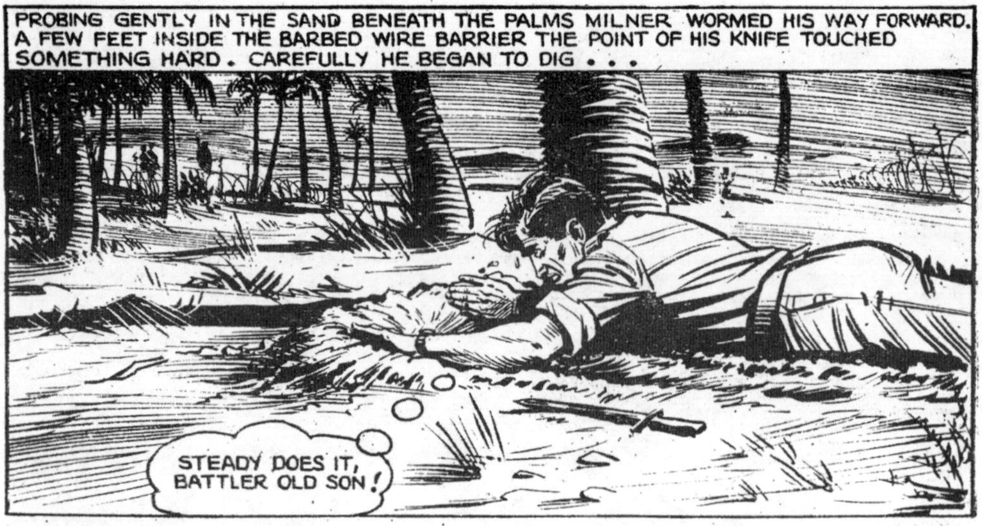
PROBING GENTLY IN THE SAND BENEATH THE PALMS MILNER WORMED HIS WAY FORWARD. A FEW FEET INSIDE THE BARBED WIRE BARRIER THE POINT OF HIS KNIFE TOUCHED SOMETHING HARD. CAREFULLY HE BEGAN TO DIG . . .
STEADY DOES IT, BATTLER OLD SON!

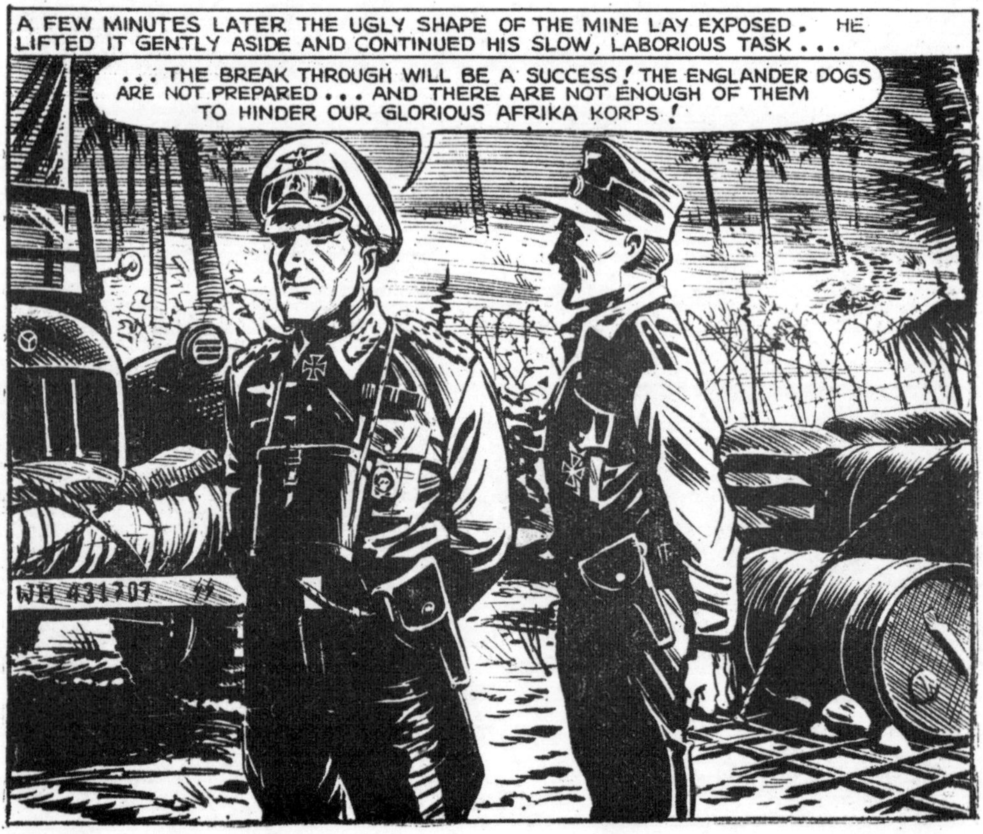
A FEW MINUTES LATER THE UGLY SHAPE OF THE MINE LAY EXPOSED. HE LIFTED IT GENTLY ASIDE AND CONTINUED HIS SLOW, LABORIOUS TASK . . .
. . . THE BREAK THROUGH WILL BE A SUCCESS! THE ENGLANDER DOGS ARE NOT PREPARED . . . AND THERE ARE NOT ENOUGH OF THEM TO HINDER OUR GLORIOUS AFRIKA KORPS!

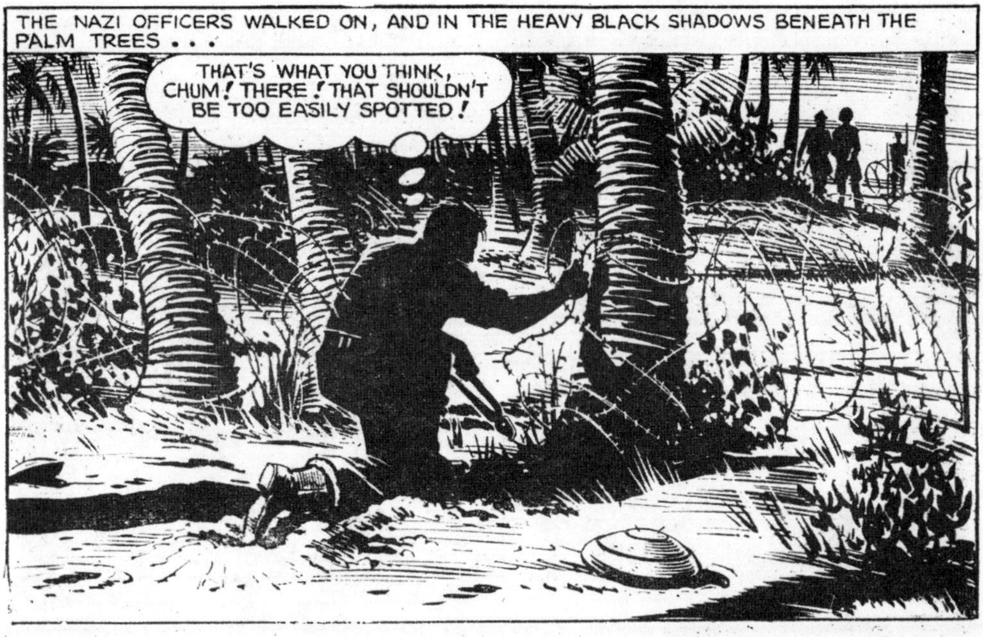
THE NAZI OFFICERS WALKED ON, AND IN THE HEAVY BLACK SHADOWS BENEATH THE PALM TREES . . .
THAT'S WHAT YOU THINK, CHUM! THERE! THAT SHOULDN'T BE TOO EASILY SPOTTED!

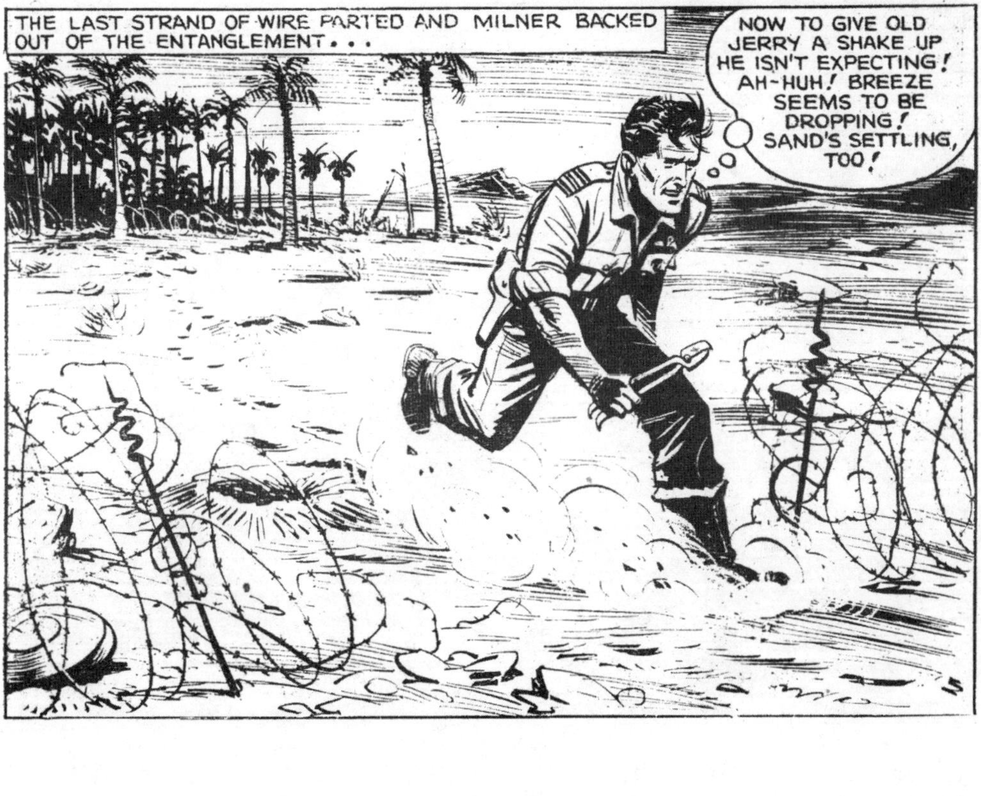
THE LAST STRAND OF WIRE PARTED AND MILNER BACKED OUT OF THE ENTANGLEMENT . . .
NOW TO GIVE OLD JERRY A SHAKE UP HE ISN'T EXPECTING! AH-HUH! BREEZE SEEMS TO BE DROPPING! SAND'S SETTLING, TOO!

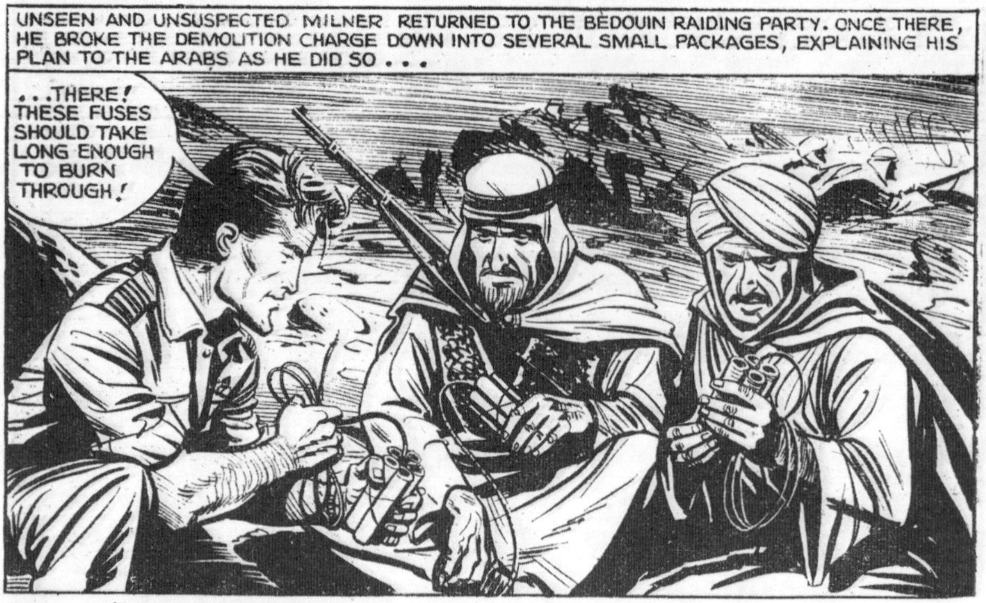
UNSEEN AND UNSUSPECTED MILNER RETURNED TO THE BEDOUIN RAIDING PARTY. ONCE THERE, HE BROKE THE DEMOLITION CHARGE DOWN INTO SEVERAL SMALL PACKAGES, EXPLAINING HIS PLAN TO THE ARABS AS HE DID SO . . .
. . .THERE! THESE FUSES SHOULD TAKE LONG ENOUGH TO BURN THROUGH!

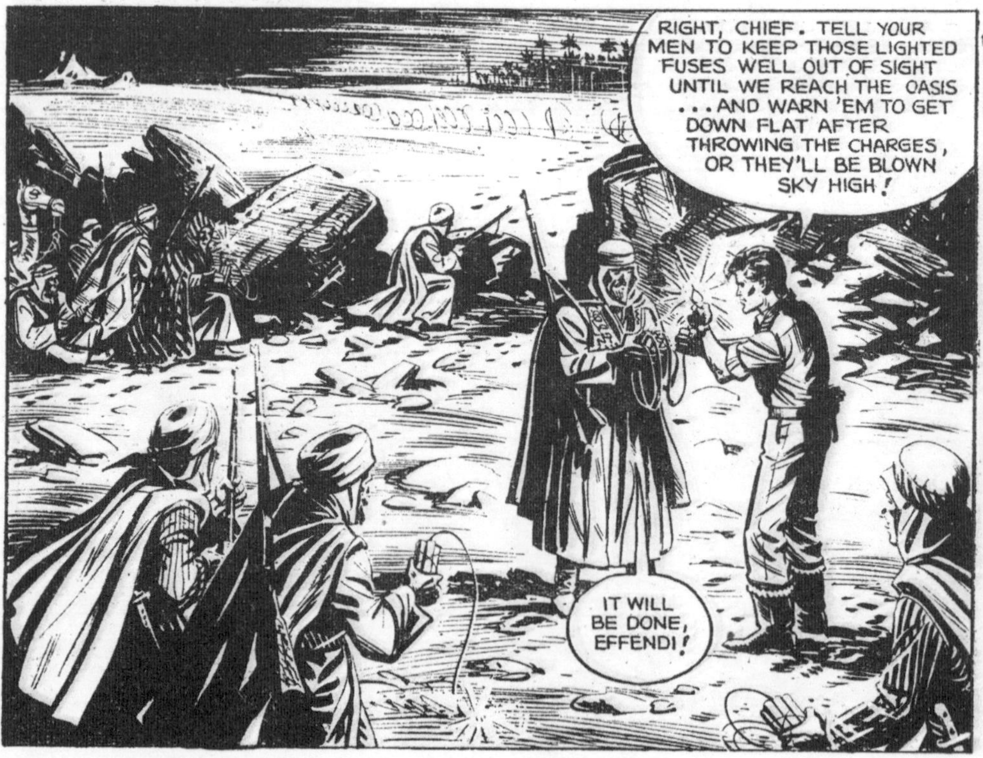
RIGHT, CHIEF. TELL YOUR MEN TO KEEP THOSE LIGHTED FUSES WELL OUT OF SIGHT UNTIL WE REACH THE OASIS . . . AND WARN 'EM TO GET DOWN FLAT AFTER THROWING THE CHARGES, OR THEY'LL BE BLOWN SKY HIGH!
IT WILL BE DONE, EFFENDI!

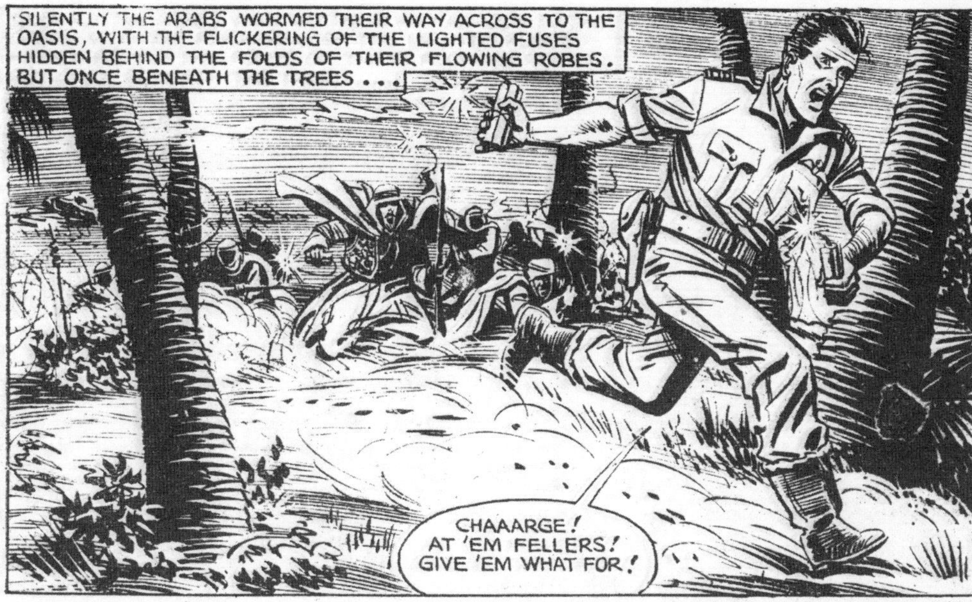
SILENTLY THE ARABS WORMED THEIR WAY ACROSS TO THE OASIS, WITH THE FLICKERING OF THE LIGHTED FUSES HIDDEN BEHIND THE FOLDS OF THEIR FLOWING ROBES. BUT ONCE BENEATH THE TREES . . .
CHAAARGE! AT 'EM FELLERS! GIVE 'EM WHAT FOR!

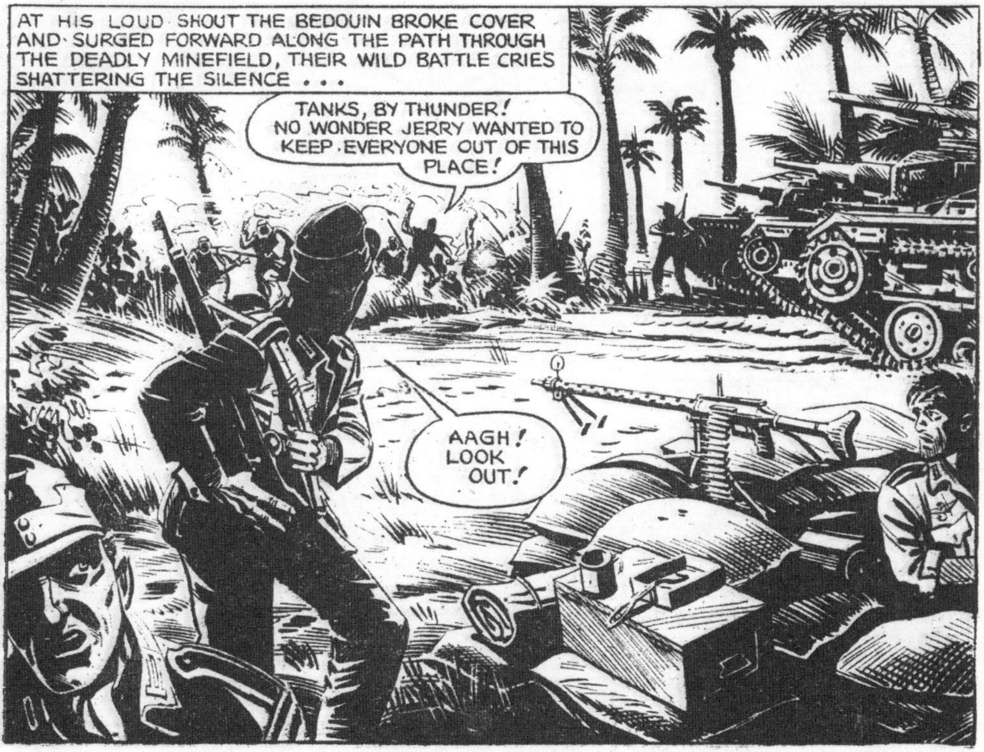
AT HIS LOUD SHOUT THE BEDOUIN BROKE COVER AND SURGED FORWARD ALONG THE PATH THROUGH THE DEADLY MINEFIELD, THEIR WILD BATTLE CRIES SHATTERING THE SILENCE . . .
TANKS, BY THUNDER! NO WONDER JERRY WANTED TO KEEP EVERYONE OUT OF THIS PLACE!
AAGH! LOOK OUT!

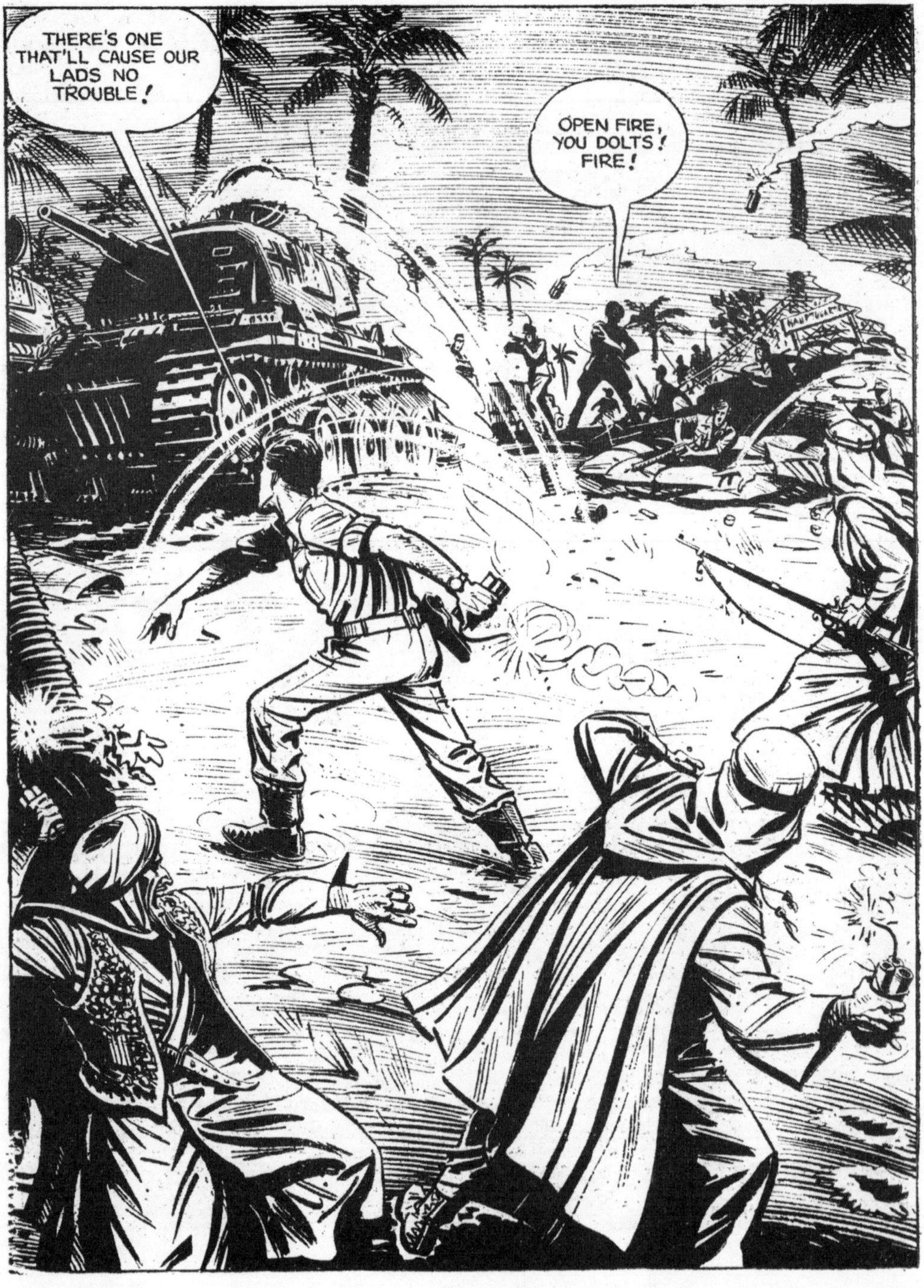
THERE'S ONE THAT'LL CAUSE OUR LADS NO TROUBLE!
OPEN FIRE, YOU DOLTS! FIRE!

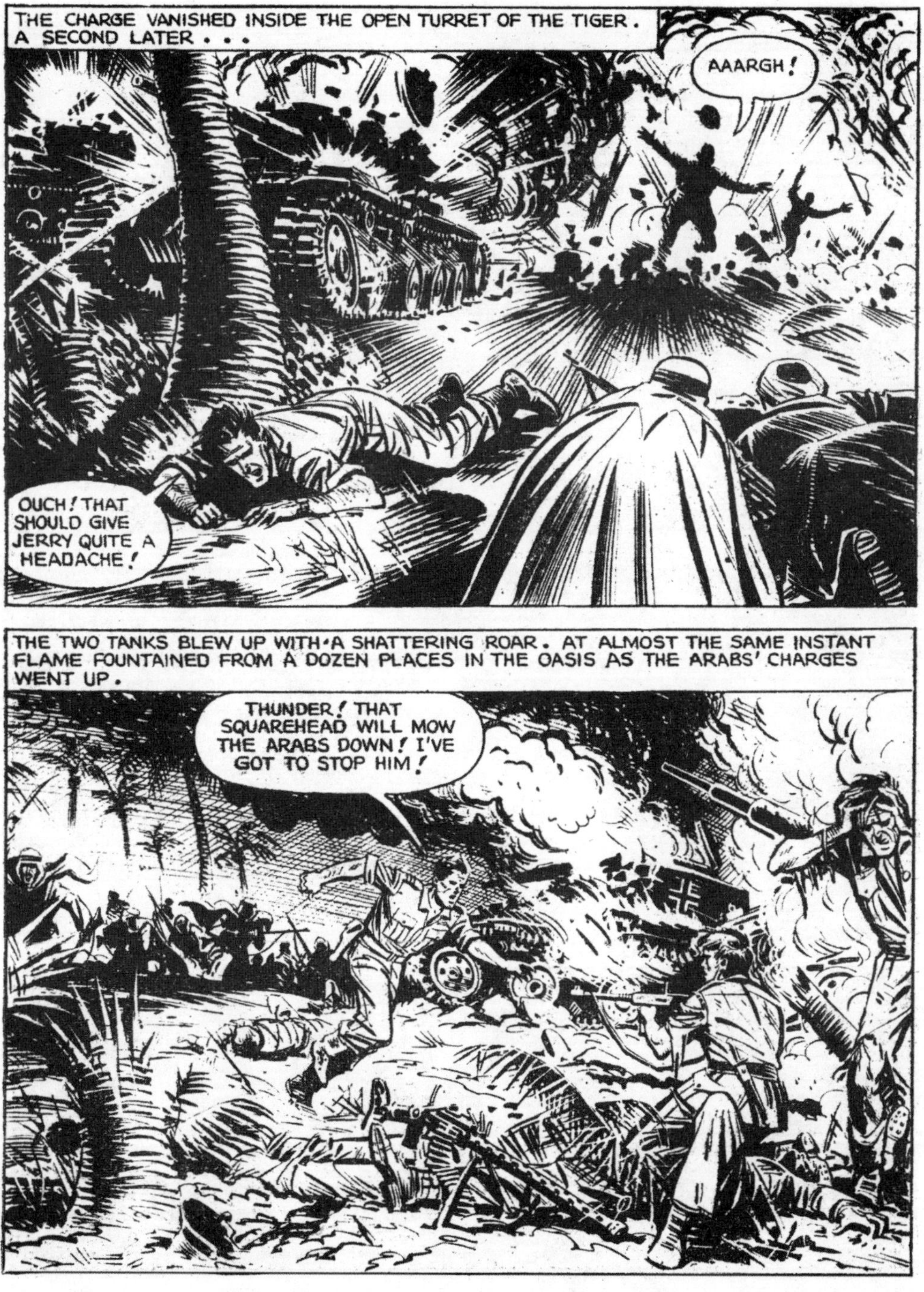
THE CHARGE VANISHED INSIDE THE OPEN TURRET OF THE TIGER. A SECOND LATER . . .
AAARGH!
OUCH! THAT SHOULD GIVE JERRY QUITE A HEADACHE!
THE TWO TANKS BLEW UP WITH A SHATTERING ROAR. AT ALMOST THE SAME INSTANT FLAME FOUNTAINED FROM A DOZEN PLACES IN THE OASIS AS THE ARABS' CHARGES WENT UP.
THUNDER! THAT SQUAREHEAD WILL MOW THE ARABS DOWN! I'VE GOT TO STOP HIM!

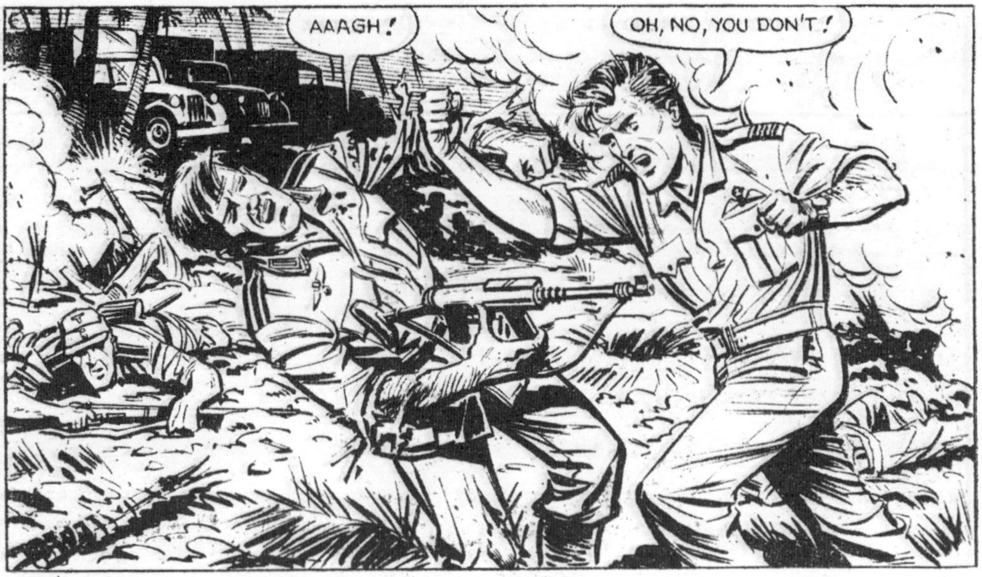
AAAGH!
OH, NO, YOU DON'T!

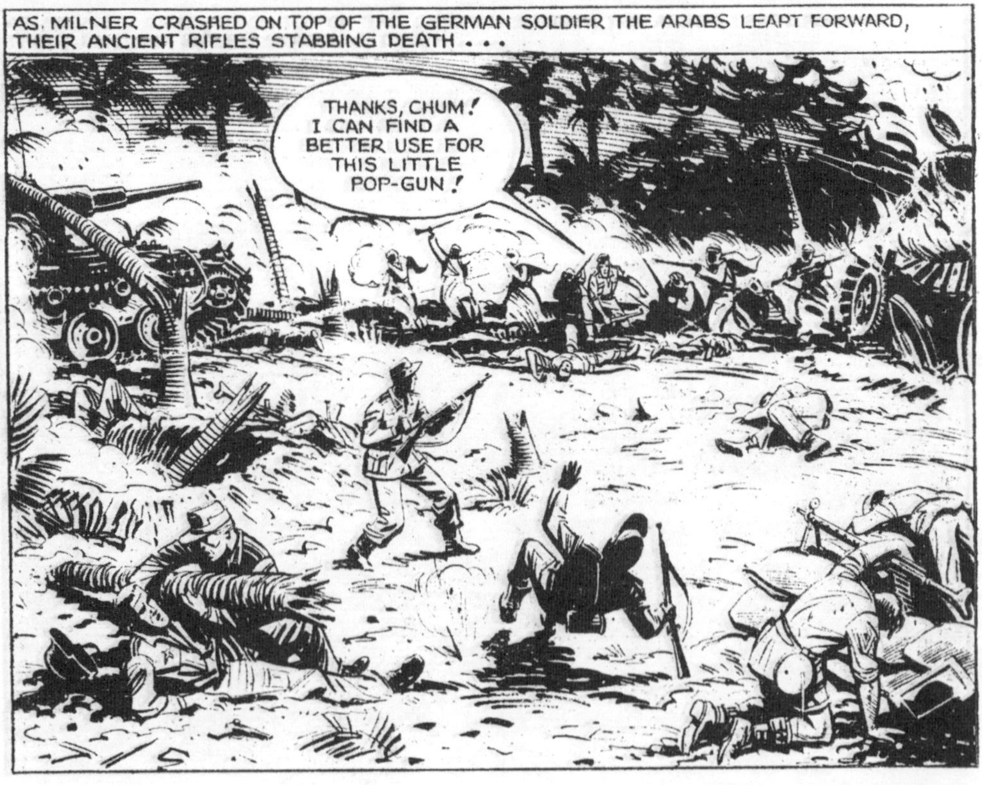
AS MILNER CRASHED ON TOP OF THE GERMAN SOLDIER THE ARABS LEAPT FORWARD, THEIR ANCIENT RIFLES STABBING DEATH . . .
THANKS, CHUM! I CAN FIND A BETTER USE FOR THIS LITTLE POP-GUN!

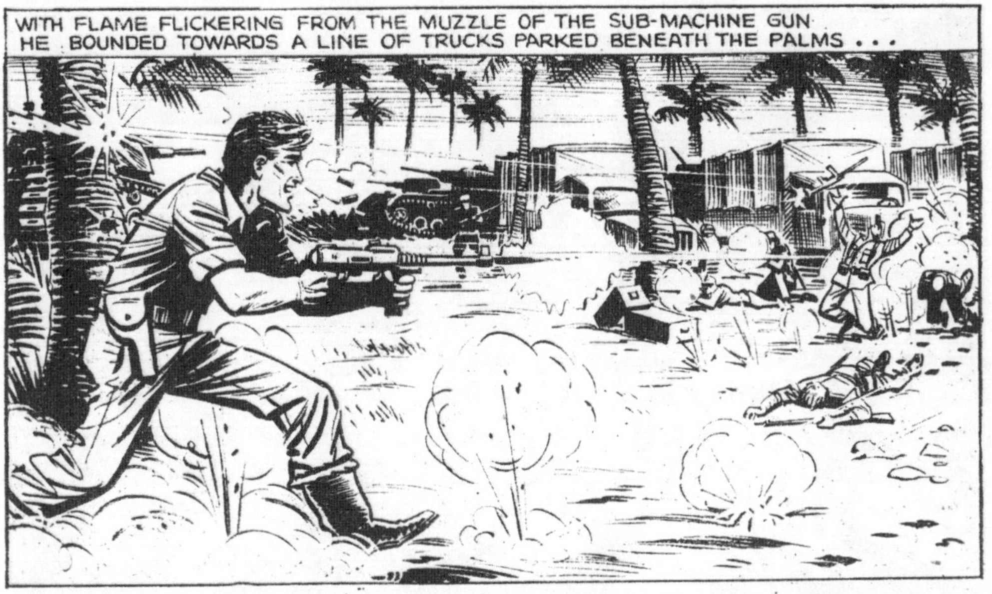
WITH FLAME FLICKERING FROM THE MUZZLE OF THE SUB-MACHINE GUN HE BOUNDED TOWARDS A LINE OF TRUCKS PARKED BENEATH THE PALMS . . .

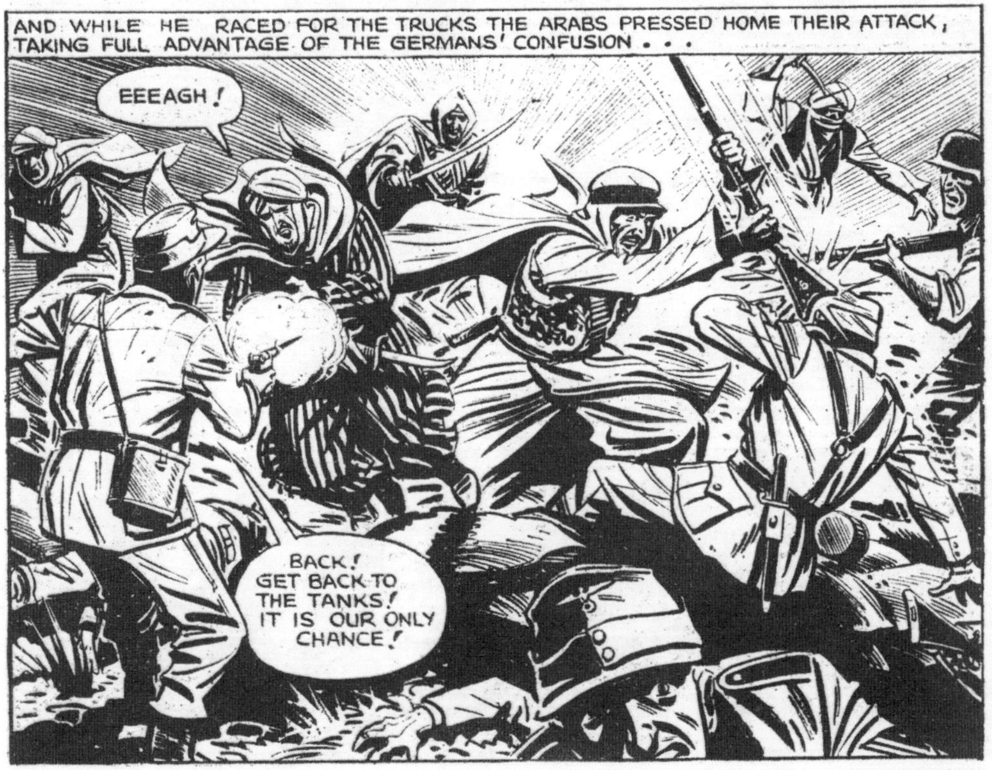
AND WHILE HE RACED FOR THE TRUCKS THE ARABS PRESSED HOME THEIR ATTACK, TAKING FULL ADVANTAGE OF THE GERMANS' CONFUSION . . .
EEEAGH!
BACK! GET BACK TO THE TANKS! IT IS OUR ONLY CHANCE!

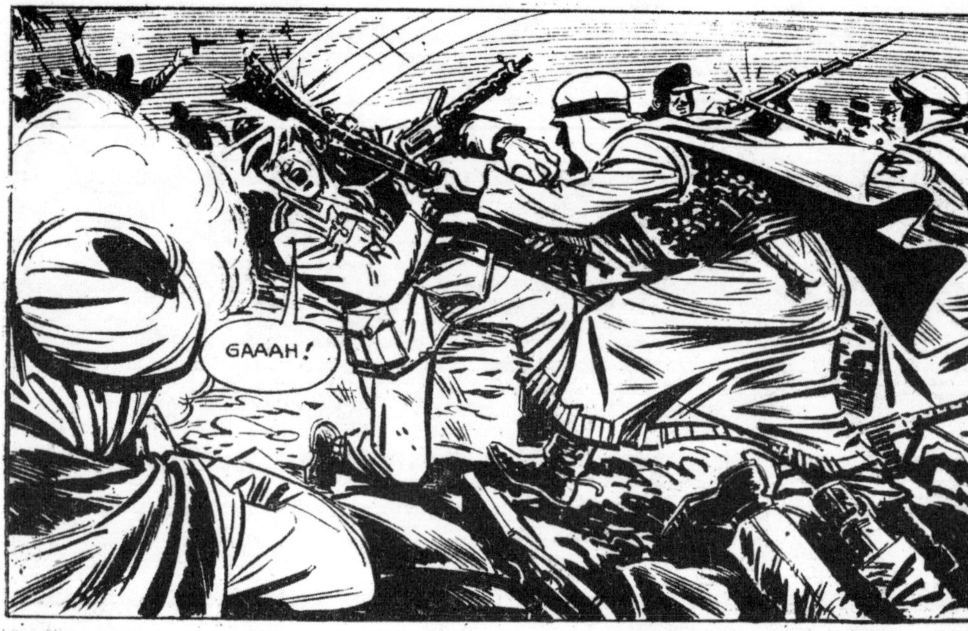
GAAAH!

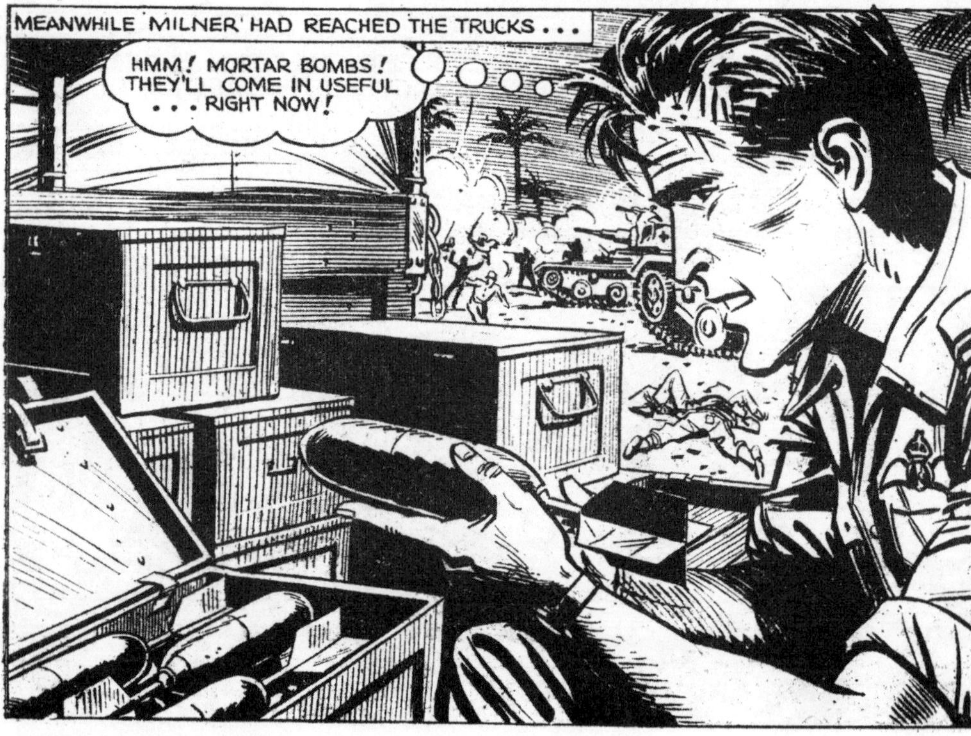
MEANWHILE MILNER HAD REACHED THE TRUCKS ...
HMM! MORTAR BOMBS! THEY'LL COME IN USEFUL ... RIGHT NOW!

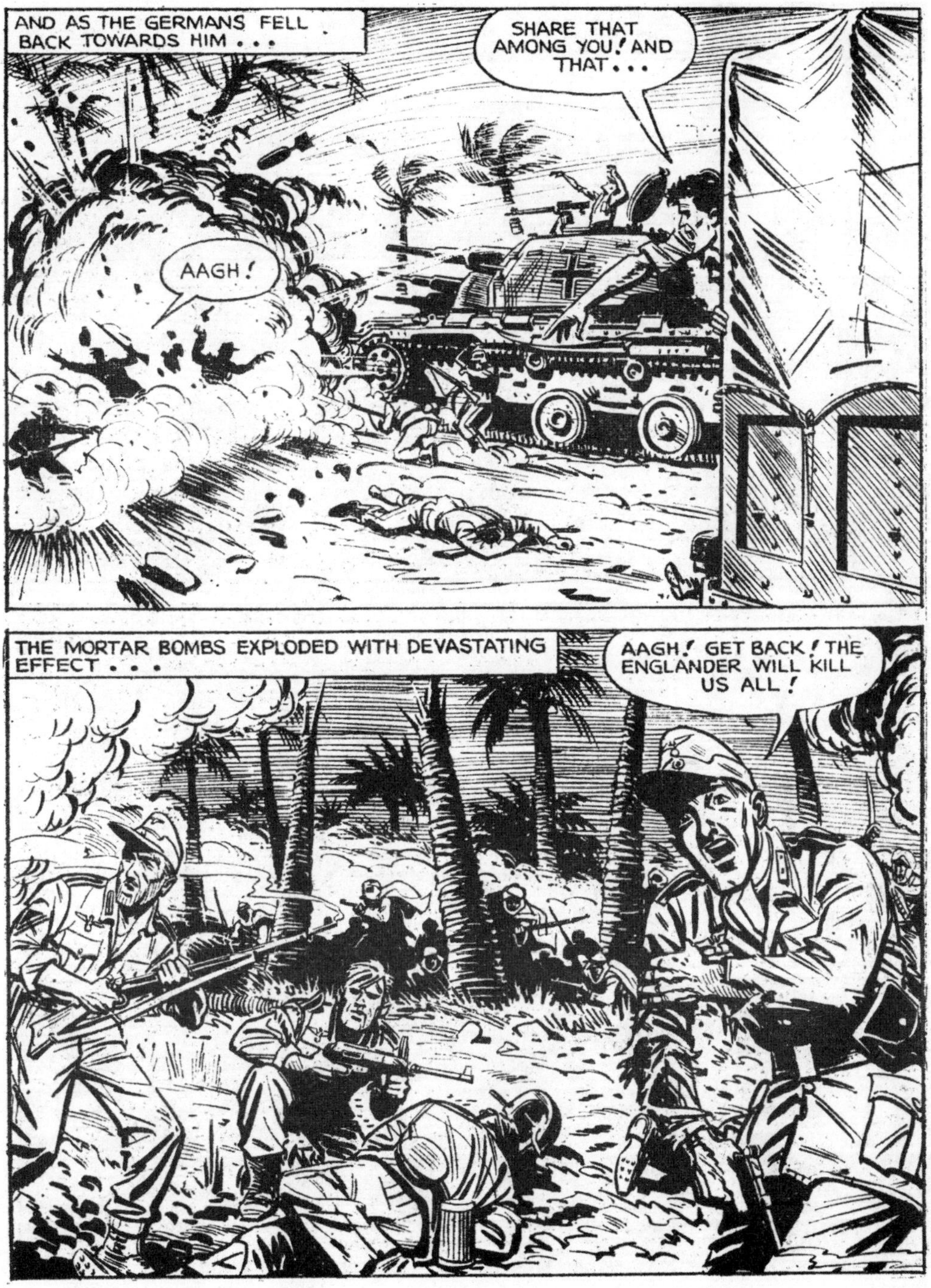
AND AS THE GERMANS FELL BACK TOWARDS HIM . . .
SHARE THAT AMONG YOU! AND THAT . . .
AAGH!
THE MORTAR BOMBS EXPLODED WITH DEVASTATING EFFECT . . .
AAGH! GET BACK! THE ENGLANDER WILL KILL US ALL!

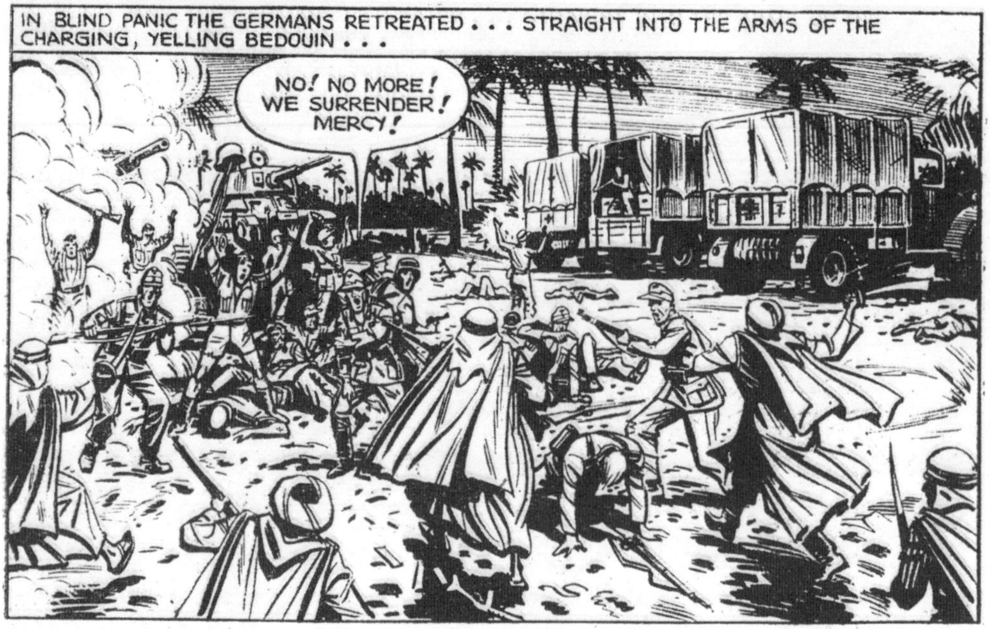
IN BLIND PANIC THE GERMANS RETREATED . . . STRAIGHT INTO THE ARMS OF THE CHARGING, YELLING BEDOUIN . . .
NO! NO MORE! WE SURRENDER! MERCY!

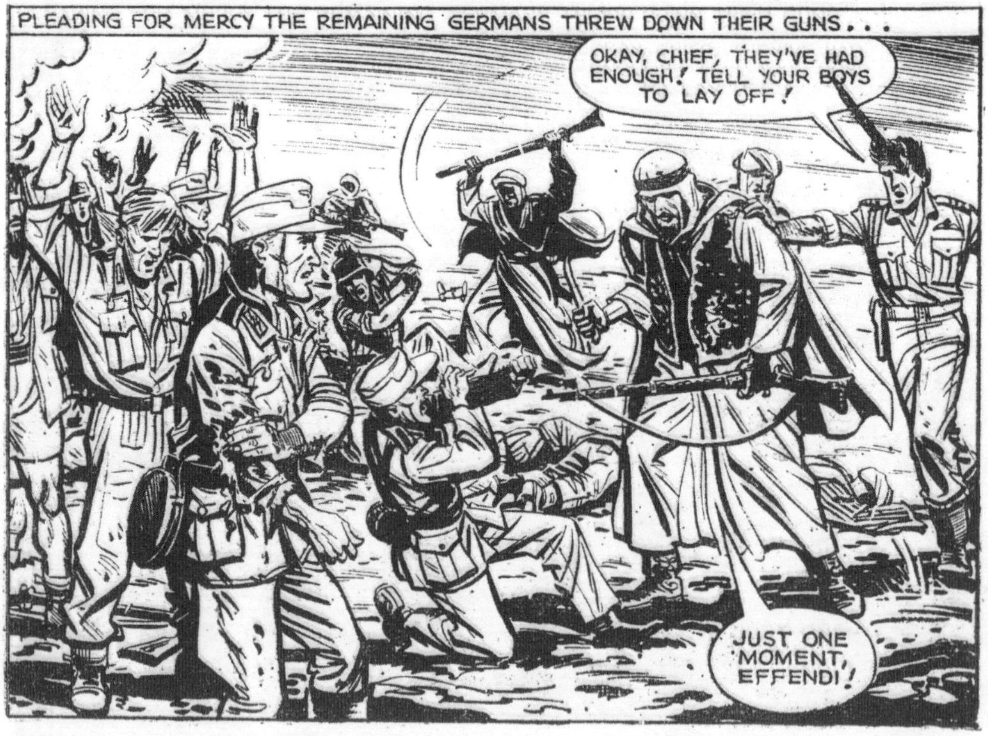
PLEADING FOR MERCY THE REMAINING GERMANS THREW DOWN THEIR GUNS . . .
OKAY, CHIEF, THEY'VE HAD ENOUGH! TELL YOUR BOYS TO LAY OFF!
JUST ONE MOMENT, EFFENDI!

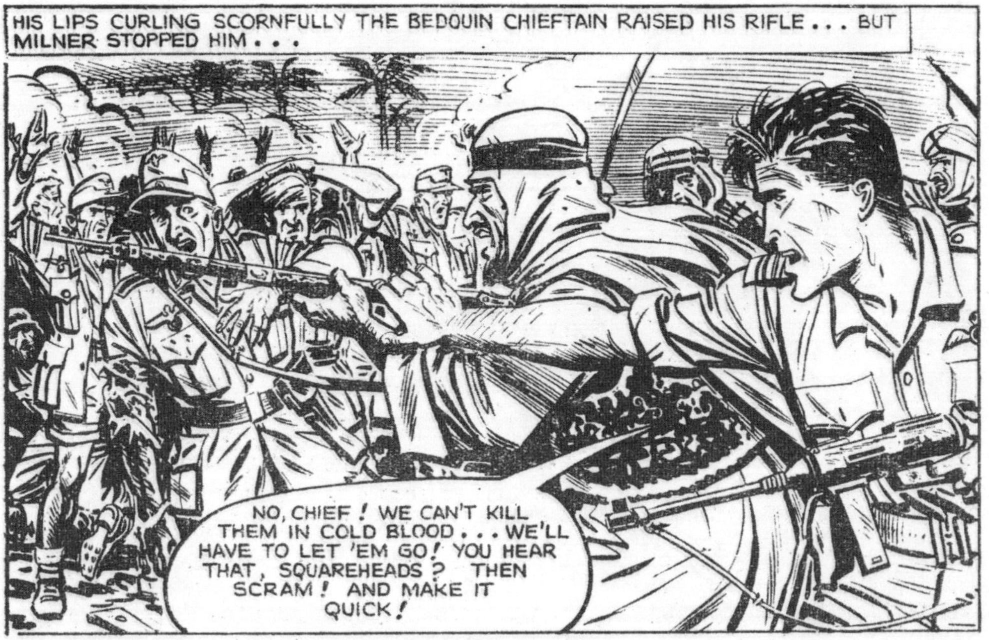
HIS LIPS CURLING SCORNFULLY THE BEDOUIN CHIEFTAIN RAISED HIS RIFLE . . . BUT MILNER STOPPED HIM . . .
NO, CHIEF ! WE CAN'T KILL THEM IN COLD BLOOD . . . WE'LL HAVE TO LET 'EM GO ! YOU HEAR THAT, SQUAREHEADS ? THEN SCRAM ! AND MAKE IT QUICK !

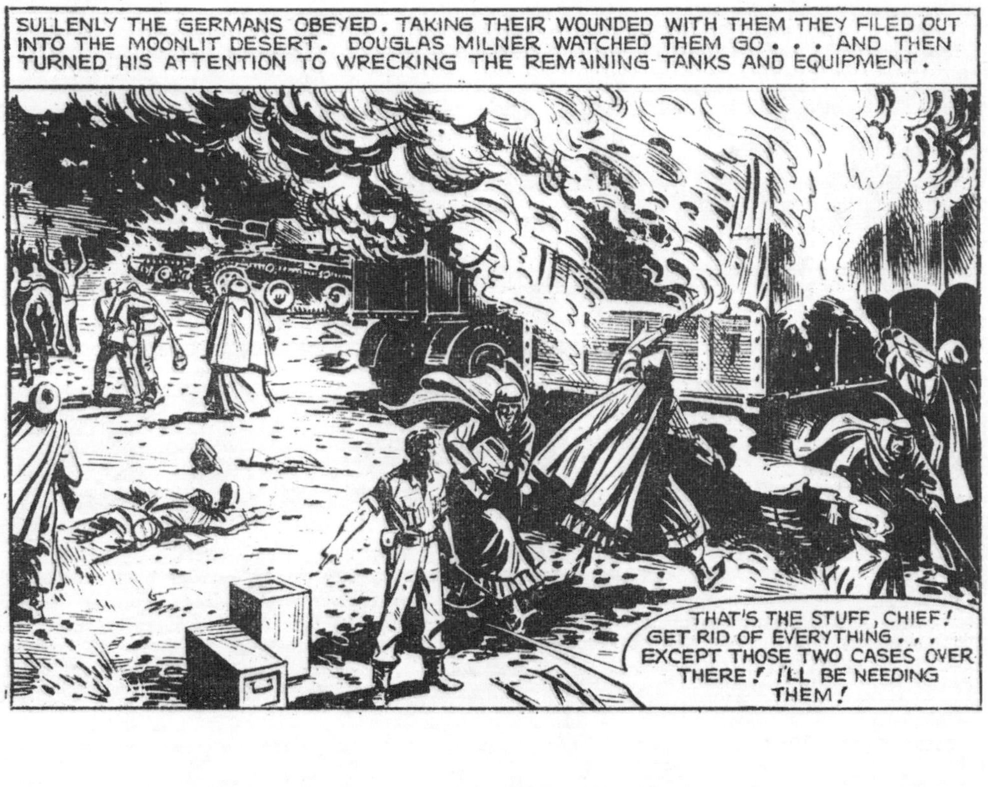
SULLENLY THE GERMANS OBEYED. TAKING THEIR WOUNDED WITH THEM THEY FILED OUT INTO THE MOONLIT DESERT. DOUGLAS MILNER WATCHED THEM GO . . . AND THEN TURNED HIS ATTENTION TO WRECKING THE REMAINING TANKS AND EQUIPMENT.
THAT'S THE STUFF, CHIEF ! GET RID OF EVERYTHING . . . EXCEPT THOSE TWO CASES OVER THERE ! I'LL BE NEEDING THEM !

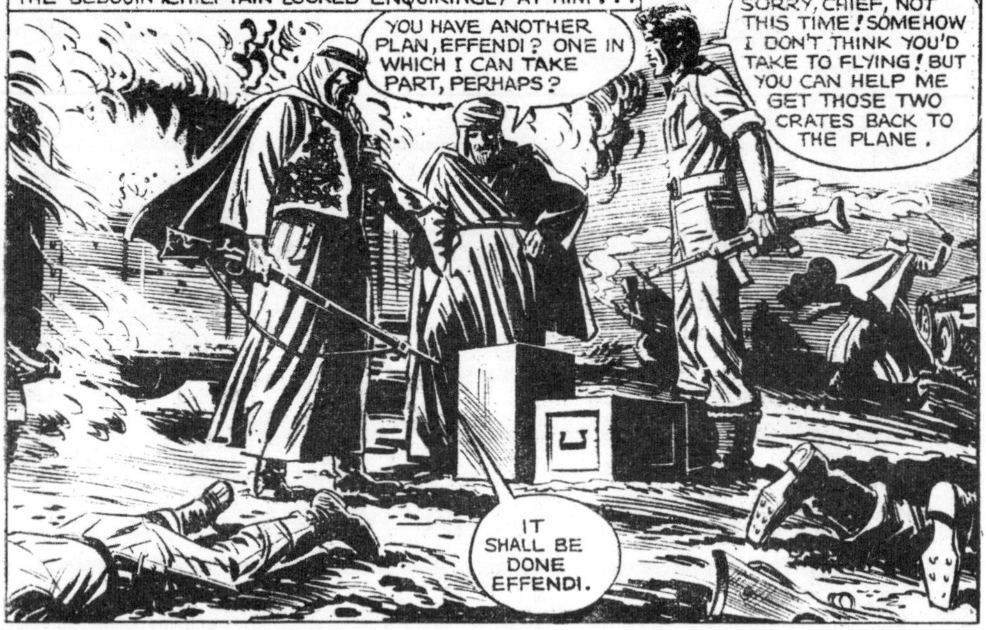
THE BEDOUIN CHIEFTAIN LOOKED ENQUIRINGLY AT HIM . . .
YOU HAVE ANOTHER PLAN, EFFENDI? ONE IN WHICH I CAN TAKE PART, PERHAPS?
SORRY, CHIEF, NOT THIS TIME! SOMEHOW I DON'T THINK YOU'D TAKE TO FLYING! BUT YOU CAN HELP ME GET THOSE TWO CRATES BACK TO THE PLANE.
IT SHALL BE DONE EFFENDI.

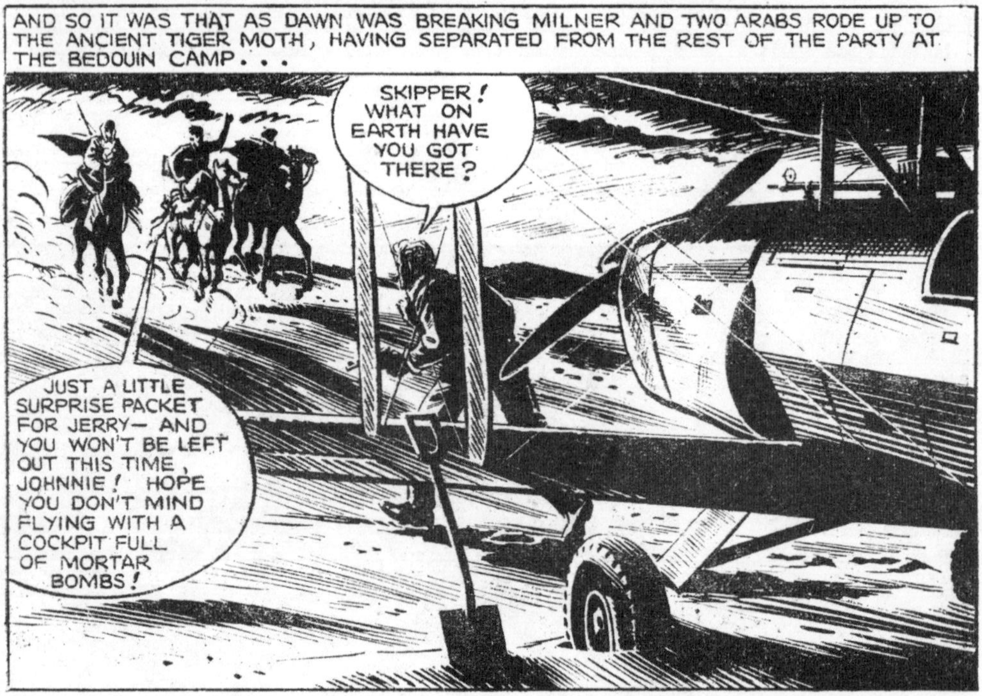
AND SO IT WAS THAT AS DAWN WAS BREAKING MILNER AND TWO ARABS RODE UP TO THE ANCIENT TIGER MOTH, HAVING SEPARATED FROM THE REST OF THE PARTY AT THE BEDOUIN CAMP . . .
SKIPPER! WHAT ON EARTH HAVE YOU GOT THERE?
JUST A LITTLE SURPRISE PACKET FOR JERRY— AND YOU WON'T BE LEFT OUT THIS TIME, JOHNNIE! HOPE YOU DON'T MIND FLYING WITH A COCKPIT FULL OF MORTAR BOMBS!

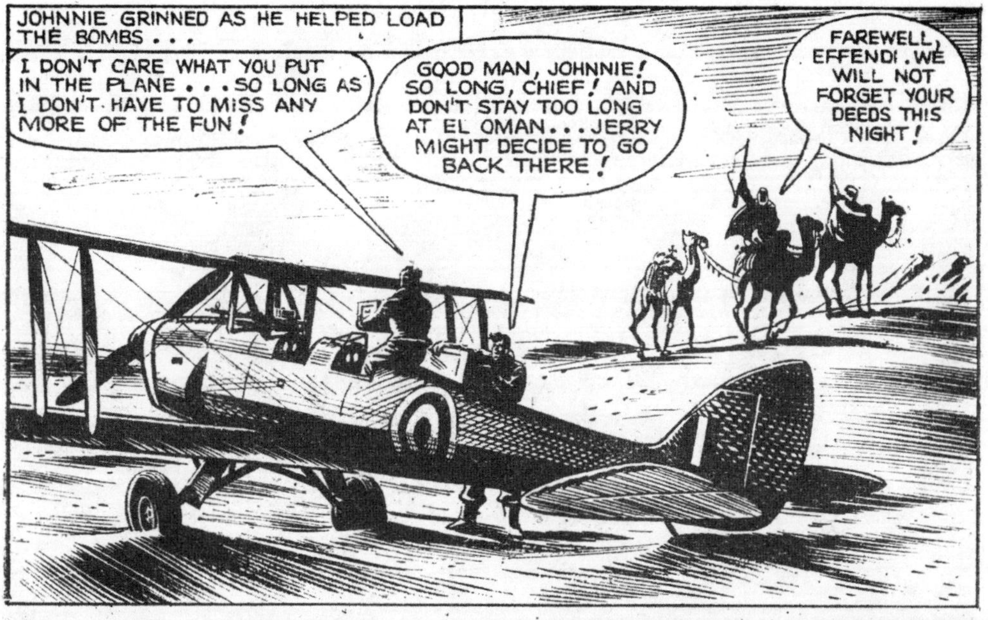
JOHNNIE GRINNED AS HE HELPED LOAD THE BOMBS . . .
I DON'T CARE WHAT YOU PUT IN THE PLANE . . . SO LONG AS I DON'T HAVE TO MISS ANY MORE OF THE FUN!
GOOD MAN, JOHNNIE! SO LONG, CHIEF! AND DON'T STAY TOO LONG AT EL OMAN . . . JERRY MIGHT DECIDE TO GO BACK THERE!
FAREWELL, EFFENDI. WE WILL NOT FORGET YOUR DEEDS THIS NIGHT!

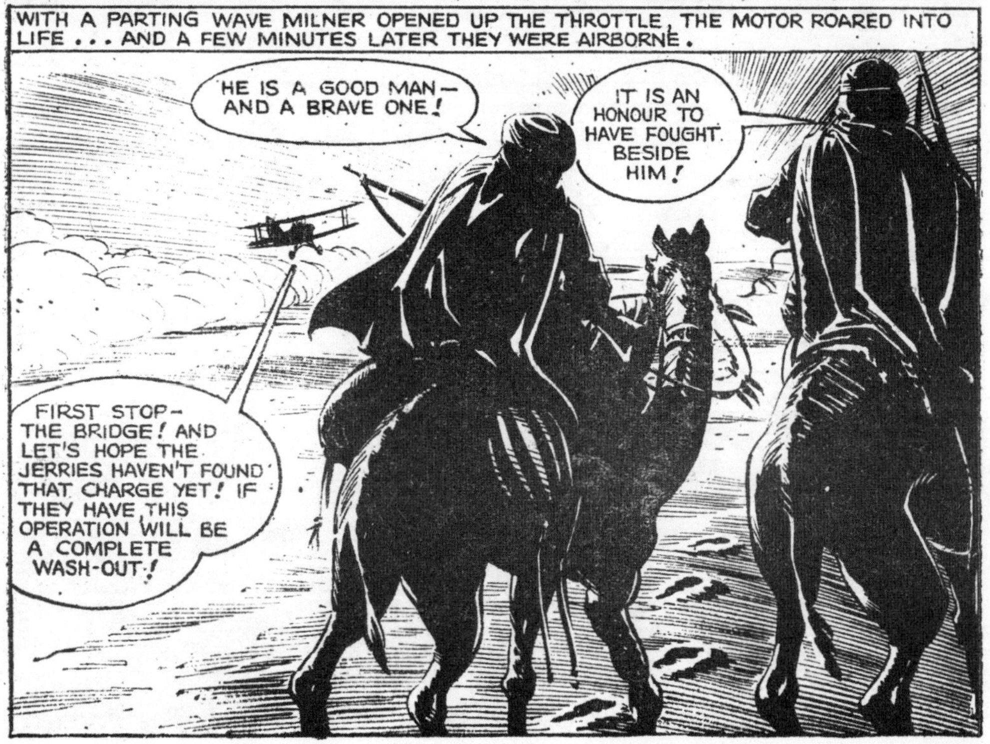
WITH A PARTING WAVE MILNER OPENED UP THE THROTTLE, THE MOTOR ROARED INTO LIFE . . . AND A FEW MINUTES LATER THEY WERE AIRBORNE.
HE IS A GOOD MAN— AND A BRAVE ONE!
IT IS AN HONOUR TO HAVE FOUGHT BESIDE HIM!
FIRST STOP— THE BRIDGE! AND LET'S HOPE THE JERRIES HAVEN'T FOUND THAT CHARGE YET! IF THEY HAVE, THIS OPERATION WILL BE A COMPLETE WASH-OUT!

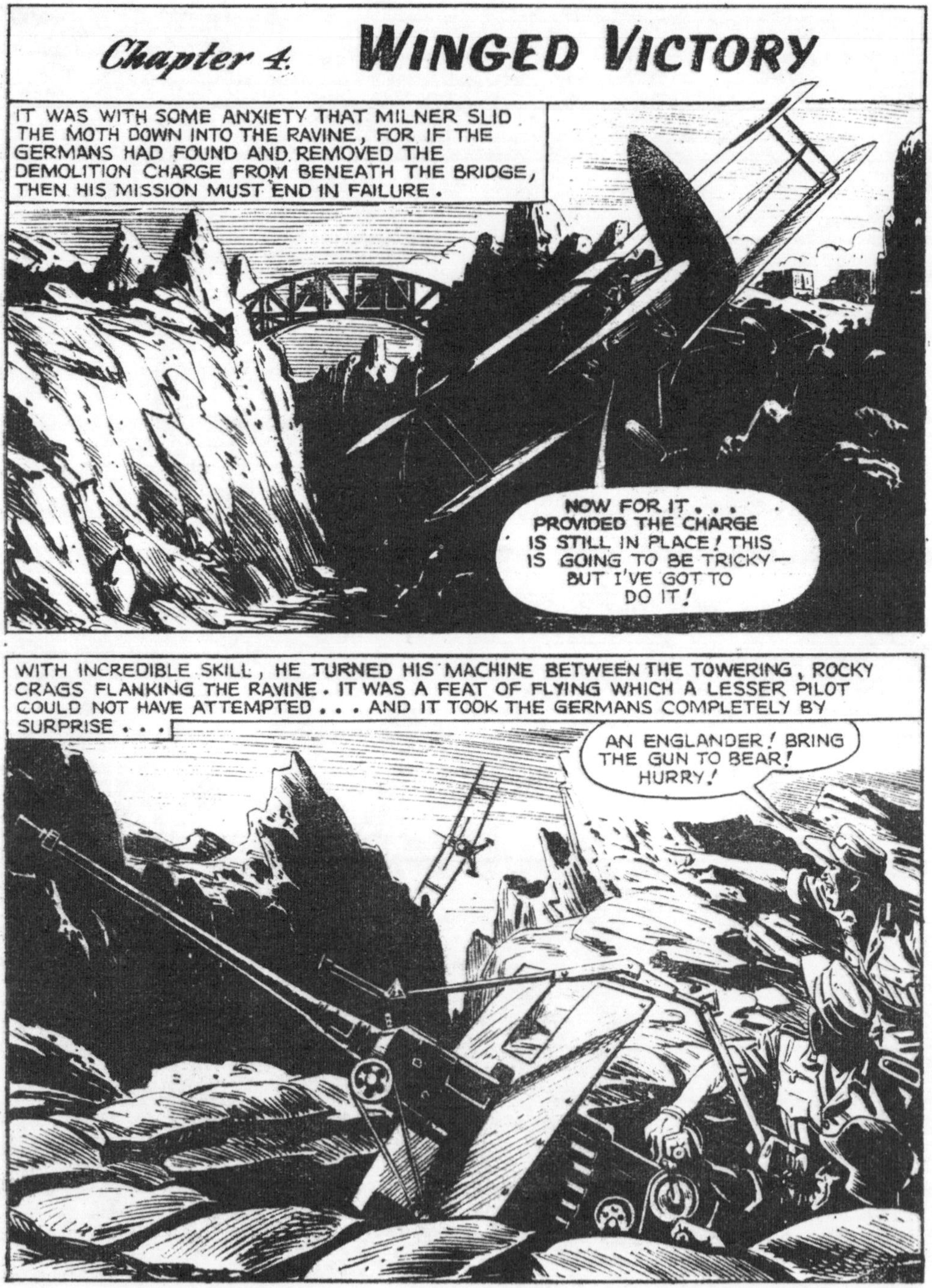
Chapter 4. WINGED VICTORY
IT WAS WITH SOME ANXIETY THAT MILNER SLID THE MOTH DOWN INTO THE RAVINE, FOR IF THE GERMANS HAD FOUND AND REMOVED THE DEMOLITION CHARGE FROM BENEATH THE BRIDGE, THEN HIS MISSION MUST END IN FAILURE.
NOW FOR IT... PROVIDED THE CHARGE IS STILL IN PLACE! THIS IS GOING TO BE TRICKY— BUT I'VE GOT TO DO IT!
WITH INCREDIBLE SKILL, HE TURNED HIS MACHINE BETWEEN THE TOWERING, ROCKY CRAGS FLANKING THE RAVINE. IT WAS A FEAT OF FLYING WHICH A LESSER PILOT COULD NOT HAVE ATTEMPTED... AND IT TOOK THE GERMANS COMPLETELY BY SURPRISE...
AN ENGLANDER! BRING THE GUN TO BEAR! HURRY!

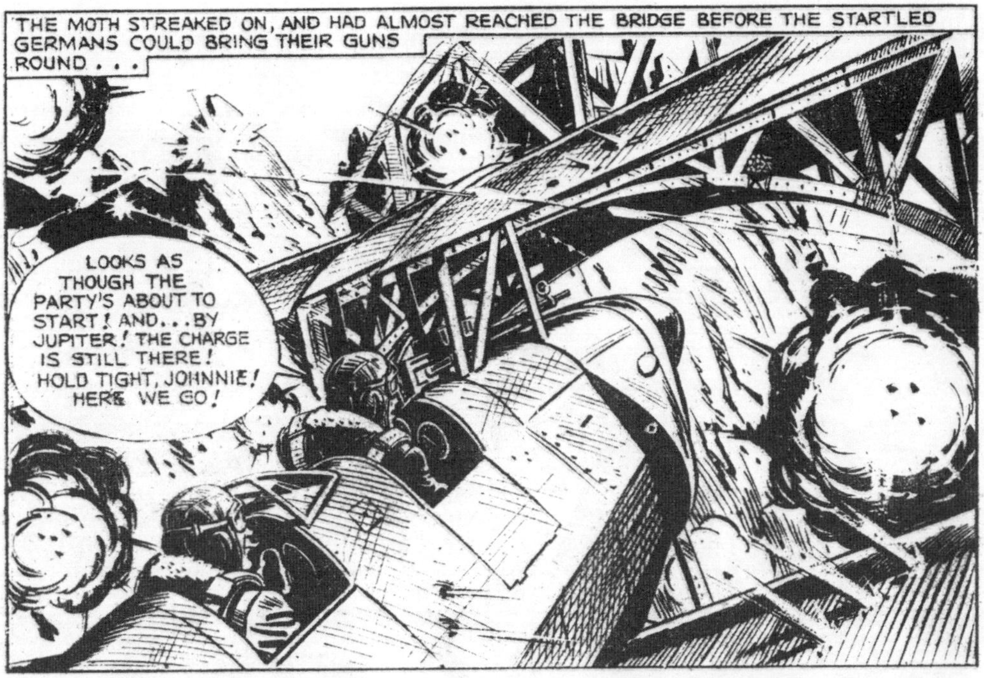
THE MOTH STREAKED ON, AND HAD ALMOST REACHED THE BRIDGE BEFORE THE STARTLED GERMANS COULD BRING THEIR GUNS ROUND . . .
LOOKS AS THOUGH THE PARTY'S ABOUT TO START! AND...BY JUPITER! THE CHARGE IS STILL THERE! HOLD TIGHT, JOHNNIE! HERE WE GO!

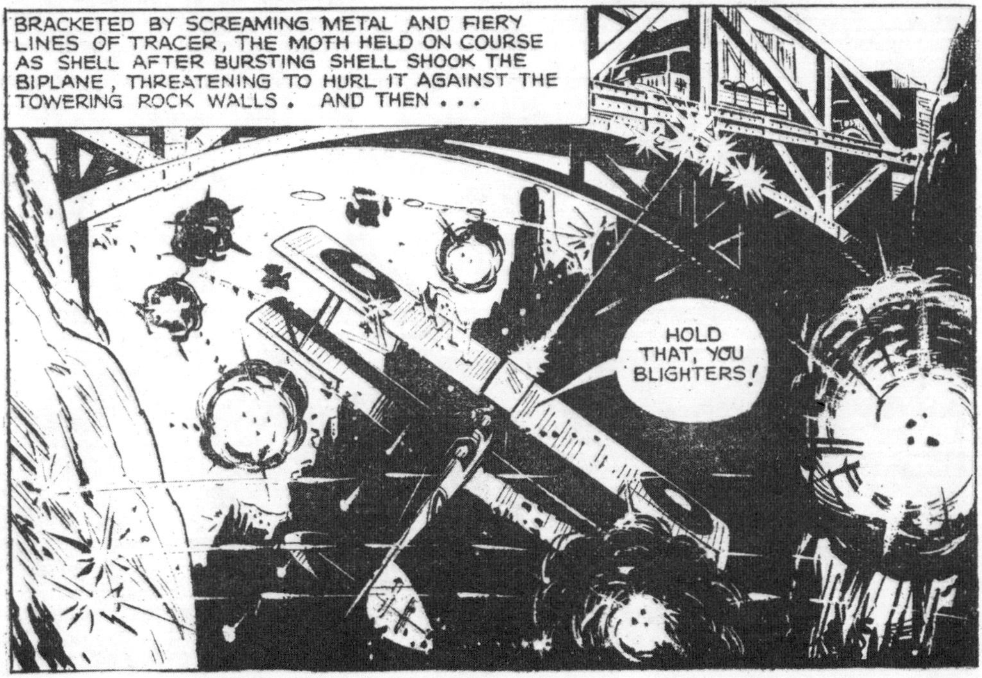
BRACKETED BY SCREAMING METAL AND FIERY LINES OF TRACER, THE MOTH HELD ON COURSE AS SHELL AFTER BURSTING SHELL SHOOK THE BIPLANE, THREATENING TO HURL IT AGAINST THE TOWERING ROCK WALLS. AND THEN . . .
HOLD THAT, YOU BLIGHTERS!

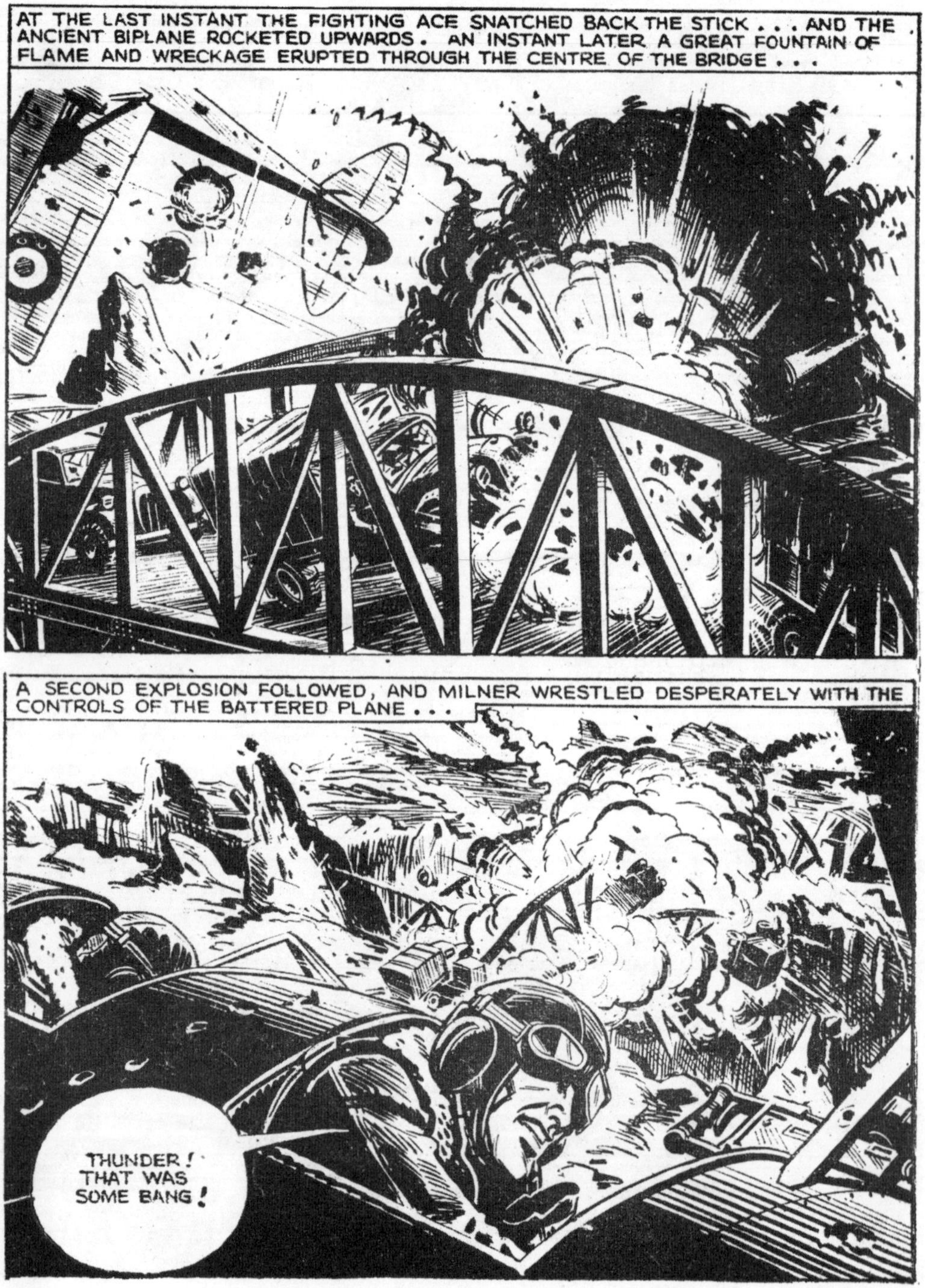
AT THE LAST INSTANT THE FIGHTING ACE SNATCHED BACK THE STICK . . . AND THE ANCIENT BIPLANE ROCKETED UPWARDS. AN INSTANT LATER A GREAT FOUNTAIN OF FLAME AND WRECKAGE ERUPTED THROUGH THE CENTRE OF THE BRIDGE . . .
A SECOND EXPLOSION FOLLOWED, AND MILNER WRESTLED DESPERATELY WITH THE CONTROLS OF THE BATTERED PLANE . . .
THUNDER! THAT WAS SOME BANG!

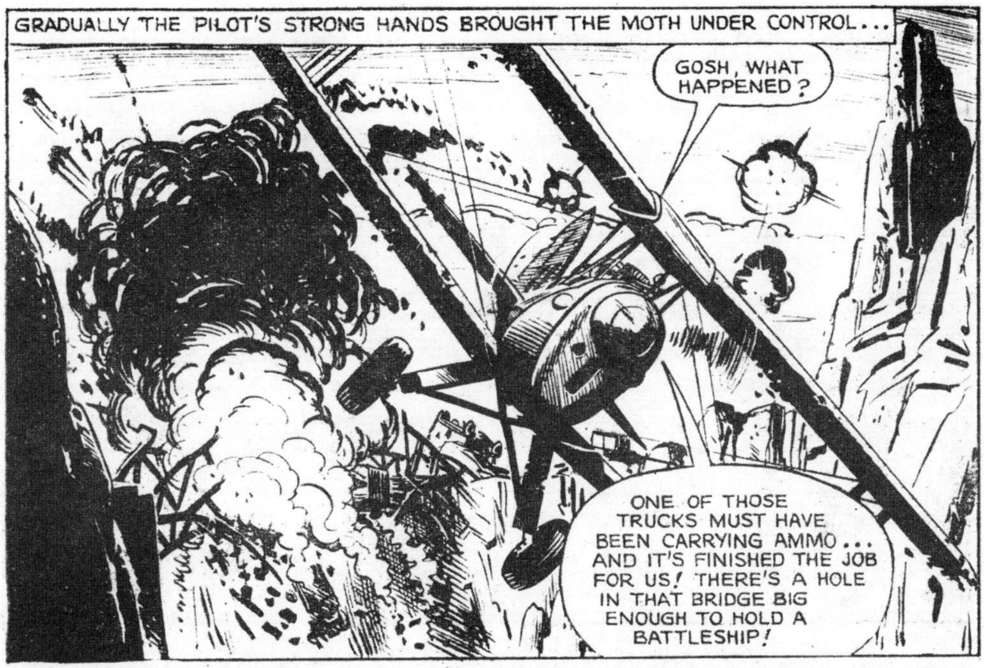
GRADUALLY THE PILOT'S STRONG HANDS BROUGHT THE MOTH UNDER CONTROL...
GOSH, WHAT HAPPENED?
ONE OF THOSE TRUCKS MUST HAVE BEEN CARRYING AMMO... AND IT'S FINISHED THE JOB FOR US! THERE'S A HOLE IN THAT BRIDGE BIG ENOUGH TO HOLD A BATTLESHIP!

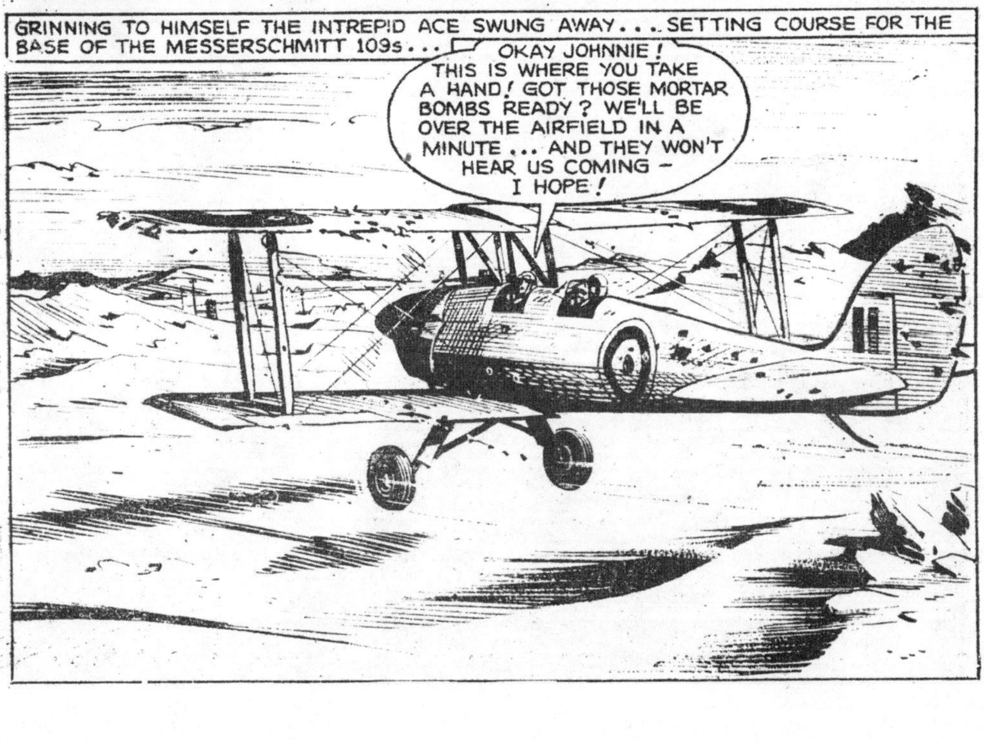
GRINNING TO HIMSELF THE INTREPID ACE SWUNG AWAY... SETTING COURSE FOR THE BASE OF THE MESSERSCHMITT 109s...
OKAY JOHNNIE! THIS IS WHERE YOU TAKE A HAND! GOT THOSE MORTAR BOMBS READY? WE'LL BE OVER THE AIRFIELD IN A MINUTE... AND THEY WON'T HEAR US COMING - I HOPE!

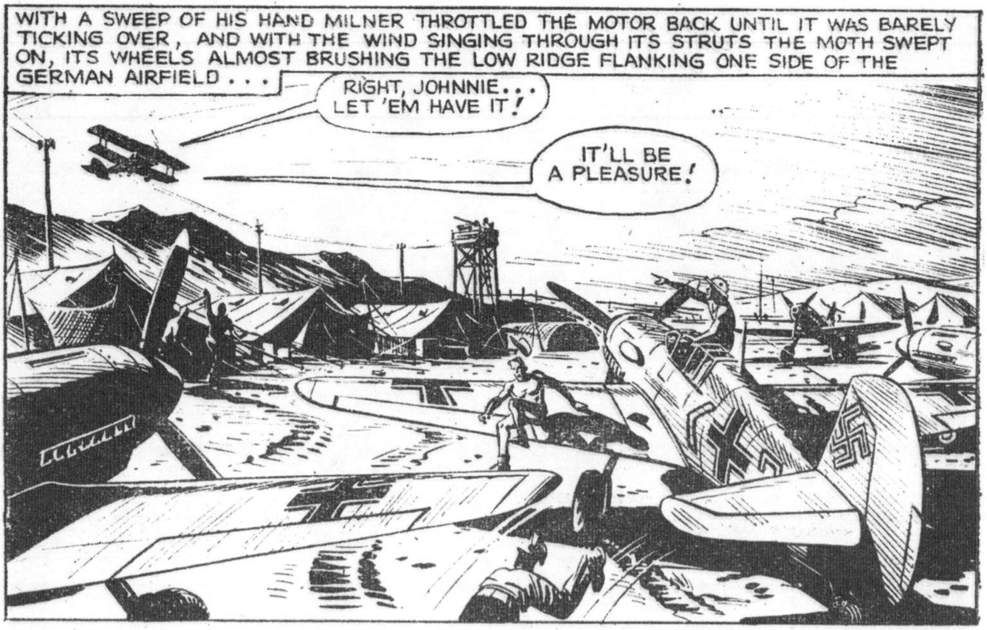
WITH A SWEEP OF HIS HAND MILNER THROTTLED THE MOTOR BACK UNTIL IT WAS BARELY TICKING OVER, AND WITH THE WIND SINGING THROUGH ITS STRUTS THE MOTH SWEPT ON, ITS WHEELS ALMOST BRUSHING THE LOW RIDGE FLANKING ONE SIDE OF THE GERMAN AIRFIELD . . .
RIGHT, JOHNNIE... LET 'EM HAVE IT!
IT'LL BE A PLEASURE!

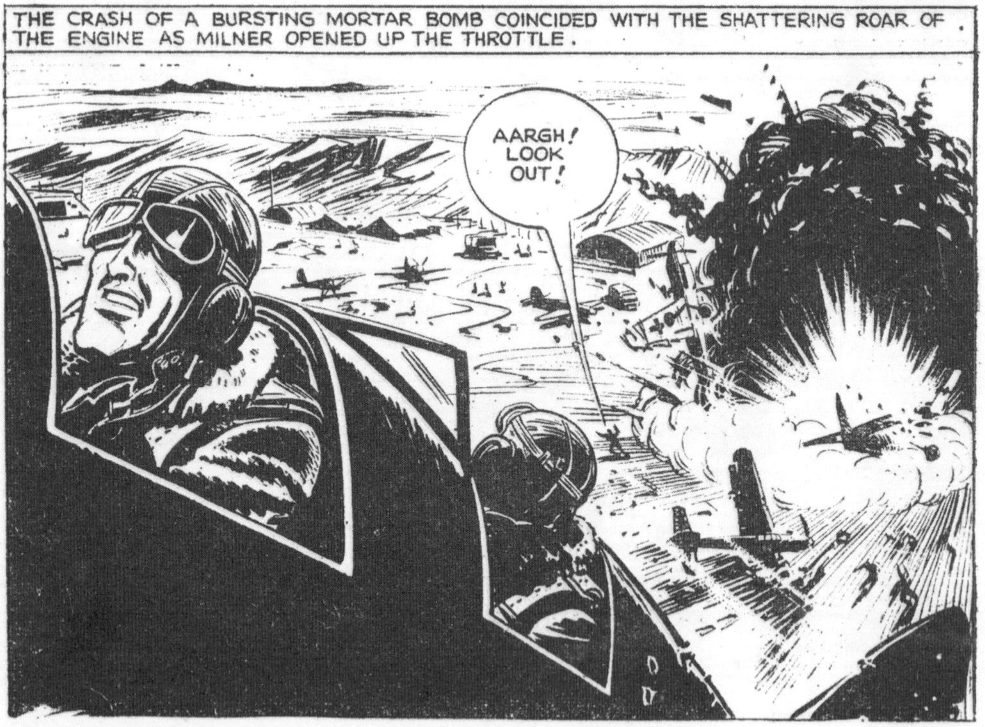
THE CRASH OF A BURSTING MORTAR BOMB COINCIDED WITH THE SHATTERING ROAR OF THE ENGINE AS MILNER OPENED UP THE THROTTLE.
AARGH! LOOK OUT!

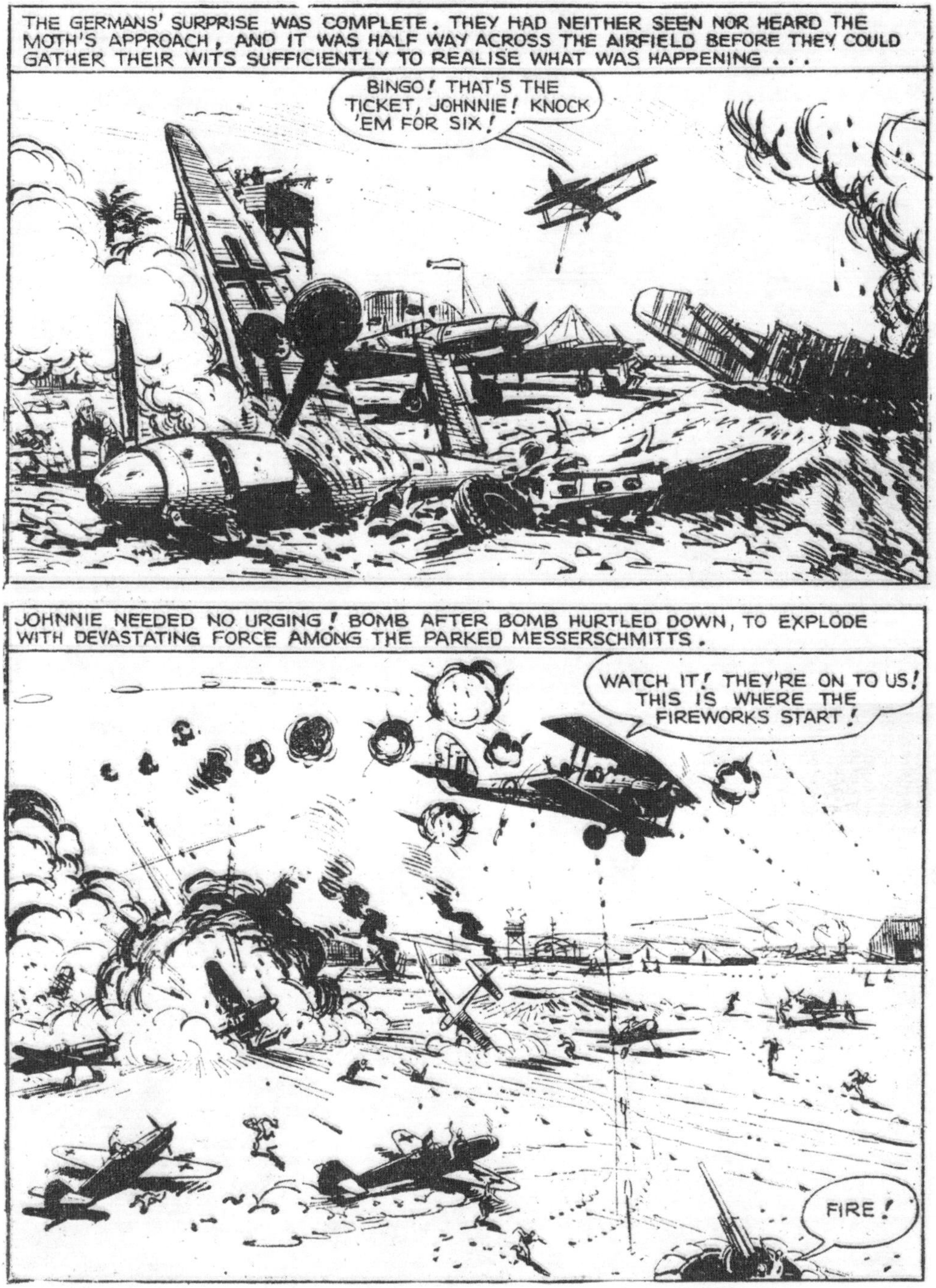
THE GERMANS' SURPRISE WAS COMPLETE. THEY HAD NEITHER SEEN NOR HEARD THE MOTH'S APPROACH, AND IT WAS HALF WAY ACROSS THE AIRFIELD BEFORE THEY COULD GATHER THEIR WITS SUFFICIENTLY TO REALISE WHAT WAS HAPPENING . . .
BINGO! THAT'S THE TICKET, JOHNNIE! KNOCK 'EM FOR SIX!
JOHNNIE NEEDED NO URGING! BOMB AFTER BOMB HURTLED DOWN, TO EXPLODE WITH DEVASTATING FORCE AMONG THE PARKED MESSERSCHMITTS.
WATCH IT! THEY'RE ON TO US! THIS IS WHERE THE FIREWORKS START!
FIRE!

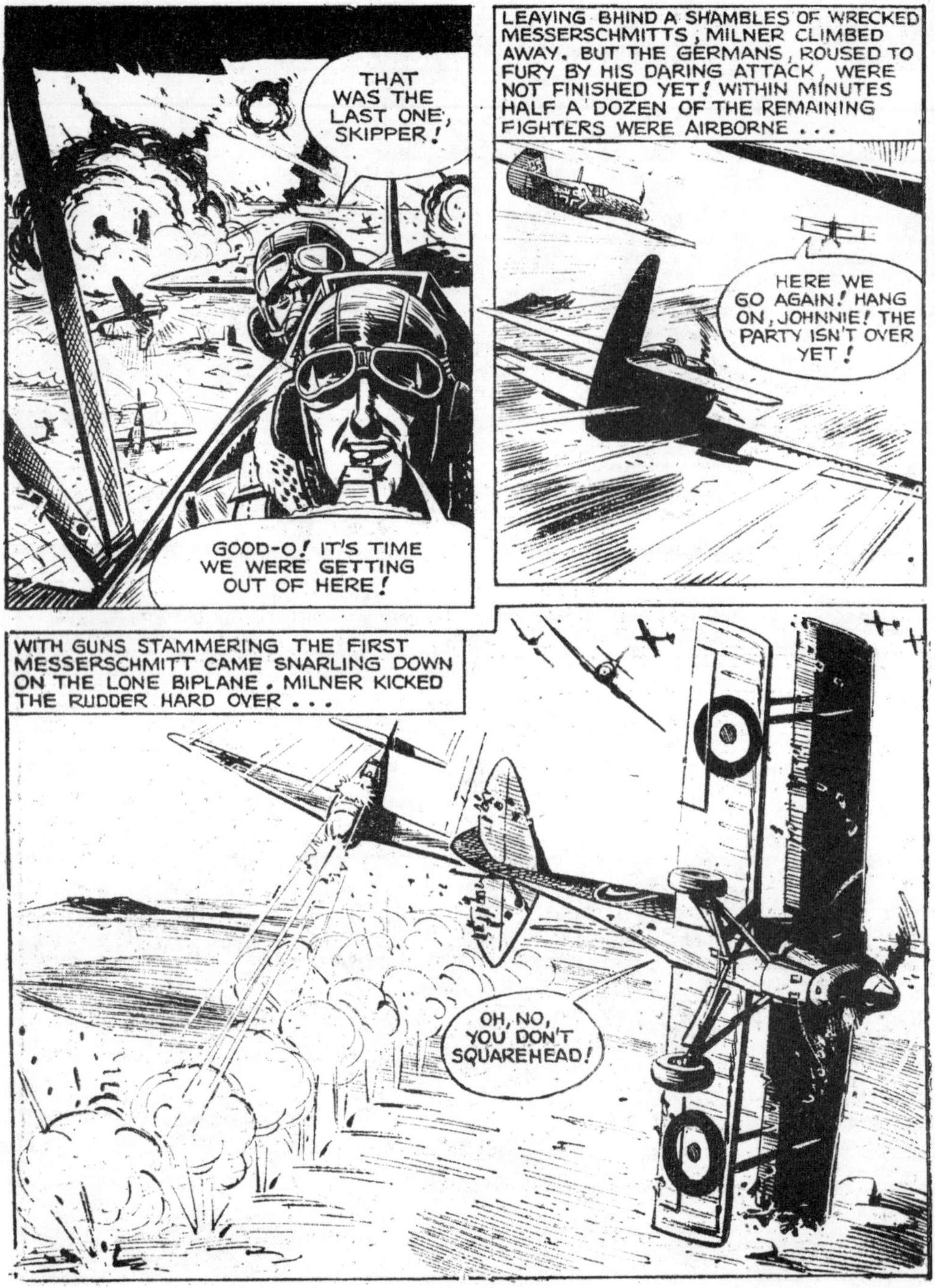
THAT WAS THE LAST ONE, SKIPPER!
GOOD-O! IT'S TIME WE WERE GETTING OUT OF HERE!
LEAVING BHIND A SHAMBLES OF WRECKED MESSERSCHMITTS, MILNER CLIMBED AWAY. BUT THE GERMANS, ROUSED TO FURY BY HIS DARING ATTACK, WERE NOT FINISHED YET! WITHIN MINUTES HALF A DOZEN OF THE REMAINING FIGHTERS WERE AIRBORNE . . .
HERE WE GO AGAIN! HANG ON, JOHNNIE! THE PARTY ISN'T OVER YET!
WITH GUNS STAMMERING THE FIRST MESSERSCHMITT CAME SNARLING DOWN ON THE LONE BIPLANE. MILNER KICKED THE RUDDER HARD OVER . . .
OH, NO, YOU DON'T SQUAREHEAD!

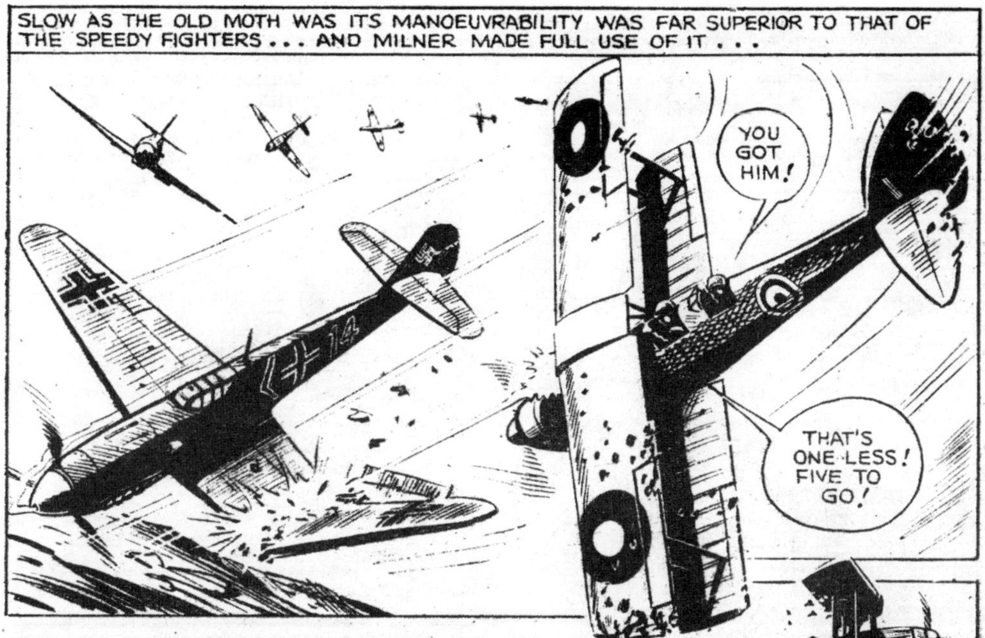
SLOW AS THE OLD MOTH WAS ITS MANOEUVRABILITY WAS FAR SUPERIOR TO THAT OF THE SPEEDY FIGHTERS . . . AND MILNER MADE FULL USE OF IT . . .
YOU GOT HIM!
THAT'S ONE LESS! FIVE TO GO!

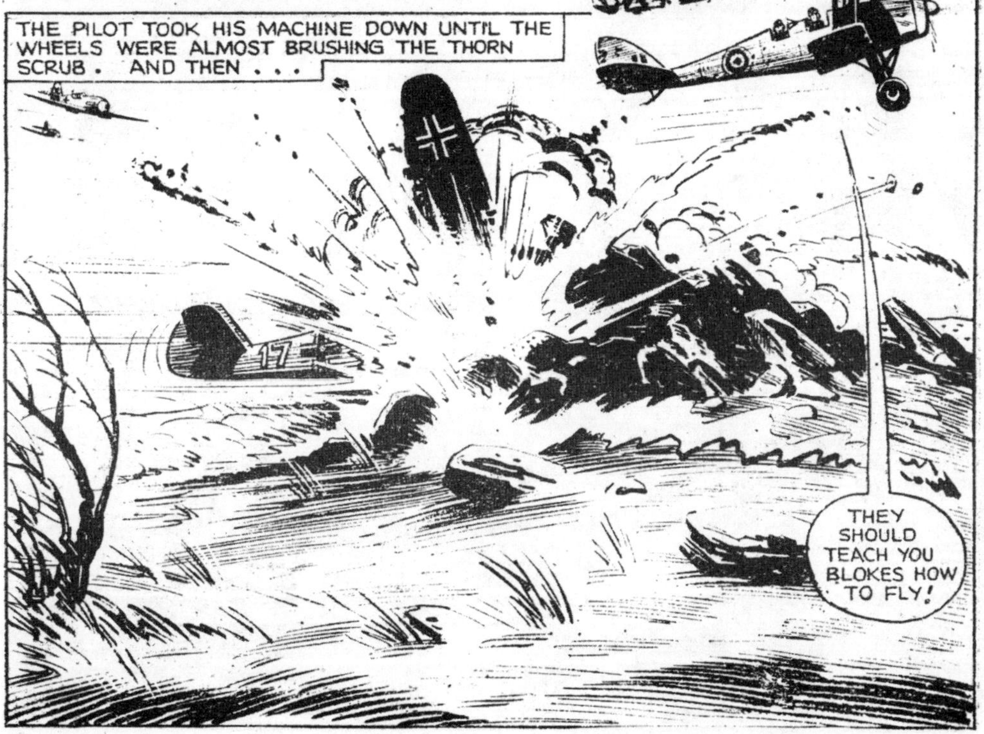
THE PILOT TOOK HIS MACHINE DOWN UNTIL THE WHEELS WERE ALMOST BRUSHING THE THORN SCRUB . AND THEN . . .
THEY SHOULD TEACH YOU BLOKES HOW TO FLY!

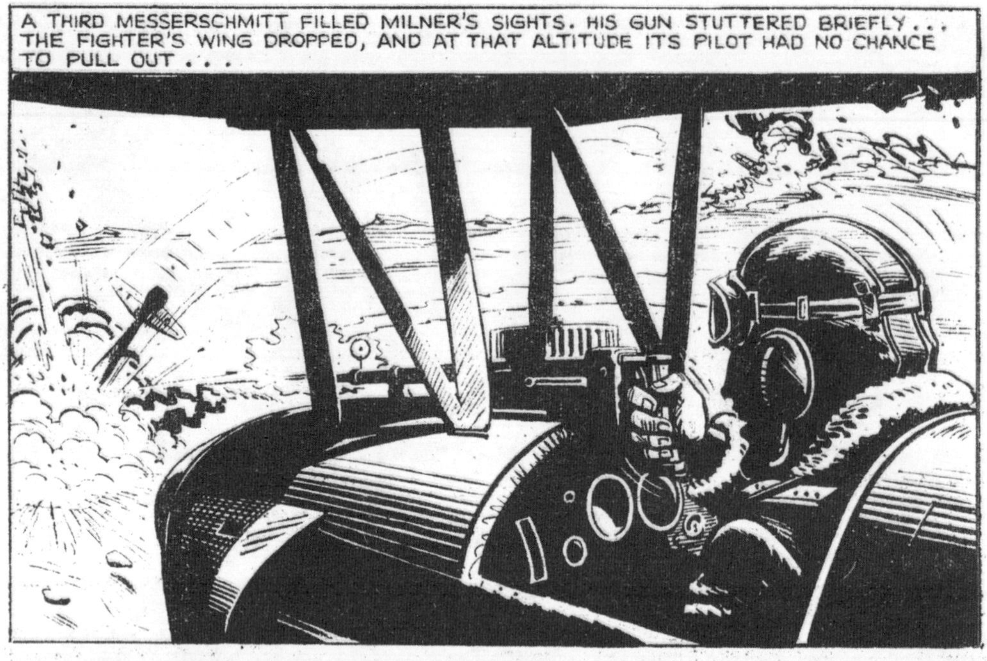
A THIRD MESSERSCHMITT FILLED MILNER'S SIGHTS. HIS GUN STUTTERED BRIEFLY . . . THE FIGHTER'S WING DROPPED, AND AT THAT ALTITUDE ITS PILOT HAD NO CHANCE TO PULL OUT . . .

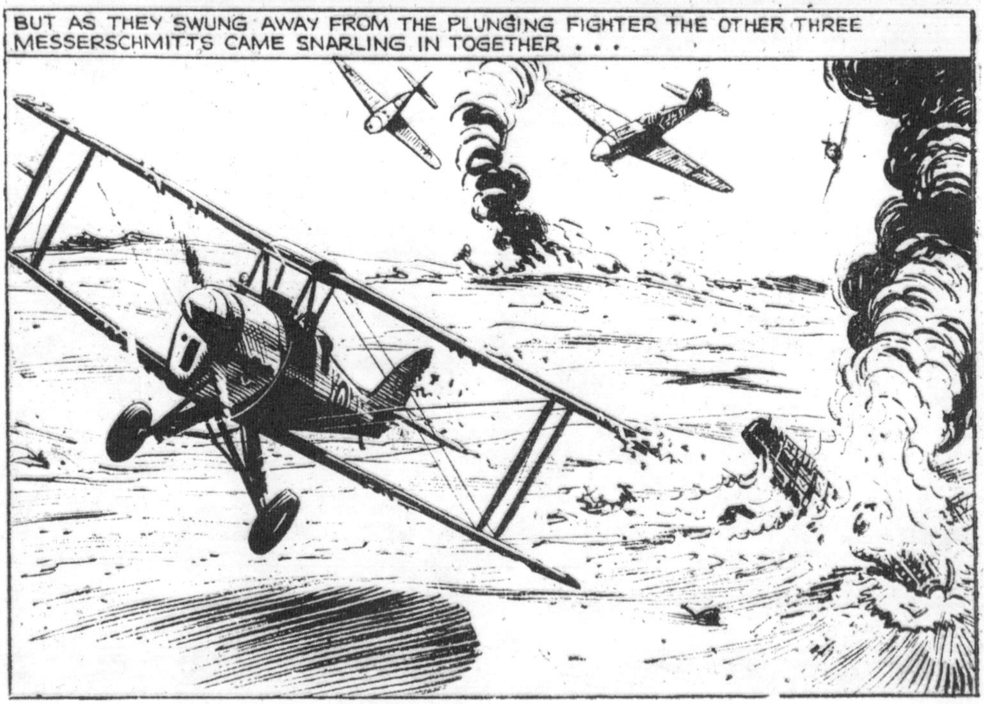
BUT AS THEY SWUNG AWAY FROM THE PLUNGING FIGHTER THE OTHER THREE MESSERSCHMITTS CAME SNARLING IN TOGETHER . . .

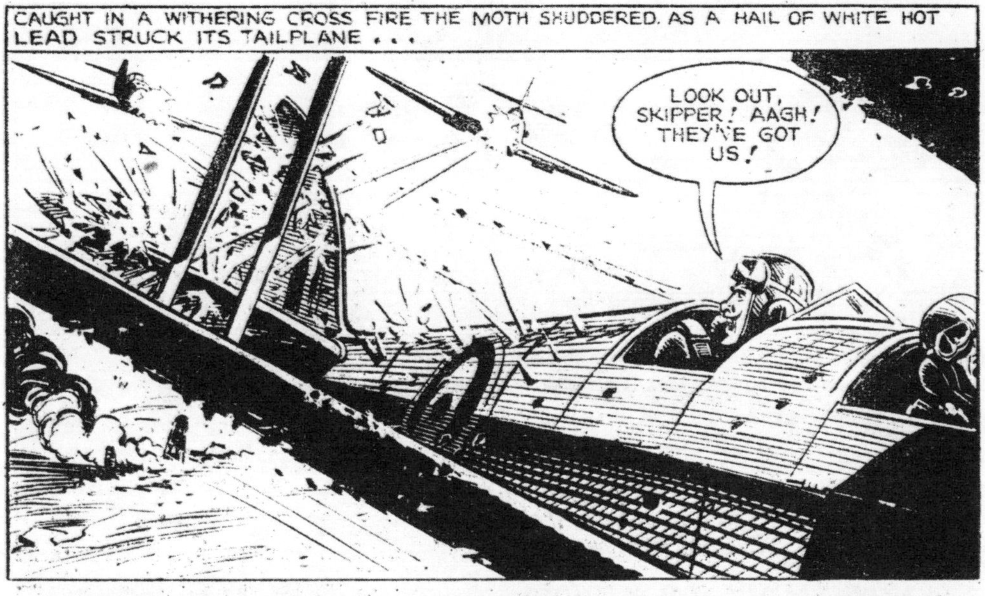
CAUGHT IN A WITHERING CROSS FIRE THE MOTH SHUDDERED. AS A HAIL OF WHITE HOT LEAD STRUCK ITS TAILPLANE . . .
LOOK OUT, SKIPPER! AAGH! THEY'VE GOT US!

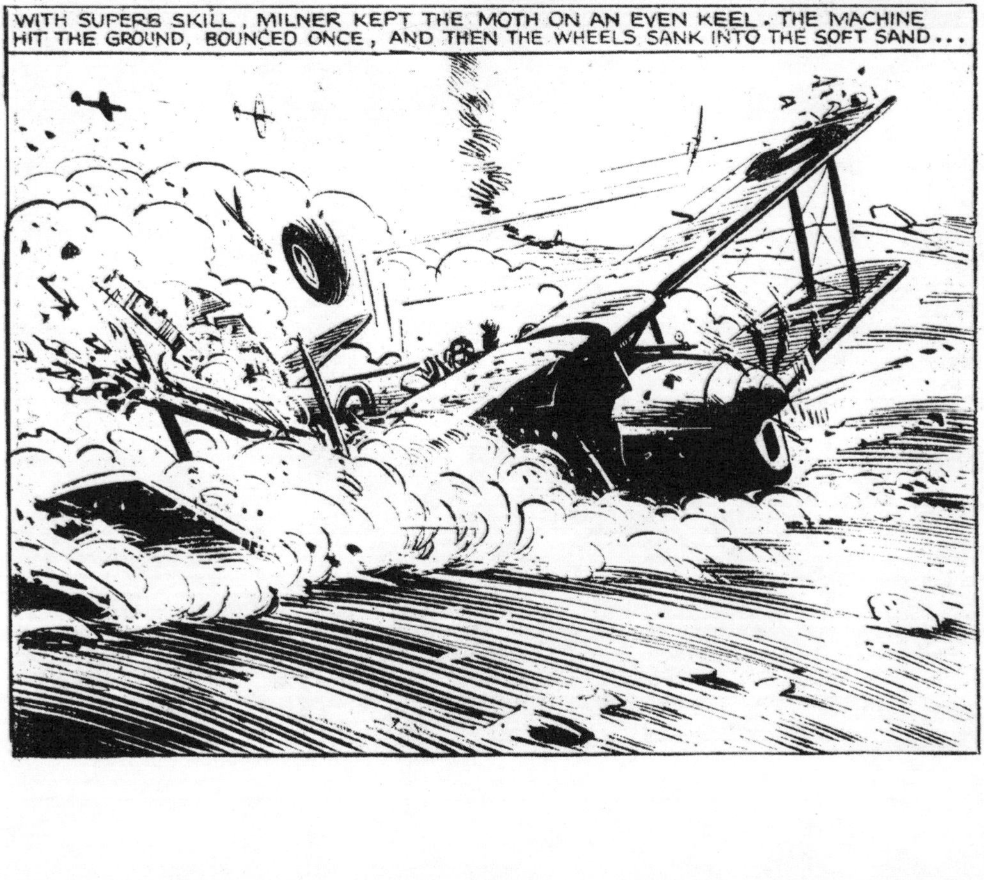
WITH SUPERB SKILL, MILNER KEPT THE MOTH ON AN EVEN KEEL. THE MACHINE HIT THE GROUND, BOUNCED ONCE, AND THEN THE WHEELS SANK INTO THE SOFT SAND...

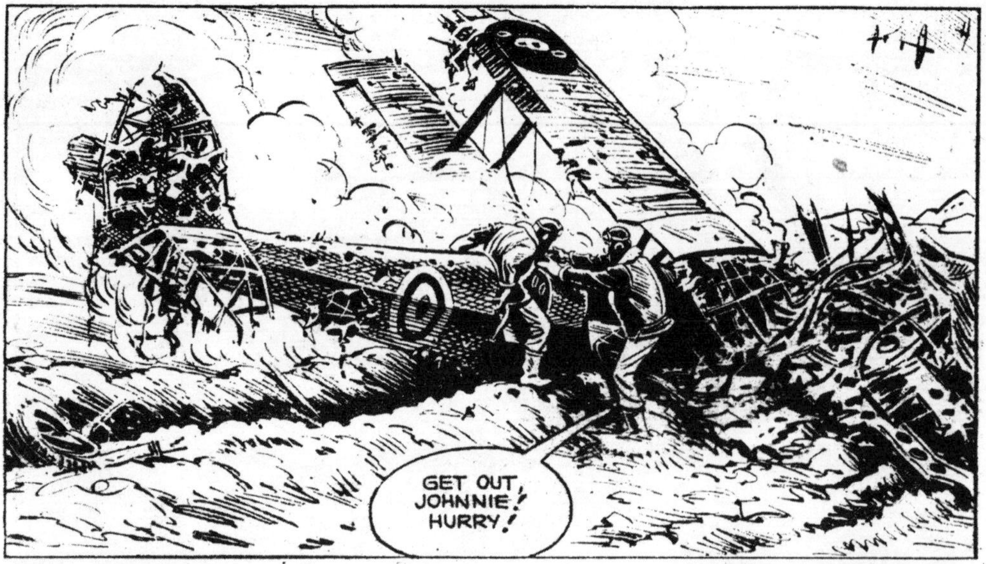
GET OUT, JOHNNIE! HURRY!

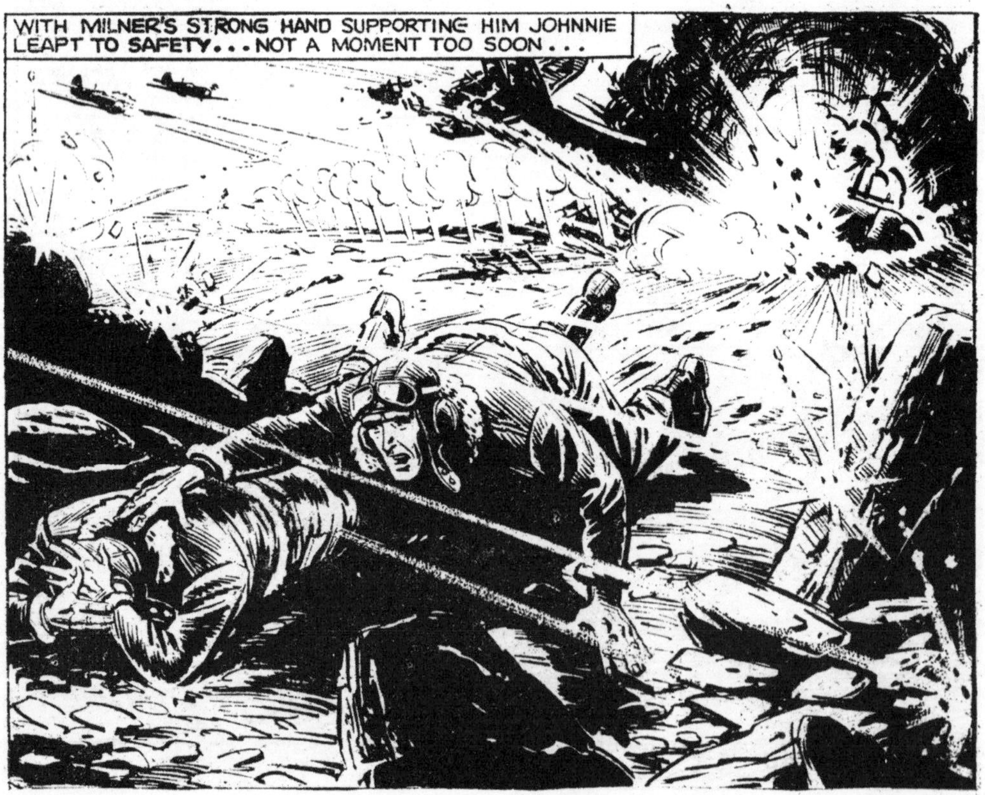
WITH MILNER'S STRONG HAND SUPPORTING HIM JOHNNIE LEAPT TO SAFETY... NOT A MOMENT TOO SOON...

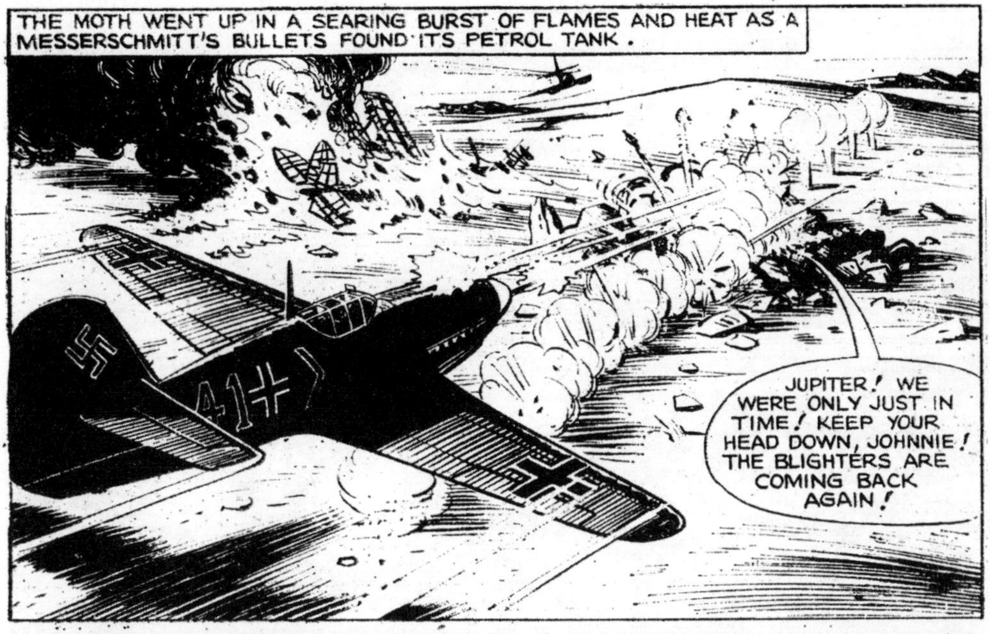
THE MOTH WENT UP IN A SEARING BURST OF FLAMES AND HEAT AS A MESSERSCHMITT'S BULLETS FOUND ITS PETROL TANK.
JUPITER! WE WERE ONLY JUST IN TIME! KEEP YOUR HEAD DOWN, JOHNNIE! THE BLIGHTERS ARE COMING BACK AGAIN!

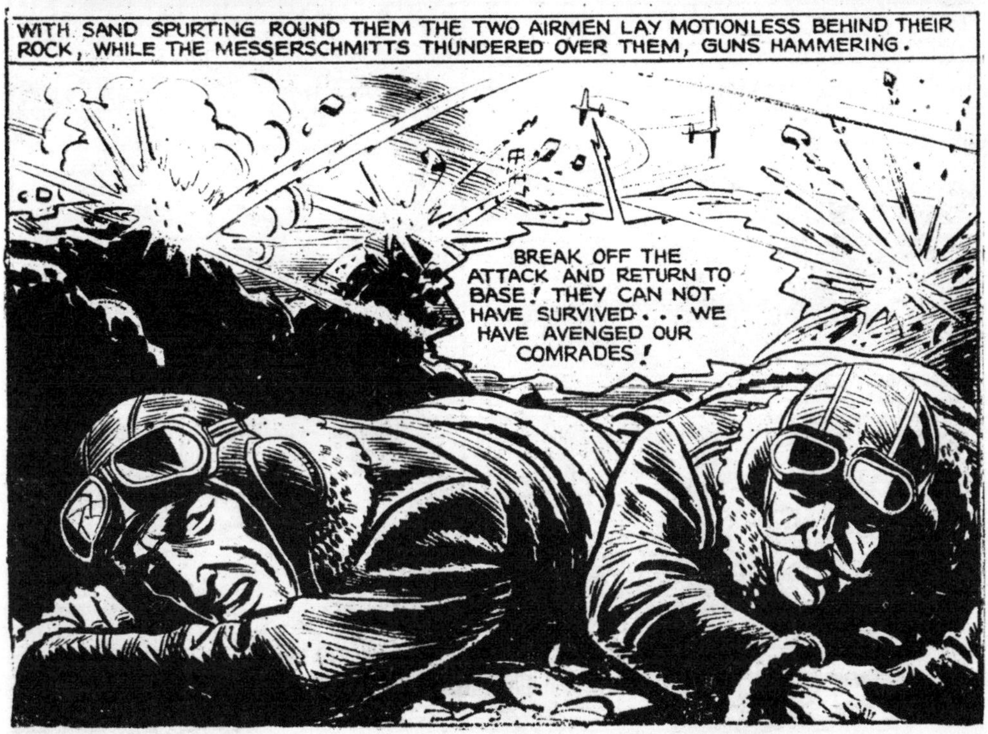
WITH SAND SPURTING ROUND THEM THE TWO AIRMEN LAY MOTIONLESS BEHIND THEIR ROCK, WHILE THE MESSERSCHMITTS THUNDERED OVER THEM, GUNS HAMMERING.
BREAK OFF THE ATTACK AND RETURN TO BASE! THEY CAN NOT HAVE SURVIVED . . . WE HAVE AVENGED OUR COMRADES!

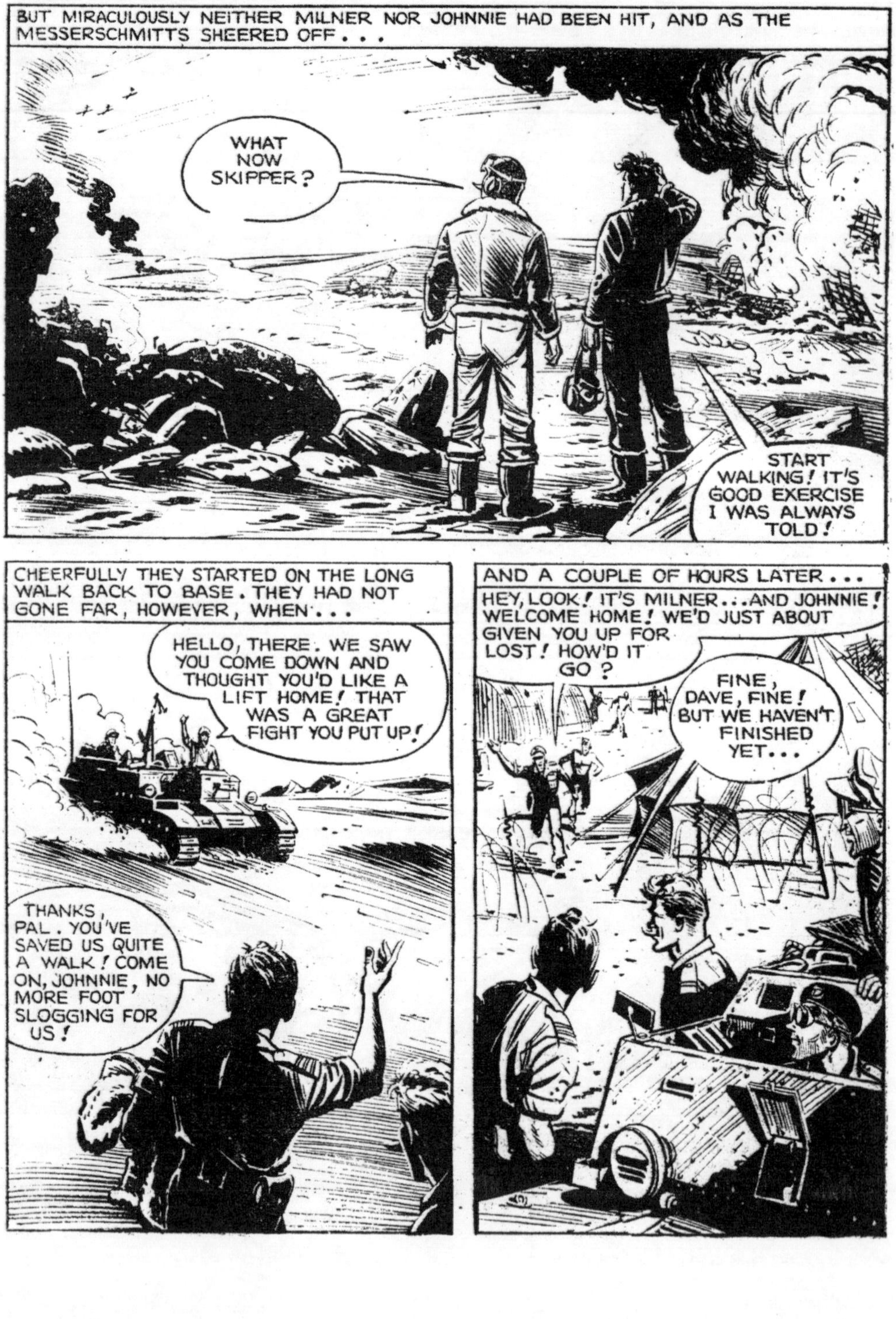
BUT MIRACULOUSLY NEITHER MILNER NOR JOHNNIE HAD BEEN HIT, AND AS THE MESSERSCHMITTS SHEERED OFF . . .
WHAT NOW SKIPPER?
START WALKING! IT'S GOOD EXERCISE I WAS ALWAYS TOLD!
CHEERFULLY THEY STARTED ON THE LONG WALK BACK TO BASE. THEY HAD NOT GONE FAR, HOWEVER, WHEN . . .
HELLO, THERE. WE SAW YOU COME DOWN AND THOUGHT YOU'D LIKE A LIFT HOME! THAT WAS A GREAT FIGHT YOU PUT UP!
THANKS, PAL. YOU'VE SAVED US QUITE A WALK! COME ON, JOHNNIE, NO MORE FOOT SLOGGING FOR US!
AND A COUPLE OF HOURS LATER . . .
HEY, LOOK! IT'S MILNER . . . AND JOHNNIE! WELCOME HOME! WE'D JUST ABOUT GIVEN YOU UP FOR LOST! HOW'D IT GO?
FINE, DAVE, FINE! BUT WE HAVEN'T FINISHED YET . . .

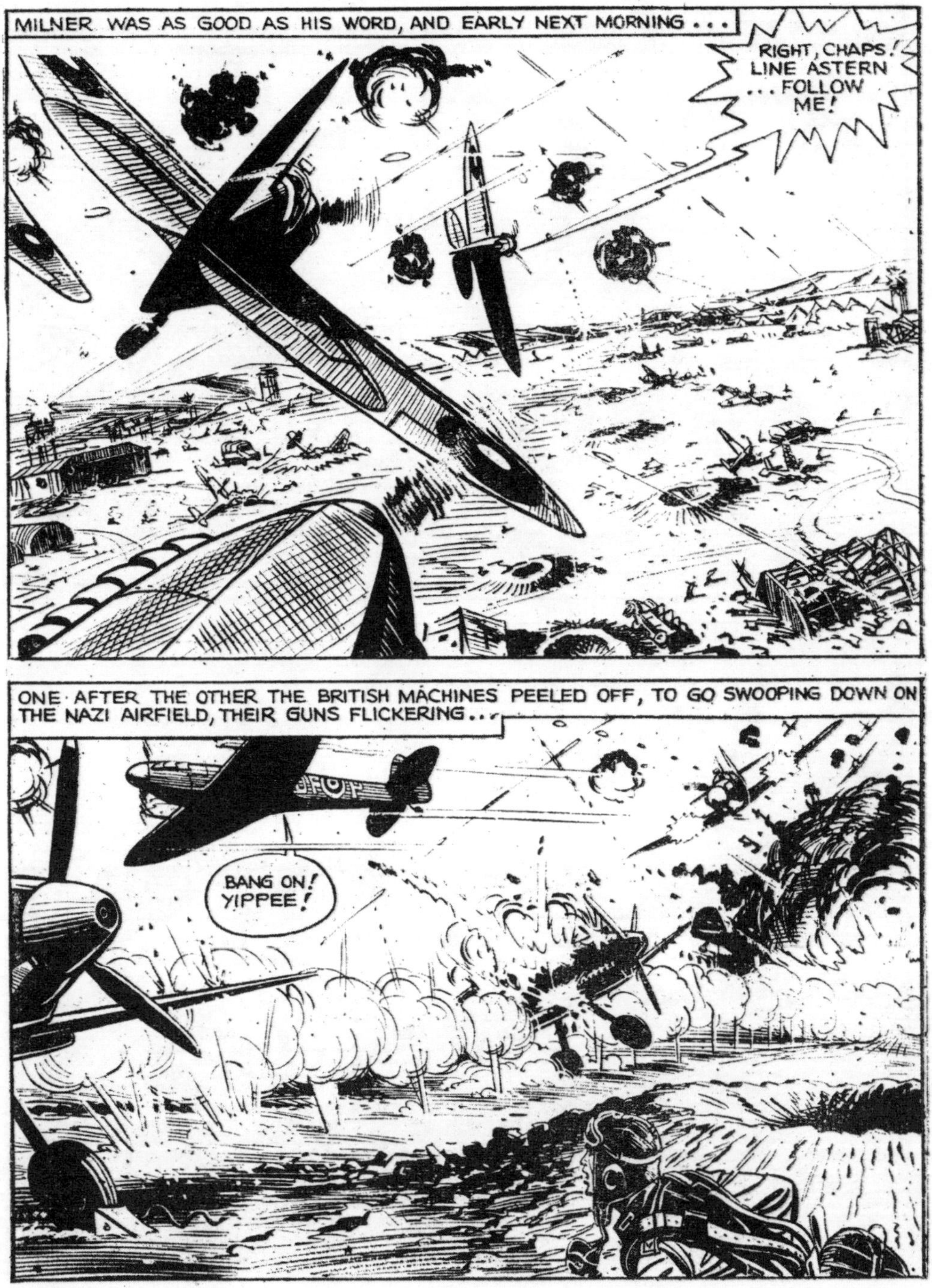
MILNER WAS AS GOOD AS HIS WORD, AND EARLY NEXT MORNING . . .
RIGHT, CHAPS! LINE ASTERN . . . FOLLOW ME!
ONE AFTER THE OTHER THE BRITISH MACHINES PEELED OFF, TO GO SWOOPING DOWN ON THE NAZI AIRFIELD, THEIR GUNS FLICKERING . . .
BANG ON! YIPPEE!

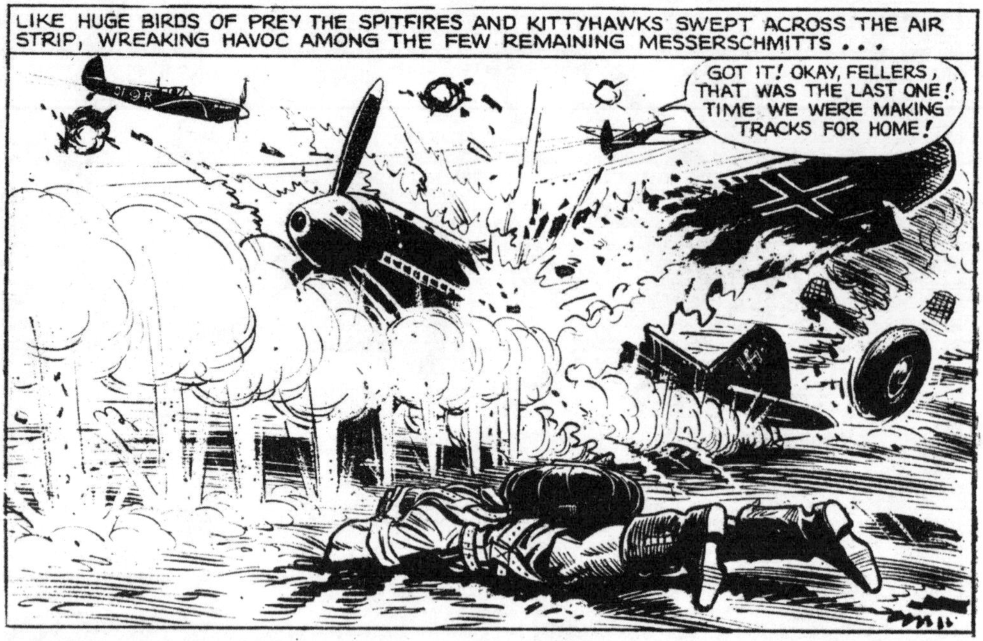
LIKE HUGE BIRDS OF PREY THE SPITFIRES AND KITTYHAWKS SWEPT ACROSS THE AIR STRIP, WREAKING HAVOC AMONG THE FEW REMAINING MESSERSCHMITTS . . .
GOT IT! OKAY, FELLERS, THAT WAS THE LAST ONE! TIME WE WERE MAKING TRACKS FOR HOME!

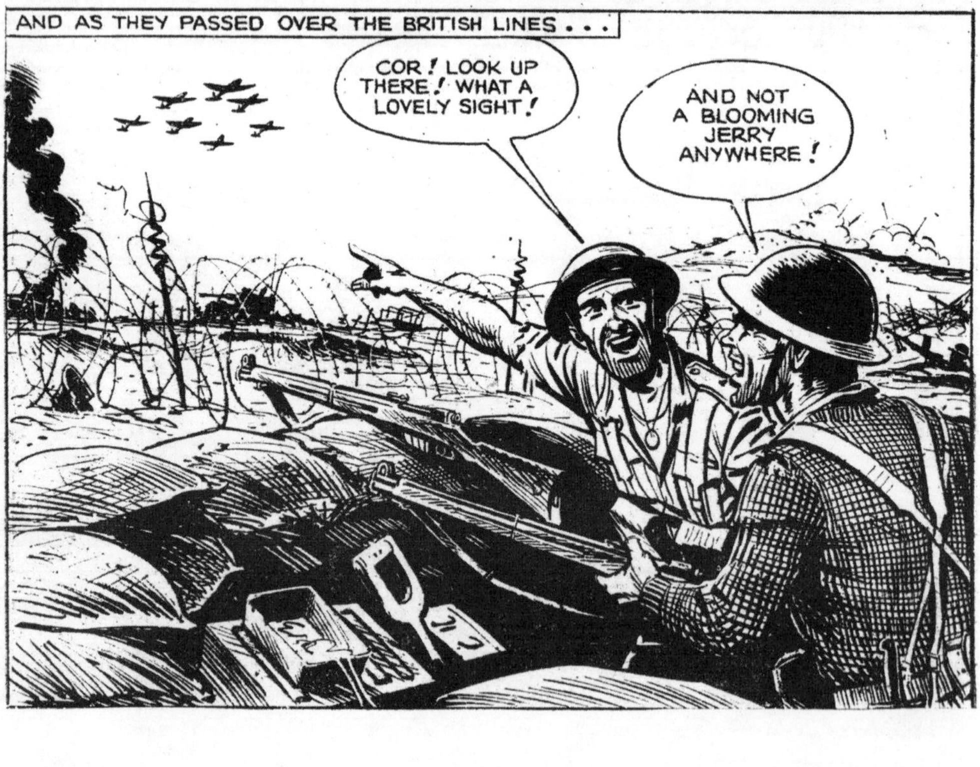
AND AS THEY PASSED OVER THE BRITISH LINES . . .
COR! LOOK UP THERE! WHAT A LOVELY SIGHT!
AND NOT A BLOOMING JERRY ANYWHERE!

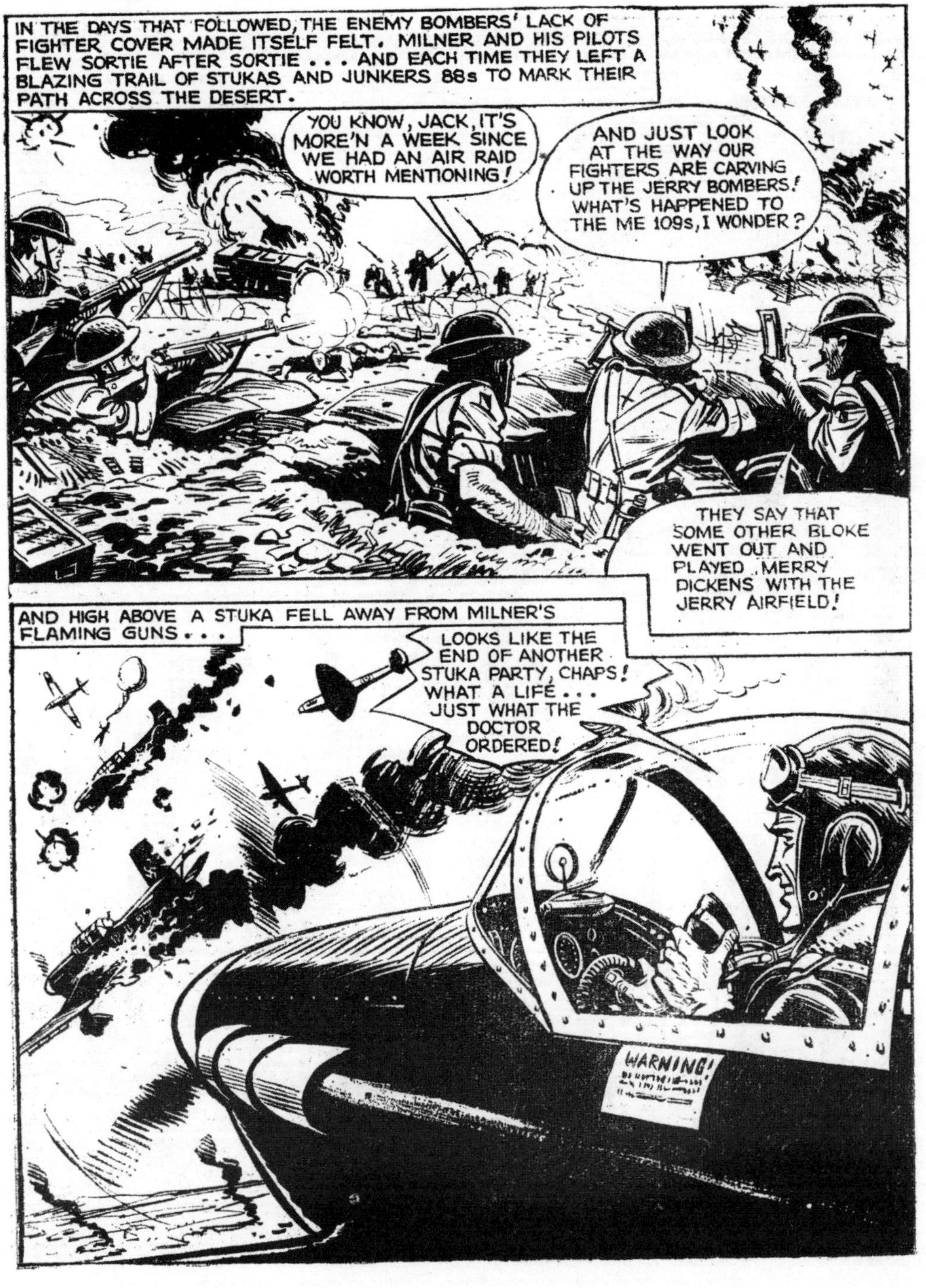
IN THE DAYS THAT FOLLOWED, THE ENEMY BOMBERS' LACK OF FIGHTER COVER MADE ITSELF FELT. MILNER AND HIS PILOTS FLEW SORTIE AFTER SORTIE . . . AND EACH TIME THEY LEFT A BLAZING TRAIL OF STUKAS AND JUNKERS 88s TO MARK THEIR PATH ACROSS THE DESERT.
YOU KNOW, JACK, IT'S MORE'N A WEEK SINCE WE HAD AN AIR RAID WORTH MENTIONING!
AND JUST LOOK AT THE WAY OUR FIGHTERS ARE CARVING UP THE JERRY BOMBERS! WHAT'S HAPPENED TO THE ME 109s, I WONDER?
THEY SAY THAT SOME OTHER BLOKE WENT OUT AND PLAYED MERRY DICKENS WITH THE JERRY AIRFIELD!
AND HIGH ABOVE A STUKA FELL AWAY FROM MILNER'S FLAMING GUNS . . .
LOOKS LIKE THE END OF ANOTHER STUKA PARTY, CHAPS! WHAT A LIFE . . . JUST WHAT THE DOCTOR ORDERED!
WARNING!

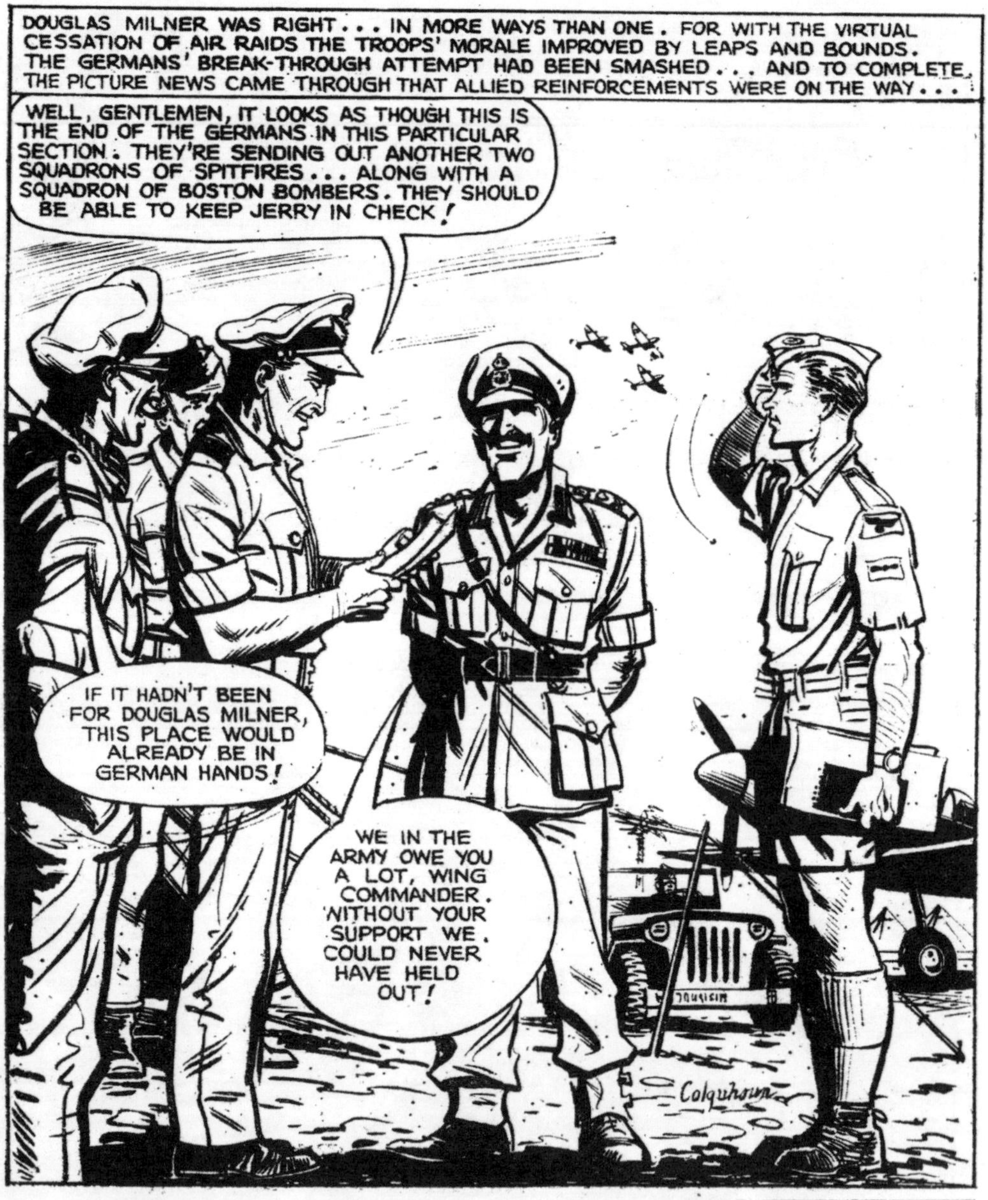
DOUGLAS MILNER WAS RIGHT . . . IN MORE WAYS THAN ONE . FOR WITH THE VIRTUAL CESSATION OF AIR RAIDS THE TROOPS' MORALE IMPROVED BY LEAPS AND BOUNDS. THE GERMANS' BREAK-THROUGH ATTEMPT HAD BEEN SMASHED . . . AND TO COMPLETE THE PICTURE NEWS CAME THROUGH THAT ALLIED REINFORCEMENTS WERE ON THE WAY . . .
WELL, GENTLEMEN, IT LOOKS AS THOUGH THIS IS THE END OF THE GERMANS IN THIS PARTICULAR SECTION. THEY'RE SENDING OUT ANOTHER TWO SQUADRONS OF SPITFIRES . . . ALONG WITH A SQUADRON OF BOSTON BOMBERS. THEY SHOULD BE ABLE TO KEEP JERRY IN CHECK!
IF IT HADN'T BEEN FOR DOUGLAS MILNER, THIS PLACE WOULD ALREADY BE IN GERMAN HANDS!
WE IN THE ARMY OWE YOU A LOT, WING COMMANDER. WITHOUT YOUR SUPPORT WE COULD NEVER HAVE HELD OUT!
Colquhoun

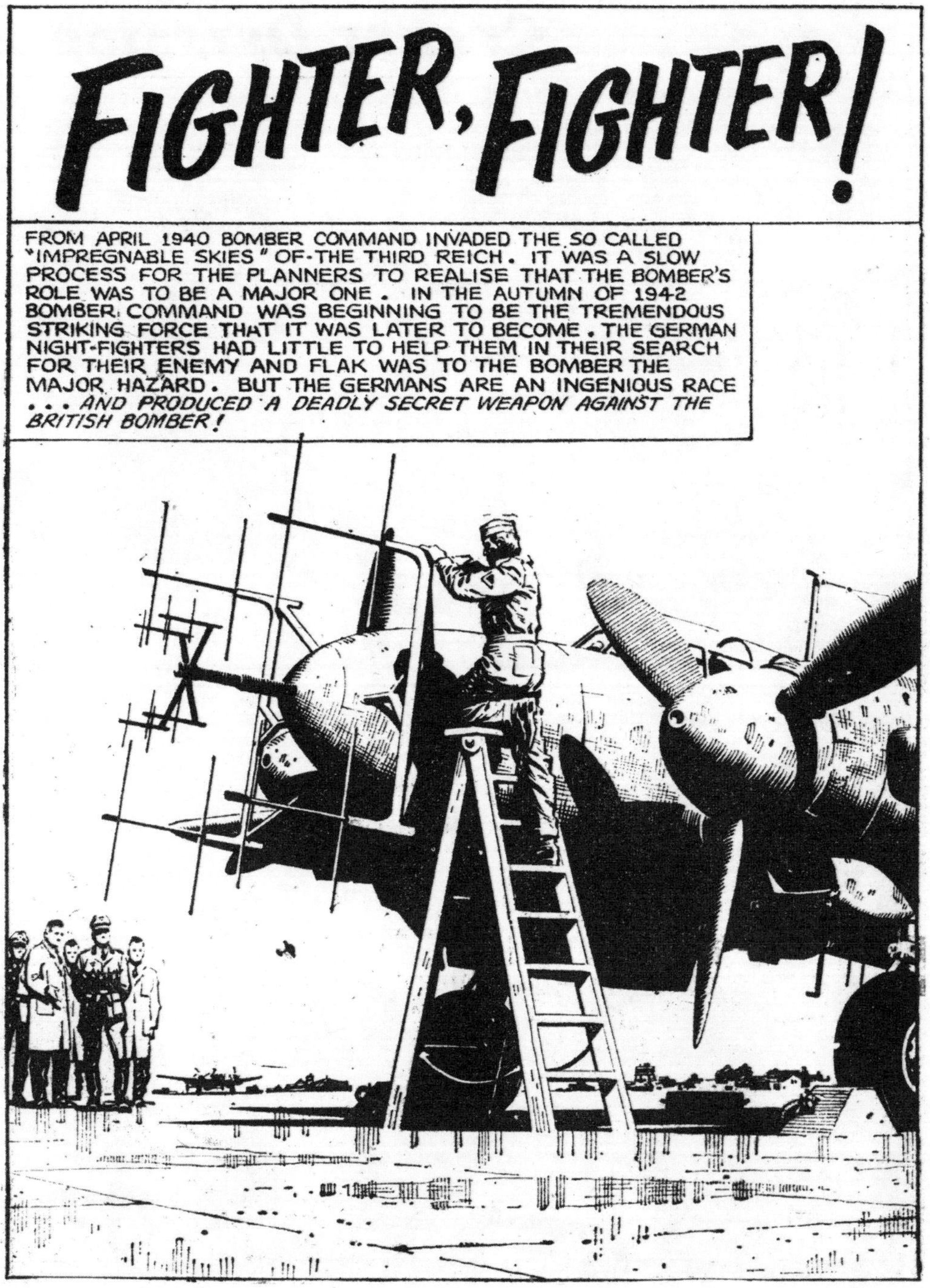
FIGHTER, FIGHTER!
FROM APRIL 1940 BOMBER COMMAND INVADED THE SO CALLED "IMPREGNABLE SKIES" OF THE THIRD REICH. IT WAS A SLOW PROCESS FOR THE PLANNERS TO REALISE THAT THE BOMBER'S ROLE WAS TO BE A MAJOR ONE. IN THE AUTUMN OF 1942 BOMBER COMMAND WAS BEGINNING TO BE THE TREMENDOUS STRIKING FORCE THAT IT WAS LATER TO BECOME. THE GERMAN NIGHT-FIGHTERS HAD LITTLE TO HELP THEM IN THEIR SEARCH FOR THEIR ENEMY AND FLAK WAS TO THE BOMBER THE MAJOR HAZARD. BUT THE GERMANS ARE AN INGENIOUS RACE ... AND PRODUCED A DEADLY SECRET WEAPON AGAINST THE BRITISH BOMBER!

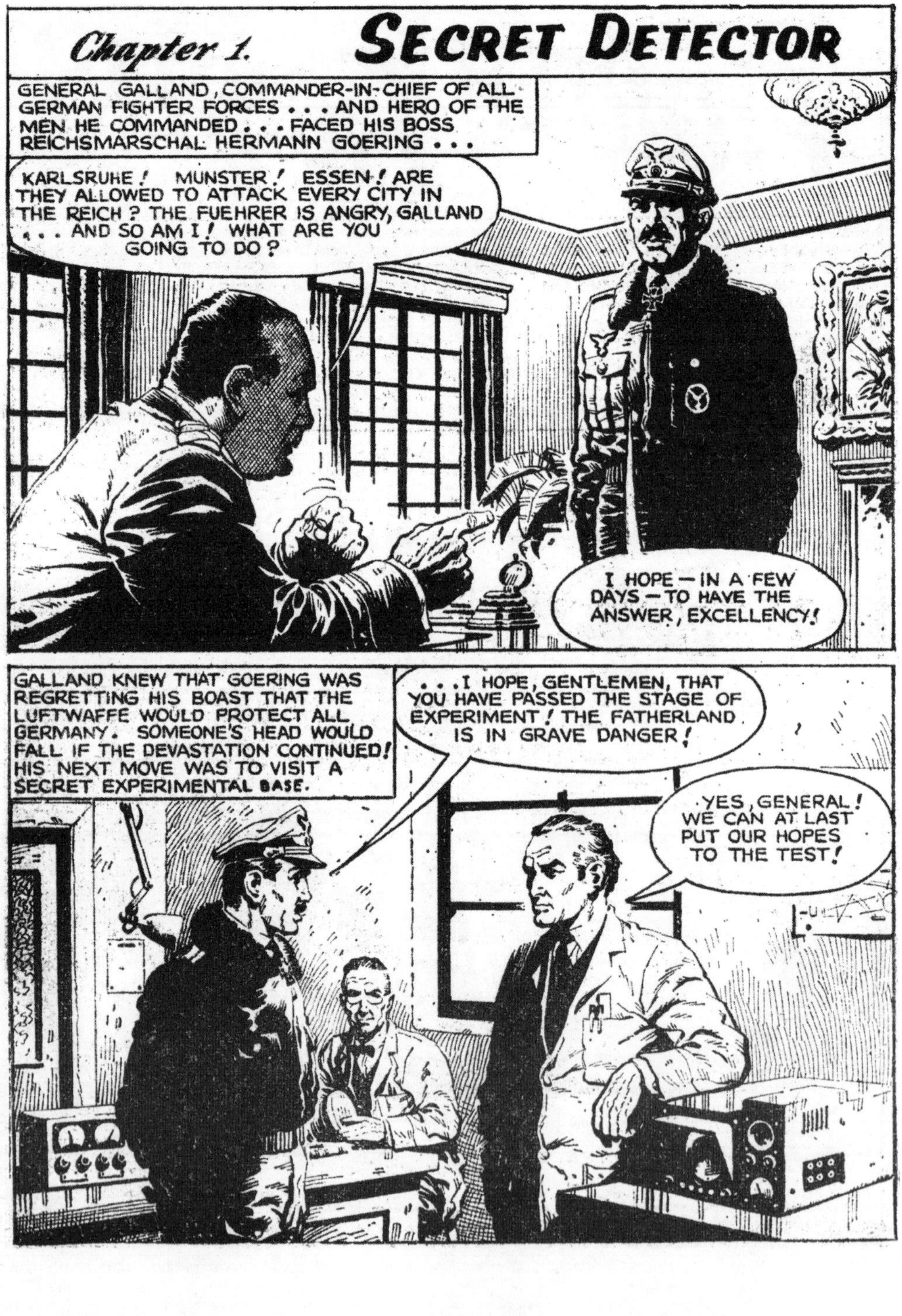
Chapter 1.
SECRET DETECTOR
GENERAL GALLAND, COMMANDER-IN-CHIEF OF ALL GERMAN FIGHTER FORCES . . . AND HERO OF THE MEN HE COMMANDED . . . FACED HIS BOSS REICHSMARSCHAL HERMANN GOERING . . .
KARLSRUHE! MUNSTER! ESSEN! ARE THEY ALLOWED TO ATTACK EVERY CITY IN THE REICH? THE FUEHRER IS ANGRY, GALLAND . . . AND SO AM I! WHAT ARE YOU GOING TO DO?
I HOPE — IN A FEW DAYS — TO HAVE THE ANSWER, EXCELLENCY!
GALLAND KNEW THAT GOERING WAS REGRETTING HIS BOAST THAT THE LUFTWAFFE WOULD PROTECT ALL GERMANY. SOMEONE'S HEAD WOULD FALL IF THE DEVASTATION CONTINUED! HIS NEXT MOVE WAS TO VISIT A SECRET EXPERIMENTAL BASE.
. . . I HOPE, GENTLEMEN, THAT YOU HAVE PASSED THE STAGE OF EXPERIMENT! THE FATHERLAND IS IN GRAVE DANGER!
YES, GENERAL! WE CAN AT LAST PUT OUR HOPES TO THE TEST!

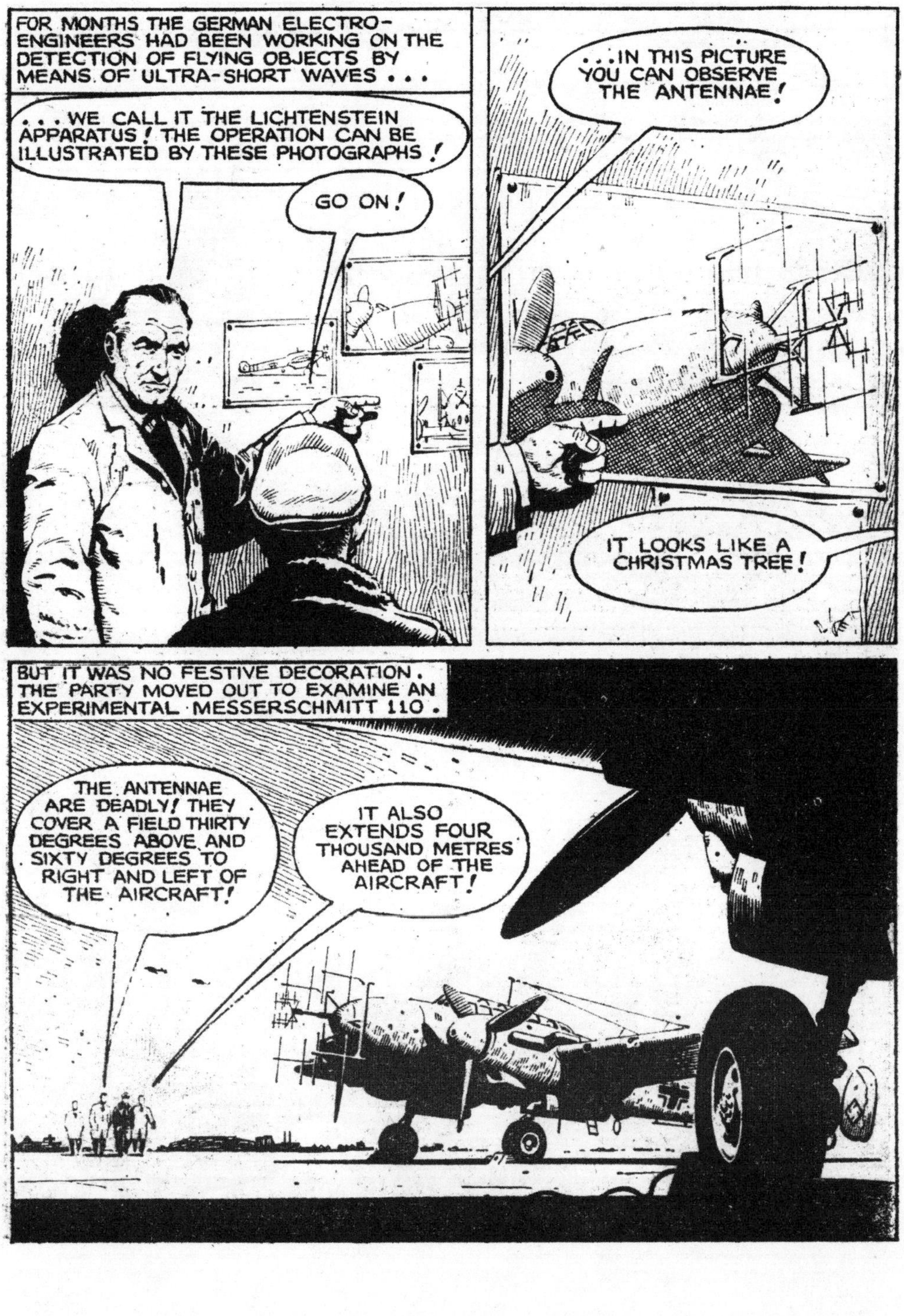
FOR MONTHS THE GERMAN ELECTRO-ENGINEERS HAD BEEN WORKING ON THE DETECTION OF FLYING OBJECTS BY MEANS OF ULTRA-SHORT WAVES . . .
. . . WE CALL IT THE LICHTENSTEIN APPARATUS! THE OPERATION CAN BE ILLUSTRATED BY THESE PHOTOGRAPHS!
GO ON!
. . . IN THIS PICTURE YOU CAN OBSERVE THE ANTENNAE!
IT LOOKS LIKE A CHRISTMAS TREE!
BUT IT WAS NO FESTIVE DECORATION. THE PARTY MOVED OUT TO EXAMINE AN EXPERIMENTAL MESSERSCHMITT 110.
THE ANTENNAE ARE DEADLY! THEY COVER A FIELD THIRTY DEGREES ABOVE AND SIXTY DEGREES TO RIGHT AND LEFT OF THE AIRCRAFT!
IT ALSO EXTENDS FOUR THOUSAND METRES AHEAD OF THE AIRCRAFT!

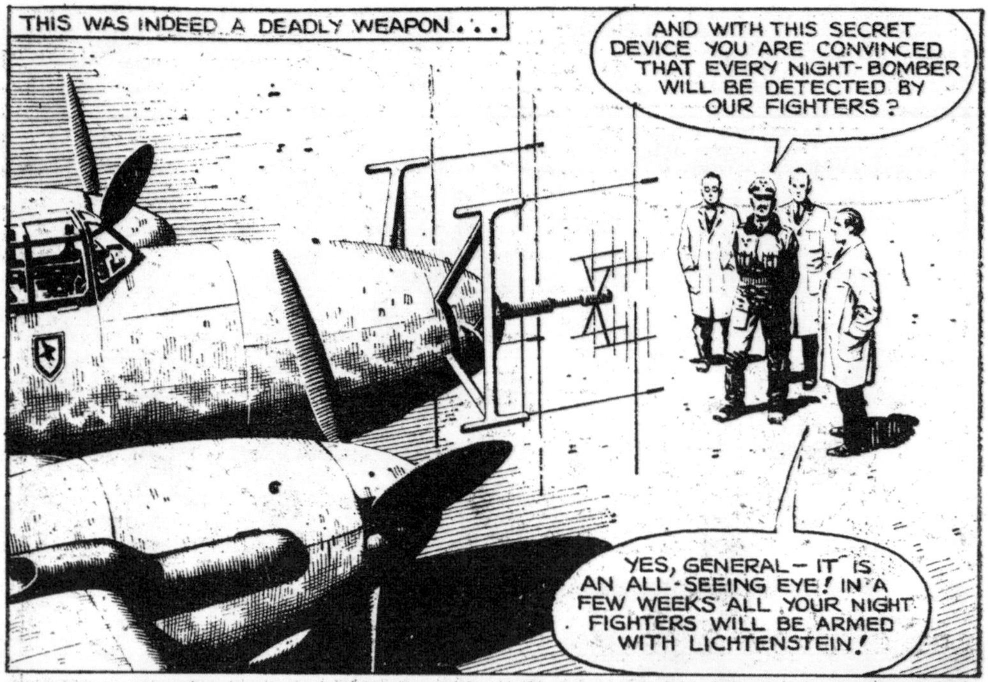
THIS WAS INDEED A DEADLY WEAPON . . .
AND WITH THIS SECRET DEVICE YOU ARE CONVINCED THAT EVERY NIGHT-BOMBER WILL BE DETECTED BY OUR FIGHTERS?
YES, GENERAL – IT IS AN ALL-SEEING EYE! IN A FEW WEEKS ALL YOUR NIGHT FIGHTERS WILL BE ARMED WITH LICHTENSTEIN!

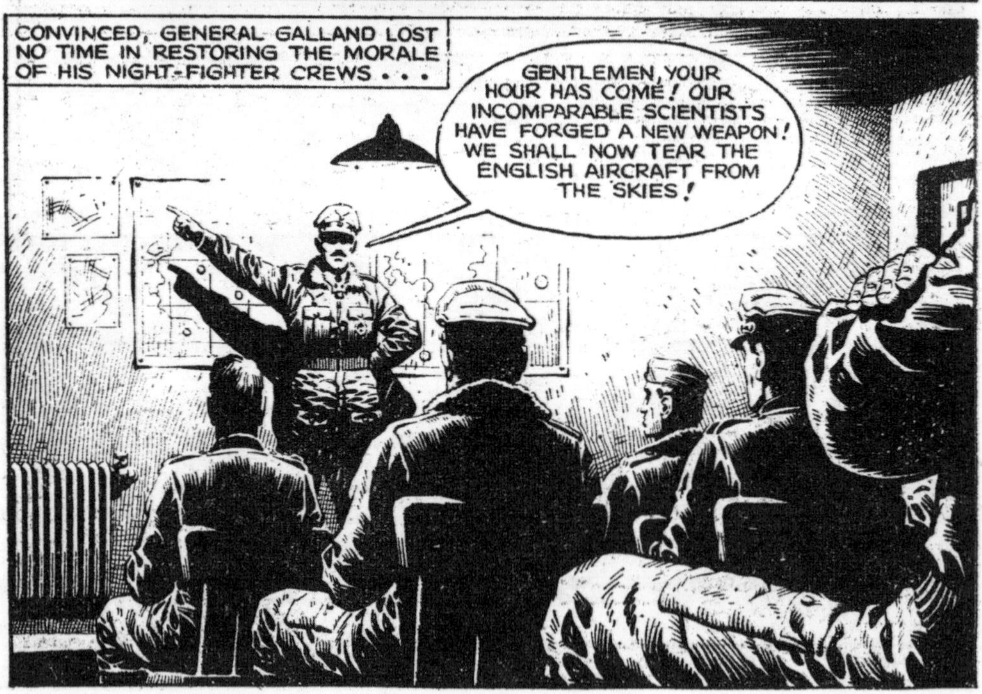
CONVINCED, GENERAL GALLAND LOST NO TIME IN RESTORING THE MORALE OF HIS NIGHT-FIGHTER CREWS . . .
GENTLEMEN, YOUR HOUR HAS COME! OUR INCOMPARABLE SCIENTISTS HAVE FORGED A NEW WEAPON! WE SHALL NOW TEAR THE ENGLISH AIRCRAFT FROM THE SKIES!

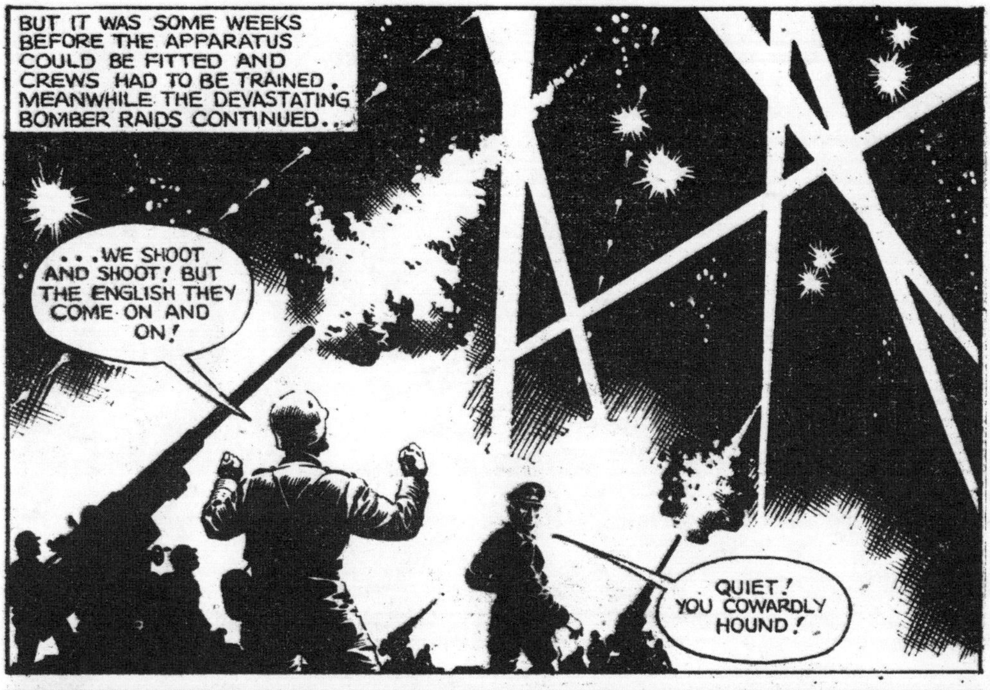
BUT IT WAS SOME WEEKS BEFORE THE APPARATUS COULD BE FITTED AND CREWS HAD TO BE TRAINED. MEANWHILE THE DEVASTATING BOMBER RAIDS CONTINUED...
...WE SHOOT AND SHOOT! BUT THE ENGLISH THEY COME ON AND ON!
QUIET! YOU COWARDLY HOUND!

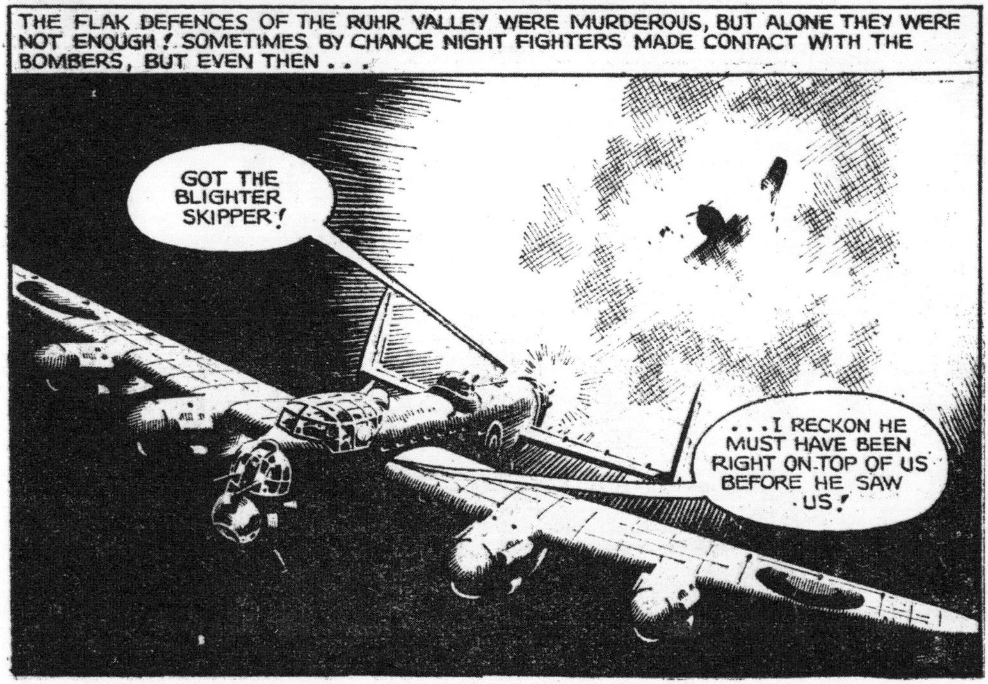
THE FLAK DEFENCES OF THE RUHR VALLEY WERE MURDEROUS, BUT ALONE THEY WERE NOT ENOUGH! SOMETIMES BY CHANCE NIGHT FIGHTERS MADE CONTACT WITH THE BOMBERS, BUT EVEN THEN...
GOT THE BLIGHTER SKIPPER!
...I RECKON HE MUST HAVE BEEN RIGHT ON TOP OF US BEFORE HE SAW US!

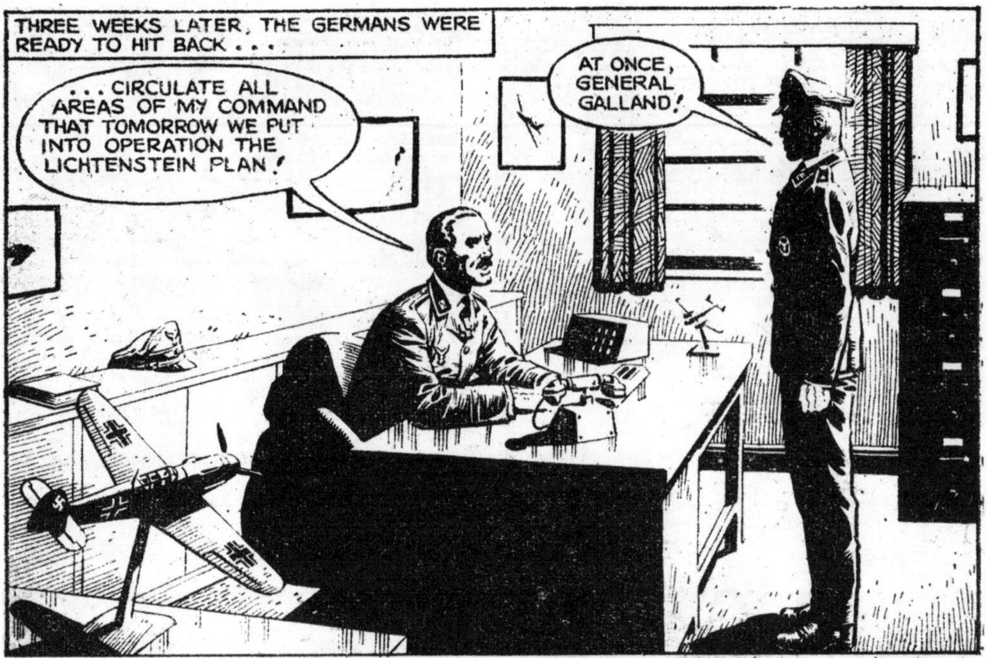
THREE WEEKS LATER, THE GERMANS WERE READY TO HIT BACK . . .
. . . CIRCULATE ALL AREAS OF MY COMMAND THAT TOMORROW WE PUT INTO OPERATION THE LICHTENSTEIN PLAN!
AT ONCE, GENERAL GALLAND!

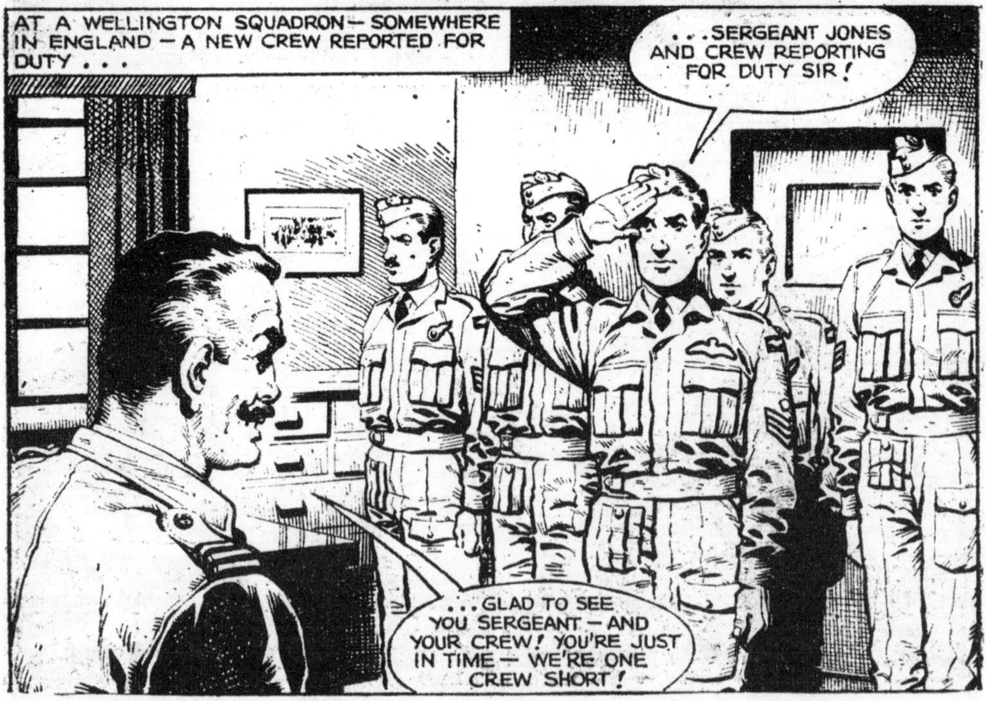
AT A WELLINGTON SQUADRON – SOMEWHERE IN ENGLAND – A NEW CREW REPORTED FOR DUTY . . .
. . . SERGEANT JONES AND CREW REPORTING FOR DUTY SIR!
. . . GLAD TO SEE YOU SERGEANT – AND YOUR CREW! YOU'RE JUST IN TIME – WE'RE ONE CREW SHORT!

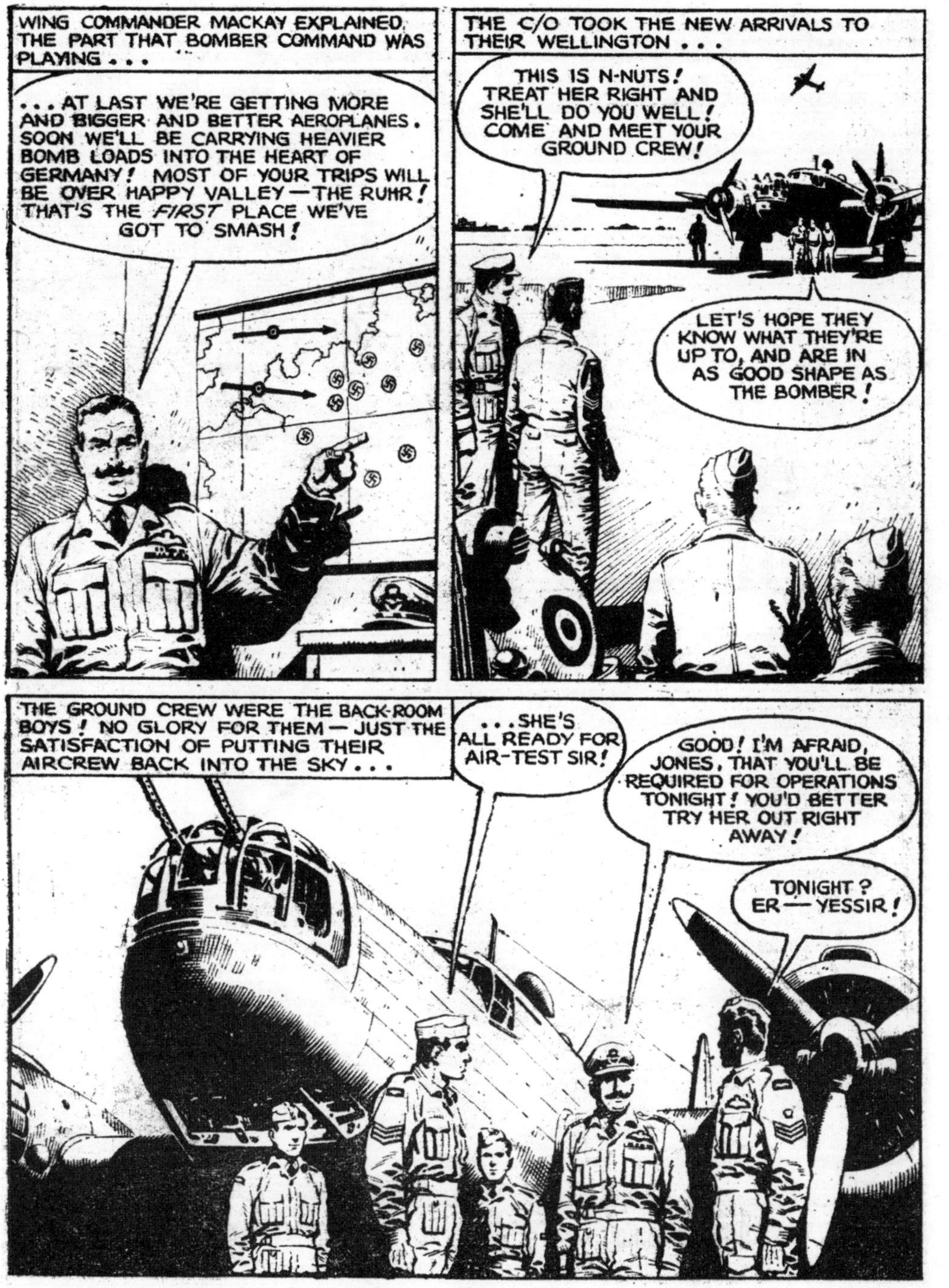
WING COMMANDER MACKAY EXPLAINED THE PART THAT BOMBER COMMAND WAS PLAYING . . .
. . . AT LAST WE'RE GETTING MORE AND BIGGER AND BETTER AEROPLANES. SOON WE'LL BE CARRYING HEAVIER BOMB LOADS INTO THE HEART OF GERMANY! MOST OF YOUR TRIPS WILL BE OVER HAPPY VALLEY — THE RUHR! THAT'S THE *FIRST* PLACE WE'VE GOT TO SMASH!
THE C/O TOOK THE NEW ARRIVALS TO THEIR WELLINGTON . . .
THIS IS N-NUTS! TREAT HER RIGHT AND SHE'LL DO YOU WELL! COME AND MEET YOUR GROUND CREW!
LET'S HOPE THEY KNOW WHAT THEY'RE UP TO, AND ARE IN AS GOOD SHAPE AS THE BOMBER!
THE GROUND CREW WERE THE BACK-ROOM BOYS! NO GLORY FOR THEM — JUST THE SATISFACTION OF PUTTING THEIR AIRCREW BACK INTO THE SKY . . .
. . . SHE'S ALL READY FOR AIR-TEST SIR!
GOOD! I'M AFRAID, JONES, THAT YOU'LL BE REQUIRED FOR OPERATIONS TONIGHT! YOU'D BETTER TRY HER OUT RIGHT AWAY!
TONIGHT? ER — YESSIR!

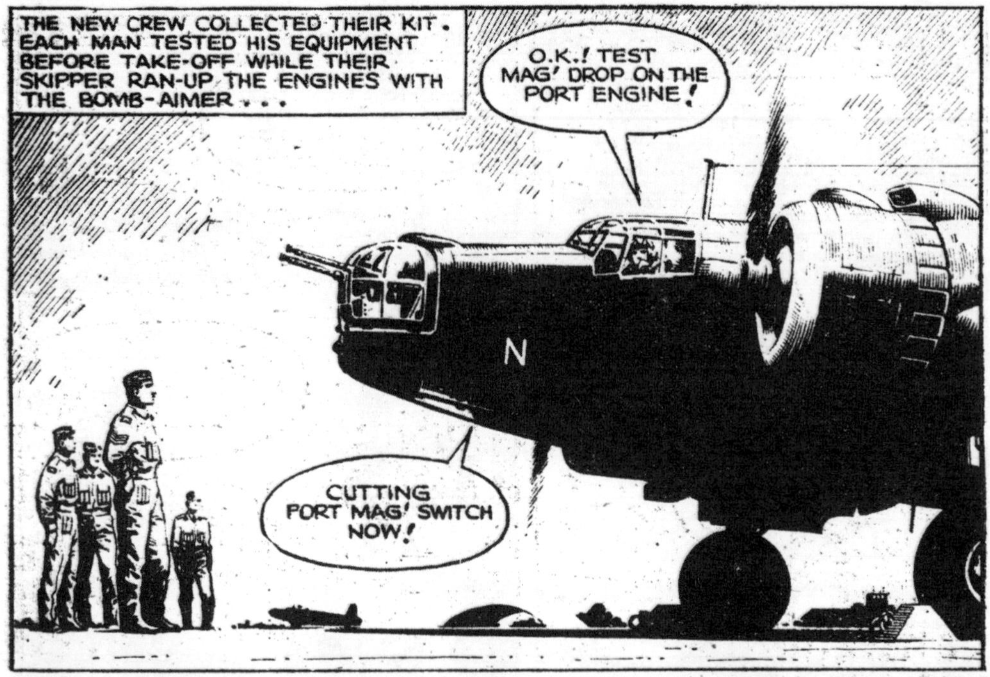
THE NEW CREW COLLECTED THEIR KIT. EACH MAN TESTED HIS EQUIPMENT BEFORE TAKE-OFF WHILE THEIR SKIPPER RAN-UP THE ENGINES WITH THE BOMB-AIMER . . .
O.K.! TEST MAG' DROP ON THE PORT ENGINE!
CUTTING PORT MAG' SWITCH NOW!

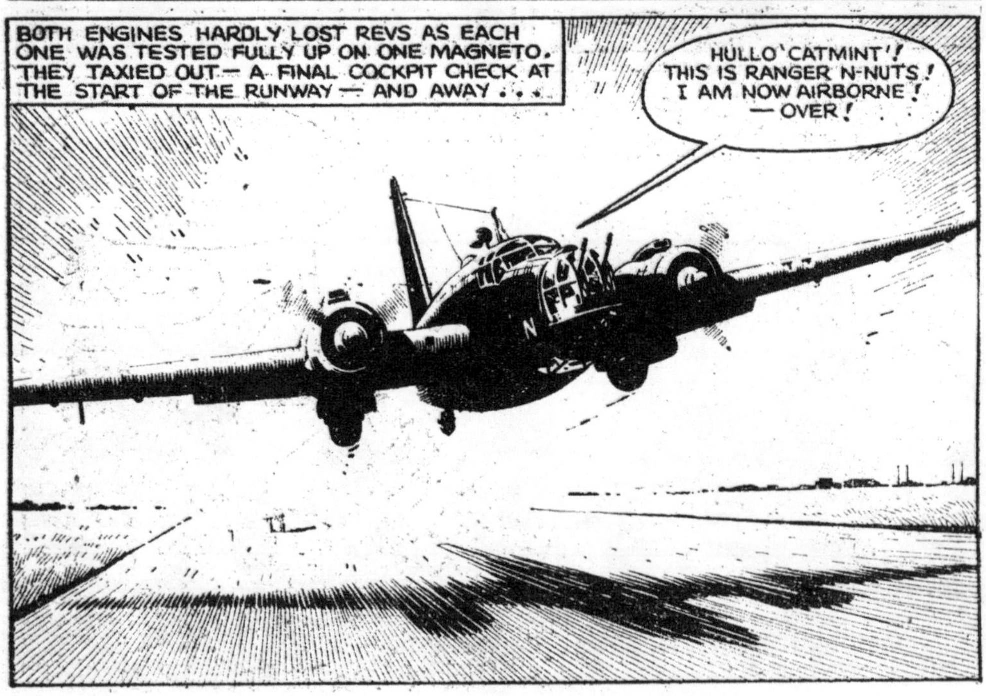
BOTH ENGINES HARDLY LOST REVS AS EACH ONE WAS TESTED FULLY UP ON ONE MAGNETO. THEY TAXIED OUT — A FINAL COCKPIT CHECK AT THE START OF THE RUNWAY — AND AWAY . . .
HULLO 'CATMINT'! THIS IS RANGER N-NUTS! I AM NOW AIRBORNE! — OVER!

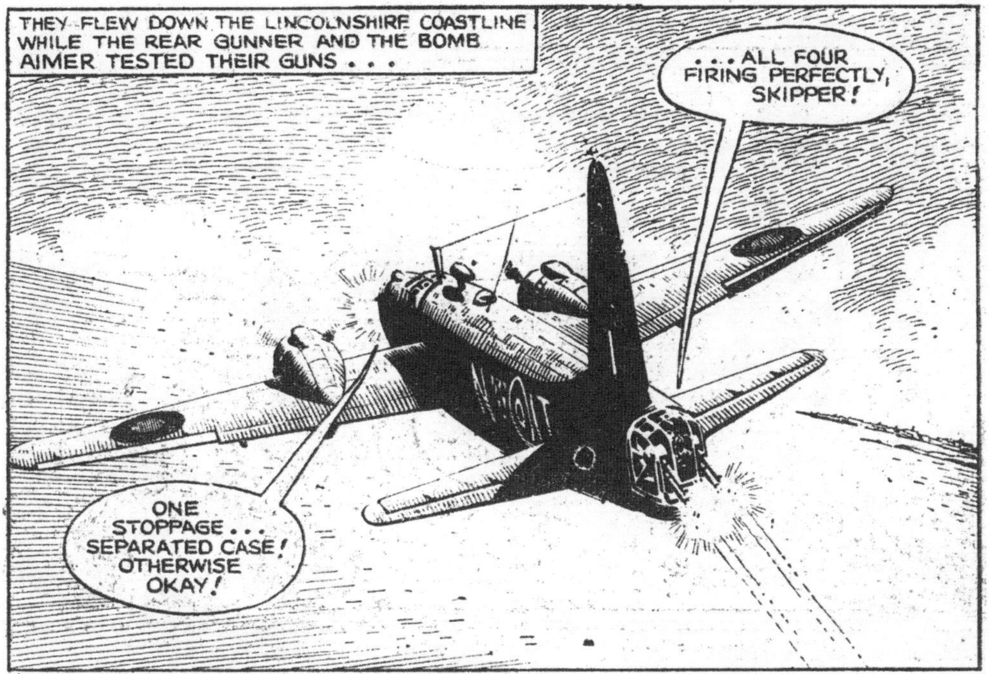
THEY FLEW DOWN THE LINCOLNSHIRE COASTLINE WHILE THE REAR GUNNER AND THE BOMB AIMER TESTED THEIR GUNS . . .
. . . ALL FOUR FIRING PERFECTLY, SKIPPER!
ONE STOPPAGE . . . SEPARATED CASE! OTHERWISE OKAY!

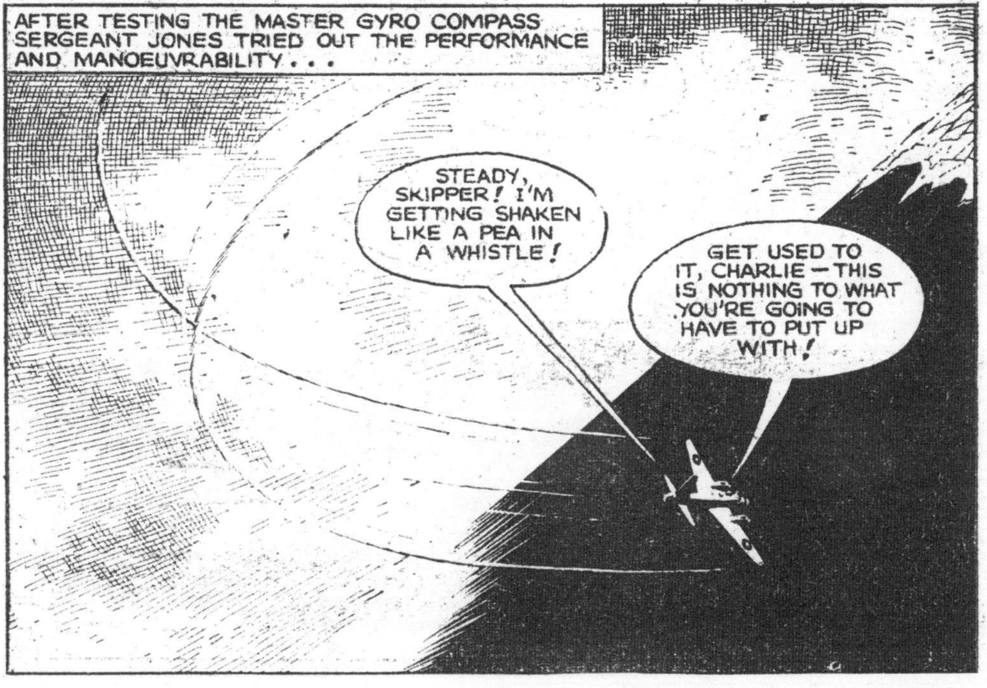
AFTER TESTING THE MASTER GYRO COMPASS SERGEANT JONES TRIED OUT THE PERFORMANCE AND MANOEUVRABILITY . . .
STEADY, SKIPPER! I'M GETTING SHAKEN LIKE A PEA IN A WHISTLE!
GET USED TO IT, CHARLIE — THIS IS NOTHING TO WHAT YOU'RE GOING TO HAVE TO PUT UP WITH!

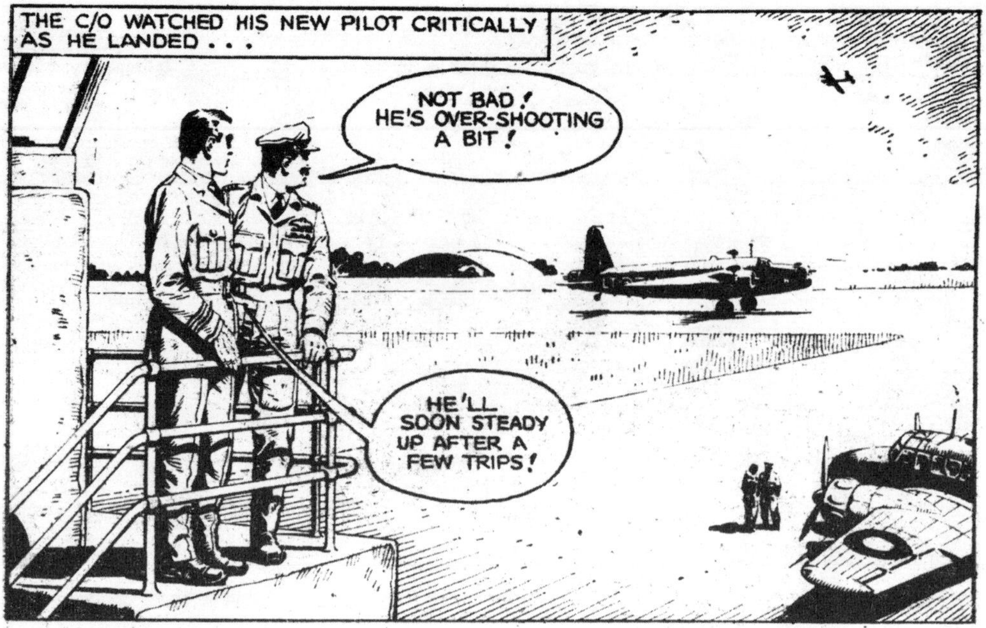
THE C/O WATCHED HIS NEW PILOT CRITICALLY AS HE LANDED . . .
NOT BAD! HE'S OVER-SHOOTING A BIT!
HE'LL SOON STEADY UP AFTER A FEW TRIPS!

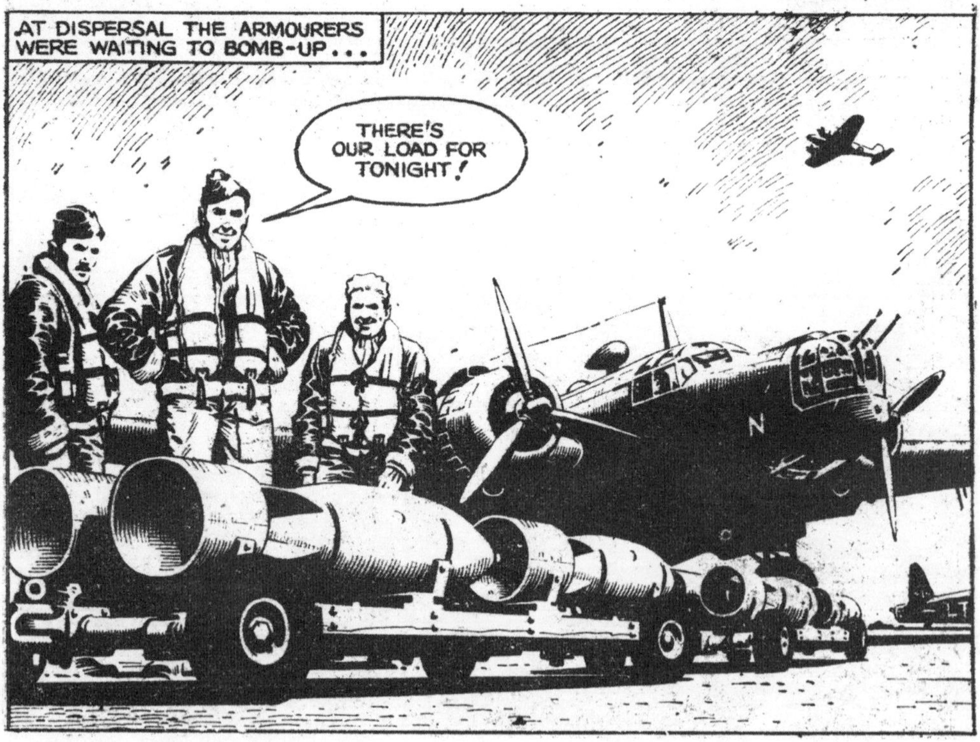
AT DISPERSAL THE ARMOURERS WERE WAITING TO BOMB-UP . . .
THERE'S OUR LOAD FOR TONIGHT!

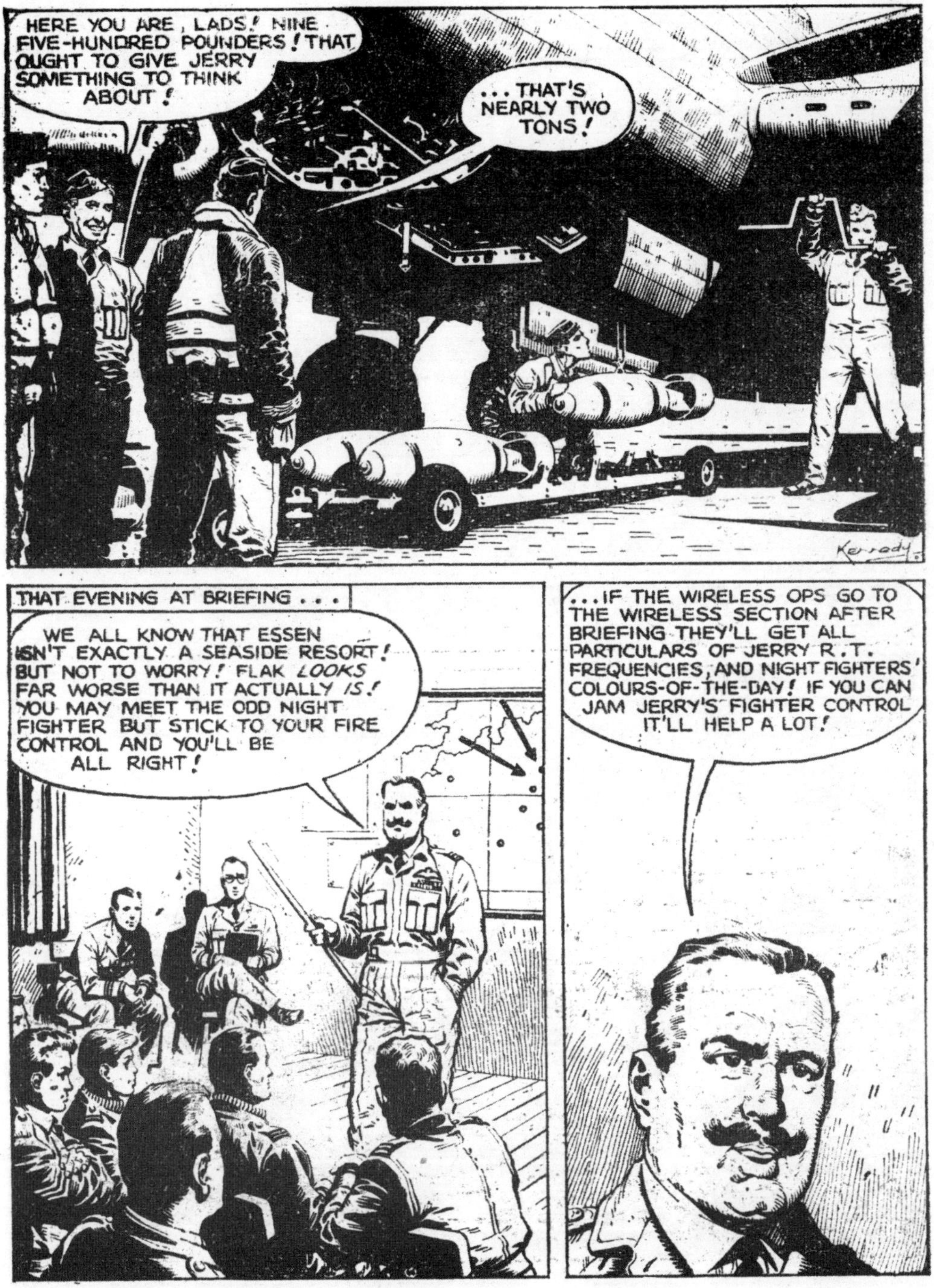
HERE YOU ARE, LADS! NINE FIVE-HUNDRED POUNDERS! THAT OUGHT TO GIVE JERRY SOMETHING TO THINK ABOUT!
... THAT'S NEARLY TWO TONS!
THAT EVENING AT BRIEFING . . .
WE ALL KNOW THAT ESSEN ISN'T EXACTLY A SEASIDE RESORT! BUT NOT TO WORRY! FLAK *LOOKS* FAR WORSE THAN IT ACTUALLY *IS*! YOU MAY MEET THE ODD NIGHT FIGHTER BUT STICK TO YOUR FIRE CONTROL AND YOU'LL BE ALL RIGHT!
...IF THE WIRELESS OPS GO TO THE WIRELESS SECTION AFTER BRIEFING THEY'LL GET ALL PARTICULARS OF JERRY R.T. FREQUENCIES, AND NIGHT FIGHTERS' COLOURS-OF-THE-DAY! IF YOU CAN JAM JERRY'S FIGHTER CONTROL IT'LL HELP A LOT!

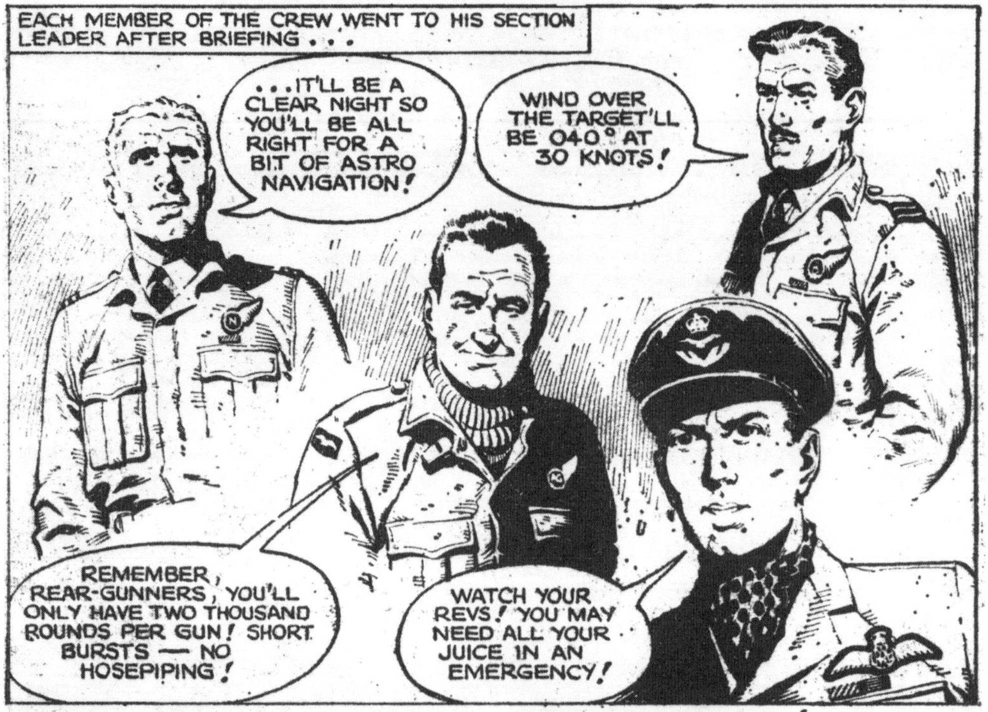
EACH MEMBER OF THE CREW WENT TO HIS SECTION LEADER AFTER BRIEFING . . .
. . . IT'LL BE A CLEAR NIGHT SO YOU'LL BE ALL RIGHT FOR A BIT OF ASTRO NAVIGATION!
WIND OVER THE TARGET'LL BE 040° AT 30 KNOTS!
REMEMBER, REAR-GUNNERS, YOU'LL ONLY HAVE TWO THOUSAND ROUNDS PER GUN! SHORT BURSTS — NO HOSEPIPING!
WATCH YOUR REVS! YOU MAY NEED ALL YOUR JUICE IN AN EMERGENCY!

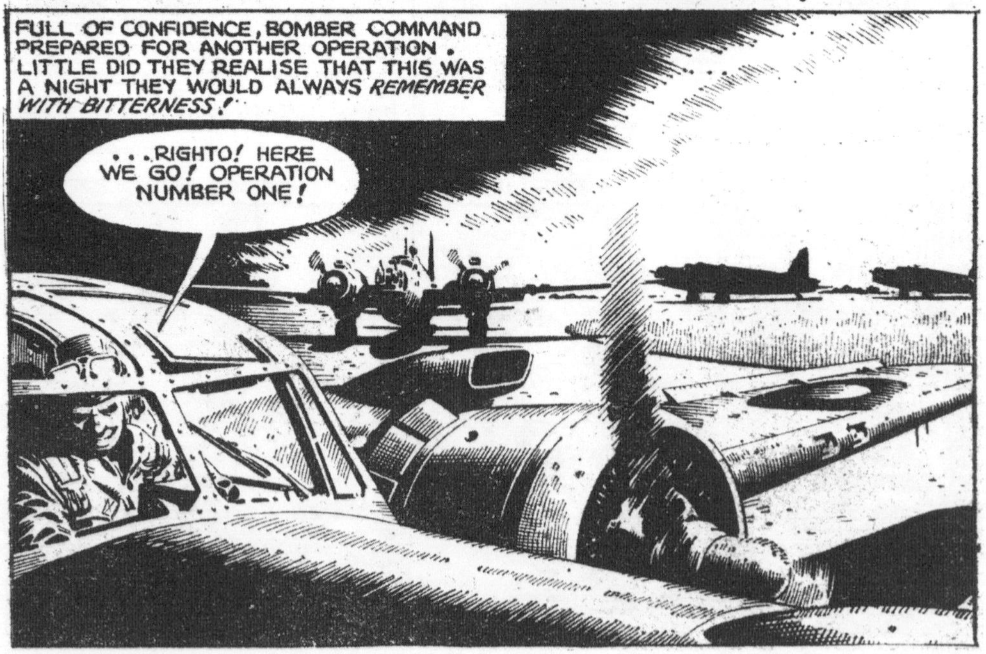
FULL OF CONFIDENCE, BOMBER COMMAND PREPARED FOR ANOTHER OPERATION. LITTLE DID THEY REALISE THAT THIS WAS A NIGHT THEY WOULD ALWAYS *REMEMBER WITH BITTERNESS!*
. . . RIGHTO! HERE WE GO! OPERATION NUMBER ONE!

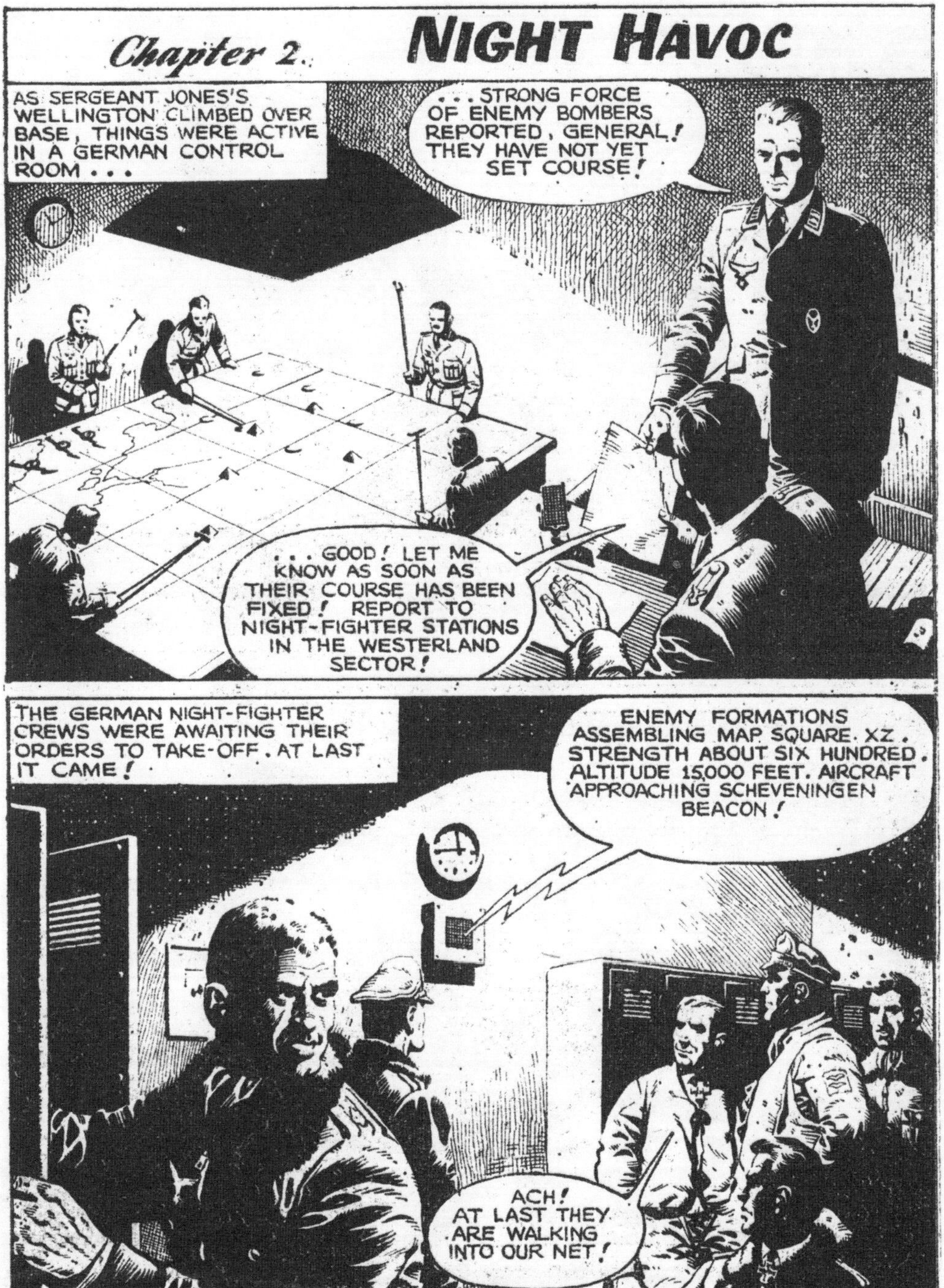
Chapter 2.
NIGHT HAVOC
AS SERGEANT JONES'S WELLINGTON CLIMBED OVER BASE, THINGS WERE ACTIVE IN A GERMAN CONTROL ROOM . . .
. . . STRONG FORCE OF ENEMY BOMBERS REPORTED, GENERAL! THEY HAVE NOT YET SET COURSE!
. . GOOD! LET ME KNOW AS SOON AS THEIR COURSE HAS BEEN FIXED! REPORT TO NIGHT-FIGHTER STATIONS IN THE WESTERLAND SECTOR!
THE GERMAN NIGHT-FIGHTER CREWS WERE AWAITING THEIR ORDERS TO TAKE-OFF. AT LAST IT CAME!
ENEMY FORMATIONS ASSEMBLING MAP SQUARE. XZ. STRENGTH ABOUT SIX HUNDRED. ALTITUDE 15,000 FEET. AIRCRAFT APPROACHING SCHEVENINGEN BEACON!
ACH! AT LAST THEY ARE WALKING INTO OUR NET!

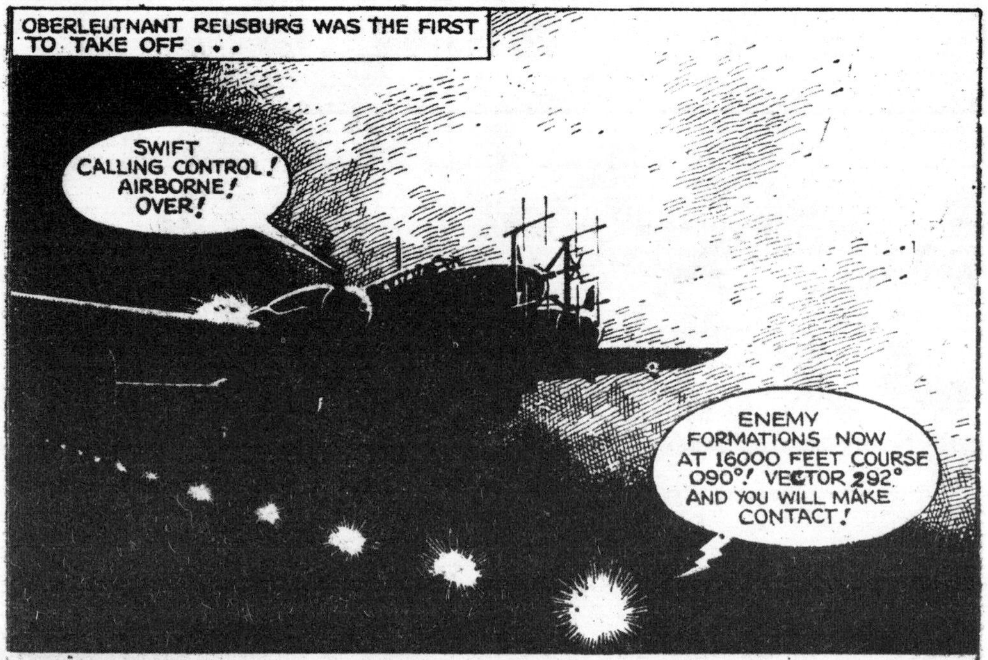
OBERLEUTNANT REUSBURG WAS THE FIRST TO TAKE OFF . . .
SWIFT CALLING CONTROL! AIRBORNE! OVER!
ENEMY FORMATIONS NOW AT 16000 FEET COURSE 090°! VECTOR 292° AND YOU WILL MAKE CONTACT!

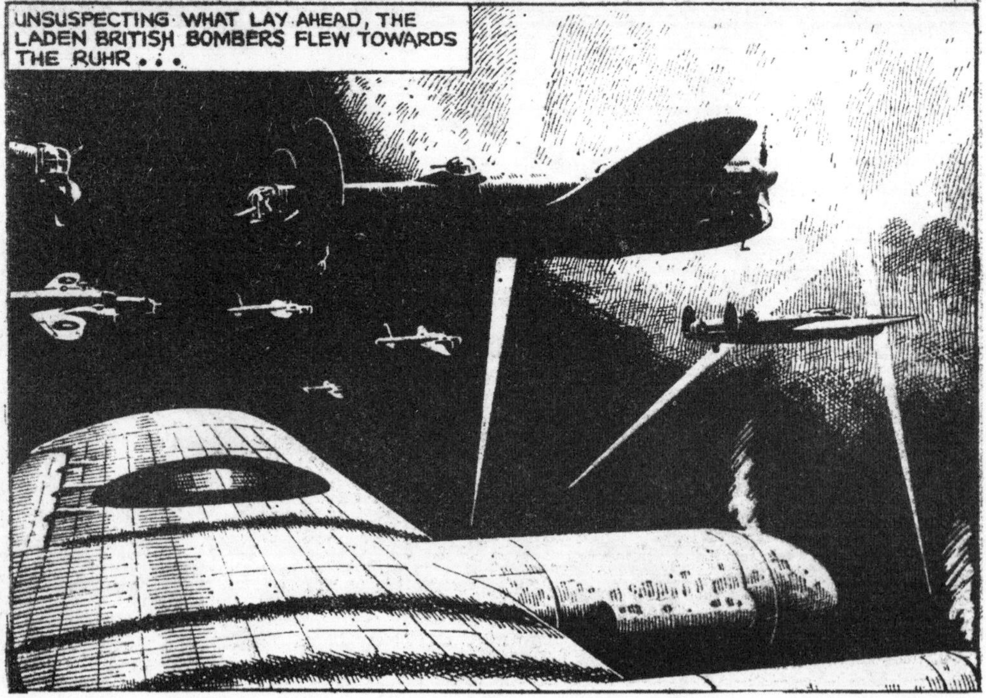
UNSUSPECTING WHAT LAY AHEAD, THE LADEN BRITISH BOMBERS FLEW TOWARDS THE RUHR . . .

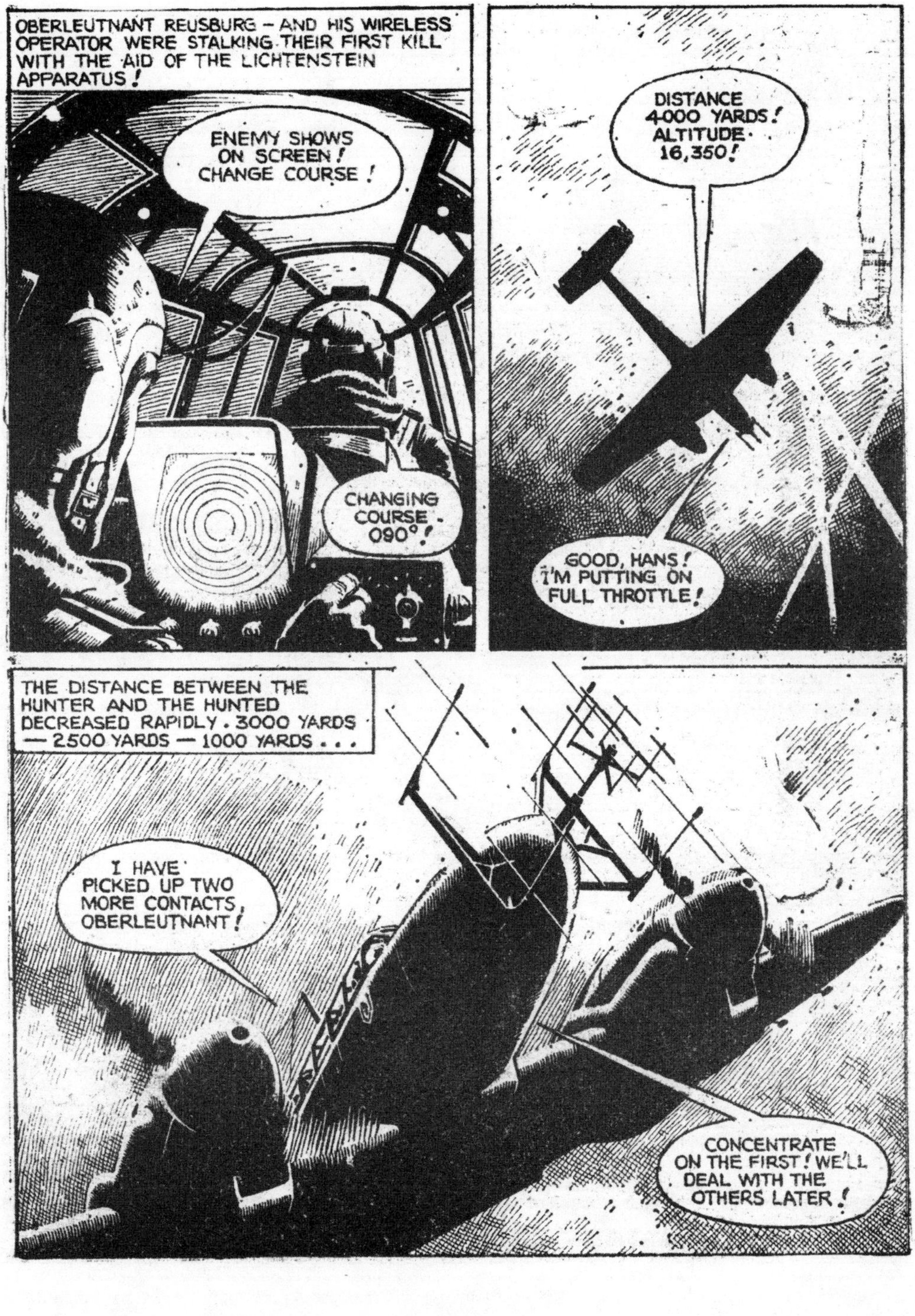
OBERLEUTNANT REUSBURG – AND HIS WIRELESS OPERATOR WERE STALKING THEIR FIRST KILL WITH THE AID OF THE LICHTENSTEIN APPARATUS!
ENEMY SHOWS ON SCREEN! CHANGE COURSE!
CHANGING COURSE 090°!
DISTANCE 4000 YARDS! ALTITUDE 16,350!
GOOD, HANS! I'M PUTTING ON FULL THROTTLE!
THE DISTANCE BETWEEN THE HUNTER AND THE HUNTED DECREASED RAPIDLY. 3000 YARDS — 2500 YARDS — 1000 YARDS . . .
I HAVE PICKED UP TWO MORE CONTACTS, OBERLEUTNANT!
CONCENTRATE ON THE FIRST! WE'LL DEAL WITH THE OTHERS LATER!

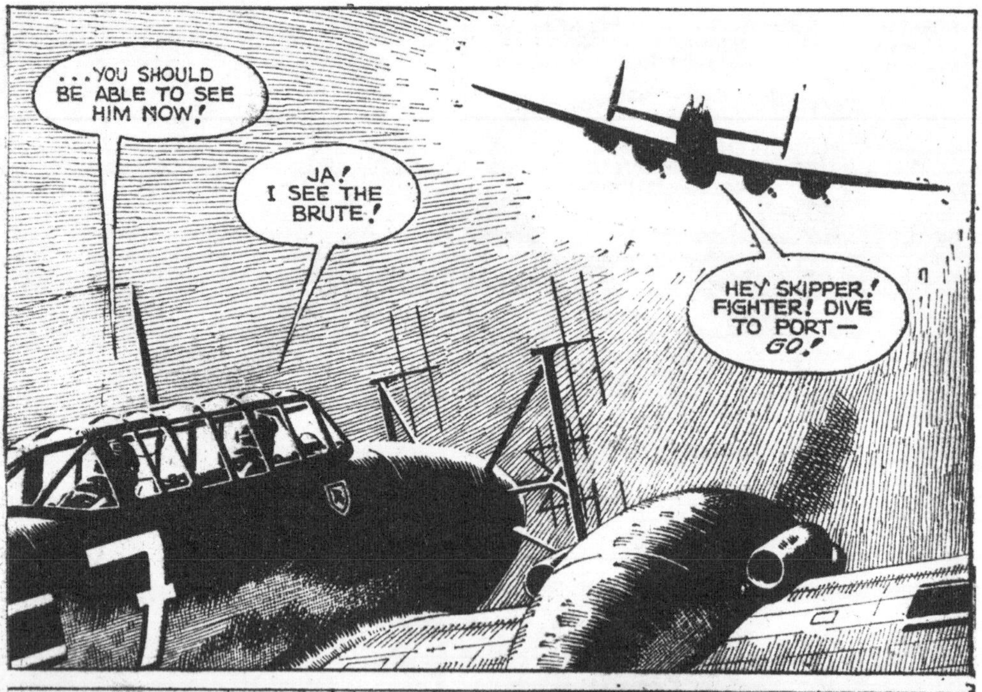
...YOU SHOULD BE ABLE TO SEE HIM NOW!
JA! I SEE THE BRUTE!
HEY SKIPPER! FIGHTER! DIVE TO PORT — GO!

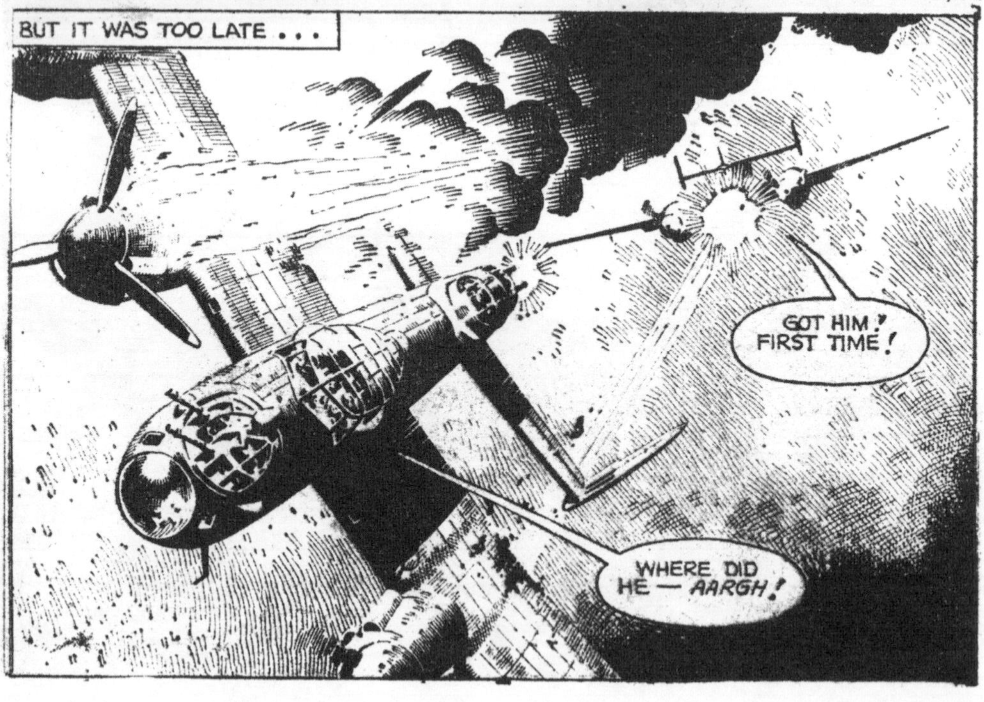
BUT IT WAS TOO LATE ...
GOT HIM! FIRST TIME!
WHERE DID HE — AARGH!

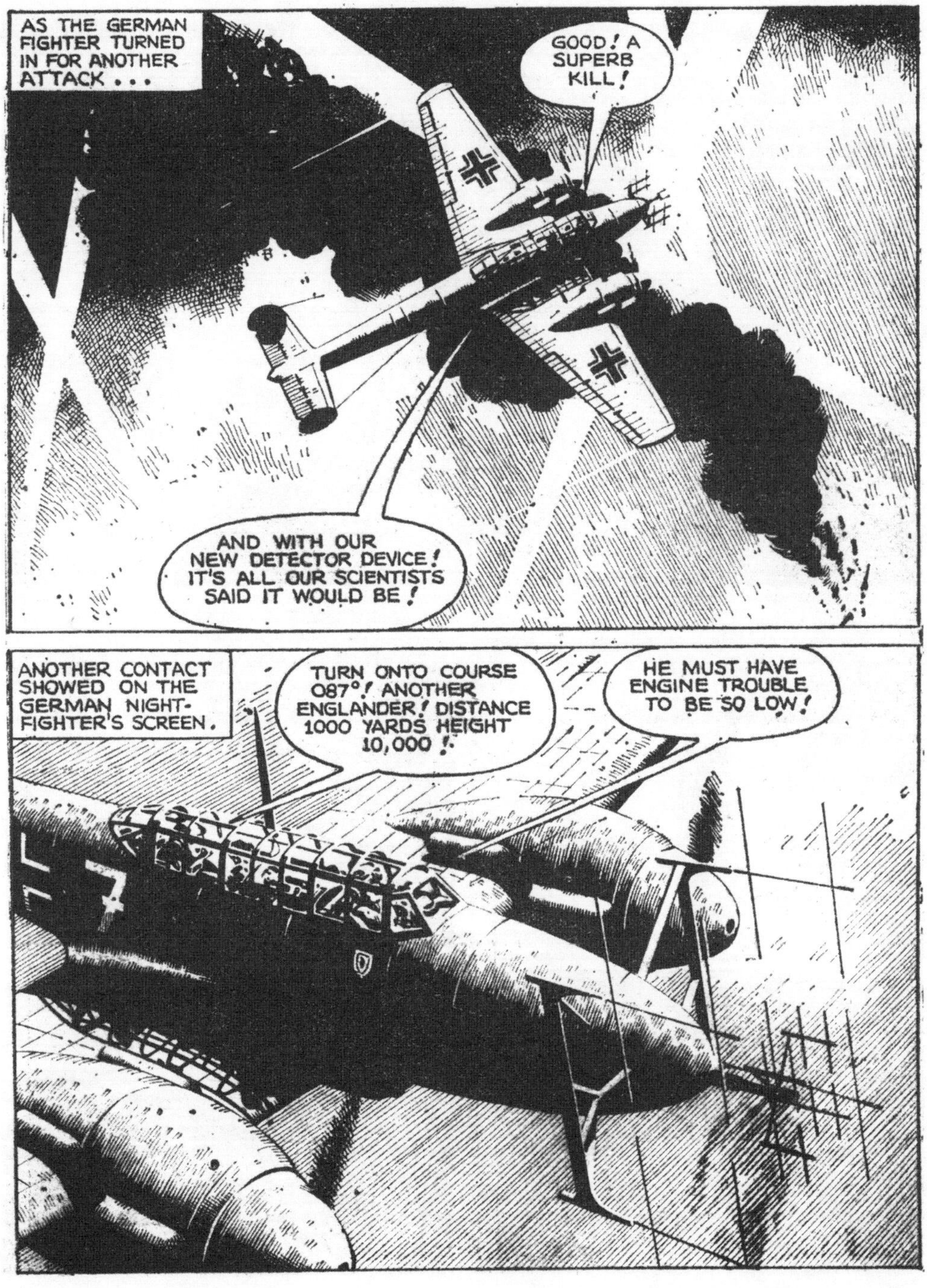
AS THE GERMAN FIGHTER TURNED IN FOR ANOTHER ATTACK . . .
GOOD! A SUPERB KILL!
AND WITH OUR NEW DETECTOR DEVICE! IT'S ALL OUR SCIENTISTS SAID IT WOULD BE!
ANOTHER CONTACT SHOWED ON THE GERMAN NIGHT-FIGHTER'S SCREEN.
TURN ONTO COURSE 087°! ANOTHER ENGLANDER! DISTANCE 1000 YARDS HEIGHT 10,000!
HE MUST HAVE ENGINE TROUBLE TO BE SO LOW!

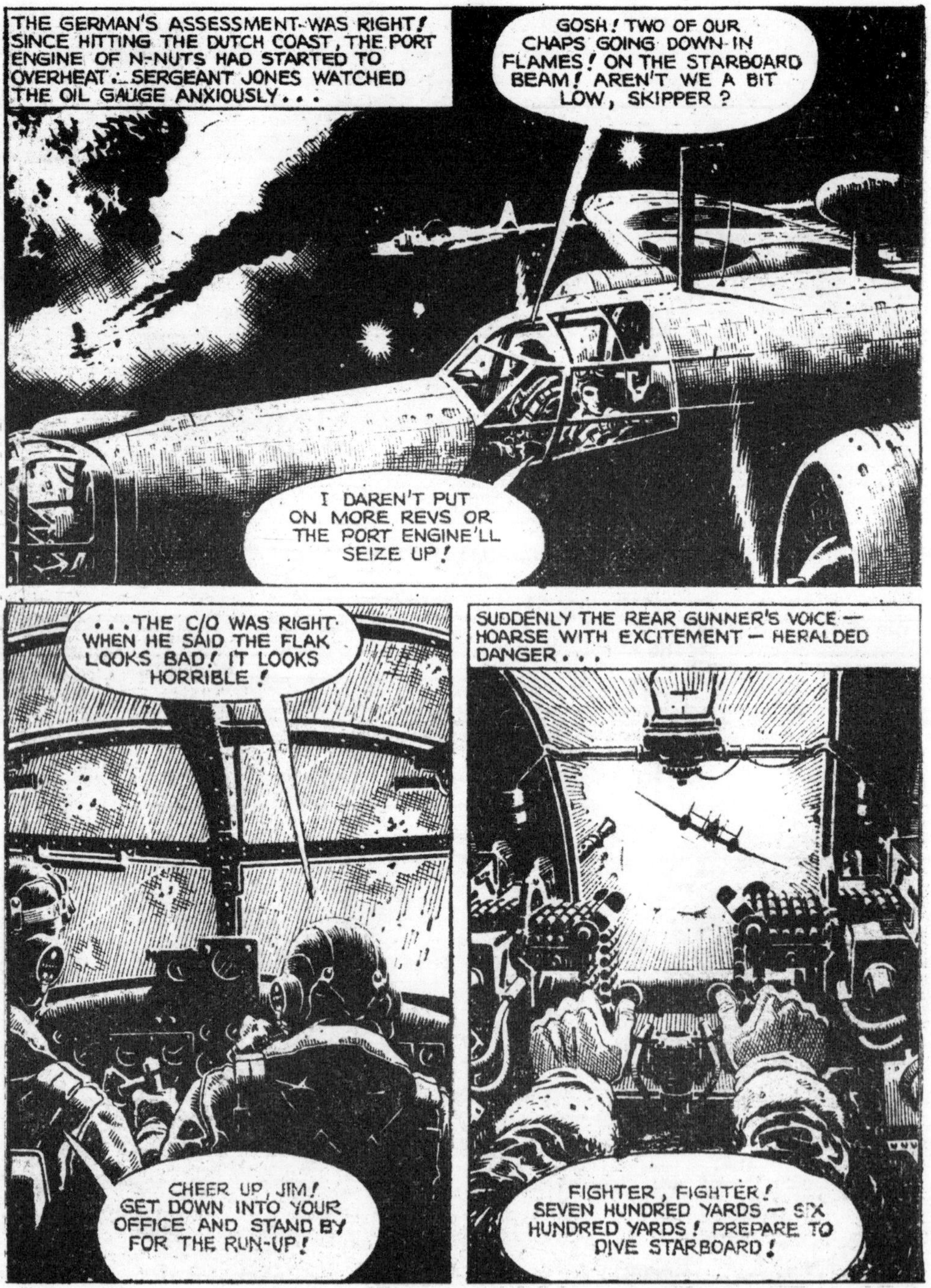
THE GERMAN'S ASSESSMENT WAS RIGHT! SINCE HITTING THE DUTCH COAST, THE PORT ENGINE OF N-NUTS HAD STARTED TO OVERHEAT... SERGEANT JONES WATCHED THE OIL GAUGE ANXIOUSLY...
GOSH! TWO OF OUR CHAPS GOING DOWN IN FLAMES! ON THE STARBOARD BEAM! AREN'T WE A BIT LOW, SKIPPER?
I DAREN'T PUT ON MORE REVS OR THE PORT ENGINE'LL SEIZE UP!
...THE C/O WAS RIGHT WHEN HE SAID THE FLAK LOOKS BAD! IT LOOKS HORRIBLE!
CHEER UP, JIM! GET DOWN INTO YOUR OFFICE AND STAND BY FOR THE RUN-UP!
SUDDENLY THE REAR GUNNER'S VOICE — HOARSE WITH EXCITEMENT — HERALDED DANGER...
FIGHTER, FIGHTER! SEVEN HUNDRED YARDS — SIX HUNDRED YARDS! PREPARE TO DIVE STARBOARD!

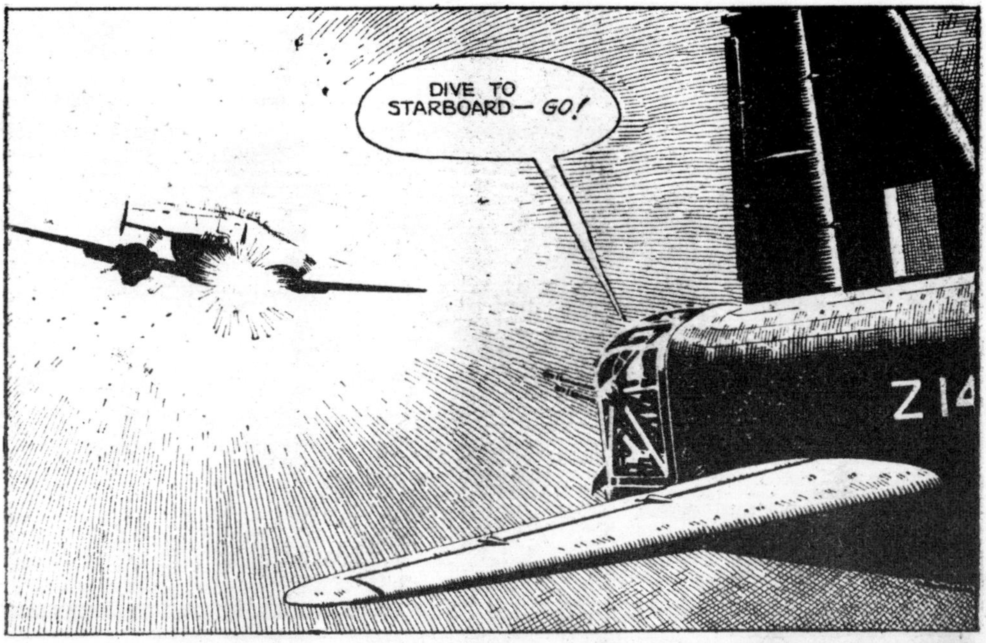
DIVE TO STARBOARD— GO!

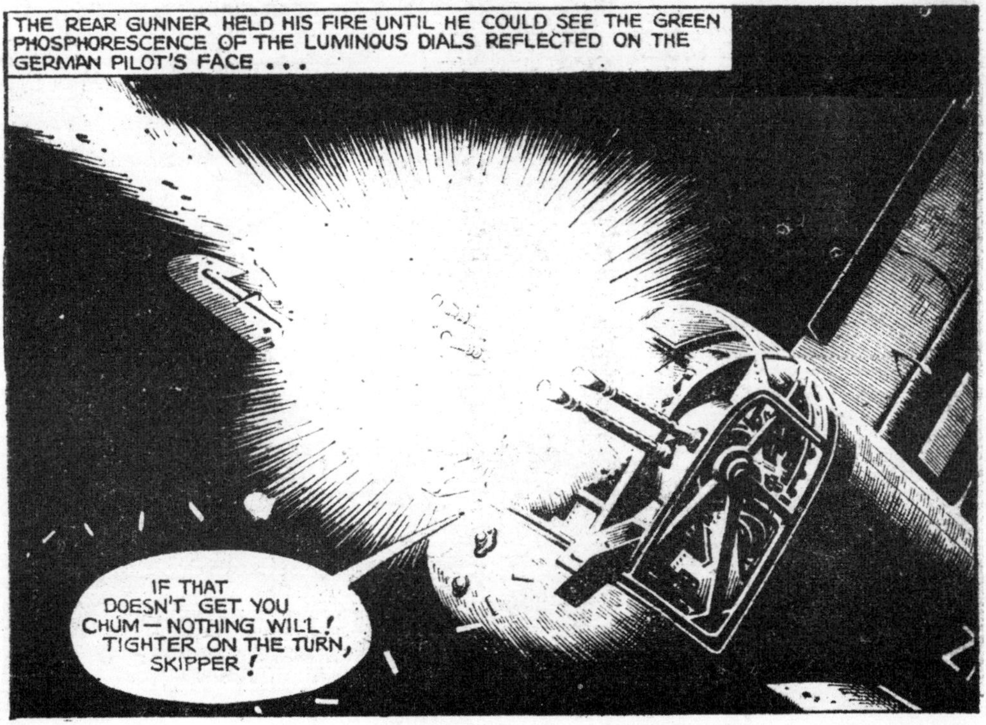
THE REAR GUNNER HELD HIS FIRE UNTIL HE COULD SEE THE GREEN PHOSPHORESCENCE OF THE LUMINOUS DIALS REFLECTED ON THE GERMAN PILOT'S FACE . . .
IF THAT DOESN'T GET YOU CHUM— NOTHING WILL! TIGHTER ON THE TURN, SKIPPER!

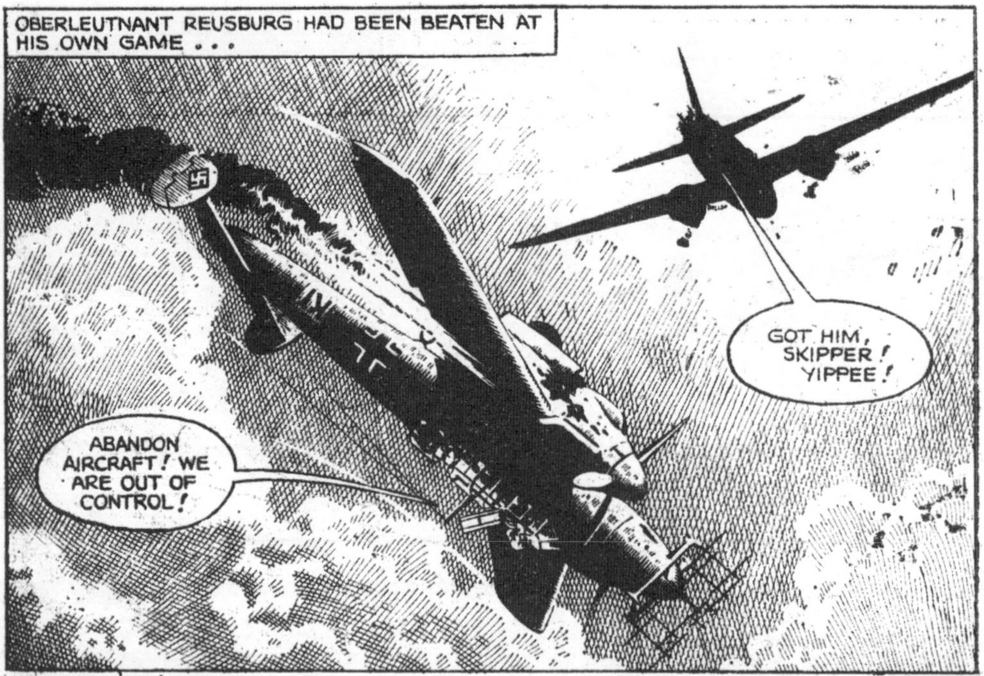
OBERLEUTNANT REUSBURG HAD BEEN BEATEN AT HIS OWN GAME . . .
GOT HIM, SKIPPER! YIPPEE!
ABANDON AIRCRAFT! WE ARE OUT OF CONTROL!

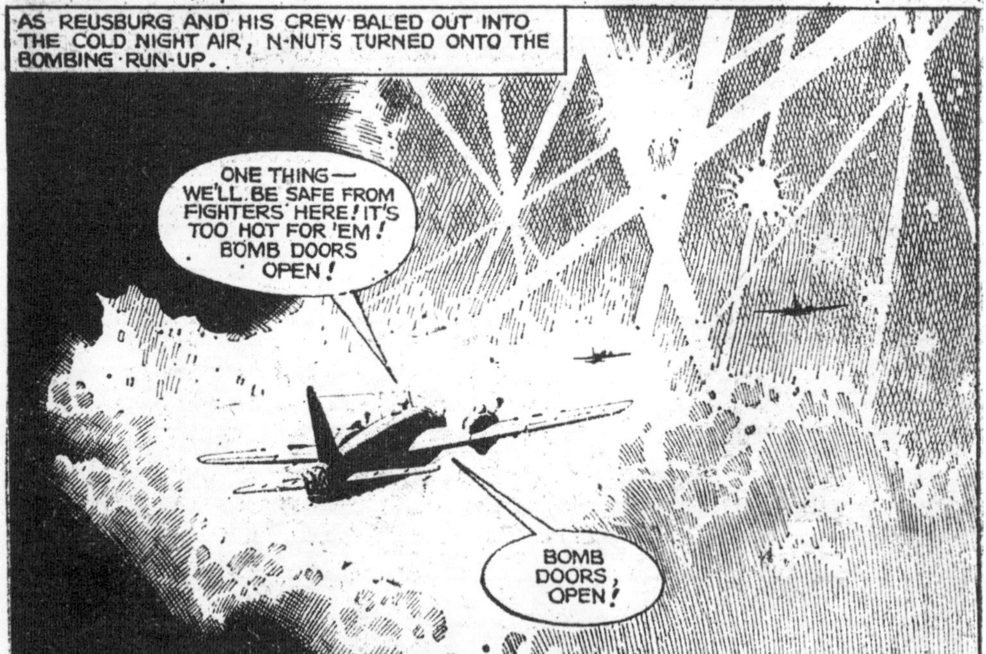
AS REUSBURG AND HIS CREW BALED OUT INTO THE COLD NIGHT AIR, N-NUTS TURNED ONTO THE BOMBING RUN-UP.
ONE THING— WE'LL BE SAFE FROM FIGHTERS HERE! IT'S TOO HOT FOR 'EM! BOMB DOORS OPEN!
BOMB DOORS, OPEN!

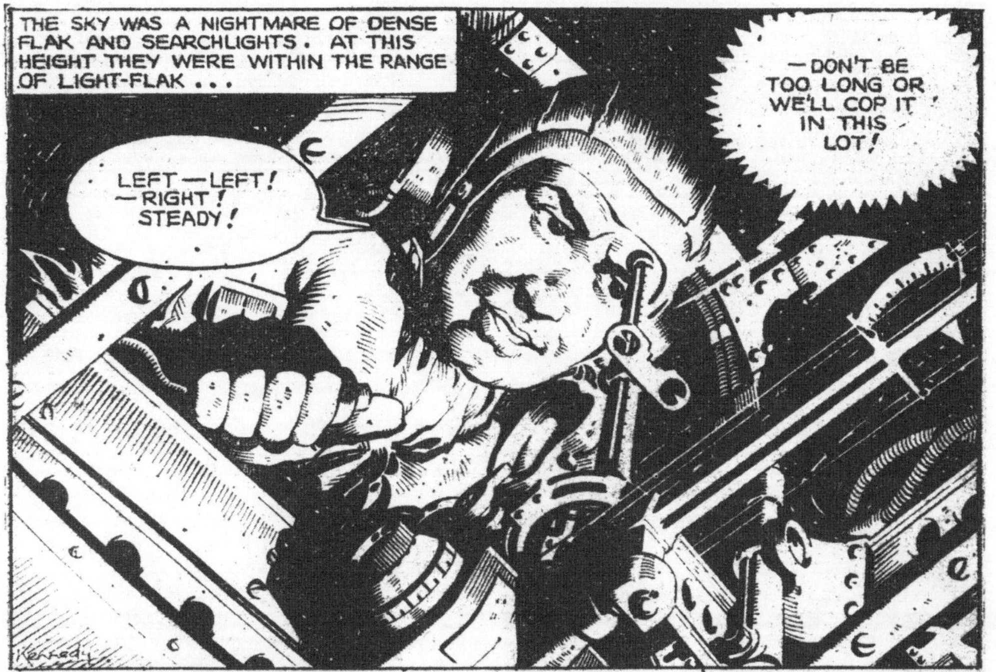
THE SKY WAS A NIGHTMARE OF DENSE FLAK AND SEARCHLIGHTS. AT THIS HEIGHT THEY WERE WITHIN THE RANGE OF LIGHT-FLAK ...
LEFT—LEFT! —RIGHT! STEADY!
—DON'T BE TOO LONG OR WE'LL COP IT IN THIS LOT!

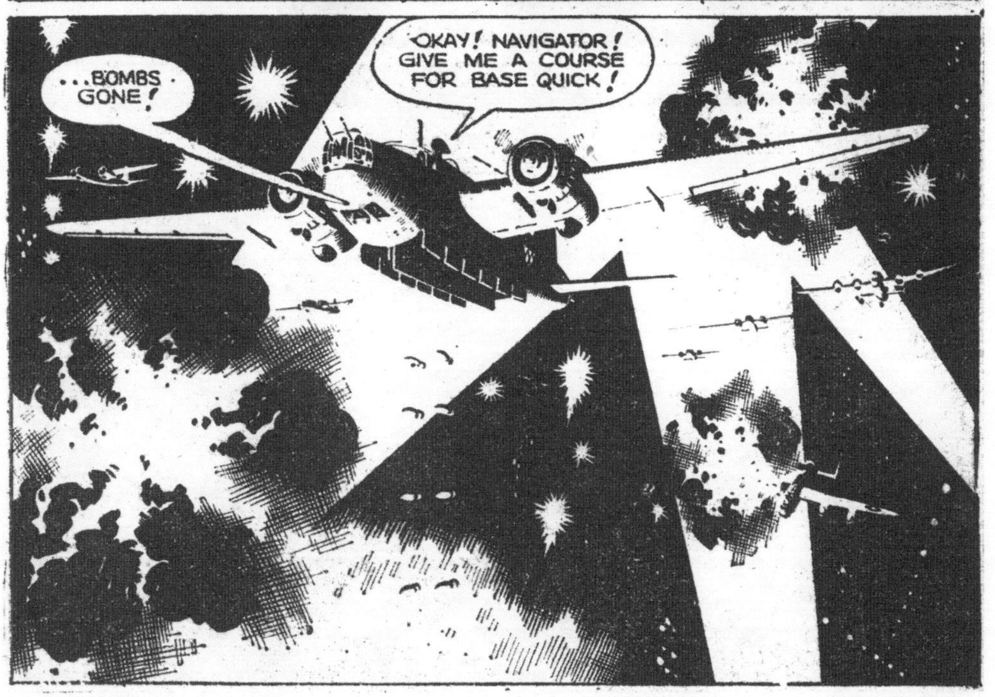
...BOMBS GONE!
OKAY! NAVIGATOR! GIVE ME A COURSE FOR BASE QUICK!

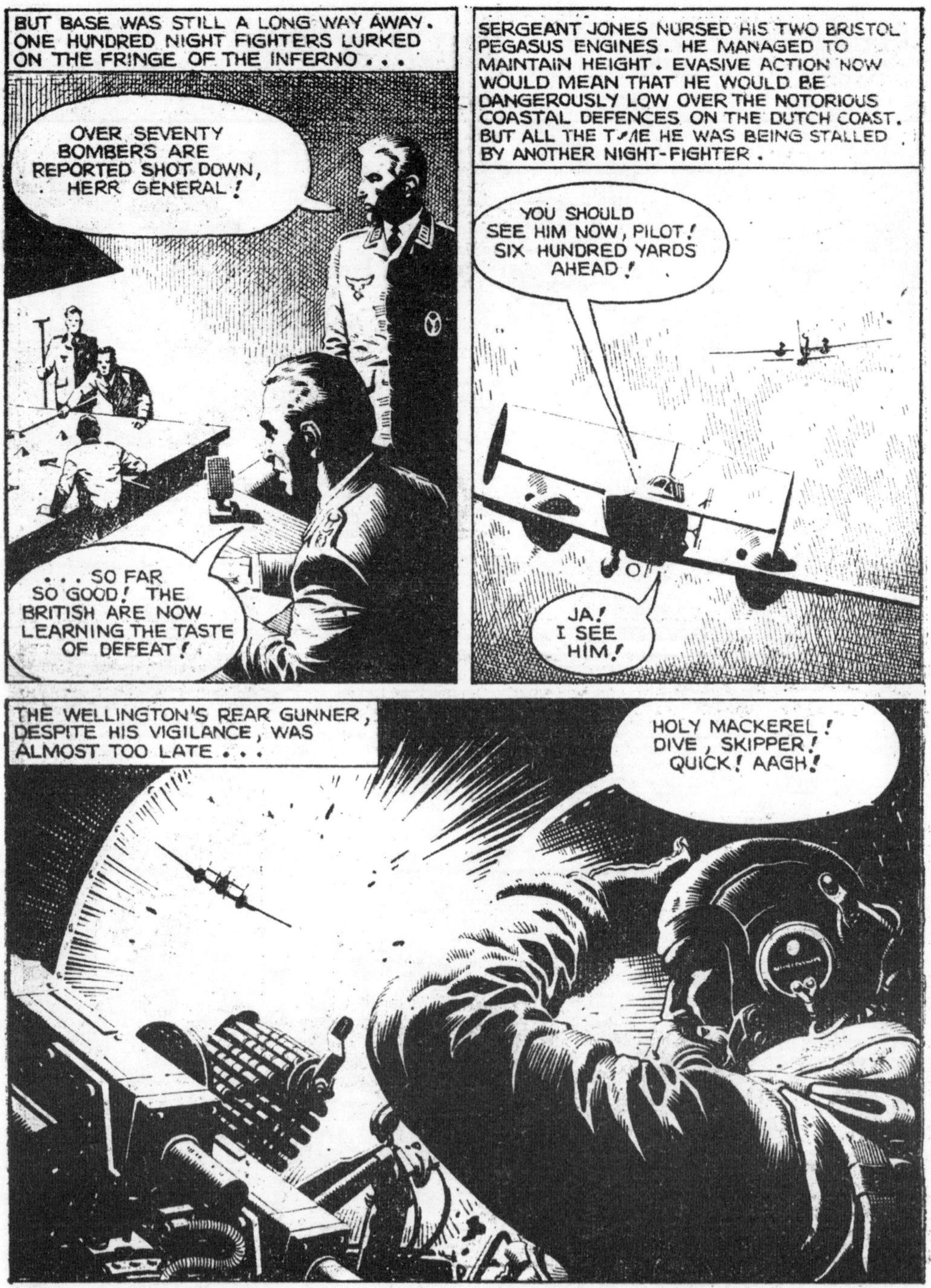
BUT BASE WAS STILL A LONG WAY AWAY. ONE HUNDRED NIGHT FIGHTERS LURKED ON THE FRINGE OF THE INFERNO . . .
OVER SEVENTY BOMBERS ARE REPORTED SHOT DOWN, HERR GENERAL!
. . . SO FAR SO GOOD! THE BRITISH ARE NOW LEARNING THE TASTE OF DEFEAT!
SERGEANT JONES NURSED HIS TWO BRISTOL PEGASUS ENGINES. HE MANAGED TO MAINTAIN HEIGHT. EVASIVE ACTION NOW WOULD MEAN THAT HE WOULD BE DANGEROUSLY LOW OVER THE NOTORIOUS COASTAL DEFENCES ON THE DUTCH COAST. BUT ALL THE TIME HE WAS BEING STALLED BY ANOTHER NIGHT-FIGHTER.
YOU SHOULD SEE HIM NOW, PILOT! SIX HUNDRED YARDS AHEAD!
JA! I SEE HIM!
THE WELLINGTON'S REAR GUNNER, DESPITE HIS VIGILANCE, WAS ALMOST TOO LATE . . .
HOLY MACKEREL! DIVE, SKIPPER! QUICK! AAGH!

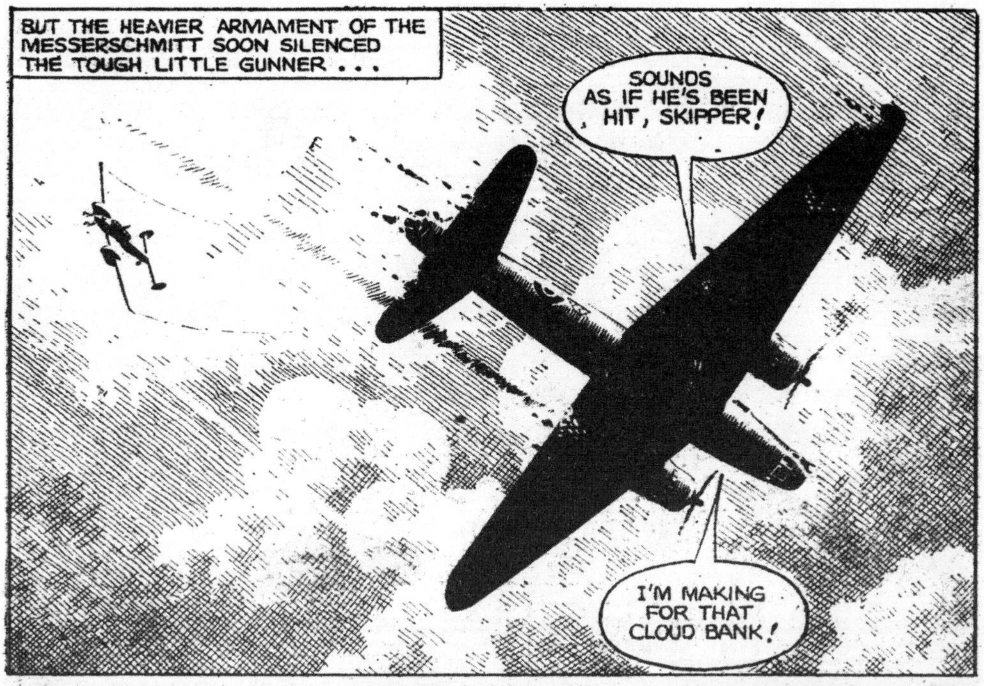
BUT THE HEAVIER ARMAMENT OF THE MESSERSCHMITT SOON SILENCED THE TOUGH LITTLE GUNNER . . .
SOUNDS AS IF HE'S BEEN HIT, SKIPPER!
I'M MAKING FOR THAT CLOUD BANK!

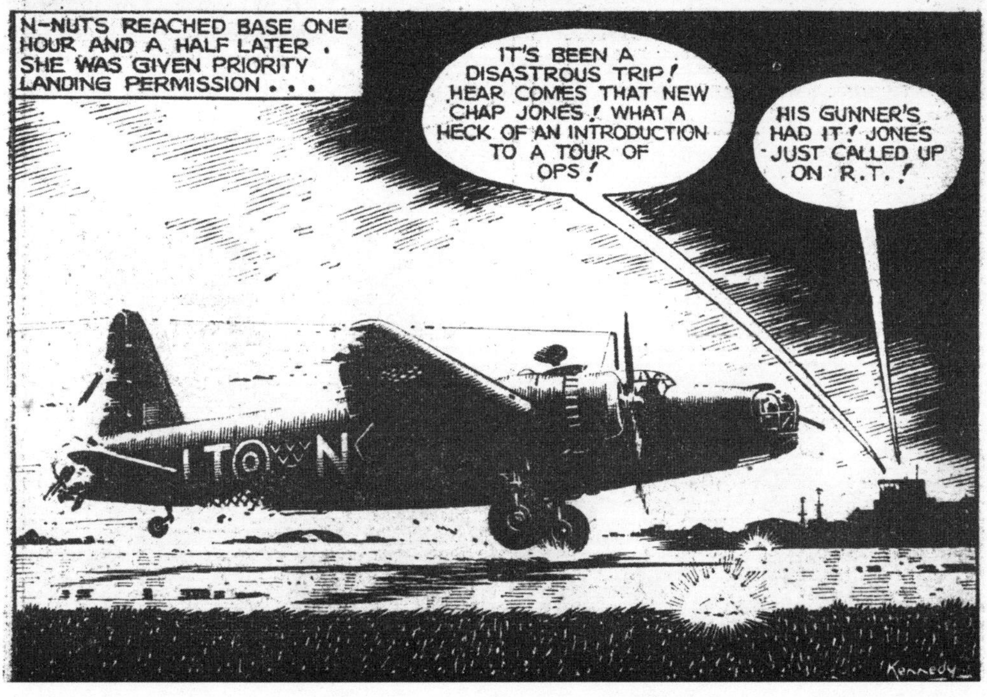
N-NUTS REACHED BASE ONE HOUR AND A HALF LATER. SHE WAS GIVEN PRIORITY LANDING PERMISSION . . .
IT'S BEEN A DISASTROUS TRIP! HEAR COMES THAT NEW CHAP JONES! WHAT A HECK OF AN INTRODUCTION TO A TOUR OF OPS!
HIS GUNNER'S HAD IT! JONES JUST CALLED UP ON R.T.!
Kennedy

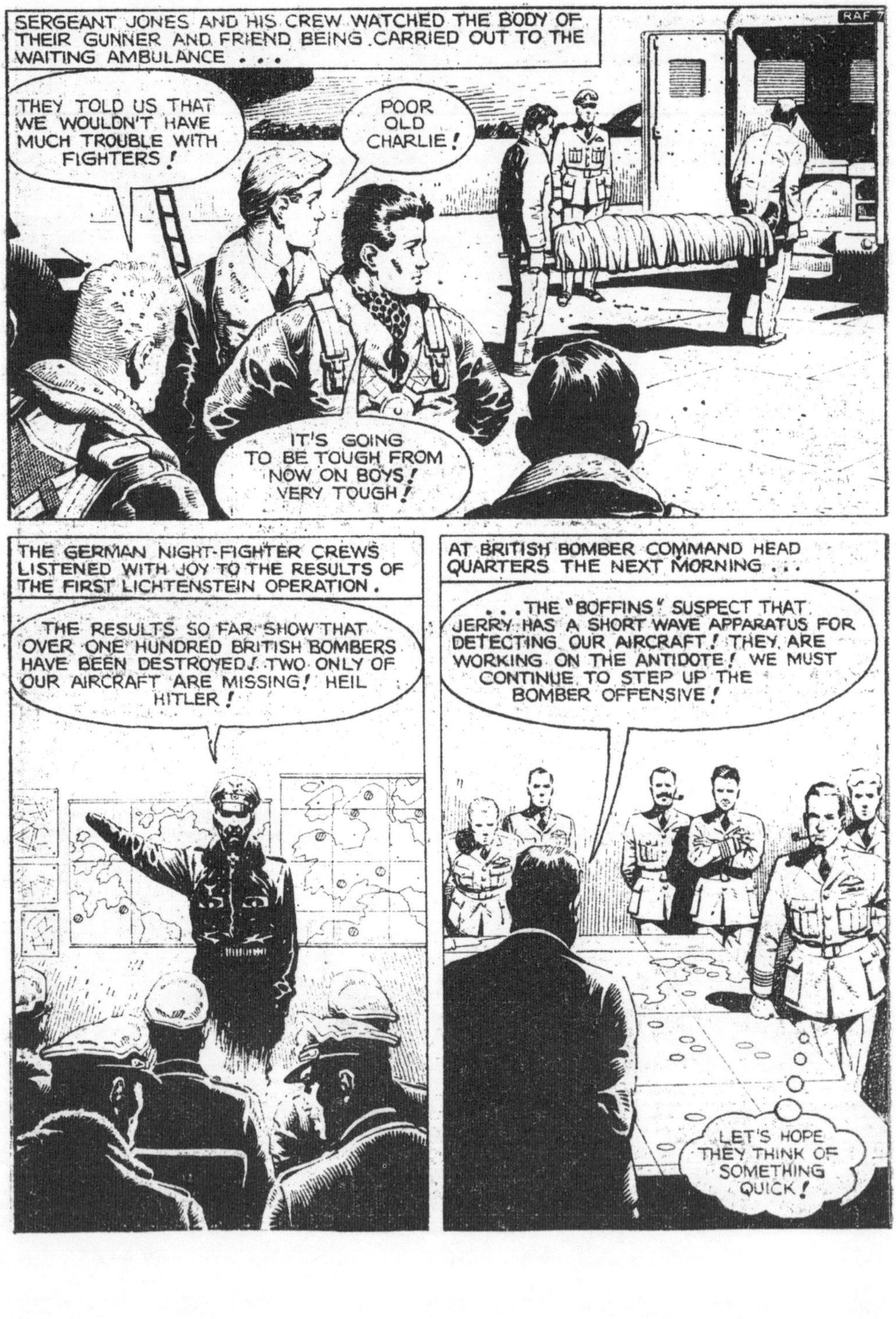
SERGEANT JONES AND HIS CREW WATCHED THE BODY OF THEIR GUNNER AND FRIEND BEING CARRIED OUT TO THE WAITING AMBULANCE . . .
THEY TOLD US THAT WE WOULDN'T HAVE MUCH TROUBLE WITH FIGHTERS!
POOR OLD CHARLIE!
IT'S GOING TO BE TOUGH FROM NOW ON BOYS! VERY TOUGH!
THE GERMAN NIGHT-FIGHTER CREWS LISTENED WITH JOY TO THE RESULTS OF THE FIRST LICHTENSTEIN OPERATION.
THE RESULTS SO FAR SHOW THAT OVER ONE HUNDRED BRITISH BOMBERS HAVE BEEN DESTROYED! TWO ONLY OF OUR AIRCRAFT ARE MISSING! HEIL HITLER!
AT BRITISH BOMBER COMMAND HEAD QUARTERS THE NEXT MORNING . . .
. . . THE "BOFFINS" SUSPECT THAT JERRY HAS A SHORT WAVE APPARATUS FOR DETECTING OUR AIRCRAFT! THEY ARE WORKING ON THE ANTIDOTE! WE MUST CONTINUE TO STEP UP THE BOMBER OFFENSIVE!
LET'S HOPE THEY THINK OF SOMETHING QUICK!

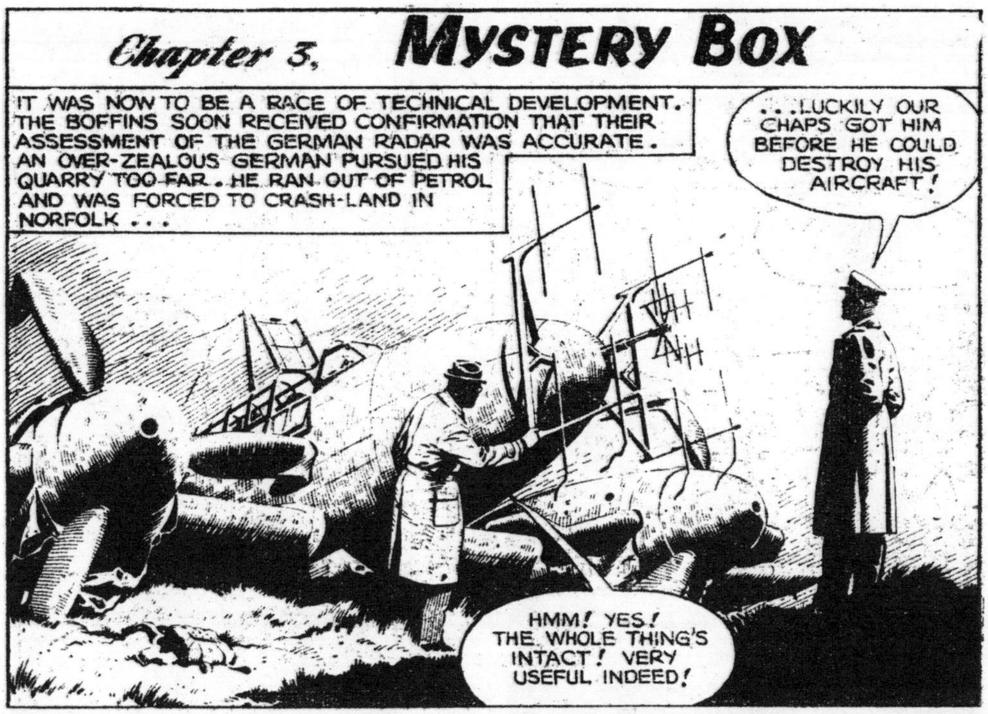
Chapter 3, MYSTERY BOX
IT WAS NOW TO BE A RACE OF TECHNICAL DEVELOPMENT. THE BOFFINS SOON RECEIVED CONFIRMATION THAT THEIR ASSESSMENT OF THE GERMAN RADAR WAS ACCURATE. AN OVER-ZEALOUS GERMAN PURSUED HIS QUARRY TOO FAR. HE RAN OUT OF PETROL AND WAS FORCED TO CRASH-LAND IN NORFOLK...
...LUCKILY OUR CHAPS GOT HIM BEFORE HE COULD DESTROY HIS AIRCRAFT!
HMM! YES! THE WHOLE THING'S INTACT! VERY USEFUL INDEED!

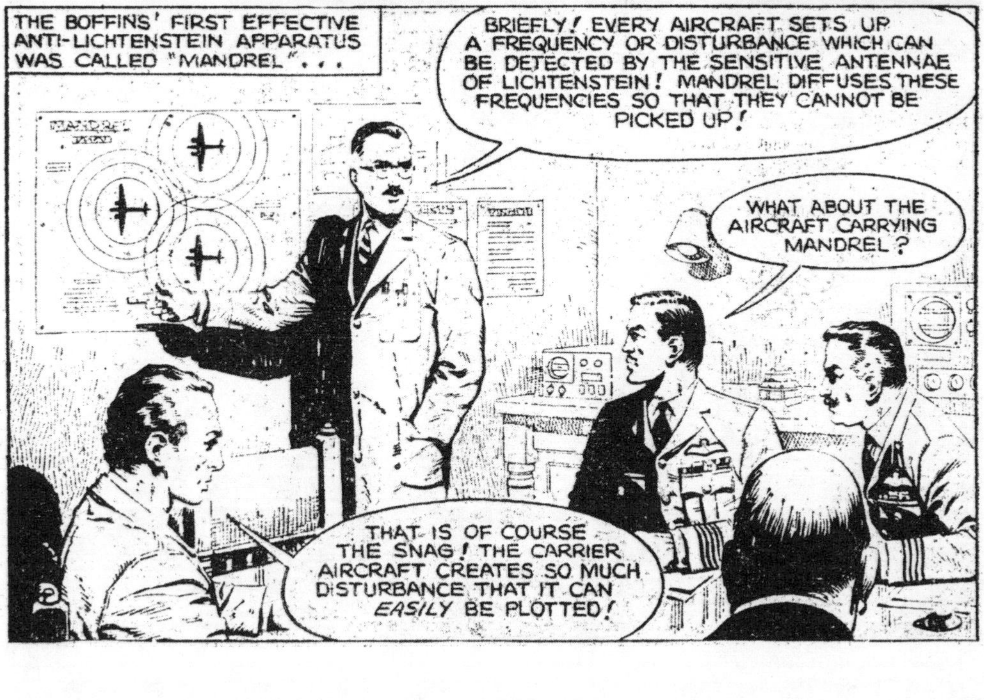
THE BOFFINS' FIRST EFFECTIVE ANTI-LICHTENSTEIN APPARATUS WAS CALLED "MANDREL"...
BRIEFLY! EVERY AIRCRAFT SETS UP A FREQUENCY OR DISTURBANCE WHICH CAN BE DETECTED BY THE SENSITIVE ANTENNAE OF LICHTENSTEIN! MANDREL DIFFUSES THESE FREQUENCIES SO THAT THEY CANNOT BE PICKED UP!
WHAT ABOUT THE AIRCRAFT CARRYING MANDREL?
THAT IS OF COURSE THE SNAG! THE CARRIER AIRCRAFT CREATES SO MUCH DISTURBANCE THAT IT CAN *EASILY* BE PLOTTED!

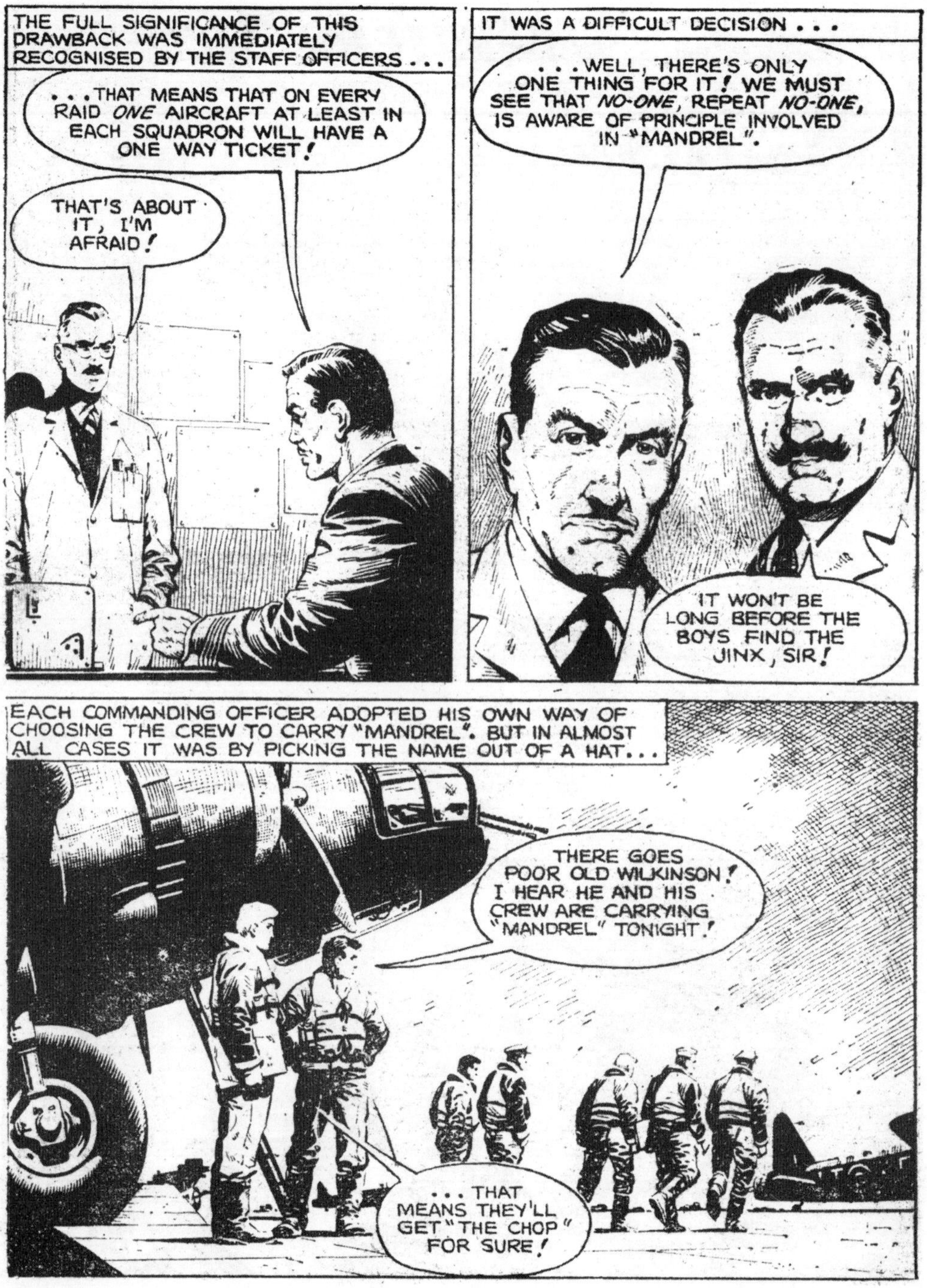
THE FULL SIGNIFICANCE OF THIS DRAWBACK WAS IMMEDIATELY RECOGNISED BY THE STAFF OFFICERS . . .
. . . THAT MEANS THAT ON EVERY RAID *ONE* AIRCRAFT AT LEAST IN EACH SQUADRON WILL HAVE A ONE WAY TICKET!
THAT'S ABOUT IT, I'M AFRAID!
IT WAS A DIFFICULT DECISION . . .
. . . WELL, THERE'S ONLY ONE THING FOR IT! WE MUST SEE THAT *NO-ONE*, REPEAT *NO-ONE*, IS AWARE OF PRINCIPLE INVOLVED IN "MANDREL".
IT WON'T BE LONG BEFORE THE BOYS FIND THE JINX, SIR!
EACH COMMANDING OFFICER ADOPTED HIS OWN WAY OF CHOOSING THE CREW TO CARRY "MANDREL". BUT IN ALMOST ALL CASES IT WAS BY PICKING THE NAME OUT OF A HAT . . .
THERE GOES POOR OLD WILKINSON! I HEAR HE AND HIS CREW ARE CARRYING "MANDREL" TONIGHT!
. . . THAT MEANS THEY'LL GET "THE CHOP" FOR SURE!

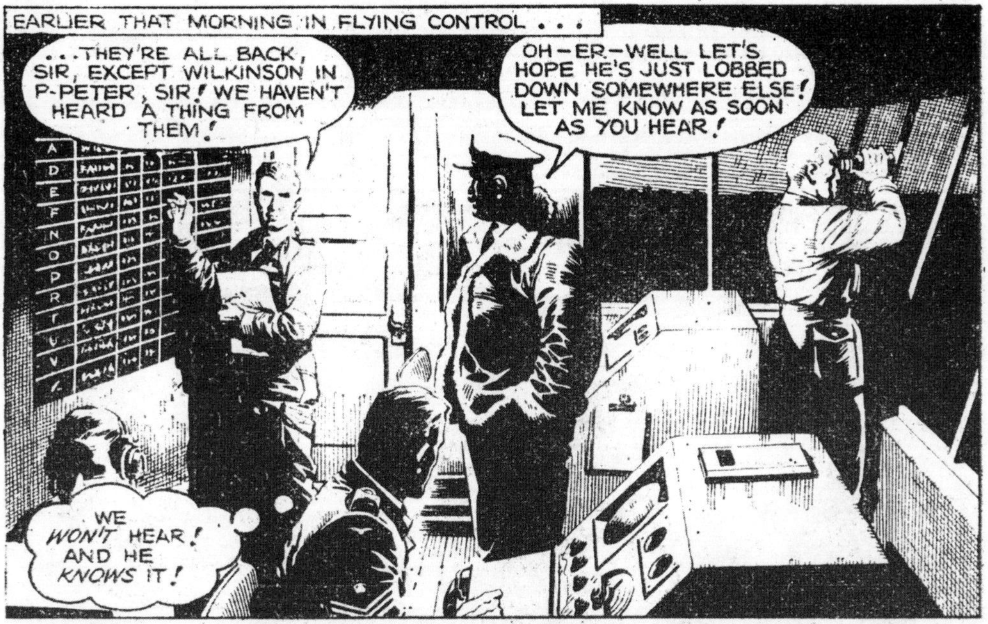
EARLIER THAT MORNING IN FLYING CONTROL . . .
. . . THEY'RE ALL BACK, SIR, EXCEPT WILKINSON IN P-PETER, SIR! WE HAVEN'T HEARD A THING FROM THEM!
OH—ER—WELL LET'S HOPE HE'S JUST LOBBED DOWN SOMEWHERE ELSE! LET ME KNOW AS SOON AS YOU HEAR!
WE *WON'T* HEAR! AND HE *KNOWS* IT!

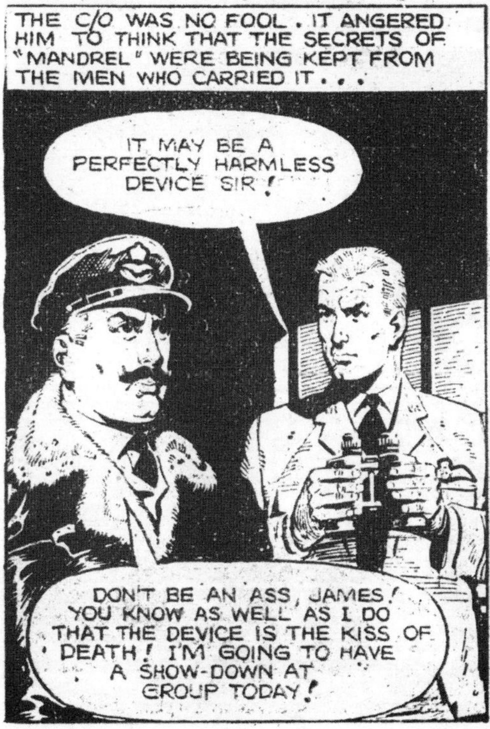
THE C/O WAS NO FOOL. IT ANGERED HIM TO THINK THAT THE SECRETS OF "MANDREL" WERE BEING KEPT FROM THE MEN WHO CARRIED IT . . .
IT MAY BE A PERFECTLY HARMLESS DEVICE SIR!
DON'T BE AN ASS, JAMES! YOU KNOW AS WELL AS I DO THAT THE DEVICE IS THE KISS OF DEATH! I'M GOING TO HAVE A SHOW-DOWN AT GROUP TODAY!

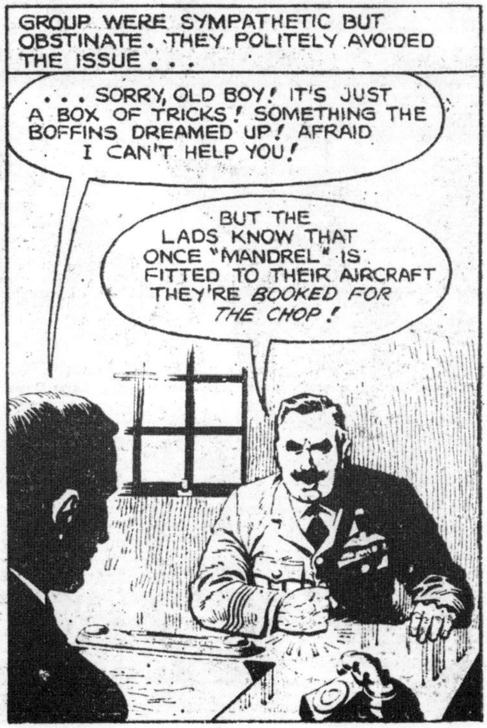
GROUP WERE SYMPATHETIC BUT OBSTINATE. THEY POLITELY AVOIDED THE ISSUE . . .
. . . SORRY, OLD BOY! IT'S JUST A BOX OF TRICKS! SOMETHING THE BOFFINS DREAMED UP! AFRAID I CAN'T HELP YOU!
BUT THE LADS KNOW THAT ONCE "MANDREL" IS FITTED TO THEIR AIRCRAFT THEY'RE *BOOKED FOR THE CHOP*!

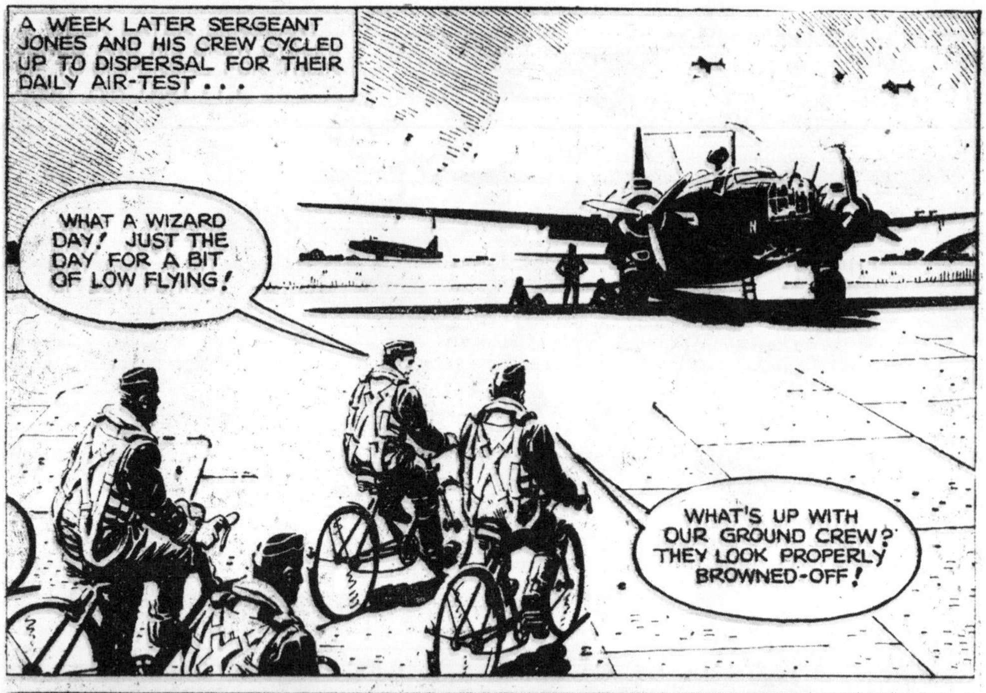
A WEEK LATER SERGEANT JONES AND HIS CREW CYCLED UP TO DISPERSAL FOR THEIR DAILY AIR-TEST . . .
WHAT A WIZARD DAY! JUST THE DAY FOR A BIT OF LOW FLYING!
WHAT'S UP WITH OUR GROUND CREW? THEY LOOK PROPERLY BROWNED-OFF!

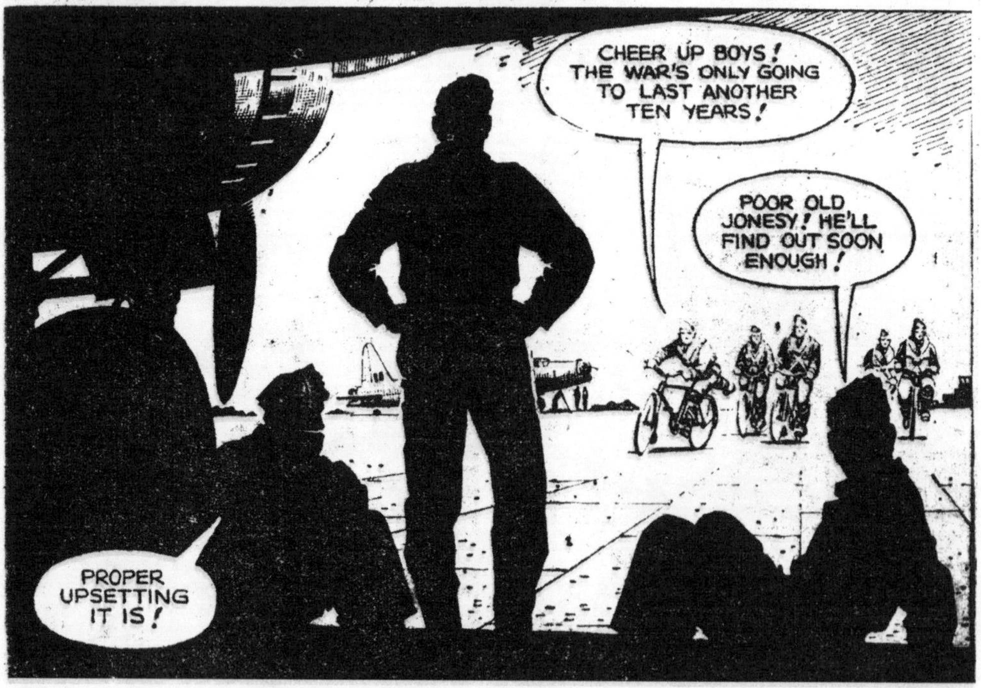
CHEER UP BOYS! THE WAR'S ONLY GOING TO LAST ANOTHER TEN YEARS!
POOR OLD JONESY! HE'LL FIND OUT SOON ENOUGH!
PROPER UPSETTING IT IS!

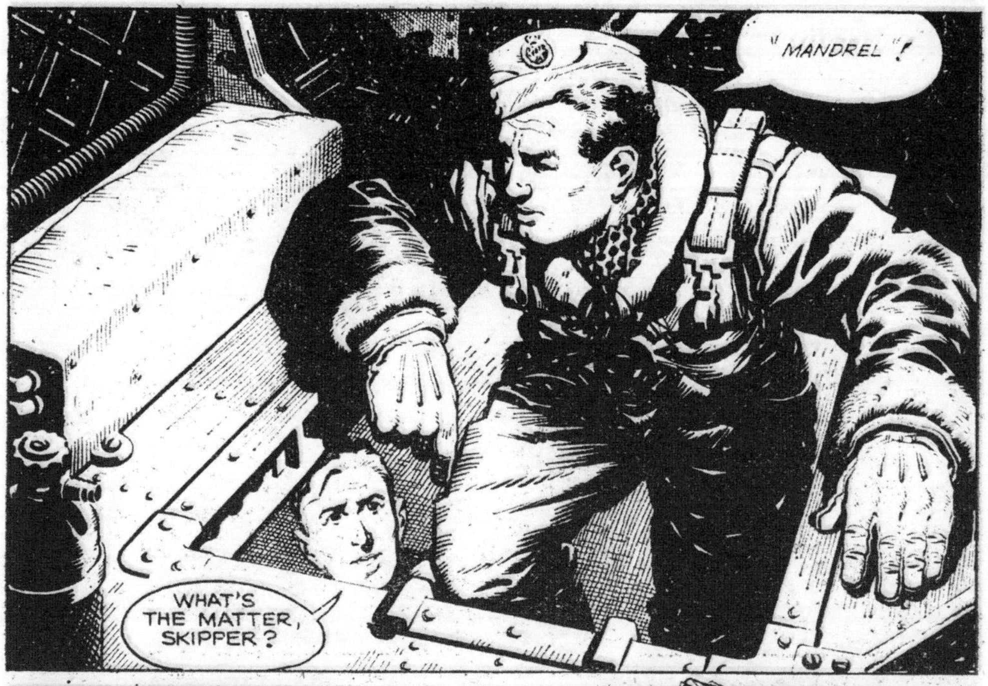
"MANDREL"!
WHAT'S THE MATTER, SKIPPER?

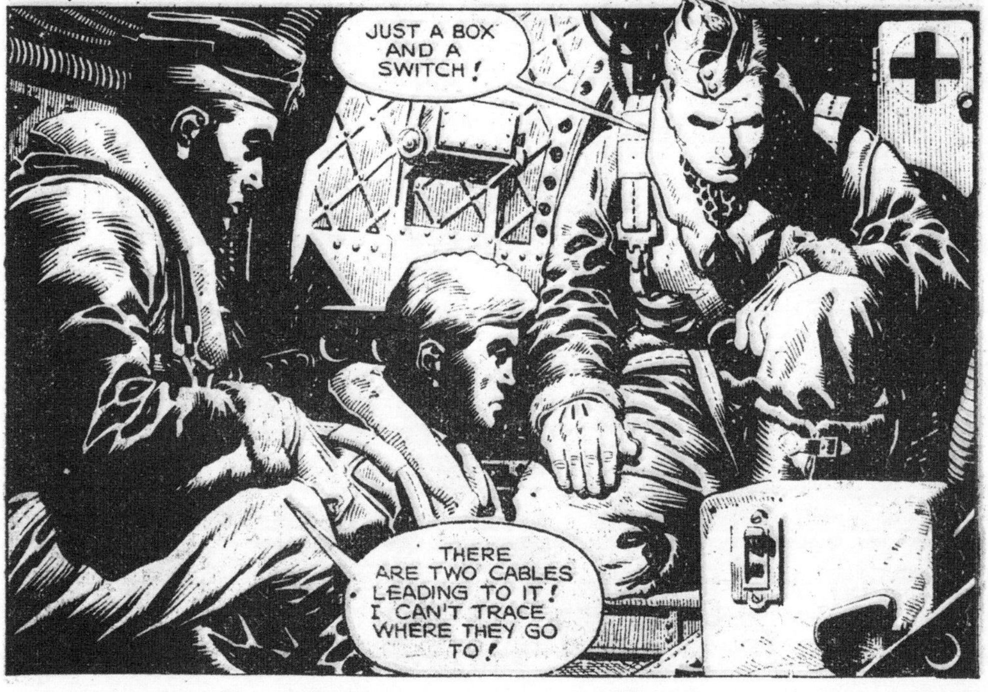
JUST A BOX AND A SWITCH!
THERE ARE TWO CABLES LEADING TO IT! I CAN'T TRACE WHERE THEY GO TO!

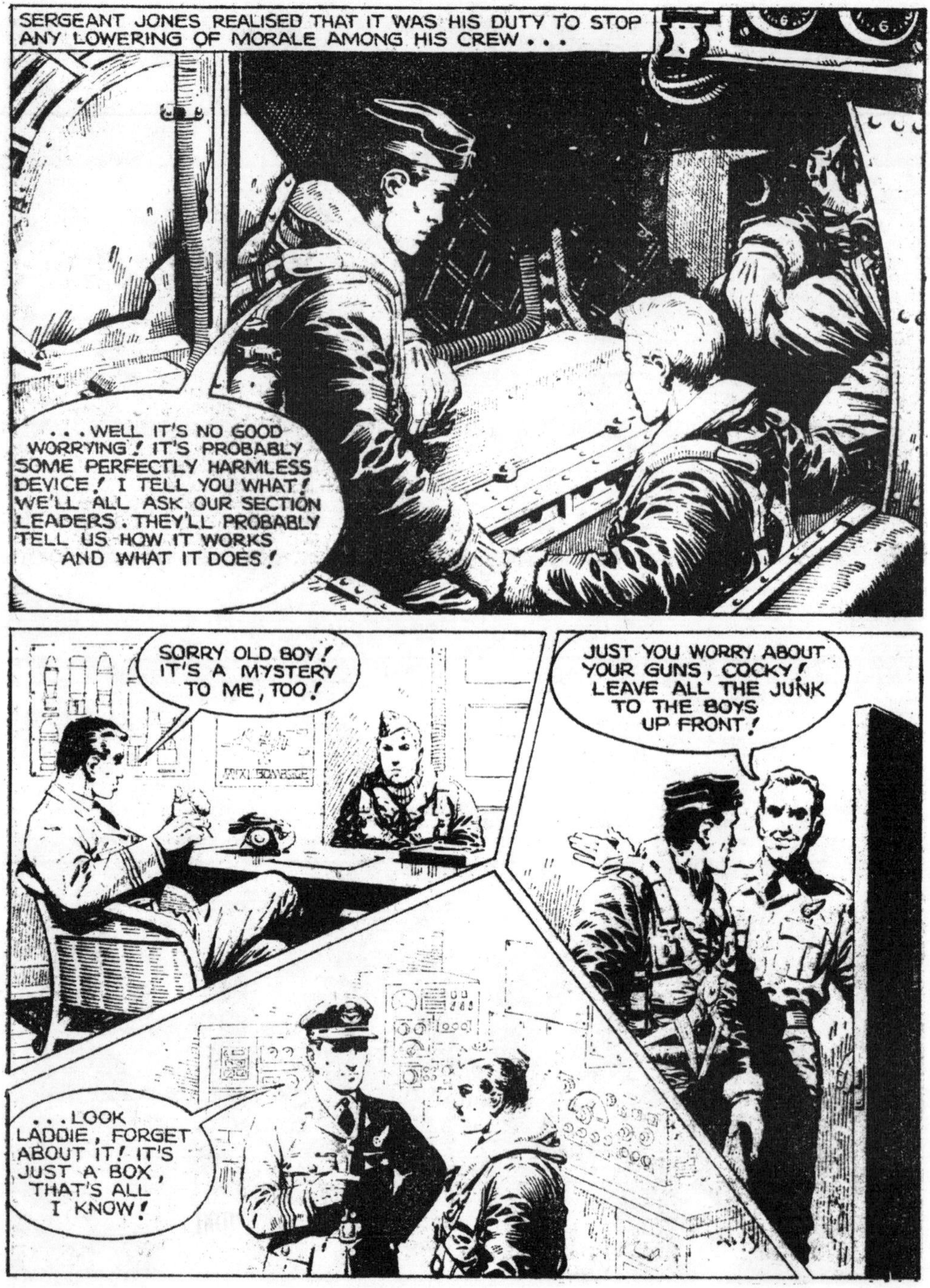
SERGEANT JONES REALISED THAT IT WAS HIS DUTY TO STOP ANY LOWERING OF MORALE AMONG HIS CREW . . .
. . . WELL IT'S NO GOOD WORRYING! IT'S PROBABLY SOME PERFECTLY HARMLESS DEVICE! I TELL YOU WHAT! WE'LL ALL ASK OUR SECTION LEADERS. THEY'LL PROBABLY TELL US HOW IT WORKS AND WHAT IT DOES!
SORRY OLD BOY! IT'S A MYSTERY TO ME, TOO!
JUST YOU WORRY ABOUT YOUR GUNS, COCKY! LEAVE ALL THE JUNK TO THE BOYS UP FRONT!
. . . LOOK LADDIE, FORGET ABOUT IT! IT'S JUST A BOX, THAT'S ALL I KNOW!

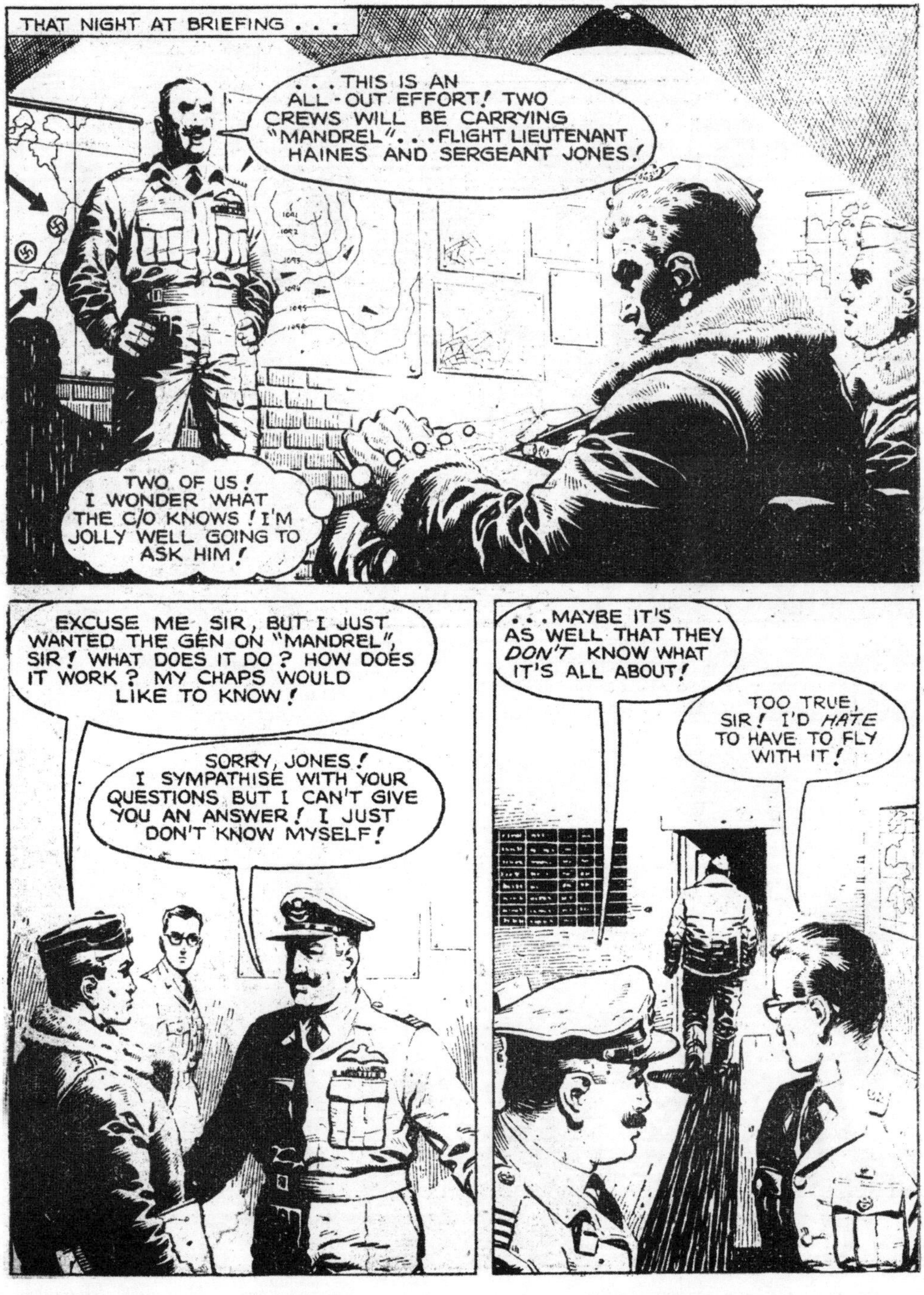
THAT NIGHT AT BRIEFING . . .
. . . THIS IS AN ALL-OUT EFFORT! TWO CREWS WILL BE CARRYING "MANDREL" . . . FLIGHT LIEUTENANT HAINES AND SERGEANT JONES!
TWO OF US! I WONDER WHAT THE C/O KNOWS! I'M JOLLY WELL GOING TO ASK HIM!
EXCUSE ME, SIR, BUT I JUST WANTED THE GEN ON "MANDREL", SIR! WHAT DOES IT DO? HOW DOES IT WORK? MY CHAPS WOULD LIKE TO KNOW!
SORRY, JONES! I SYMPATHISE WITH YOUR QUESTIONS BUT I CAN'T GIVE YOU AN ANSWER! I JUST DON'T KNOW MYSELF!
. . . MAYBE IT'S AS WELL THAT THEY DON'T KNOW WHAT IT'S ALL ABOUT!
TOO TRUE, SIR! I'D HATE TO HAVE TO FLY WITH IT!

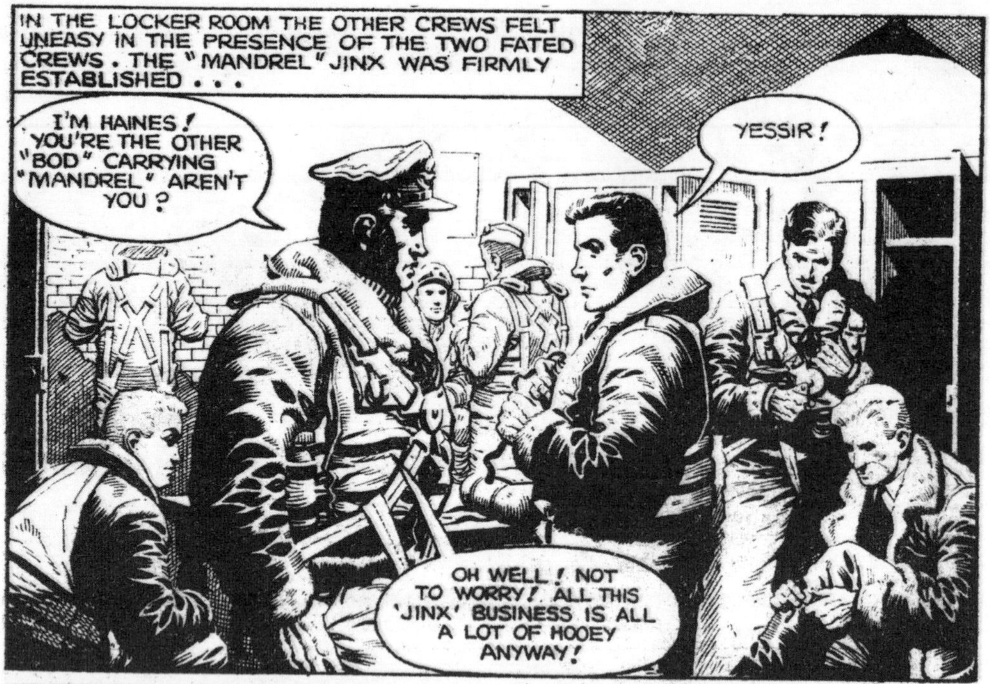
IN THE LOCKER ROOM THE OTHER CREWS FELT UNEASY IN THE PRESENCE OF THE TWO FATED CREWS. THE "MANDREL" JINX WAS FIRMLY ESTABLISHED . . .
I'M HAINES! YOU'RE THE OTHER "BOD" CARRYING "MANDREL" AREN'T YOU?
YESSIR!
OH WELL! NOT TO WORRY! ALL THIS 'JINX' BUSINESS IS ALL A LOT OF HOOEY ANYWAY!

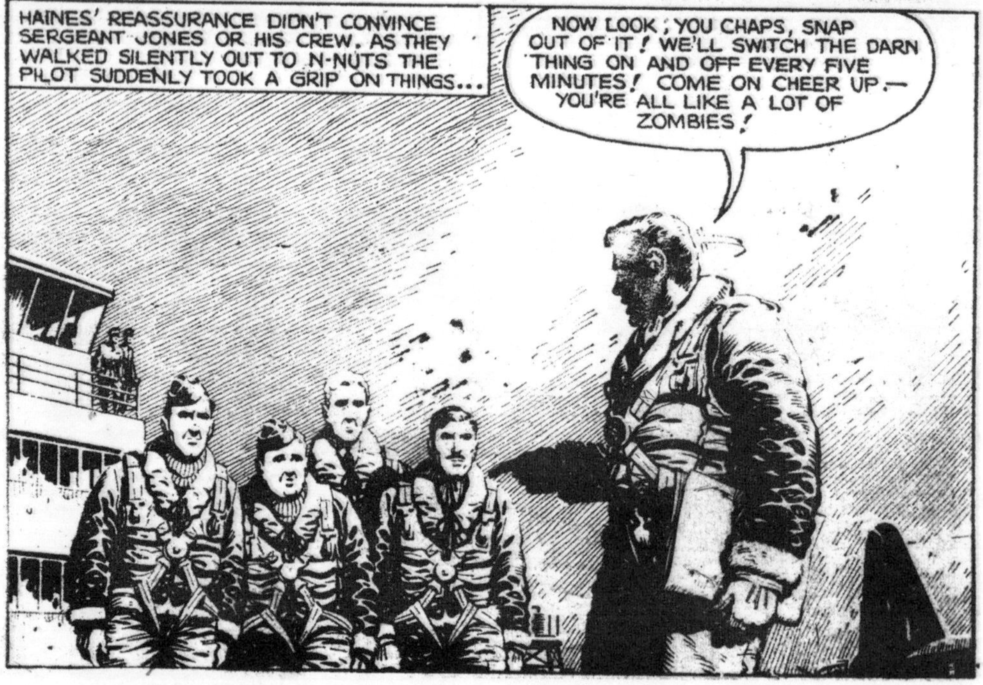
HAINES' REASSURANCE DIDN'T CONVINCE SERGEANT JONES OR HIS CREW. AS THEY WALKED SILENTLY OUT TO N-NUTS THE PILOT SUDDENLY TOOK A GRIP ON THINGS...
NOW LOOK; YOU CHAPS, SNAP OUT OF IT! WE'LL SWITCH THE DARN THING ON AND OFF EVERY FIVE MINUTES! COME ON CHEER UP.— YOU'RE ALL LIKE A LOT OF ZOMBIES!

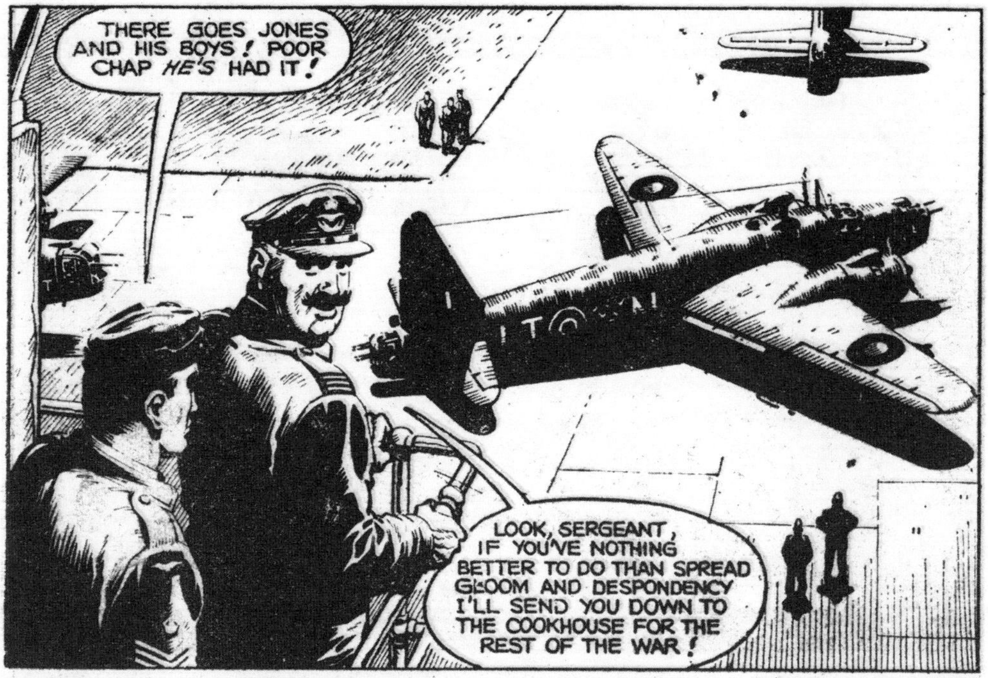
THERE GOES JONES AND HIS BOYS! POOR CHAP HE'S HAD IT!
LOOK, SERGEANT, IF YOU'VE NOTHING BETTER TO DO THAN SPREAD GLOOM AND DESPONDENCY I'LL SEND YOU DOWN TO THE COOKHOUSE FOR THE REST OF THE WAR!

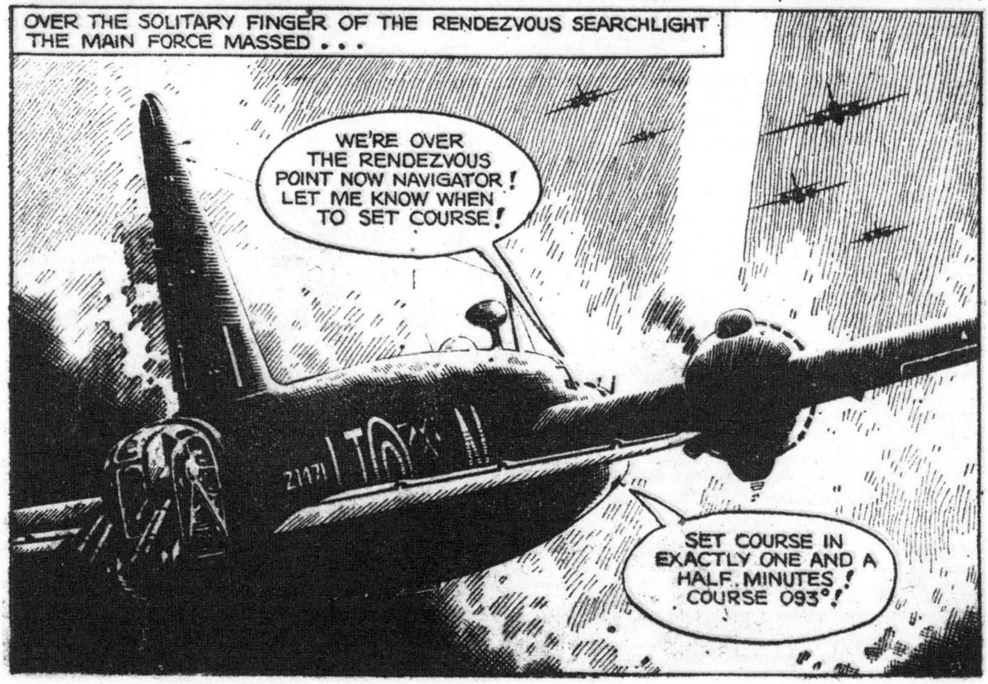
OVER THE SOLITARY FINGER OF THE RENDEZVOUS SEARCHLIGHT THE MAIN FORCE MASSED . . .
WE'RE OVER THE RENDEZVOUS POINT NOW NAVIGATOR! LET ME KNOW WHEN TO SET COURSE!
SET COURSE IN EXACTLY ONE AND A HALF MINUTES! COURSE 093°!

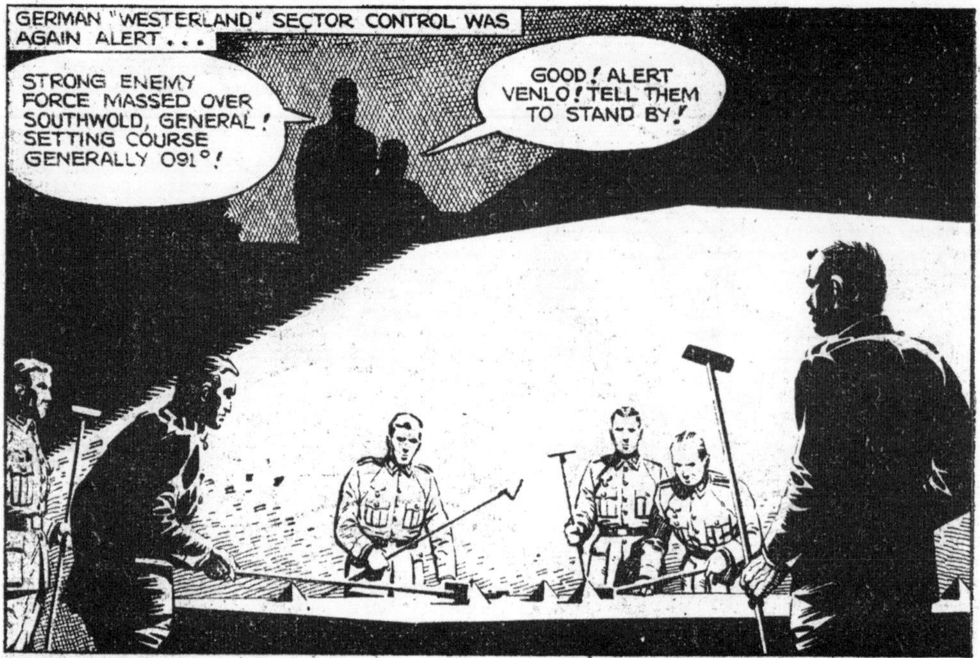
GERMAN "WESTERLAND" SECTOR CONTROL WAS AGAIN ALERT . . .
STRONG ENEMY FORCE MASSED OVER SOUTHWOLD, GENERAL! SETTING COURSE GENERALLY 091°!
GOOD! ALERT VENLO! TELL THEM TO STAND BY!

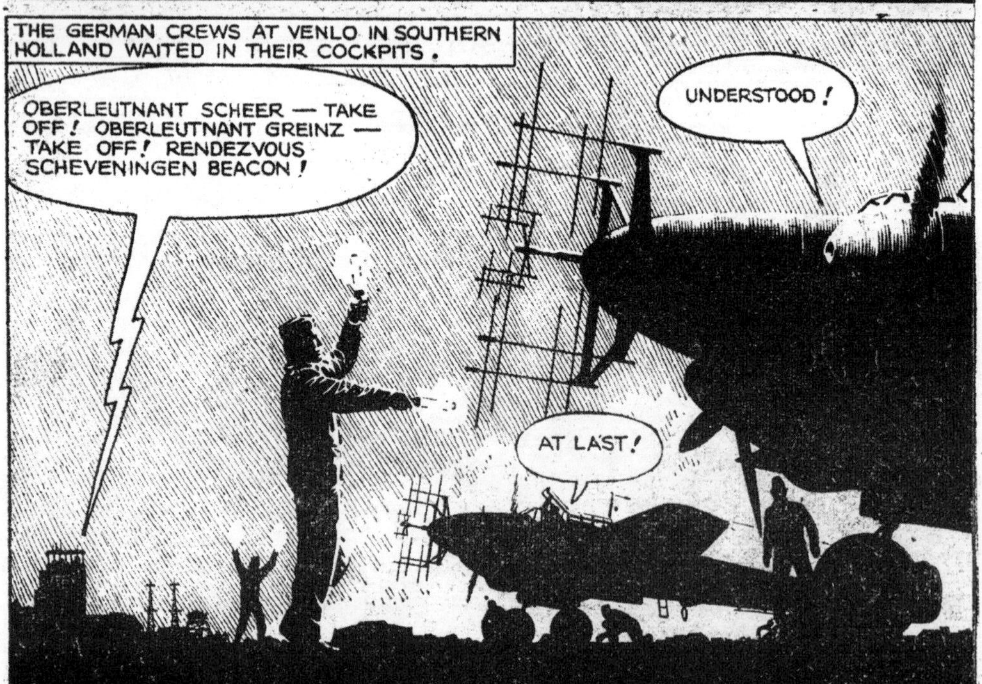
THE GERMAN CREWS AT VENLO IN SOUTHERN HOLLAND WAITED IN THEIR COCKPITS.
OBERLEUTNANT SCHEER — TAKE OFF! OBERLEUTNANT GREINZ — TAKE OFF! RENDEZVOUS SCHEVENINGEN BEACON!
UNDERSTOOD!
AT LAST!

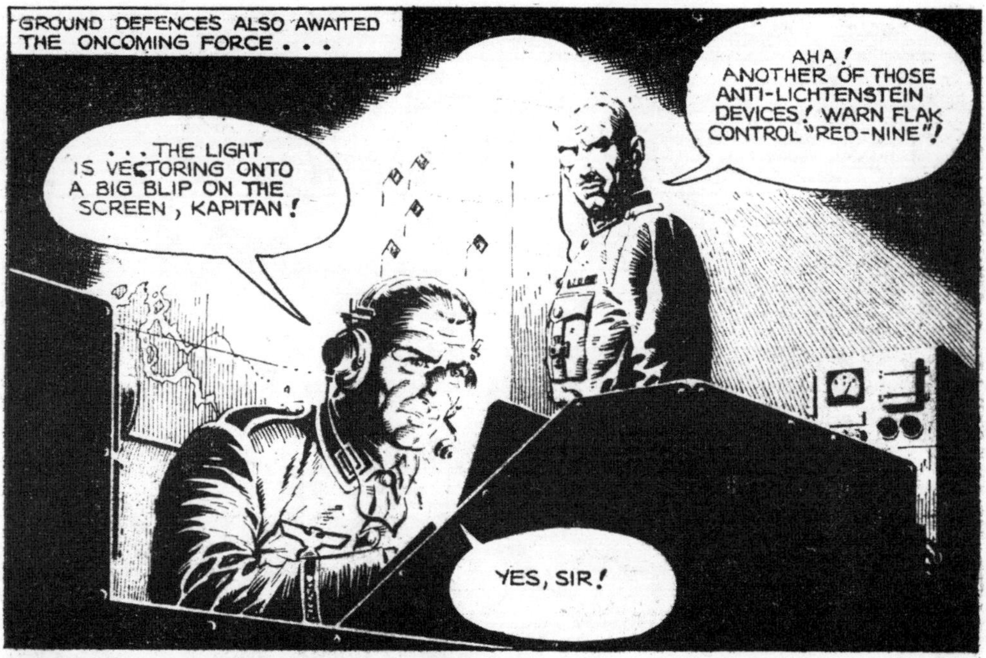
GROUND DEFENCES ALSO AWAITED THE ONCOMING FORCE . . .
. . . THE LIGHT IS VECTORING ONTO A BIG BLIP ON THE SCREEN, KAPITAN!
AHA! ANOTHER OF THOSE ANTI-LICHTENSTEIN DEVICES! WARN FLAK CONTROL "RED-NINE"!
YES, SIR!

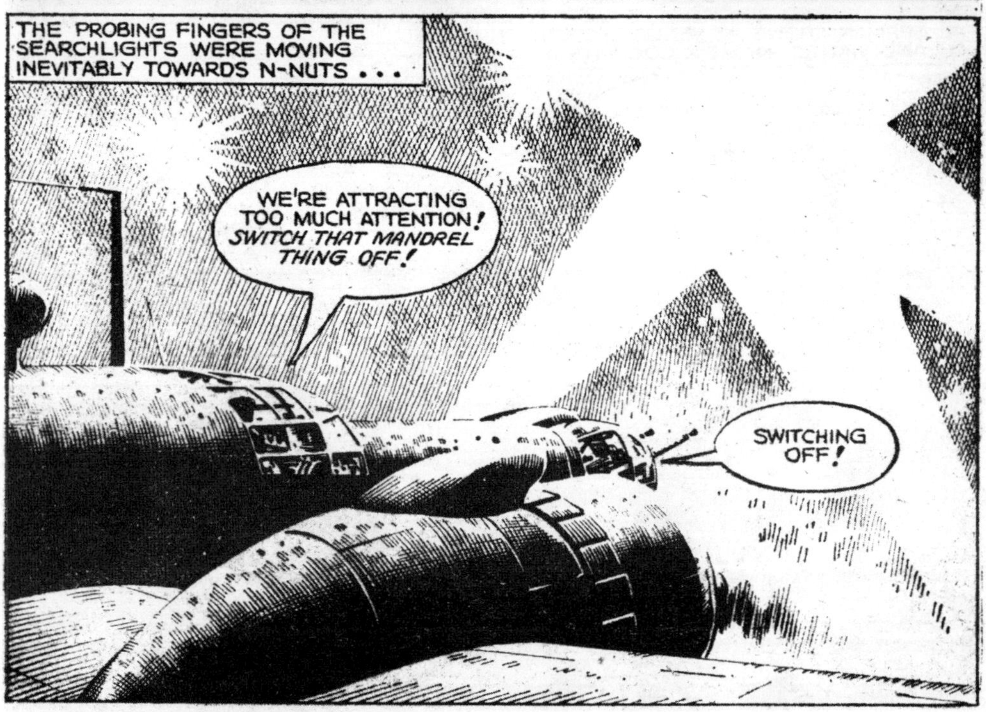
THE PROBING FINGERS OF THE SEARCHLIGHTS WERE MOVING INEVITABLY TOWARDS N-NUTS . . .
WE'RE ATTRACTING TOO MUCH ATTENTION! *SWITCH THAT MANDREL THING OFF!*
SWITCHING OFF!

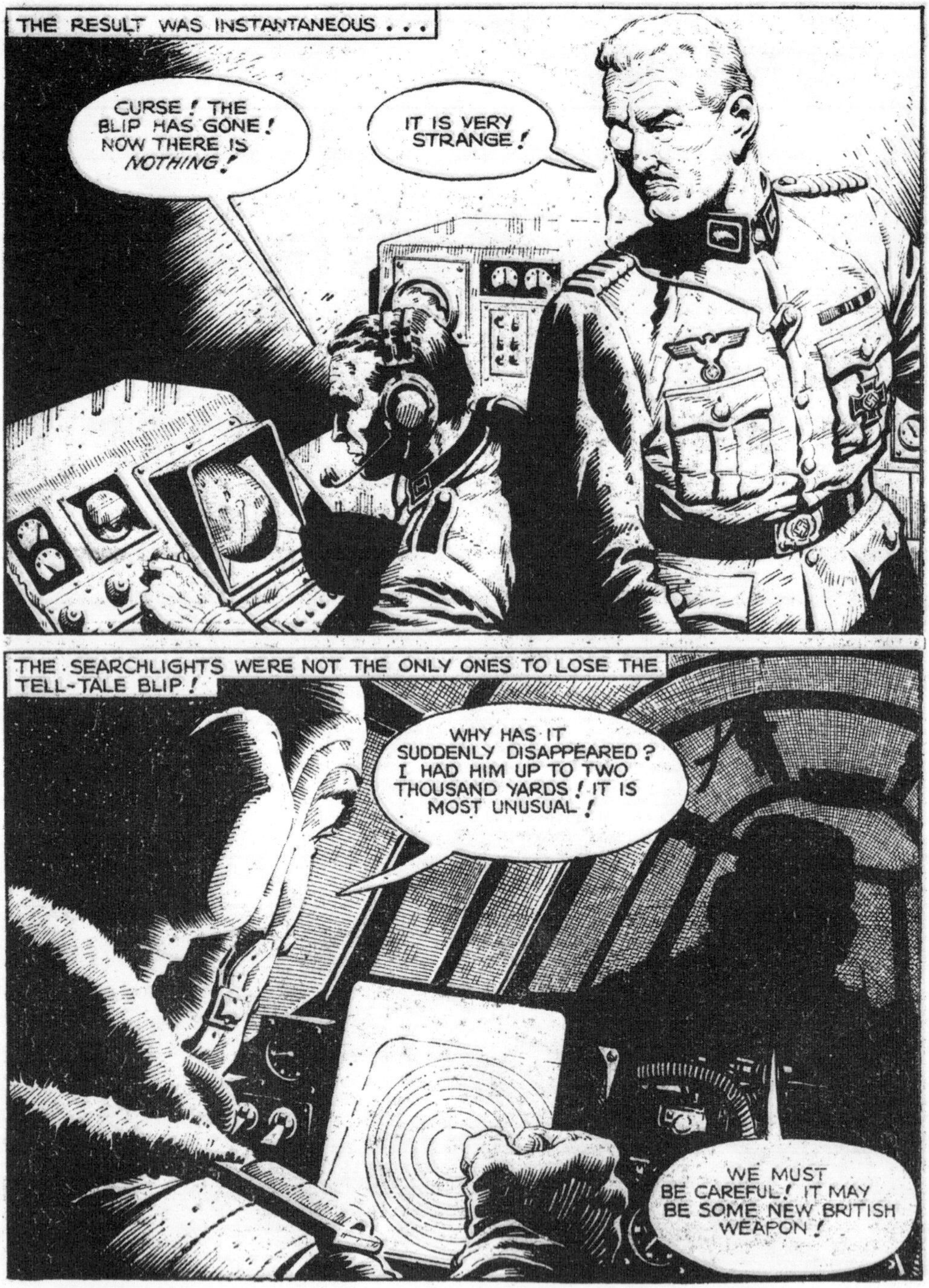
THE RESULT WAS INSTANTANEOUS . . .
CURSE! THE BLIP HAS GONE! NOW THERE IS *NOTHING!*
IT IS VERY STRANGE!
THE SEARCHLIGHTS WERE NOT THE ONLY ONES TO LOSE THE TELL-TALE BLIP!
WHY HAS IT SUDDENLY DISAPPEARED? I HAD HIM UP TO TWO THOUSAND YARDS! IT IS MOST UNUSUAL!
WE MUST BE CAREFUL! IT MAY BE SOME NEW BRITISH WEAPON!

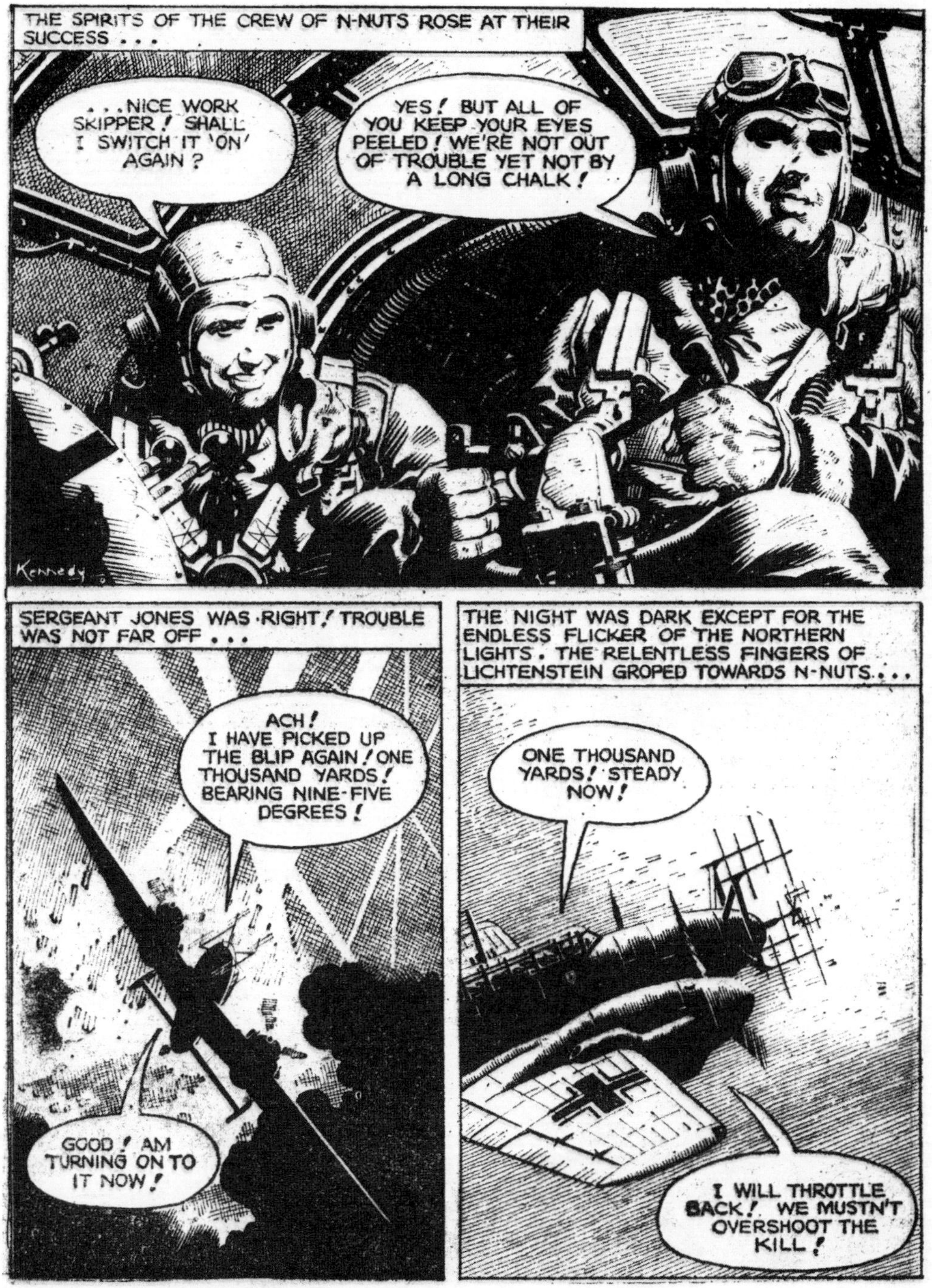
THE SPIRITS OF THE CREW OF N-NUTS ROSE AT THEIR SUCCESS . . .
. . . NICE WORK SKIPPER! SHALL I SWITCH IT 'ON' AGAIN?
YES! BUT ALL OF YOU KEEP YOUR EYES PEELED! WE'RE NOT OUT OF TROUBLE YET NOT BY A LONG CHALK!
Kennedy
SERGEANT JONES WAS RIGHT! TROUBLE WAS NOT FAR OFF . . .
ACH! I HAVE PICKED UP THE BLIP AGAIN! ONE THOUSAND YARDS! BEARING NINE-FIVE DEGREES!
GOOD! AM TURNING ON TO IT NOW!
THE NIGHT WAS DARK EXCEPT FOR THE ENDLESS FLICKER OF THE NORTHERN LIGHTS. THE RELENTLESS FINGERS OF LICHTENSTEIN GROPED TOWARDS N-NUTS . . .
ONE THOUSAND YARDS! STEADY NOW!
I WILL THROTTLE BACK! WE MUSTN'T OVERSHOOT THE KILL!

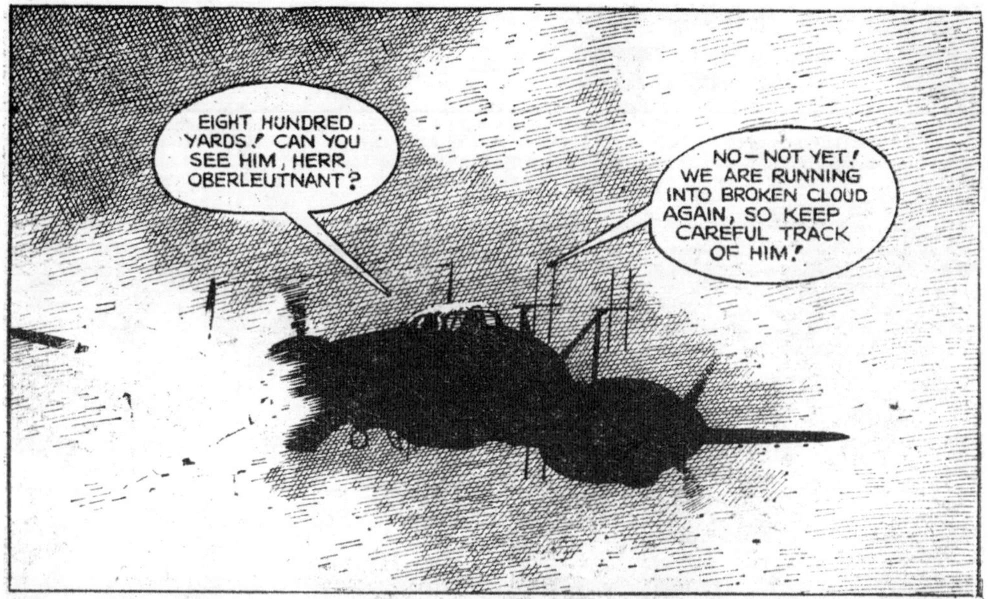
EIGHT HUNDRED YARDS! CAN YOU SEE HIM, HERR OBERLEUTNANT?
NO—NOT YET! WE ARE RUNNING INTO BROKEN CLOUD AGAIN, SO KEEP CAREFUL TRACK OF HIM!

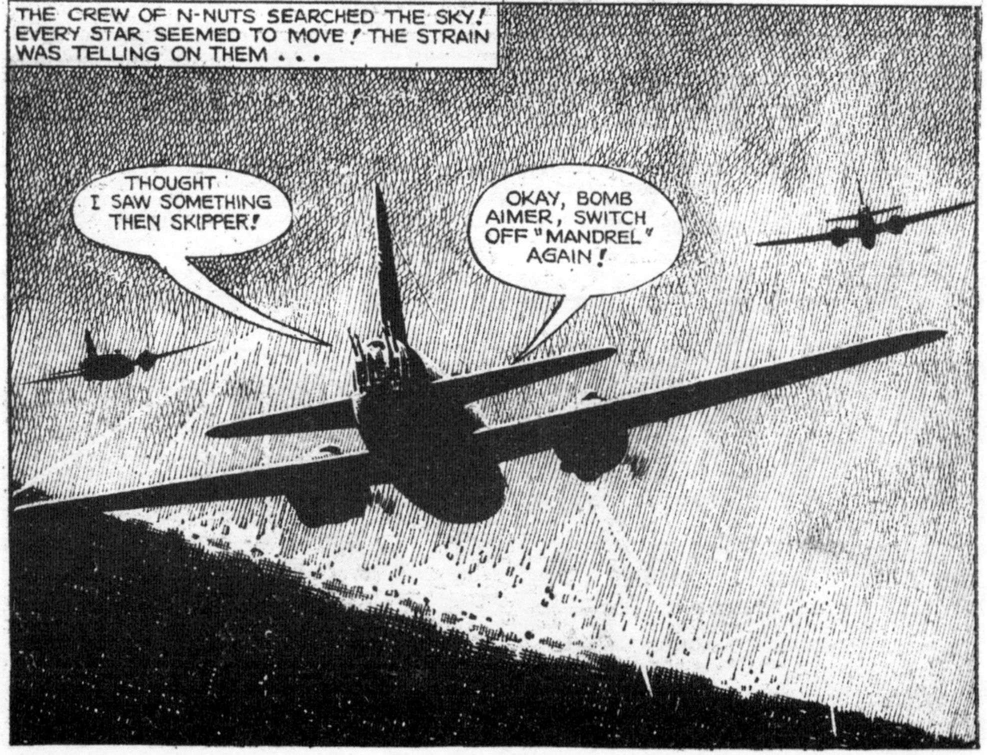
THE CREW OF N-NUTS SEARCHED THE SKY! EVERY STAR SEEMED TO MOVE! THE STRAIN WAS TELLING ON THEM . . .
THOUGHT I SAW SOMETHING THEN SKIPPER!
OKAY, BOMB AIMER, SWITCH OFF "MANDREL" AGAIN!

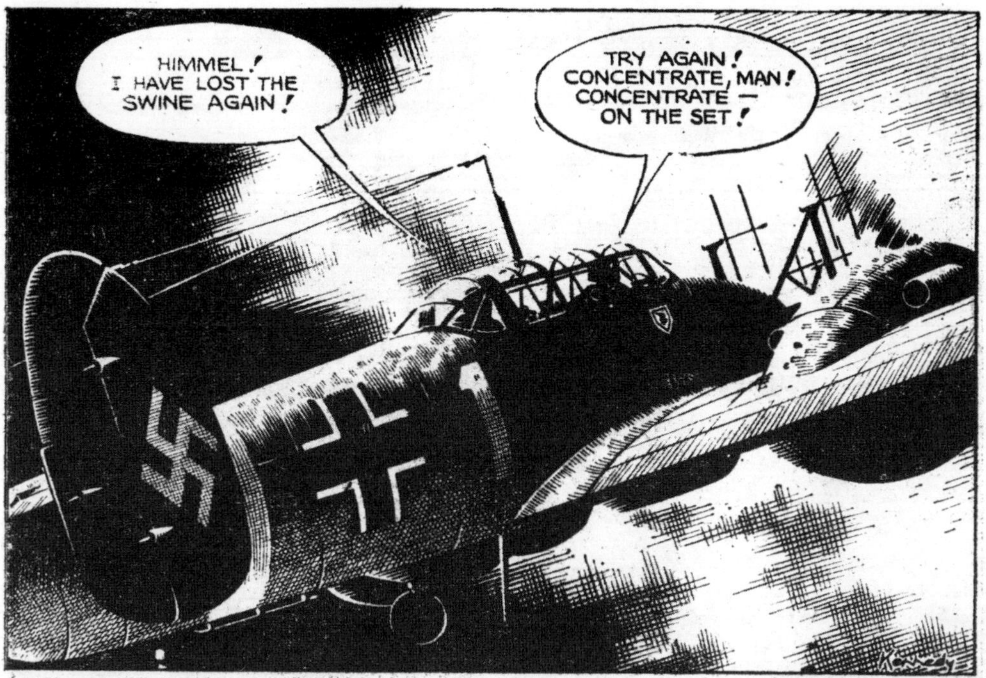
HIMMEL! I HAVE LOST THE SWINE AGAIN!
TRY AGAIN! CONCENTRATE, MAN! CONCENTRATE — ON THE SET!

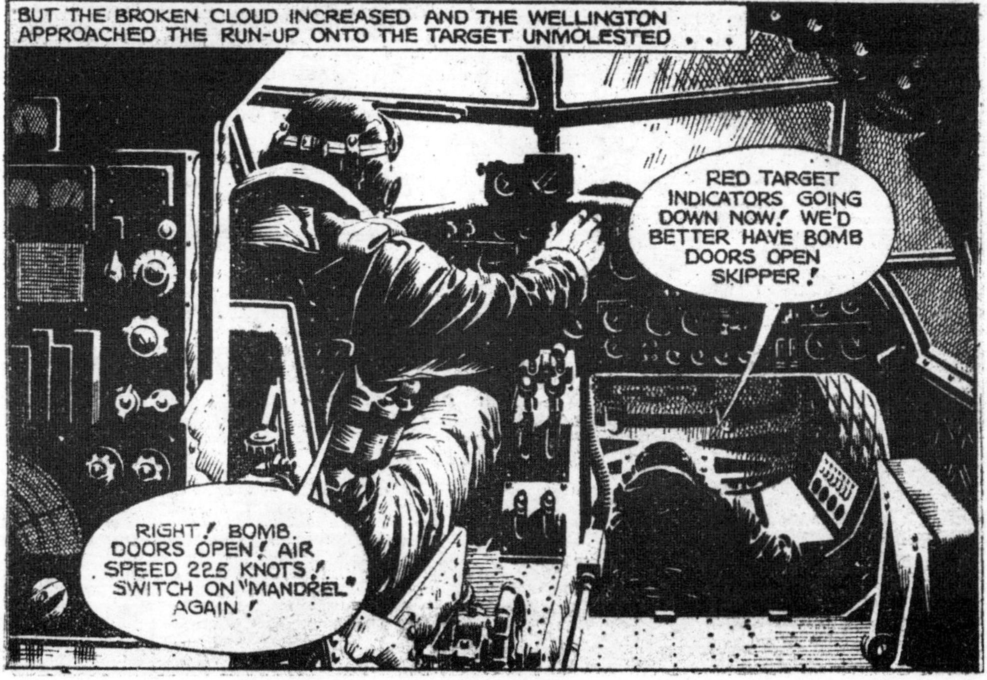
BUT THE BROKEN CLOUD INCREASED AND THE WELLINGTON APPROACHED THE RUN-UP ONTO THE TARGET UNMOLESTED . . .
RED TARGET INDICATORS GOING DOWN NOW! WE'D BETTER HAVE BOMB DOORS OPEN SKIPPER!
RIGHT! BOMB DOORS OPEN! AIR SPEED 225 KNOTS! SWITCH ON "MANDREL" AGAIN!

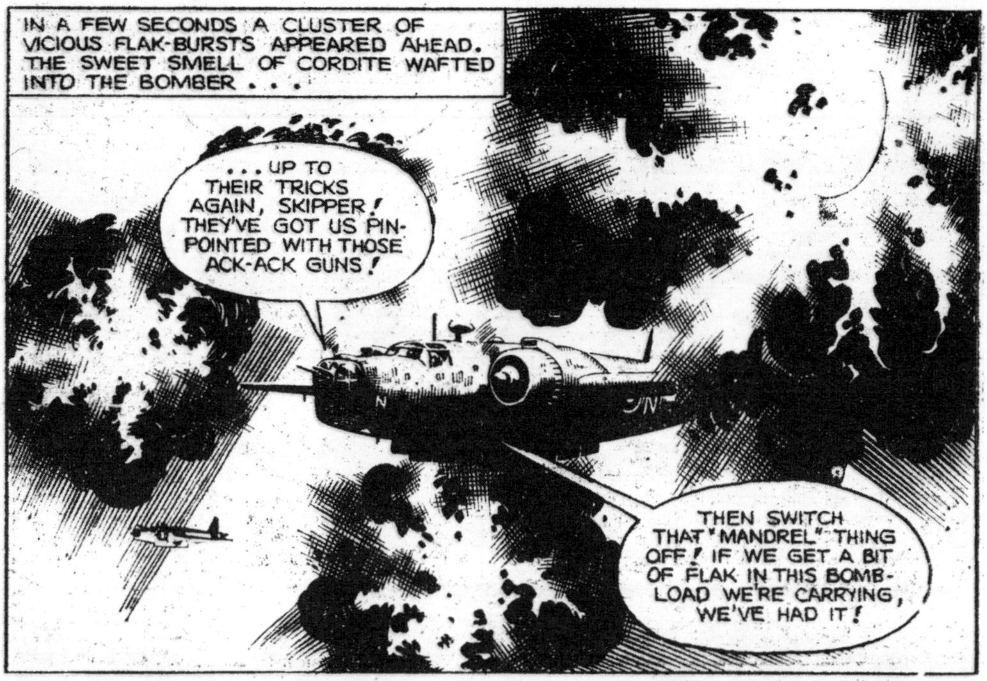
IN A FEW SECONDS A CLUSTER OF VICIOUS FLAK-BURSTS APPEARED AHEAD. THE SWEET SMELL OF CORDITE WAFTED INTO THE BOMBER . . .
. . . UP TO THEIR TRICKS AGAIN, SKIPPER! THEY'VE GOT US PIN-POINTED WITH THOSE ACK-ACK GUNS!
THEN SWITCH THAT "MANDREL" THING OFF! IF WE GET A BIT OF FLAK IN THIS BOMB-LOAD WE'RE CARRYING, WE'VE HAD IT!

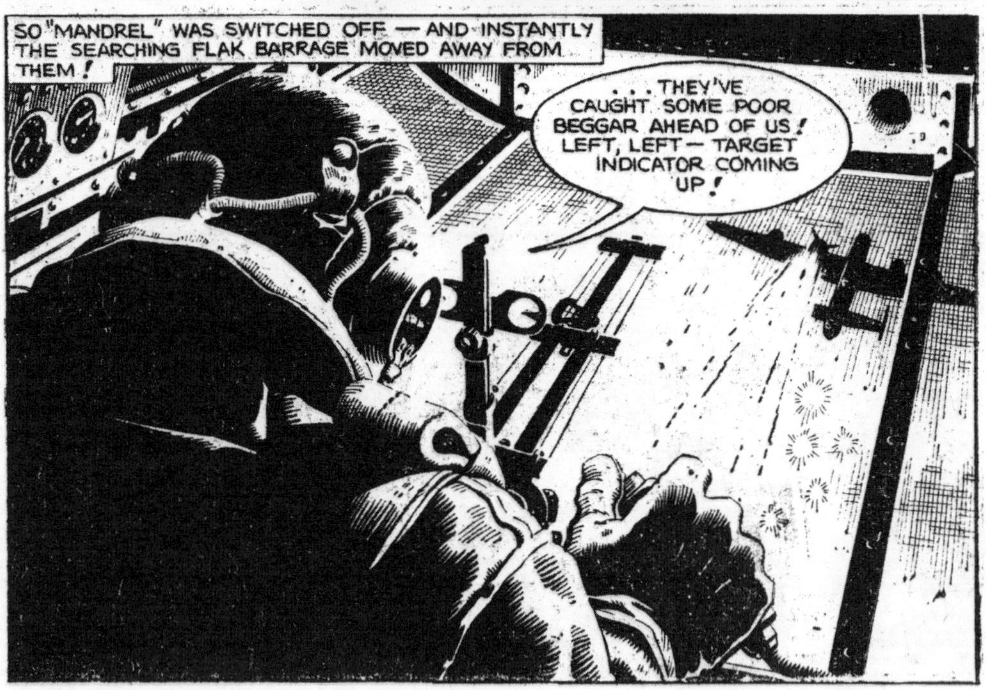
SO "MANDREL" WAS SWITCHED OFF — AND INSTANTLY THE SEARCHING FLAK BARRAGE MOVED AWAY FROM THEM!
. . . THEY'VE CAUGHT SOME POOR BEGGAR AHEAD OF US! LEFT, LEFT — TARGET INDICATOR COMING UP!

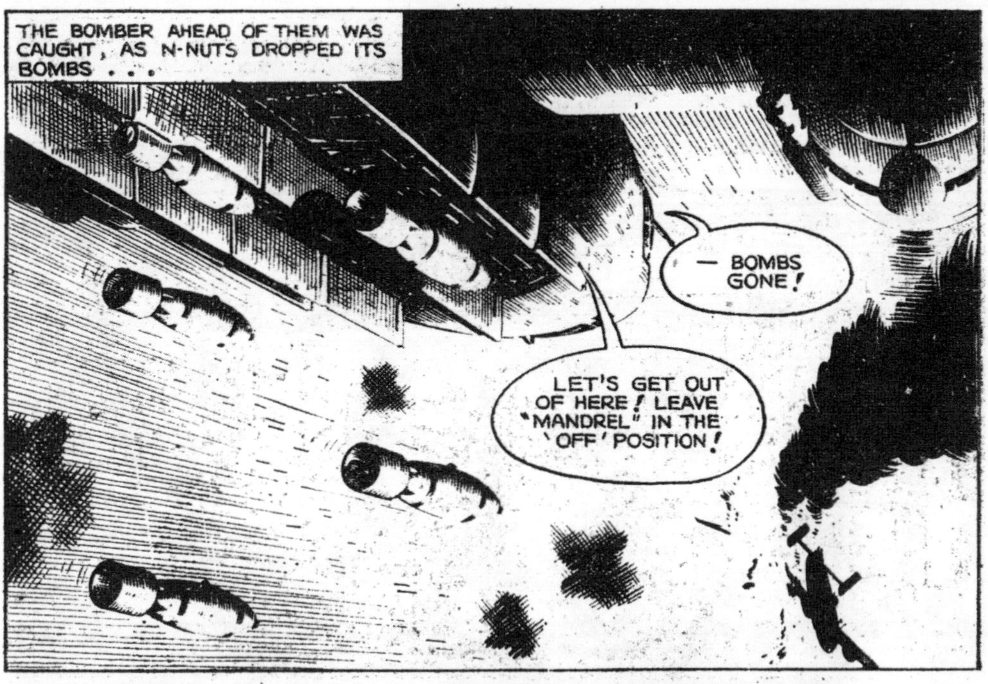
THE BOMBER AHEAD OF THEM WAS CAUGHT, AS N-NUTS DROPPED ITS BOMBS . . .
— BOMBS GONE!
LET'S GET OUT OF HERE! LEAVE "MANDREL" IN THE 'OFF' POSITION!

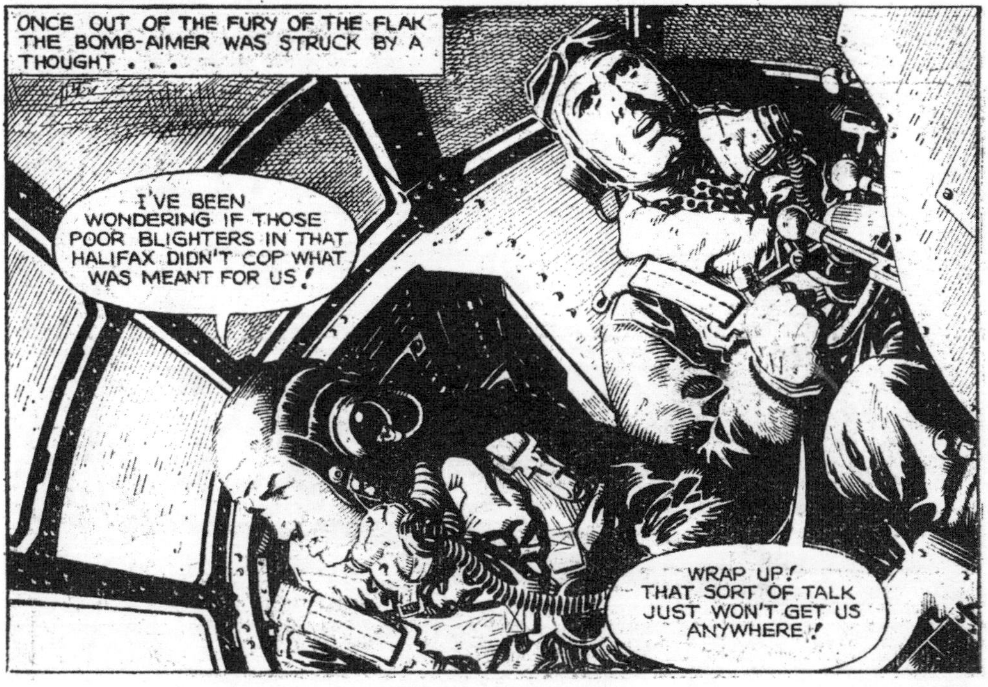
ONCE OUT OF THE FURY OF THE FLAK THE BOMB-AIMER WAS STRUCK BY A THOUGHT . . .
I'VE BEEN WONDERING IF THOSE POOR BLIGHTERS IN THAT HALIFAX DIDN'T COP WHAT WAS MEANT FOR US!
WRAP UP! THAT SORT OF TALK JUST WON'T GET US ANYWHERE!

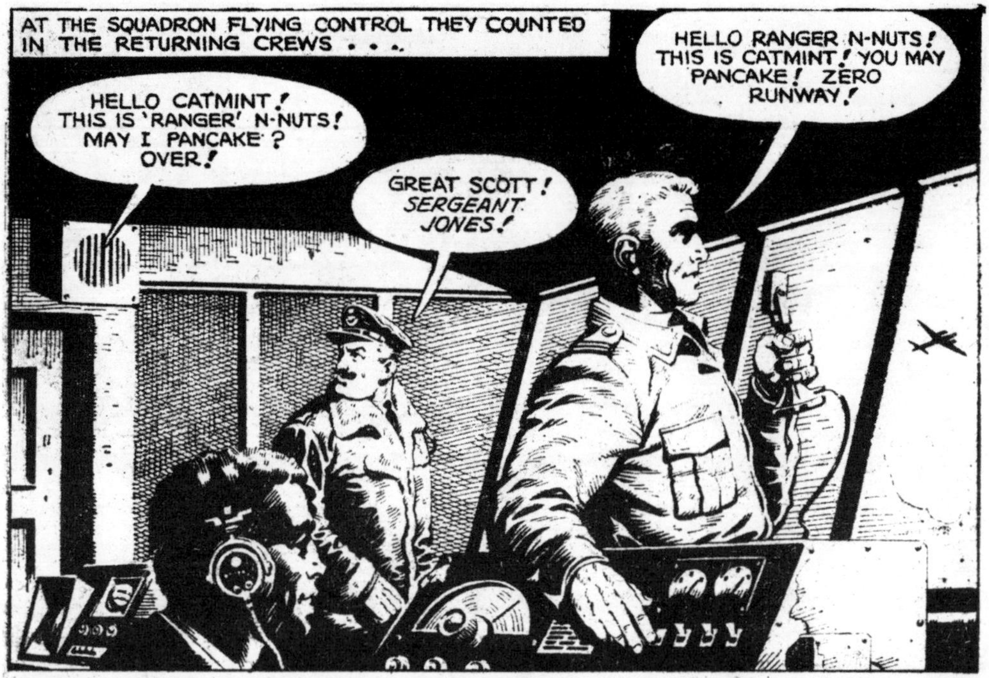
AT THE SQUADRON FLYING CONTROL THEY COUNTED IN THE RETURNING CREWS . . .
HELLO CATMINT! THIS IS 'RANGER' N-NUTS! MAY I PANCAKE? OVER!
GREAT SCOTT! SERGEANT JONES!
HELLO RANGER N-NUTS! THIS IS CATMINT! YOU MAY PANCAKE! ZERO RUNWAY!

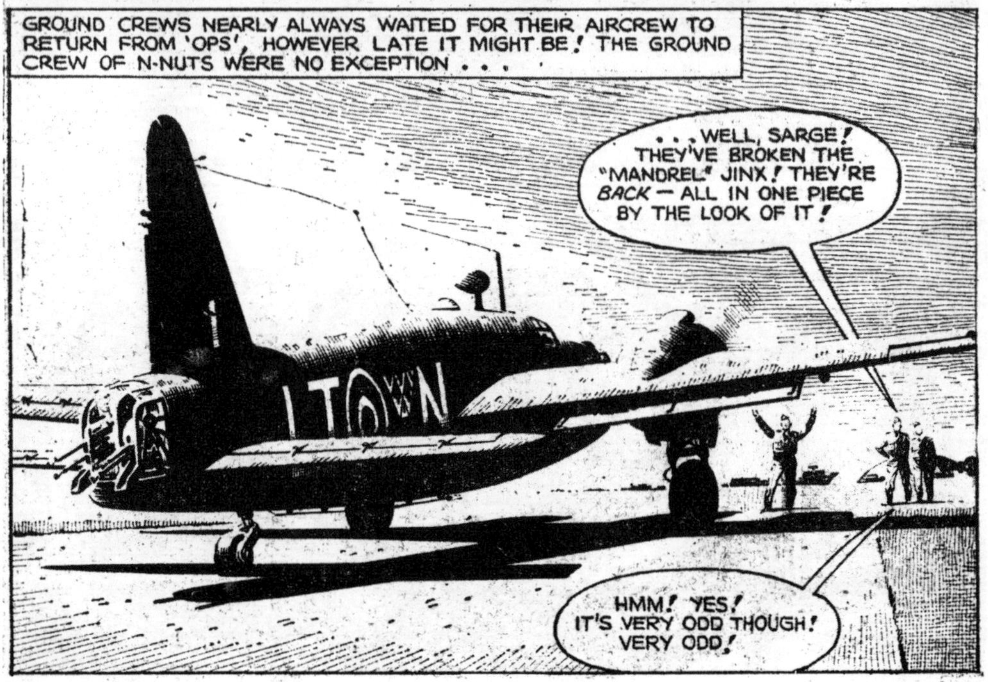
GROUND CREWS NEARLY ALWAYS WAITED FOR THEIR AIRCREW TO RETURN FROM 'OPS', HOWEVER LATE IT MIGHT BE! THE GROUND CREW OF N-NUTS WERE NO EXCEPTION . . .
. . . WELL, SARGE! THEY'VE BROKEN THE "MANDREL" JINX! THEY'RE BACK — ALL IN ONE PIECE BY THE LOOK OF IT!
HMM! YES! IT'S VERY ODD THOUGH! VERY ODD!

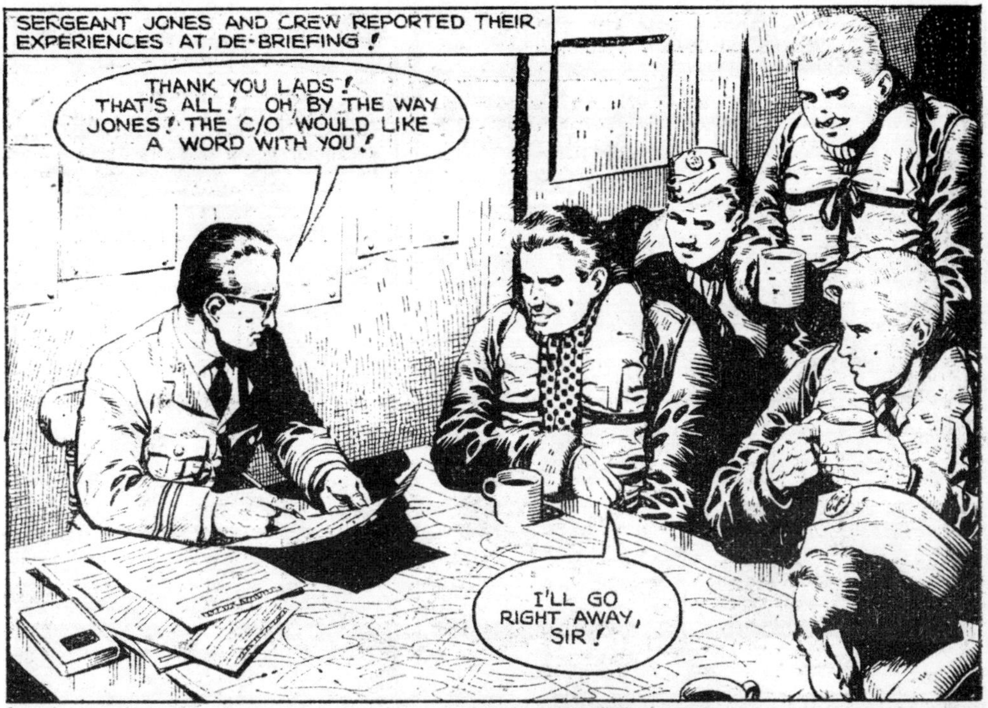
SERGEANT JONES AND CREW REPORTED THEIR EXPERIENCES AT DE-BRIEFING!
THANK YOU LADS! THAT'S ALL! OH, BY THE WAY JONES! THE C/O WOULD LIKE A WORD WITH YOU!
I'LL GO RIGHT AWAY, SIR!

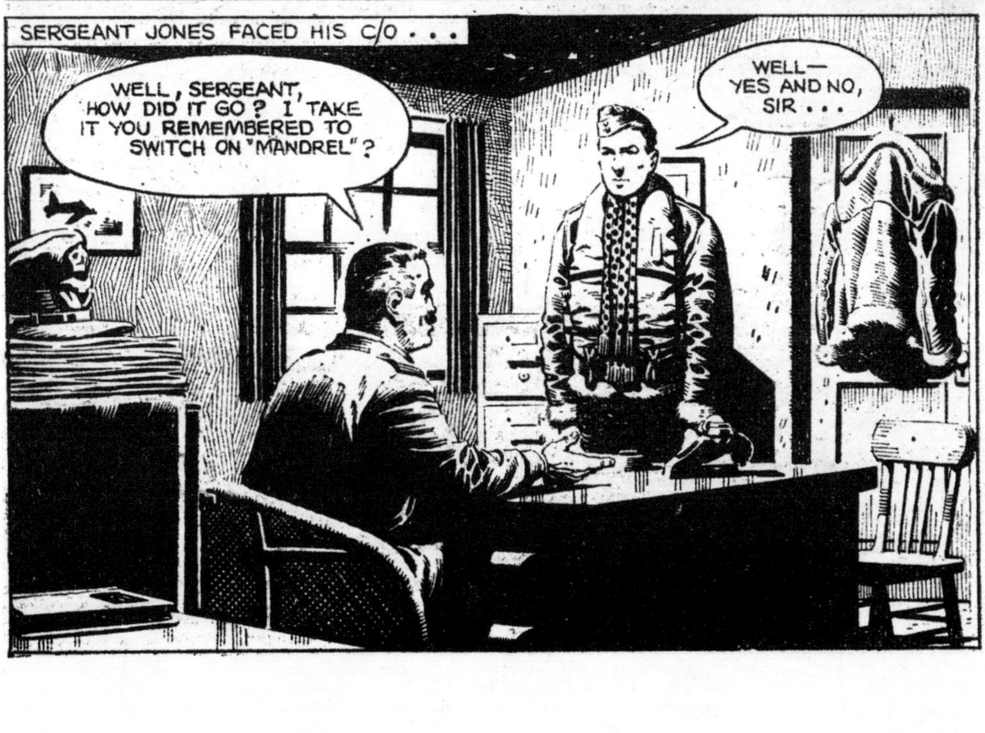
SERGEANT JONES FACED HIS C/O . . .
WELL, SERGEANT, HOW DID IT GO? I TAKE IT YOU REMEMBERED TO SWITCH ON "MANDREL"?
WELL— YES AND NO, SIR . . .

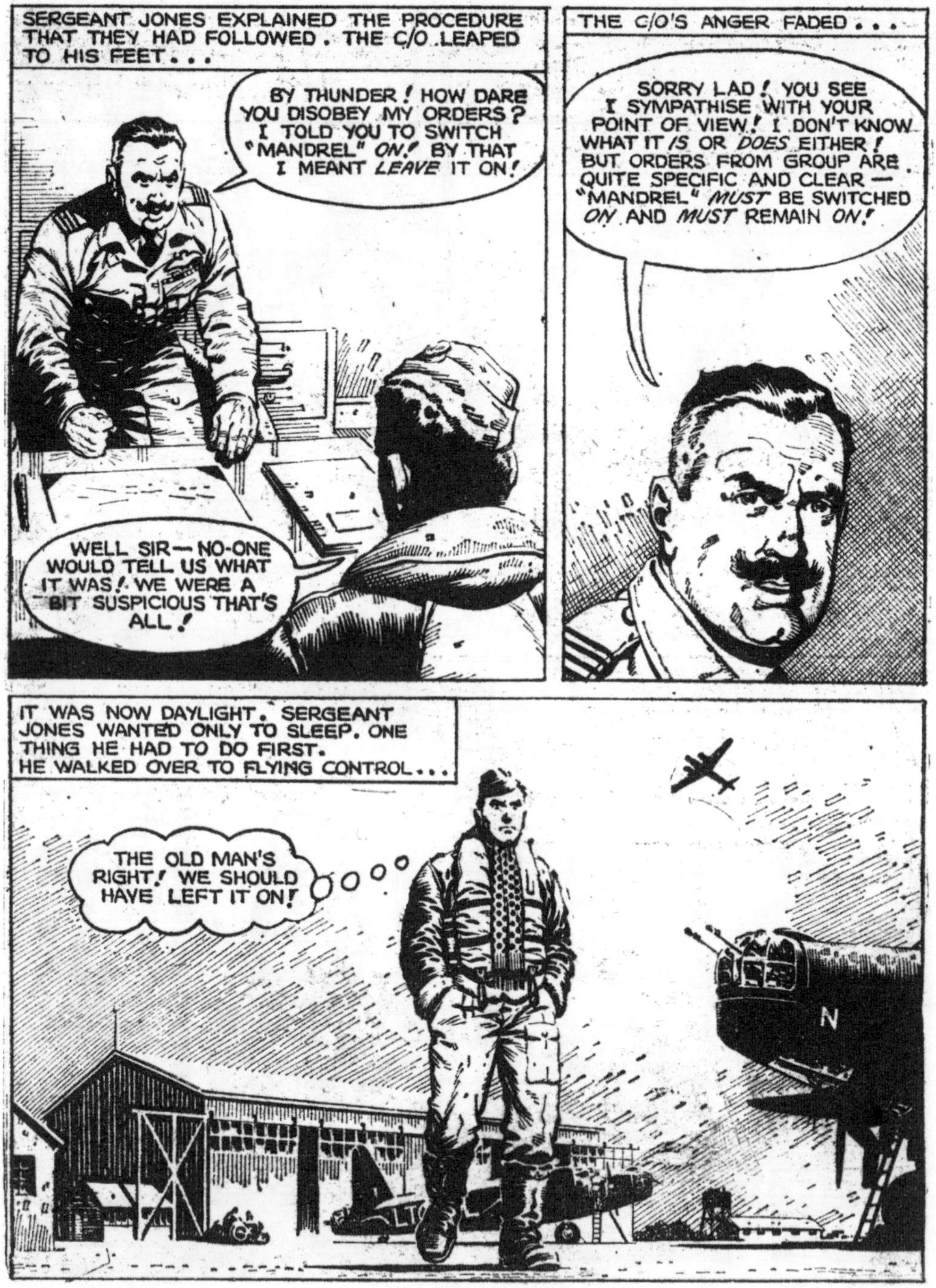
SERGEANT JONES EXPLAINED THE PROCEDURE THAT THEY HAD FOLLOWED. THE C/O LEAPED TO HIS FEET...
BY THUNDER! HOW DARE YOU DISOBEY MY ORDERS? I TOLD YOU TO SWITCH "MANDREL" ON! BY THAT I MEANT LEAVE IT ON!
WELL SIR—NO-ONE WOULD TELL US WHAT IT WAS! WE WERE A BIT SUSPICIOUS THAT'S ALL!
THE C/O'S ANGER FADED...
SORRY LAD! YOU SEE I SYMPATHISE WITH YOUR POINT OF VIEW! I DON'T KNOW WHAT IT IS OR DOES EITHER! BUT ORDERS FROM GROUP ARE QUITE SPECIFIC AND CLEAR—"MANDREL" MUST BE SWITCHED ON AND MUST REMAIN ON!
IT WAS NOW DAYLIGHT. SERGEANT JONES WANTED ONLY TO SLEEP. ONE THING HE HAD TO DO FIRST. HE WALKED OVER TO FLYING CONTROL...
THE OLD MAN'S RIGHT! WE SHOULD HAVE LEFT IT ON!

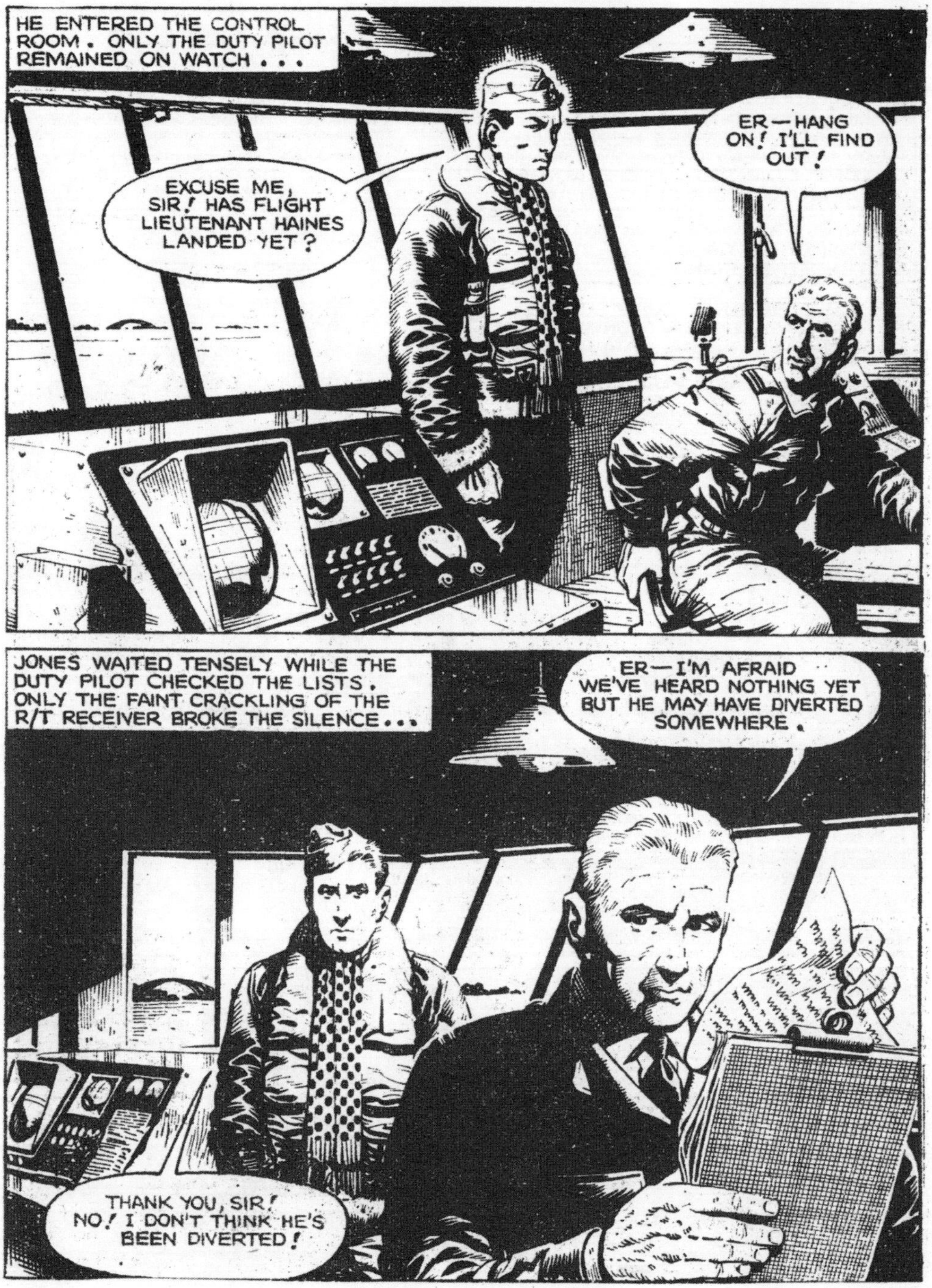
HE ENTERED THE CONTROL ROOM. ONLY THE DUTY PILOT REMAINED ON WATCH...
EXCUSE ME, SIR! HAS FLIGHT LIEUTENANT HAINES LANDED YET?
ER—HANG ON! I'LL FIND OUT!
JONES WAITED TENSELY WHILE THE DUTY PILOT CHECKED THE LISTS. ONLY THE FAINT CRACKLING OF THE R/T RECEIVER BROKE THE SILENCE...
ER—I'M AFRAID WE'VE HEARD NOTHING YET BUT HE MAY HAVE DIVERTED SOMEWHERE.
THANK YOU, SIR! NO! I DON'T THINK HE'S BEEN DIVERTED!

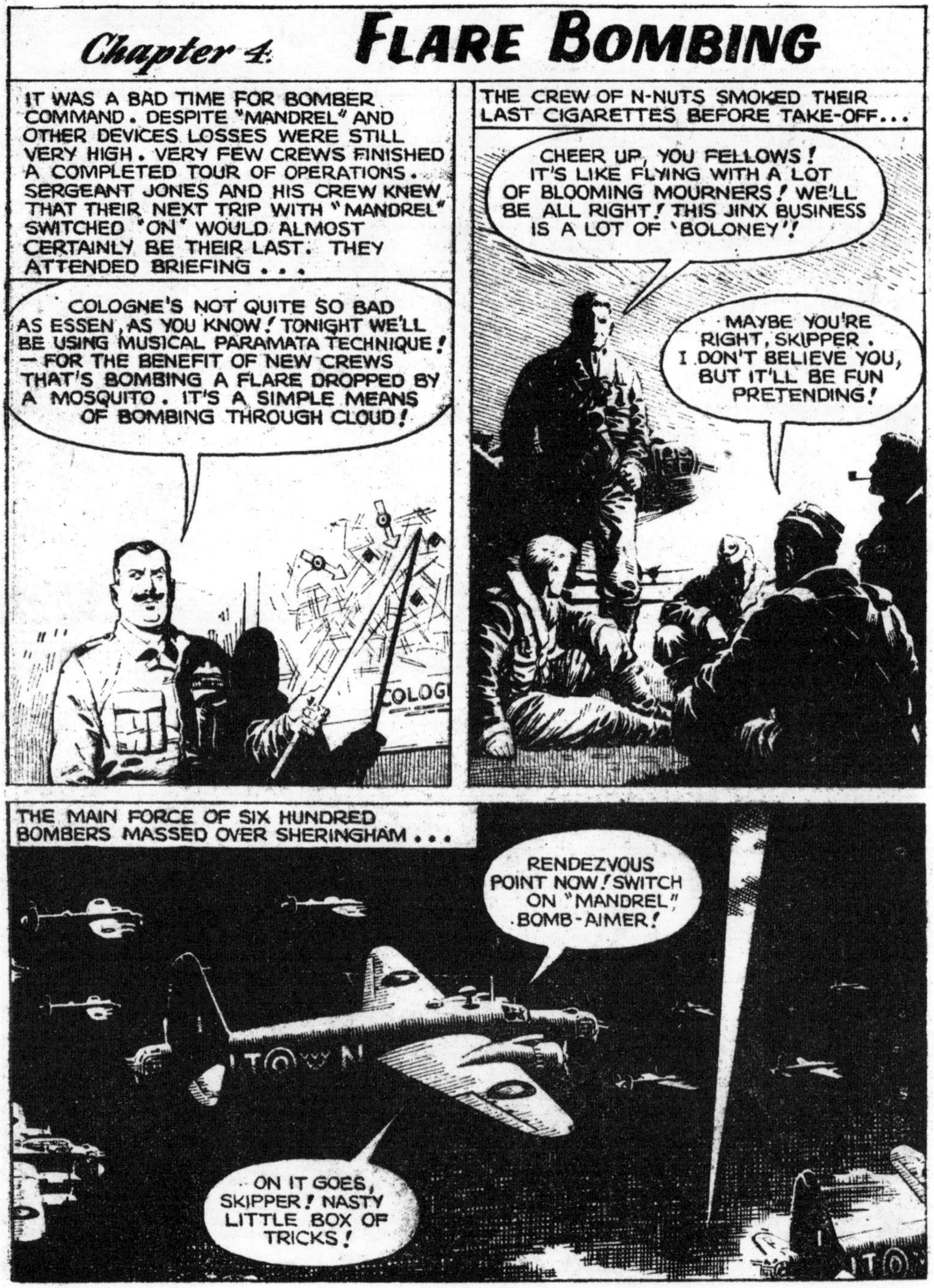
Chapter 4: FLARE BOMBING
IT WAS A BAD TIME FOR BOMBER COMMAND. DESPITE "MANDREL" AND OTHER DEVICES LOSSES WERE STILL VERY HIGH. VERY FEW CREWS FINISHED A COMPLETED TOUR OF OPERATIONS. SERGEANT JONES AND HIS CREW KNEW THAT THEIR NEXT TRIP WITH "MANDREL" SWITCHED "ON" WOULD ALMOST CERTAINLY BE THEIR LAST. THEY ATTENDED BRIEFING . . .
COLOGNE'S NOT QUITE SO BAD AS ESSEN, AS YOU KNOW! TONIGHT WE'LL BE USING MUSICAL PARAMATA TECHNIQUE! — FOR THE BENEFIT OF NEW CREWS THAT'S BOMBING A FLARE DROPPED BY A MOSQUITO. IT'S A SIMPLE MEANS OF BOMBING THROUGH CLOUD!
COLOG
THE CREW OF N-NUTS SMOKED THEIR LAST CIGARETTES BEFORE TAKE-OFF...
CHEER UP, YOU FELLOWS! IT'S LIKE FLYING WITH A LOT OF BLOOMING MOURNERS! WE'LL BE ALL RIGHT! THIS JINX BUSINESS IS A LOT OF 'BOLONEY'!
MAYBE YOU'RE RIGHT, SKIPPER. I DON'T BELIEVE YOU, BUT IT'LL BE FUN PRETENDING!
THE MAIN FORCE OF SIX HUNDRED BOMBERS MASSED OVER SHERINGHAM...
RENDEZVOUS POINT NOW! SWITCH ON "MANDREL," BOMB-AIMER!
ON IT GOES, SKIPPER! NASTY LITTLE BOX OF TRICKS!

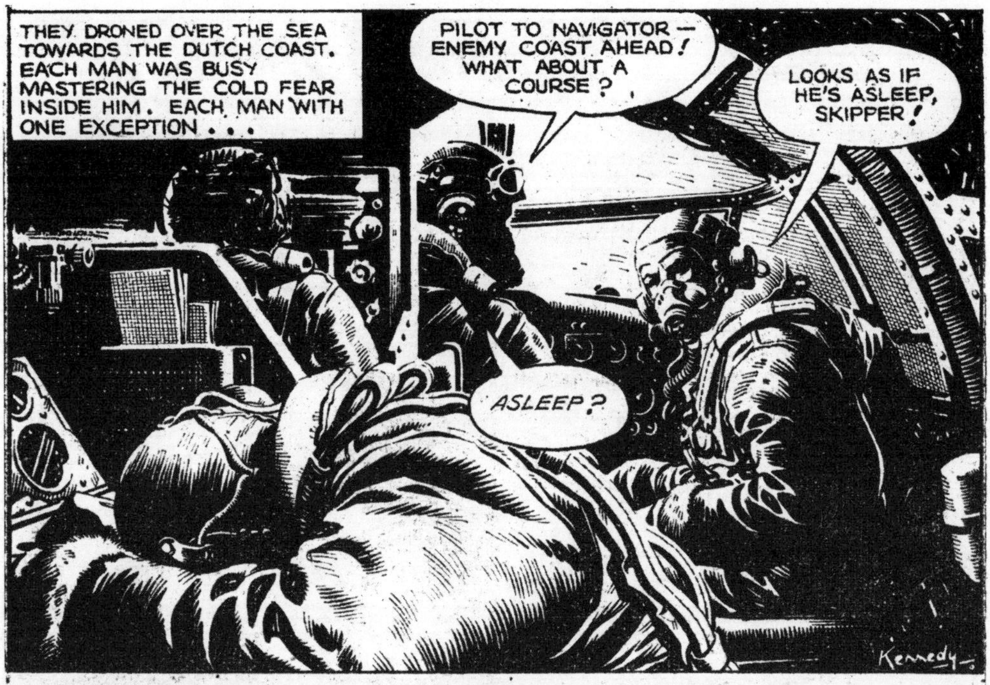
THEY DRONED OVER THE SEA TOWARDS THE DUTCH COAST. EACH MAN WAS BUSY MASTERING THE COLD FEAR INSIDE HIM. EACH MAN WITH ONE EXCEPTION . . .
PILOT TO NAVIGATOR — ENEMY COAST AHEAD! WHAT ABOUT A COURSE?
LOOKS AS IF HE'S ASLEEP, SKIPPER!
ASLEEP?
Kennedy

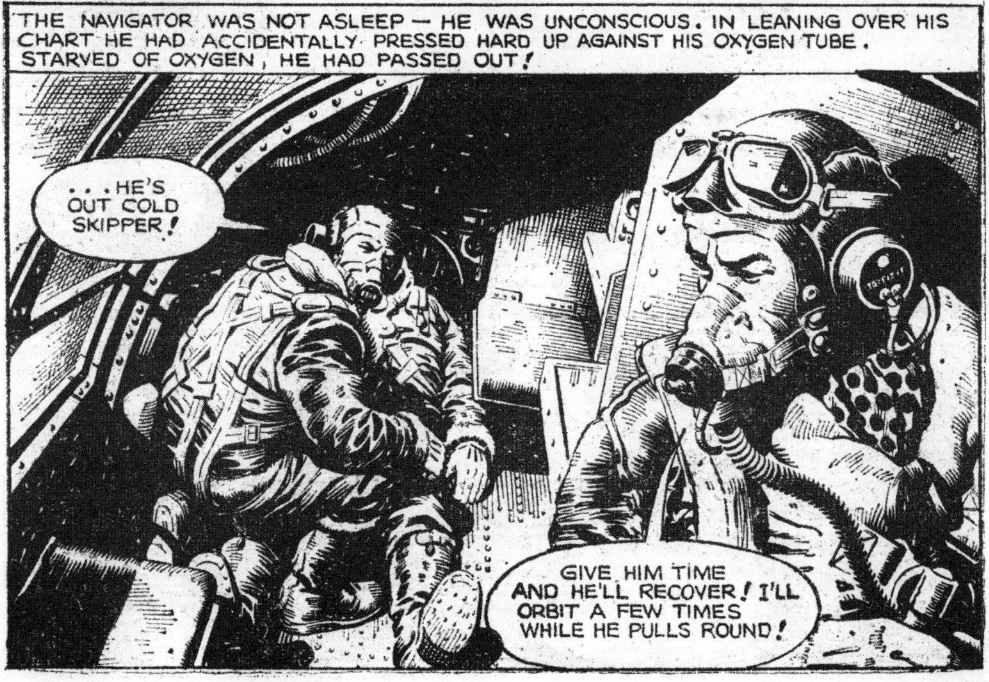
THE NAVIGATOR WAS NOT ASLEEP — HE WAS UNCONSCIOUS. IN LEANING OVER HIS CHART HE HAD ACCIDENTALLY PRESSED HARD UP AGAINST HIS OXYGEN TUBE. STARVED OF OXYGEN, HE HAD PASSED OUT!
. . . HE'S OUT COLD SKIPPER!
GIVE HIM TIME AND HE'LL RECOVER! I'LL ORBIT A FEW TIMES WHILE HE PULLS ROUND!

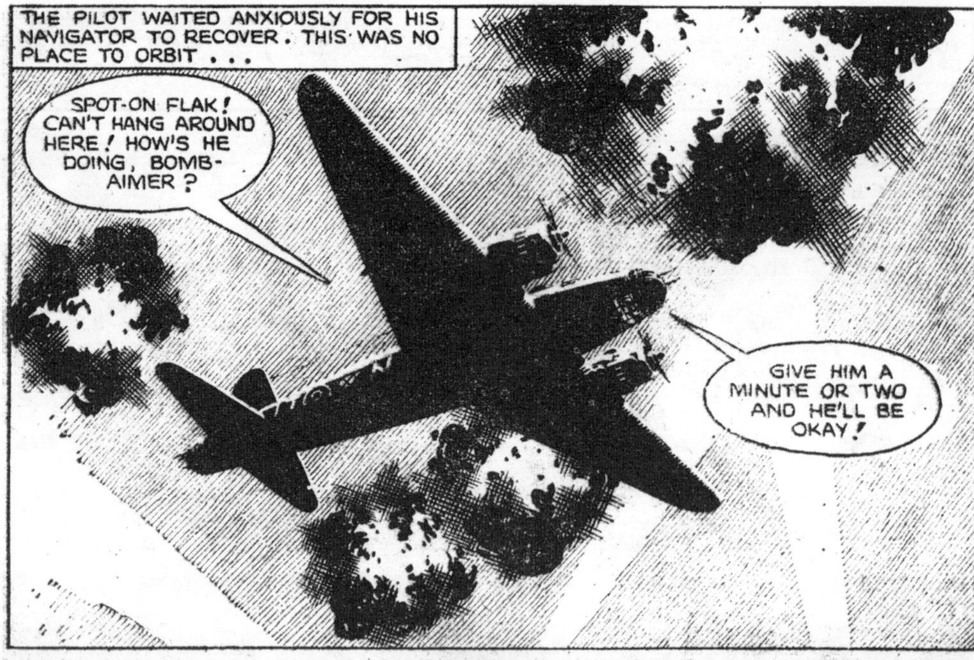
THE PILOT WAITED ANXIOUSLY FOR HIS NAVIGATOR TO RECOVER. THIS WAS NO PLACE TO ORBIT . . .
SPOT-ON FLAK! CAN'T HANG AROUND HERE! HOW'S HE DOING, BOMB-AIMER?
GIVE HIM A MINUTE OR TWO AND HE'LL BE OKAY!

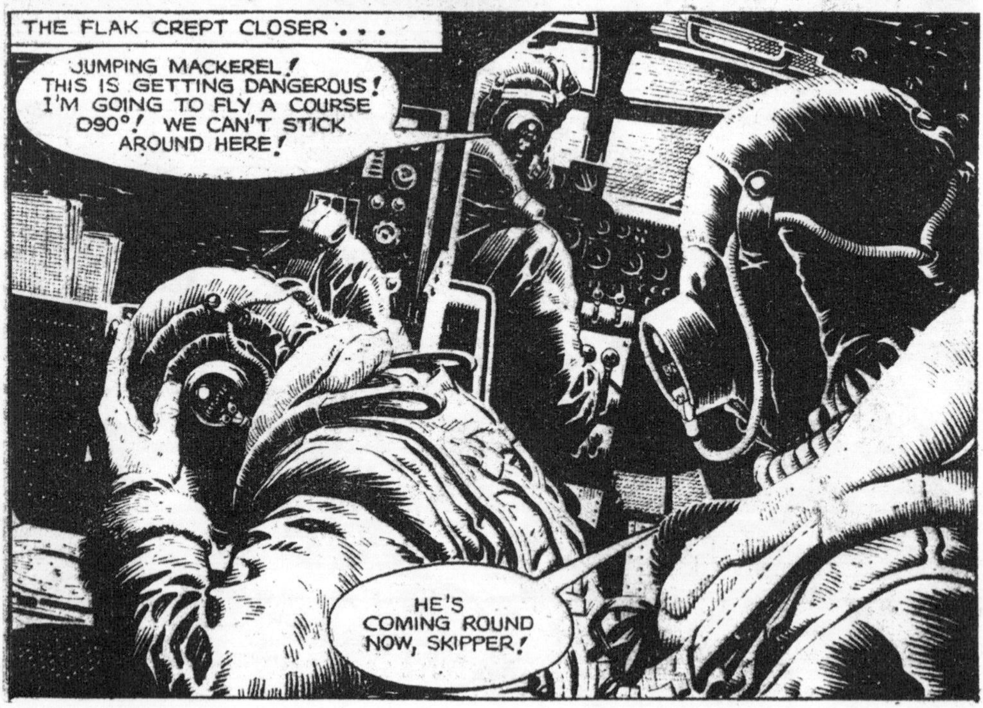
THE FLAK CREPT CLOSER . . .
JUMPING MACKEREL! THIS IS GETTING DANGEROUS! I'M GOING TO FLY A COURSE 090°! WE CAN'T STICK AROUND HERE!
HE'S COMING ROUND NOW, SKIPPER!

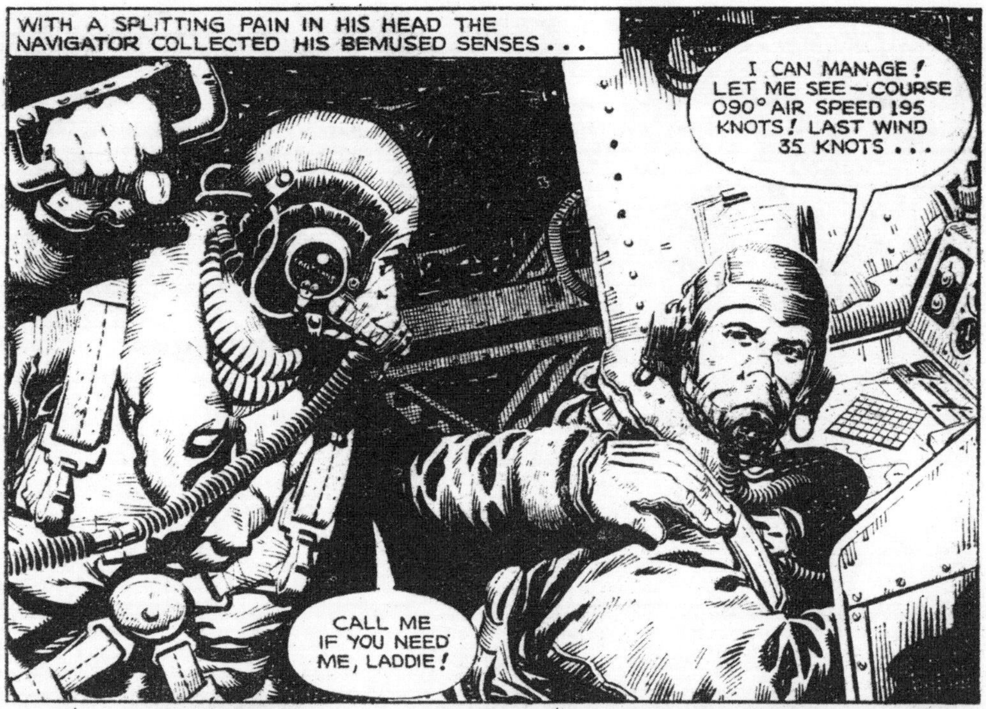
WITH A SPLITTING PAIN IN HIS HEAD THE NAVIGATOR COLLECTED HIS BEMUSED SENSES . . .
I CAN MANAGE! LET ME SEE—COURSE 090° AIR SPEED 195 KNOTS! LAST WIND 35 KNOTS . . .
CALL ME IF YOU NEED ME, LADDIE!

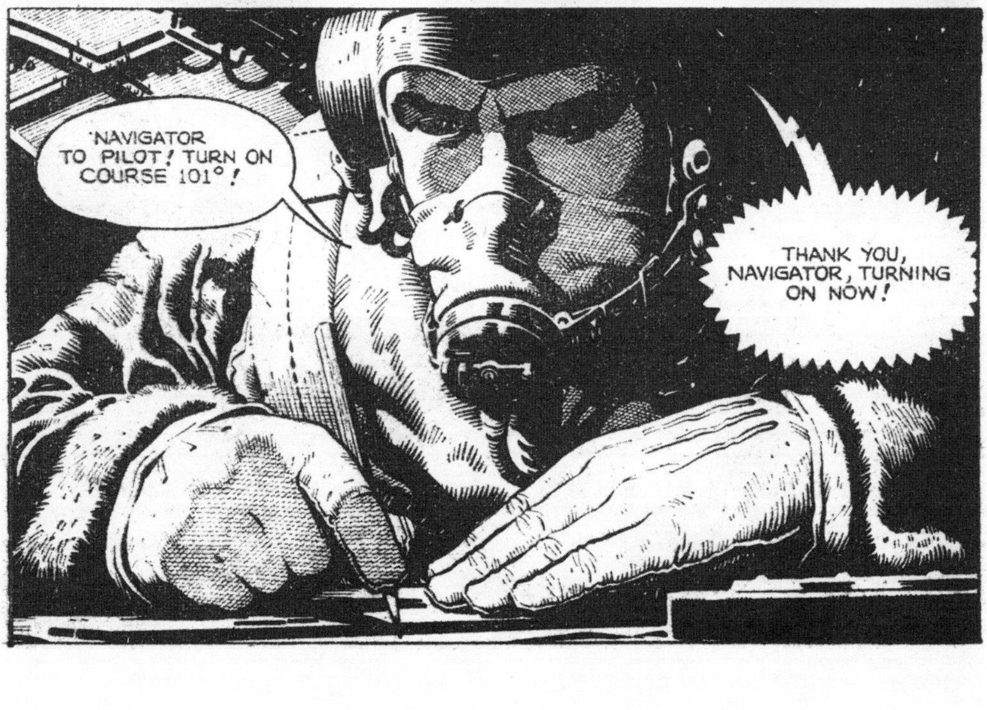
'NAVIGATOR TO PILOT! TURN ON COURSE 101°!
THANK YOU, NAVIGATOR, TURNING ON NOW!

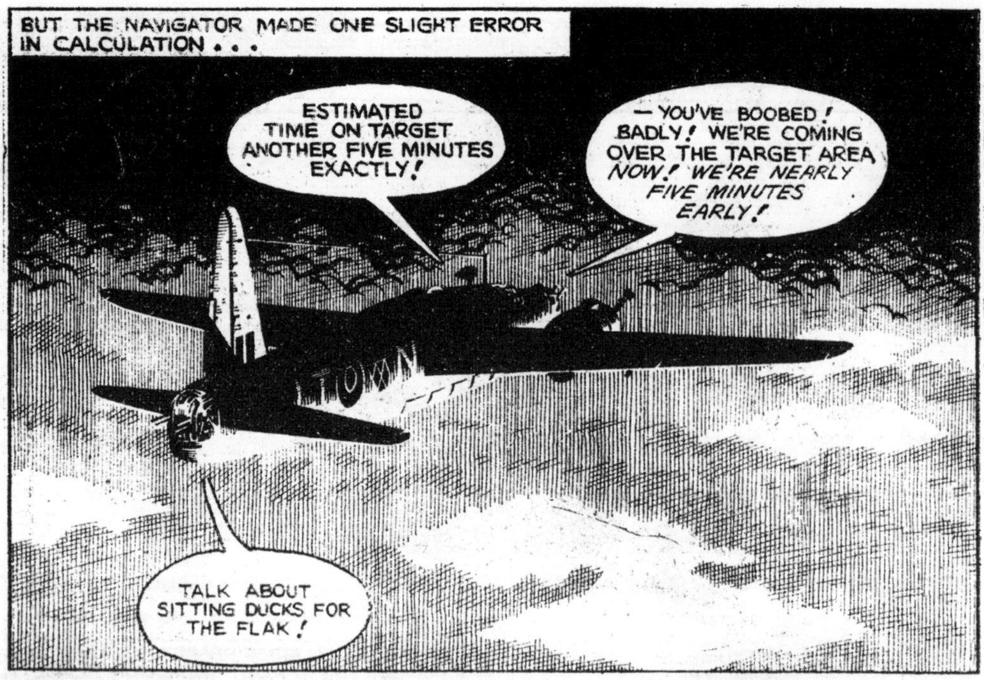
BUT THE NAVIGATOR MADE ONE SLIGHT ERROR IN CALCULATION . . .
ESTIMATED TIME ON TARGET ANOTHER FIVE MINUTES EXACTLY!
—YOU'VE BOOBED! BADLY! WE'RE COMING OVER THE TARGET AREA NOW! WE'RE NEARLY FIVE MINUTES EARLY!
TALK ABOUT SITTING DUCKS FOR THE FLAK!

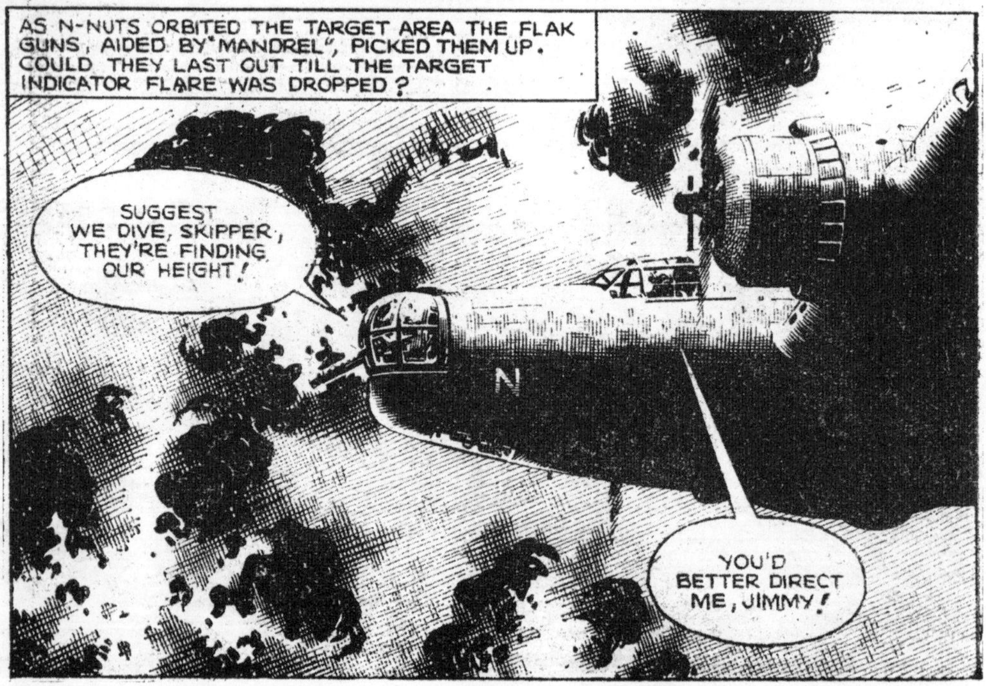
AS N-NUTS ORBITED THE TARGET AREA THE FLAK GUNS, AIDED BY "MANDREL", PICKED THEM UP. COULD THEY LAST OUT TILL THE TARGET INDICATOR FLARE WAS DROPPED?
SUGGEST WE DIVE, SKIPPER, THEY'RE FINDING OUR HEIGHT!
YOU'D BETTER DIRECT ME, JIMMY!

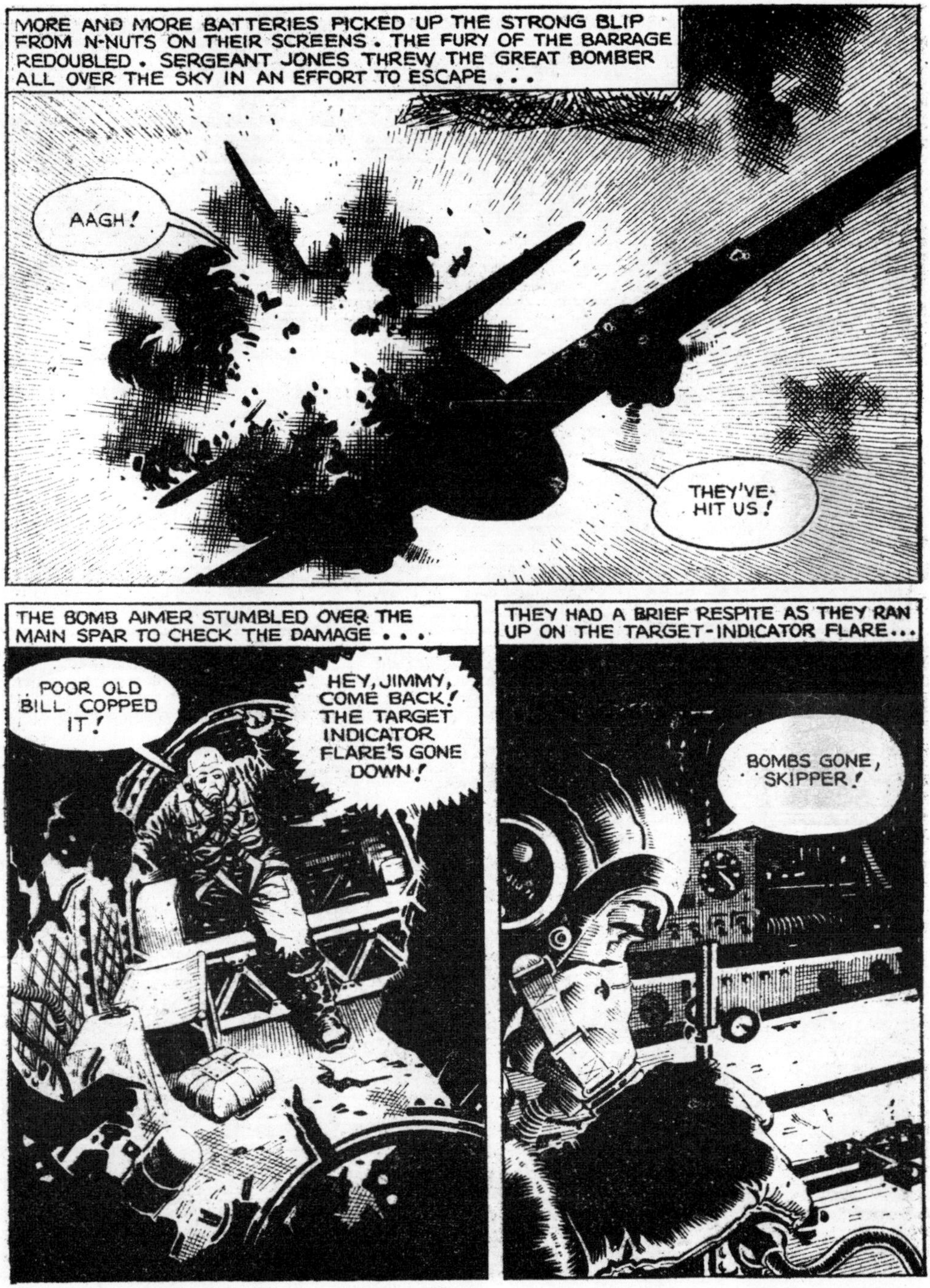
MORE AND MORE BATTERIES PICKED UP THE STRONG BLIP FROM N-NUTS ON THEIR SCREENS. THE FURY OF THE BARRAGE REDOUBLED. SERGEANT JONES THREW THE GREAT BOMBER ALL OVER THE SKY IN AN EFFORT TO ESCAPE ...
AAGH!
THEY'VE HIT US!
THE BOMB AIMER STUMBLED OVER THE MAIN SPAR TO CHECK THE DAMAGE ...
POOR OLD BILL COPPED IT!
HEY, JIMMY, COME BACK! THE TARGET INDICATOR FLARE'S GONE DOWN!
THEY HAD A BRIEF RESPITE AS THEY RAN UP ON THE TARGET-INDICATOR FLARE...
BOMBS GONE, SKIPPER!

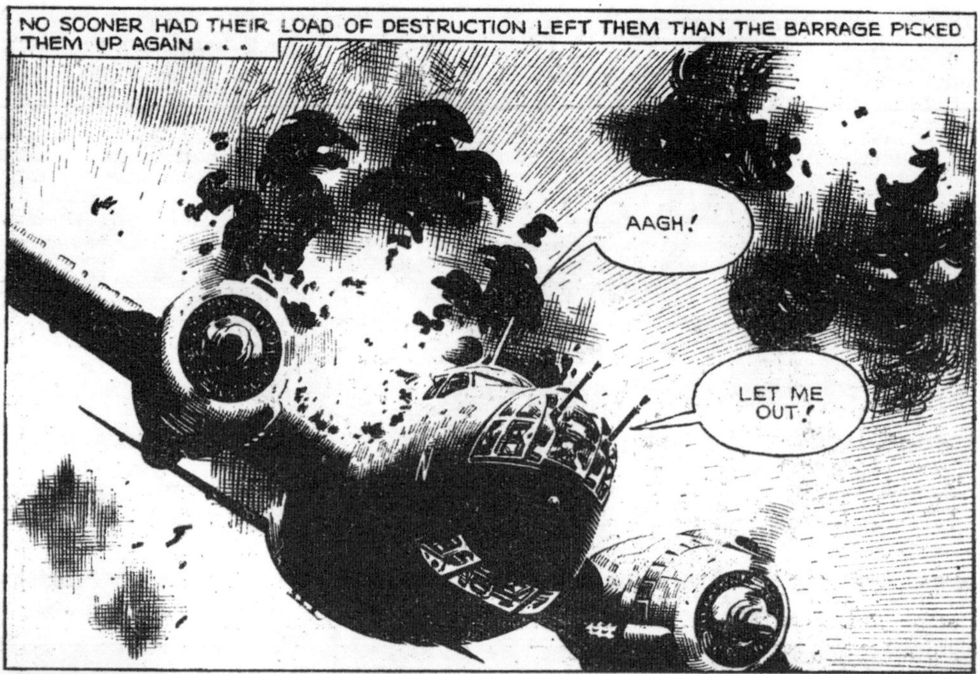
NO SOONER HAD THEIR LOAD OF DESTRUCTION LEFT THEM THAN THE BARRAGE PICKED THEM UP AGAIN . . .
AAGH!
LET ME OUT!

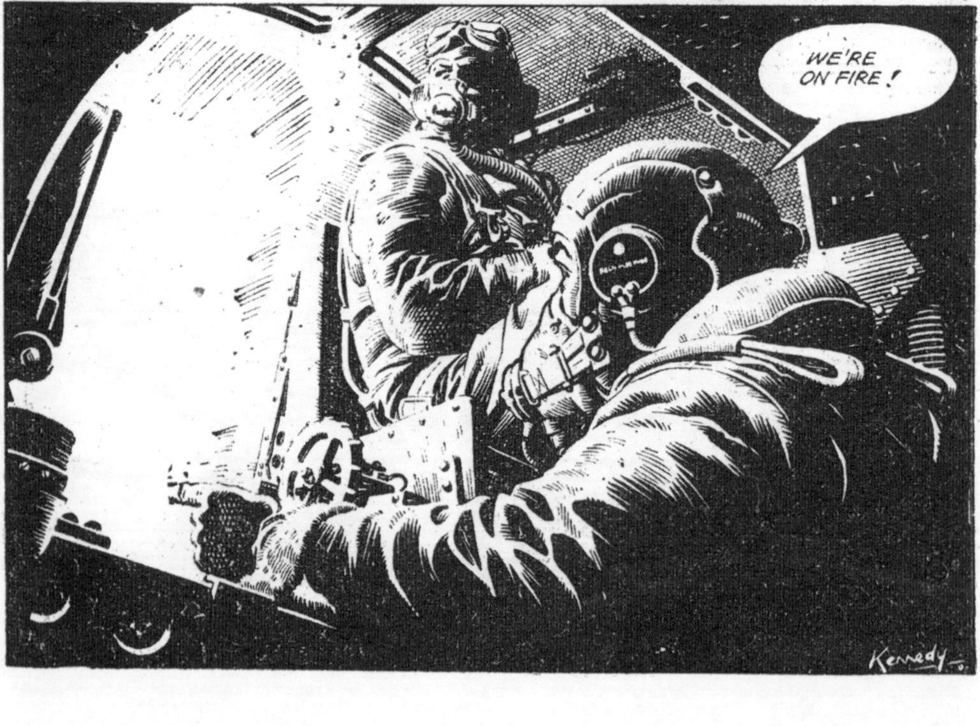
WE'RE ON FIRE!
Kennedy

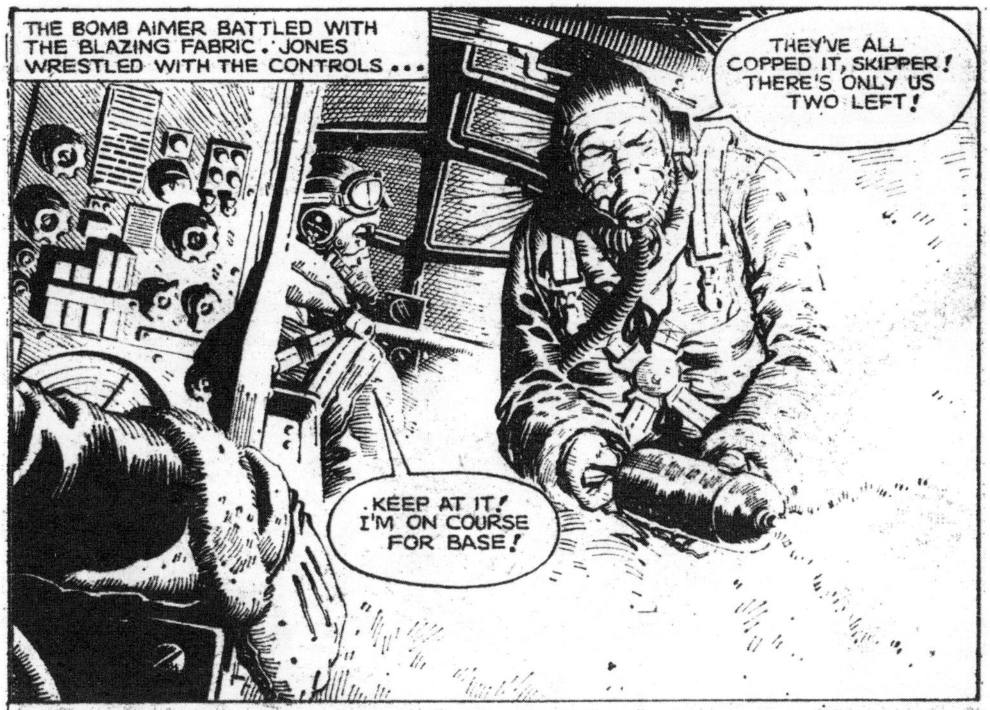
THE BOMB AIMER BATTLED WITH THE BLAZING FABRIC. JONES WRESTLED WITH THE CONTROLS...
THEY'VE ALL COPPED IT, SKIPPER! THERE'S ONLY US TWO LEFT!
KEEP AT IT! I'M ON COURSE FOR BASE!

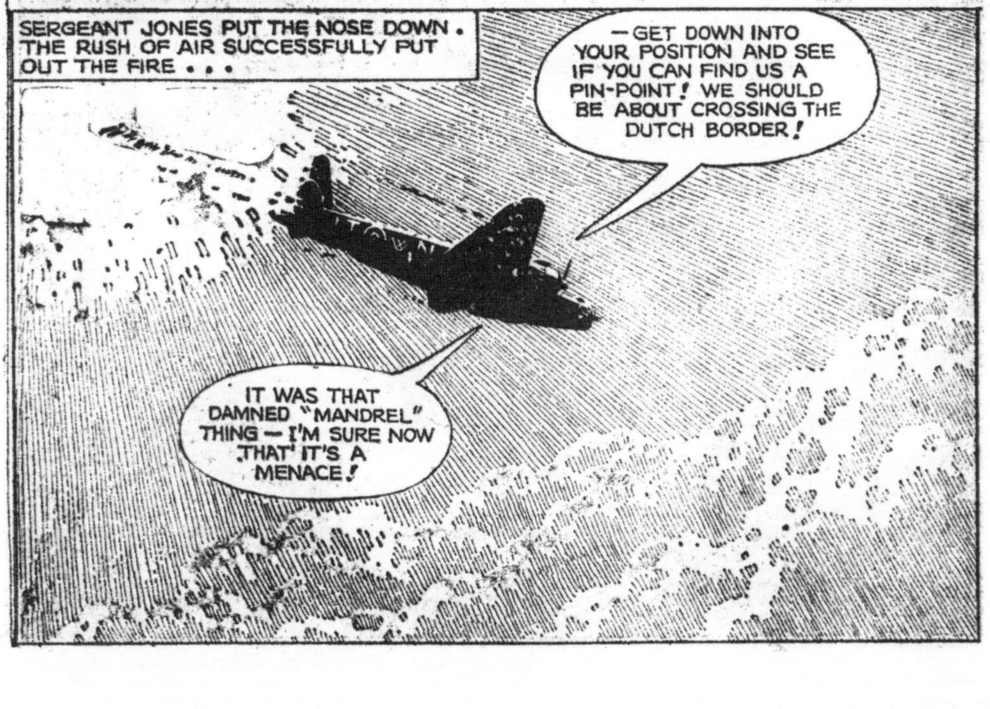
SERGEANT JONES PUT THE NOSE DOWN. THE RUSH OF AIR SUCCESSFULLY PUT OUT THE FIRE...
—GET DOWN INTO YOUR POSITION AND SEE IF YOU CAN FIND US A PIN-POINT! WE SHOULD BE ABOUT CROSSING THE DUTCH BORDER!
IT WAS THAT DAMNED "MANDREL" THING—I'M SURE NOW THAT IT'S A MENACE!

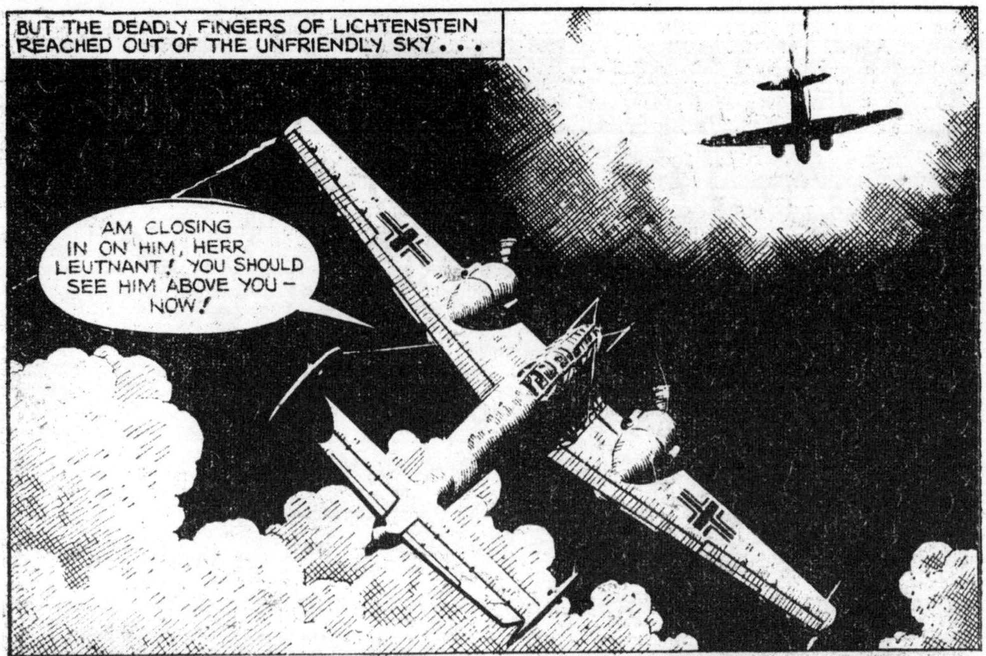
BUT THE DEADLY FINGERS OF LICHTENSTEIN REACHED OUT OF THE UNFRIENDLY SKY . . .
AM CLOSING IN ON HIM, HERR LEUTNANT! YOU SHOULD SEE HIM ABOVE YOU – NOW!

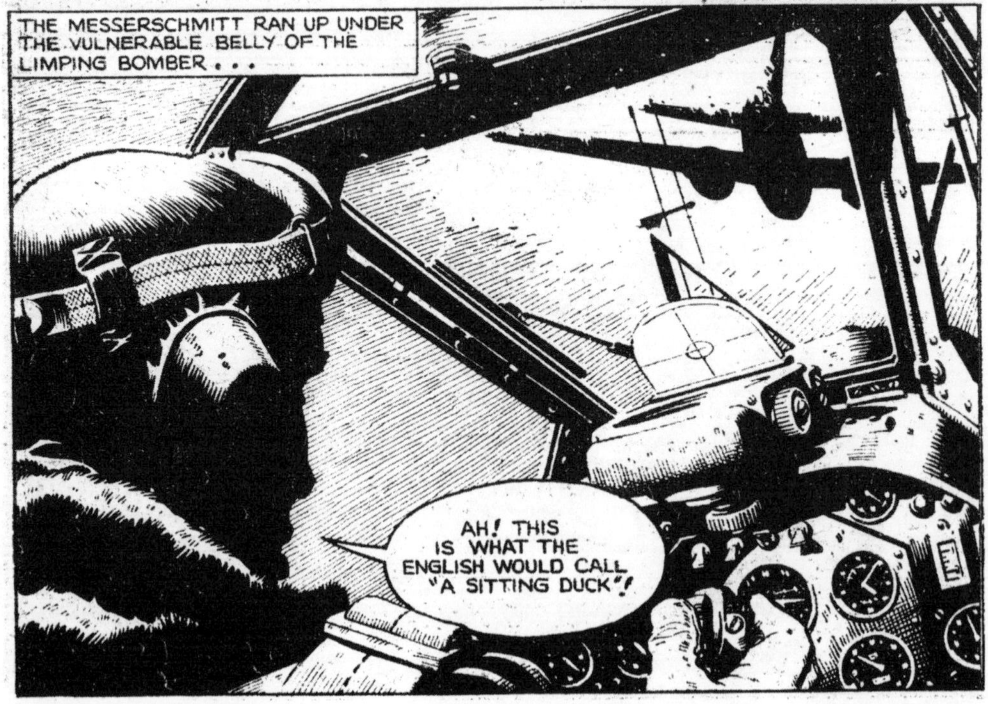
THE MESSERSCHMITT RAN UP UNDER THE VULNERABLE BELLY OF THE LIMPING BOMBER . . .
AH! THIS IS WHAT THE ENGLISH WOULD CALL "A SITTING DUCK"!

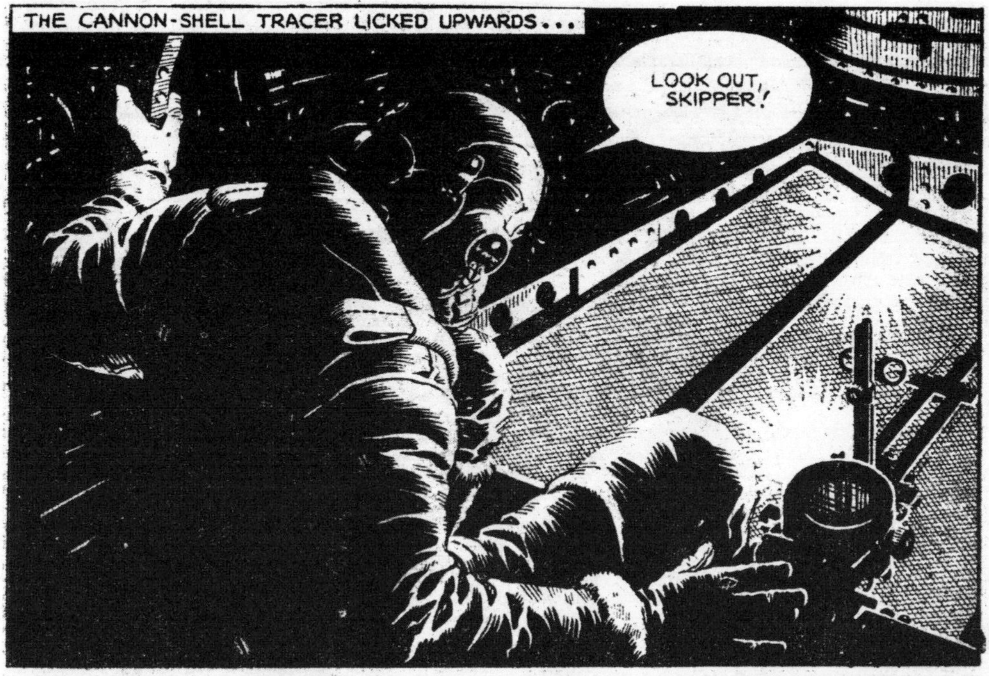
THE CANNON-SHELL TRACER LICKED UPWARDS...
LOOK OUT, SKIPPER!

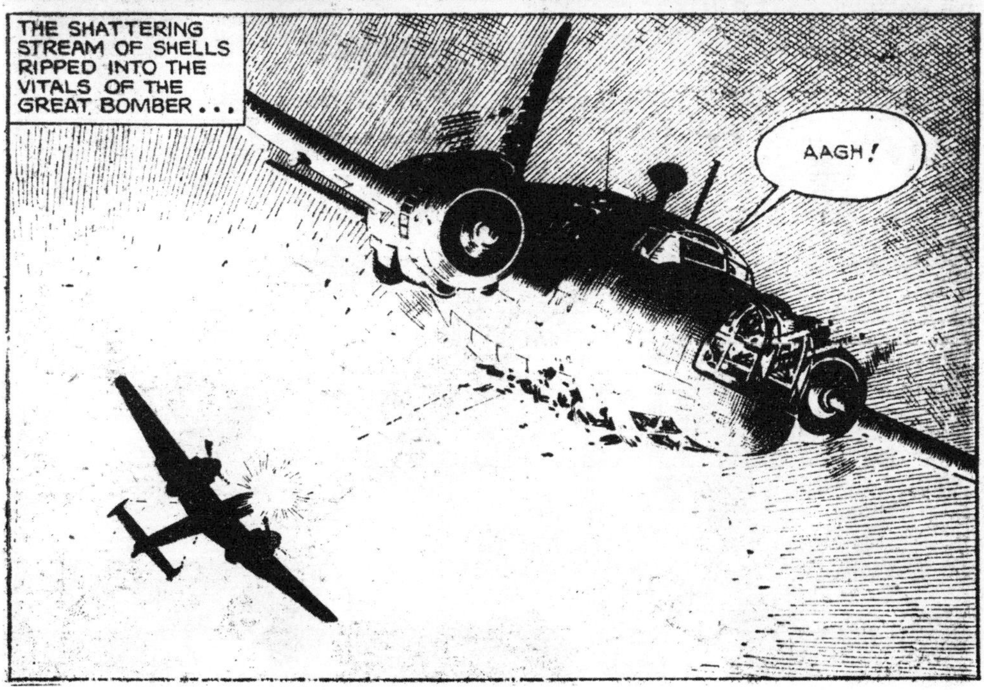
THE SHATTERING STREAM OF SHELLS RIPPED INTO THE VITALS OF THE GREAT BOMBER...
AAGH!

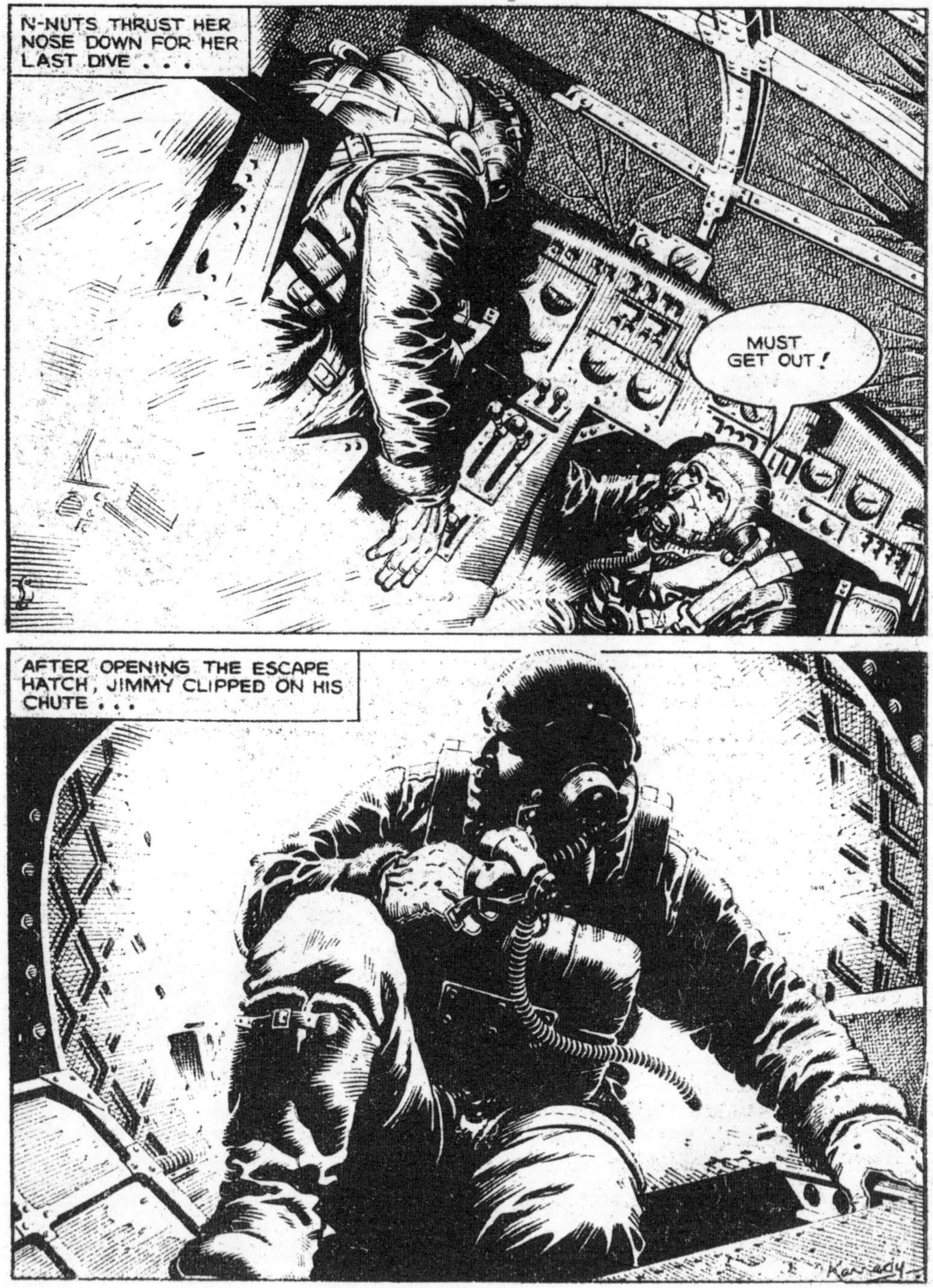
N-NUTS THRUST HER NOSE DOWN FOR HER LAST DIVE . . .
MUST GET OUT!
AFTER OPENING THE ESCAPE HATCH, JIMMY CLIPPED ON HIS CHUTE . . .

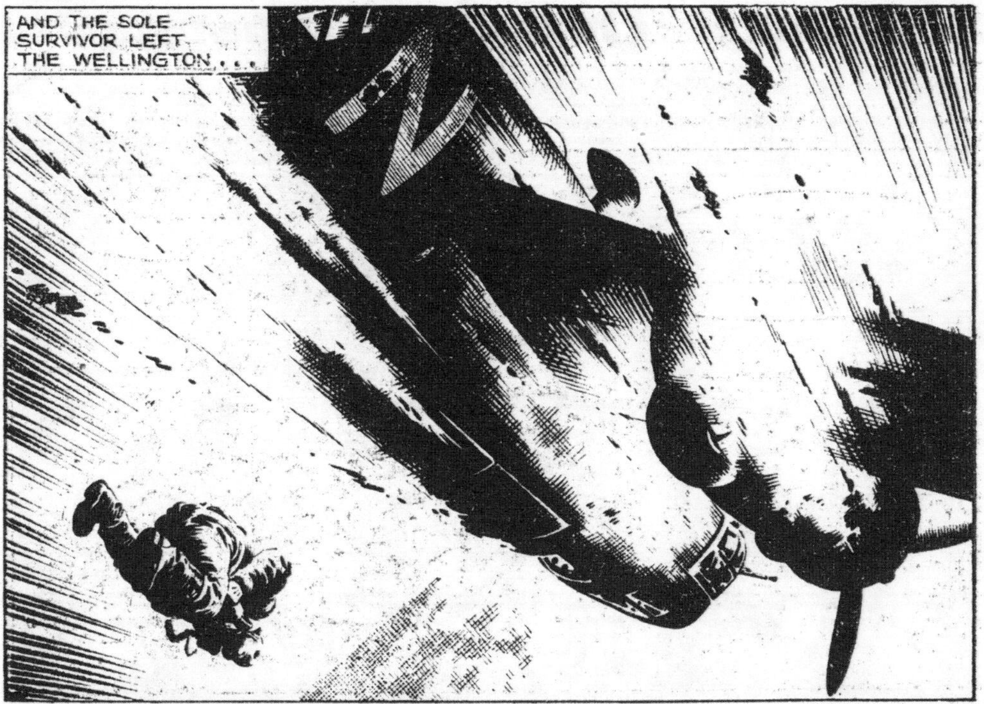
AND THE SOLE SURVIVOR LEFT THE WELLINGTON...

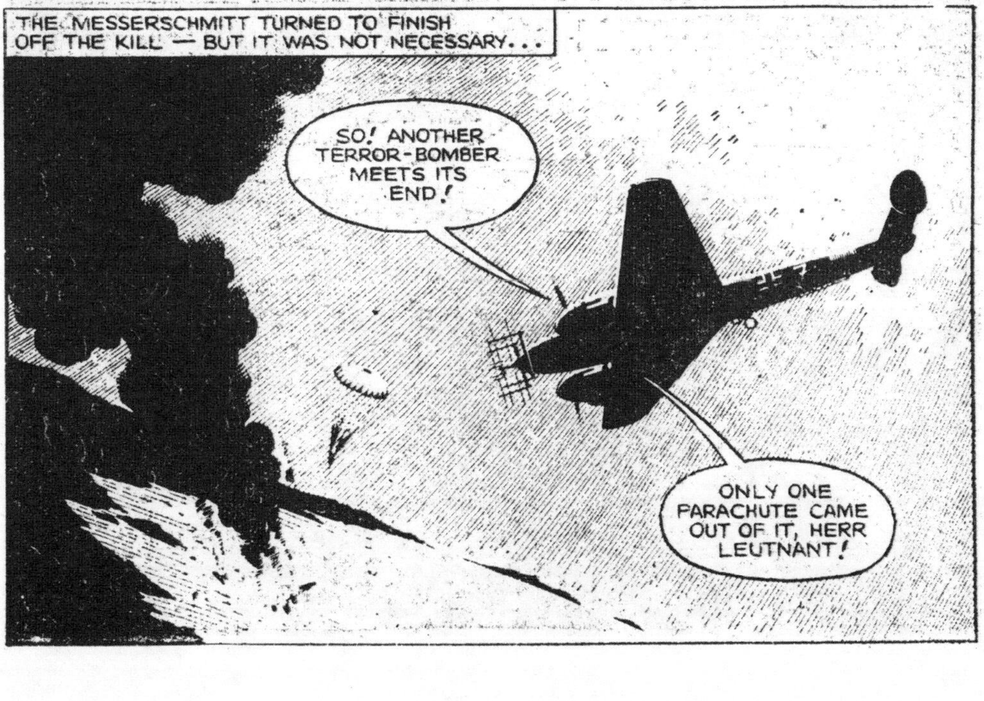
THE MESSERSCHMITT TURNED TO FINISH OFF THE KILL — BUT IT WAS NOT NECESSARY...
SO! ANOTHER TERROR-BOMBER MEETS ITS END!
ONLY ONE PARACHUTE CAME OUT OF IT, HERR LEUTNANT!

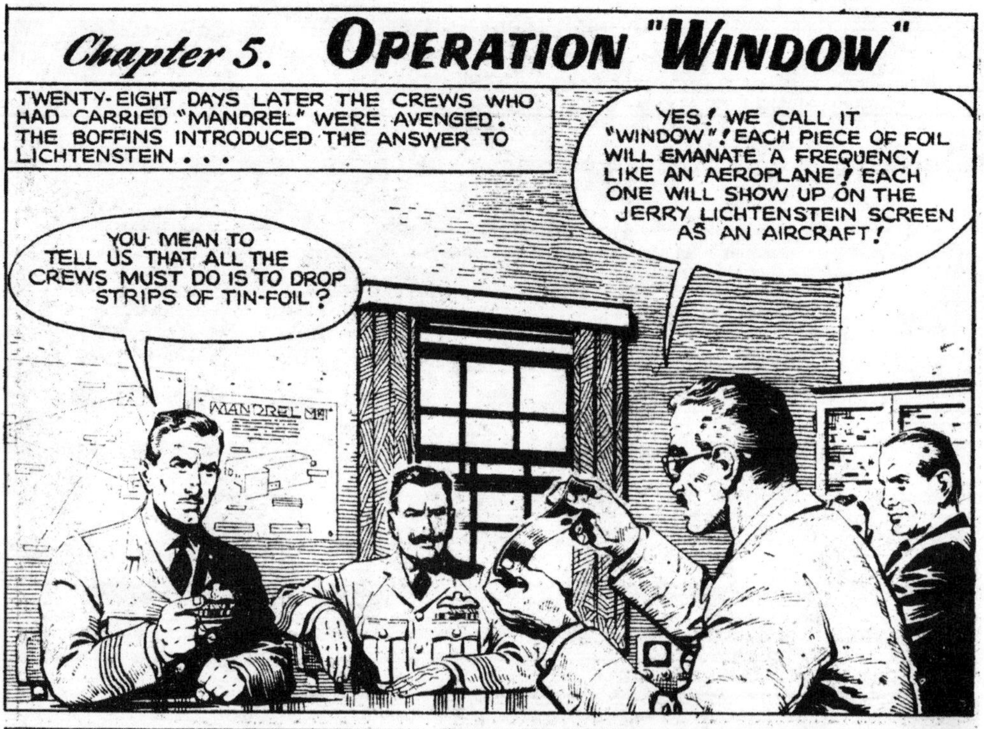
Chapter 5. OPERATION "WINDOW"
TWENTY-EIGHT DAYS LATER THE CREWS WHO HAD CARRIED "MANDREL" WERE AVENGED. THE BOFFINS INTRODUCED THE ANSWER TO LICHTENSTEIN . . .
YOU MEAN TO TELL US THAT ALL THE CREWS MUST DO IS TO DROP STRIPS OF TIN-FOIL?
YES! WE CALL IT "WINDOW"! EACH PIECE OF FOIL WILL EMANATE A FREQUENCY LIKE AN AEROPLANE! EACH ONE WILL SHOW UP ON THE JERRY LICHTENSTEIN SCREEN AS AN AIRCRAFT!
MANDREL

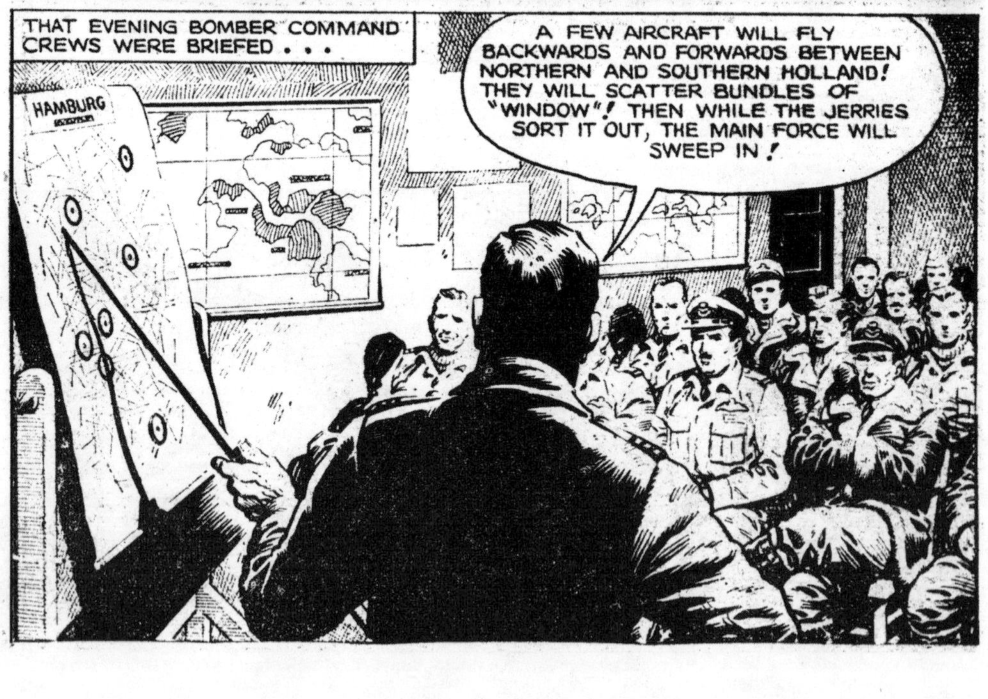
THAT EVENING BOMBER COMMAND CREWS WERE BRIEFED . . .
A FEW AIRCRAFT WILL FLY BACKWARDS AND FORWARDS BETWEEN NORTHERN AND SOUTHERN HOLLAND! THEY WILL SCATTER BUNDLES OF "WINDOW"! THEN WHILE THE JERRIES SORT IT OUT, THE MAIN FORCE WILL SWEEP IN!
HAMBURG

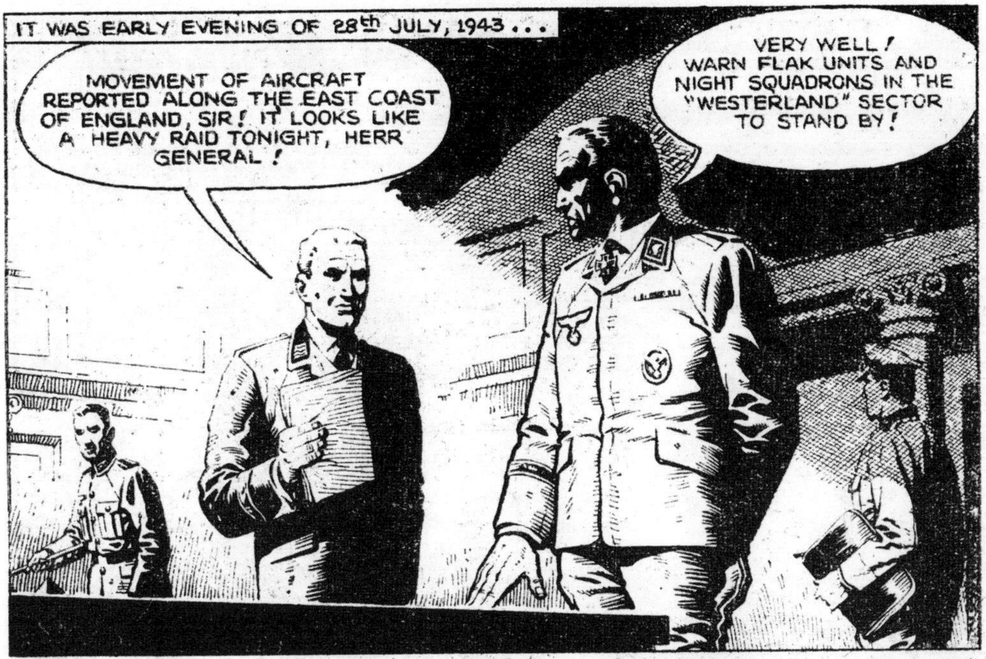
IT WAS EARLY EVENING OF 28th JULY, 1943 . . .
MOVEMENT OF AIRCRAFT REPORTED ALONG THE EAST COAST OF ENGLAND, SIR! IT LOOKS LIKE A HEAVY RAID TONIGHT, HERR GENERAL!
VERY WELL! WARN FLAK UNITS AND NIGHT SQUADRONS IN THE "WESTERLAND" SECTOR TO STAND BY!

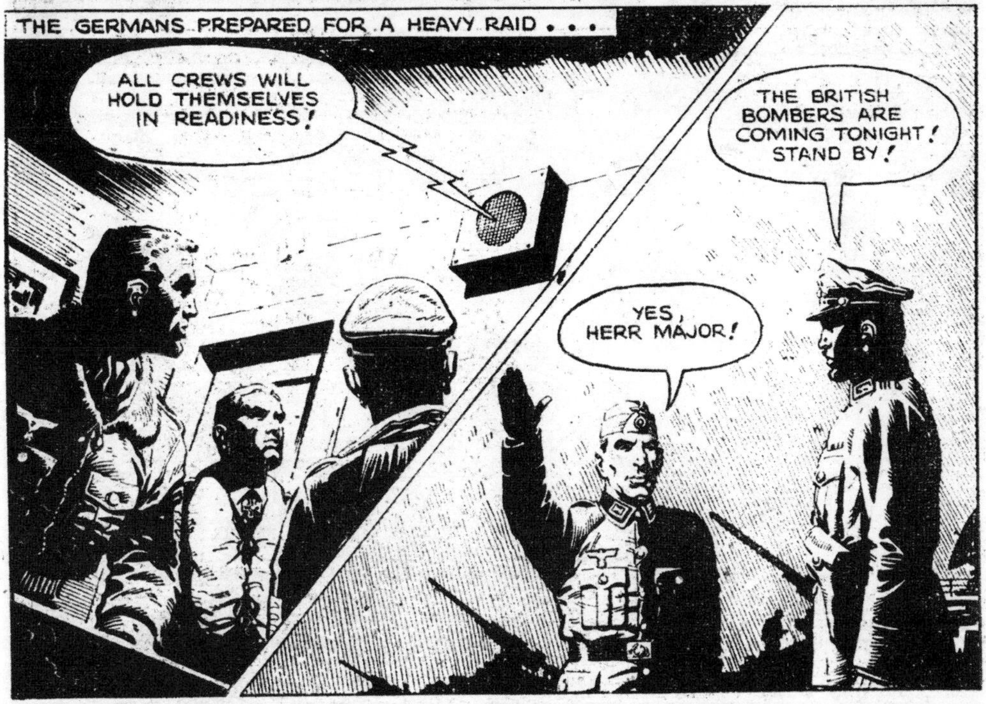
THE GERMANS PREPARED FOR A HEAVY RAID . . .
ALL CREWS WILL HOLD THEMSELVES IN READINESS!
THE BRITISH BOMBERS ARE COMING TONIGHT! STAND BY!
YES, HERR MAJOR!

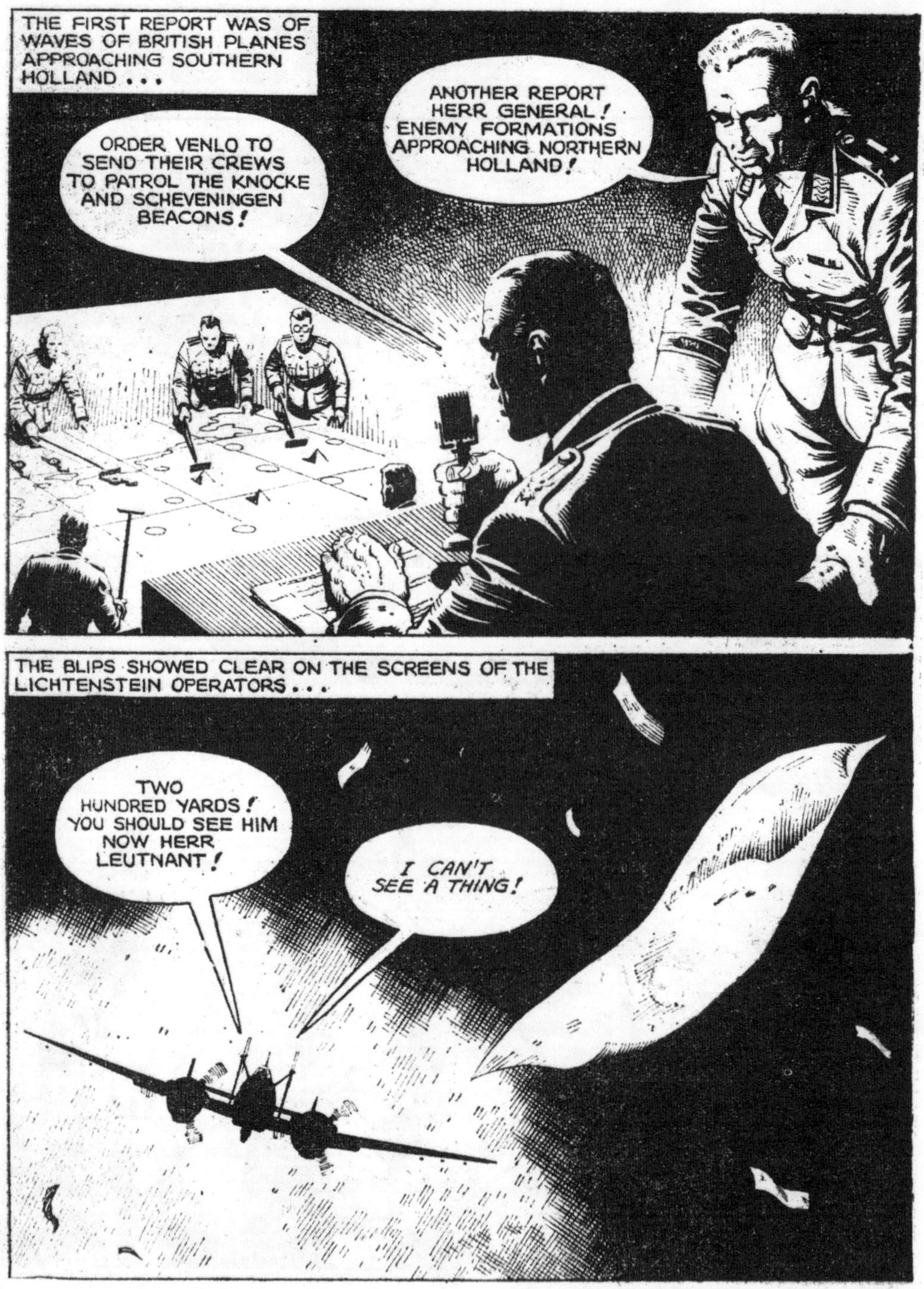
THE FIRST REPORT WAS OF WAVES OF BRITISH PLANES APPROACHING SOUTHERN HOLLAND ...
ANOTHER REPORT HERR GENERAL! ENEMY FORMATIONS APPROACHING NORTHERN HOLLAND!
ORDER VENLO TO SEND THEIR CREWS TO PATROL THE KNOCKE AND SCHEVENINGEN BEACONS!
THE BLIPS SHOWED CLEAR ON THE SCREENS OF THE LICHTENSTEIN OPERATORS ...
TWO HUNDRED YARDS! YOU SHOULD SEE HIM NOW HERR LEUTNANT!
I CAN'T SEE A THING!

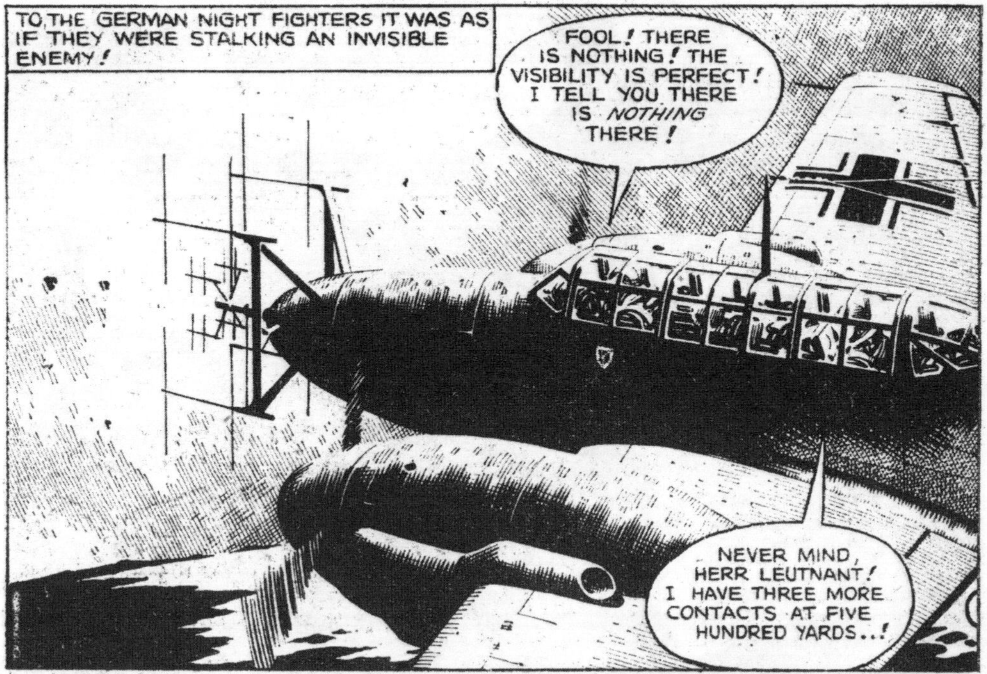
TO THE GERMAN NIGHT FIGHTERS IT WAS AS IF THEY WERE STALKING AN INVISIBLE ENEMY!
FOOL! THERE IS NOTHING! THE VISIBILITY IS PERFECT! I TELL YOU THERE IS *NOTHING* THERE!
NEVER MIND, HERR LEUTNANT! I HAVE THREE MORE CONTACTS AT FIVE HUNDRED YARDS..!

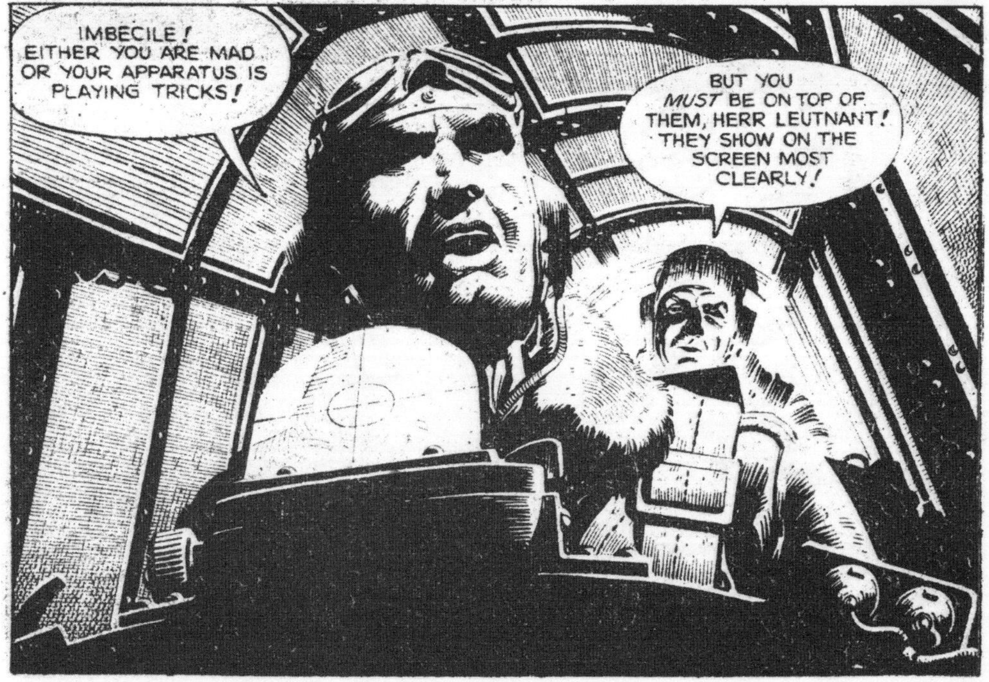
IMBECILE! EITHER YOU ARE MAD OR YOUR APPARATUS IS PLAYING TRICKS!
BUT YOU *MUST* BE ON TOP OF THEM, HERR LEUTNANT! THEY SHOW ON THE SCREEN MOST CLEARLY!

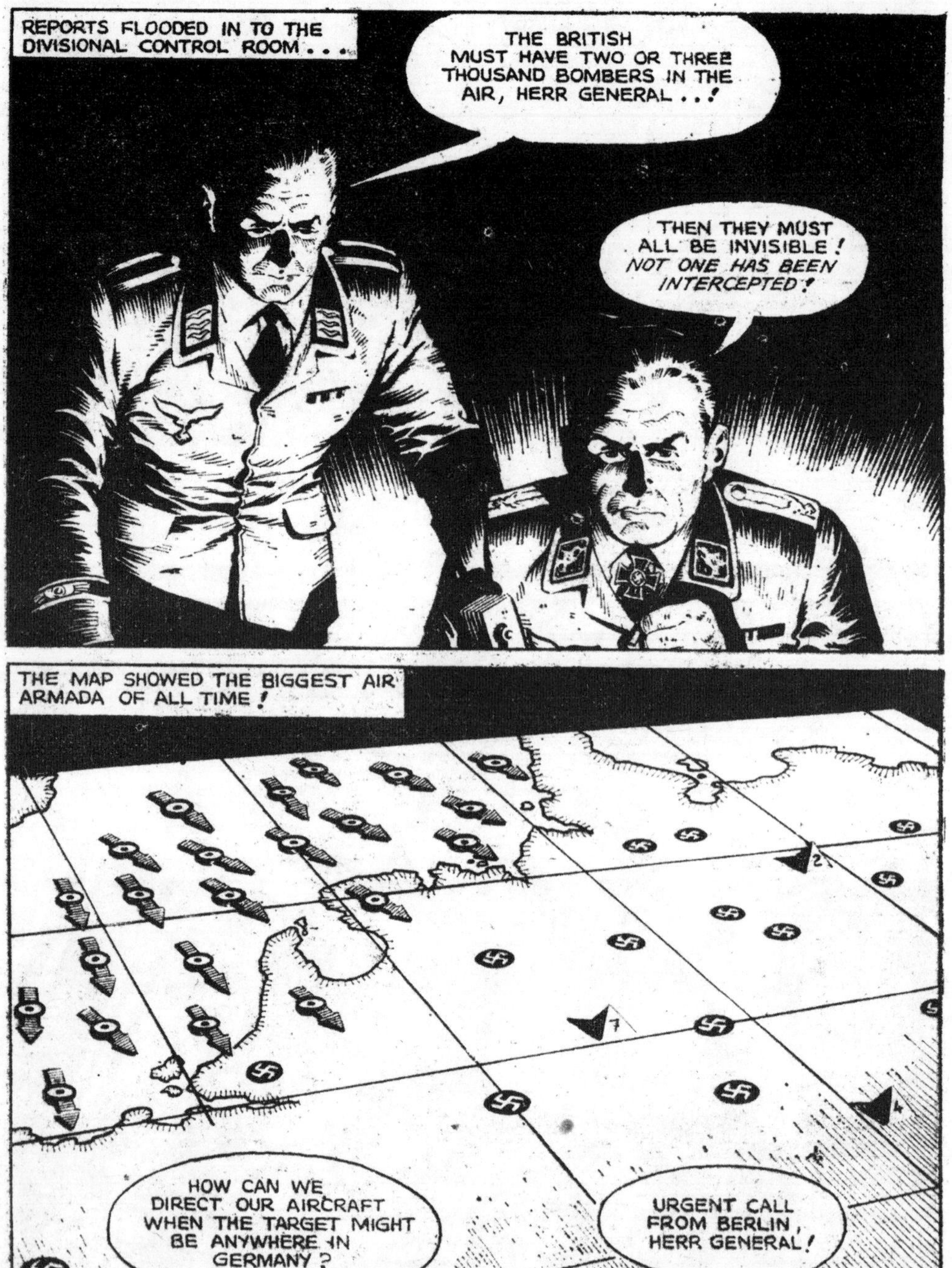
REPORTS FLOODED IN TO THE DIVISIONAL CONTROL ROOM . . .
THE BRITISH MUST HAVE TWO OR THREE THOUSAND BOMBERS IN THE AIR, HERR GENERAL . . !
THEN THEY MUST ALL BE INVISIBLE! NOT ONE HAS BEEN INTERCEPTED!
THE MAP SHOWED THE BIGGEST AIR ARMADA OF ALL TIME!
HOW CAN WE DIRECT OUR AIRCRAFT WHEN THE TARGET MIGHT BE ANYWHERE IN GERMANY?
URGENT CALL FROM BERLIN, HERR GENERAL!

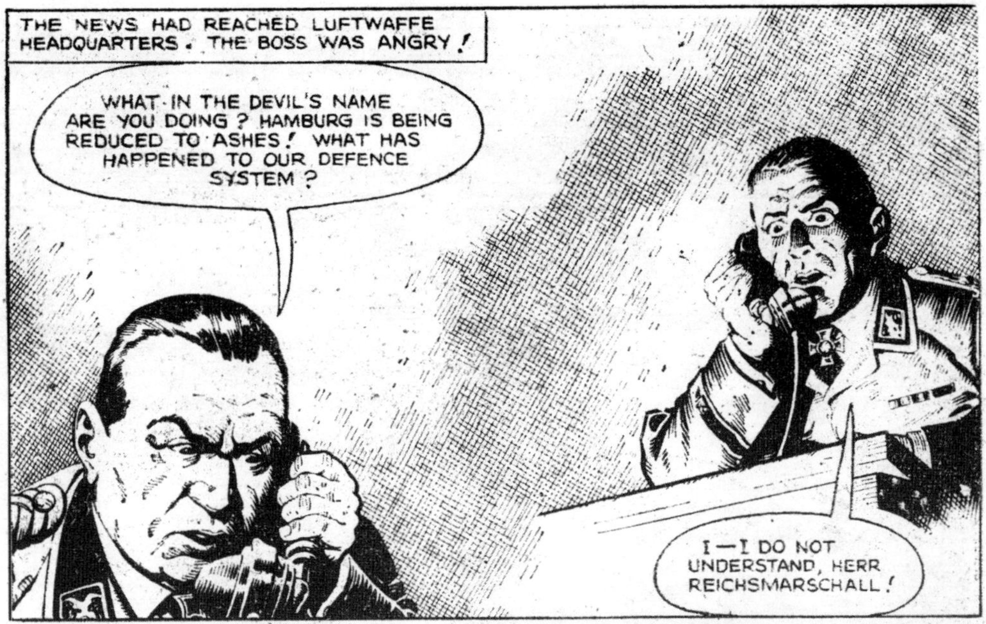
THE NEWS HAD REACHED LUFTWAFFE HEADQUARTERS. THE BOSS WAS ANGRY!
WHAT IN THE DEVIL'S NAME ARE YOU DOING? HAMBURG IS BEING REDUCED TO ASHES! WHAT HAS HAPPENED TO OUR DEFENCE SYSTEM?
I—I DO NOT UNDERSTAND, HERR REICHSMARSCHALL!

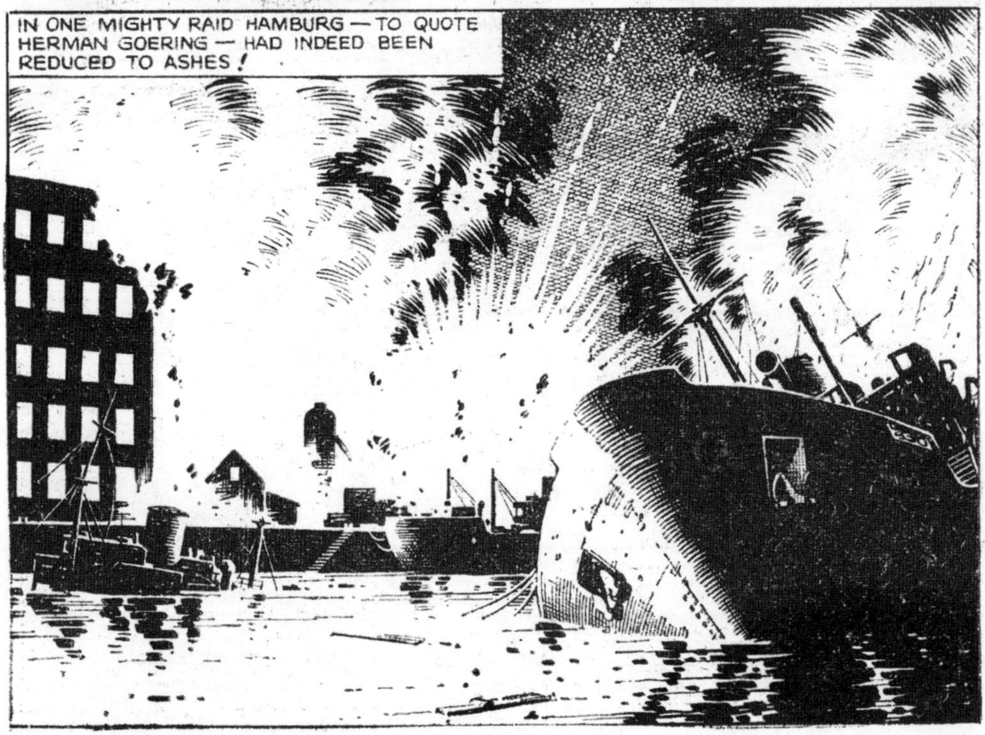
IN ONE MIGHTY RAID HAMBURG — TO QUOTE HERMAN GOERING — HAD INDEED BEEN REDUCED TO ASHES!

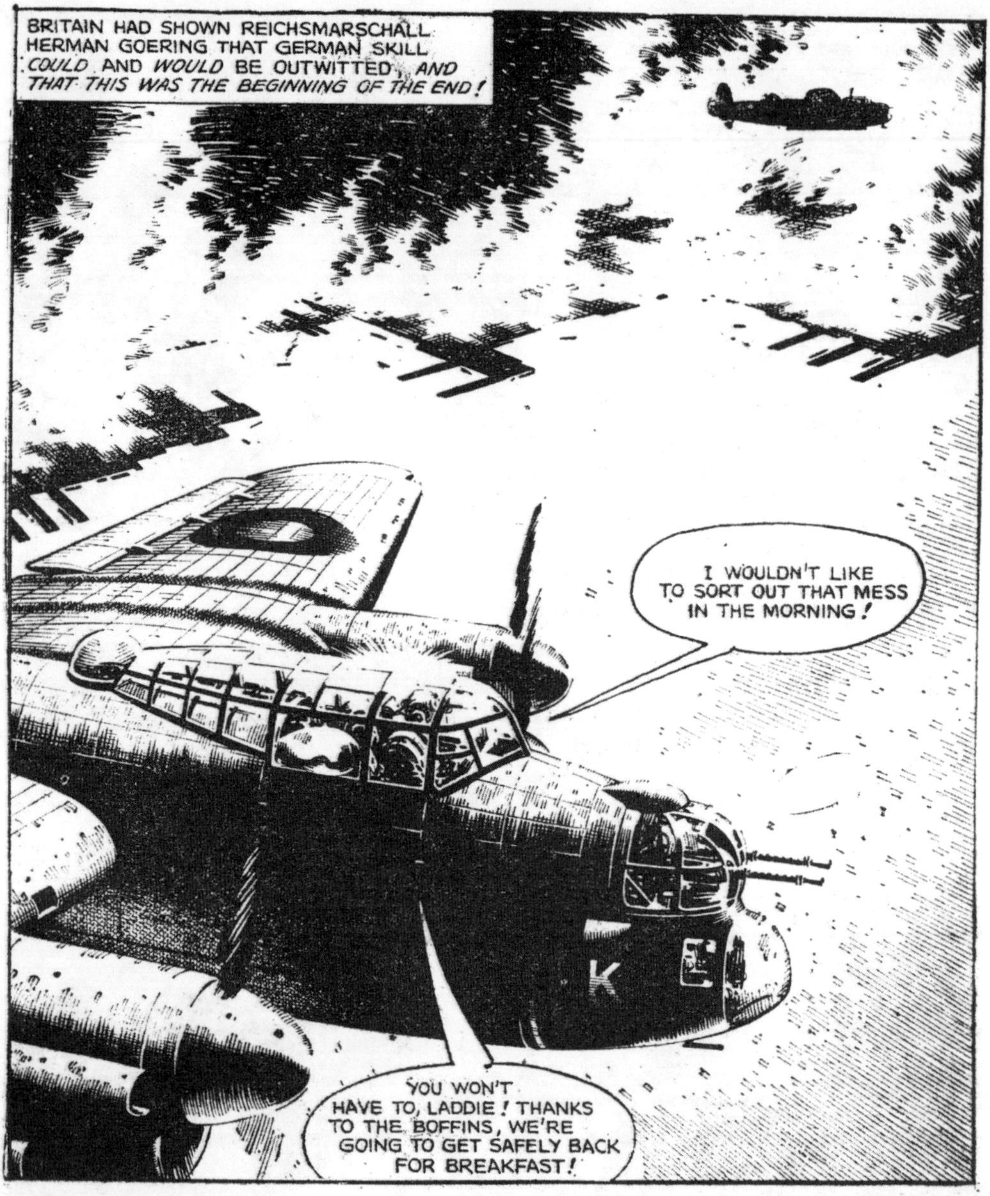
BRITAIN HAD SHOWN REICHSMARSCHALL HERMAN GOERING THAT GERMAN SKILL COULD AND WOULD BE OUTWITTED, AND THAT THIS WAS THE BEGINNING OF THE END!
I WOULDN'T LIKE TO SORT OUT THAT MESS IN THE MORNING!
YOU WON'T HAVE TO, LADDIE! THANKS TO THE BOFFINS, WE'RE GOING TO GET SAFELY BACK FOR BREAKFAST!
K

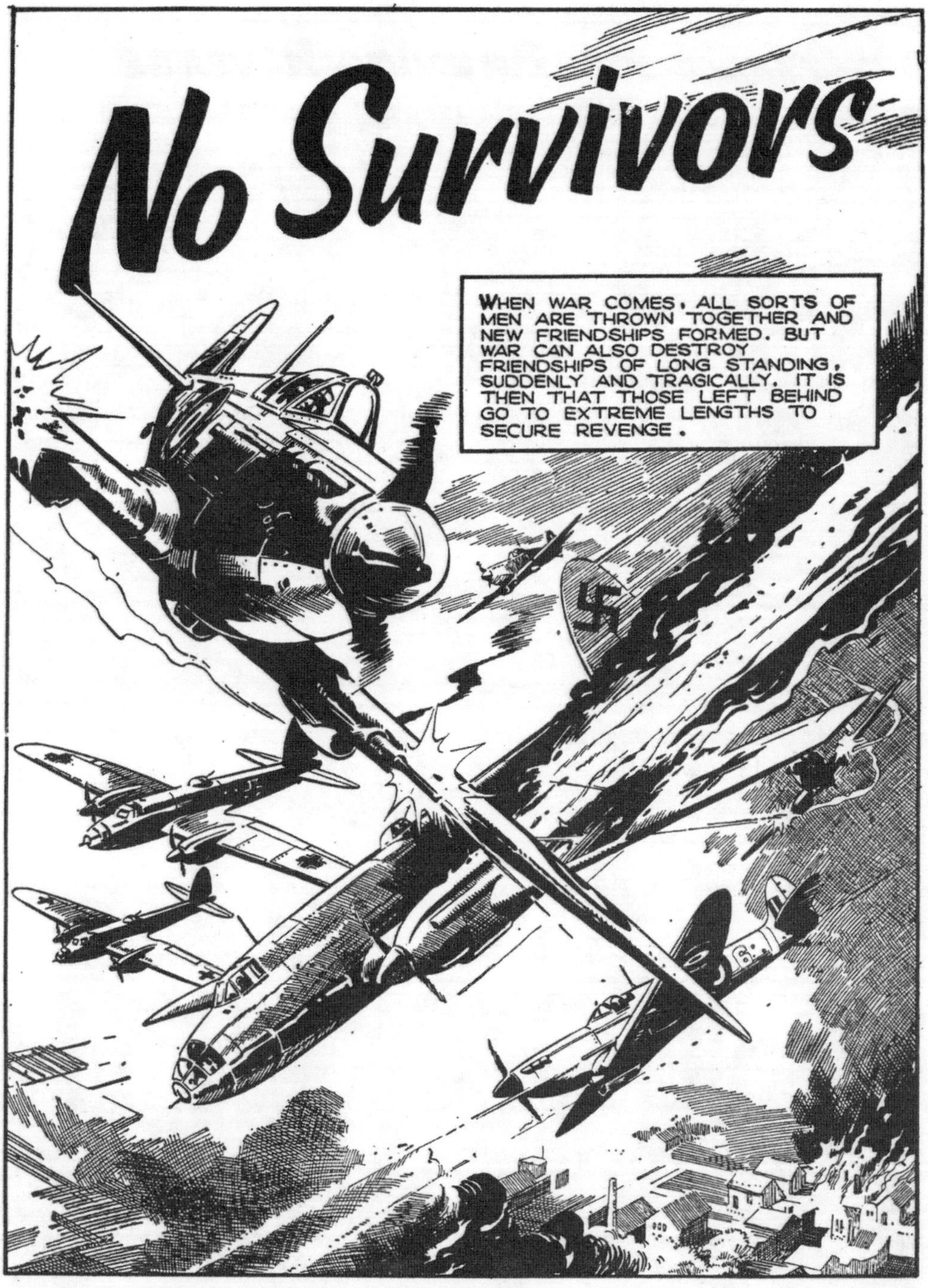
No Survivors
WHEN WAR COMES, ALL SORTS OF MEN ARE THROWN TOGETHER AND NEW FRIENDSHIPS FORMED. BUT WAR CAN ALSO DESTROY FRIENDSHIPS OF LONG STANDING, SUDDENLY AND TRAGICALLY. IT IS THEN THAT THOSE LEFT BEHIND GO TO EXTREME LENGTHS TO SECURE REVENGE.

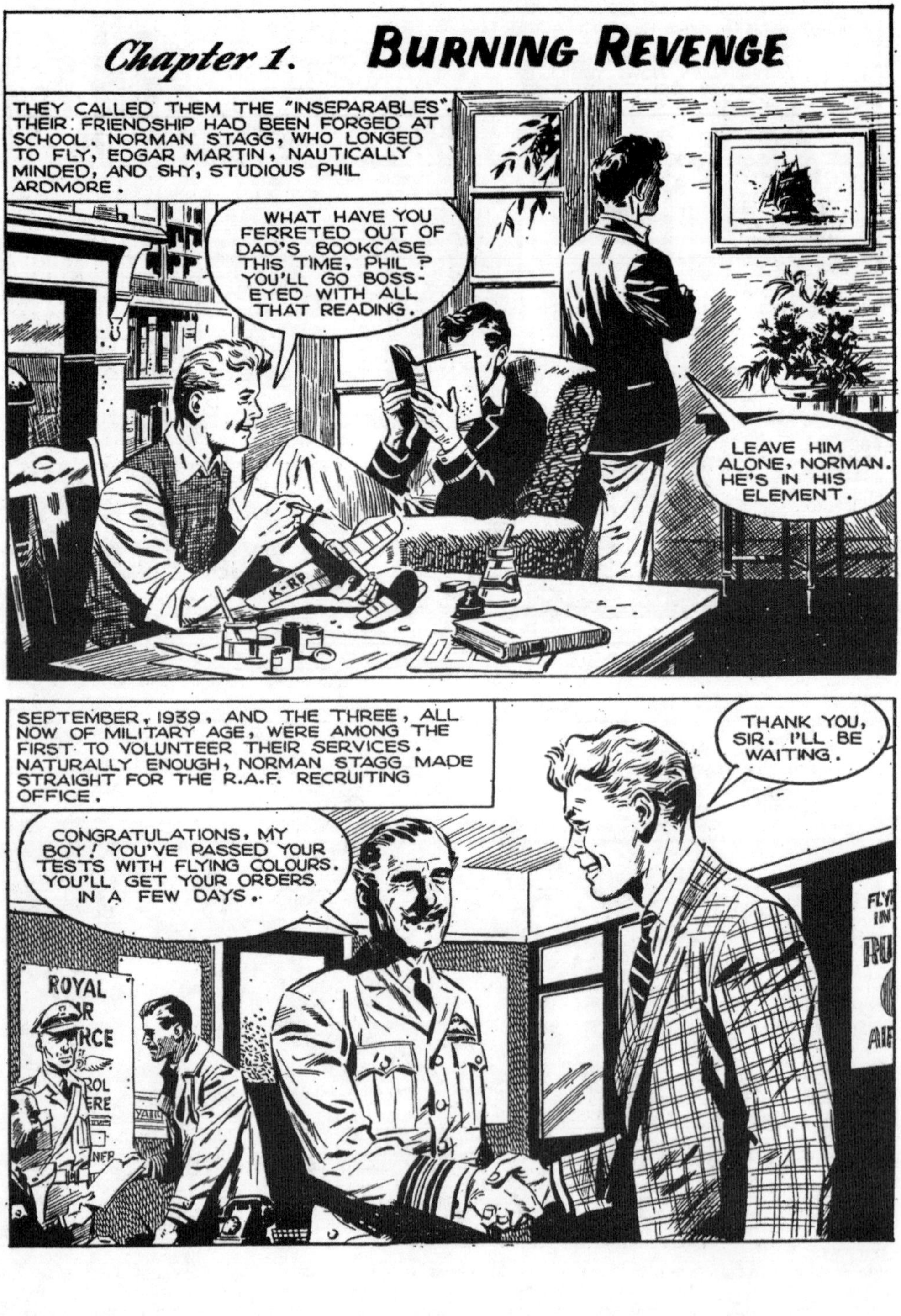
Chapter 1. BURNING REVENGE
THEY CALLED THEM THE "INSEPARABLES". THEIR FRIENDSHIP HAD BEEN FORGED AT SCHOOL. NORMAN STAGG, WHO LONGED TO FLY, EDGAR MARTIN, NAUTICALLY MINDED, AND SHY, STUDIOUS PHIL ARDMORE.
WHAT HAVE YOU FERRETED OUT OF DAD'S BOOKCASE THIS TIME, PHIL? YOU'LL GO BOSS-EYED WITH ALL THAT READING.
LEAVE HIM ALONE, NORMAN. HE'S IN HIS ELEMENT.
K-RP
SEPTEMBER, 1939, AND THE THREE, ALL NOW OF MILITARY AGE, WERE AMONG THE FIRST TO VOLUNTEER THEIR SERVICES. NATURALLY ENOUGH, NORMAN STAGG MADE STRAIGHT FOR THE R.A.F. RECRUITING OFFICE.
CONGRATULATIONS, MY BOY! YOU'VE PASSED YOUR TESTS WITH FLYING COLOURS. YOU'LL GET YOUR ORDERS IN A FEW DAYS.
THANK YOU, SIR. I'LL BE WAITING.

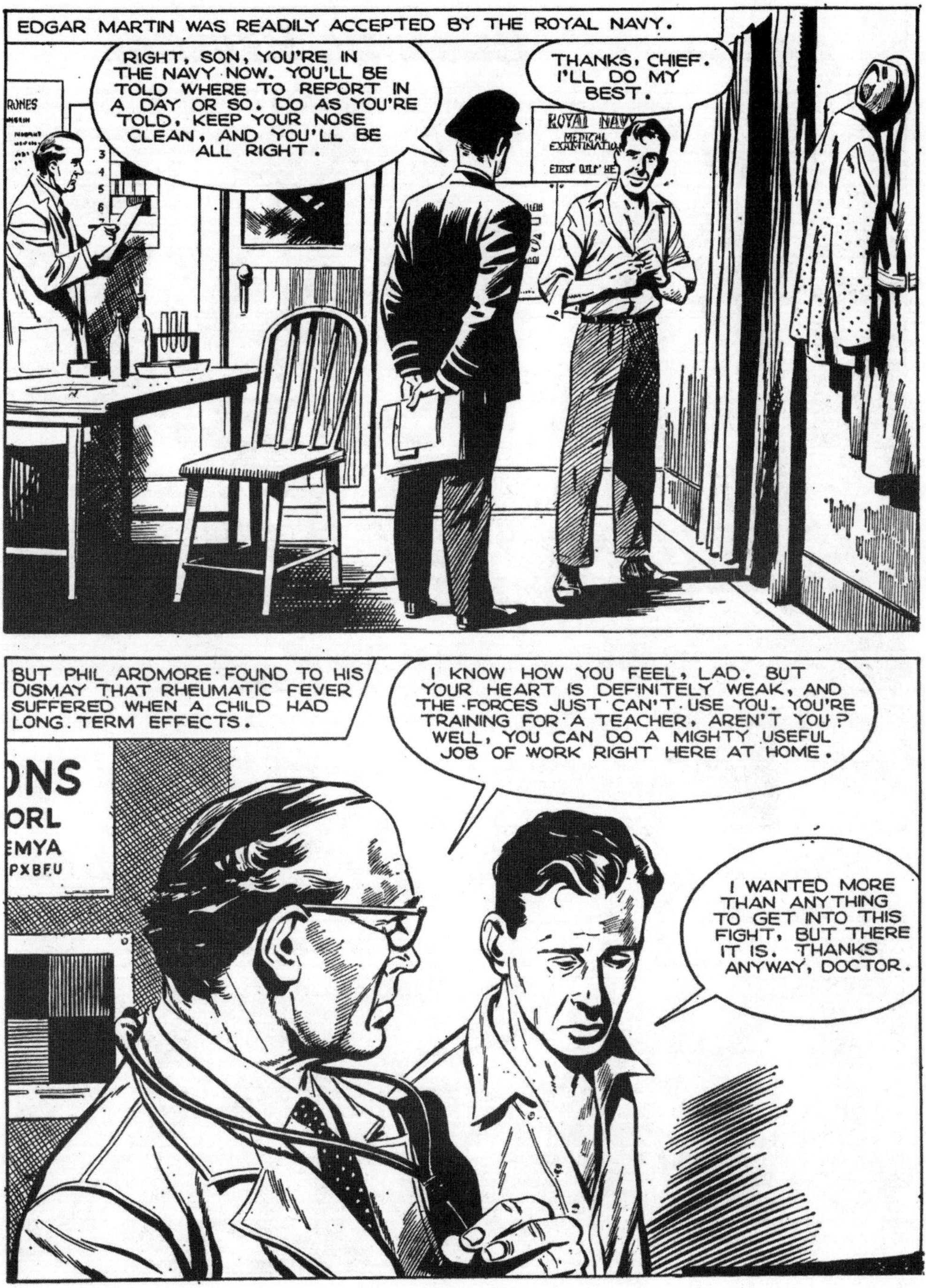
EDGAR MARTIN WAS READILY ACCEPTED BY THE ROYAL NAVY.
RIGHT, SON, YOU'RE IN THE NAVY NOW. YOU'LL BE TOLD WHERE TO REPORT IN A DAY OR SO. DO AS YOU'RE TOLD, KEEP YOUR NOSE CLEAN, AND YOU'LL BE ALL RIGHT.
THANKS, CHIEF. I'LL DO MY BEST.
BUT PHIL ARDMORE FOUND TO HIS DISMAY THAT RHEUMATIC FEVER SUFFERED WHEN A CHILD HAD LONG TERM EFFECTS.
I KNOW HOW YOU FEEL, LAD. BUT YOUR HEART IS DEFINITELY WEAK, AND THE FORCES JUST CAN'T USE YOU. YOU'RE TRAINING FOR A TEACHER, AREN'T YOU? WELL, YOU CAN DO A MIGHTY USEFUL JOB OF WORK RIGHT HERE AT HOME.
I WANTED MORE THAN ANYTHING TO GET INTO THIS FIGHT, BUT THERE IT IS. THANKS ANYWAY, DOCTOR.

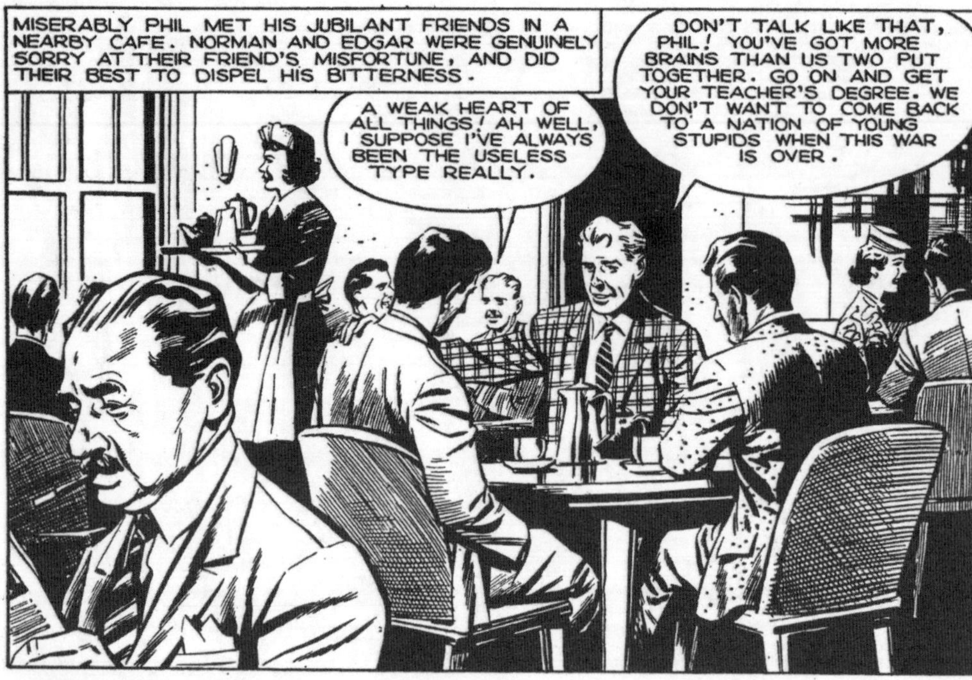
MISERABLY PHIL MET HIS JUBILANT FRIENDS IN A NEARBY CAFE. NORMAN AND EDGAR WERE GENUINELY SORRY AT THEIR FRIEND'S MISFORTUNE, AND DID THEIR BEST TO DISPEL HIS BITTERNESS.
A WEAK HEART OF ALL THINGS! AH WELL, I SUPPOSE I'VE ALWAYS BEEN THE USELESS TYPE REALLY.
DON'T TALK LIKE THAT, PHIL! YOU'VE GOT MORE BRAINS THAN US TWO PUT TOGETHER. GO ON AND GET YOUR TEACHER'S DEGREE. WE DON'T WANT TO COME BACK TO A NATION OF YOUNG STUPIDS WHEN THIS WAR IS OVER.

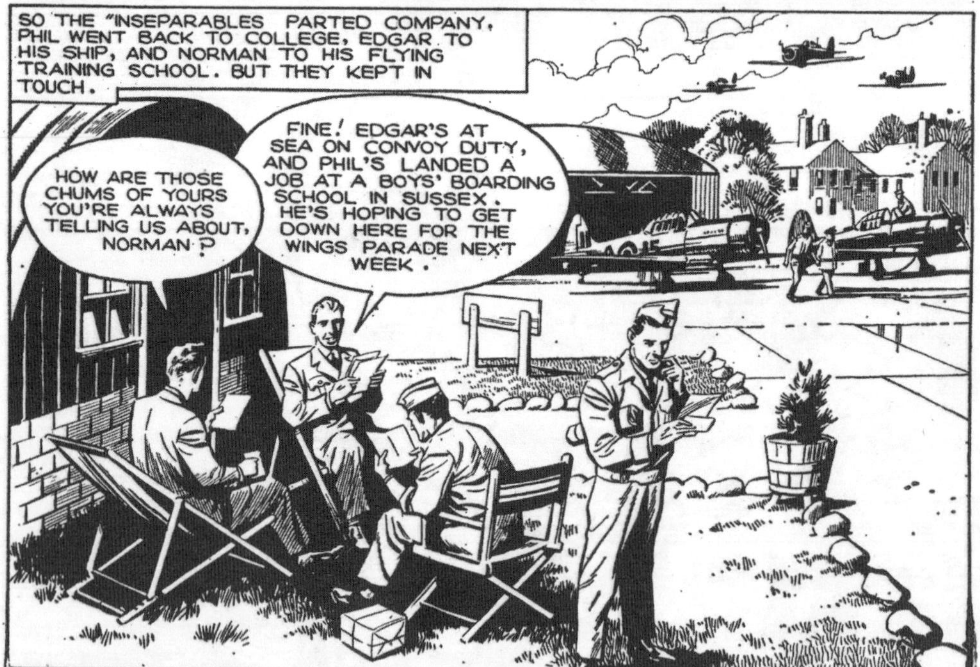
SO THE "INSEPARABLES PARTED COMPANY, PHIL WENT BACK TO COLLEGE, EDGAR TO HIS SHIP, AND NORMAN TO HIS FLYING TRAINING SCHOOL. BUT THEY KEPT IN TOUCH.
HOW ARE THOSE CHUMS OF YOURS YOU'RE ALWAYS TELLING US ABOUT, NORMAN?
FINE! EDGAR'S AT SEA ON CONVOY DUTY, AND PHIL'S LANDED A JOB AT A BOYS' BOARDING SCHOOL IN SUSSEX. HE'S HOPING TO GET DOWN HERE FOR THE WINGS PARADE NEXT WEEK.

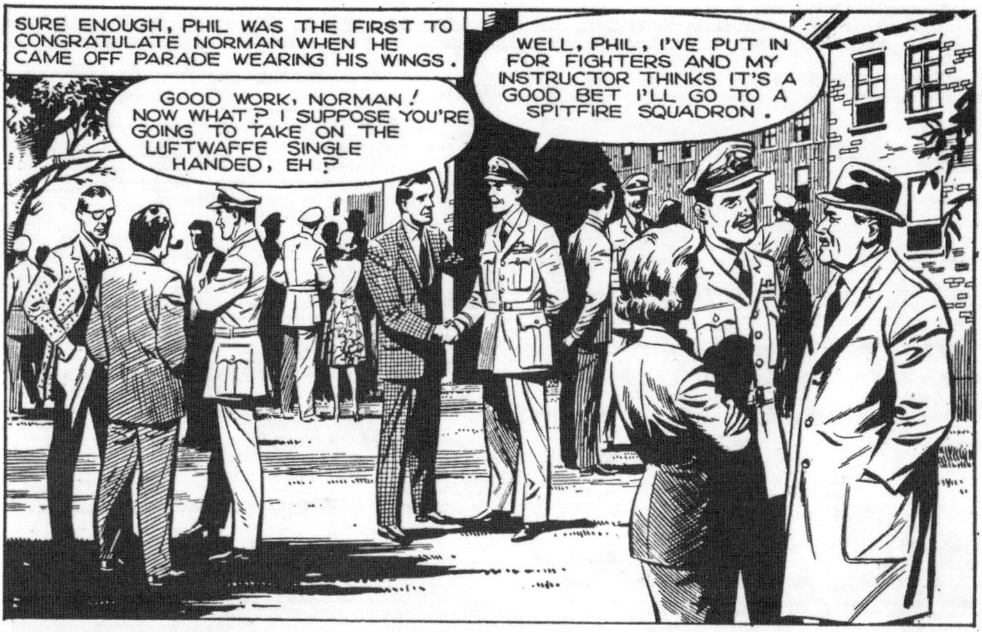
SURE ENOUGH, PHIL WAS THE FIRST TO CONGRATULATE NORMAN WHEN HE CAME OFF PARADE WEARING HIS WINGS.
GOOD WORK, NORMAN! NOW WHAT? I SUPPOSE YOU'RE GOING TO TAKE ON THE LUFTWAFFE SINGLE HANDED, EH?
WELL, PHIL, I'VE PUT IN FOR FIGHTERS AND MY INSTRUCTOR THINKS IT'S A GOOD BET I'LL GO TO A SPITFIRE SQUADRON.

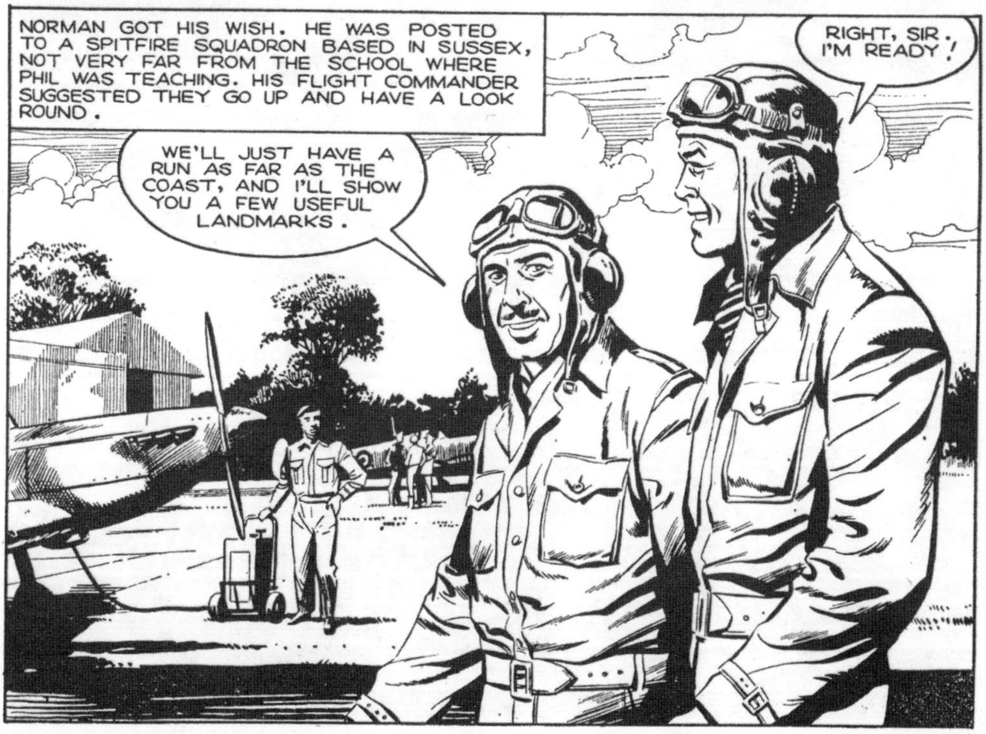
NORMAN GOT HIS WISH. HE WAS POSTED TO A SPITFIRE SQUADRON BASED IN SUSSEX, NOT VERY FAR FROM THE SCHOOL WHERE PHIL WAS TEACHING. HIS FLIGHT COMMANDER SUGGESTED THEY GO UP AND HAVE A LOOK ROUND.
WE'LL JUST HAVE A RUN AS FAR AS THE COAST, AND I'LL SHOW YOU A FEW USEFUL LANDMARKS.
RIGHT, SIR. I'M READY!

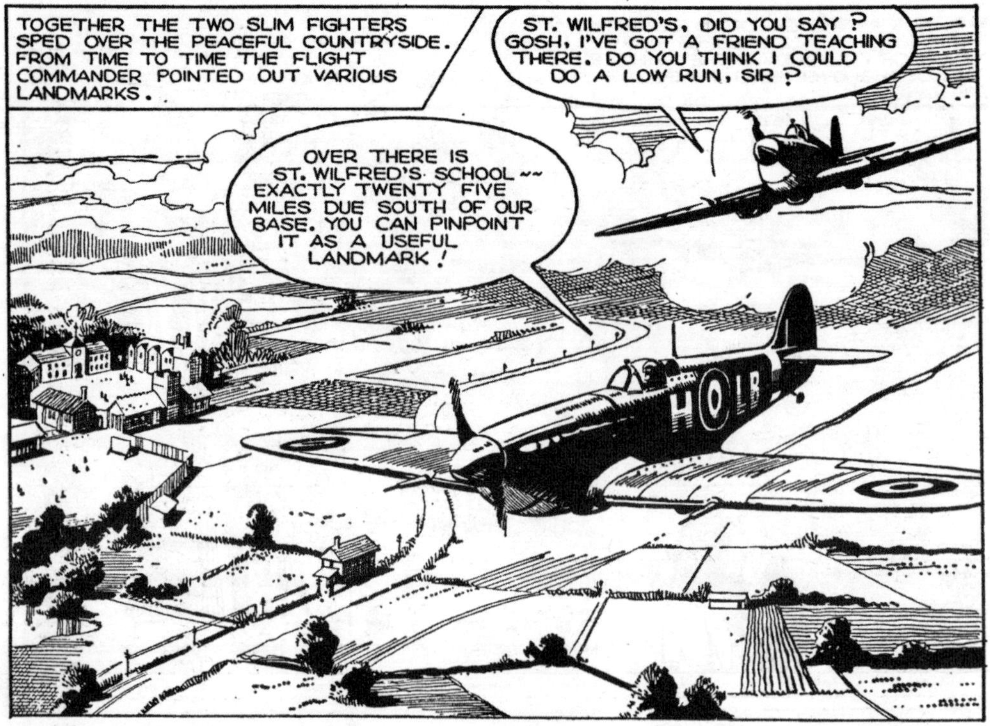
TOGETHER THE TWO SLIM FIGHTERS SPED OVER THE PEACEFUL COUNTRYSIDE. FROM TIME TO TIME THE FLIGHT COMMANDER POINTED OUT VARIOUS LANDMARKS . .
ST. WILFRED'S, DID YOU SAY ? GOSH, I'VE GOT A FRIEND TEACHING THERE. DO YOU THINK I COULD DO A LOW RUN, SIR ?
OVER THERE IS ST. WILFRED'S SCHOOL ~~ EXACTLY TWENTY FIVE MILES DUE SOUTH OF OUR BASE. YOU CAN PINPOINT IT AS A USEFUL LANDMARK !

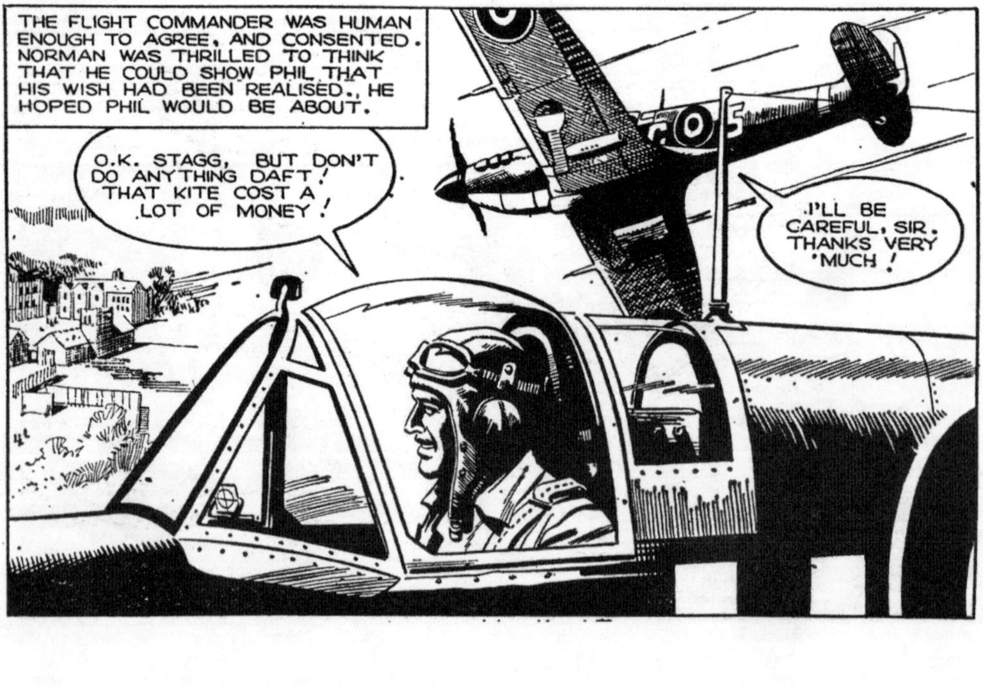
THE FLIGHT COMMANDER WAS HUMAN ENOUGH TO AGREE, AND CONSENTED. NORMAN WAS THRILLED TO THINK THAT HE COULD SHOW PHIL THAT HIS WISH HAD BEEN REALISED., HE HOPED PHIL WOULD BE ABOUT.
O.K. STAGG, BUT DON'T DO ANYTHING DAFT ! THAT KITE COST A LOT OF MONEY !
I'LL BE CAREFUL, SIR. THANKS VERY MUCH !

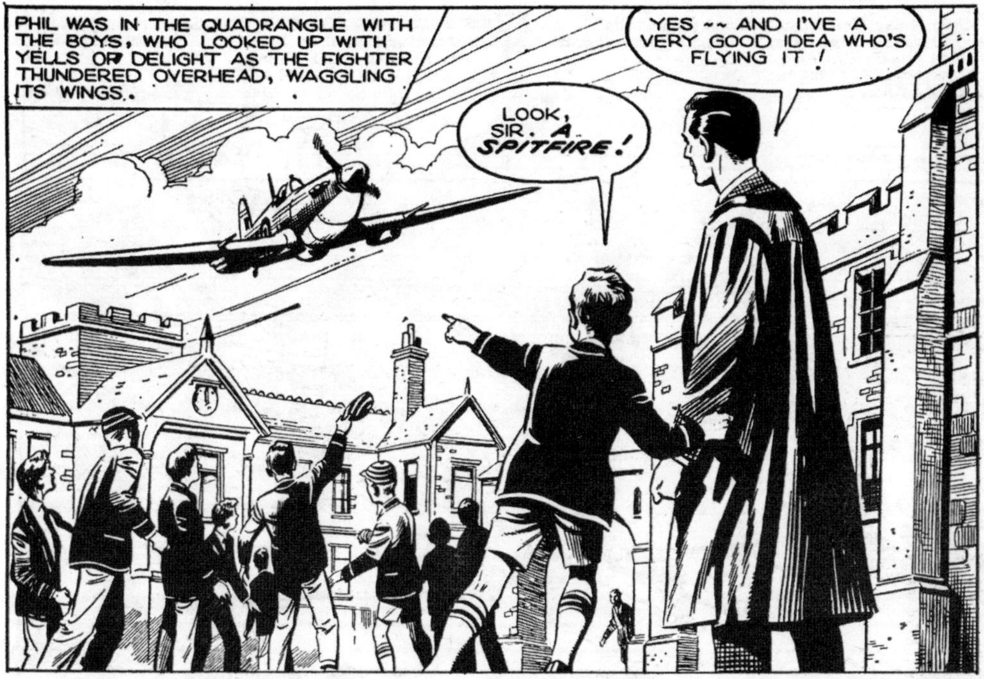
PHIL WAS IN THE QUADRANGLE WITH THE BOYS, WHO LOOKED UP WITH YELLS OF DELIGHT AS THE FIGHTER THUNDERED OVERHEAD, WAGGLING ITS WINGS. .
LOOK, SIR. A SPITFIRE!
YES -- AND I'VE A VERY GOOD IDEA WHO'S FLYING IT!

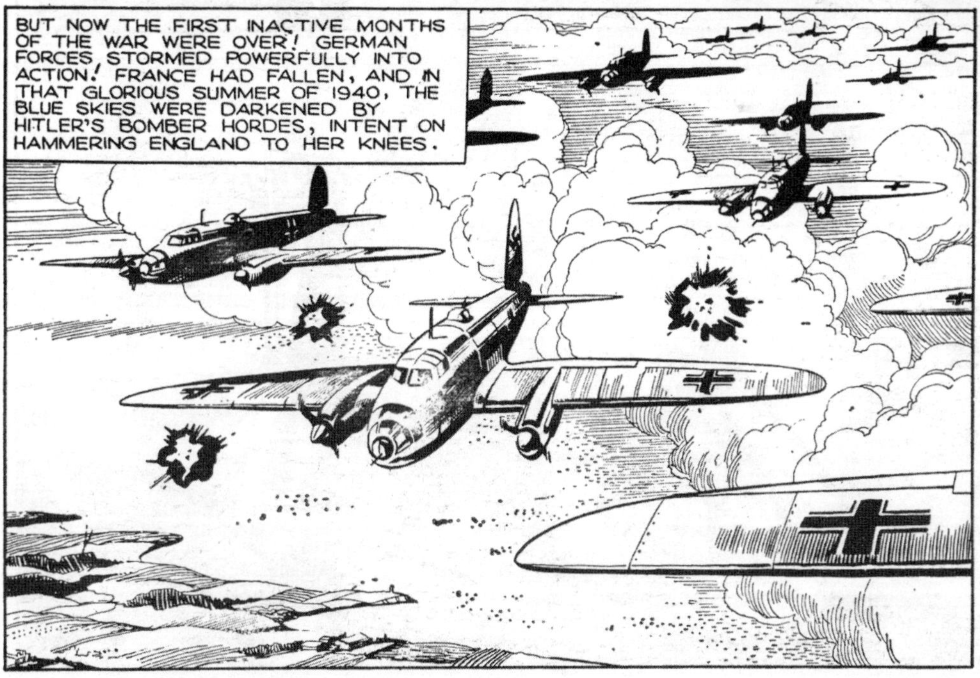
BUT NOW THE FIRST INACTIVE MONTHS OF THE WAR WERE OVER! GERMAN FORCES STORMED POWERFULLY INTO ACTION! FRANCE HAD FALLEN, AND IN THAT GLORIOUS SUMMER OF 1940, THE BLUE SKIES WERE DARKENED BY HITLER'S BOMBER HORDES, INTENT ON HAMMERING ENGLAND TO HER KNEES.

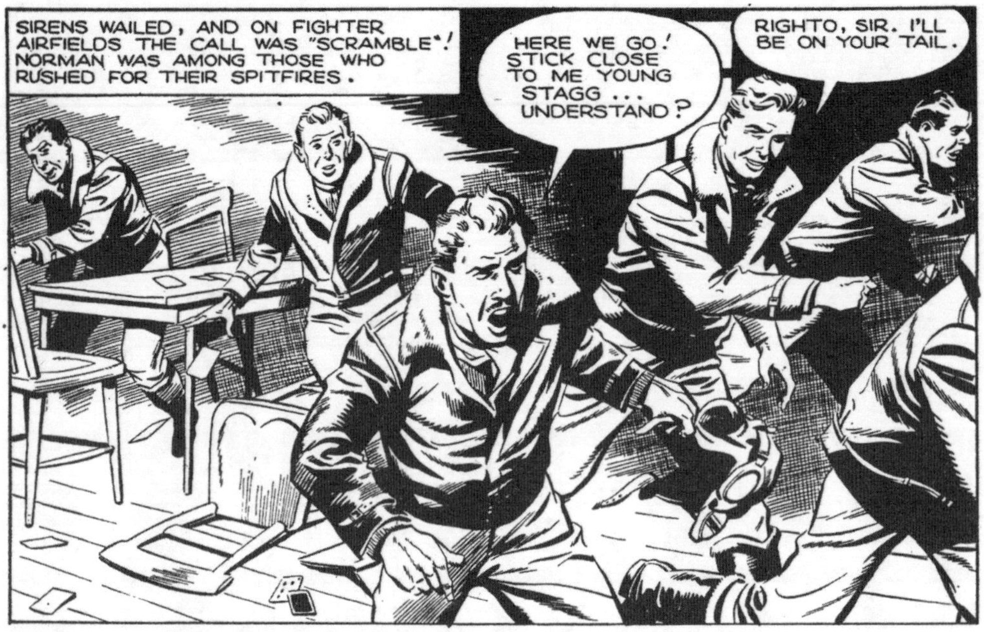
SIRENS WAILED, AND ON FIGHTER AIRFIELDS THE CALL WAS "SCRAMBLE"! NORMAN WAS AMONG THOSE WHO RUSHED FOR THEIR SPITFIRES.
HERE WE GO! STICK CLOSE TO ME YOUNG STAGG ... UNDERSTAND?
RIGHTO, SIR. I'LL BE ON YOUR TAIL.

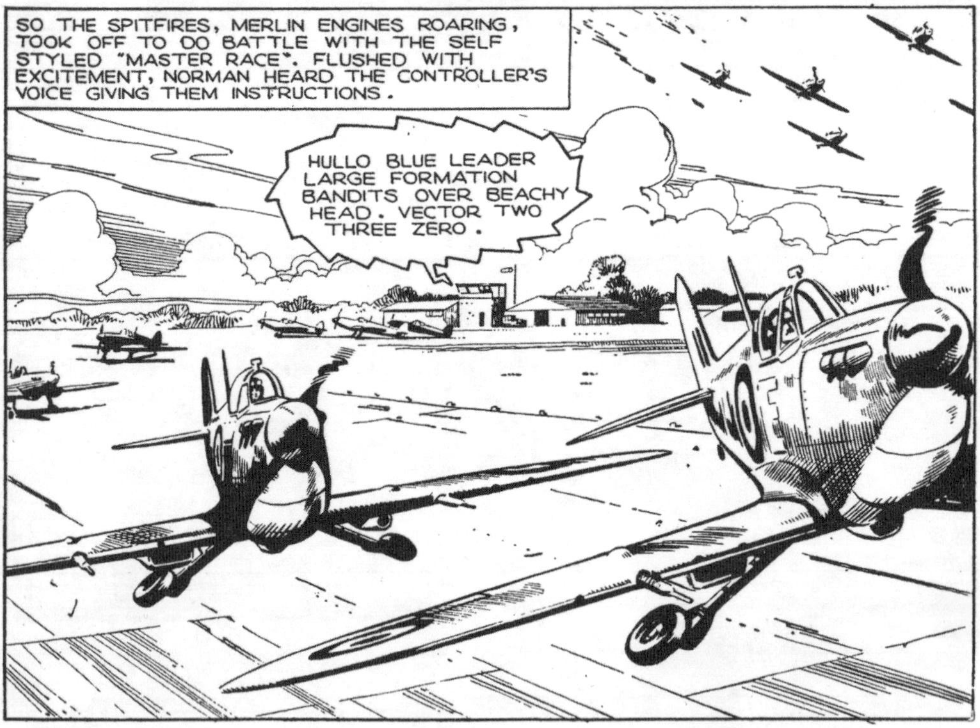
SO THE SPITFIRES, MERLIN ENGINES ROARING, TOOK OFF TO DO BATTLE WITH THE SELF STYLED "MASTER RACE". FLUSHED WITH EXCITEMENT, NORMAN HEARD THE CONTROLLER'S VOICE GIVING THEM INSTRUCTIONS.
HULLO BLUE LEADER LARGE FORMATION BANDITS OVER BEACHY HEAD. VECTOR TWO THREE ZERO.

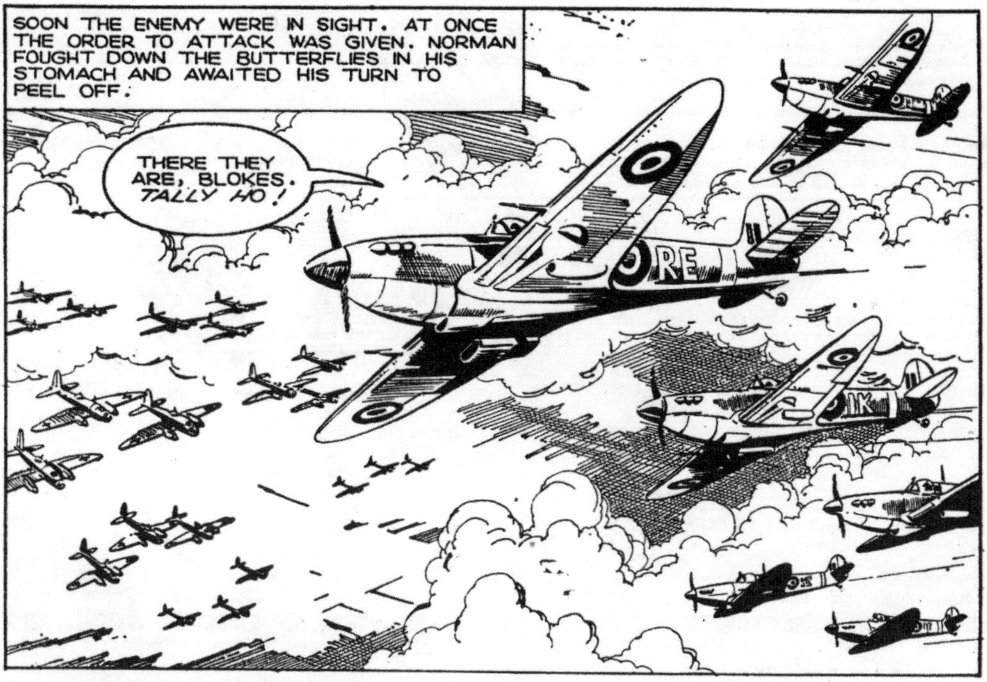
SOON THE ENEMY WERE IN SIGHT. AT ONCE THE ORDER TO ATTACK WAS GIVEN. NORMAN FOUGHT DOWN THE BUTTERFLIES IN HIS STOMACH AND AWAITED HIS TURN TO PEEL OFF.
THERE THEY ARE, BLOKES. TALLY HO!
RE

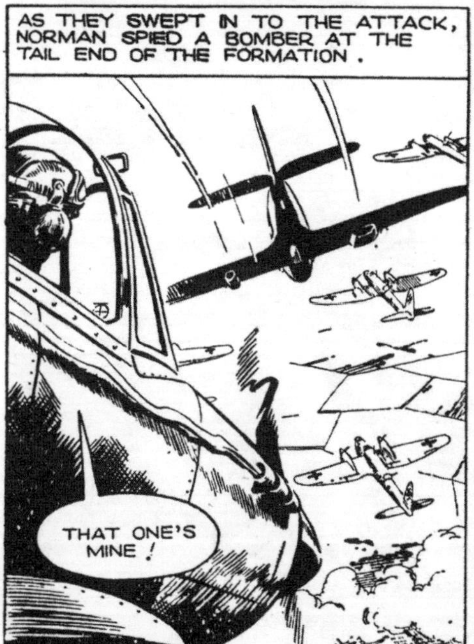
AS THEY SWEPT IN TO THE ATTACK, NORMAN SPIED A BOMBER AT THE TAIL END OF THE FORMATION.
THAT ONE'S MINE!

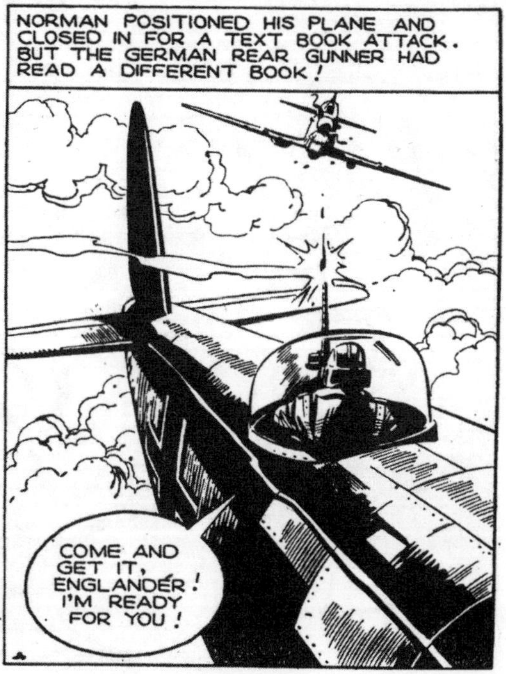
NORMAN POSITIONED HIS PLANE AND CLOSED IN FOR A TEXT BOOK ATTACK. BUT THE GERMAN REAR GUNNER HAD READ A DIFFERENT BOOK!
COME AND GET IT, ENGLANDER! I'M READY FOR YOU!

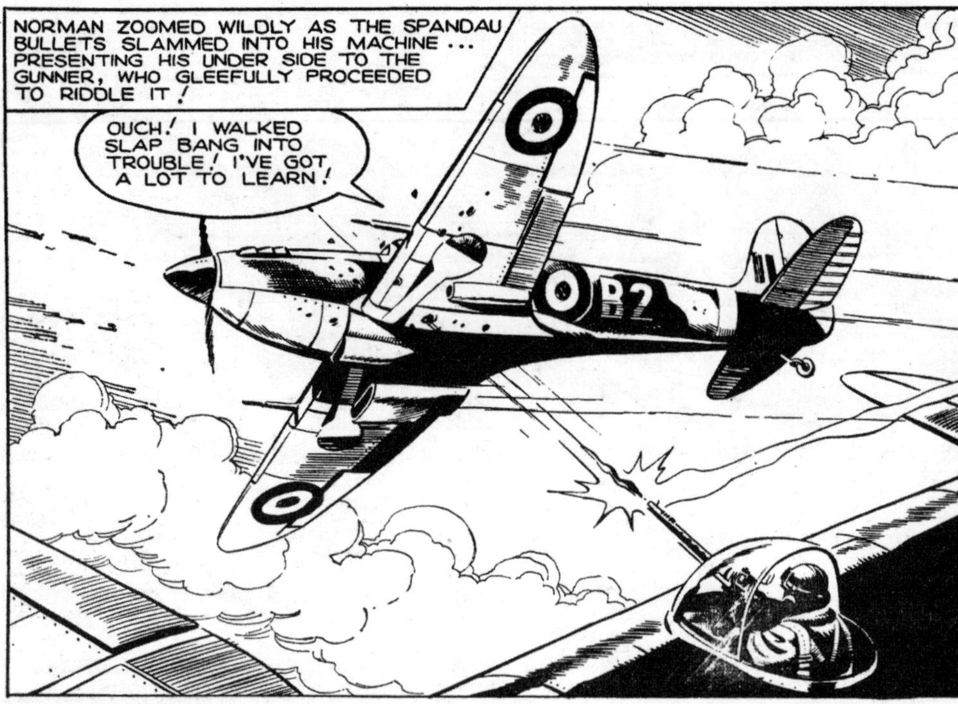
NORMAN ZOOMED WILDLY AS THE SPANDAU BULLETS SLAMMED INTO HIS MACHINE ... PRESENTING HIS UNDER SIDE TO THE GUNNER, WHO GLEEFULLY PROCEEDED TO RIDDLE IT!
OUCH! I WALKED SLAP BANG INTO TROUBLE! I'VE GOT A LOT TO LEARN!
B2

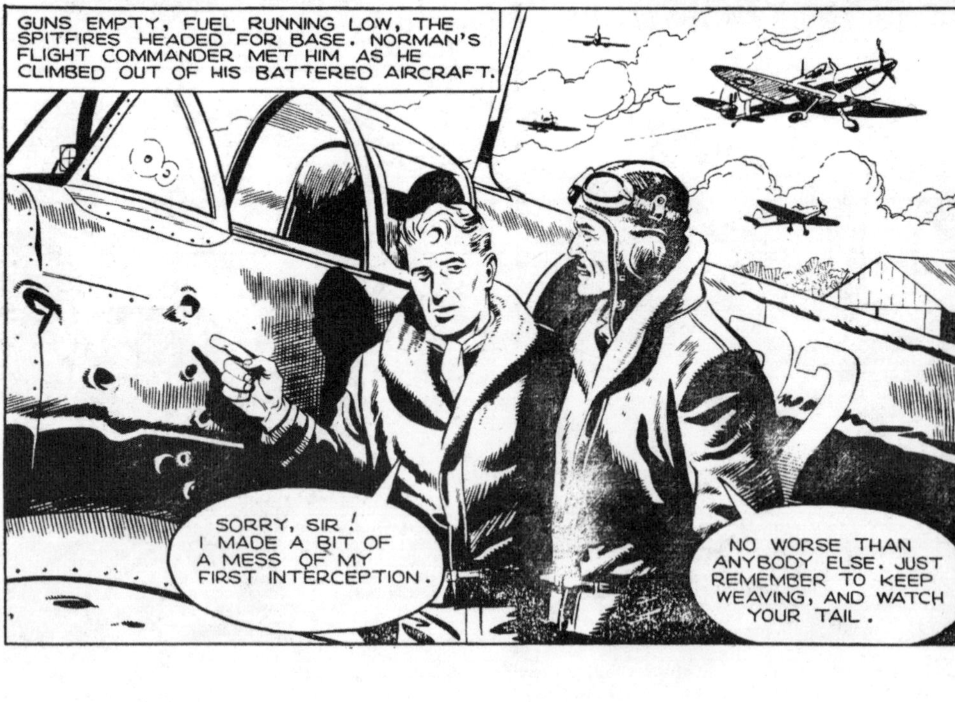
GUNS EMPTY, FUEL RUNNING LOW, THE SPITFIRES HEADED FOR BASE. NORMAN'S FLIGHT COMMANDER MET HIM AS HE CLIMBED OUT OF HIS BATTERED AIRCRAFT.
SORRY, SIR! I MADE A BIT OF A MESS OF MY FIRST INTERCEPTION.
NO WORSE THAN ANYBODY ELSE. JUST REMEMBER TO KEEP WEAVING, AND WATCH YOUR TAIL.

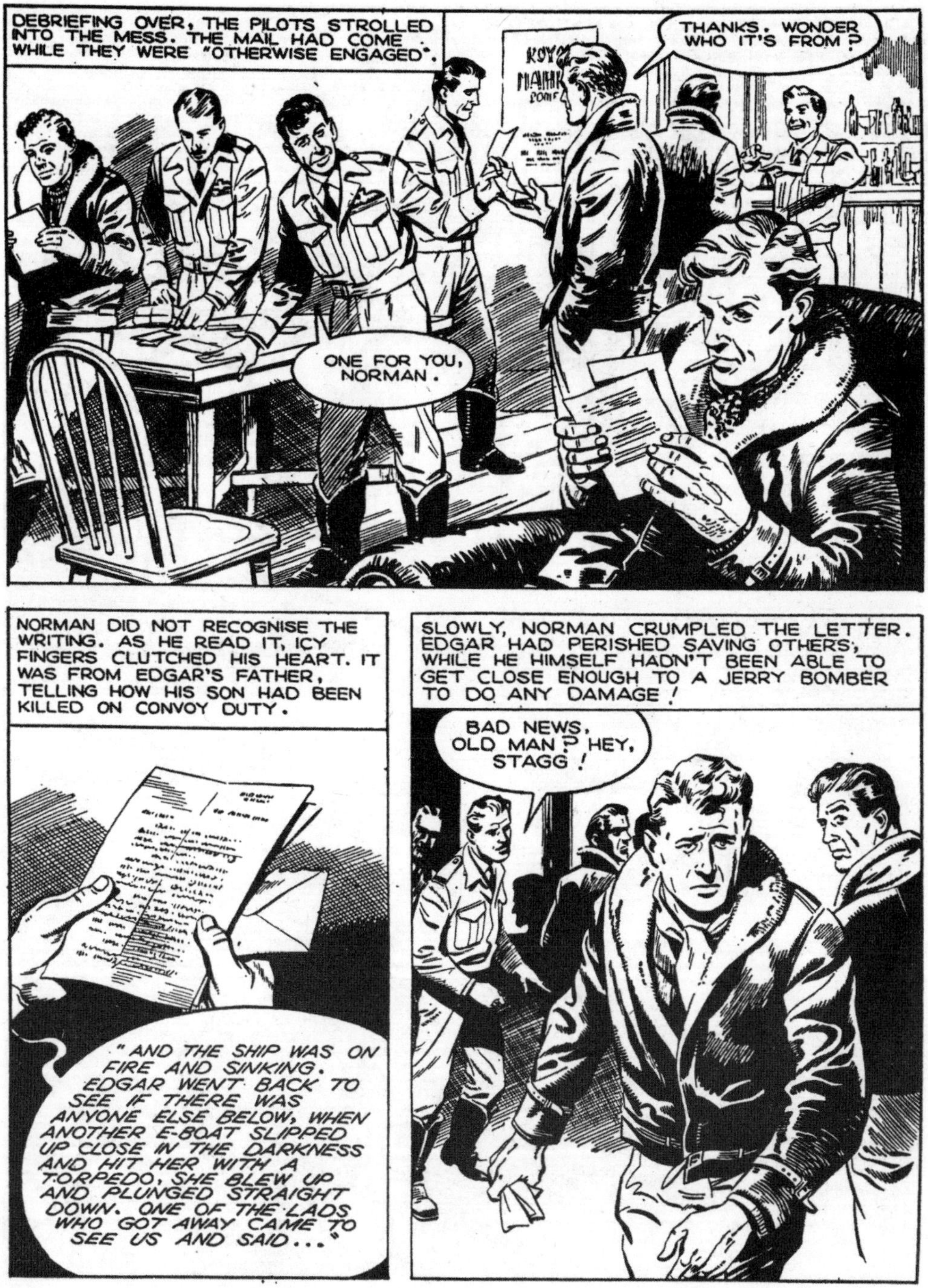
DEBRIEFING OVER, THE PILOTS STROLLED INTO THE MESS. THE MAIL HAD COME WHILE THEY WERE "OTHERWISE ENGAGED".
THANKS. WONDER WHO IT'S FROM?
ONE FOR YOU, NORMAN.
NORMAN DID NOT RECOGNISE THE WRITING. AS HE READ IT, ICY FINGERS CLUTCHED HIS HEART. IT WAS FROM EDGAR'S FATHER, TELLING HOW HIS SON HAD BEEN KILLED ON CONVOY DUTY.
"AND THE SHIP WAS ON FIRE AND SINKING. EDGAR WENT BACK TO SEE IF THERE WAS ANYONE ELSE BELOW, WHEN ANOTHER E-BOAT SLIPPED UP CLOSE IN THE DARKNESS AND HIT HER WITH A TORPEDO. SHE BLEW UP AND PLUNGED STRAIGHT DOWN. ONE OF THE LADS WHO GOT AWAY CAME TO SEE US AND SAID..."
SLOWLY, NORMAN CRUMPLED THE LETTER. EDGAR HAD PERISHED SAVING OTHERS, WHILE HE HIMSELF HADN'T BEEN ABLE TO GET CLOSE ENOUGH TO A JERRY BOMBER TO DO ANY DAMAGE!
BAD NEWS, OLD MAN? HEY, STAGG!

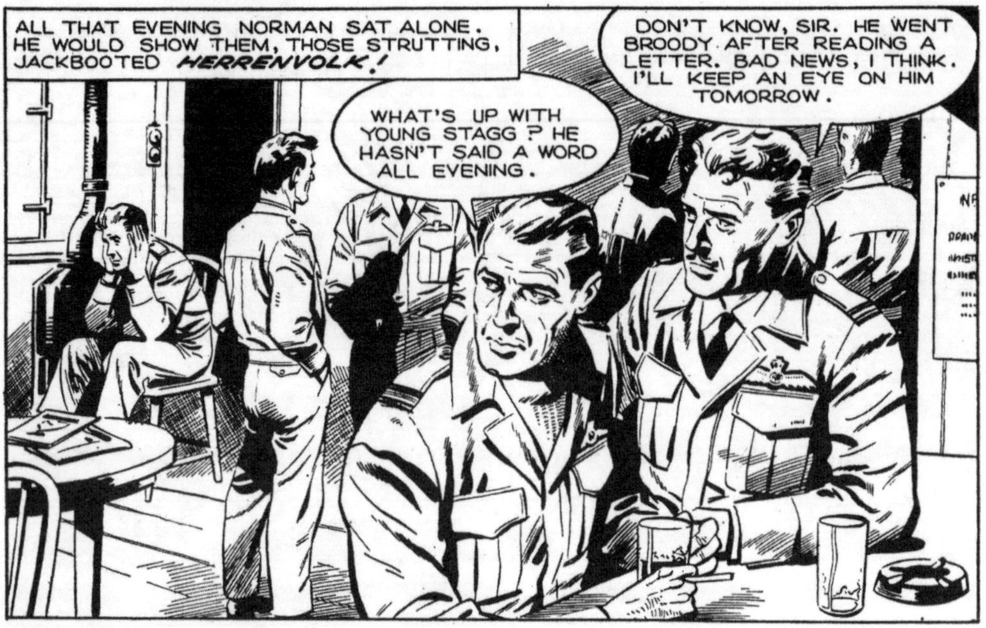
ALL THAT EVENING NORMAN SAT ALONE. HE WOULD SHOW THEM, THOSE STRUTTING, JACKBOOTED HERRENVOLK!
WHAT'S UP WITH YOUNG STAGG? HE HASN'T SAID A WORD ALL EVENING.
DON'T KNOW, SIR. HE WENT BROODY AFTER READING A LETTER. BAD NEWS, I THINK. I'LL KEEP AN EYE ON HIM TOMORROW.

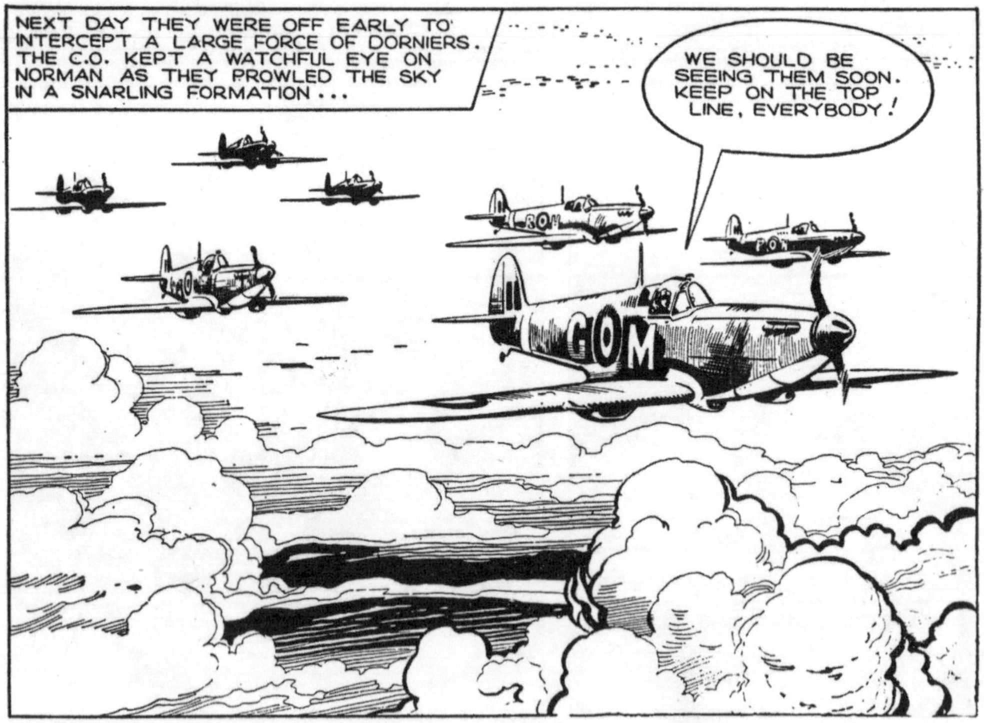
NEXT DAY THEY WERE OFF EARLY TO INTERCEPT A LARGE FORCE OF DORNIERS. THE C.O. KEPT A WATCHFUL EYE ON NORMAN AS THEY PROWLED THE SKY IN A SNARLING FORMATION...
WE SHOULD BE SEEING THEM SOON. KEEP ON THE TOP LINE, EVERYBODY!
GOM

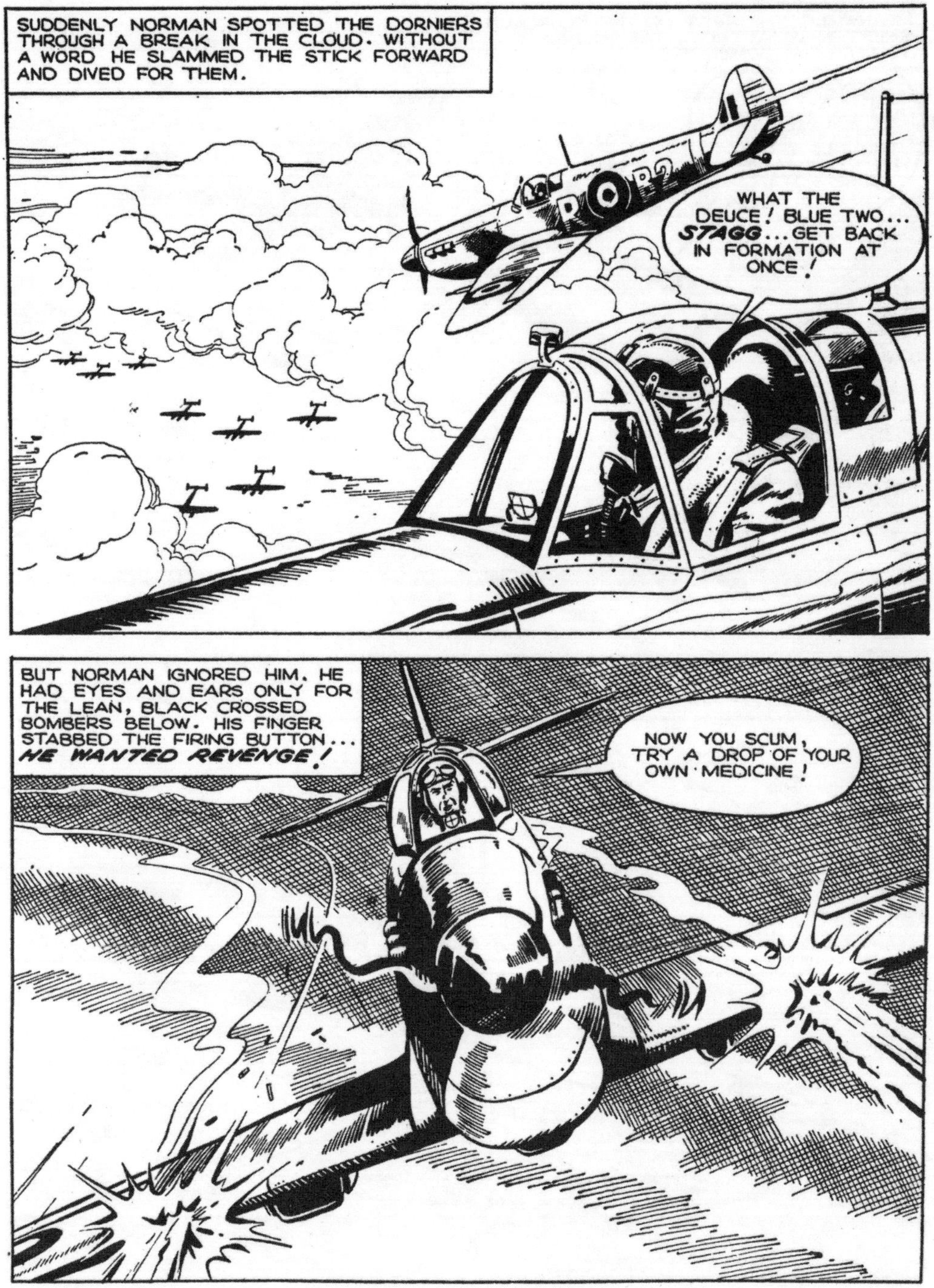
SUDDENLY NORMAN SPOTTED THE DORNIERS THROUGH A BREAK IN THE CLOUD. WITHOUT A WORD HE SLAMMED THE STICK FORWARD AND DIVED FOR THEM.
WHAT THE DEUCE! BLUE TWO... STAGG... GET BACK IN FORMATION AT ONCE!
BUT NORMAN IGNORED HIM. HE HAD EYES AND EARS ONLY FOR THE LEAN, BLACK CROSSED BOMBERS BELOW. HIS FINGER STABBED THE FIRING BUTTON... HE WANTED REVENGE!
NOW YOU SCUM, TRY A DROP OF YOUR OWN MEDICINE!

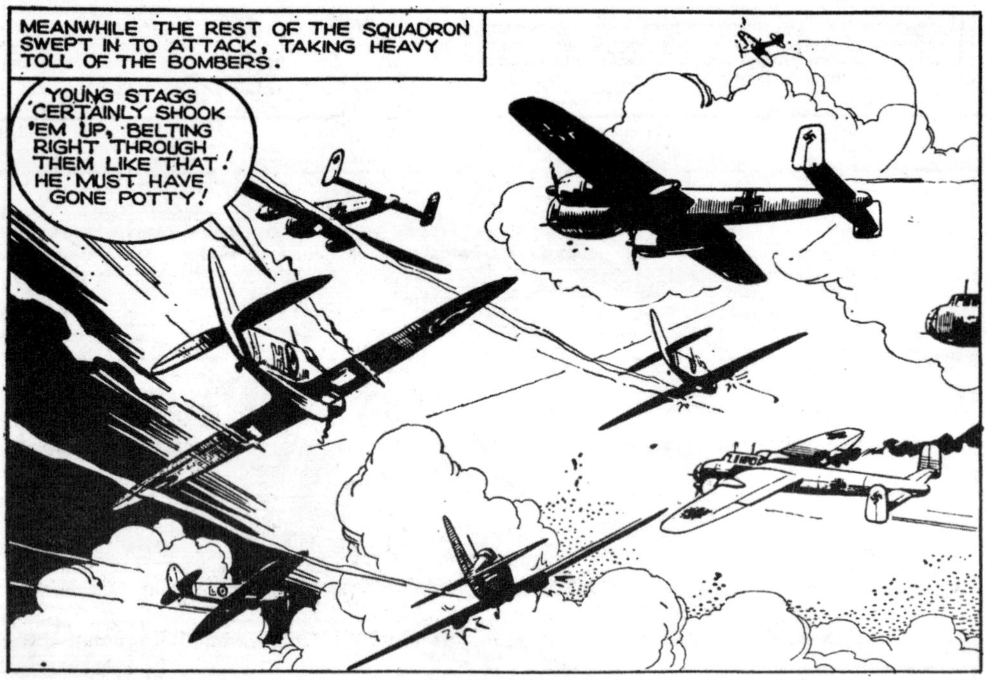
MEANWHILE THE REST OF THE SQUADRON SWEPT IN TO ATTACK, TAKING HEAVY TOLL OF THE BOMBERS.
YOUNG STAGG CERTAINLY SHOOK 'EM UP, BELTING RIGHT THROUGH THEM LIKE THAT! HE MUST HAVE GONE POTTY!

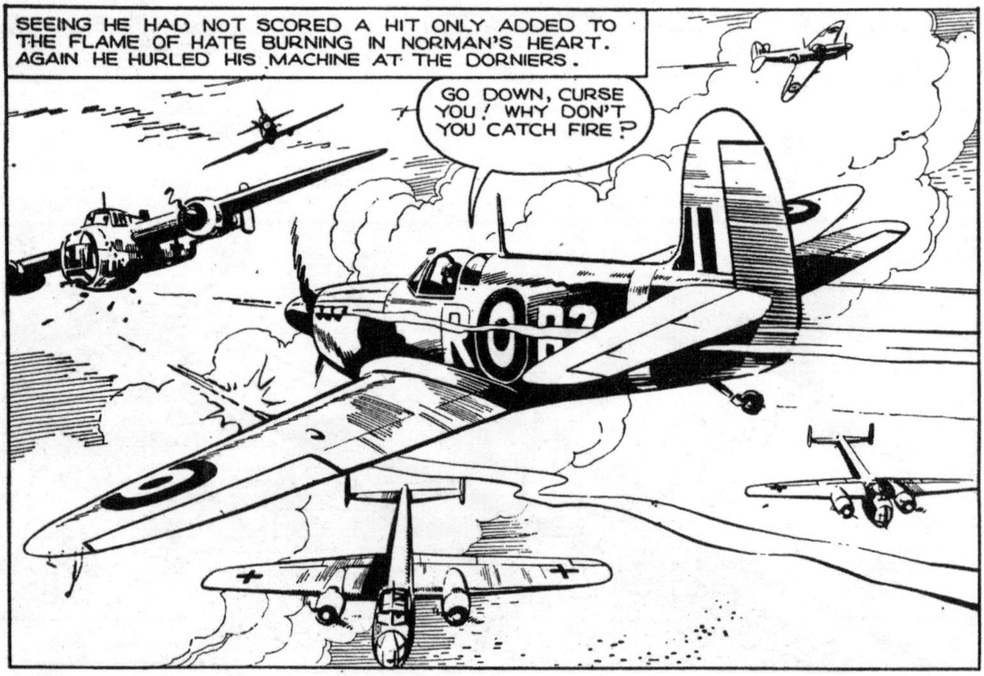
SEEING HE HAD NOT SCORED A HIT ONLY ADDED TO THE FLAME OF HATE BURNING IN NORMAN'S HEART. AGAIN HE HURLED HIS MACHINE AT THE DORNIERS.
GO DOWN, CURSE YOU! WHY DON'T YOU CATCH FIRE?

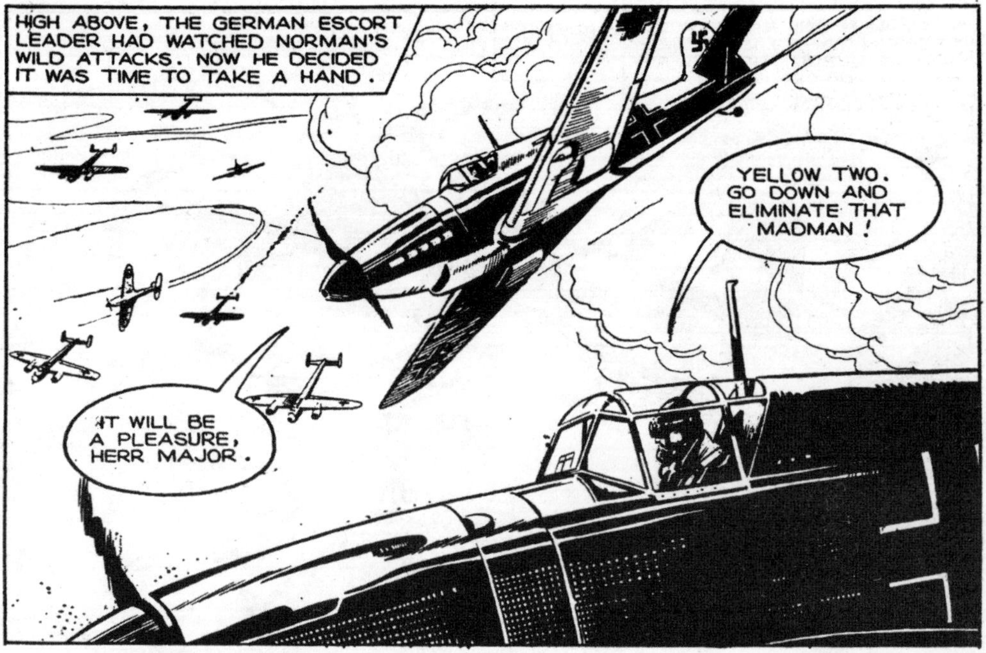
HIGH ABOVE, THE GERMAN ESCORT LEADER HAD WATCHED NORMAN'S WILD ATTACKS. NOW HE DECIDED IT WAS TIME TO TAKE A HAND.
YELLOW TWO. GO DOWN AND ELIMINATE THAT MADMAN!
IT WILL BE A PLEASURE, HERR MAJOR.

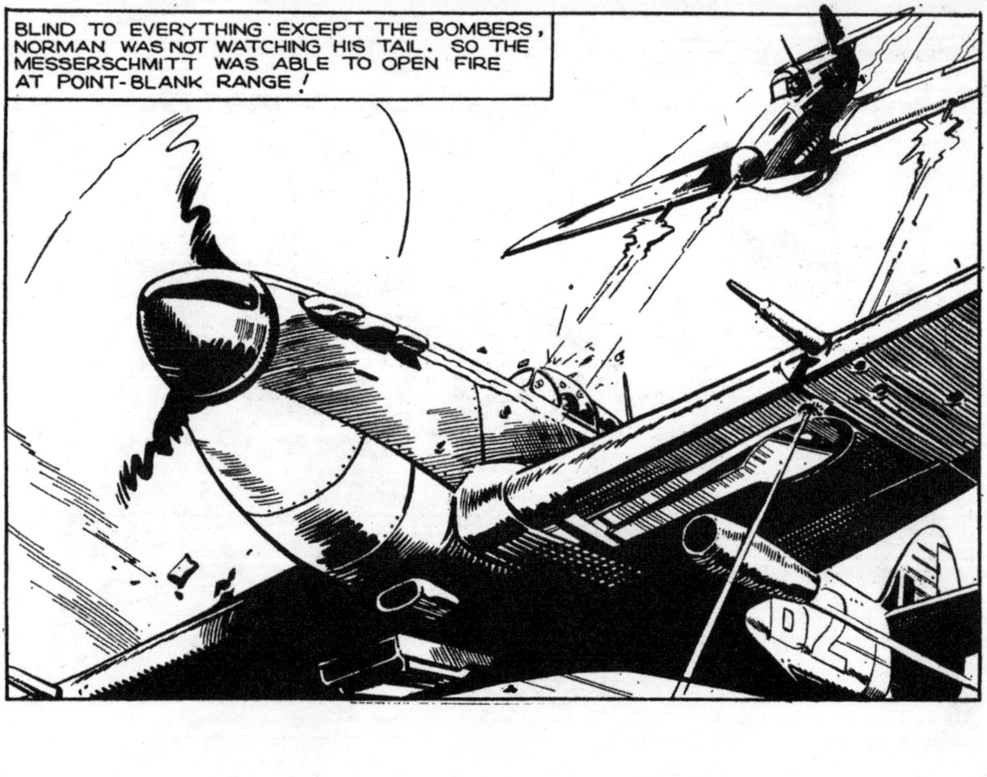
BLIND TO EVERYTHING EXCEPT THE BOMBERS, NORMAN WAS NOT WATCHING HIS TAIL. SO THE MESSERSCHMITT WAS ABLE TO OPEN FIRE AT POINT-BLANK RANGE!

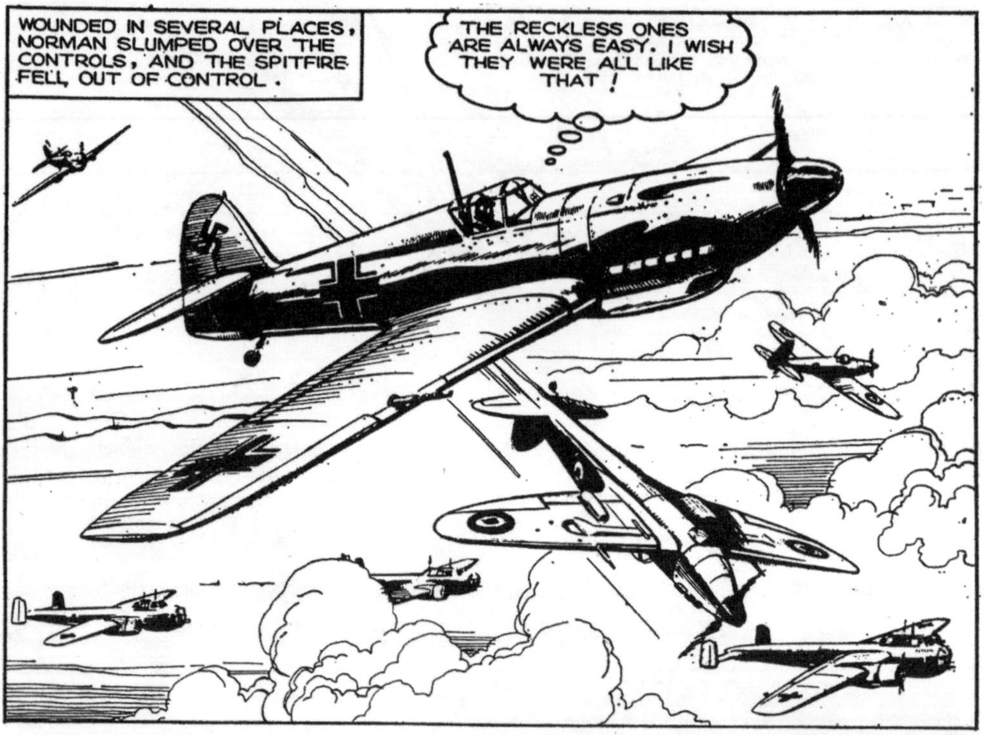
WOUNDED IN SEVERAL PLACES, NORMAN SLUMPED OVER THE CONTROLS, AND THE SPITFIRE FELL OUT OF CONTROL.
THE RECKLESS ONES ARE ALWAYS EASY. I WISH THEY WERE ALL LIKE THAT!

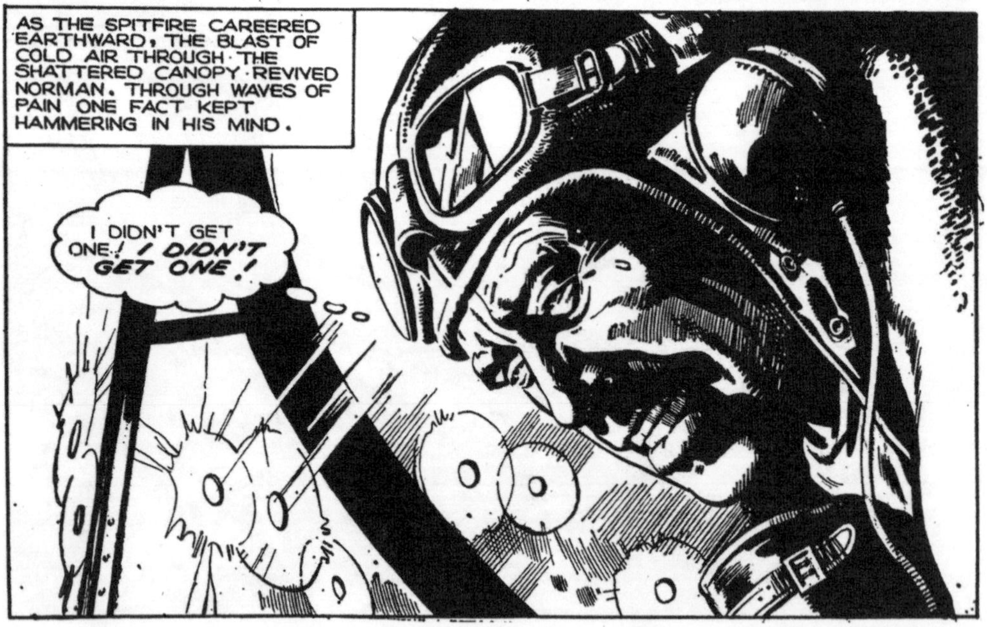
AS THE SPITFIRE CAREERED EARTHWARD, THE BLAST OF COLD AIR THROUGH THE SHATTERED CANOPY REVIVED NORMAN. THROUGH WAVES OF PAIN ONE FACT KEPT HAMMERING IN HIS MIND.
I DIDN'T GET ONE! I DIDN'T GET ONE!

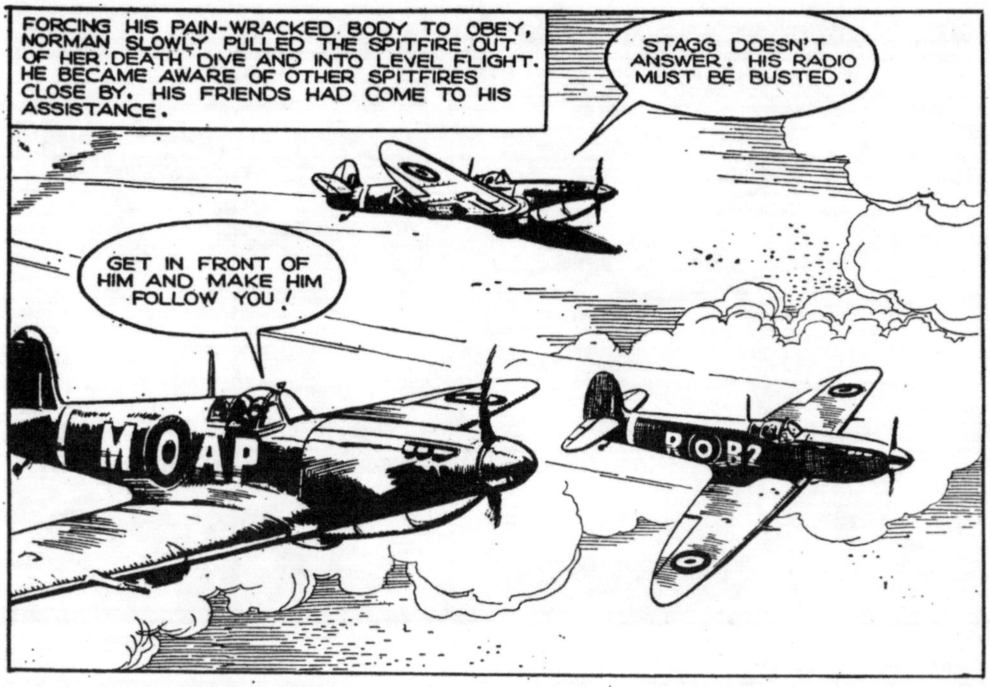
FORCING HIS PAIN-WRACKED BODY TO OBEY, NORMAN SLOWLY PULLED THE SPITFIRE OUT OF HER DEATH DIVE AND INTO LEVEL FLIGHT. HE BECAME AWARE OF OTHER SPITFIRES CLOSE BY. HIS FRIENDS HAD COME TO HIS ASSISTANCE.
STAGG DOESN'T ANSWER. HIS RADIO MUST BE BUSTED.
GET IN FRONT OF HIM AND MAKE HIM FOLLOW YOU!
M O AP
R O B 2

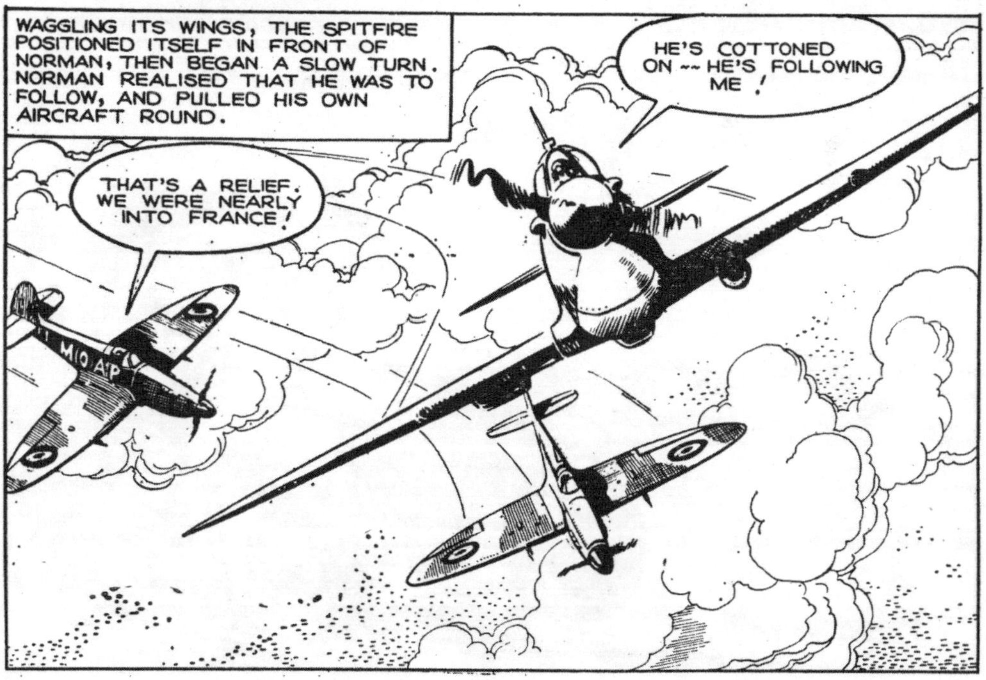
WAGGLING ITS WINGS, THE SPITFIRE POSITIONED ITSELF IN FRONT OF NORMAN, THEN BEGAN A SLOW TURN. NORMAN REALISED THAT HE WAS TO FOLLOW, AND PULLED HIS OWN AIRCRAFT ROUND.
HE'S COTTONED ON -- HE'S FOLLOWING ME!
THAT'S A RELIEF. WE WERE NEARLY INTO FRANCE!
M O AP

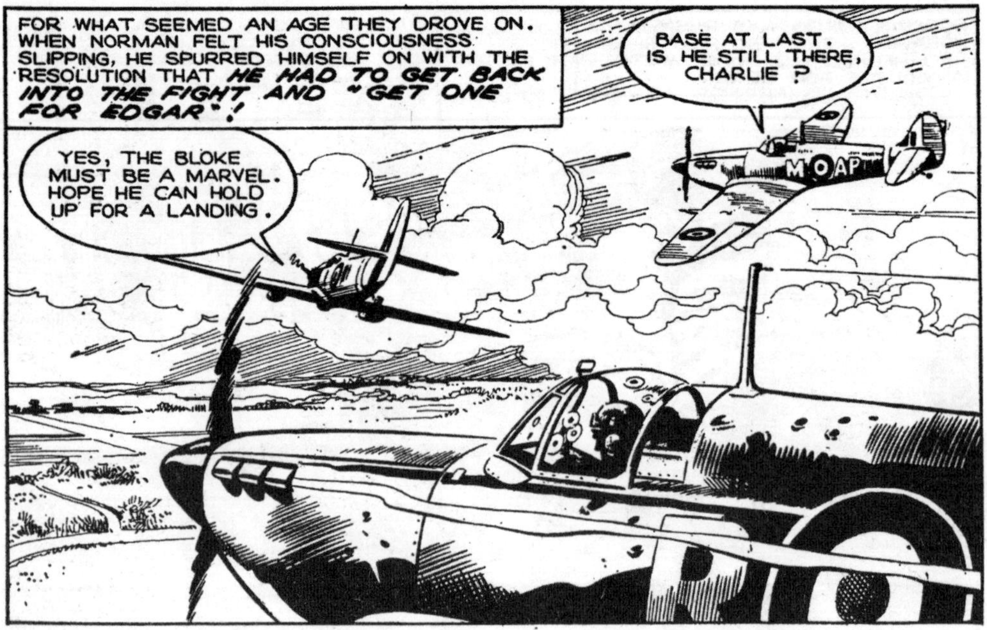
FOR WHAT SEEMED AN AGE THEY DROVE ON. WHEN NORMAN FELT HIS CONSCIOUSNESS SLIPPING, HE SPURRED HIMSELF ON WITH THE RESOLUTION THAT HE HAD TO GET BACK INTO THE FIGHT AND "GET ONE FOR EDGAR"!
BASE AT LAST. IS HE STILL THERE, CHARLIE ?
YES, THE BLOKE MUST BE A MARVEL. HOPE HE CAN HOLD UP FOR A LANDING.
M O AP

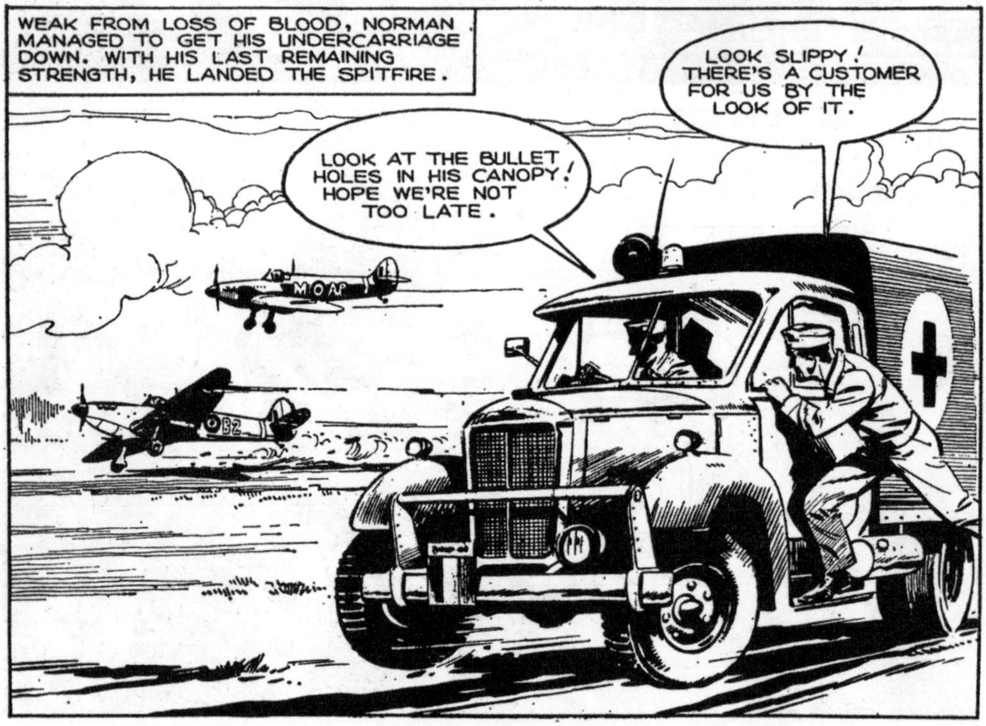
WEAK FROM LOSS OF BLOOD, NORMAN MANAGED TO GET HIS UNDERCARRIAGE DOWN. WITH HIS LAST REMAINING STRENGTH, HE LANDED THE SPITFIRE.
LOOK SLIPPY! THERE'S A CUSTOMER FOR US BY THE LOOK OF IT.
LOOK AT THE BULLET HOLES IN HIS CANOPY! HOPE WE'RE NOT TOO LATE.
M O AP

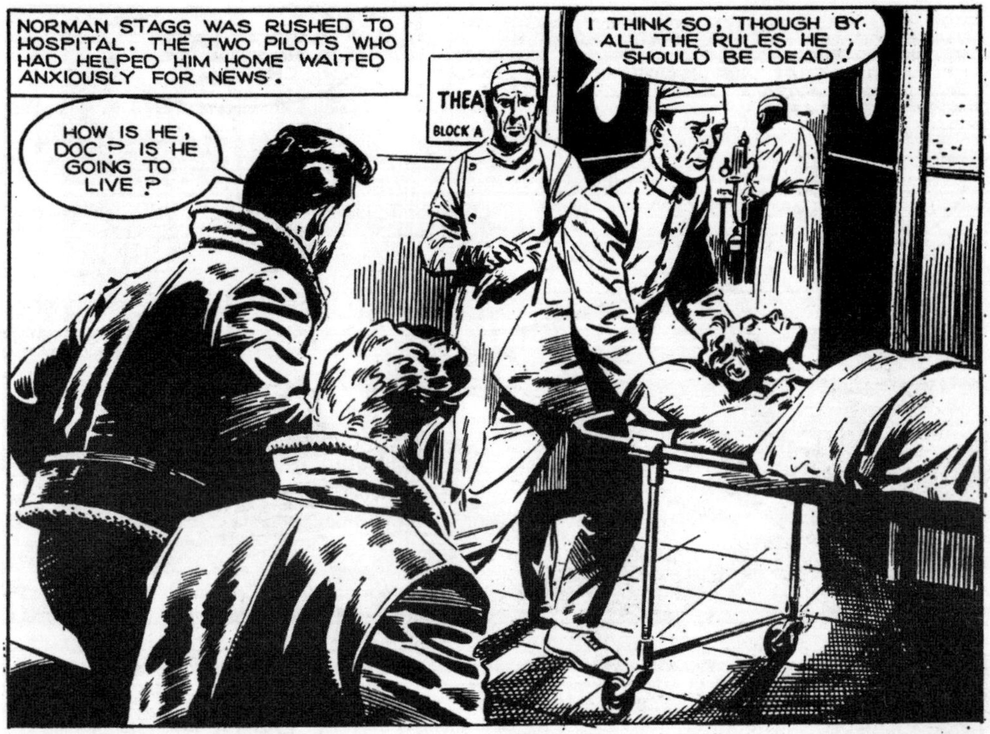
NORMAN STAGG WAS RUSHED TO HOSPITAL. THE TWO PILOTS WHO HAD HELPED HIM HOME WAITED ANXIOUSLY FOR NEWS.
HOW IS HE, DOC? IS HE GOING TO LIVE?
I THINK SO, THOUGH BY ALL THE RULES HE SHOULD BE DEAD!
THEATRE
BLOCK A

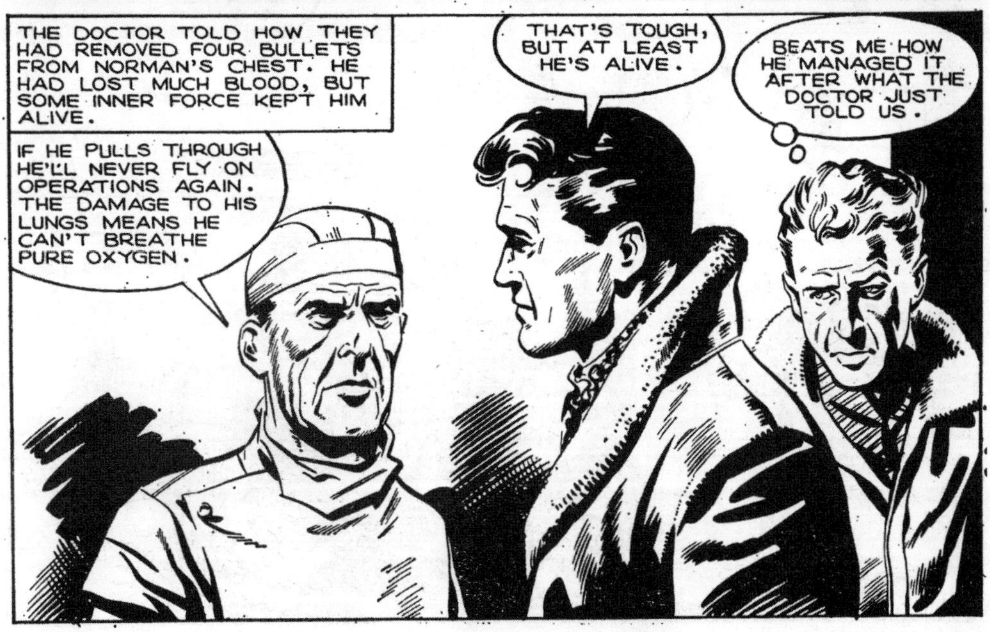
THE DOCTOR TOLD HOW THEY HAD REMOVED FOUR BULLETS FROM NORMAN'S CHEST. HE HAD LOST MUCH BLOOD, BUT SOME INNER FORCE KEPT HIM ALIVE.
IF HE PULLS THROUGH HE'LL NEVER FLY ON OPERATIONS AGAIN. THE DAMAGE TO HIS LUNGS MEANS HE CAN'T BREATHE PURE OXYGEN.
THAT'S TOUGH, BUT AT LEAST HE'S ALIVE.
BEATS ME HOW HE MANAGED IT AFTER WHAT THE DOCTOR JUST TOLD US.

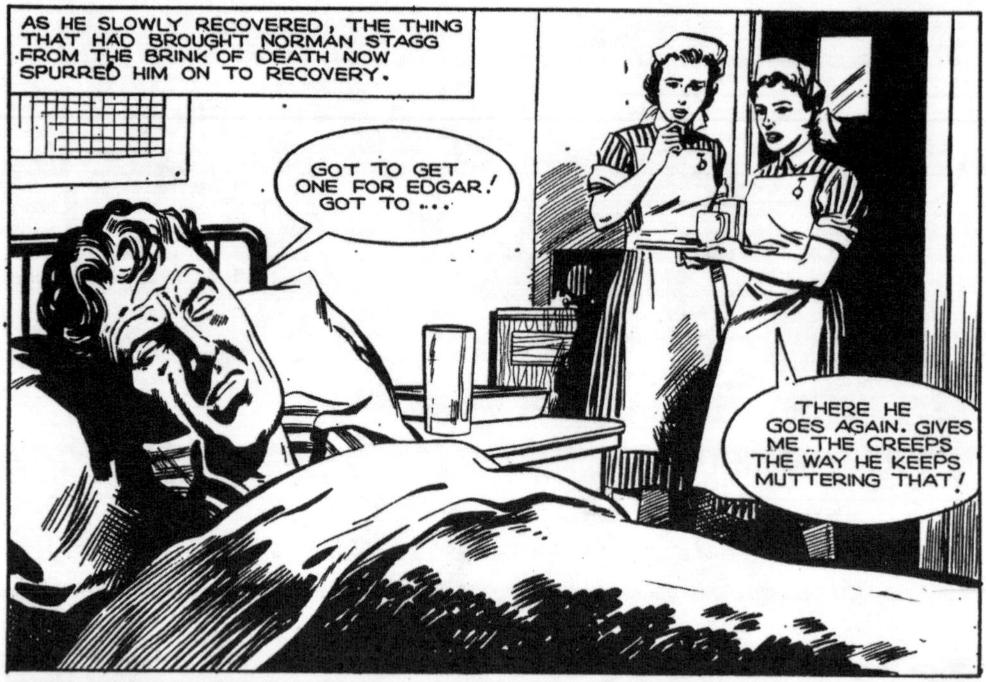
AS HE SLOWLY RECOVERED, THE THING THAT HAD BROUGHT NORMAN STAGG FROM THE BRINK OF DEATH NOW SPURRED HIM ON TO RECOVERY.
GOT TO GET ONE FOR EDGAR! GOT TO ....
THERE HE GOES AGAIN. GIVES ME THE CREEPS THE WAY HE KEEPS MUTTERING THAT!

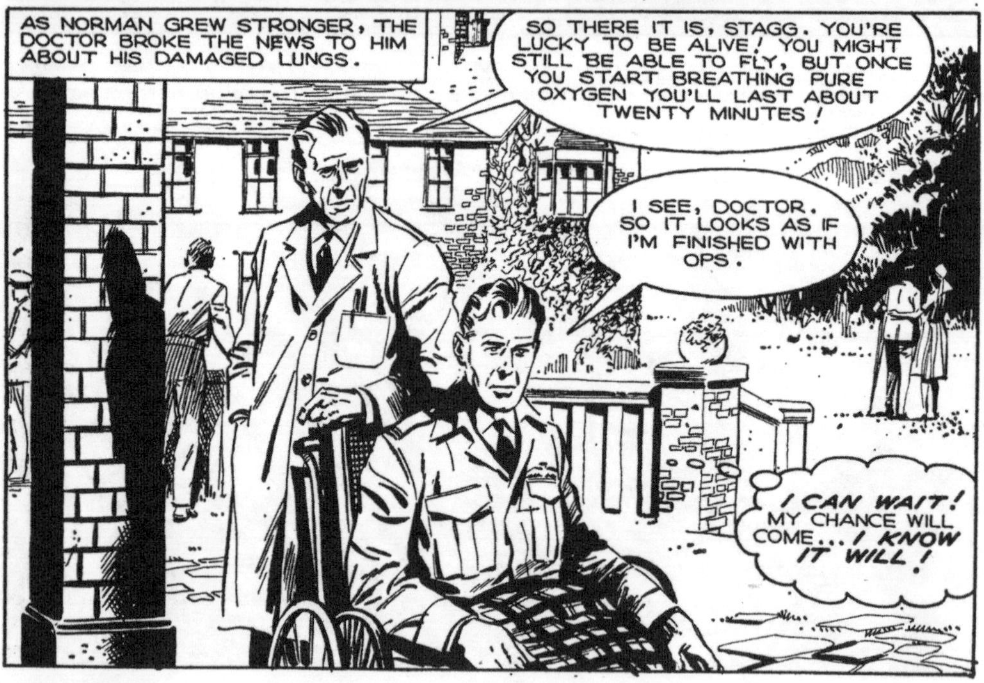
AS NORMAN GREW STRONGER, THE DOCTOR BROKE THE NEWS TO HIM ABOUT HIS DAMAGED LUNGS.
SO THERE IT IS, STAGG. YOU'RE LUCKY TO BE ALIVE! YOU MIGHT STILL BE ABLE TO FLY, BUT ONCE YOU START BREATHING PURE OXYGEN YOU'LL LAST ABOUT TWENTY MINUTES!
I SEE, DOCTOR. SO IT LOOKS AS IF I'M FINISHED WITH OPS.
I CAN WAIT! MY CHANCE WILL COME... I KNOW IT WILL!

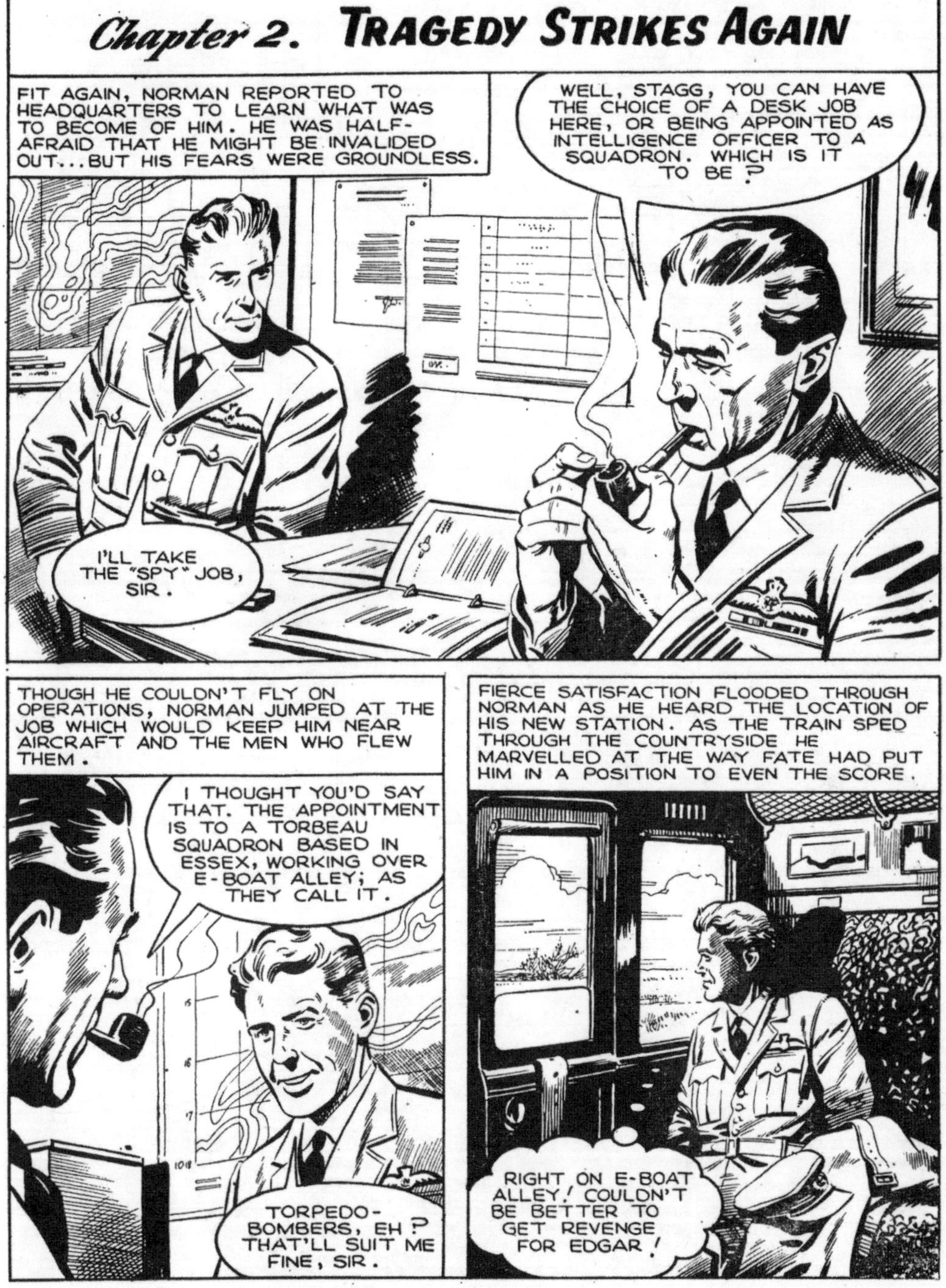
Chapter 2. TRAGEDY STRIKES AGAIN
FIT AGAIN, NORMAN REPORTED TO HEADQUARTERS TO LEARN WHAT WAS TO BECOME OF HIM. HE WAS HALF-AFRAID THAT HE MIGHT BE INVALIDED OUT... BUT HIS FEARS WERE GROUNDLESS.
WELL, STAGG, YOU CAN HAVE THE CHOICE OF A DESK JOB HERE, OR BEING APPOINTED AS INTELLIGENCE OFFICER TO A SQUADRON. WHICH IS IT TO BE?
I'LL TAKE THE "SPY" JOB, SIR.
THOUGH HE COULDN'T FLY ON OPERATIONS, NORMAN JUMPED AT THE JOB WHICH WOULD KEEP HIM NEAR AIRCRAFT AND THE MEN WHO FLEW THEM.
I THOUGHT YOU'D SAY THAT. THE APPOINTMENT IS TO A TORBEAU SQUADRON BASED IN ESSEX, WORKING OVER E-BOAT ALLEY, AS THEY CALL IT.
TORPEDO-BOMBERS, EH? THAT'LL SUIT ME FINE, SIR.
FIERCE SATISFACTION FLOODED THROUGH NORMAN AS HE HEARD THE LOCATION OF HIS NEW STATION. AS THE TRAIN SPED THROUGH THE COUNTRYSIDE HE MARVELLED AT THE WAY FATE HAD PUT HIM IN A POSITION TO EVEN THE SCORE.
RIGHT ON E-BOAT ALLEY! COULDN'T BE BETTER TO GET REVENGE FOR EDGAR!

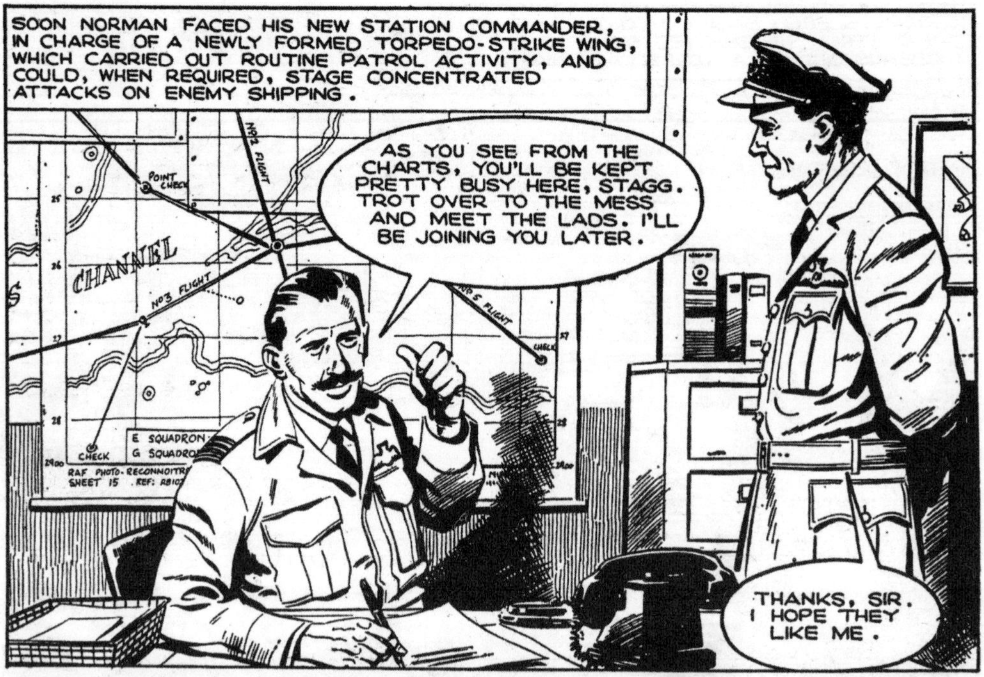
SOON NORMAN FACED HIS NEW STATION COMMANDER, IN CHARGE OF A NEWLY FORMED TORPEDO-STRIKE WING, WHICH CARRIED OUT ROUTINE PATROL ACTIVITY, AND COULD, WHEN REQUIRED, STAGE CONCENTRATED ATTACKS ON ENEMY SHIPPING.
AS YOU SEE FROM THE CHARTS, YOU'LL BE KEPT PRETTY BUSY HERE, STAGG. TROT OVER TO THE MESS AND MEET THE LADS. I'LL BE JOINING YOU LATER.
THANKS, SIR. I HOPE THEY LIKE ME.

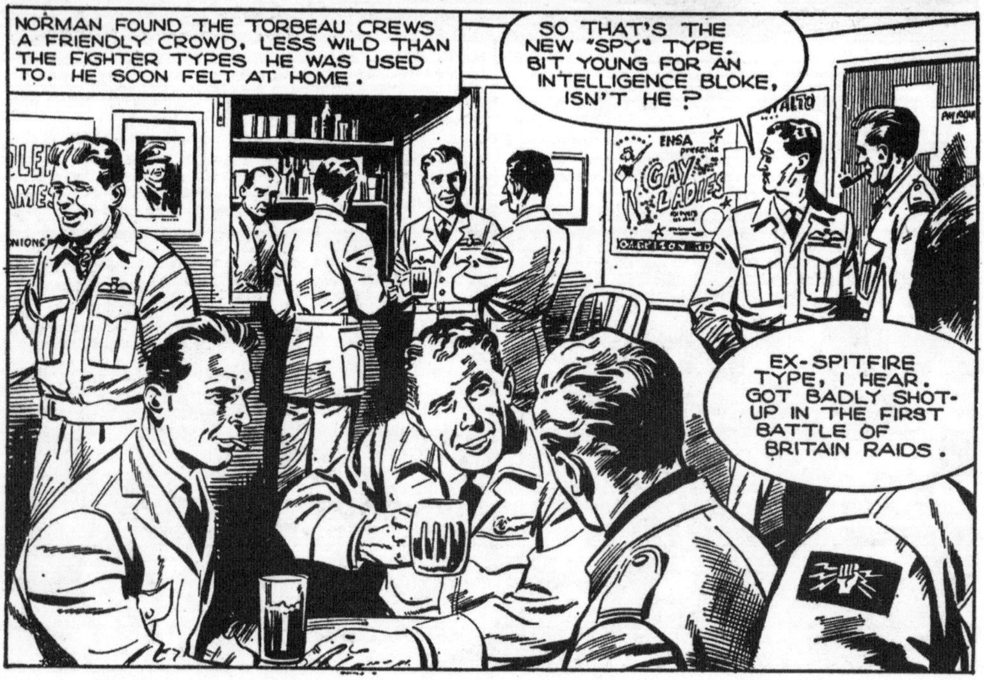
NORMAN FOUND THE TORBEAU CREWS A FRIENDLY CROWD, LESS WILD THAN THE FIGHTER TYPES HE WAS USED TO. HE SOON FELT AT HOME.
SO THAT'S THE NEW "SPY" TYPE. BIT YOUNG FOR AN INTELLIGENCE BLOKE, ISN'T HE?
EX-SPITFIRE TYPE, I HEAR. GOT BADLY SHOT-UP IN THE FIRST BATTLE OF BRITAIN RAIDS.

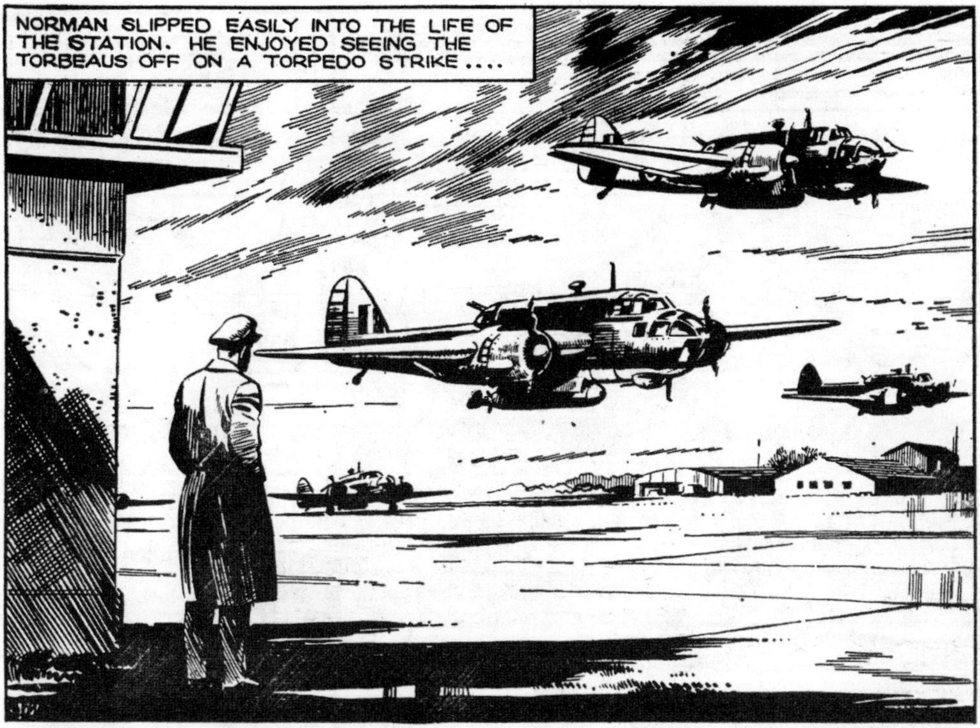
NORMAN SLIPPED EASILY INTO THE LIFE OF THE STATION. HE ENJOYED SEEING THE TORBEAUS OFF ON A TORPEDO STRIKE....

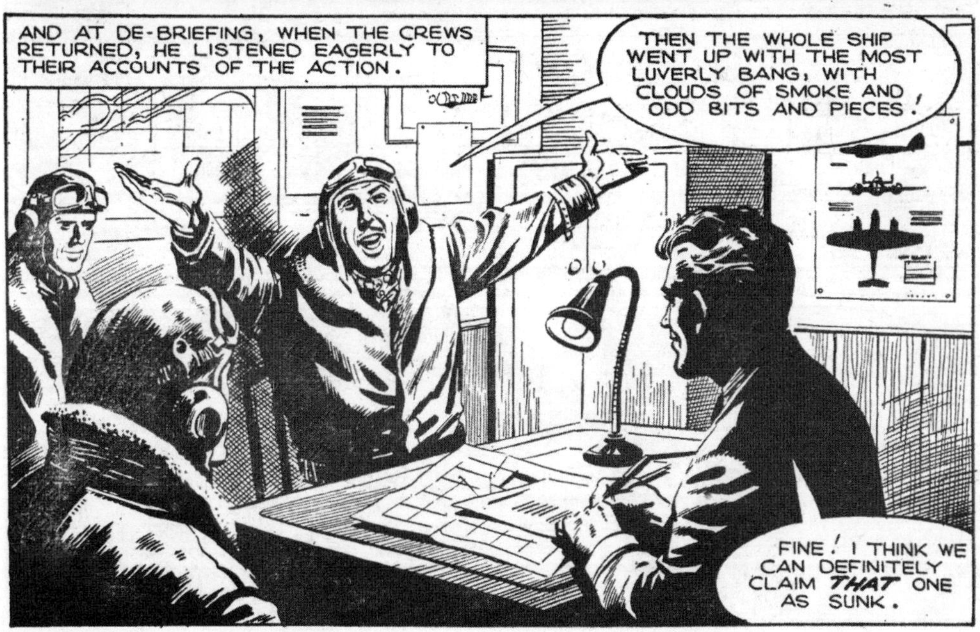
AND AT DE-BRIEFING, WHEN THE CREWS RETURNED, HE LISTENED EAGERLY TO THEIR ACCOUNTS OF THE ACTION.
THEN THE WHOLE SHIP WENT UP WITH THE MOST LUVERLY BANG, WITH CLOUDS OF SMOKE AND ODD BITS AND PIECES!
FINE! I THINK WE CAN DEFINITELY CLAIM THAT ONE AS SUNK.

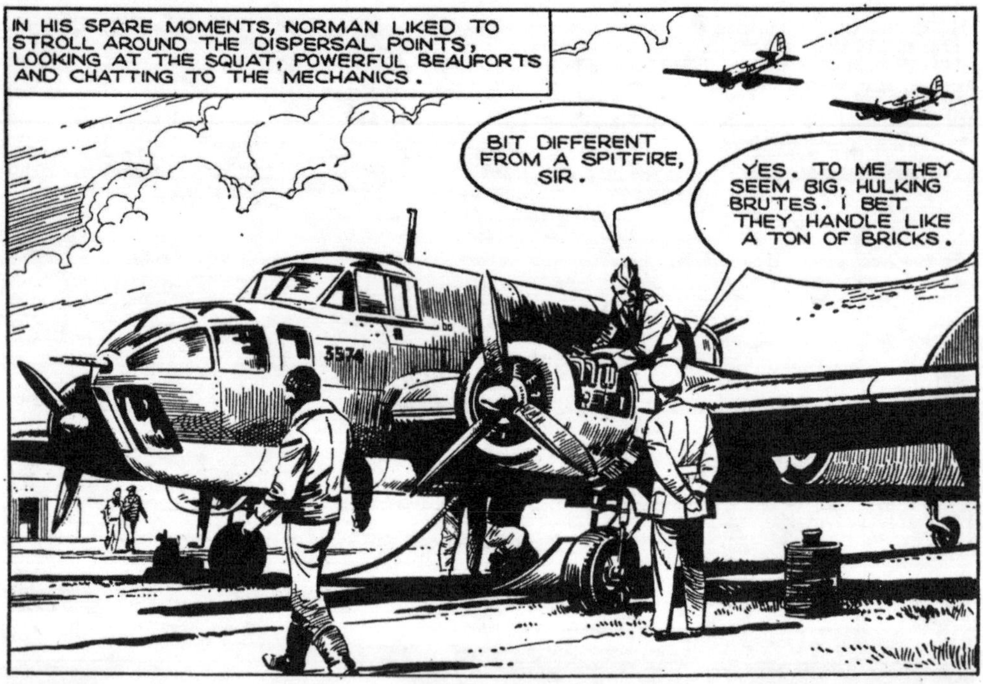
IN HIS SPARE MOMENTS, NORMAN LIKED TO STROLL AROUND THE DISPERSAL POINTS, LOOKING AT THE SQUAT, POWERFUL BEAUFORTS AND CHATTING TO THE MECHANICS.
BIT DIFFERENT FROM A SPITFIRE, SIR.
YES. TO ME THEY SEEM BIG, HULKING BRUTES. I BET THEY HANDLE LIKE A TON OF BRICKS.

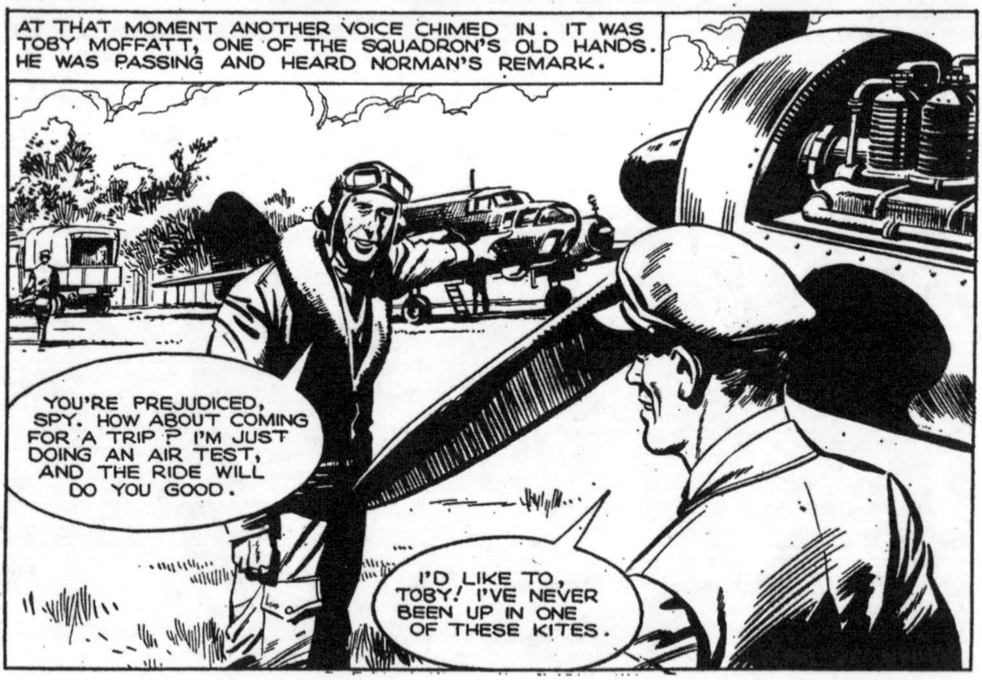
AT THAT MOMENT ANOTHER VOICE CHIMED IN. IT WAS TOBY MOFFATT, ONE OF THE SQUADRON'S OLD HANDS. HE WAS PASSING AND HEARD NORMAN'S REMARK.
YOU'RE PREJUDICED, SPY. HOW ABOUT COMING FOR A TRIP? I'M JUST DOING AN AIR TEST, AND THE RIDE WILL DO YOU GOOD.
I'D LIKE TO, TOBY! I'VE NEVER BEEN UP IN ONE OF THESE KITES.

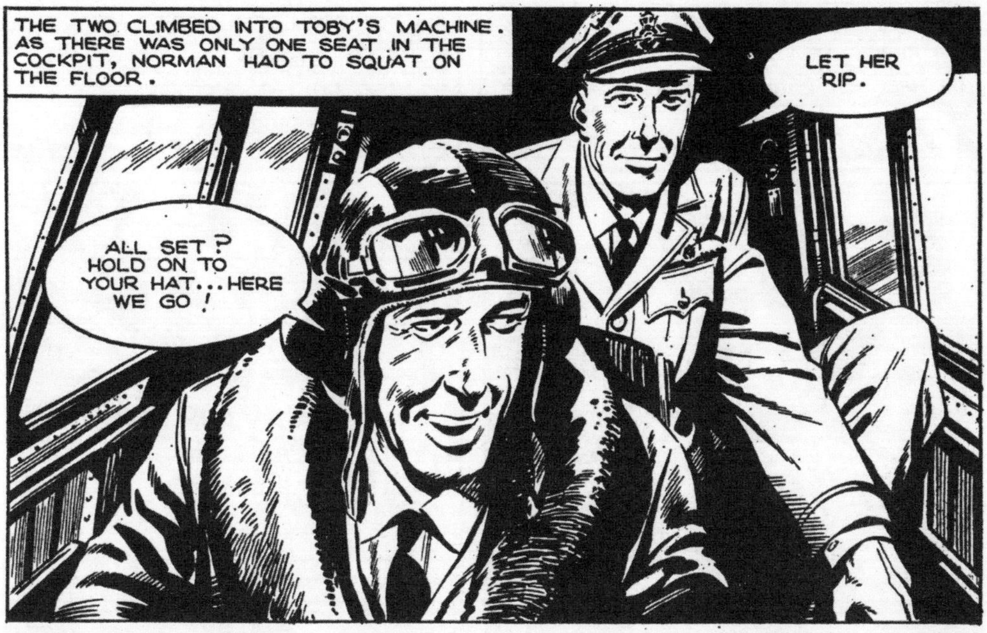
THE TWO CLIMBED INTO TOBY'S MACHINE. AS THERE WAS ONLY ONE SEAT IN THE COCKPIT, NORMAN HAD TO SQUAT ON THE FLOOR.
LET HER RIP.
ALL SET? HOLD ON TO YOUR HAT... HERE WE GO!

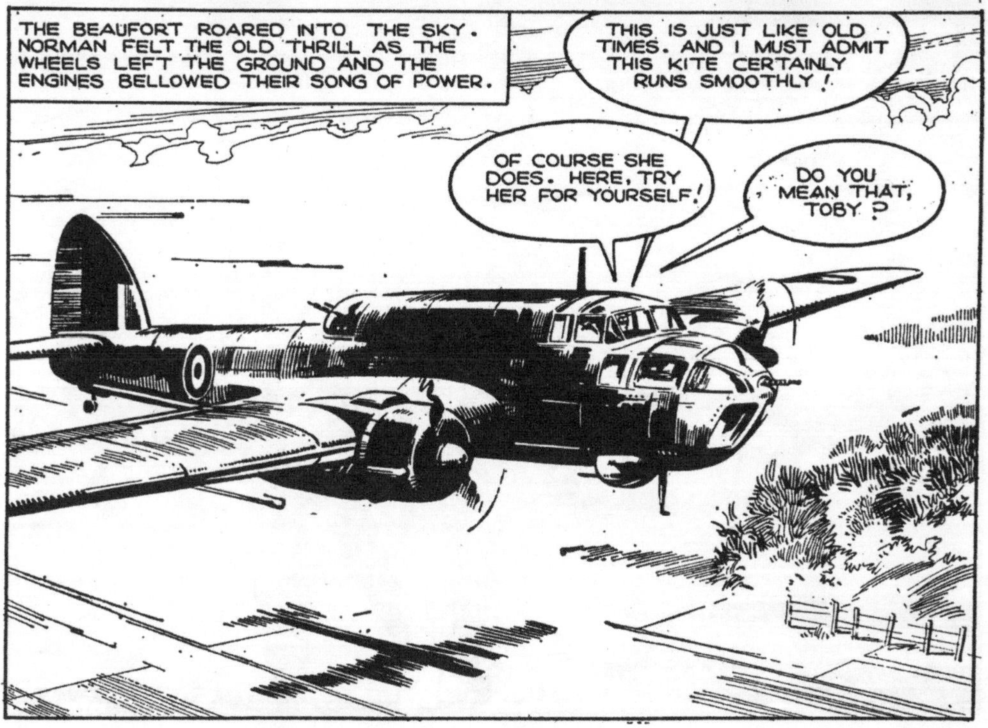
THE BEAUFORT ROARED INTO THE SKY. NORMAN FELT THE OLD THRILL AS THE WHEELS LEFT THE GROUND AND THE ENGINES BELLOWED THEIR SONG OF POWER.
THIS IS JUST LIKE OLD TIMES. AND I MUST ADMIT THIS KITE CERTAINLY RUNS SMOOTHLY!
OF COURSE SHE DOES. HERE, TRY HER FOR YOURSELF!
DO YOU MEAN THAT, TOBY?

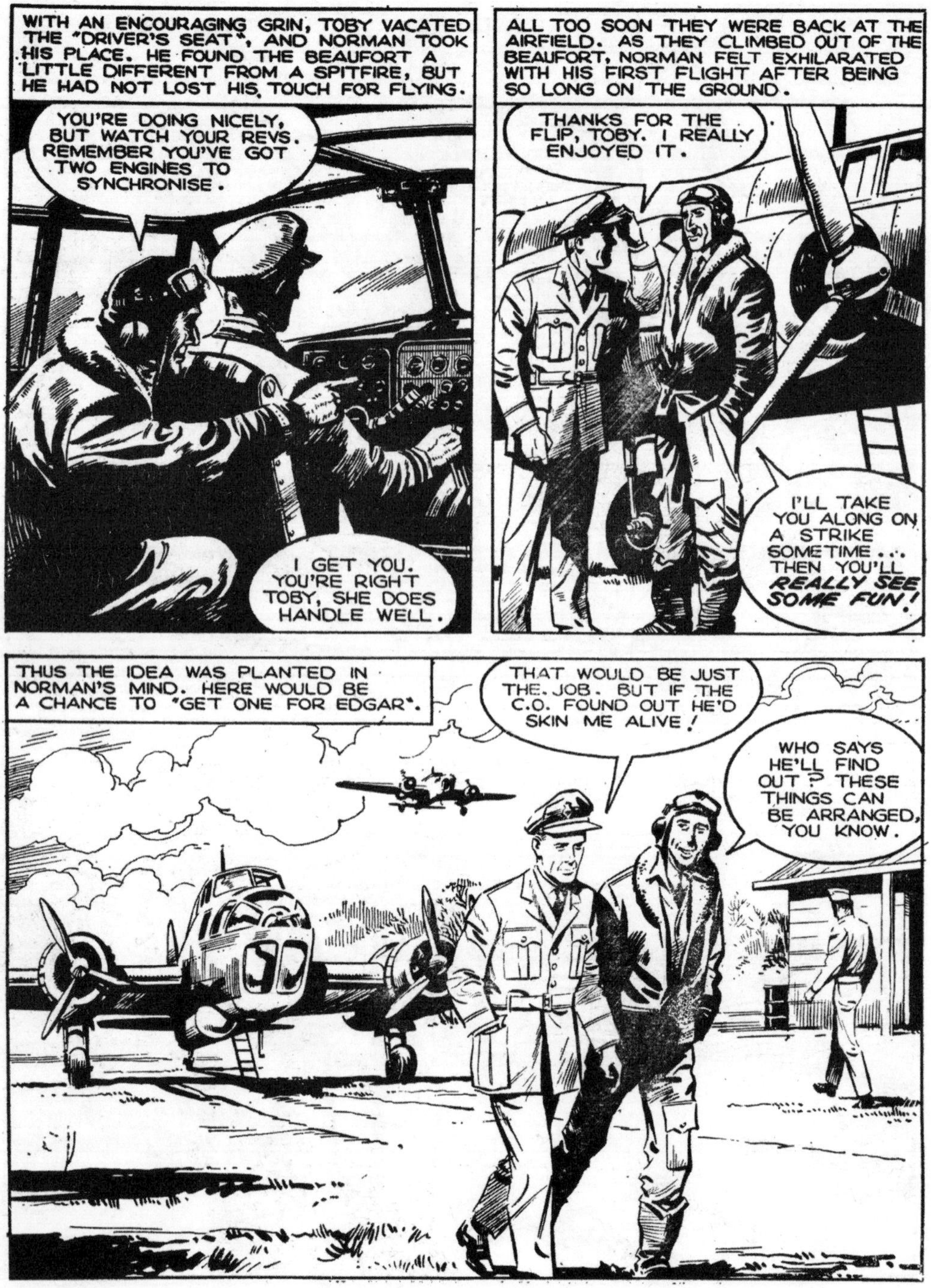
WITH AN ENCOURAGING GRIN, TOBY VACATED THE "DRIVER'S SEAT", AND NORMAN TOOK HIS PLACE. HE FOUND THE BEAUFORT A LITTLE DIFFERENT FROM A SPITFIRE, BUT HE HAD NOT LOST HIS TOUCH FOR FLYING.
YOU'RE DOING NICELY, BUT WATCH YOUR REVS. REMEMBER YOU'VE GOT TWO ENGINES TO SYNCHRONISE.
I GET YOU. YOU'RE RIGHT TOBY, SHE DOES HANDLE WELL.
ALL TOO SOON THEY WERE BACK AT THE AIRFIELD. AS THEY CLIMBED OUT OF THE BEAUFORT, NORMAN FELT EXHILARATED WITH HIS FIRST FLIGHT AFTER BEING SO LONG ON THE GROUND.
THANKS FOR THE FLIP, TOBY. I REALLY ENJOYED IT.
I'LL TAKE YOU ALONG ON A STRIKE SOMETIME ... THEN YOU'LL REALLY SEE SOME FUN!
THUS THE IDEA WAS PLANTED IN NORMAN'S MIND. HERE WOULD BE A CHANCE TO "GET ONE FOR EDGAR".
THAT WOULD BE JUST THE JOB. BUT IF THE C.O. FOUND OUT HE'D SKIN ME ALIVE!
WHO SAYS HE'LL FIND OUT? THESE THINGS CAN BE ARRANGED, YOU KNOW.

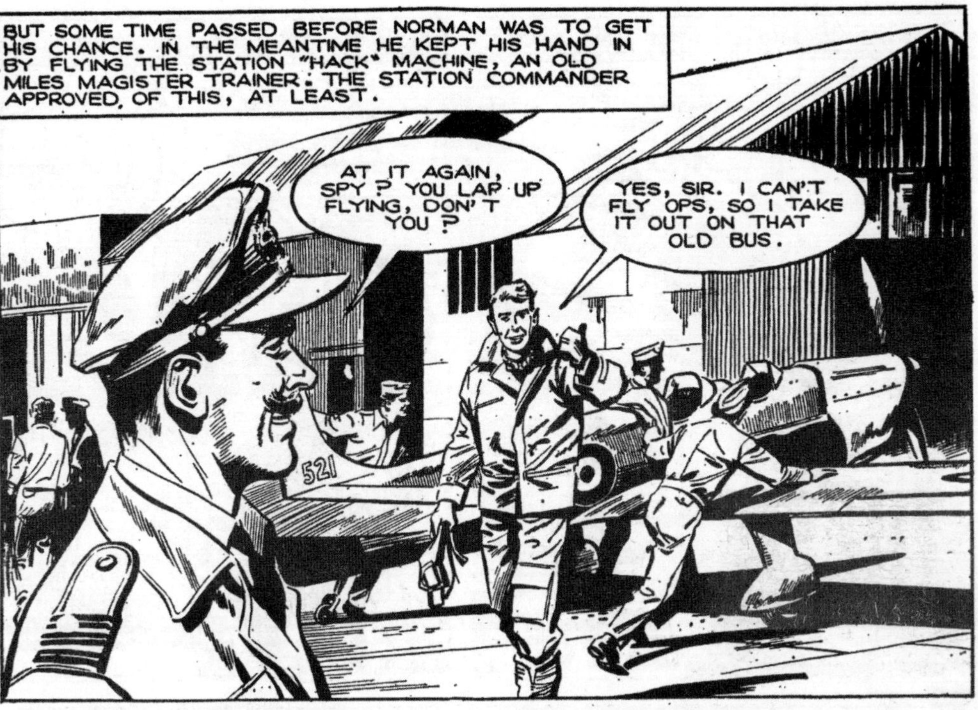
BUT SOME TIME PASSED BEFORE NORMAN WAS TO GET HIS CHANCE. IN THE MEANTIME HE KEPT HIS HAND IN BY FLYING THE STATION "HACK" MACHINE, AN OLD MILES MAGISTER TRAINER. THE STATION COMMANDER APPROVED, OF THIS, AT LEAST.
AT IT AGAIN, SPY ? YOU LAP UP FLYING, DON'T YOU ?
YES, SIR. I CAN'T FLY OPS, SO I TAKE IT OUT ON THAT OLD BUS.
521

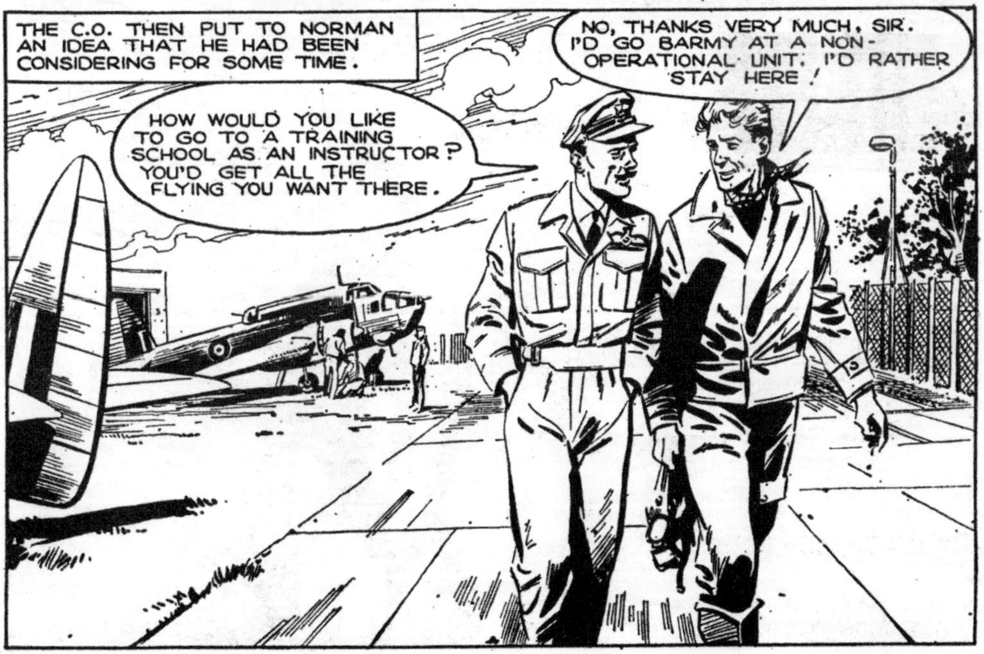
THE C.O. THEN PUT TO NORMAN AN IDEA THAT HE HAD BEEN CONSIDERING FOR SOME TIME.
HOW WOULD YOU LIKE TO GO TO A TRAINING SCHOOL AS AN INSTRUCTOR ? YOU'D GET ALL THE FLYING YOU WANT THERE.
NO, THANKS VERY MUCH, SIR. I'D GO BARMY AT A NON-OPERATIONAL UNIT. I'D RATHER STAY HERE !

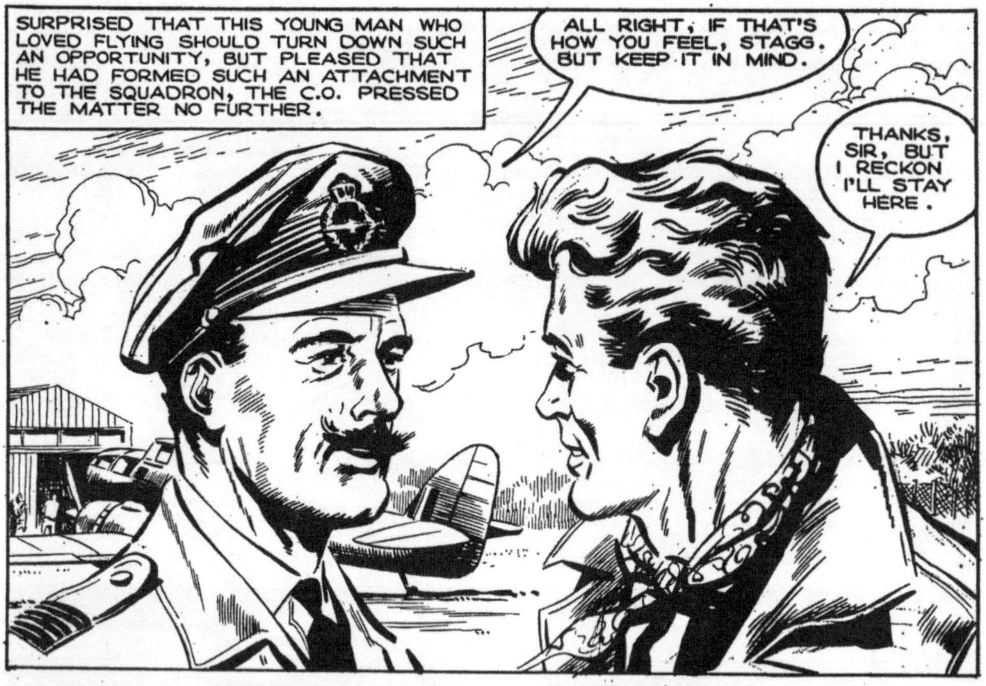
SURPRISED THAT THIS YOUNG MAN WHO LOVED FLYING SHOULD TURN DOWN SUCH AN OPPORTUNITY, BUT PLEASED THAT HE HAD FORMED SUCH AN ATTACHMENT TO THE SQUADRON, THE C.O. PRESSED THE MATTER NO FURTHER.
THANKS, SIR, BUT I RECKON I'LL STAY HERE.
ALL RIGHT, IF THAT'S HOW YOU FEEL, STAGG. BUT KEEP IT IN MIND.

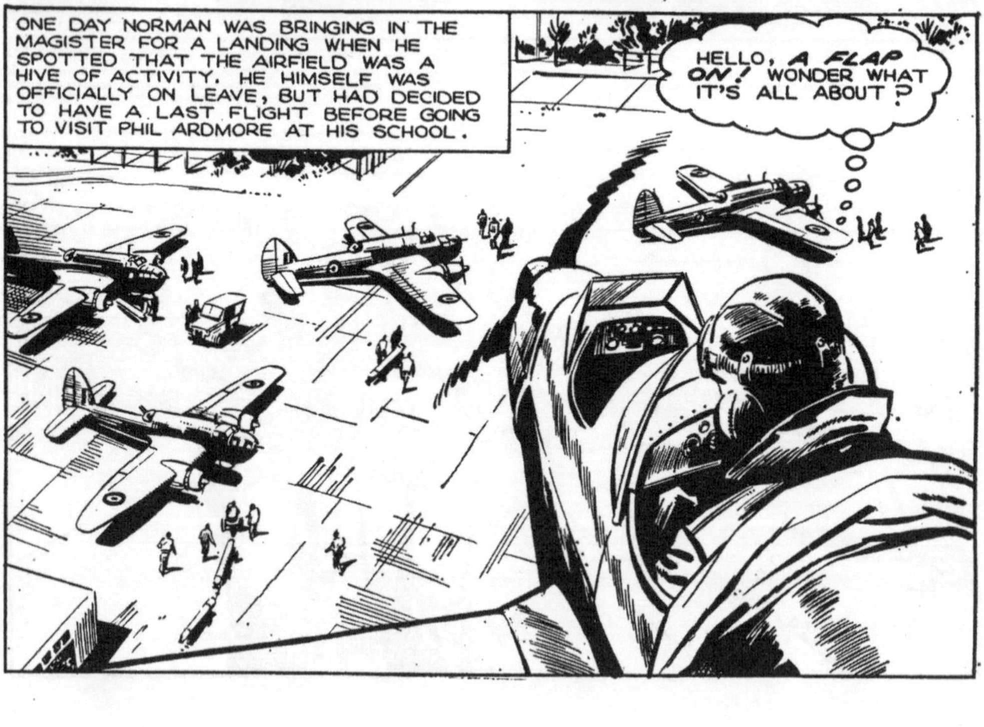
ONE DAY NORMAN WAS BRINGING IN THE MAGISTER FOR A LANDING WHEN HE SPOTTED THAT THE AIRFIELD WAS A HIVE OF ACTIVITY. HE HIMSELF WAS OFFICIALLY ON LEAVE, BUT HAD DECIDED TO HAVE A LAST FLIGHT BEFORE GOING TO VISIT PHIL ARDMORE AT HIS SCHOOL.
HELLO, A FLAP ON! WONDER WHAT IT'S ALL ABOUT?

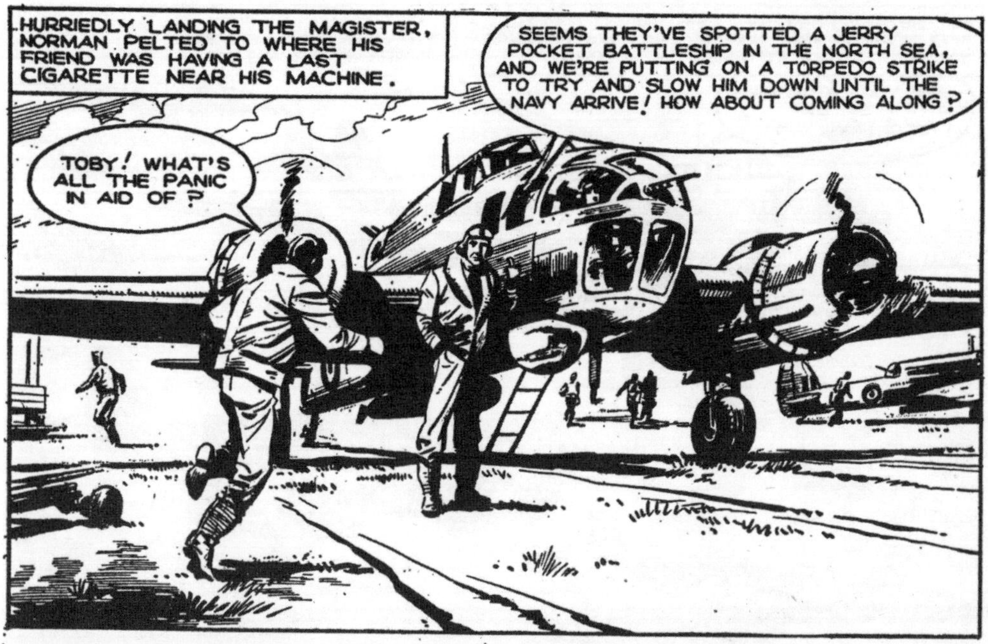
HURRIEDLY LANDING THE MAGISTER, NORMAN PELTED TO WHERE HIS FRIEND WAS HAVING A LAST CIGARETTE NEAR HIS MACHINE.
TOBY! WHAT'S ALL THE PANIC IN AID OF?
SEEMS THEY'VE SPOTTED A JERRY POCKET BATTLESHIP IN THE NORTH SEA, AND WE'RE PUTTING ON A TORPEDO STRIKE TO TRY AND SLOW HIM DOWN UNTIL THE NAVY ARRIVE! HOW ABOUT COMING ALONG?

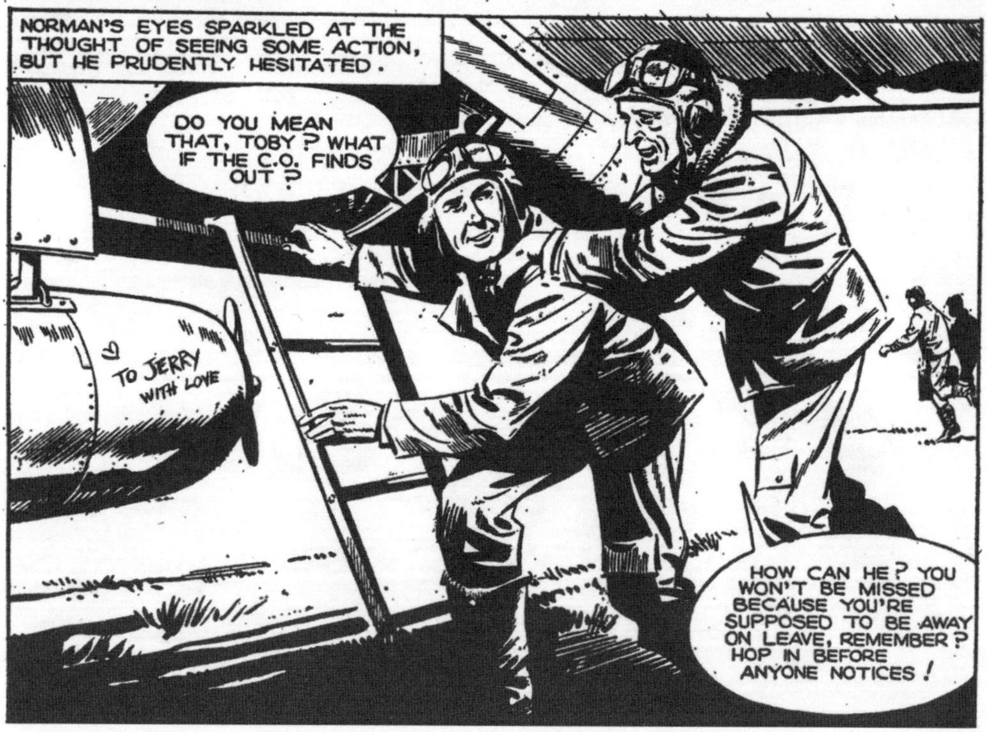
NORMAN'S EYES SPARKLED AT THE THOUGHT OF SEEING SOME ACTION, BUT HE PRUDENTLY HESITATED.
DO YOU MEAN THAT, TOBY? WHAT IF THE C.O. FINDS OUT?
TO JERRY WITH LOVE
HOW CAN HE? YOU WON'T BE MISSED BECAUSE YOU'RE SUPPOSED TO BE AWAY ON LEAVE, REMEMBER? HOP IN BEFORE ANYONE NOTICES!

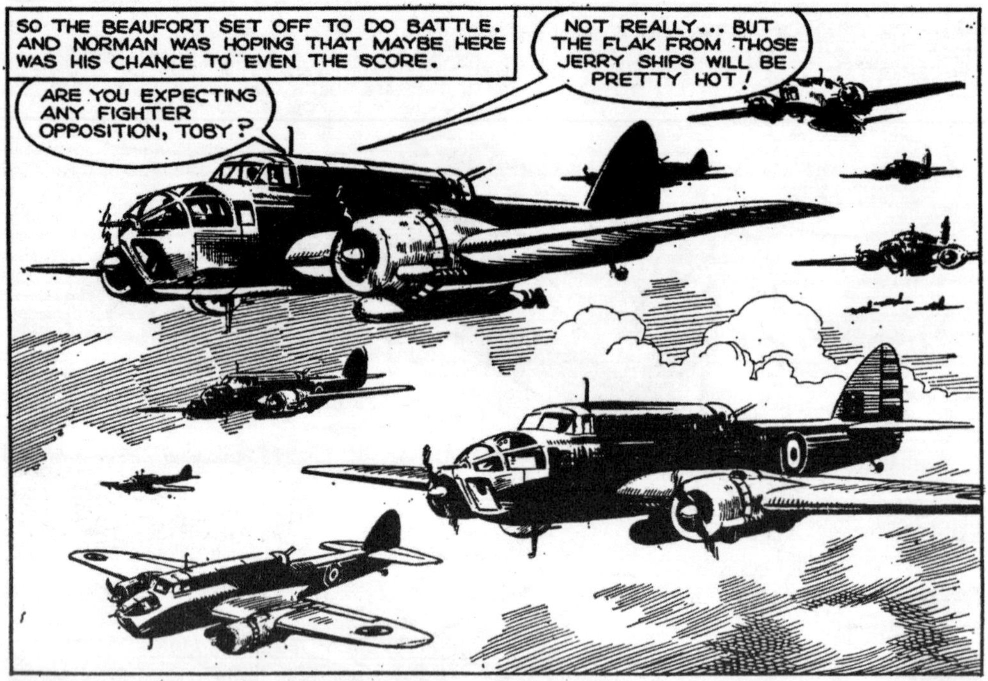
SO THE BEAUFORT SET OFF TO DO BATTLE. AND NORMAN WAS HOPING THAT MAYBE HERE WAS HIS CHANCE TO EVEN THE SCORE.
ARE YOU EXPECTING ANY FIGHTER OPPOSITION, TOBY?
NOT REALLY... BUT THE FLAK FROM THOSE JERRY SHIPS WILL BE PRETTY HOT!

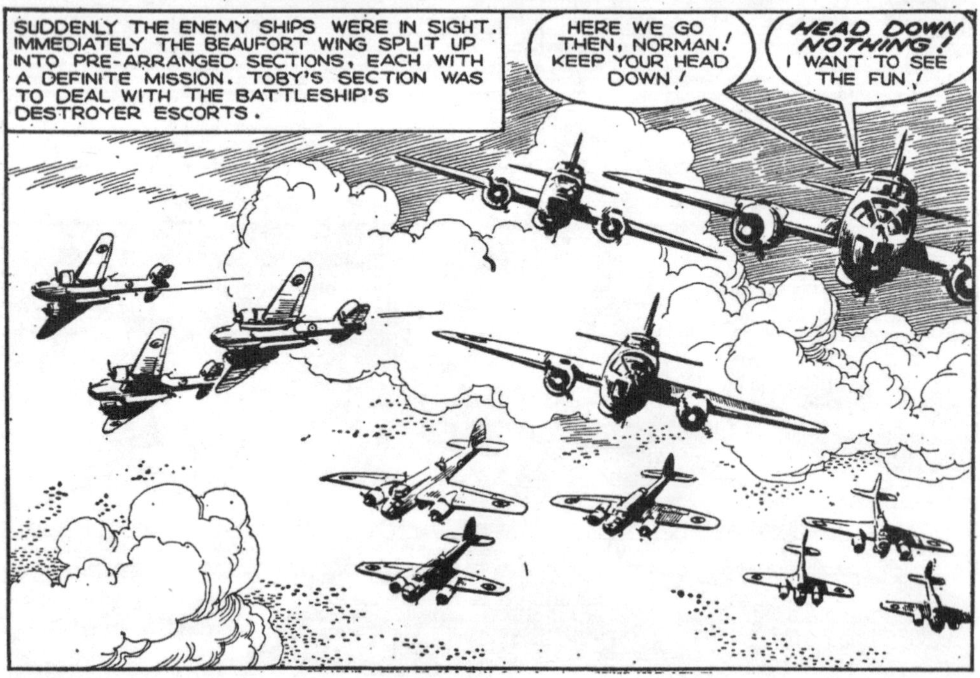
SUDDENLY THE ENEMY SHIPS WERE IN SIGHT. IMMEDIATELY THE BEAUFORT WING SPLIT UP INTO PRE-ARRANGED SECTIONS, EACH WITH A DEFINITE MISSION. TOBY'S SECTION WAS TO DEAL WITH THE BATTLESHIP'S DESTROYER ESCORTS.
HERE WE GO THEN, NORMAN! KEEP YOUR HEAD DOWN!
HEAD DOWN NOTHING! I WANT TO SEE THE FUN!

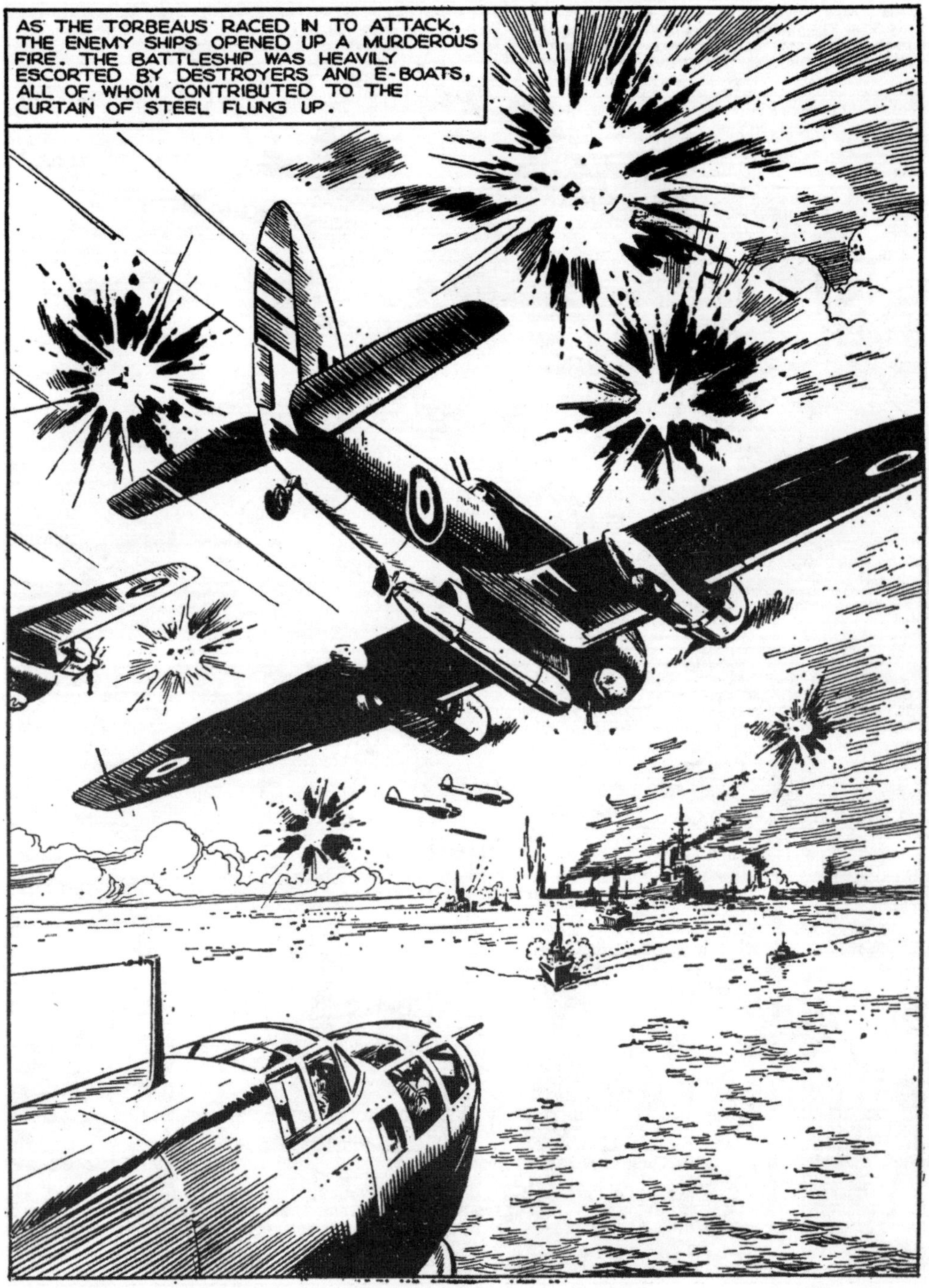
AS THE TORBEAUS RACED IN TO ATTACK, THE ENEMY SHIPS OPENED UP A MURDEROUS FIRE. THE BATTLESHIP WAS HEAVILY ESCORTED BY DESTROYERS AND E-BOATS, ALL OF WHOM CONTRIBUTED TO THE CURTAIN OF STEEL FLUNG UP.

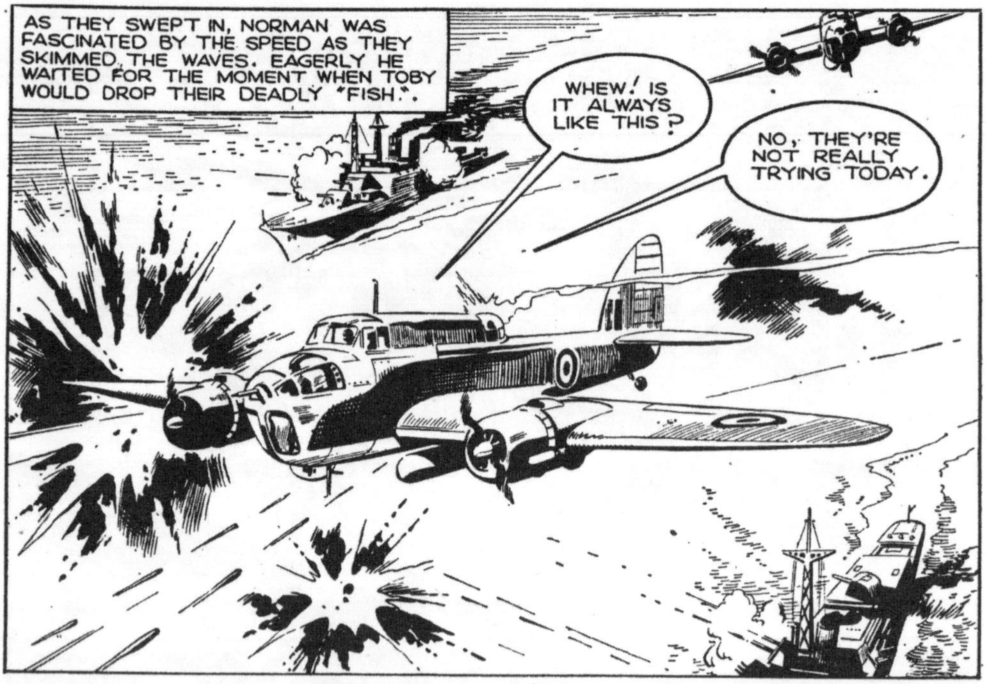
AS THEY SWEPT IN, NORMAN WAS FASCINATED BY THE SPEED AS THEY SKIMMED THE WAVES. EAGERLY HE WAITED FOR THE MOMENT WHEN TOBY WOULD DROP THEIR DEADLY "FISH".
WHEW! IS IT ALWAYS LIKE THIS?
NO, THEY'RE NOT REALLY TRYING TODAY.

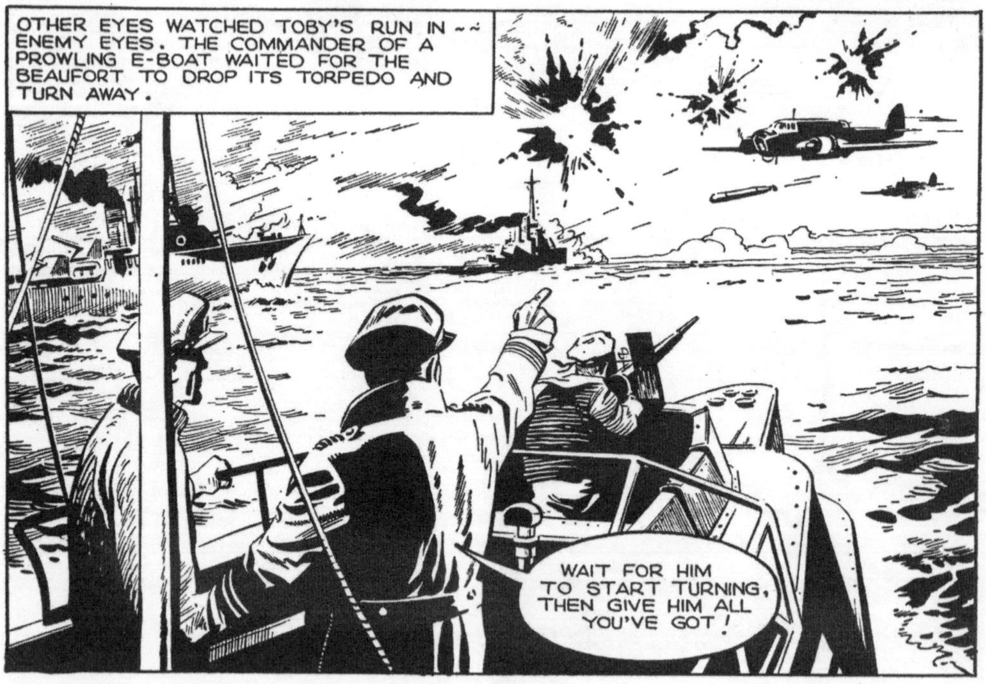
OTHER EYES WATCHED TOBY'S RUN IN ~~ ENEMY EYES. THE COMMANDER OF A PROWLING E-BOAT WAITED FOR THE BEAUFORT TO DROP ITS TORPEDO AND TURN AWAY.
WAIT FOR HIM TO START TURNING, THEN GIVE HIM ALL YOU'VE GOT!

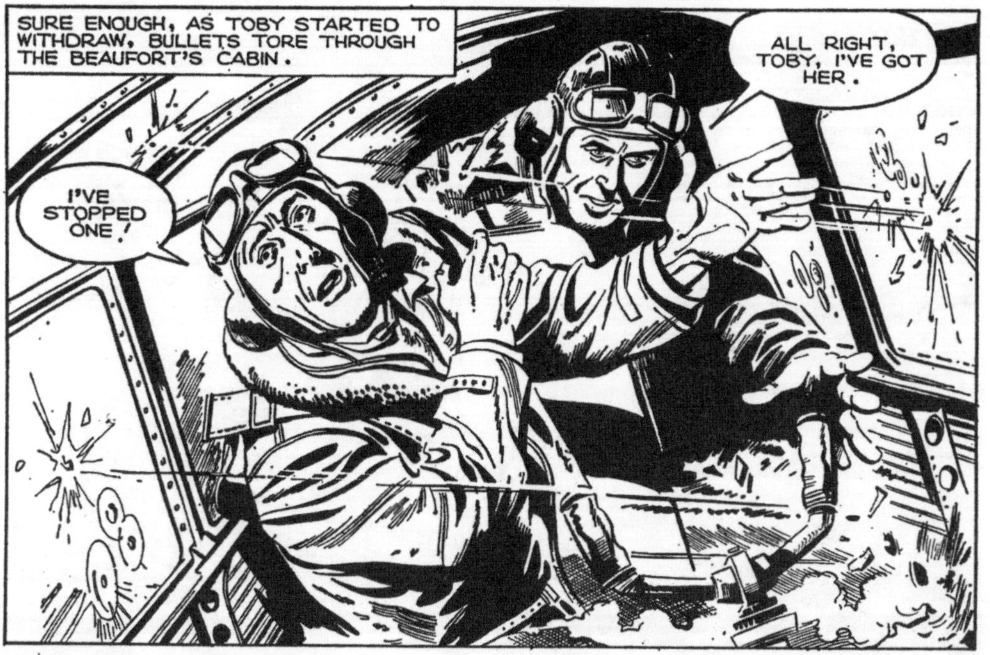
SURE ENOUGH, AS TOBY STARTED TO WITHDRAW, BULLETS TORE THROUGH THE BEAUFORT'S CABIN.
ALL RIGHT, TOBY, I'VE GOT HER.
I'VE STOPPED ONE!

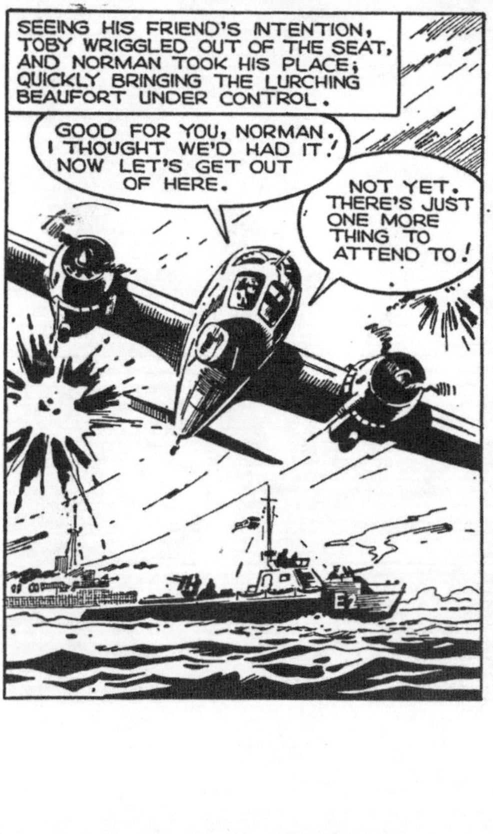
SEEING HIS FRIEND'S INTENTION, TOBY WRIGGLED OUT OF THE SEAT, AND NORMAN TOOK HIS PLACE, QUICKLY BRINGING THE LURCHING BEAUFORT UNDER CONTROL.
GOOD FOR YOU, NORMAN. I THOUGHT WE'D HAD IT! NOW LET'S GET OUT OF HERE.
NOT YET. THERE'S JUST ONE MORE THING TO ATTEND TO!

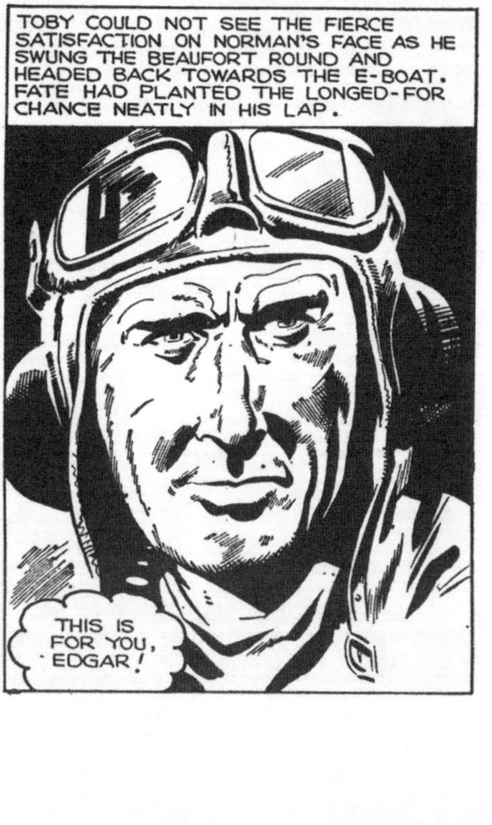
TOBY COULD NOT SEE THE FIERCE SATISFACTION ON NORMAN'S FACE AS HE SWUNG THE BEAUFORT ROUND AND HEADED BACK TOWARDS THE E-BOAT. FATE HAD PLANTED THE LONGED-FOR CHANCE NEATLY IN HIS LAP.
THIS IS FOR YOU, EDGAR!

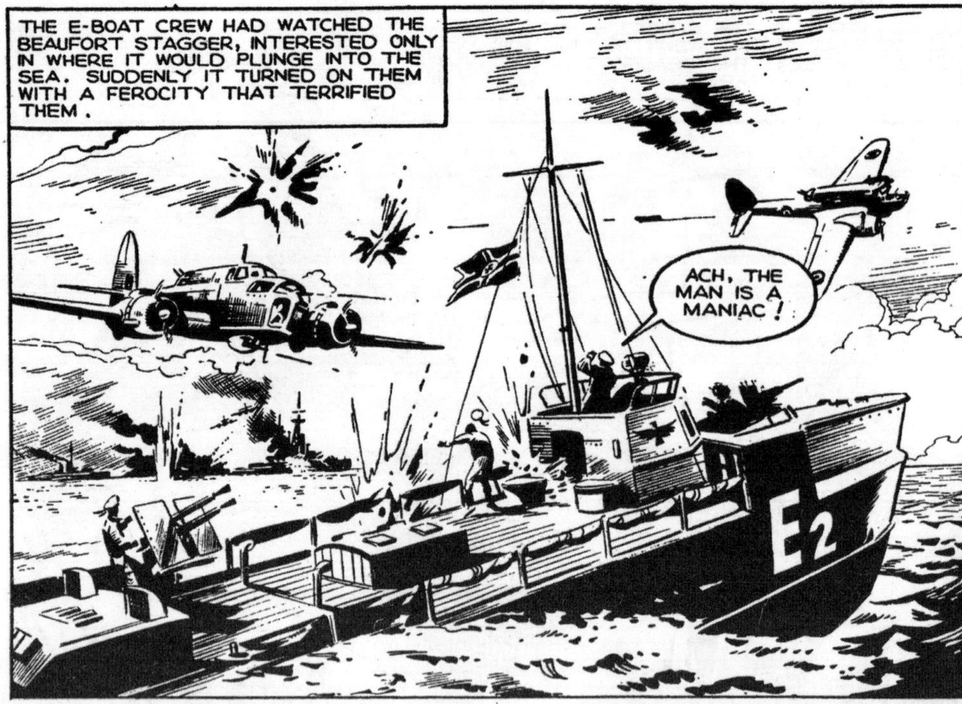
THE E-BOAT CREW HAD WATCHED THE BEAUFORT STAGGER, INTERESTED ONLY IN WHERE IT WOULD PLUNGE INTO THE SEA. SUDDENLY IT TURNED ON THEM WITH A FEROCITY THAT TERRIFIED THEM.
ACH, THE MAN IS A MANIAC!
E2

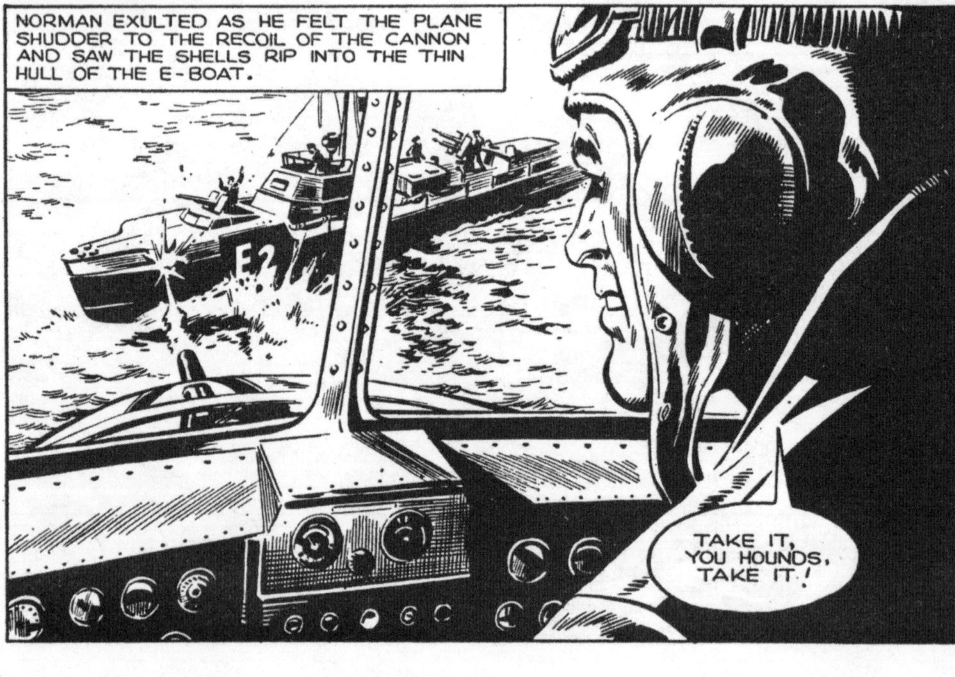
NORMAN EXULTED AS HE FELT THE PLANE SHUDDER TO THE RECOIL OF THE CANNON AND SAW THE SHELLS RIP INTO THE THIN HULL OF THE E-BOAT.
E2
TAKE IT, YOU HOUNDS, TAKE IT!

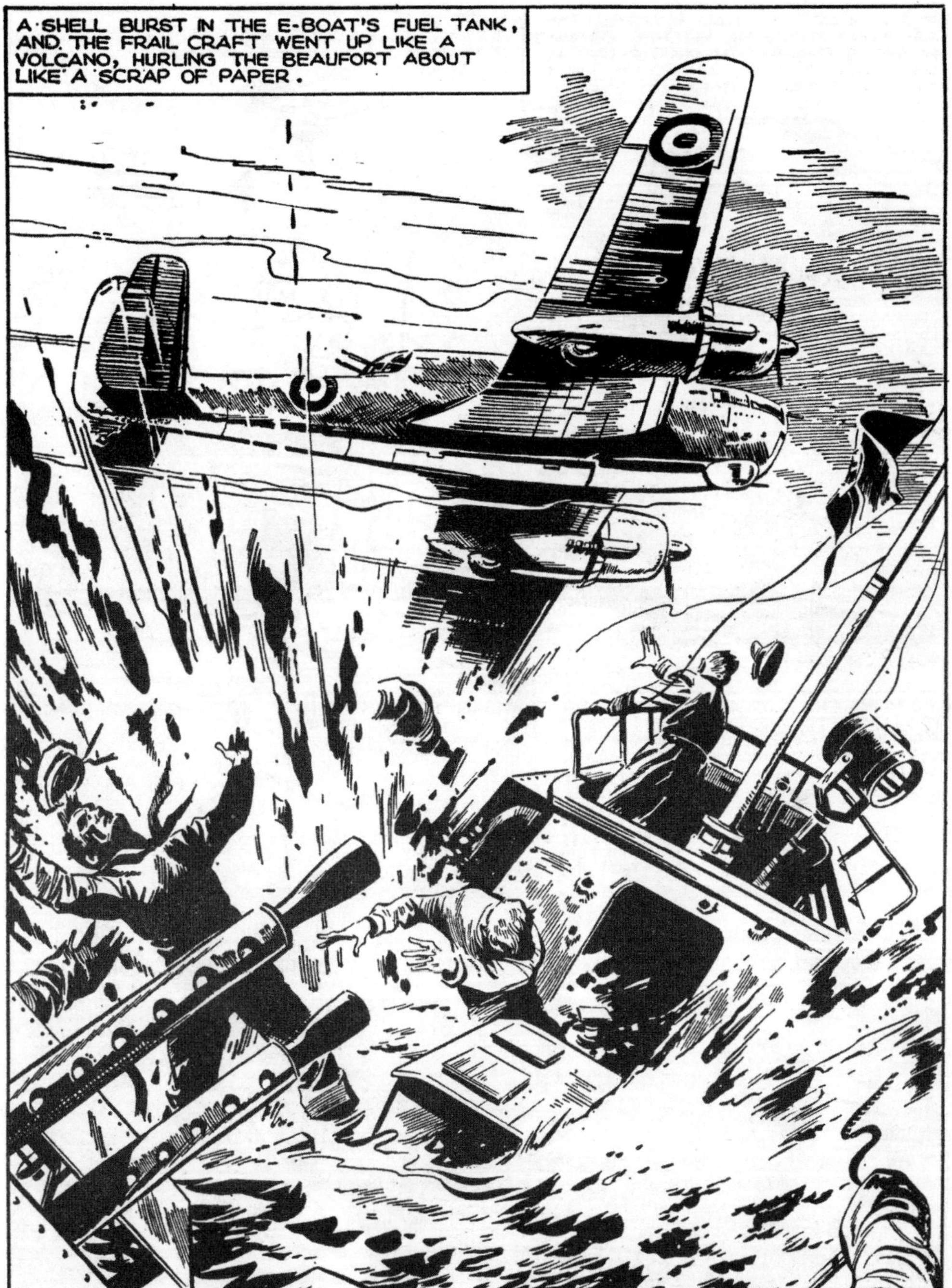
A SHELL BURST IN THE E-BOAT'S FUEL TANK, AND THE FRAIL CRAFT WENT UP LIKE A VOLCANO, HURLING THE BEAUFORT ABOUT LIKE A SCRAP OF PAPER.

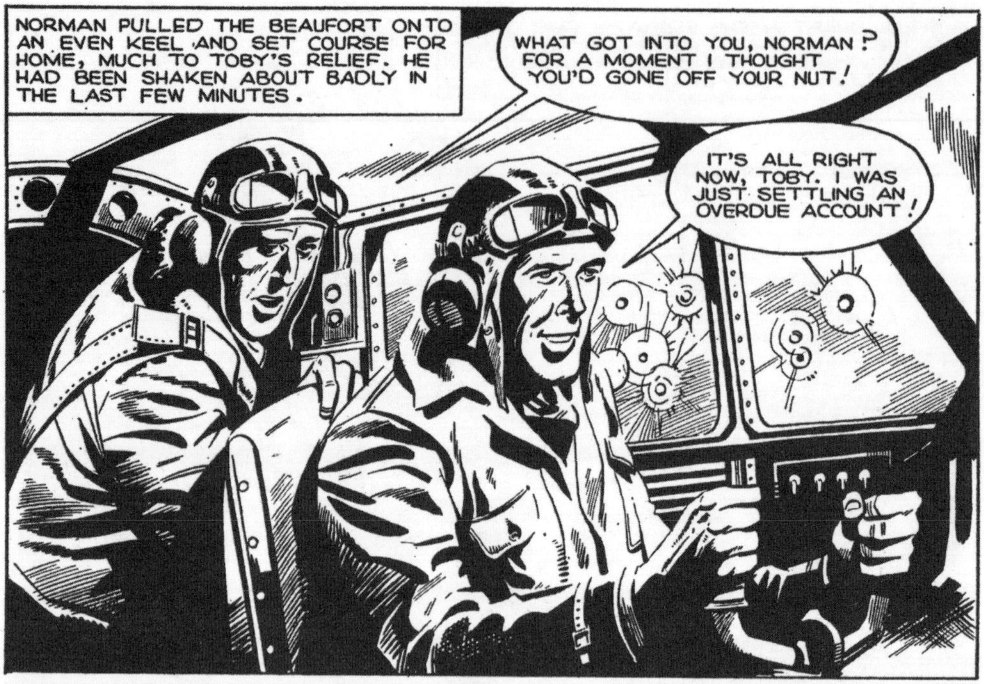
NORMAN PULLED THE BEAUFORT ONTO AN EVEN KEEL AND SET COURSE FOR HOME, MUCH TO TOBY'S RELIEF. HE HAD BEEN SHAKEN ABOUT BADLY IN THE LAST FEW MINUTES.
WHAT GOT INTO YOU, NORMAN? FOR A MOMENT I THOUGHT YOU'D GONE OFF YOUR NUT!
IT'S ALL RIGHT NOW, TOBY. I WAS JUST SETTLING AN OVERDUE ACCOUNT!

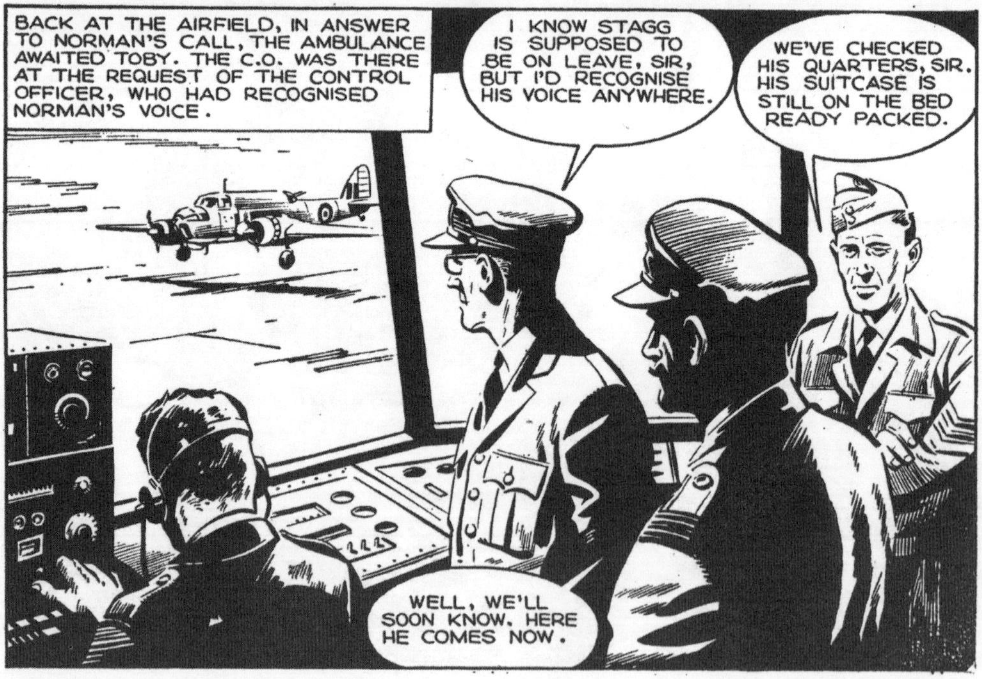
BACK AT THE AIRFIELD, IN ANSWER TO NORMAN'S CALL, THE AMBULANCE AWAITED TOBY. THE C.O. WAS THERE AT THE REQUEST OF THE CONTROL OFFICER, WHO HAD RECOGNISED NORMAN'S VOICE.
I KNOW STAGG IS SUPPOSED TO BE ON LEAVE, SIR, BUT I'D RECOGNISE HIS VOICE ANYWHERE.
WE'VE CHECKED HIS QUARTERS, SIR. HIS SUITCASE IS STILL ON THE BED READY PACKED.
WELL, WE'LL SOON KNOW. HERE HE COMES NOW.

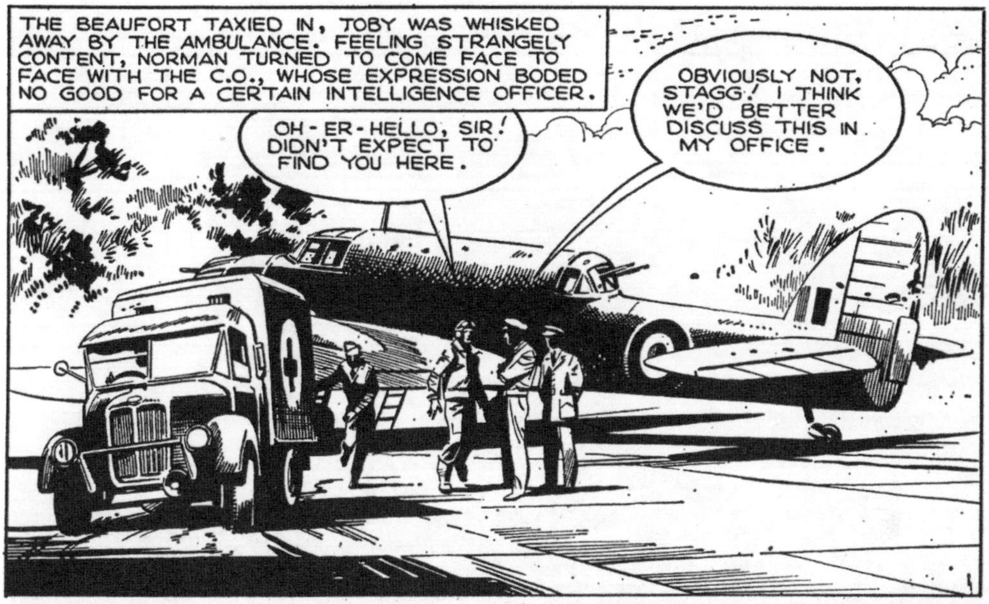
THE BEAUFORT TAXIED IN, TOBY WAS WHISKED AWAY BY THE AMBULANCE. FEELING STRANGELY CONTENT, NORMAN TURNED TO COME FACE TO FACE WITH THE C.O., WHOSE EXPRESSION BODED NO GOOD FOR A CERTAIN INTELLIGENCE OFFICER.
OH-ER-HELLO, SIR! DIDN'T EXPECT TO FIND YOU HERE.
OBVIOUSLY NOT, STAGG! I THINK WE'D BETTER DISCUSS THIS IN MY OFFICE.

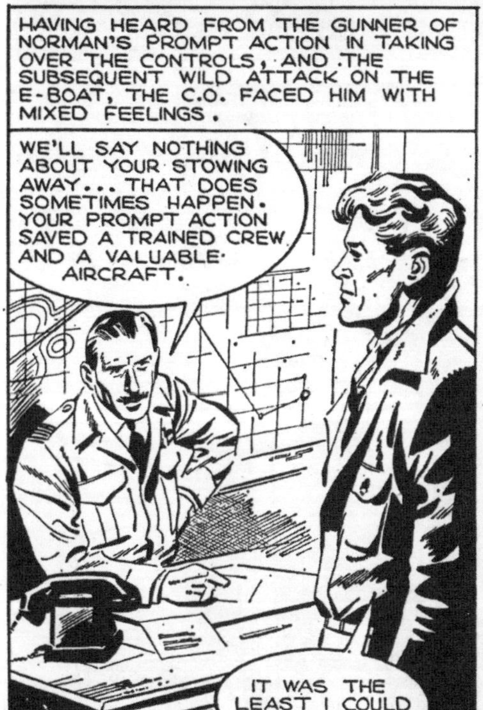
HAVING HEARD FROM THE GUNNER OF NORMAN'S PROMPT ACTION IN TAKING OVER THE CONTROLS, AND THE SUBSEQUENT WILD ATTACK ON THE E-BOAT, THE C.O. FACED HIM WITH MIXED FEELINGS.
WE'LL SAY NOTHING ABOUT YOUR STOWING AWAY... THAT DOES SOMETIMES HAPPEN. YOUR PROMPT ACTION SAVED A TRAINED CREW AND A VALUABLE AIRCRAFT.
IT WAS THE LEAST I COULD DO, SIR.

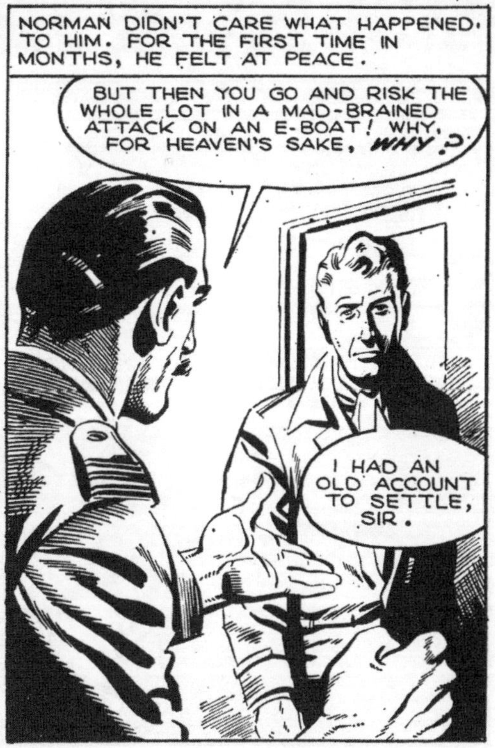
NORMAN DIDN'T CARE WHAT HAPPENED TO HIM. FOR THE FIRST TIME IN MONTHS, HE FELT AT PEACE.
BUT THEN YOU GO AND RISK THE WHOLE LOT IN A MAD-BRAINED ATTACK ON AN E-BOAT! WHY, FOR HEAVEN'S SAKE, WHY?
I HAD AN OLD ACCOUNT TO SETTLE, SIR.

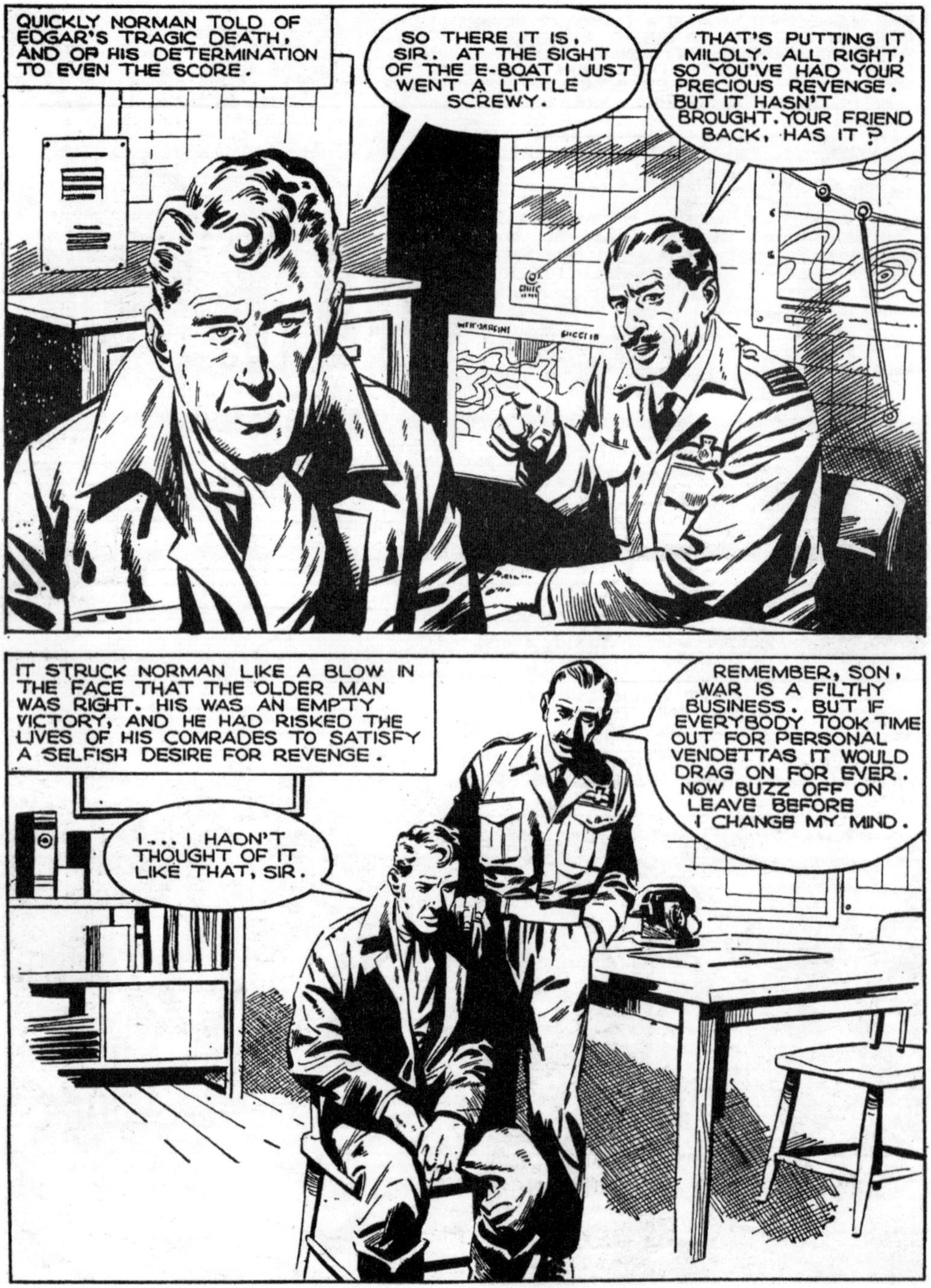
QUICKLY NORMAN TOLD OF EDGAR'S TRAGIC DEATH, AND OF HIS DETERMINATION TO EVEN THE SCORE.
SO THERE IT IS, SIR. AT THE SIGHT OF THE E-BOAT I JUST WENT A LITTLE SCREWY.
THAT'S PUTTING IT MILDLY. ALL RIGHT, SO YOU'VE HAD YOUR PRECIOUS REVENGE. BUT IT HASN'T BROUGHT YOUR FRIEND BACK, HAS IT?
IT STRUCK NORMAN LIKE A BLOW IN THE FACE THAT THE OLDER MAN WAS RIGHT. HIS WAS AN EMPTY VICTORY, AND HE HAD RISKED THE LIVES OF HIS COMRADES TO SATISFY A SELFISH DESIRE FOR REVENGE.
REMEMBER, SON, WAR IS A FILTHY BUSINESS. BUT IF EVERYBODY TOOK TIME OUT FOR PERSONAL VENDETTAS IT WOULD DRAG ON FOR EVER. NOW BUZZ OFF ON LEAVE BEFORE I CHANGE MY MIND.
I... I HADN'T THOUGHT OF IT LIKE THAT, SIR.

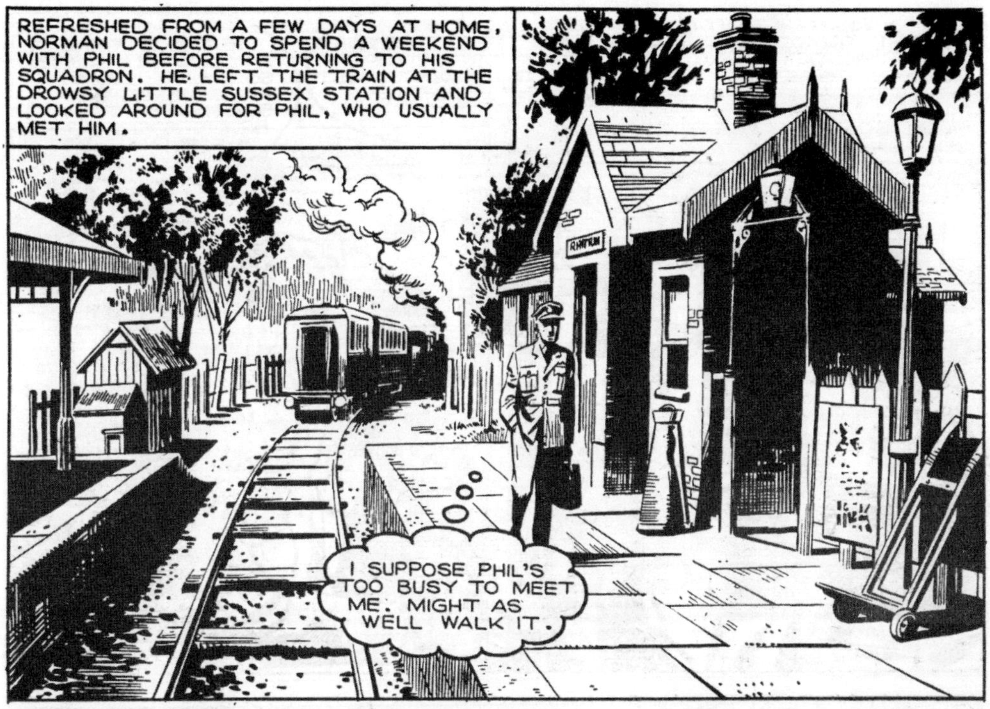
REFRESHED FROM A FEW DAYS AT HOME, NORMAN DECIDED TO SPEND A WEEKEND WITH PHIL BEFORE RETURNING TO HIS SQUADRON. HE LEFT THE TRAIN AT THE DROWSY LITTLE SUSSEX STATION AND LOOKED AROUND FOR PHIL, WHO USUALLY MET HIM.
I SUPPOSE PHIL'S TOO BUSY TO MEET ME. MIGHT AS WELL WALK IT.

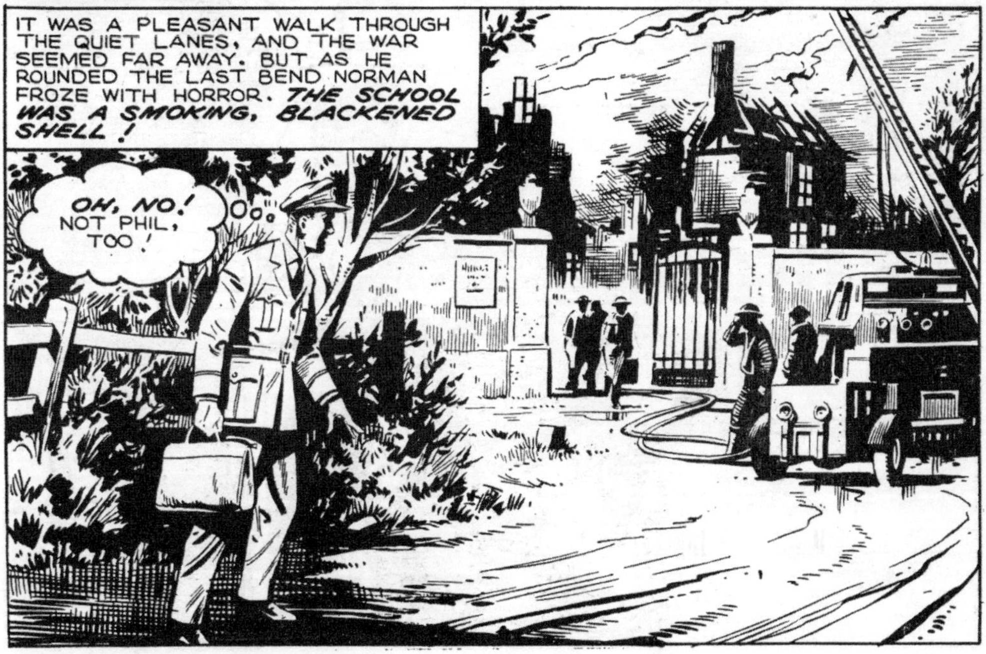
IT WAS A PLEASANT WALK THROUGH THE QUIET LANES, AND THE WAR SEEMED FAR AWAY. BUT AS HE ROUNDED THE LAST BEND NORMAN FROZE WITH HORROR. *THE SCHOOL WAS A SMOKING, BLACKENED SHELL!*
OH, NO! NOT PHIL, TOO!

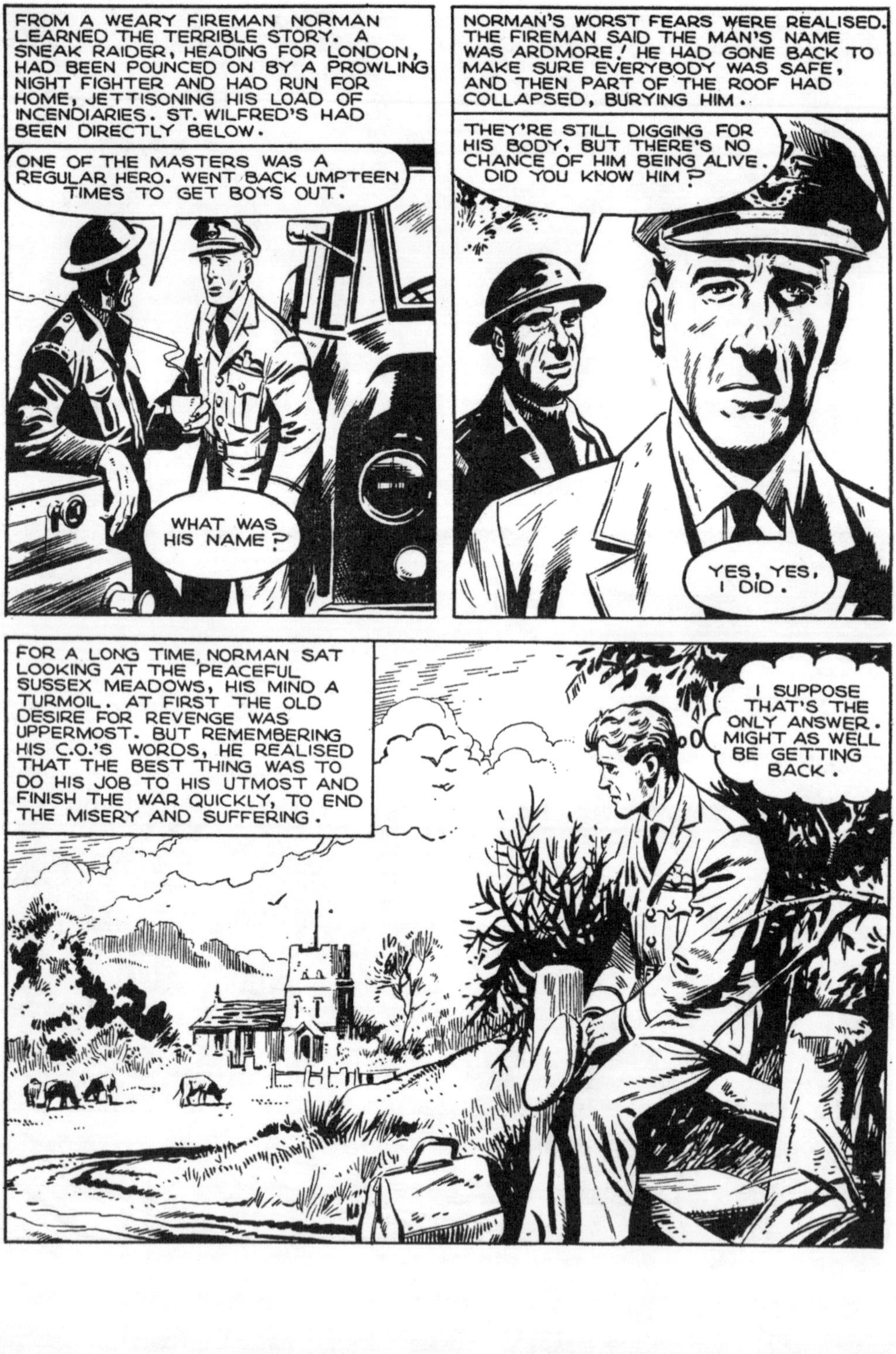
FROM A WEARY FIREMAN NORMAN LEARNED THE TERRIBLE STORY. A SNEAK RAIDER, HEADING FOR LONDON, HAD BEEN POUNCED ON BY A PROWLING NIGHT FIGHTER AND HAD RUN FOR HOME, JETTISONING HIS LOAD OF INCENDIARIES. ST. WILFRED'S HAD BEEN DIRECTLY BELOW.
ONE OF THE MASTERS WAS A REGULAR HERO. WENT BACK UMPTEEN TIMES TO GET BOYS OUT.
WHAT WAS HIS NAME?
NORMAN'S WORST FEARS WERE REALISED. THE FIREMAN SAID THE MAN'S NAME WAS ARDMORE! HE HAD GONE BACK TO MAKE SURE EVERYBODY WAS SAFE, AND THEN PART OF THE ROOF HAD COLLAPSED, BURYING HIM.
THEY'RE STILL DIGGING FOR HIS BODY, BUT THERE'S NO CHANCE OF HIM BEING ALIVE. DID YOU KNOW HIM?
YES, YES, I DID.
FOR A LONG TIME, NORMAN SAT LOOKING AT THE PEACEFUL SUSSEX MEADOWS, HIS MIND A TURMOIL. AT FIRST THE OLD DESIRE FOR REVENGE WAS UPPERMOST. BUT REMEMBERING HIS C.O.'S WORDS, HE REALISED THAT THE BEST THING WAS TO DO HIS JOB TO HIS UTMOST AND FINISH THE WAR QUICKLY, TO END THE MISERY AND SUFFERING.
I SUPPOSE THAT'S THE ONLY ANSWER. MIGHT AS WELL BE GETTING BACK.

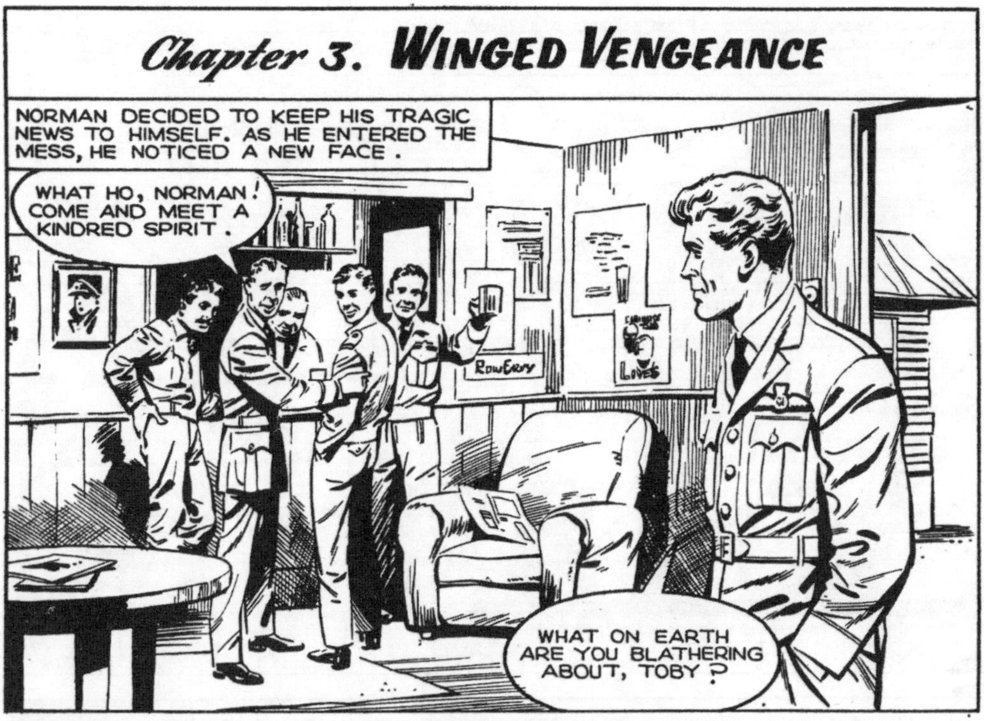
Chapter 3. WINGED VENGEANCE
NORMAN DECIDED TO KEEP HIS TRAGIC NEWS TO HIMSELF. AS HE ENTERED THE MESS, HE NOTICED A NEW FACE.
WHAT HO, NORMAN! COME AND MEET A KINDRED SPIRIT.
WHAT ON EARTH ARE YOU BLATHERING ABOUT, TOBY?

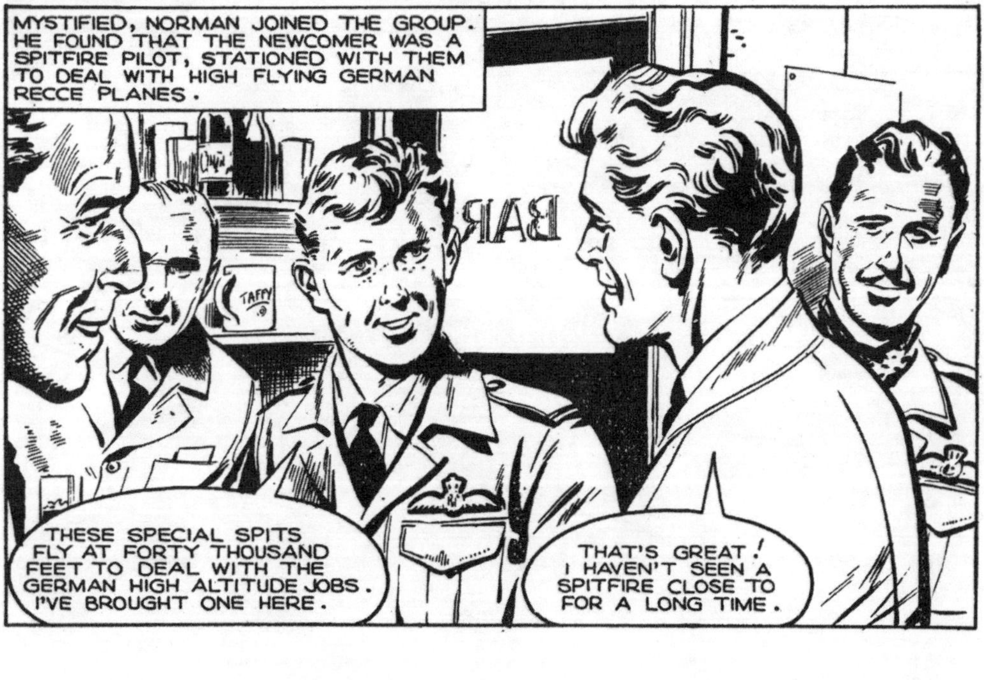
MYSTIFIED, NORMAN JOINED THE GROUP. HE FOUND THAT THE NEWCOMER WAS A SPITFIRE PILOT, STATIONED WITH THEM TO DEAL WITH HIGH FLYING GERMAN RECCE PLANES.
THESE SPECIAL SPITS FLY AT FORTY THOUSAND FEET TO DEAL WITH THE GERMAN HIGH ALTITUDE JOBS. I'VE BROUGHT ONE HERE.
THAT'S GREAT! I HAVEN'T SEEN A SPITFIRE CLOSE TO FOR A LONG TIME.

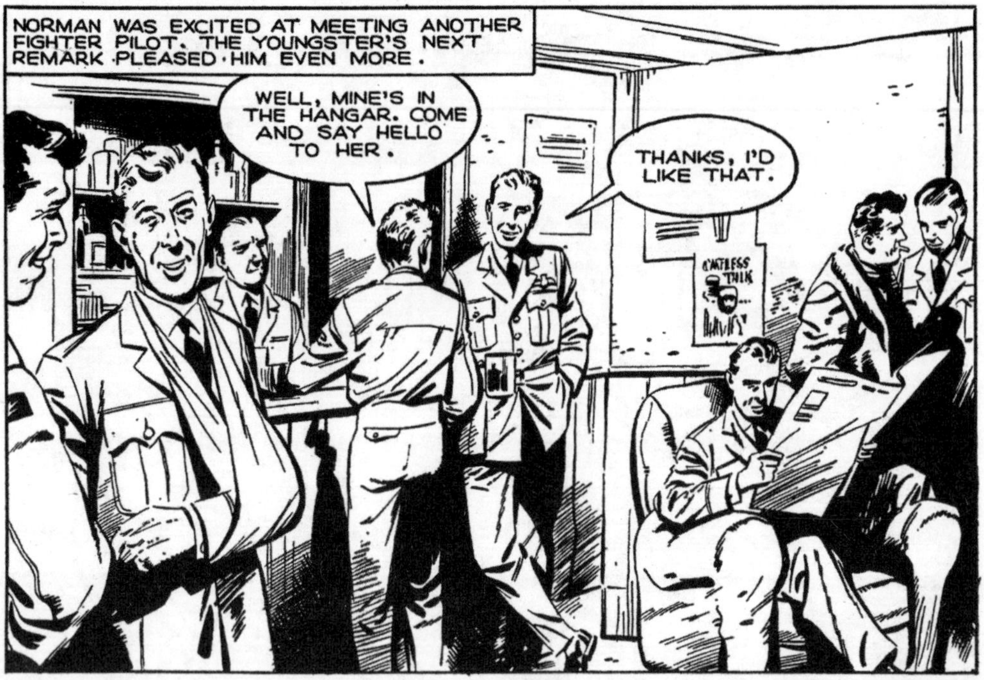
NORMAN WAS EXCITED AT MEETING ANOTHER FIGHTER PILOT. THE YOUNGSTER'S NEXT REMARK PLEASED HIM EVEN MORE.
WELL, MINE'S IN THE HANGAR. COME AND SAY HELLO TO HER.
THANKS, I'D LIKE THAT.

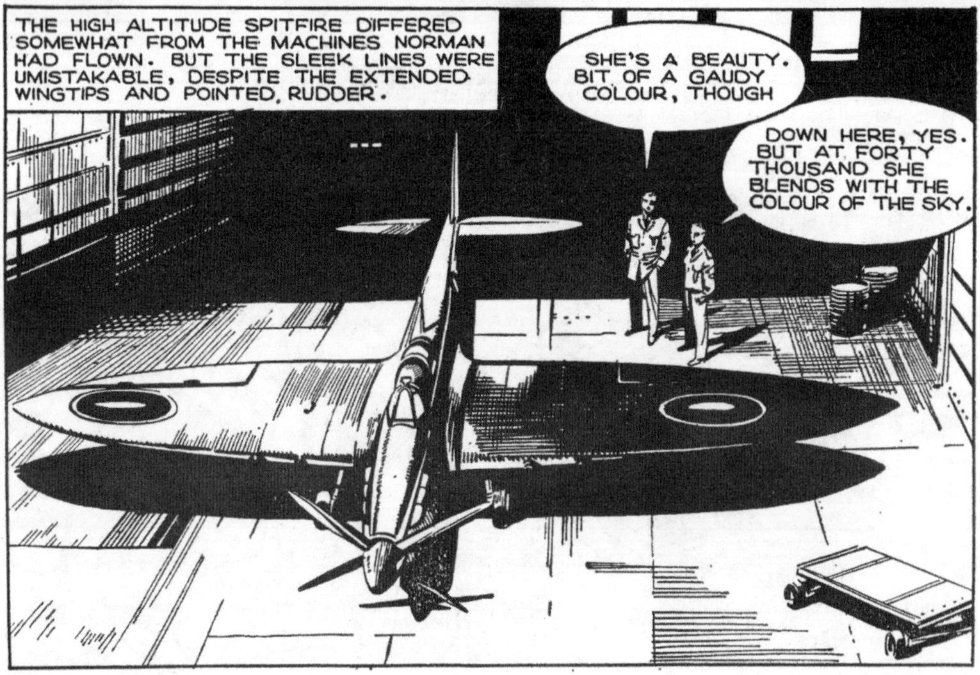
THE HIGH ALTITUDE SPITFIRE DIFFERED SOMEWHAT FROM THE MACHINES NORMAN HAD FLOWN. BUT THE SLEEK LINES WERE UMISTAKABLE, DESPITE THE EXTENDED WINGTIPS AND POINTED RUDDER.
SHE'S A BEAUTY. BIT OF A GAUDY COLOUR, THOUGH
DOWN HERE, YES. BUT AT FORTY THOUSAND SHE BLENDS WITH THE COLOUR OF THE SKY.

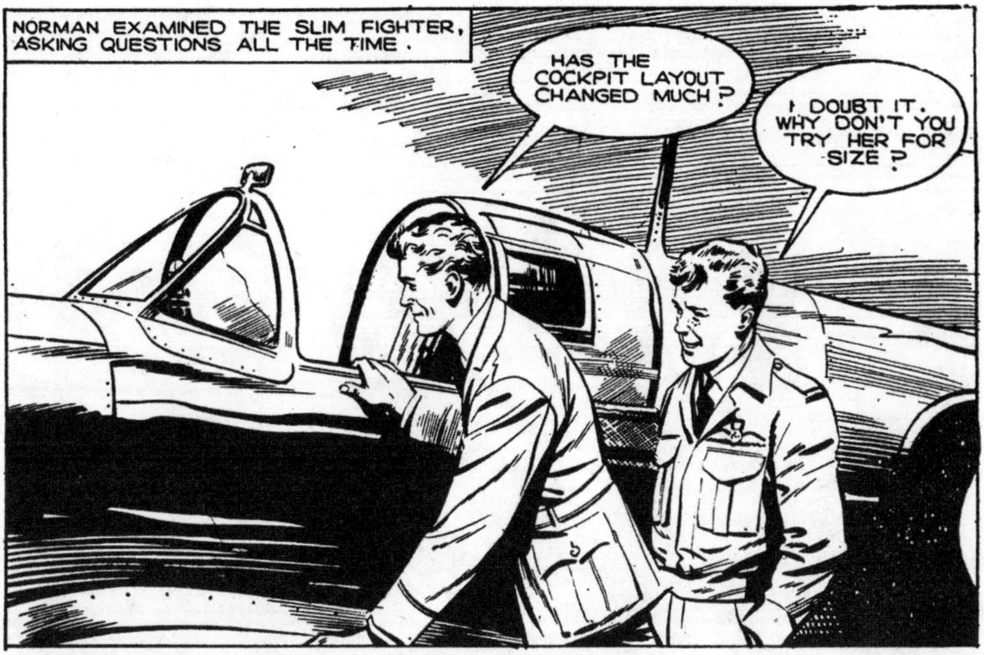
NORMAN EXAMINED THE SLIM FIGHTER, ASKING QUESTIONS ALL THE TIME.
HAS THE COCKPIT LAYOUT CHANGED MUCH?
I DOUBT IT. WHY DON'T YOU TRY HER FOR SIZE?

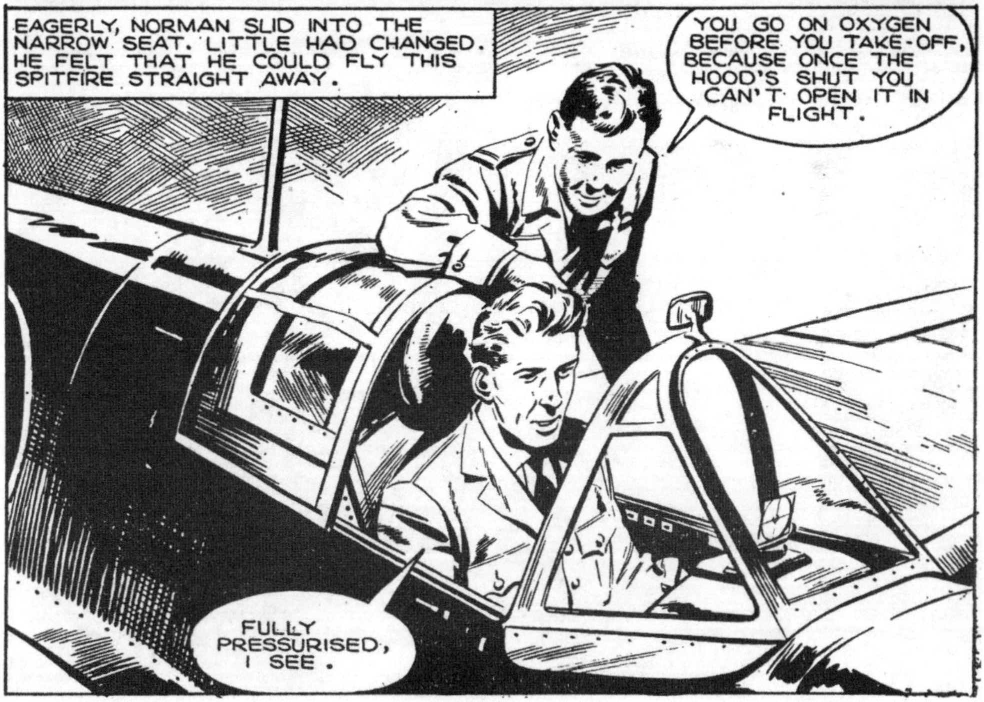
EAGERLY, NORMAN SLID INTO THE NARROW SEAT. LITTLE HAD CHANGED. HE FELT THAT HE COULD FLY THIS SPITFIRE STRAIGHT AWAY.
YOU GO ON OXYGEN BEFORE YOU TAKE-OFF, BECAUSE ONCE THE HOOD'S SHUT YOU CAN'T OPEN IT IN FLIGHT.
FULLY PRESSURISED, I SEE.

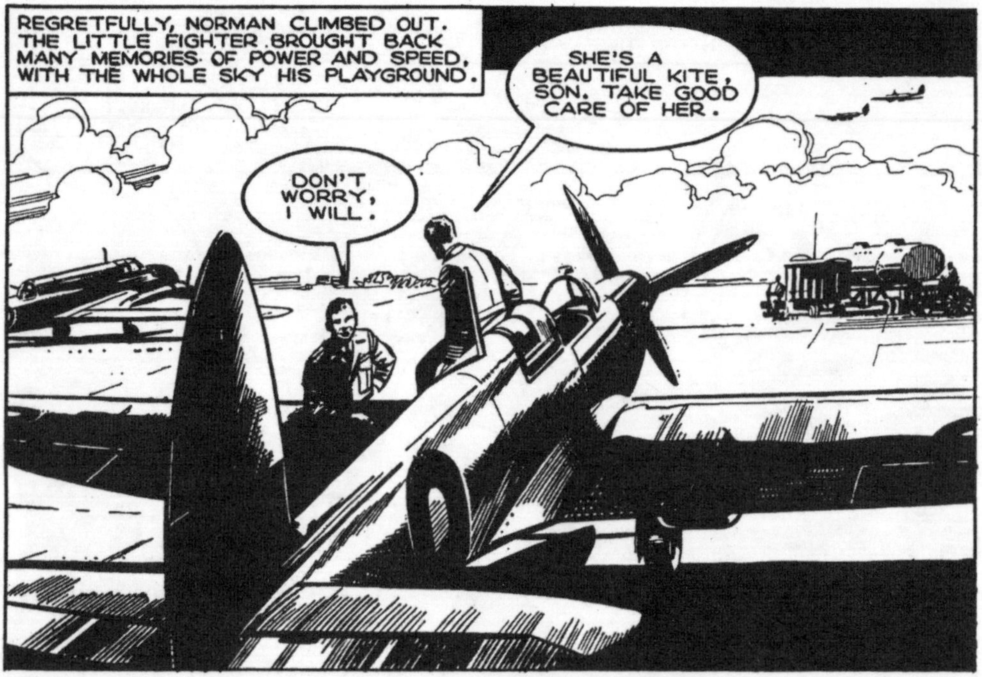
REGRETFULLY, NORMAN CLIMBED OUT. THE LITTLE FIGHTER BROUGHT BACK MANY MEMORIES OF POWER AND SPEED, WITH THE WHOLE SKY HIS PLAYGROUND.
SHE'S A BEAUTIFUL KITE, SON. TAKE GOOD CARE OF HER.
DON'T WORRY, I WILL.

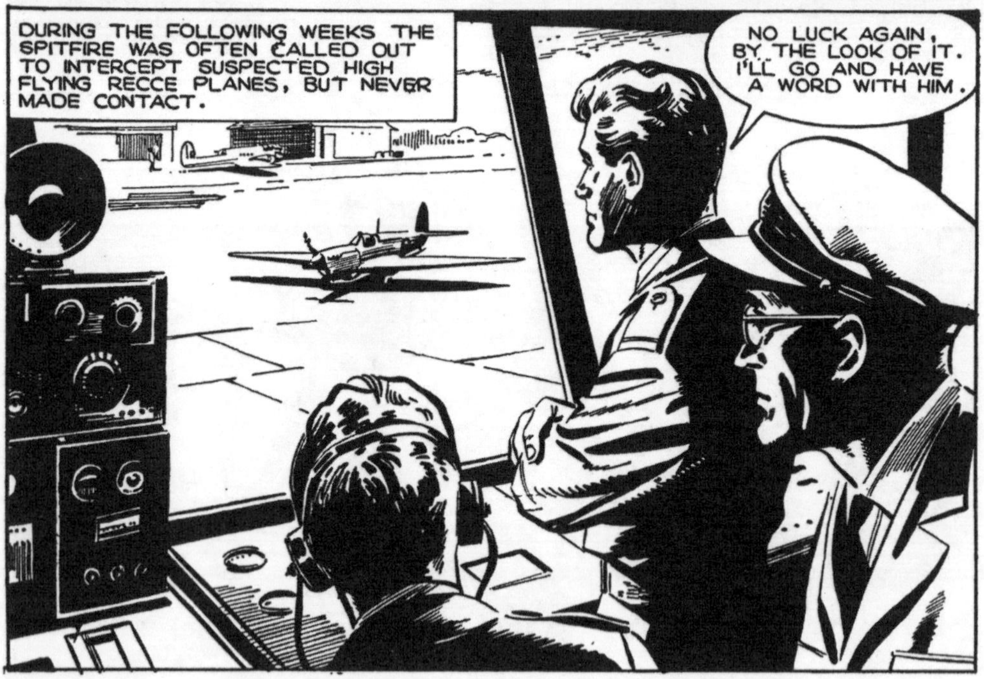
DURING THE FOLLOWING WEEKS THE SPITFIRE WAS OFTEN CALLED OUT TO INTERCEPT SUSPECTED HIGH FLYING RECCE PLANES, BUT NEVER MADE CONTACT.
NO LUCK AGAIN, BY THE LOOK OF IT. I'LL GO AND HAVE A WORD WITH HIM.

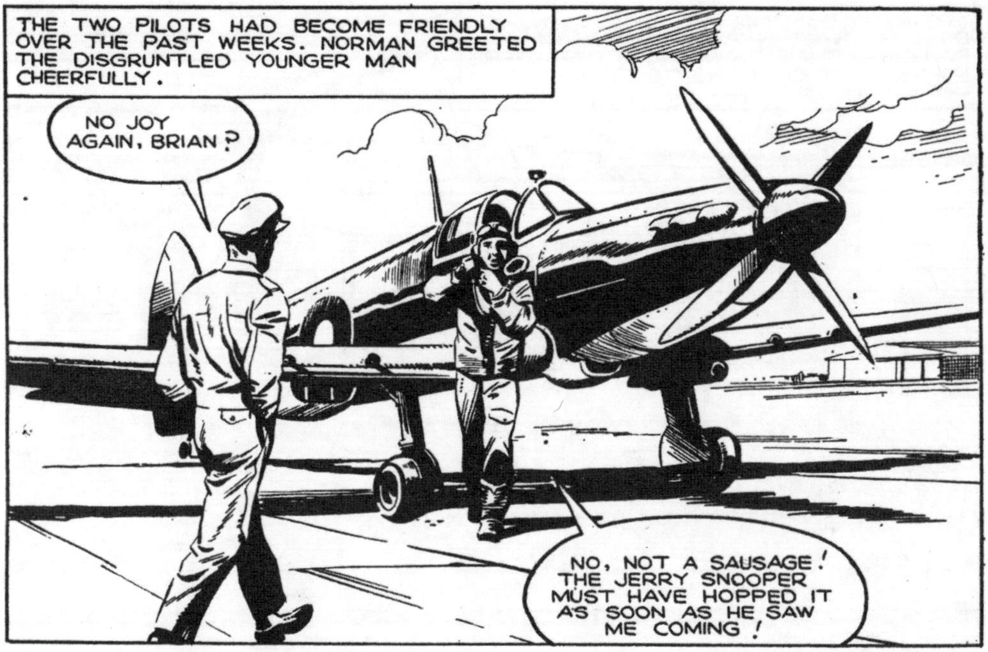
THE TWO PILOTS HAD BECOME FRIENDLY OVER THE PAST WEEKS. NORMAN GREETED THE DISGRUNTLED YOUNGER MAN CHEERFULLY.
NO JOY AGAIN, BRIAN?
NO, NOT A SAUSAGE! THE JERRY SNOOPER MUST HAVE HOPPED IT AS SOON AS HE SAW ME COMING!

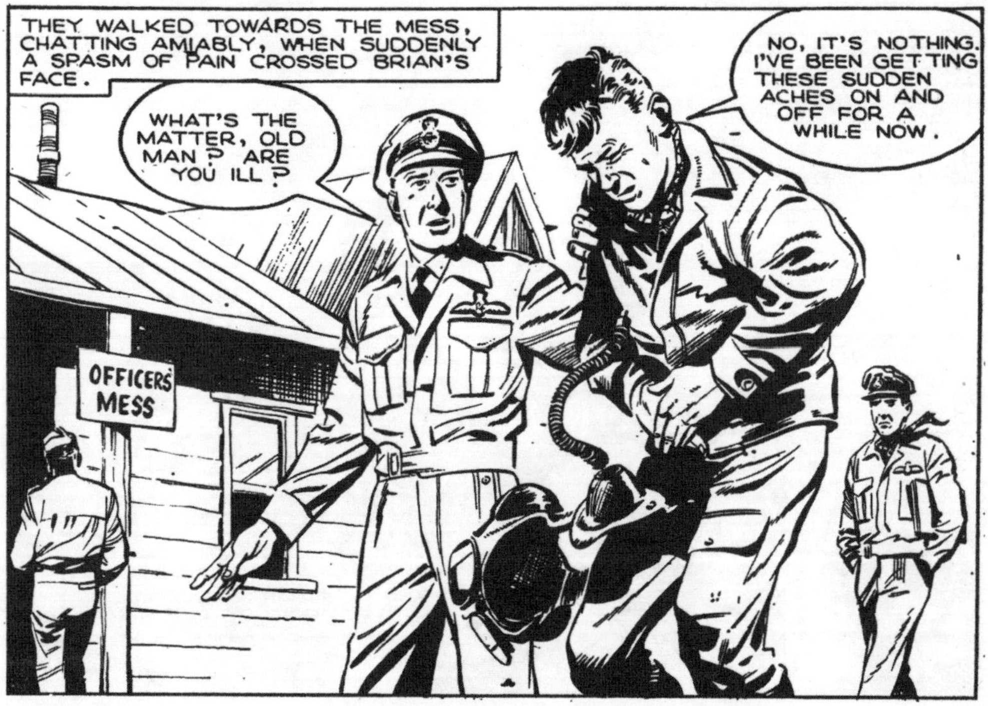
THEY WALKED TOWARDS THE MESS, CHATTING AMIABLY, WHEN SUDDENLY A SPASM OF PAIN CROSSED BRIAN'S FACE.
WHAT'S THE MATTER, OLD MAN? ARE YOU ILL?
NO, IT'S NOTHING. I'VE BEEN GETTING THESE SUDDEN ACHES ON AND OFF FOR A WHILE NOW.
OFFICERS MESS

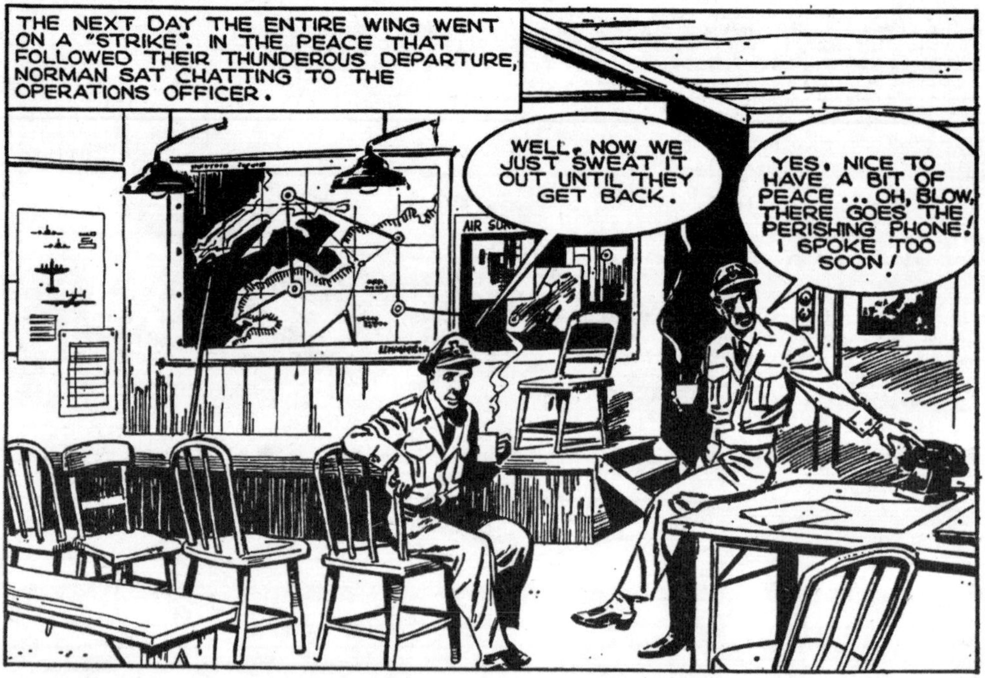
THE NEXT DAY THE ENTIRE WING WENT ON A "STRIKE". IN THE PEACE THAT FOLLOWED THEIR THUNDEROUS DEPARTURE, NORMAN SAT CHATTING TO THE OPERATIONS OFFICER.
WELL, NOW WE JUST SWEAT IT OUT UNTIL THEY GET BACK.
YES. NICE TO HAVE A BIT OF PEACE ... OH, BLOW, THERE GOES THE PERISHING PHONE! I SPOKE TOO SOON!

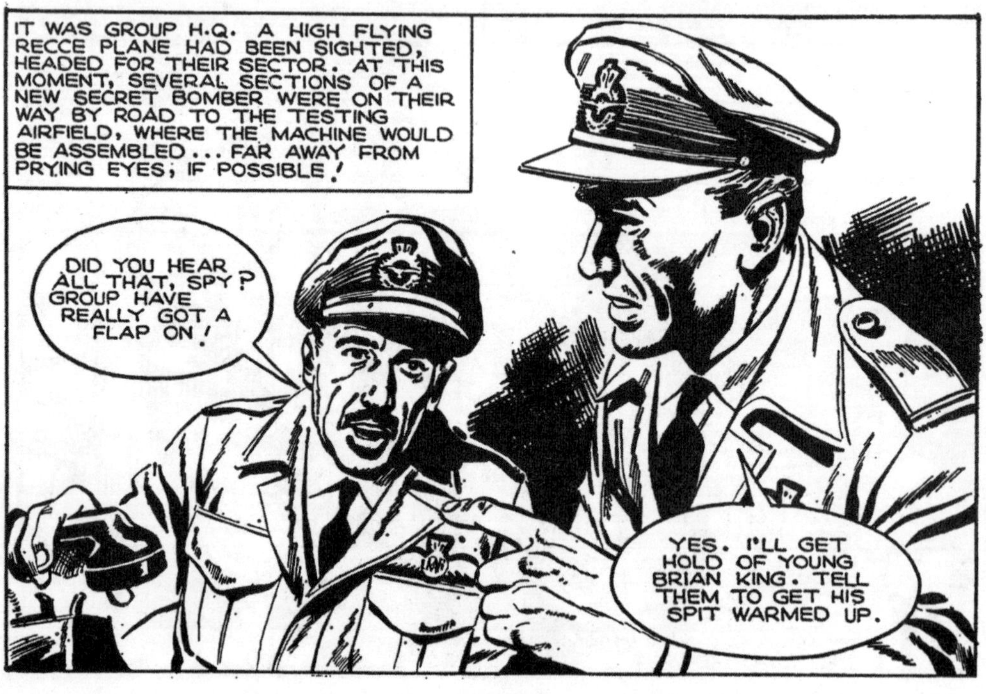
IT WAS GROUP H.Q. A HIGH FLYING RECCE PLANE HAD BEEN SIGHTED, HEADED FOR THEIR SECTOR. AT THIS MOMENT, SEVERAL SECTIONS OF A NEW SECRET BOMBER WERE ON THEIR WAY BY ROAD TO THE TESTING AIRFIELD, WHERE THE MACHINE WOULD BE ASSEMBLED ... FAR AWAY FROM PRYING EYES, IF POSSIBLE!
DID YOU HEAR ALL THAT, SPY? GROUP HAVE REALLY GOT A FLAP ON!
YES. I'LL GET HOLD OF YOUNG BRIAN KING. TELL THEM TO GET HIS SPIT WARMED UP.

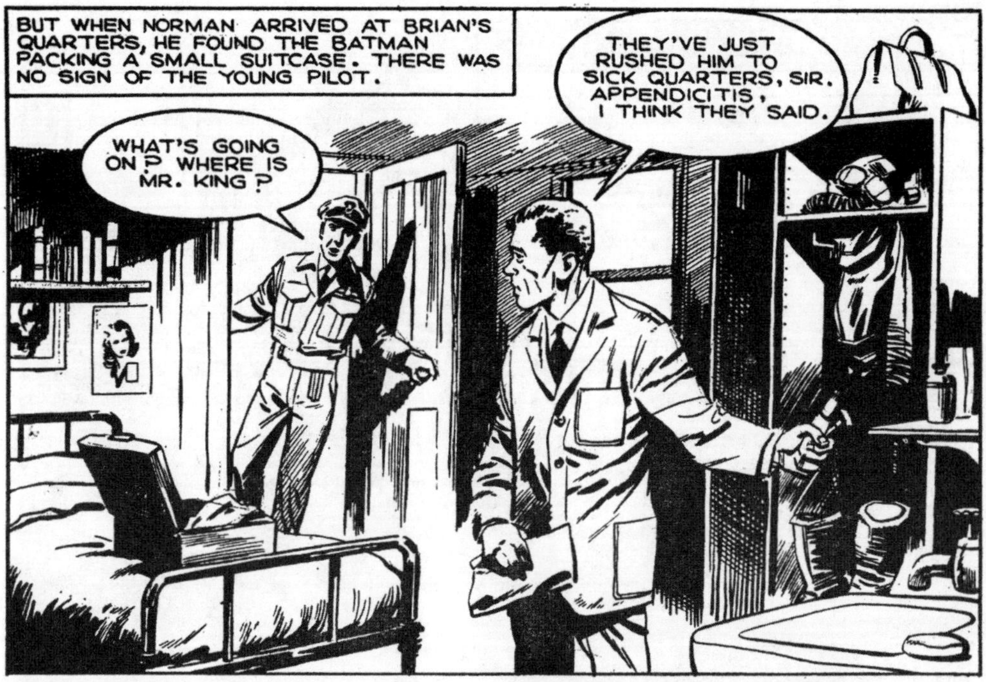
BUT WHEN NORMAN ARRIVED AT BRIAN'S QUARTERS, HE FOUND THE BATMAN PACKING A SMALL SUITCASE. THERE WAS NO SIGN OF THE YOUNG PILOT.
WHAT'S GOING ON? WHERE IS MR. KING?
THEY'VE JUST RUSHED HIM TO SICK QUARTERS, SIR. APPENDICITIS, I THINK THEY SAID.

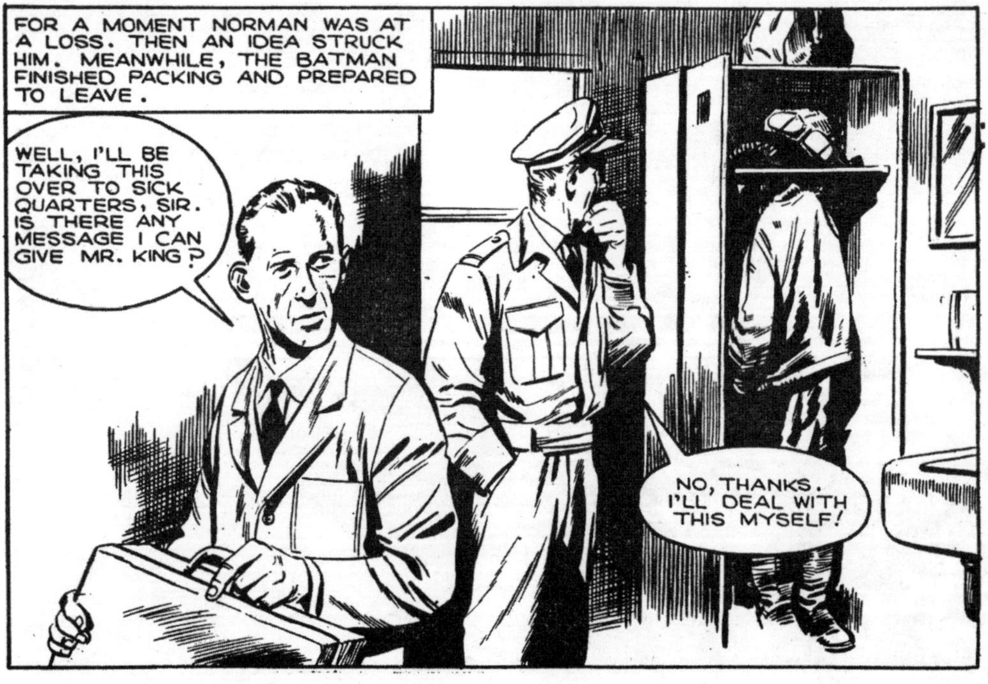
FOR A MOMENT NORMAN WAS AT A LOSS. THEN AN IDEA STRUCK HIM. MEANWHILE, THE BATMAN FINISHED PACKING AND PREPARED TO LEAVE.
WELL, I'LL BE TAKING THIS OVER TO SICK QUARTERS, SIR. IS THERE ANY MESSAGE I CAN GIVE MR. KING?
NO, THANKS. I'LL DEAL WITH THIS MYSELF!

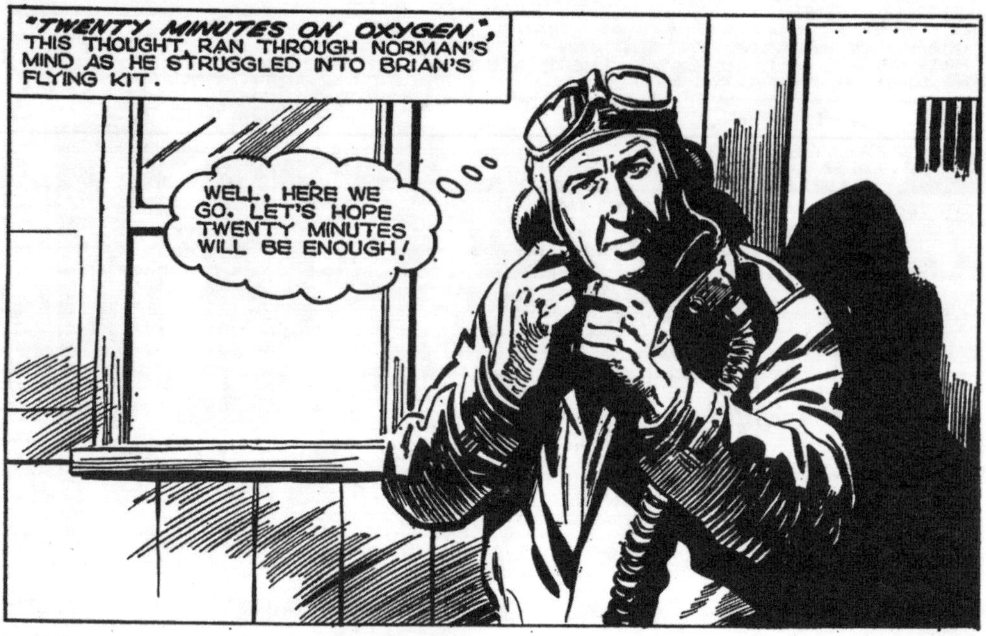
"TWENTY MINUTES ON OXYGEN", THIS THOUGHT RAN THROUGH NORMAN'S MIND AS HE STRUGGLED INTO BRIAN'S FLYING KIT.
WELL, HERE WE GO. LET'S HOPE TWENTY MINUTES WILL BE ENOUGH!

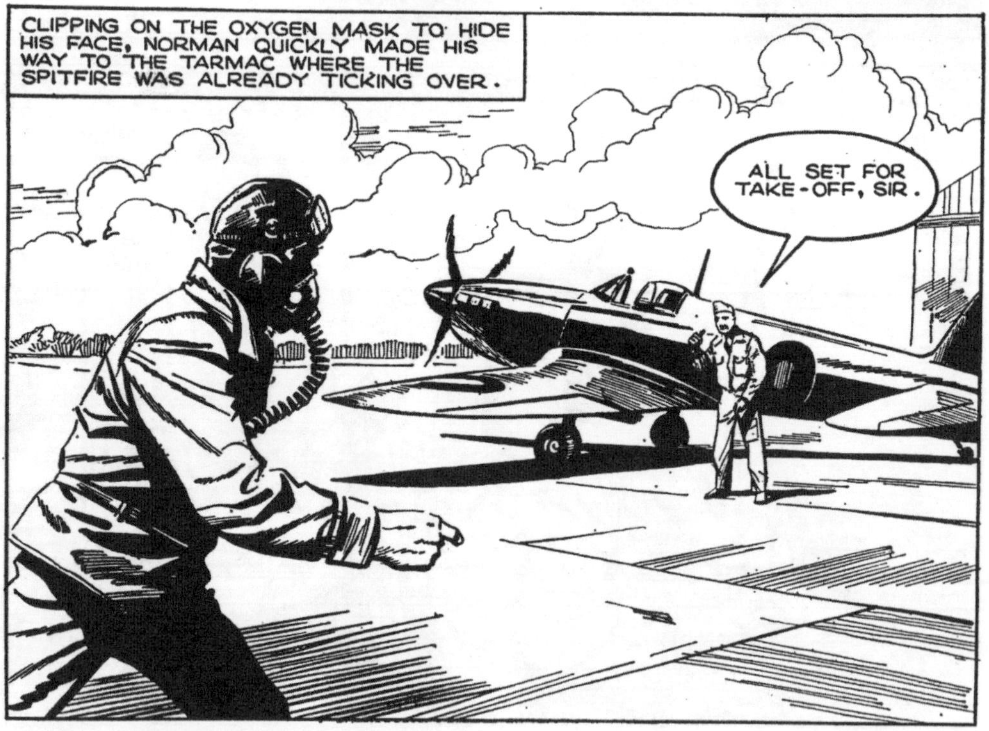
CLIPPING ON THE OXYGEN MASK TO HIDE HIS FACE, NORMAN QUICKLY MADE HIS WAY TO THE TARMAC WHERE THE SPITFIRE WAS ALREADY TICKING OVER.
ALL SET FOR TAKE-OFF, SIR.

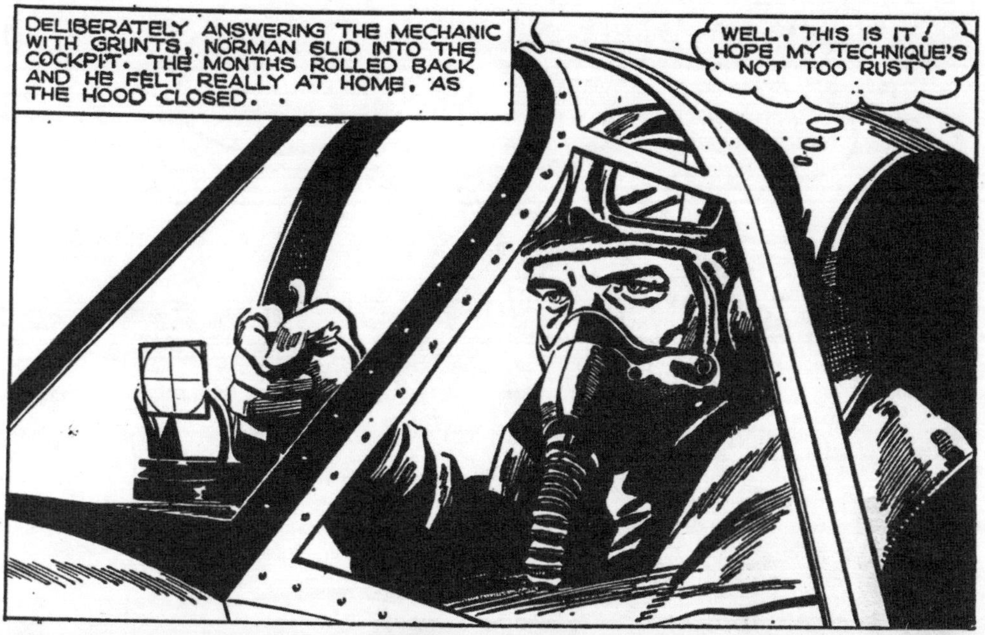
DELIBERATELY ANSWERING THE MECHANIC WITH GRUNTS, NORMAN SLID INTO THE COCKPIT. THE MONTHS ROLLED BACK AND HE FELT REALLY AT HOME, AS THE HOOD CLOSED.
WELL, THIS IS IT! HOPE MY TECHNIQUE'S NOT TOO RUSTY.

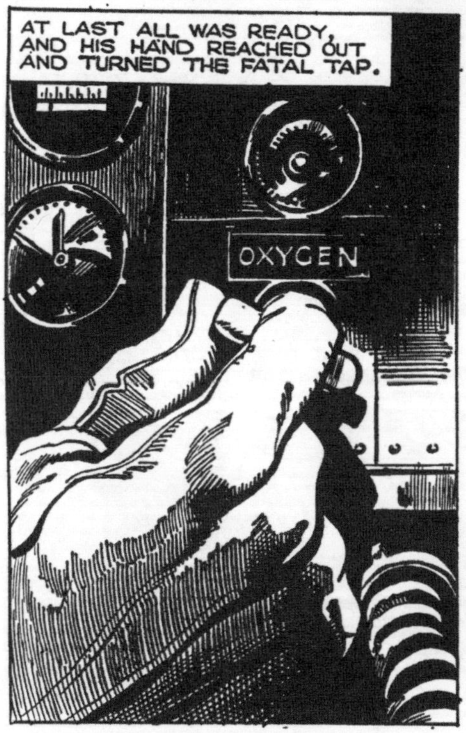
AT LAST ALL WAS READY, AND HIS HAND REACHED OUT AND TURNED THE FATAL TAP.
OXYGEN

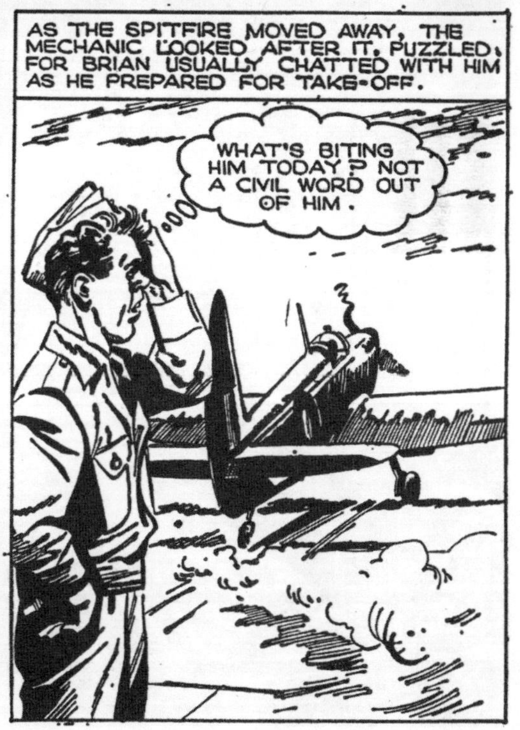
AS THE SPITFIRE MOVED AWAY, THE MECHANIC LOOKED AFTER IT, PUZZLED, FOR BRIAN USUALLY CHATTED WITH HIM AS HE PREPARED FOR TAKE-OFF.
WHAT'S BITING HIM TODAY? NOT A CIVIL WORD OUT OF HIM.

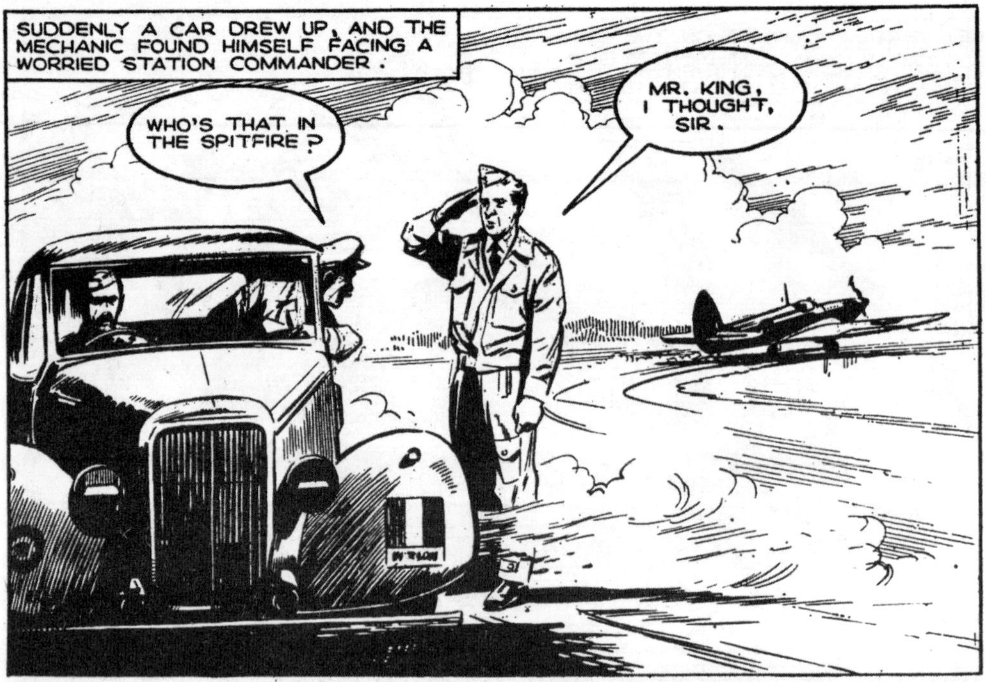
SUDDENLY A CAR DREW UP, AND THE MECHANIC FOUND HIMSELF FACING A WORRIED STATION COMMANDER.
WHO'S THAT IN THE SPITFIRE?
MR. KING, I THOUGHT, SIR.

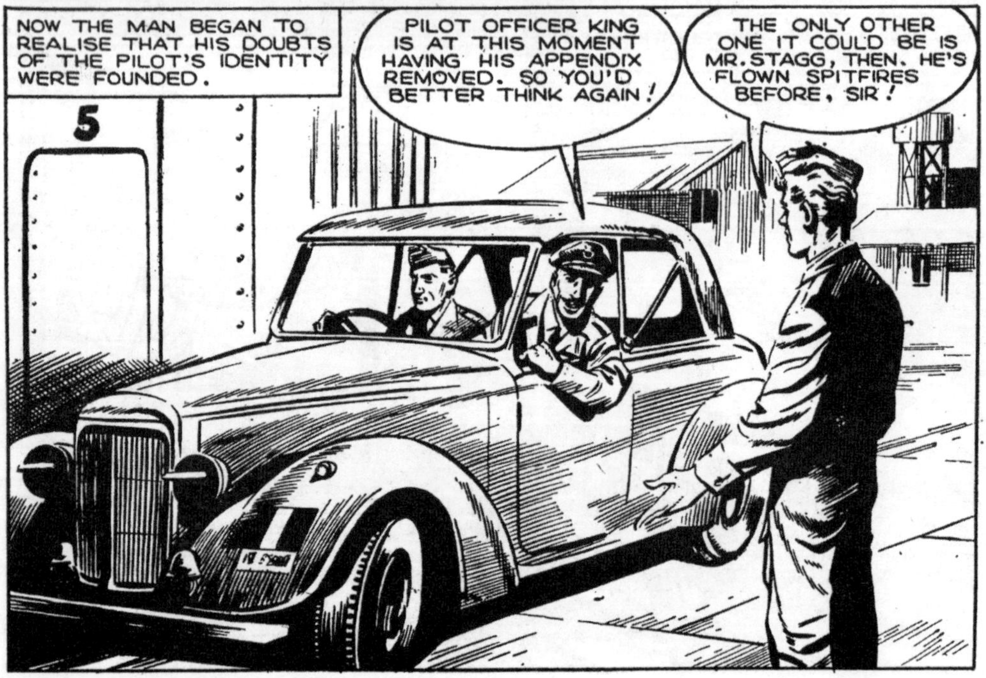
NOW THE MAN BEGAN TO REALISE THAT HIS DOUBTS OF THE PILOT'S IDENTITY WERE FOUNDED.
PILOT OFFICER KING IS AT THIS MOMENT HAVING HIS APPENDIX REMOVED. SO YOU'D BETTER THINK AGAIN!
THE ONLY OTHER ONE IT COULD BE IS MR. STAGG, THEN. HE'S FLOWN SPITFIRES BEFORE, SIR!
5

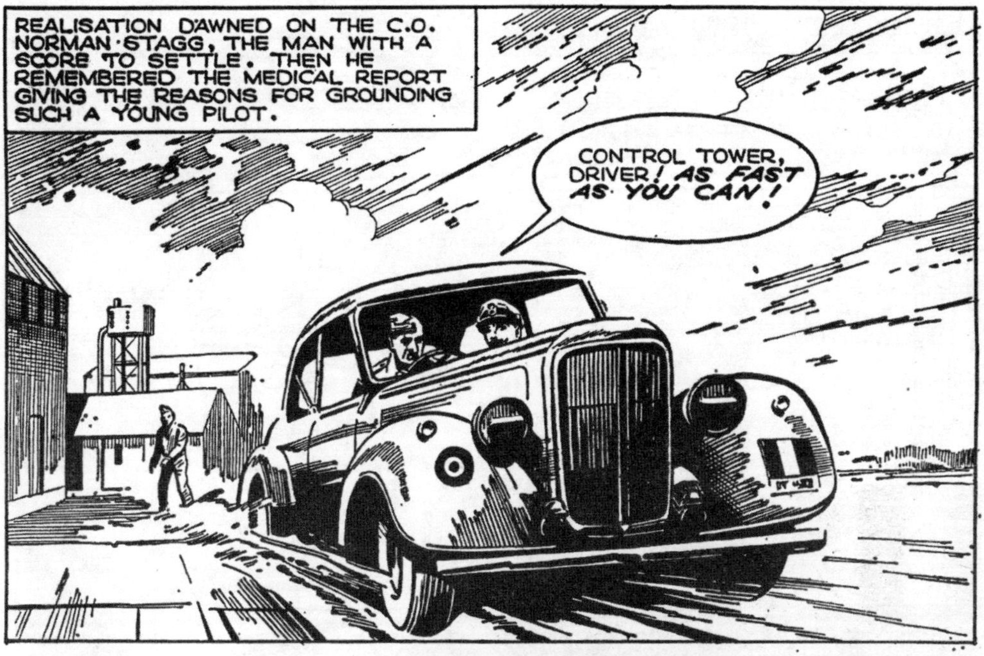
REALISATION DAWNED ON THE C.O. NORMAN STAGG, THE MAN WITH A SCORE TO SETTLE. THEN HE REMEMBERED THE MEDICAL REPORT GIVING THE REASONS FOR GROUNDING SUCH A YOUNG PILOT.
CONTROL TOWER, DRIVER! AS FAST AS YOU CAN!

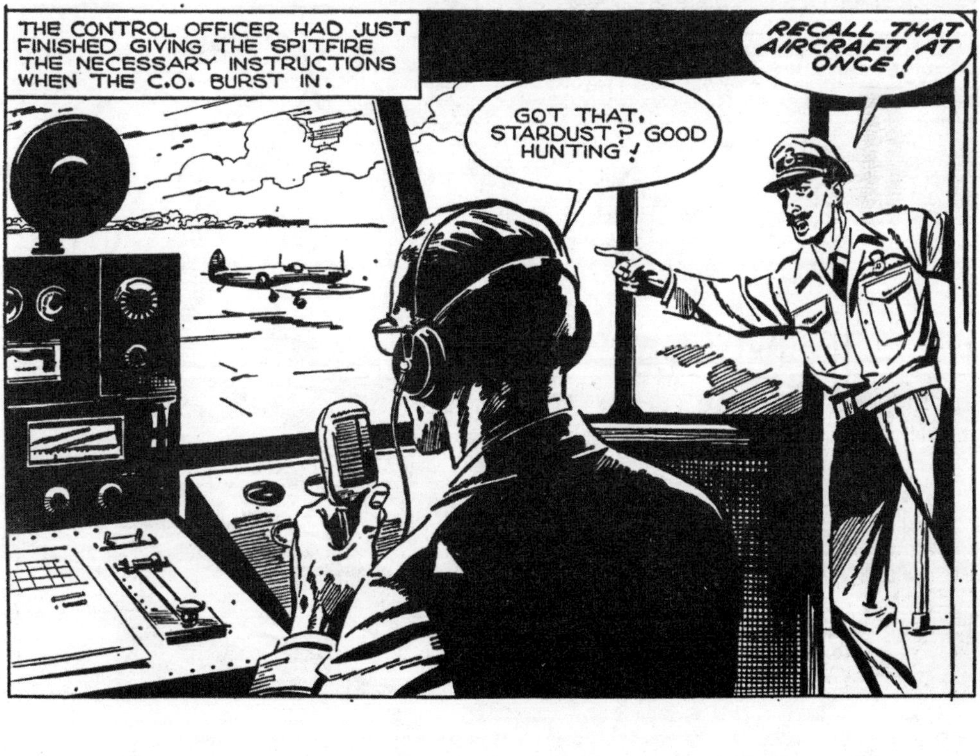
THE CONTROL OFFICER HAD JUST FINISHED GIVING THE SPITFIRE THE NECESSARY INSTRUCTIONS WHEN THE C.O. BURST IN.
GOT THAT, STARDUST? GOOD HUNTING!
RECALL THAT AIRCRAFT AT ONCE!

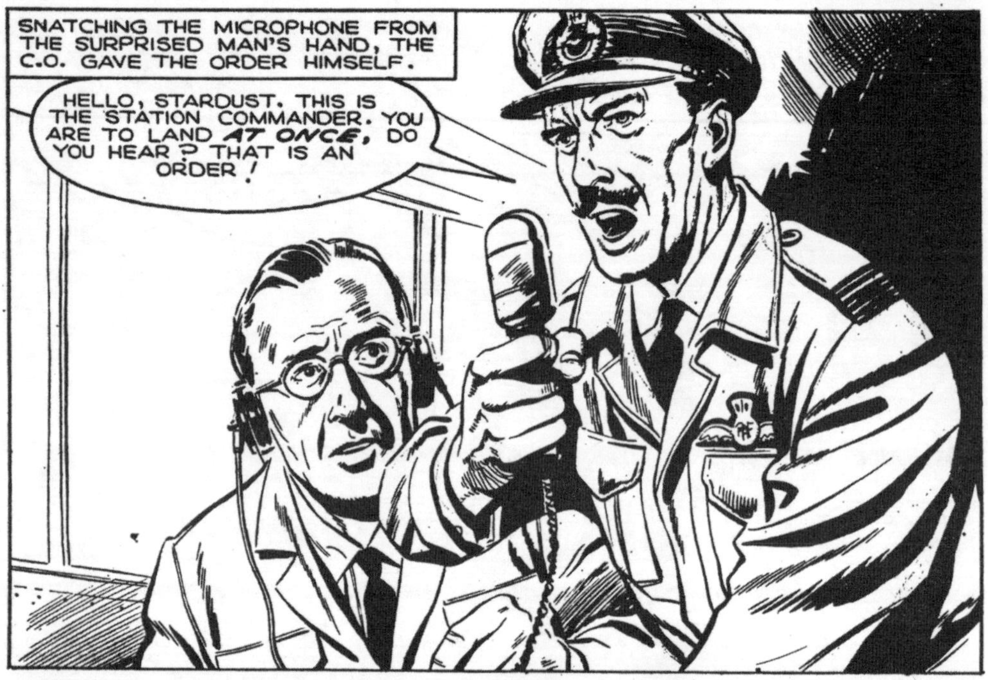
SNATCHING THE MICROPHONE FROM THE SURPRISED MAN'S HAND, THE C.O. GAVE THE ORDER HIMSELF.
HELLO, STARDUST. THIS IS THE STATION COMMANDER. YOU ARE TO LAND AT ONCE, DO YOU HEAR? THAT IS AN ORDER!

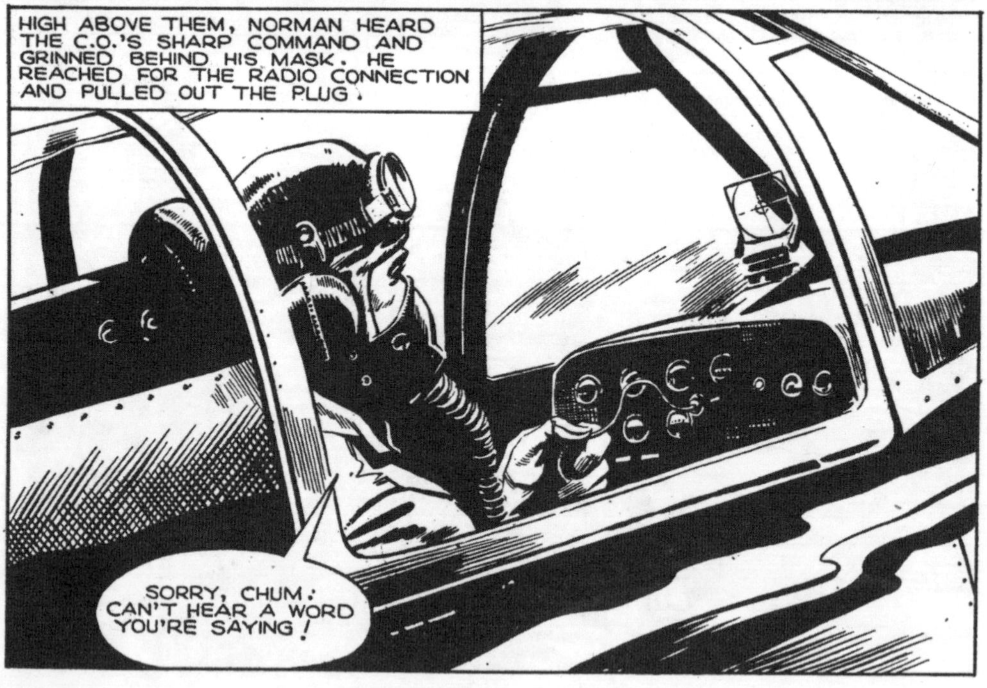
HIGH ABOVE THEM, NORMAN HEARD THE C.O.'S SHARP COMMAND AND GRINNED BEHIND HIS MASK. HE REACHED FOR THE RADIO CONNECTION AND PULLED OUT THE PLUG.
SORRY, CHUM: CAN'T HEAR A WORD YOU'RE SAYING!

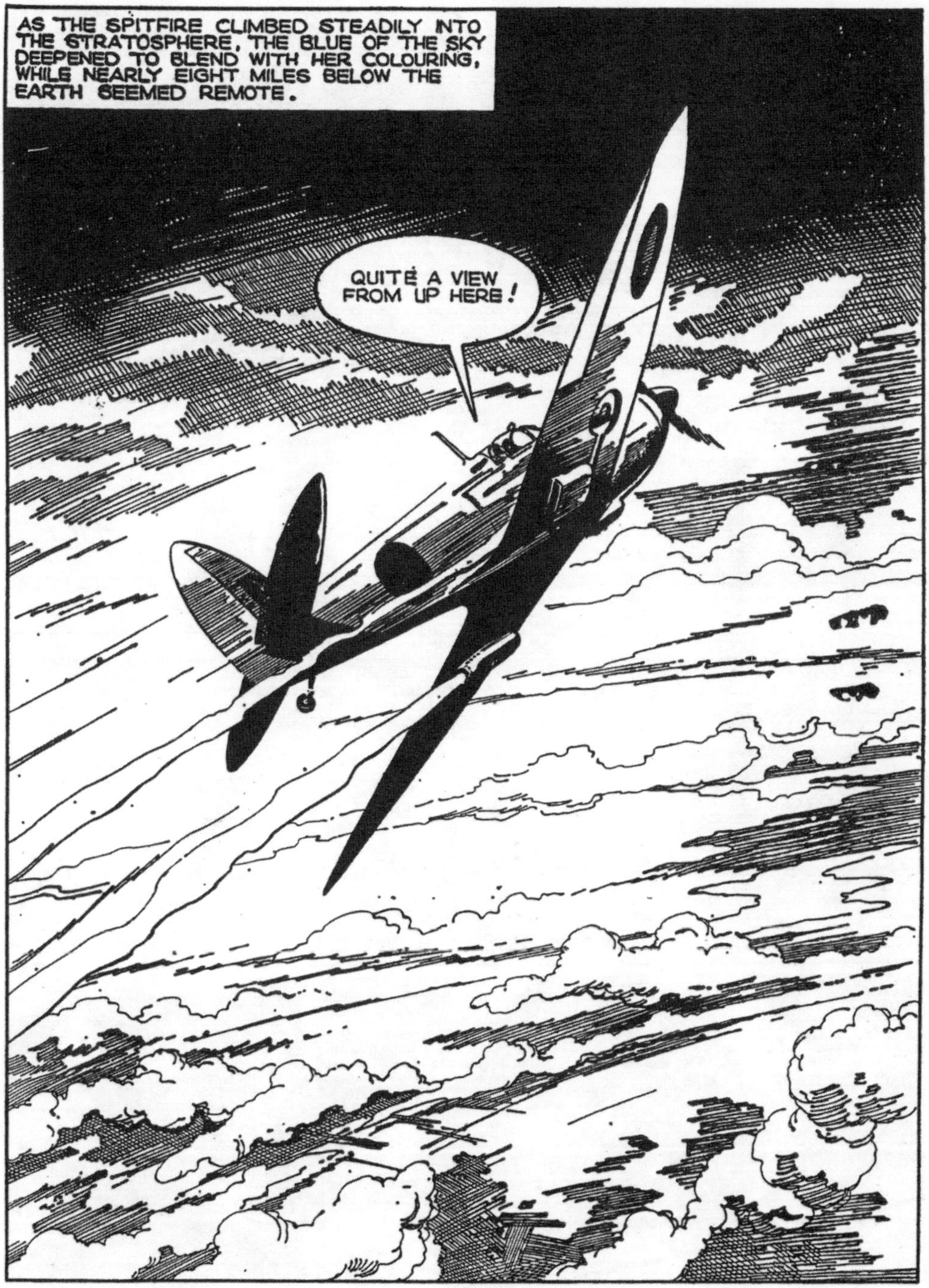
AS THE SPITFIRE CLIMBED STEADILY INTO THE STRATOSPHERE, THE BLUE OF THE SKY DEEPENED TO BLEND WITH HER COLOURING, WHILE NEARLY EIGHT MILES BELOW THE EARTH SEEMED REMOTE.
QUITE A VIEW FROM UP HERE!

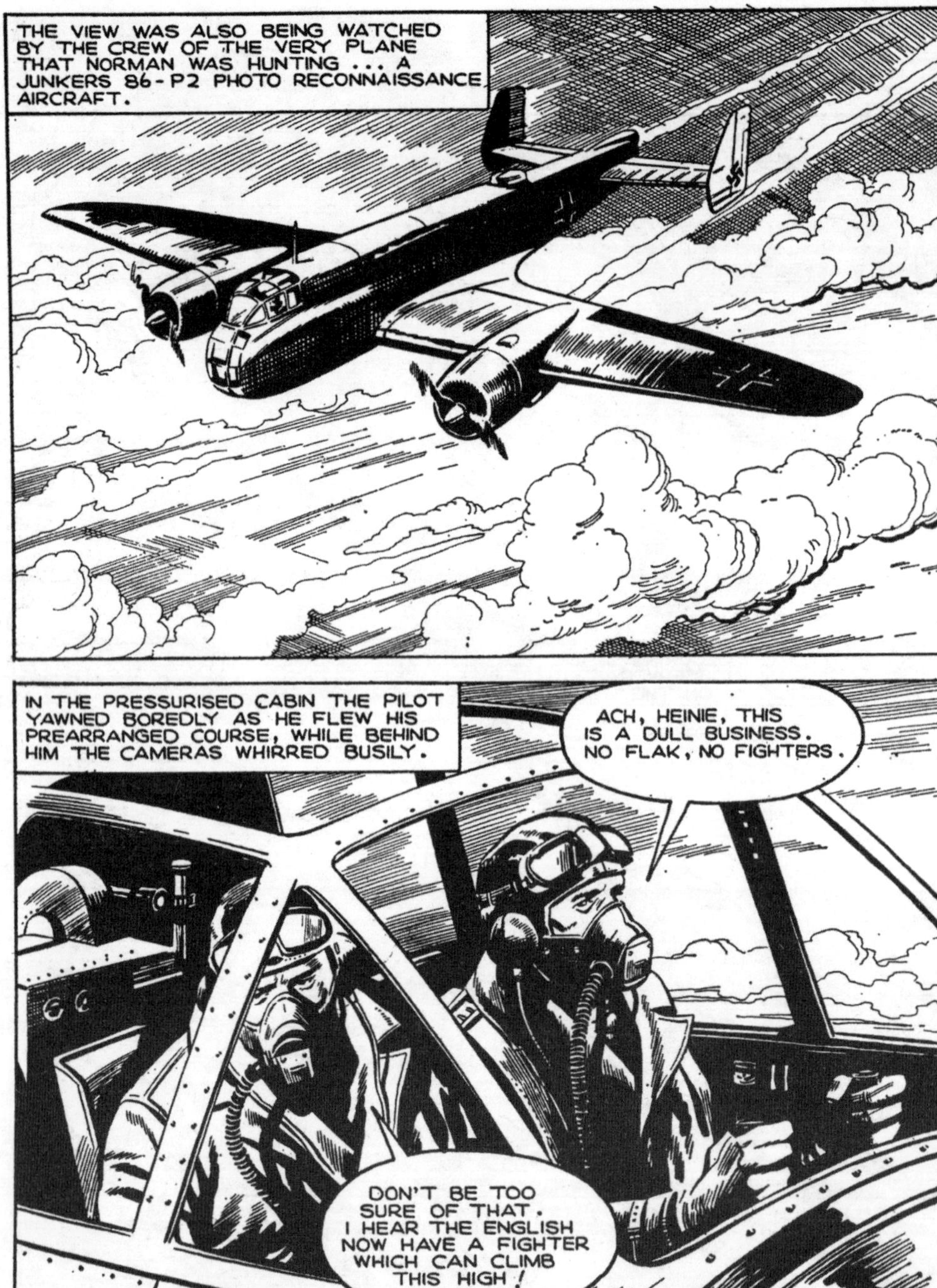
THE VIEW WAS ALSO BEING WATCHED BY THE CREW OF THE VERY PLANE THAT NORMAN WAS HUNTING ... A JUNKERS 86-P2 PHOTO RECONNAISSANCE AIRCRAFT.
IN THE PRESSURISED CABIN THE PILOT YAWNED BOREDLY AS HE FLEW HIS PREARRANGED COURSE, WHILE BEHIND HIM THE CAMERAS WHIRRED BUSILY.
ACH, HEINIE, THIS IS A DULL BUSINESS. NO FLAK, NO FIGHTERS.
DON'T BE TOO SURE OF THAT. I HEAR THE ENGLISH NOW HAVE A FIGHTER WHICH CAN CLIMB THIS HIGH!

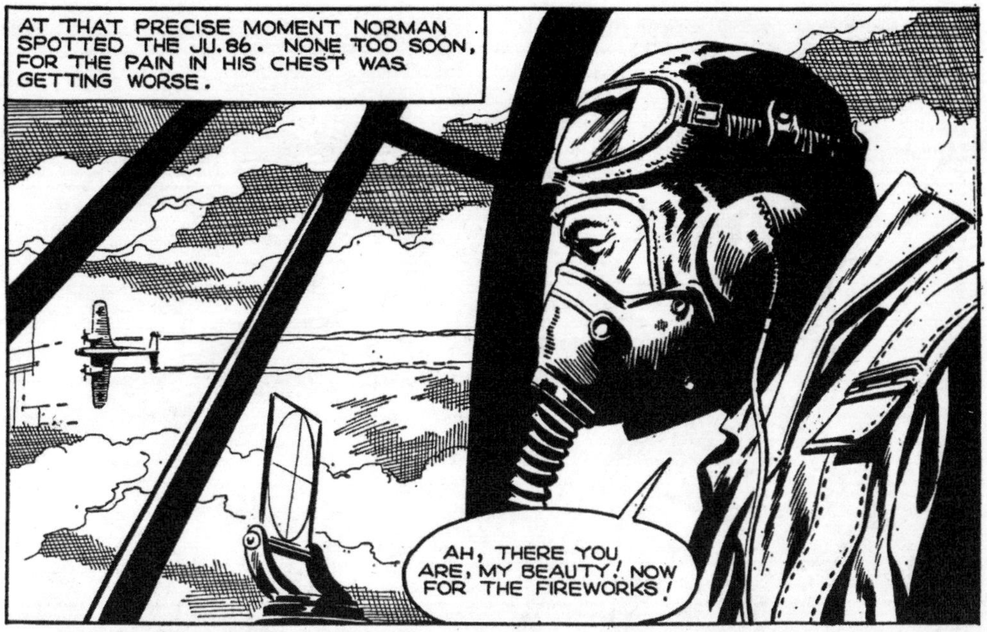
AT THAT PRECISE MOMENT NORMAN SPOTTED THE JU.86. NONE TOO SOON, FOR THE PAIN IN HIS CHEST WAS GETTING WORSE.
AH, THERE YOU ARE, MY BEAUTY! NOW FOR THE FIREWORKS!

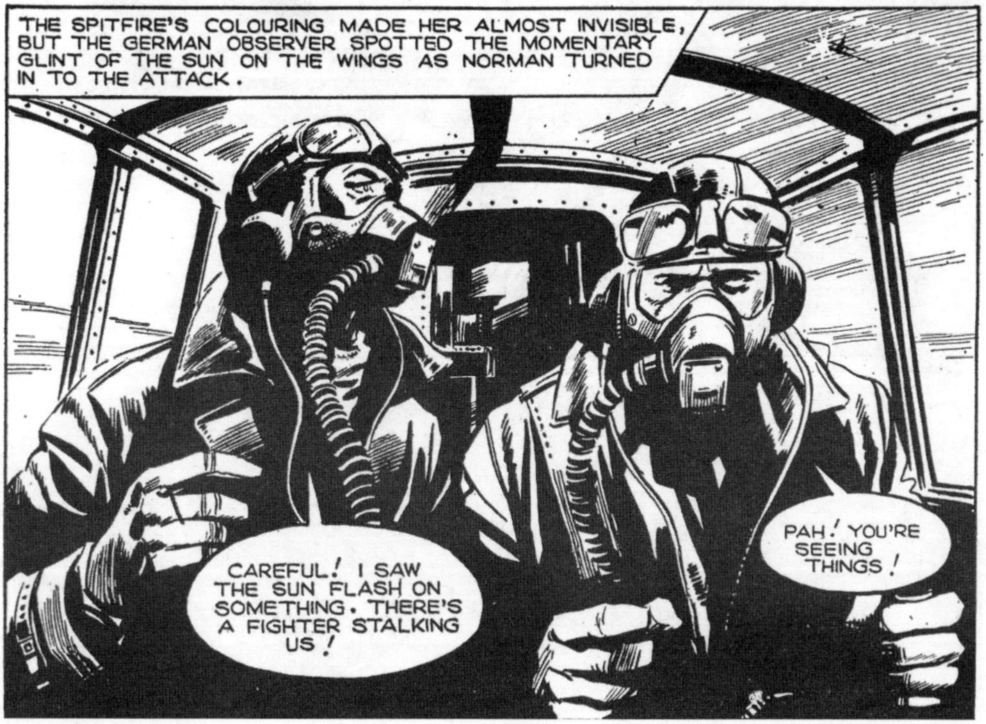
THE SPITFIRE'S COLOURING MADE HER ALMOST INVISIBLE, BUT THE GERMAN OBSERVER SPOTTED THE MOMENTARY GLINT OF THE SUN ON THE WINGS AS NORMAN TURNED IN TO THE ATTACK.
CAREFUL! I SAW THE SUN FLASH ON SOMETHING. THERE'S A FIGHTER STALKING US!
PAH! YOU'RE SEEING THINGS!

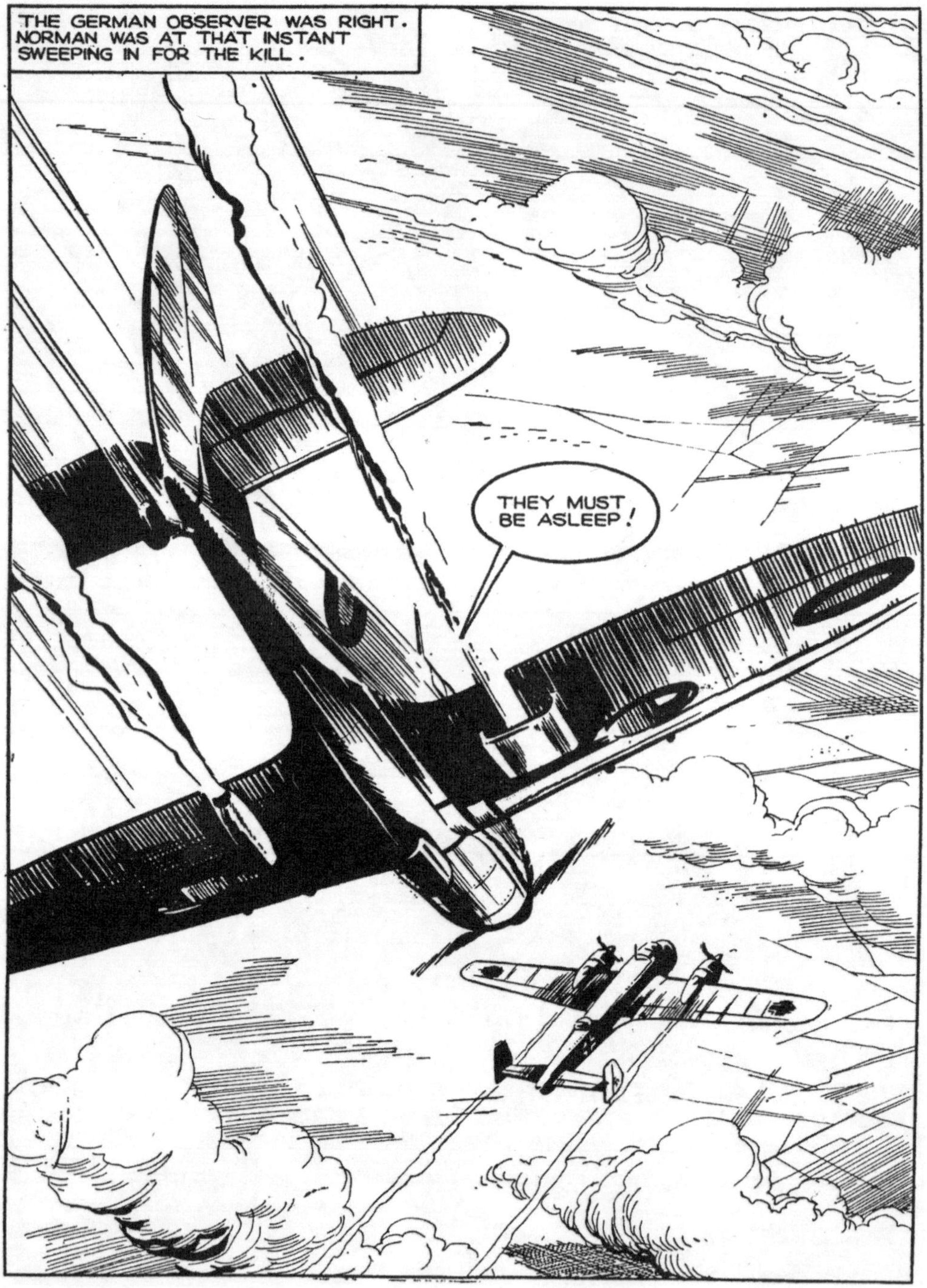
THE GERMAN OBSERVER WAS RIGHT. NORMAN WAS AT THAT INSTANT SWEEPING IN FOR THE KILL.
THEY MUST BE ASLEEP!

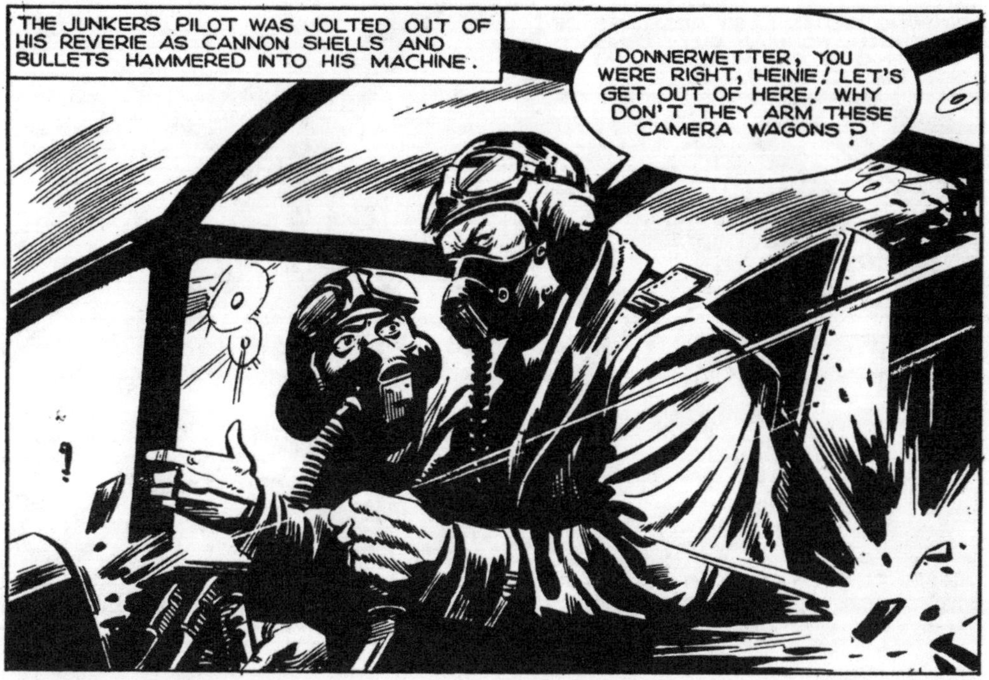
THE JUNKERS PILOT WAS JOLTED OUT OF HIS REVERIE AS CANNON SHELLS AND BULLETS HAMMERED INTO HIS MACHINE.
DONNERWETTER, YOU WERE RIGHT, HEINIE! LET'S GET OUT OF HERE! WHY DON'T THEY ARM THESE CAMERA WAGONS?

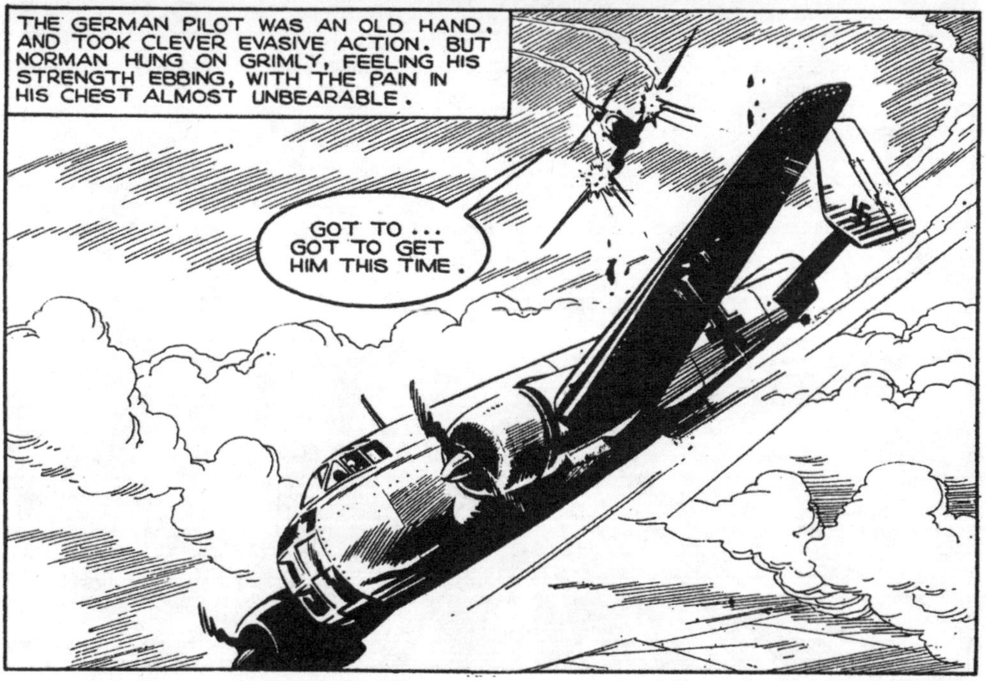
THE GERMAN PILOT WAS AN OLD HAND, AND TOOK CLEVER EVASIVE ACTION. BUT NORMAN HUNG ON GRIMLY, FEELING HIS STRENGTH EBBING, WITH THE PAIN IN HIS CHEST ALMOST UNBEARABLE.
GOT TO ... GOT TO GET HIM THIS TIME.

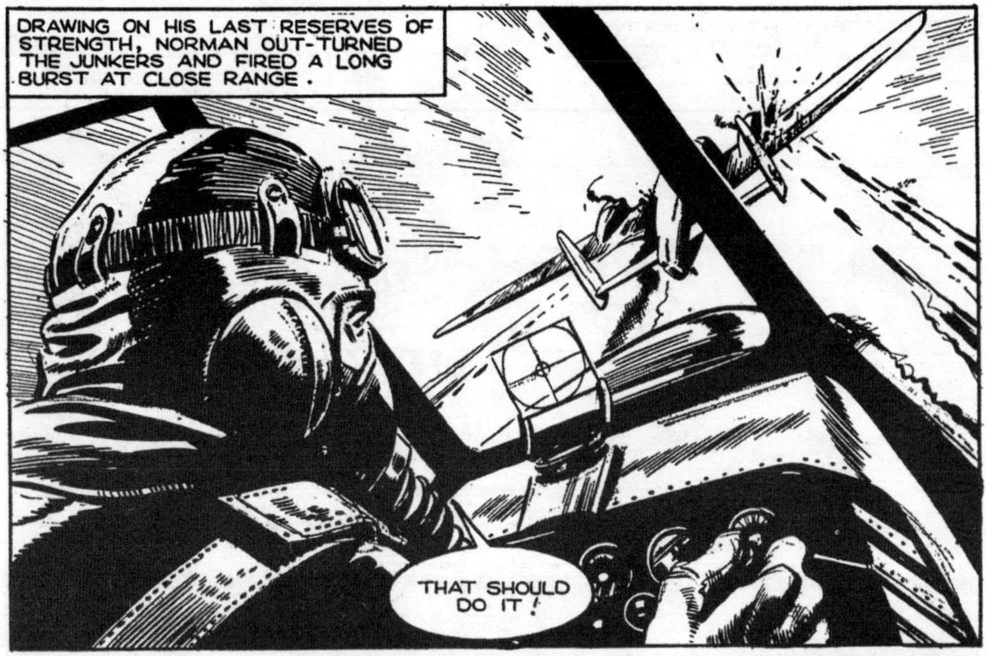
DRAWING ON HIS LAST RESERVES OF STRENGTH, NORMAN OUT-TURNED THE JUNKERS AND FIRED A LONG BURST AT CLOSE RANGE.
THAT SHOULD DO IT!

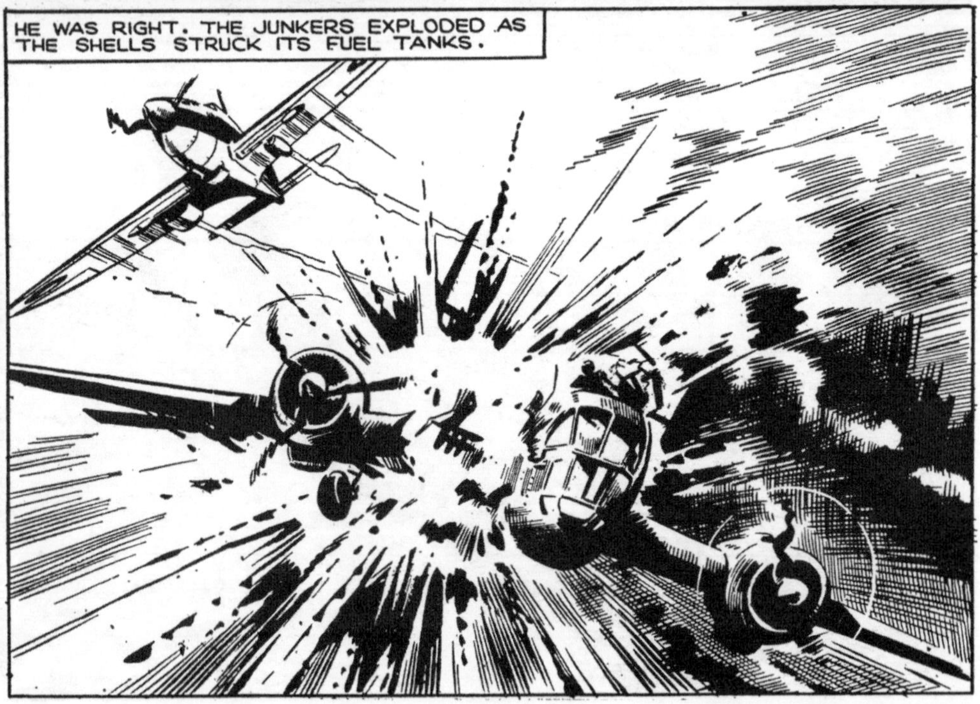
HE WAS RIGHT. THE JUNKERS EXPLODED AS THE SHELLS STRUCK ITS FUEL TANKS.

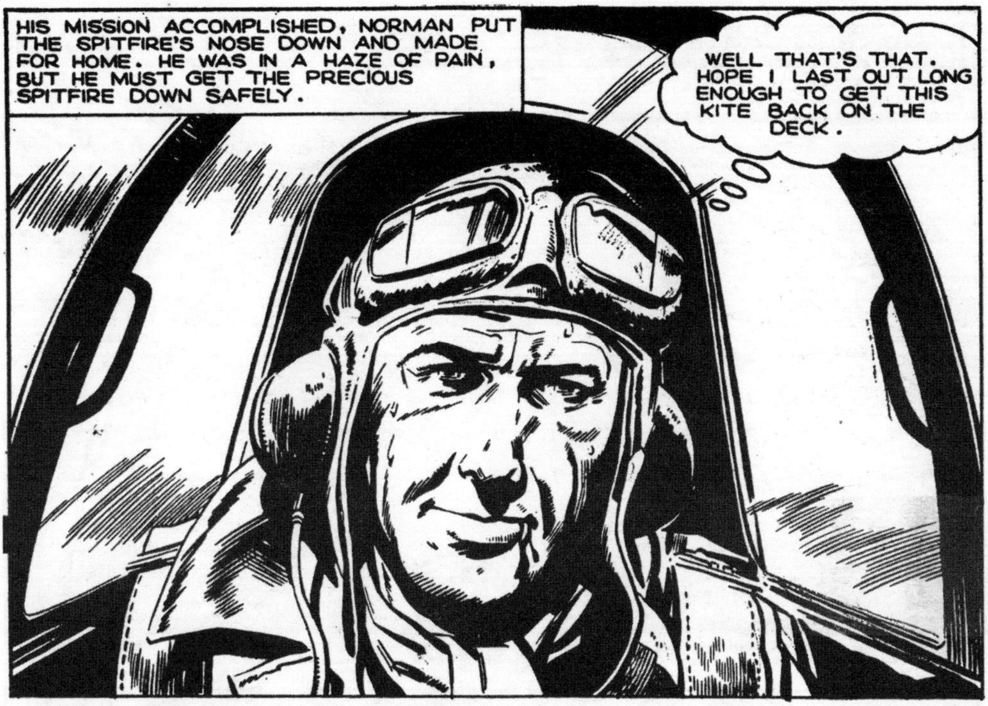
HIS MISSION ACCOMPLISHED, NORMAN PUT THE SPITFIRE'S NOSE DOWN AND MADE FOR HOME. HE WAS IN A HAZE OF PAIN, BUT HE MUST GET THE PRECIOUS SPITFIRE DOWN SAFELY.
WELL THAT'S THAT. HOPE I LAST OUT LONG ENOUGH TO GET THIS KITE BACK ON THE DECK.

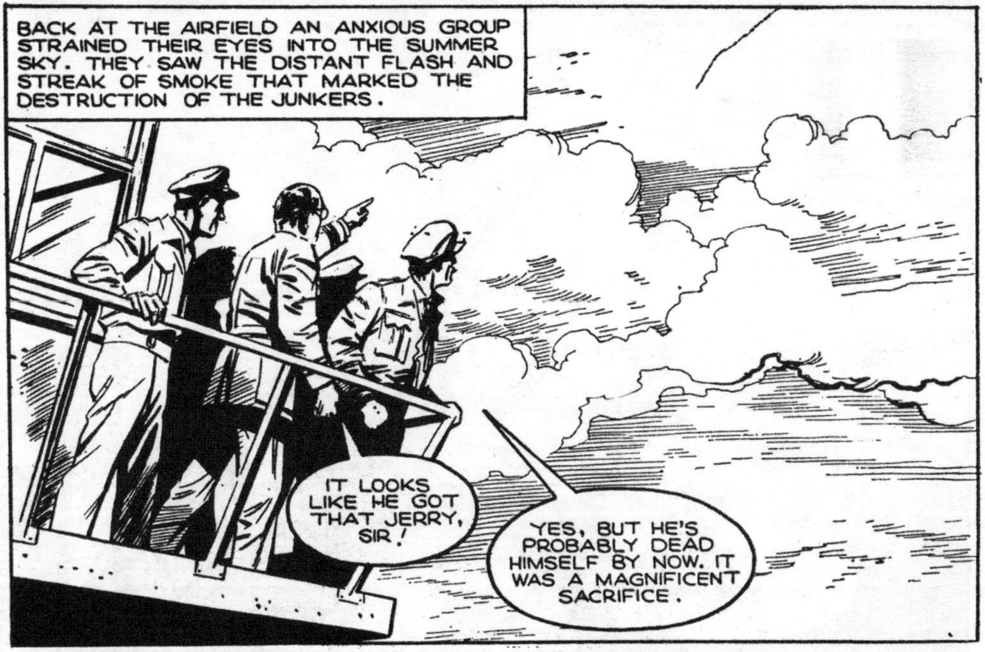
BACK AT THE AIRFIELD AN ANXIOUS GROUP STRAINED THEIR EYES INTO THE SUMMER SKY. THEY SAW THE DISTANT FLASH AND STREAK OF SMOKE THAT MARKED THE DESTRUCTION OF THE JUNKERS.
IT LOOKS LIKE HE GOT THAT JERRY, SIR!
YES, BUT HE'S PROBABLY DEAD HIMSELF BY NOW. IT WAS A MAGNIFICENT SACRIFICE.

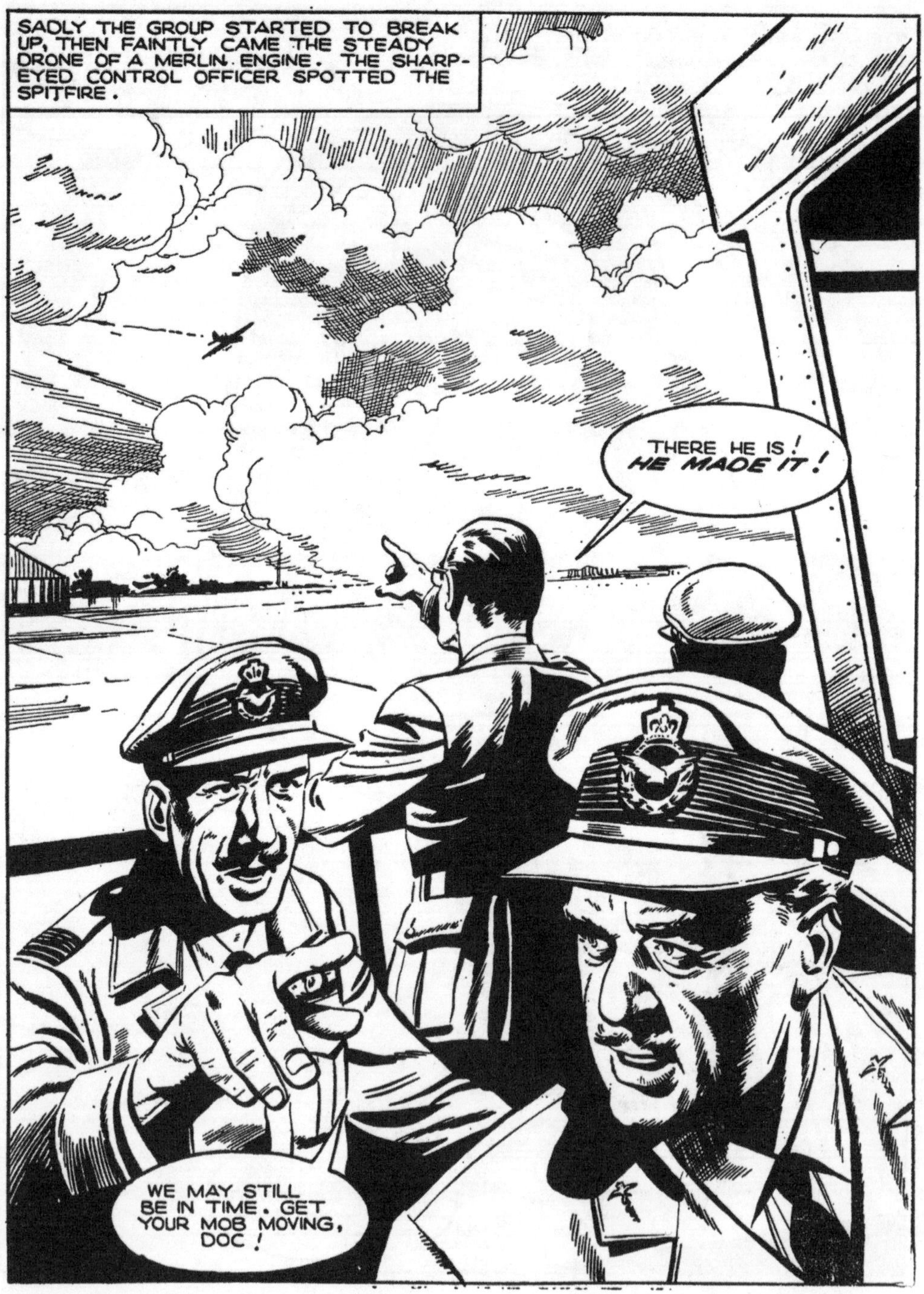
SADLY THE GROUP STARTED TO BREAK UP, THEN FAINTLY CAME THE STEADY DRONE OF A MERLIN ENGINE. THE SHARP-EYED CONTROL OFFICER SPOTTED THE SPITFIRE.
THERE HE IS! HE MADE IT!
WE MAY STILL BE IN TIME. GET YOUR MOB MOVING, DOC!

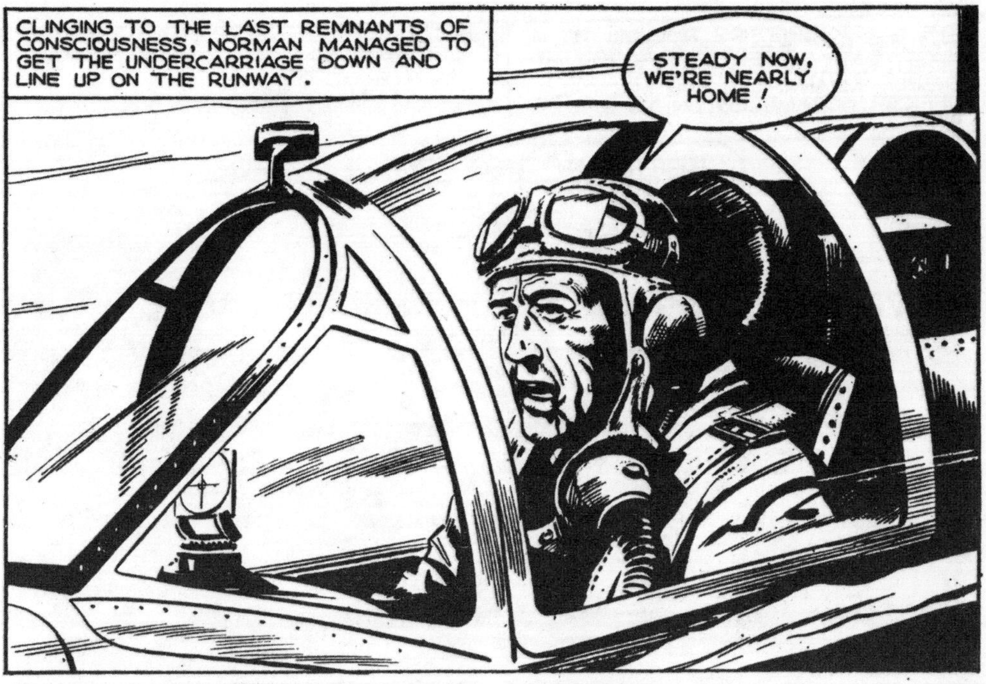
CLINGING TO THE LAST REMNANTS OF CONSCIOUSNESS, NORMAN MANAGED TO GET THE UNDERCARRIAGE DOWN AND LINE UP ON THE RUNWAY.
STEADY NOW, WE'RE NEARLY HOME!

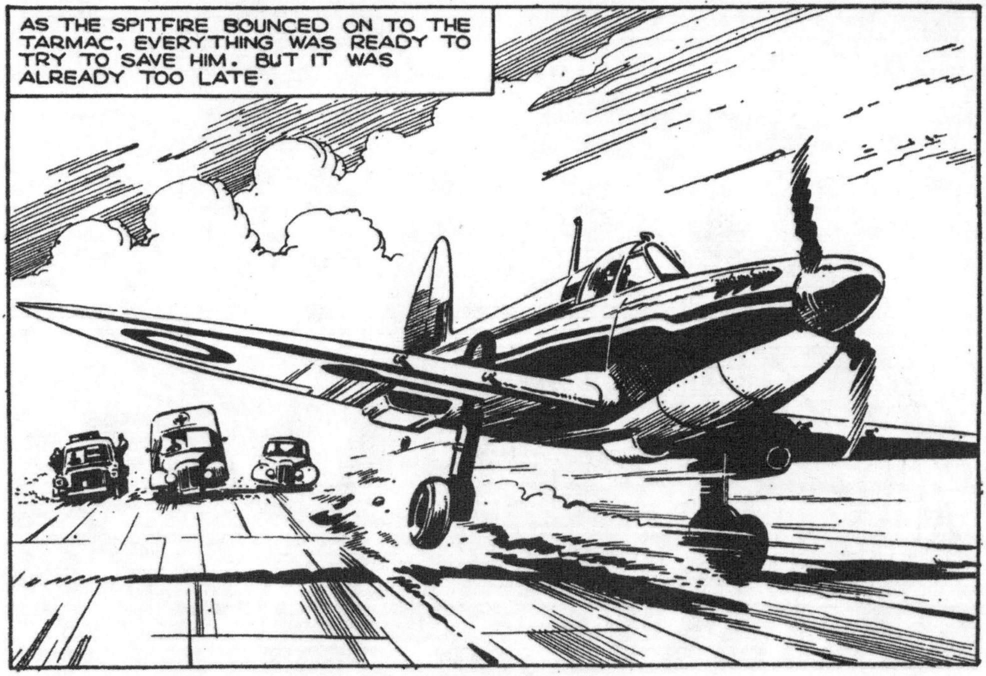
AS THE SPITFIRE BOUNCED ON TO THE TARMAC, EVERYTHING WAS READY TO TRY TO SAVE HIM. BUT IT WAS ALREADY TOO LATE.

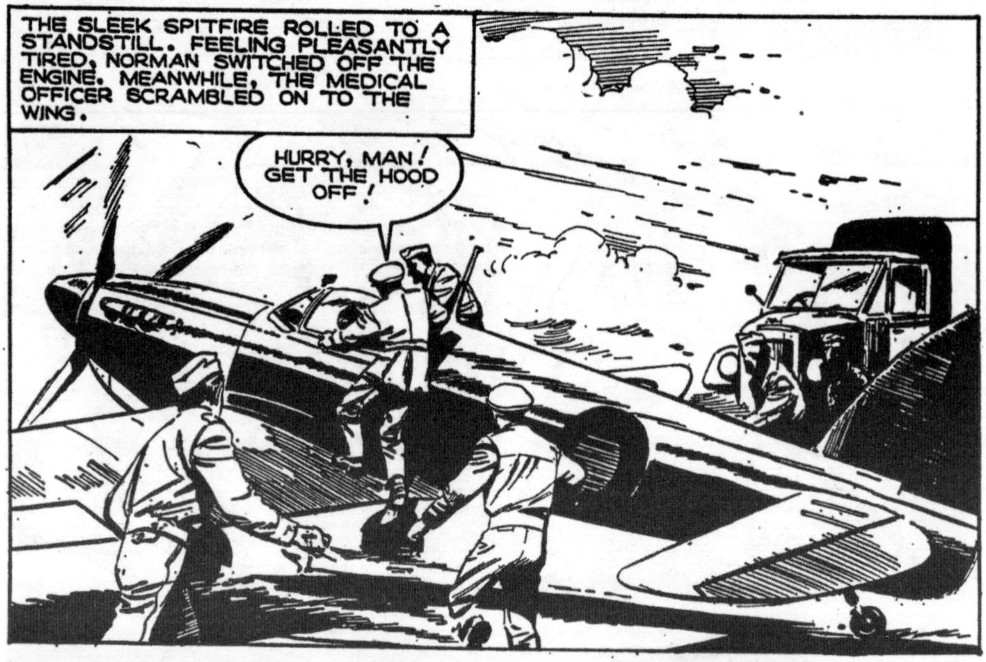
THE SLEEK SPITFIRE ROLLED TO A STANDSTILL. FEELING PLEASANTLY TIRED, NORMAN SWITCHED OFF THE ENGINE. MEANWHILE, THE MEDICAL OFFICER SCRAMBLED ON TO THE WING.
HURRY, MAN! GET THE HOOD OFF!

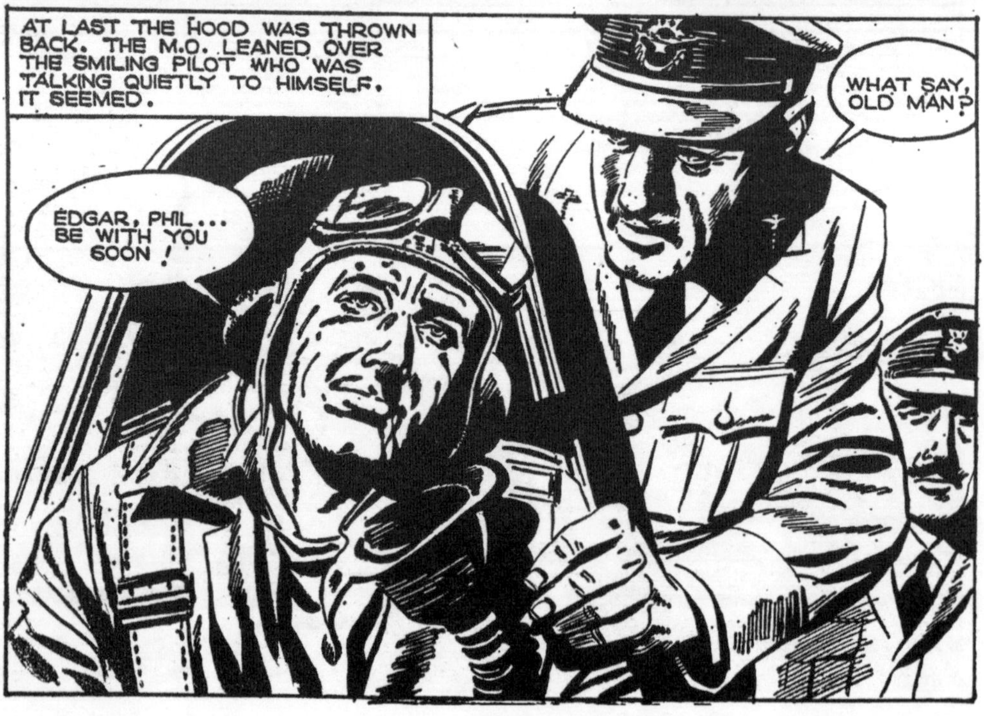
AT LAST THE HOOD WAS THROWN BACK. THE M.O. LEANED OVER THE SMILING PILOT WHO WAS TALKING QUIETLY TO HIMSELF, IT SEEMED.
WHAT SAY, OLD MAN?
EDGAR, PHIL... BE WITH YOU SOON!

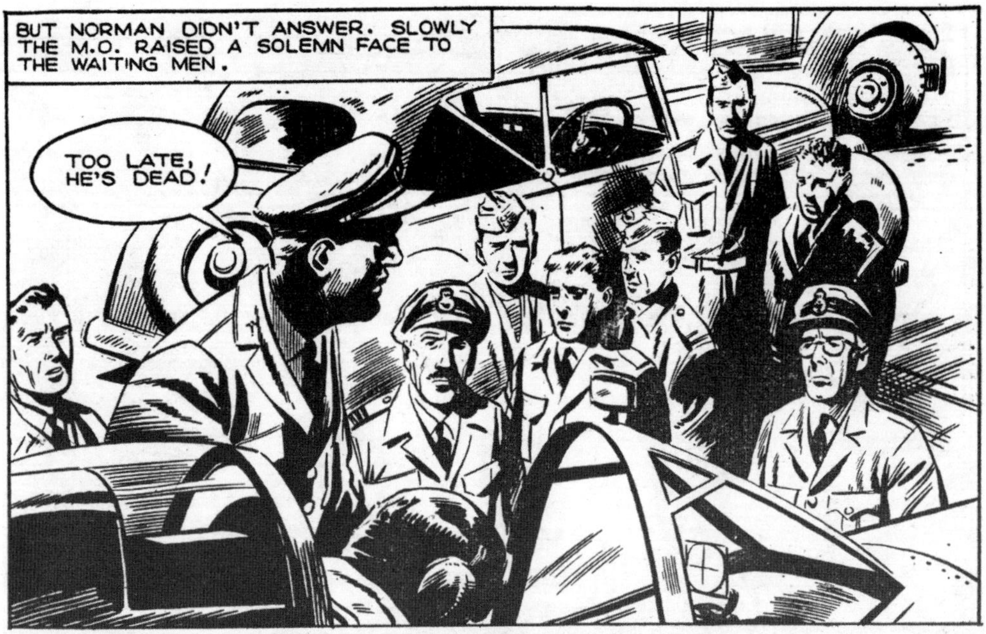
BUT NORMAN DIDN'T ANSWER. SLOWLY THE M.O. RAISED A SOLEMN FACE TO THE WAITING MEN.
TOO LATE, HE'S DEAD!

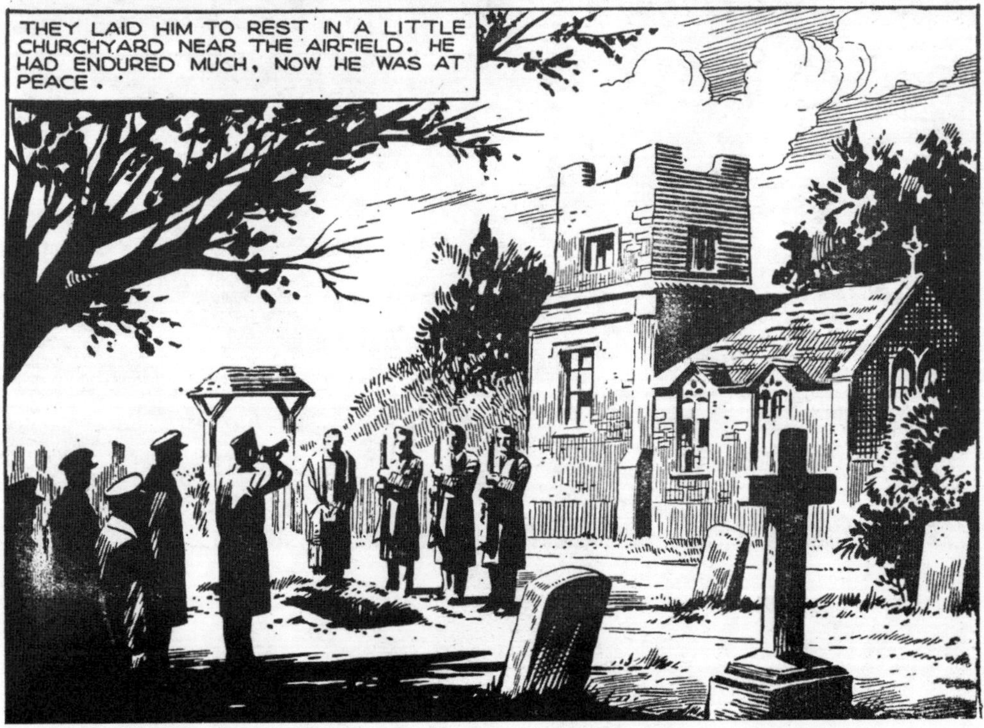
THEY LAID HIM TO REST IN A LITTLE CHURCHYARD NEAR THE AIRFIELD. HE HAD ENDURED MUCH, NOW HE WAS AT PEACE.

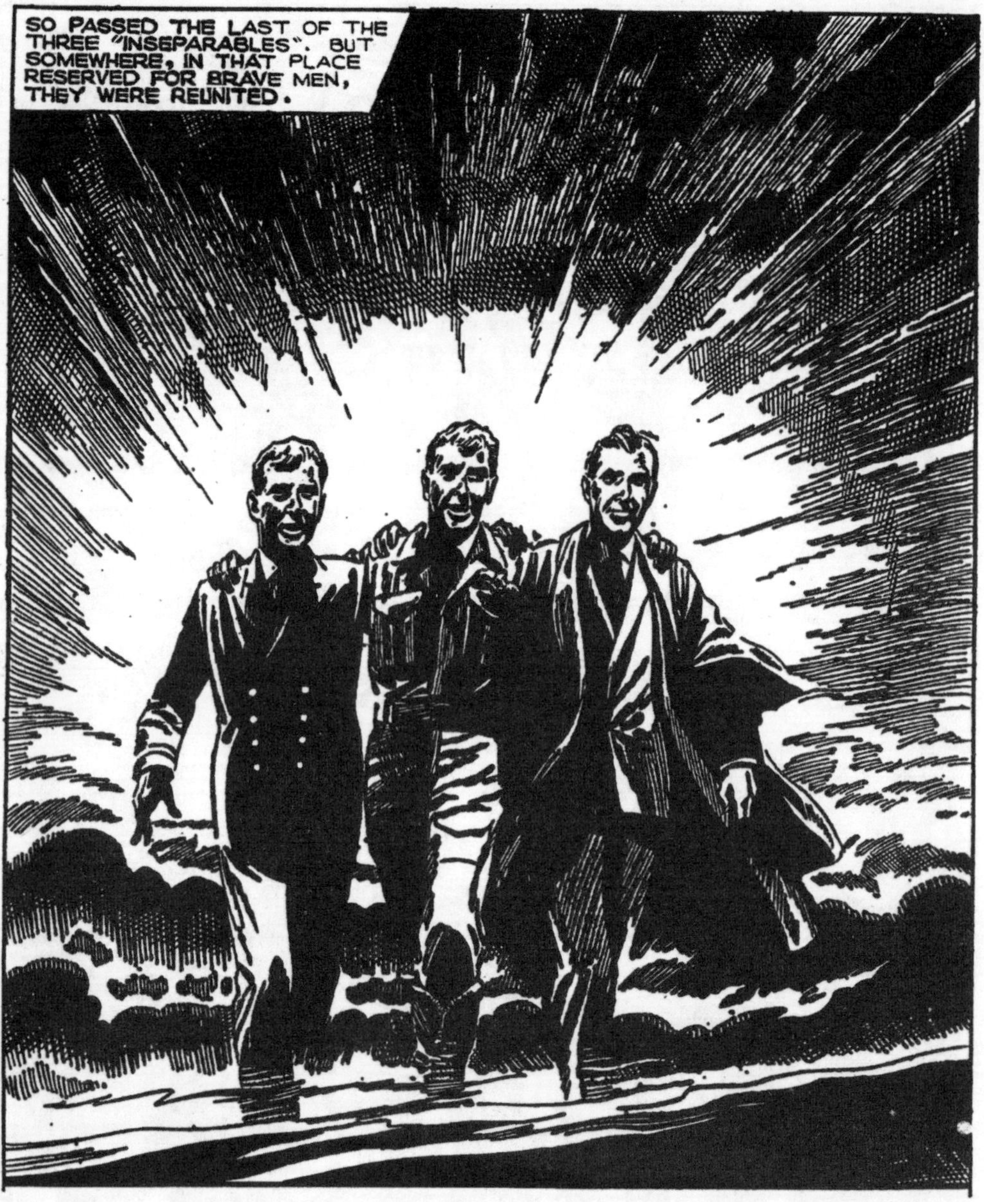
SO PASSED THE LAST OF THE THREE "INSEPARABLES". BUT SOMEWHERE, IN THAT PLACE RESERVED FOR BRAVE MEN, THEY WERE REUNITED.

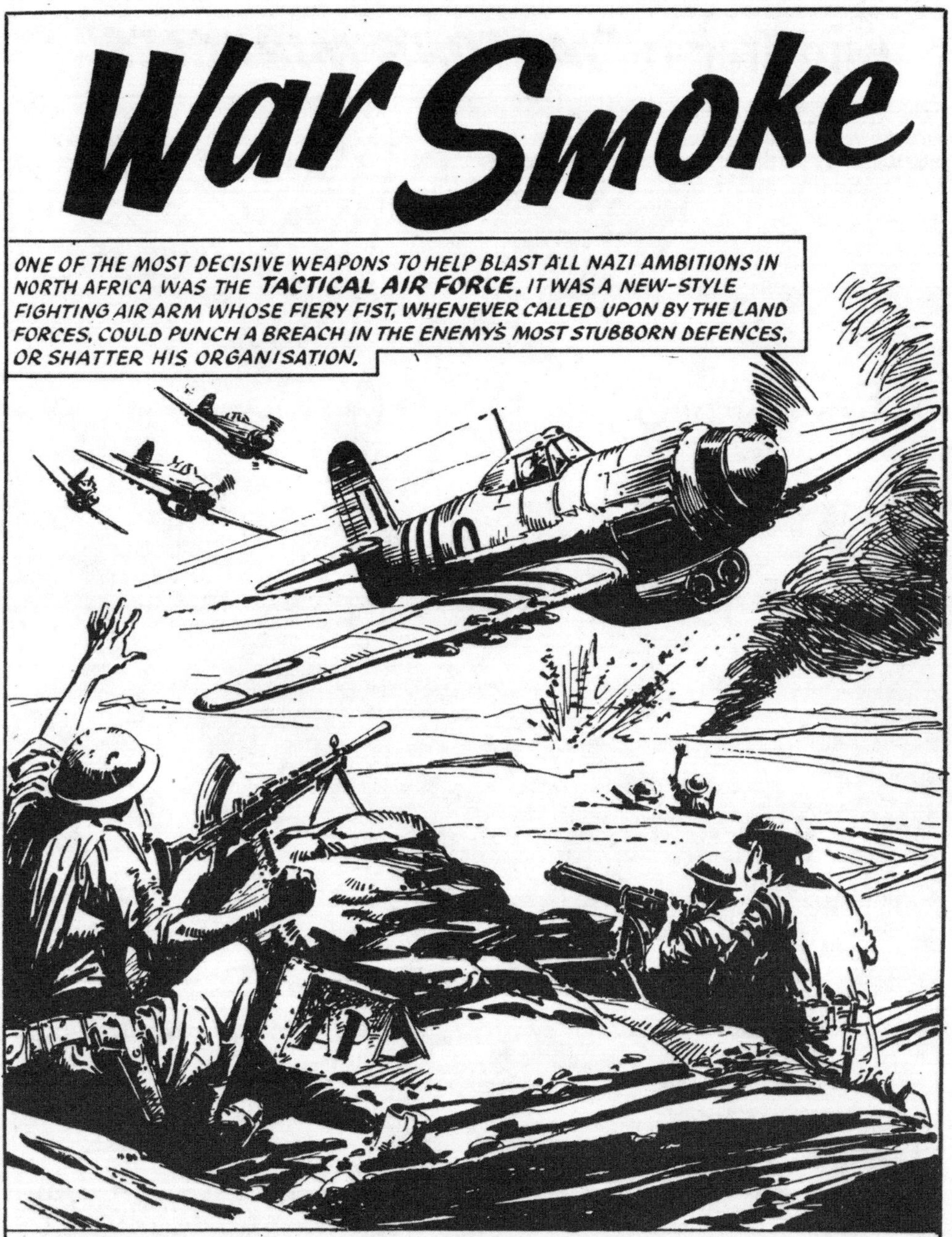
War Smoke
ONE OF THE MOST DECISIVE WEAPONS TO HELP BLAST ALL NAZI AMBITIONS IN NORTH AFRICA WAS THE TACTICAL AIR FORCE. IT WAS A NEW-STYLE FIGHTING AIR ARM WHOSE FIERY FIST, WHENEVER CALLED UPON BY THE LAND FORCES, COULD PUNCH A BREACH IN THE ENEMY'S MOST STUBBORN DEFENCES, OR SHATTER HIS ORGANISATION.
AND DEADLY AMONGST THE DEADLIEST AT THIS SPECIALISED FORM OF AIR-TO-GROUND FIGHTING WAS THE POWERFUL HAWKER TYPHOON, CARRIER OF THE FIERCE NEW ROCKET BOMBS, INTRODUCED IN JUNE, 1943.

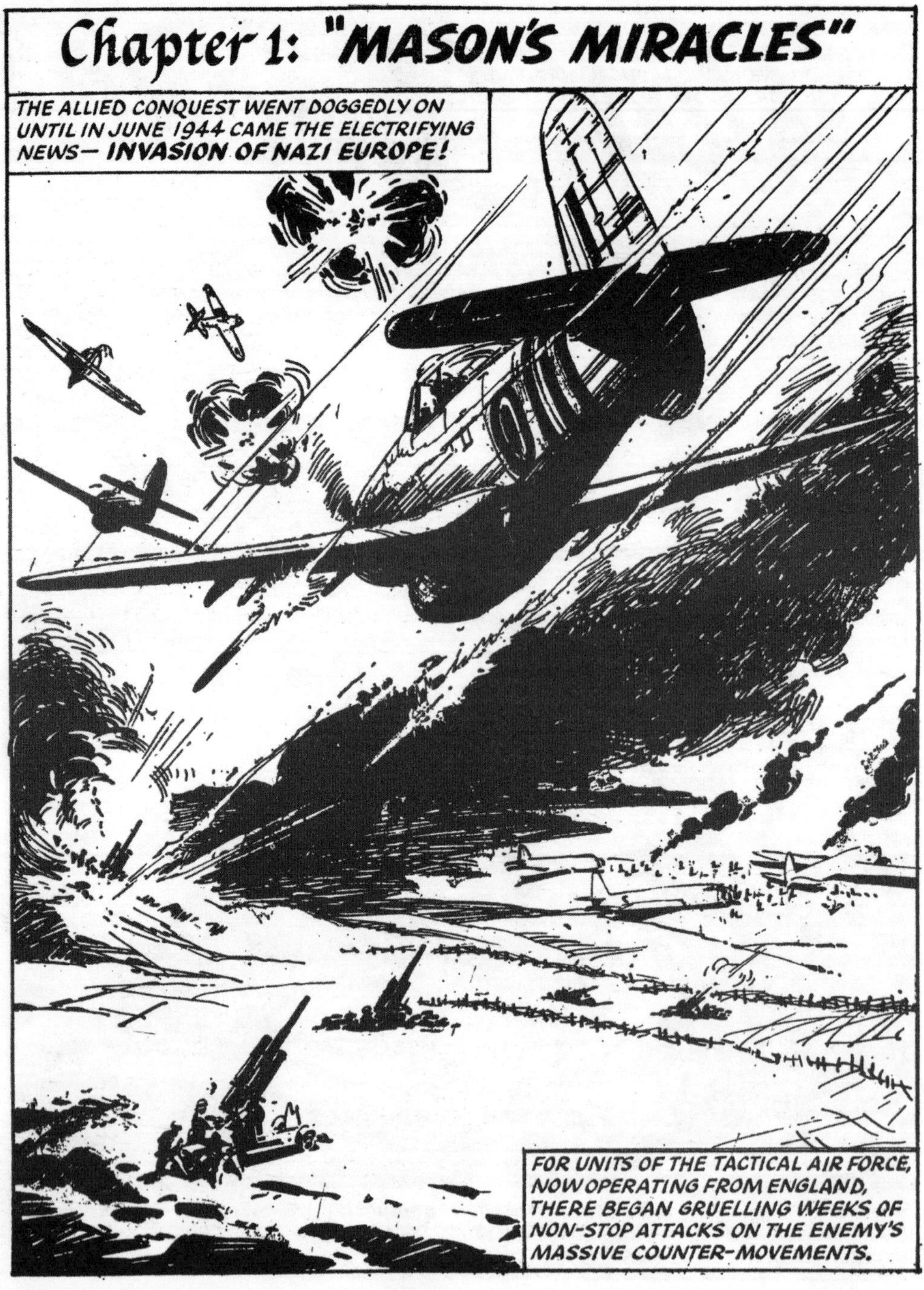
Chapter 1: "MASON'S MIRACLES"
THE ALLIED CONQUEST WENT DOGGEDLY ON UNTIL IN JUNE 1944 CAME THE ELECTRIFYING NEWS— INVASION OF NAZI EUROPE!
FOR UNITS OF THE TACTICAL AIR FORCE, NOW OPERATING FROM ENGLAND, THERE BEGAN GRUELLING WEEKS OF NON-STOP ATTACKS ON THE ENEMY'S MASSIVE COUNTER-MOVEMENTS.

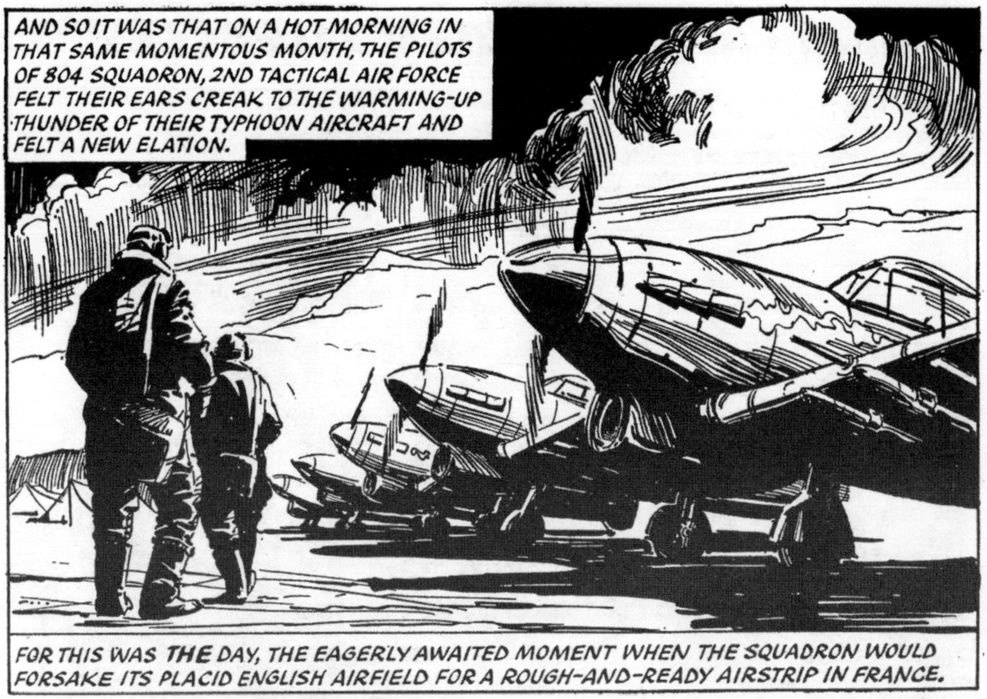
AND SO IT WAS THAT ON A HOT MORNING IN THAT SAME MOMENTOUS MONTH, THE PILOTS OF 804 SQUADRON, 2ND TACTICAL AIR FORCE FELT THEIR EARS CREAK TO THE WARMING-UP THUNDER OF THEIR TYPHOON AIRCRAFT AND FELT A NEW ELATION.
FOR THIS WAS THE DAY, THE EAGERLY AWAITED MOMENT WHEN THE SQUADRON WOULD FORSAKE ITS PLACID ENGLISH AIRFIELD FOR A ROUGH-AND-READY AIRSTRIP IN FRANCE.

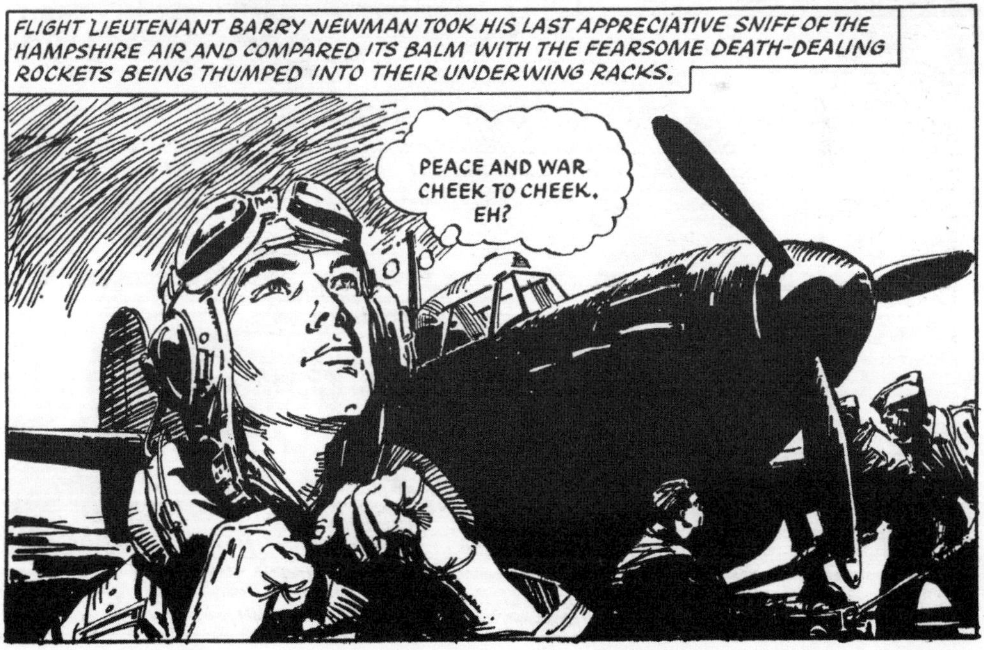
FLIGHT LIEUTENANT BARRY NEWMAN TOOK HIS LAST APPRECIATIVE SNIFF OF THE HAMPSHIRE AIR AND COMPARED ITS BALM WITH THE FEARSOME DEATH-DEALING ROCKETS BEING THUMPED INTO THEIR UNDERWING RACKS.
PEACE AND WAR CHEEK TO CHEEK, EH?

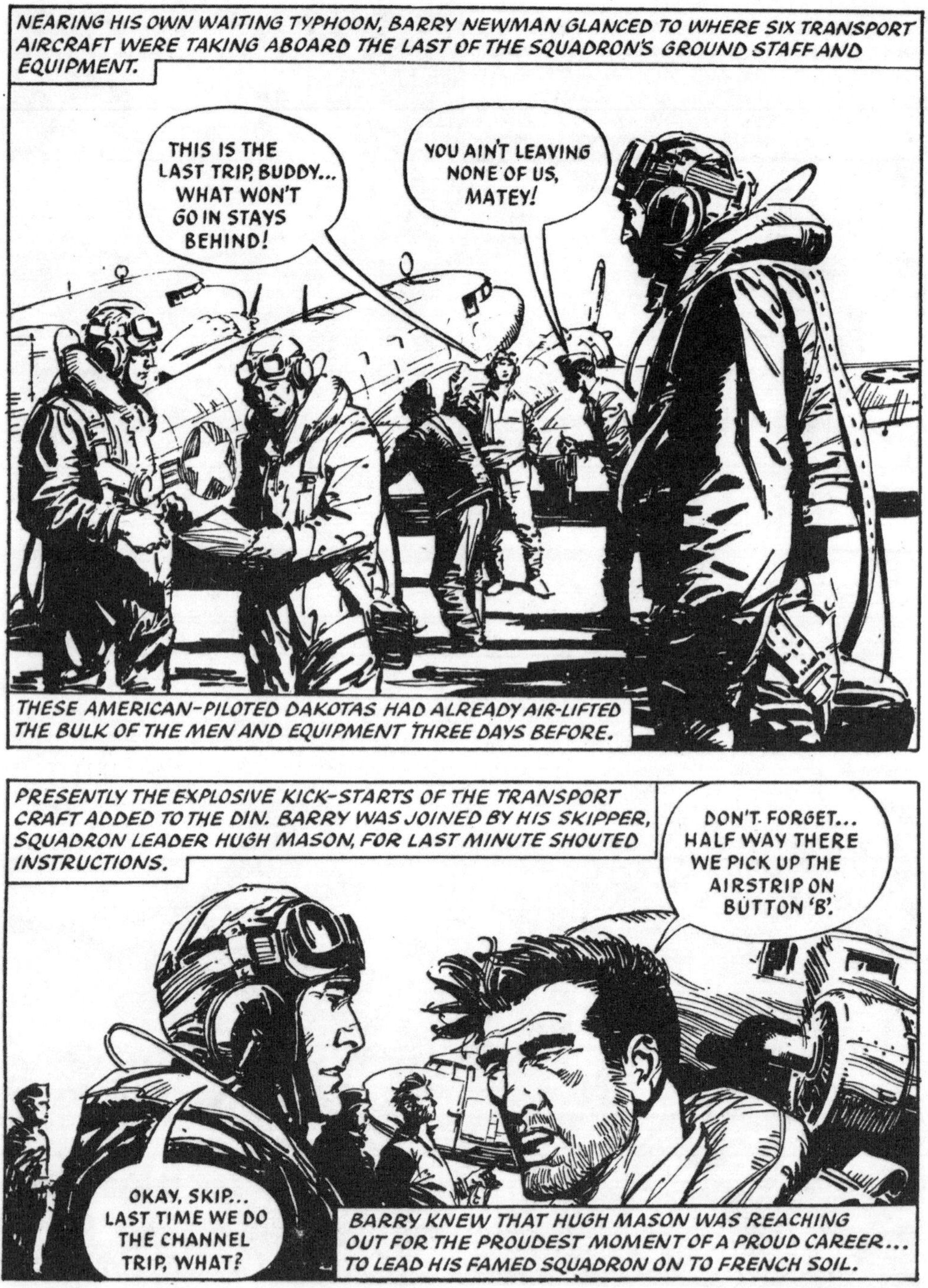
NEARING HIS OWN WAITING TYPHOON, BARRY NEWMAN GLANCED TO WHERE SIX TRANSPORT AIRCRAFT WERE TAKING ABOARD THE LAST OF THE SQUADRON'S GROUND STAFF AND EQUIPMENT.
THIS IS THE LAST TRIP, BUDDY... WHAT WON'T GO IN STAYS BEHIND!
YOU AIN'T LEAVING NONE OF US, MATEY!
THESE AMERICAN-PILOTED DAKOTAS HAD ALREADY AIR-LIFTED THE BULK OF THE MEN AND EQUIPMENT THREE DAYS BEFORE.
PRESENTLY THE EXPLOSIVE KICK-STARTS OF THE TRANSPORT CRAFT ADDED TO THE DIN. BARRY WAS JOINED BY HIS SKIPPER, SQUADRON LEADER HUGH MASON, FOR LAST MINUTE SHOUTED INSTRUCTIONS.
DON'T FORGET... HALF WAY THERE WE PICK UP THE AIRSTRIP ON BUTTON 'B'.
OKAY, SKIP... LAST TIME WE DO THE CHANNEL TRIP, WHAT?
BARRY KNEW THAT HUGH MASON WAS REACHING OUT FOR THE PROUDEST MOMENT OF A PROUD CAREER... TO LEAD HIS FAMED SQUADRON ON TO FRENCH SOIL.

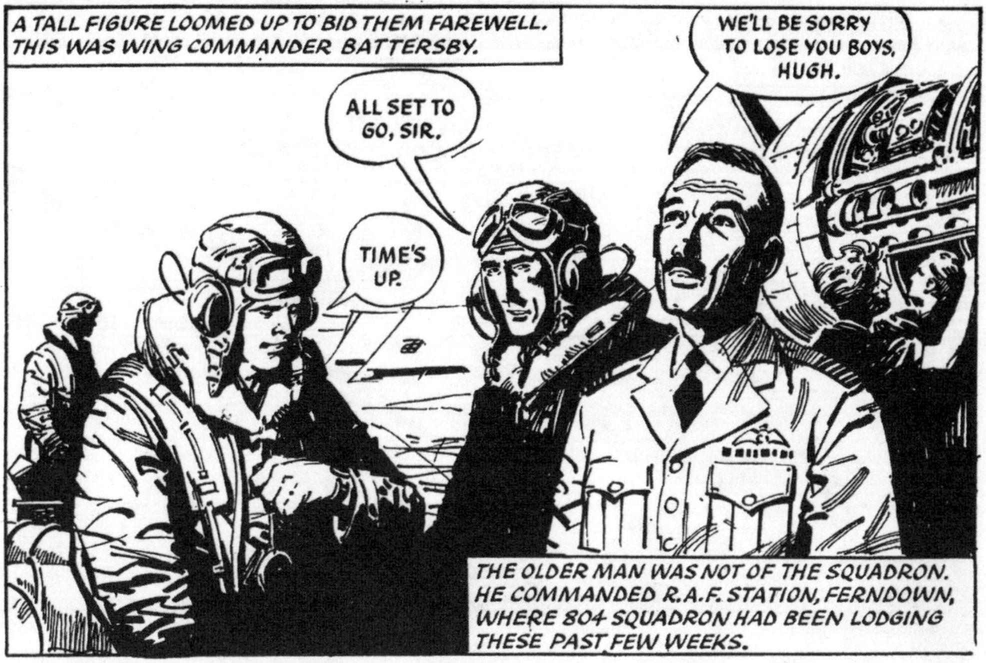
A TALL FIGURE LOOMED UP TO BID THEM FAREWELL. THIS WAS WING COMMANDER BATTERSBY.
ALL SET TO GO, SIR.
WE'LL BE SORRY TO LOSE YOU BOYS, HUGH.
TIME'S UP.
THE OLDER MAN WAS NOT OF THE SQUADRON. HE COMMANDED R.A.F. STATION, FERNDOWN, WHERE 804 SQUADRON HAD BEEN LODGING THESE PAST FEW WEEKS.

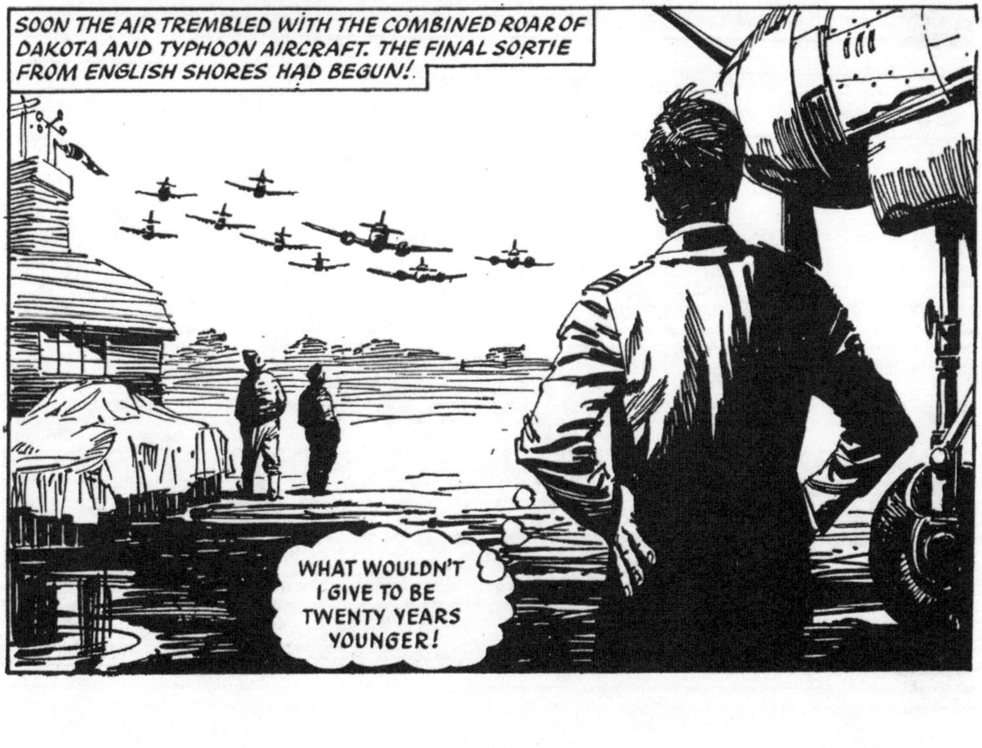
SOON THE AIR TREMBLED WITH THE COMBINED ROAR OF DAKOTA AND TYPHOON AIRCRAFT. THE FINAL SORTIE FROM ENGLISH SHORES HAD BEGUN!
WHAT WOULDN'T I GIVE TO BE TWENTY YEARS YOUNGER!

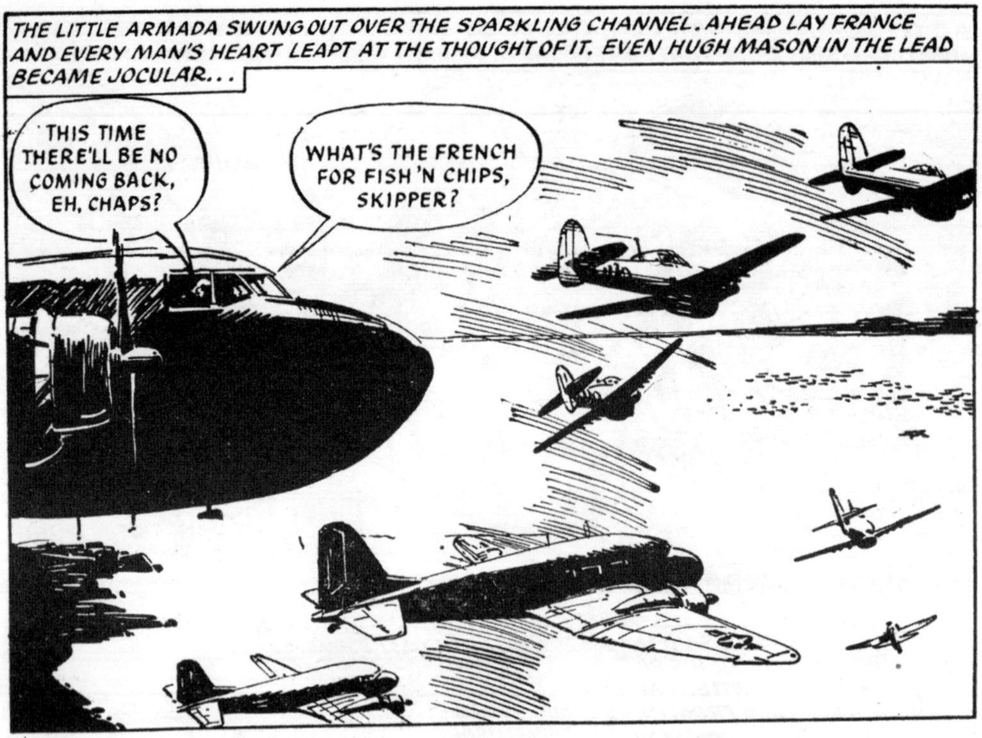
THE LITTLE ARMADA SWUNG OUT OVER THE SPARKLING CHANNEL. AHEAD LAY FRANCE AND EVERY MAN'S HEART LEAPT AT THE THOUGHT OF IT. EVEN HUGH MASON IN THE LEAD BECAME JOCULAR...
THIS TIME THERE'LL BE NO COMING BACK, EH, CHAPS?
WHAT'S THE FRENCH FOR FISH 'N CHIPS, SKIPPER?

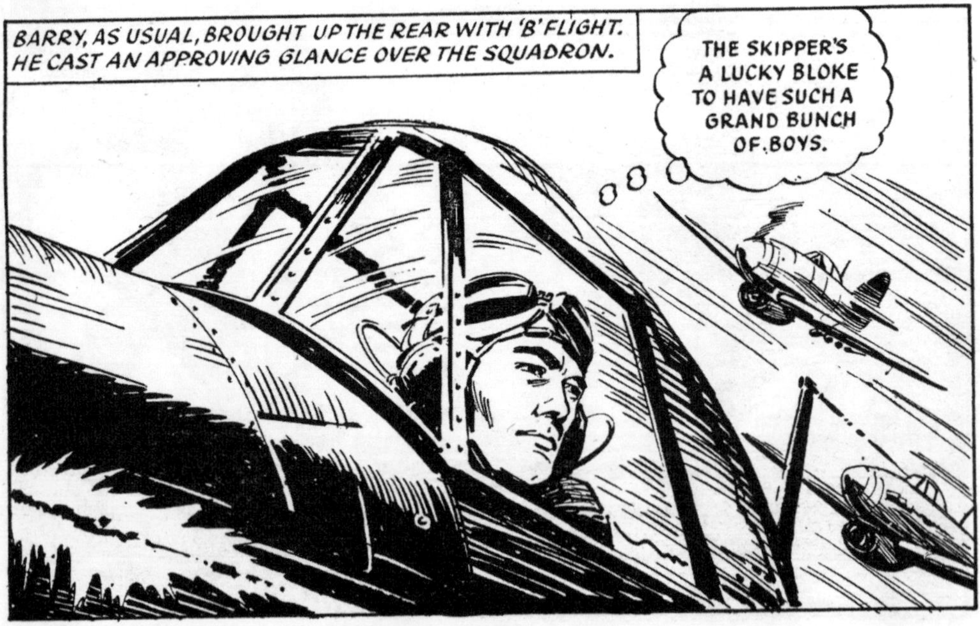
BARRY, AS USUAL, BROUGHT UP THE REAR WITH 'B' FLIGHT. HE CAST AN APPROVING GLANCE OVER THE SQUADRON.
THE SKIPPER'S A LUCKY BLOKE TO HAVE SUCH A GRAND BUNCH OF BOYS.

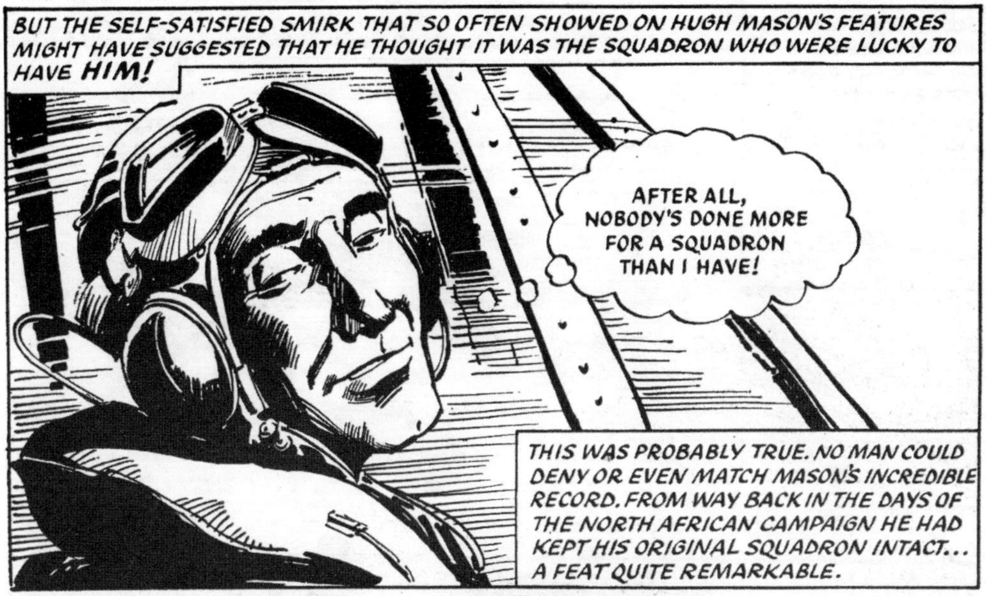
BUT THE SELF-SATISFIED SMIRK THAT SO OFTEN SHOWED ON HUGH MASON'S FEATURES MIGHT HAVE SUGGESTED THAT HE THOUGHT IT WAS THE SQUADRON WHO WERE LUCKY TO HAVE HIM!
AFTER ALL, NOBODY'S DONE MORE FOR A SQUADRON THAN I HAVE!
THIS WAS PROBABLY TRUE. NO MAN COULD DENY OR EVEN MATCH MASON'S INCREDIBLE RECORD. FROM WAY BACK IN THE DAYS OF THE NORTH AFRICAN CAMPAIGN HE HAD KEPT HIS ORIGINAL SQUADRON INTACT... A FEAT QUITE REMARKABLE.

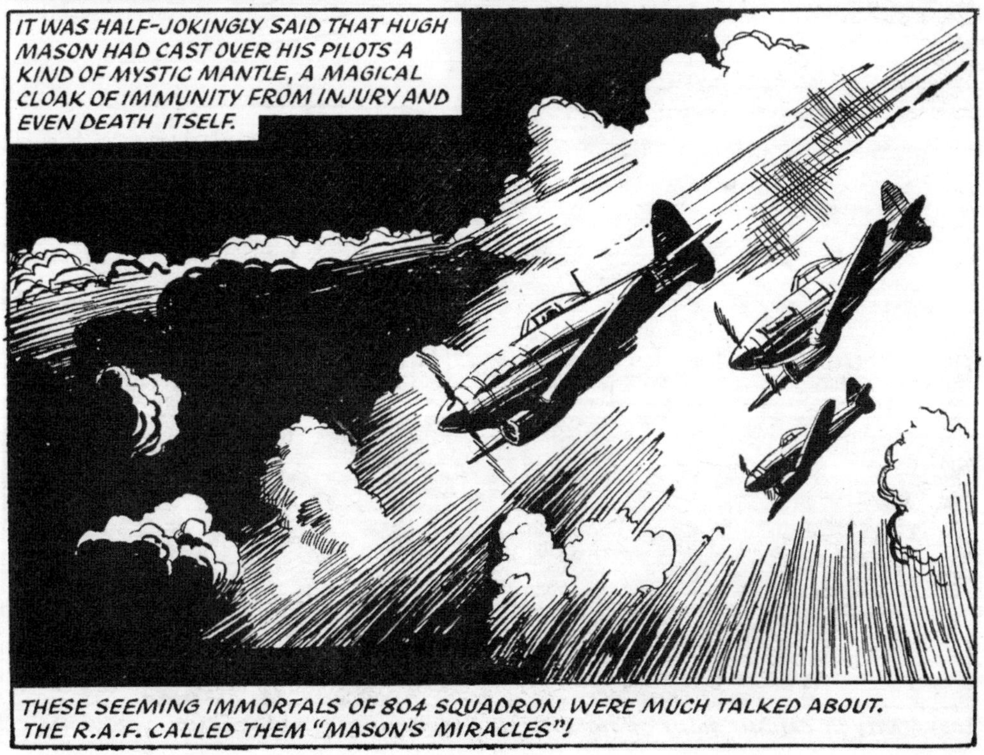
IT WAS HALF-JOKINGLY SAID THAT HUGH MASON HAD CAST OVER HIS PILOTS A KIND OF MYSTIC MANTLE, A MAGICAL CLOAK OF IMMUNITY FROM INJURY AND EVEN DEATH ITSELF.
THESE SEEMING IMMORTALS OF 804 SQUADRON WERE MUCH TALKED ABOUT. THE R.A.F. CALLED THEM "MASON'S MIRACLES"!

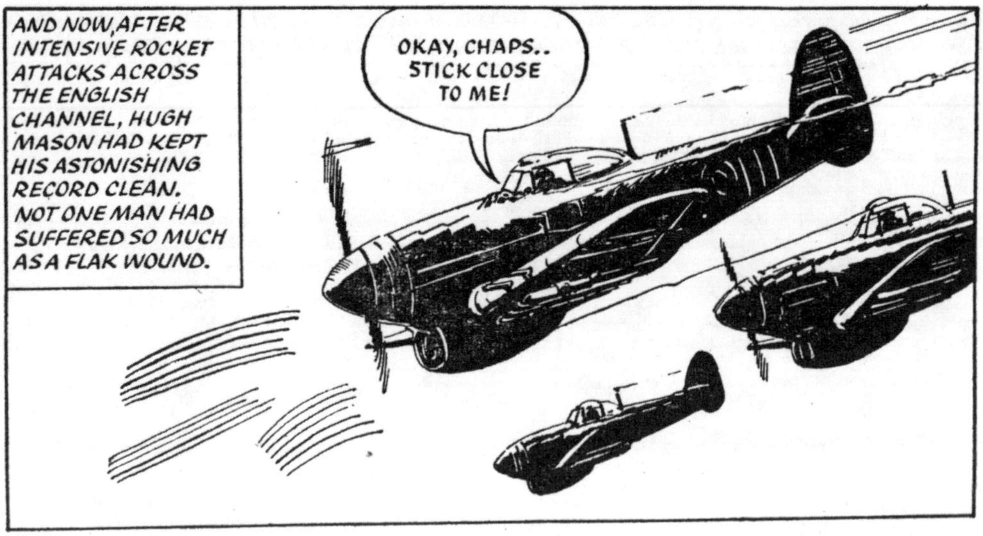
AND NOW, AFTER INTENSIVE ROCKET ATTACKS ACROSS THE ENGLISH CHANNEL, HUGH MASON HAD KEPT HIS ASTONISHING RECORD CLEAN. NOT ONE MAN HAD SUFFERED SO MUCH AS A FLAK WOUND.
OKAY, CHAPS.. STICK CLOSE TO ME!

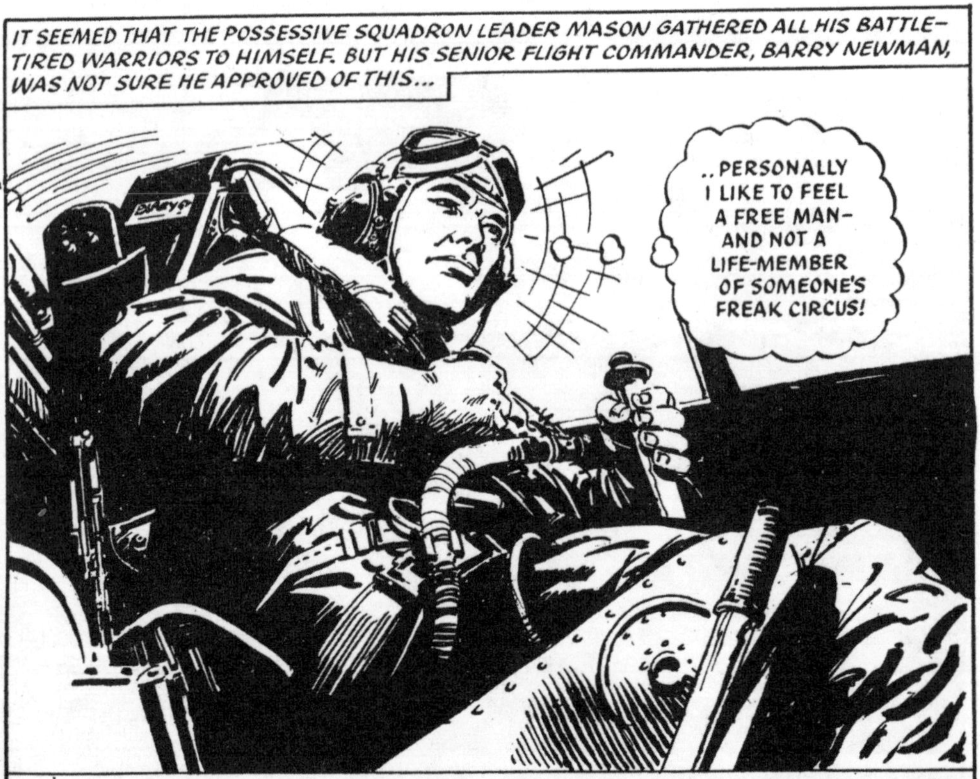
IT SEEMED THAT THE POSSESSIVE SQUADRON LEADER MASON GATHERED ALL HIS BATTLE-TIRED WARRIORS TO HIMSELF. BUT HIS SENIOR FLIGHT COMMANDER, BARRY NEWMAN, WAS NOT SURE HE APPROVED OF THIS...
..PERSONALLY I LIKE TO FEEL A FREE MAN- AND NOT A LIFE-MEMBER OF SOMEONE'S FREAK CIRCUS!
PRESENTLY HE CAUGHT SIGHT OF THE BATTLE-SCARRED DUNES OF ARROMANCHES IN FRANCE.

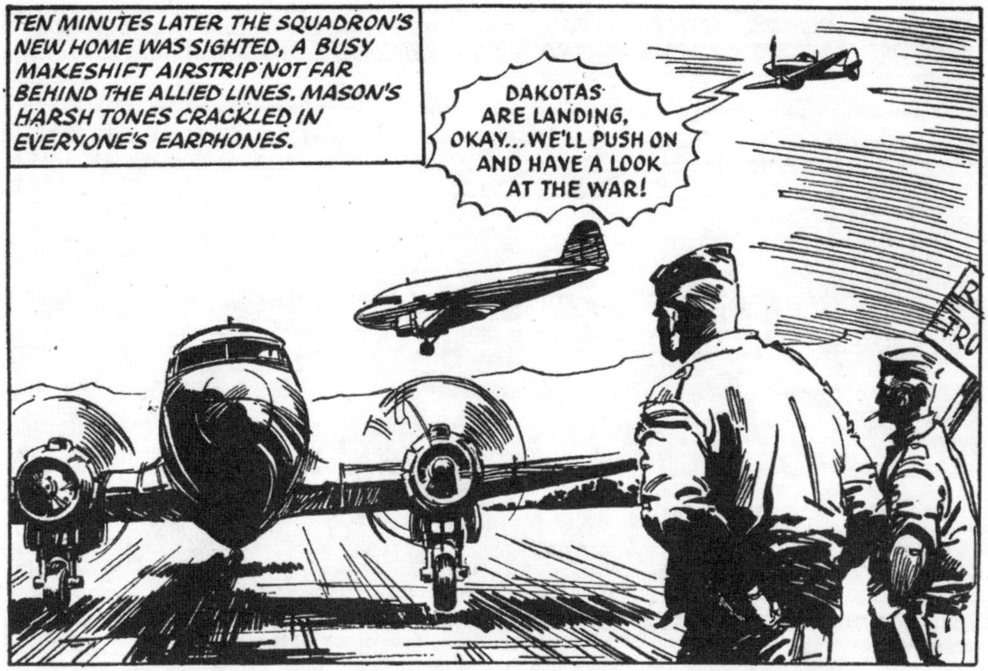
TEN MINUTES LATER THE SQUADRON'S NEW HOME WAS SIGHTED, A BUSY MAKESHIFT AIRSTRIP NOT FAR BEHIND THE ALLIED LINES. MASON'S HARSH TONES CRACKLED IN EVERYONE'S EARPHONES.
DAKOTAS ARE LANDING, OKAY... WE'LL PUSH ON AND HAVE A LOOK AT THE WAR!

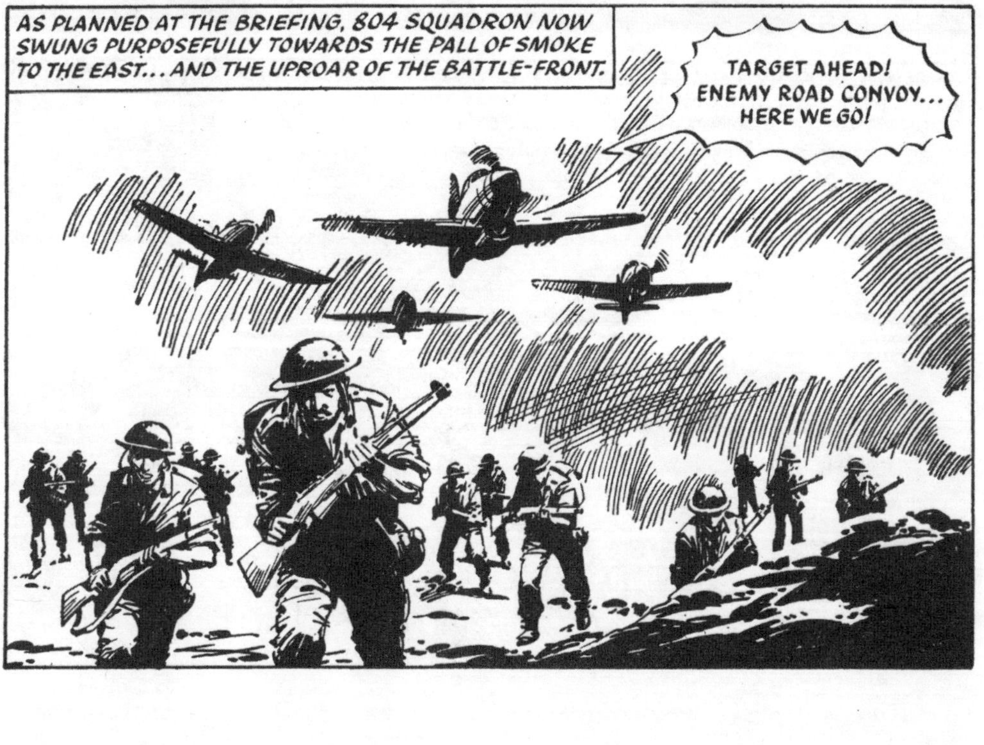
AS PLANNED AT THE BRIEFING, 804 SQUADRON NOW SWUNG PURPOSEFULLY TOWARDS THE PALL OF SMOKE TO THE EAST... AND THE UPROAR OF THE BATTLE-FRONT.
TARGET AHEAD! ENEMY ROAD CONVOY... HERE WE GO!

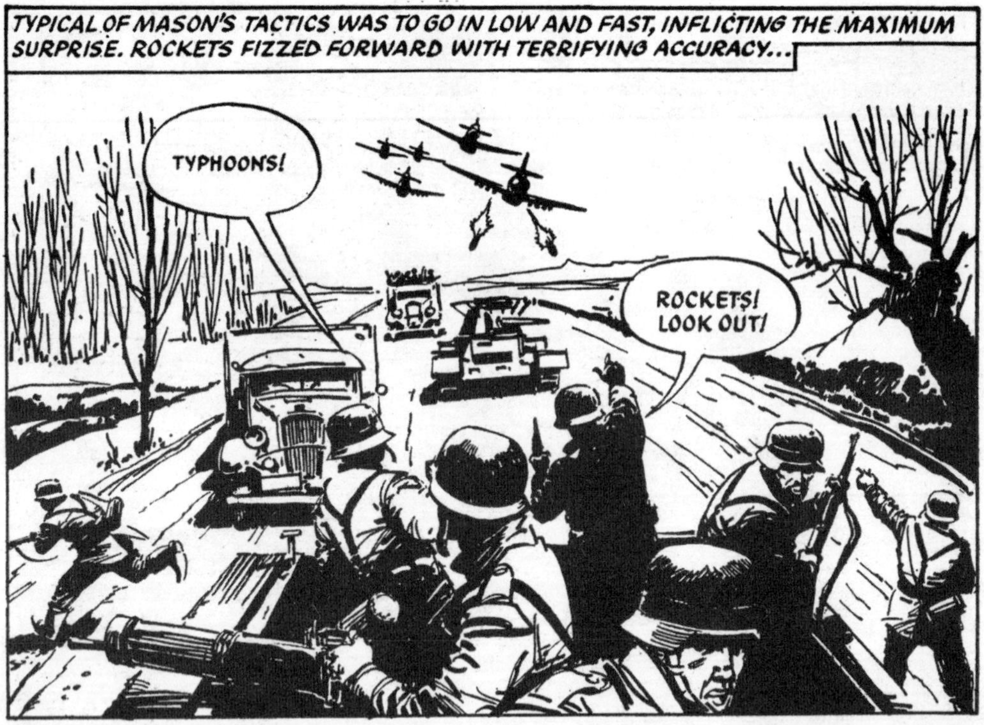
TYPICAL OF MASON'S TACTICS WAS TO GO IN LOW AND FAST, INFLICTING THE MAXIMUM SURPRISE. ROCKETS FIZZED FORWARD WITH TERRIFYING ACCURACY...
TYPHOONS!
ROCKETS! LOOK OUT!

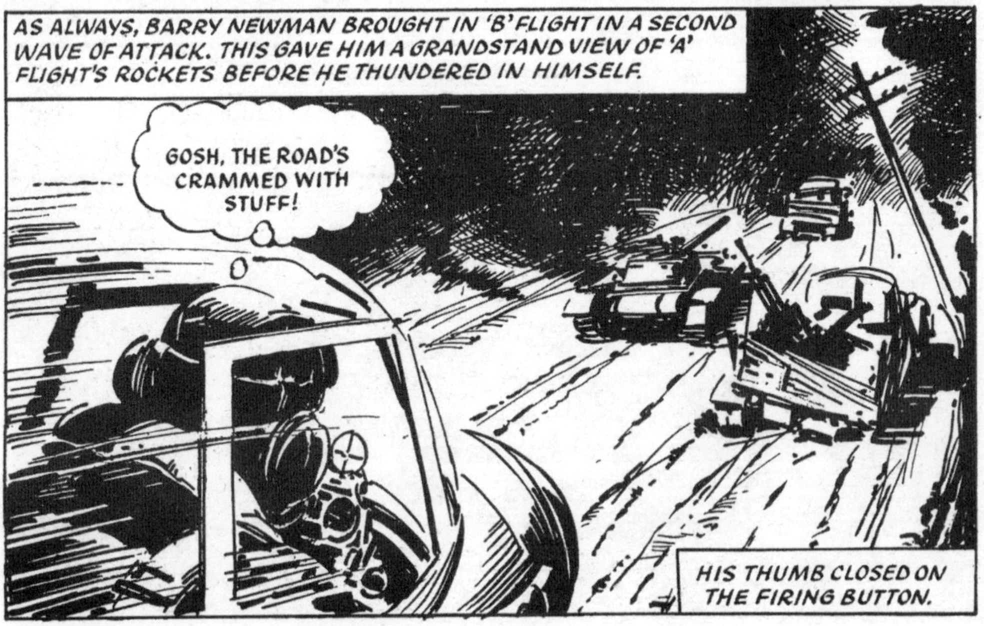
AS ALWAYS, BARRY NEWMAN BROUGHT IN 'B' FLIGHT IN A SECOND WAVE OF ATTACK. THIS GAVE HIM A GRANDSTAND VIEW OF 'A' FLIGHT'S ROCKETS BEFORE HE THUNDERED IN HIMSELF.
GOSH, THE ROAD'S CRAMMED WITH STUFF!
HIS THUMB CLOSED ON THE FIRING BUTTON.

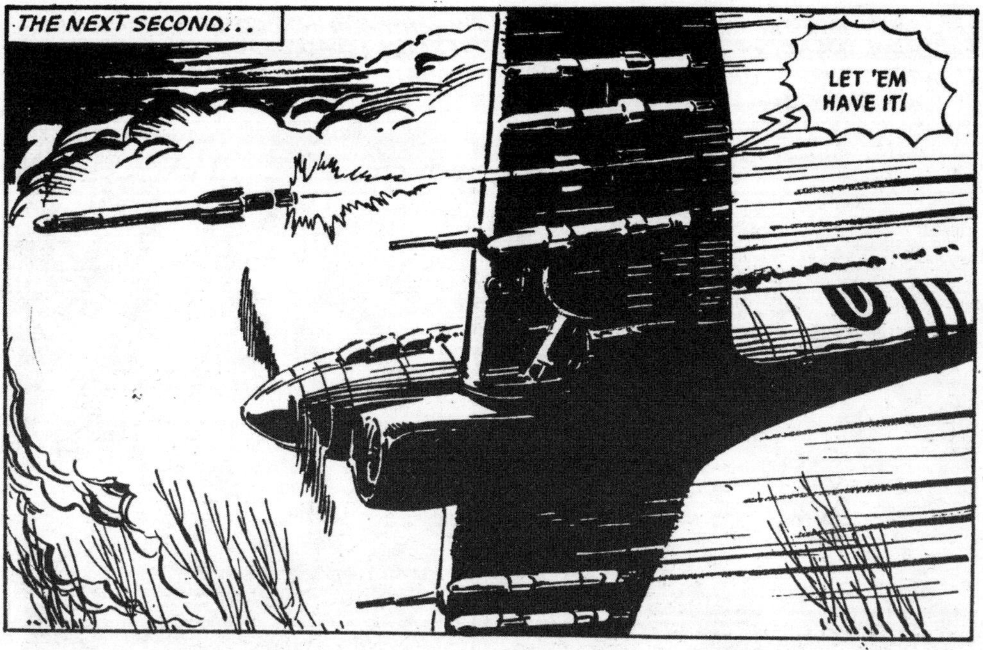
THE NEXT SECOND...
LET 'EM HAVE IT!

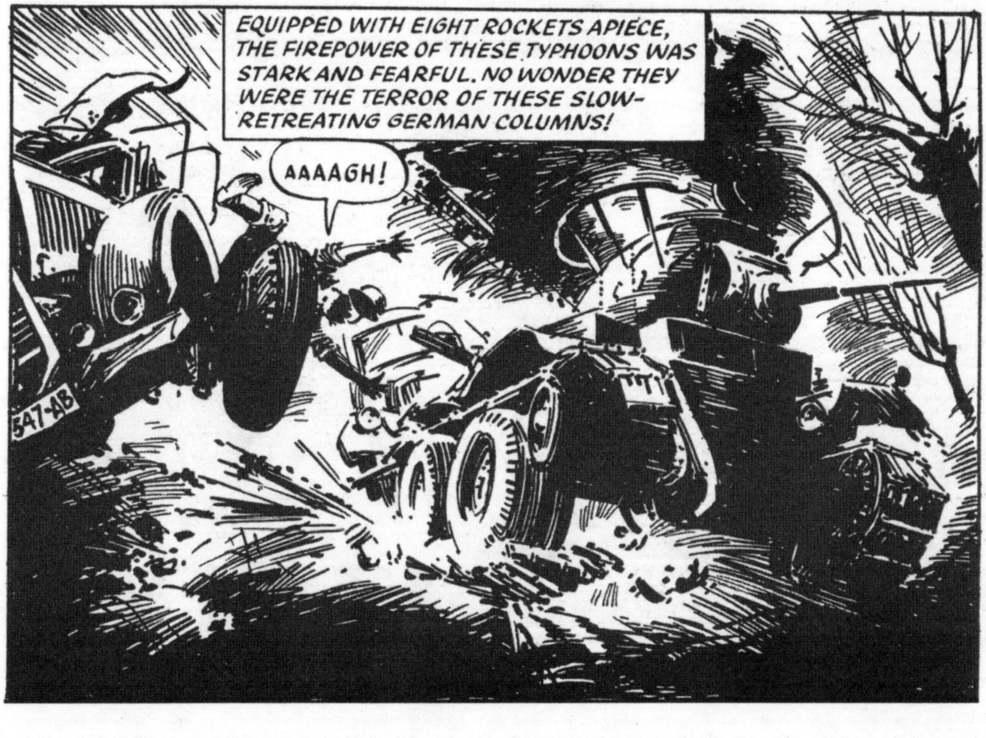
EQUIPPED WITH EIGHT ROCKETS APIECE, THE FIREPOWER OF THESE TYPHOONS WAS STARK AND FEARFUL. NO WONDER THEY WERE THE TERROR OF THESE SLOW-RETREATING GERMAN COLUMNS!
AAAAGH!
547-AB

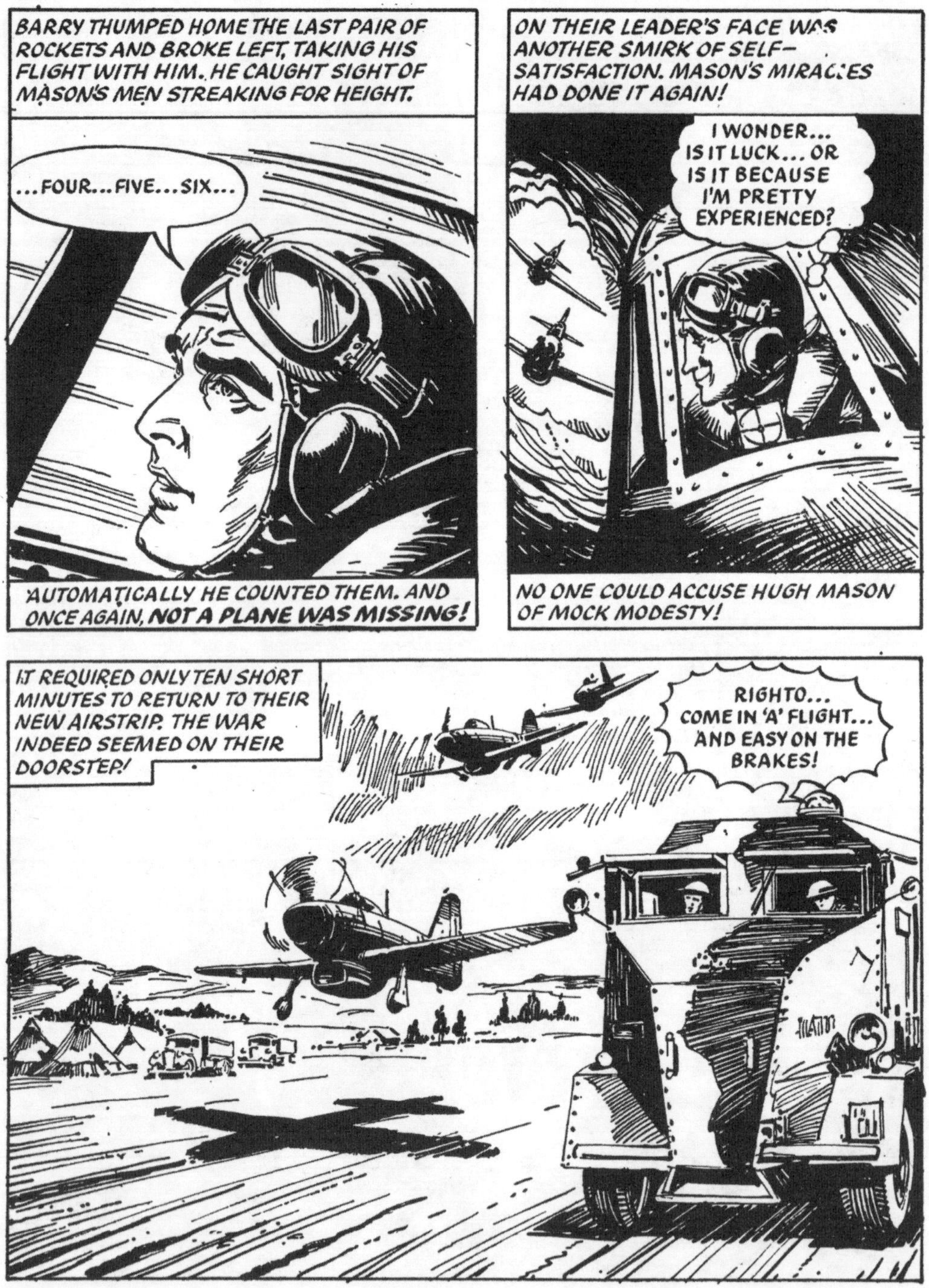
BARRY THUMPED HOME THE LAST PAIR OF ROCKETS AND BROKE LEFT, TAKING HIS FLIGHT WITH HIM. HE CAUGHT SIGHT OF MASON'S MEN STREAKING FOR HEIGHT.
...FOUR...FIVE...SIX...
AUTOMATICALLY HE COUNTED THEM. AND ONCE AGAIN, NOT A PLANE WAS MISSING!
ON THEIR LEADER'S FACE WAS ANOTHER SMIRK OF SELF-SATISFACTION. MASON'S MIRACLES HAD DONE IT AGAIN!
I WONDER... IS IT LUCK... OR IS IT BECAUSE I'M PRETTY EXPERIENCED?
NO ONE COULD ACCUSE HUGH MASON OF MOCK MODESTY!
IT REQUIRED ONLY TEN SHORT MINUTES TO RETURN TO THEIR NEW AIRSTRIP. THE WAR INDEED SEEMED ON THEIR DOORSTEP!
RIGHTO... COME IN 'A' FLIGHT... AND EASY ON THE BRAKES!

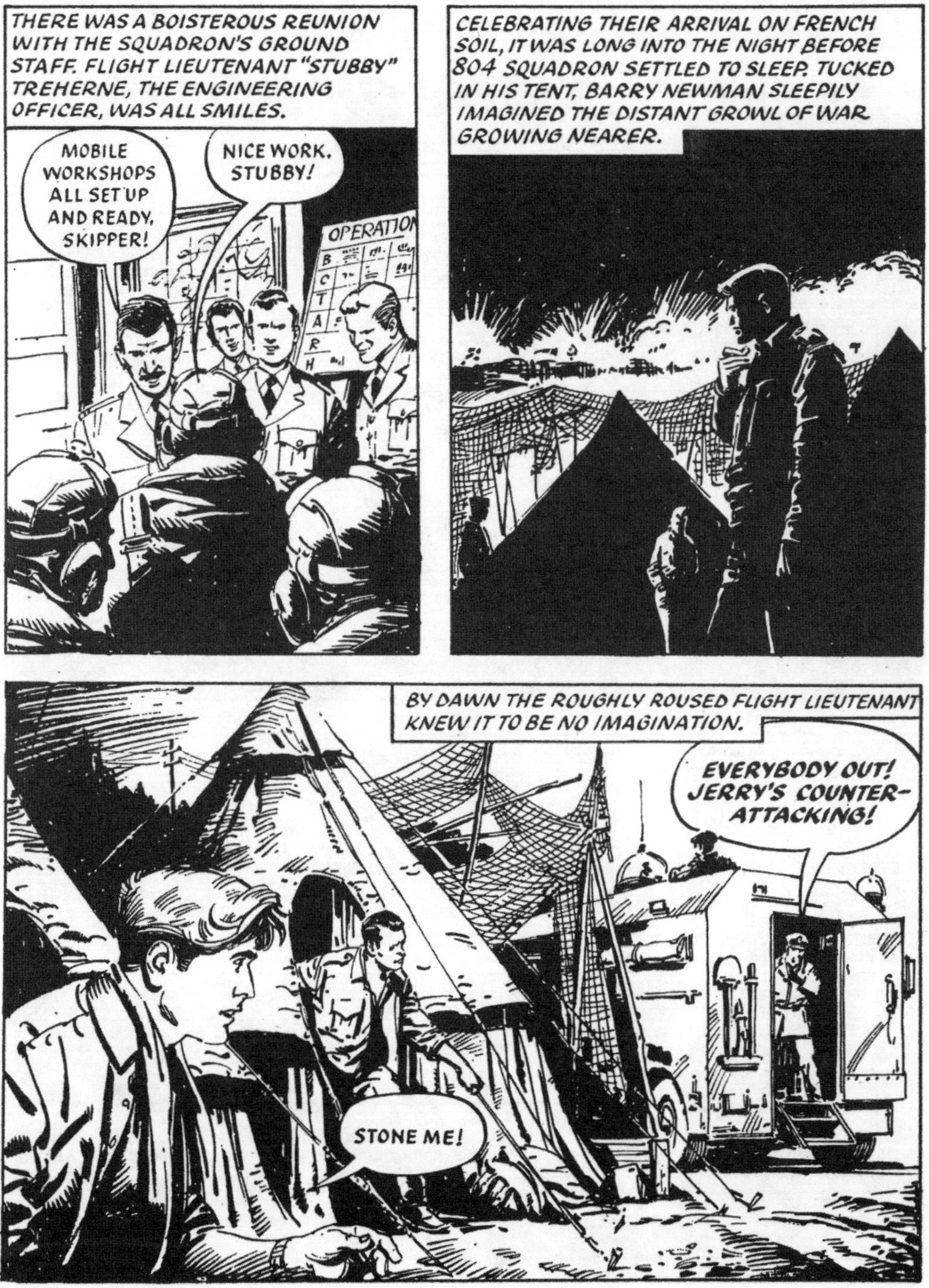
THERE WAS A BOISTEROUS REUNION WITH THE SQUADRON'S GROUND STAFF. FLIGHT LIEUTENANT "STUBBY" TREHERNE, THE ENGINEERING OFFICER, WAS ALL SMILES.
MOBILE WORKSHOPS ALL SET UP AND READY, SKIPPER!
NICE WORK, STUBBY!
OPERATION
CELEBRATING THEIR ARRIVAL ON FRENCH SOIL, IT WAS LONG INTO THE NIGHT BEFORE 804 SQUADRON SETTLED TO SLEEP. TUCKED IN HIS TENT, BARRY NEWMAN SLEEPILY IMAGINED THE DISTANT GROWL OF WAR GROWING NEARER.
BY DAWN THE ROUGHLY ROUSED FLIGHT LIEUTENANT KNEW IT TO BE NO IMAGINATION.
EVERYBODY OUT! JERRY'S COUNTER-ATTACKING!
STONE ME!

Chapter 2: RAIN OF DEATH

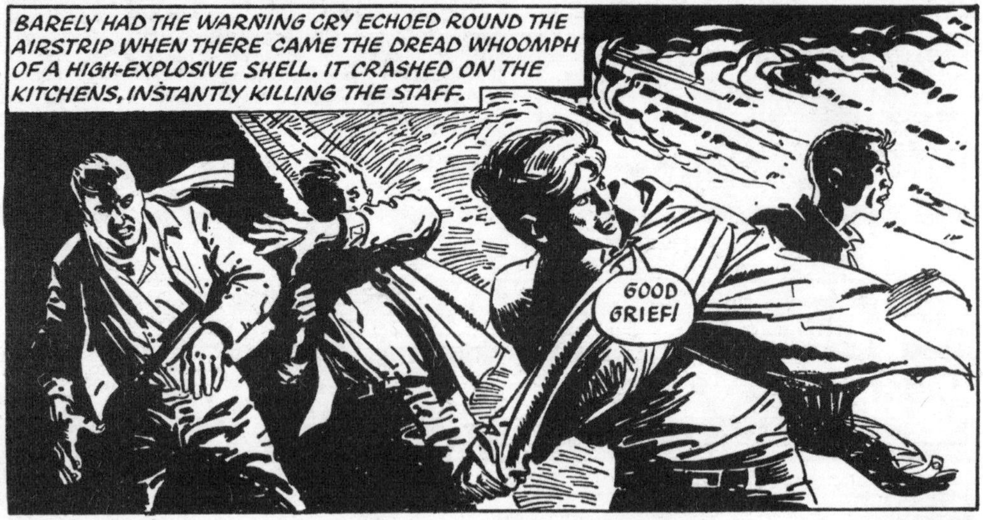
BARELY HAD THE WARNING CRY ECHOED ROUND THE AIRSTRIP WHEN THERE CAME THE DREAD WHOOMPH OF A HIGH-EXPLOSIVE SHELL. IT CRASHED ON THE KITCHENS, INSTANTLY KILLING THE STAFF.
GOOD GRIEF!

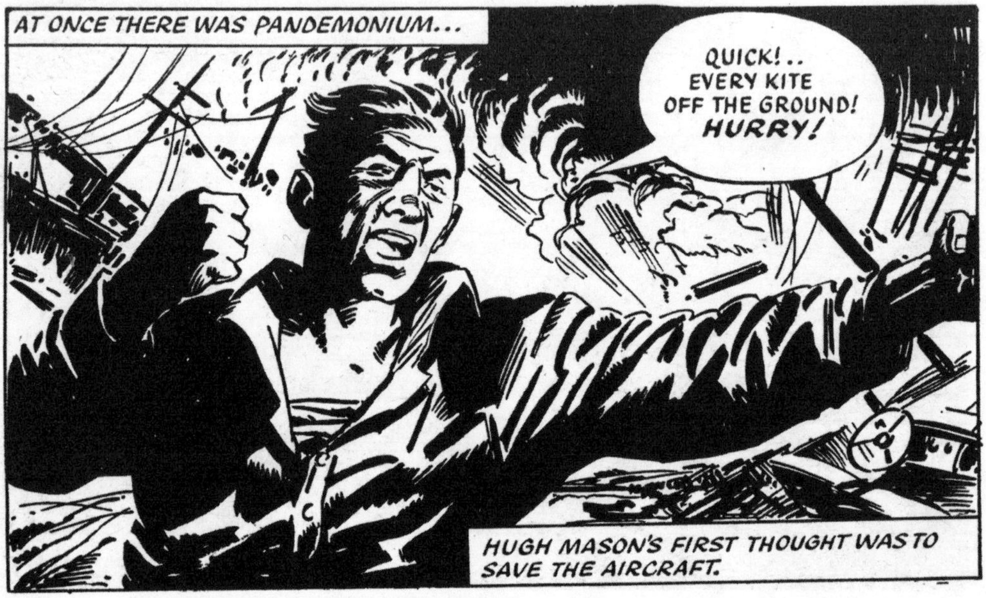
AT ONCE THERE WAS PANDEMONIUM...
QUICK!.. EVERY KITE OFF THE GROUND! HURRY!
HUGH MASON'S FIRST THOUGHT WAS TO SAVE THE AIRCRAFT.

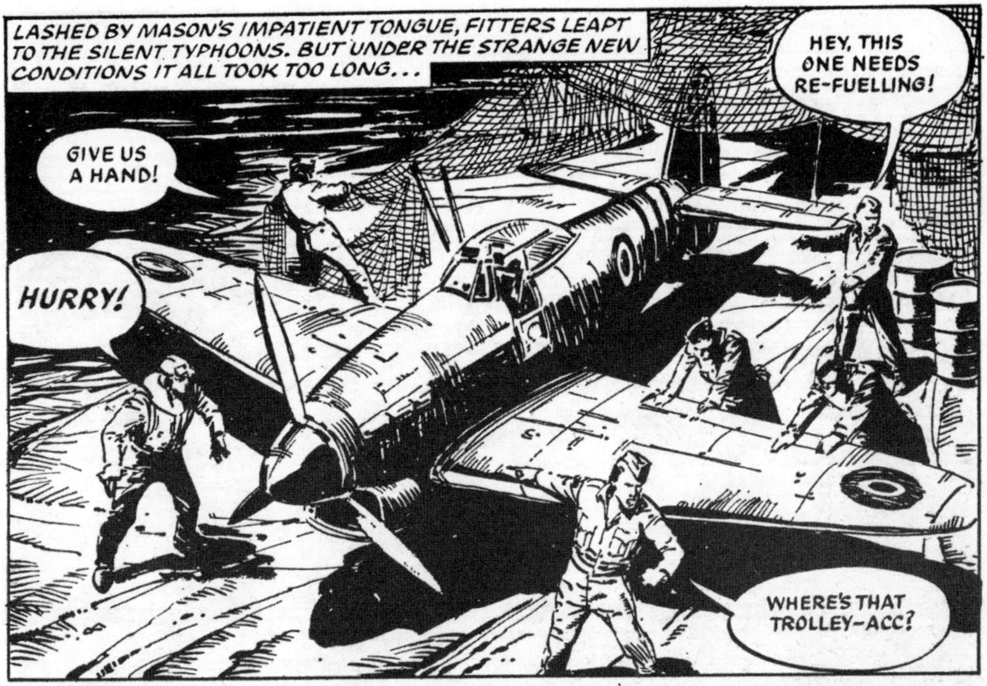
LASHED BY MASON'S IMPATIENT TONGUE, FITTERS LEAPT TO THE SILENT TYPHOONS. BUT UNDER THE STRANGE NEW CONDITIONS IT ALL TOOK TOO LONG...
HEY, THIS ONE NEEDS RE-FUELLING!
GIVE US A HAND!
HURRY!
WHERE'S THAT TROLLEY-ACC?

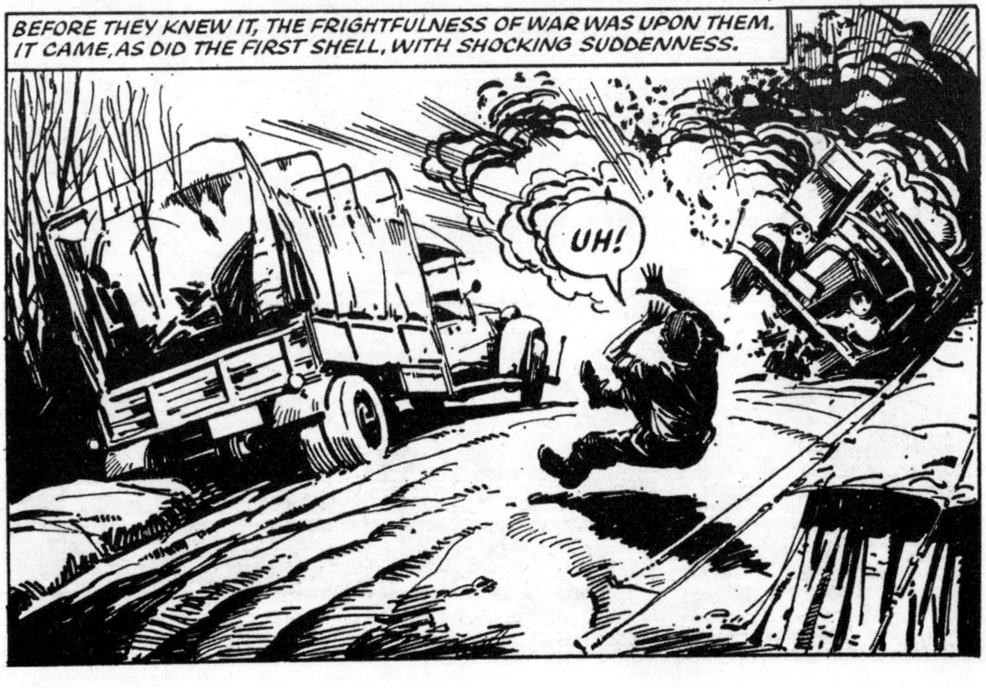
BEFORE THEY KNEW IT, THE FRIGHTFULNESS OF WAR WAS UPON THEM. IT CAME, AS DID THE FIRST SHELL, WITH SHOCKING SUDDENNESS.
UH!

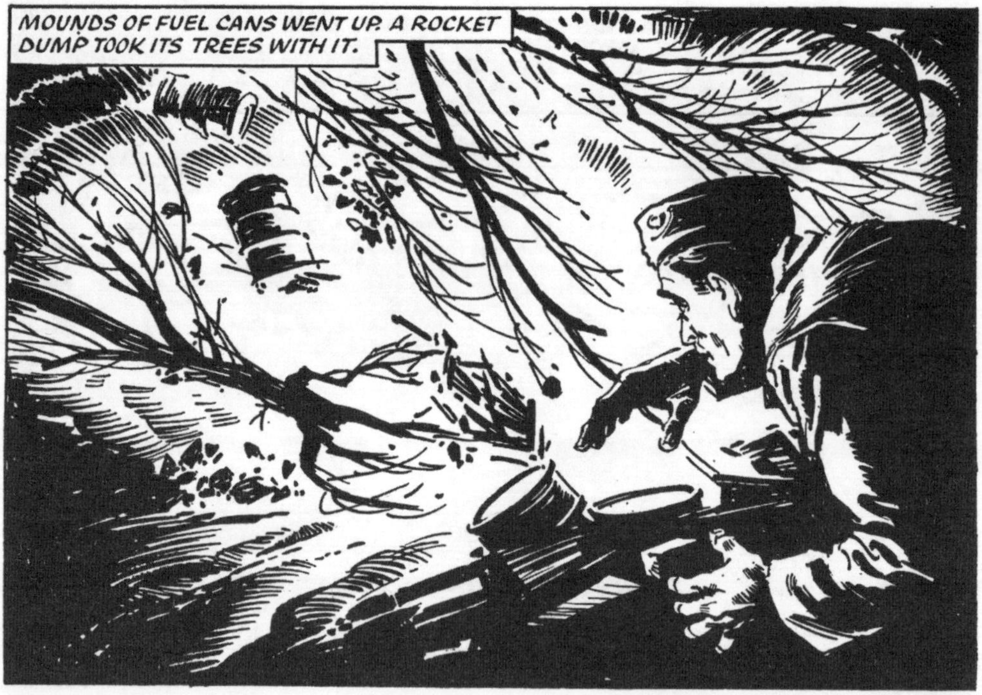
MOUNDS OF FUEL CANS WENT UP. A ROCKET DUMP TOOK ITS TREES WITH IT.

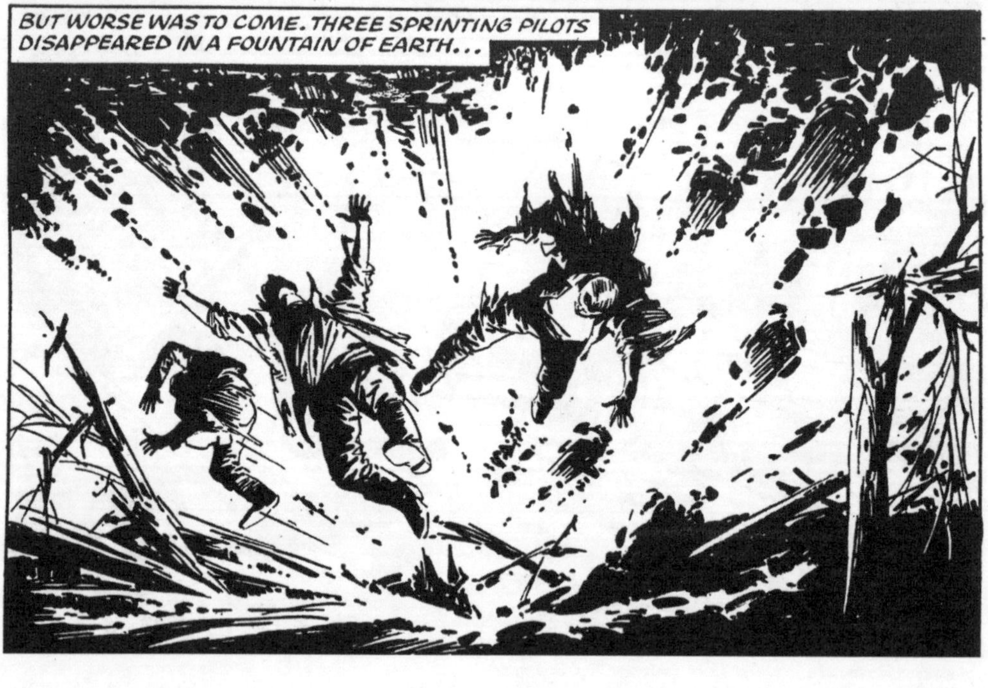
BUT WORSE WAS TO COME. THREE SPRINTING PILOTS DISAPPEARED IN A FOUNTAIN OF EARTH...

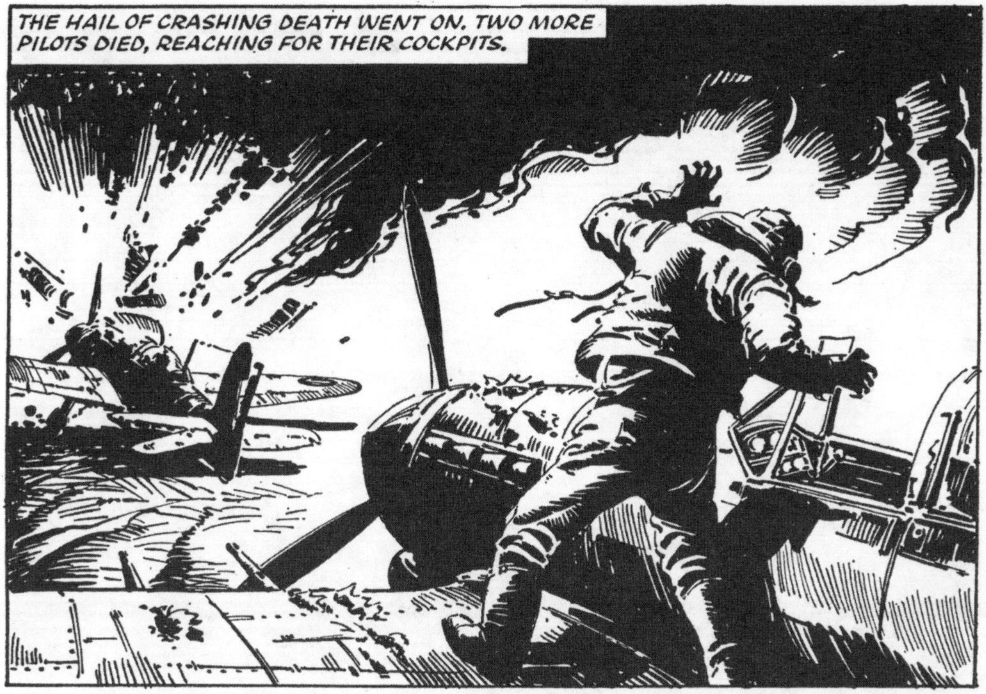
THE HAIL OF CRASHING DEATH WENT ON. TWO MORE PILOTS DIED, REACHING FOR THEIR COCKPITS.

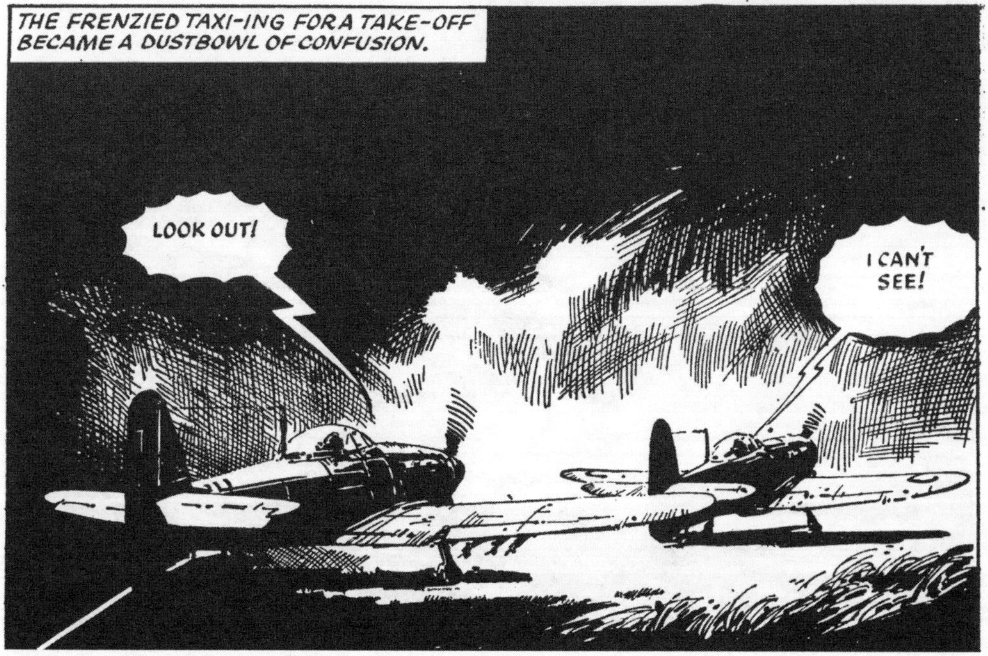
THE FRENZIED TAXI-ING FOR A TAKE-OFF BECAME A DUSTBOWL OF CONFUSION.
LOOK OUT!
I CAN'T SEE!

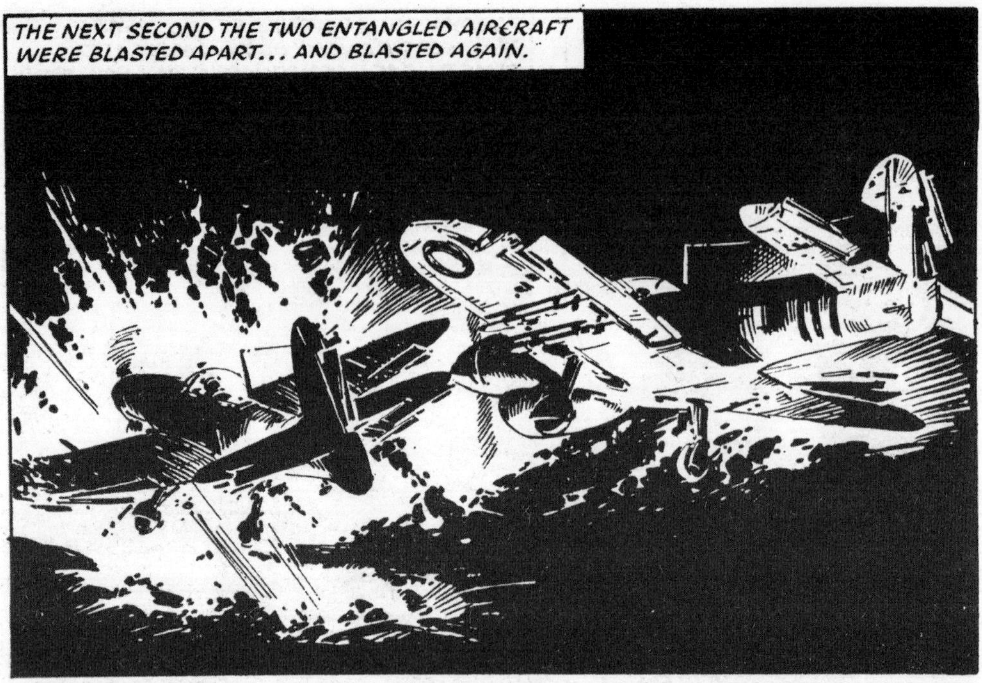
THE NEXT SECOND THE TWO ENTANGLED AIRCRAFT WERE BLASTED APART... AND BLASTED AGAIN.

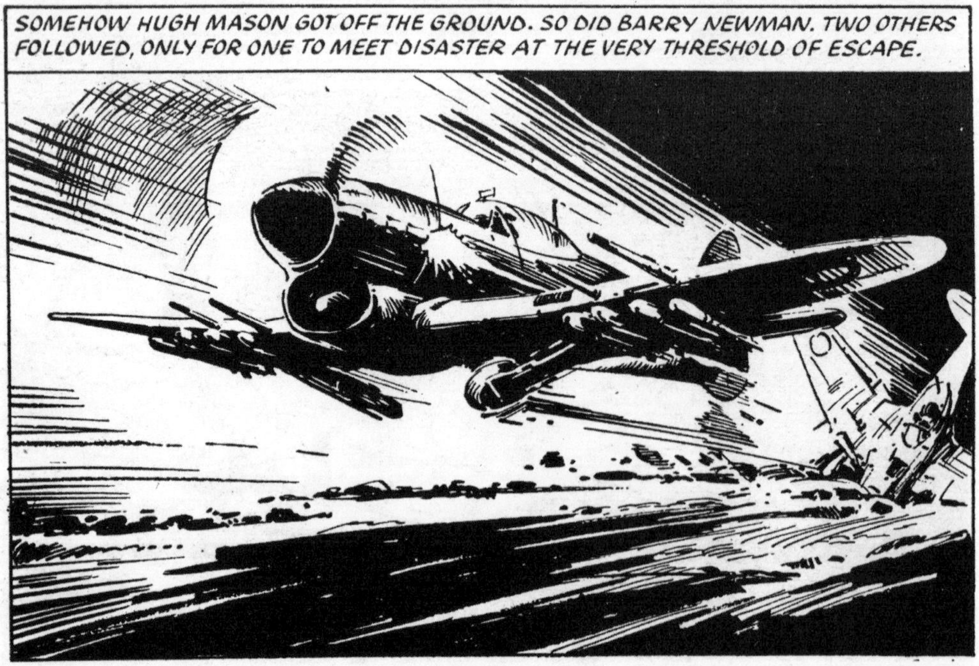
SOMEHOW HUGH MASON GOT OFF THE GROUND. SO DID BARRY NEWMAN. TWO OTHERS FOLLOWED, ONLY FOR ONE TO MEET DISASTER AT THE VERY THRESHOLD OF ESCAPE.

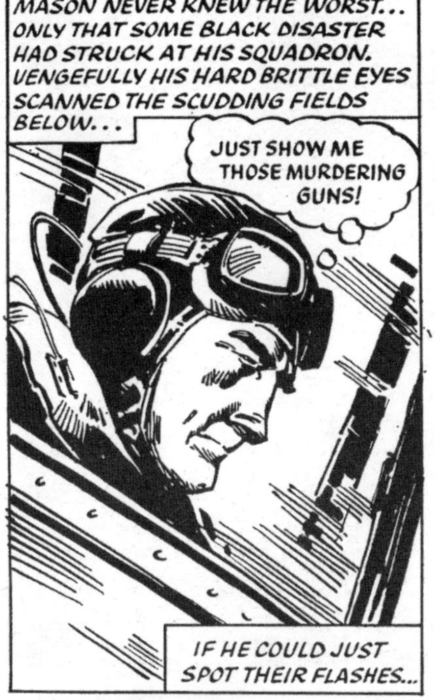
MASON NEVER KNEW THE WORST... ONLY THAT SOME BLACK DISASTER HAD STRUCK AT HIS SQUADRON. VENGEFULLY HIS HARD BRITTLE EYES SCANNED THE SCUDDING FIELDS BELOW...
JUST SHOW ME THOSE MURDERING GUNS!
IF HE COULD JUST SPOT THEIR FLASHES...

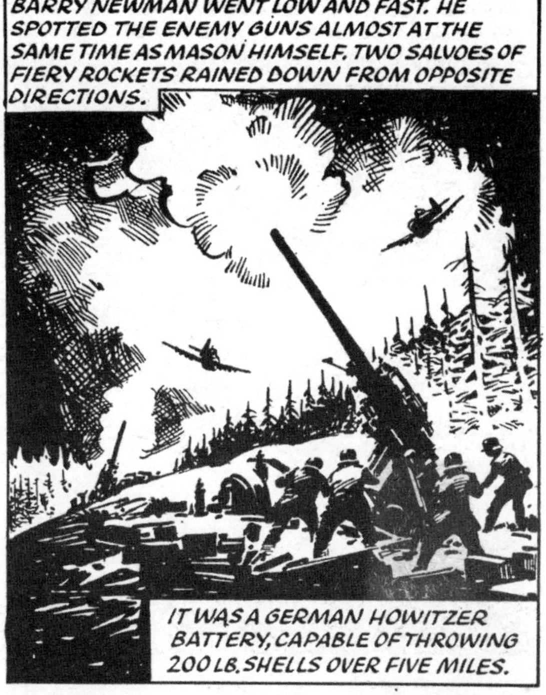
BARRY NEWMAN WENT LOW AND FAST. HE SPOTTED THE ENEMY GUNS ALMOST AT THE SAME TIME AS MASON HIMSELF. TWO SALVOES OF FIERY ROCKETS RAINED DOWN FROM OPPOSITE DIRECTIONS.
IT WAS A GERMAN HOWITZER BATTERY, CAPABLE OF THROWING 200 LB. SHELLS OVER FIVE MILES.

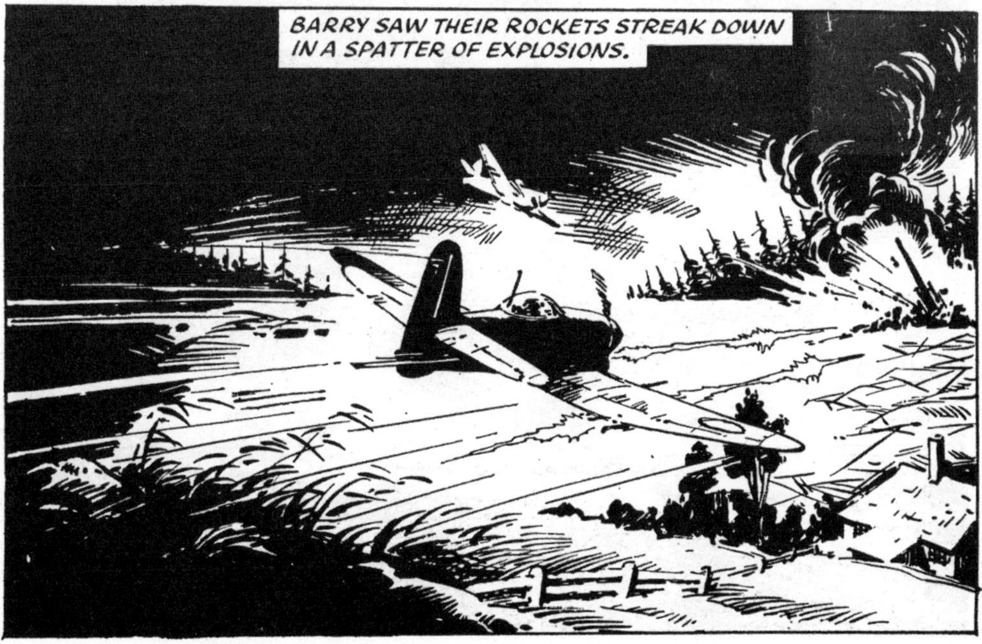
BARRY SAW THEIR ROCKETS STREAK DOWN IN A SPATTER OF EXPLOSIONS.

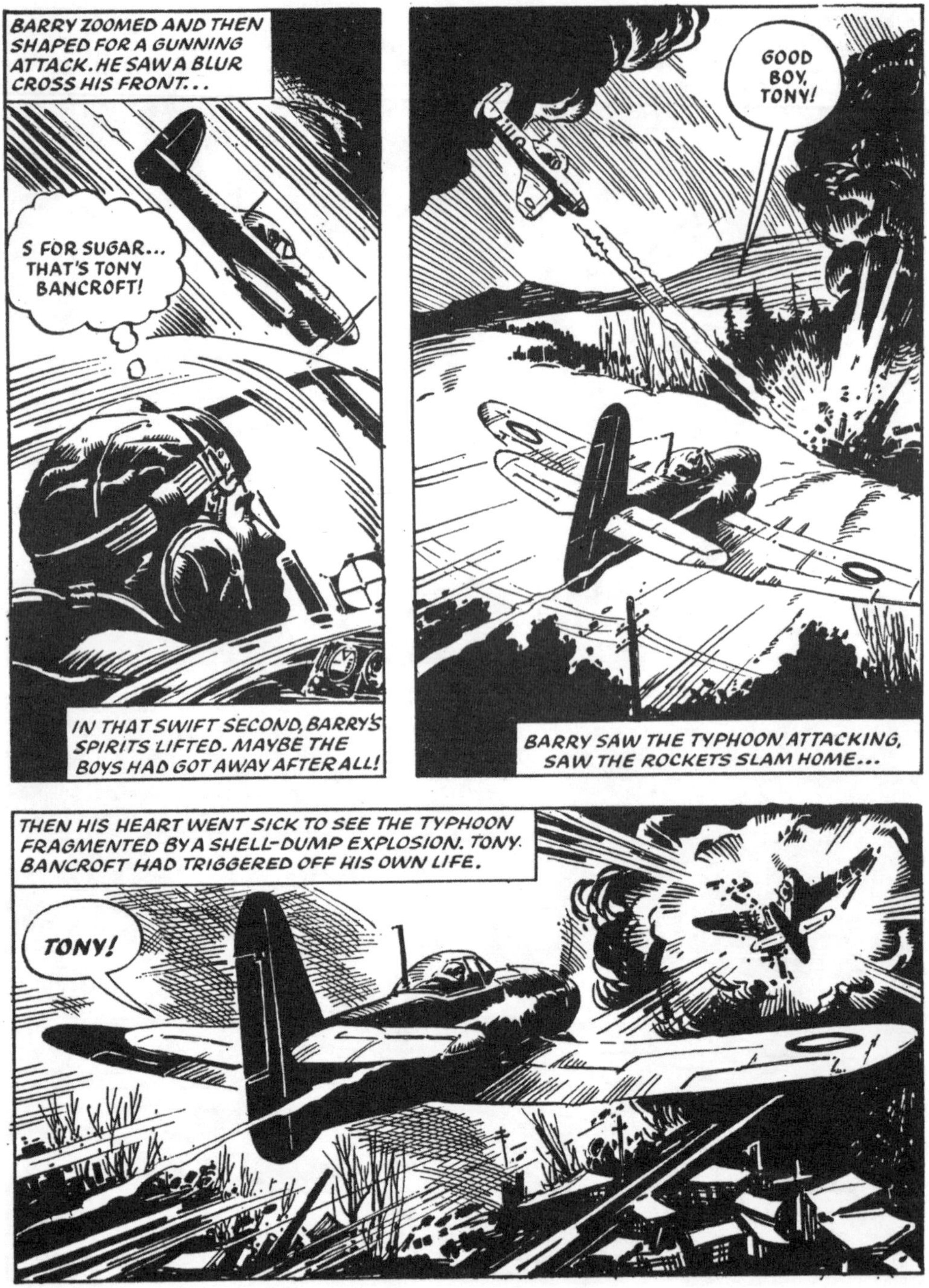
BARRY ZOOMED AND THEN SHAPED FOR A GUNNING ATTACK. HE SAW A BLUR CROSS HIS FRONT...
S FOR SUGAR... THAT'S TONY BANCROFT!
IN THAT SWIFT SECOND, BARRY'S SPIRITS LIFTED. MAYBE THE BOYS HAD GOT AWAY AFTER ALL!
GOOD BOY, TONY!
BARRY SAW THE TYPHOON ATTACKING, SAW THE ROCKETS SLAM HOME...
THEN HIS HEART WENT SICK TO SEE THE TYPHOON FRAGMENTED BY A SHELL-DUMP EXPLOSION. TONY BANCROFT HAD TRIGGERED OFF HIS OWN LIFE.
TONY!

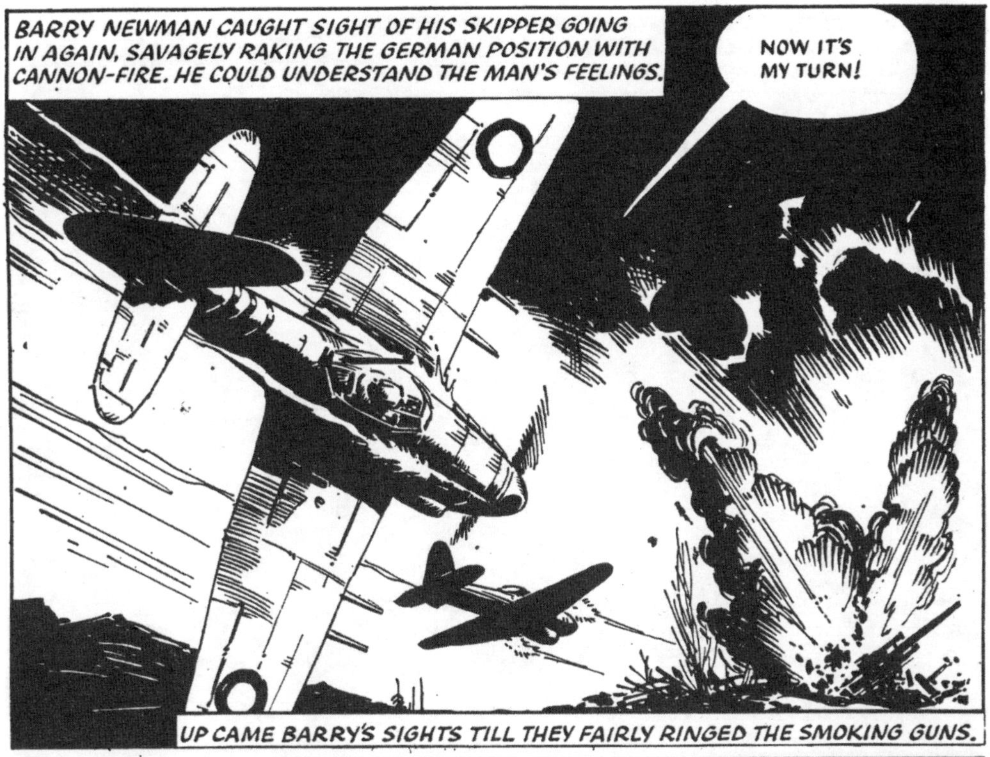
BARRY NEWMAN CAUGHT SIGHT OF HIS SKIPPER GOING IN AGAIN, SAVAGELY RAKING THE GERMAN POSITION WITH CANNON-FIRE. HE COULD UNDERSTAND THE MAN'S FEELINGS.
NOW IT'S MY TURN!
UP CAME BARRY'S SIGHTS TILL THEY FAIRLY RINGED THE SMOKING GUNS.

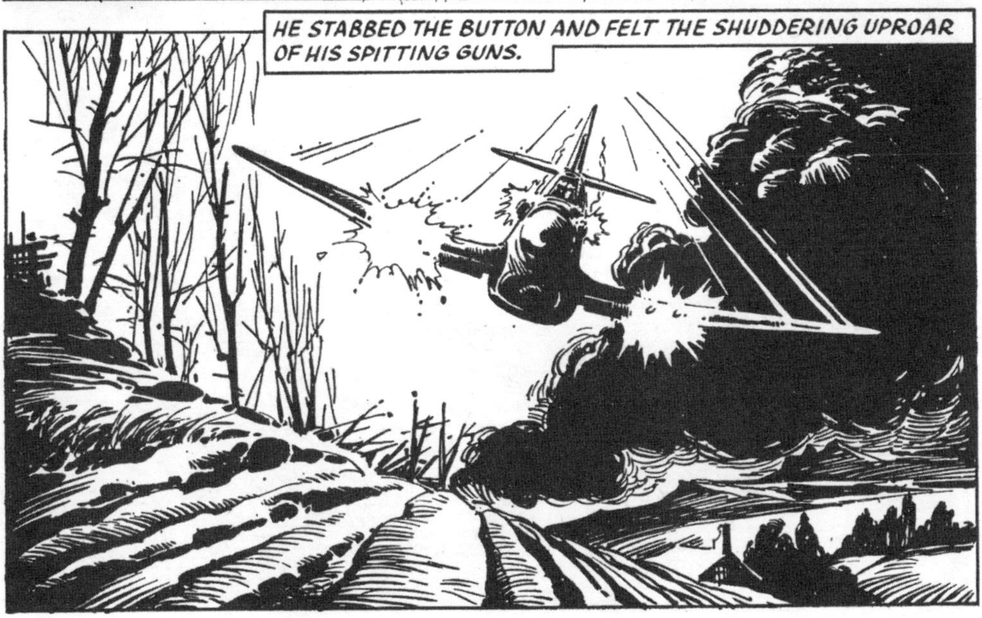
HE STABBED THE BUTTON AND FELT THE SHUDDERING UPROAR OF HIS SPITTING GUNS.

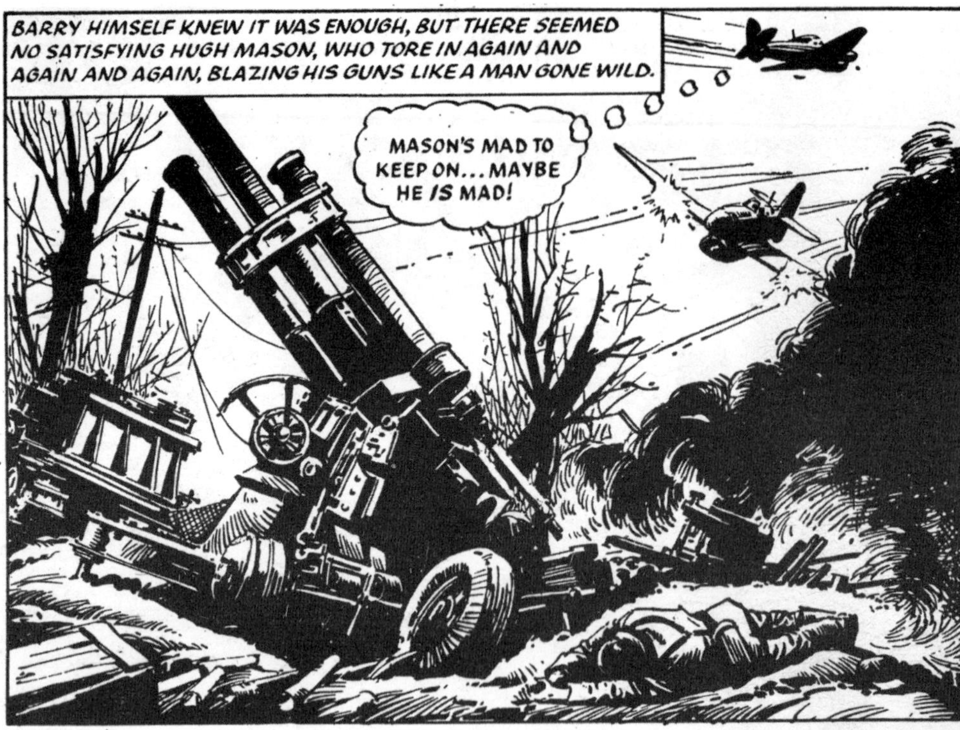
BARRY HIMSELF KNEW IT WAS ENOUGH, BUT THERE SEEMED NO SATISFYING HUGH MASON, WHO TORE IN AGAIN AND AGAIN AND AGAIN, BLAZING HIS GUNS LIKE A MAN GONE WILD.
MASON'S MAD TO KEEP ON... MAYBE HE IS MAD!

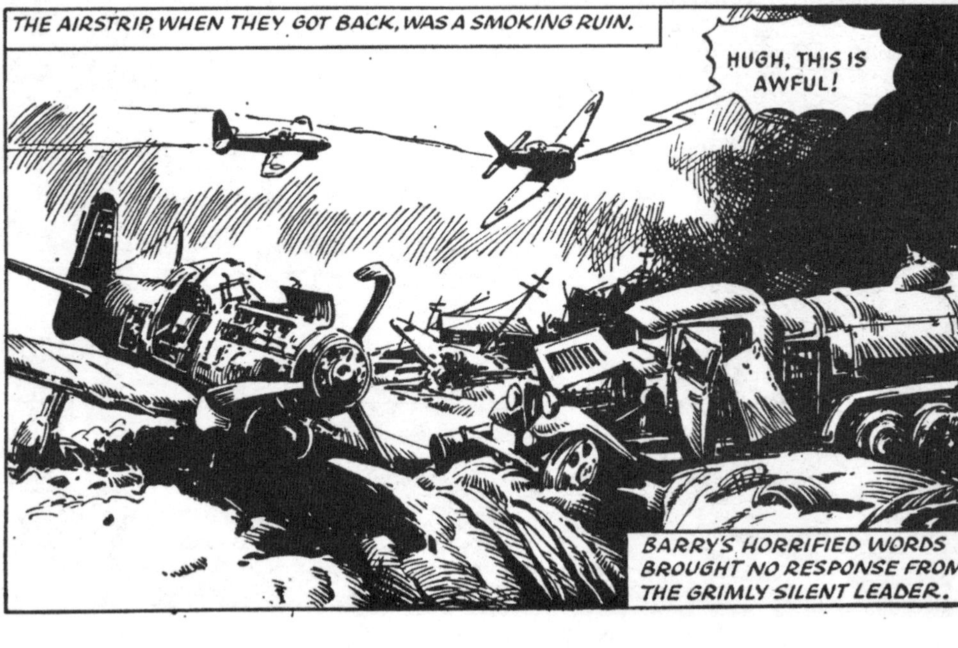
THE AIRSTRIP, WHEN THEY GOT BACK, WAS A SMOKING RUIN.
HUGH, THIS IS AWFUL!
BARRY'S HORRIFIED WORDS BROUGHT NO RESPONSE FROM THE GRIMLY SILENT LEADER.

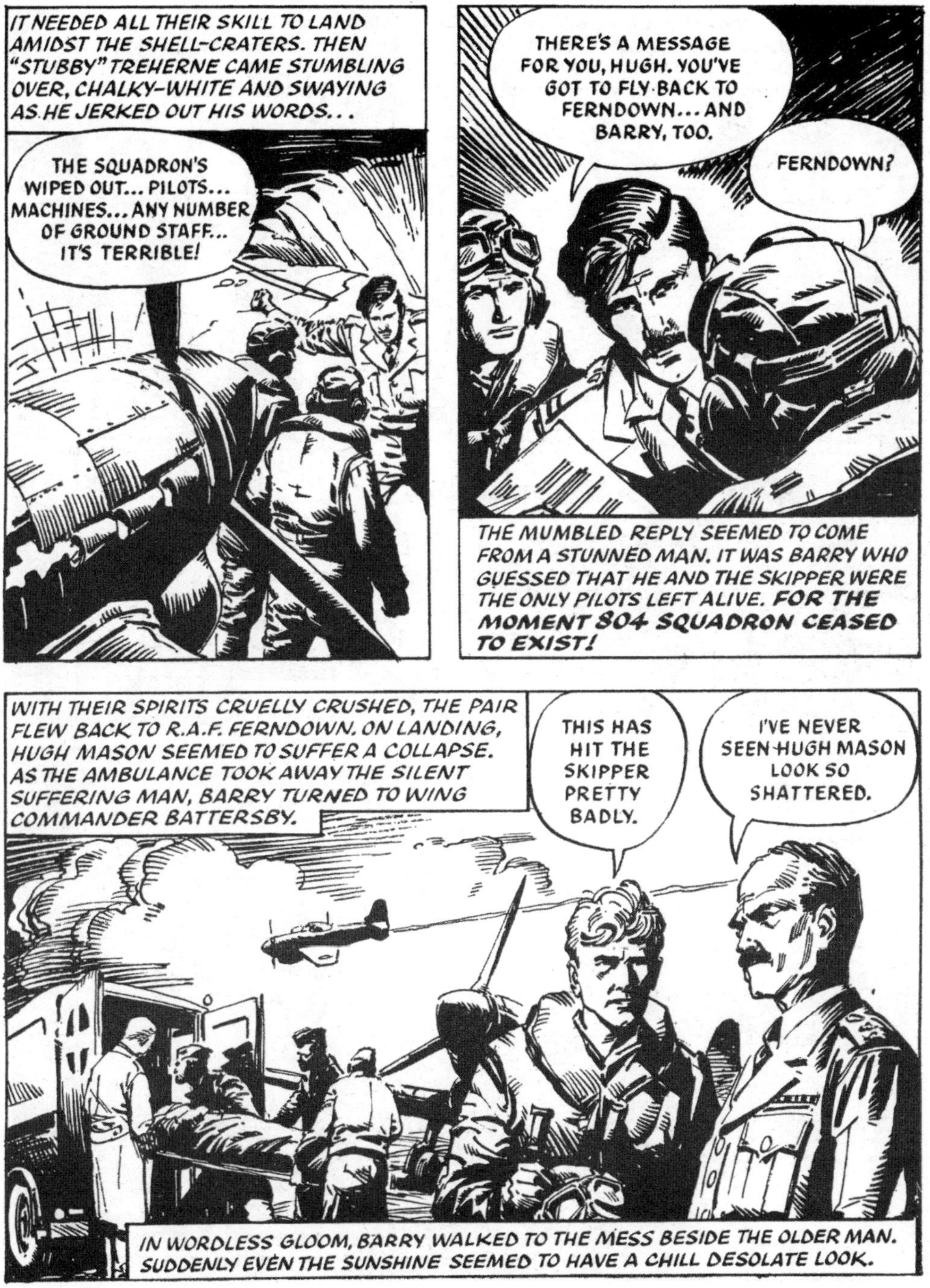
IT NEEDED ALL THEIR SKILL TO LAND AMIDST THE SHELL-CRATERS. THEN "STUBBY" TREHERNE CAME STUMBLING OVER, CHALKY-WHITE AND SWAYING AS HE JERKED OUT HIS WORDS. . .
THE SQUADRON'S WIPED OUT... PILOTS... MACHINES... ANY NUMBER OF GROUND STAFF... IT'S TERRIBLE!
THERE'S A MESSAGE FOR YOU, HUGH. YOU'VE GOT TO FLY BACK TO FERNDOWN... AND BARRY, TOO.
FERNDOWN?
THE MUMBLED REPLY SEEMED TO COME FROM A STUNNED MAN. IT WAS BARRY WHO GUESSED THAT HE AND THE SKIPPER WERE THE ONLY PILOTS LEFT ALIVE. FOR THE MOMENT 804 SQUADRON CEASED TO EXIST!
WITH THEIR SPIRITS CRUELLY CRUSHED, THE PAIR FLEW BACK TO R.A.F. FERNDOWN. ON LANDING, HUGH MASON SEEMED TO SUFFER A COLLAPSE. AS THE AMBULANCE TOOK AWAY THE SILENT SUFFERING MAN, BARRY TURNED TO WING COMMANDER BATTERSBY.
THIS HAS HIT THE SKIPPER PRETTY BADLY.
I'VE NEVER SEEN HUGH MASON LOOK SO SHATTERED.
IN WORDLESS GLOOM, BARRY WALKED TO THE MESS BESIDE THE OLDER MAN. SUDDENLY EVEN THE SUNSHINE SEEMED TO HAVE A CHILL DESOLATE LOOK.

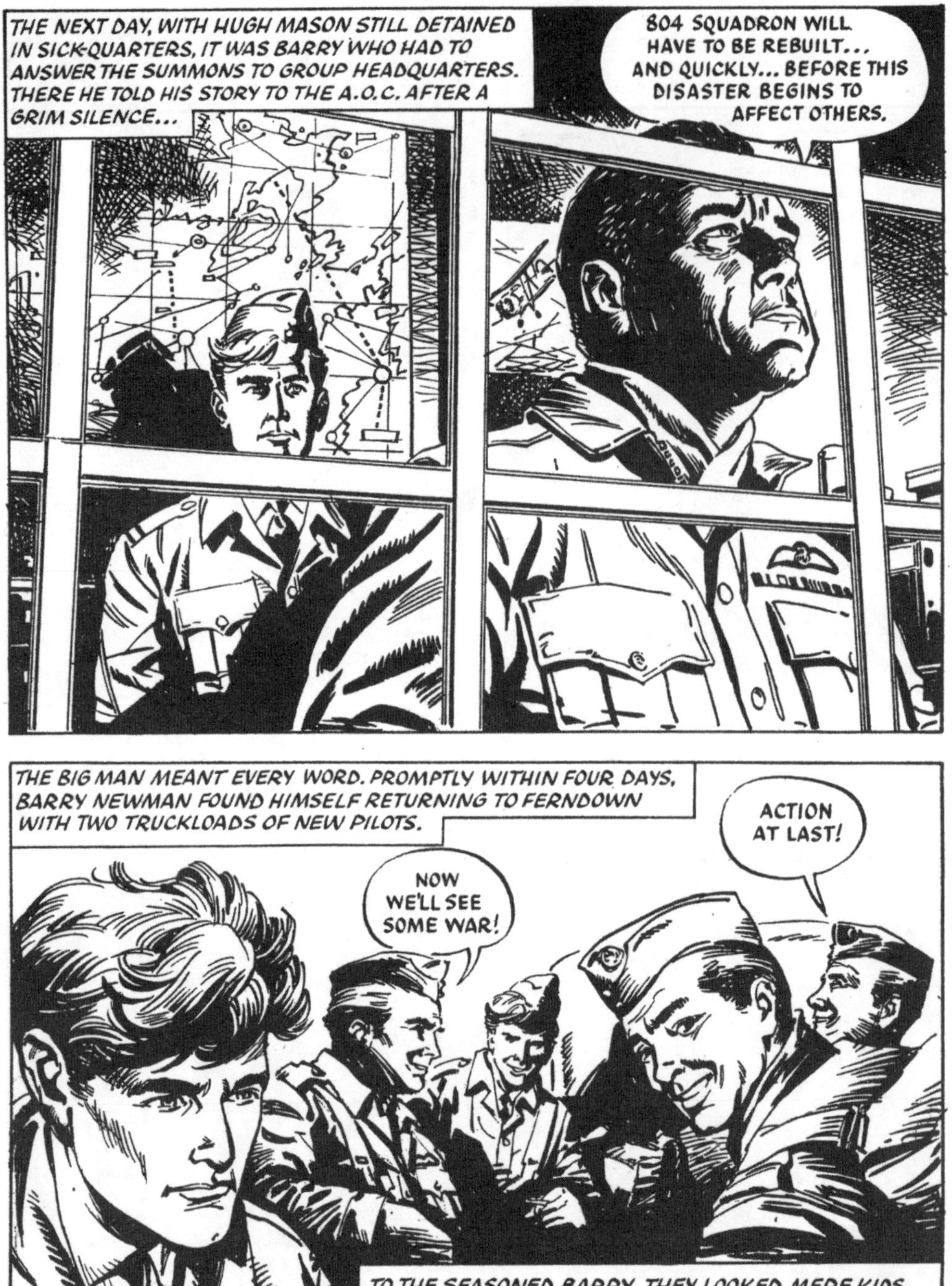
THE NEXT DAY, WITH HUGH MASON STILL DETAINED IN SICK-QUARTERS, IT WAS BARRY WHO HAD TO ANSWER THE SUMMONS TO GROUP HEADQUARTERS. THERE HE TOLD HIS STORY TO THE A.O.C. AFTER A GRIM SILENCE...
804 SQUADRON WILL HAVE TO BE REBUILT... AND QUICKLY... BEFORE THIS DISASTER BEGINS TO AFFECT OTHERS.
THE BIG MAN MEANT EVERY WORD. PROMPTLY WITHIN FOUR DAYS, BARRY NEWMAN FOUND HIMSELF RETURNING TO FERNDOWN WITH TWO TRUCKLOADS OF NEW PILOTS.
NOW WE'LL SEE SOME WAR!
ACTION AT LAST!
TO THE SEASONED BARRY, THEY LOOKED MERE KIDS.

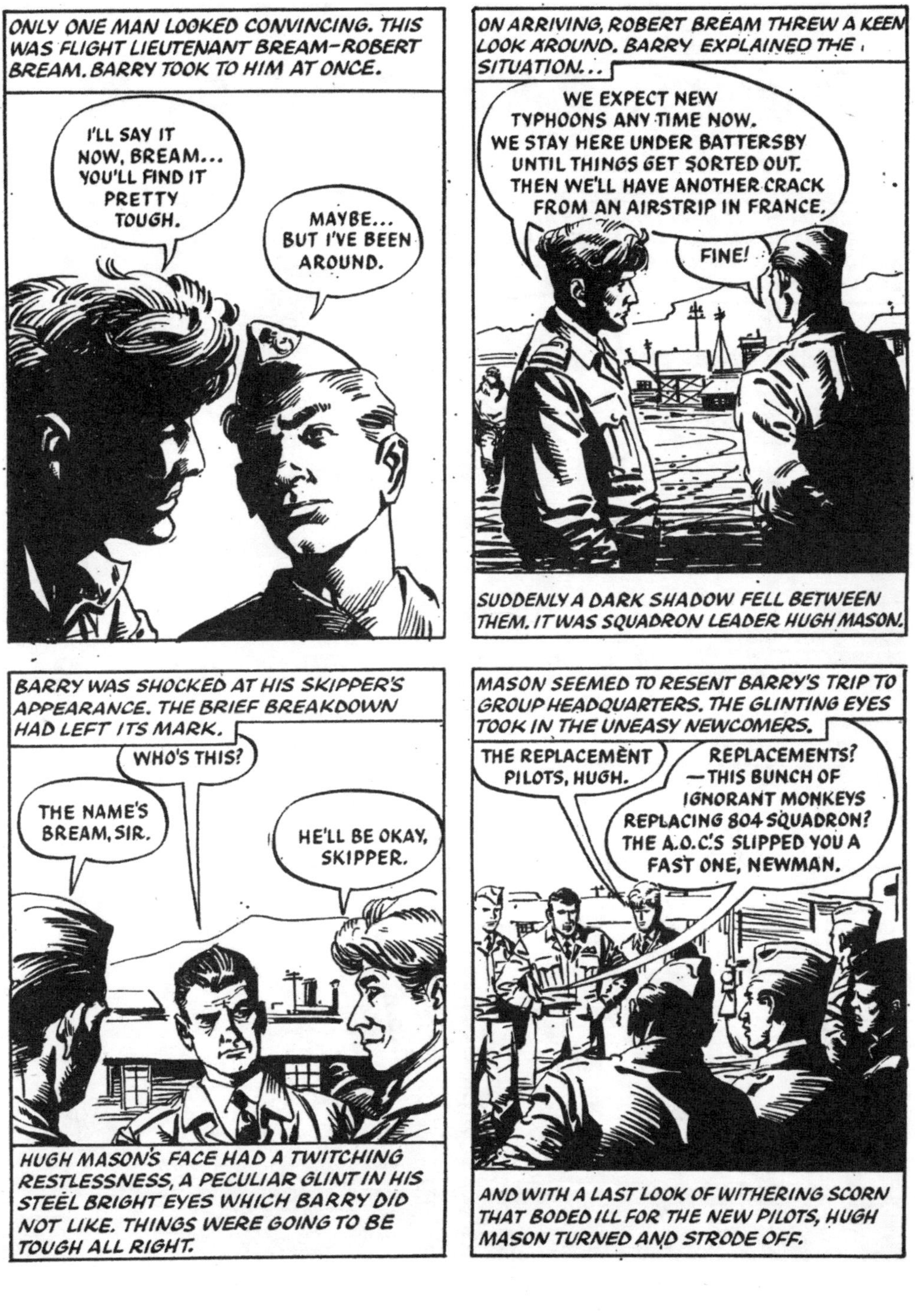
ONLY ONE MAN LOOKED CONVINCING. THIS WAS FLIGHT LIEUTENANT BREAM—ROBERT BREAM. BARRY TOOK TO HIM AT ONCE.
I'LL SAY IT NOW, BREAM... YOU'LL FIND IT PRETTY TOUGH.
MAYBE... BUT I'VE BEEN AROUND.
ON ARRIVING, ROBERT BREAM THREW A KEEN LOOK AROUND. BARRY EXPLAINED THE SITUATION...
WE EXPECT NEW TYPHOONS ANY TIME NOW. WE STAY HERE UNDER BATTERSBY UNTIL THINGS GET SORTED OUT. THEN WE'LL HAVE ANOTHER CRACK FROM AN AIRSTRIP IN FRANCE.
FINE!
SUDDENLY A DARK SHADOW FELL BETWEEN THEM. IT WAS SQUADRON LEADER HUGH MASON.
BARRY WAS SHOCKED AT HIS SKIPPER'S APPEARANCE. THE BRIEF BREAKDOWN HAD LEFT ITS MARK.
WHO'S THIS?
THE NAME'S BREAM, SIR.
HE'LL BE OKAY, SKIPPER.
HUGH MASON'S FACE HAD A TWITCHING RESTLESSNESS, A PECULIAR GLINT IN HIS STEEL BRIGHT EYES WHICH BARRY DID NOT LIKE. THINGS WERE GOING TO BE TOUGH ALL RIGHT.
MASON SEEMED TO RESENT BARRY'S TRIP TO GROUP HEADQUARTERS. THE GLINTING EYES TOOK IN THE UNEASY NEWCOMERS.
THE REPLACEMENT PILOTS, HUGH.
REPLACEMENTS? —THIS BUNCH OF IGNORANT MONKEYS REPLACING 804 SQUADRON? THE A.O.C.'S SLIPPED YOU A FAST ONE, NEWMAN.
AND WITH A LAST LOOK OF WITHERING SCORN THAT BODED ILL FOR THE NEW PILOTS, HUGH MASON TURNED AND STRODE OFF.

Chapter 3: THE AVENGER

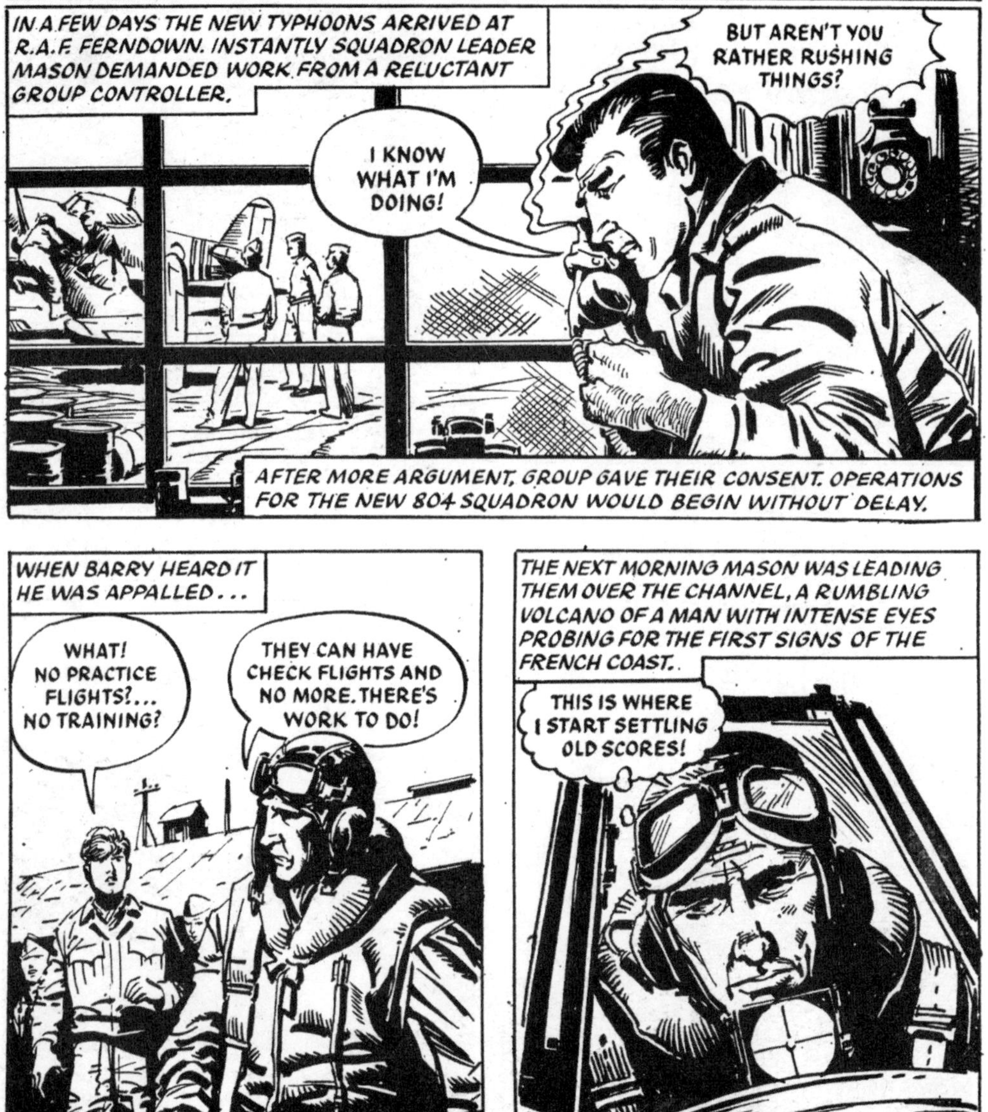
IN A FEW DAYS THE NEW TYPHOONS ARRIVED AT R.A.F. FERNDOWN. INSTANTLY SQUADRON LEADER MASON DEMANDED WORK FROM A RELUCTANT GROUP CONTROLLER.
BUT AREN'T YOU RATHER RUSHING THINGS?
I KNOW WHAT I'M DOING!
AFTER MORE ARGUMENT, GROUP GAVE THEIR CONSENT. OPERATIONS FOR THE NEW 804 SQUADRON WOULD BEGIN WITHOUT DELAY.
WHEN BARRY HEARD IT HE WAS APPALLED...
WHAT! NO PRACTICE FLIGHTS?... NO TRAINING?
THEY CAN HAVE CHECK FLIGHTS AND NO MORE. THERE'S WORK TO DO!
THE NEXT MORNING MASON WAS LEADING THEM OVER THE CHANNEL, A RUMBLING VOLCANO OF A MAN WITH INTENSE EYES PROBING FOR THE FIRST SIGNS OF THE FRENCH COAST.
THIS IS WHERE I START SETTLING OLD SCORES!

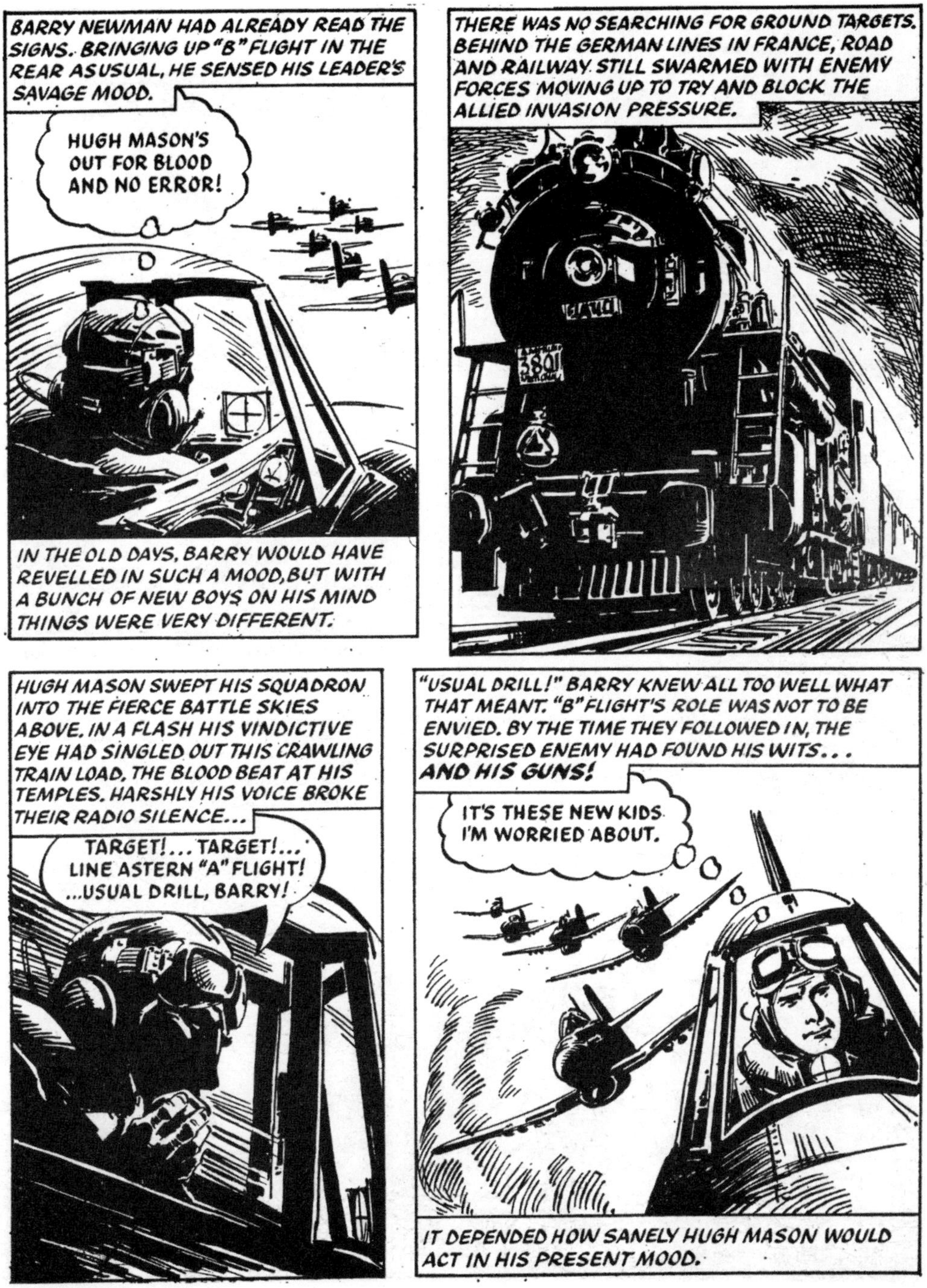
BARRY NEWMAN HAD ALREADY READ THE SIGNS. BRINGING UP "B" FLIGHT IN THE REAR AS USUAL, HE SENSED HIS LEADER'S SAVAGE MOOD.
HUGH MASON'S OUT FOR BLOOD AND NO ERROR!
IN THE OLD DAYS, BARRY WOULD HAVE REVELLED IN SUCH A MOOD, BUT WITH A BUNCH OF NEW BOYS ON HIS MIND THINGS WERE VERY DIFFERENT.
THERE WAS NO SEARCHING FOR GROUND TARGETS. BEHIND THE GERMAN LINES IN FRANCE, ROAD AND RAILWAY STILL SWARMED WITH ENEMY FORCES MOVING UP TO TRY AND BLOCK THE ALLIED INVASION PRESSURE.
HUGH MASON SWEPT HIS SQUADRON INTO THE FIERCE BATTLE SKIES ABOVE. IN A FLASH HIS VINDICTIVE EYE HAD SINGLED OUT THIS CRAWLING TRAIN LOAD. THE BLOOD BEAT AT HIS TEMPLES. HARSHLY HIS VOICE BROKE THEIR RADIO SILENCE...
TARGET!... TARGET!... LINE ASTERN "A" FLIGHT! ...USUAL DRILL, BARRY!
"USUAL DRILL!" BARRY KNEW ALL TOO WELL WHAT THAT MEANT. "B" FLIGHT'S ROLE WAS NOT TO BE ENVIED. BY THE TIME THEY FOLLOWED IN, THE SURPRISED ENEMY HAD FOUND HIS WITS... AND HIS GUNS!
IT'S THESE NEW KIDS I'M WORRIED ABOUT.
IT DEPENDED HOW SANELY HUGH MASON WOULD ACT IN HIS PRESENT MOOD.

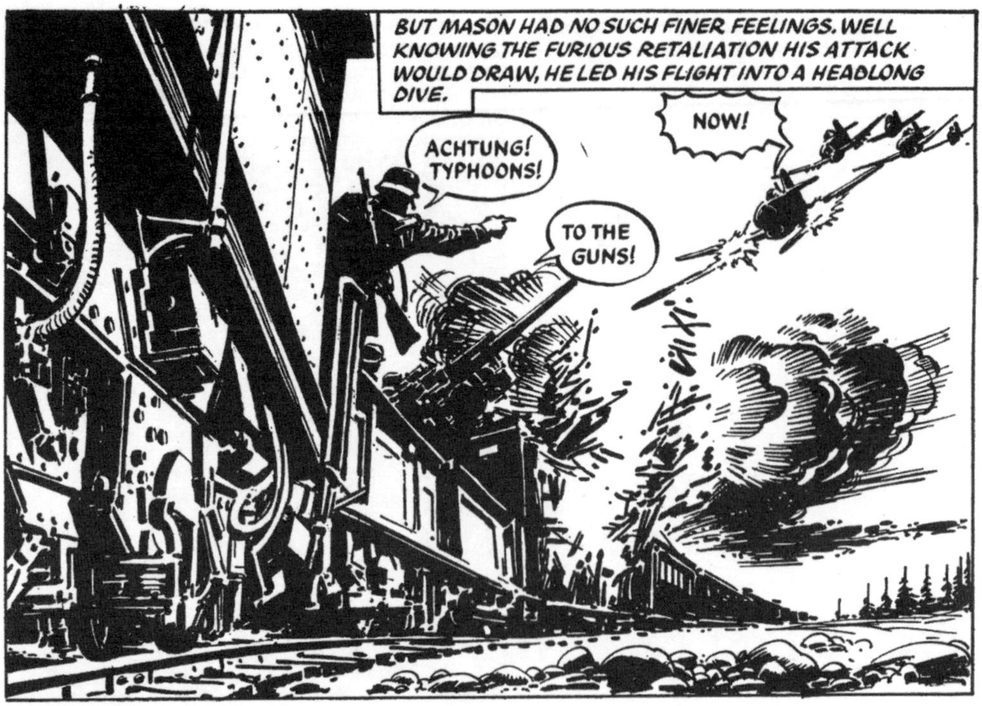
BUT MASON HAD NO SUCH FINER FEELINGS. WELL KNOWING THE FURIOUS RETALIATION HIS ATTACK WOULD DRAW, HE LED HIS FLIGHT INTO A HEADLONG DIVE.
NOW!
ACHTUNG! TYPHOONS!
TO THE GUNS!

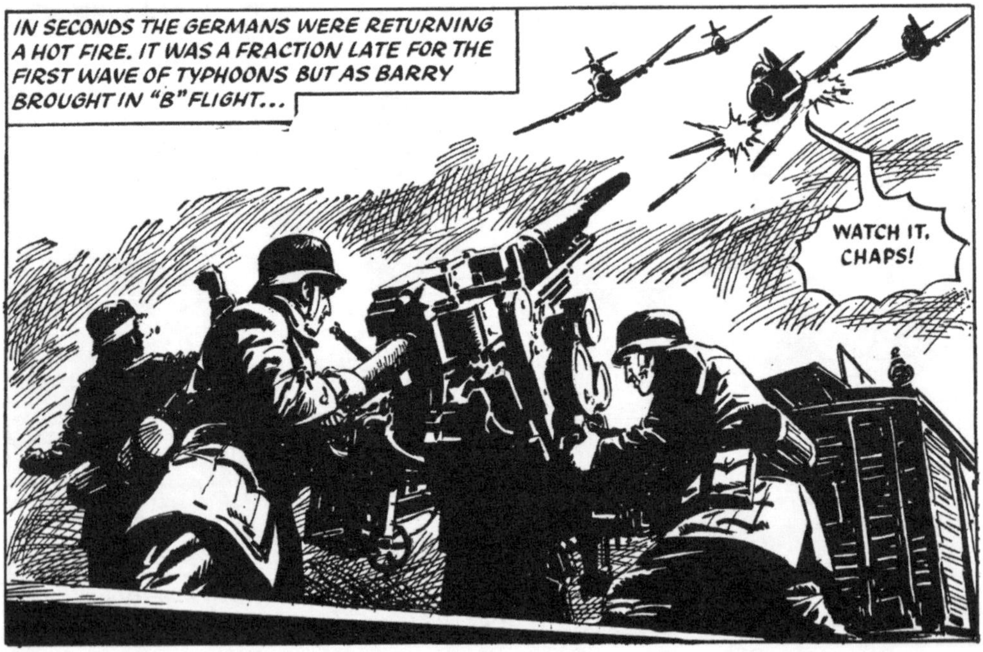
IN SECONDS THE GERMANS WERE RETURNING A HOT FIRE. IT WAS A FRACTION LATE FOR THE FIRST WAVE OF TYPHOONS BUT AS BARRY BROUGHT IN "B" FLIGHT...
WATCH IT, CHAPS!

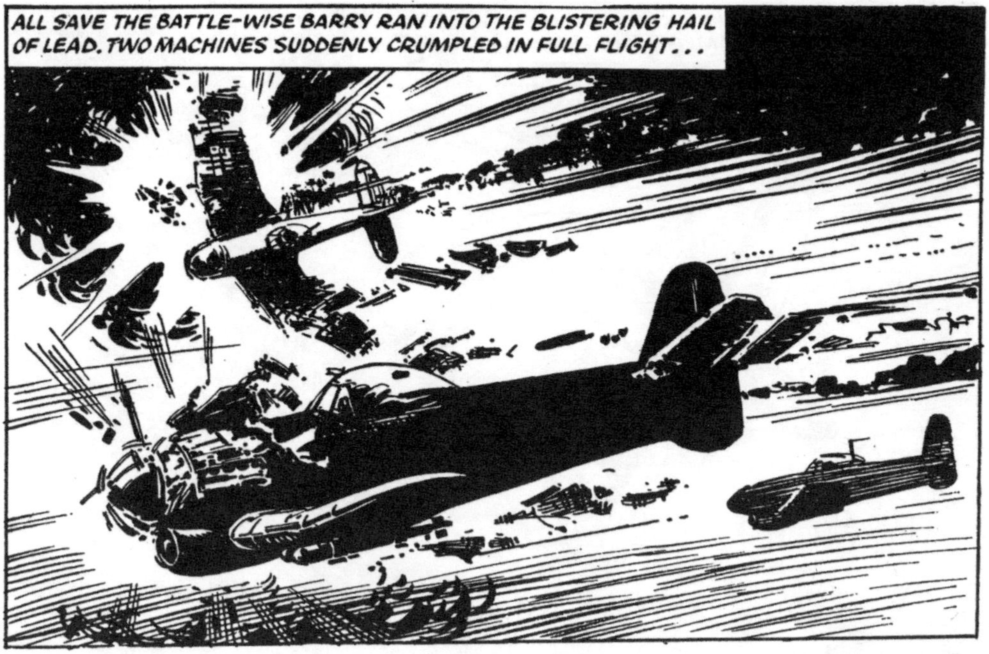
ALL SAVE THE BATTLE-WISE BARRY RAN INTO THE BLISTERING HAIL OF LEAD. TWO MACHINES SUDDENLY CRUMPLED IN FULL FLIGHT...

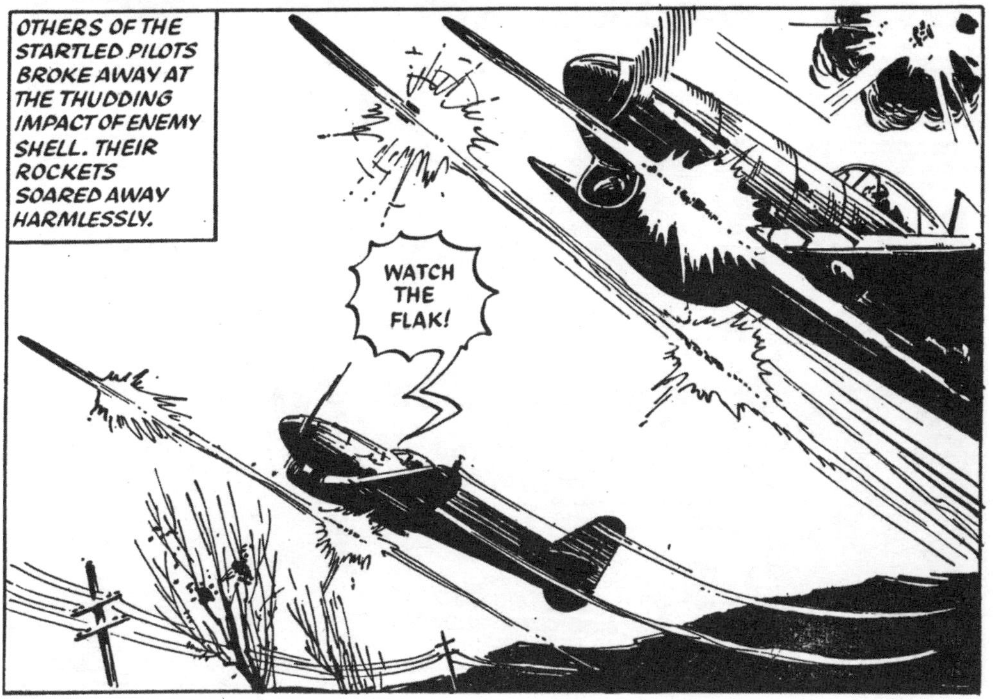
OTHERS OF THE STARTLED PILOTS BROKE AWAY AT THE THUDDING IMPACT OF ENEMY SHELL. THEIR ROCKETS SOARED AWAY HARMLESSLY.
WATCH THE FLAK!

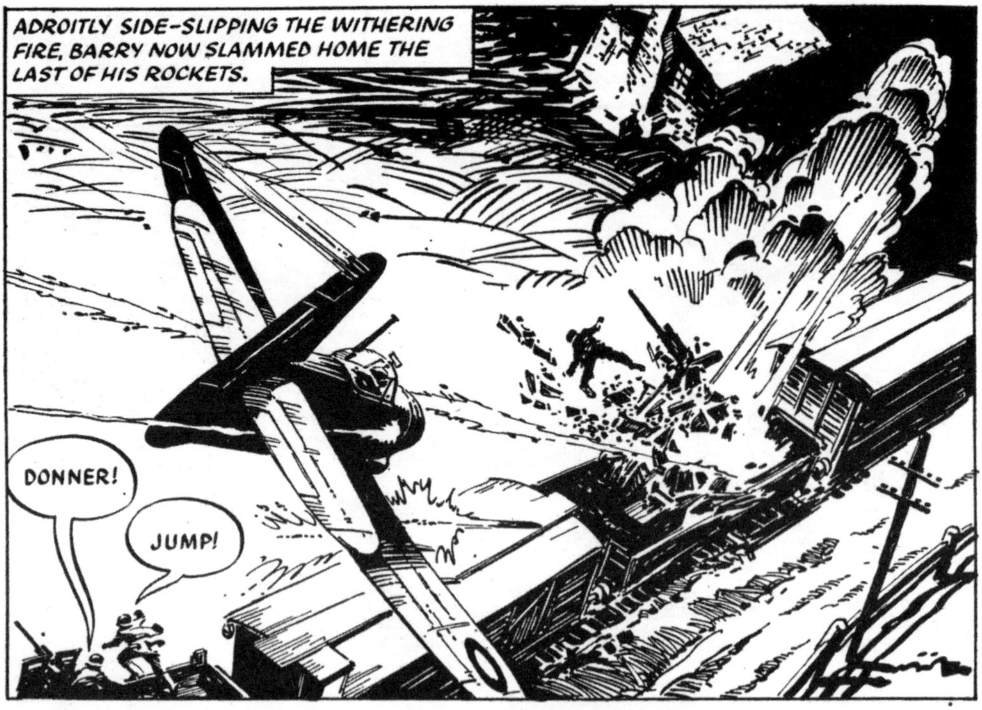
ADROITLY SIDE-SLIPPING THE WITHERING FIRE, BARRY NOW SLAMMED HOME THE LAST OF HIS ROCKETS.
DONNER!
JUMP!

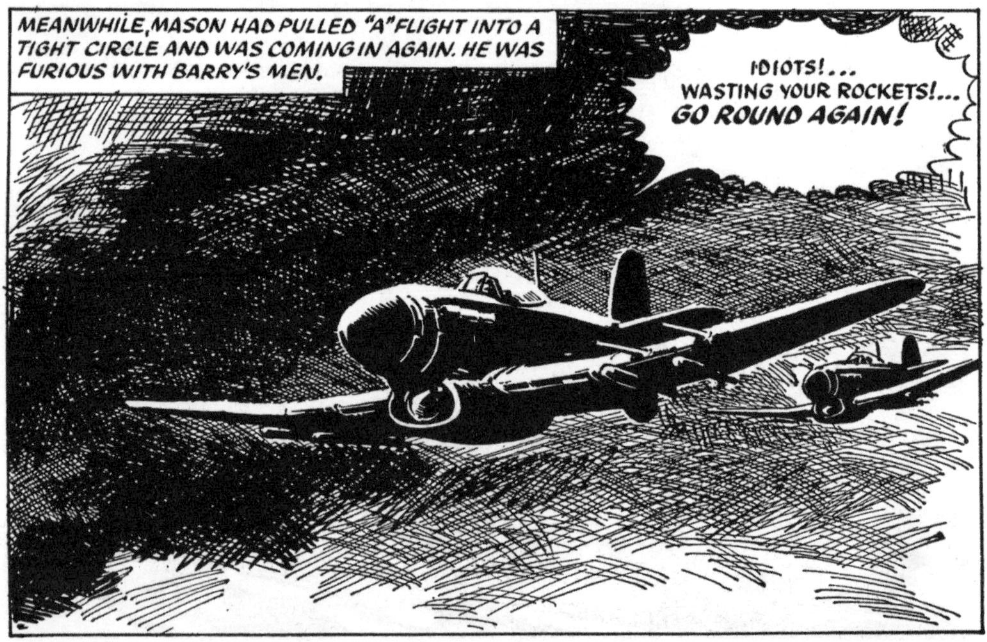
MEANWHILE, MASON HAD PULLED "A" FLIGHT INTO A TIGHT CIRCLE AND WAS COMING IN AGAIN. HE WAS FURIOUS WITH BARRY'S MEN.
IDIOTS!... WASTING YOUR ROCKETS!... GO ROUND AGAIN!

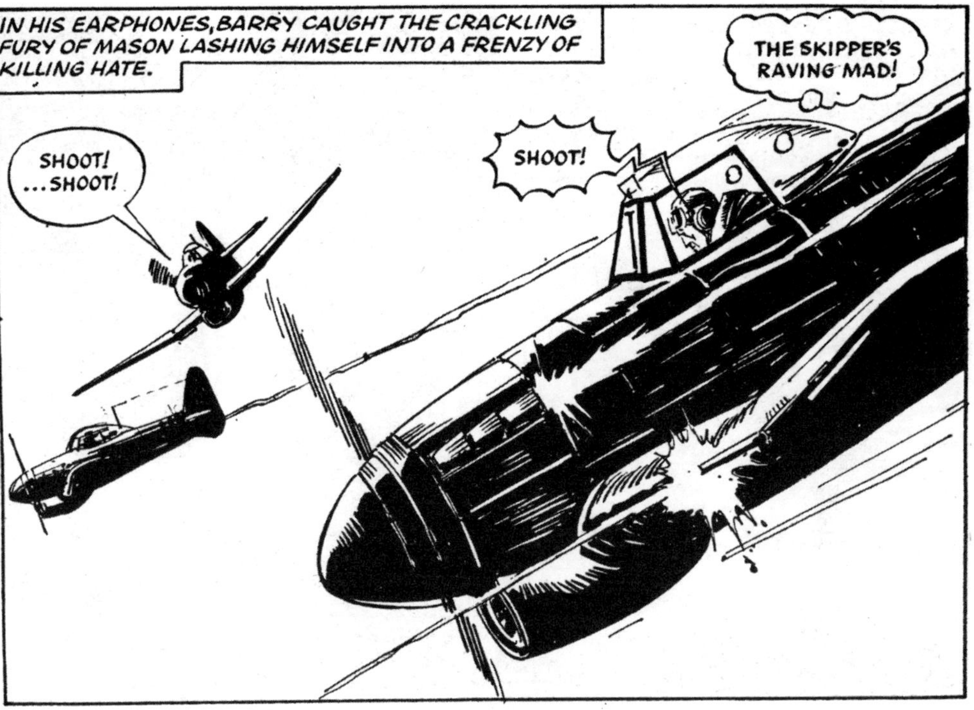
IN HIS EARPHONES, BARRY CAUGHT THE CRACKLING FURY OF MASON LASHING HIMSELF INTO A FRENZY OF KILLING HATE.
THE SKIPPER'S RAVING MAD!
SHOOT! ...SHOOT!
SHOOT!

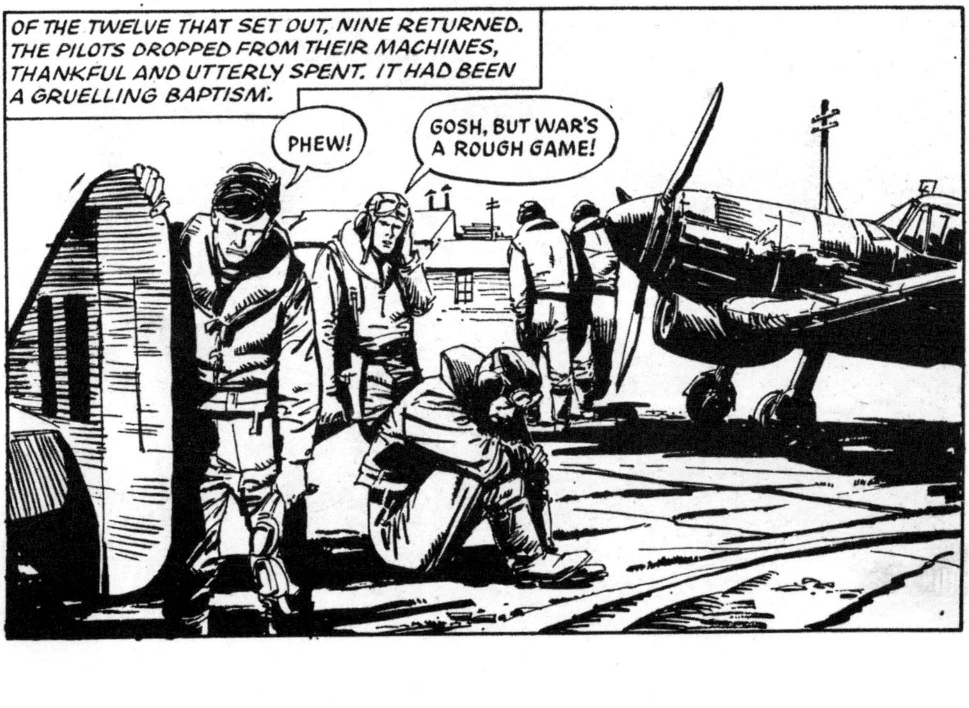
OF THE TWELVE THAT SET OUT, NINE RETURNED. THE PILOTS DROPPED FROM THEIR MACHINES, THANKFUL AND UTTERLY SPENT. IT HAD BEEN A GRUELLING BAPTISM.
PHEW!
GOSH, BUT WAR'S A ROUGH GAME!

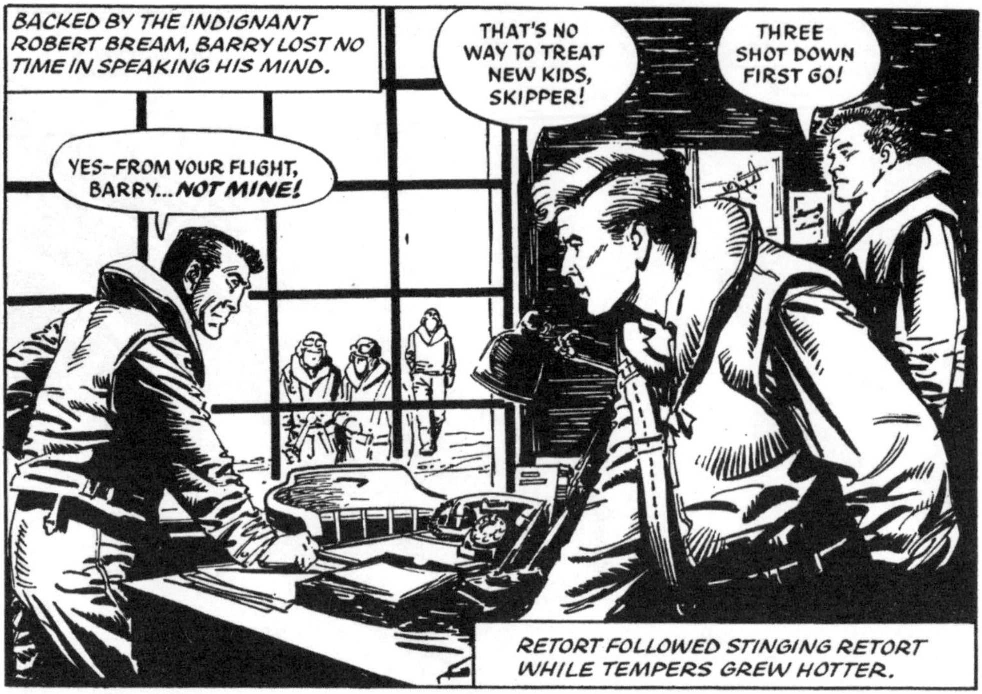
BACKED BY THE INDIGNANT ROBERT BREAM, BARRY LOST NO TIME IN SPEAKING HIS MIND.
THAT'S NO WAY TO TREAT NEW KIDS, SKIPPER!
THREE SHOT DOWN FIRST GO!
YES–FROM YOUR FLIGHT, BARRY... NOT MINE!
RETORT FOLLOWED STINGING RETORT WHILE TEMPERS GREW HOTTER.

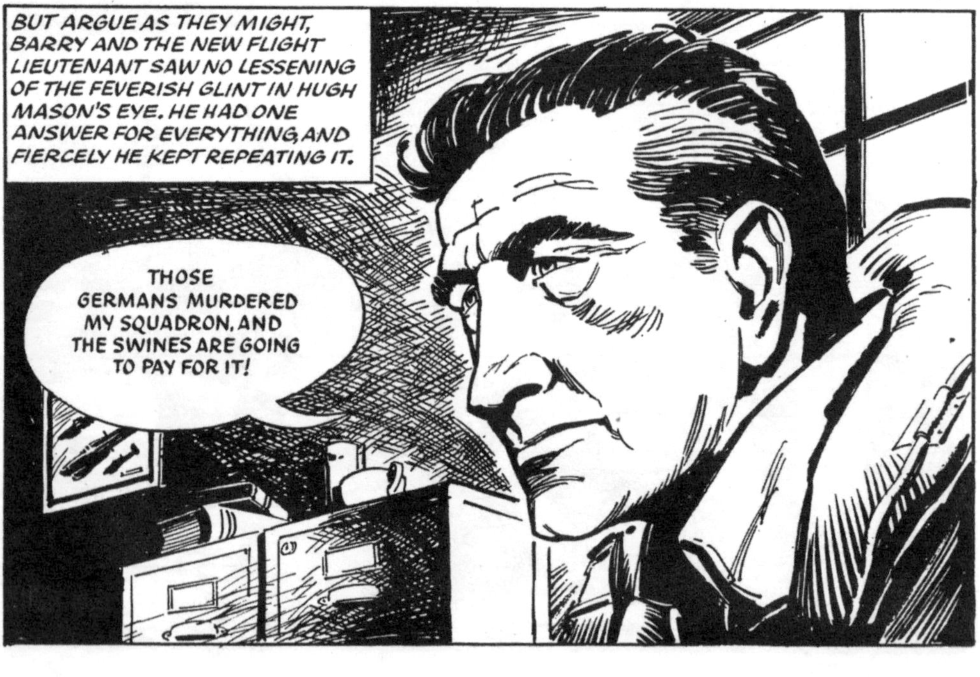
BUT ARGUE AS THEY MIGHT, BARRY AND THE NEW FLIGHT LIEUTENANT SAW NO LESSENING OF THE FEVERISH GLINT IN HUGH MASON'S EYE. HE HAD ONE ANSWER FOR EVERYTHING, AND FIERCELY HE KEPT REPEATING IT.
THOSE GERMANS MURDERED MY SQUADRON, AND THE SWINES ARE GOING TO PAY FOR IT!

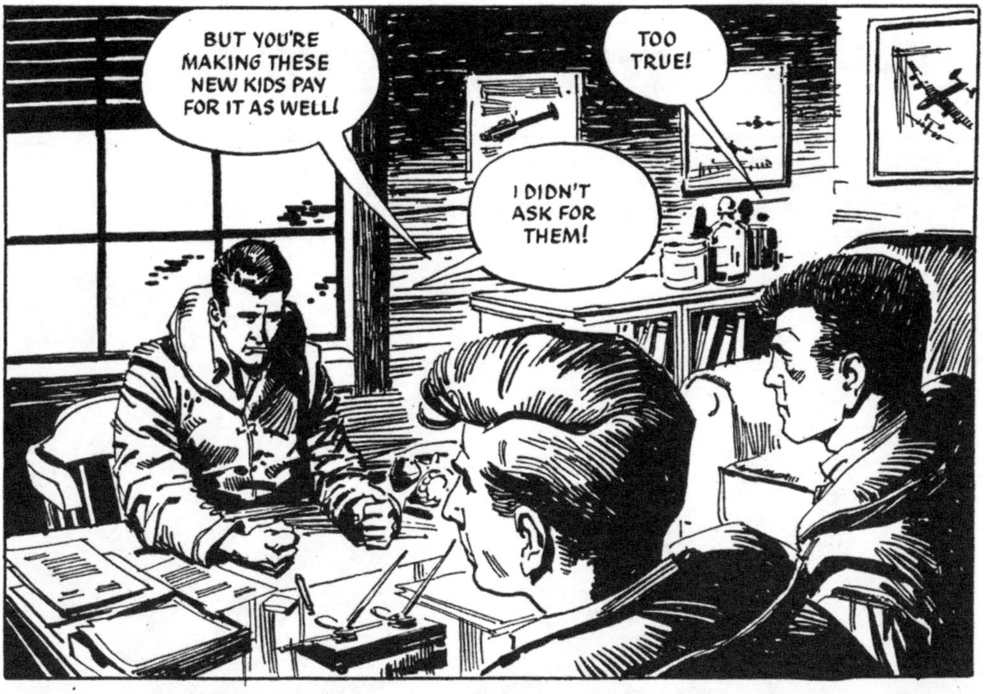
BUT YOU'RE MAKING THESE NEW KIDS PAY FOR IT AS WELL!
TOO TRUE!
I DIDN'T ASK FOR THEM!

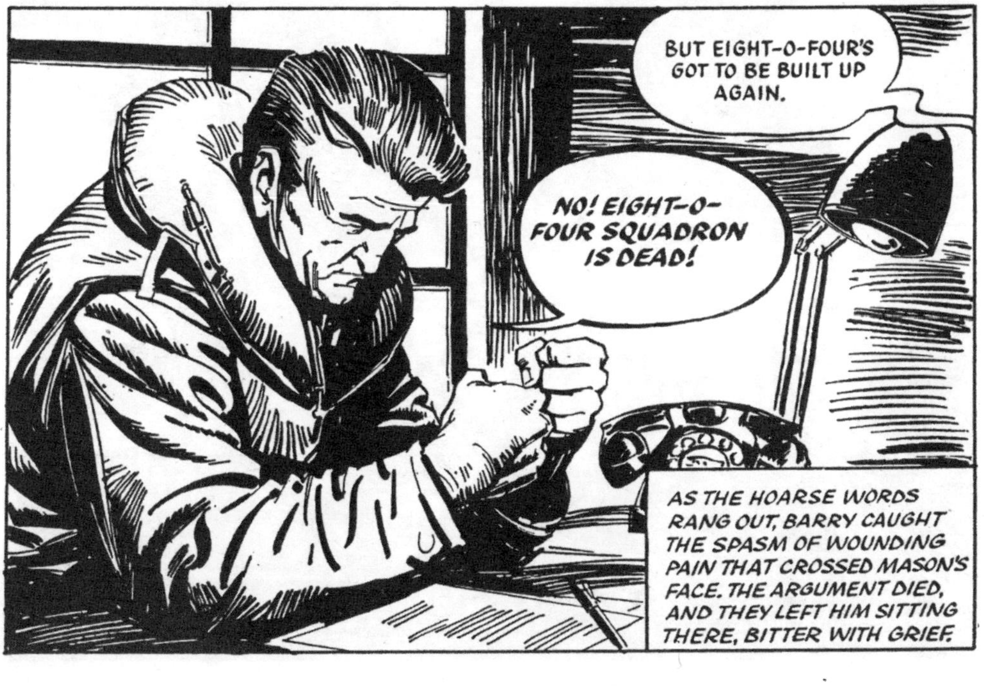
BUT EIGHT-O-FOUR'S GOT TO BE BUILT UP AGAIN.
NO! EIGHT-O-FOUR SQUADRON IS DEAD!
AS THE HOARSE WORDS RANG OUT, BARRY CAUGHT THE SPASM OF WOUNDING PAIN THAT CROSSED MASON'S FACE. THE ARGUMENT DIED, AND THEY LEFT HIM SITTING THERE, BITTER WITH GRIEF.

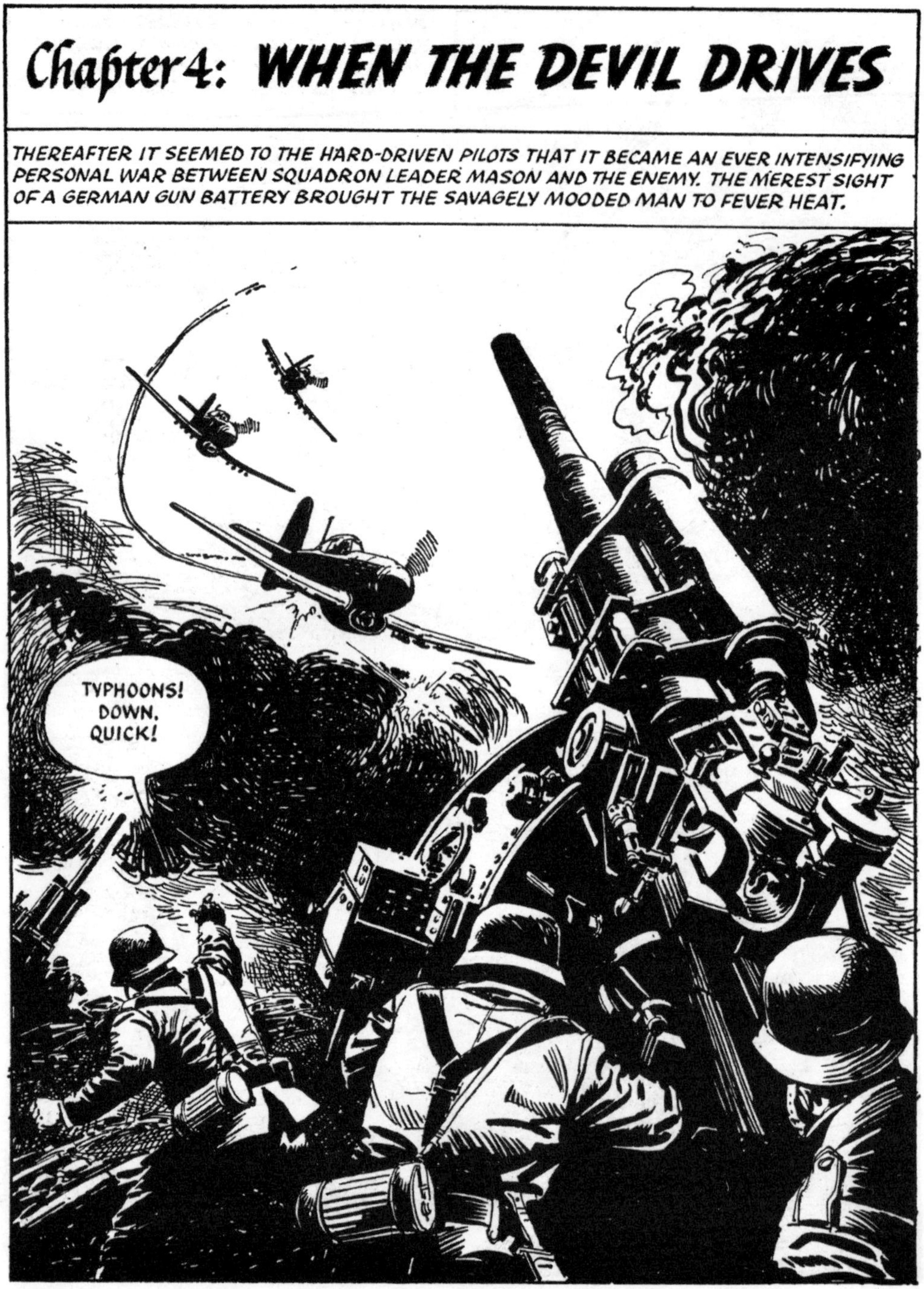
Chapter 4: WHEN THE DEVIL DRIVES
THEREAFTER IT SEEMED TO THE HARD-DRIVEN PILOTS THAT IT BECAME AN EVER INTENSIFYING PERSONAL WAR BETWEEN SQUADRON LEADER MASON AND THE ENEMY. THE MEREST SIGHT OF A GERMAN GUN BATTERY BROUGHT THE SAVAGELY MOODED MAN TO FEVER HEAT.
TYPHOONS! DOWN, QUICK!

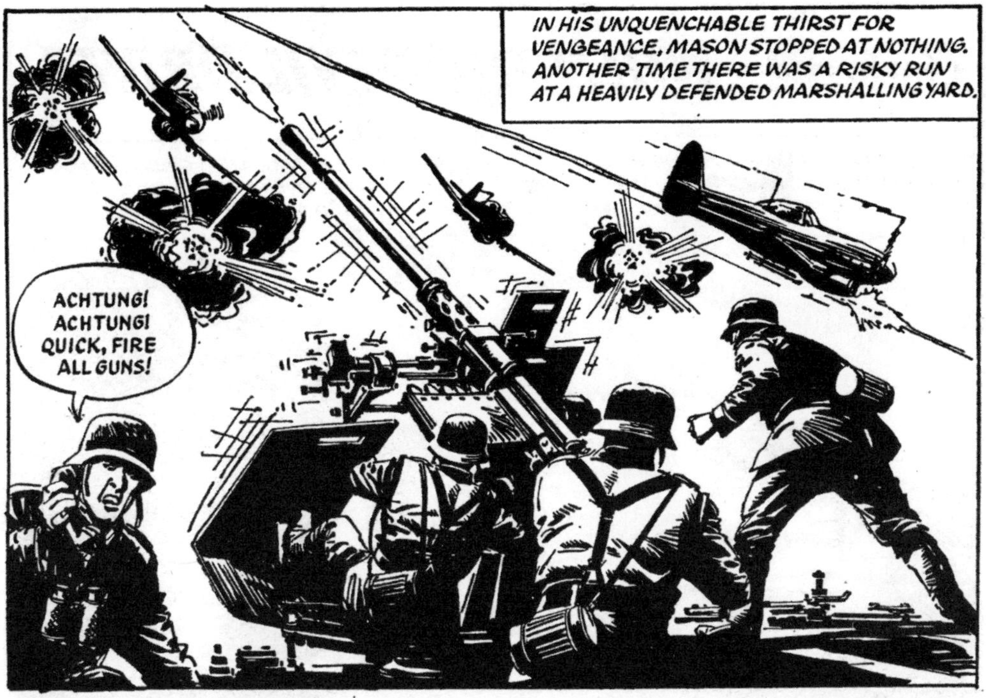
IN HIS UNQUENCHABLE THIRST FOR VENGEANCE, MASON STOPPED AT NOTHING. ANOTHER TIME THERE WAS A RISKY RUN AT A HEAVILY DEFENDED MARSHALLING YARD.
ACHTUNG! ACHTUNG! QUICK, FIRE ALL GUNS!

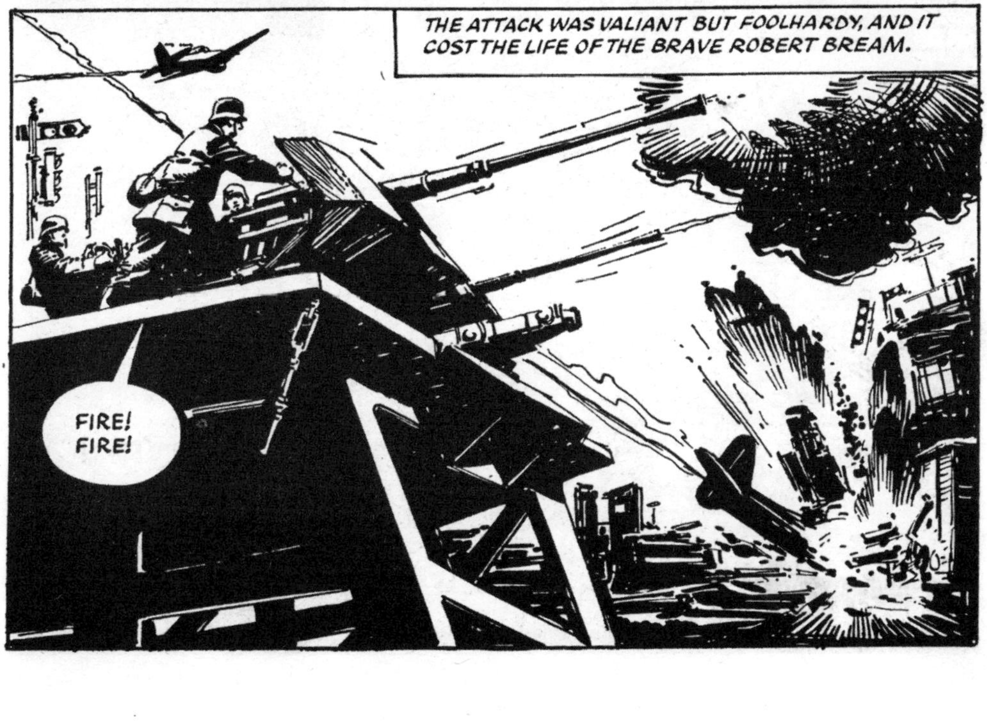
THE ATTACK WAS VALIANT BUT FOOLHARDY, AND IT COST THE LIFE OF THE BRAVE ROBERT BREAM.
FIRE! FIRE!

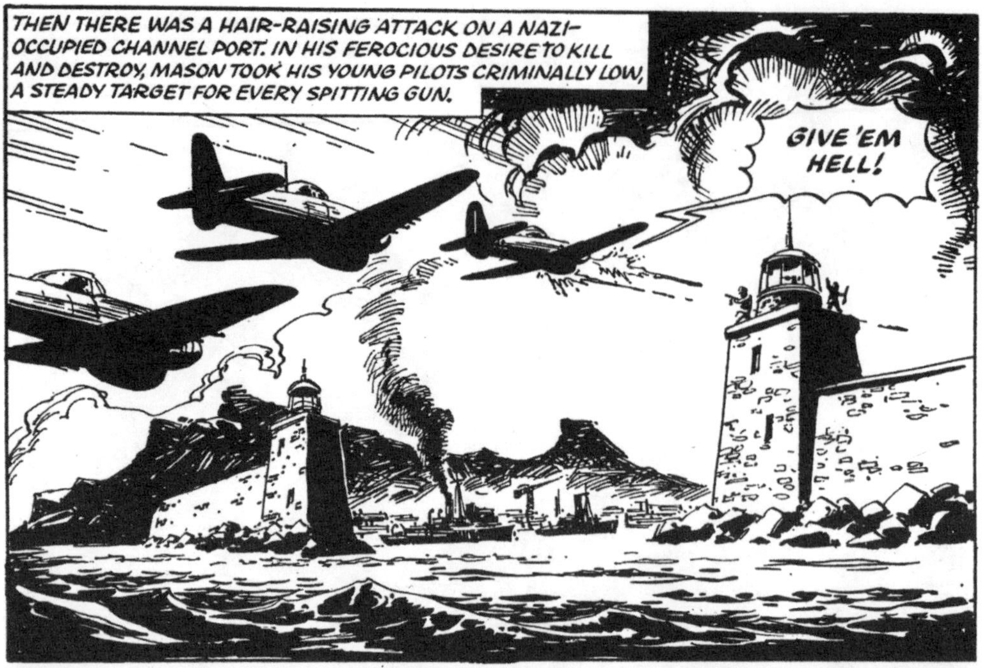
THEN THERE WAS A HAIR-RAISING ATTACK ON A NAZI-OCCUPIED CHANNEL PORT. IN HIS FEROCIOUS DESIRE TO KILL AND DESTROY, MASON TOOK HIS YOUNG PILOTS CRIMINALLY LOW, A STEADY TARGET FOR EVERY SPITTING GUN.
GIVE 'EM HELL!

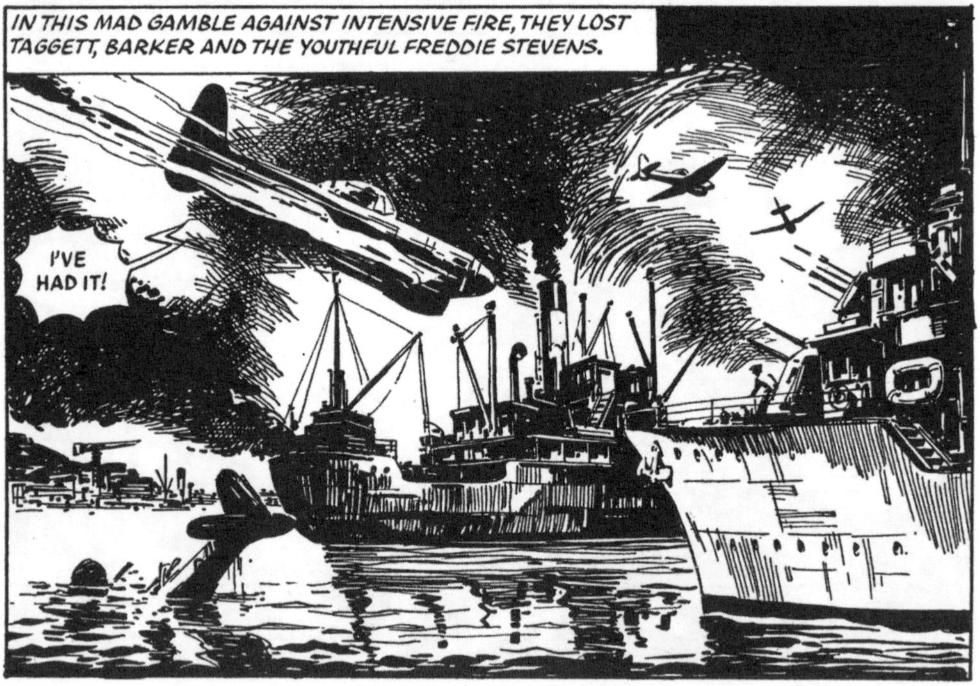
IN THIS MAD GAMBLE AGAINST INTENSIVE FIRE, THEY LOST TAGGETT, BARKER AND THE YOUTHFUL FREDDIE STEVENS.
I'VE HAD IT!

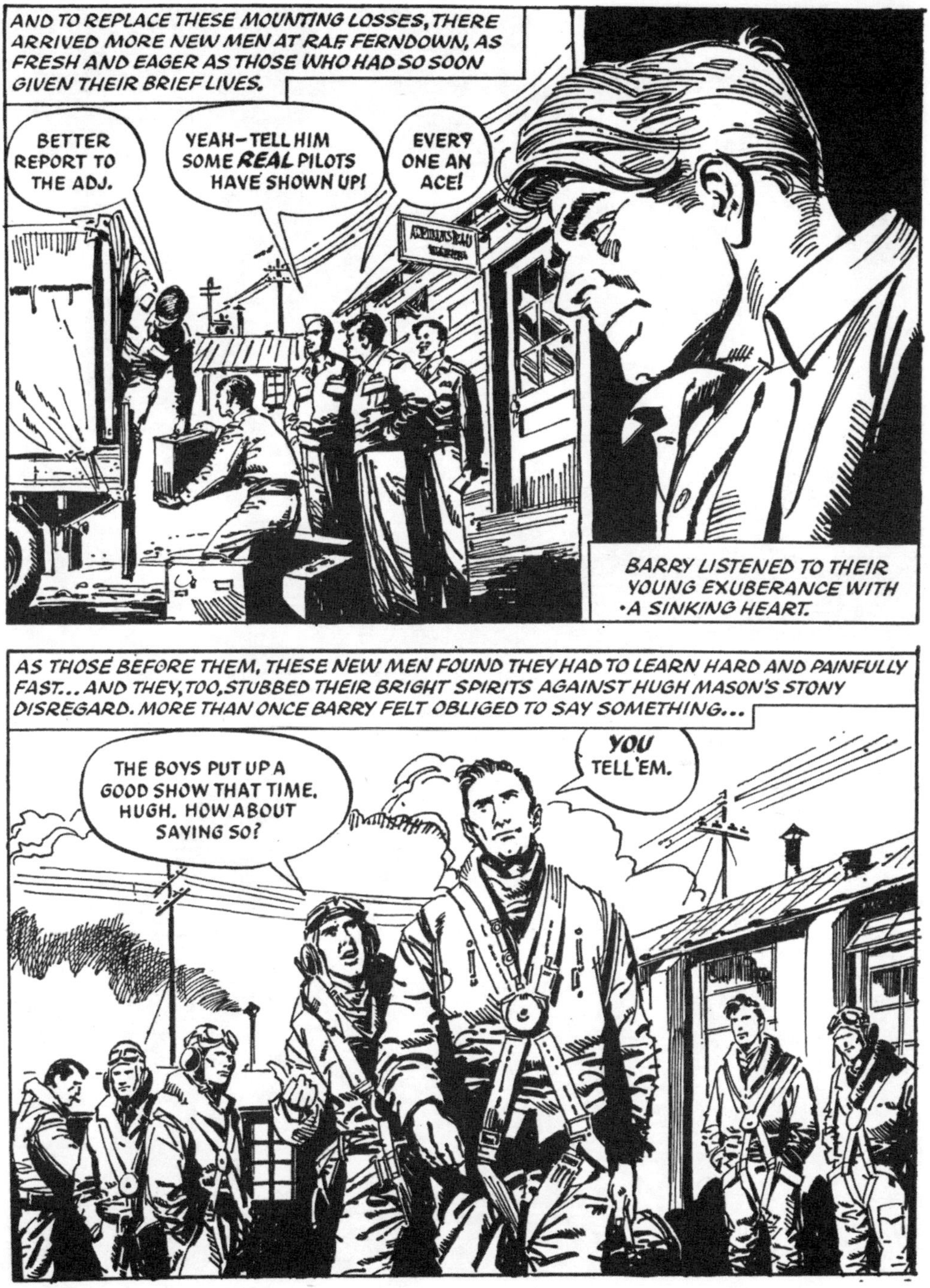
AND TO REPLACE THESE MOUNTING LOSSES, THERE ARRIVED MORE NEW MEN AT R.A.F. FERNDOWN, AS FRESH AND EAGER AS THOSE WHO HAD SO SOON GIVEN THEIR BRIEF LIVES.
BETTER REPORT TO THE ADJ.
YEAH—TELL HIM SOME REAL PILOTS HAVE SHOWN UP!
EVERY ONE AN ACE!
BARRY LISTENED TO THEIR YOUNG EXUBERANCE WITH A SINKING HEART.
AS THOSE BEFORE THEM, THESE NEW MEN FOUND THEY HAD TO LEARN HARD AND PAINFULLY FAST... AND THEY, TOO, STUBBED THEIR BRIGHT SPIRITS AGAINST HUGH MASON'S STONY DISREGARD. MORE THAN ONCE BARRY FELT OBLIGED TO SAY SOMETHING...
THE BOYS PUT UP A GOOD SHOW THAT TIME, HUGH. HOW ABOUT SAYING SO?
YOU TELL 'EM.

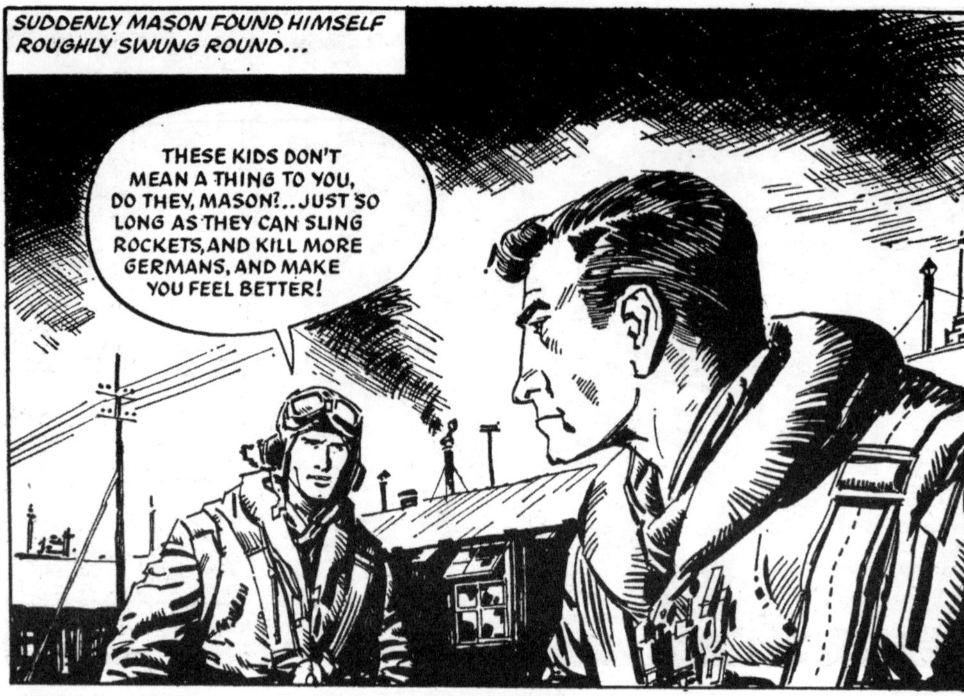
SUDDENLY MASON FOUND HIMSELF ROUGHLY SWUNG ROUND...
THESE KIDS DON'T MEAN A THING TO YOU, DO THEY, MASON?..JUST SO LONG AS THEY CAN SLING ROCKETS, AND KILL MORE GERMANS, AND MAKE YOU FEEL BETTER!

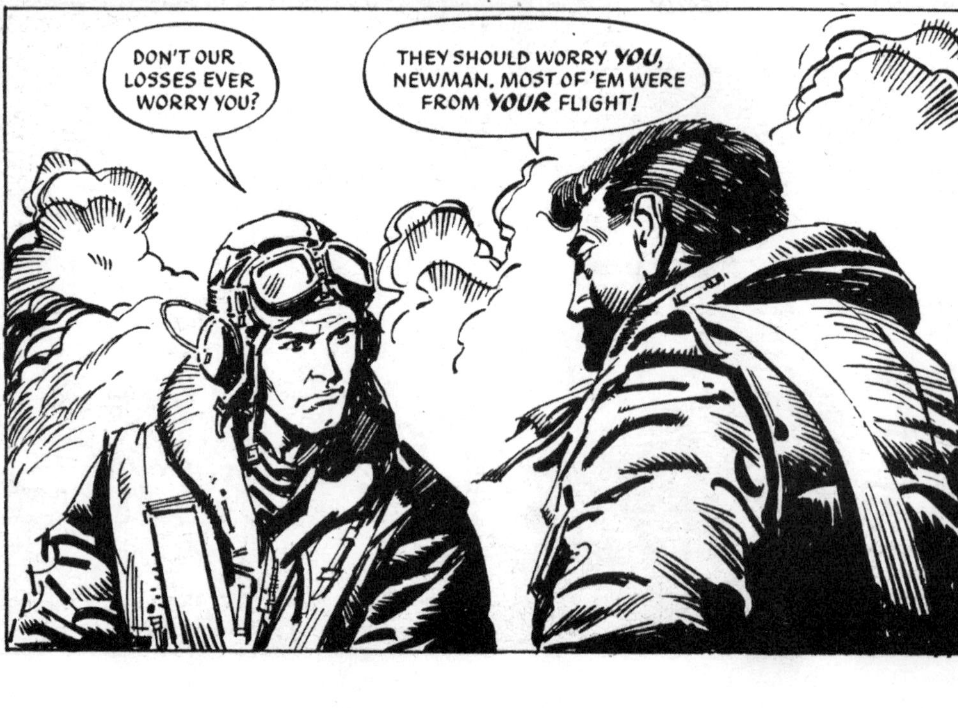
DON'T OUR LOSSES EVER WORRY YOU?
THEY SHOULD WORRY YOU, NEWMAN. MOST OF 'EM WERE FROM YOUR FLIGHT!

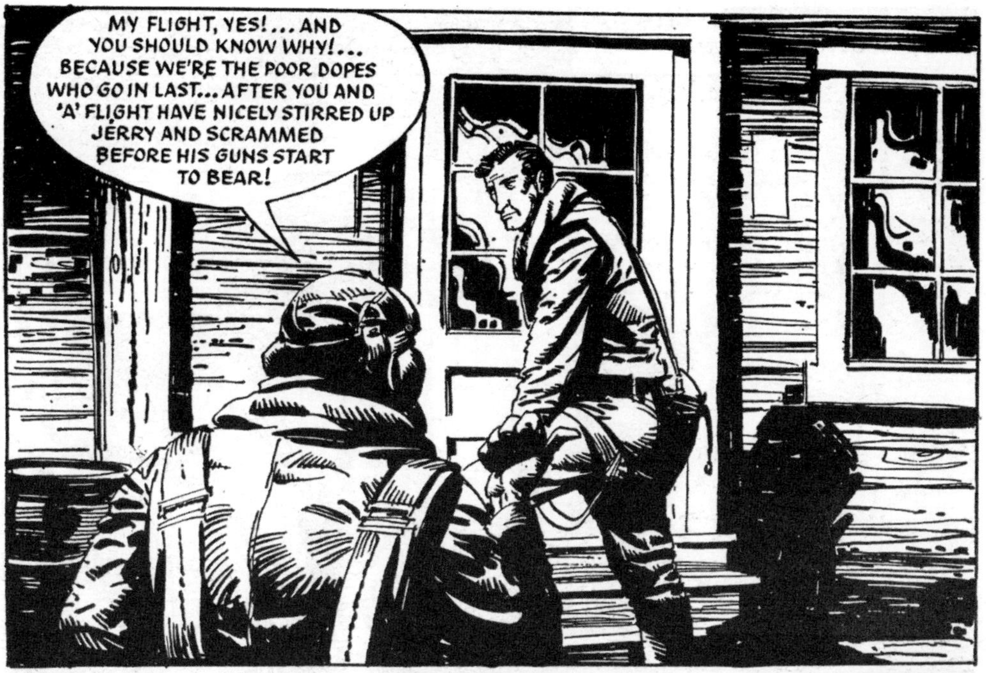
MY FLIGHT, YES!... AND YOU SHOULD KNOW WHY!... BECAUSE WE'RE THE POOR DOPES WHO GO IN LAST... AFTER YOU AND 'A' FLIGHT HAVE NICELY STIRRED UP JERRY AND SCRAMMED BEFORE HIS GUNS START TO BEAR!

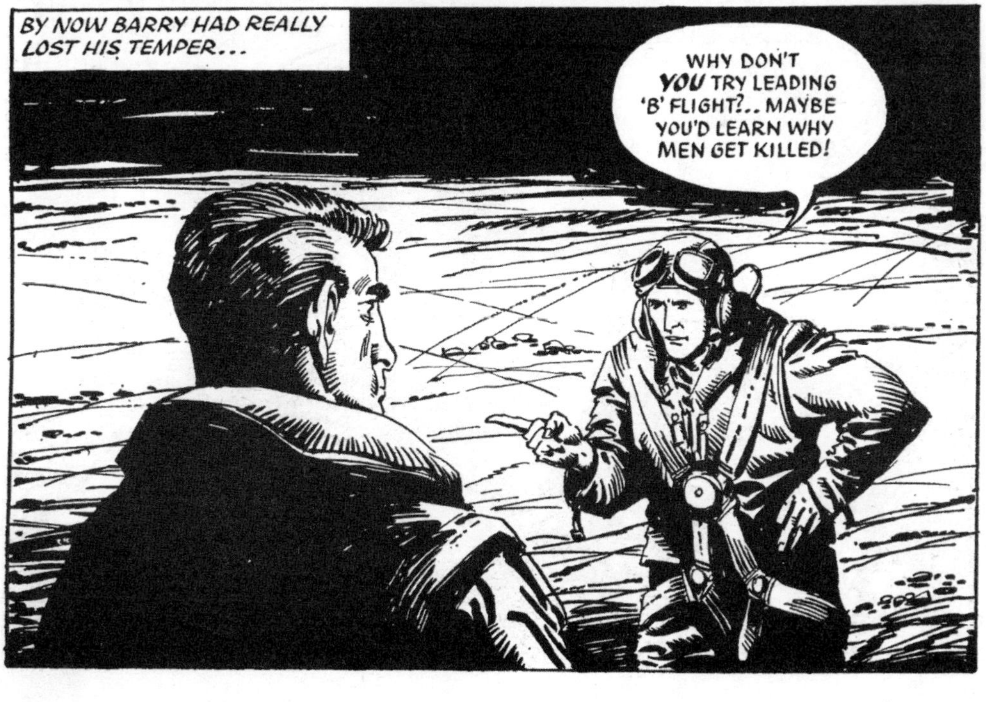
BY NOW BARRY HAD REALLY LOST HIS TEMPER...
WHY DON'T YOU TRY LEADING 'B' FLIGHT?.. MAYBE YOU'D LEARN WHY MEN GET KILLED!

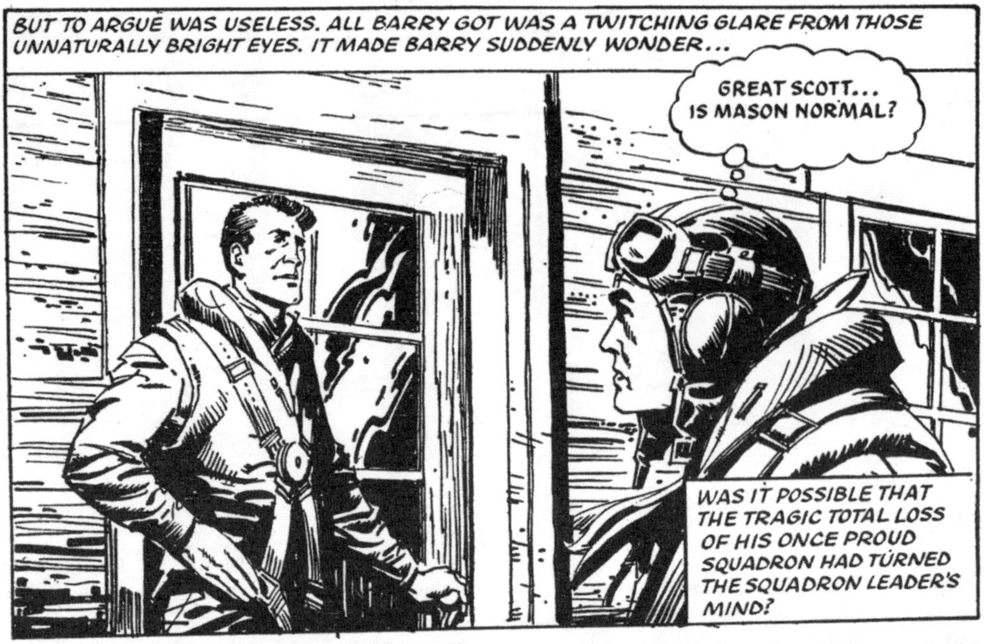
BUT TO ARGUE WAS USELESS. ALL BARRY GOT WAS A TWITCHING GLARE FROM THOSE UNNATURALLY BRIGHT EYES. IT MADE BARRY SUDDENLY WONDER...
GREAT SCOTT... IS MASON NORMAL?
WAS IT POSSIBLE THAT THE TRAGIC TOTAL LOSS OF HIS ONCE PROUD SQUADRON HAD TURNED THE SQUADRON LEADER'S MIND?

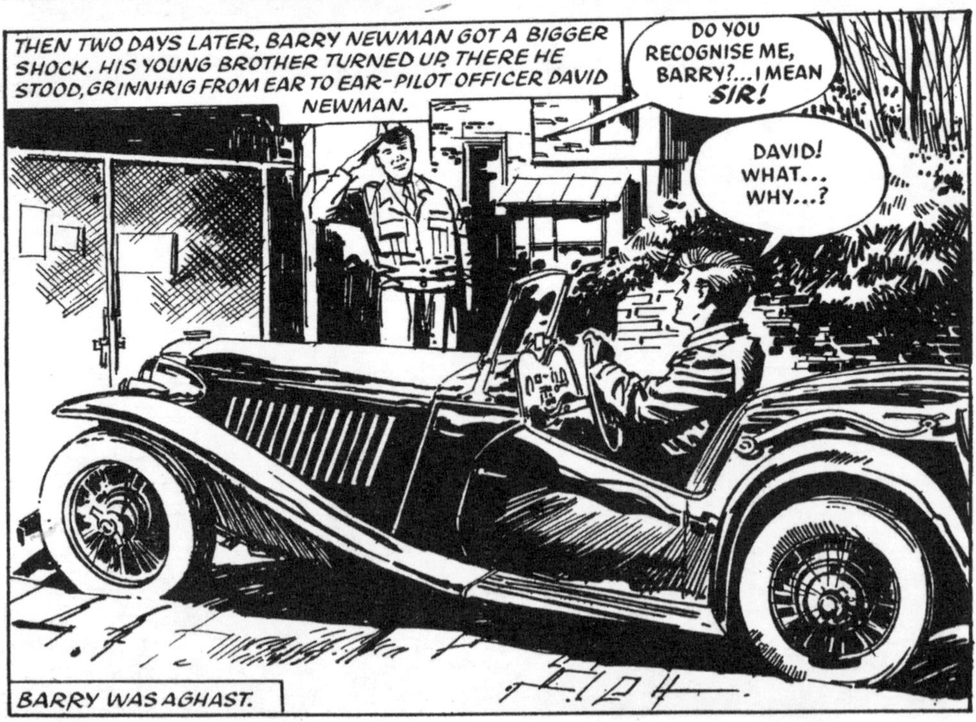
THEN TWO DAYS LATER, BARRY NEWMAN GOT A BIGGER SHOCK. HIS YOUNG BROTHER TURNED UP. THERE HE STOOD, GRINNING FROM EAR TO EAR-PILOT OFFICER DAVID NEWMAN.
DO YOU RECOGNISE ME, BARRY?...I MEAN SIR!
DAVID! WHAT... WHY...?
BARRY WAS AGHAST.

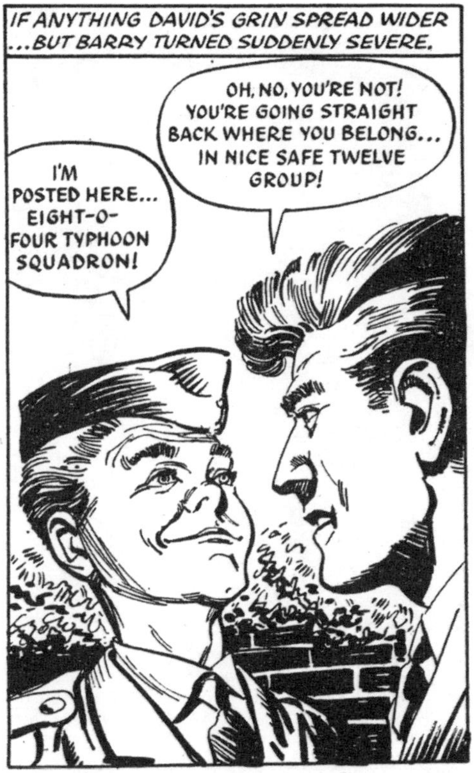
IF ANYTHING DAVID'S GRIN SPREAD WIDER ...BUT BARRY TURNED SUDDENLY SEVERE.
I'M POSTED HERE... EIGHT-O-FOUR TYPHOON SQUADRON!
OH, NO, YOU'RE NOT! YOU'RE GOING STRAIGHT BACK WHERE YOU BELONG... IN NICE SAFE TWELVE GROUP!

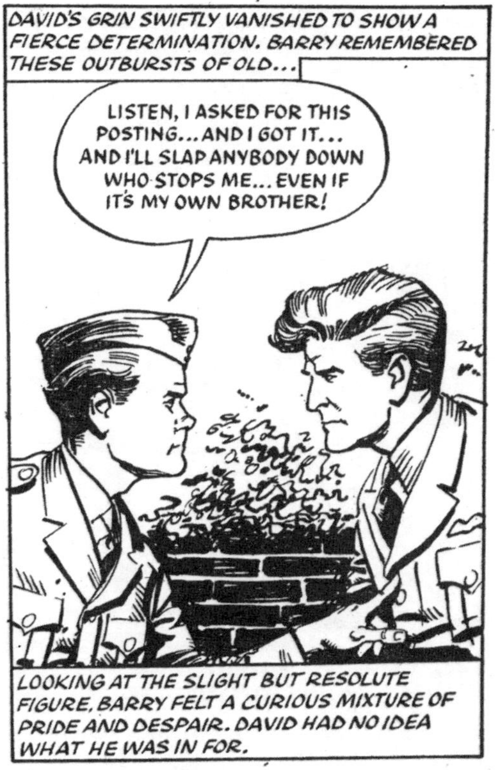
DAVID'S GRIN SWIFTLY VANISHED TO SHOW A FIERCE DETERMINATION. BARRY REMEMBERED THESE OUTBURSTS OF OLD...
LISTEN, I ASKED FOR THIS POSTING... AND I GOT IT... AND I'LL SLAP ANYBODY DOWN WHO STOPS ME... EVEN IF IT'S MY OWN BROTHER!
LOOKING AT THE SLIGHT BUT RESOLUTE FIGURE, BARRY FELT A CURIOUS MIXTURE OF PRIDE AND DESPAIR. DAVID HAD NO IDEA WHAT HE WAS IN FOR.

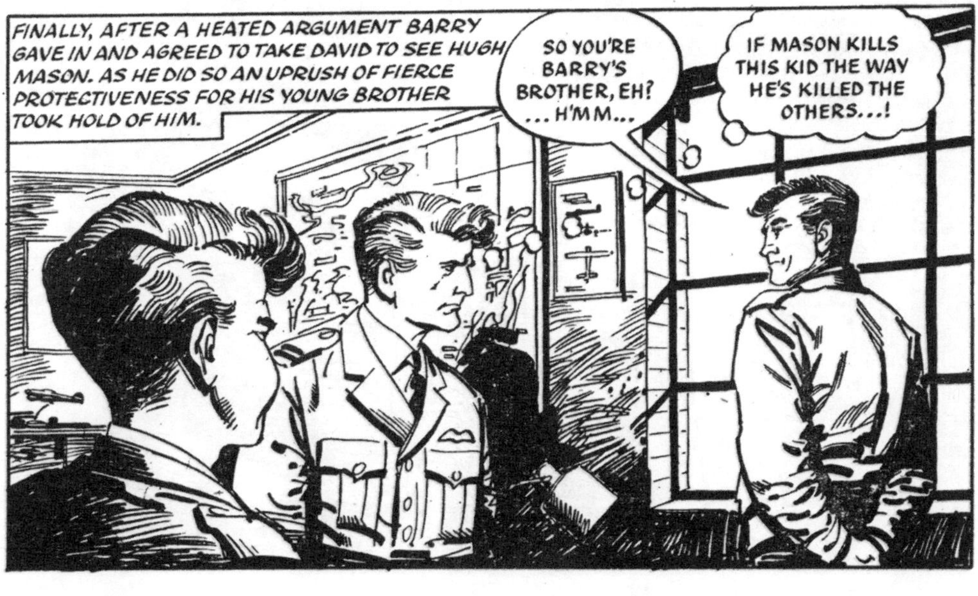
FINALLY, AFTER A HEATED ARGUMENT BARRY GAVE IN AND AGREED TO TAKE DAVID TO SEE HUGH MASON. AS HE DID SO AN UPRUSH OF FIERCE PROTECTIVENESS FOR HIS YOUNG BROTHER TOOK HOLD OF HIM.
SO YOU'RE BARRY'S BROTHER, EH? ... H'MM...
IF MASON KILLS THIS KID THE WAY HE'S KILLED THE OTHERS...!

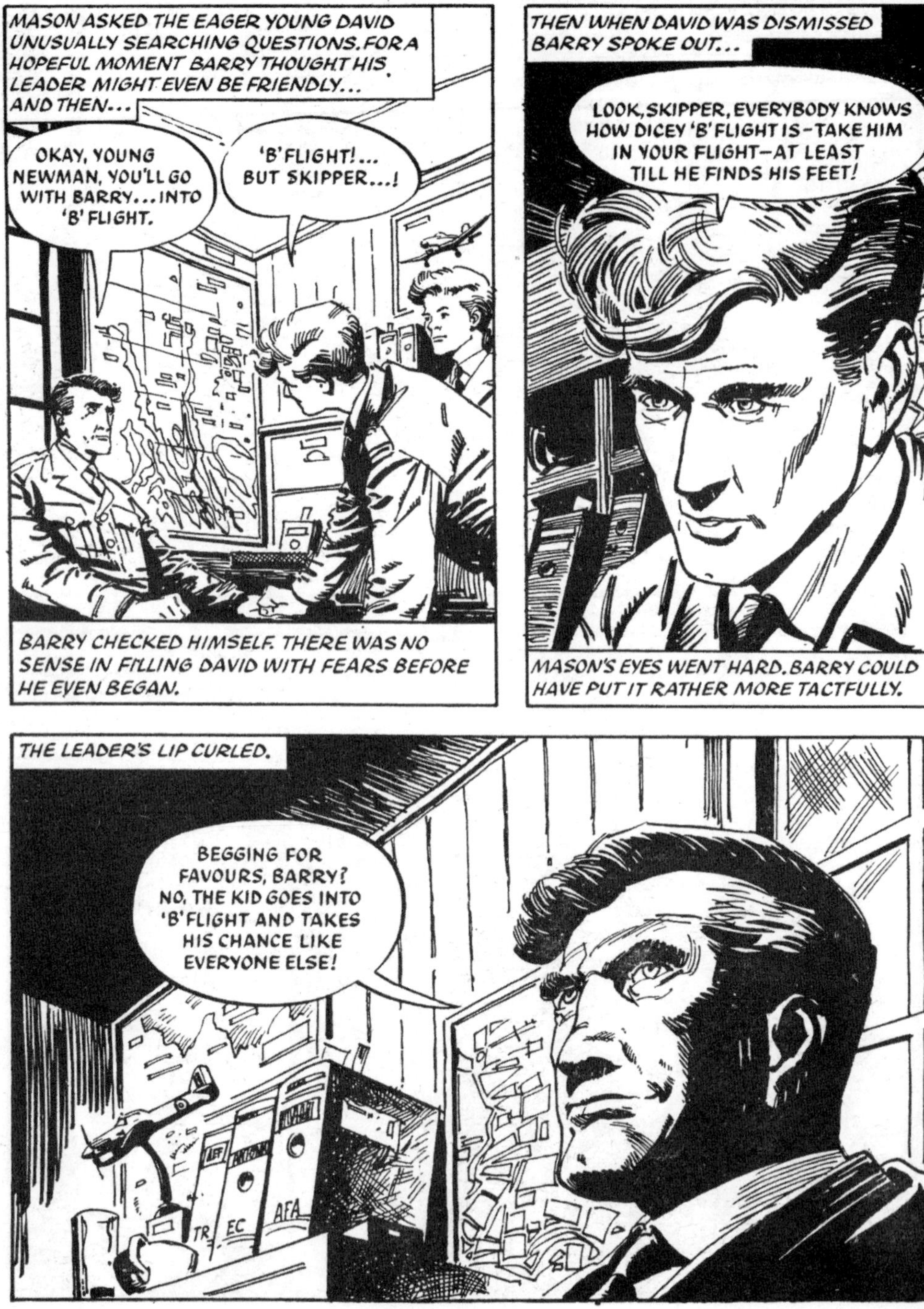
MASON ASKED THE EAGER YOUNG DAVID UNUSUALLY SEARCHING QUESTIONS. FOR A HOPEFUL MOMENT BARRY THOUGHT HIS LEADER MIGHT EVEN BE FRIENDLY... AND THEN...
OKAY, YOUNG NEWMAN, YOU'LL GO WITH BARRY... INTO 'B' FLIGHT.
'B' FLIGHT!... BUT SKIPPER...!
BARRY CHECKED HIMSELF. THERE WAS NO SENSE IN FILLING DAVID WITH FEARS BEFORE HE EVEN BEGAN.
THEN WHEN DAVID WAS DISMISSED BARRY SPOKE OUT...
LOOK, SKIPPER, EVERYBODY KNOWS HOW DICEY 'B' FLIGHT IS—TAKE HIM IN YOUR FLIGHT—AT LEAST TILL HE FINDS HIS FEET!
MASON'S EYES WENT HARD. BARRY COULD HAVE PUT IT RATHER MORE TACTFULLY.
THE LEADER'S LIP CURLED.
BEGGING FOR FAVOURS, BARRY? NO, THE KID GOES INTO 'B' FLIGHT AND TAKES HIS CHANCE LIKE EVERYONE ELSE!

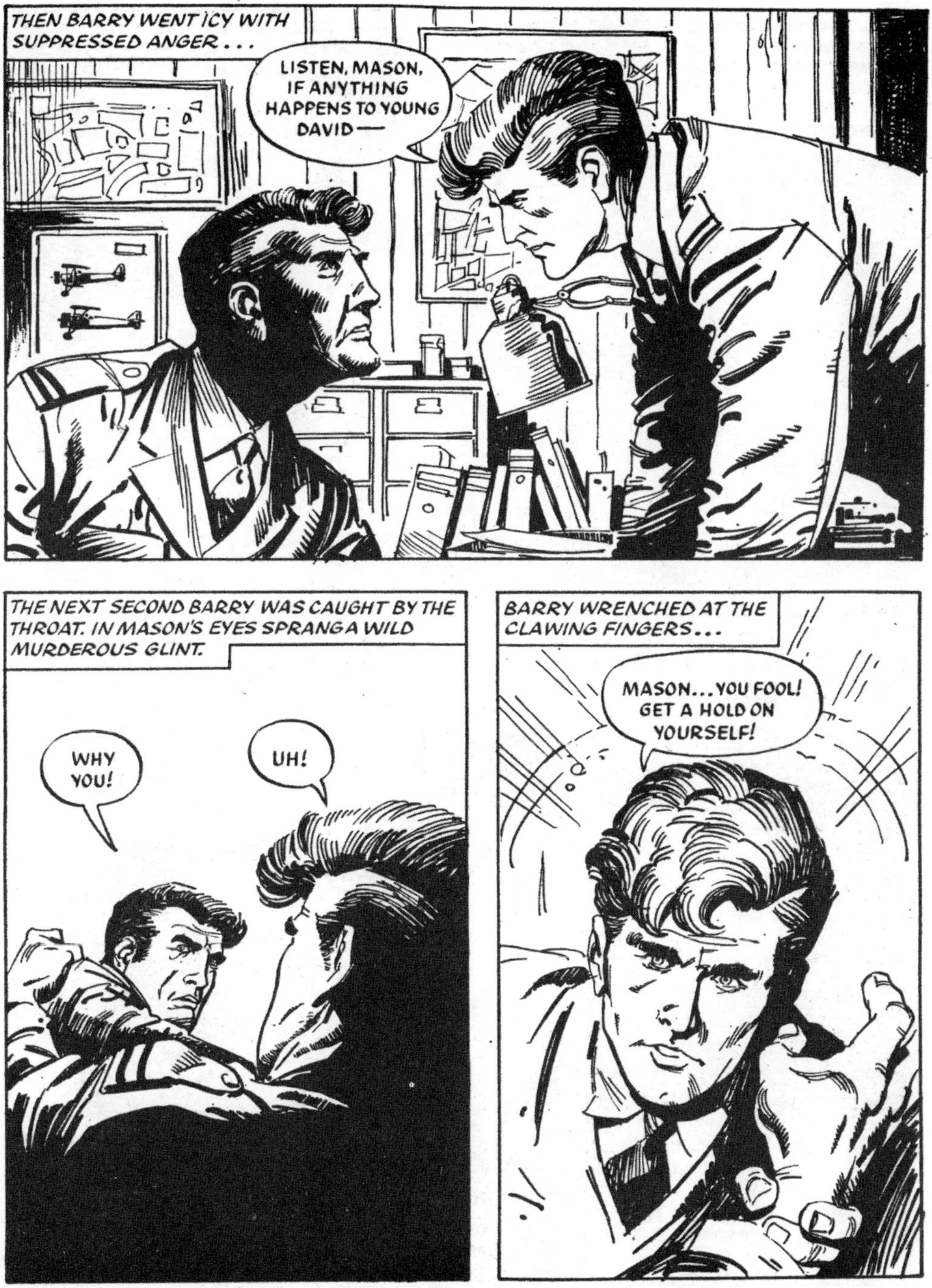
THEN BARRY WENT ICY WITH SUPPRESSED ANGER . . .
LISTEN, MASON, IF ANYTHING HAPPENS TO YOUNG DAVID —
THE NEXT SECOND BARRY WAS CAUGHT BY THE THROAT. IN MASON'S EYES SPRANG A WILD MURDEROUS GLINT.
WHY YOU!
UH!
BARRY WRENCHED AT THE CLAWING FINGERS...
MASON... YOU FOOL! GET A HOLD ON YOURSELF!

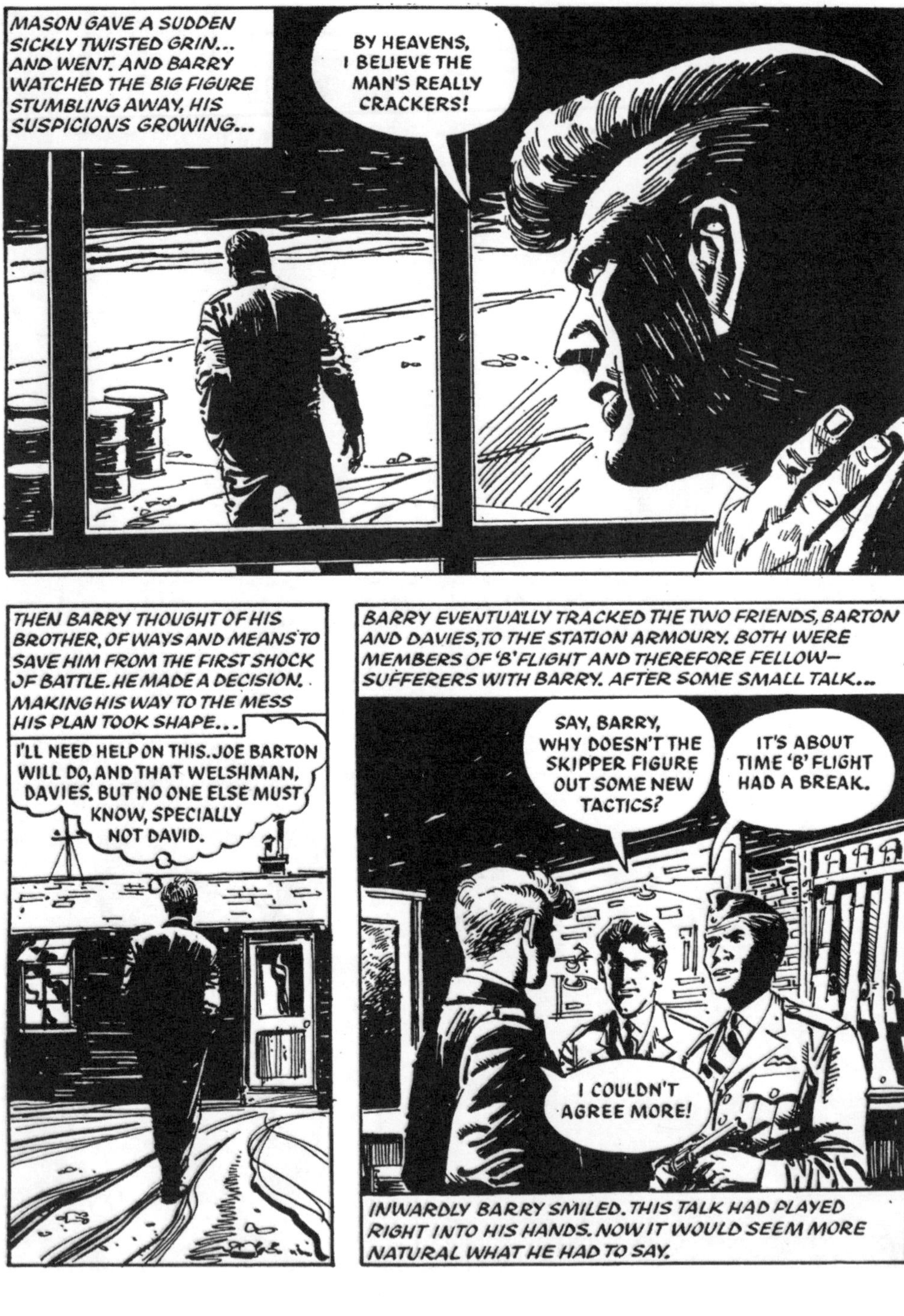
MASON GAVE A SUDDEN SICKLY TWISTED GRIN... AND WENT. AND BARRY WATCHED THE BIG FIGURE STUMBLING AWAY, HIS SUSPICIONS GROWING...
BY HEAVENS, I BELIEVE THE MAN'S REALLY CRACKERS!
THEN BARRY THOUGHT OF HIS BROTHER, OF WAYS AND MEANS TO SAVE HIM FROM THE FIRST SHOCK OF BATTLE. HE MADE A DECISION. MAKING HIS WAY TO THE MESS HIS PLAN TOOK SHAPE...
I'LL NEED HELP ON THIS. JOE BARTON WILL DO, AND THAT WELSHMAN, DAVIES. BUT NO ONE ELSE MUST KNOW, SPECIALLY NOT DAVID.
BARRY EVENTUALLY TRACKED THE TWO FRIENDS, BARTON AND DAVIES, TO THE STATION ARMOURY. BOTH WERE MEMBERS OF 'B' FLIGHT AND THEREFORE FELLOW-SUFFERERS WITH BARRY. AFTER SOME SMALL TALK...
SAY, BARRY, WHY DOESN'T THE SKIPPER FIGURE OUT SOME NEW TACTICS?
IT'S ABOUT TIME 'B' FLIGHT HAD A BREAK.
I COULDN'T AGREE MORE!
INWARDLY BARRY SMILED. THIS TALK HAD PLAYED RIGHT INTO HIS HANDS. NOW IT WOULD SEEM MORE NATURAL WHAT HE HAD TO SAY.

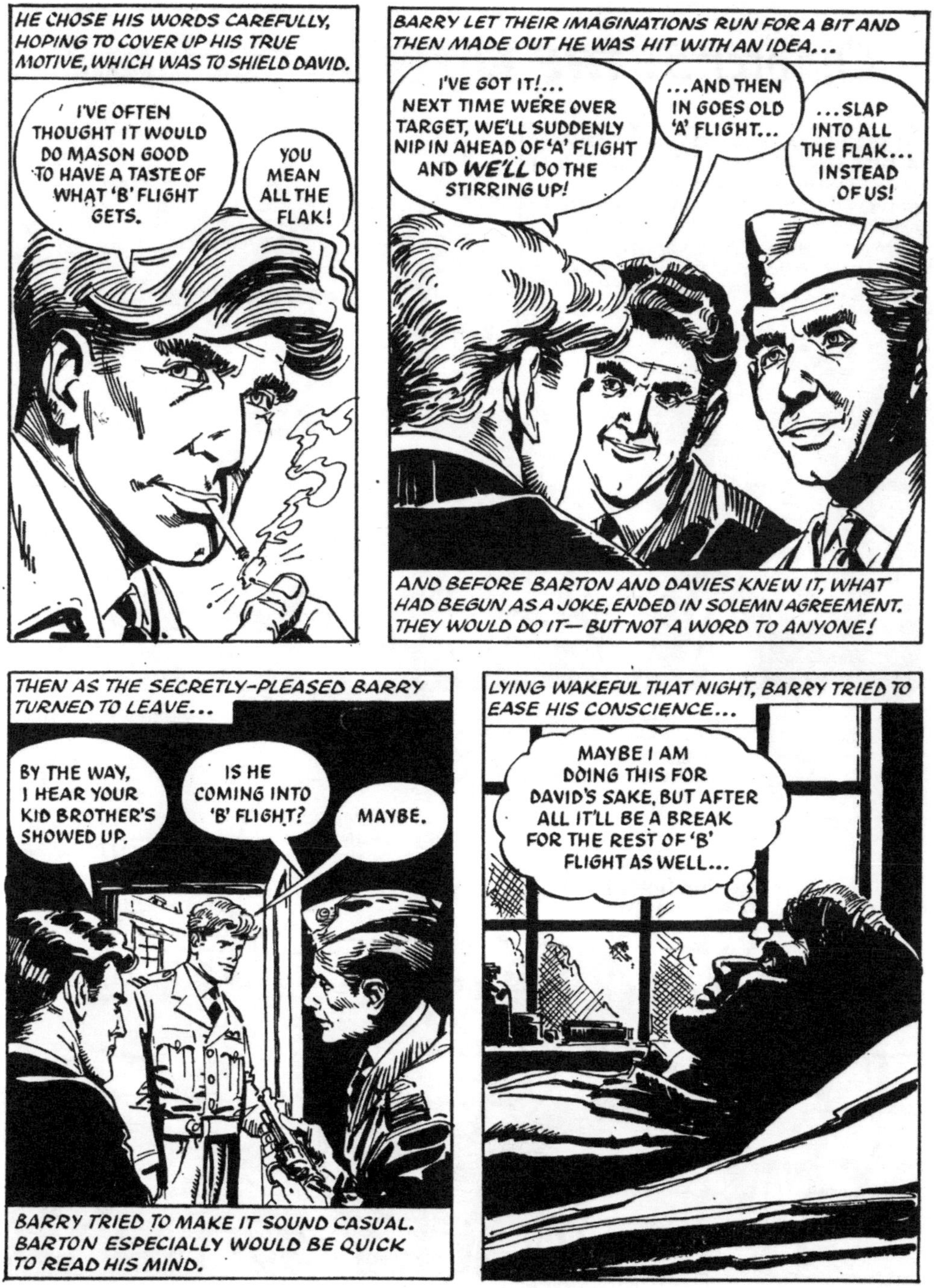
HE CHOSE HIS WORDS CAREFULLY, HOPING TO COVER UP HIS TRUE MOTIVE, WHICH WAS TO SHIELD DAVID.
I'VE OFTEN THOUGHT IT WOULD DO MASON GOOD TO HAVE A TASTE OF WHAT 'B' FLIGHT GETS.
YOU MEAN ALL THE FLAK!
BARRY LET THEIR IMAGINATIONS RUN FOR A BIT AND THEN MADE OUT HE WAS HIT WITH AN IDEA...
I'VE GOT IT!... NEXT TIME WE'RE OVER TARGET, WE'LL SUDDENLY NIP IN AHEAD OF 'A' FLIGHT AND WE'LL DO THE STIRRING UP!
...AND THEN IN GOES OLD 'A' FLIGHT...
...SLAP INTO ALL THE FLAK... INSTEAD OF US!
AND BEFORE BARTON AND DAVIES KNEW IT, WHAT HAD BEGUN AS A JOKE, ENDED IN SOLEMN AGREEMENT. THEY WOULD DO IT— BUT NOT A WORD TO ANYONE!
THEN AS THE SECRETLY-PLEASED BARRY TURNED TO LEAVE...
BY THE WAY, I HEAR YOUR KID BROTHER'S SHOWED UP.
IS HE COMING INTO 'B' FLIGHT?
MAYBE.
BARRY TRIED TO MAKE IT SOUND CASUAL. BARTON ESPECIALLY WOULD BE QUICK TO READ HIS MIND.
LYING WAKEFUL THAT NIGHT, BARRY TRIED TO EASE HIS CONSCIENCE...
MAYBE I AM DOING THIS FOR DAVID'S SAKE, BUT AFTER ALL IT'LL BE A BREAK FOR THE REST OF 'B' FLIGHT AS WELL...

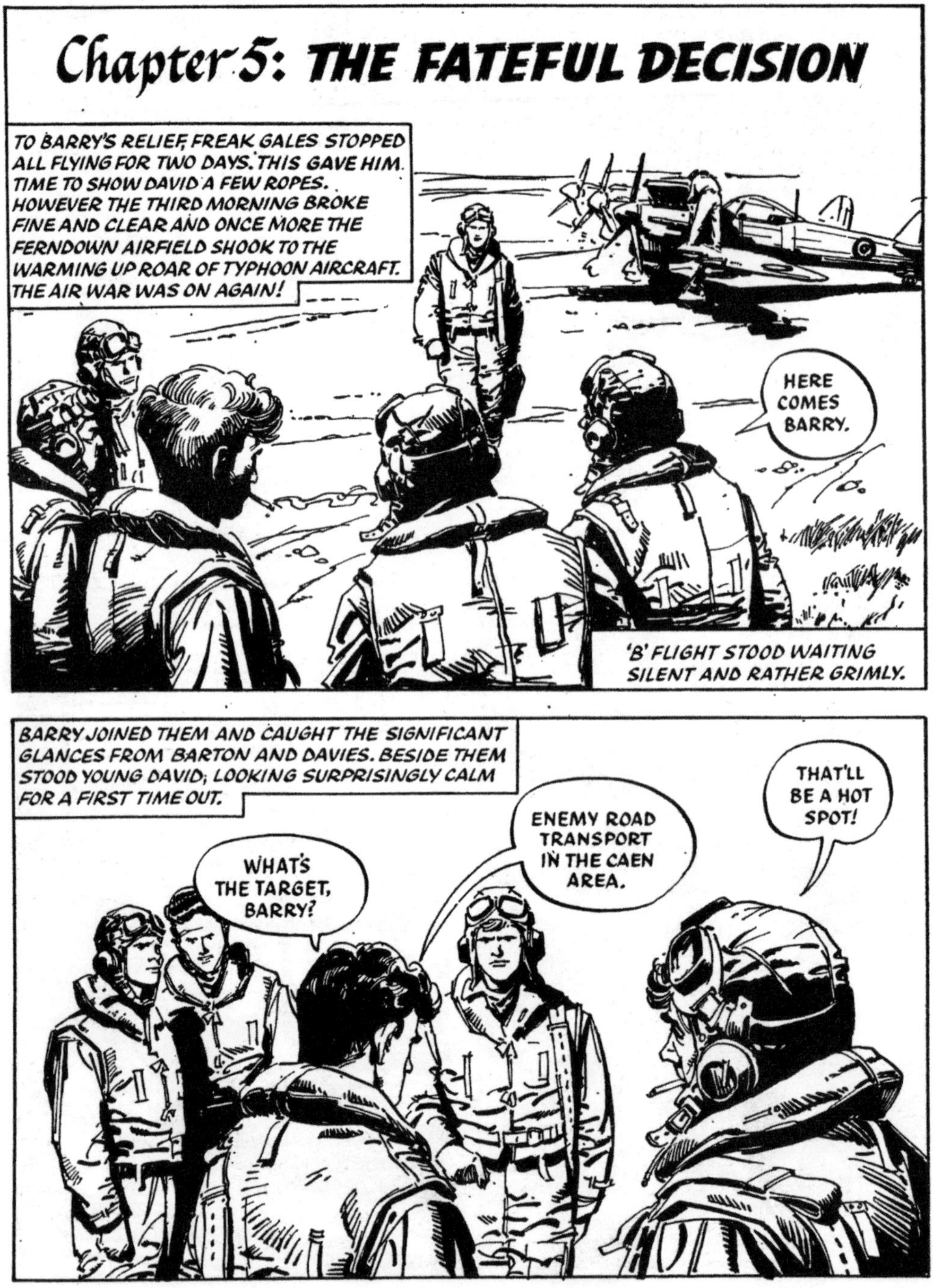
Chapter 5: THE FATEFUL DECISION
TO BARRY'S RELIEF, FREAK GALES STOPPED ALL FLYING FOR TWO DAYS. THIS GAVE HIM TIME TO SHOW DAVID A FEW ROPES. HOWEVER THE THIRD MORNING BROKE FINE AND CLEAR AND ONCE MORE THE FERNDOWN AIRFIELD SHOOK TO THE WARMING UP ROAR OF TYPHOON AIRCRAFT. THE AIR WAR WAS ON AGAIN!
HERE COMES BARRY.
'B' FLIGHT STOOD WAITING SILENT AND RATHER GRIMLY.
BARRY JOINED THEM AND CAUGHT THE SIGNIFICANT GLANCES FROM BARTON AND DAVIES. BESIDE THEM STOOD YOUNG DAVID; LOOKING SURPRISINGLY CALM FOR A FIRST TIME OUT.
WHAT'S THE TARGET, BARRY?
ENEMY ROAD TRANSPORT IN THE CAEN AREA.
THAT'LL BE A HOT SPOT!

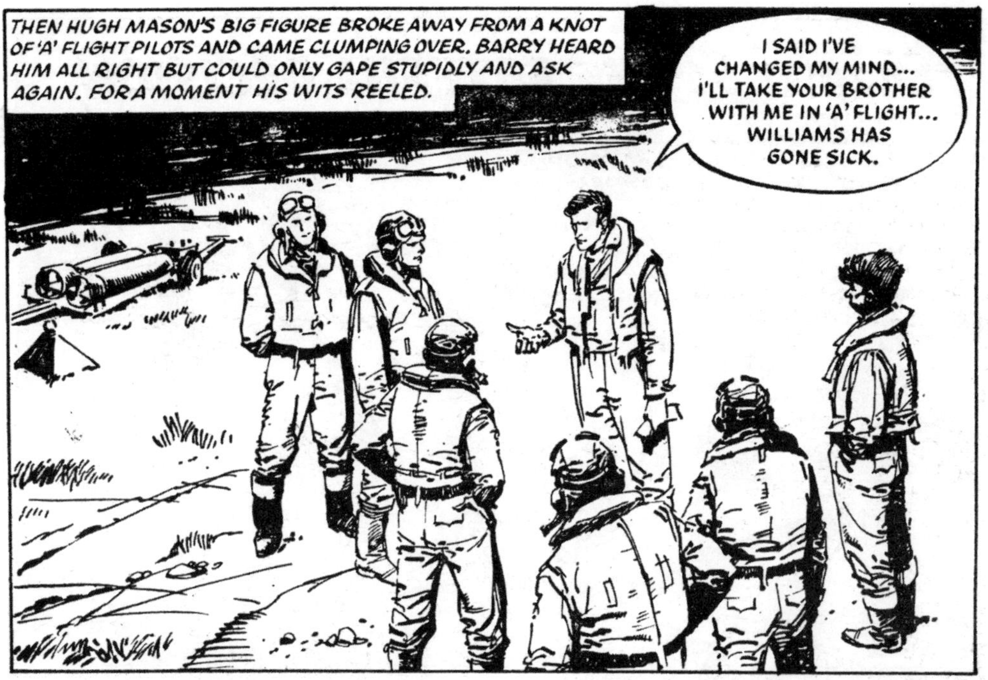
THEN HUGH MASON'S BIG FIGURE BROKE AWAY FROM A KNOT OF 'A' FLIGHT PILOTS AND CAME CLUMPING OVER. BARRY HEARD HIM ALL RIGHT BUT COULD ONLY GAPE STUPIDLY AND ASK AGAIN. FOR A MOMENT HIS WITS REELED.
I SAID I'VE CHANGED MY MIND... I'LL TAKE YOUR BROTHER WITH ME IN 'A' FLIGHT... WILLIAMS HAS GONE SICK.

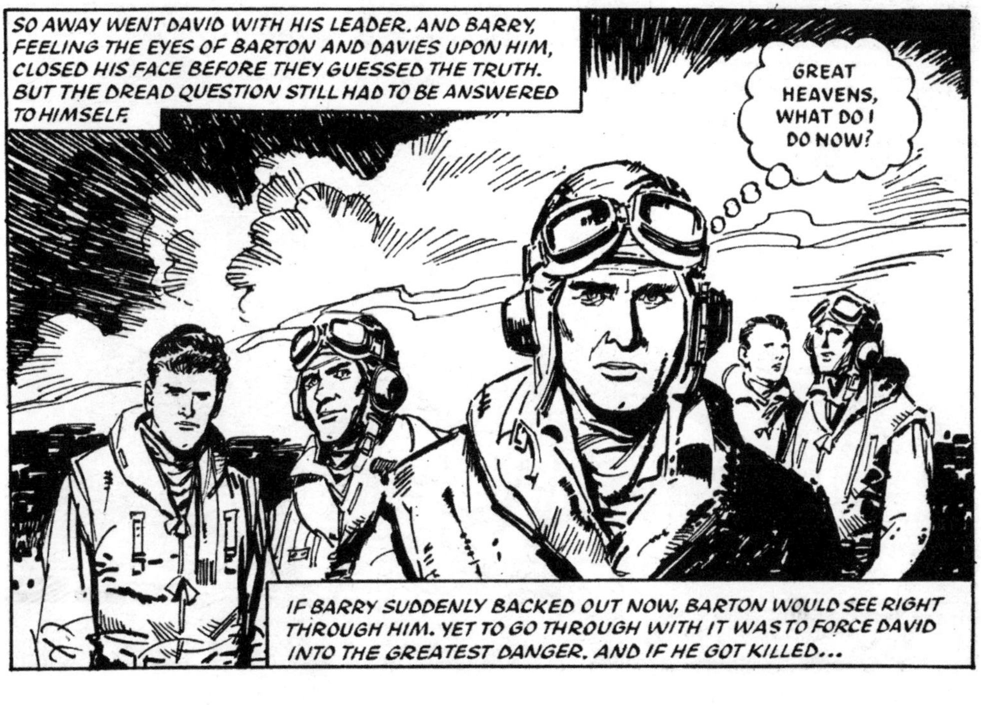
SO AWAY WENT DAVID WITH HIS LEADER. AND BARRY, FEELING THE EYES OF BARTON AND DAVIES UPON HIM, CLOSED HIS FACE BEFORE THEY GUESSED THE TRUTH. BUT THE DREAD QUESTION STILL HAD TO BE ANSWERED TO HIMSELF.
GREAT HEAVENS, WHAT DO I DO NOW?
IF BARRY SUDDENLY BACKED OUT NOW, BARTON WOULD SEE RIGHT THROUGH HIM. YET TO GO THROUGH WITH IT WAS TO FORCE DAVID INTO THE GREATEST DANGER. AND IF HE GOT KILLED...

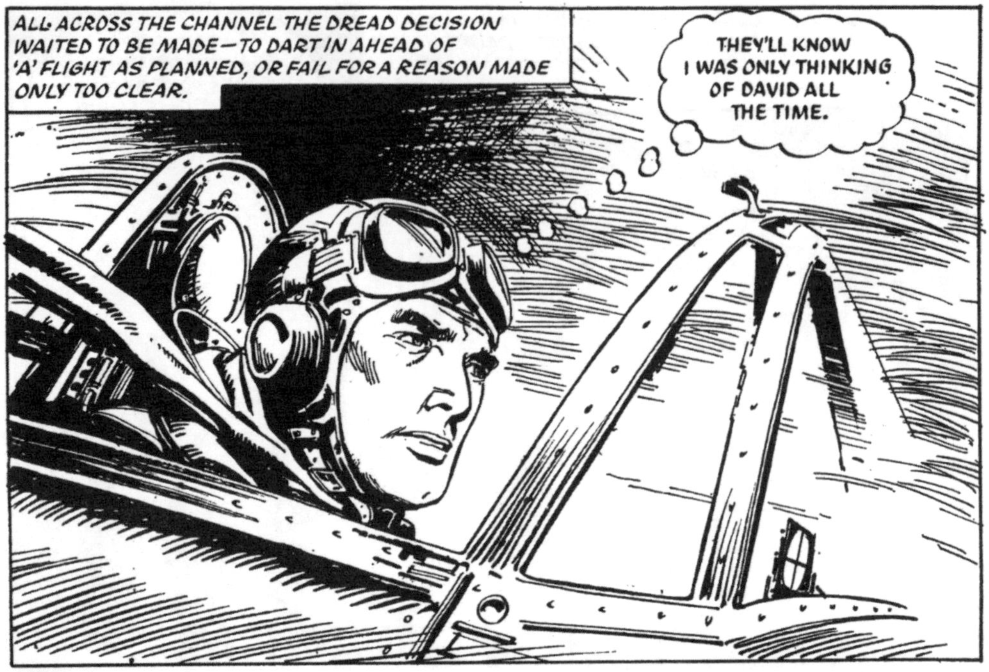
ALL ACROSS THE CHANNEL THE DREAD DECISION WAITED TO BE MADE—TO DART IN AHEAD OF 'A' FLIGHT AS PLANNED, OR FAIL FOR A REASON MADE ONLY TOO CLEAR.
THEY'LL KNOW I WAS ONLY THINKING OF DAVID ALL THE TIME.

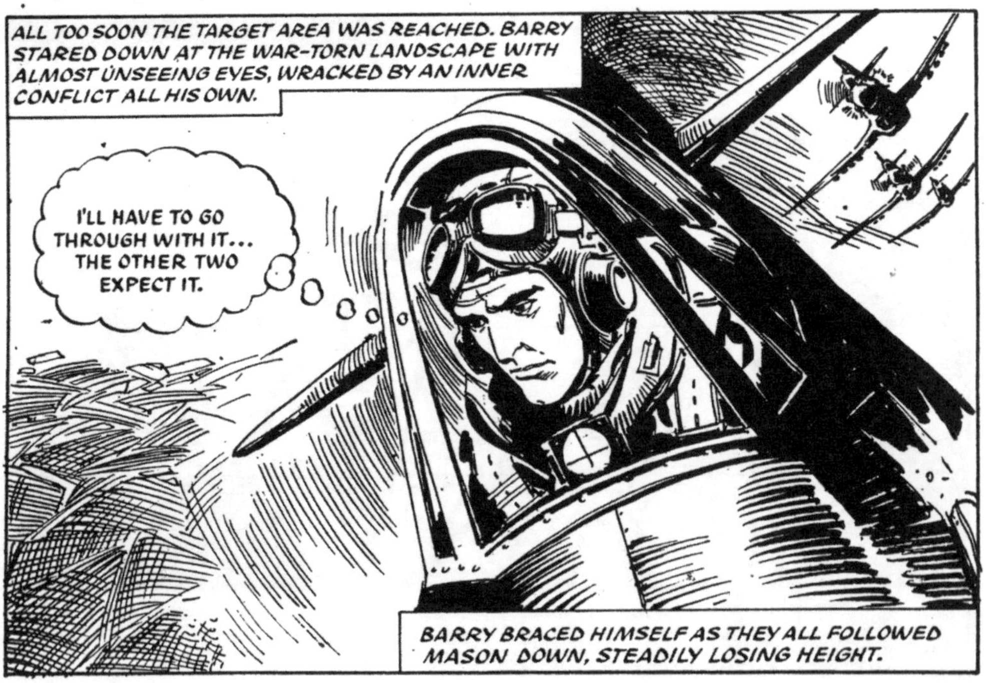
ALL TOO SOON THE TARGET AREA WAS REACHED. BARRY STARED DOWN AT THE WAR-TORN LANDSCAPE WITH ALMOST UNSEEING EYES, WRACKED BY AN INNER CONFLICT ALL HIS OWN.
I'LL HAVE TO GO THROUGH WITH IT... THE OTHER TWO EXPECT IT.
BARRY BRACED HIMSELF AS THEY ALL FOLLOWED MASON DOWN, STEADILY LOSING HEIGHT.

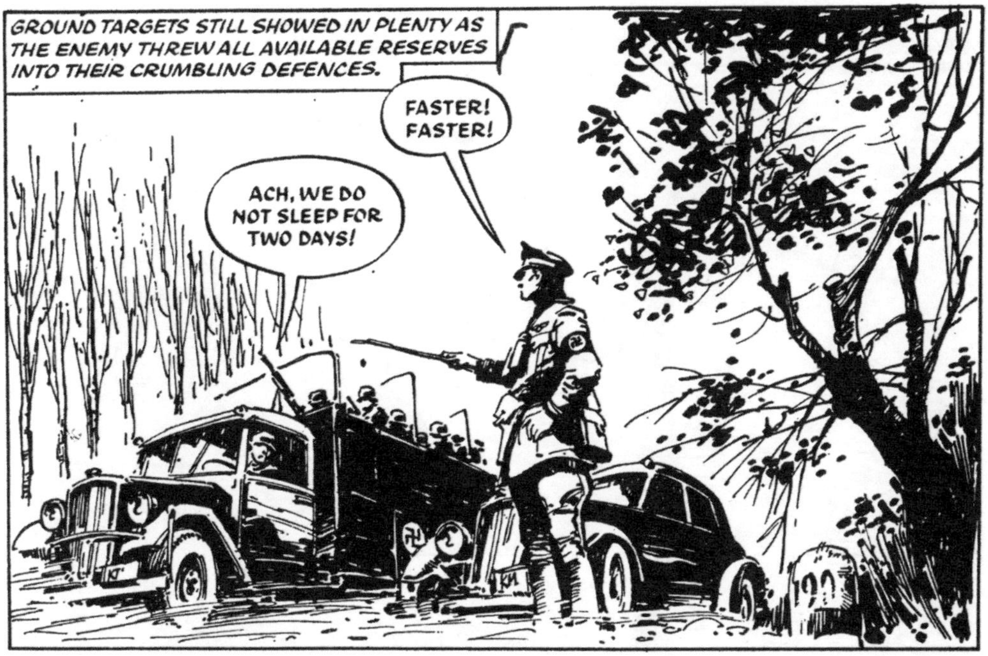
GROUND TARGETS STILL SHOWED IN PLENTY AS THE ENEMY THREW ALL AVAILABLE RESERVES INTO THEIR CRUMBLING DEFENCES.
ACH, WE DO NOT SLEEP FOR TWO DAYS!
FASTER! FASTER!

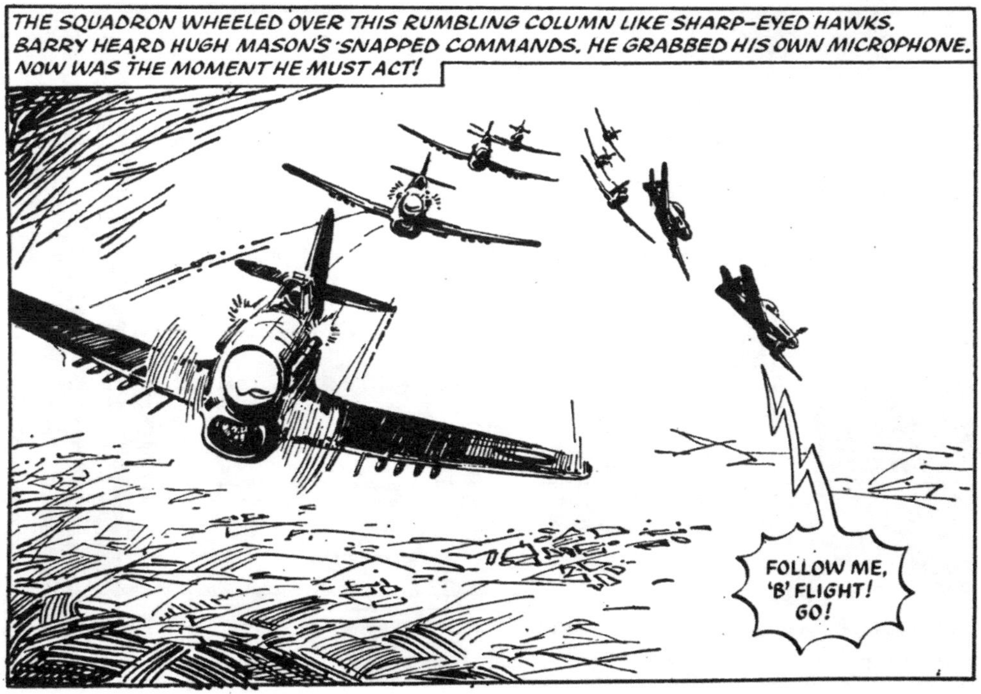
THE SQUADRON WHEELED OVER THIS RUMBLING COLUMN LIKE SHARP-EYED HAWKS. BARRY HEARD HUGH MASON'S SNAPPED COMMANDS. HE GRABBED HIS OWN MICROPHONE. NOW WAS THE MOMENT HE MUST ACT!
FOLLOW ME, 'B' FLIGHT! GO!

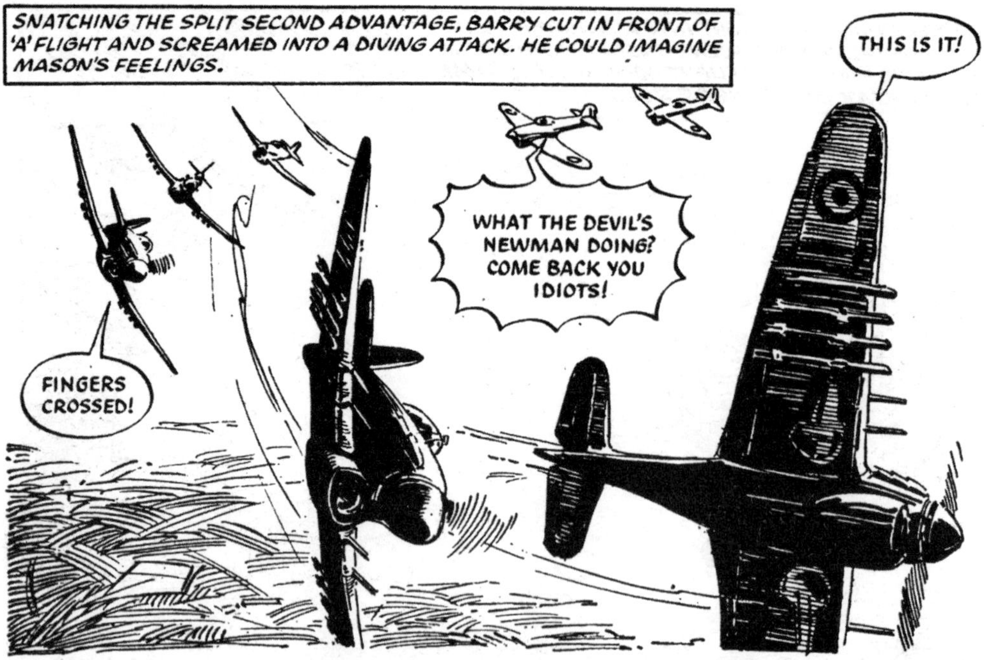
SNATCHING THE SPLIT SECOND ADVANTAGE, BARRY CUT IN FRONT OF 'A' FLIGHT AND SCREAMED INTO A DIVING ATTACK. HE COULD IMAGINE MASON'S FEELINGS.
THIS IS IT!
WHAT THE DEVIL'S NEWMAN DOING? COME BACK YOU IDIOTS!
FINGERS CROSSED!

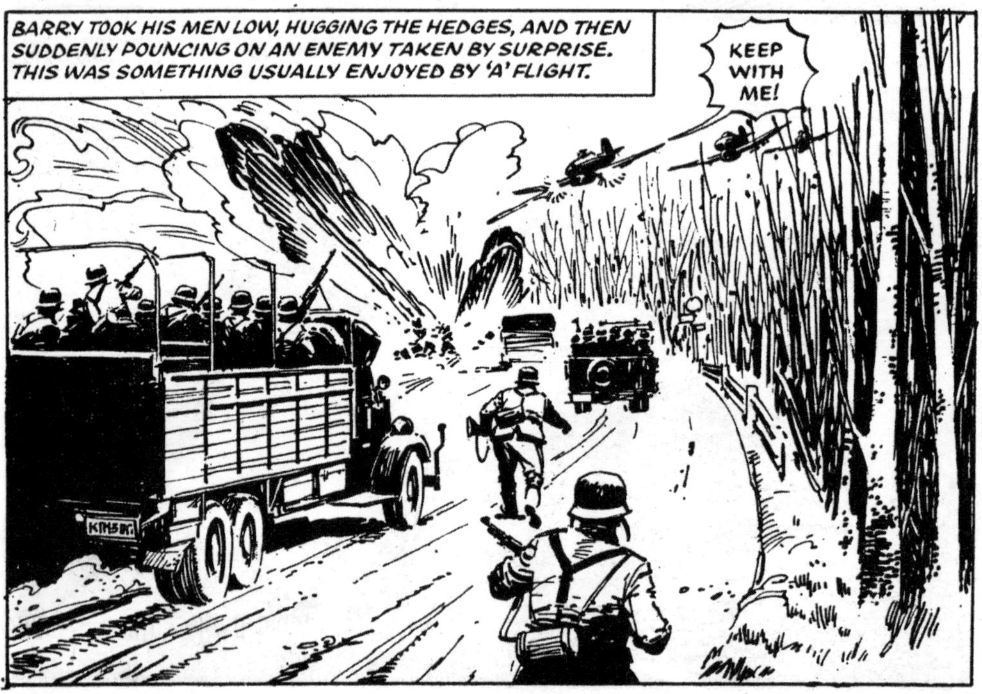
BARRY TOOK HIS MEN LOW, HUGGING THE HEDGES, AND THEN SUDDENLY POUNCING ON AN ENEMY TAKEN BY SURPRISE. THIS WAS SOMETHING USUALLY ENJOYED BY 'A' FLIGHT.
KEEP WITH ME!

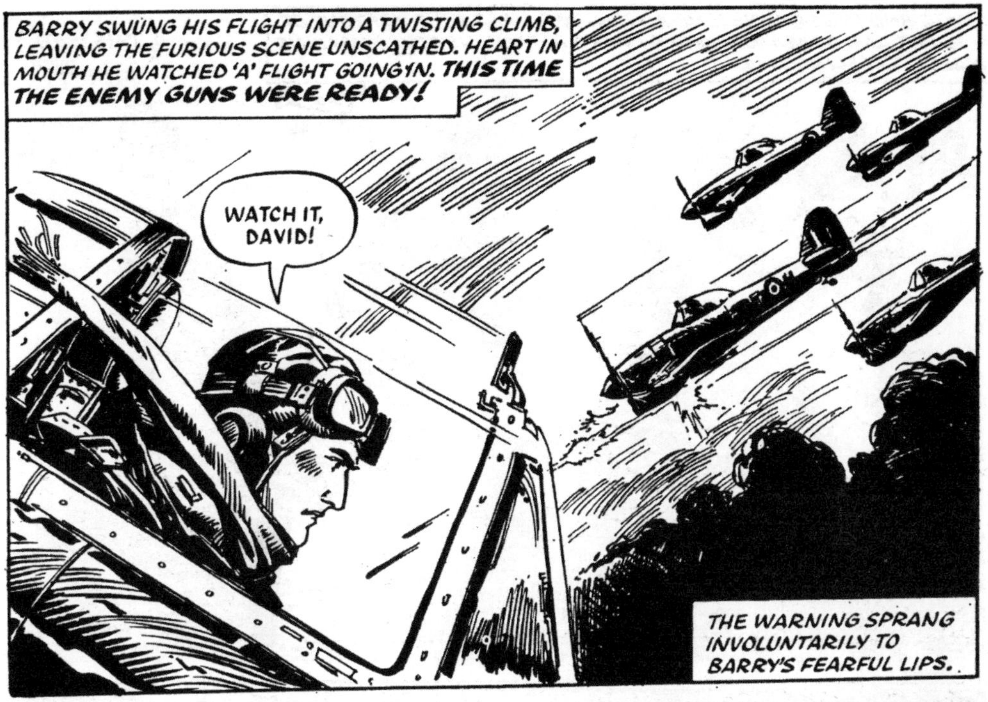
BARRY SWUNG HIS FLIGHT INTO A TWISTING CLIMB, LEAVING THE FURIOUS SCENE UNSCATHED. HEART IN MOUTH HE WATCHED 'A' FLIGHT GOING IN. THIS TIME THE ENEMY GUNS WERE READY!
WATCH IT, DAVID!
THE WARNING SPRANG INVOLUNTARILY TO BARRY'S FEARFUL LIPS.

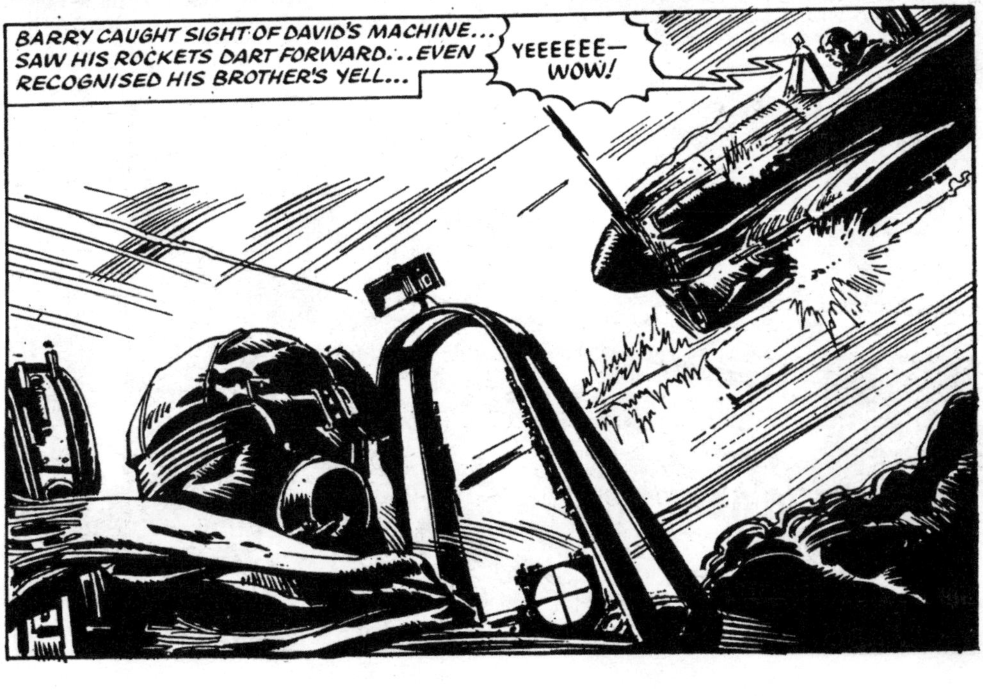
BARRY CAUGHT SIGHT OF DAVID'S MACHINE... SAW HIS ROCKETS DART FORWARD...EVEN RECOGNISED HIS BROTHER'S YELL...
YEEEEEE—WOW!

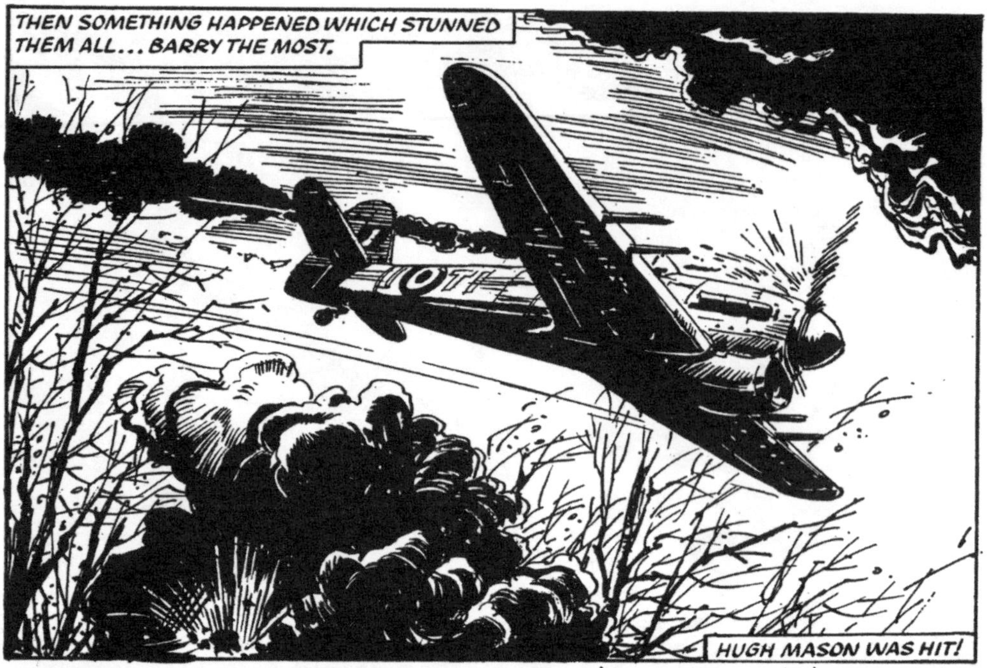
THEN SOMETHING HAPPENED WHICH STUNNED THEM ALL... BARRY THE MOST.
HUGH MASON WAS HIT!

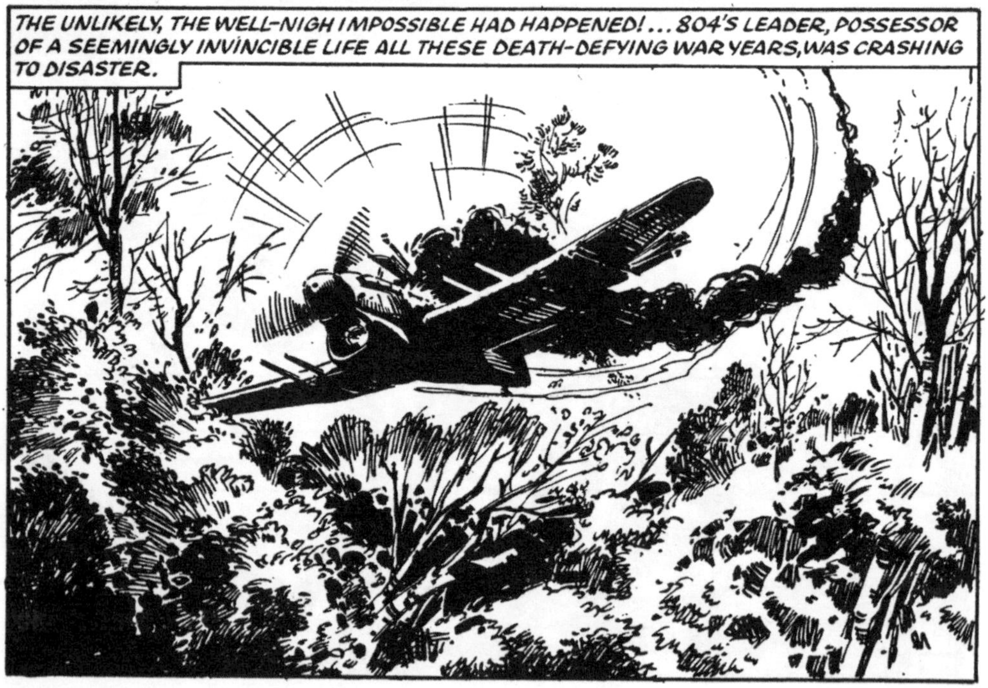
THE UNLIKELY, THE WELL-NIGH IMPOSSIBLE HAD HAPPENED! ... 804'S LEADER, POSSESSOR OF A SEEMINGLY INVINCIBLE LIFE ALL THESE DEATH-DEFYING WAR YEARS, WAS CRASHING TO DISASTER.

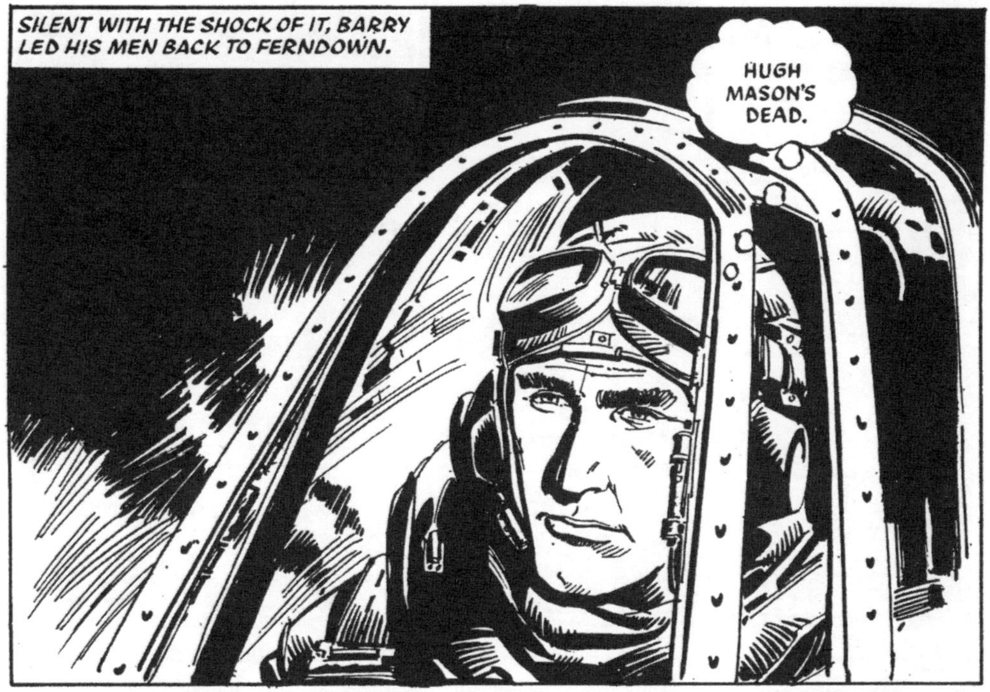
SILENT WITH THE SHOCK OF IT, BARRY LED HIS MEN BACK TO FERNDOWN.
HUGH MASON'S DEAD.

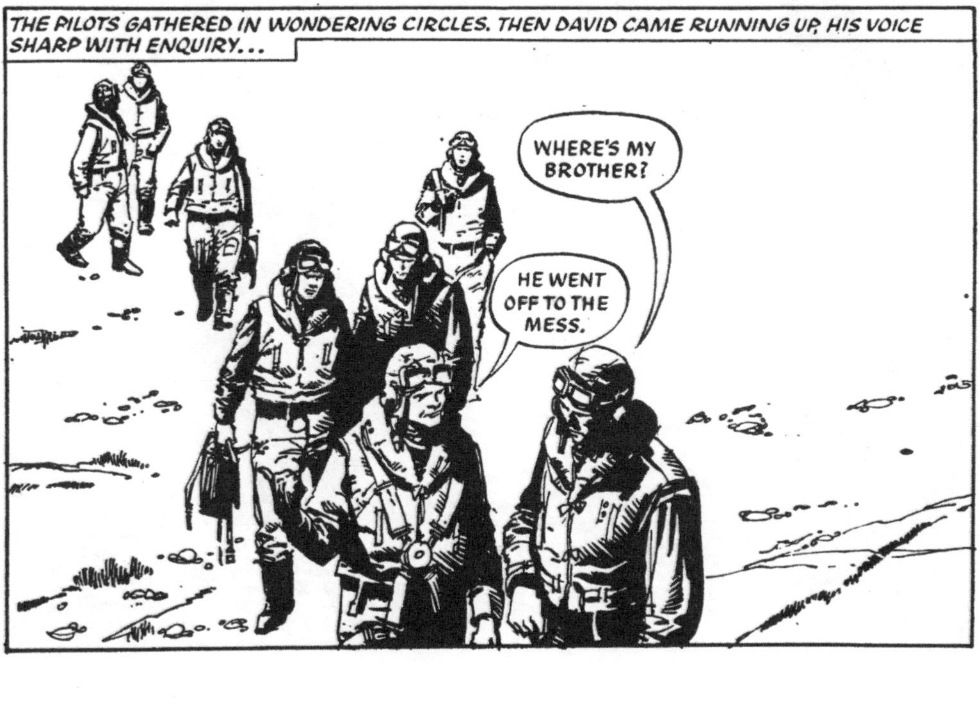
THE PILOTS GATHERED IN WONDERING CIRCLES. THEN DAVID CAME RUNNING UP, HIS VOICE SHARP WITH ENQUIRY...
WHERE'S MY BROTHER?
HE WENT OFF TO THE MESS.

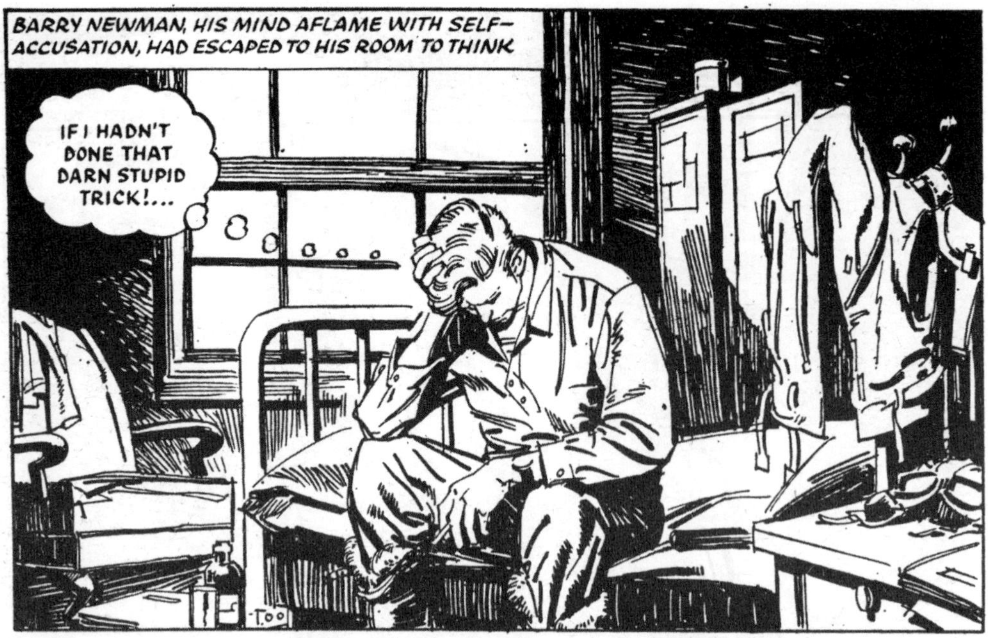
BARRY NEWMAN, HIS MIND AFLAME WITH SELF-ACCUSATION, HAD ESCAPED TO HIS ROOM TO THINK
IF I HADN'T DONE THAT DARN STUPID TRICK!...

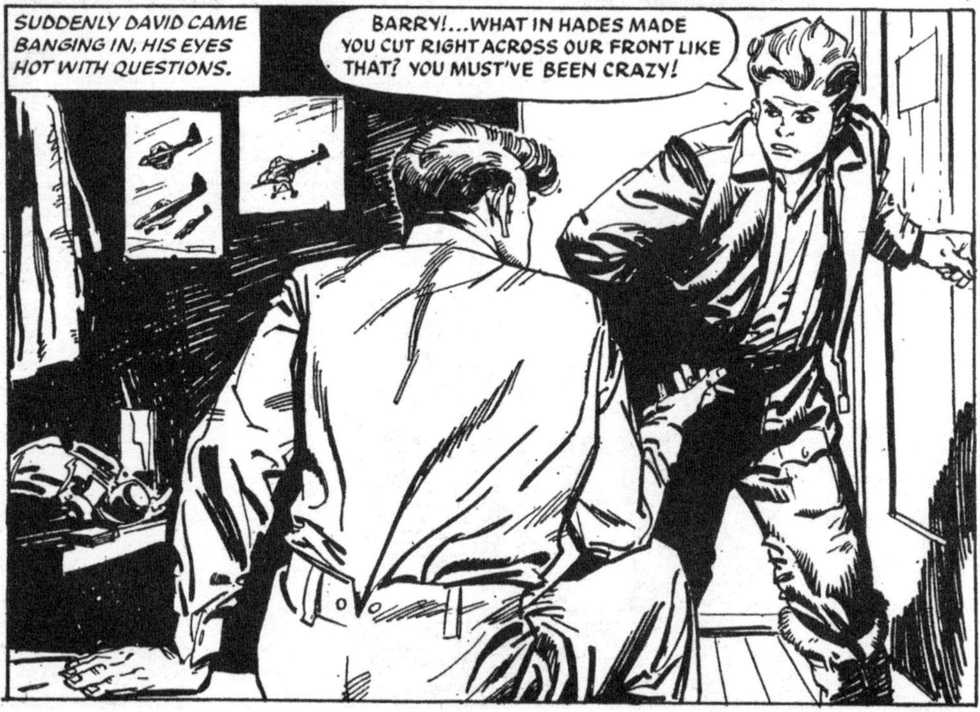
SUDDENLY DAVID CAME BANGING IN, HIS EYES HOT WITH QUESTIONS.
BARRY!...WHAT IN HADES MADE YOU CUT RIGHT ACROSS OUR FRONT LIKE THAT? YOU MUST'VE BEEN CRAZY!

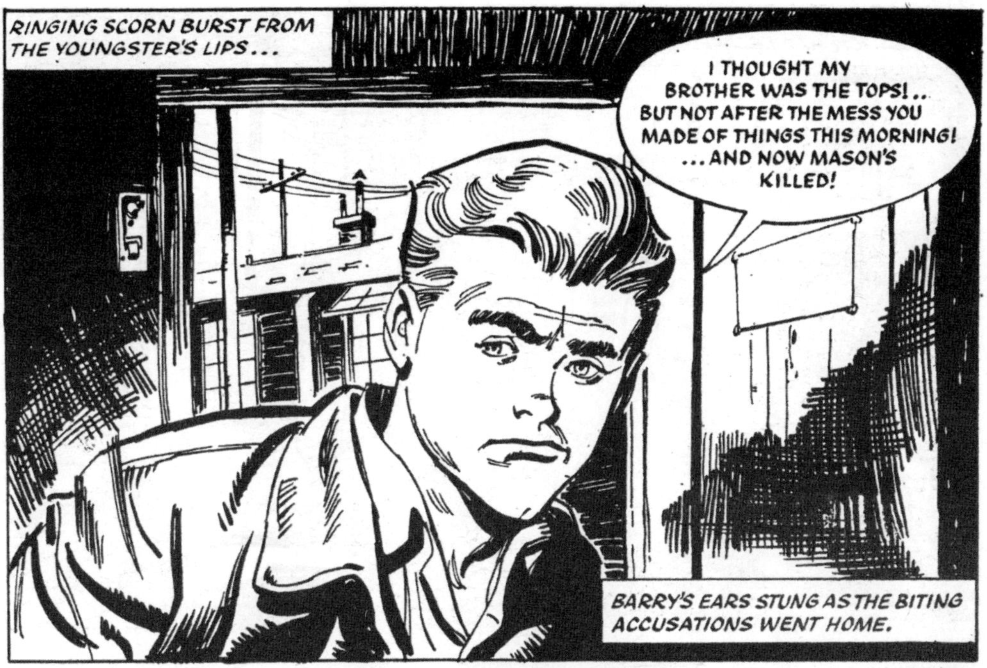
RINGING SCORN BURST FROM THE YOUNGSTER'S LIPS...
I THOUGHT MY BROTHER WAS THE TOPS!.. BUT NOT AFTER THE MESS YOU MADE OF THINGS THIS MORNING! ...AND NOW MASON'S KILLED!
BARRY'S EARS STUNG AS THE BITING ACCUSATIONS WENT HOME.

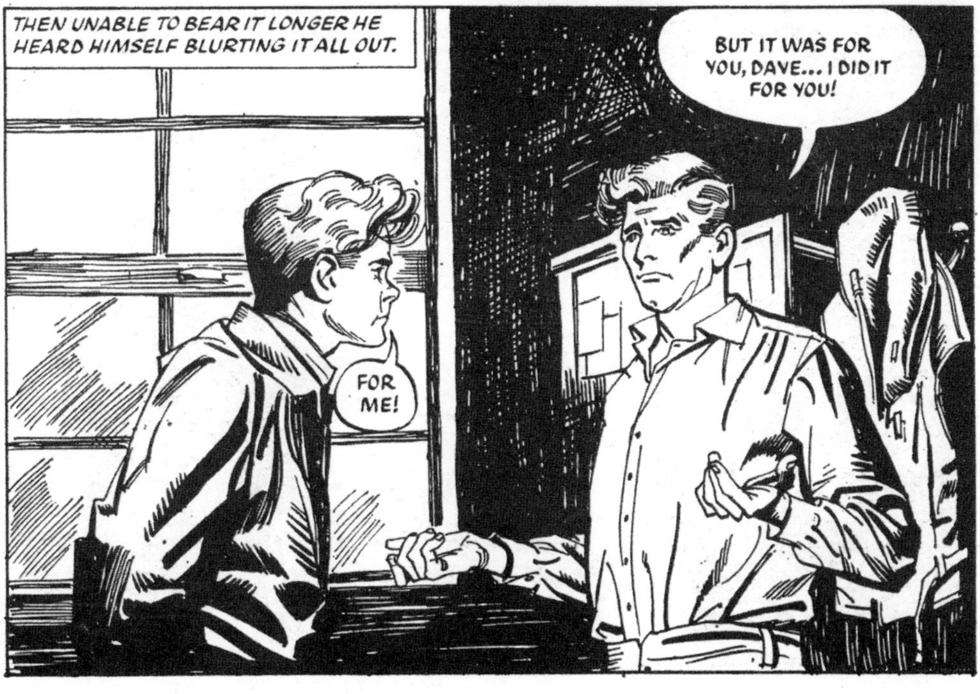
THEN UNABLE TO BEAR IT LONGER HE HEARD HIMSELF BLURTING IT ALL OUT.
BUT IT WAS FOR YOU, DAVE... I DID IT FOR YOU!
FOR ME!

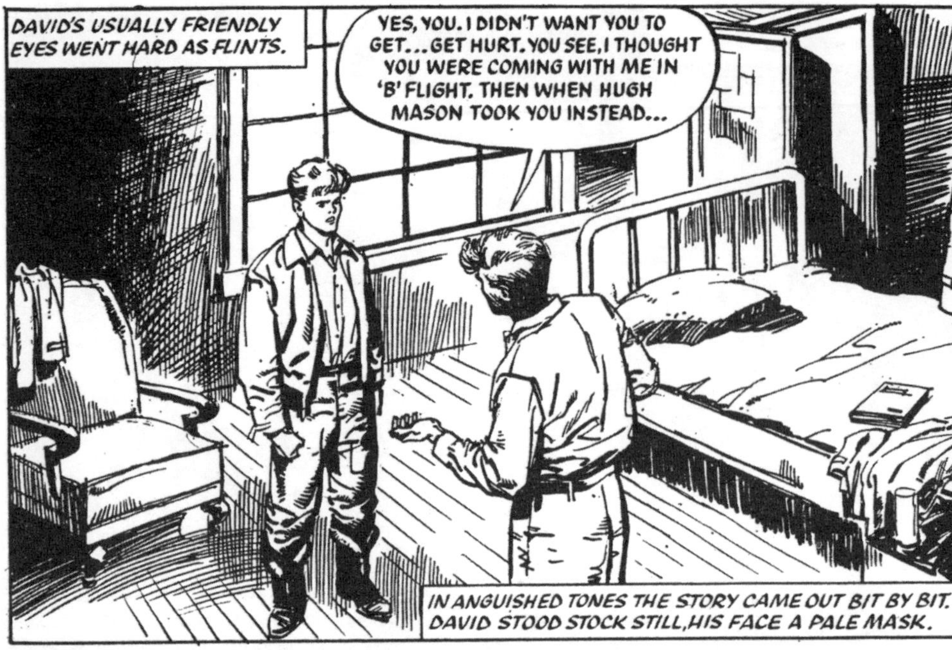
DAVID'S USUALLY FRIENDLY EYES WENT HARD AS FLINTS.
YES, YOU. I DIDN'T WANT YOU TO GET... GET HURT. YOU SEE, I THOUGHT YOU WERE COMING WITH ME IN 'B' FLIGHT. THEN WHEN HUGH MASON TOOK YOU INSTEAD...
IN ANGUISHED TONES THE STORY CAME OUT BIT BY BIT. DAVID STOOD STOCK STILL, HIS FACE A PALE MASK.

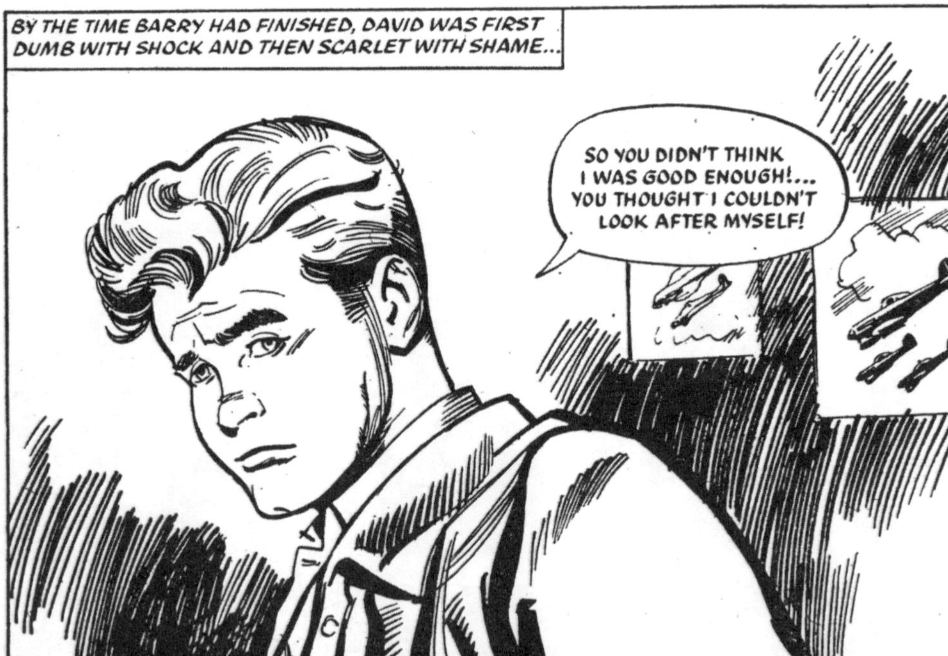
BY THE TIME BARRY HAD FINISHED, DAVID WAS FIRST DUMB WITH SHOCK AND THEN SCARLET WITH SHAME...
SO YOU DIDN'T THINK I WAS GOOD ENOUGH!... YOU THOUGHT I COULDN'T LOOK AFTER MYSELF!

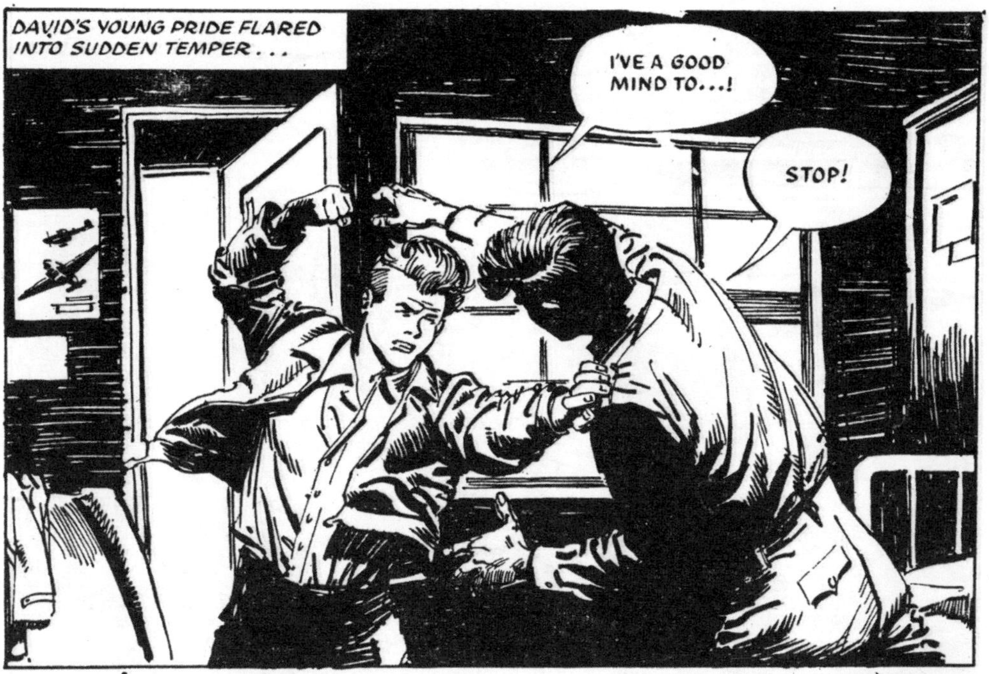
DAVID'S YOUNG PRIDE FLARED INTO SUDDEN TEMPER . . .
I'VE A GOOD MIND TO...!
STOP!

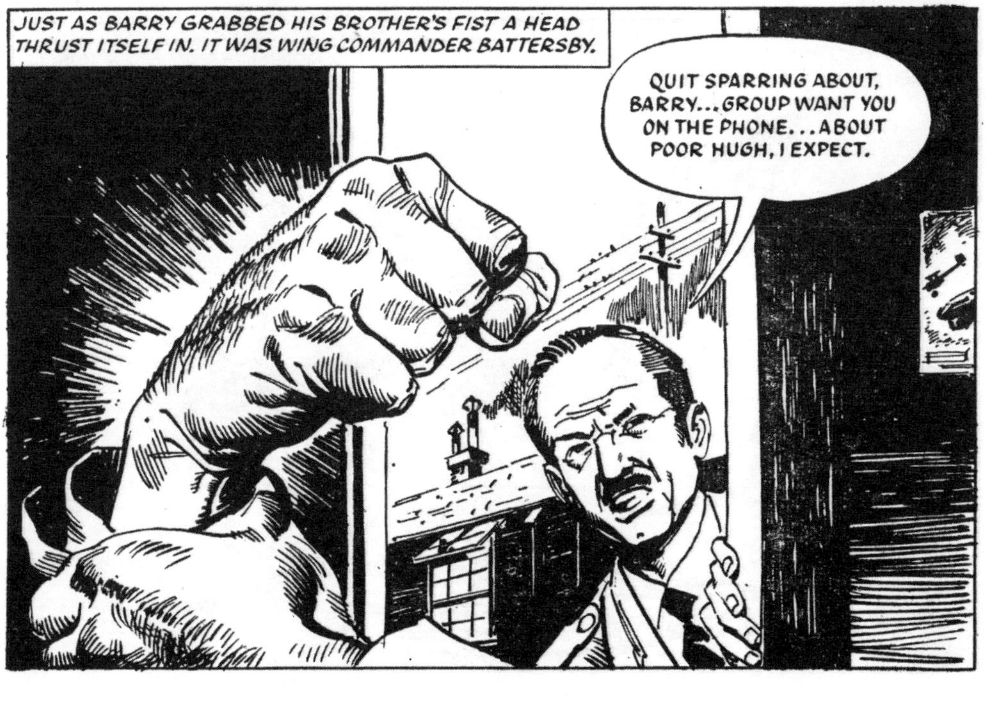
JUST AS BARRY GRABBED HIS BROTHER'S FIST A HEAD THRUST ITSELF IN. IT WAS WING COMMANDER BATTERSBY.
QUIT SPARRING ABOUT, BARRY...GROUP WANT YOU ON THE PHONE...ABOUT POOR HUGH, I EXPECT.

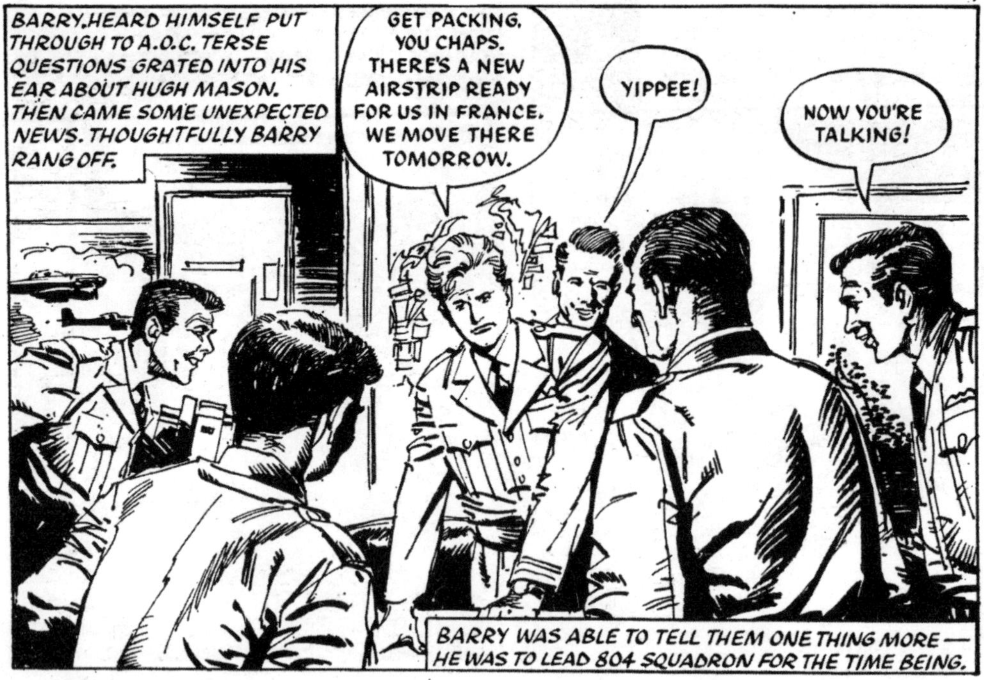
BARRY HEARD HIMSELF PUT THROUGH TO A.O.C. TERSE QUESTIONS GRATED INTO HIS EAR ABOUT HUGH MASON. THEN CAME SOME UNEXPECTED NEWS. THOUGHTFULLY BARRY RANG OFF.
GET PACKING, YOU CHAPS. THERE'S A NEW AIRSTRIP READY FOR US IN FRANCE. WE MOVE THERE TOMORROW.
YIPPEE!
NOW YOU'RE TALKING!
BARRY WAS ABLE TO TELL THEM ONE THING MORE — HE WAS TO LEAD 804 SQUADRON FOR THE TIME BEING.

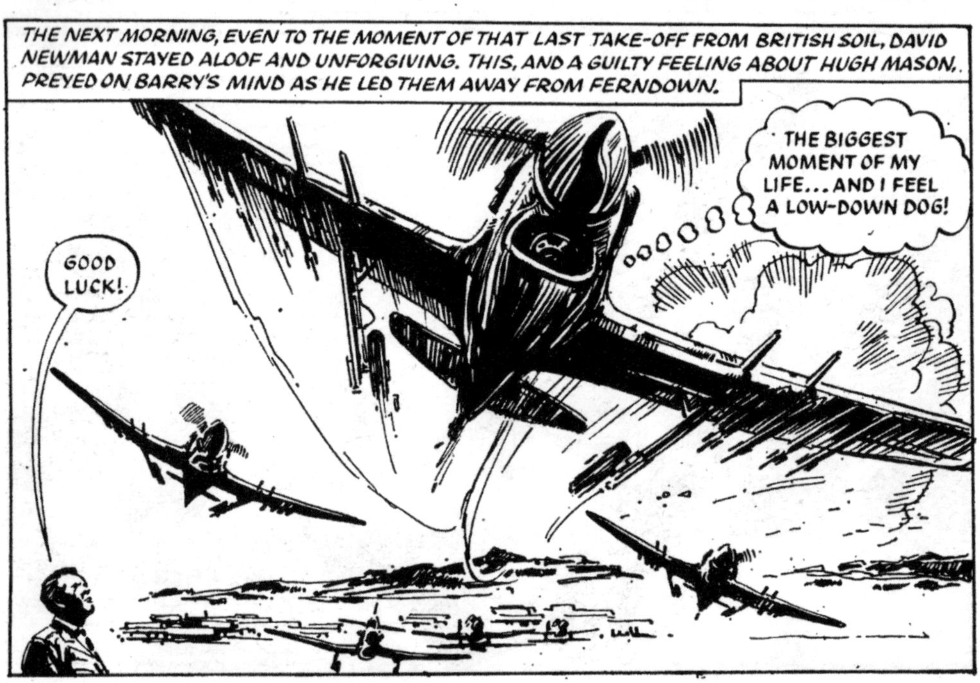
THE NEXT MORNING, EVEN TO THE MOMENT OF THAT LAST TAKE-OFF FROM BRITISH SOIL, DAVID NEWMAN STAYED ALOOF AND UNFORGIVING. THIS, AND A GUILTY FEELING ABOUT HUGH MASON, PREYED ON BARRY'S MIND AS HE LED THEM AWAY FROM FERNDOWN.
GOOD LUCK!
THE BIGGEST MOMENT OF MY LIFE... AND I FEEL A LOW-DOWN DOG!

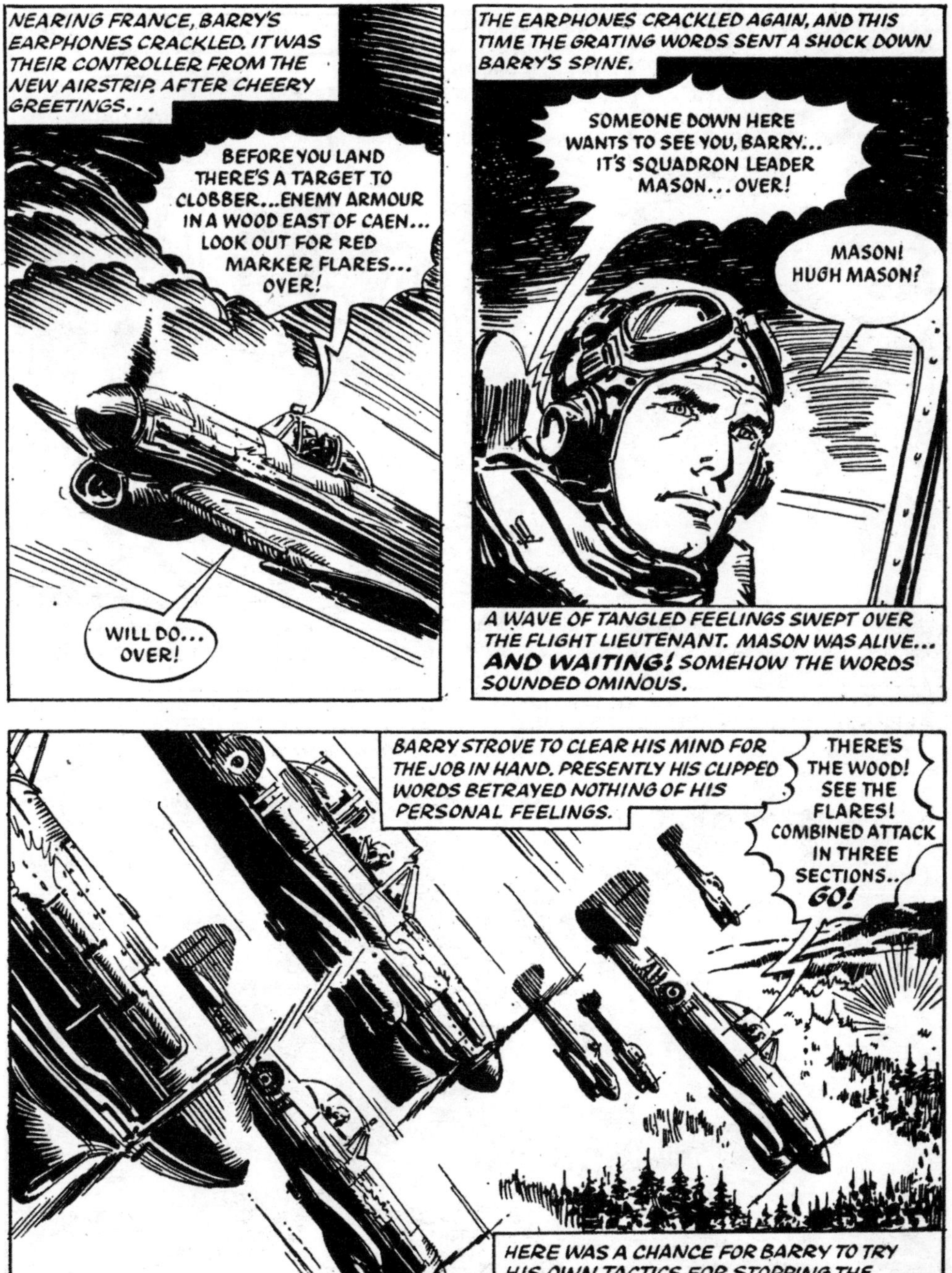
NEARING FRANCE, BARRY'S EARPHONES CRACKLED. IT WAS THEIR CONTROLLER FROM THE NEW AIRSTRIP. AFTER CHEERY GREETINGS...
BEFORE YOU LAND THERE'S A TARGET TO CLOBBER...ENEMY ARMOUR IN A WOOD EAST OF CAEN... LOOK OUT FOR RED MARKER FLARES... OVER!
WILL DO... OVER!
THE EARPHONES CRACKLED AGAIN, AND THIS TIME THE GRATING WORDS SENT A SHOCK DOWN BARRY'S SPINE.
SOMEONE DOWN HERE WANTS TO SEE YOU, BARRY... IT'S SQUADRON LEADER MASON... OVER!
MASON! HUGH MASON?
A WAVE OF TANGLED FEELINGS SWEPT OVER THE FLIGHT LIEUTENANT. MASON WAS ALIVE... AND WAITING! SOMEHOW THE WORDS SOUNDED OMINOUS.
BARRY STROVE TO CLEAR HIS MIND FOR THE JOB IN HAND. PRESENTLY HIS CLIPPED WORDS BETRAYED NOTHING OF HIS PERSONAL FEELINGS.
THERE'S THE WOOD! SEE THE FLARES! COMBINED ATTACK IN THREE SECTIONS.. GO!
HERE WAS A CHANCE FOR BARRY TO TRY HIS OWN TACTICS FOR STOPPING THE CRUEL RUN OF CASUALTIES.

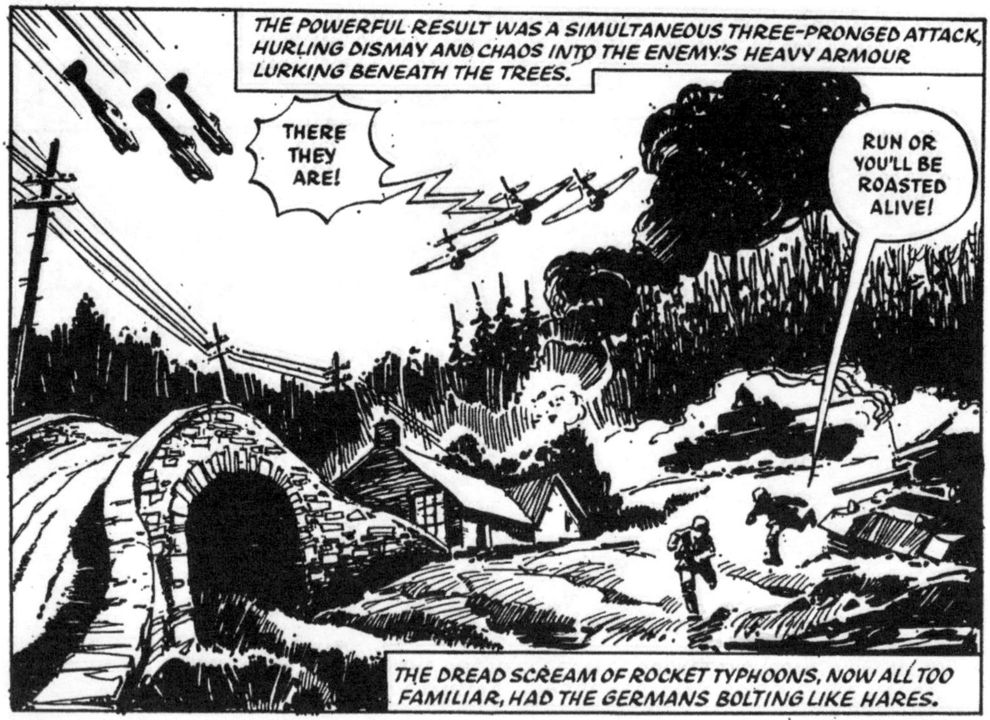
THE POWERFUL RESULT WAS A SIMULTANEOUS THREE-PRONGED ATTACK, HURLING DISMAY AND CHAOS INTO THE ENEMY'S HEAVY ARMOUR LURKING BENEATH THE TREES.
THERE THEY ARE!
RUN OR YOU'LL BE ROASTED ALIVE!
THE DREAD SCREAM OF ROCKET TYPHOONS, NOW ALL TOO FAMILIAR, HAD THE GERMANS BOLTING LIKE HARES.

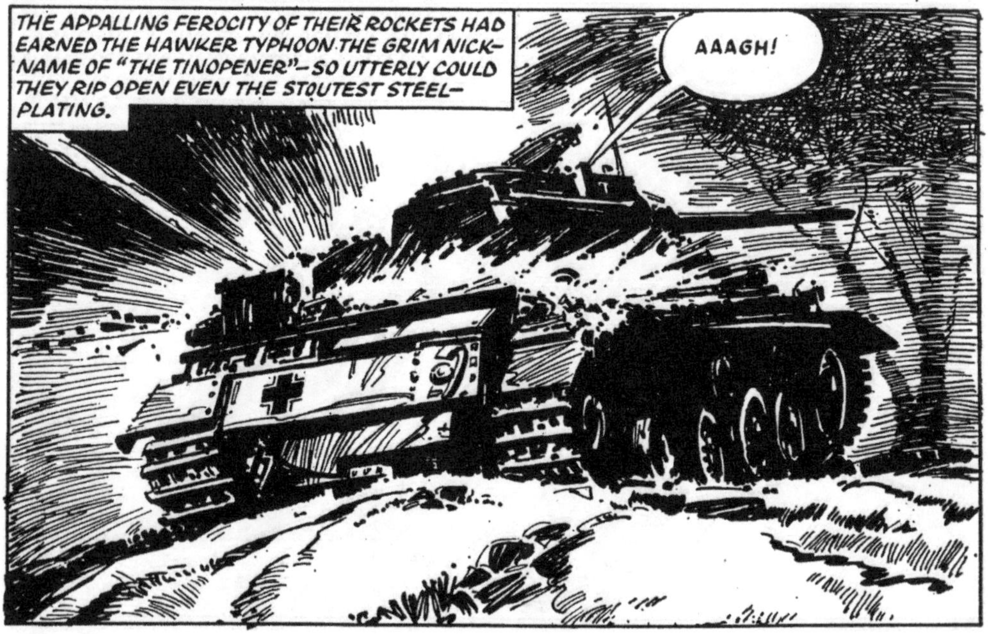
THE APPALLING FEROCITY OF THEIR ROCKETS HAD EARNED THE HAWKER TYPHOON THE GRIM NICK-NAME OF "THE TINOPENER"– SO UTTERLY COULD THEY RIP OPEN EVEN THE STOUTEST STEEL-PLATING.
AAAGH!

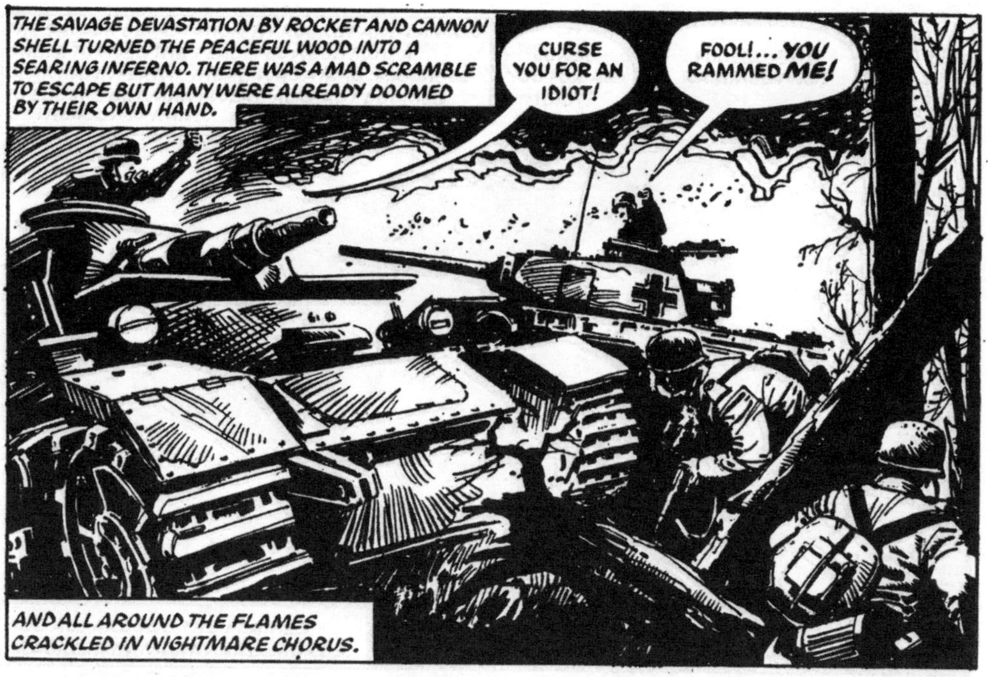
THE SAVAGE DEVASTATION BY ROCKET AND CANNON SHELL TURNED THE PEACEFUL WOOD INTO A SEARING INFERNO. THERE WAS A MAD SCRAMBLE TO ESCAPE BUT MANY WERE ALREADY DOOMED BY THEIR OWN HAND.
CURSE YOU FOR AN IDIOT!
FOOL!... YOU RAMMED ME!
AND ALL AROUND THE FLAMES CRACKLED IN NIGHTMARE CHORUS.

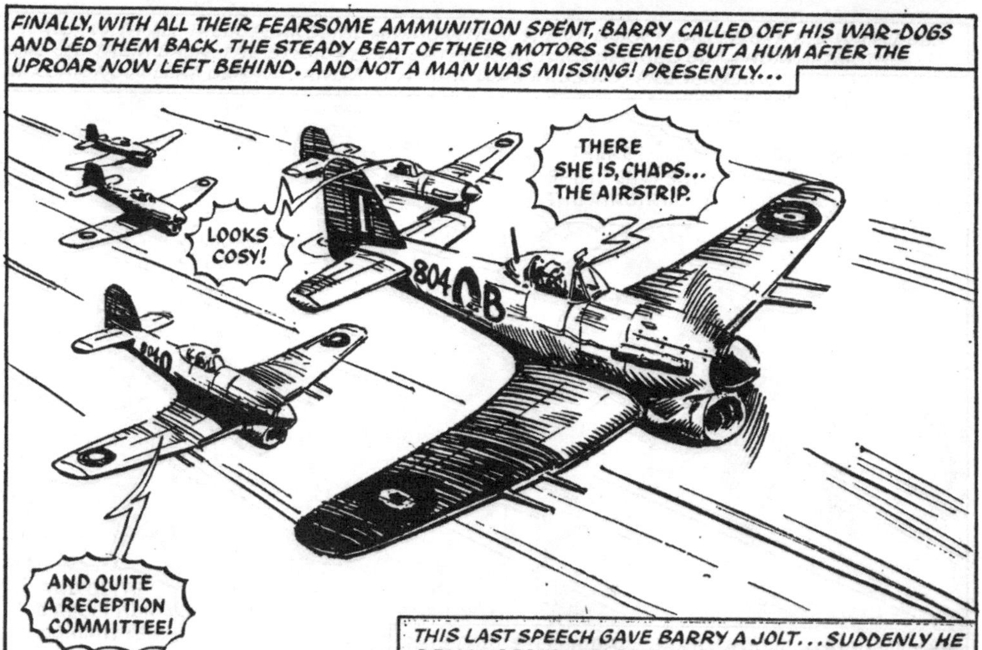
FINALLY, WITH ALL THEIR FEARSOME AMMUNITION SPENT, BARRY CALLED OFF HIS WAR-DOGS AND LED THEM BACK. THE STEADY BEAT OF THEIR MOTORS SEEMED BUT A HUM AFTER THE UPROAR NOW LEFT BEHIND. AND NOT A MAN WAS MISSING! PRESENTLY...
THERE SHE IS, CHAPS... THE AIRSTRIP.
LOOKS COSY!
AND QUITE A RECEPTION COMMITTEE!
THIS LAST SPEECH GAVE BARRY A JOLT... SUDDENLY HE REMEMBERED—HUGH MASON WOULD BE DOWN THERE!

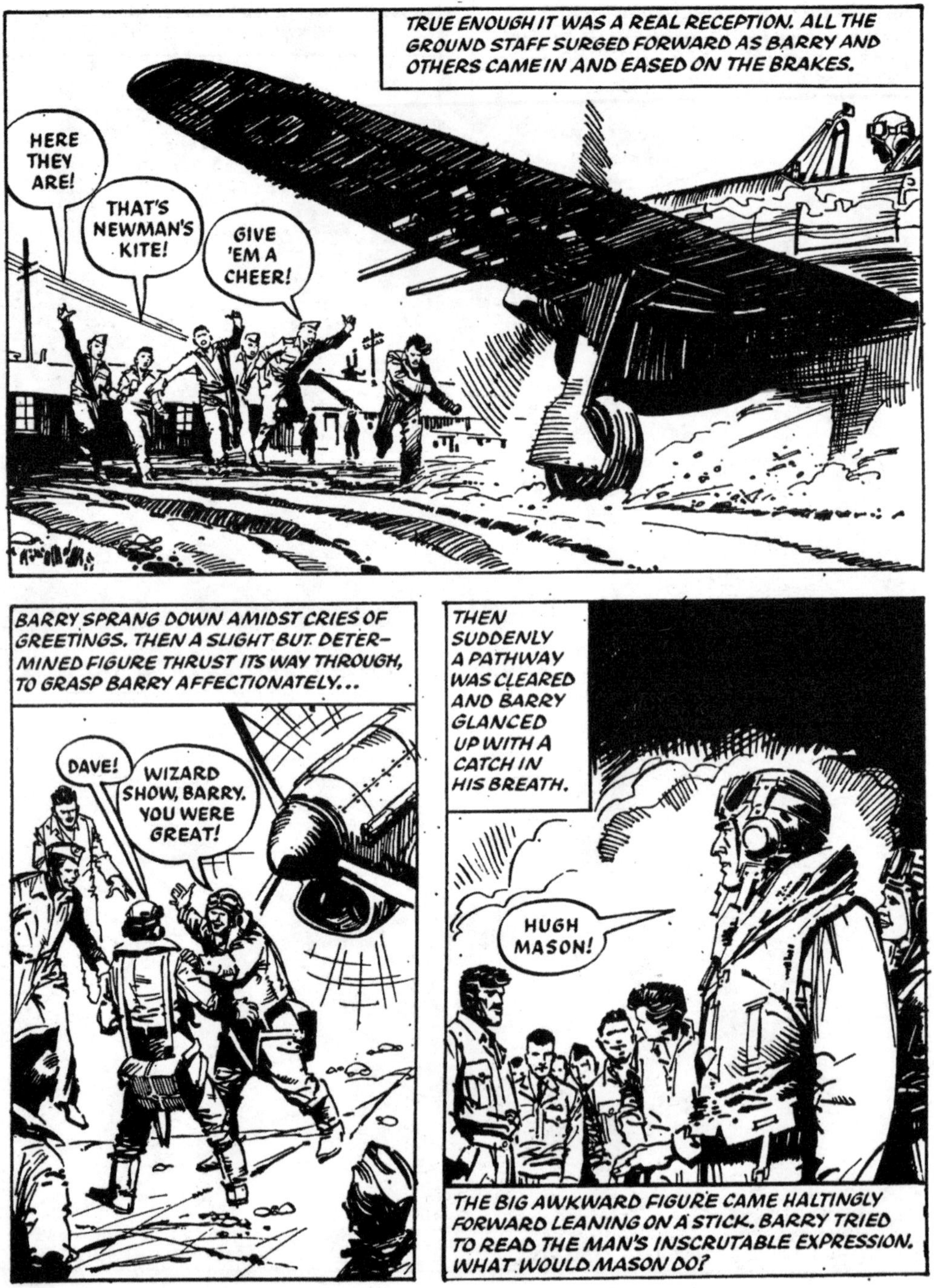
TRUE ENOUGH IT WAS A REAL RECEPTION. ALL THE GROUND STAFF SURGED FORWARD AS BARRY AND OTHERS CAME IN AND EASED ON THE BRAKES.
HERE THEY ARE!
THAT'S NEWMAN'S KITE!
GIVE 'EM A CHEER!
BARRY SPRANG DOWN AMIDST CRIES OF GREETINGS. THEN A SLIGHT BUT DETERMINED FIGURE THRUST ITS WAY THROUGH, TO GRASP BARRY AFFECTIONATELY...
DAVE!
WIZARD SHOW, BARRY. YOU WERE GREAT!
THEN SUDDENLY A PATHWAY WAS CLEARED AND BARRY GLANCED UP WITH A CATCH IN HIS BREATH.
HUGH MASON!
THE BIG AWKWARD FIGURE CAME HALTINGLY FORWARD LEANING ON A STICK. BARRY TRIED TO READ THE MAN'S INSCRUTABLE EXPRESSION. WHAT WOULD MASON DO?

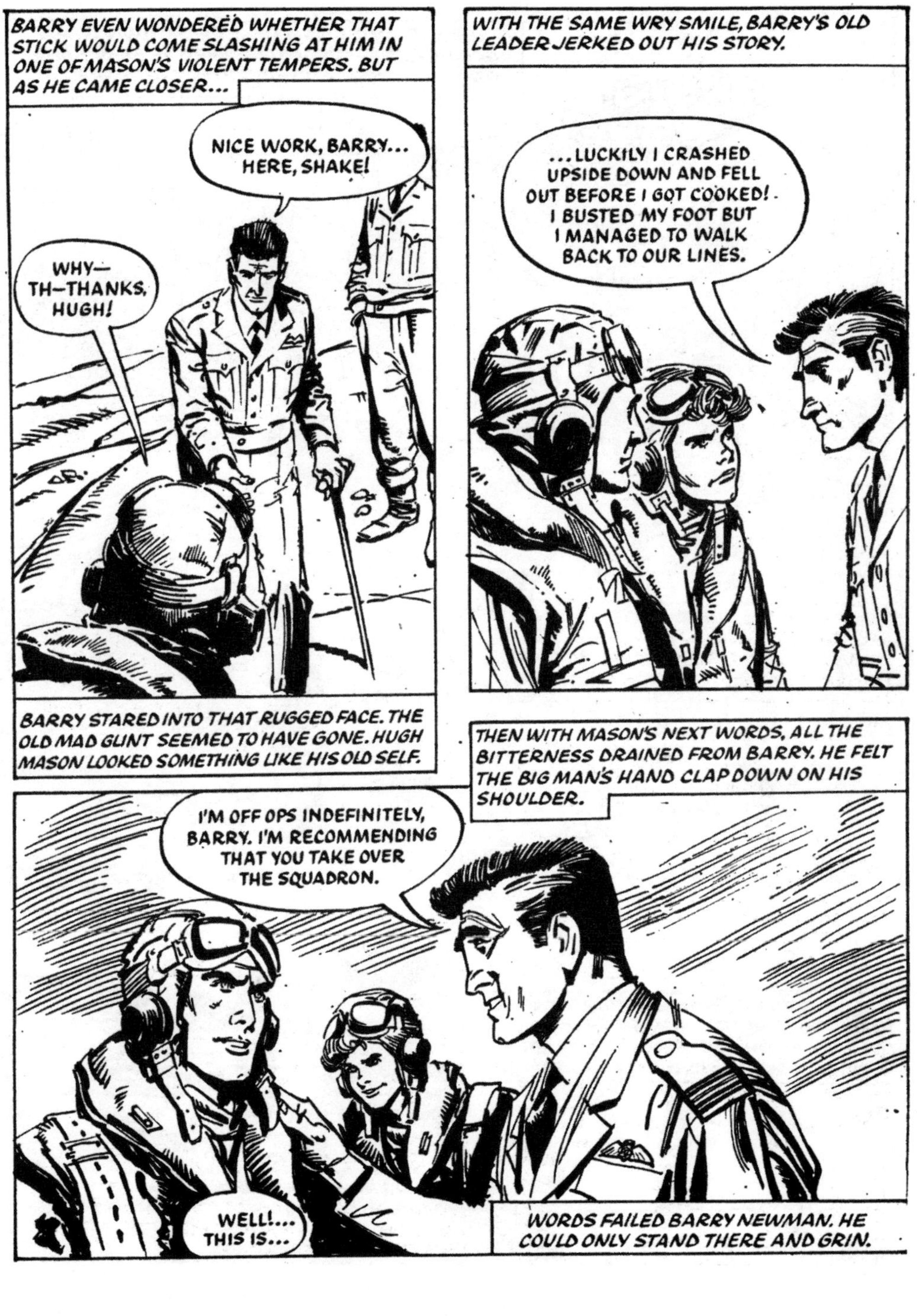
BARRY EVEN WONDERED WHETHER THAT STICK WOULD COME SLASHING AT HIM IN ONE OF MASON'S VIOLENT TEMPERS. BUT AS HE CAME CLOSER...
NICE WORK, BARRY... HERE, SHAKE!
WHY— TH—THANKS, HUGH!
BARRY STARED INTO THAT RUGGED FACE. THE OLD MAD GLINT SEEMED TO HAVE GONE. HUGH MASON LOOKED SOMETHING LIKE HIS OLD SELF.
WITH THE SAME WRY SMILE, BARRY'S OLD LEADER JERKED OUT HIS STORY.
...LUCKILY I CRASHED UPSIDE DOWN AND FELL OUT BEFORE I GOT COOKED! I BUSTED MY FOOT BUT I MANAGED TO WALK BACK TO OUR LINES.
THEN WITH MASON'S NEXT WORDS, ALL THE BITTERNESS DRAINED FROM BARRY. HE FELT THE BIG MAN'S HAND CLAP DOWN ON HIS SHOULDER.
I'M OFF OPS INDEFINITELY, BARRY. I'M RECOMMENDING THAT YOU TAKE OVER THE SQUADRON.
WELL!... THIS IS...
WORDS FAILED BARRY NEWMAN. HE COULD ONLY STAND THERE AND GRIN.

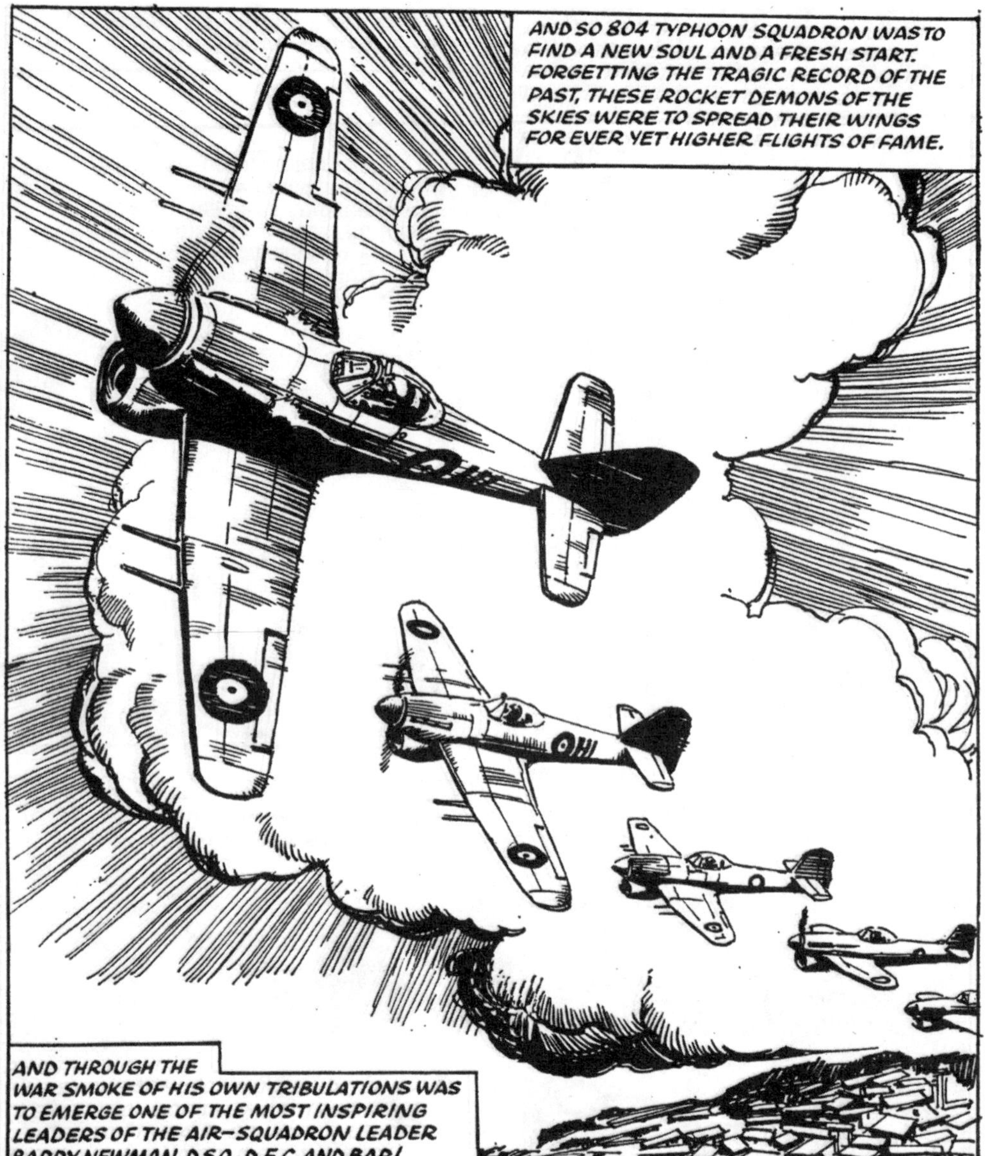
AND SO 804 TYPHOON SQUADRON WAS TO FIND A NEW SOUL AND A FRESH START. FORGETTING THE TRAGIC RECORD OF THE PAST, THESE ROCKET DEMONS OF THE SKIES WERE TO SPREAD THEIR WINGS FOR EVER YET HIGHER FLIGHTS OF FAME.
AND THROUGH THE WAR SMOKE OF HIS OWN TRIBULATIONS WAS TO EMERGE ONE OF THE MOST INSPIRING LEADERS OF THE AIR–SQUADRON LEADER BARRY NEWMAN, D.S.O., D.F.C. AND BAR!

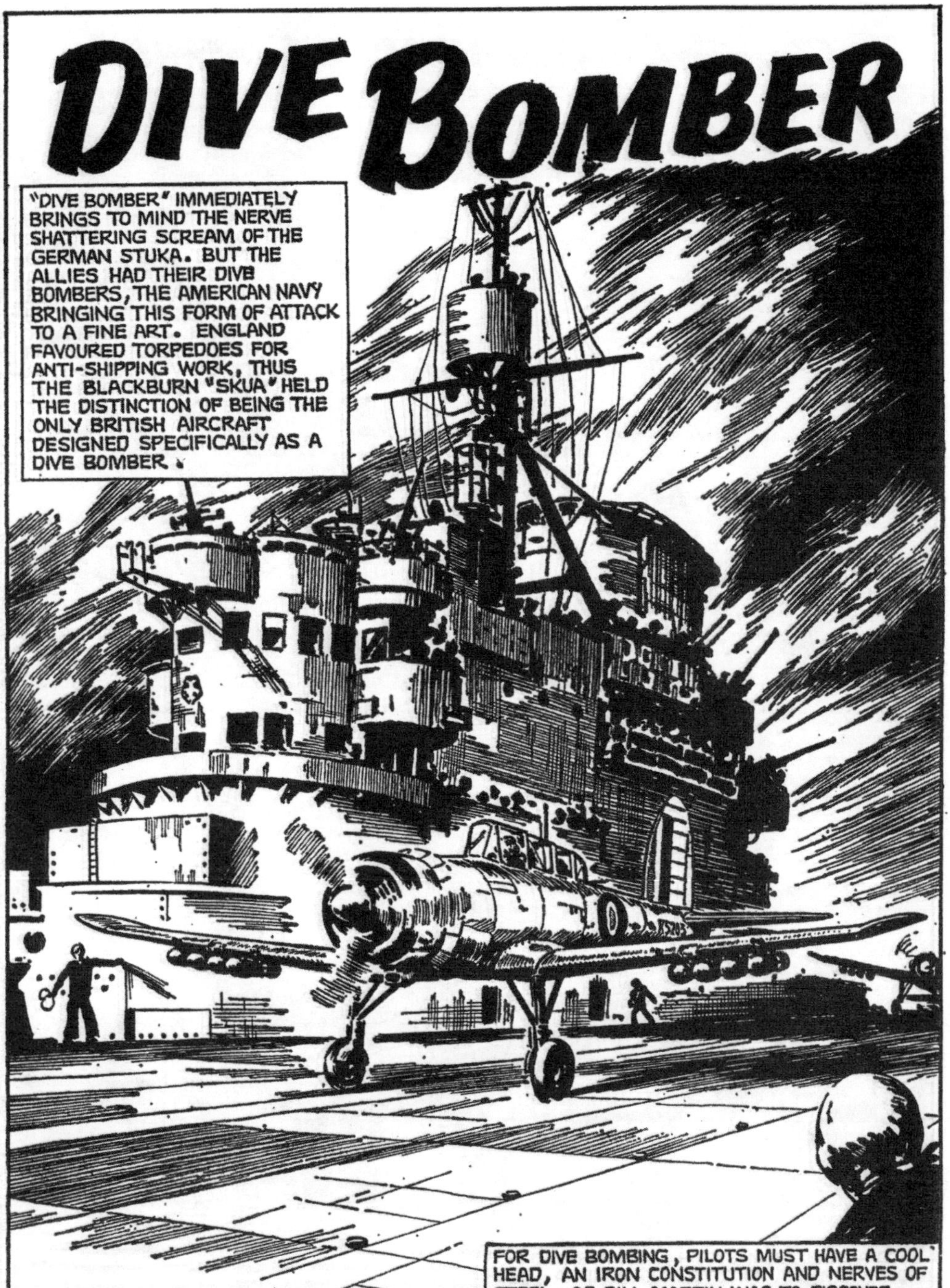
DIVE BOMBER
"DIVE BOMBER" IMMEDIATELY BRINGS TO MIND THE NERVE SHATTERING SCREAM OF THE GERMAN STUKA. BUT THE ALLIES HAD THEIR DIVE BOMBERS, THE AMERICAN NAVY BRINGING THIS FORM OF ATTACK TO A FINE ART. ENGLAND FAVOURED TORPEDOES FOR ANTI-SHIPPING WORK, THUS THE BLACKBURN "SKUA" HELD THE DISTINCTION OF BEING THE ONLY BRITISH AIRCRAFT DESIGNED SPECIFICALLY AS A DIVE BOMBER.
FOR DIVE BOMBING, PILOTS MUST HAVE A COOL HEAD, AN IRON CONSTITUTION AND NERVES OF STEEL, AS BILL MARTIN WAS TO DISCOVER ...

Chapter 1. HOT-HEADED COURAGE

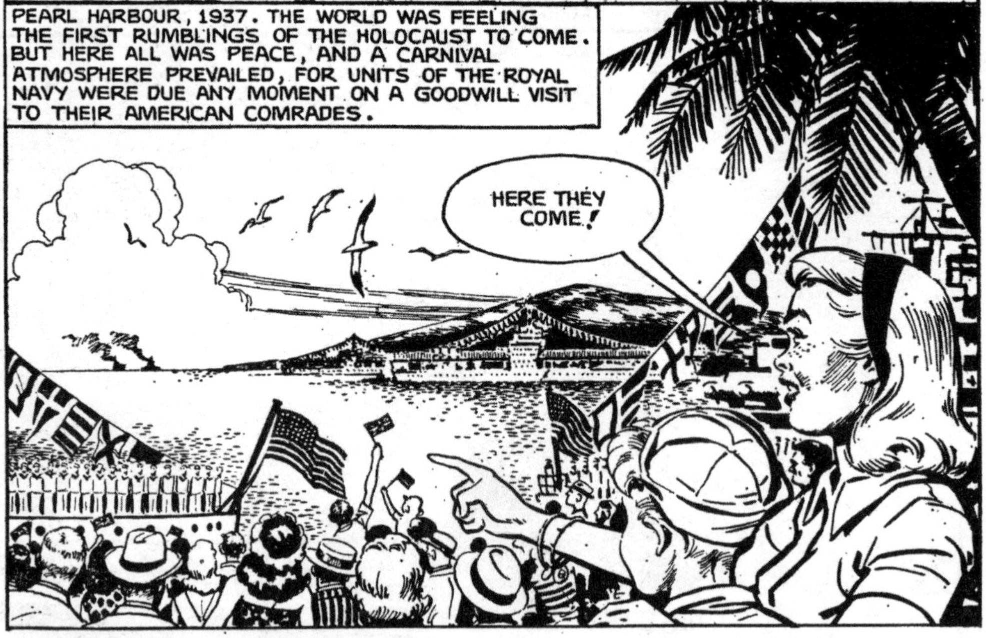
PEARL HARBOUR, 1937. THE WORLD WAS FEELING THE FIRST RUMBLINGS OF THE HOLOCAUST TO COME. BUT HERE ALL WAS PEACE, AND A CARNIVAL ATMOSPHERE PREVAILED, FOR UNITS OF THE ROYAL NAVY WERE DUE ANY MOMENT ON A GOODWILL VISIT TO THEIR AMERICAN COMRADES.
HERE THEY COME!

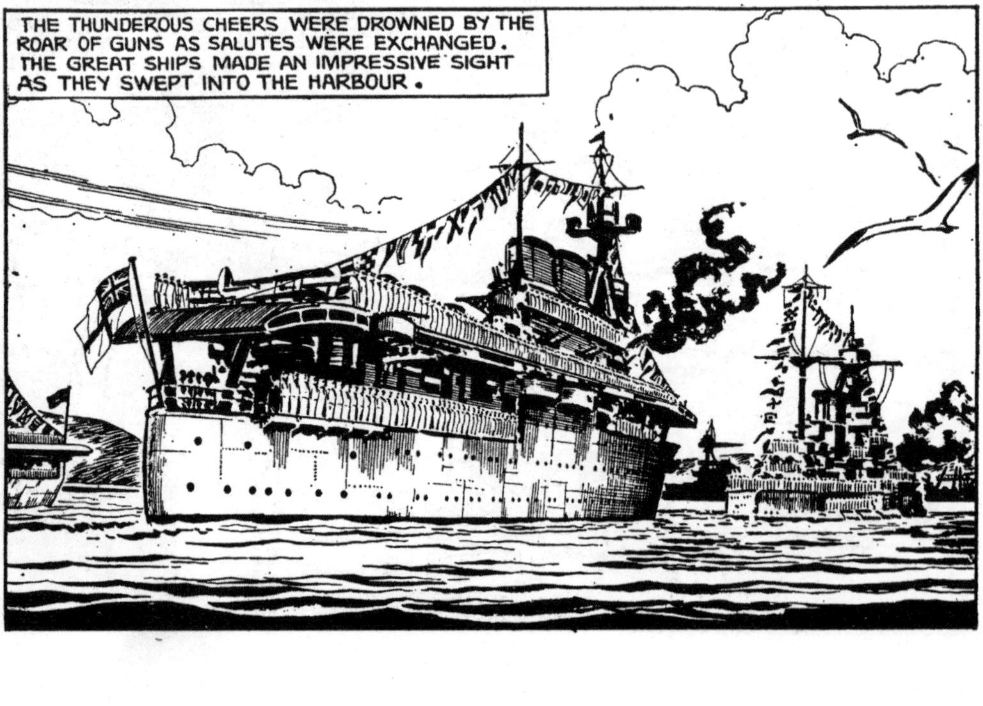
THE THUNDEROUS CHEERS WERE DROWNED BY THE ROAR OF GUNS AS SALUTES WERE EXCHANGED. THE GREAT SHIPS MADE AN IMPRESSIVE SIGHT AS THEY SWEPT INTO THE HARBOUR.

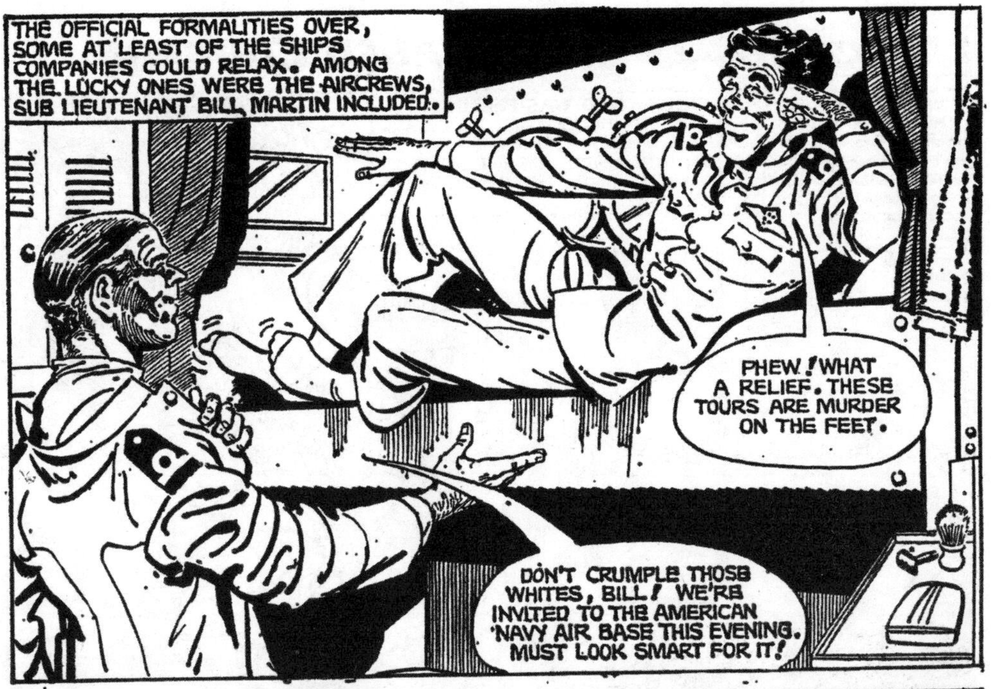
THE OFFICIAL FORMALITIES OVER, SOME AT LEAST OF THE SHIPS COMPANIES COULD RELAX. AMONG THE LUCKY ONES WERE THE AIRCREWS, SUB LIEUTENANT BILL MARTIN INCLUDED.
PHEW! WHAT A RELIEF. THESE TOURS ARE MURDER ON THE FEET.
DON'T CRUMPLE THOSE WHITES, BILL! WE'RE INVITED TO THE AMERICAN NAVY AIR BASE THIS EVENING. MUST LOOK SMART FOR IT!

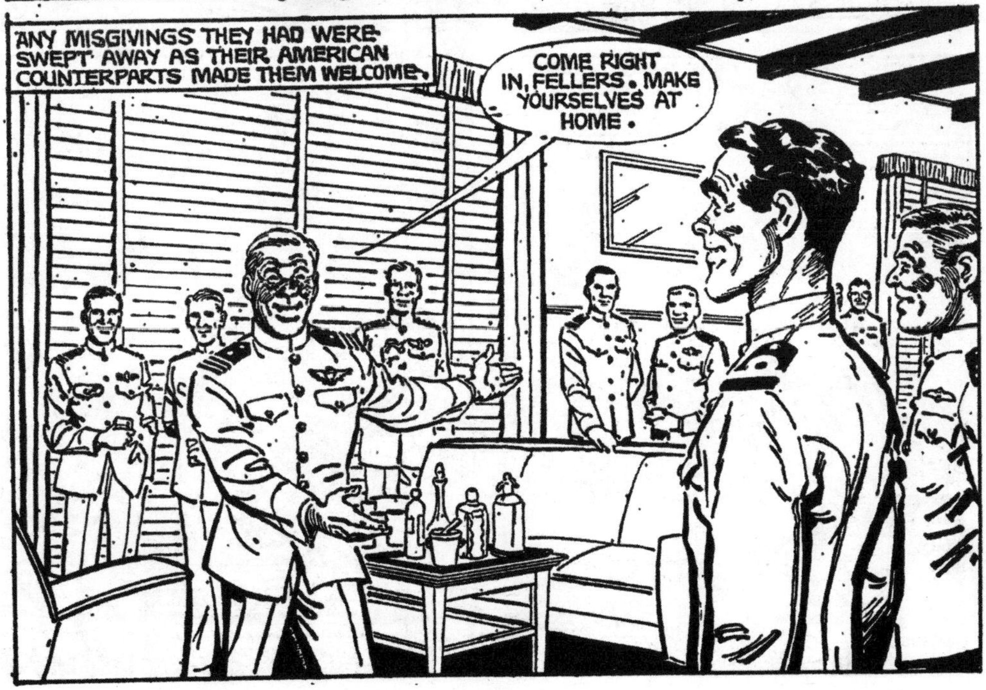
ANY MISGIVINGS THEY HAD WERE SWEPT AWAY AS THEIR AMERICAN COUNTERPARTS MADE THEM WELCOME.
COME RIGHT IN, FELLERS. MAKE YOURSELVES AT HOME.

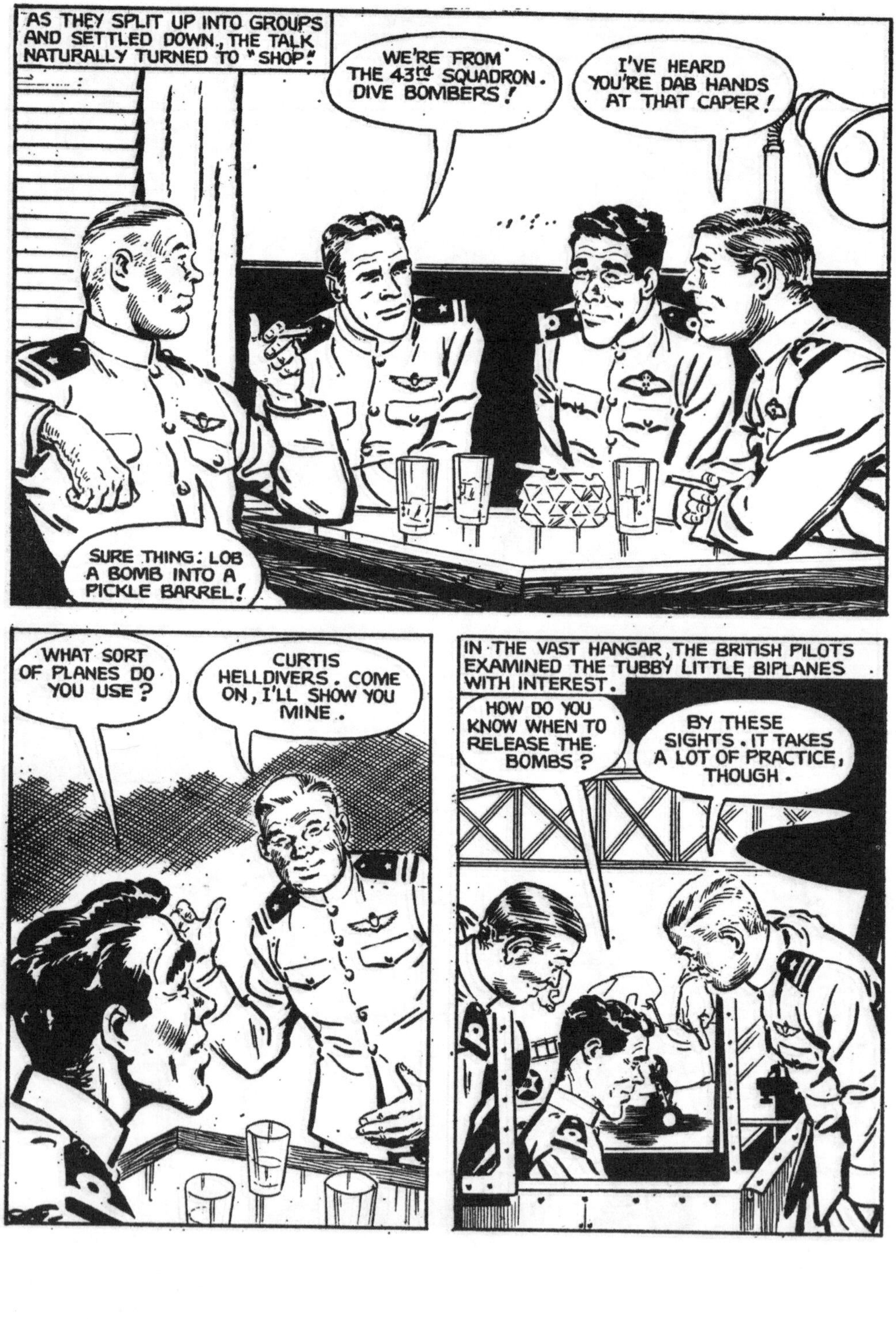
AS THEY SPLIT UP INTO GROUPS AND SETTLED DOWN, THE TALK NATURALLY TURNED TO "SHOP!"
WE'RE FROM THE 43rd SQUADRON. DIVE BOMBERS!
I'VE HEARD YOU'RE DAB HANDS AT THAT CAPER!
SURE THING: LOB A BOMB INTO A PICKLE BARREL!
WHAT SORT OF PLANES DO YOU USE?
CURTIS HELLDIVERS. COME ON, I'LL SHOW YOU MINE.
IN THE VAST HANGAR, THE BRITISH PILOTS EXAMINED THE TUBBY LITTLE BIPLANES WITH INTEREST.
HOW DO YOU KNOW WHEN TO RELEASE THE BOMBS?
BY THESE SIGHTS. IT TAKES A LOT OF PRACTICE, THOUGH.

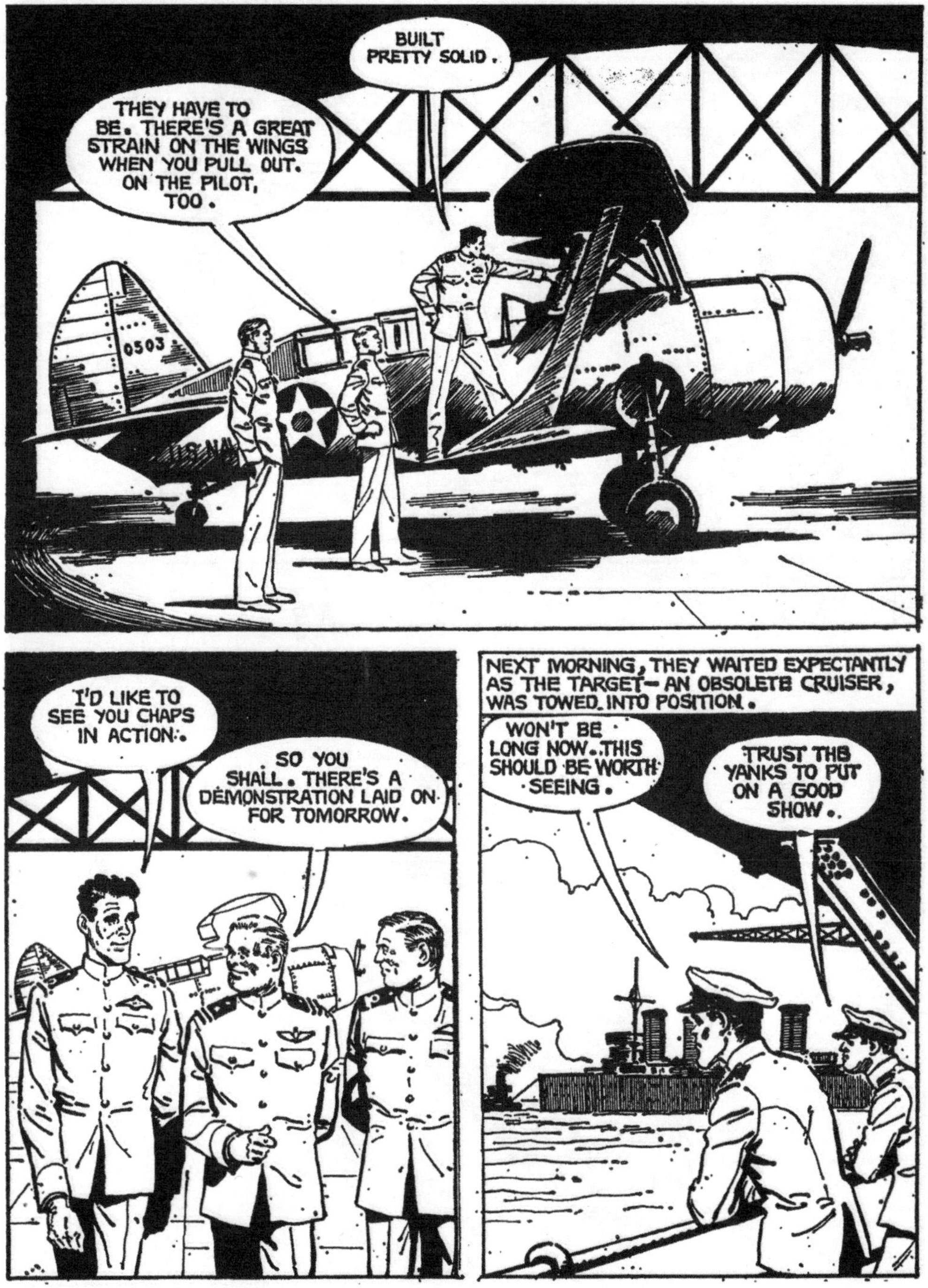
BUILT PRETTY SOLID.
THEY HAVE TO BE. THERE'S A GREAT STRAIN ON THE WINGS WHEN YOU PULL OUT. ON THE PILOT, TOO.
0503
I'D LIKE TO SEE YOU CHAPS IN ACTION.
SO YOU SHALL. THERE'S A DEMONSTRATION LAID ON FOR TOMORROW.
NEXT MORNING, THEY WAITED EXPECTANTLY AS THE TARGET— AN OBSOLETE CRUISER, WAS TOWED INTO POSITION.
WON'T BE LONG NOW. THIS SHOULD BE WORTH SEEING.
TRUST THE YANKS TO PUT ON A GOOD SHOW.

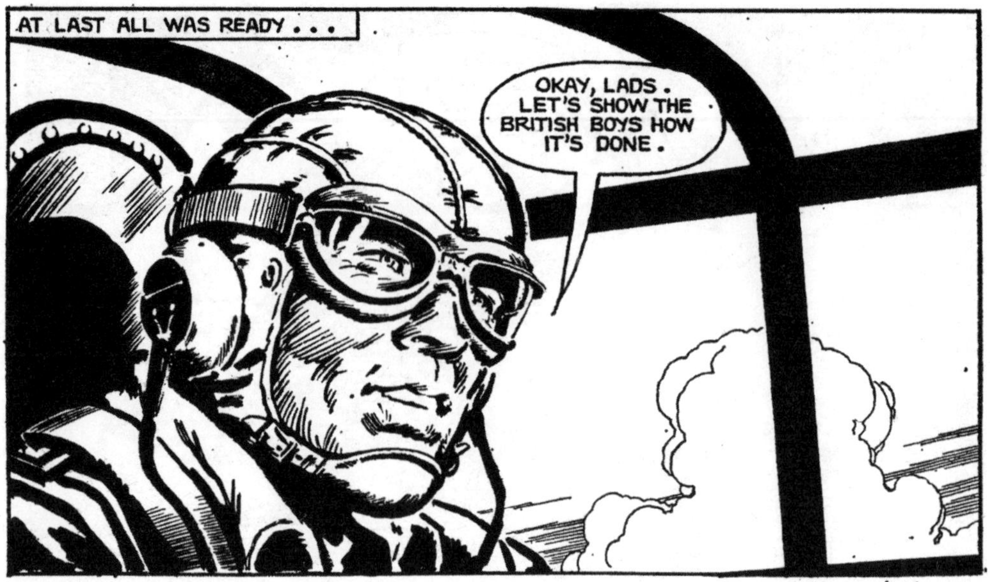
AT LAST ALL WAS READY . . .
OKAY, LADS. LET'S SHOW THE BRITISH BOYS HOW IT'S DONE.

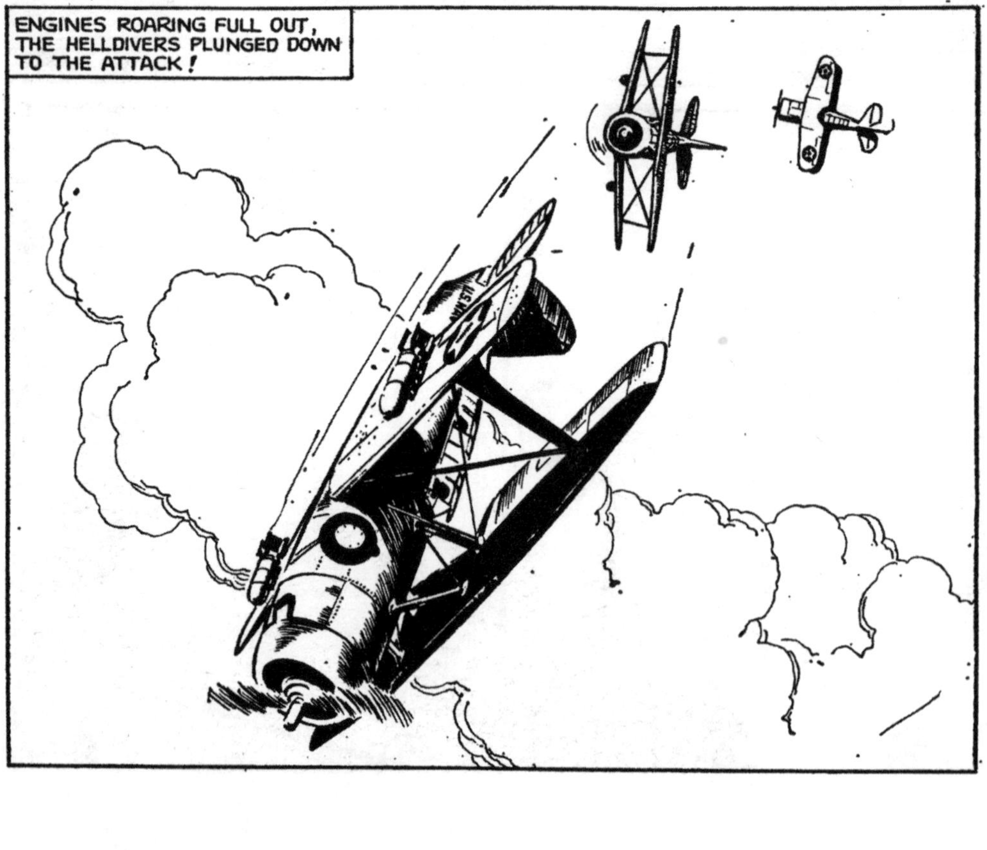
ENGINES ROARING FULL OUT, THE HELLDIVERS PLUNGED DOWN TO THE ATTACK!

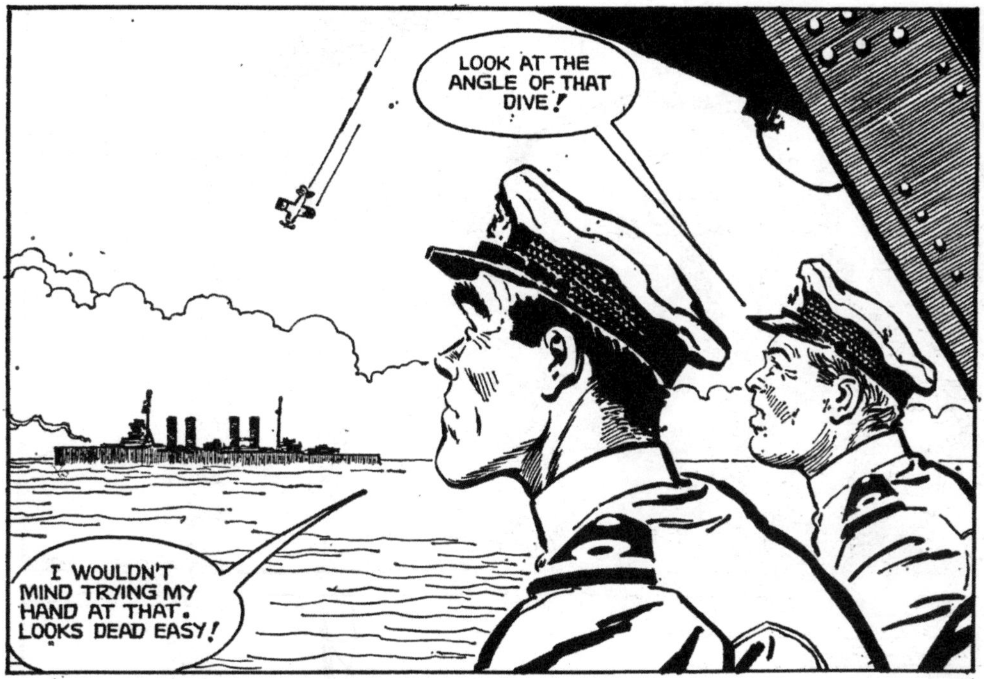
LOOK AT THE ANGLE OF THAT DIVE!
I WOULDN'T MIND TRYING MY HAND AT THAT. LOOKS DEAD EASY!

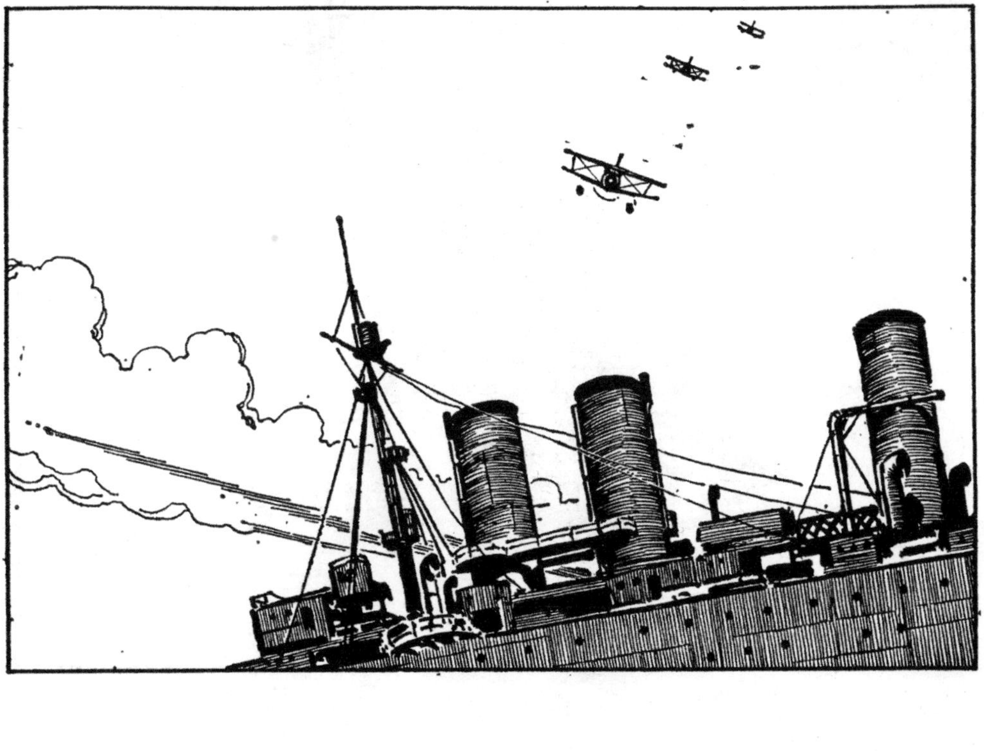

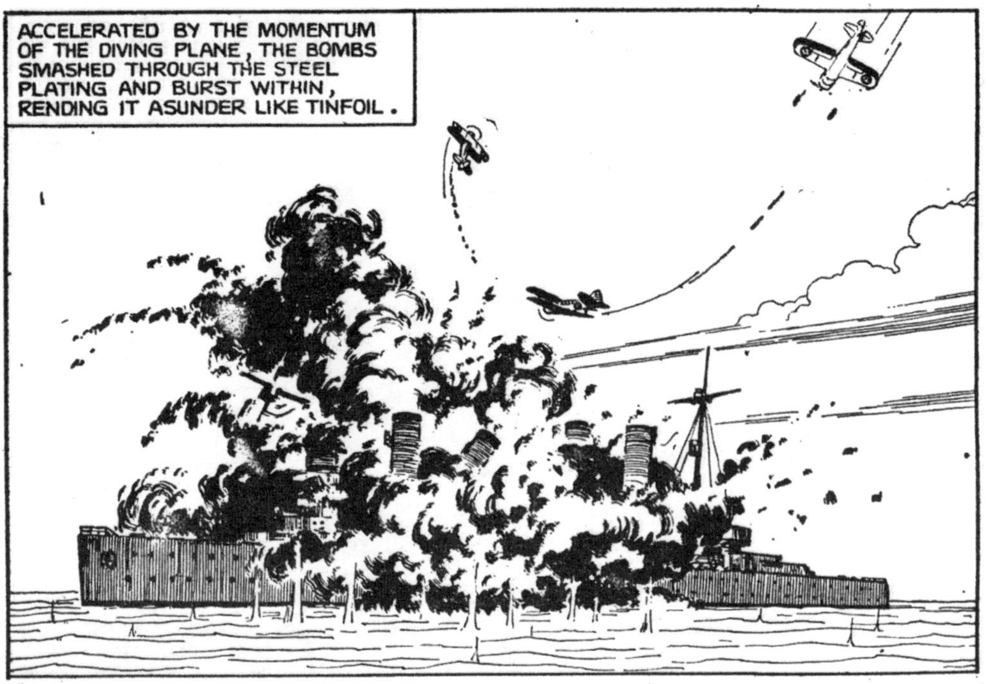
ACCELERATED BY THE MOMENTUM OF THE DIVING PLANE, THE BOMBS SMASHED THROUGH THE STEEL PLATING AND BURST WITHIN, RENDING IT ASUNDER LIKE TINFOIL.

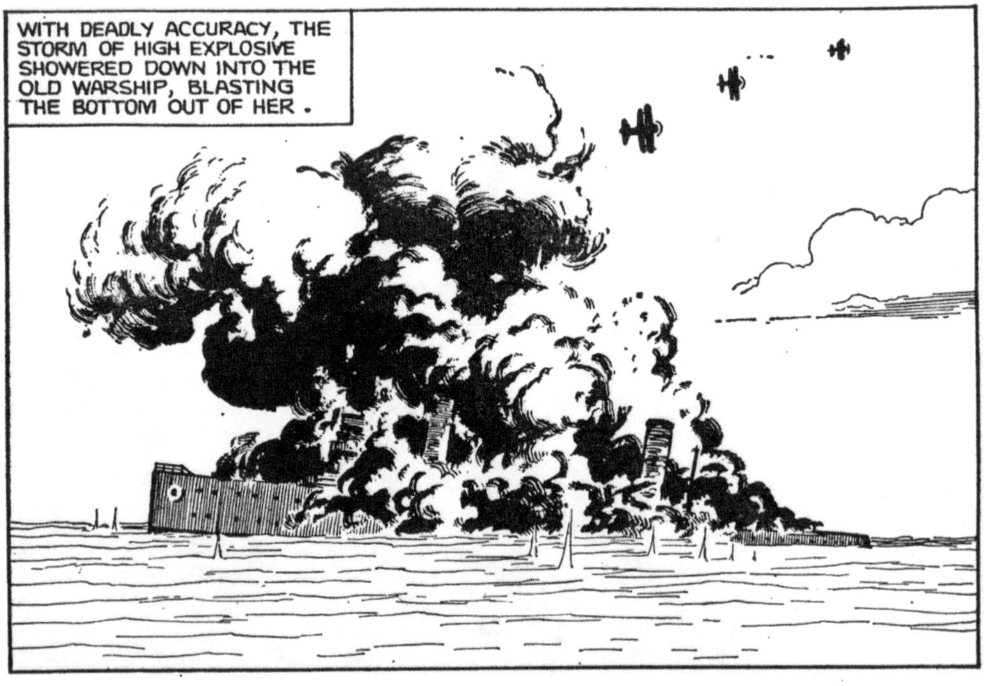
WITH DEADLY ACCURACY, THE STORM OF HIGH EXPLOSIVE SHOWERED DOWN INTO THE OLD WARSHIP, BLASTING THE BOTTOM OUT OF HER.

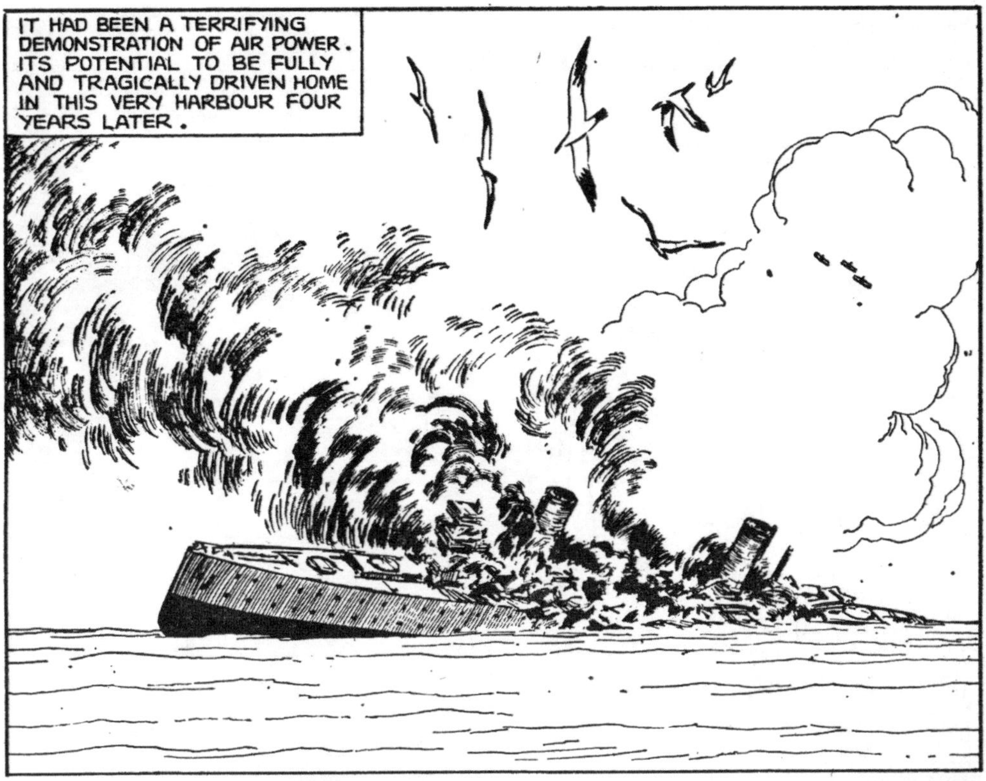
IT HAD BEEN A TERRIFYING DEMONSTRATION OF AIR POWER. ITS POTENTIAL TO BE FULLY AND TRAGICALLY DRIVEN HOME IN THIS VERY HARBOUR FOUR YEARS LATER.

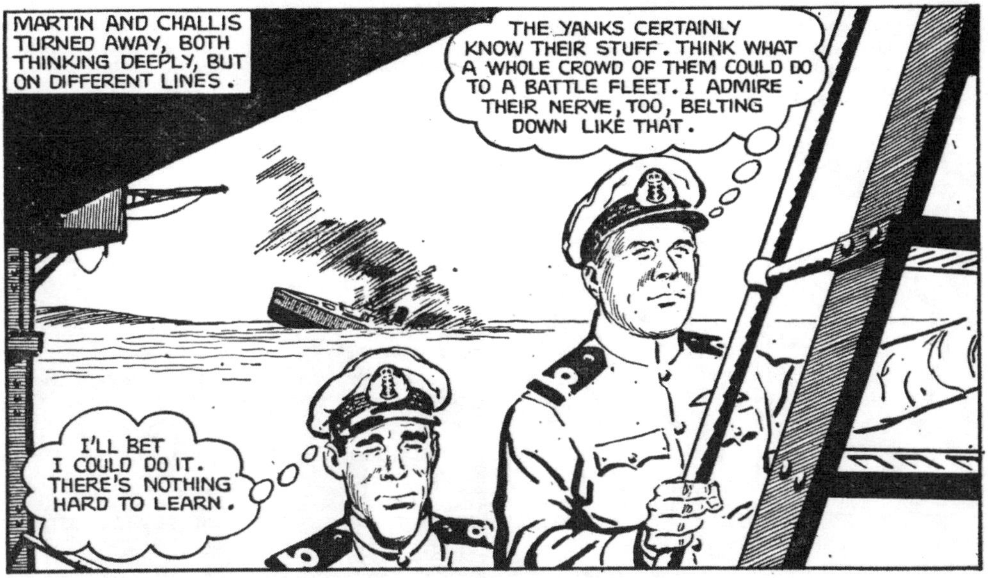
MARTIN AND CHALLIS TURNED AWAY, BOTH THINKING DEEPLY, BUT ON DIFFERENT LINES.
THE YANKS CERTAINLY KNOW THEIR STUFF. THINK WHAT A WHOLE CROWD OF THEM COULD DO TO A BATTLE FLEET. I ADMIRE THEIR NERVE, TOO, BELTING DOWN LIKE THAT.
I'LL BET I COULD DO IT. THERE'S NOTHING HARD TO LEARN.

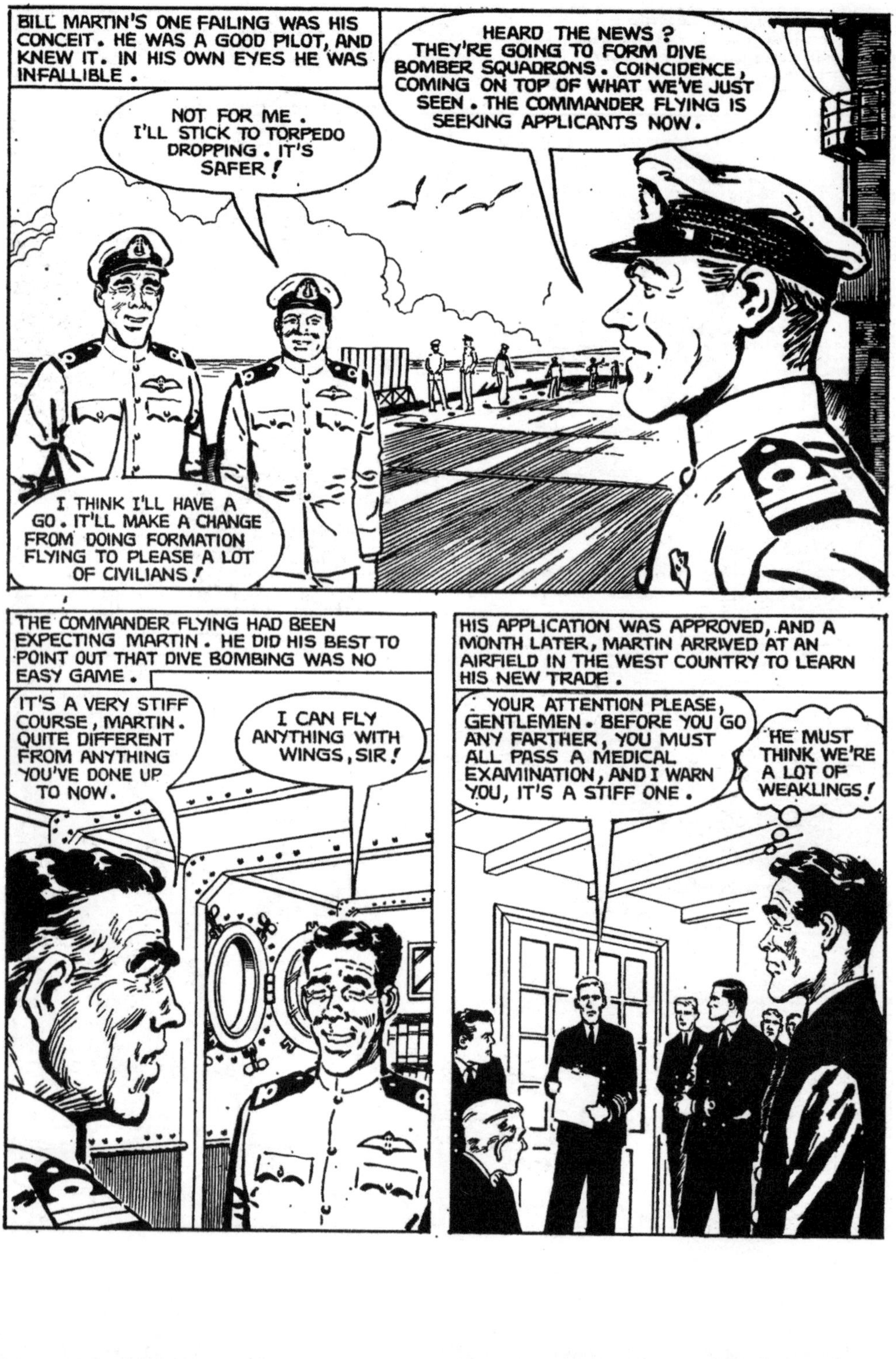
BILL MARTIN'S ONE FAILING WAS HIS CONCEIT. HE WAS A GOOD PILOT, AND KNEW IT. IN HIS OWN EYES HE WAS INFALLIBLE.
HEARD THE NEWS? THEY'RE GOING TO FORM DIVE BOMBER SQUADRONS. COINCIDENCE, COMING ON TOP OF WHAT WE'VE JUST SEEN. THE COMMANDER FLYING IS SEEKING APPLICANTS NOW.
NOT FOR ME. I'LL STICK TO TORPEDO DROPPING. IT'S SAFER!
I THINK I'LL HAVE A GO. IT'LL MAKE A CHANGE FROM DOING FORMATION FLYING TO PLEASE A LOT OF CIVILIANS!
THE COMMANDER FLYING HAD BEEN EXPECTING MARTIN. HE DID HIS BEST TO POINT OUT THAT DIVE BOMBING WAS NO EASY GAME.
IT'S A VERY STIFF COURSE, MARTIN. QUITE DIFFERENT FROM ANYTHING YOU'VE DONE UP TO NOW.
I CAN FLY ANYTHING WITH WINGS, SIR!
HIS APPLICATION WAS APPROVED, AND A MONTH LATER, MARTIN ARRIVED AT AN AIRFIELD IN THE WEST COUNTRY TO LEARN HIS NEW TRADE.
YOUR ATTENTION PLEASE, GENTLEMEN. BEFORE YOU GO ANY FARTHER, YOU MUST ALL PASS A MEDICAL EXAMINATION, AND I WARN YOU, IT'S A STIFF ONE.
HE MUST THINK WE'RE A LOT OF WEAKLINGS!

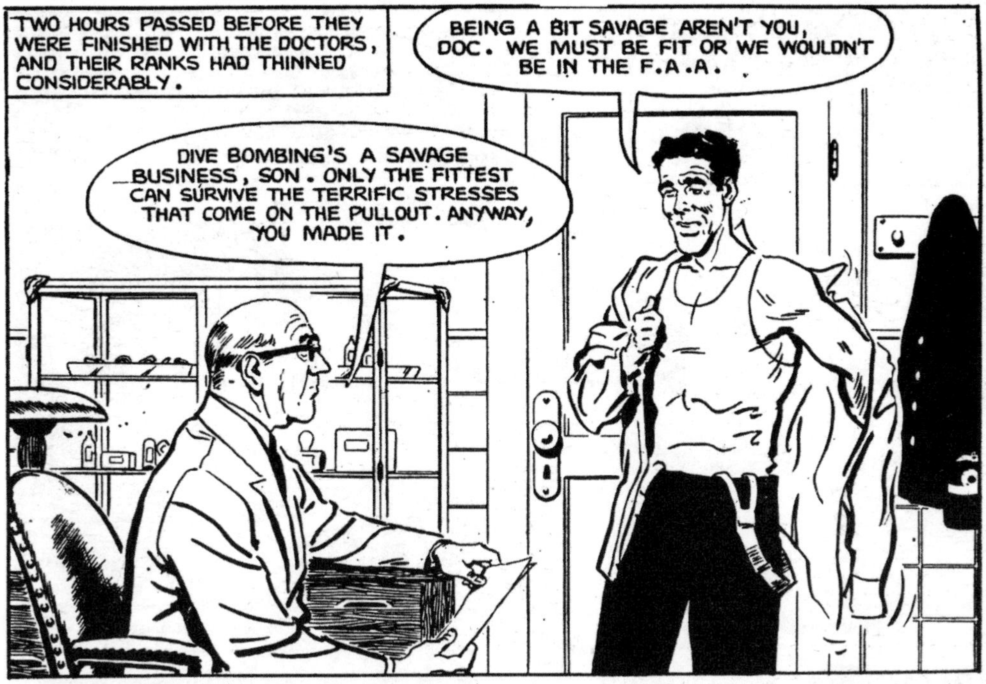
TWO HOURS PASSED BEFORE THEY WERE FINISHED WITH THE DOCTORS, AND THEIR RANKS HAD THINNED CONSIDERABLY.
BEING A BIT SAVAGE AREN'T YOU, DOC. WE MUST BE FIT OR WE WOULDN'T BE IN THE F.A.A.
DIVE BOMBING'S A SAVAGE BUSINESS, SON. ONLY THE FITTEST CAN SURVIVE THE TERRIFIC STRESSES THAT COME ON THE PULLOUT. ANYWAY, YOU MADE IT.

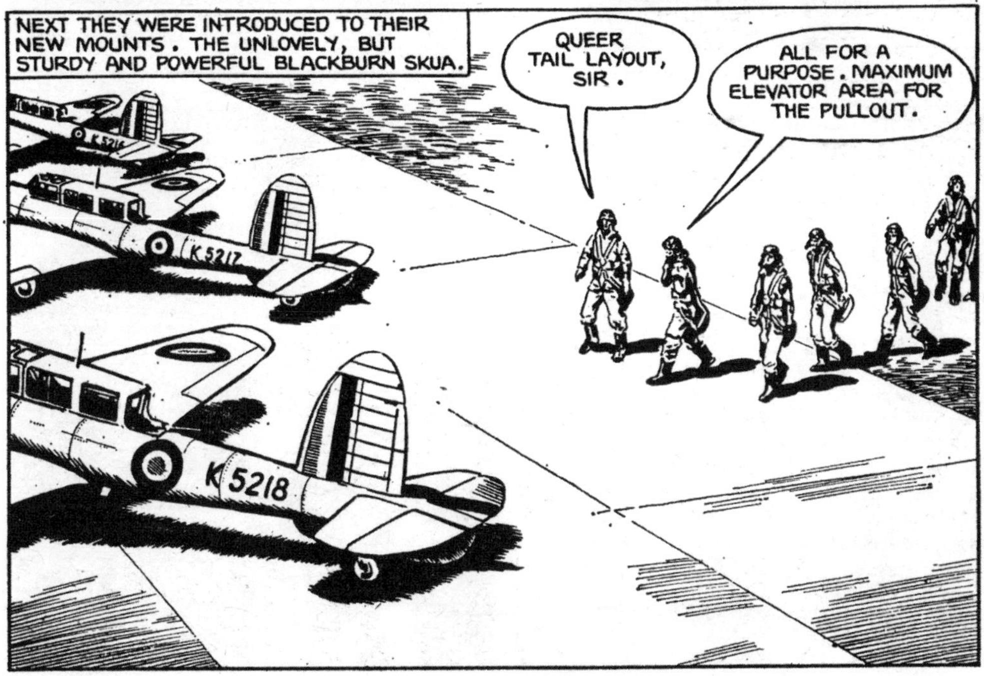
NEXT THEY WERE INTRODUCED TO THEIR NEW MOUNTS. THE UNLOVELY, BUT STURDY AND POWERFUL BLACKBURN SKUA.
QUEER TAIL LAYOUT, SIR.
ALL FOR A PURPOSE. MAXIMUM ELEVATOR AREA FOR THE PULLOUT.
K 5217
K 5218

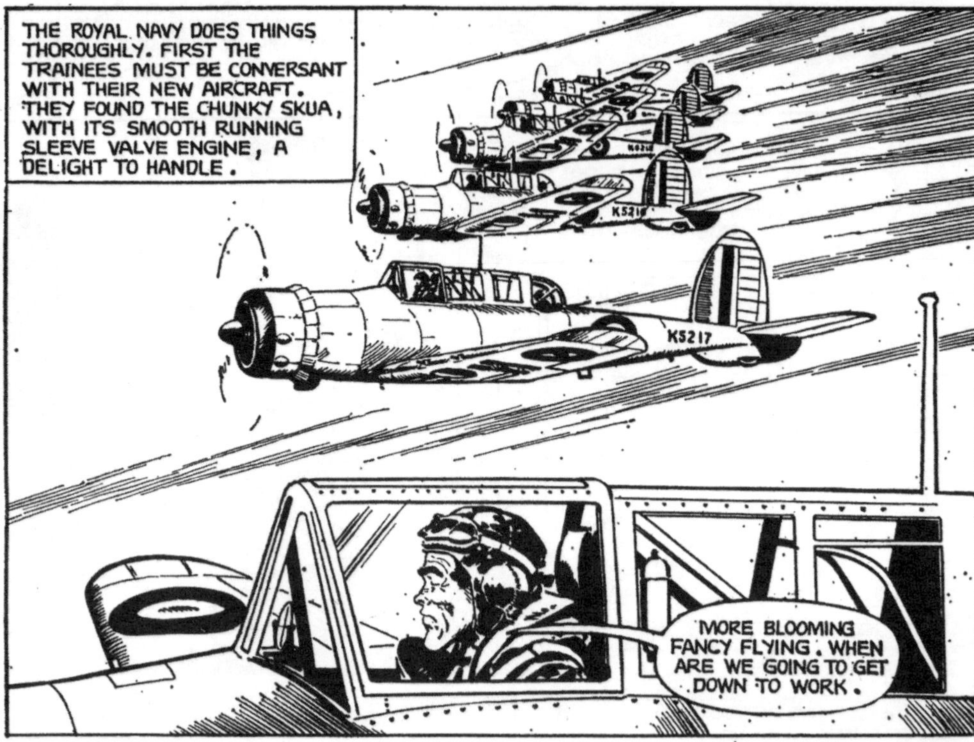
THE ROYAL NAVY DOES THINGS THOROUGHLY. FIRST THE TRAINEES MUST BE CONVERSANT WITH THEIR NEW AIRCRAFT. THEY FOUND THE CHUNKY SKUA, WITH ITS SMOOTH RUNNING SLEEVE VALVE ENGINE, A DELIGHT TO HANDLE.
K5217
MORE BLOOMING FANCY FLYING. WHEN ARE WE GOING TO GET DOWN TO WORK.

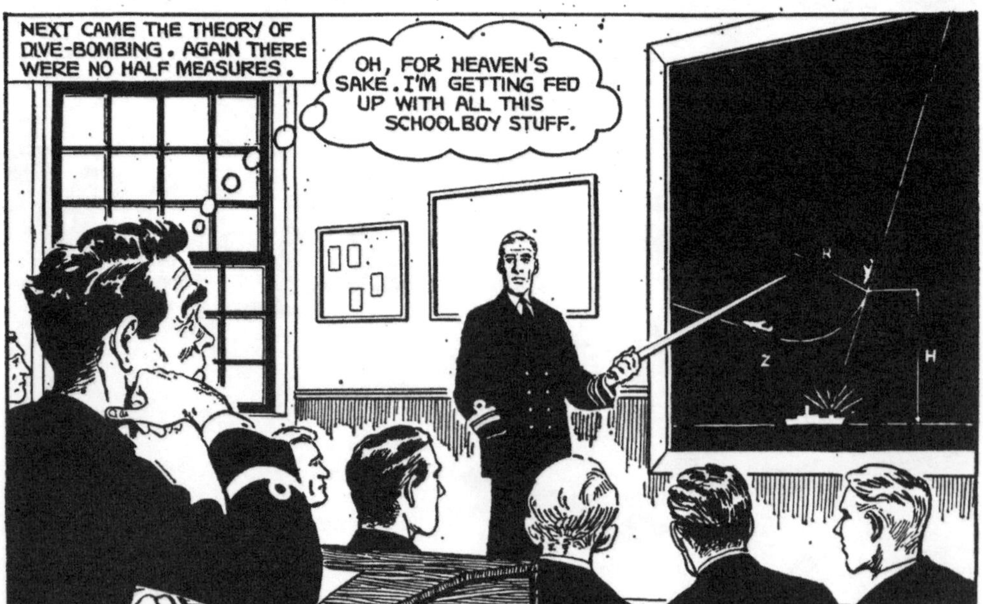
NEXT CAME THE THEORY OF DIVE-BOMBING. AGAIN THERE WERE NO HALF MEASURES.
OH, FOR HEAVEN'S SAKE. I'M GETTING FED UP WITH ALL THIS SCHOOLBOY STUFF.

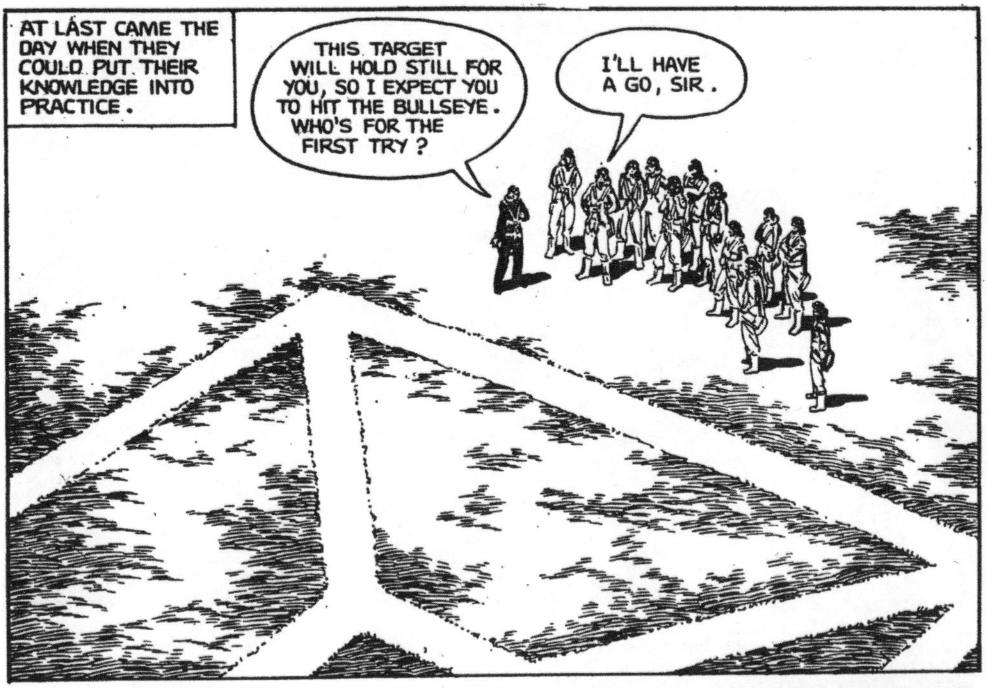
AT LAST CAME THE DAY WHEN THEY COULD PUT THEIR KNOWLEDGE INTO PRACTICE.
THIS TARGET WILL HOLD STILL FOR YOU, SO I EXPECT YOU TO HIT THE BULLSEYE. WHO'S FOR THE FIRST TRY?
I'LL HAVE A GO, SIR.

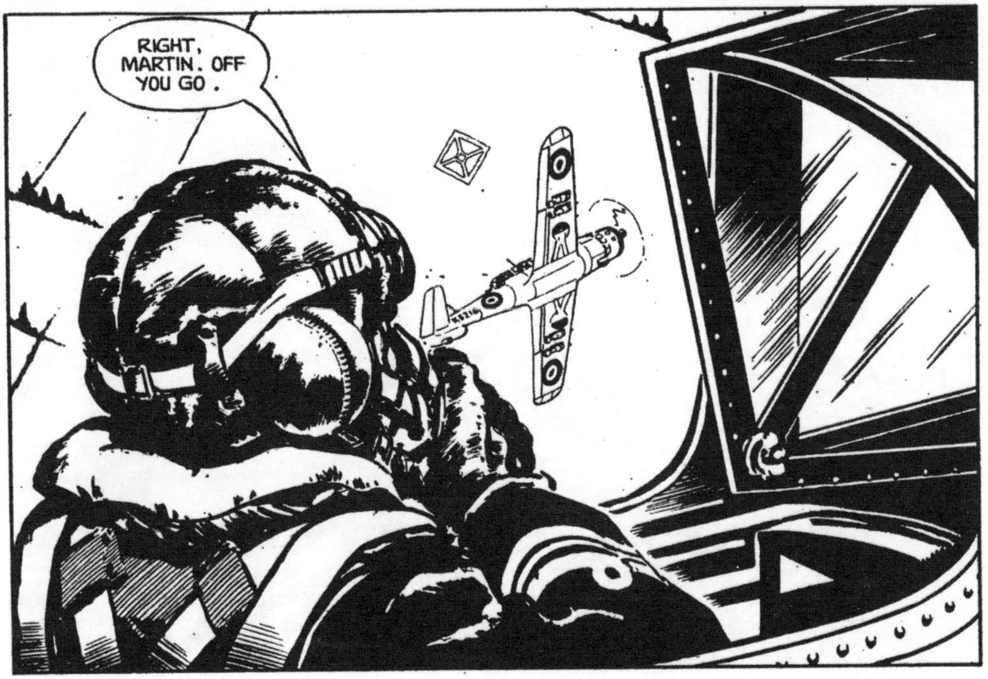
RIGHT, MARTIN. OFF YOU GO.

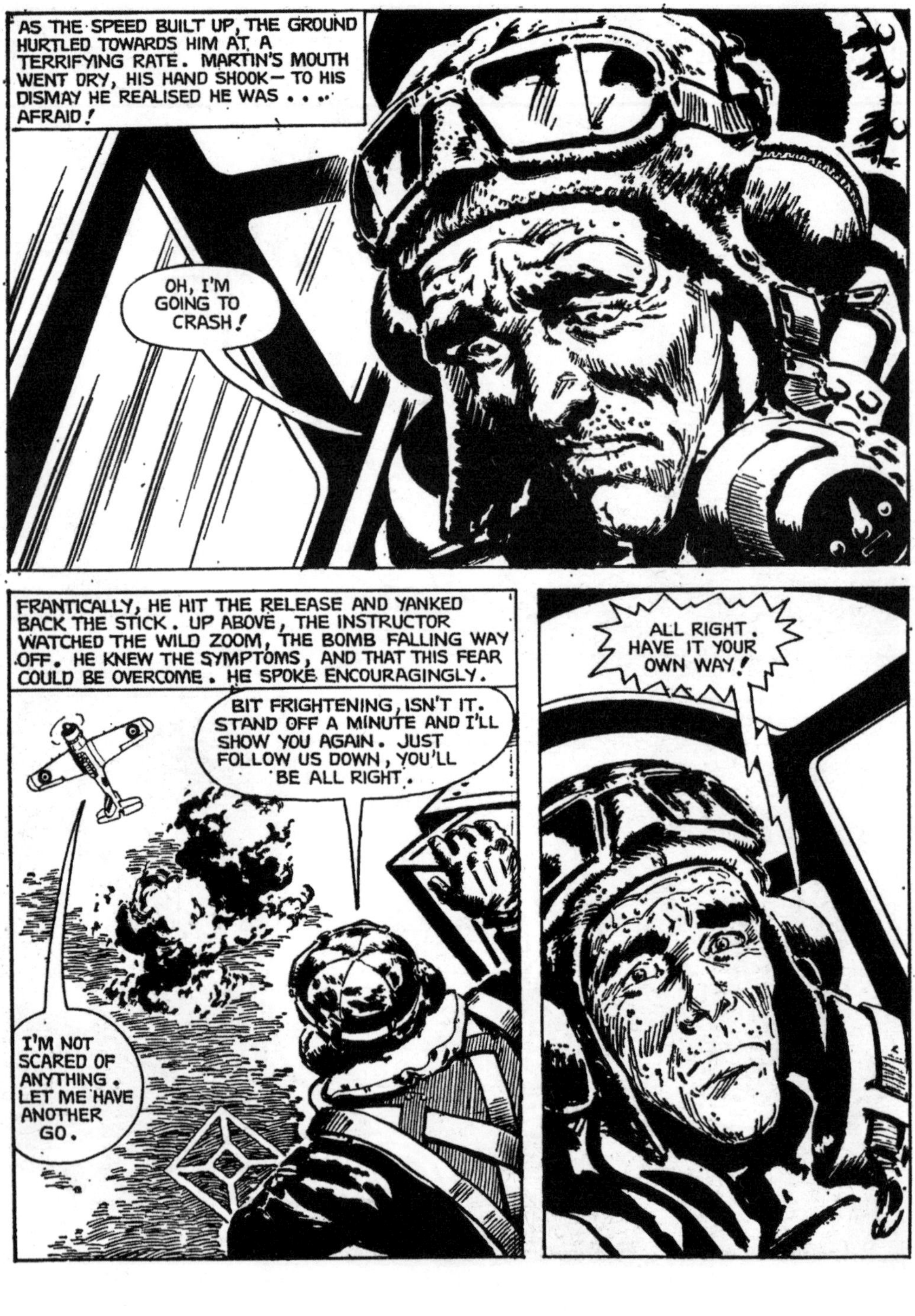
AS THE SPEED BUILT UP, THE GROUND HURTLED TOWARDS HIM AT A TERRIFYING RATE. MARTIN'S MOUTH WENT DRY, HIS HAND SHOOK— TO HIS DISMAY HE REALISED HE WAS . . . AFRAID!
OH, I'M GOING TO CRASH!
FRANTICALLY, HE HIT THE RELEASE AND YANKED BACK THE STICK. UP ABOVE, THE INSTRUCTOR WATCHED THE WILD ZOOM, THE BOMB FALLING WAY OFF. HE KNEW THE SYMPTOMS, AND THAT THIS FEAR COULD BE OVERCOME. HE SPOKE ENCOURAGINGLY.
BIT FRIGHTENING, ISN'T IT. STAND OFF A MINUTE AND I'LL SHOW YOU AGAIN. JUST FOLLOW US DOWN, YOU'LL BE ALL RIGHT.
I'M NOT SCARED OF ANYTHING. LET ME HAVE ANOTHER GO.
ALL RIGHT. HAVE IT YOUR OWN WAY!

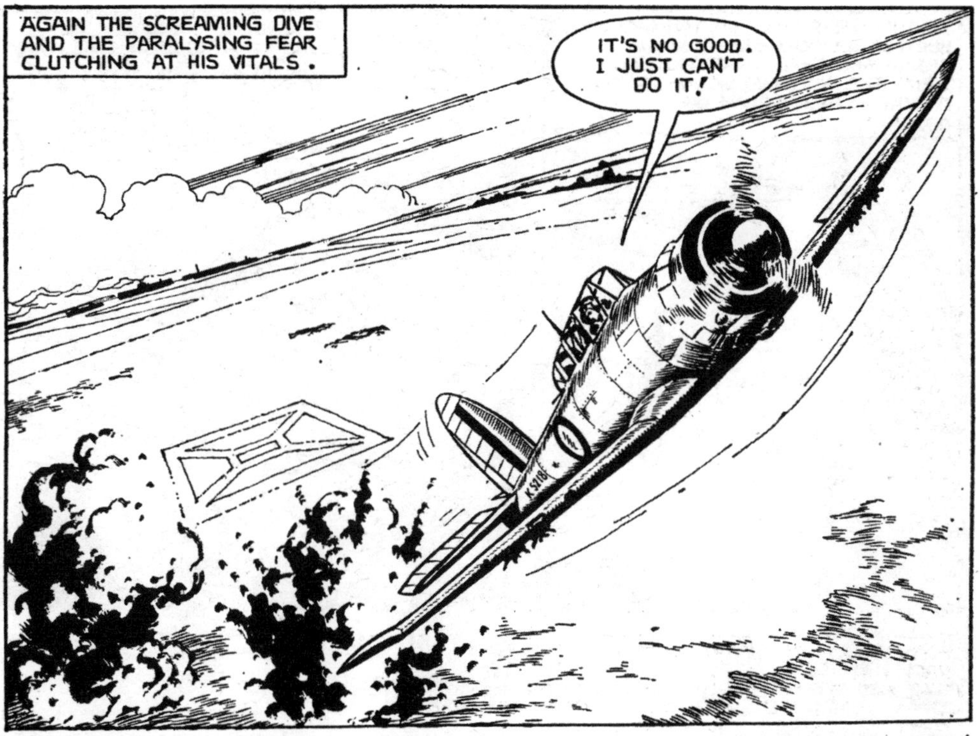
AGAIN THE SCREAMING DIVE AND THE PARALYSING FEAR CLUTCHING AT HIS VITALS.
IT'S NO GOOD. I JUST CAN'T DO IT!

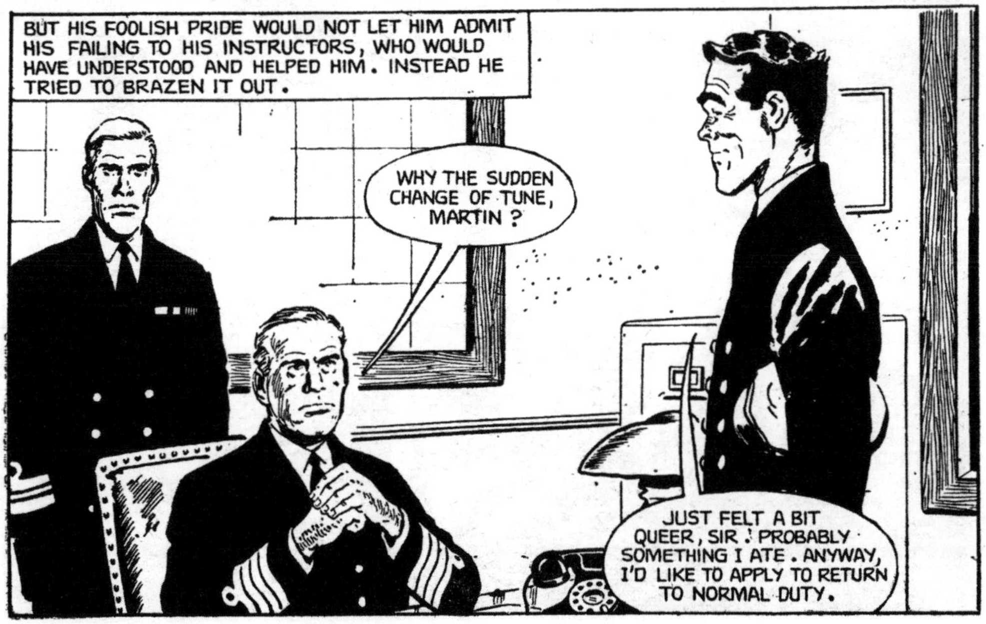
BUT HIS FOOLISH PRIDE WOULD NOT LET HIM ADMIT HIS FAILING TO HIS INSTRUCTORS, WHO WOULD HAVE UNDERSTOOD AND HELPED HIM. INSTEAD HE TRIED TO BRAZEN IT OUT.
WHY THE SUDDEN CHANGE OF TUNE, MARTIN?
JUST FELT A BIT QUEER, SIR! PROBABLY SOMETHING I ATE. ANYWAY, I'D LIKE TO APPLY TO RETURN TO NORMAL DUTY.

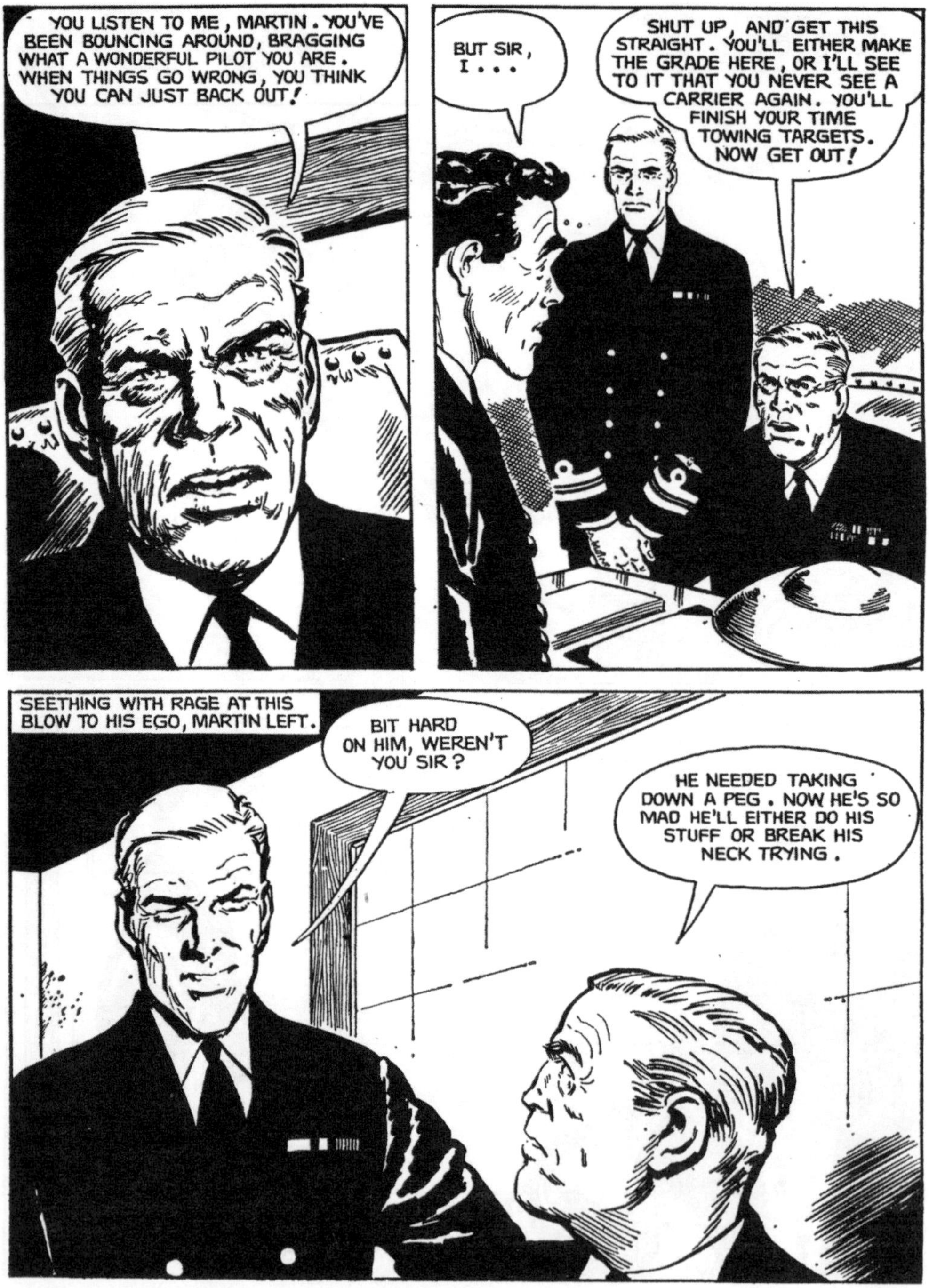
YOU LISTEN TO ME, MARTIN. YOU'VE BEEN BOUNCING AROUND, BRAGGING WHAT A WONDERFUL PILOT YOU ARE. WHEN THINGS GO WRONG, YOU THINK YOU CAN JUST BACK OUT!
BUT SIR, I . . .
SHUT UP, AND GET THIS STRAIGHT. YOU'LL EITHER MAKE THE GRADE HERE, OR I'LL SEE TO IT THAT YOU NEVER SEE A CARRIER AGAIN. YOU'LL FINISH YOUR TIME TOWING TARGETS. NOW GET OUT!
SEETHING WITH RAGE AT THIS BLOW TO HIS EGO, MARTIN LEFT.
BIT HARD ON HIM, WEREN'T YOU SIR?
HE NEEDED TAKING DOWN A PEG. NOW HE'S SO MAD HE'LL EITHER DO HIS STUFF OR BREAK HIS NECK TRYING.

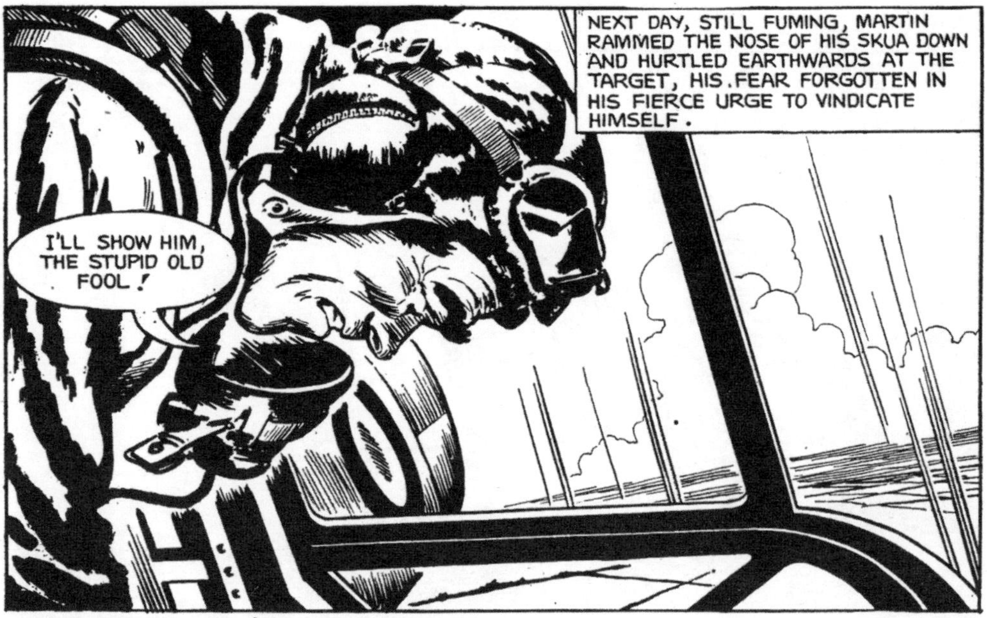
NEXT DAY, STILL FUMING, MARTIN RAMMED THE NOSE OF HIS SKUA DOWN AND HURTLED EARTHWARDS AT THE TARGET, HIS FEAR FORGOTTEN IN HIS FIERCE URGE TO VINDICATE HIMSELF.
I'LL SHOW HIM, THE STUPID OLD FOOL!

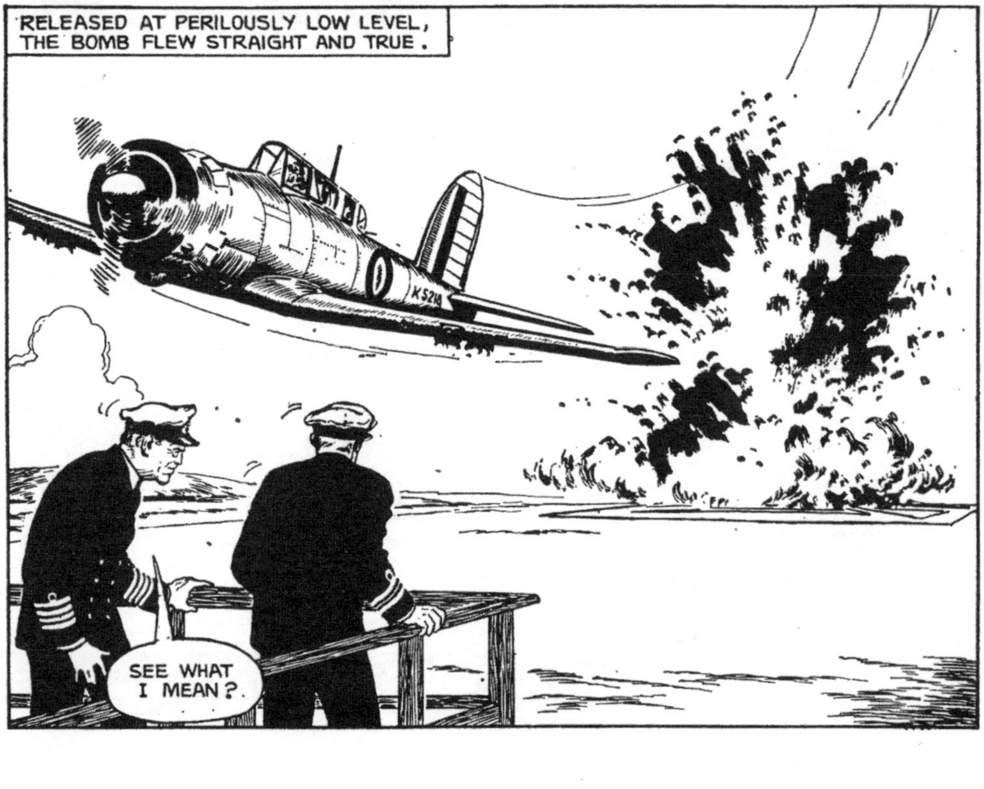
RELEASED AT PERILOUSLY LOW LEVEL, THE BOMB FLEW STRAIGHT AND TRUE.
SEE WHAT I MEAN?

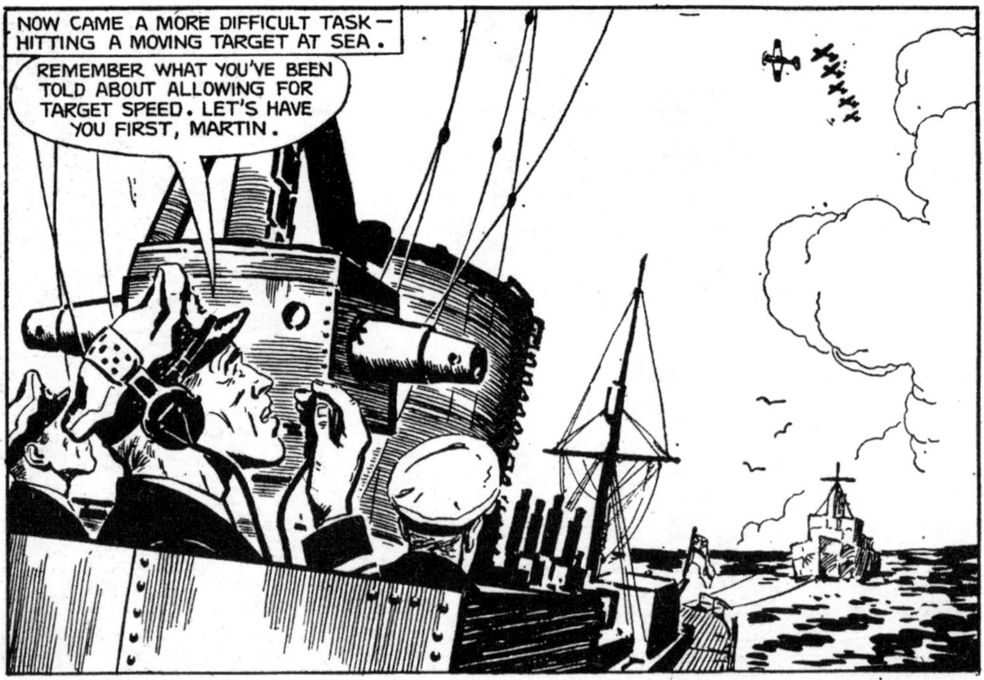
NOW CAME A MORE DIFFICULT TASK— HITTING A MOVING TARGET AT SEA.
REMEMBER WHAT YOU'VE BEEN TOLD ABOUT ALLOWING FOR TARGET SPEED. LET'S HAVE YOU FIRST, MARTIN.

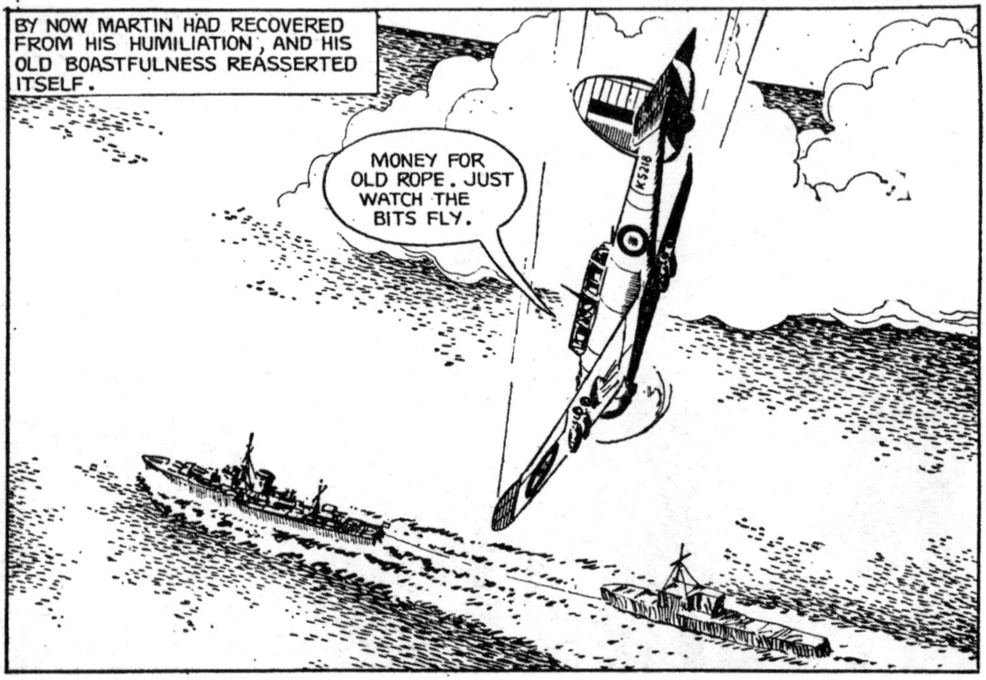
BY NOW MARTIN HAD RECOVERED FROM HIS HUMILIATION, AND HIS OLD BOASTFULNESS REASSERTED ITSELF.
MONEY FOR OLD ROPE. JUST WATCH THE BITS FLY.

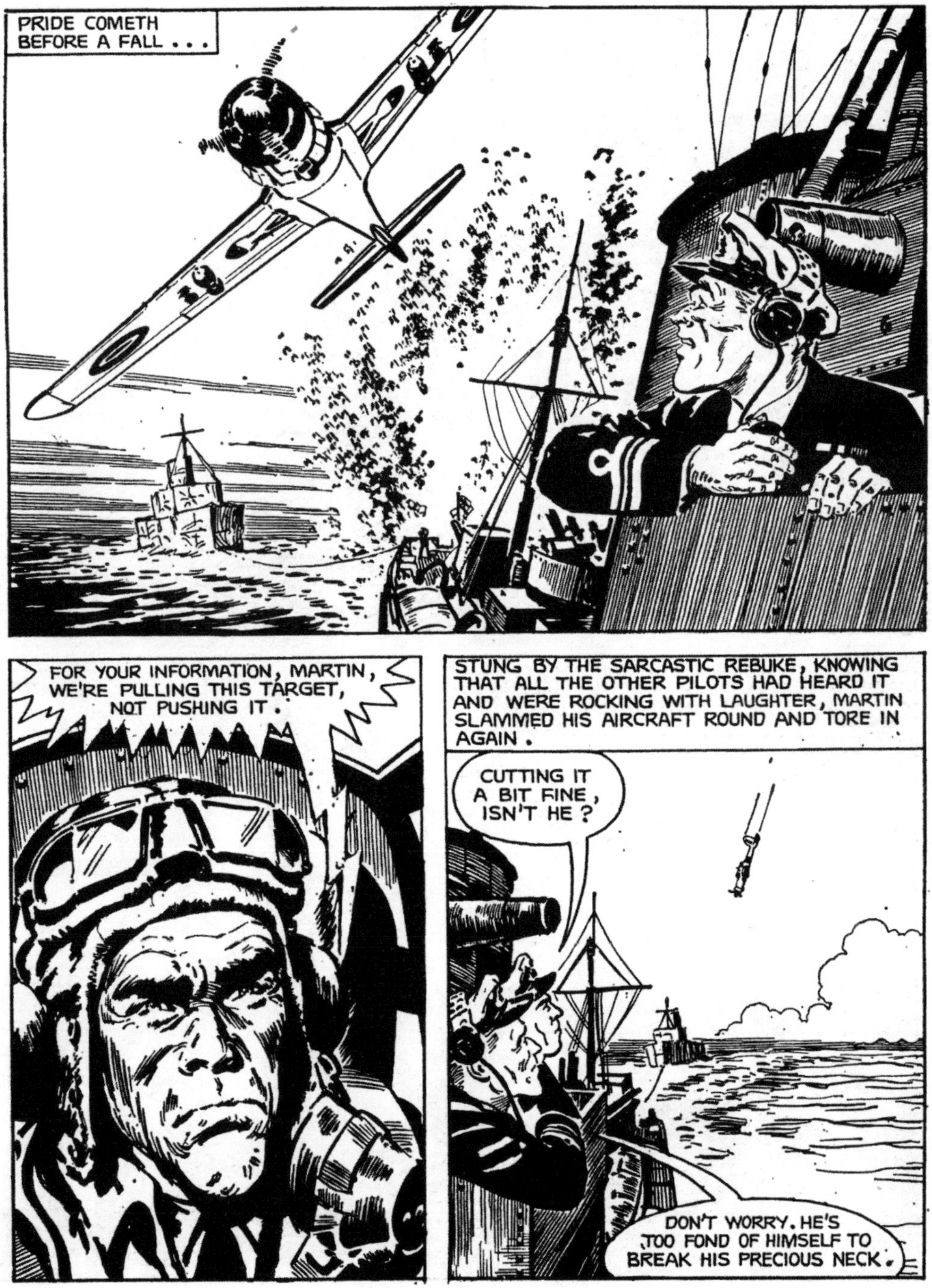
PRIDE COMETH BEFORE A FALL . . .
FOR YOUR INFORMATION, MARTIN, WE'RE PULLING THIS TARGET, NOT PUSHING IT.
STUNG BY THE SARCASTIC REBUKE, KNOWING THAT ALL THE OTHER PILOTS HAD HEARD IT AND WERE ROCKING WITH LAUGHTER, MARTIN SLAMMED HIS AIRCRAFT ROUND AND TORE IN AGAIN.
CUTTING IT A BIT FINE, ISN'T HE ?
DON'T WORRY. HE'S TOO FOND OF HIMSELF TO BREAK HIS PRECIOUS NECK.

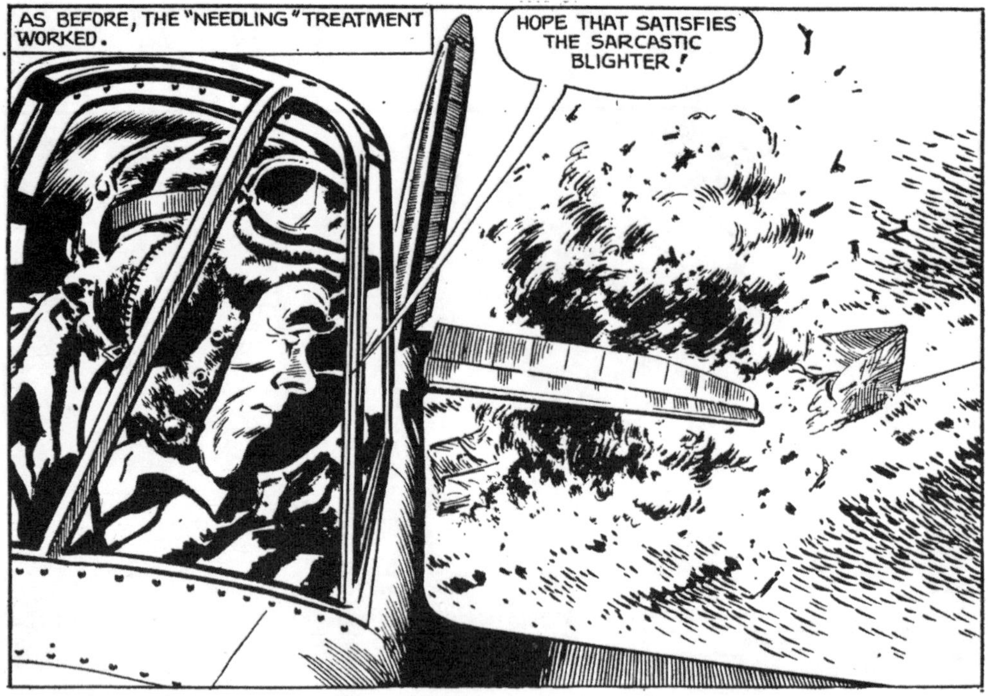
AS BEFORE, THE "NEEDLING" TREATMENT WORKED.
HOPE THAT SATISFIES THE SARCASTIC BLIGHTER!

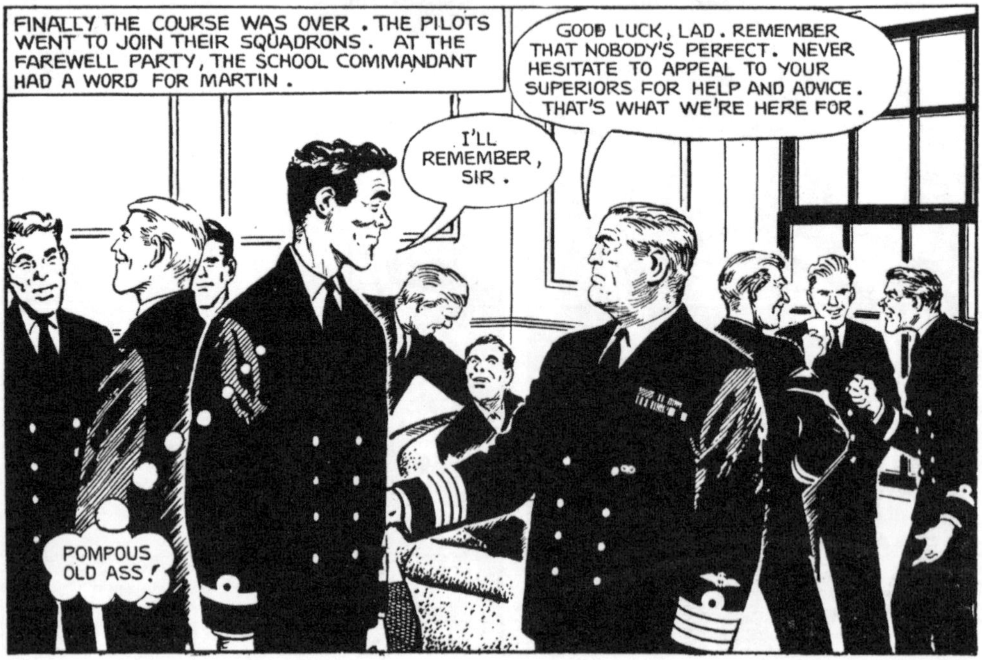
FINALLY THE COURSE WAS OVER. THE PILOTS WENT TO JOIN THEIR SQUADRONS. AT THE FAREWELL PARTY, THE SCHOOL COMMANDANT HAD A WORD FOR MARTIN.
GOOD LUCK, LAD. REMEMBER THAT NOBODY'S PERFECT. NEVER HESITATE TO APPEAL TO YOUR SUPERIORS FOR HELP AND ADVICE. THAT'S WHAT WE'RE HERE FOR.
I'LL REMEMBER, SIR.
POMPOUS OLD ASS!

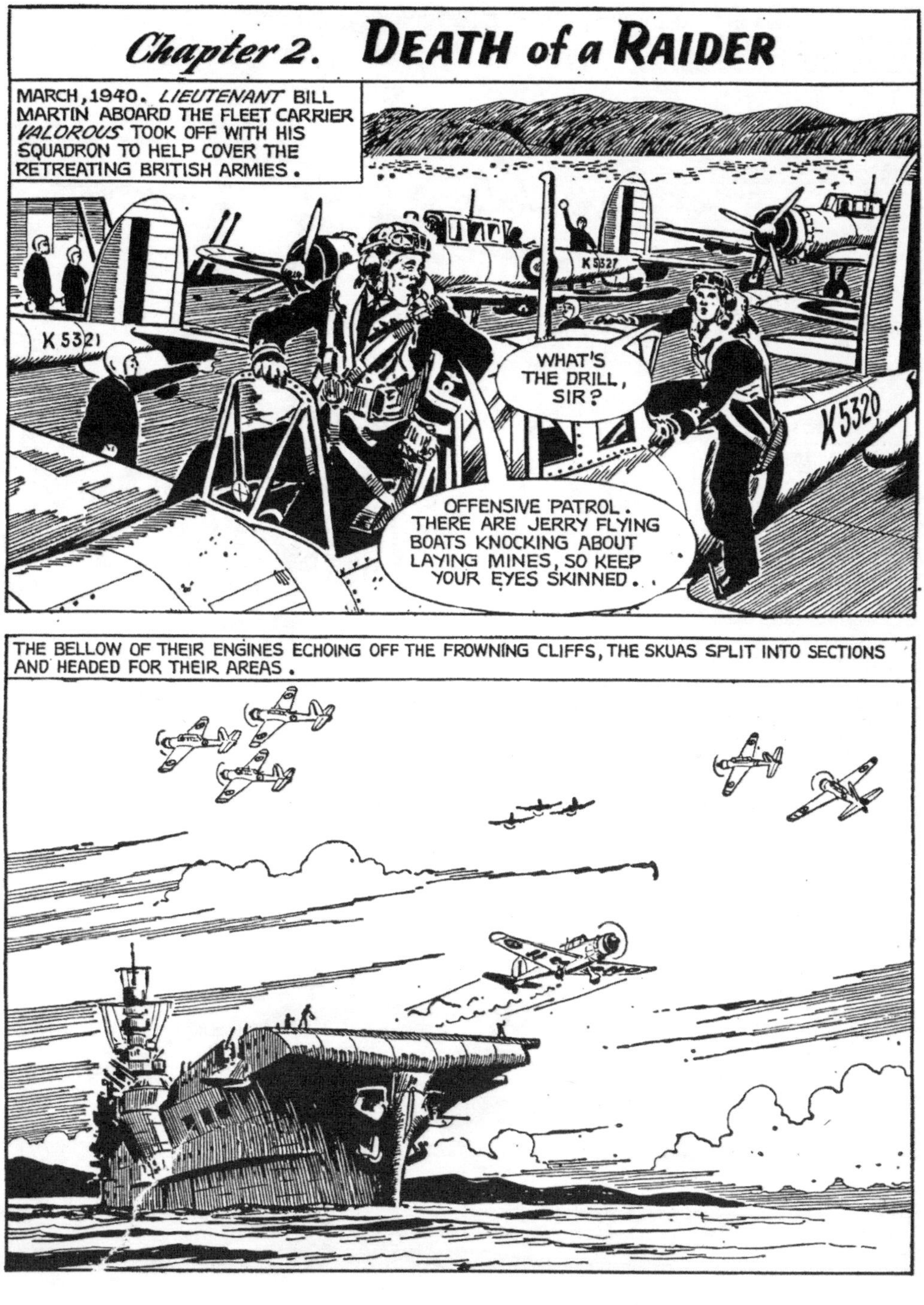
Chapter 2. DEATH of a RAIDER
MARCH, 1940. LIEUTENANT BILL MARTIN ABOARD THE FLEET CARRIER VALOROUS TOOK OFF WITH HIS SQUADRON TO HELP COVER THE RETREATING BRITISH ARMIES.
K 5321
K 5320
WHAT'S THE DRILL, SIR?
OFFENSIVE PATROL. THERE ARE JERRY FLYING BOATS KNOCKING ABOUT LAYING MINES, SO KEEP YOUR EYES SKINNED.
THE BELLOW OF THEIR ENGINES ECHOING OFF THE FROWNING CLIFFS, THE SKUAS SPLIT INTO SECTIONS AND HEADED FOR THEIR AREAS.

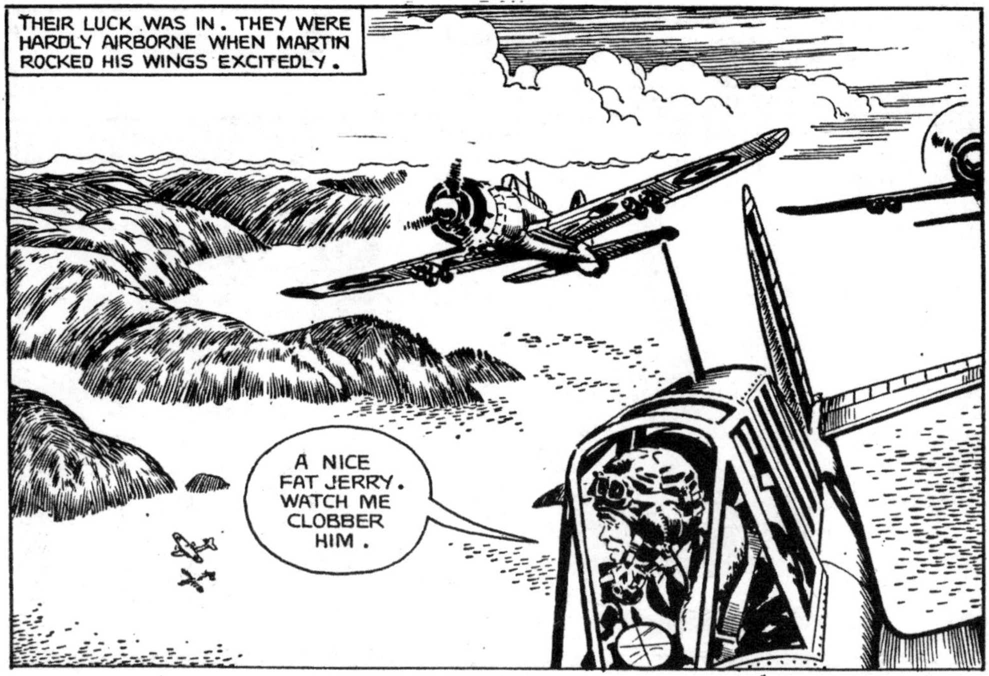
THEIR LUCK WAS IN. THEY WERE HARDLY AIRBORNE WHEN MARTIN ROCKED HIS WINGS EXCITEDLY.
A NICE FAT JERRY. WATCH ME CLOBBER HIM.

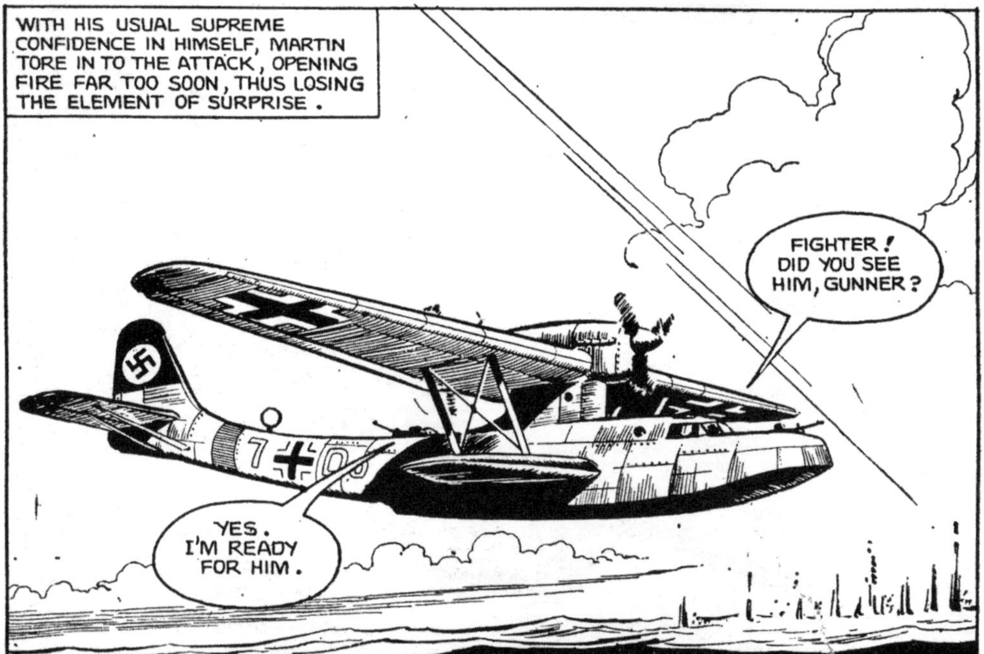
WITH HIS USUAL SUPREME CONFIDENCE IN HIMSELF, MARTIN TORE IN TO THE ATTACK, OPENING FIRE FAR TOO SOON, THUS LOSING THE ELEMENT OF SURPRISE.
FIGHTER! DID YOU SEE HIM, GUNNER?
YES. I'M READY FOR HIM.

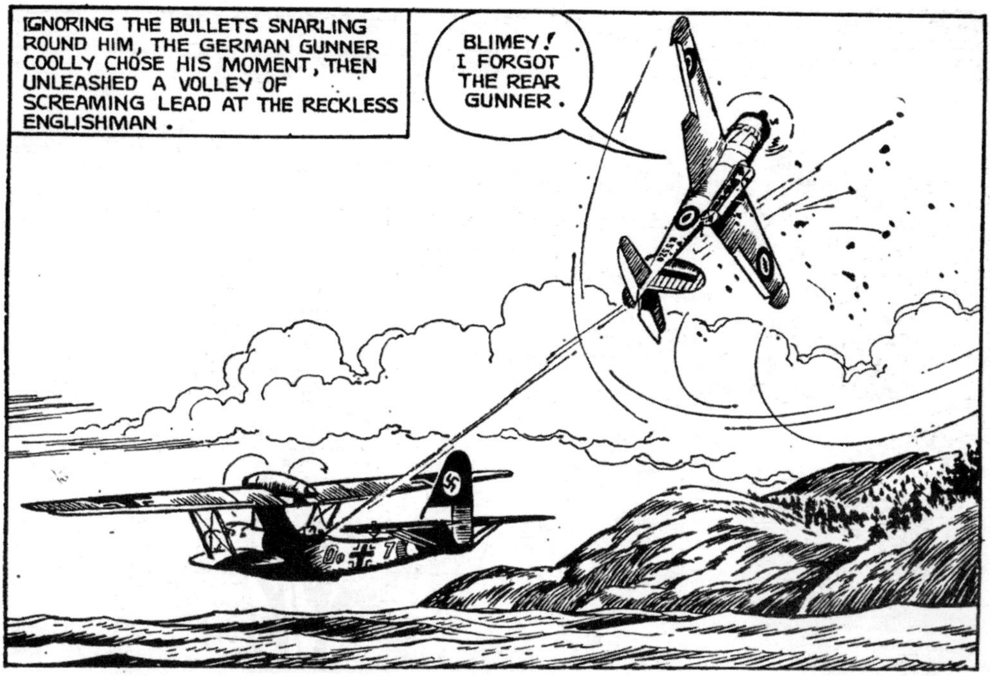
IGNORING THE BULLETS SNARLING ROUND HIM, THE GERMAN GUNNER COOLLY CHOSE HIS MOMENT, THEN UNLEASHED A VOLLEY OF SCREAMING LEAD AT THE RECKLESS ENGLISHMAN.
BLIMEY! I FORGOT THE REAR GUNNER.

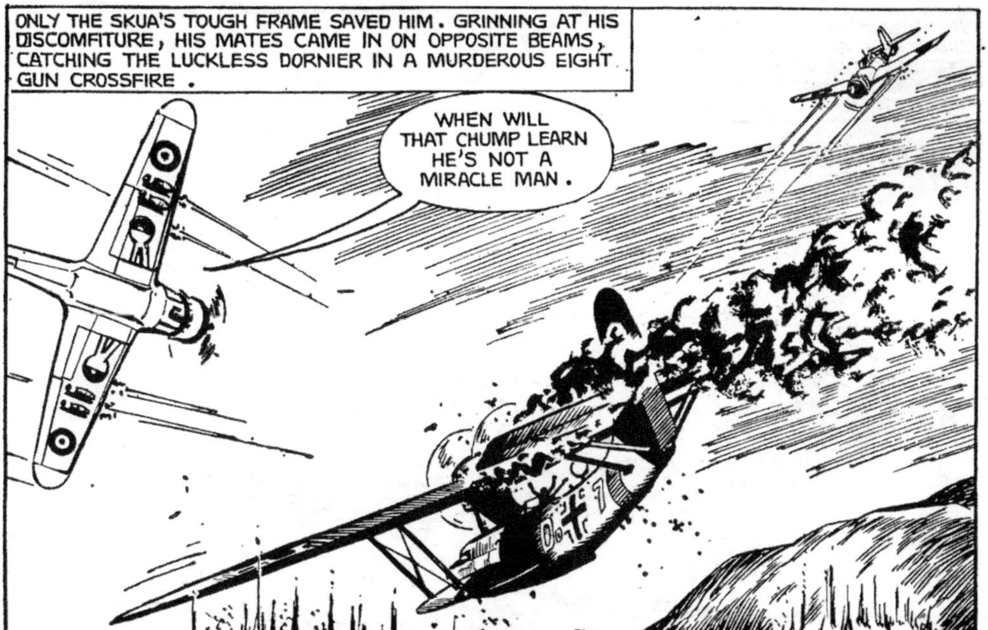
ONLY THE SKUA'S TOUGH FRAME SAVED HIM. GRINNING AT HIS DISCOMFITURE, HIS MATES CAME IN ON OPPOSITE BEAMS, CATCHING THE LUCKLESS DORNIER IN A MURDEROUS EIGHT GUN CROSSFIRE.
WHEN WILL THAT CHUMP LEARN HE'S NOT A MIRACLE MAN.

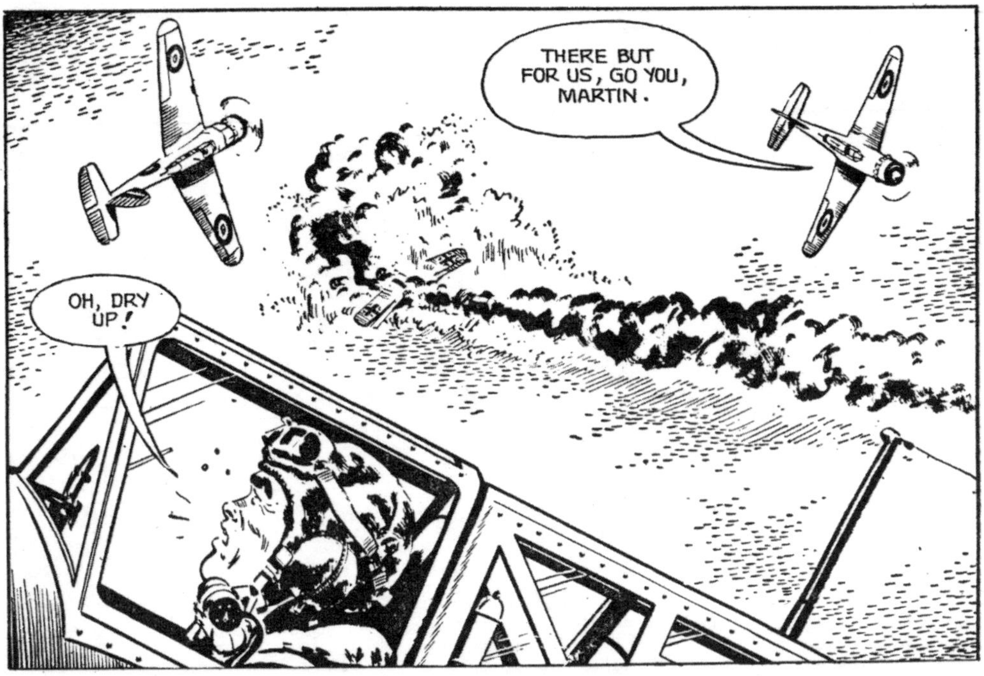
THERE BUT FOR US, GO YOU, MARTIN.
OH, DRY UP!

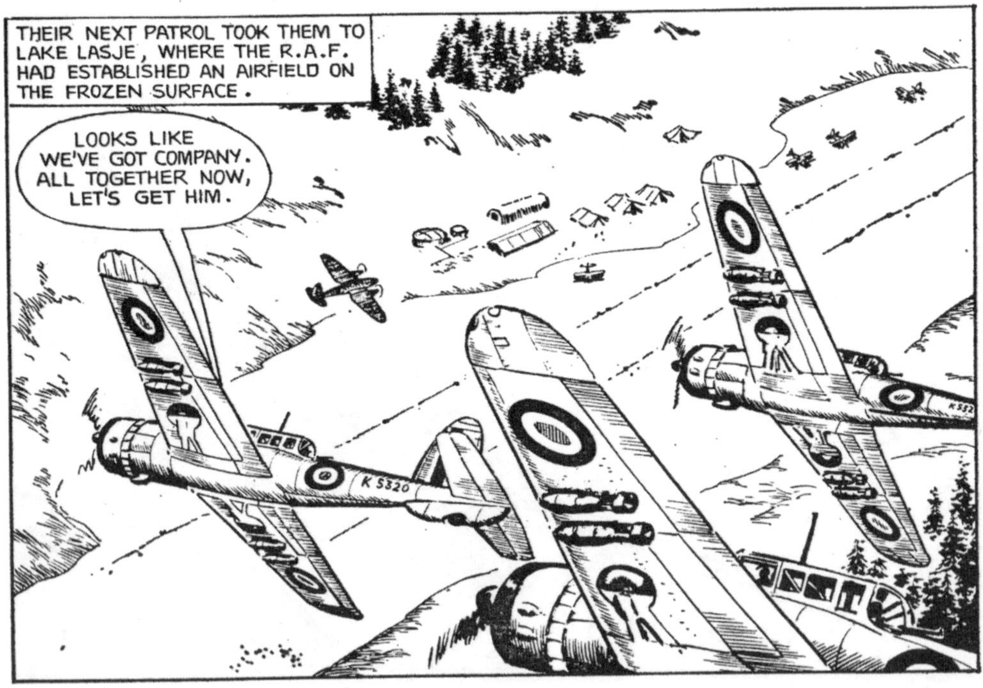
THEIR NEXT PATROL TOOK THEM TO LAKE LASJE, WHERE THE R.A.F. HAD ESTABLISHED AN AIRFIELD ON THE FROZEN SURFACE.
LOOKS LIKE WE'VE GOT COMPANY. ALL TOGETHER NOW, LET'S GET HIM.
K 5320

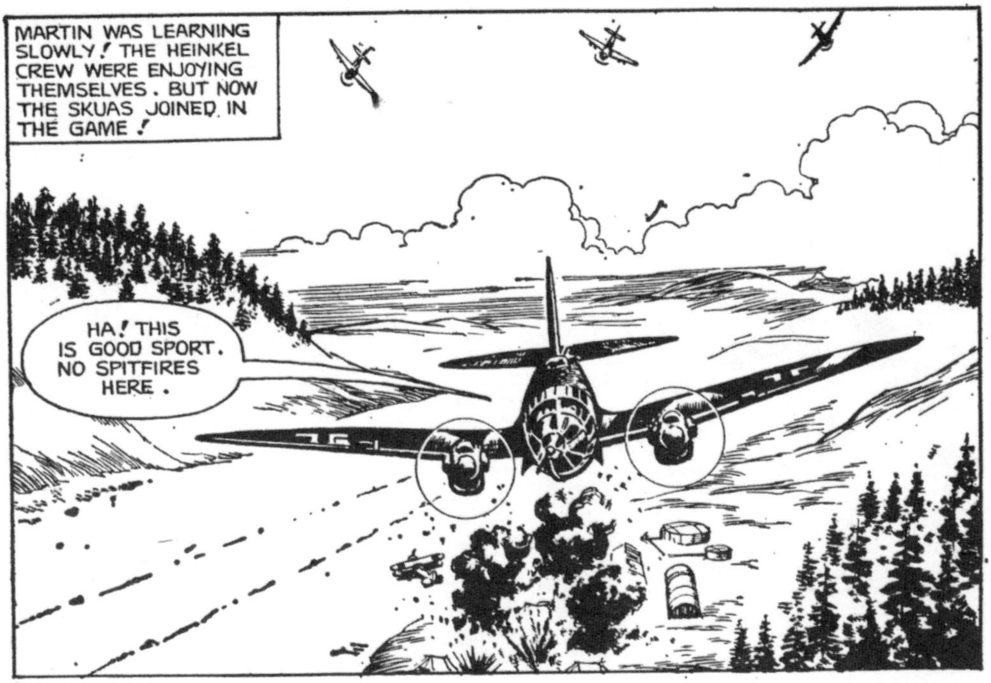
MARTIN WAS LEARNING SLOWLY! THE HEINKEL CREW WERE ENJOYING THEMSELVES. BUT NOW THE SKUAS JOINED IN THE GAME!
HA! THIS IS GOOD SPORT. NO SPITFIRES HERE.

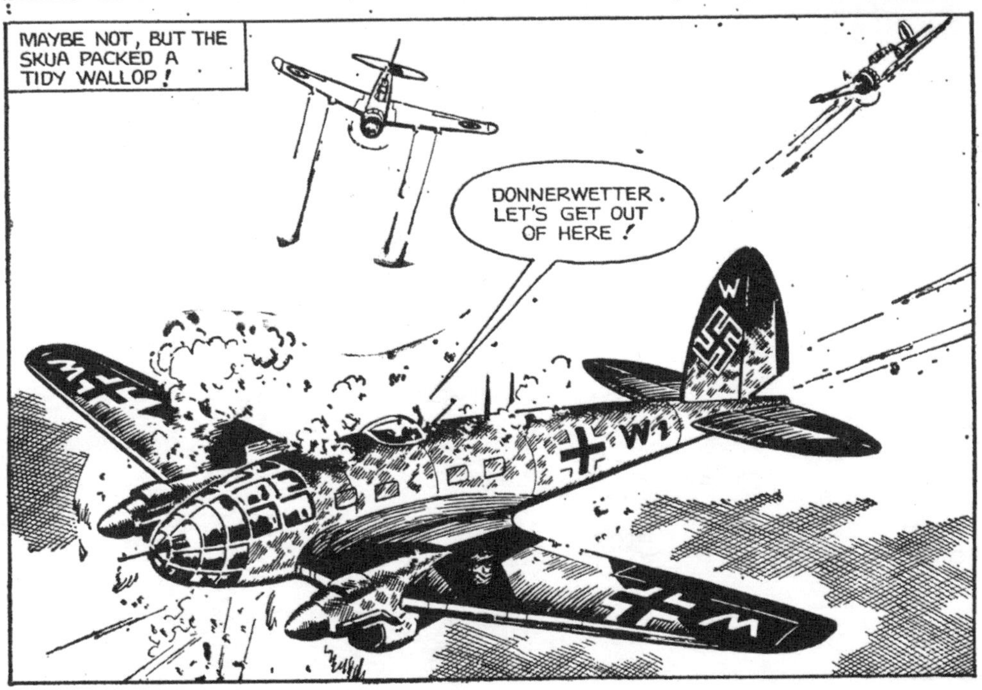
MAYBE NOT, BUT THE SKUA PACKED A TIDY WALLOP!
DONNERWETTER. LET'S GET OUT OF HERE!

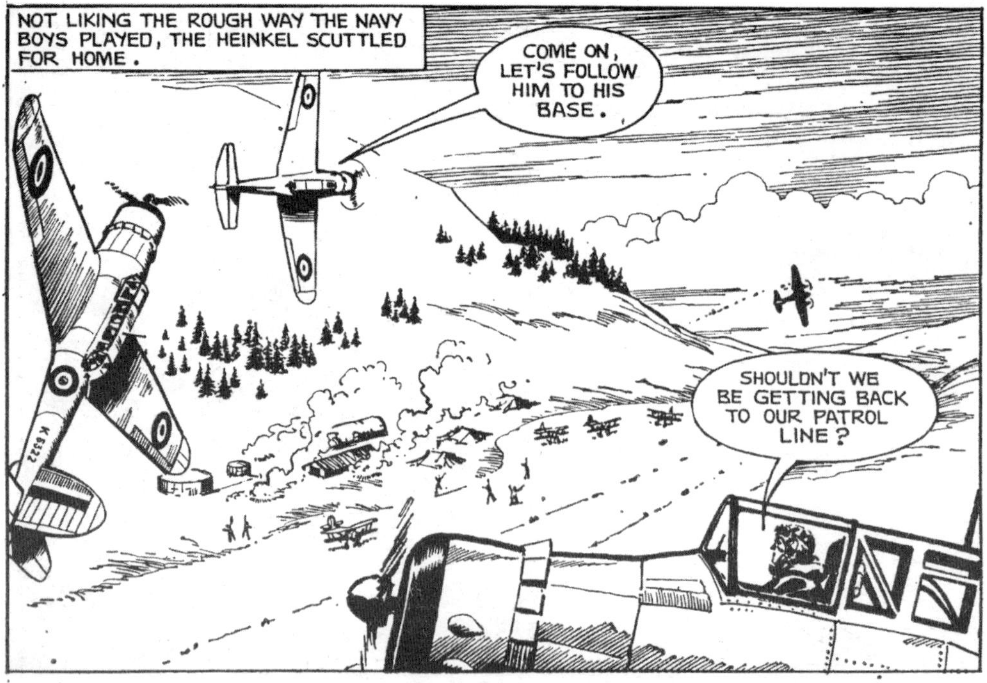
NOT LIKING THE ROUGH WAY THE NAVY BOYS PLAYED, THE HEINKEL SCUTTLED FOR HOME.
COME ON, LET'S FOLLOW HIM TO HIS BASE.
SHOULDN'T WE BE GETTING BACK TO OUR PATROL LINE?

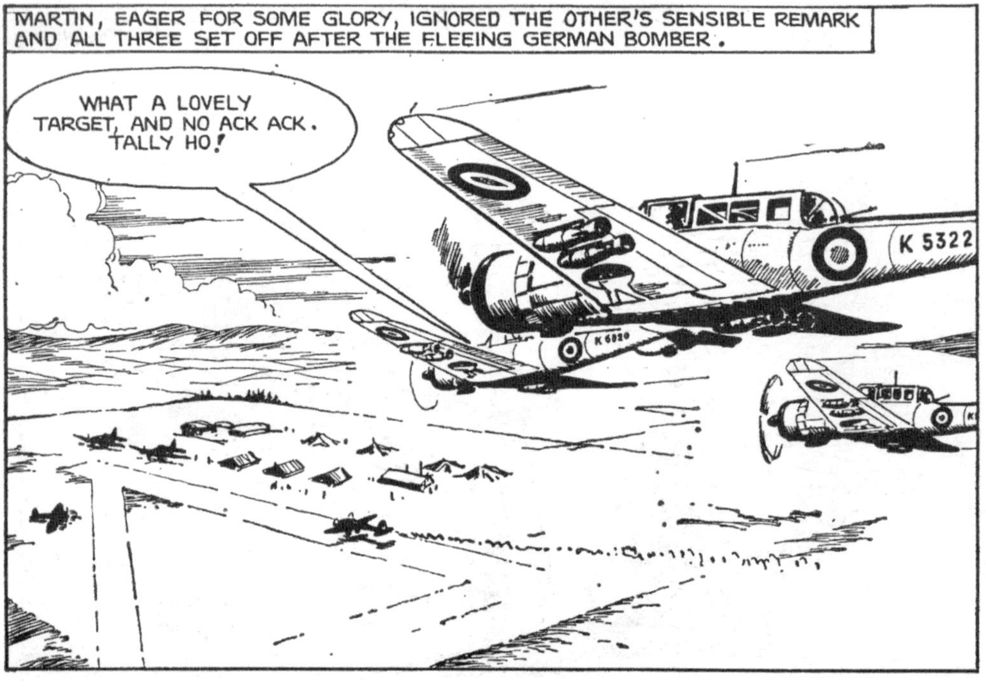
MARTIN, EAGER FOR SOME GLORY, IGNORED THE OTHER'S SENSIBLE REMARK AND ALL THREE SET OFF AFTER THE FLEEING GERMAN BOMBER.
WHAT A LOVELY TARGET, AND NO ACK ACK. TALLY HO!
K 5322

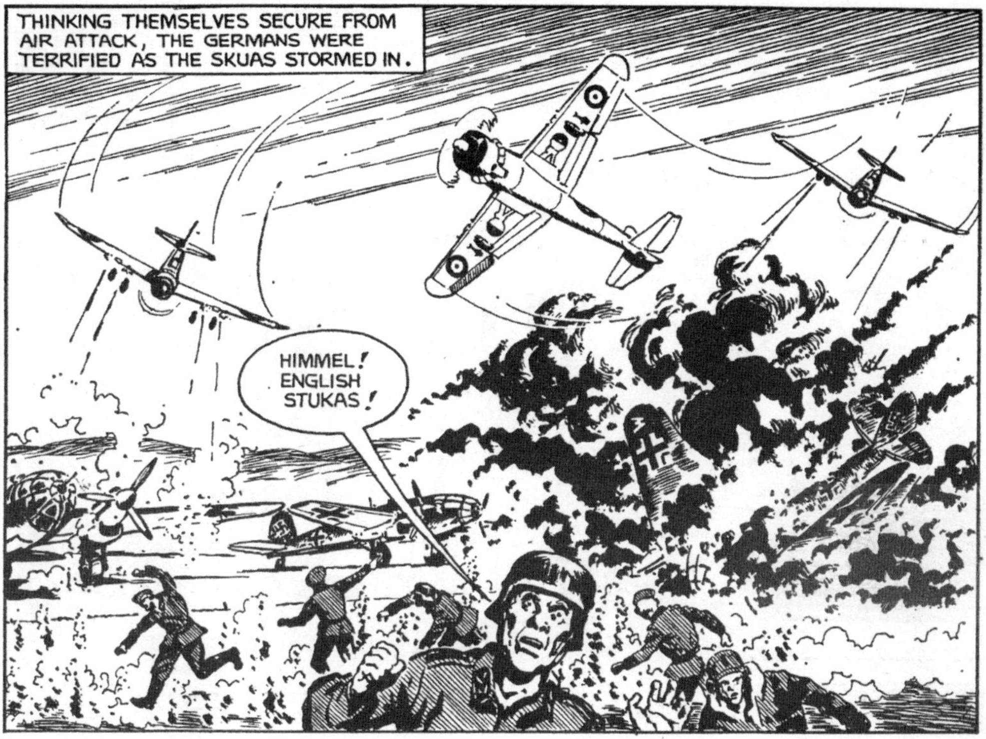
THINKING THEMSELVES SECURE FROM AIR ATTACK, THE GERMANS WERE TERRIFIED AS THE SKUAS STORMED IN.
HIMMEL! ENGLISH STUKAS!

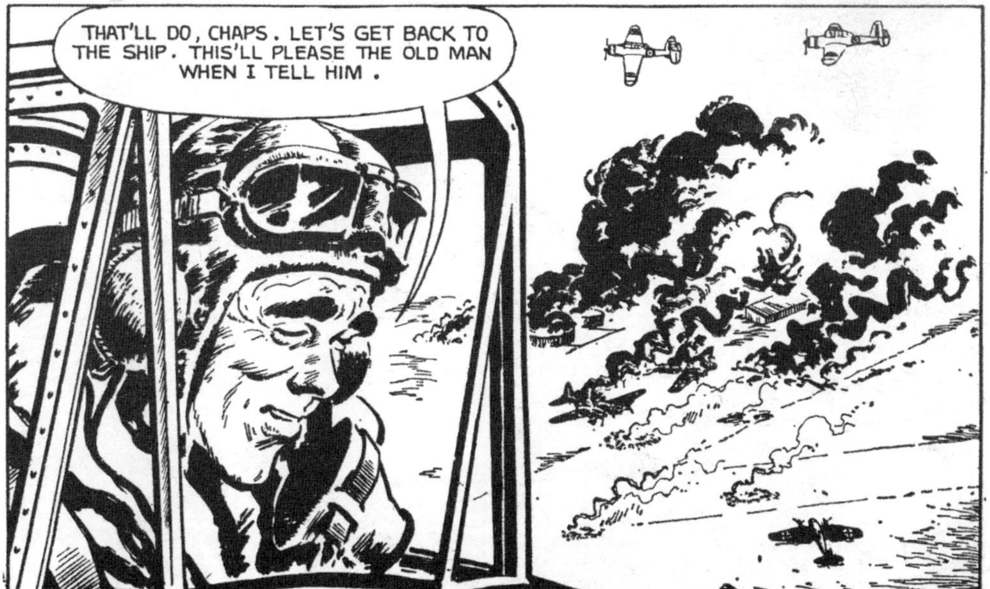
THAT'LL DO, CHAPS. LET'S GET BACK TO THE SHIP. THIS'LL PLEASE THE OLD MAN WHEN I TELL HIM.

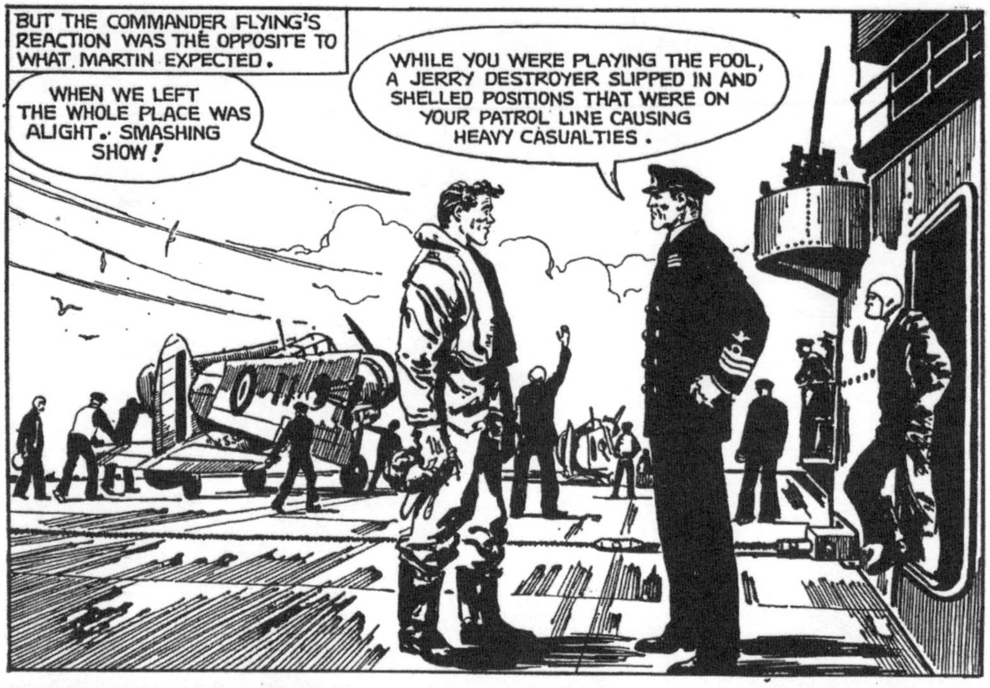
BUT THE COMMANDER FLYING'S REACTION WAS THE OPPOSITE TO WHAT MARTIN EXPECTED.
WHEN WE LEFT THE WHOLE PLACE WAS ALIGHT. SMASHING SHOW!
WHILE YOU WERE PLAYING THE FOOL, A JERRY DESTROYER SLIPPED IN AND SHELLED POSITIONS THAT WERE ON YOUR PATROL LINE CAUSING HEAVY CASUALTIES.

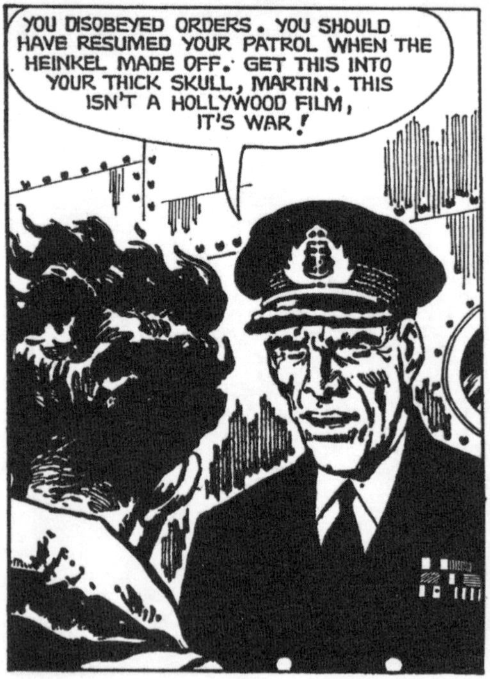
YOU DISOBEYED ORDERS. YOU SHOULD HAVE RESUMED YOUR PATROL WHEN THE HEINKEL MADE OFF. GET THIS INTO YOUR THICK SKULL, MARTIN. THIS ISN'T A HOLLYWOOD FILM, IT'S WAR!

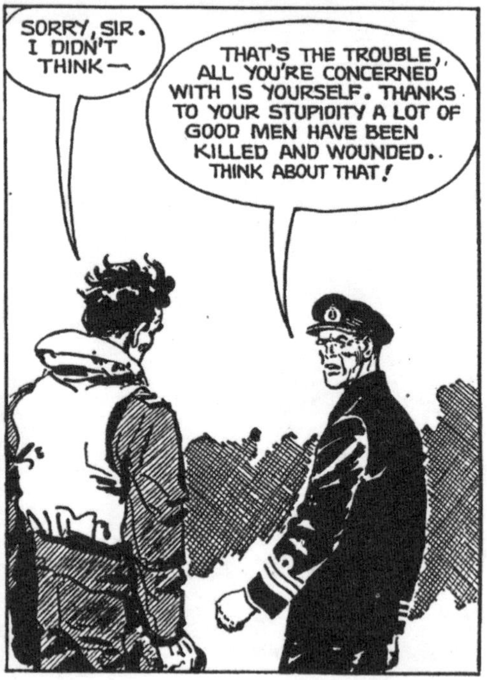
SORRY, SIR. I DIDN'T THINK—
THAT'S THE TROUBLE, ALL YOU'RE CONCERNED WITH IS YOURSELF. THANKS TO YOUR STUPIDITY A LOT OF GOOD MEN HAVE BEEN KILLED AND WOUNDED.. THINK ABOUT THAT!

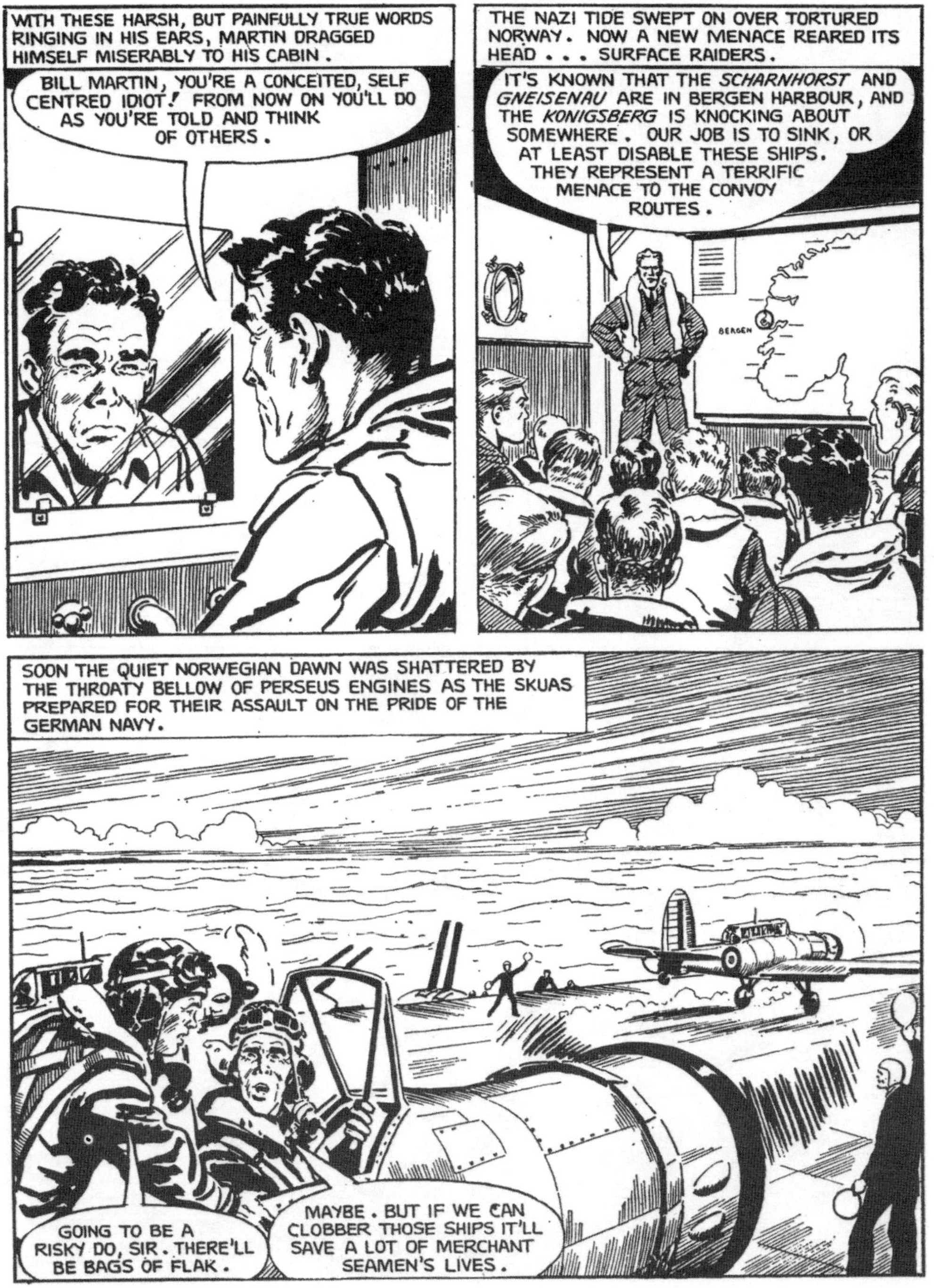
WITH THESE HARSH, BUT PAINFULLY TRUE WORDS RINGING IN HIS EARS, MARTIN DRAGGED HIMSELF MISERABLY TO HIS CABIN.
BILL MARTIN, YOU'RE A CONCEITED, SELF CENTRED IDIOT! FROM NOW ON YOU'LL DO AS YOU'RE TOLD AND THINK OF OTHERS.
THE NAZI TIDE SWEPT ON OVER TORTURED NORWAY. NOW A NEW MENACE REARED ITS HEAD . . . SURFACE RAIDERS.
IT'S KNOWN THAT THE *SCHARNHORST* AND *GNEISENAU* ARE IN BERGEN HARBOUR, AND THE *KONIGSBERG* IS KNOCKING ABOUT SOMEWHERE. OUR JOB IS TO SINK, OR AT LEAST DISABLE THESE SHIPS. THEY REPRESENT A TERRIFIC MENACE TO THE CONVOY ROUTES.
BERGEN
SOON THE QUIET NORWEGIAN DAWN WAS SHATTERED BY THE THROATY BELLOW OF PERSEUS ENGINES AS THE SKUAS PREPARED FOR THEIR ASSAULT ON THE PRIDE OF THE GERMAN NAVY.
GOING TO BE A RISKY DO, SIR. THERE'LL BE BAGS OF FLAK.
MAYBE. BUT IF WE CAN CLOBBER THOSE SHIPS IT'LL SAVE A LOT OF MERCHANT SEAMEN'S LIVES.

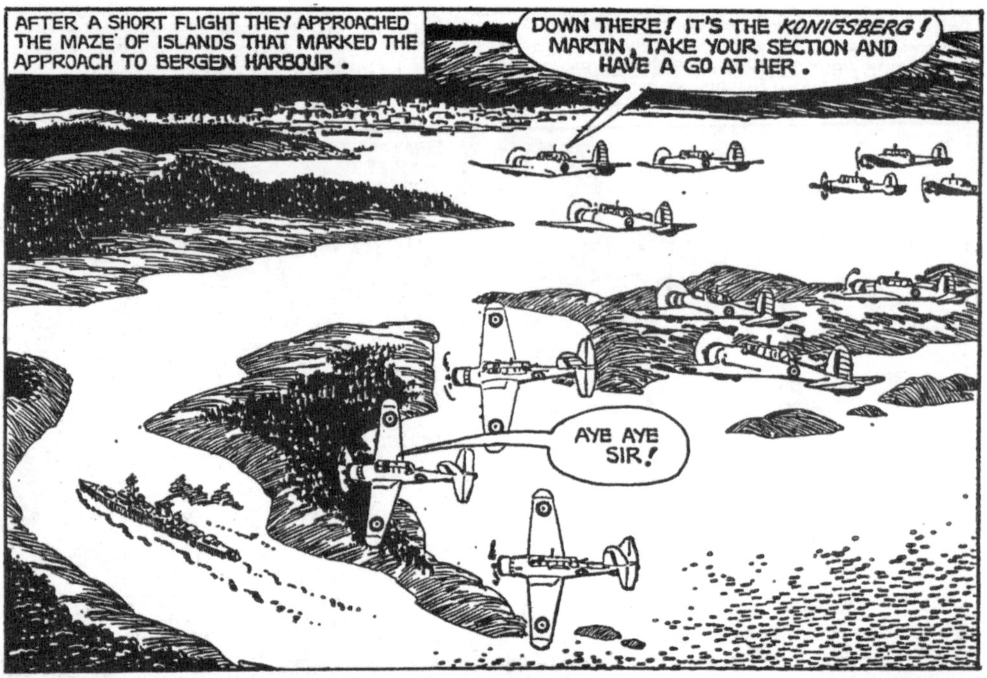
AFTER A SHORT FLIGHT THEY APPROACHED THE MAZE OF ISLANDS THAT MARKED THE APPROACH TO BERGEN HARBOUR.
DOWN THERE! IT'S THE *KONIGSBERG*! MARTIN, TAKE YOUR SECTION AND HAVE A GO AT HER.
AYE AYE SIR!

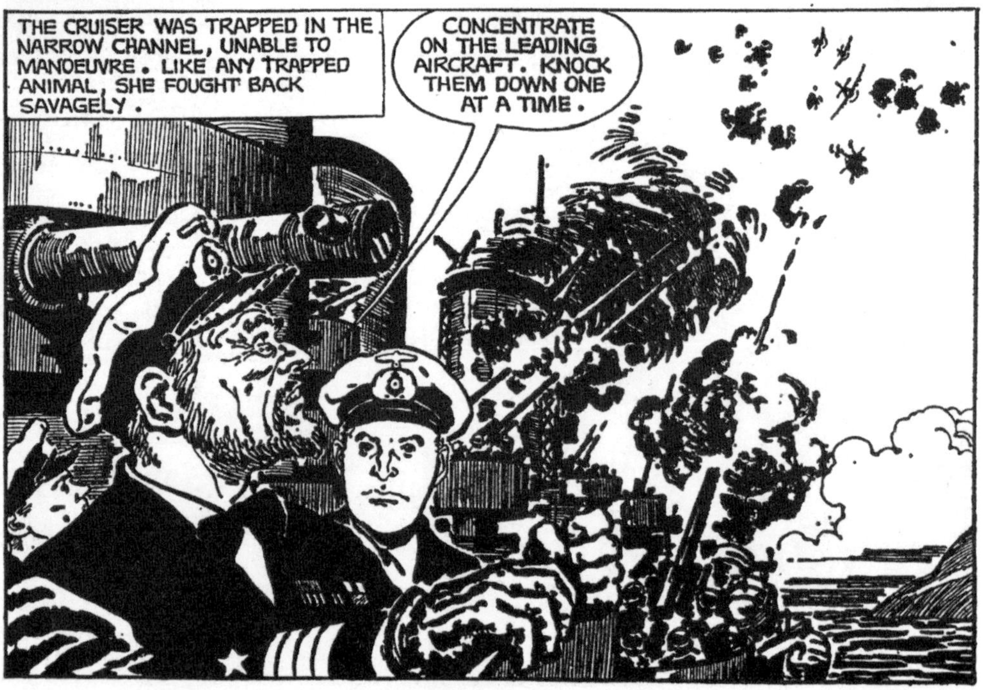
THE CRUISER WAS TRAPPED IN THE NARROW CHANNEL, UNABLE TO MANOEUVRE. LIKE ANY TRAPPED ANIMAL, SHE FOUGHT BACK SAVAGELY.
CONCENTRATE ON THE LEADING AIRCRAFT. KNOCK THEM DOWN ONE AT A TIME.

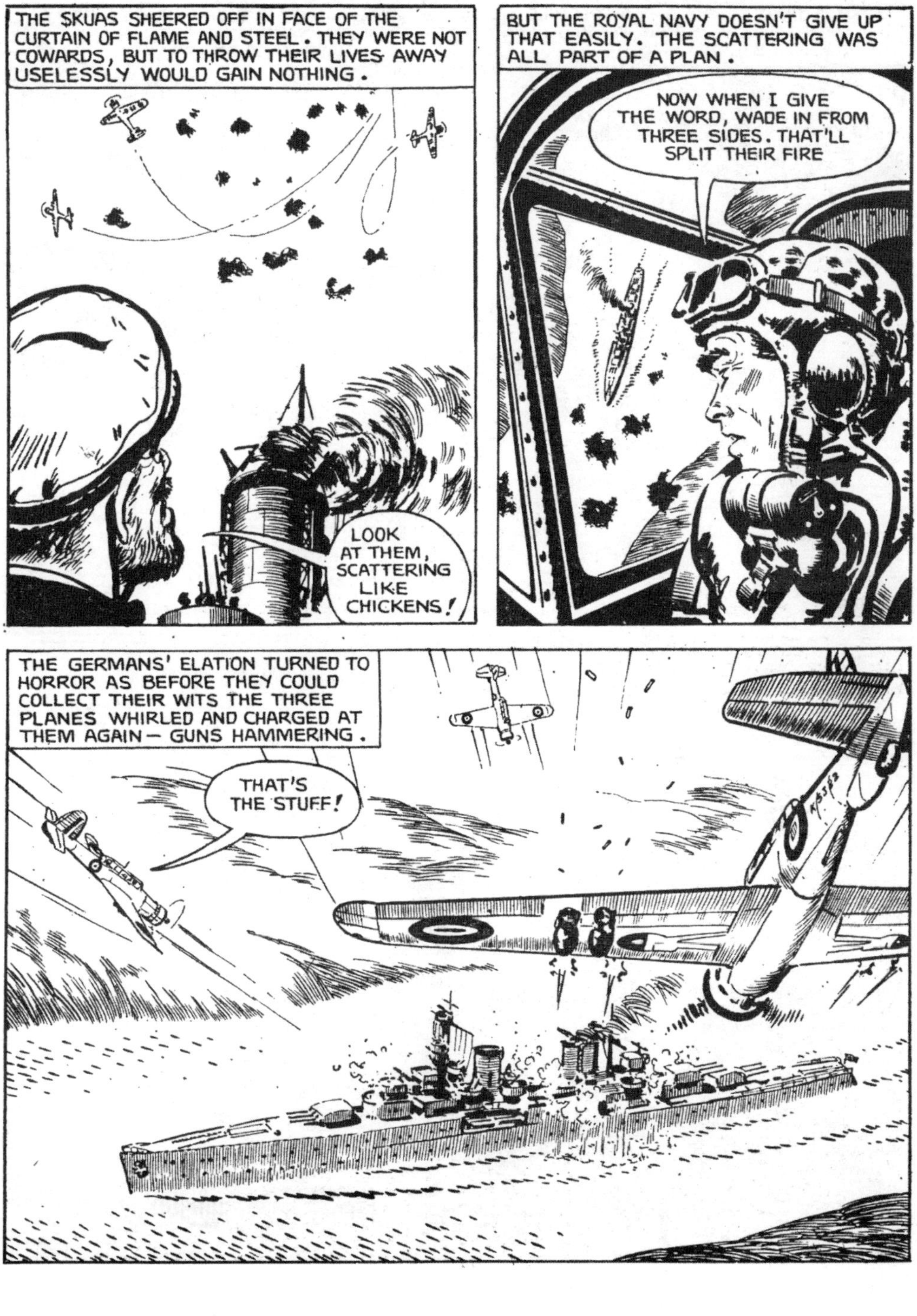
THE SKUAS SHEERED OFF IN FACE OF THE CURTAIN OF FLAME AND STEEL. THEY WERE NOT COWARDS, BUT TO THROW THEIR LIVES AWAY USELESSLY WOULD GAIN NOTHING.
LOOK AT THEM, SCATTERING LIKE CHICKENS!
BUT THE ROYAL NAVY DOESN'T GIVE UP THAT EASILY. THE SCATTERING WAS ALL PART OF A PLAN.
NOW WHEN I GIVE THE WORD, WADE IN FROM THREE SIDES. THAT'LL SPLIT THEIR FIRE
THE GERMANS' ELATION TURNED TO HORROR AS BEFORE THEY COULD COLLECT THEIR WITS THE THREE PLANES WHIRLED AND CHARGED AT THEM AGAIN — GUNS HAMMERING.
THAT'S THE STUFF!

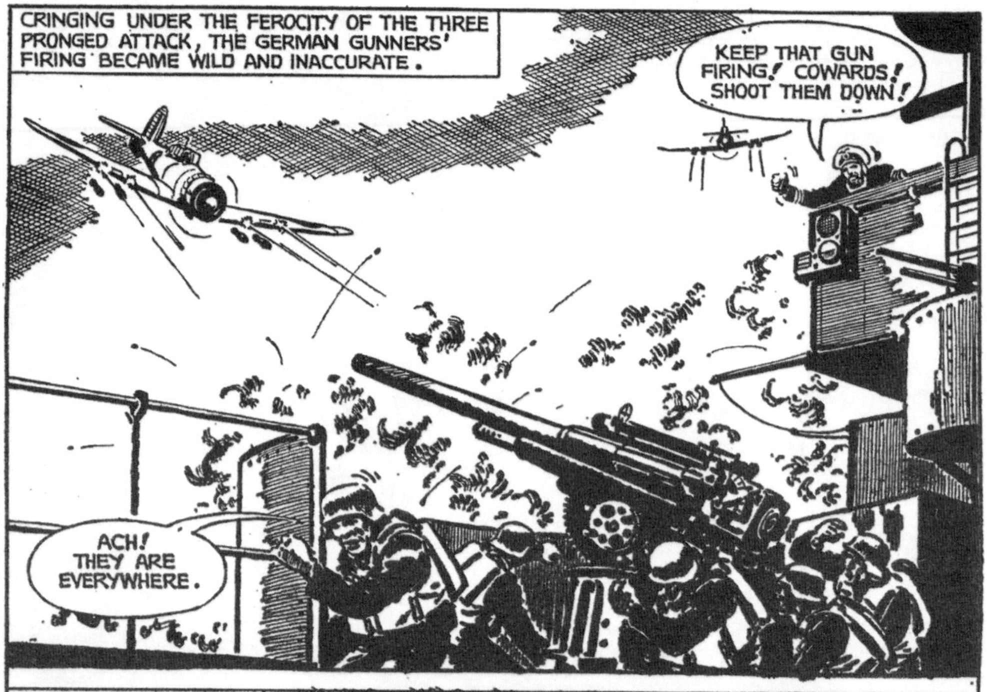
CRINGING UNDER THE FEROCITY OF THE THREE PRONGED ATTACK, THE GERMAN GUNNERS' FIRING BECAME WILD AND INACCURATE.
KEEP THAT GUN FIRING! COWARDS! SHOOT THEM DOWN!
ACH! THEY ARE EVERYWHERE.

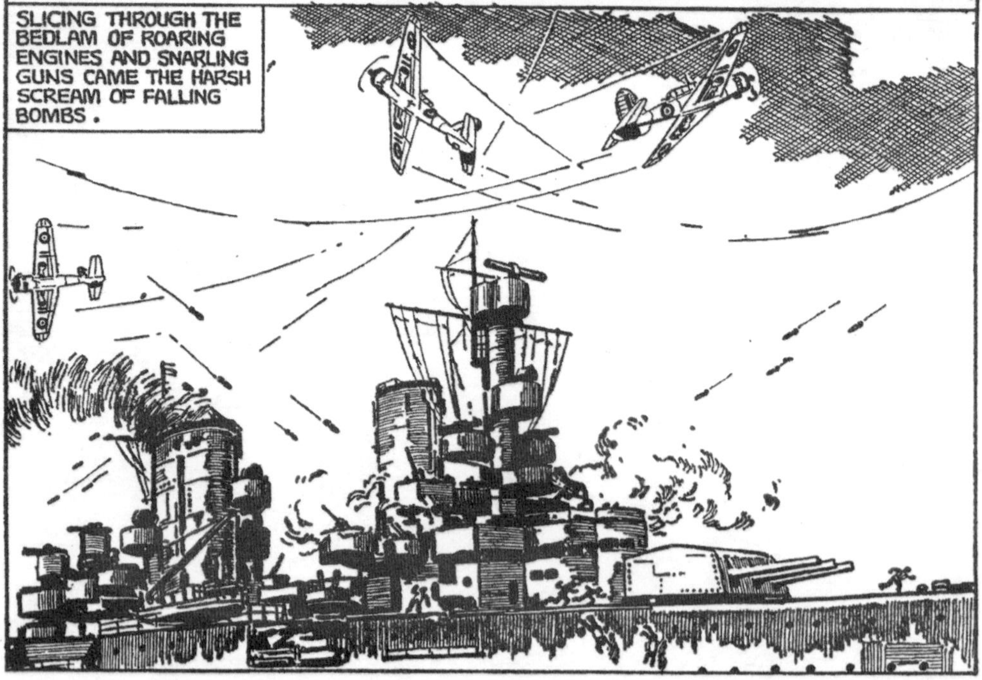
SLICING THROUGH THE BEDLAM OF ROARING ENGINES AND SNARLING GUNS CAME THE HARSH SCREAM OF FALLING BOMBS.

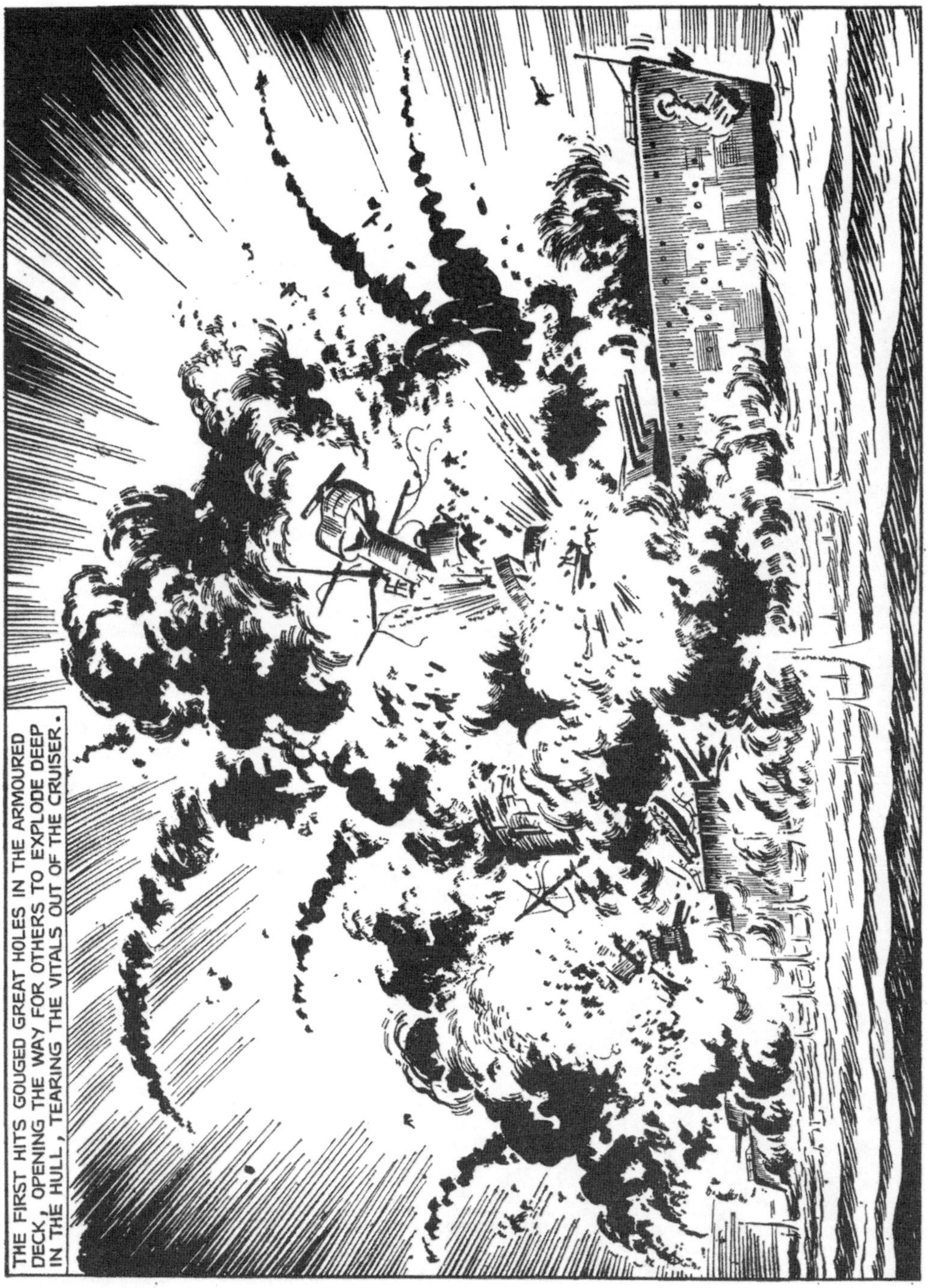
THE FIRST HITS GOUGED GREAT HOLES IN THE ARMOURED
DECK, OPENING THE WAY FOR OTHERS TO EXPLODE DEEP
IN THE HULL, TEARING THE VITALS OUT OF THE CRUISER.

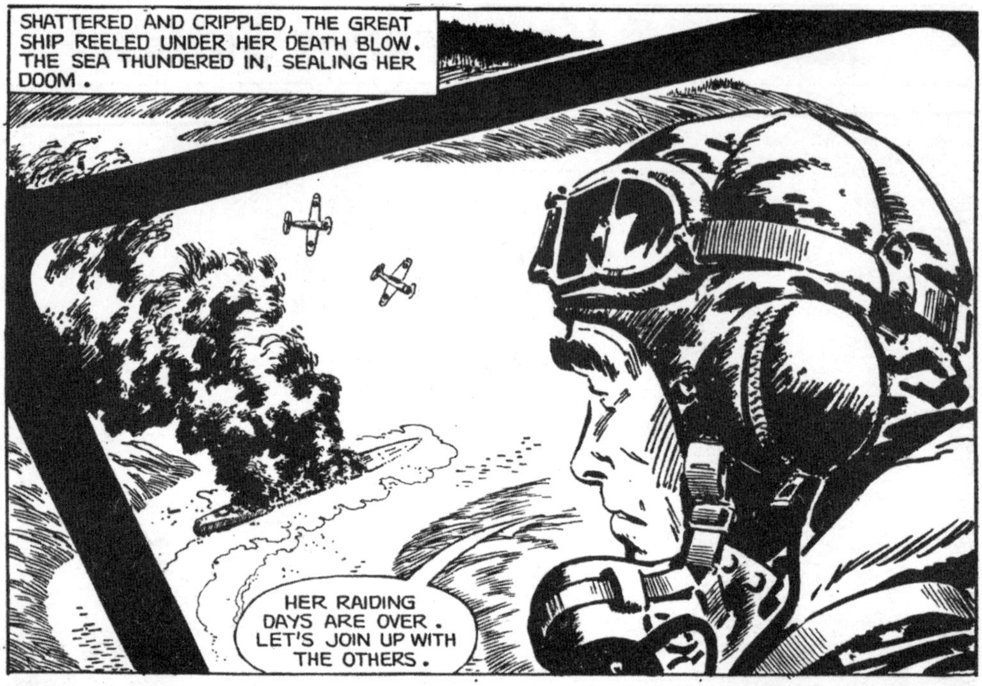
SHATTERED AND CRIPPLED, THE GREAT SHIP REELED UNDER HER DEATH BLOW. THE SEA THUNDERED IN, SEALING HER DOOM.
HER RAIDING DAYS ARE OVER. LET'S JOIN UP WITH THE OTHERS.

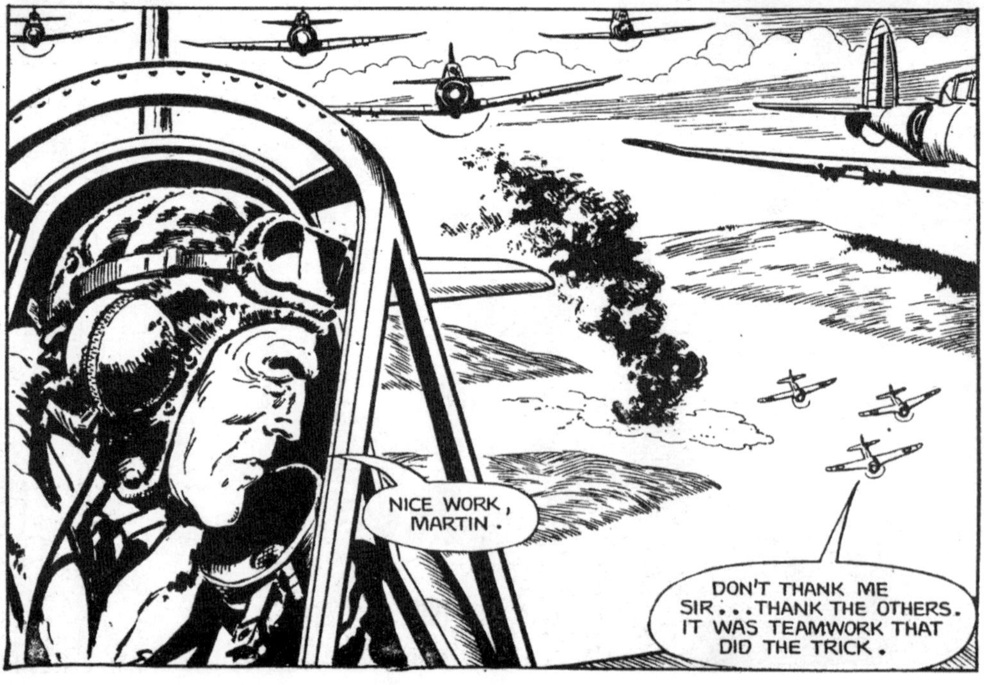
NICE WORK, MARTIN.
DON'T THANK ME SIR...THANK THE OTHERS. IT WAS TEAMWORK THAT DID THE TRICK.

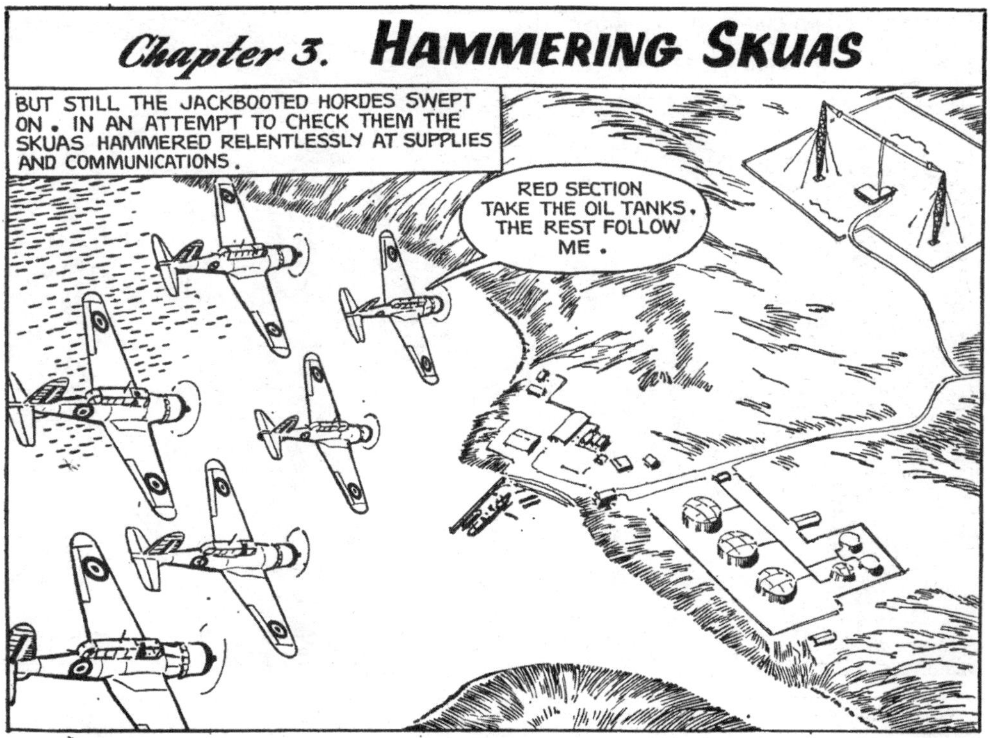
Chapter 3. HAMMERING SKUAS
BUT STILL THE JACKBOOTED HORDES SWEPT ON. IN AN ATTEMPT TO CHECK THEM THE SKUAS HAMMERED RELENTLESSLY AT SUPPLIES AND COMMUNICATIONS.
RED SECTION TAKE THE OIL TANKS. THE REST FOLLOW ME.

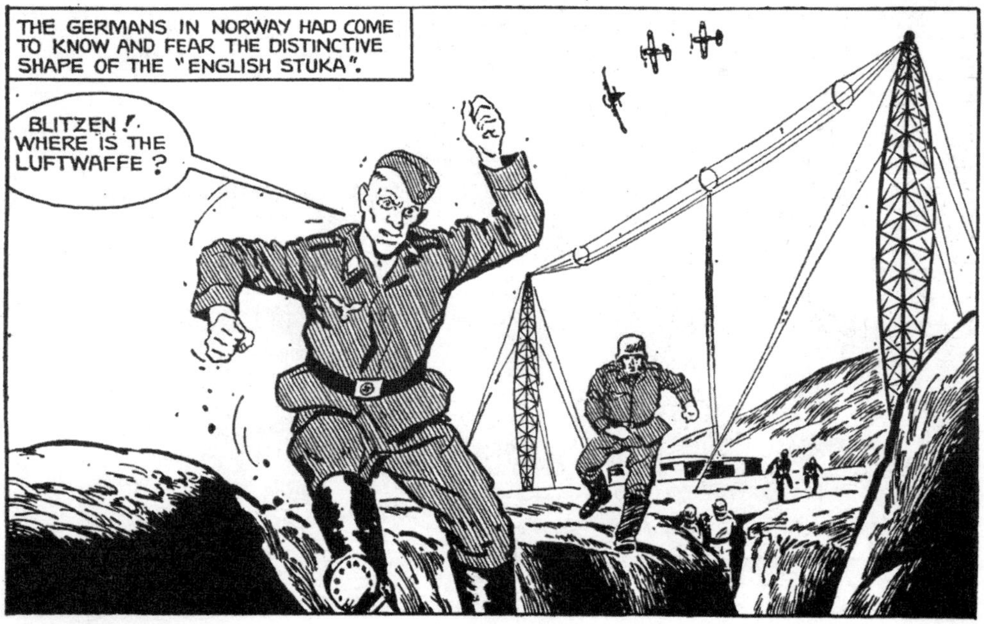
THE GERMANS IN NORWAY HAD COME TO KNOW AND FEAR THE DISTINCTIVE SHAPE OF THE "ENGLISH STUKA".
BLITZEN! WHERE IS THE LUFTWAFFE?

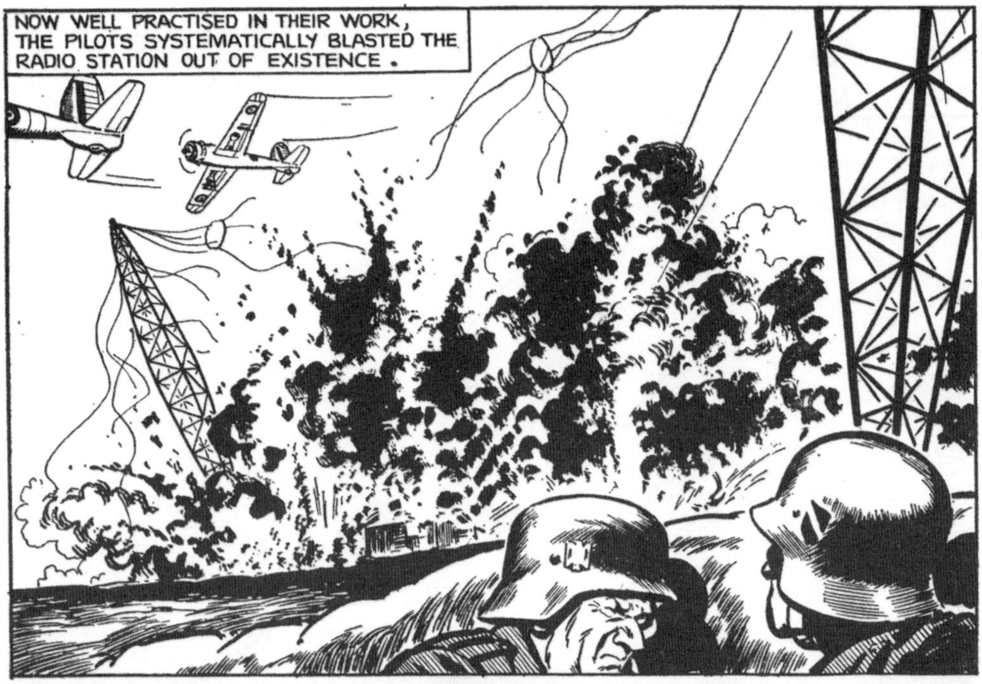
NOW WELL PRACTISED IN THEIR WORK, THE PILOTS SYSTEMATICALLY BLASTED THE RADIO STATION OUT OF EXISTENCE.

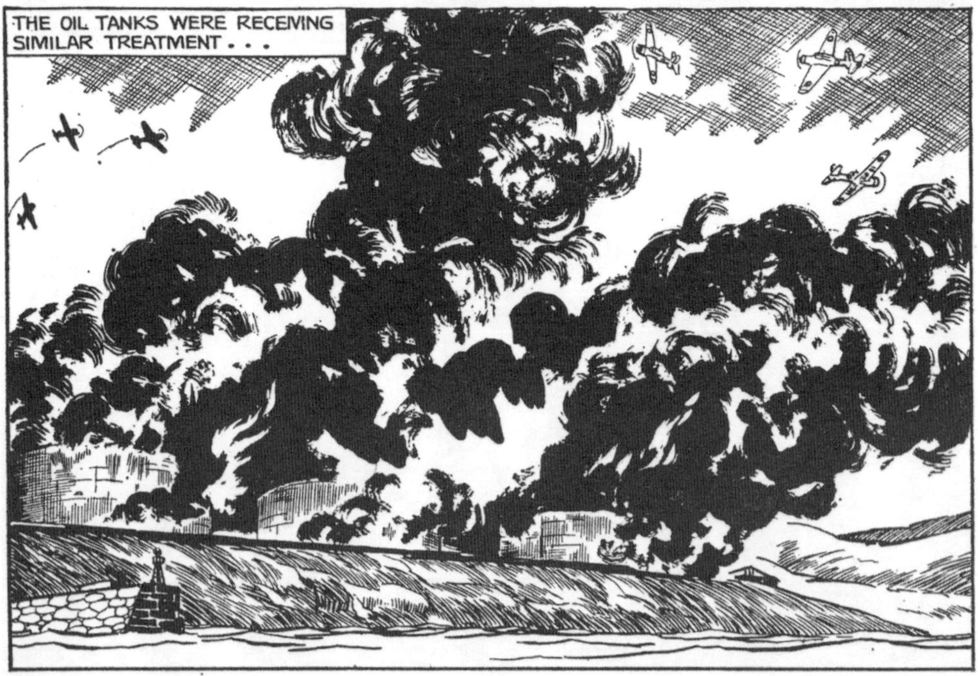
THE OIL TANKS WERE RECEIVING SIMILAR TREATMENT . . .

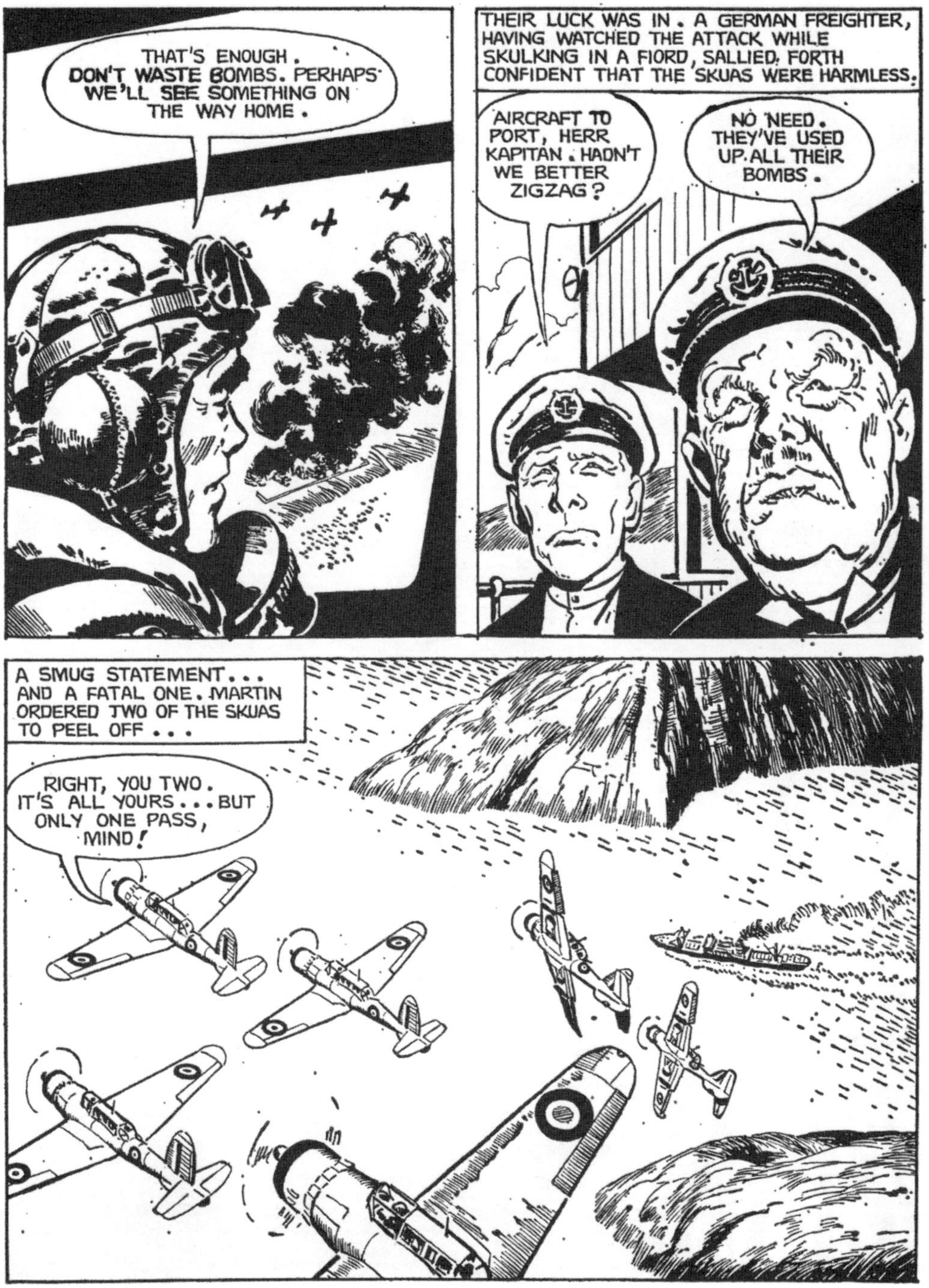
THAT'S ENOUGH. DON'T WASTE BOMBS. PERHAPS WE'LL SEE SOMETHING ON THE WAY HOME.
THEIR LUCK WAS IN. A GERMAN FREIGHTER, HAVING WATCHED THE ATTACK WHILE SKULKING IN A FIORD, SALLIED FORTH CONFIDENT THAT THE SKUAS WERE HARMLESS.
AIRCRAFT TO PORT, HERR KAPITAN. HADN'T WE BETTER ZIGZAG?
NO NEED. THEY'VE USED UP ALL THEIR BOMBS.
A SMUG STATEMENT... AND A FATAL ONE. MARTIN ORDERED TWO OF THE SKUAS TO PEEL OFF...
RIGHT, YOU TWO. IT'S ALL YOURS... BUT ONLY ONE PASS, MIND!

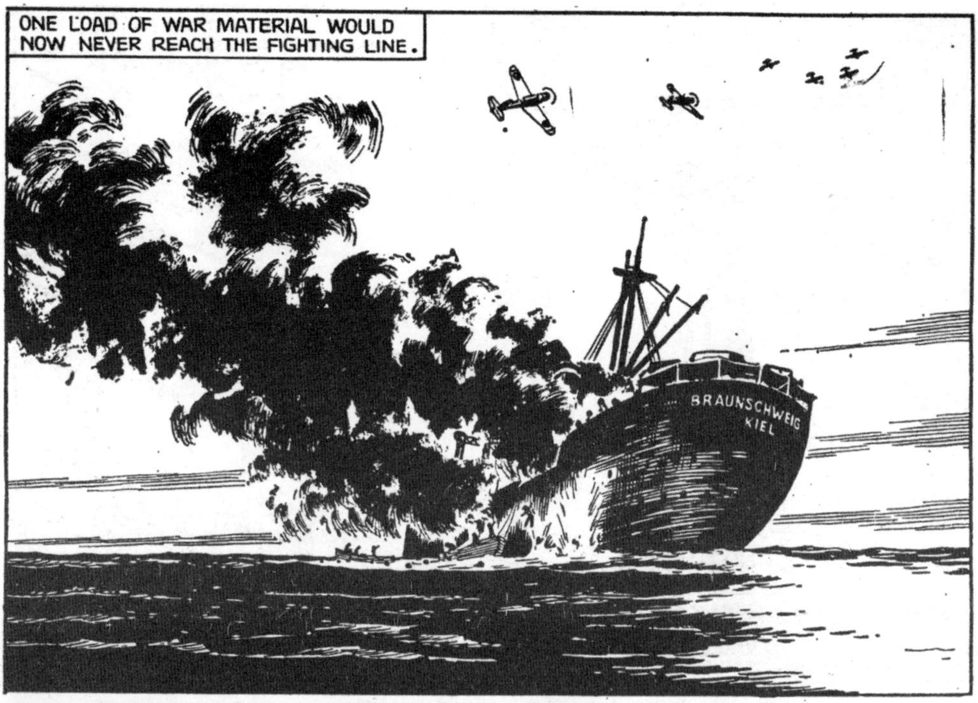
ONE LOAD OF WAR MATERIAL WOULD NOW NEVER REACH THE FIGHTING LINE.
BRAUNSCHWEIG KIEL

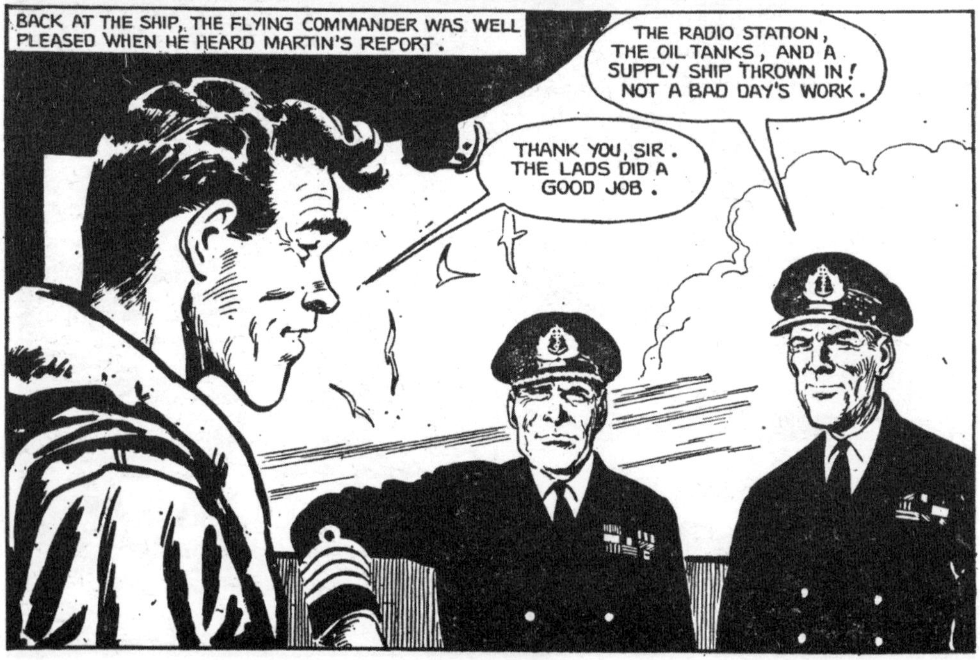
BACK AT THE SHIP, THE FLYING COMMANDER WAS WELL PLEASED WHEN HE HEARD MARTIN'S REPORT.
THE RADIO STATION, THE OIL TANKS, AND A SUPPLY SHIP THROWN IN! NOT A BAD DAY'S WORK.
THANK YOU, SIR. THE LADS DID A GOOD JOB.

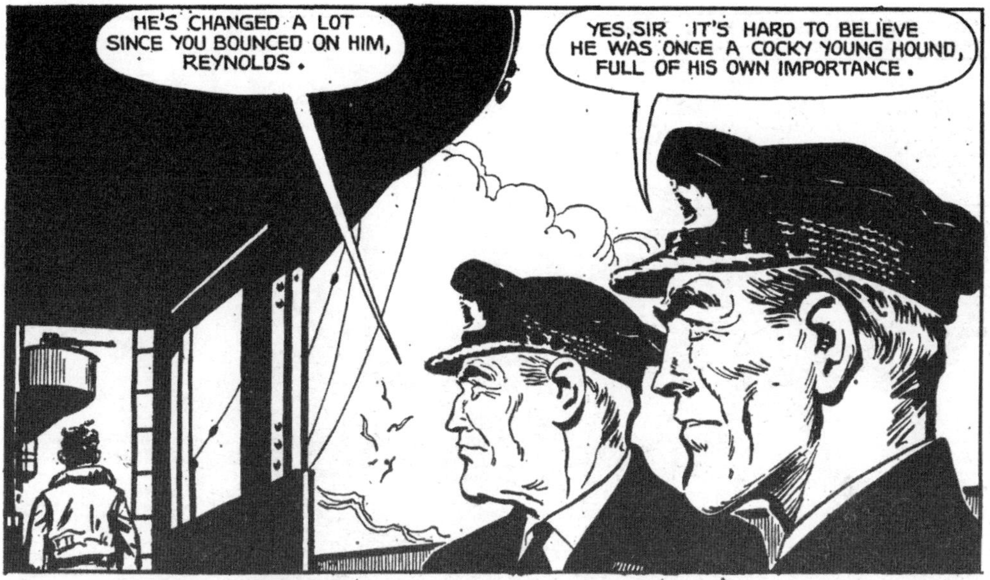
HE'S CHANGED A LOT SINCE YOU BOUNCED ON HIM, REYNOLDS.
YES, SIR. IT'S HARD TO BELIEVE HE WAS ONCE A COCKY YOUNG HOUND, FULL OF HIS OWN IMPORTANCE.

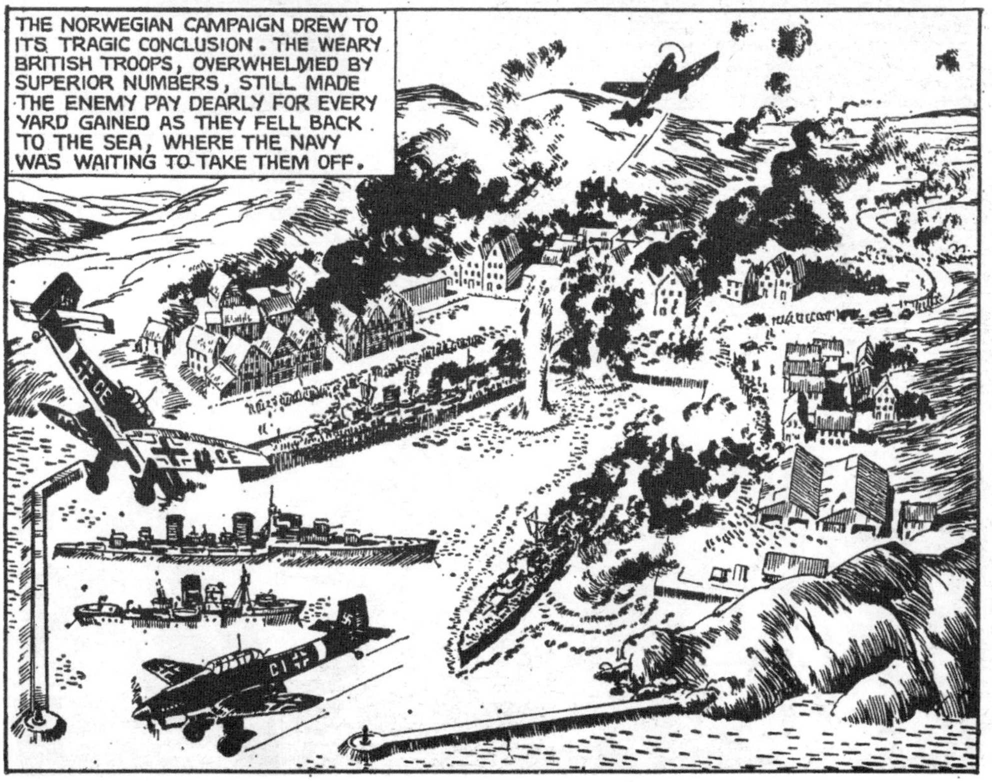
THE NORWEGIAN CAMPAIGN DREW TO ITS TRAGIC CONCLUSION. THE WEARY BRITISH TROOPS, OVERWHELMED BY SUPERIOR NUMBERS, STILL MADE THE ENEMY PAY DEARLY FOR EVERY YARD GAINED AS THEY FELL BACK TO THE SEA, WHERE THE NAVY WAS WAITING TO TAKE THEM OFF.

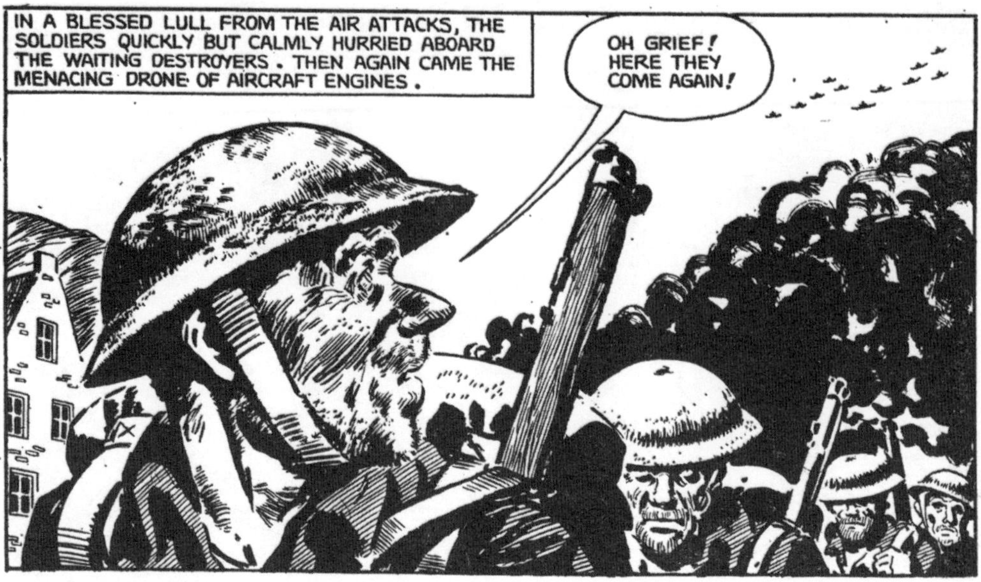
IN A BLESSED LULL FROM THE AIR ATTACKS, THE SOLDIERS QUICKLY BUT CALMLY HURRIED ABOARD THE WAITING DESTROYERS. THEN AGAIN CAME THE MENACING DRONE OF AIRCRAFT ENGINES.
OH GRIEF! HERE THEY COME AGAIN!

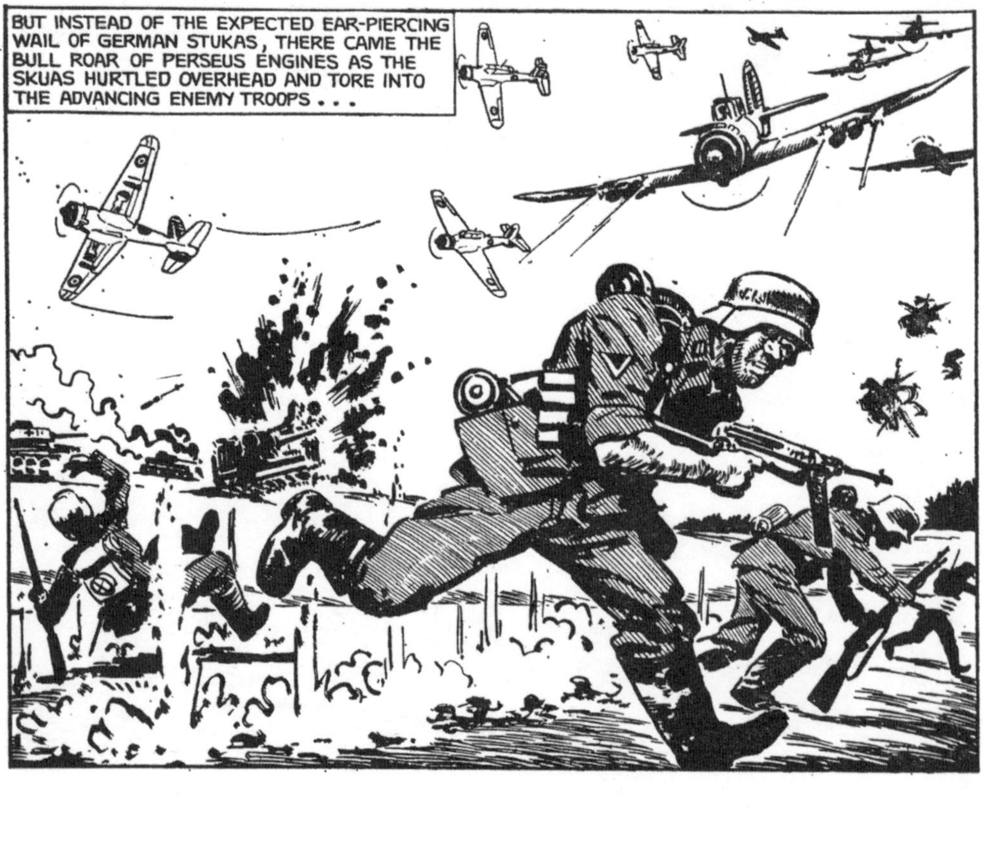
BUT INSTEAD OF THE EXPECTED EAR-PIERCING WAIL OF GERMAN STUKAS, THERE CAME THE BULL ROAR OF PERSEUS ENGINES AS THE SKUAS HURTLED OVERHEAD AND TORE INTO THE ADVANCING ENEMY TROOPS...

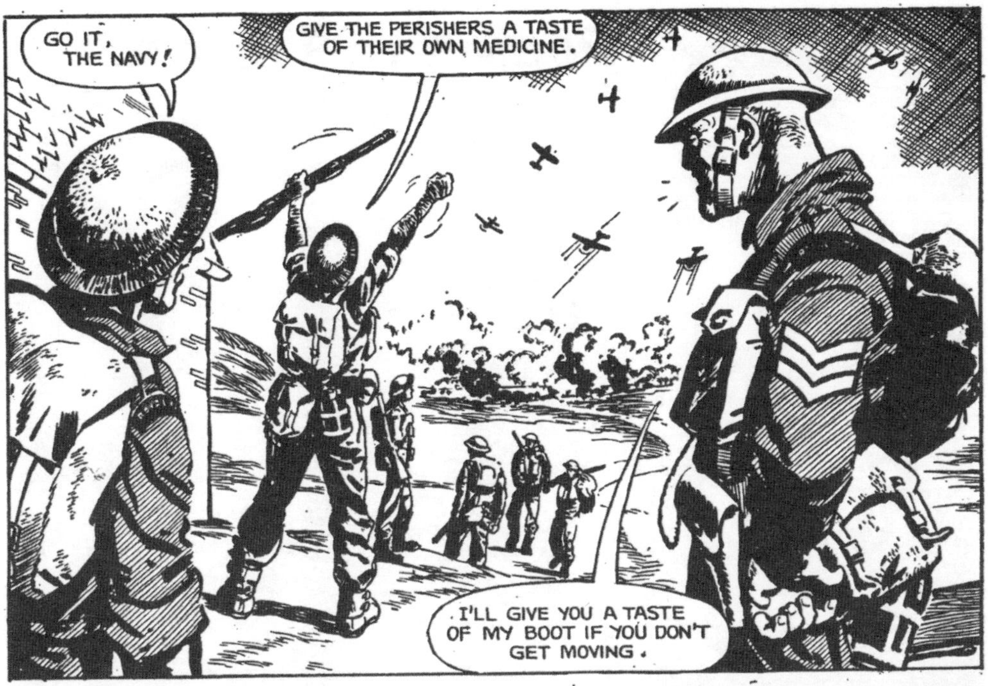
GO IT, THE NAVY!
GIVE THE PERISHERS A TASTE OF THEIR OWN MEDICINE.
I'LL GIVE YOU A TASTE OF MY BOOT IF YOU DON'T GET MOVING.

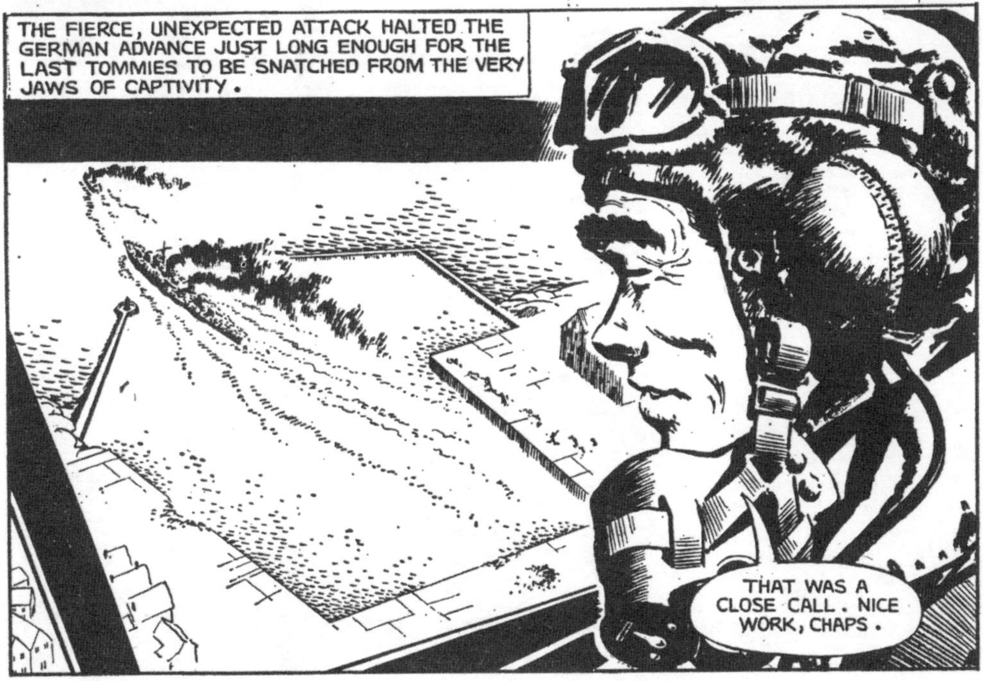
THE FIERCE, UNEXPECTED ATTACK HALTED THE GERMAN ADVANCE JUST LONG ENOUGH FOR THE LAST TOMMIES TO BE SNATCHED FROM THE VERY JAWS OF CAPTIVITY.
THAT WAS A CLOSE CALL. NICE WORK, CHAPS.

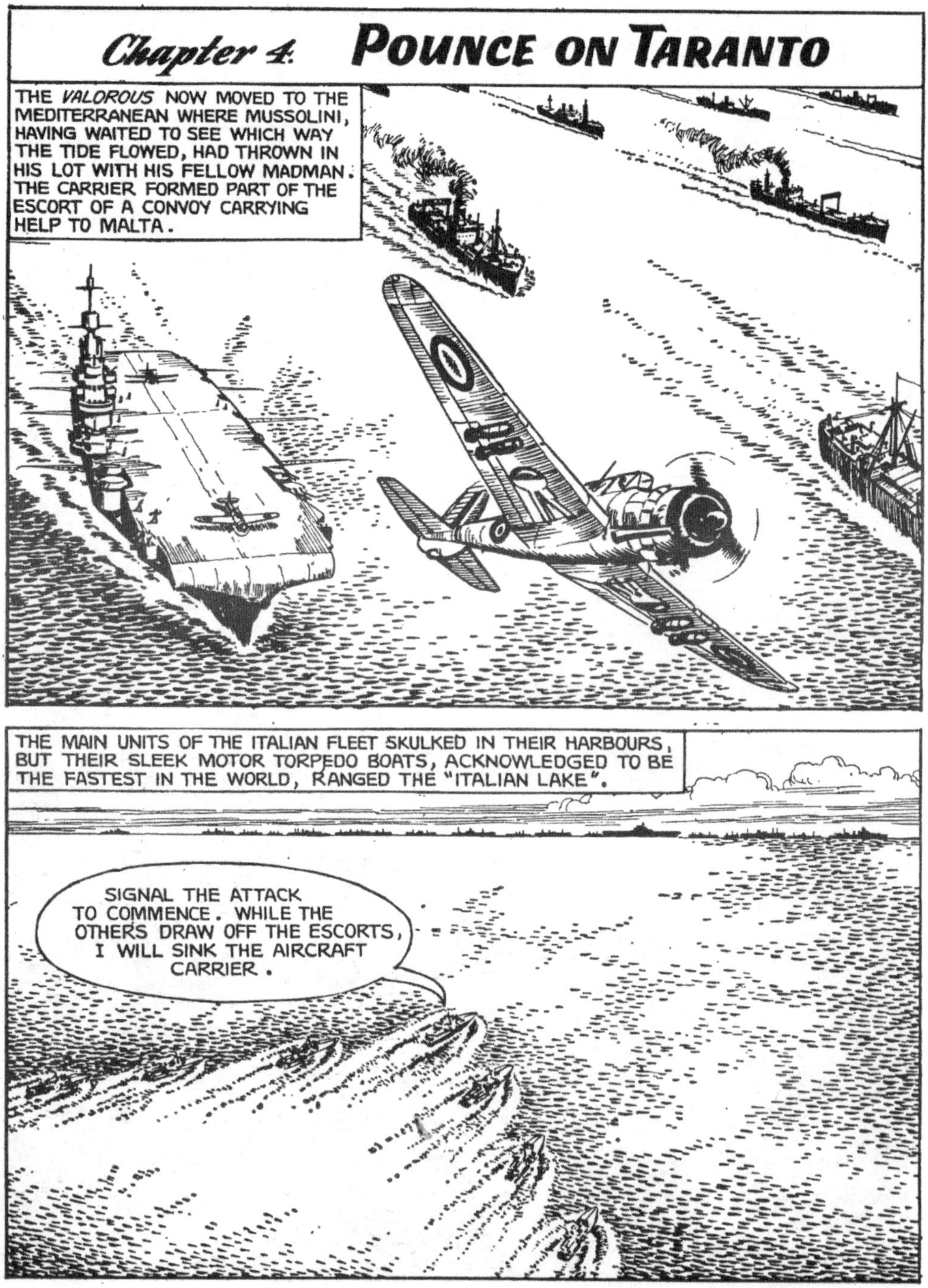
Chapter 4: POUNCE ON TARANTO
THE VALOROUS NOW MOVED TO THE MEDITERRANEAN WHERE MUSSOLINI, HAVING WAITED TO SEE WHICH WAY THE TIDE FLOWED, HAD THROWN IN HIS LOT WITH HIS FELLOW MADMAN. THE CARRIER FORMED PART OF THE ESCORT OF A CONVOY CARRYING HELP TO MALTA.
THE MAIN UNITS OF THE ITALIAN FLEET SKULKED IN THEIR HARBOURS, BUT THEIR SLEEK MOTOR TORPEDO BOATS, ACKNOWLEDGED TO BE THE FASTEST IN THE WORLD, RANGED THE "ITALIAN LAKE".
SIGNAL THE ATTACK TO COMMENCE. WHILE THE OTHERS DRAW OFF THE ESCORTS, I WILL SINK THE AIRCRAFT CARRIER.

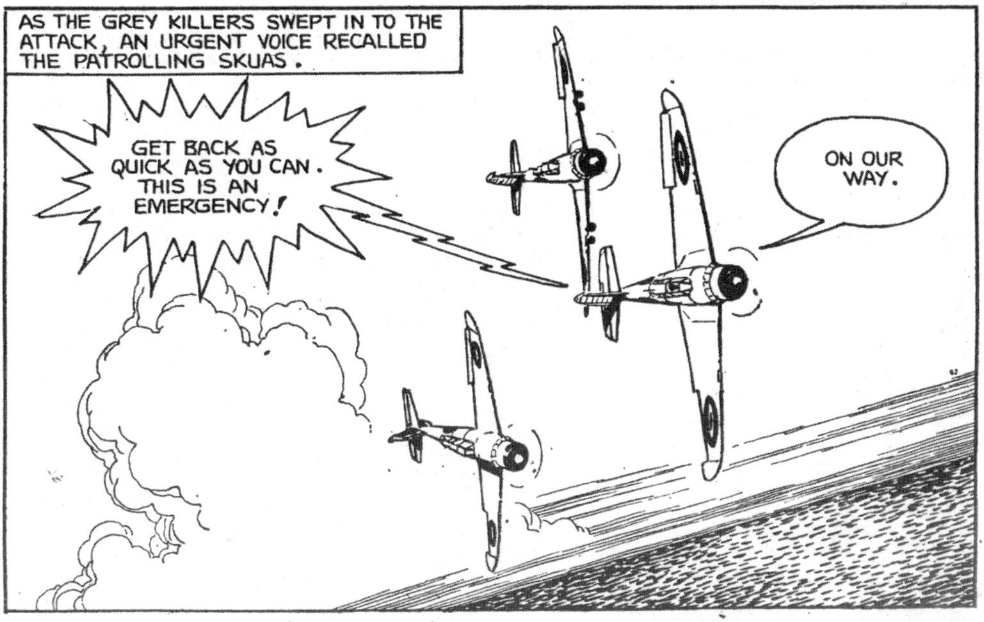
AS THE GREY KILLERS SWEPT IN TO THE ATTACK, AN URGENT VOICE RECALLED THE PATROLLING SKUAS.
GET BACK AS QUICK AS YOU CAN. THIS IS AN EMERGENCY!
ON OUR WAY.

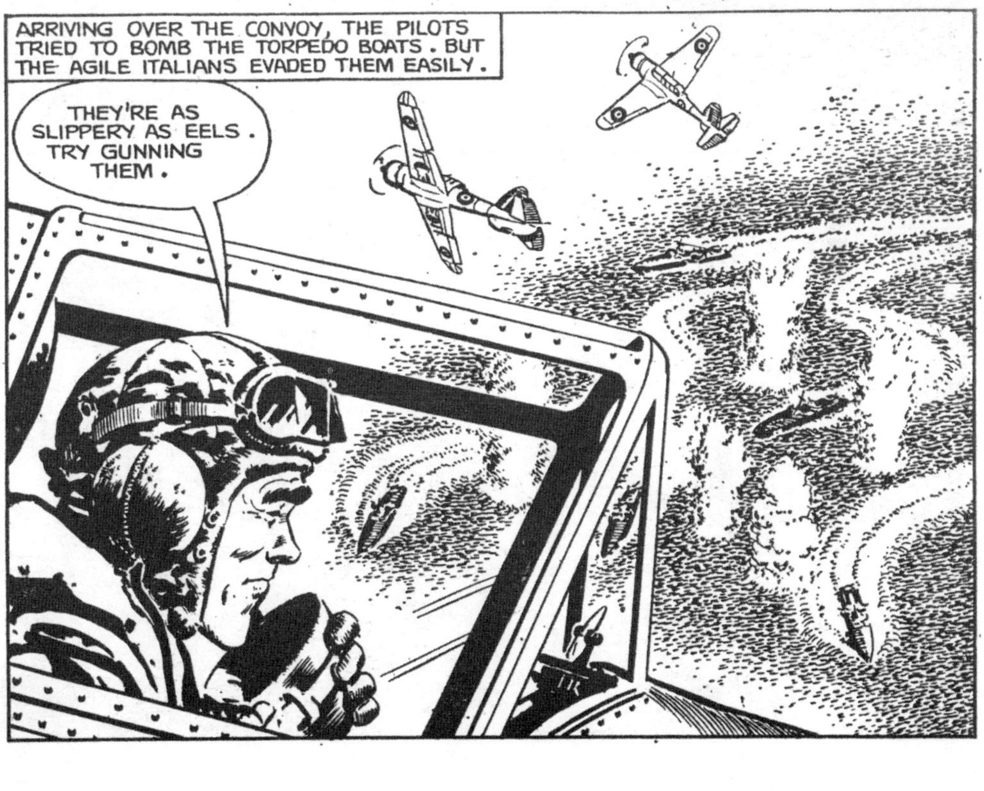
ARRIVING OVER THE CONVOY, THE PILOTS TRIED TO BOMB THE TORPEDO BOATS. BUT THE AGILE ITALIANS EVADED THEM EASILY.
THEY'RE AS SLIPPERY AS EELS. TRY GUNNING THEM.

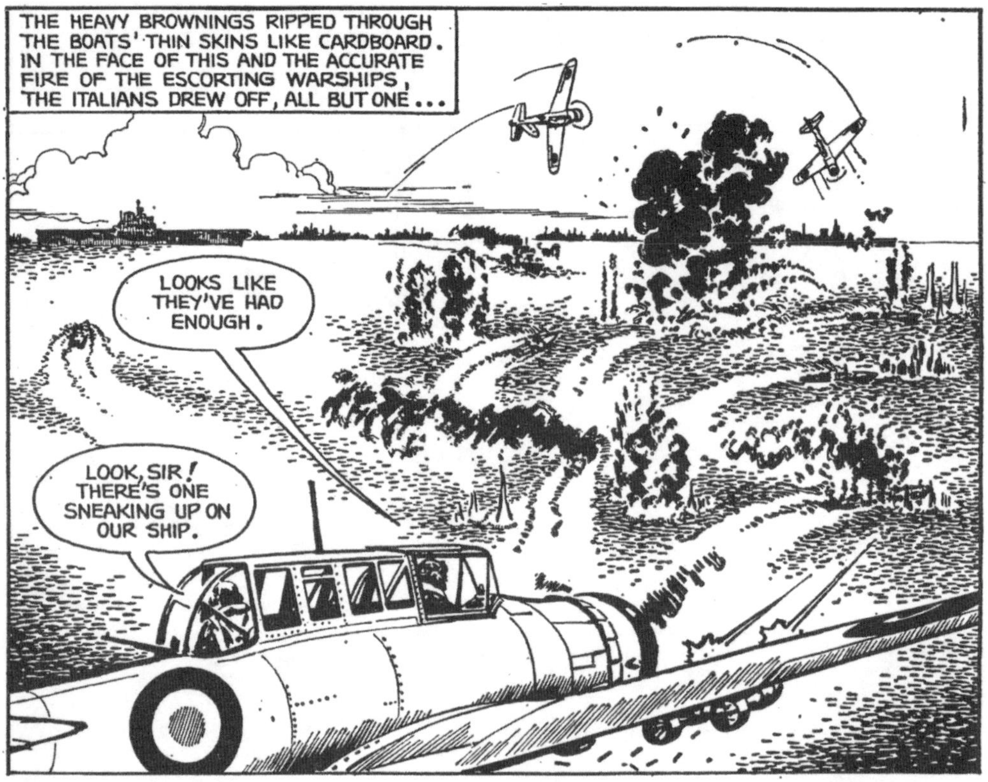
THE HEAVY BROWNINGS RIPPED THROUGH THE BOATS' THIN SKINS LIKE CARDBOARD. IN THE FACE OF THIS AND THE ACCURATE FIRE OF THE ESCORTING WARSHIPS, THE ITALIANS DREW OFF, ALL BUT ONE...
LOOKS LIKE THEY'VE HAD ENOUGH.
LOOK, SIR! THERE'S ONE SNEAKING UP ON OUR SHIP.

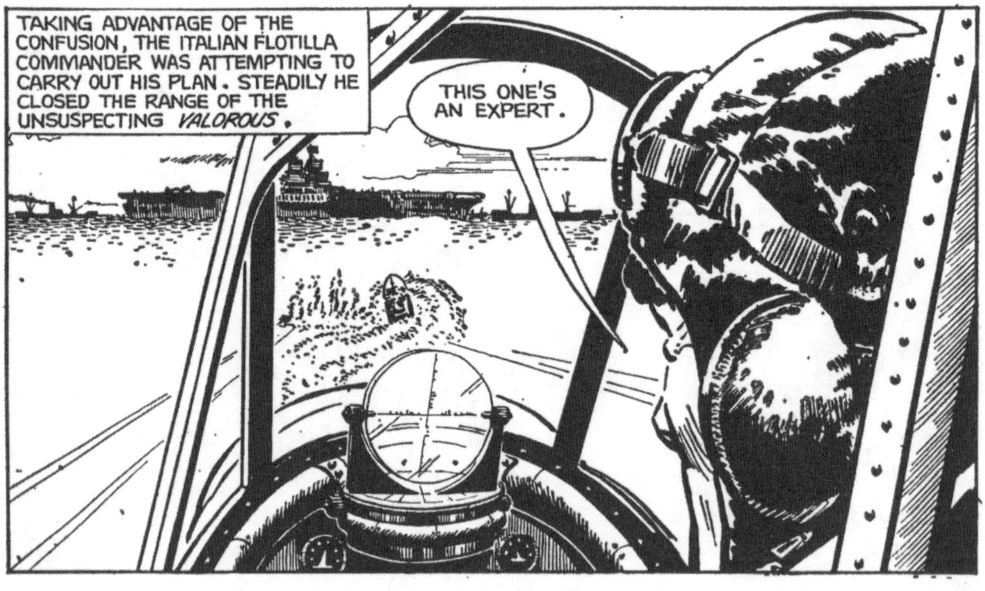
TAKING ADVANTAGE OF THE CONFUSION, THE ITALIAN FLOTILLA COMMANDER WAS ATTEMPTING TO CARRY OUT HIS PLAN. STEADILY HE CLOSED THE RANGE OF THE UNSUSPECTING *VALOROUS*.
THIS ONE'S AN EXPERT.

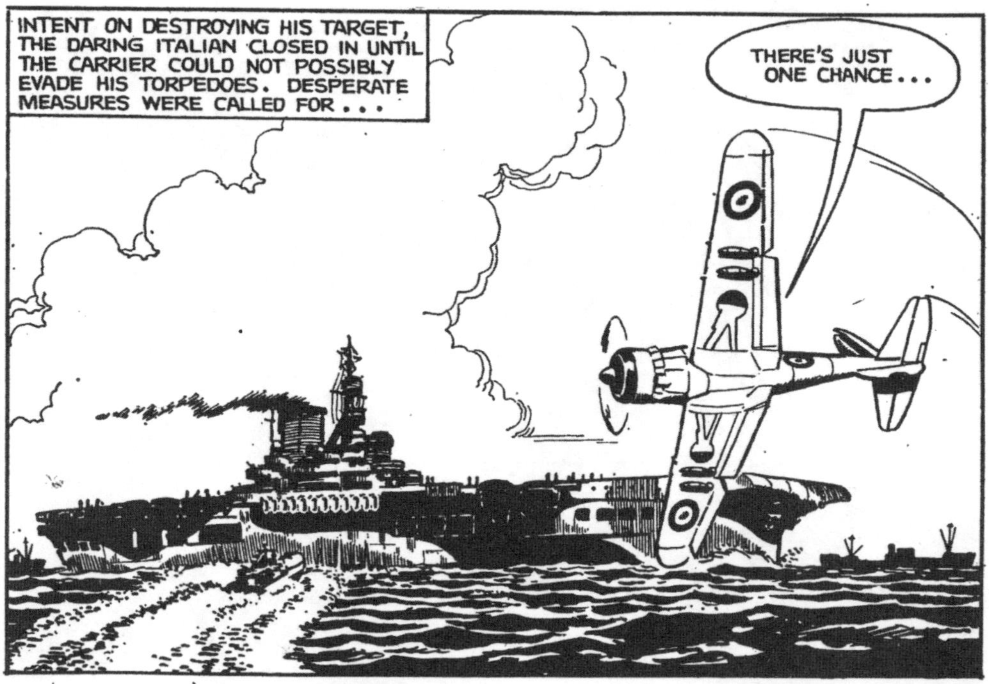
INTENT ON DESTROYING HIS TARGET, THE DARING ITALIAN CLOSED IN UNTIL THE CARRIER COULD NOT POSSIBLY EVADE HIS TORPEDOES. DESPERATE MEASURES WERE CALLED FOR...
THERE'S JUST ONE CHANCE...

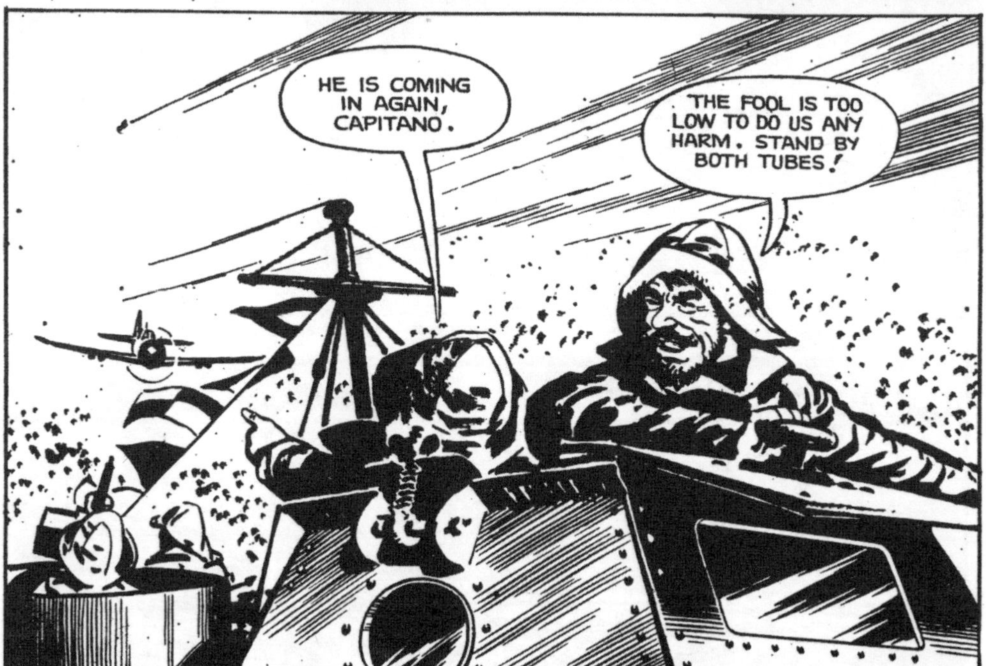
HE IS COMING IN AGAIN, CAPITANO.
THE FOOL IS TOO LOW TO DO US ANY HARM. STAND BY BOTH TUBES!

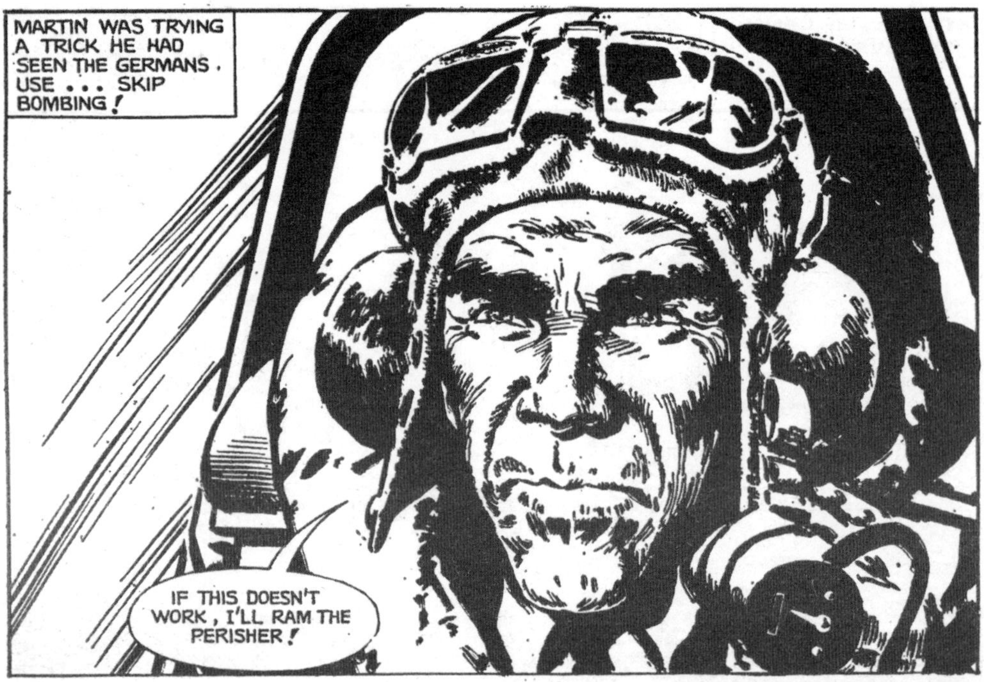
MARTIN WAS TRYING A TRICK HE HAD SEEN THE GERMANS USE ... SKIP BOMBING!
IF THIS DOESN'T WORK, I'LL RAM THE PERISHER!

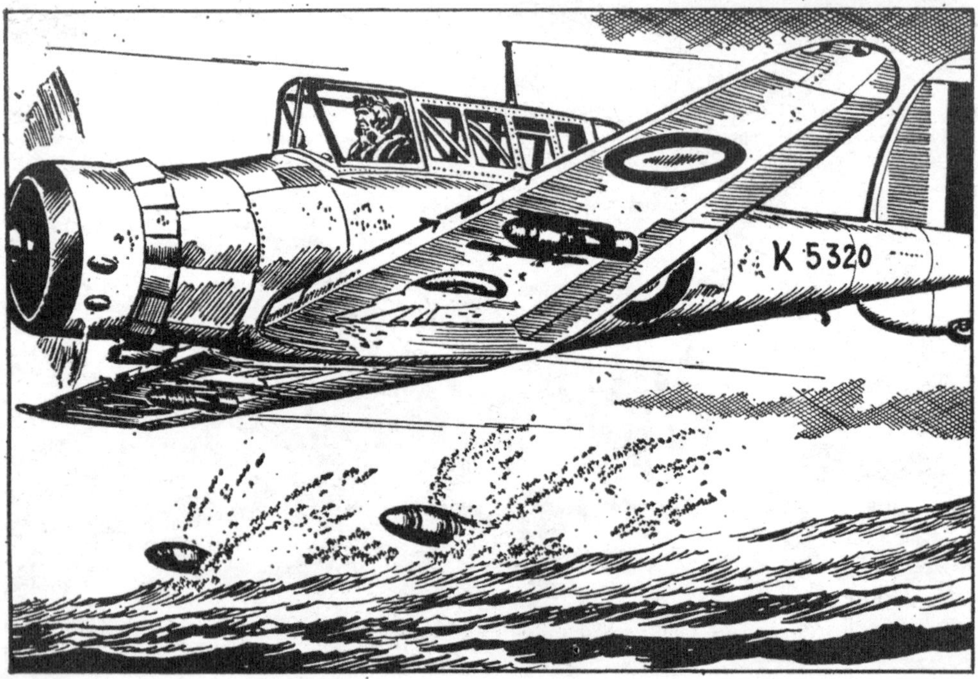
K 5320

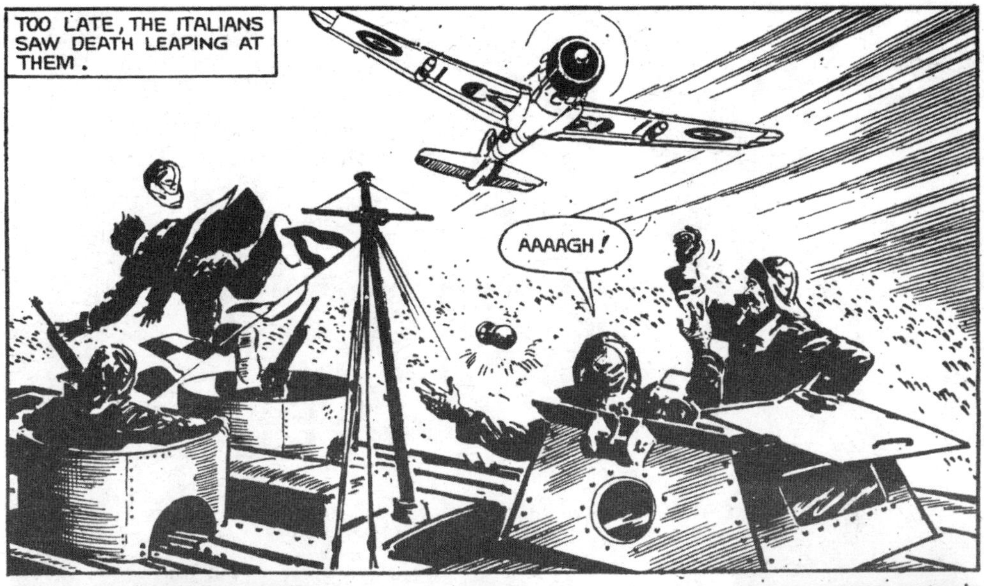
TOO LATE, THE ITALIANS SAW DEATH LEAPING AT THEM.
AAAAGH!

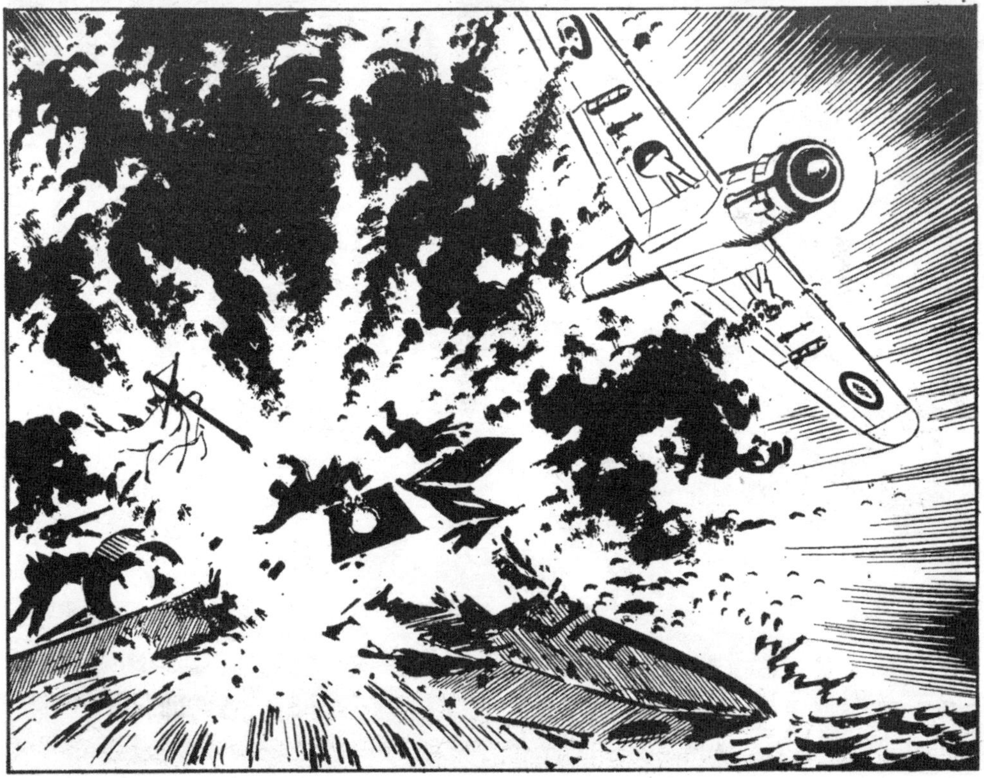

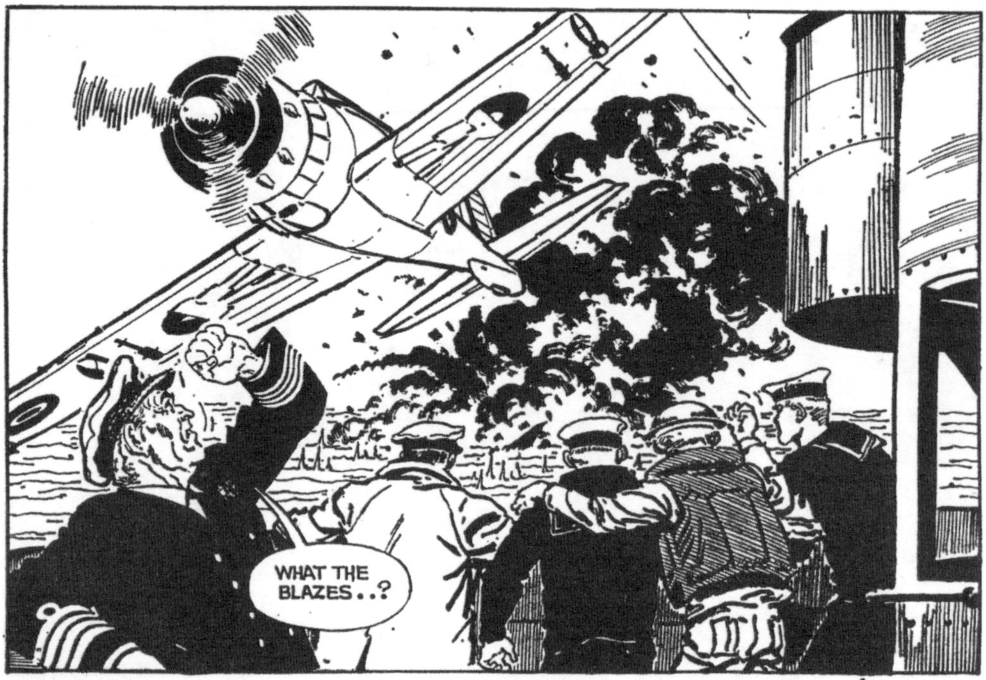
WHAT THE BLAZES..?

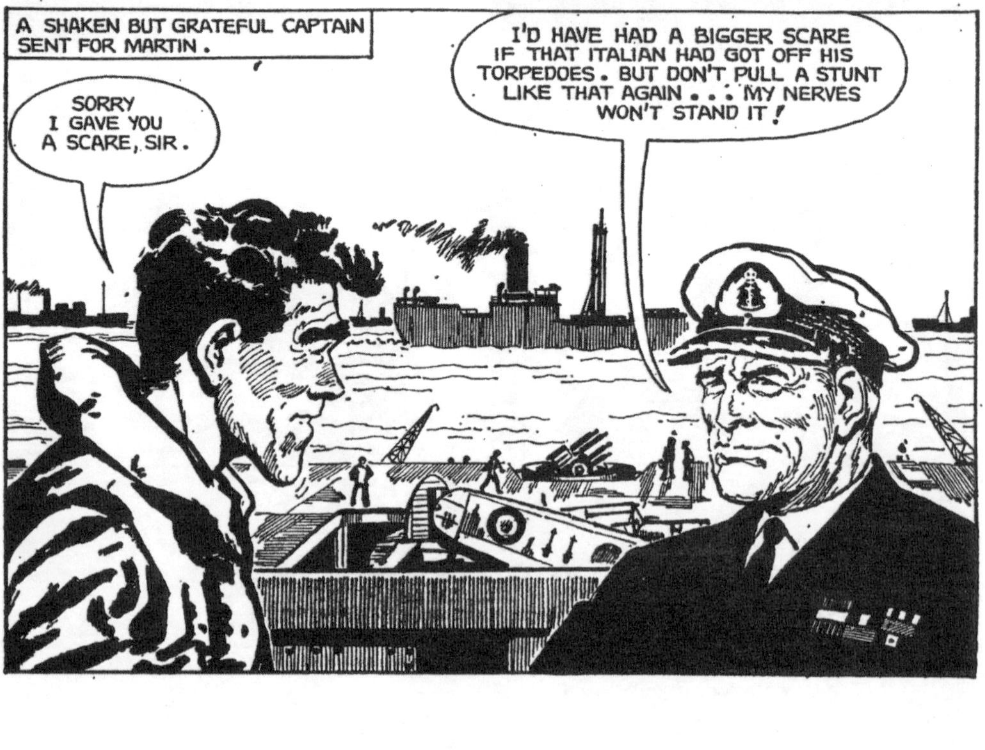
A SHAKEN BUT GRATEFUL CAPTAIN SENT FOR MARTIN.
SORRY I GAVE YOU A SCARE, SIR.
I'D HAVE HAD A BIGGER SCARE IF THAT ITALIAN HAD GOT OFF HIS TORPEDOES. BUT DON'T PULL A STUNT LIKE THAT AGAIN... MY NERVES WON'T STAND IT!

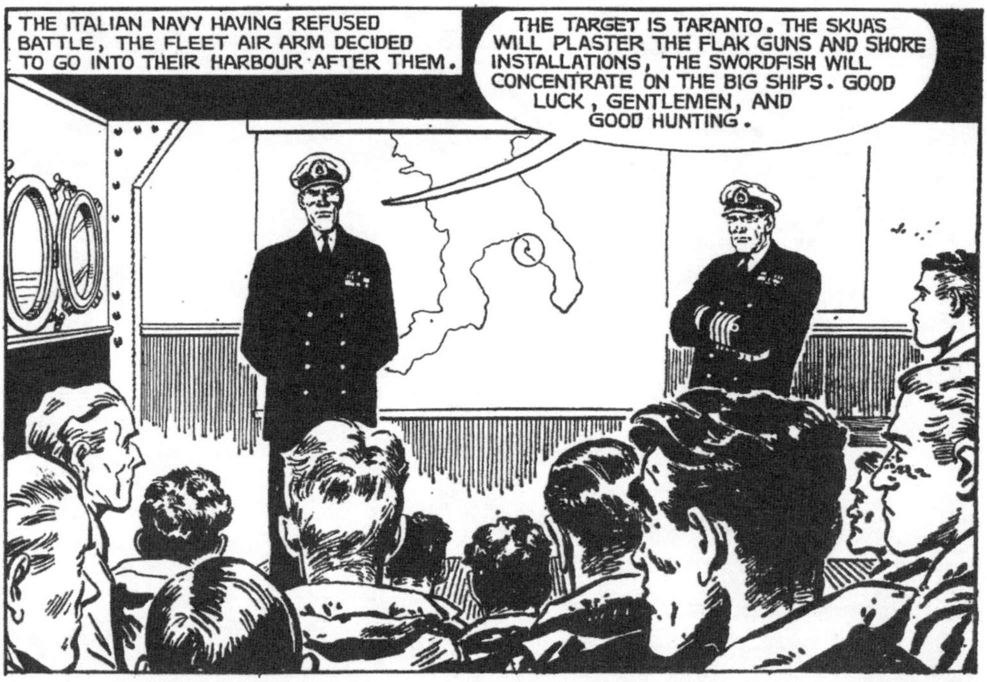
THE ITALIAN NAVY HAVING REFUSED BATTLE, THE FLEET AIR ARM DECIDED TO GO INTO THEIR HARBOUR AFTER THEM.
THE TARGET IS TARANTO. THE SKUAS WILL PLASTER THE FLAK GUNS AND SHORE INSTALLATIONS, THE SWORDFISH WILL CONCENTRATE ON THE BIG SHIPS. GOOD LUCK, GENTLEMEN, AND GOOD HUNTING.

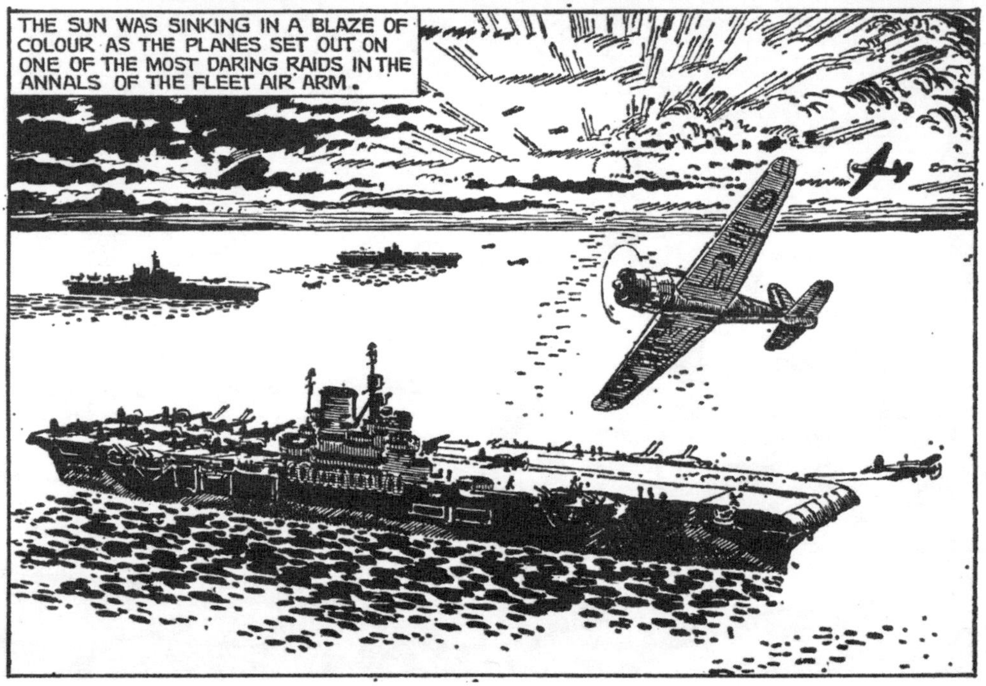
THE SUN WAS SINKING IN A BLAZE OF COLOUR AS THE PLANES SET OUT ON ONE OF THE MOST DARING RAIDS IN THE ANNALS OF THE FLEET AIR ARM.

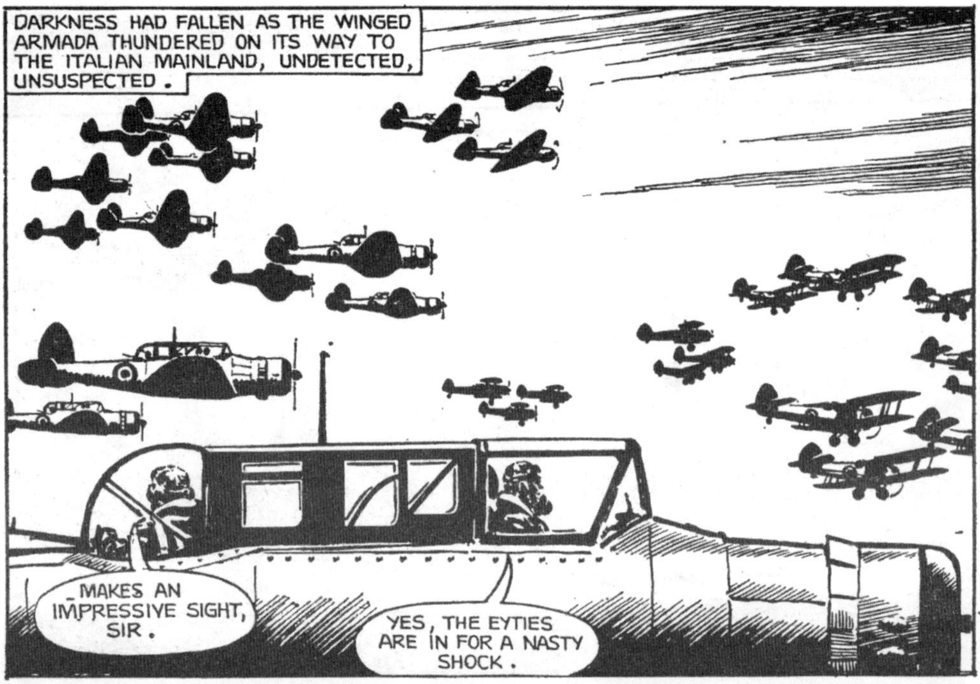
DARKNESS HAD FALLEN AS THE WINGED ARMADA THUNDERED ON ITS WAY TO THE ITALIAN MAINLAND, UNDETECTED, UNSUSPECTED.
_MAKES AN IMPRESSIVE SIGHT, SIR.
YES, THE EYTIES ARE IN FOR A NASTY SHOCK.

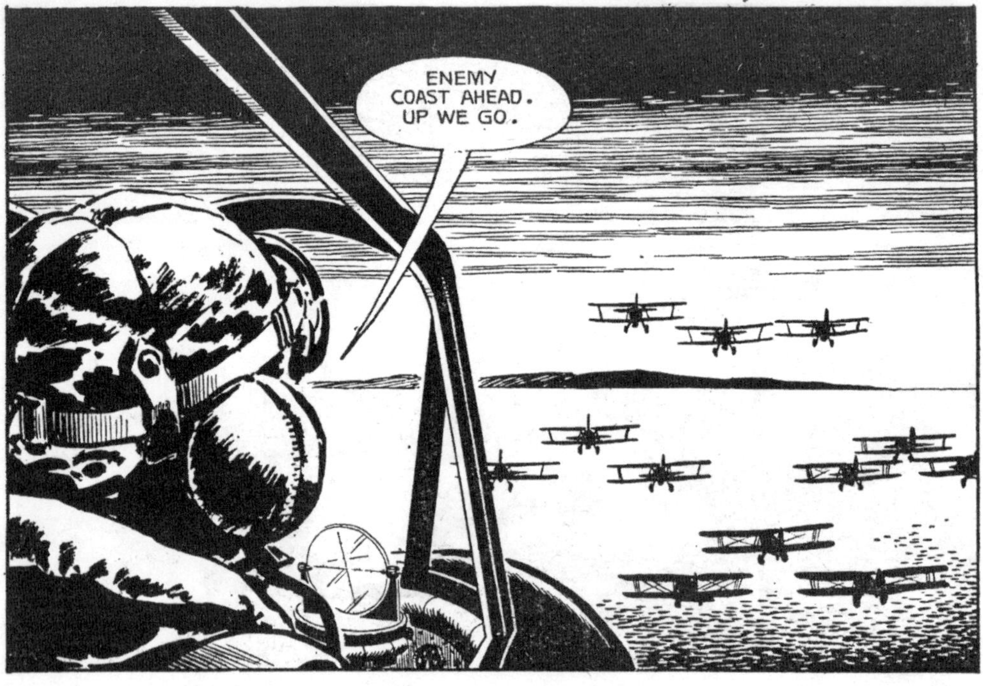
ENEMY COAST AHEAD. UP WE GO.

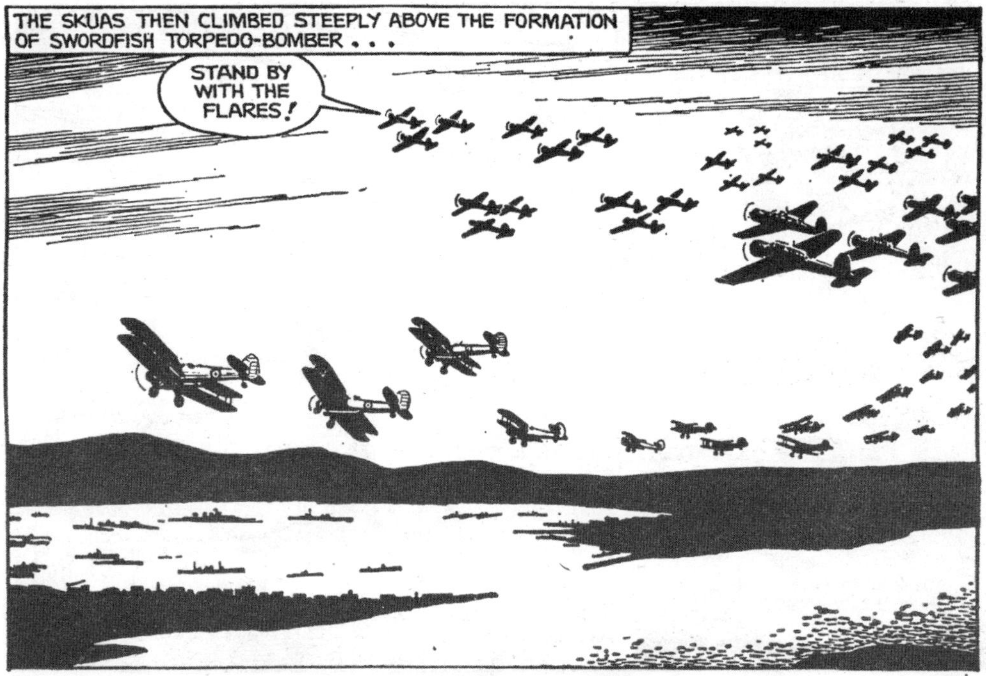
THE SKUAS THEN CLIMBED STEEPLY ABOVE THE FORMATION OF SWORDFISH TORPEDO-BOMBER . . .
STAND BY WITH THE FLARES!

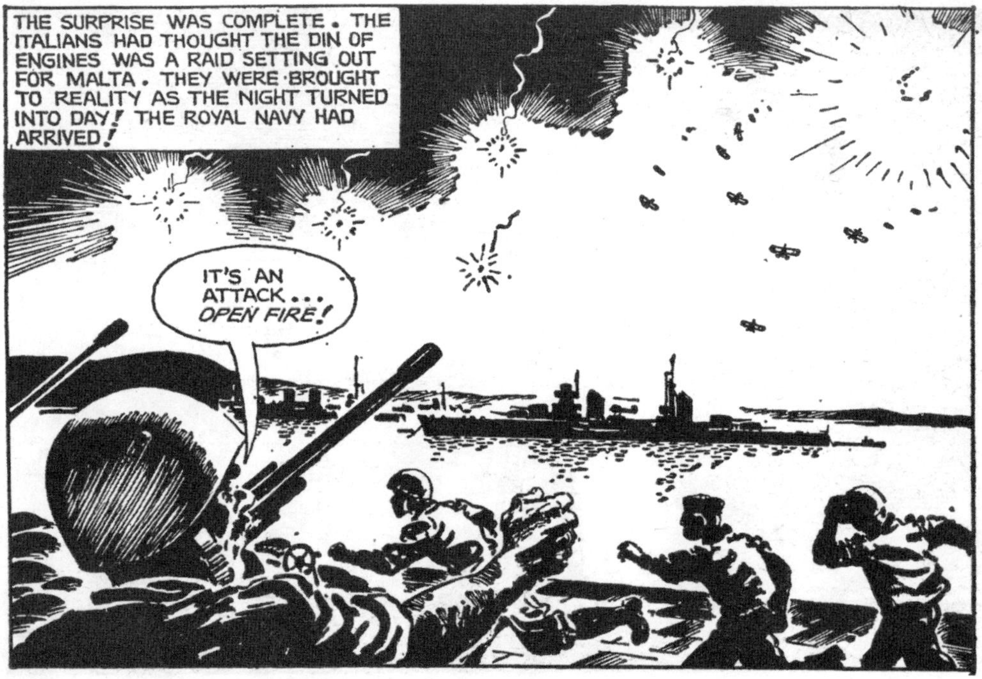
THE SURPRISE WAS COMPLETE. THE ITALIANS HAD THOUGHT THE DIN OF ENGINES WAS A RAID SETTING OUT FOR MALTA. THEY WERE BROUGHT TO REALITY AS THE NIGHT TURNED INTO DAY! THE ROYAL NAVY HAD ARRIVED!
IT'S AN ATTACK... *OPEN FIRE!*

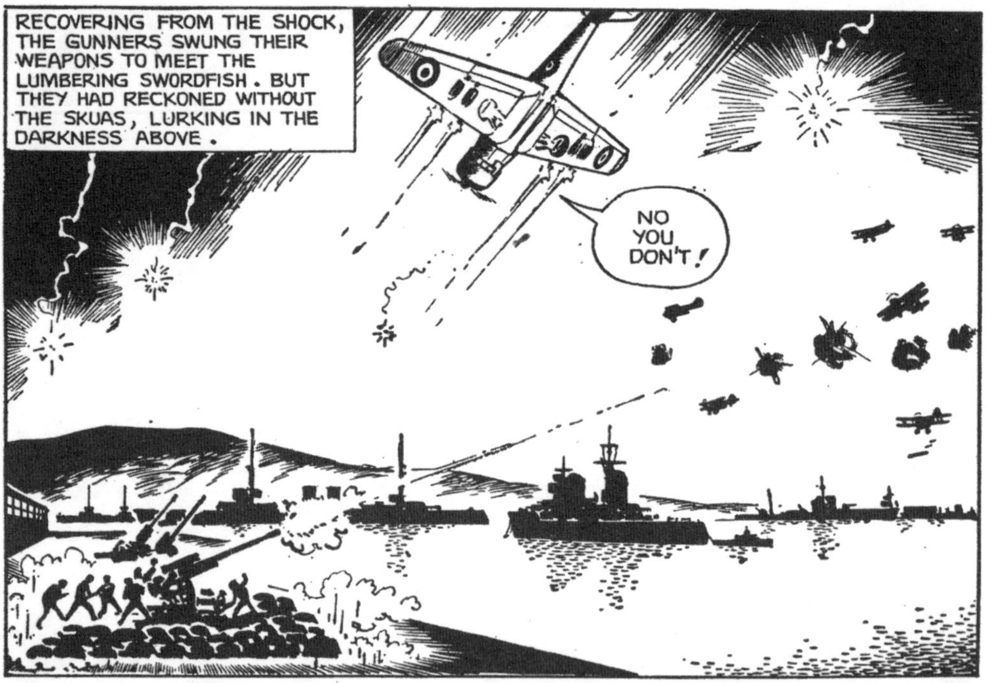
RECOVERING FROM THE SHOCK, THE GUNNERS SWUNG THEIR WEAPONS TO MEET THE LUMBERING SWORDFISH. BUT THEY HAD RECKONED WITHOUT THE SKUAS, LURKING IN THE DARKNESS ABOVE.
NO YOU DON'T!

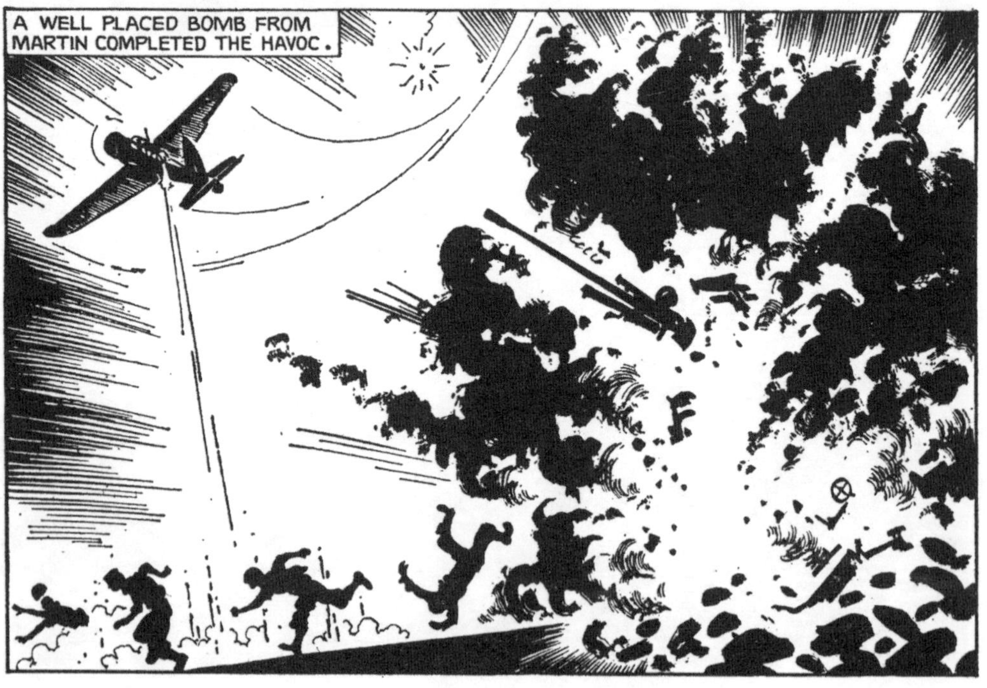
A WELL PLACED BOMB FROM MARTIN COMPLETED THE HAVOC.

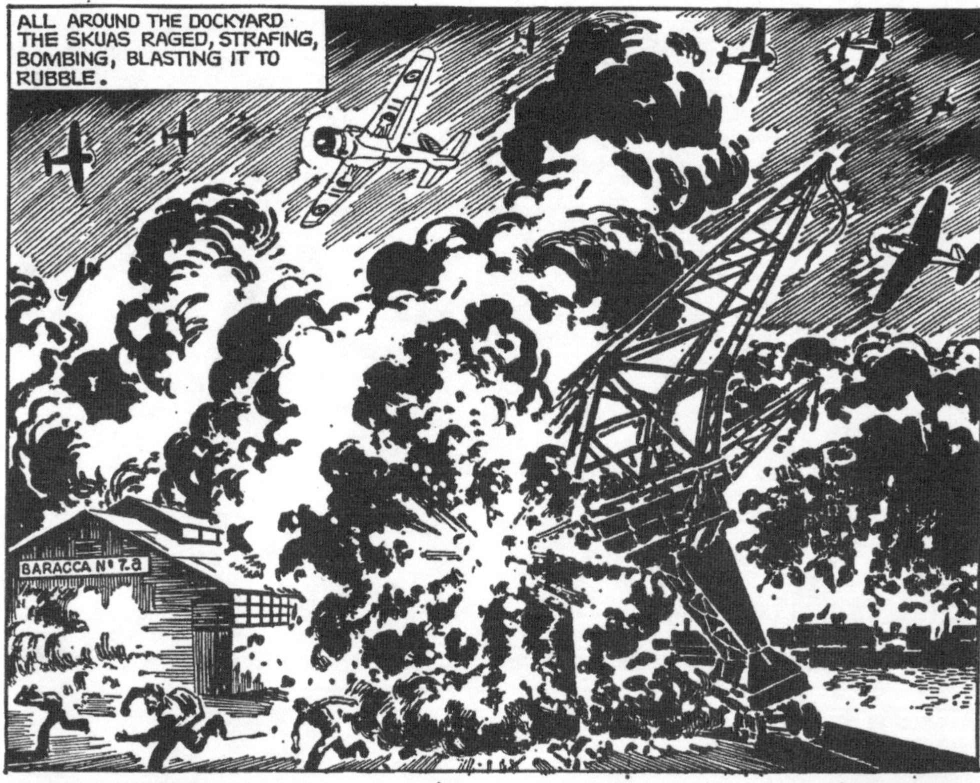
ALL AROUND THE DOCKYARD THE SKUAS RAGED, STRAFING, BOMBING, BLASTING IT TO RUBBLE.
BARACCA Nº 7.a

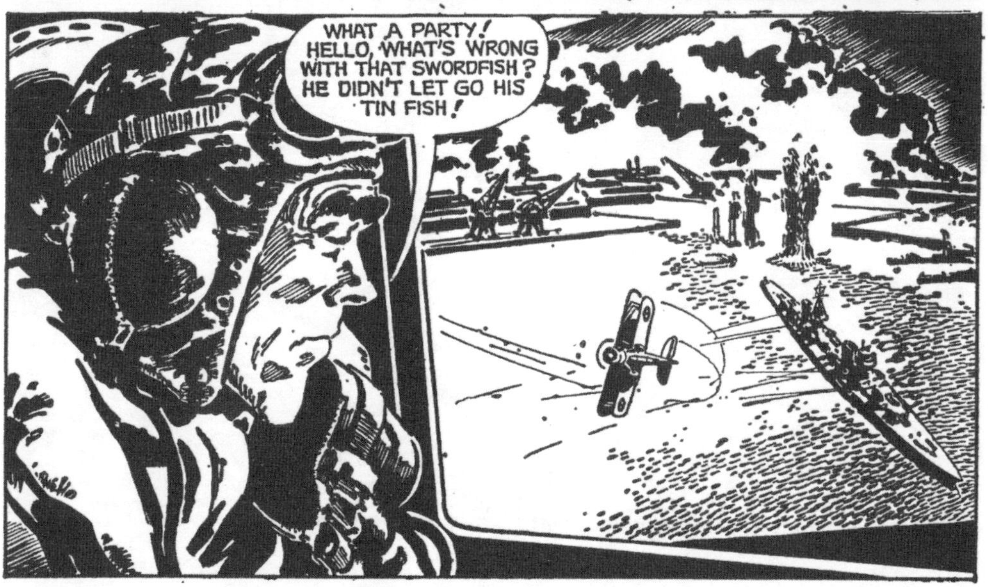
WHAT A PARTY! HELLO, WHAT'S WRONG WITH THAT SWORDFISH? HE DIDN'T LET GO HIS TIN FISH!

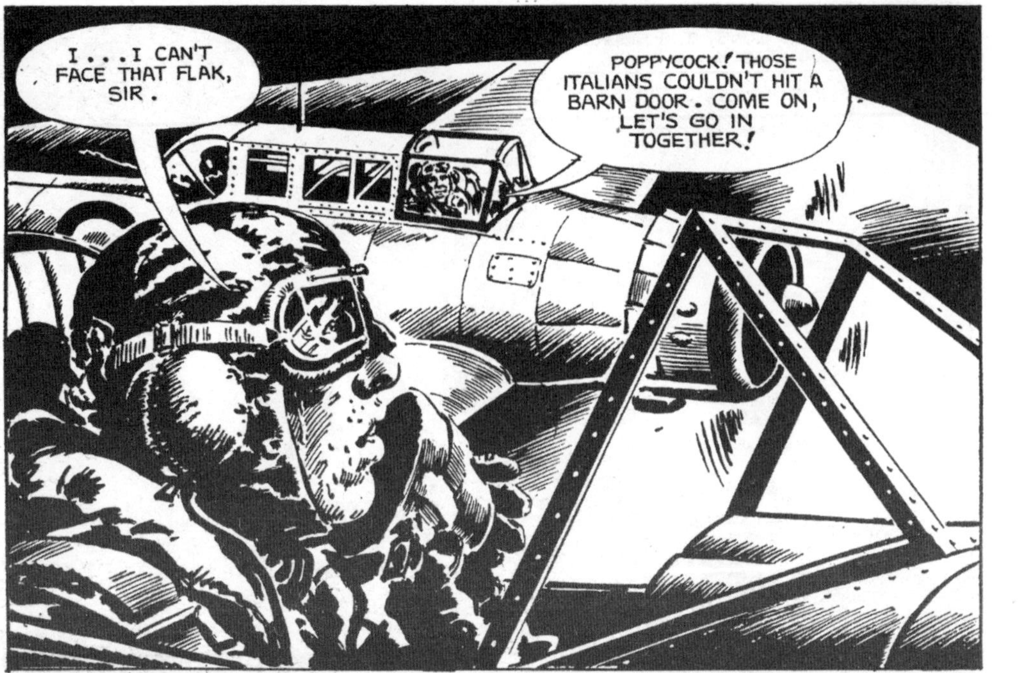
I . . . I CAN'T FACE THAT FLAK, SIR.
POPPYCOCK! THOSE ITALIANS COULDN'T HIT A BARN DOOR. COME ON, LET'S GO IN TOGETHER!

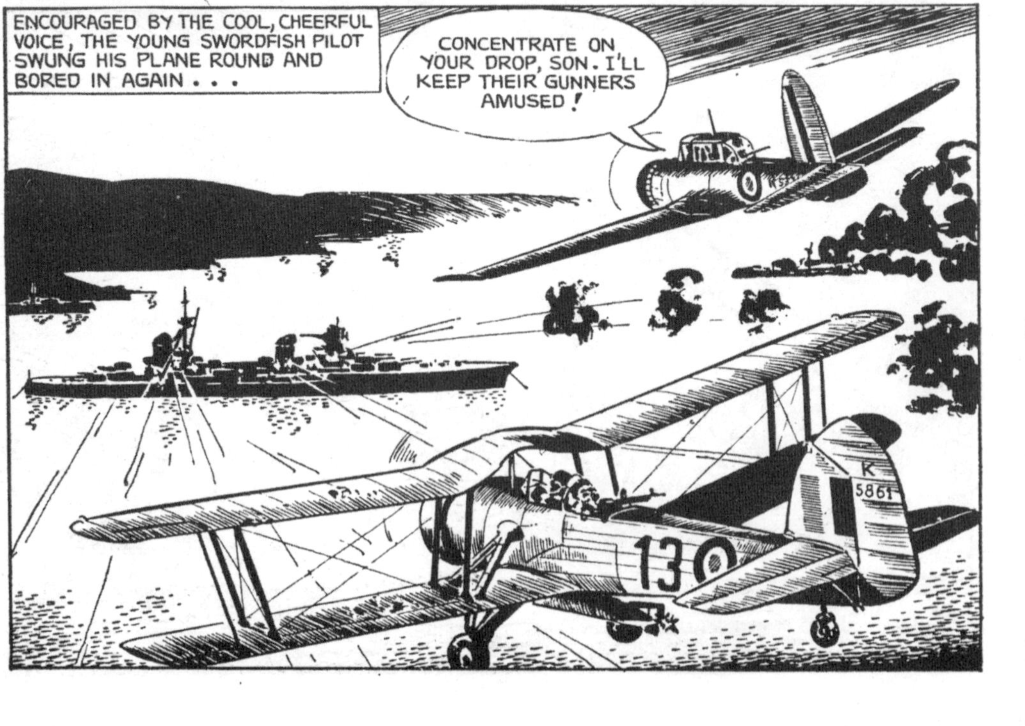
ENCOURAGED BY THE COOL, CHEERFUL VOICE, THE YOUNG SWORDFISH PILOT SWUNG HIS PLANE ROUND AND BORED IN AGAIN . . .
CONCENTRATE ON YOUR DROP, SON. I'LL KEEP THEIR GUNNERS AMUSED!
K 5861
13

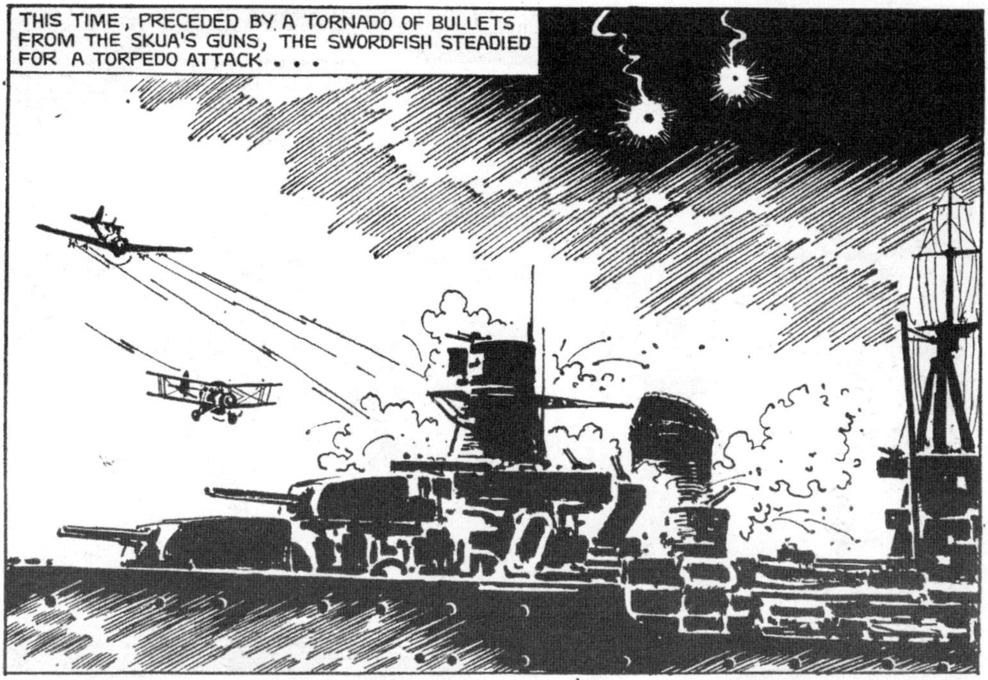
THIS TIME, PRECEDED BY A TORNADO OF BULLETS FROM THE SKUA'S GUNS, THE SWORDFISH STEADIED FOR A TORPEDO ATTACK . . .

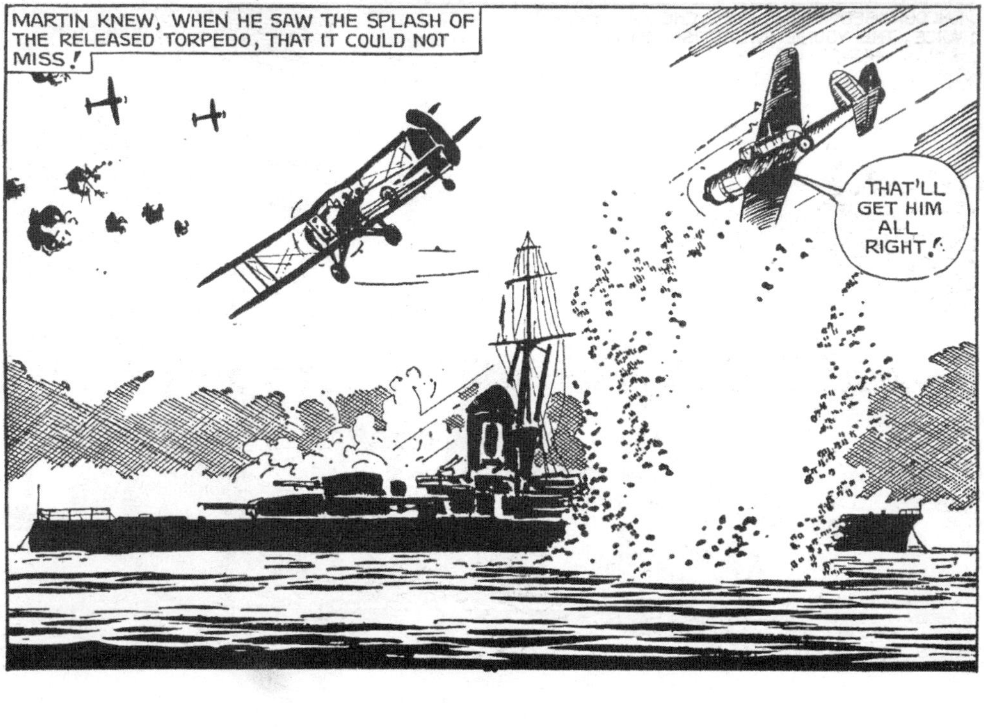
MARTIN KNEW, WHEN HE SAW THE SPLASH OF THE RELEASED TORPEDO, THAT IT COULD NOT MISS!
THAT'LL GET HIM ALL RIGHT!

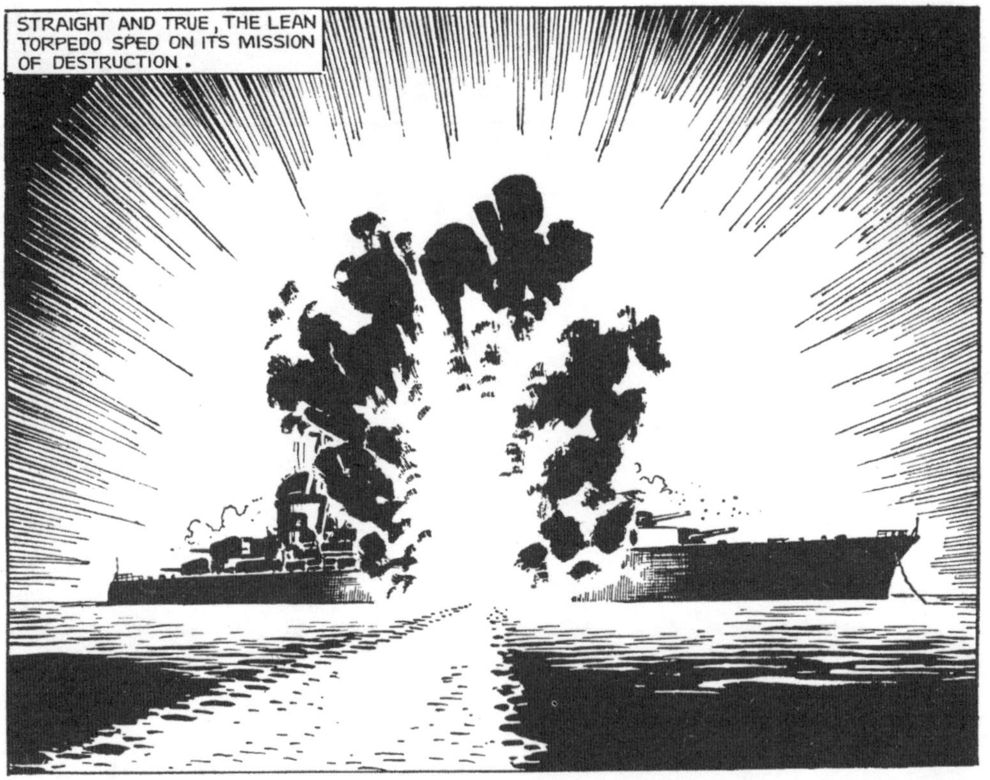
STRAIGHT AND TRUE, THE LEAN TORPEDO SPED ON ITS MISSION OF DESTRUCTION.

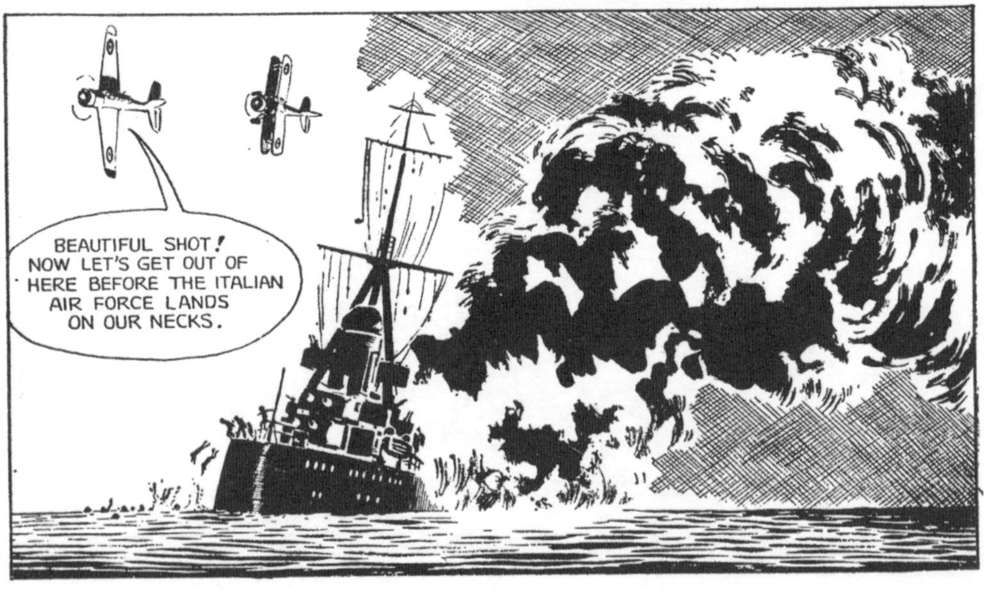
BEAUTIFUL SHOT! NOW LET'S GET OUT OF HERE BEFORE THE ITALIAN AIR FORCE LANDS ON OUR NECKS.

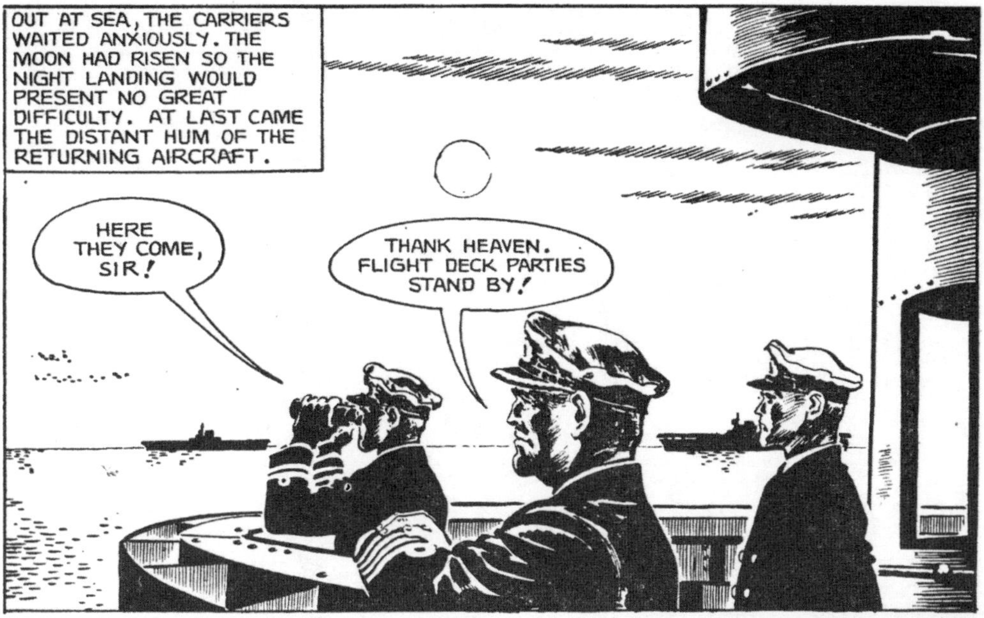
OUT AT SEA, THE CARRIERS WAITED ANXIOUSLY. THE MOON HAD RISEN SO THE NIGHT LANDING WOULD PRESENT NO GREAT DIFFICULTY. AT LAST CAME THE DISTANT HUM OF THE RETURNING AIRCRAFT.
HERE THEY COME, SIR!
THANK HEAVEN. FLIGHT DECK PARTIES STAND BY!

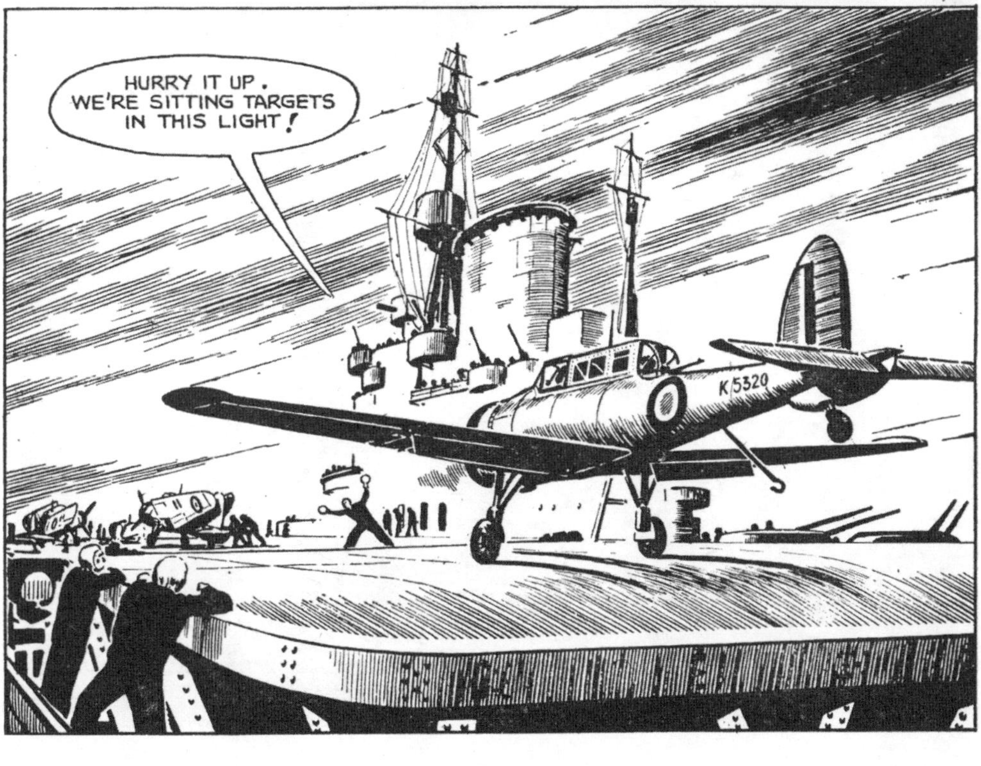
HURRY IT UP. WE'RE SITTING TARGETS IN THIS LIGHT!
K5320

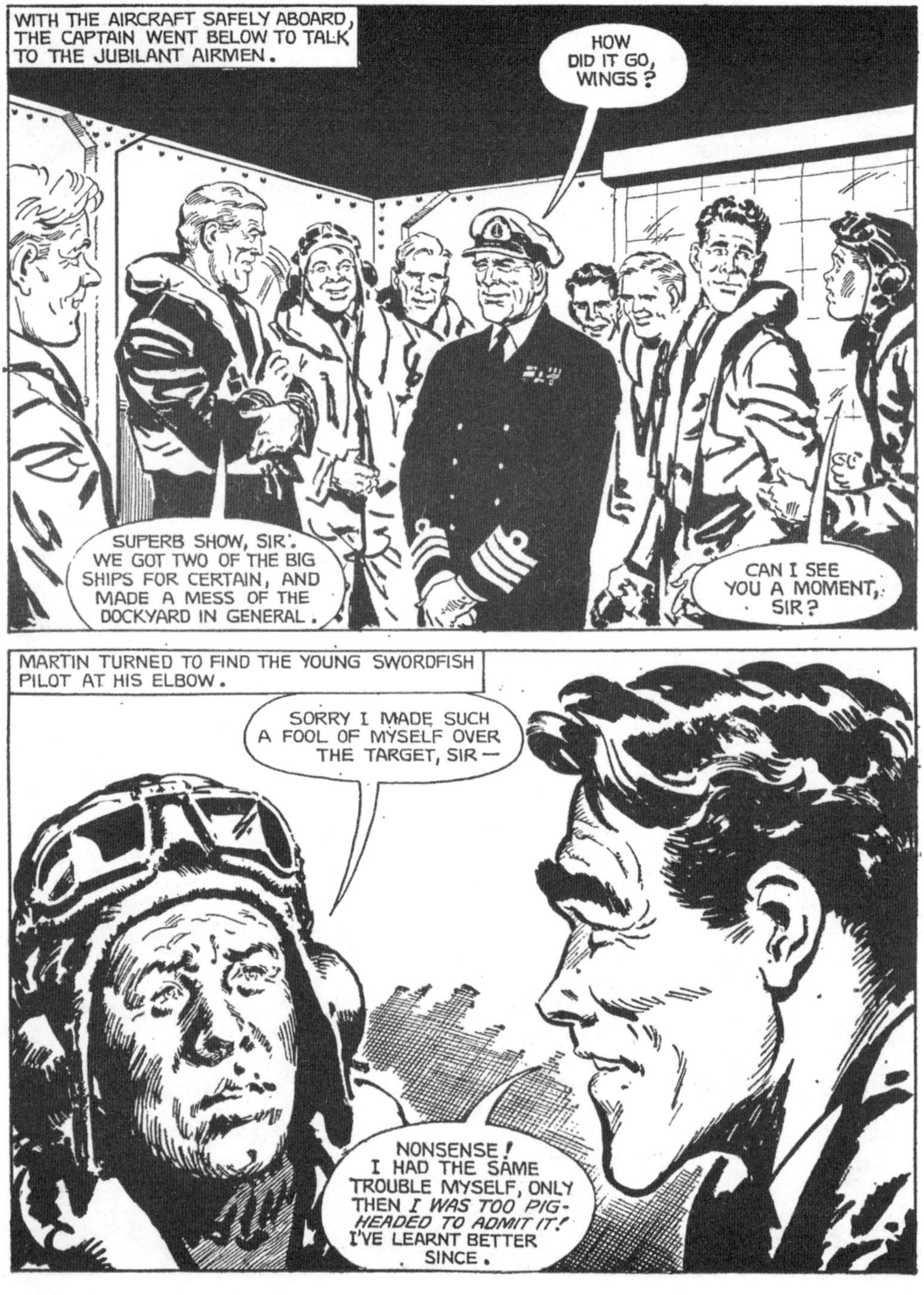
WITH THE AIRCRAFT SAFELY ABOARD, THE CAPTAIN WENT BELOW TO TALK TO THE JUBILANT AIRMEN.
HOW DID IT GO, WINGS?
SUPERB SHOW, SIR. WE GOT TWO OF THE BIG SHIPS FOR CERTAIN, AND MADE A MESS OF THE DOCKYARD IN GENERAL.
CAN I SEE YOU A MOMENT, SIR?
MARTIN TURNED TO FIND THE YOUNG SWORDFISH PILOT AT HIS ELBOW.
SORRY I MADE SUCH A FOOL OF MYSELF OVER THE TARGET, SIR —
NONSENSE! I HAD THE SAME TROUBLE MYSELF, ONLY THEN *I WAS TOO PIG-HEADED TO ADMIT IT!* I'VE LEARNT BETTER SINCE.

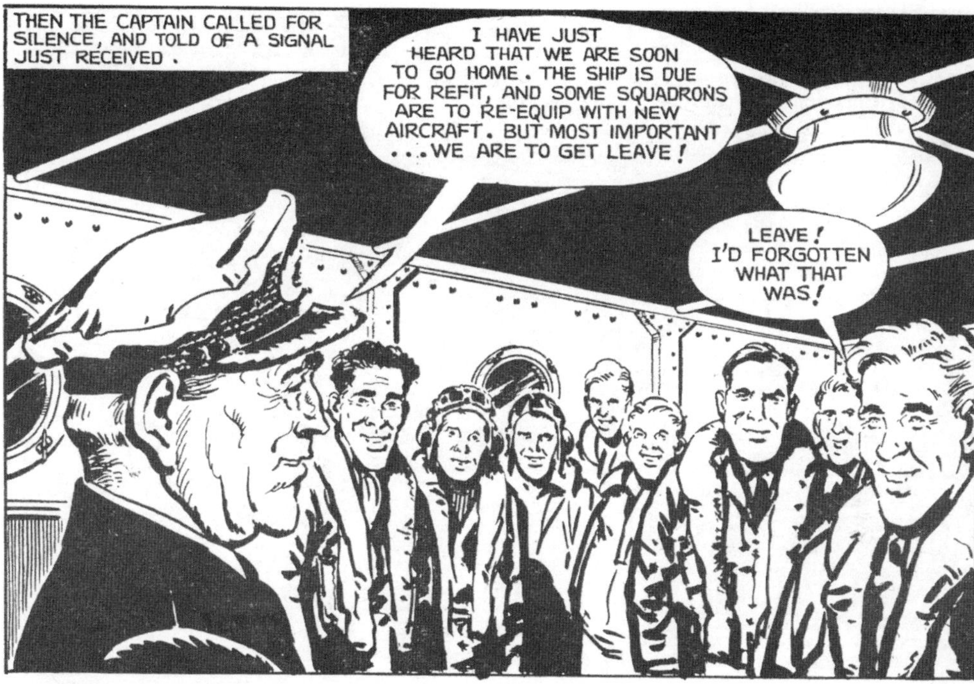
THEN THE CAPTAIN CALLED FOR SILENCE, AND TOLD OF A SIGNAL JUST RECEIVED.
I HAVE JUST HEARD THAT WE ARE SOON TO GO HOME. THE SHIP IS DUE FOR REFIT, AND SOME SQUADRONS ARE TO RE-EQUIP WITH NEW AIRCRAFT. BUT MOST IMPORTANT ...WE ARE TO GET LEAVE!
LEAVE! I'D FORGOTTEN WHAT THAT WAS!

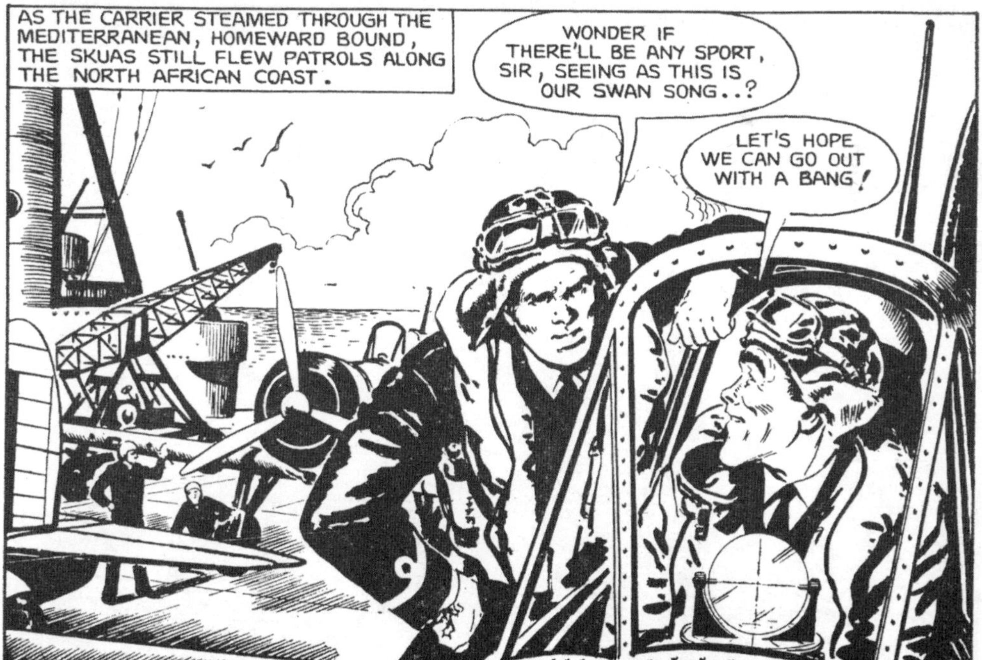
AS THE CARRIER STEAMED THROUGH THE MEDITERRANEAN, HOMEWARD BOUND, THE SKUAS STILL FLEW PATROLS ALONG THE NORTH AFRICAN COAST.
WONDER IF THERE'LL BE ANY SPORT, SIR, SEEING AS THIS IS OUR SWAN SONG..?
LET'S HOPE WE CAN GO OUT WITH A BANG!

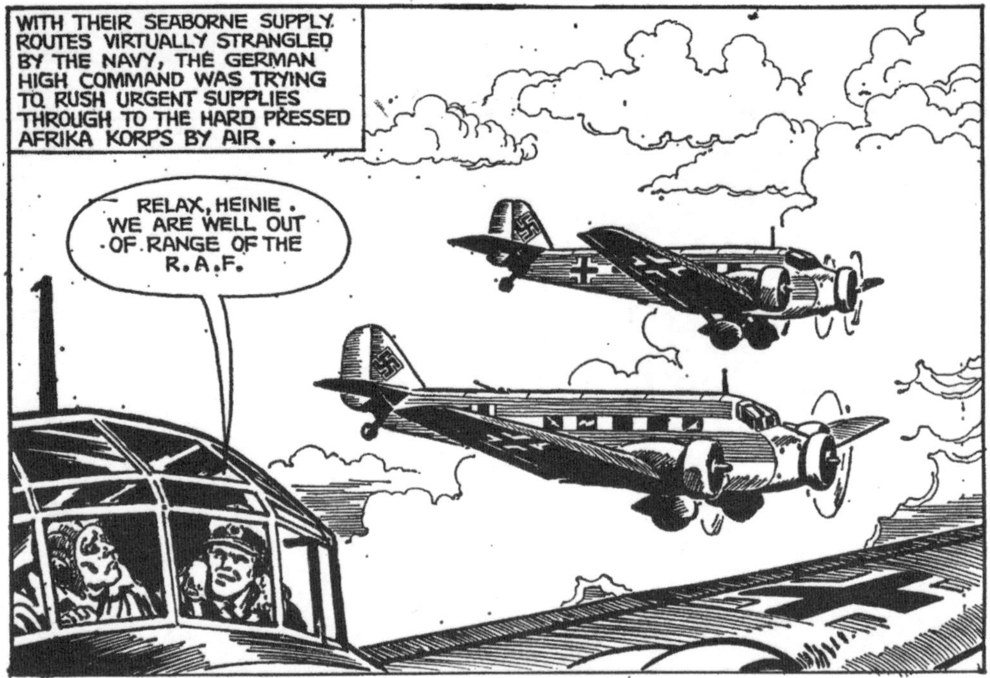
WITH THEIR SEABORNE SUPPLY ROUTES VIRTUALLY STRANGLED BY THE NAVY, THE GERMAN HIGH COMMAND WAS TRYING TO RUSH URGENT SUPPLIES THROUGH TO THE HARD PRESSED AFRIKA KORPS BY AIR.
RELAX, HEINIE. WE ARE WELL OUT OF RANGE OF THE R.A.F.

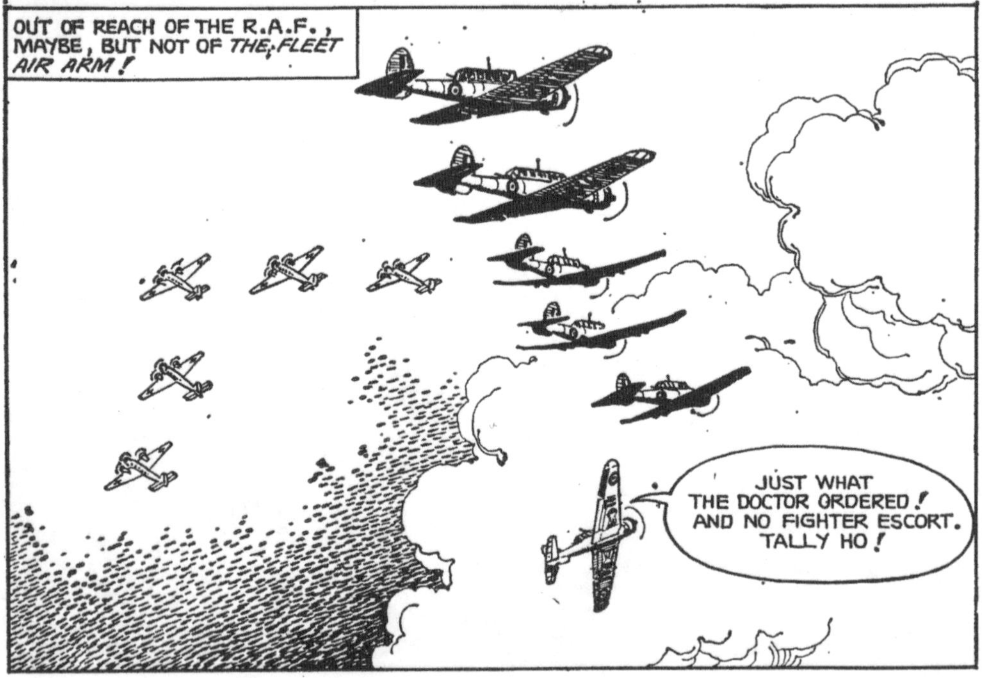
OUT OF REACH OF THE R.A.F., MAYBE, BUT NOT OF *THE FLEET AIR ARM!*
JUST WHAT THE DOCTOR ORDERED! AND NO FIGHTER ESCORT. TALLY HO!

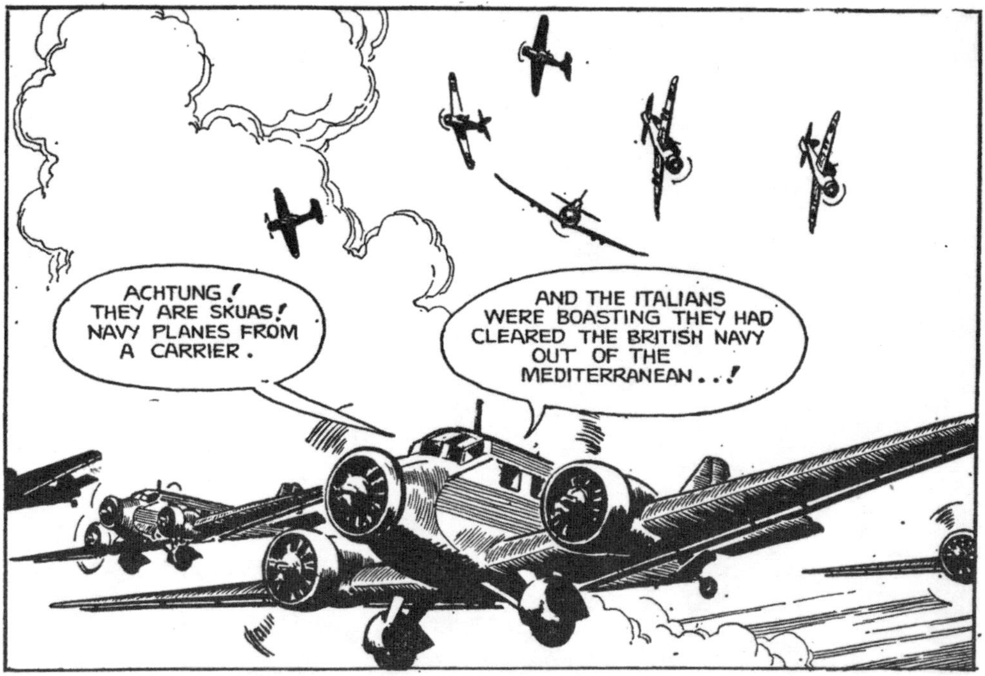
ACHTUNG! THEY ARE SKUAS! NAVY PLANES FROM A CARRIER.
AND THE ITALIANS WERE BOASTING THEY HAD CLEARED THE BRITISH NAVY OUT OF THE MEDITERRANEAN..!

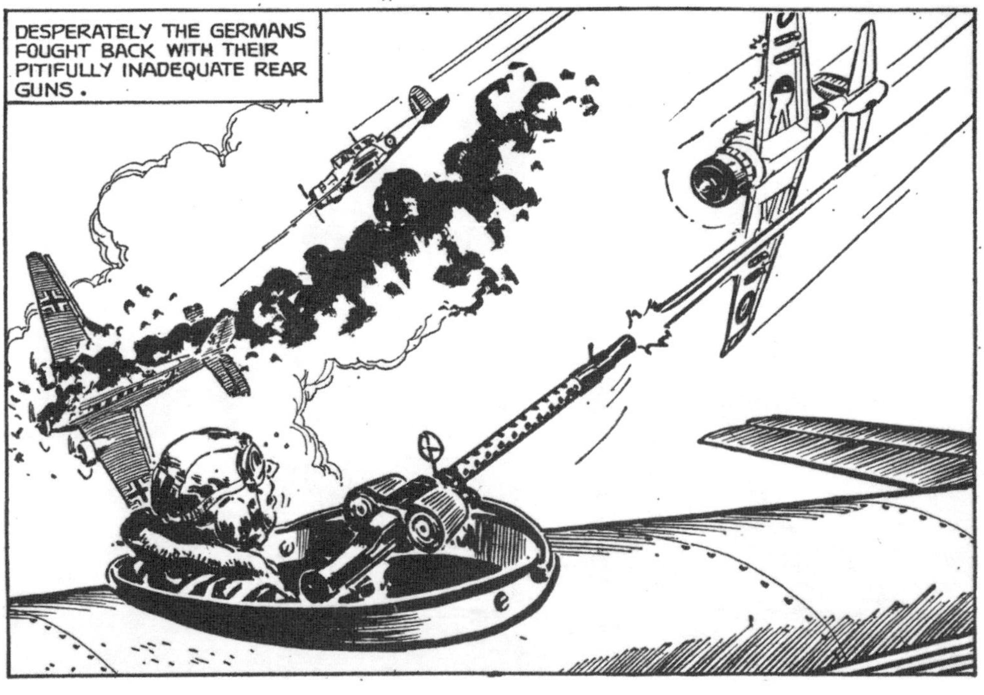
DESPERATELY THE GERMANS FOUGHT BACK WITH THEIR PITIFULLY INADEQUATE REAR GUNS.

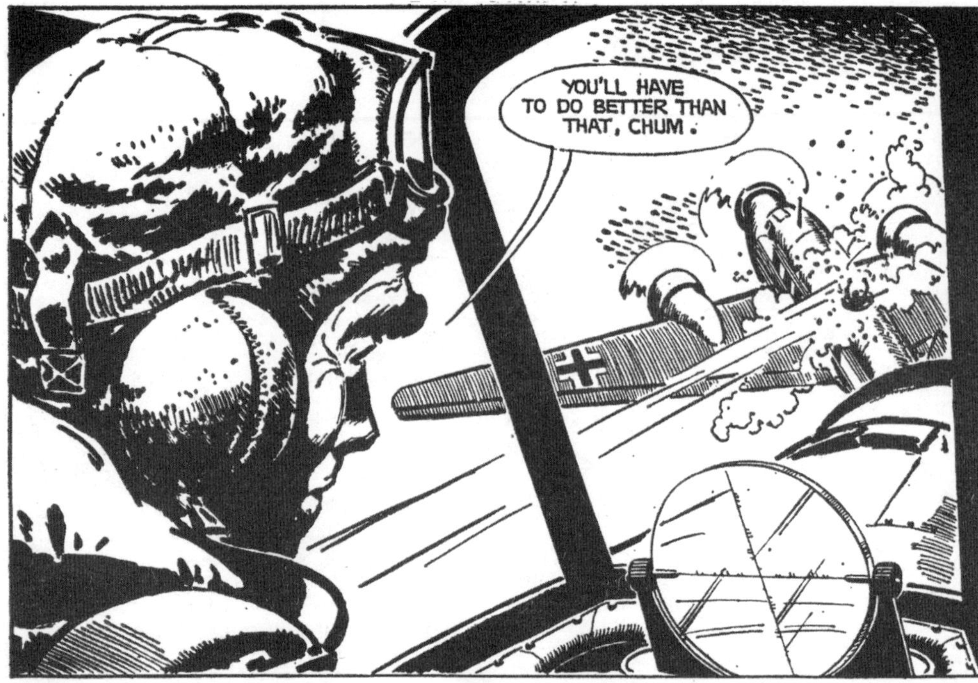
YOU'LL HAVE TO DO BETTER THAN THAT, CHUM.

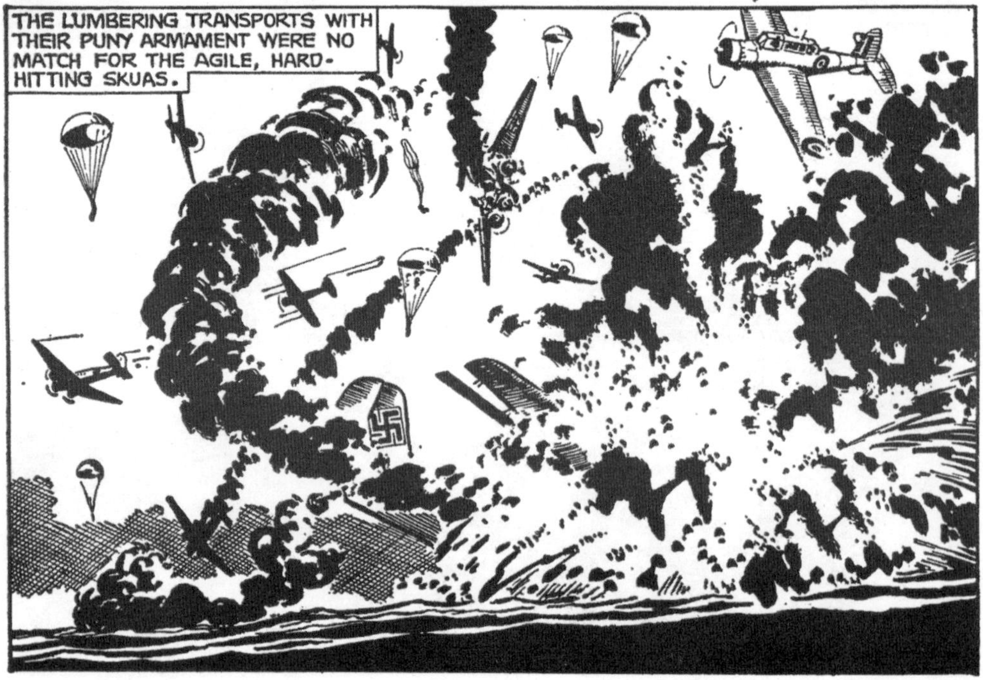
THE LUMBERING TRANSPORTS WITH THEIR PUNY ARMAMENT WERE NO MATCH FOR THE AGILE, HARD-HITTING SKUAS.

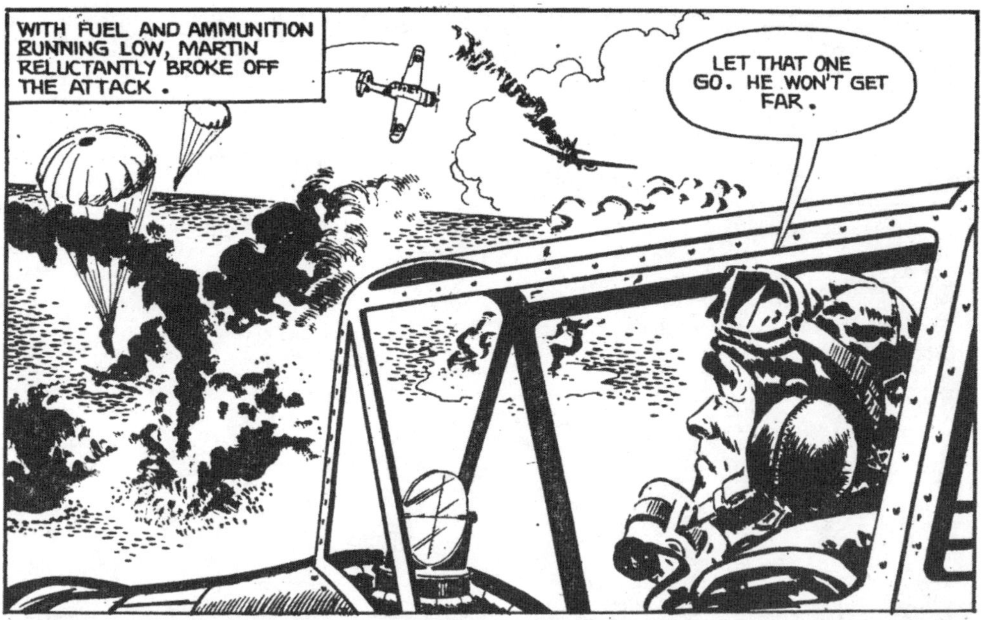
WITH FUEL AND AMMUNITION RUNNING LOW, MARTIN RELUCTANTLY BROKE OFF THE ATTACK.
LET THAT ONE GO. HE WON'T GET FAR.

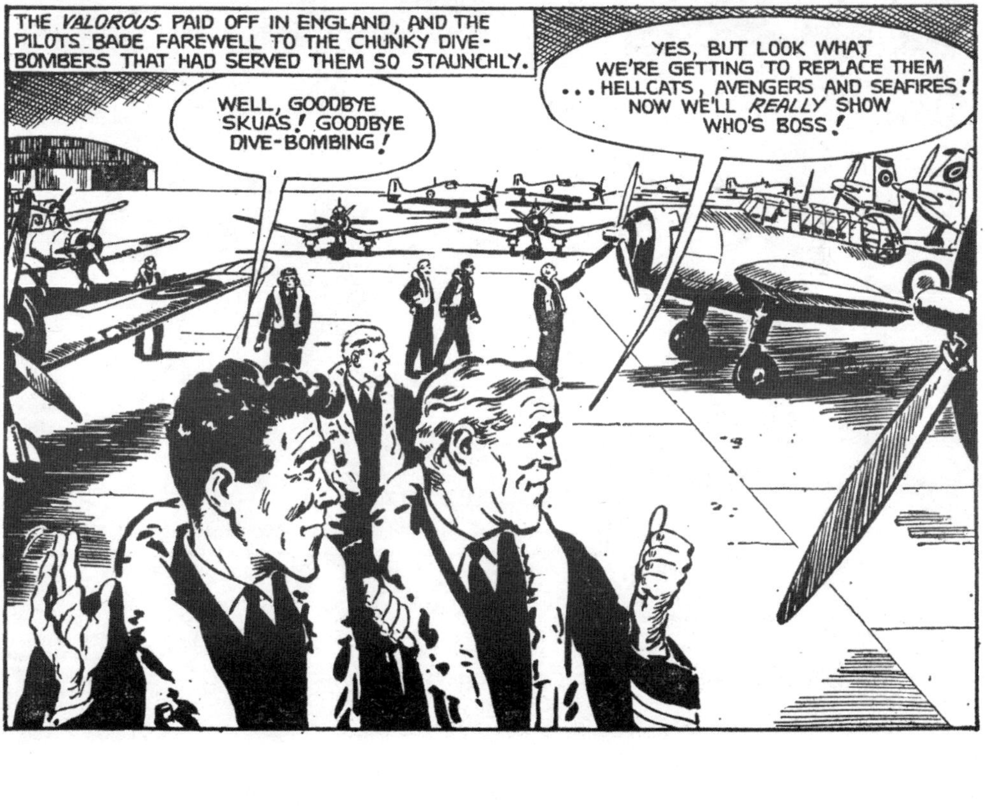
THE *VALOROUS* PAID OFF IN ENGLAND, AND THE PILOTS BADE FAREWELL TO THE CHUNKY DIVE-BOMBERS THAT HAD SERVED THEM SO STAUNCHLY.
WELL, GOODBYE SKUAS! GOODBYE DIVE-BOMBING!
YES, BUT LOOK WHAT WE'RE GETTING TO REPLACE THEM ...HELLCATS, AVENGERS AND SEAFIRES! NOW WE'LL *REALLY* SHOW WHO'S BOSS!

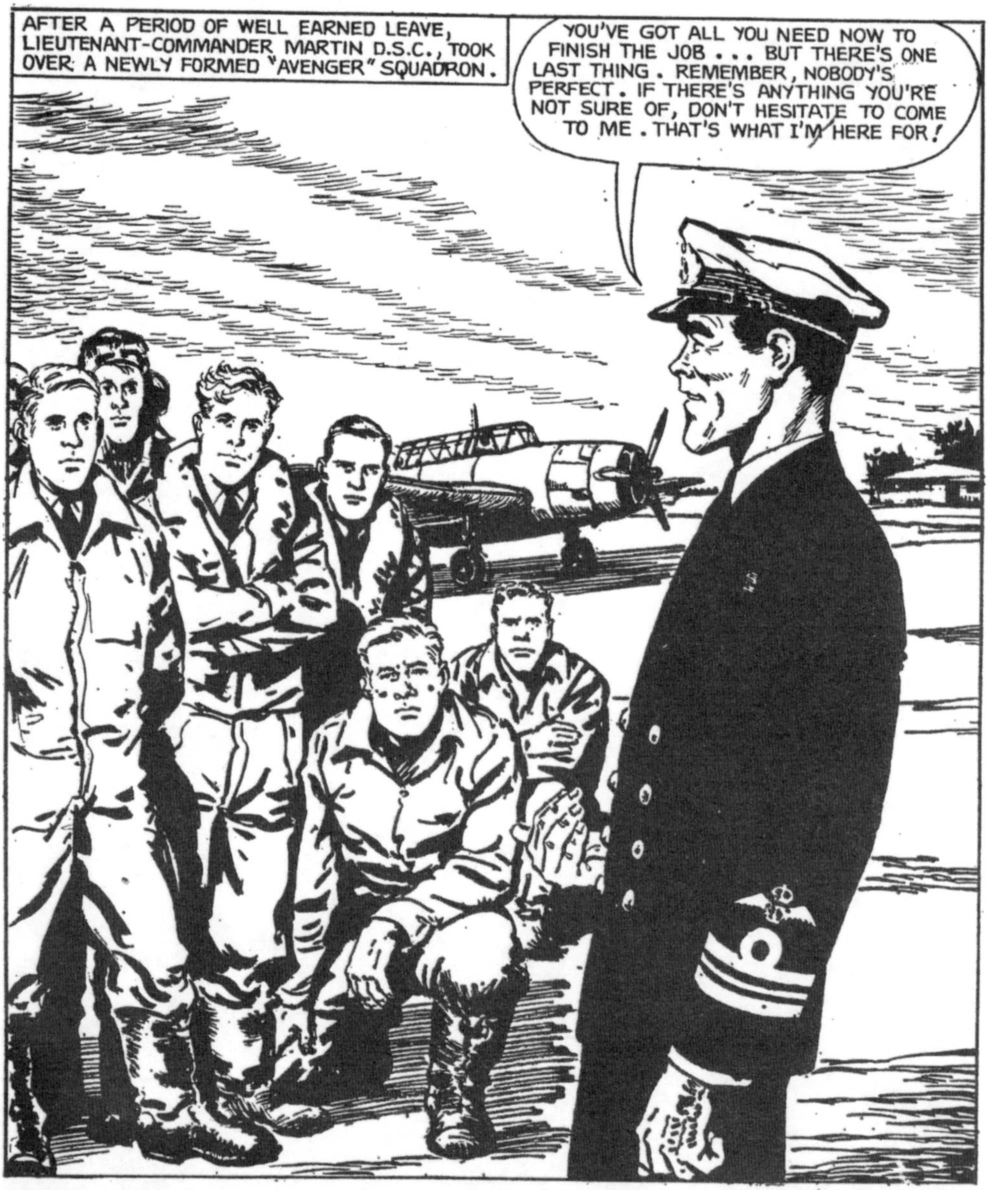
AFTER A PERIOD OF WELL EARNED LEAVE, LIEUTENANT-COMMANDER MARTIN D.S.C., TOOK OVER A NEWLY FORMED "AVENGER" SQUADRON.
YOU'VE GOT ALL YOU NEED NOW TO FINISH THE JOB . . . BUT THERE'S ONE LAST THING. REMEMBER, NOBODY'S PERFECT. IF THERE'S ANYTHING YOU'RE NOT SURE OF, DON'T HESITATE TO COME TO ME. THAT'S WHAT I'M HERE FOR!

Printed in England and published each month by Fleetway Publications Ltd., Fleetway House, Farringdon Street, London, E.C.4. Sole Agents: Australasia, Messrs. Gordon & Gotch, Ltd.; South Africa, Central News Agency, Ltd.; Federation of Rhodesia and Nyasaland, Messrs. Kingstons, Ltd.

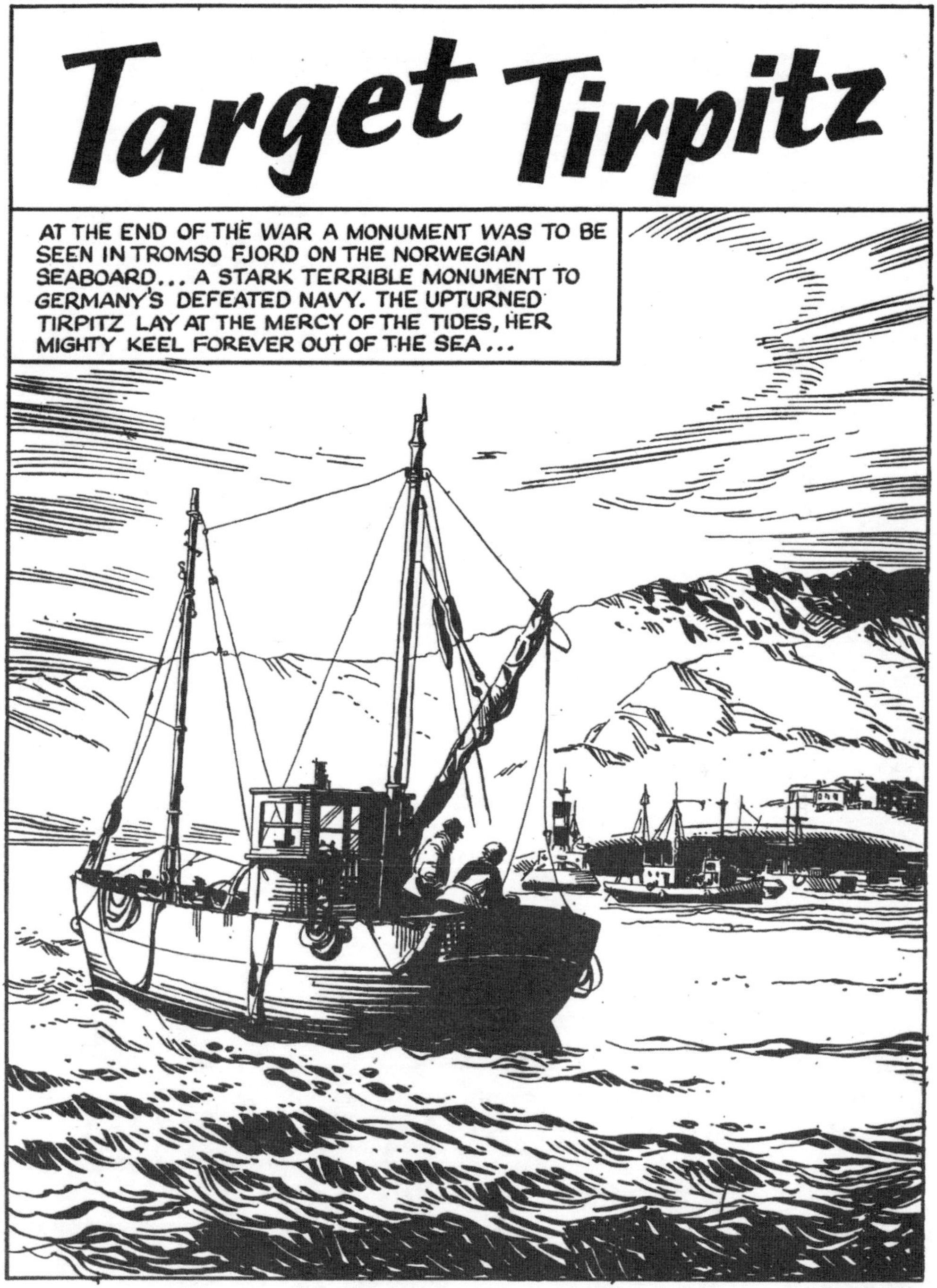
Target Tirpitz
AT THE END OF THE WAR A MONUMENT WAS TO BE SEEN IN TROMSO FJORD ON THE NORWEGIAN SEABOARD... A STARK TERRIBLE MONUMENT TO GERMANY'S DEFEATED NAVY. THE UPTURNED TIRPITZ LAY AT THE MERCY OF THE TIDES, HER MIGHTY KEEL FOREVER OUT OF THE SEA...

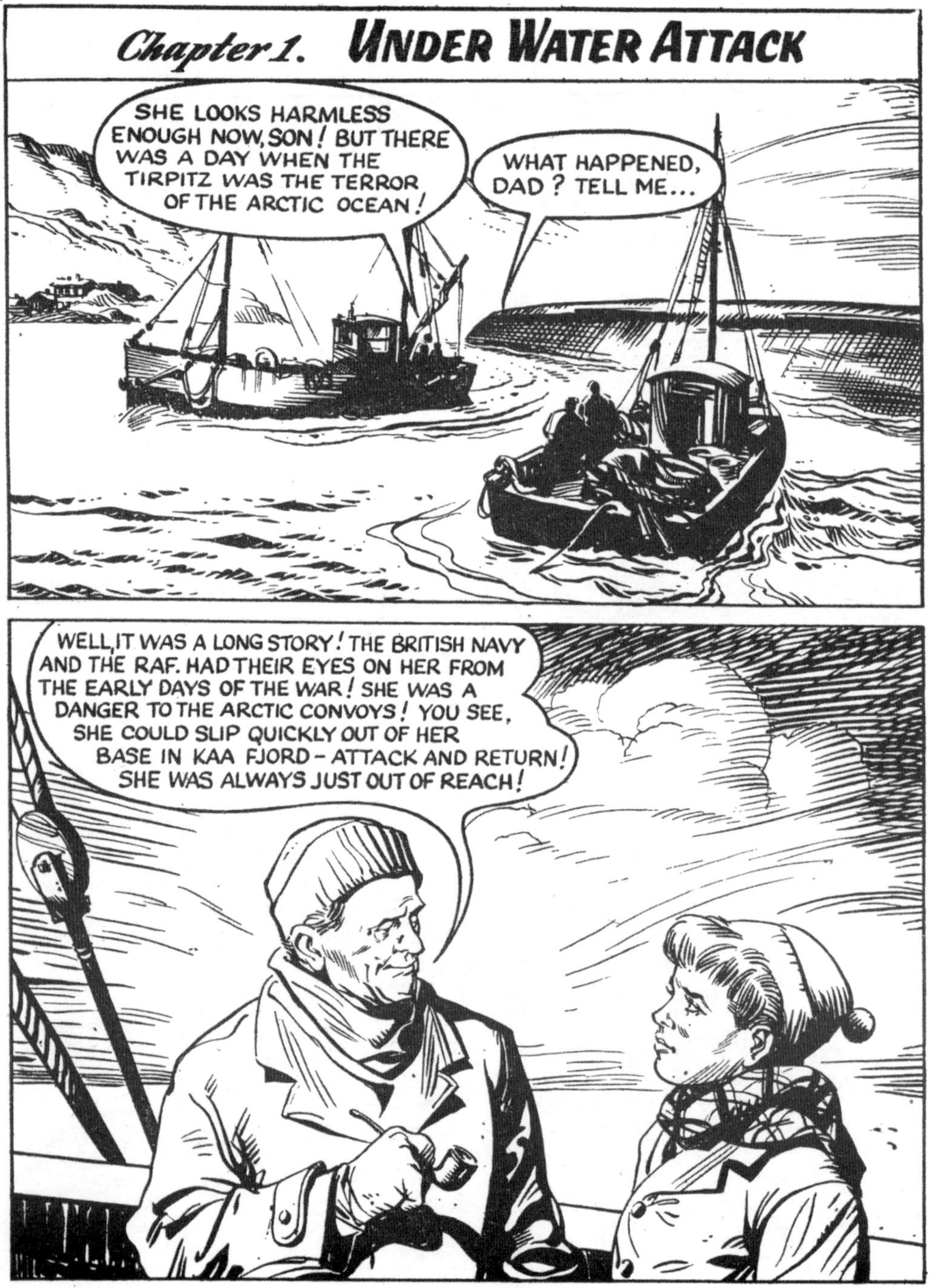
Chapter 1. UNDER WATER ATTACK
SHE LOOKS HARMLESS ENOUGH NOW, SON! BUT THERE WAS A DAY WHEN THE TIRPITZ WAS THE TERROR OF THE ARCTIC OCEAN!
WHAT HAPPENED, DAD? TELL ME...
WELL, IT WAS A LONG STORY! THE BRITISH NAVY AND THE RAF. HAD THEIR EYES ON HER FROM THE EARLY DAYS OF THE WAR! SHE WAS A DANGER TO THE ARCTIC CONVOYS! YOU SEE, SHE COULD SLIP QUICKLY OUT OF HER BASE IN KAA FJORD – ATTACK AND RETURN! SHE WAS ALWAYS JUST OUT OF REACH!

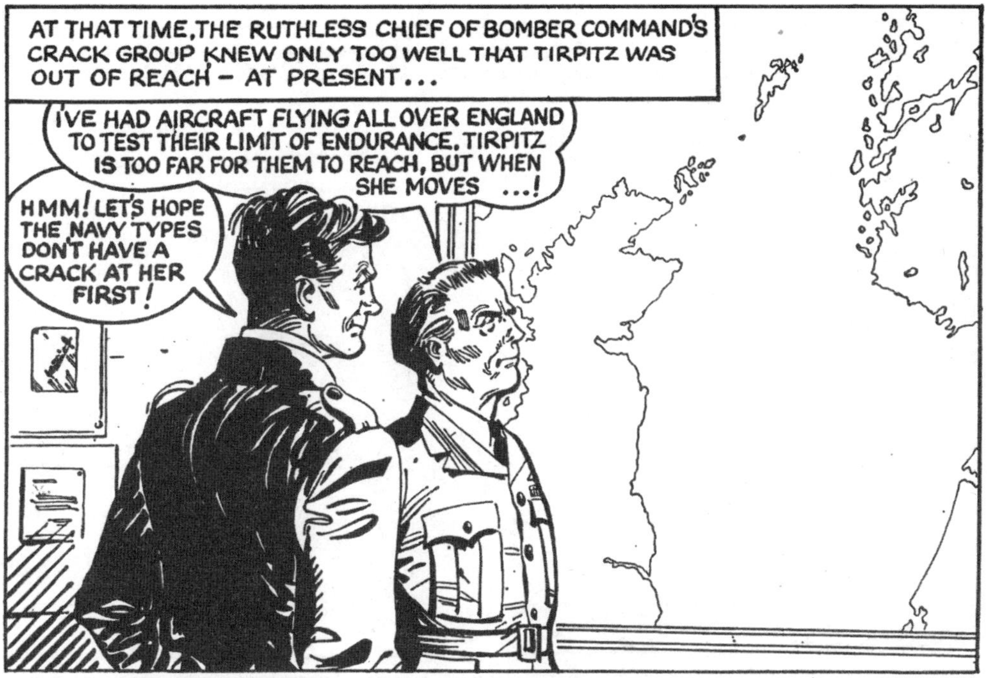
AT THAT TIME, THE RUTHLESS CHIEF OF BOMBER COMMAND'S CRACK GROUP KNEW ONLY TOO WELL THAT TIRPITZ WAS OUT OF REACH – AT PRESENT...
I'VE HAD AIRCRAFT FLYING ALL OVER ENGLAND TO TEST THEIR LIMIT OF ENDURANCE. TIRPITZ IS TOO FAR FOR THEM TO REACH, BUT WHEN SHE MOVES ...!
HMM! LET'S HOPE THE NAVY TYPES DON'T HAVE A CRACK AT HER FIRST!

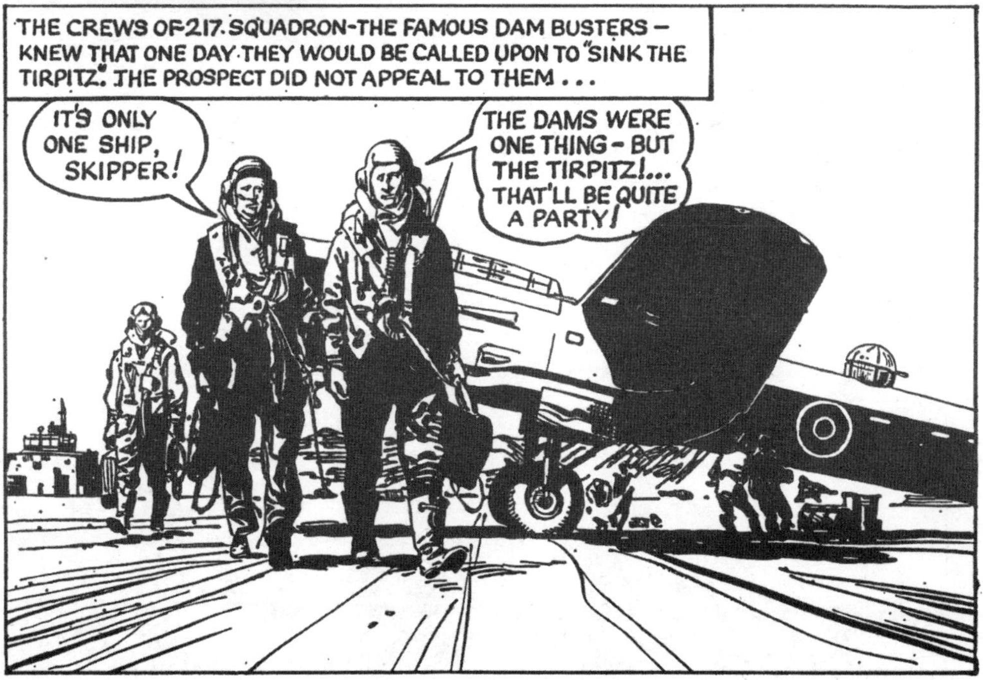
THE CREWS OF 217 SQUADRON – THE FAMOUS DAM BUSTERS – KNEW THAT ONE DAY THEY WOULD BE CALLED UPON TO "SINK THE TIRPITZ." THE PROSPECT DID NOT APPEAL TO THEM...
IT'S ONLY ONE SHIP, SKIPPER!
THE DAMS WERE ONE THING – BUT THE TIRPITZ!... THAT'LL BE QUITE A PARTY!

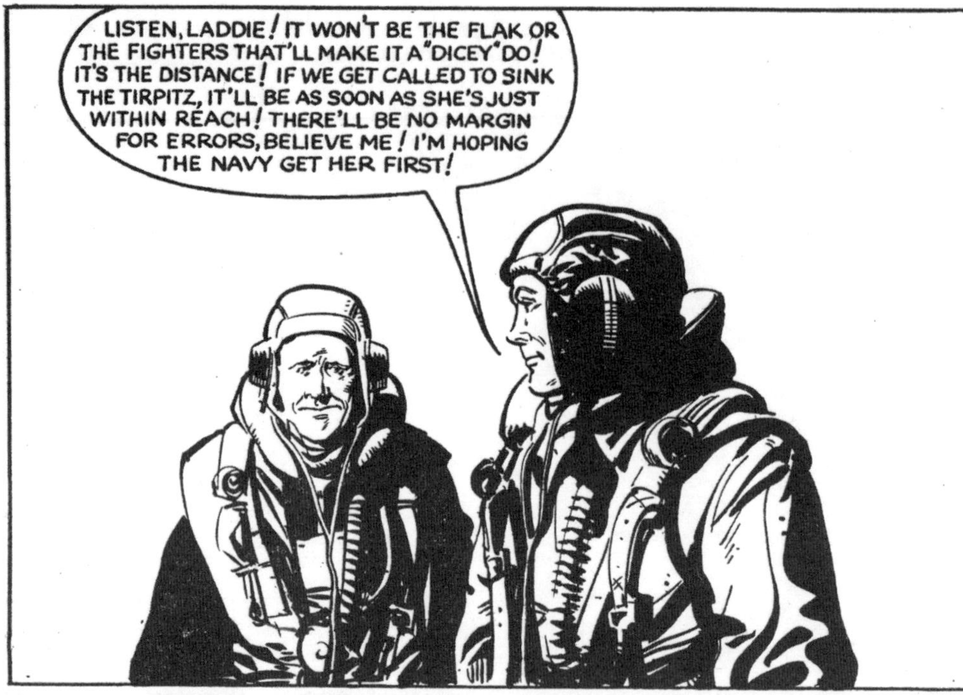
LISTEN, LADDIE! IT WON'T BE THE FLAK OR THE FIGHTERS THAT'LL MAKE IT A "DICEY" DO! IT'S THE DISTANCE! IF WE GET CALLED TO SINK THE TIRPITZ, IT'LL BE AS SOON AS SHE'S JUST WITHIN REACH! THERE'LL BE NO MARGIN FOR ERRORS, BELIEVE ME! I'M HOPING THE NAVY GET HER FIRST!

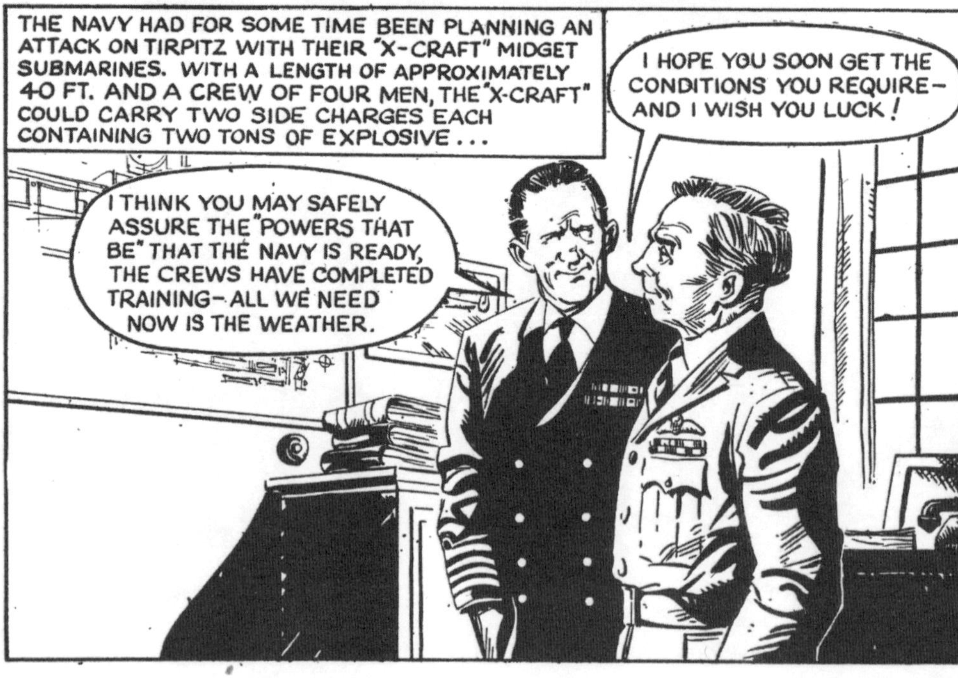
THE NAVY HAD FOR SOME TIME BEEN PLANNING AN ATTACK ON TIRPITZ WITH THEIR "X-CRAFT" MIDGET SUBMARINES. WITH A LENGTH OF APPROXIMATELY 40 FT. AND A CREW OF FOUR MEN, THE "X-CRAFT" COULD CARRY TWO SIDE CHARGES EACH CONTAINING TWO TONS OF EXPLOSIVE...
I THINK YOU MAY SAFELY ASSURE THE "POWERS THAT BE" THAT THE NAVY IS READY, THE CREWS HAVE COMPLETED TRAINING– ALL WE NEED NOW IS THE WEATHER.
I HOPE YOU SOON GET THE CONDITIONS YOU REQUIRE– AND I WISH YOU LUCK!

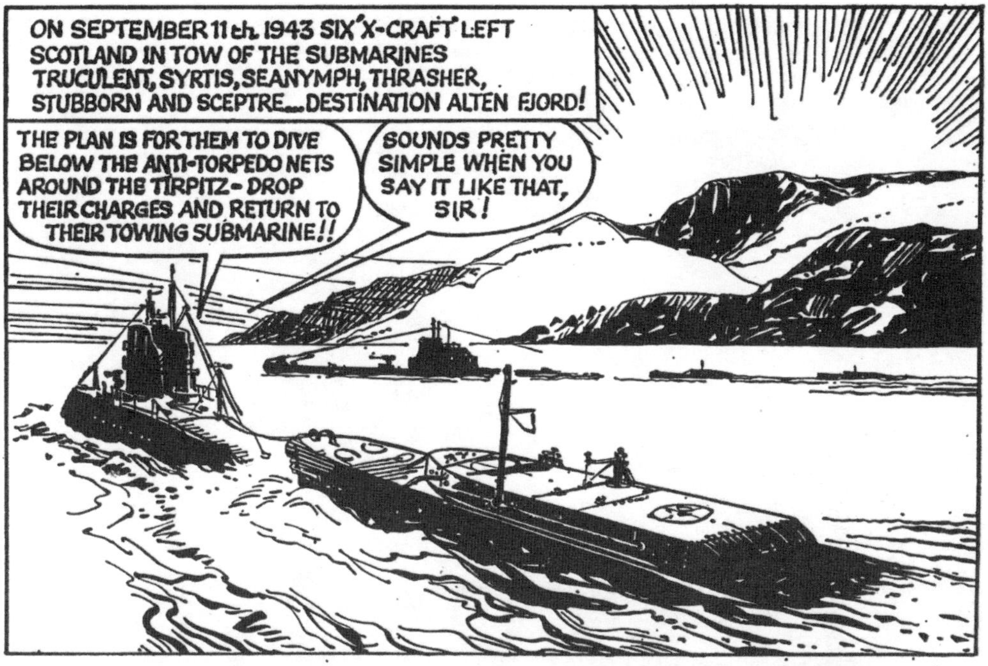
ON SEPTEMBER 11th 1943 SIX 'X-CRAFT' LEFT SCOTLAND IN TOW OF THE SUBMARINES TRUCULENT, SYRTIS, SEANYMPH, THRASHER, STUBBORN AND SCEPTRE...DESTINATION ALTEN FJORD!
THE PLAN IS FOR THEM TO DIVE BELOW THE ANTI-TORPEDO NETS AROUND THE TIRPITZ - DROP THEIR CHARGES AND RETURN TO THEIR TOWING SUBMARINE!!
SOUNDS PRETTY SIMPLE WHEN YOU SAY IT LIKE THAT, SIR!

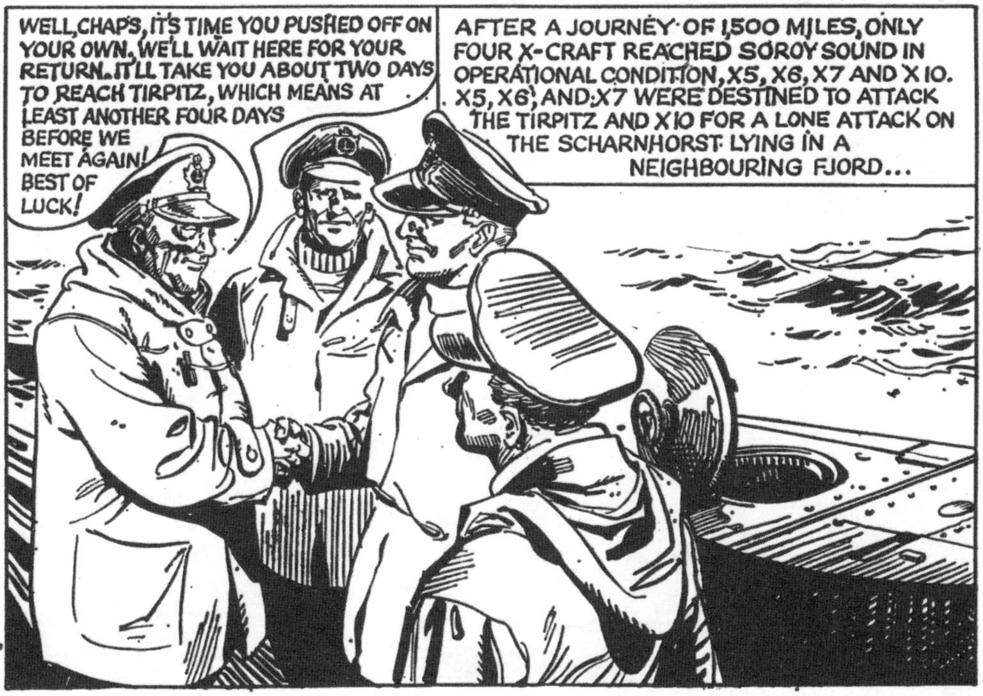
WELL, CHAPS, IT'S TIME YOU PUSHED OFF ON YOUR OWN. WE'LL WAIT HERE FOR YOUR RETURN. IT'LL TAKE YOU ABOUT TWO DAYS TO REACH TIRPITZ, WHICH MEANS AT LEAST ANOTHER FOUR DAYS BEFORE WE MEET AGAIN! BEST OF LUCK!
AFTER A JOURNEY OF 1,500 MILES, ONLY FOUR X-CRAFT REACHED SOROY SOUND IN OPERATIONAL CONDITION, X5, X6, X7 AND X10. X5, X6, AND X7 WERE DESTINED TO ATTACK THE TIRPITZ AND X10 FOR A LONE ATTACK ON THE SCHARNHORST LYING IN A NEIGHBOURING FJORD...

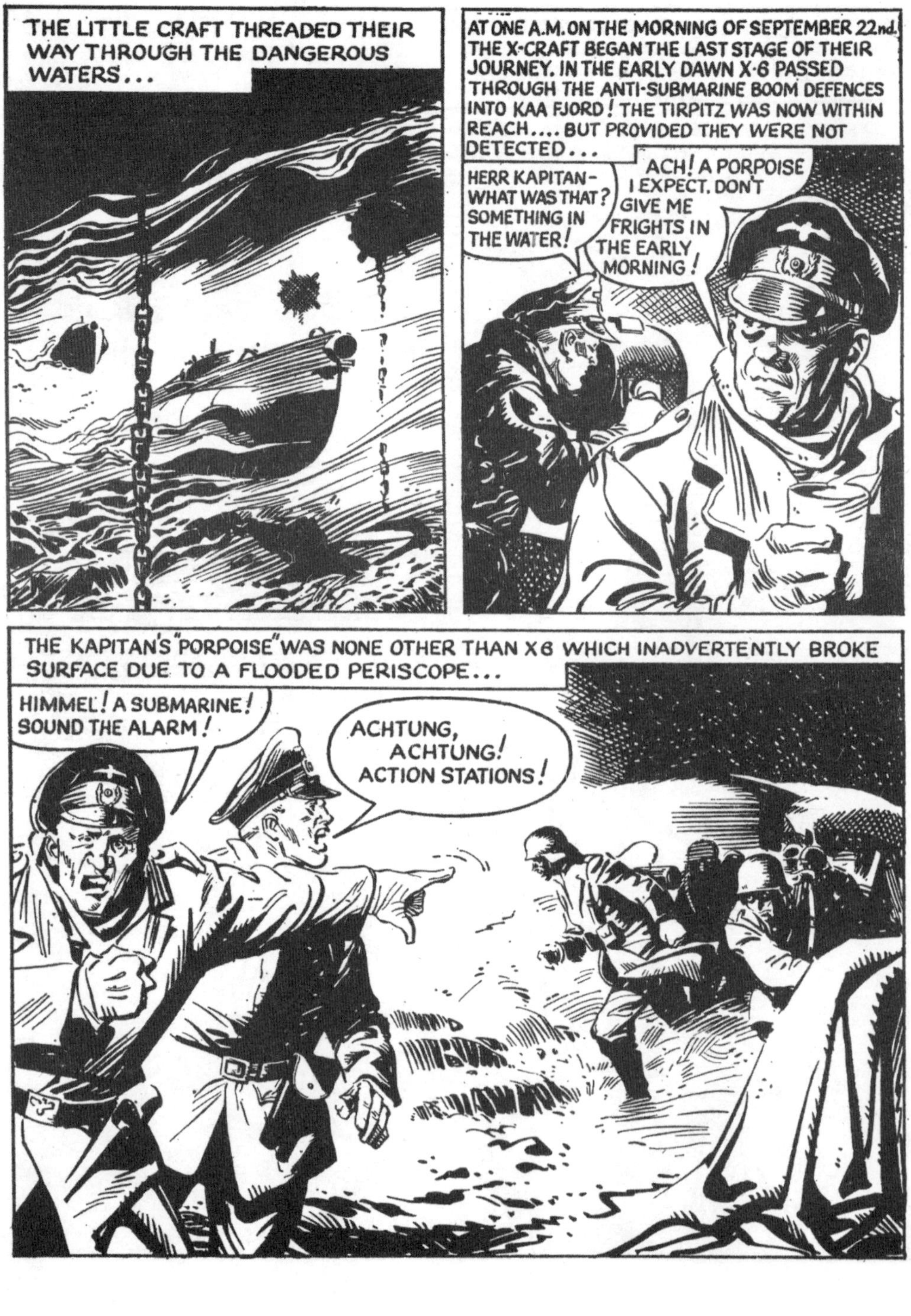

THE LITTLE CRAFT THREADED THEIR WAY THROUGH THE DANGEROUS WATERS...
AT ONE A.M. ON THE MORNING OF SEPTEMBER 22nd. THE X-CRAFT BEGAN THE LAST STAGE OF THEIR JOURNEY. IN THE EARLY DAWN X-6 PASSED THROUGH THE ANTI-SUBMARINE BOOM DEFENCES INTO KAA FJORD! THE TIRPITZ WAS NOW WITHIN REACH.... BUT PROVIDED THEY WERE NOT DETECTED...
HERR KAPITAN– WHAT WAS THAT? SOMETHING IN THE WATER!
ACH! A PORPOISE I EXPECT. DON'T GIVE ME FRIGHTS IN THE EARLY MORNING!
THE KAPITAN'S "PORPOISE" WAS NONE OTHER THAN X6 WHICH INADVERTENTLY BROKE SURFACE DUE TO A FLOODED PERISCOPE...
HIMMEL! A SUBMARINE! SOUND THE ALARM!
ACHTUNG, ACHTUNG! ACTION STATIONS!

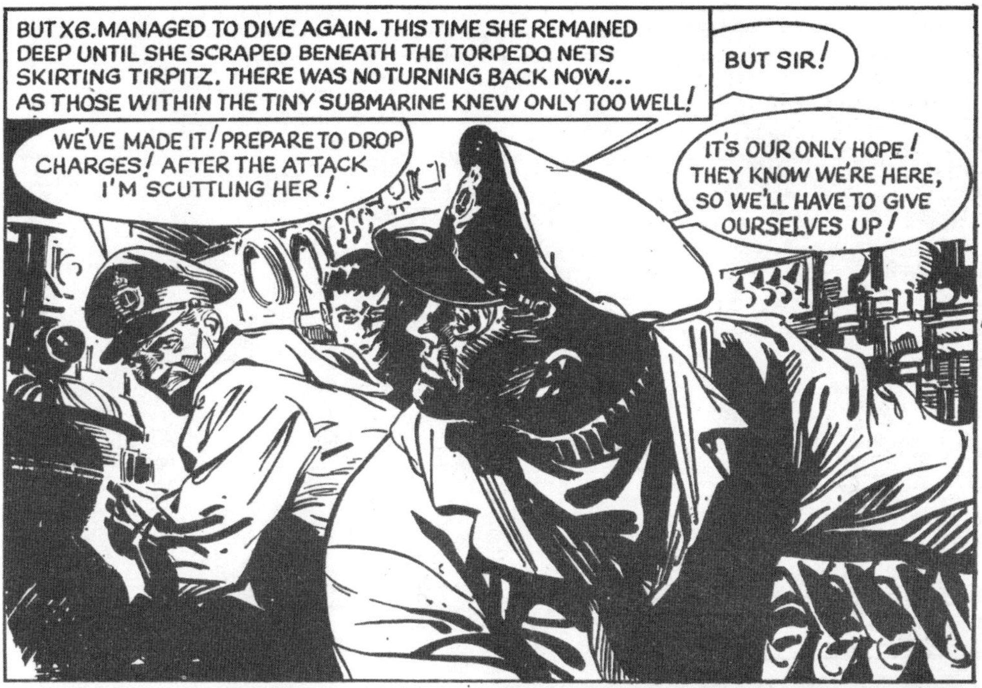
BUT X6. MANAGED TO DIVE AGAIN. THIS TIME SHE REMAINED DEEP UNTIL SHE SCRAPED BENEATH THE TORPEDO NETS SKIRTING TIRPITZ. THERE WAS NO TURNING BACK NOW... AS THOSE WITHIN THE TINY SUBMARINE KNEW ONLY TOO WELL!
WE'VE MADE IT! PREPARE TO DROP CHARGES! AFTER THE ATTACK I'M SCUTTLING HER!
BUT SIR!
IT'S OUR ONLY HOPE! THEY KNOW WE'RE HERE, SO WE'LL HAVE TO GIVE OURSELVES UP!

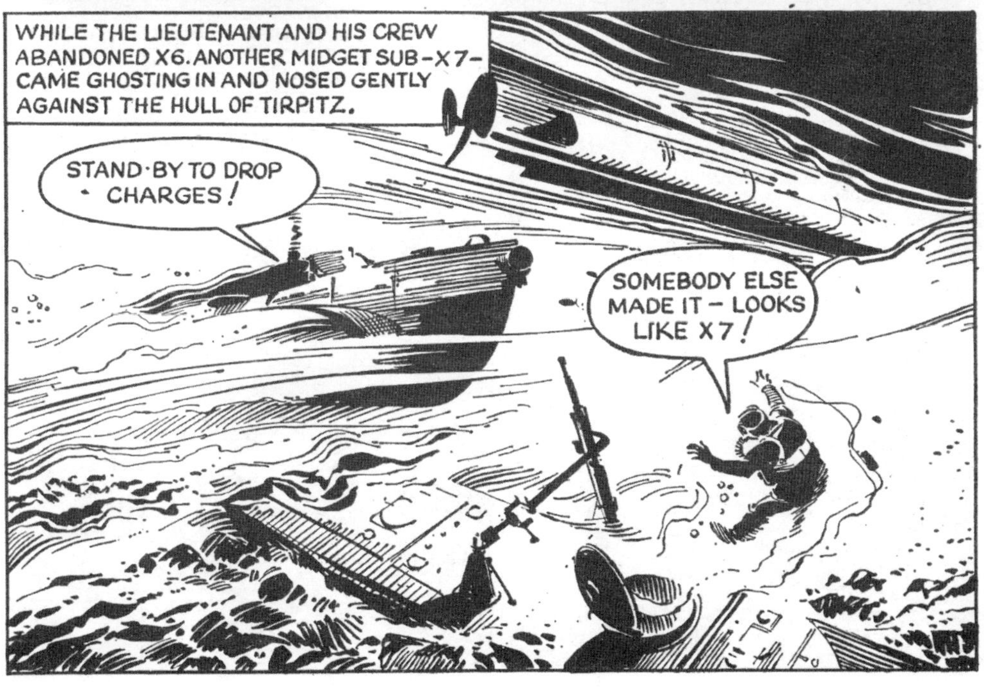
WHILE THE LIEUTENANT AND HIS CREW ABANDONED X6. ANOTHER MIDGET SUB - X7 - CAME GHOSTING IN AND NOSED GENTLY AGAINST THE HULL OF TIRPITZ.
STAND-BY TO DROP CHARGES!
SOMEBODY ELSE MADE IT - LOOKS LIKE X7!

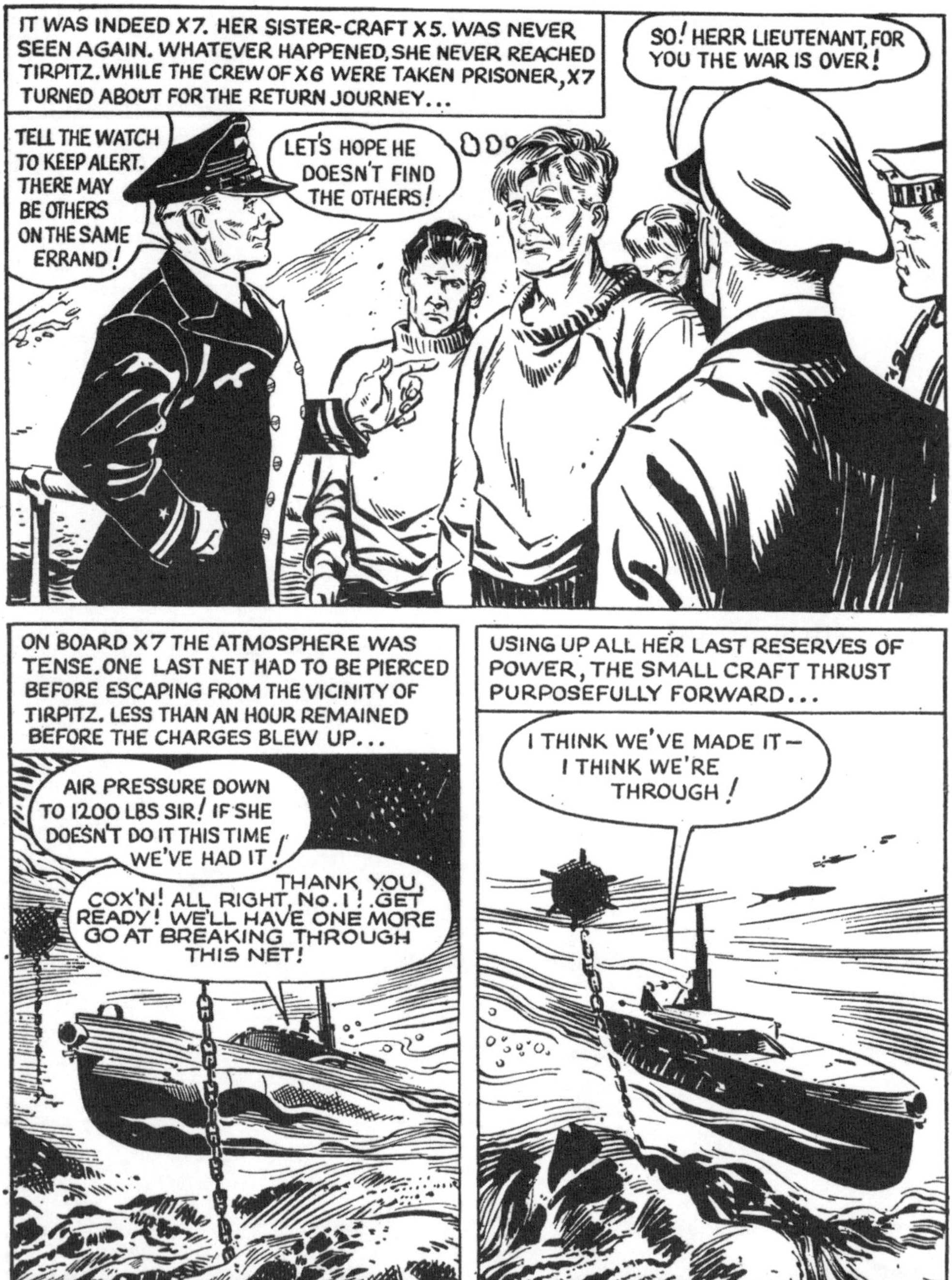
IT WAS INDEED X7. HER SISTER-CRAFT X5. WAS NEVER SEEN AGAIN. WHATEVER HAPPENED, SHE NEVER REACHED TIRPITZ. WHILE THE CREW OF X6 WERE TAKEN PRISONER, X7 TURNED ABOUT FOR THE RETURN JOURNEY...
SO! HERR LIEUTENANT, FOR YOU THE WAR IS OVER!
TELL THE WATCH TO KEEP ALERT. THERE MAY BE OTHERS ON THE SAME ERRAND!
LET'S HOPE HE DOESN'T FIND THE OTHERS!
ON BOARD X7 THE ATMOSPHERE WAS TENSE. ONE LAST NET HAD TO BE PIERCED BEFORE ESCAPING FROM THE VICINITY OF TIRPITZ. LESS THAN AN HOUR REMAINED BEFORE THE CHARGES BLEW UP...
AIR PRESSURE DOWN TO 1200 LBS SIR! IF SHE DOESN'T DO IT THIS TIME WE'VE HAD IT!
THANK YOU, COX'N! ALL RIGHT, No. 1! GET READY! WE'LL HAVE ONE MORE GO AT BREAKING THROUGH THIS NET!
USING UP ALL HER LAST RESERVES OF POWER, THE SMALL CRAFT THRUST PURPOSEFULLY FORWARD...
I THINK WE'VE MADE IT – I THINK WE'RE THROUGH!

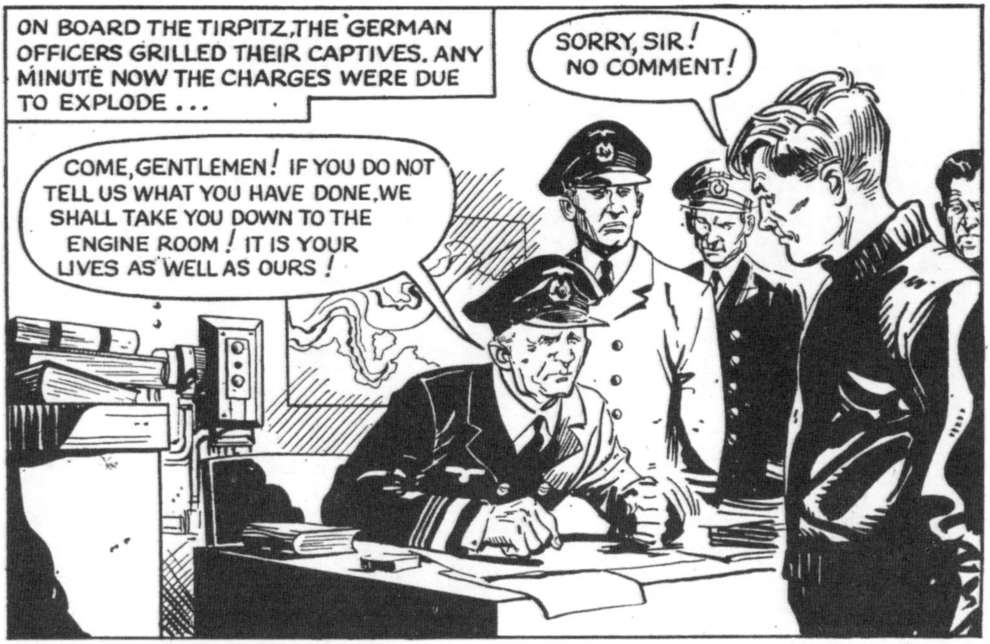
ON BOARD THE TIRPITZ, THE GERMAN OFFICERS GRILLED THEIR CAPTIVES. ANY MINUTE NOW THE CHARGES WERE DUE TO EXPLODE ...
SORRY, SIR! NO COMMENT!
COME, GENTLEMEN! IF YOU DO NOT TELL US WHAT YOU HAVE DONE, WE SHALL TAKE YOU DOWN TO THE ENGINE ROOM! IT IS YOUR LIVES AS WELL AS OURS!

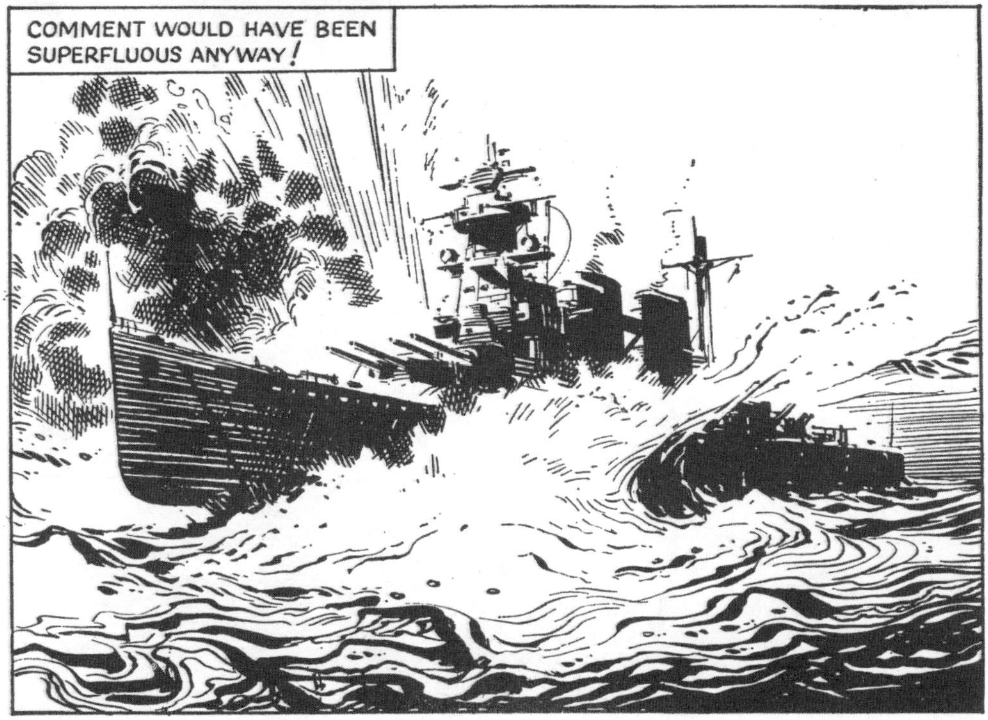
COMMENT WOULD HAVE BEEN SUPERFLUOUS ANYWAY!

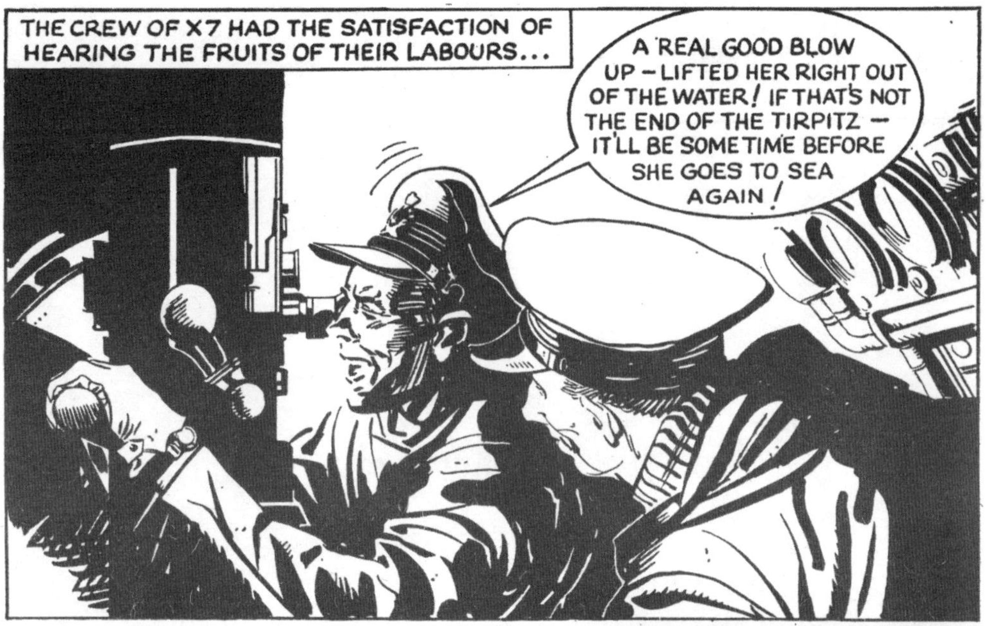
THE CREW OF X7 HAD THE SATISFACTION OF HEARING THE FRUITS OF THEIR LABOURS...
A REAL GOOD BLOW UP – LIFTED HER RIGHT OUT OF THE WATER! IF THAT'S NOT THE END OF THE TIRPITZ – IT'LL BE SOME TIME BEFORE SHE GOES TO SEA AGAIN!

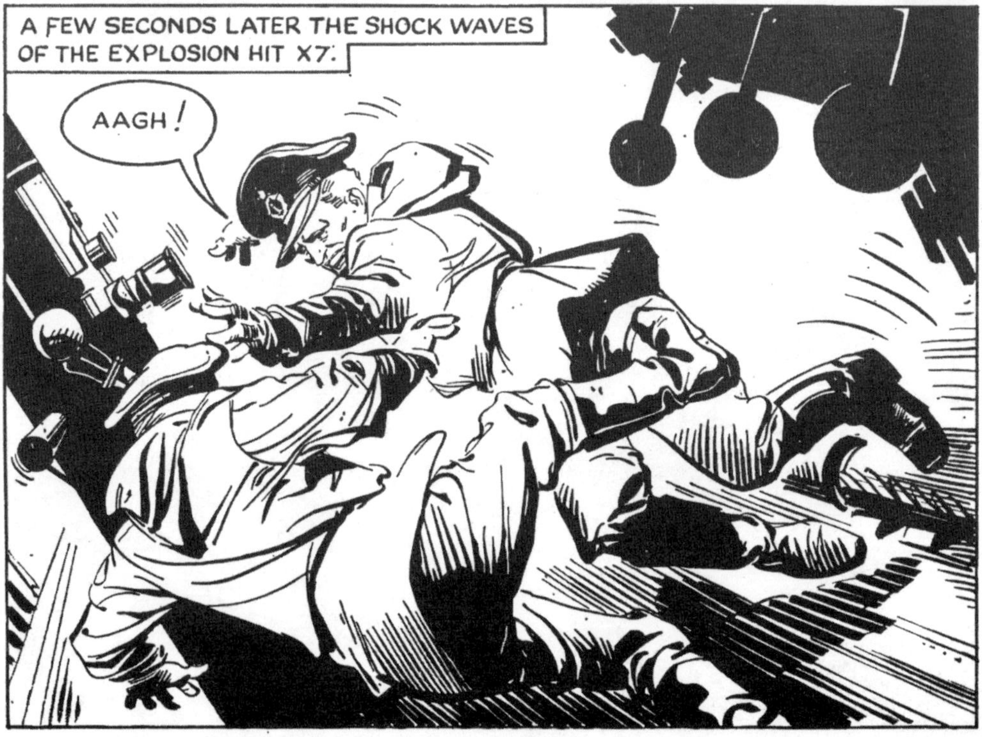
A FEW SECONDS LATER THE SHOCK WAVES OF THE EXPLOSION HIT X7.
AAGH!

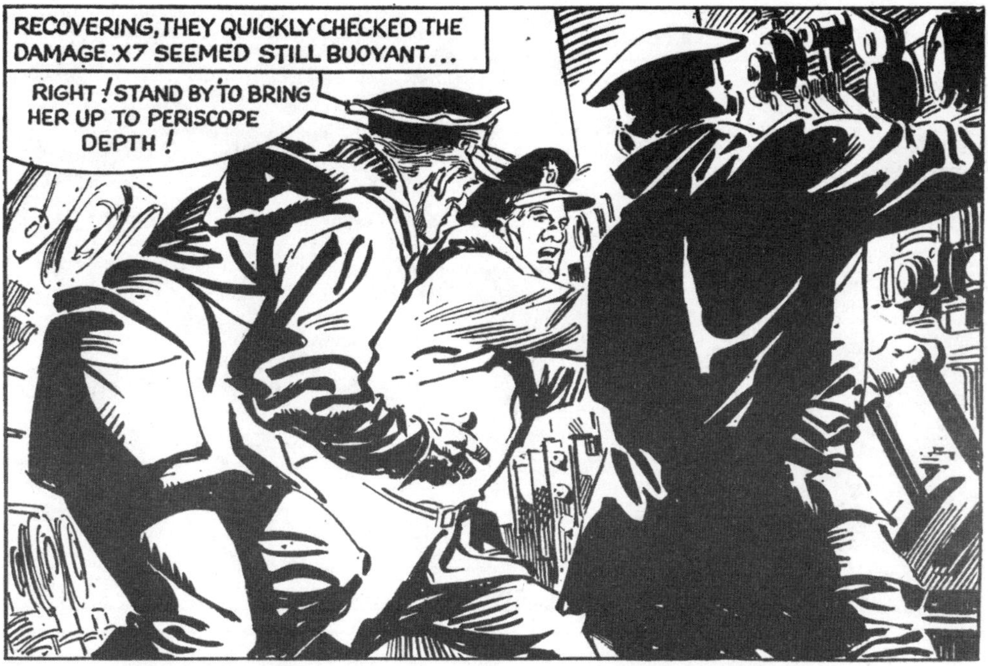
RECOVERING, THEY QUICKLY CHECKED THE DAMAGE. X7 SEEMED STILL BUOYANT...
RIGHT! STAND BY TO BRING HER UP TO PERISCOPE DEPTH!

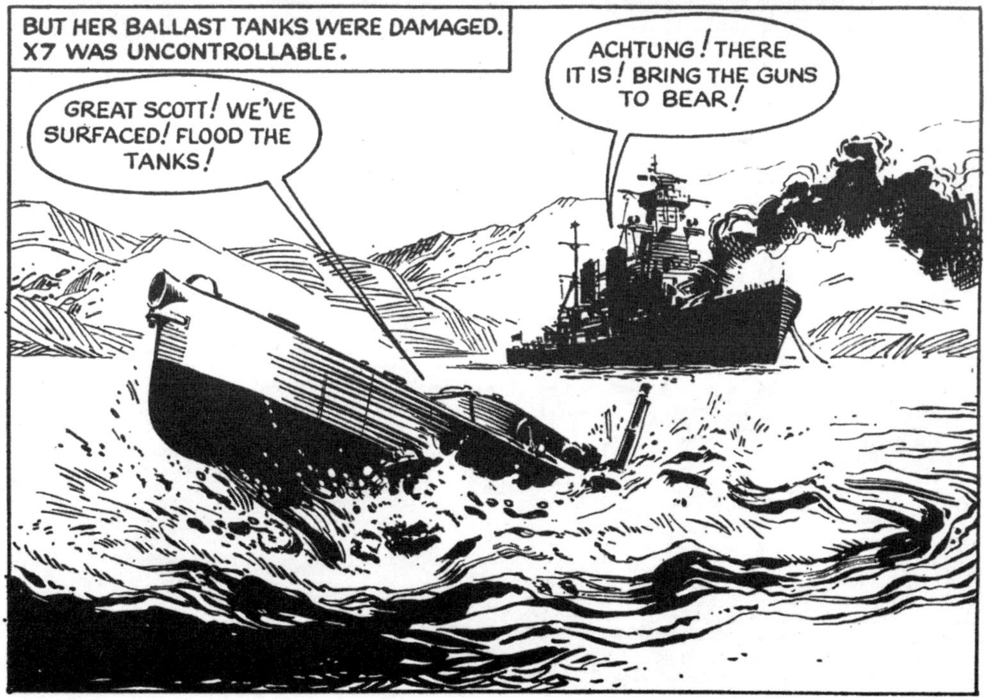
BUT HER BALLAST TANKS WERE DAMAGED. X7 WAS UNCONTROLLABLE.
GREAT SCOTT! WE'VE SURFACED! FLOOD THE TANKS!
ACHTUNG! THERE IT IS! BRING THE GUNS TO BEAR!

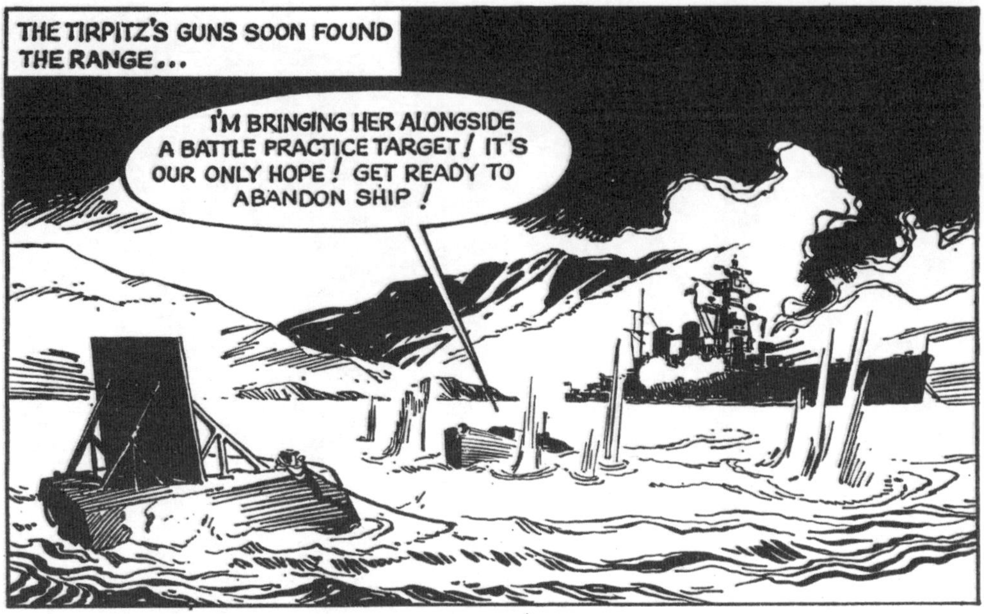
THE TIRPITZ'S GUNS SOON FOUND THE RANGE...
I'M BRINGING HER ALONGSIDE A BATTLE PRACTICE TARGET! IT'S OUR ONLY HOPE! GET READY TO ABANDON SHIP!

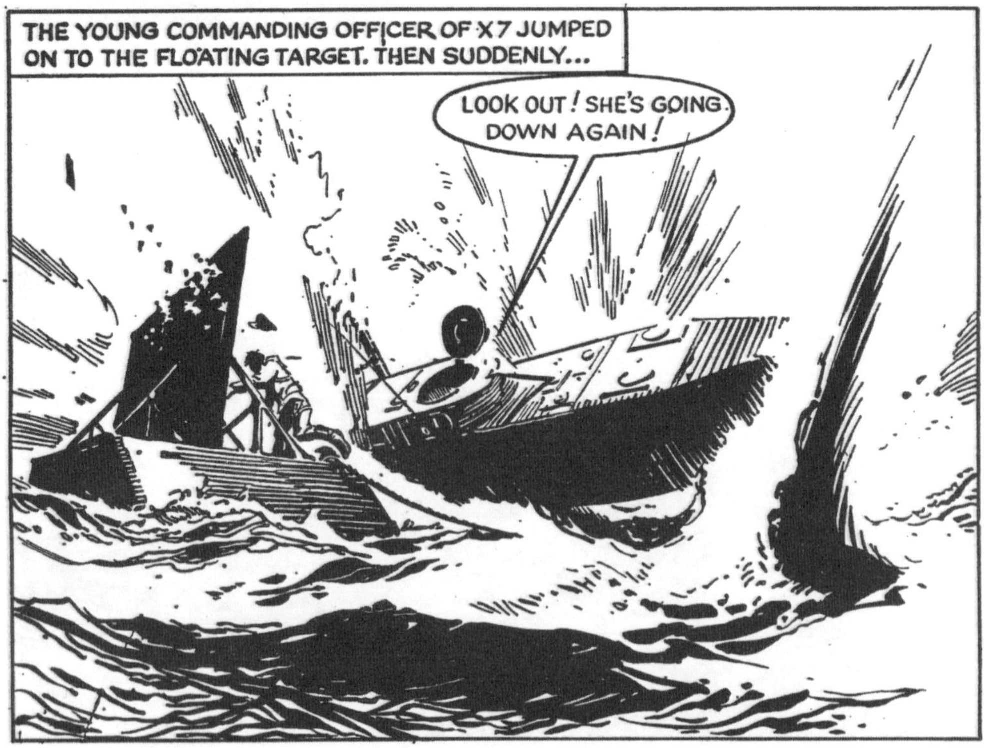
THE YOUNG COMMANDING OFFICER OF X7 JUMPED ON TO THE FLOATING TARGET. THEN SUDDENLY...
LOOK OUT! SHE'S GOING DOWN AGAIN!

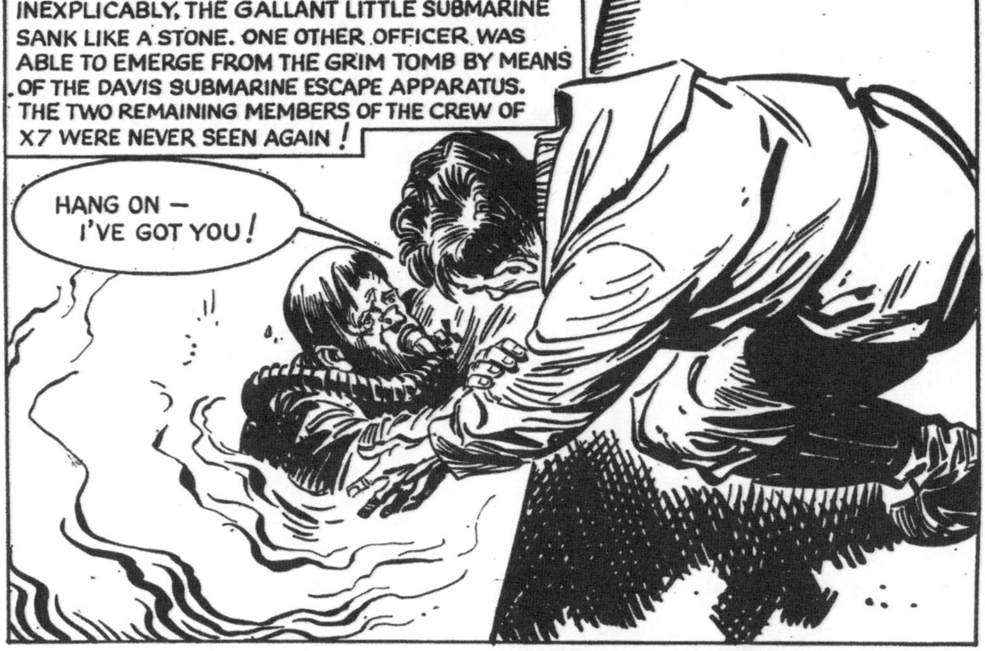
INEXPLICABLY, THE GALLANT LITTLE SUBMARINE SANK LIKE A STONE. ONE OTHER OFFICER WAS ABLE TO EMERGE FROM THE GRIM TOMB BY MEANS OF THE DAVIS SUBMARINE ESCAPE APPARATUS. THE TWO REMAINING MEMBERS OF THE CREW OF X7 WERE NEVER SEEN AGAIN!
HANG ON — I'VE GOT YOU!

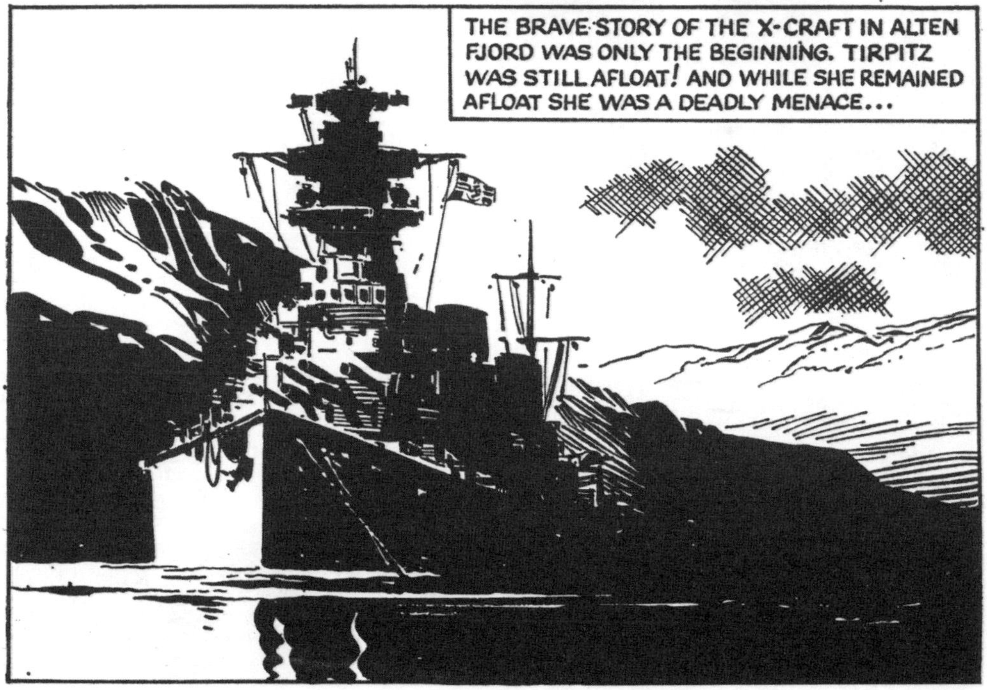
THE BRAVE STORY OF THE X-CRAFT IN ALTEN FJORD WAS ONLY THE BEGINNING. TIRPITZ WAS STILL AFLOAT! AND WHILE SHE REMAINED AFLOAT SHE WAS A DEADLY MENACE...

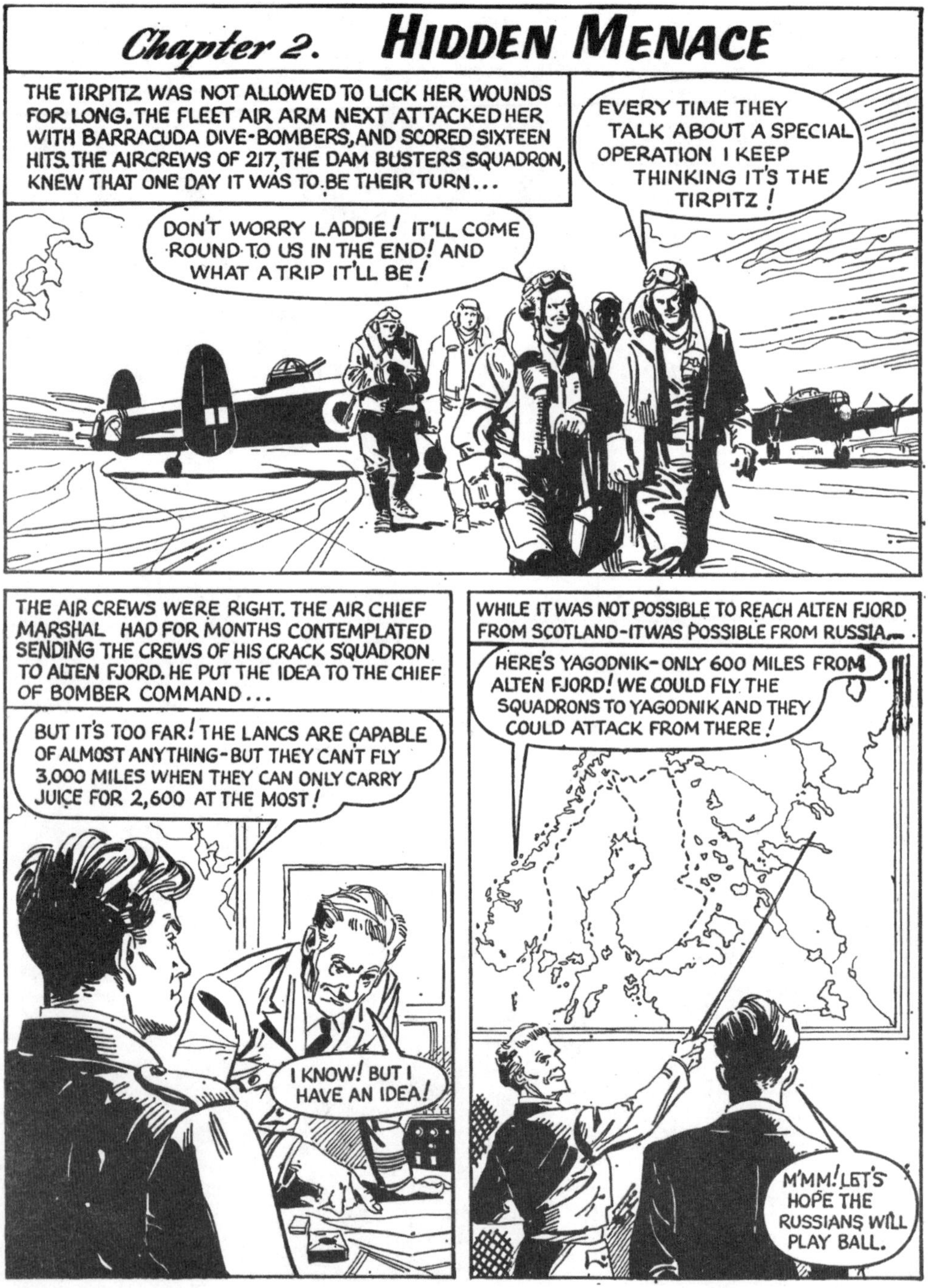
Chapter 2. HIDDEN MENACE
THE TIRPITZ WAS NOT ALLOWED TO LICK HER WOUNDS FOR LONG. THE FLEET AIR ARM NEXT ATTACKED HER WITH BARRACUDA DIVE-BOMBERS, AND SCORED SIXTEEN HITS. THE AIRCREWS OF 217, THE DAM BUSTERS SQUADRON, KNEW THAT ONE DAY IT WAS TO BE THEIR TURN...
EVERY TIME THEY TALK ABOUT A SPECIAL OPERATION I KEEP THINKING IT'S THE TIRPITZ!
DON'T WORRY LADDIE! IT'LL COME ROUND TO US IN THE END! AND WHAT A TRIP IT'LL BE!
THE AIR CREWS WERE RIGHT. THE AIR CHIEF MARSHAL HAD FOR MONTHS CONTEMPLATED SENDING THE CREWS OF HIS CRACK SQUADRON TO ALTEN FJORD. HE PUT THE IDEA TO THE CHIEF OF BOMBER COMMAND...
BUT IT'S TOO FAR! THE LANCS ARE CAPABLE OF ALMOST ANYTHING-BUT THEY CAN'T FLY 3,000 MILES WHEN THEY CAN ONLY CARRY JUICE FOR 2,600 AT THE MOST!
I KNOW! BUT I HAVE AN IDEA!
WHILE IT WAS NOT POSSIBLE TO REACH ALTEN FJORD FROM SCOTLAND-IT WAS POSSIBLE FROM RUSSIA...
HERE'S YAGODNIK-ONLY 600 MILES FROM ALTEN FJORD! WE COULD FLY THE SQUADRONS TO YAGODNIK AND THEY COULD ATTACK FROM THERE!
M'MM! LET'S HOPE THE RUSSIANS WILL PLAY BALL.

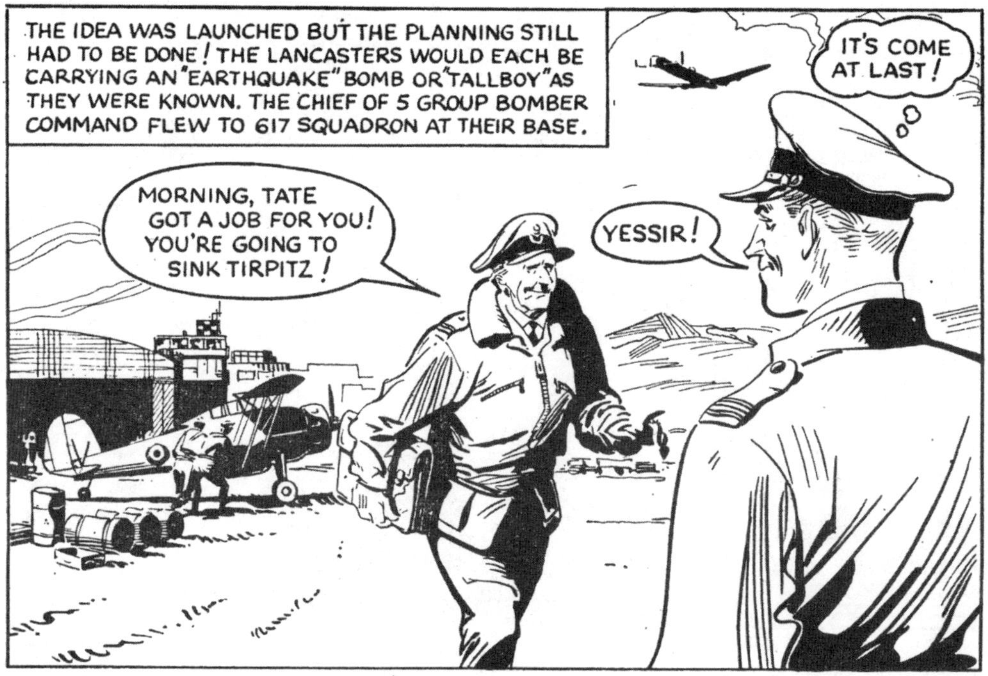
THE IDEA WAS LAUNCHED BUT THE PLANNING STILL HAD TO BE DONE! THE LANCASTERS WOULD EACH BE CARRYING AN "EARTHQUAKE" BOMB OR "TALLBOY" AS THEY WERE KNOWN. THE CHIEF OF 5 GROUP BOMBER COMMAND FLEW TO 617 SQUADRON AT THEIR BASE.
IT'S COME AT LAST!
MORNING, TATE GOT A JOB FOR YOU! YOU'RE GOING TO SINK TIRPITZ!
YESSIR!

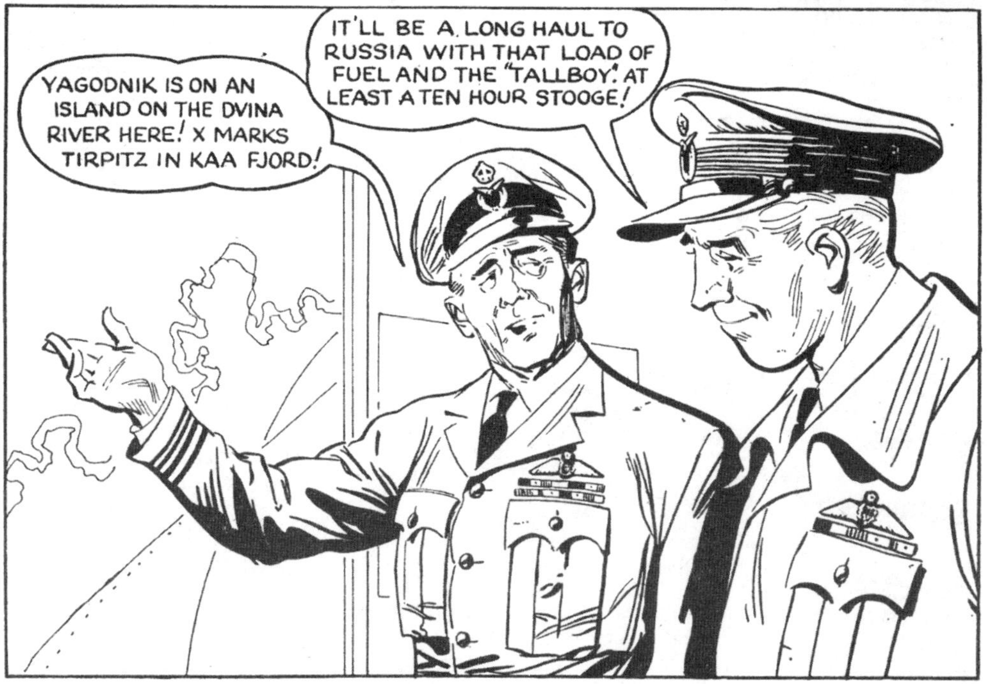
YAGODNIK IS ON AN ISLAND ON THE DVINA RIVER HERE! X MARKS TIRPITZ IN KAA FJORD!
IT'LL BE A LONG HAUL TO RUSSIA WITH THAT LOAD OF FUEL AND THE "TALLBOY" AT LEAST A TEN HOUR STOOGE!

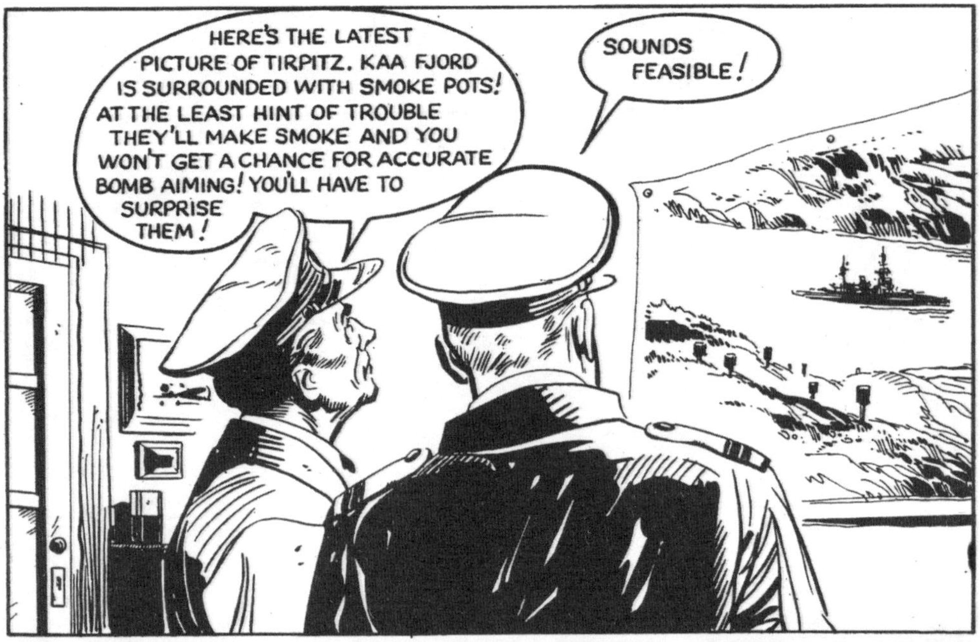
HERE'S THE LATEST PICTURE OF TIRPITZ. KAA FJORD IS SURROUNDED WITH SMOKE POTS! AT THE LEAST HINT OF TROUBLE THEY'LL MAKE SMOKE AND YOU WON'T GET A CHANCE FOR ACCURATE BOMB AIMING! YOU'LL HAVE TO SURPRISE THEM!
SOUNDS FEASIBLE!

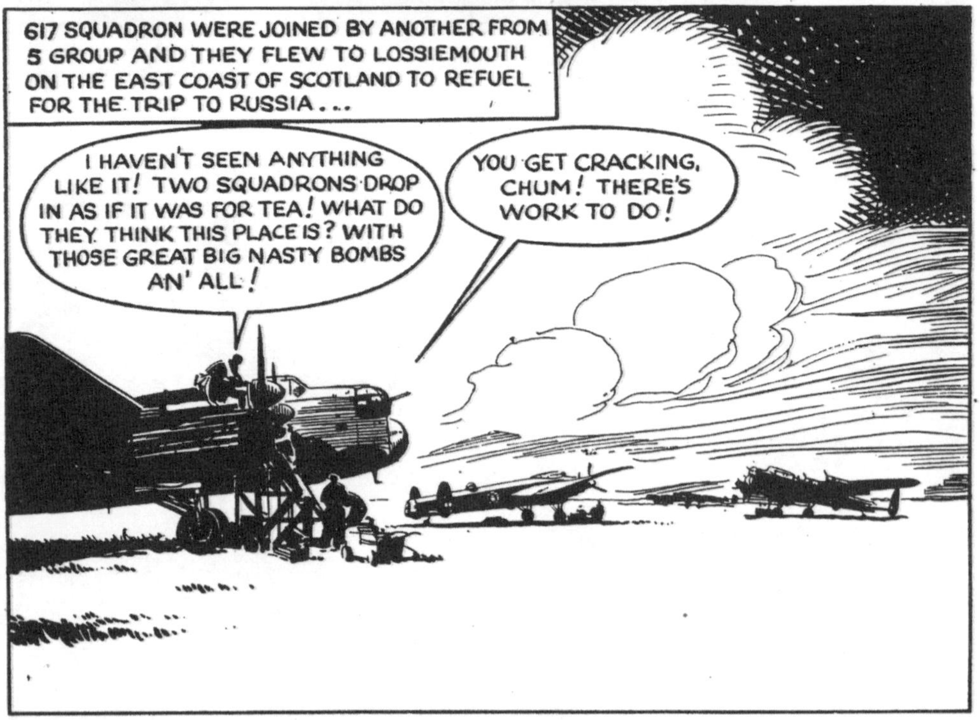
617 SQUADRON WERE JOINED BY ANOTHER FROM 5 GROUP AND THEY FLEW TO LOSSIEMOUTH ON THE EAST COAST OF SCOTLAND TO REFUEL FOR THE TRIP TO RUSSIA...
I HAVEN'T SEEN ANYTHING LIKE IT! TWO SQUADRONS DROP IN AS IF IT WAS FOR TEA! WHAT DO THEY THINK THIS PLACE IS? WITH THOSE GREAT BIG NASTY BOMBS AN' ALL!
YOU GET CRACKING, CHUM! THERE'S WORK TO DO!

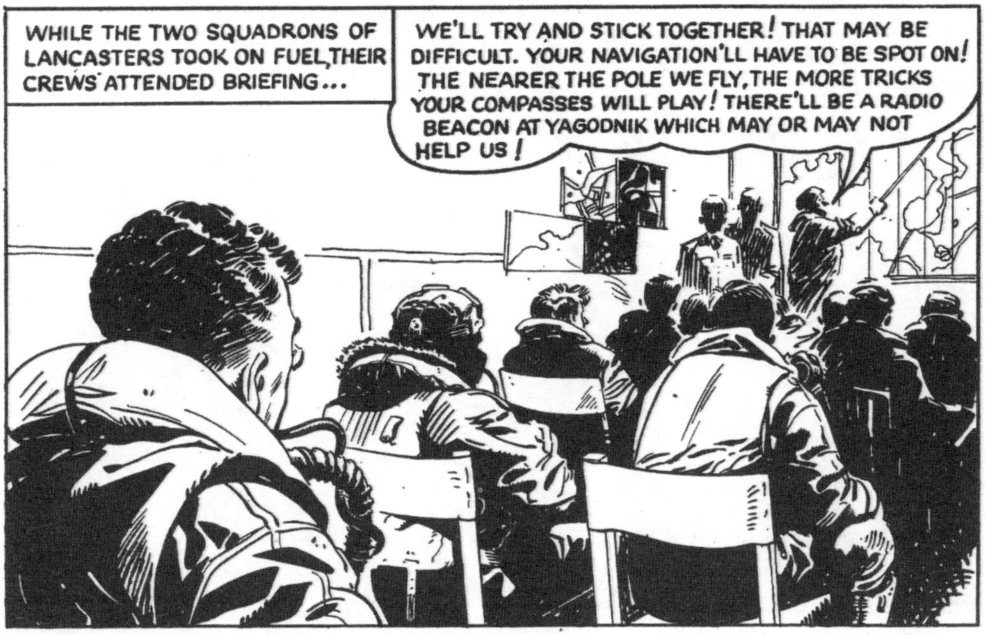
WHILE THE TWO SQUADRONS OF LANCASTERS TOOK ON FUEL,THEIR CREWS ATTENDED BRIEFING...
WE'LL TRY AND STICK TOGETHER! THAT MAY BE DIFFICULT. YOUR NAVIGATION'LL HAVE TO BE SPOT ON! THE NEARER THE POLE WE FLY, THE MORE TRICKS YOUR COMPASSES WILL PLAY! THERE'LL BE A RADIO BEACON AT YAGODNIK WHICH MAY OR MAY NOT HELP US!

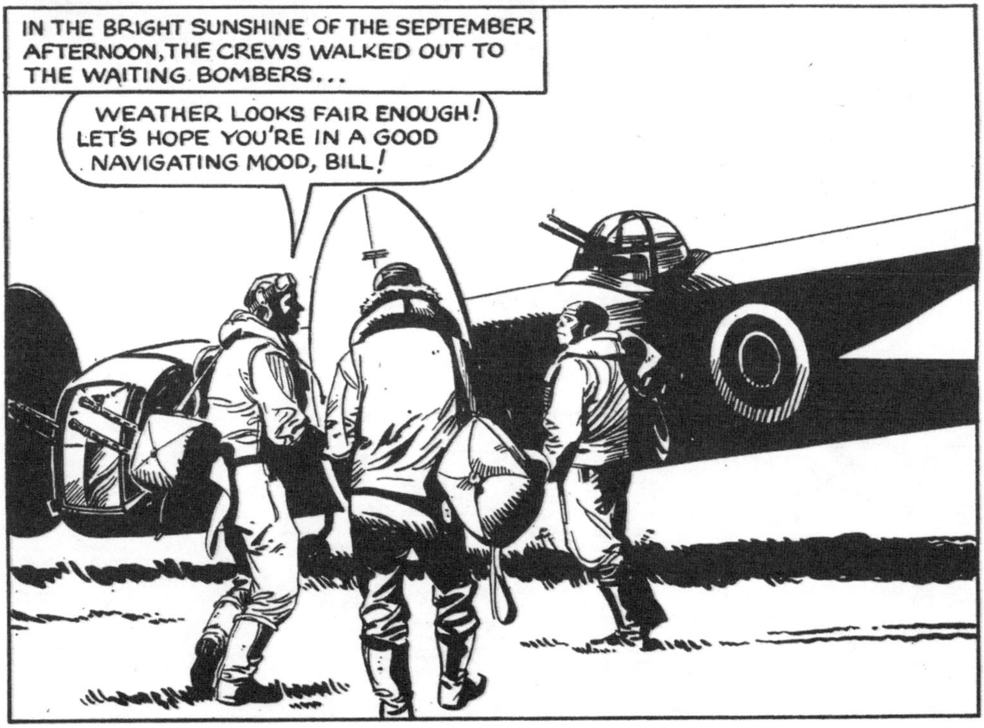
IN THE BRIGHT SUNSHINE OF THE SEPTEMBER AFTERNOON, THE CREWS WALKED OUT TO THE WAITING BOMBERS...
WEATHER LOOKS FAIR ENOUGH! LET'S HOPE YOU'RE IN A GOOD NAVIGATING MOOD, BILL!

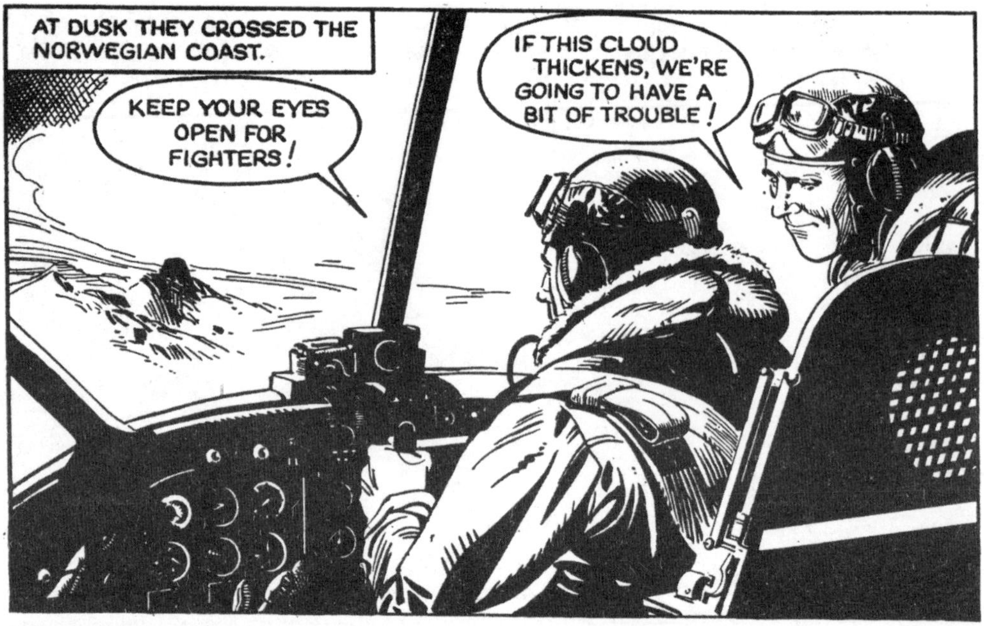
AT DUSK THEY CROSSED THE NORWEGIAN COAST.
KEEP YOUR EYES OPEN FOR FIGHTERS!
IF THIS CLOUD THICKENS, WE'RE GOING TO HAVE A BIT OF TROUBLE!

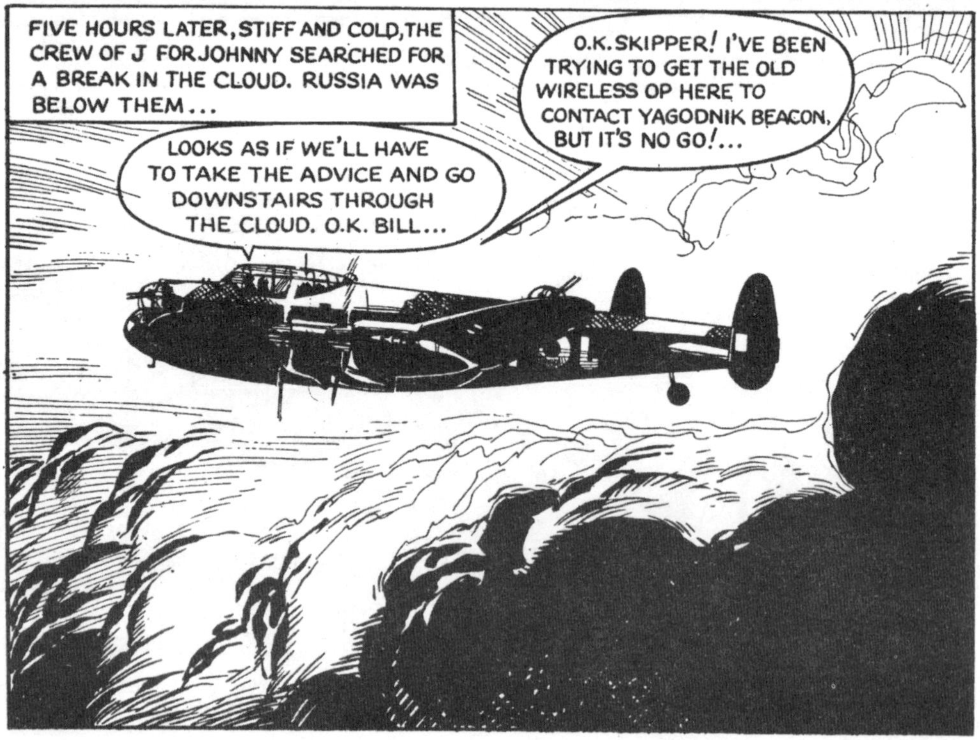
FIVE HOURS LATER, STIFF AND COLD, THE CREW OF J FOR JOHNNY SEARCHED FOR A BREAK IN THE CLOUD. RUSSIA WAS BELOW THEM...
O.K. SKIPPER! I'VE BEEN TRYING TO GET THE OLD WIRELESS OP HERE TO CONTACT YAGODNIK BEACON, BUT IT'S NO GO!...
LOOKS AS IF WE'LL HAVE TO TAKE THE ADVICE AND GO DOWNSTAIRS THROUGH THE CLOUD. O.K. BILL...

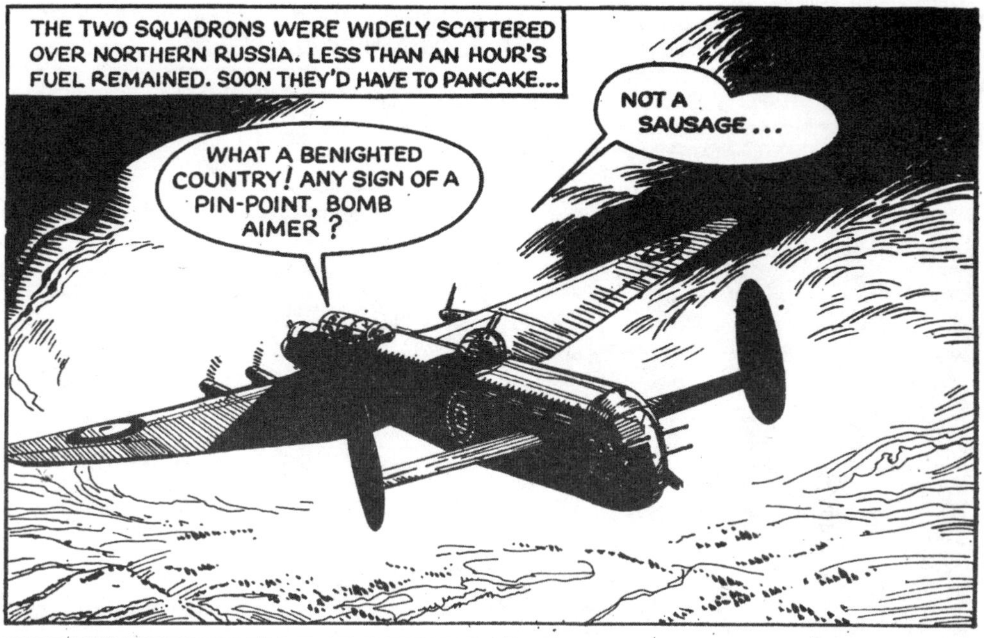
THE TWO SQUADRONS WERE WIDELY SCATTERED OVER NORTHERN RUSSIA. LESS THAN AN HOUR'S FUEL REMAINED. SOON THEY'D HAVE TO PANCAKE...
WHAT A BENIGHTED COUNTRY! ANY SIGN OF A PIN-POINT, BOMB AIMER?
NOT A SAUSAGE...

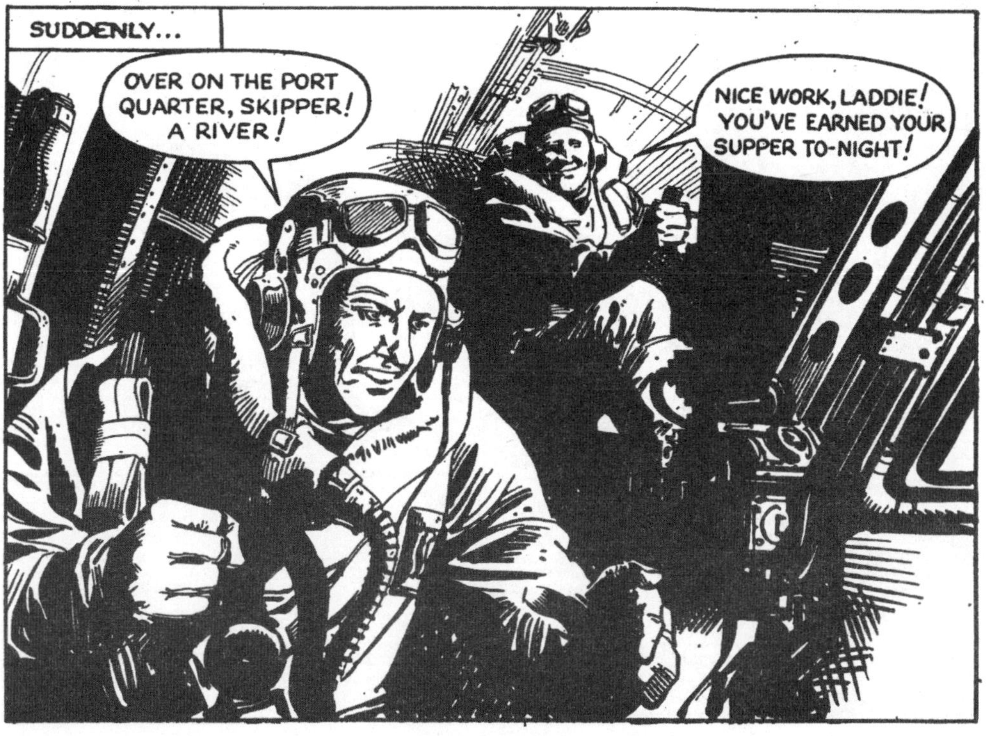
SUDDENLY...
OVER ON THE PORT QUARTER, SKIPPER! A RIVER!
NICE WORK, LADDIE! YOU'VE EARNED YOUR SUPPER TO-NIGHT!

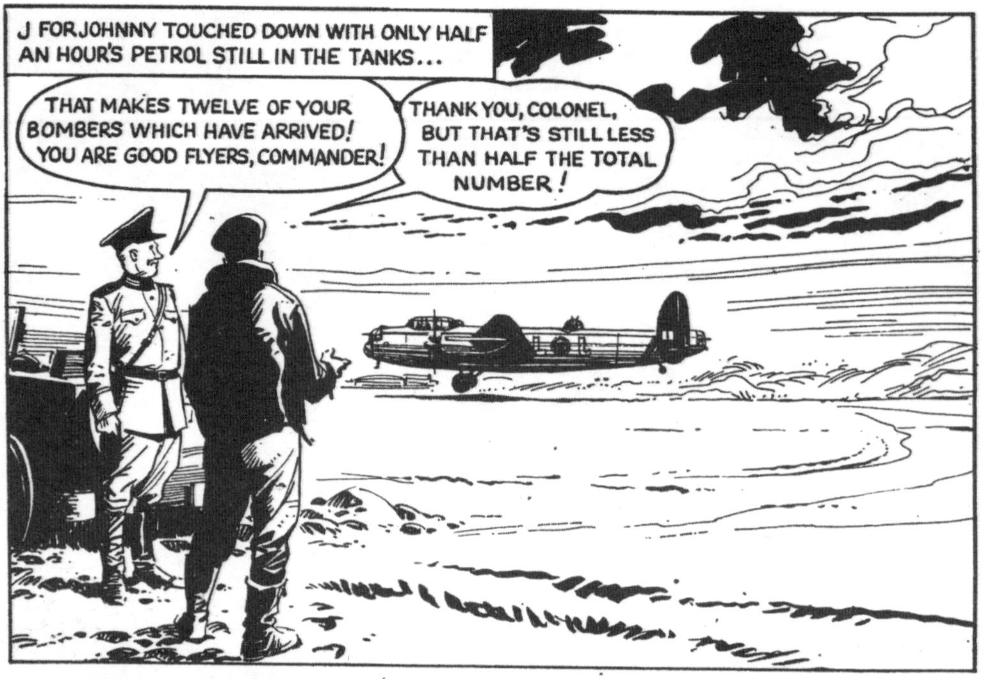
J FOR JOHNNY TOUCHED DOWN WITH ONLY HALF AN HOUR'S PETROL STILL IN THE TANKS...
THAT MAKES TWELVE OF YOUR BOMBERS WHICH HAVE ARRIVED! YOU ARE GOOD FLYERS, COMMANDER!
THANK YOU, COLONEL, BUT THAT'S STILL LESS THAN HALF THE TOTAL NUMBER!

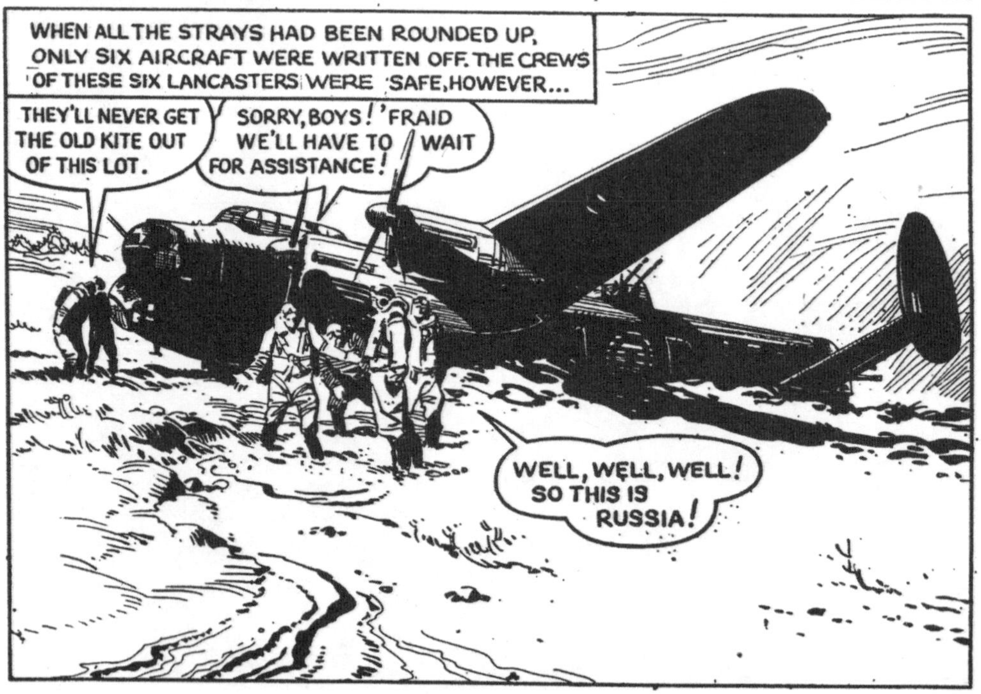
WHEN ALL THE STRAYS HAD BEEN ROUNDED UP, ONLY SIX AIRCRAFT WERE WRITTEN OFF. THE CREWS OF THESE SIX LANCASTERS WERE SAFE, HOWEVER...
THEY'LL NEVER GET THE OLD KITE OUT OF THIS LOT.
SORRY, BOYS! 'FRAID WE'LL HAVE TO WAIT FOR ASSISTANCE!
WELL, WELL, WELL! SO THIS IS RUSSIA!

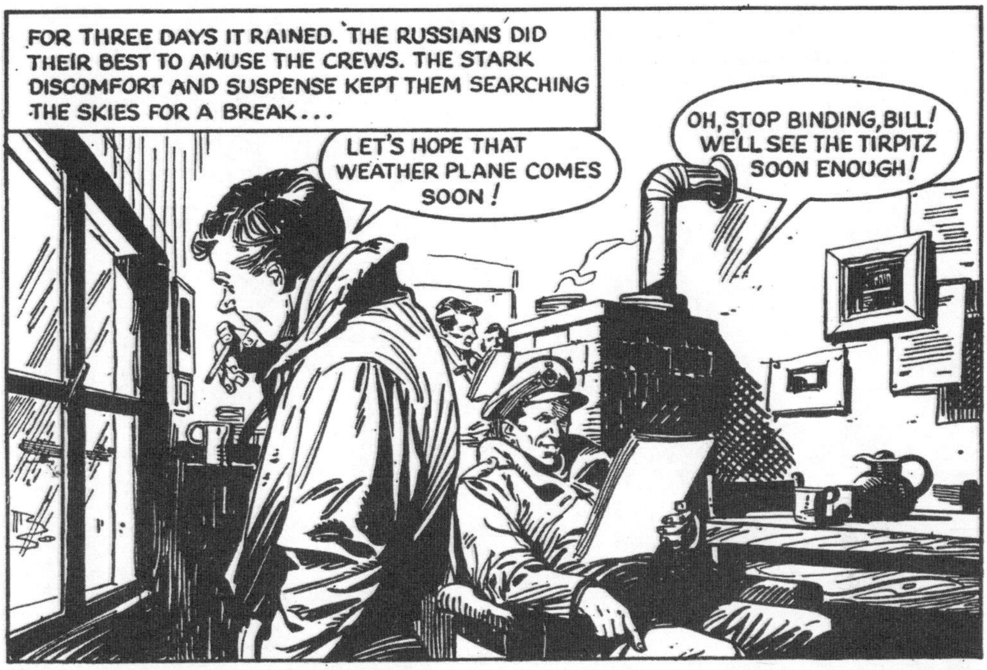
FOR THREE DAYS IT RAINED. THE RUSSIANS DID THEIR BEST TO AMUSE THE CREWS. THE STARK DISCOMFORT AND SUSPENSE KEPT THEM SEARCHING THE SKIES FOR A BREAK...
LET'S HOPE THAT WEATHER PLANE COMES SOON!
OH, STOP BINDING, BILL! WE'LL SEE THE TIRPITZ SOON ENOUGH!

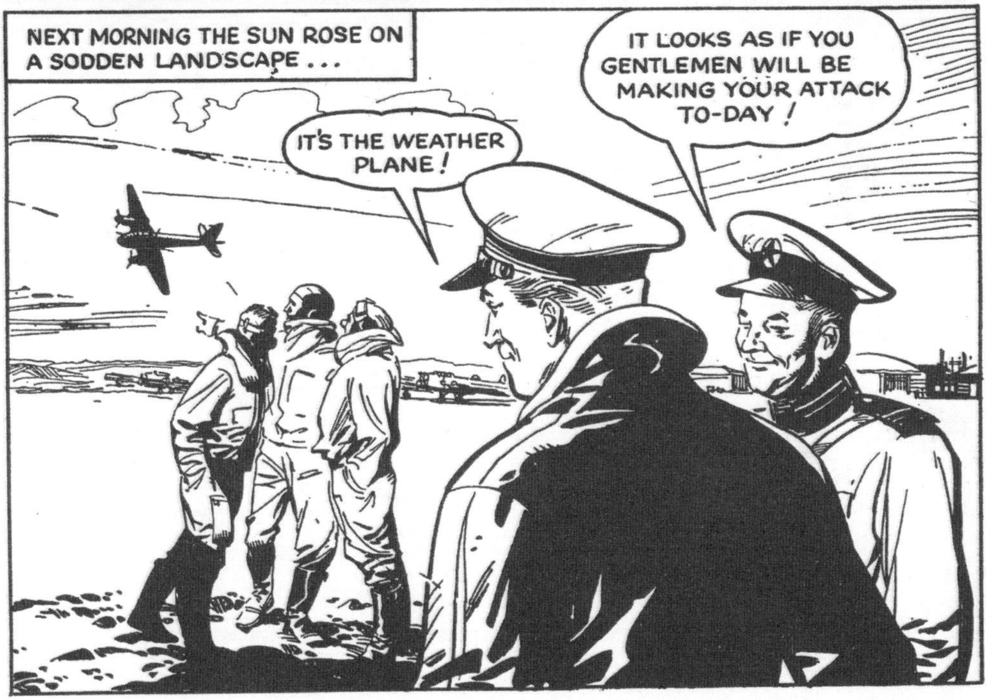
NEXT MORNING THE SUN ROSE ON A SODDEN LANDSCAPE...
IT'S THE WEATHER PLANE!
IT LOOKS AS IF YOU GENTLEMEN WILL BE MAKING YOUR ATTACK TO-DAY!

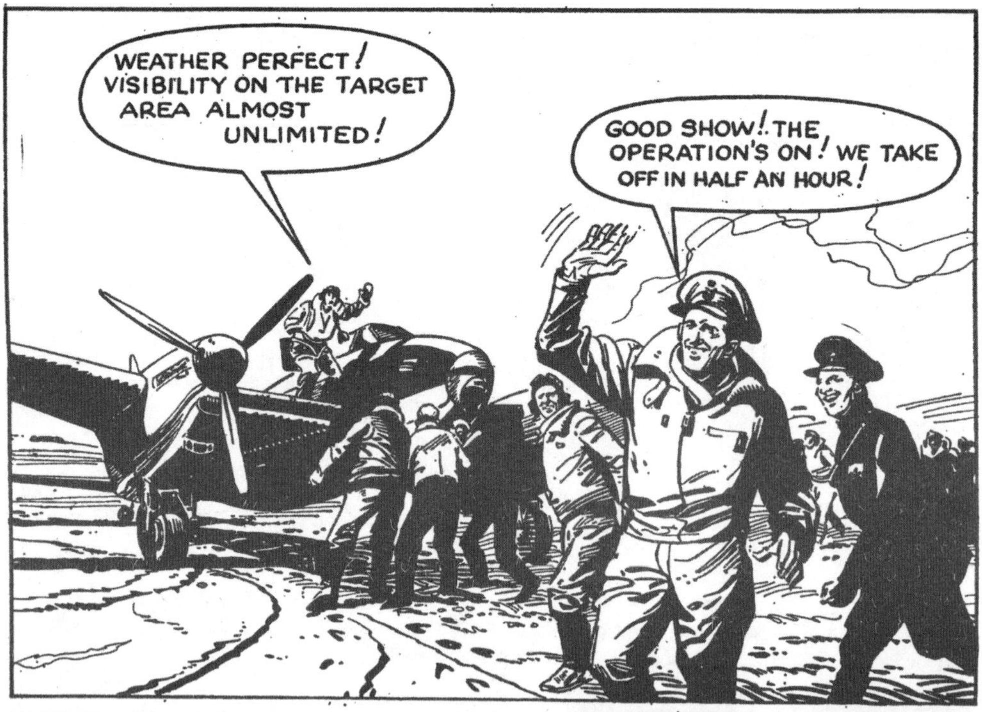
WEATHER PERFECT! VISIBILITY ON THE TARGET AREA ALMOST UNLIMITED!
GOOD SHOW! THE OPERATION'S ON! WE TAKE OFF IN HALF AN HOUR!

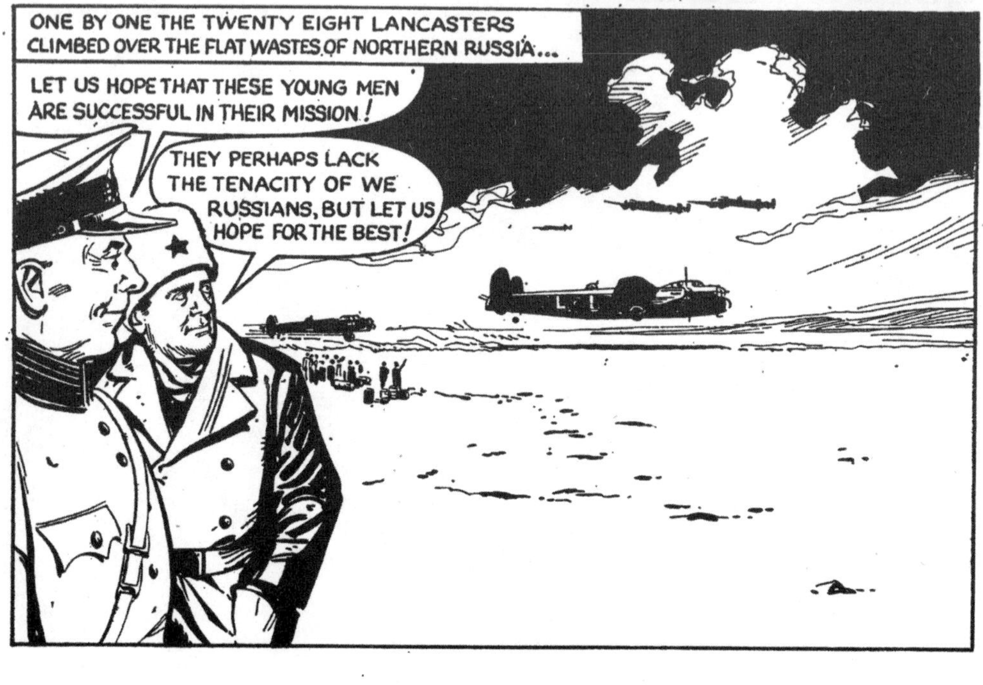
ONE BY ONE THE TWENTY EIGHT LANCASTERS CLIMBED OVER THE FLAT WASTES OF NORTHERN RUSSIA...
LET US HOPE THAT THESE YOUNG MEN ARE SUCCESSFUL IN THEIR MISSION!
THEY PERHAPS LACK THE TENACITY OF WE RUSSIANS, BUT LET US HOPE FOR THE BEST!

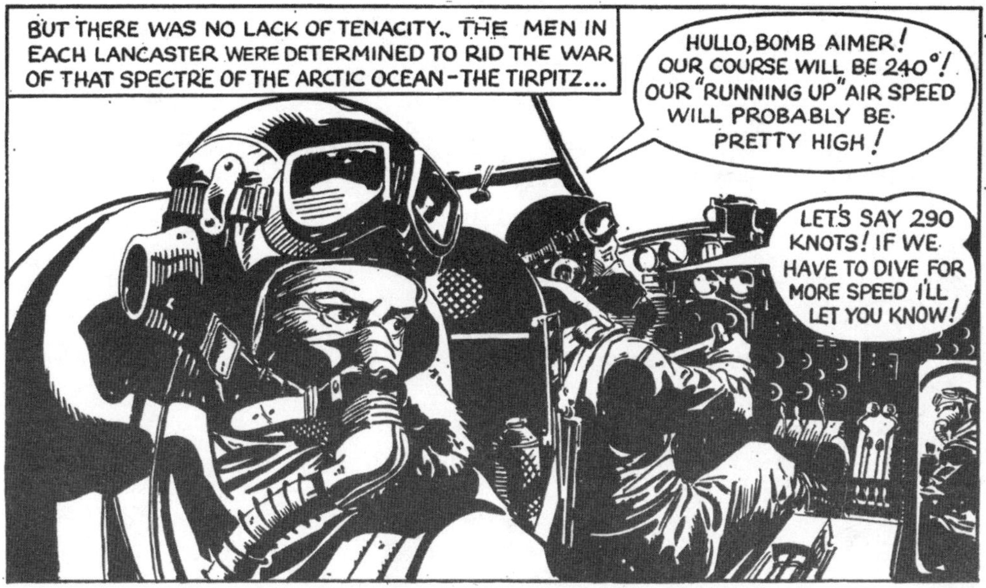
BUT THERE WAS NO LACK OF TENACITY.. THE MEN IN EACH LANCASTER WERE DETERMINED TO RID THE WAR OF THAT SPECTRE OF THE ARCTIC OCEAN – THE TIRPITZ...
HULLO, BOMB AIMER! OUR COURSE WILL BE 240°! OUR "RUNNING UP" AIR SPEED WILL PROBABLY BE PRETTY HIGH!
LET'S SAY 290 KNOTS! IF WE HAVE TO DIVE FOR MORE SPEED I'LL LET YOU KNOW!

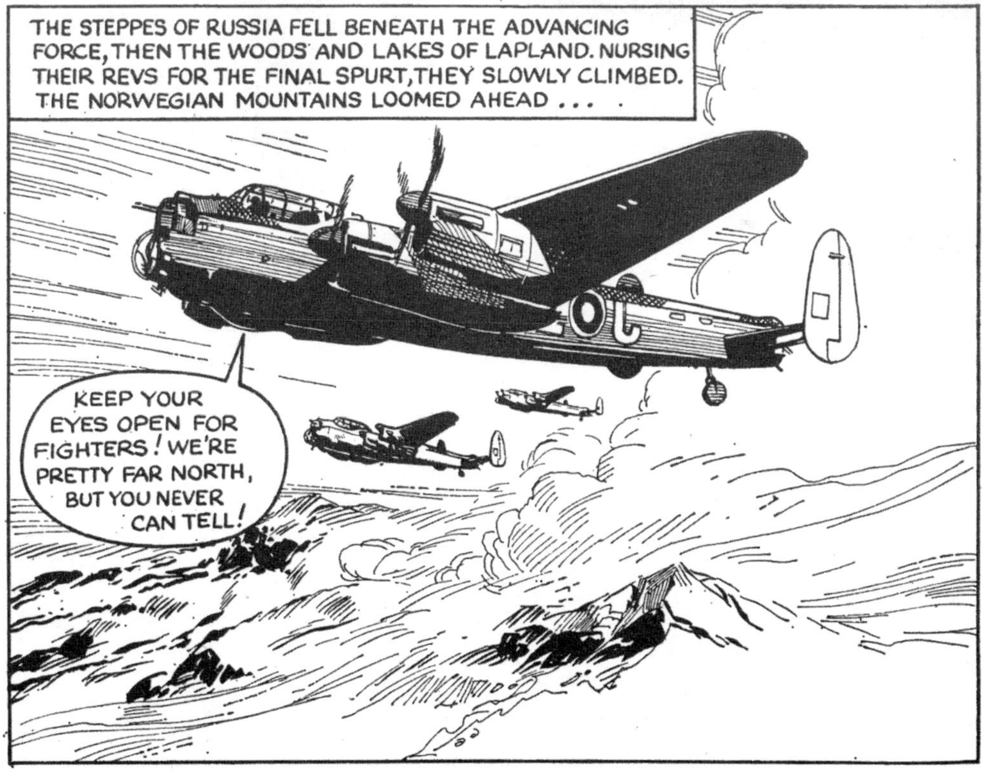
THE STEPPES OF RUSSIA FELL BENEATH THE ADVANCING FORCE, THEN THE WOODS AND LAKES OF LAPLAND. NURSING THEIR REVS FOR THE FINAL SPURT, THEY SLOWLY CLIMBED. THE NORWEGIAN MOUNTAINS LOOMED AHEAD ...
KEEP YOUR EYES OPEN FOR FIGHTERS! WE'RE PRETTY FAR NORTH, BUT YOU NEVER CAN TELL!

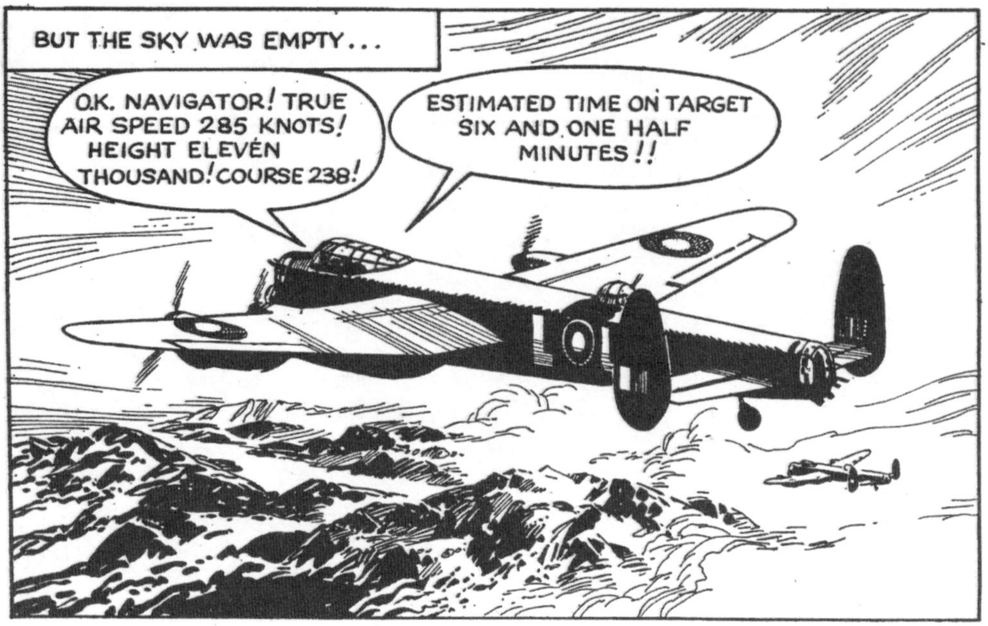
BUT THE SKY WAS EMPTY...
O.K. NAVIGATOR! TRUE AIR SPEED 285 KNOTS! HEIGHT ELEVEN THOUSAND! COURSE 238!
ESTIMATED TIME ON TARGET SIX AND ONE HALF MINUTES!!

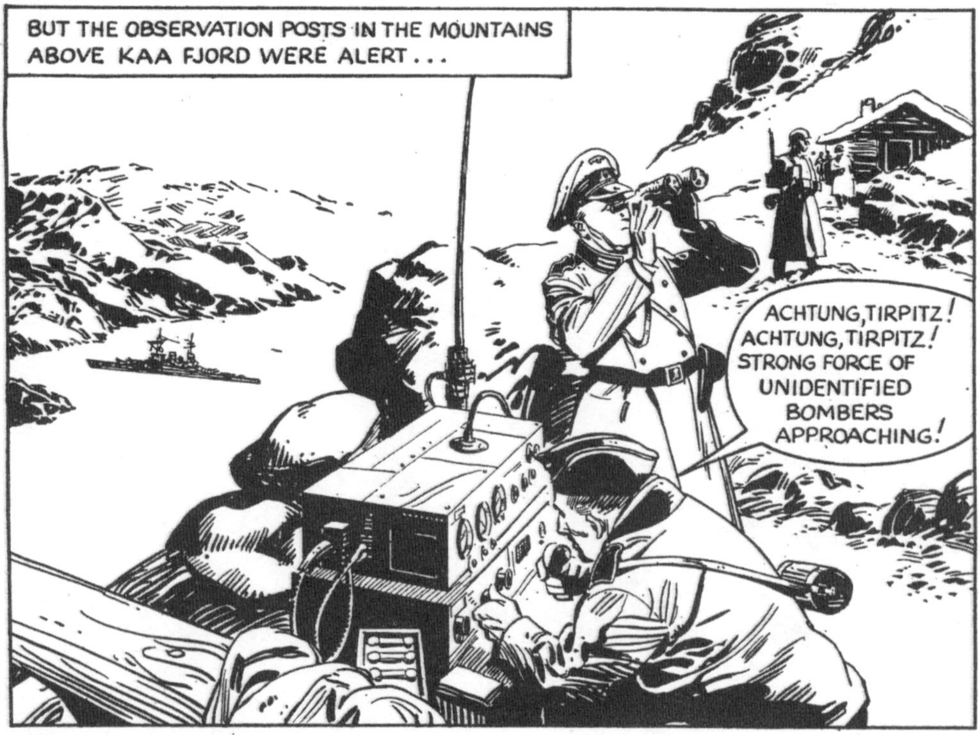
BUT THE OBSERVATION POSTS IN THE MOUNTAINS ABOVE KAA FJORD WERE ALERT...
ACHTUNG, TIRPITZ! ACHTUNG, TIRPITZ! STRONG FORCE OF UNIDENTIFIED BOMBERS APPROACHING!

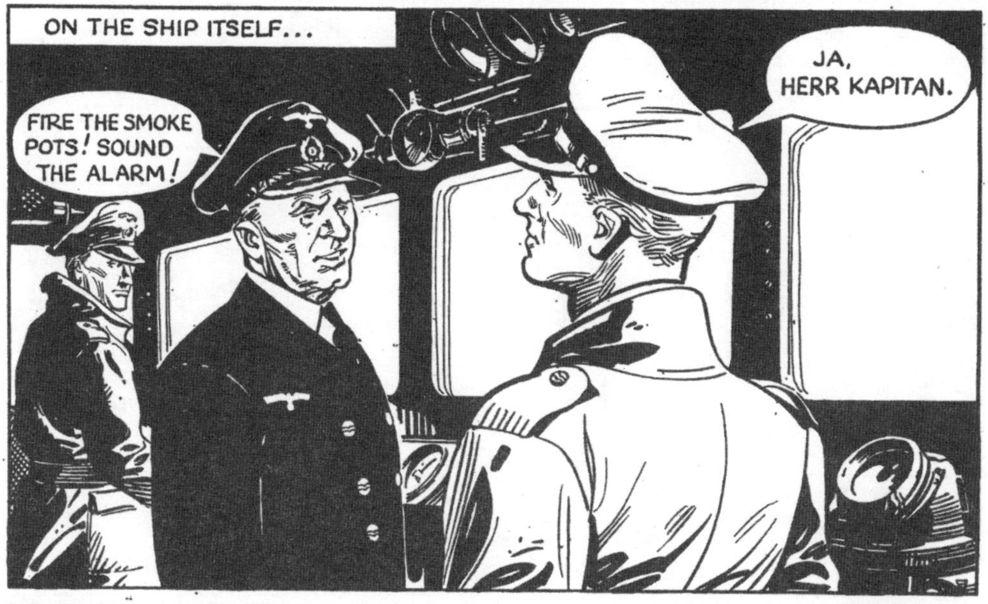
ON THE SHIP ITSELF...
FIRE THE SMOKE POTS! SOUND THE ALARM!
JA, HERR KAPITAN.

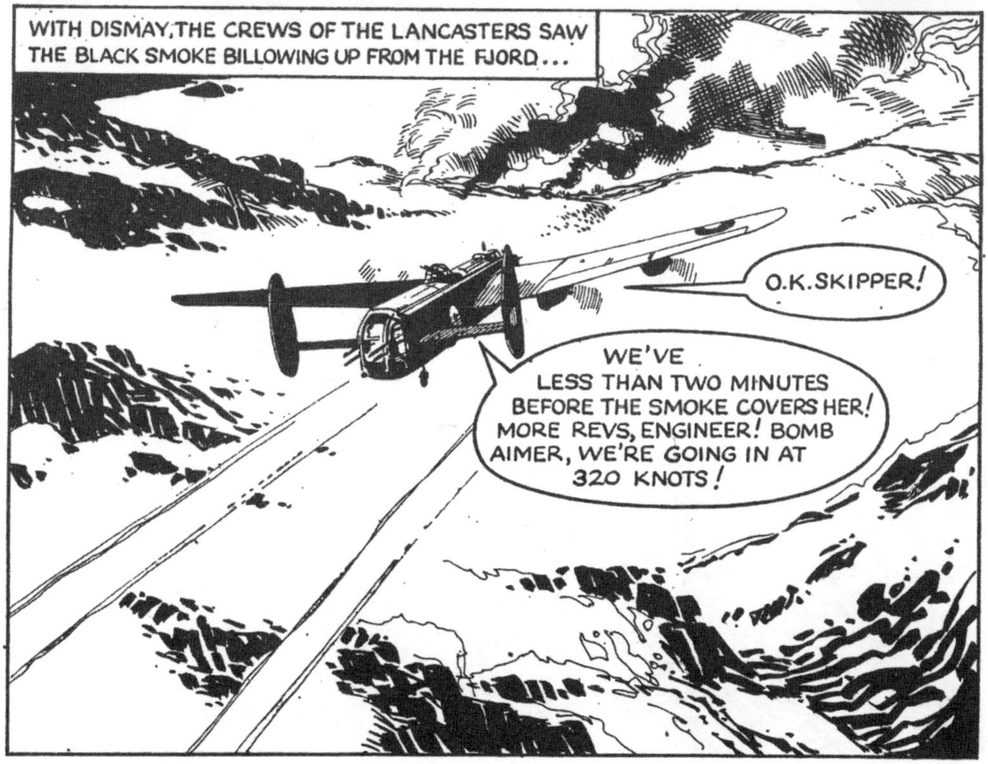
WITH DISMAY, THE CREWS OF THE LANCASTERS SAW THE BLACK SMOKE BILLOWING UP FROM THE FJORD...
WE'VE LESS THAN TWO MINUTES BEFORE THE SMOKE COVERS HER! MORE REVS, ENGINEER! BOMB AIMER, WE'RE GOING IN AT 320 KNOTS!
O.K. SKIPPER!

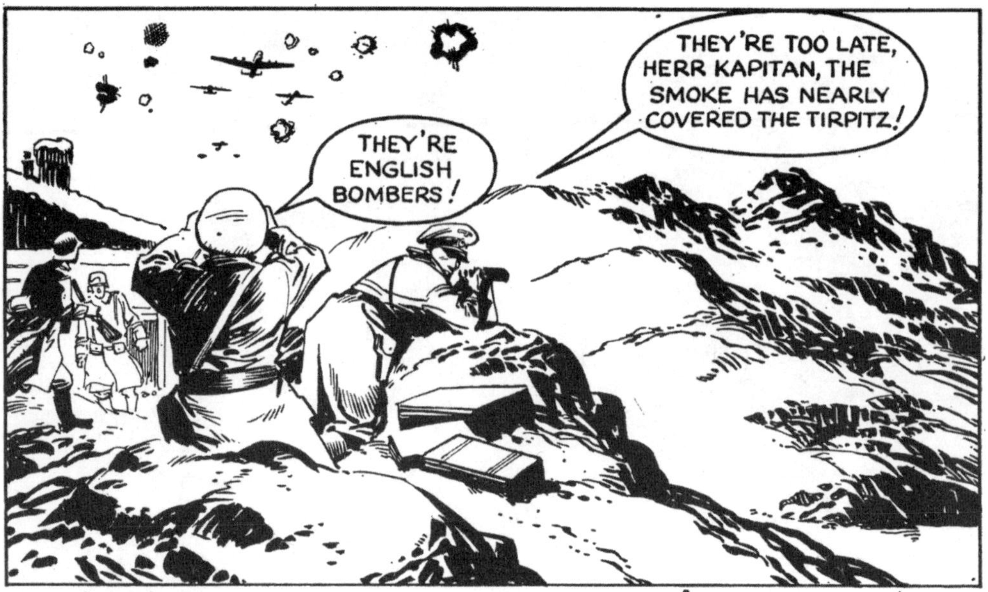
THEY'RE ENGLISH BOMBERS!
THEY'RE TOO LATE, HERR KAPITAN, THE SMOKE HAS NEARLY COVERED THE TIRPITZ!

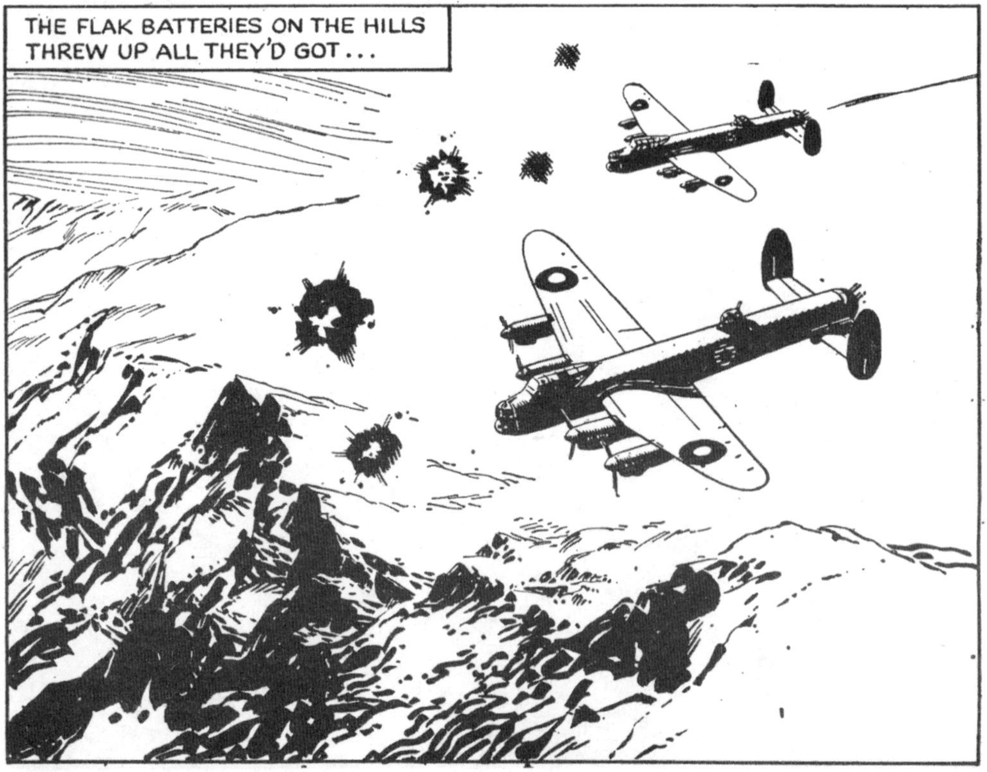
THE FLAK BATTERIES ON THE HILLS THREW UP ALL THEY'D GOT...

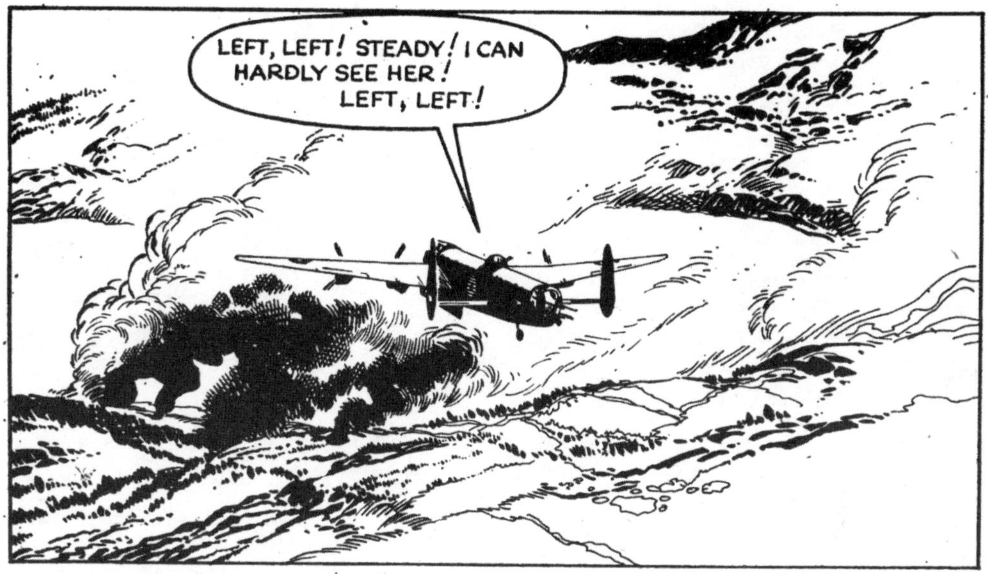
LEFT, LEFT! STEADY! I CAN HARDLY SEE HER! LEFT, LEFT!

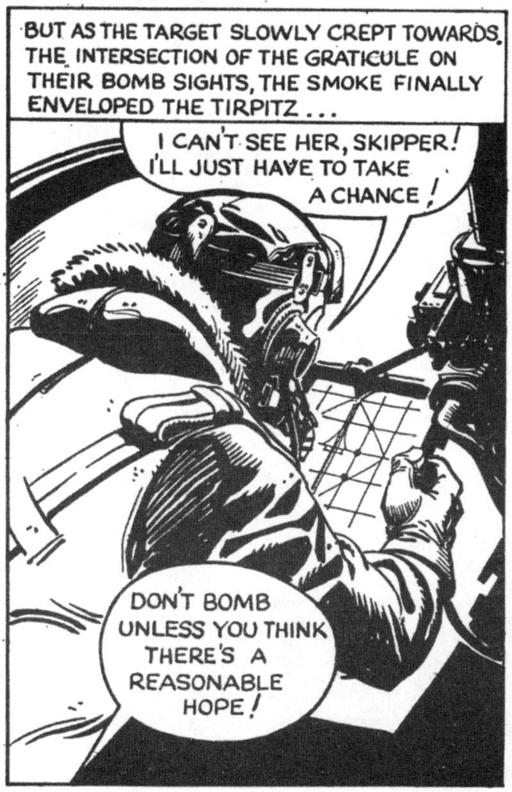
BUT AS THE TARGET SLOWLY CREPT TOWARDS THE INTERSECTION OF THE GRATICULE ON THEIR BOMB SIGHTS, THE SMOKE FINALLY ENVELOPED THE TIRPITZ...
I CAN'T SEE HER, SKIPPER! I'LL JUST HAVE TO TAKE A CHANCE!
DON'T BOMB UNLESS YOU THINK THERE'S A REASONABLE HOPE!

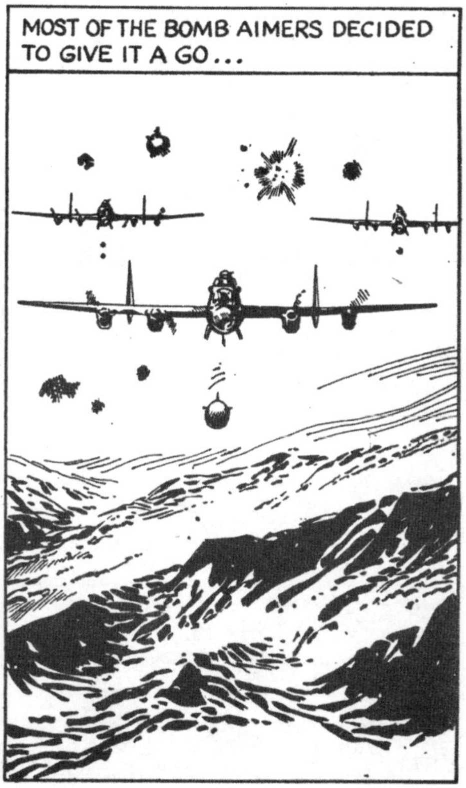
MOST OF THE BOMB AIMERS DECIDED TO GIVE IT A GO...

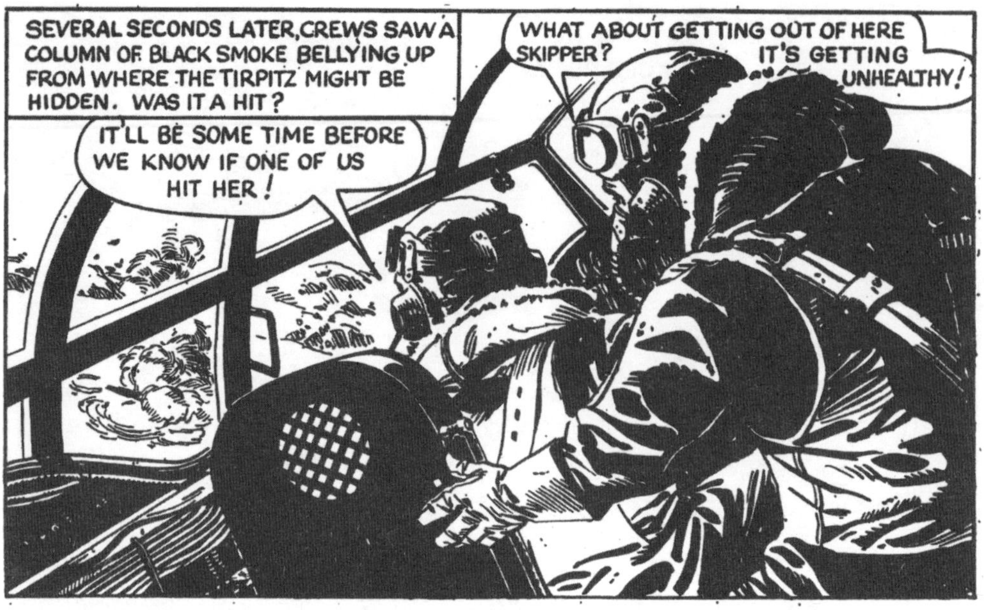
SEVERAL SECONDS LATER, CREWS SAW A COLUMN OF BLACK SMOKE BELLYING UP FROM WHERE THE TIRPITZ MIGHT BE HIDDEN. WAS IT A HIT?
WHAT ABOUT GETTING OUT OF HERE SKIPPER? IT'S GETTING UNHEALTHY!
IT'LL BE SOME TIME BEFORE WE KNOW IF ONE OF US HIT HER!

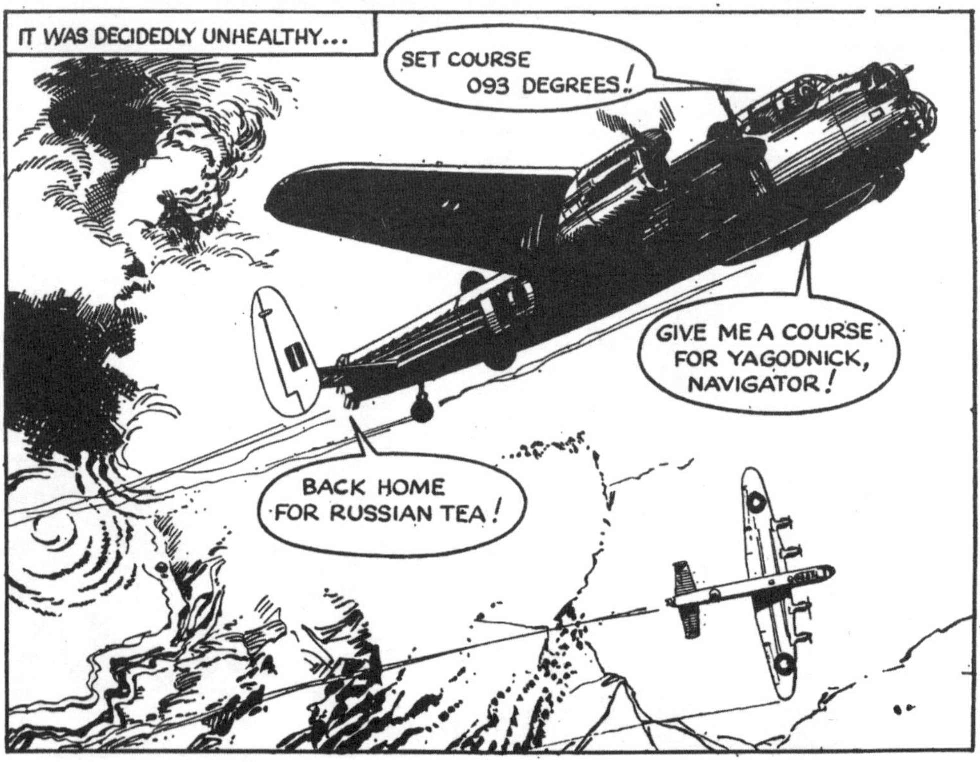
IT WAS DECIDEDLY UNHEALTHY...
GIVE ME A COURSE FOR YAGODNICK, NAVIGATOR!
SET COURSE 093 DEGREES!
BACK HOME FOR RUSSIAN TEA!

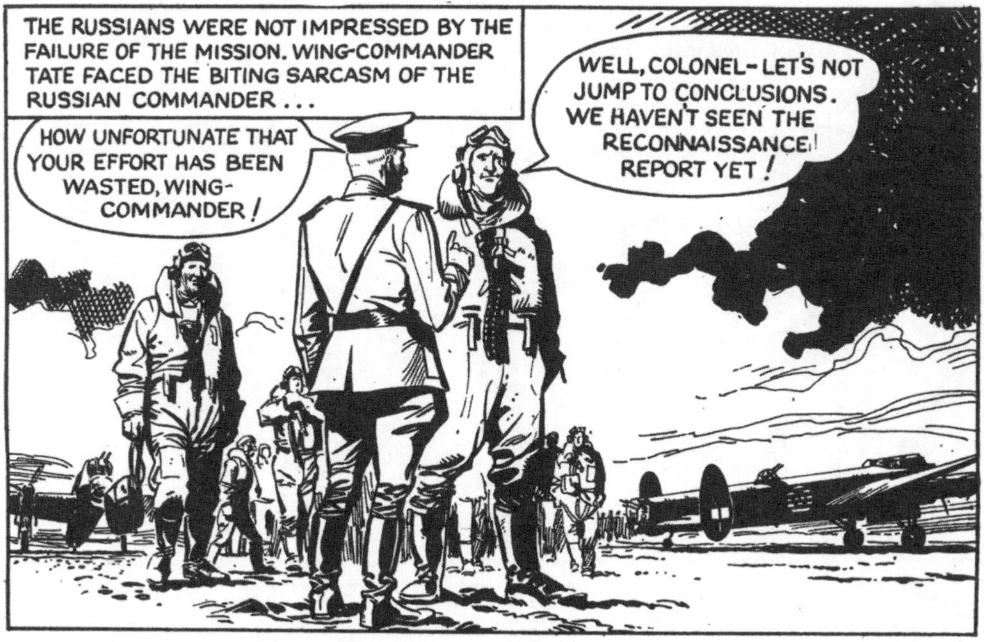
THE RUSSIANS WERE NOT IMPRESSED BY THE FAILURE OF THE MISSION. WING-COMMANDER TATE FACED THE BITING SARCASM OF THE RUSSIAN COMMANDER . . .
HOW UNFORTUNATE THAT YOUR EFFORT HAS BEEN WASTED, WING-COMMANDER!
WELL, COLONEL - LET'S NOT JUMP TO CONCLUSIONS. WE HAVEN'T SEEN THE RECONNAISSANCE REPORT YET!

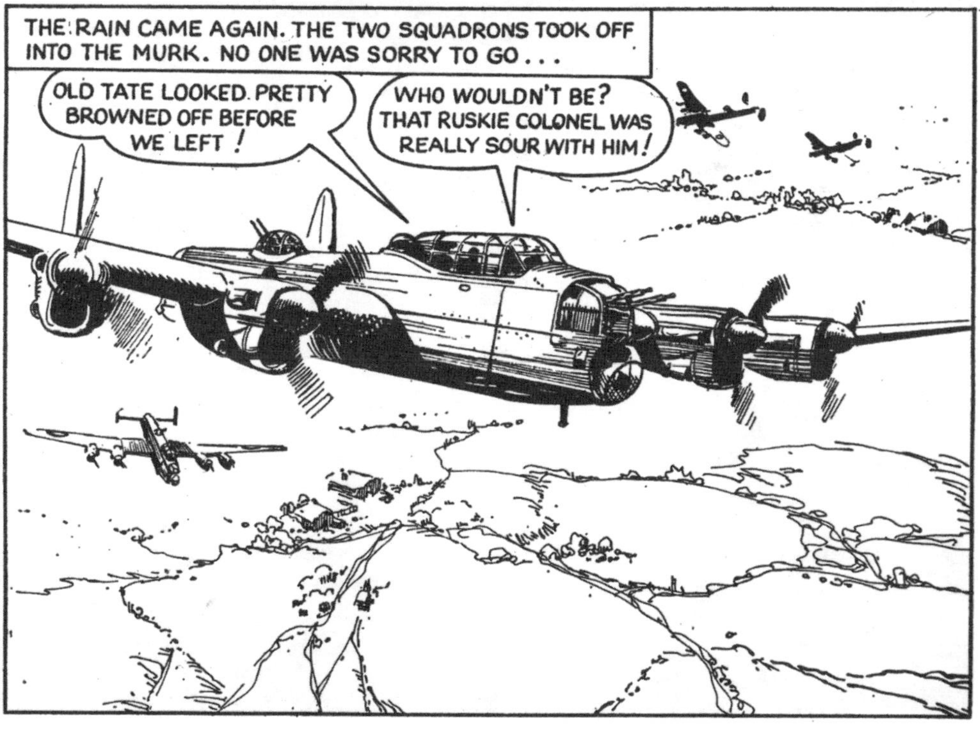
THE RAIN CAME AGAIN. THE TWO SQUADRONS TOOK OFF INTO THE MURK. NO ONE WAS SORRY TO GO . . .
OLD TATE LOOKED PRETTY BROWNED OFF BEFORE WE LEFT!
WHO WOULDN'T BE? THAT RUSKIE COLONEL WAS REALLY SOUR WITH HIM!

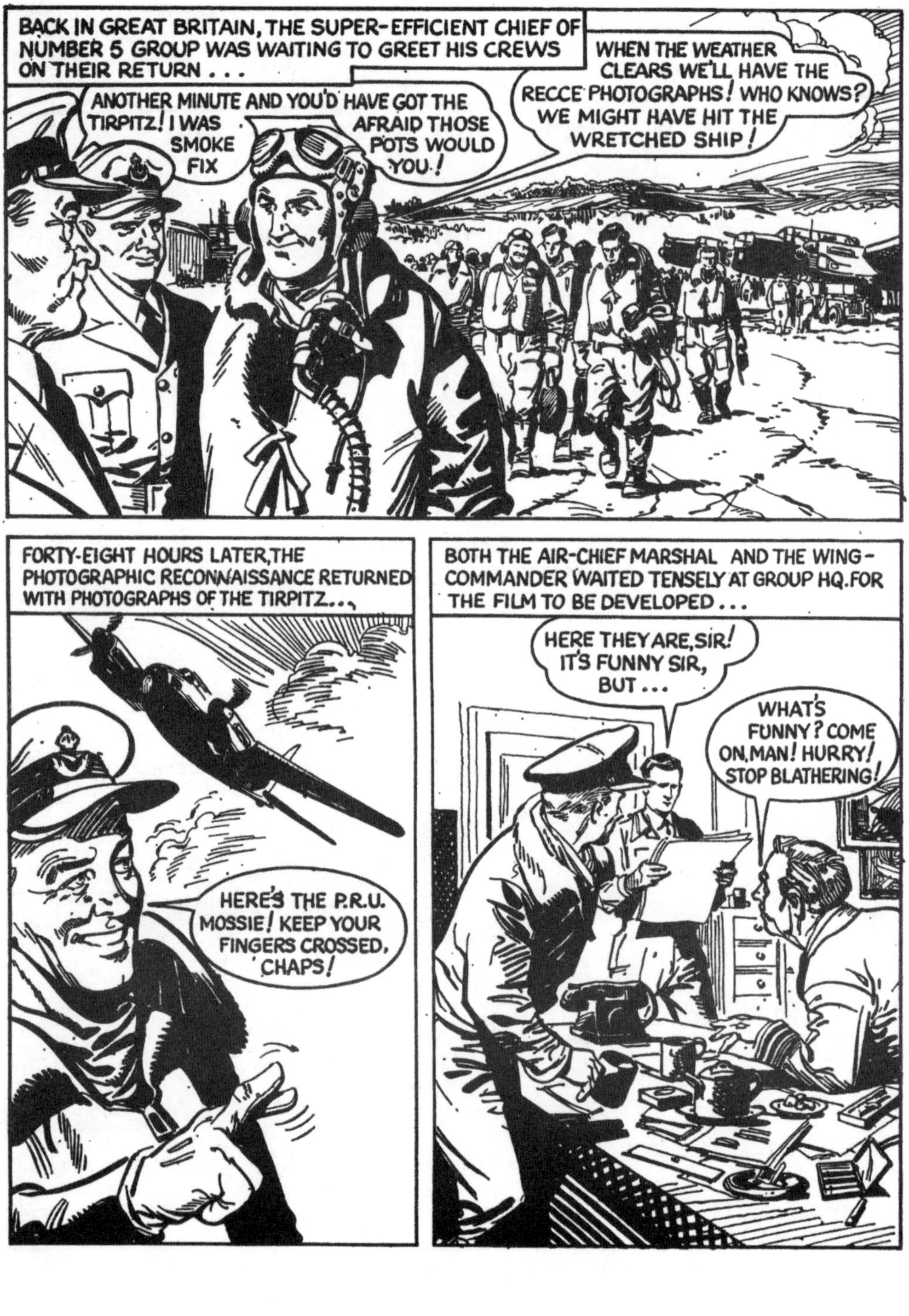
BACK IN GREAT BRITAIN, THE SUPER-EFFICIENT CHIEF OF NUMBER 5 GROUP WAS WAITING TO GREET HIS CREWS ON THEIR RETURN . . .
ANOTHER MINUTE AND YOU'D HAVE GOT THE TIRPITZ! I WAS AFRAID THOSE SMOKE POTS WOULD FIX YOU!
WHEN THE WEATHER CLEARS WE'LL HAVE THE RECCE PHOTOGRAPHS! WHO KNOWS? WE MIGHT HAVE HIT THE WRETCHED SHIP!
FORTY-EIGHT HOURS LATER, THE PHOTOGRAPHIC RECONNAISSANCE RETURNED WITH PHOTOGRAPHS OF THE TIRPITZ...
HERE'S THE P.R.U. MOSSIE! KEEP YOUR FINGERS CROSSED, CHAPS!
BOTH THE AIR-CHIEF MARSHAL AND THE WING-COMMANDER WAITED TENSELY AT GROUP HQ. FOR THE FILM TO BE DEVELOPED . . .
HERE THEY ARE, SIR! IT'S FUNNY SIR, BUT . . .
WHAT'S FUNNY? COME ON, MAN! HURRY! STOP BLATHERING!

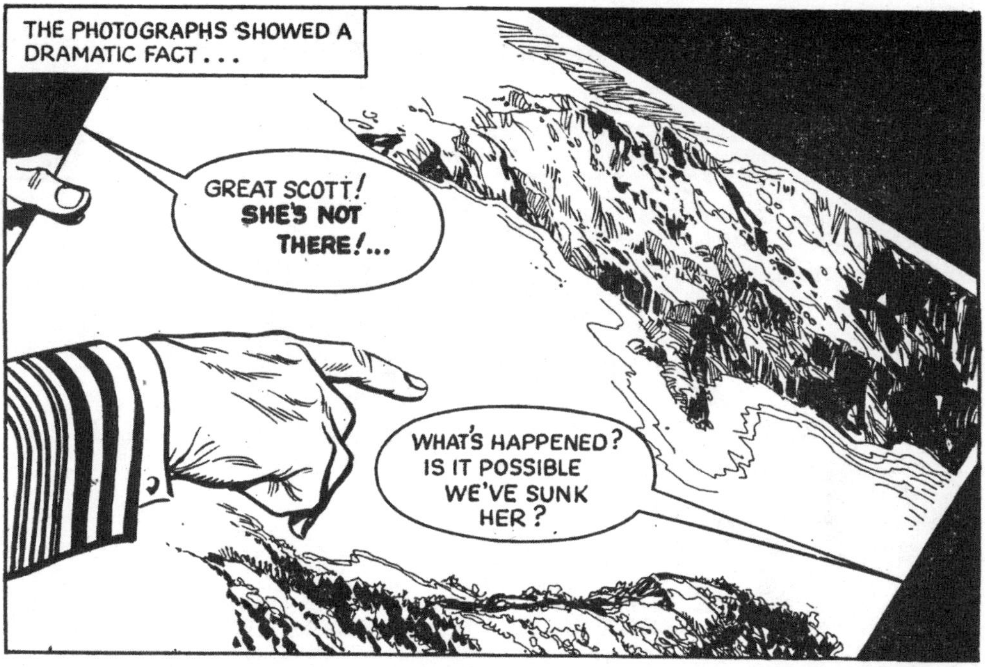
THE PHOTOGRAPHS SHOWED A DRAMATIC FACT . . .
GREAT SCOTT! **SHE'S NOT THERE!...**
WHAT'S HAPPENED? IS IT POSSIBLE WE'VE SUNK HER?

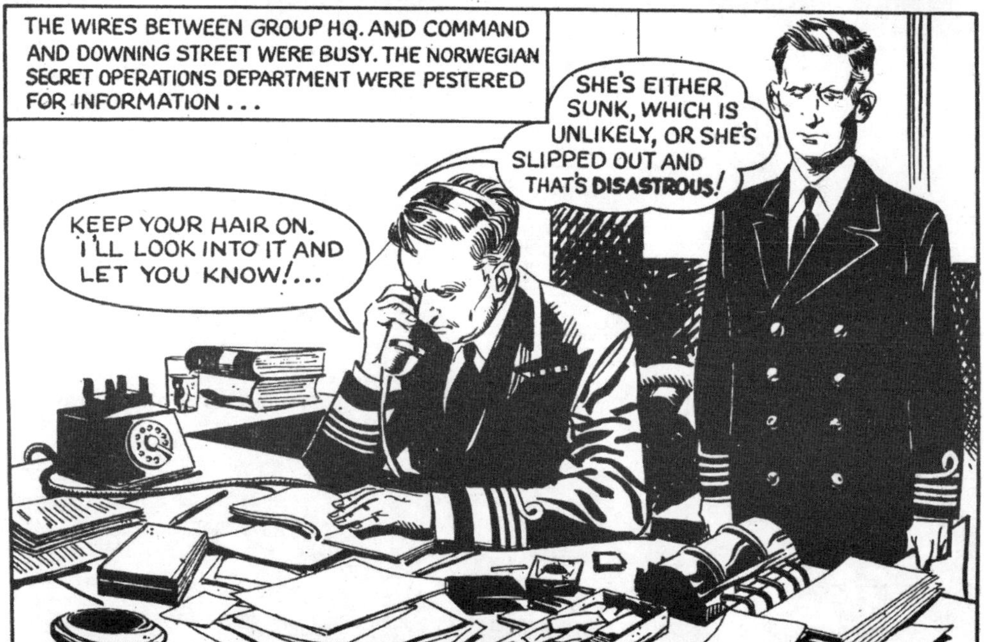
THE WIRES BETWEEN GROUP HQ. AND COMMAND AND DOWNING STREET WERE BUSY. THE NORWEGIAN SECRET OPERATIONS DEPARTMENT WERE PESTERED FOR INFORMATION . . .
SHE'S EITHER SUNK, WHICH IS UNLIKELY, OR SHE'S SLIPPED OUT AND THAT'S **DISASTROUS**!
KEEP YOUR HAIR ON. I'LL LOOK INTO IT AND LET YOU KNOW!...

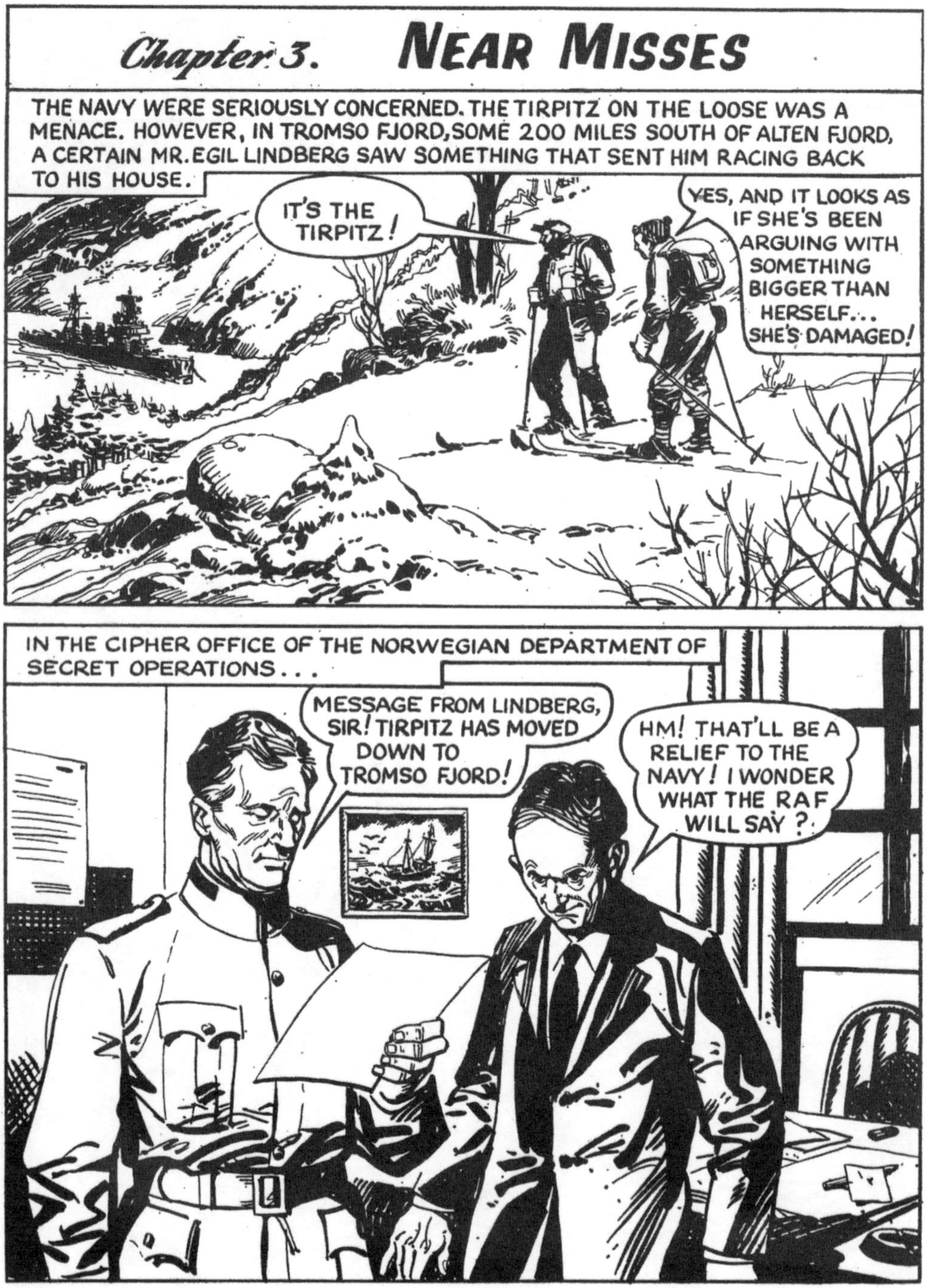
Chapter 3. NEAR MISSES
THE NAVY WERE SERIOUSLY CONCERNED. THE TIRPITZ ON THE LOOSE WAS A MENACE. HOWEVER, IN TROMSO FJORD, SOME 200 MILES SOUTH OF ALTEN FJORD, A CERTAIN MR. EGIL LINDBERG SAW SOMETHING THAT SENT HIM RACING BACK TO HIS HOUSE.
IT'S THE TIRPITZ!
YES, AND IT LOOKS AS IF SHE'S BEEN ARGUING WITH SOMETHING BIGGER THAN HERSELF... SHE'S DAMAGED!
IN THE CIPHER OFFICE OF THE NORWEGIAN DEPARTMENT OF SECRET OPERATIONS...
MESSAGE FROM LINDBERG, SIR! TIRPITZ HAS MOVED DOWN TO TROMSO FJORD!
HM! THAT'LL BE A RELIEF TO THE NAVY! I WONDER WHAT THE RAF WILL SAY?

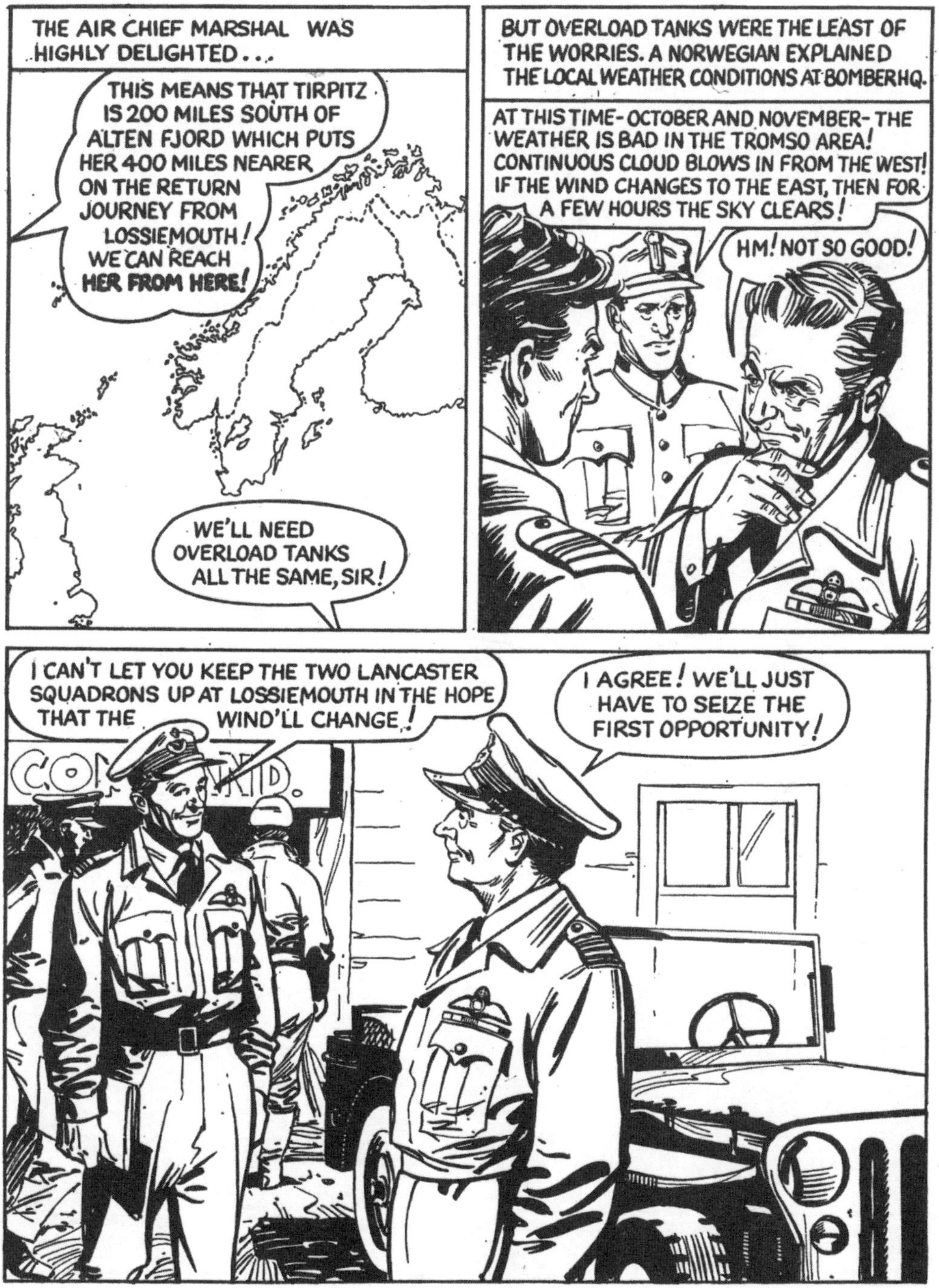
THE AIR CHIEF MARSHAL WAS HIGHLY DELIGHTED...
THIS MEANS THAT TIRPITZ IS 200 MILES SOUTH OF ALTEN FJORD WHICH PUTS HER 400 MILES NEARER ON THE RETURN JOURNEY FROM LOSSIEMOUTH! WE CAN REACH HER FROM HERE!
WE'LL NEED OVERLOAD TANKS ALL THE SAME, SIR!
BUT OVERLOAD TANKS WERE THE LEAST OF THE WORRIES. A NORWEGIAN EXPLAINED THE LOCAL WEATHER CONDITIONS AT BOMBER HQ.
AT THIS TIME- OCTOBER AND NOVEMBER- THE WEATHER IS BAD IN THE TROMSO AREA! CONTINUOUS CLOUD BLOWS IN FROM THE WEST! IF THE WIND CHANGES TO THE EAST, THEN FOR A FEW HOURS THE SKY CLEARS!
HM! NOT SO GOOD!
I CAN'T LET YOU KEEP THE TWO LANCASTER SQUADRONS UP AT LOSSIEMOUTH IN THE HOPE THAT THE WIND'LL CHANGE!
I AGREE! WE'LL JUST HAVE TO SEIZE THE FIRST OPPORTUNITY!

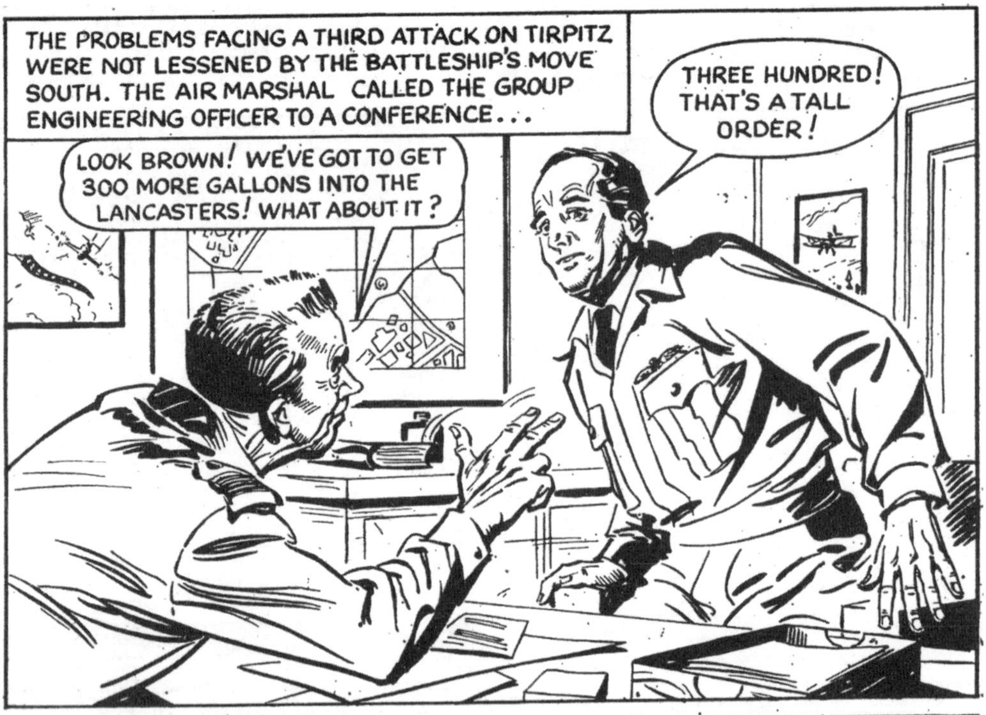
THE PROBLEMS FACING A THIRD ATTACK ON TIRPITZ WERE NOT LESSENED BY THE BATTLESHIP'S MOVE SOUTH. THE AIR MARSHAL CALLED THE GROUP ENGINEERING OFFICER TO A CONFERENCE...
LOOK BROWN! WE'VE GOT TO GET 300 MORE GALLONS INTO THE LANCASTERS! WHAT ABOUT IT?
THREE HUNDRED! THAT'S A TALL ORDER!

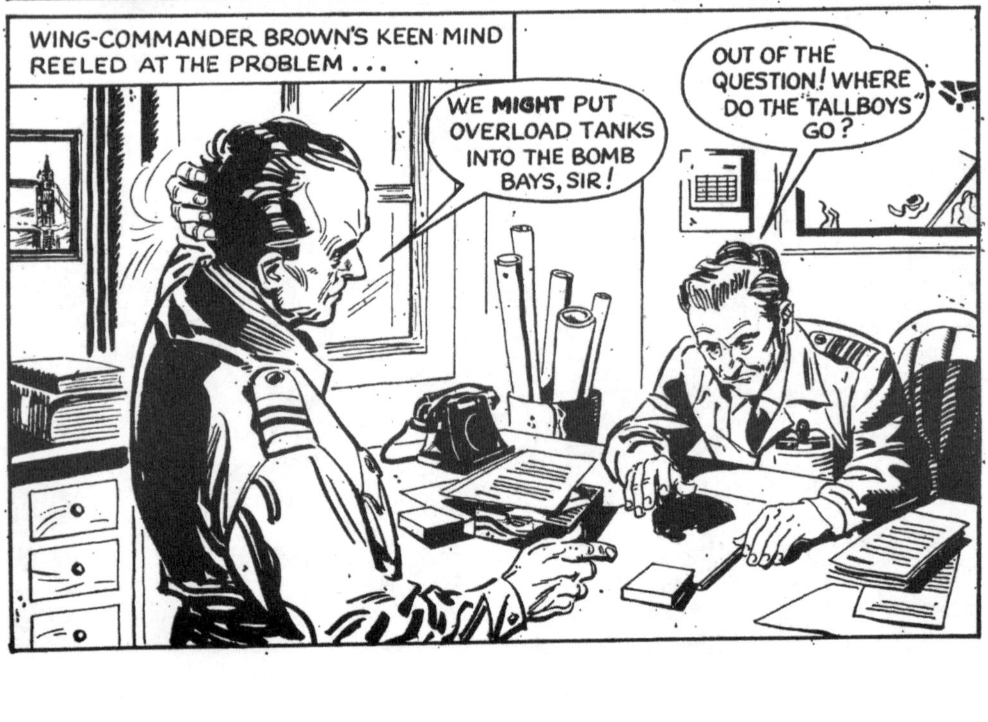
WING-COMMANDER BROWN'S KEEN MIND REELED AT THE PROBLEM...
WE **MIGHT** PUT OVERLOAD TANKS INTO THE BOMB BAYS, SIR!
OUT OF THE QUESTION! WHERE DO THE "TALLBOYS" GO?

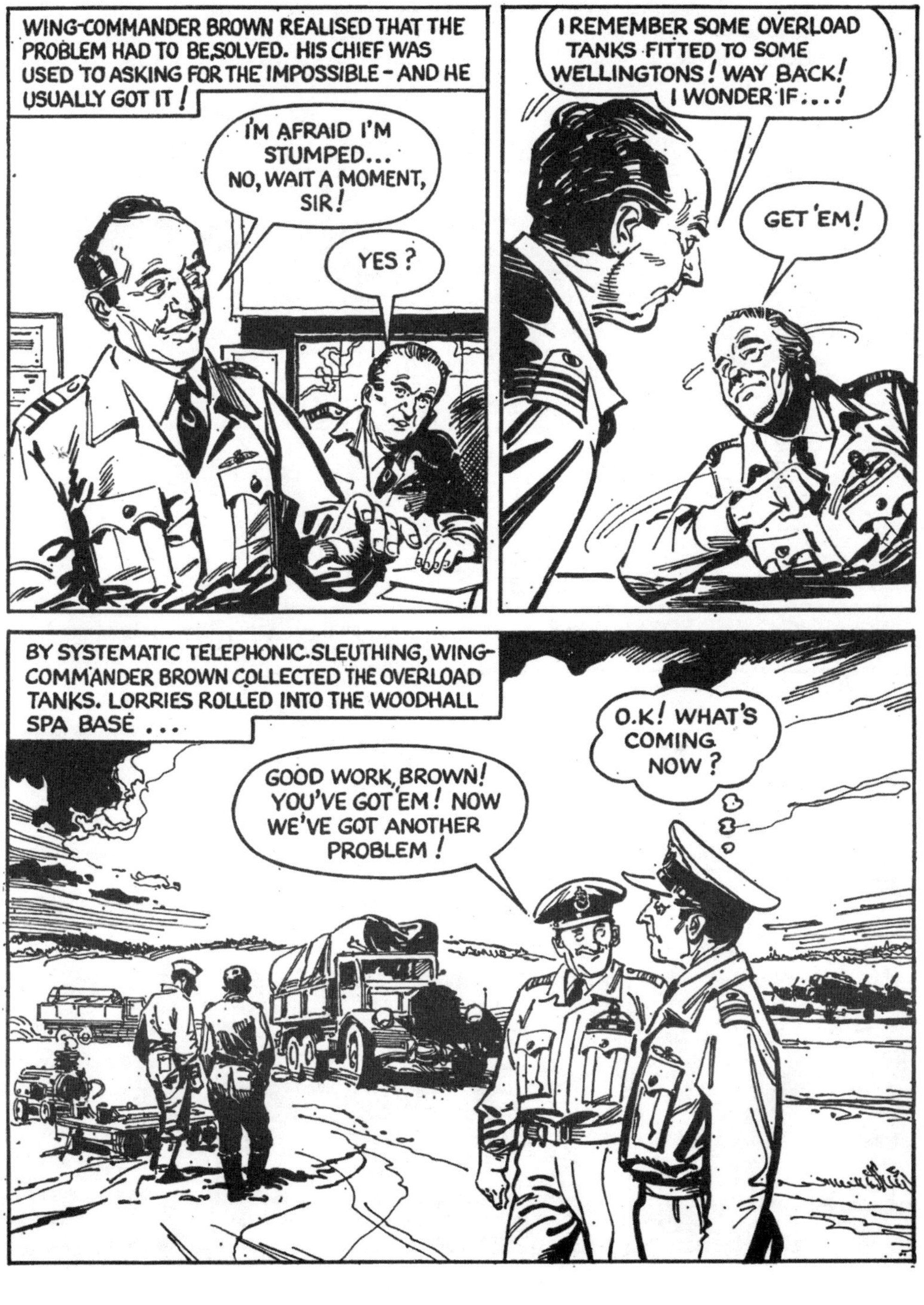
WING-COMMANDER BROWN REALISED THAT THE PROBLEM HAD TO BE SOLVED. HIS CHIEF WAS USED TO ASKING FOR THE IMPOSSIBLE - AND HE USUALLY GOT IT!
I'M AFRAID I'M STUMPED... NO, WAIT A MOMENT, SIR!
YES?
I REMEMBER SOME OVERLOAD TANKS FITTED TO SOME WELLINGTONS! WAY BACK! I WONDER IF...!
GET 'EM!
BY SYSTEMATIC TELEPHONIC SLEUTHING, WING-COMMANDER BROWN COLLECTED THE OVERLOAD TANKS. LORRIES ROLLED INTO THE WOODHALL SPA BASE...
GOOD WORK, BROWN! YOU'VE GOT 'EM! NOW WE'VE GOT ANOTHER PROBLEM!
O.K! WHAT'S COMING NOW?

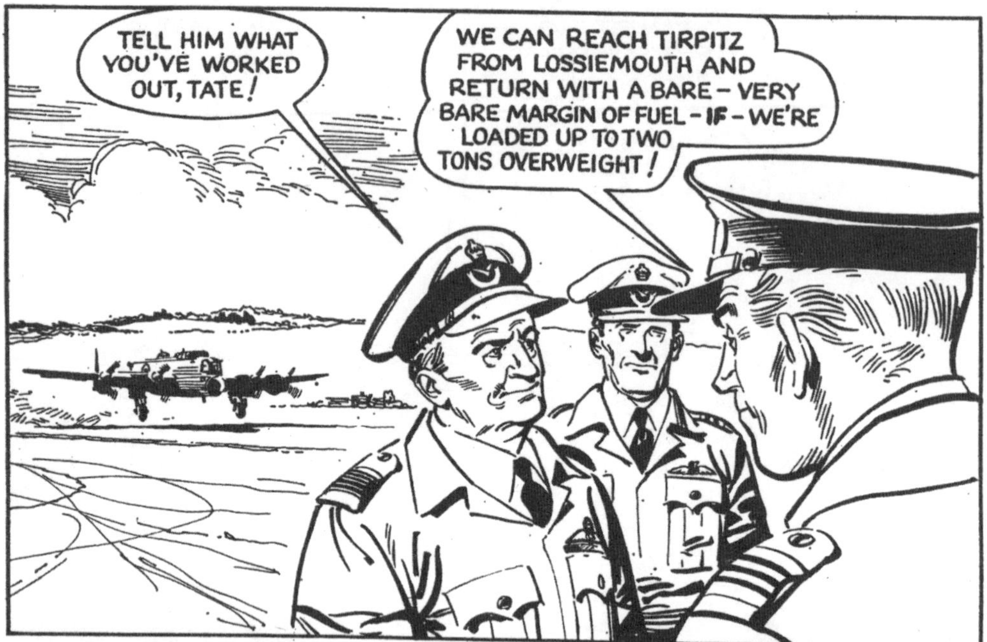
TELL HIM WHAT YOU'VE WORKED OUT, TATE!
WE CAN REACH TIRPITZ FROM LOSSIEMOUTH AND RETURN WITH A BARE - VERY BARE MARGIN OF FUEL - IF - WE'RE LOADED UP TO TWO TONS OVERWEIGHT!

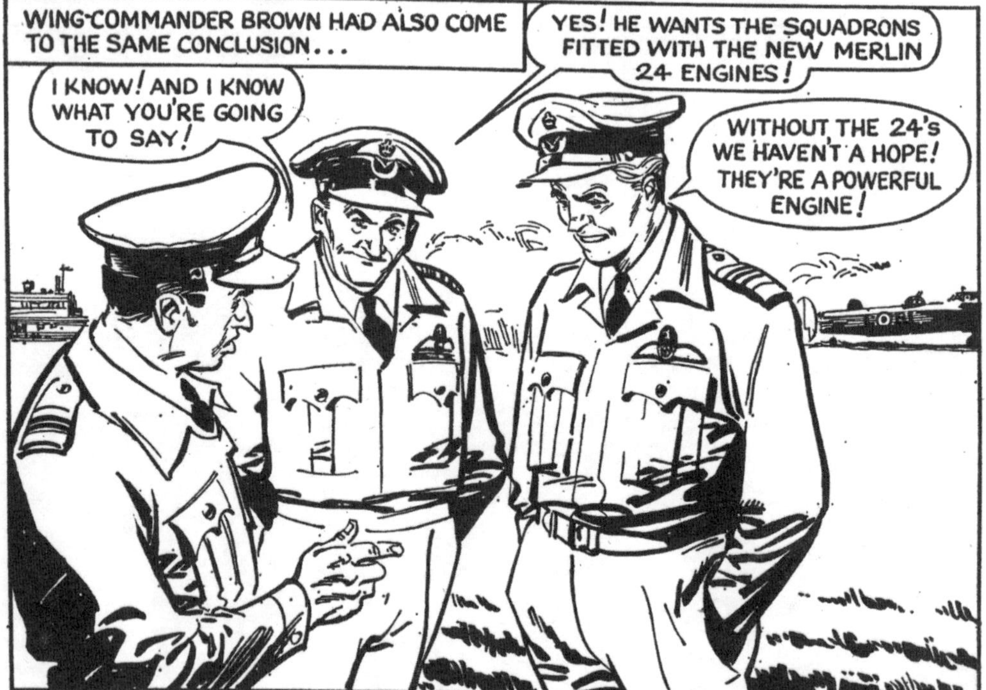
WING-COMMANDER BROWN HAD ALSO COME TO THE SAME CONCLUSION...
I KNOW! AND I KNOW WHAT YOU'RE GOING TO SAY!
YES! HE WANTS THE SQUADRONS FITTED WITH THE NEW MERLIN 24 ENGINES!
WITHOUT THE 24'S WE HAVEN'T A HOPE! THEY'RE A POWERFUL ENGINE!

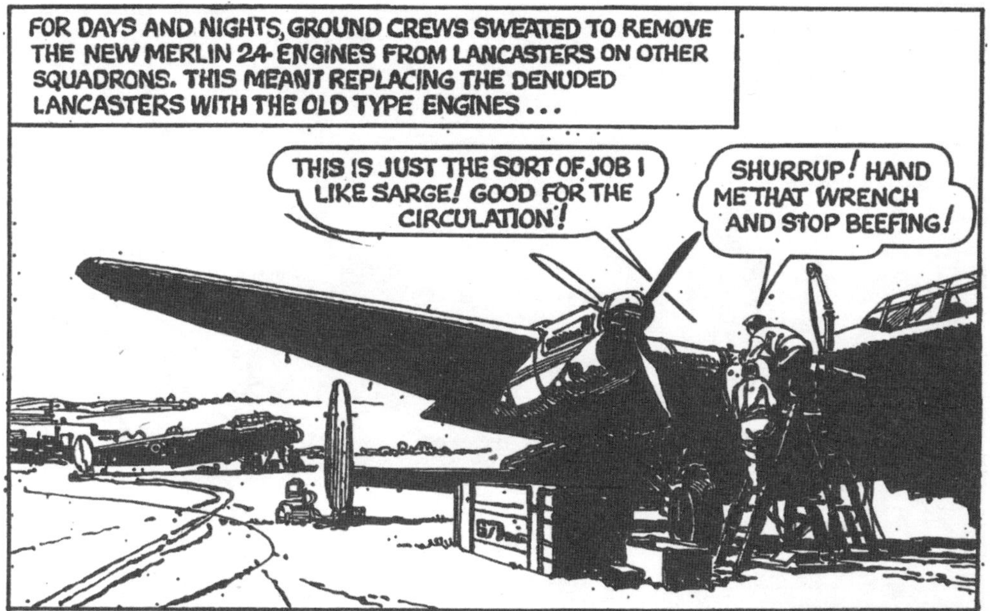
FOR DAYS AND NIGHTS, GROUND CREWS SWEATED TO REMOVE THE NEW MERLIN 24 ENGINES FROM LANCASTERS ON OTHER SQUADRONS. THIS MEANT REPLACING THE DENUDED LANCASTERS WITH THE OLD TYPE ENGINES . . .
THIS IS JUST THE SORT OF JOB I LIKE SARGE! GOOD FOR THE CIRCULATION!
SHURRUP! HAND ME THAT WRENCH AND STOP BEEFING!

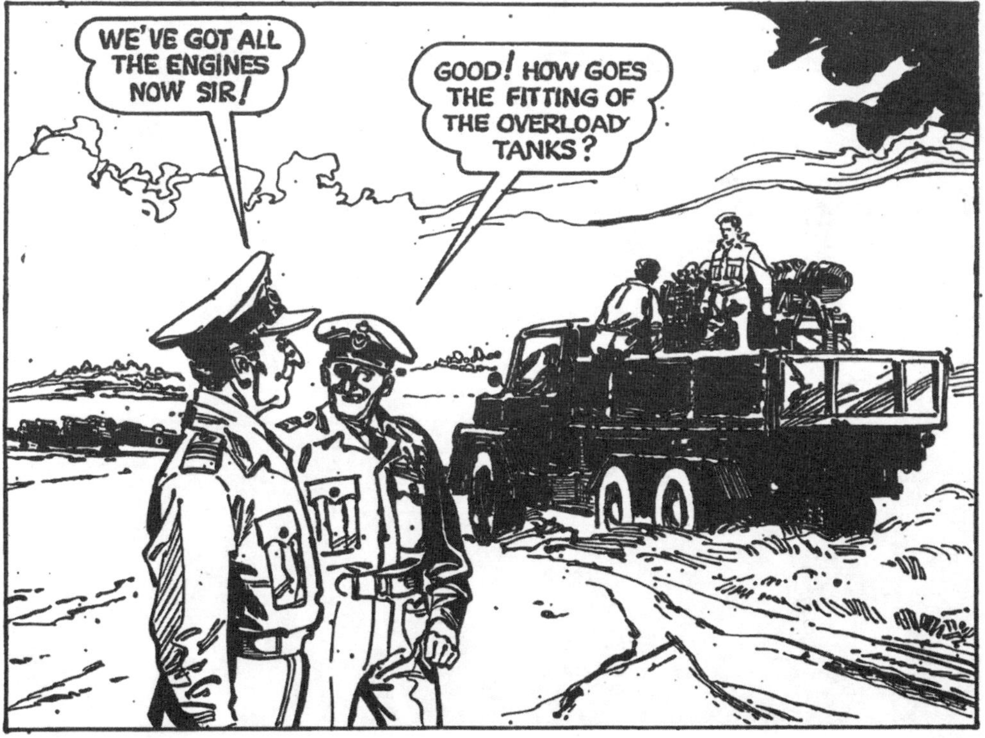
WE'VE GOT ALL THE ENGINES NOW SIR!
GOOD! HOW GOES THE FITTING OF THE OVERLOAD TANKS?

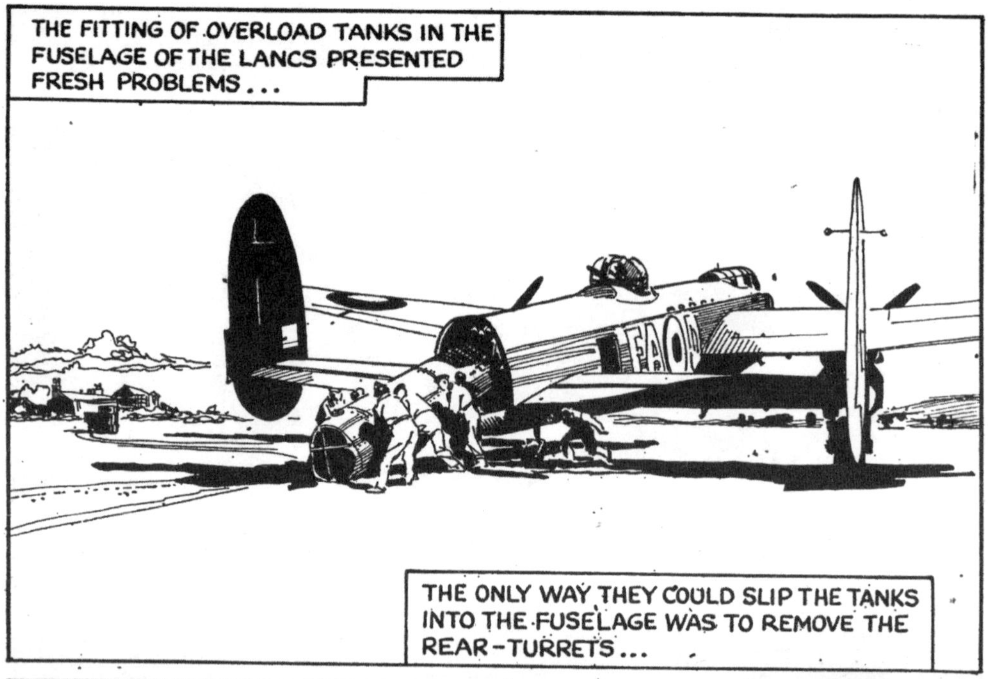
THE FITTING OF OVERLOAD TANKS IN THE FUSELAGE OF THE LANCS PRESENTED FRESH PROBLEMS...
THE ONLY WAY THEY COULD SLIP THE TANKS INTO THE FUSELAGE WAS TO REMOVE THE REAR-TURRETS...

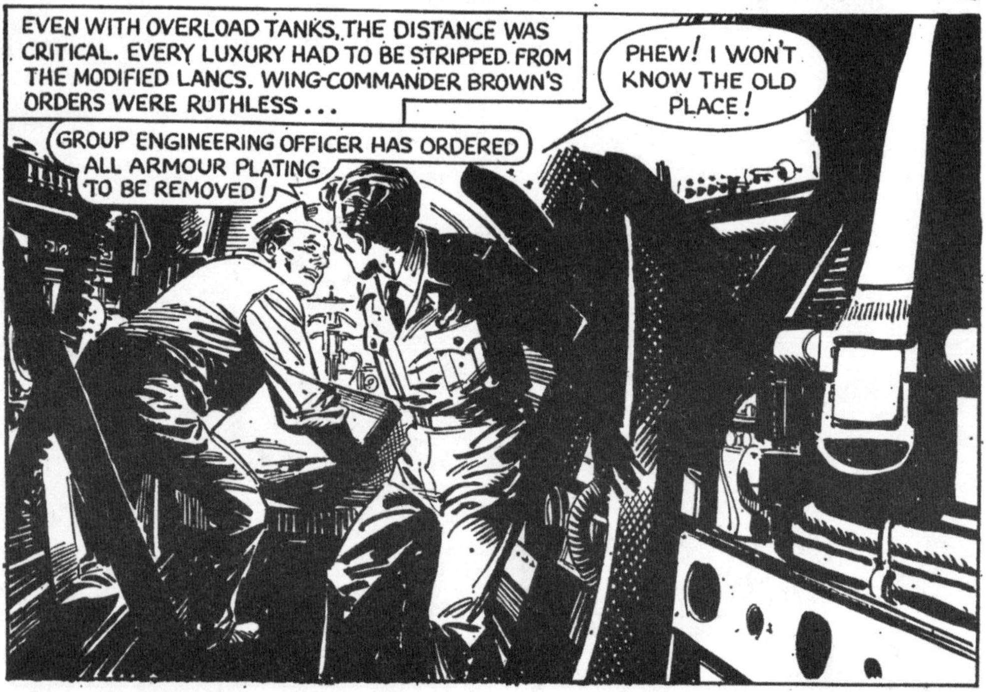
EVEN WITH OVERLOAD TANKS, THE DISTANCE WAS CRITICAL. EVERY LUXURY HAD TO BE STRIPPED FROM THE MODIFIED LANCS. WING-COMMANDER BROWN'S ORDERS WERE RUTHLESS...
GROUP ENGINEERING OFFICER HAS ORDERED ALL ARMOUR PLATING TO BE REMOVED!
PHEW! I WON'T KNOW THE OLD PLACE!

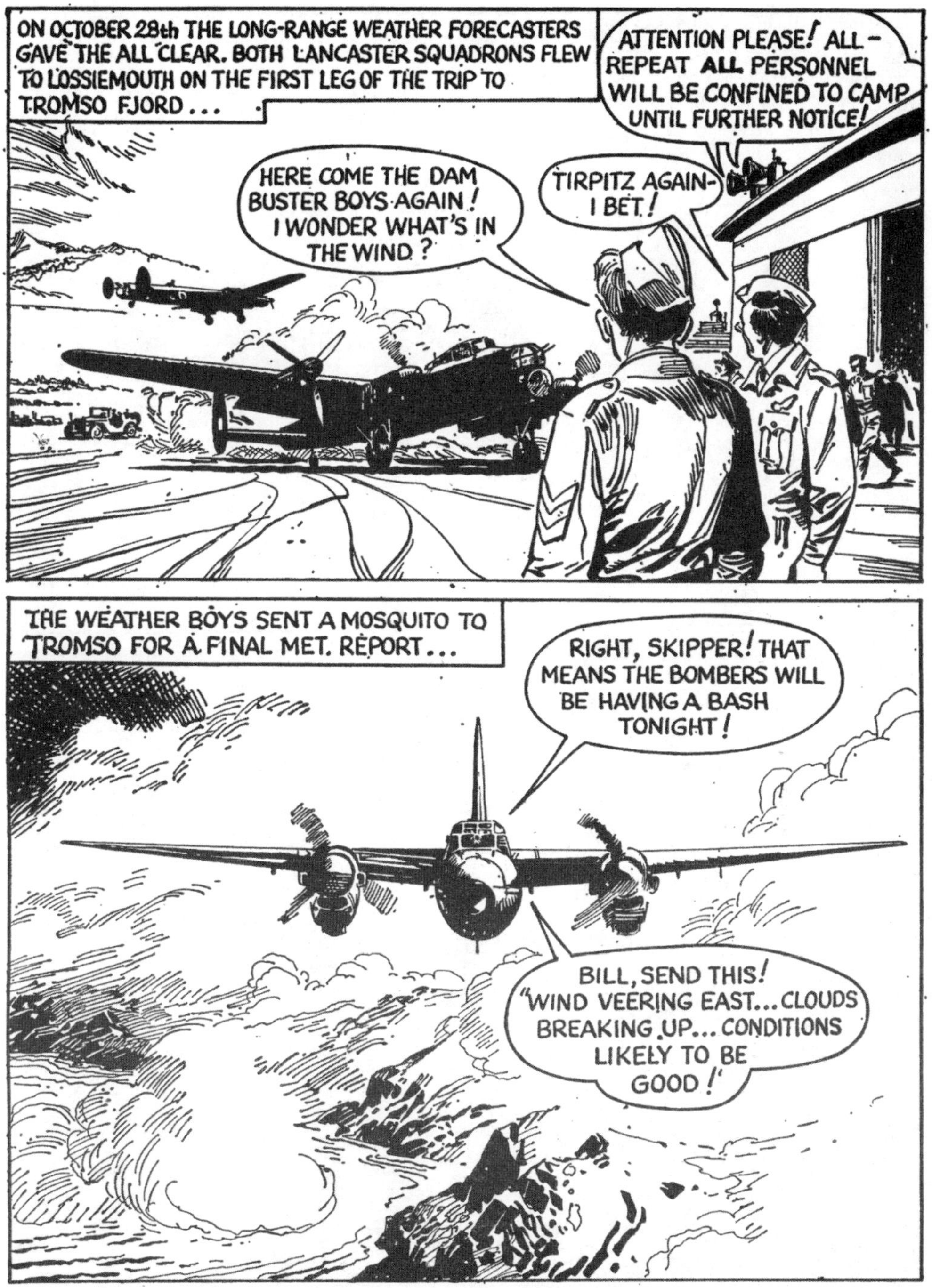
ON OCTOBER 28th THE LONG-RANGE WEATHER FORECASTERS GAVE THE ALL CLEAR. BOTH LANCASTER SQUADRONS FLEW TO LOSSIEMOUTH ON THE FIRST LEG OF THE TRIP TO TROMSO FJORD...
ATTENTION PLEASE! ALL - REPEAT ALL PERSONNEL WILL BE CONFINED TO CAMP UNTIL FURTHER NOTICE!
HERE COME THE DAM BUSTER BOYS AGAIN! I WONDER WHAT'S IN THE WIND?
TIRPITZ AGAIN - I BET!
THE WEATHER BOYS SENT A MOSQUITO TO TROMSO FOR A FINAL MET. REPORT...
BILL, SEND THIS! "WIND VEERING EAST... CLOUDS BREAKING UP... CONDITIONS LIKELY TO BE GOOD!"
RIGHT, SKIPPER! THAT MEANS THE BOMBERS WILL BE HAVING A BASH TONIGHT!

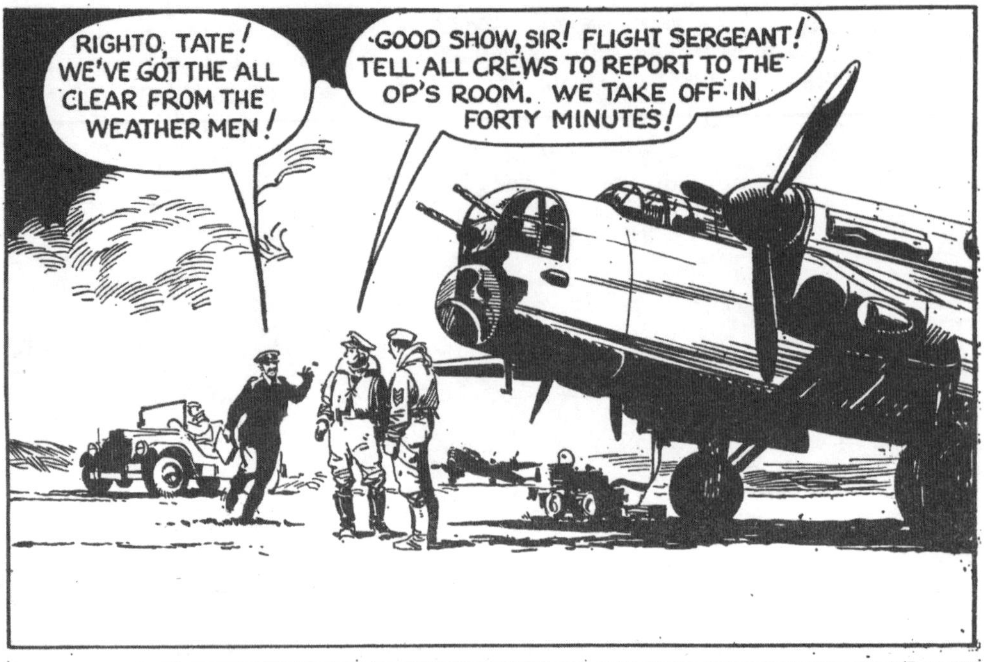
RIGHTO, TATE! WE'VE GOT THE ALL CLEAR FROM THE WEATHER MEN!
GOOD SHOW, SIR! FLIGHT SERGEANT! TELL ALL CREWS TO REPORT TO THE OP'S ROOM. WE TAKE OFF IN FORTY MINUTES!

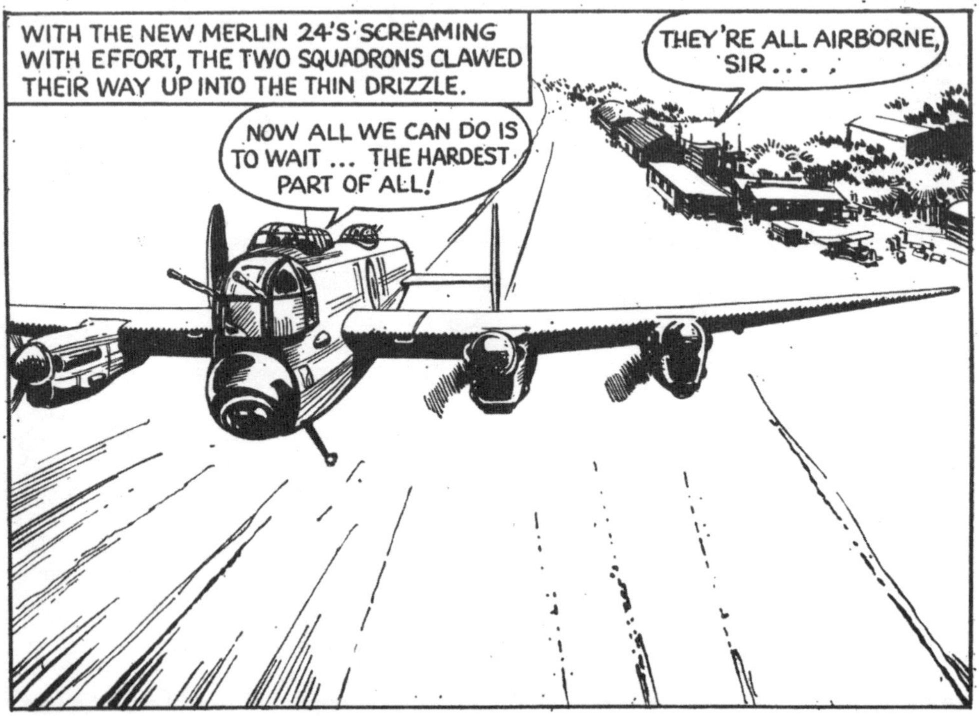
WITH THE NEW MERLIN 24'S SCREAMING WITH EFFORT, THE TWO SQUADRONS CLAWED THEIR WAY UP INTO THE THIN DRIZZLE.
THEY'RE ALL AIRBORNE, SIR . . . ,
NOW ALL WE CAN DO IS TO WAIT ... THE HARDEST PART OF ALL!

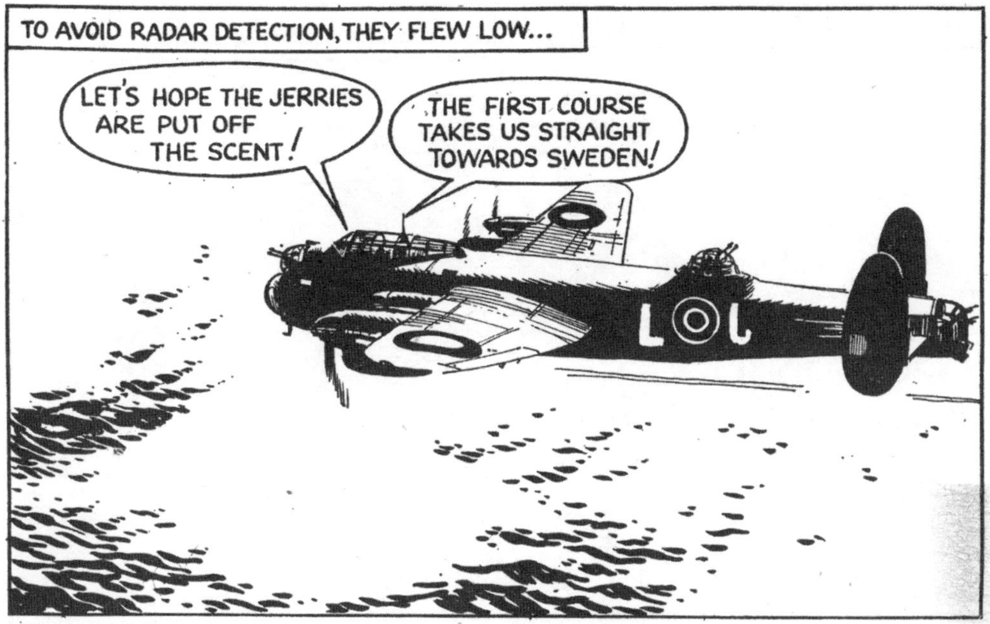
TO AVOID RADAR DETECTION, THEY FLEW LOW...
LET'S HOPE THE JERRIES ARE PUT OFF THE SCENT!
THE FIRST COURSE TAKES US STRAIGHT TOWARDS SWEDEN!

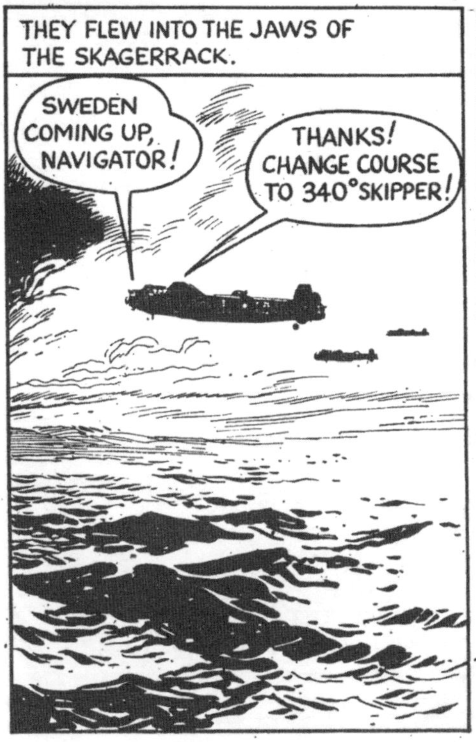
THEY FLEW INTO THE JAWS OF THE SKAGERRACK.
SWEDEN COMING UP, NAVIGATOR!
THANKS! CHANGE COURSE TO 340° SKIPPER!

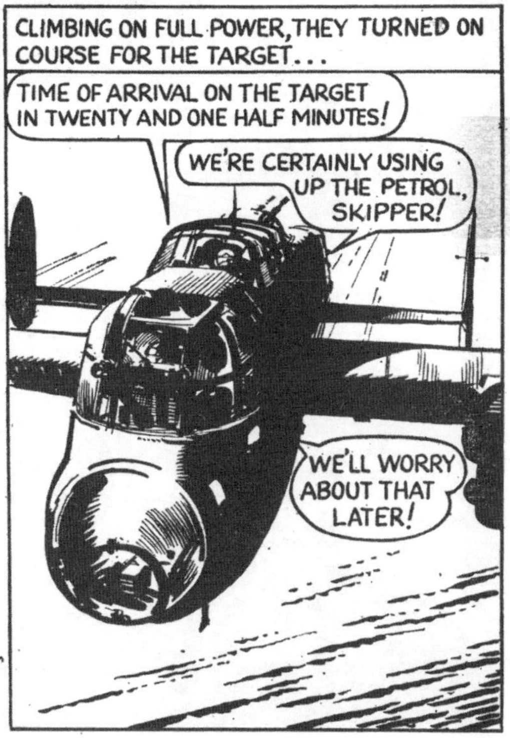
CLIMBING ON FULL POWER, THEY TURNED ON COURSE FOR THE TARGET...
TIME OF ARRIVAL ON THE TARGET IN TWENTY AND ONE HALF MINUTES!
WE'RE CERTAINLY USING UP THE PETROL, SKIPPER!
WE'LL WORRY ABOUT THAT LATER!

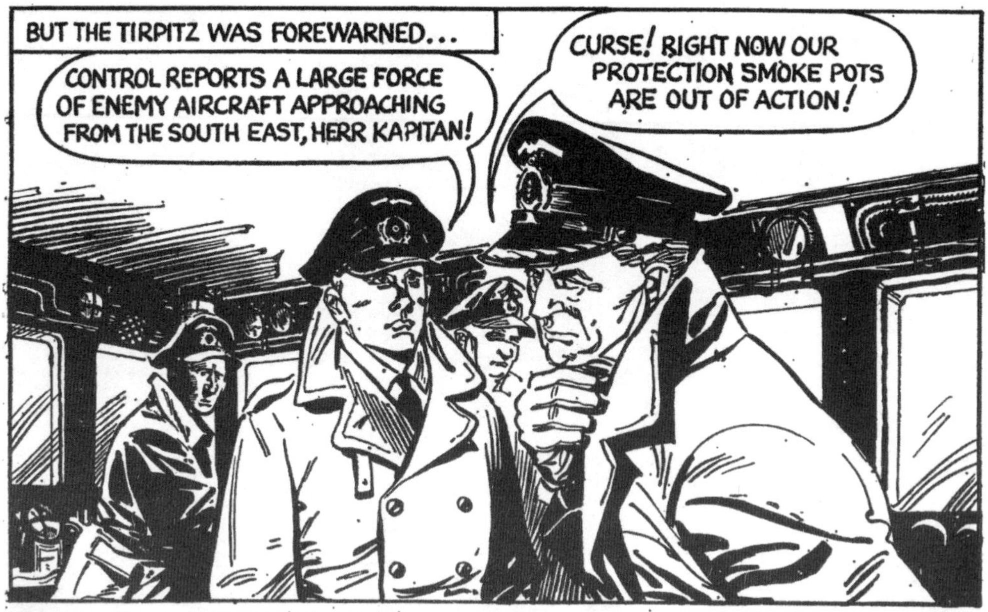
BUT THE TIRPITZ WAS FOREWARNED...
CONTROL REPORTS A LARGE FORCE OF ENEMY AIRCRAFT APPROACHING FROM THE SOUTH EAST, HERR KAPITAN!
CURSE! RIGHT NOW OUR PROTECTION SMOKE POTS ARE OUT OF ACTION!

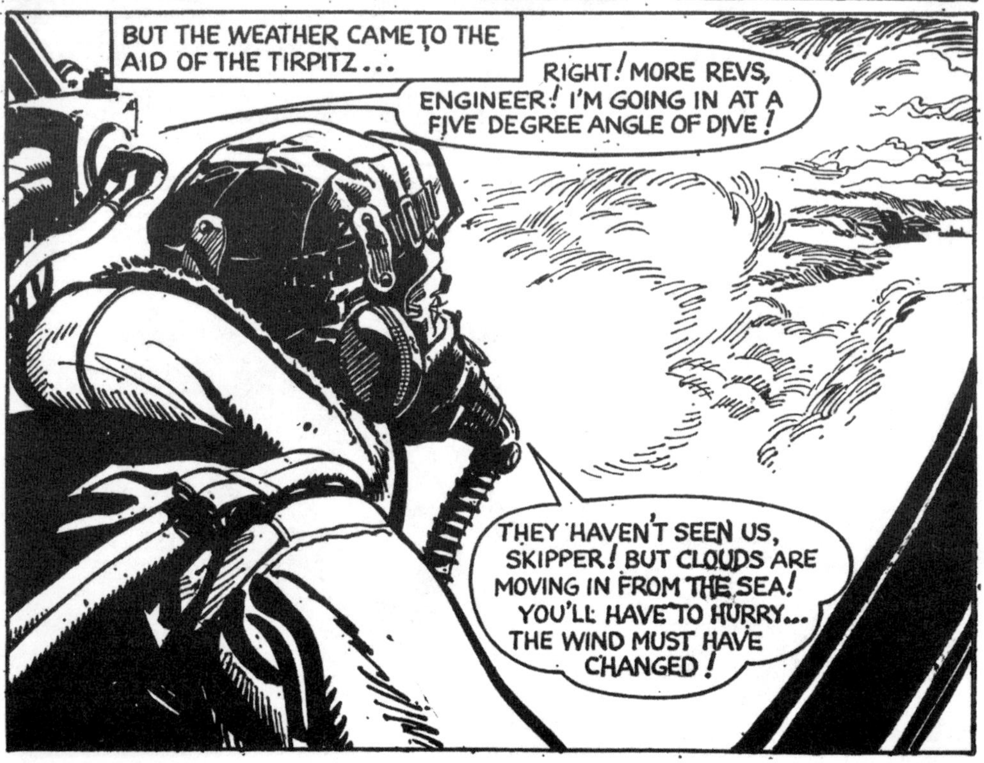
BUT THE WEATHER CAME TO THE AID OF THE TIRPITZ...
RIGHT! MORE REVS, ENGINEER! I'M GOING IN AT A FIVE DEGREE ANGLE OF DIVE!
THEY HAVEN'T SEEN US, SKIPPER! BUT CLOUDS ARE MOVING IN FROM THE SEA! YOU'LL HAVE TO HURRY... THE WIND MUST HAVE CHANGED!

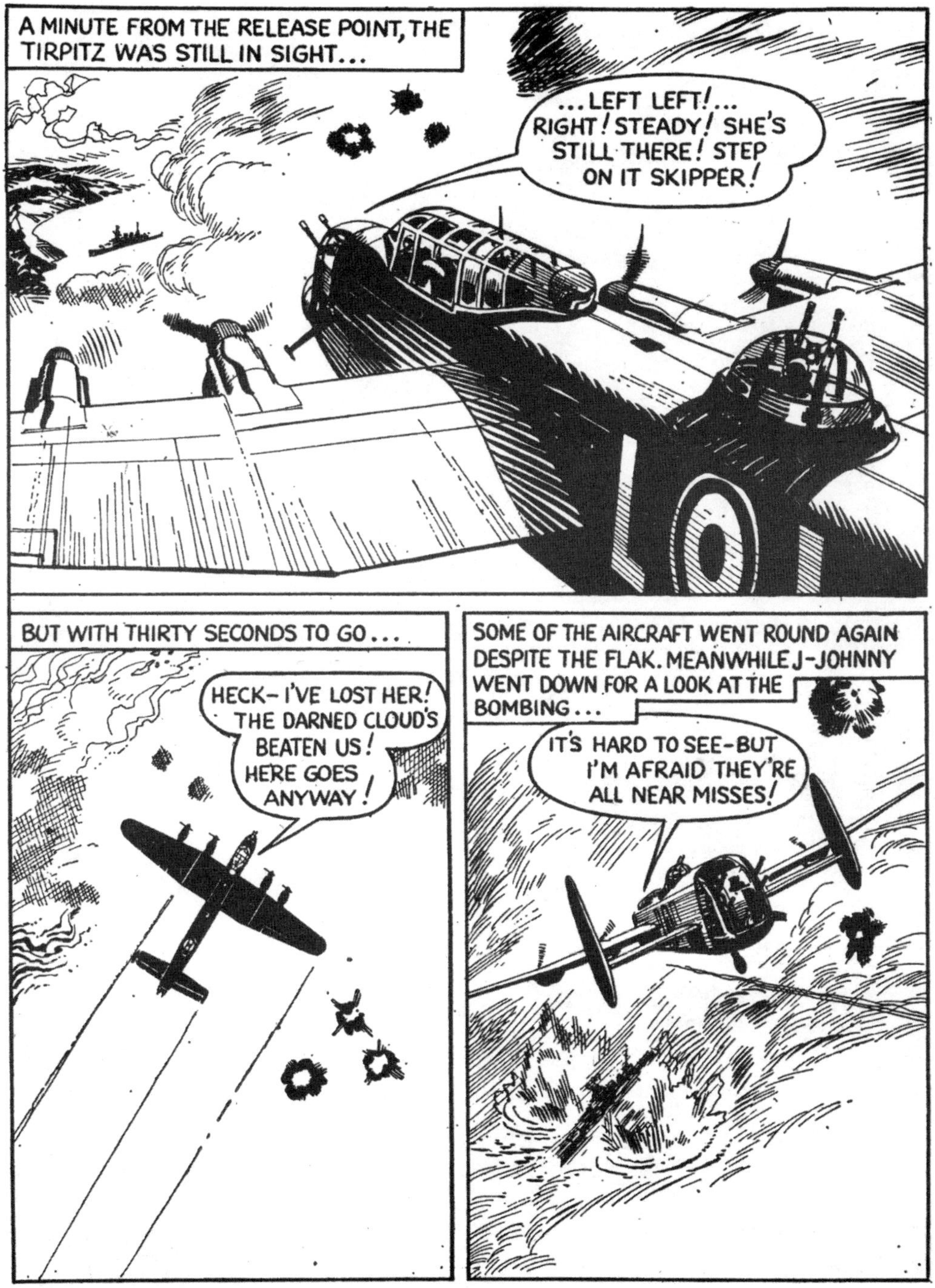
A MINUTE FROM THE RELEASE POINT, THE TIRPITZ WAS STILL IN SIGHT...
...LEFT LEFT!... RIGHT! STEADY! SHE'S STILL THERE! STEP ON IT SKIPPER!
BUT WITH THIRTY SECONDS TO GO...
HECK– I'VE LOST HER! THE DARNED CLOUD'S BEATEN US! HERE GOES ANYWAY!
SOME OF THE AIRCRAFT WENT ROUND AGAIN DESPITE THE FLAK. MEANWHILE J-JOHNNY WENT DOWN FOR A LOOK AT THE BOMBING...
IT'S HARD TO SEE–BUT I'M AFRAID THEY'RE ALL NEAR MISSES!

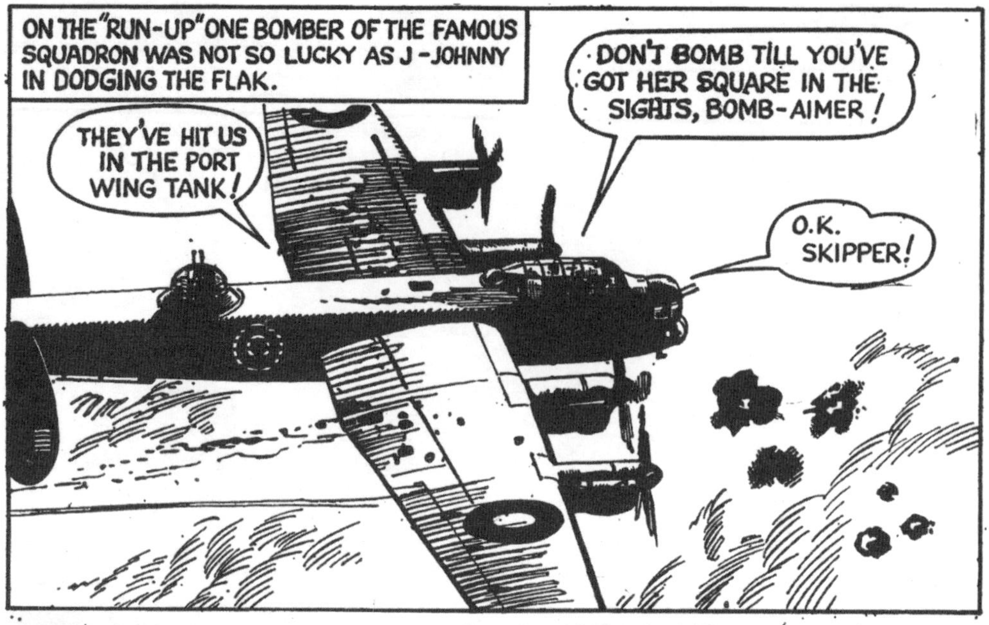
ON THE "RUN-UP" ONE BOMBER OF THE FAMOUS SQUADRON WAS NOT SO LUCKY AS J-JOHNNY IN DODGING THE FLAK.
THEY'VE HIT US IN THE PORT WING TANK!
DON'T BOMB TILL YOU'VE GOT HER SQUARE IN THE SIGHTS, BOMB-AIMER!
O.K. SKIPPER!

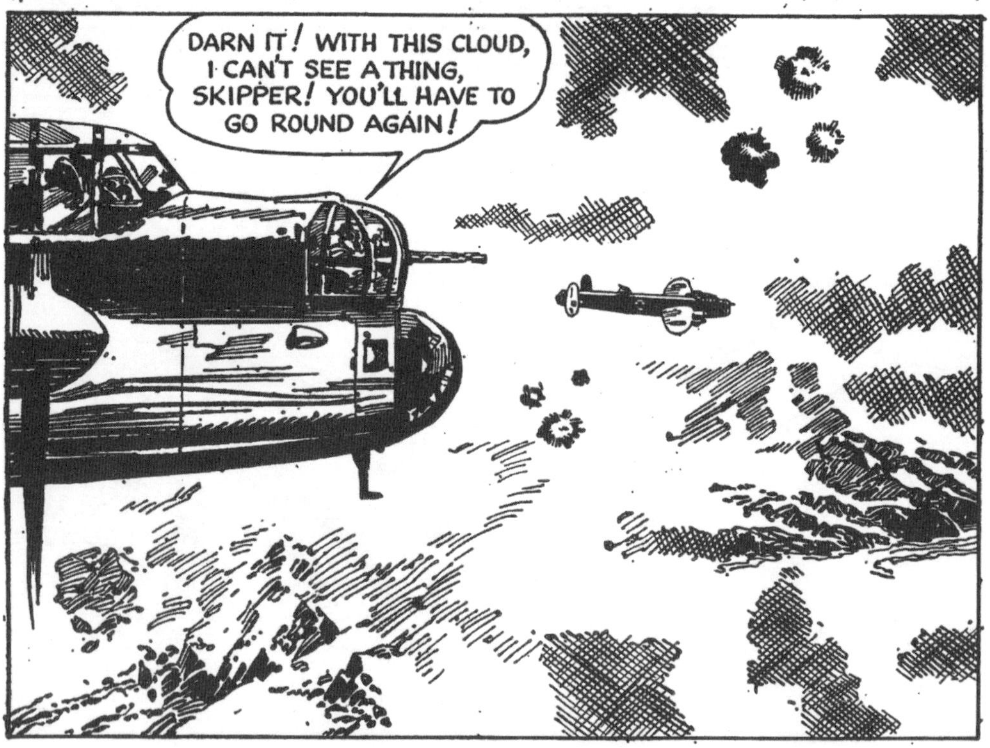
DARN IT! WITH THIS CLOUD, I CAN'T SEE A THING, SKIPPER! YOU'LL HAVE TO GO ROUND AGAIN!

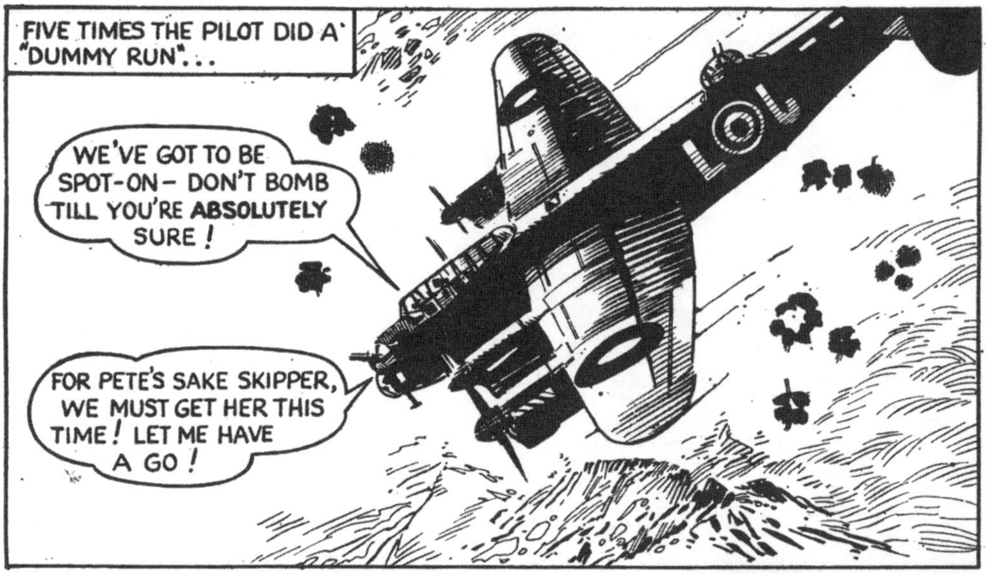
FIVE TIMES THE PILOT DID A "DUMMY RUN"...
WE'VE GOT TO BE SPOT-ON – DON'T BOMB TILL YOU'RE ABSOLUTELY SURE!
FOR PETE'S SAKE SKIPPER, WE MUST GET HER THIS TIME! LET ME HAVE A GO!

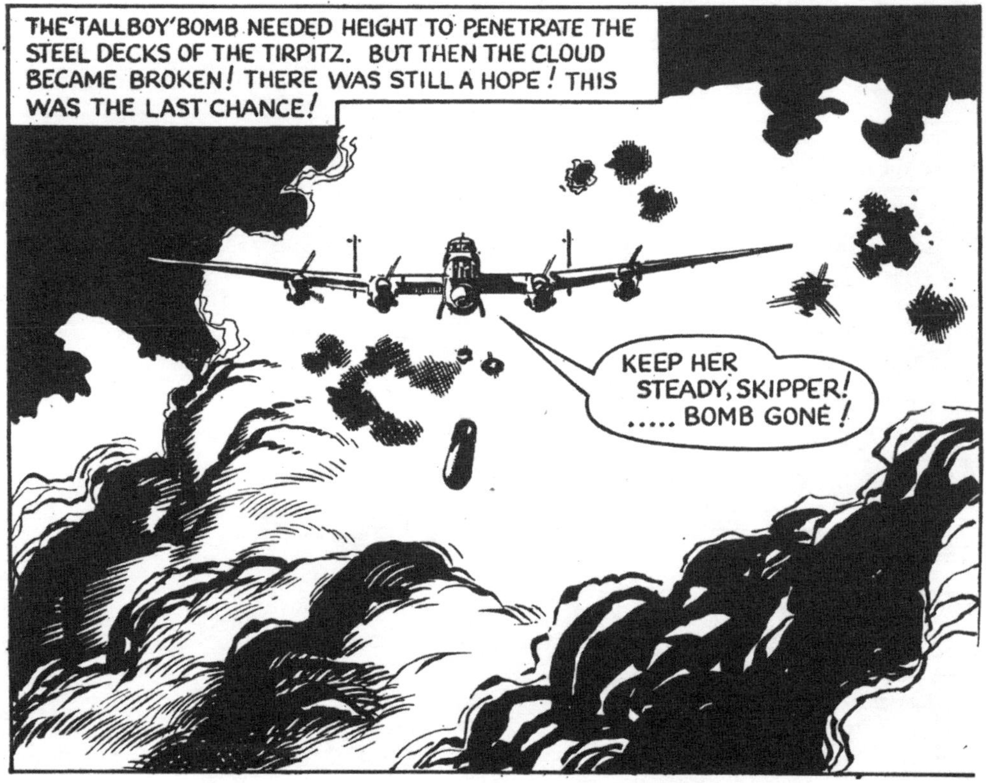
THE 'TALLBOY' BOMB NEEDED HEIGHT TO PENETRATE THE STEEL DECKS OF THE TIRPITZ. BUT THEN THE CLOUD BECAME BROKEN! THERE WAS STILL A HOPE! THIS WAS THE LAST CHANCE!
KEEP HER STEADY, SKIPPER! ..... BOMB GONE!

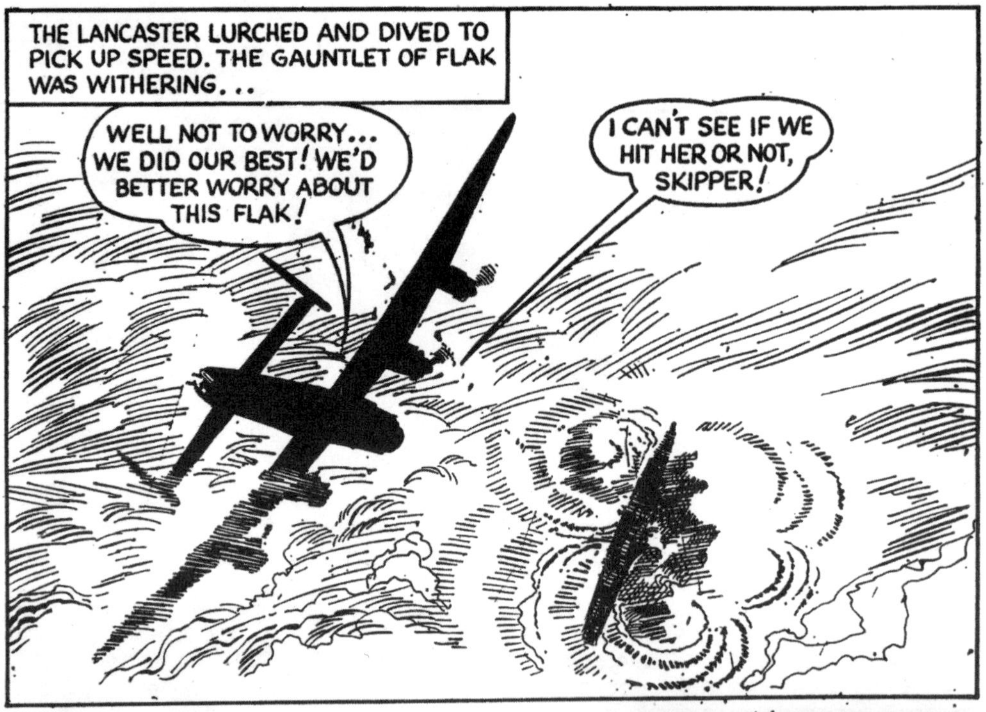
THE LANCASTER LURCHED AND DIVED TO PICK UP SPEED. THE GAUNTLET OF FLAK WAS WITHERING...
I CAN'T SEE IF WE HIT HER OR NOT, SKIPPER!
WELL NOT TO WORRY... WE DID OUR BEST! WE'D BETTER WORRY ABOUT THIS FLAK!

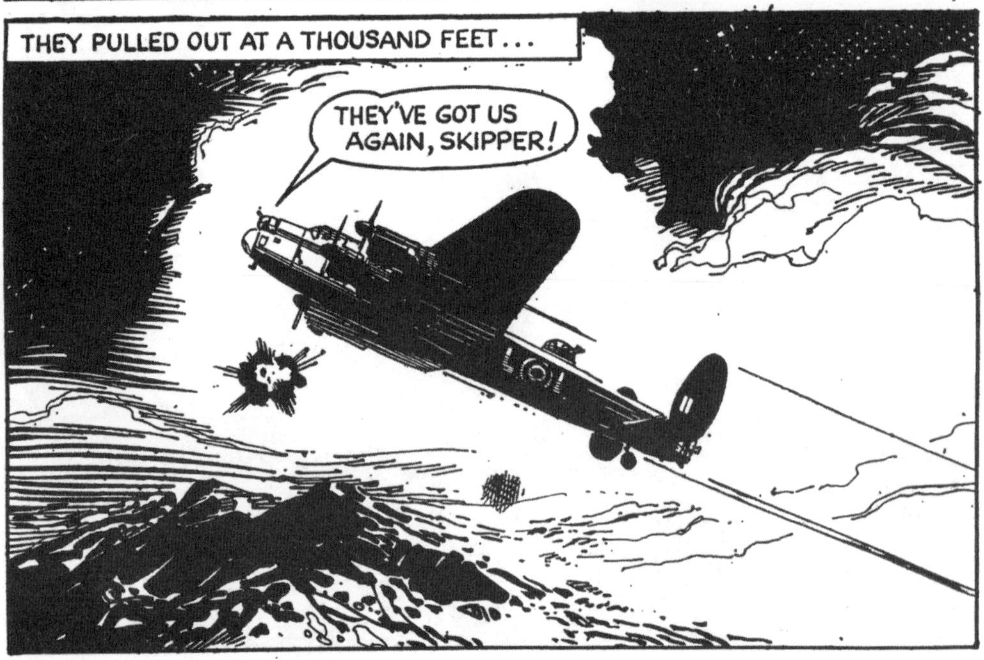
THEY PULLED OUT AT A THOUSAND FEET...
THEY'VE GOT US AGAIN, SKIPPER!

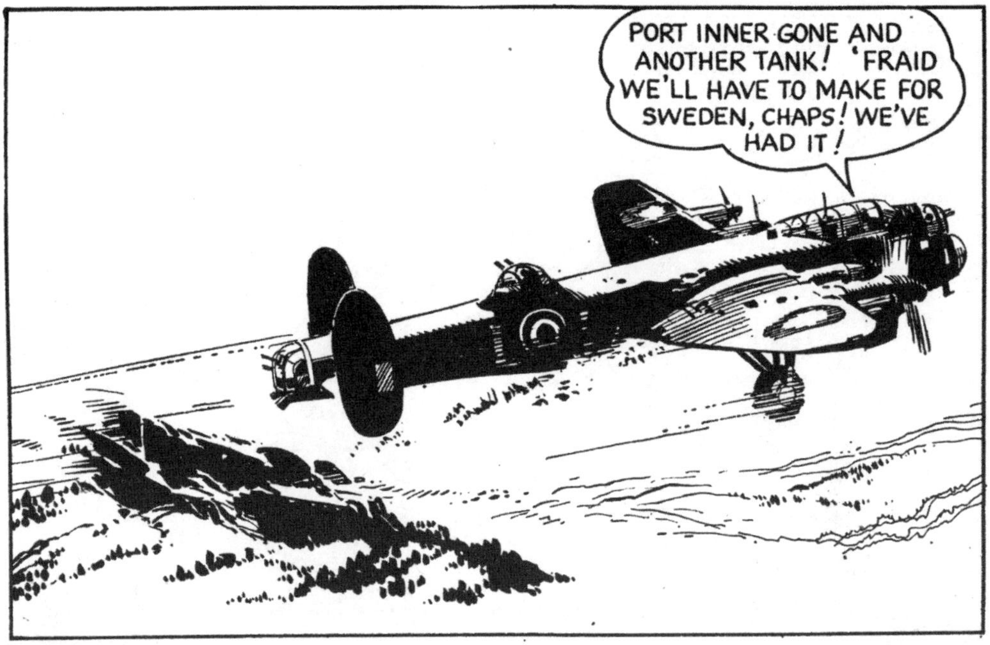
PORT INNER GONE AND ANOTHER TANK! 'FRAID WE'LL HAVE TO MAKE FOR SWEDEN, CHAPS! WE'VE HAD IT!

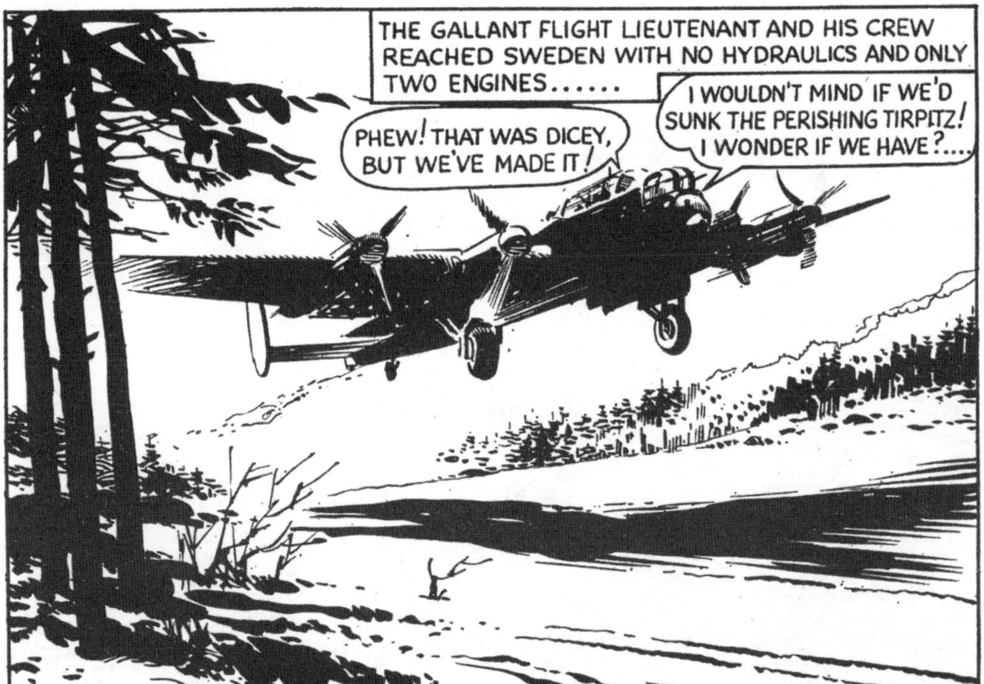
THE GALLANT FLIGHT LIEUTENANT AND HIS CREW REACHED SWEDEN WITH NO HYDRAULICS AND ONLY TWO ENGINES......
PHEW! THAT WAS DICEY, BUT WE'VE MADE IT!
I WOULDN'T MIND IF WE'D SUNK THE PERISHING TIRPITZ! I WONDER IF WE HAVE?...

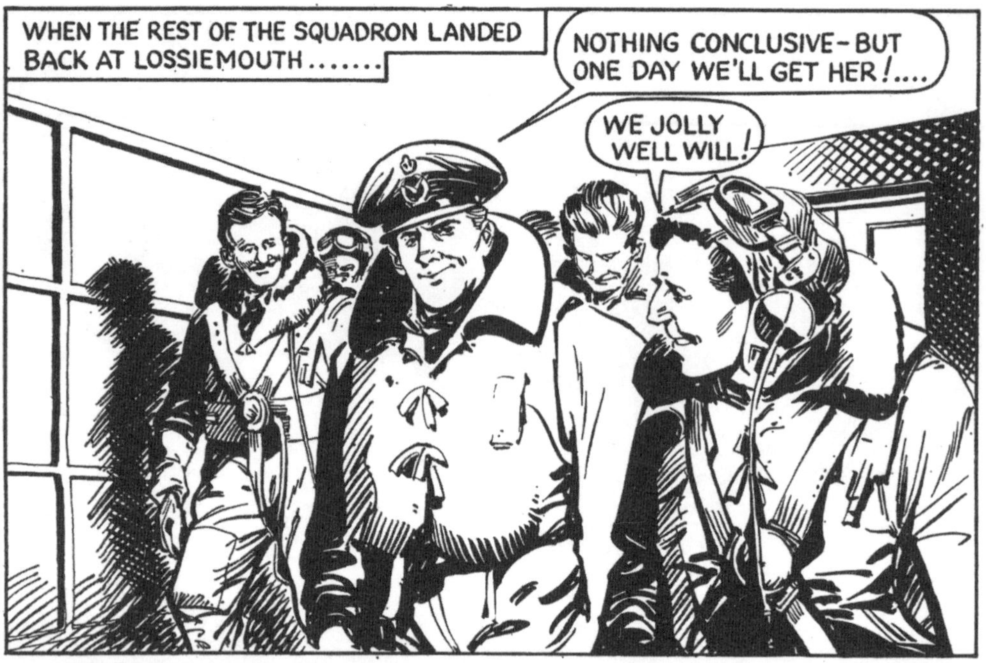
WHEN THE REST OF THE SQUADRON LANDED BACK AT LOSSIEMOUTH.......
NOTHING CONCLUSIVE - BUT ONE DAY WE'LL GET HER!....
WE JOLLY WELL WILL!

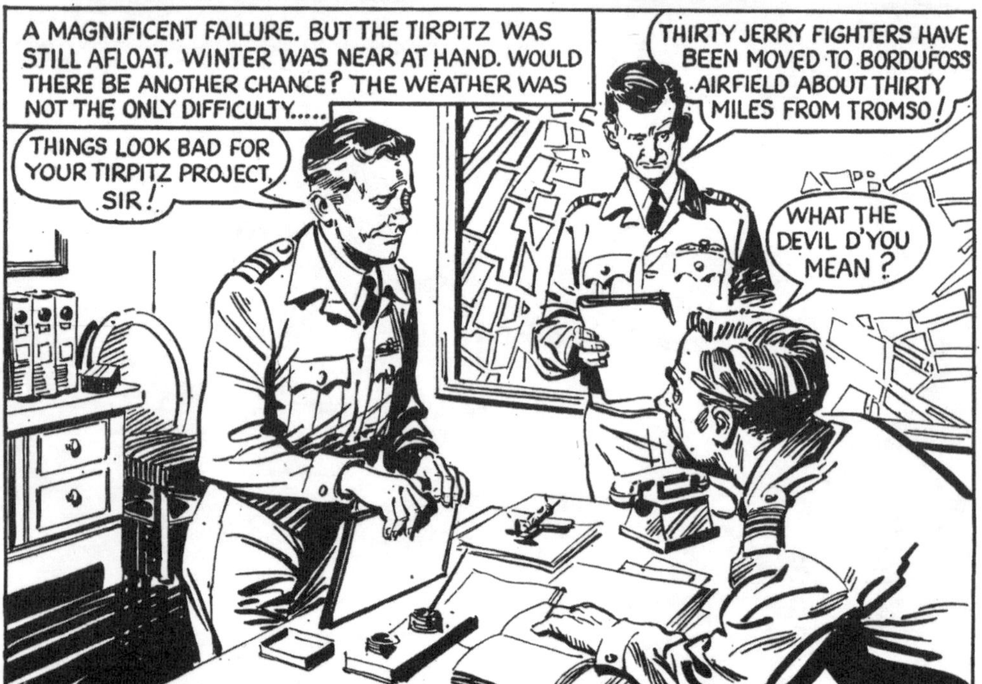
A MAGNIFICENT FAILURE. BUT THE TIRPITZ WAS STILL AFLOAT. WINTER WAS NEAR AT HAND. WOULD THERE BE ANOTHER CHANCE? THE WEATHER WAS NOT THE ONLY DIFFICULTY.....
THINGS LOOK BAD FOR YOUR TIRPITZ PROJECT, SIR!
THIRTY JERRY FIGHTERS HAVE BEEN MOVED TO BORDUFOSS AIRFIELD ABOUT THIRTY MILES FROM TROMSO!
WHAT THE DEVIL D'YOU MEAN?

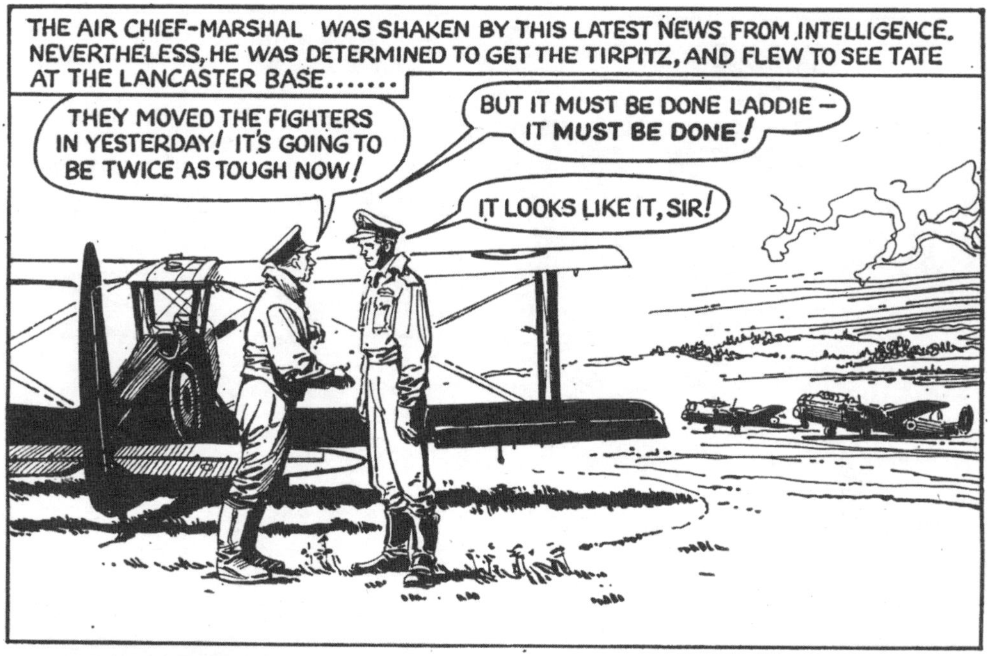
THE AIR CHIEF-MARSHAL WAS SHAKEN BY THIS LATEST NEWS FROM INTELLIGENCE. NEVERTHELESS, HE WAS DETERMINED TO GET THE TIRPITZ, AND FLEW TO SEE TATE AT THE LANCASTER BASE.......
THEY MOVED THE FIGHTERS IN YESTERDAY! IT'S GOING TO BE TWICE AS TOUGH NOW!
BUT IT MUST BE DONE LADDIE — IT MUST BE DONE!
IT LOOKS LIKE IT, SIR!

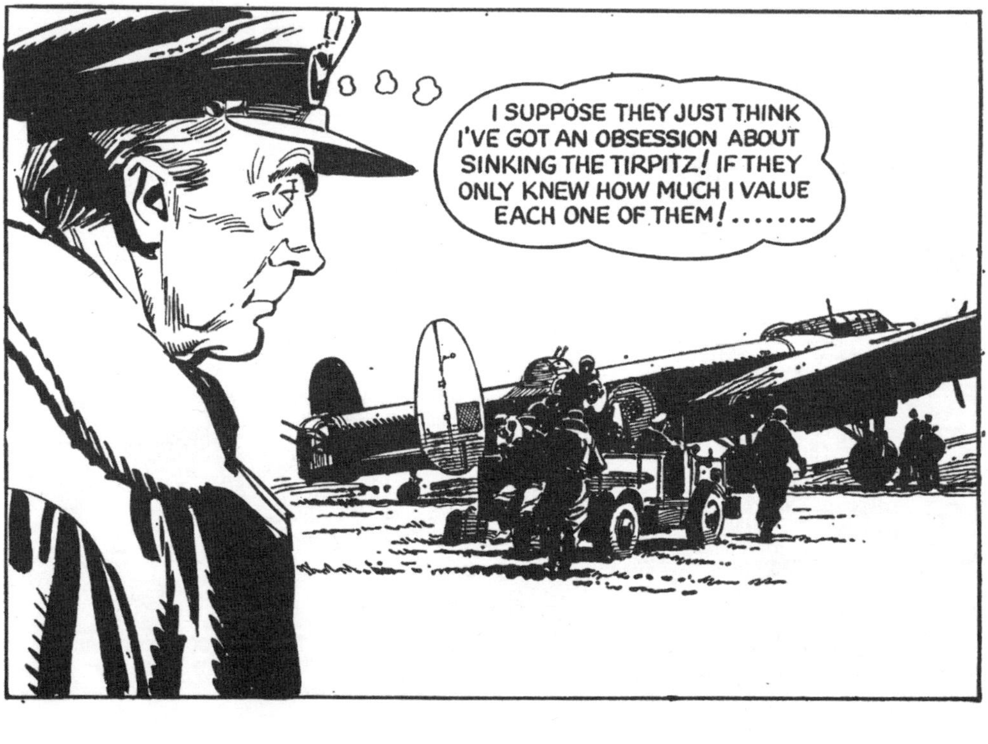
I SUPPOSE THEY JUST THINK I'VE GOT AN OBSESSION ABOUT SINKING THE TIRPITZ! IF THEY ONLY KNEW HOW MUCH I VALUE EACH ONE OF THEM!........

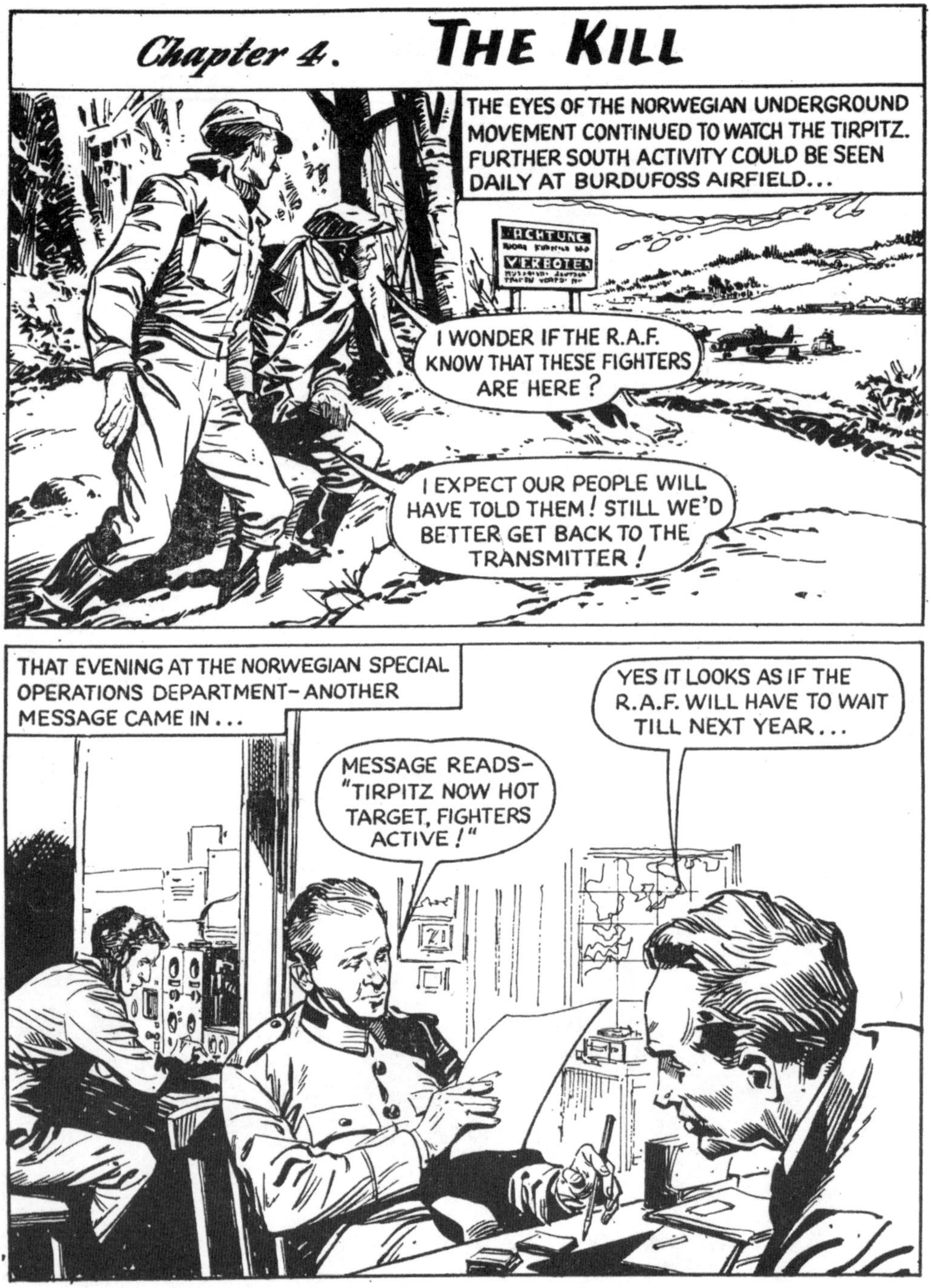
Chapter 4. THE KILL
THE EYES OF THE NORWEGIAN UNDERGROUND MOVEMENT CONTINUED TO WATCH THE TIRPITZ. FURTHER SOUTH ACTIVITY COULD BE SEEN DAILY AT BURDUFOSS AIRFIELD...
I WONDER IF THE R.A.F. KNOW THAT THESE FIGHTERS ARE HERE?
I EXPECT OUR PEOPLE WILL HAVE TOLD THEM! STILL WE'D BETTER GET BACK TO THE TRANSMITTER!
THAT EVENING AT THE NORWEGIAN SPECIAL OPERATIONS DEPARTMENT-ANOTHER MESSAGE CAME IN...
MESSAGE READS- "TIRPITZ NOW HOT TARGET, FIGHTERS ACTIVE!"
YES IT LOOKS AS IF THE R.A.F. WILL HAVE TO WAIT TILL NEXT YEAR...

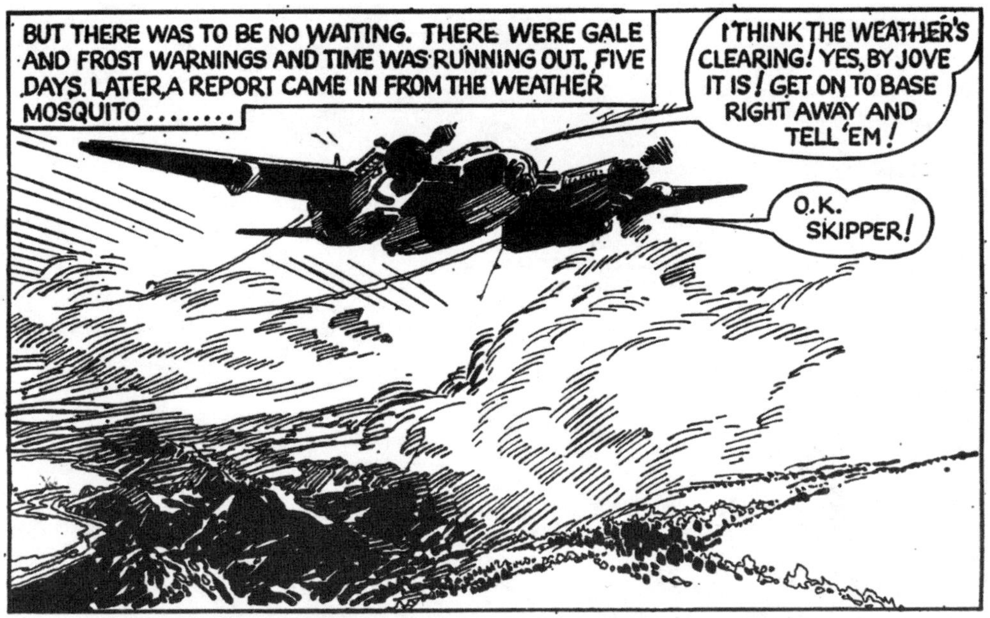
BUT THERE WAS TO BE NO WAITING. THERE WERE GALE AND FROST WARNINGS AND TIME WAS RUNNING OUT. FIVE DAYS. LATER, A REPORT CAME IN FROM THE WEATHER MOSQUITO ....
I THINK THE WEATHER'S CLEARING! YES, BY JOVE IT IS! GET ON TO BASE RIGHT AWAY AND TELL 'EM!
O.K. SKIPPER!

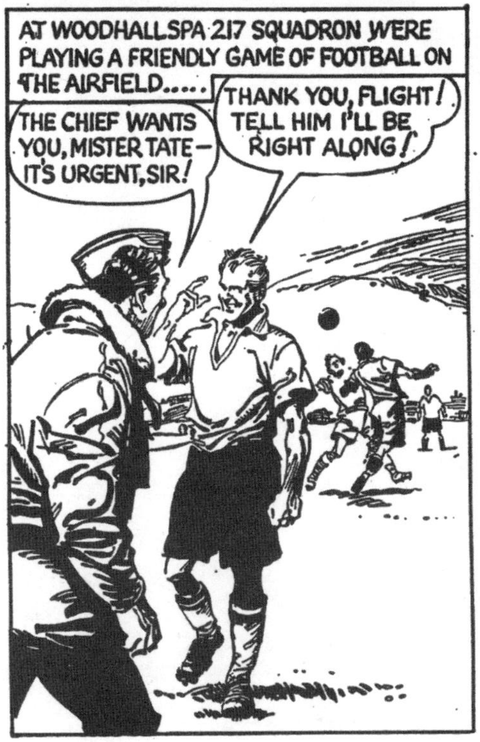
AT WOODHALL SPA 217 SQUADRON WERE PLAYING A FRIENDLY GAME OF FOOTBALL ON THE AIRFIELD.....
THE CHIEF WANTS YOU, MISTER TATE— IT'S URGENT, SIR!
THANK YOU, FLIGHT! TELL HIM I'LL BE RIGHT ALONG!

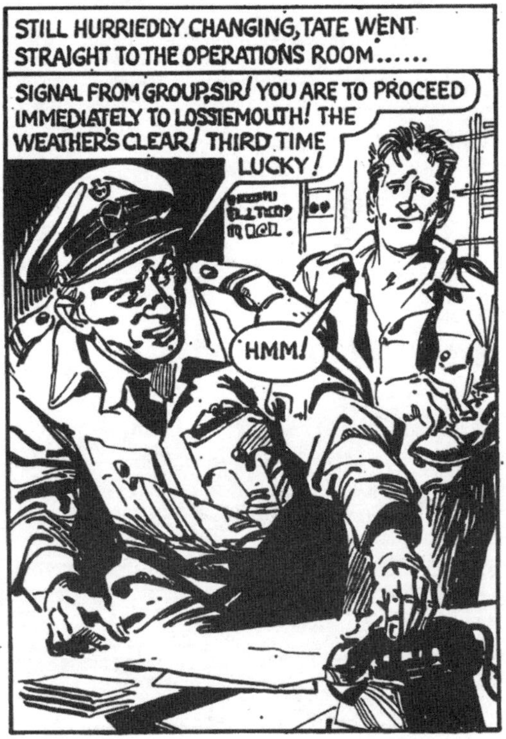
STILL HURRIEDLY CHANGING, TATE WENT STRAIGHT TO THE OPERATIONS ROOM......
SIGNAL FROM GROUP, SIR! YOU ARE TO PROCEED IMMEDIATELY TO LOSSIEMOUTH! THE WEATHER'S CLEAR! THIRD TIME LUCKY!
HMM!

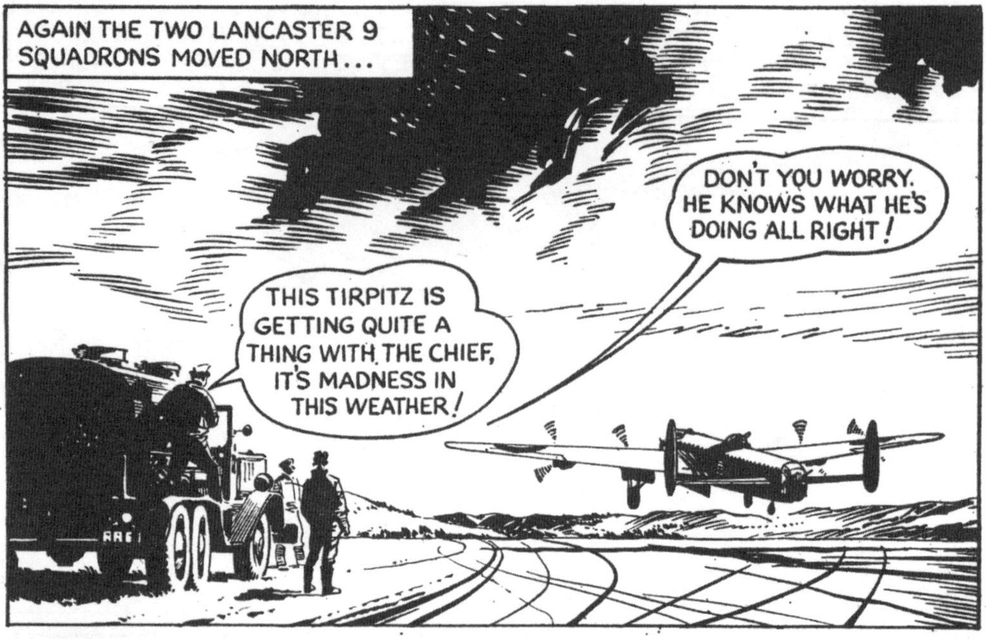
AGAIN THE TWO LANCASTER 9 SQUADRONS MOVED NORTH...
THIS TIRPITZ IS GETTING QUITE A THING WITH THE CHIEF, IT'S MADNESS IN THIS WEATHER!
DON'T YOU WORRY. HE KNOWS WHAT HE'S DOING ALL RIGHT!

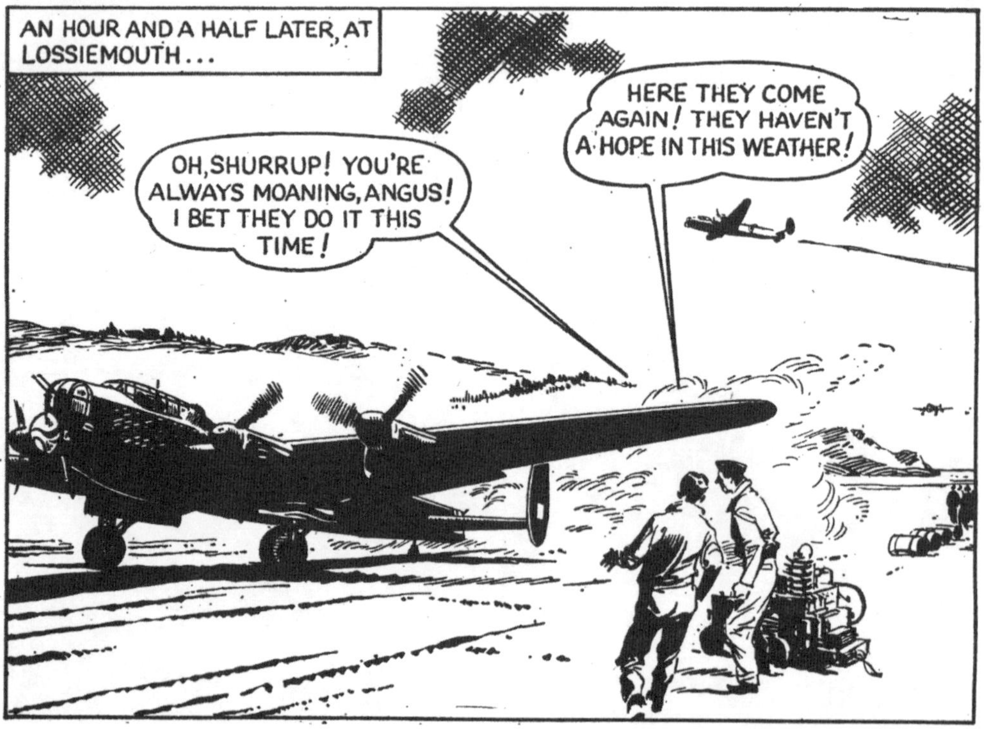
AN HOUR AND A HALF LATER, AT LOSSIEMOUTH...
HERE THEY COME AGAIN! THEY HAVEN'T A HOPE IN THIS WEATHER!
OH, SHURRUP! YOU'RE ALWAYS MOANING, ANGUS! I BET THEY DO IT THIS TIME!

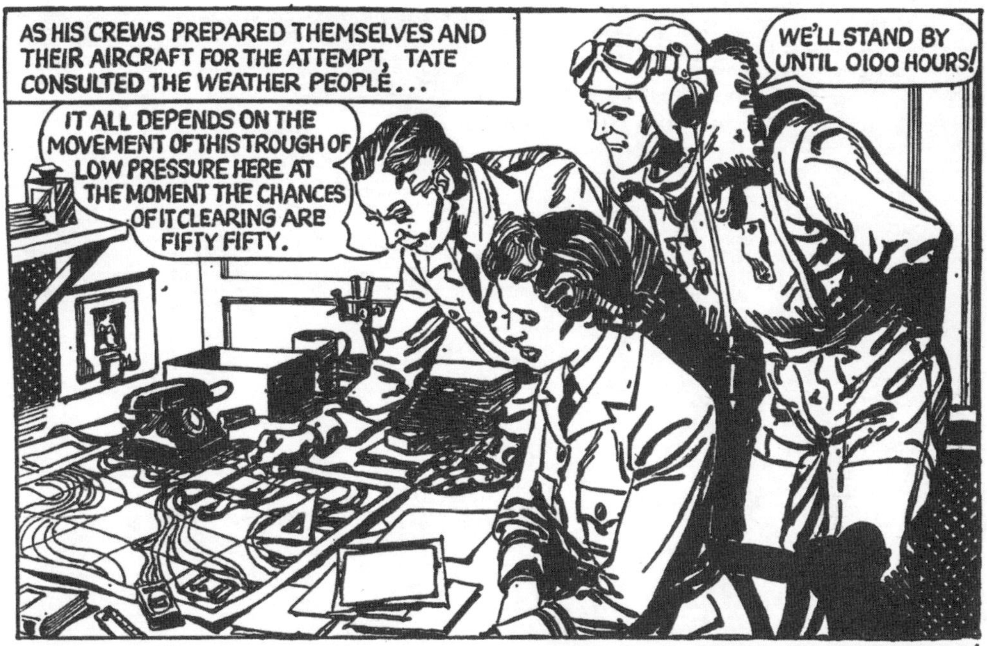
AS HIS CREWS PREPARED THEMSELVES AND THEIR AIRCRAFT FOR THE ATTEMPT, TATE CONSULTED THE WEATHER PEOPLE...
IT ALL DEPENDS ON THE MOVEMENT OF THIS TROUGH OF LOW PRESSURE HERE AT THE MOMENT THE CHANCES OF IT CLEARING ARE FIFTY FIFTY.
WE'LL STAND BY UNTIL 0100 HOURS!

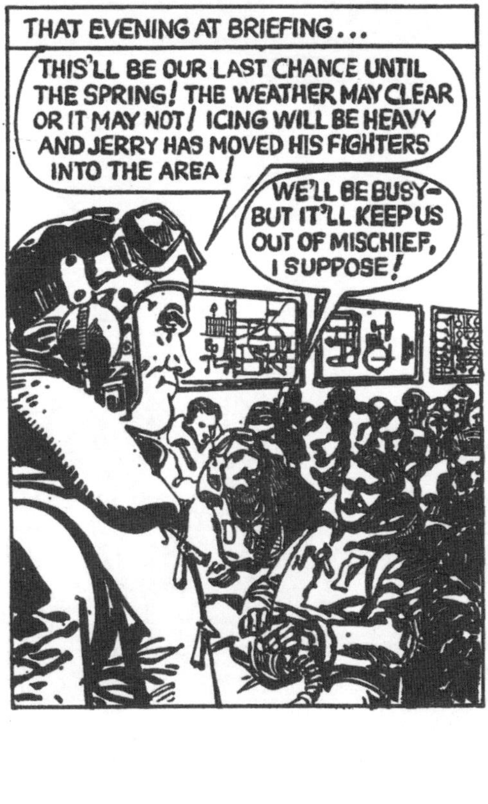
THAT EVENING AT BRIEFING...
THIS'LL BE OUR LAST CHANCE UNTIL THE SPRING! THE WEATHER MAY CLEAR OR IT MAY NOT! ICING WILL BE HEAVY AND JERRY HAS MOVED HIS FIGHTERS INTO THE AREA!
WE'LL BE BUSY—BUT IT'LL KEEP US OUT OF MISCHIEF, I SUPPOSE!

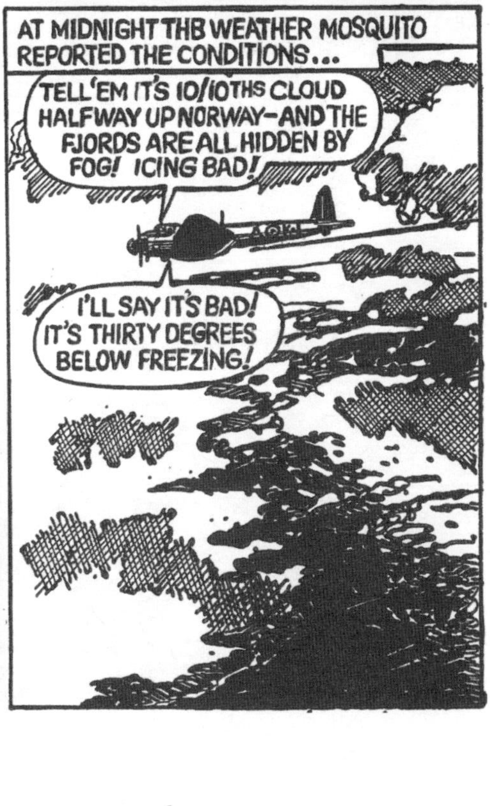
AT MIDNIGHT THB WEATHER MOSQUITO REPORTED THE CONDITIONS...
TELL'EM IT'S 10/10THS CLOUD HALFWAY UP NORWAY—AND THE FJORDS ARE ALL HIDDEN BY FOG! ICING BAD!
I'LL SAY IT'S BAD! IT'S THIRTY DEGREES BELOW FREEZING!

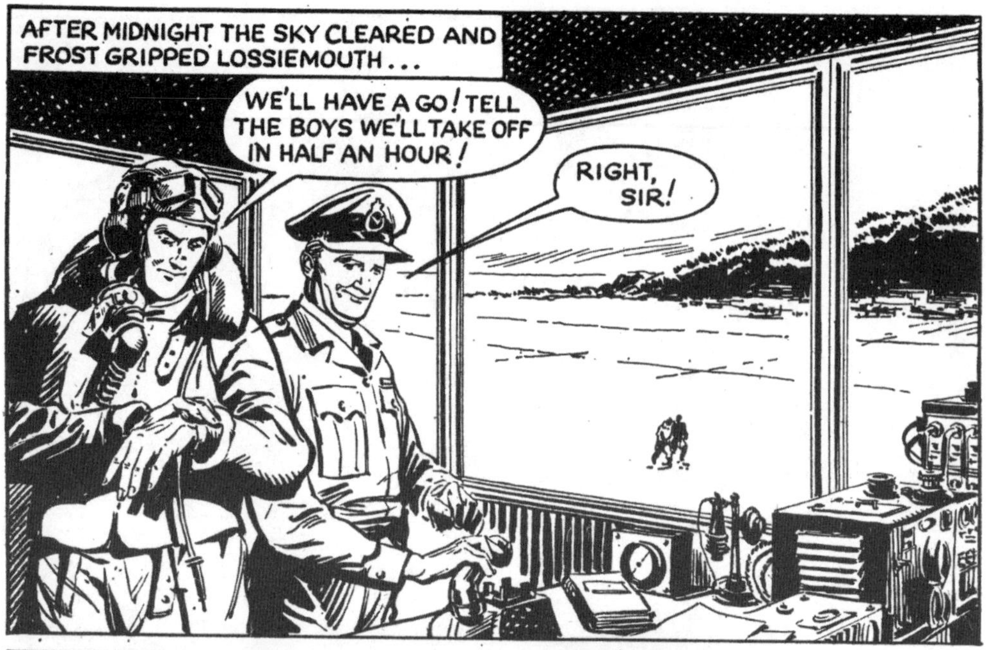
AFTER MIDNIGHT THE SKY CLEARED AND FROST GRIPPED LOSSIEMOUTH...
WE'LL HAVE A GO! TELL THE BOYS WE'LL TAKE OFF IN HALF AN HOUR!
RIGHT, SIR!

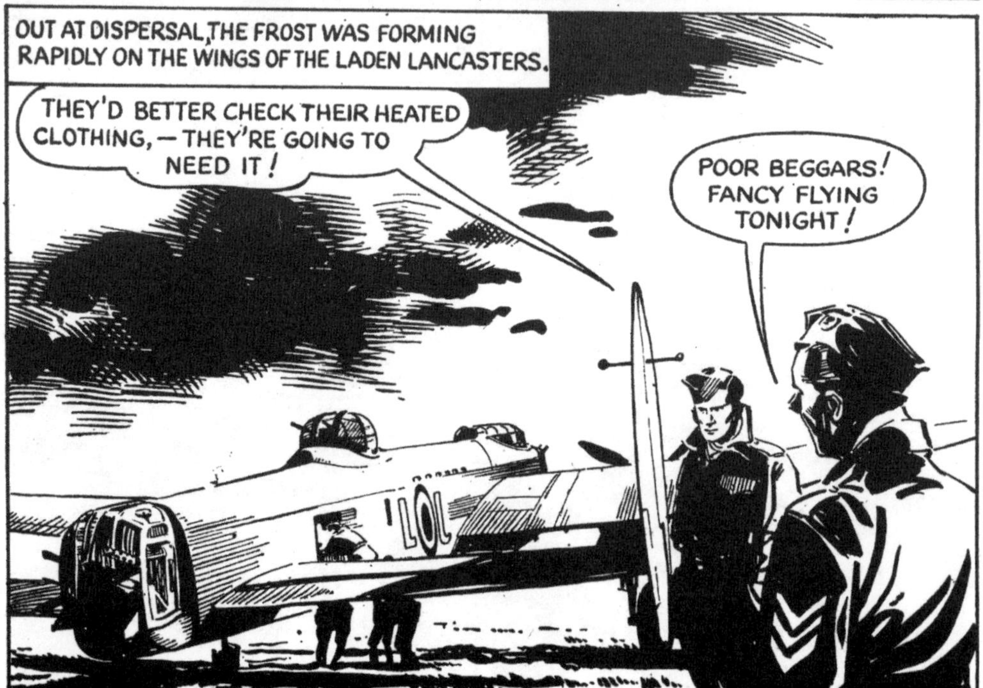
OUT AT DISPERSAL, THE FROST WAS FORMING RAPIDLY ON THE WINGS OF THE LADEN LANCASTERS.
THEY'D BETTER CHECK THEIR HEATED CLOTHING, — THEY'RE GOING TO NEED IT!
POOR BEGGARS! FANCY FLYING TONIGHT!

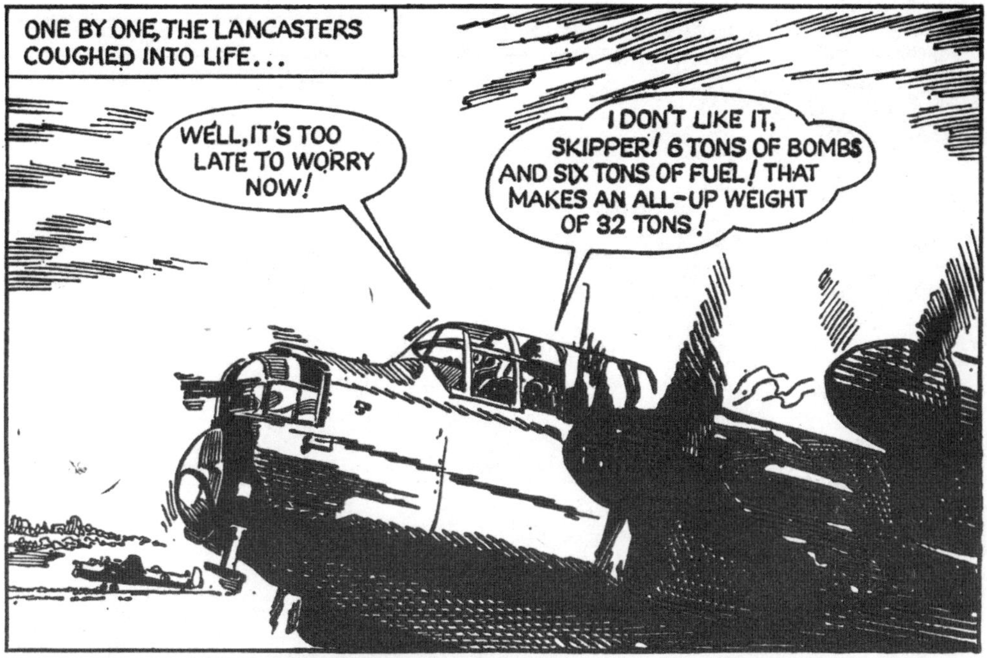
ONE BY ONE, THE LANCASTERS COUGHED INTO LIFE...
WELL, IT'S TOO LATE TO WORRY NOW!
I DON'T LIKE IT, SKIPPER! 6 TONS OF BOMBS AND SIX TONS OF FUEL! THAT MAKES AN ALL-UP WEIGHT OF 32 TONS!

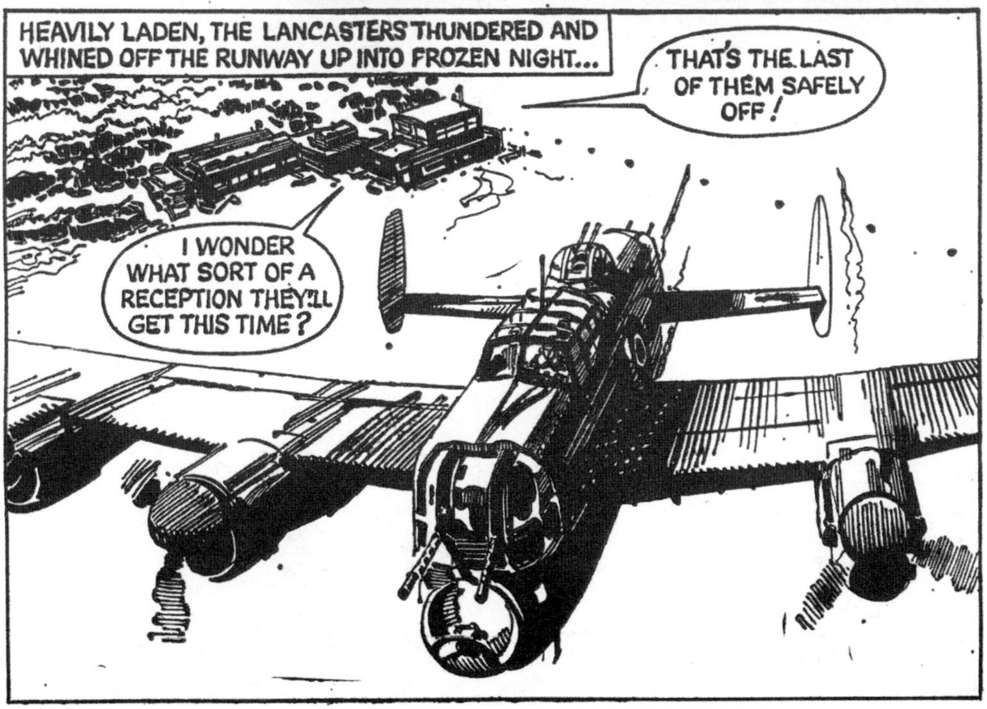
HEAVILY LADEN, THE LANCASTERS THUNDERED AND WHINED OFF THE RUNWAY UP INTO FROZEN NIGHT...
THAT'S THE LAST OF THEM SAFELY OFF!
I WONDER WHAT SORT OF A RECEPTION THEY'LL GET THIS TIME?

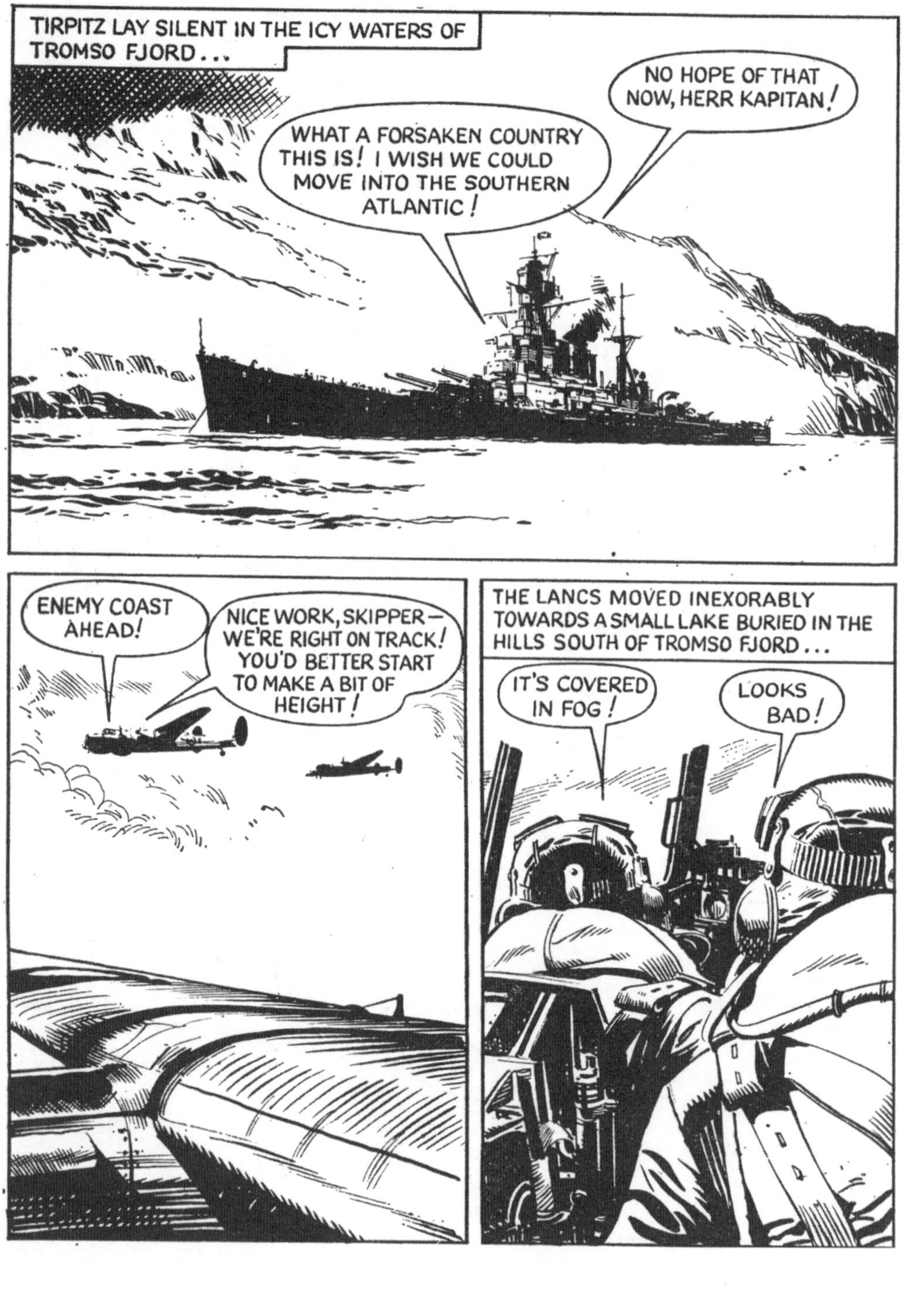
TIRPITZ LAY SILENT IN THE ICY WATERS OF TROMSO FJORD...
WHAT A FORSAKEN COUNTRY THIS IS! I WISH WE COULD MOVE INTO THE SOUTHERN ATLANTIC!
NO HOPE OF THAT NOW, HERR KAPITAN!
ENEMY COAST AHEAD!
NICE WORK, SKIPPER— WE'RE RIGHT ON TRACK! YOU'D BETTER START TO MAKE A BIT OF HEIGHT!
THE LANCS MOVED INEXORABLY TOWARDS A SMALL LAKE BURIED IN THE HILLS SOUTH OF TROMSO FJORD...
IT'S COVERED IN FOG!
LOOKS BAD!

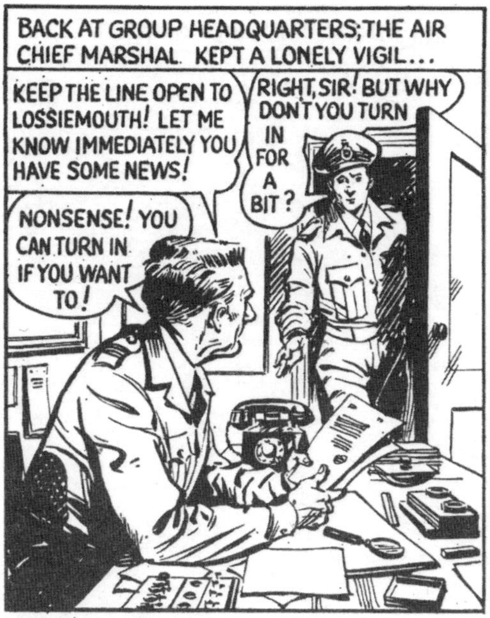
BACK AT GROUP HEADQUARTERS; THE AIR CHIEF MARSHAL KEPT A LONELY VIGIL...
KEEP THE LINE OPEN TO LOSSIEMOUTH! LET ME KNOW IMMEDIATELY YOU HAVE SOME NEWS!
RIGHT, SIR! BUT WHY DON'T YOU TURN IN FOR A BIT?
NONSENSE! YOU CAN TURN IN IF YOU WANT TO!

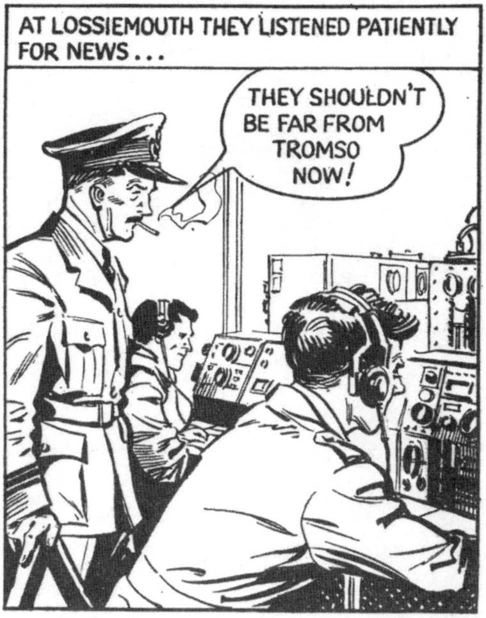
AT LOSSIEMOUTH THEY LISTENED PATIENTLY FOR NEWS...
THEY SHOULDN'T BE FAR FROM TROMSO NOW!

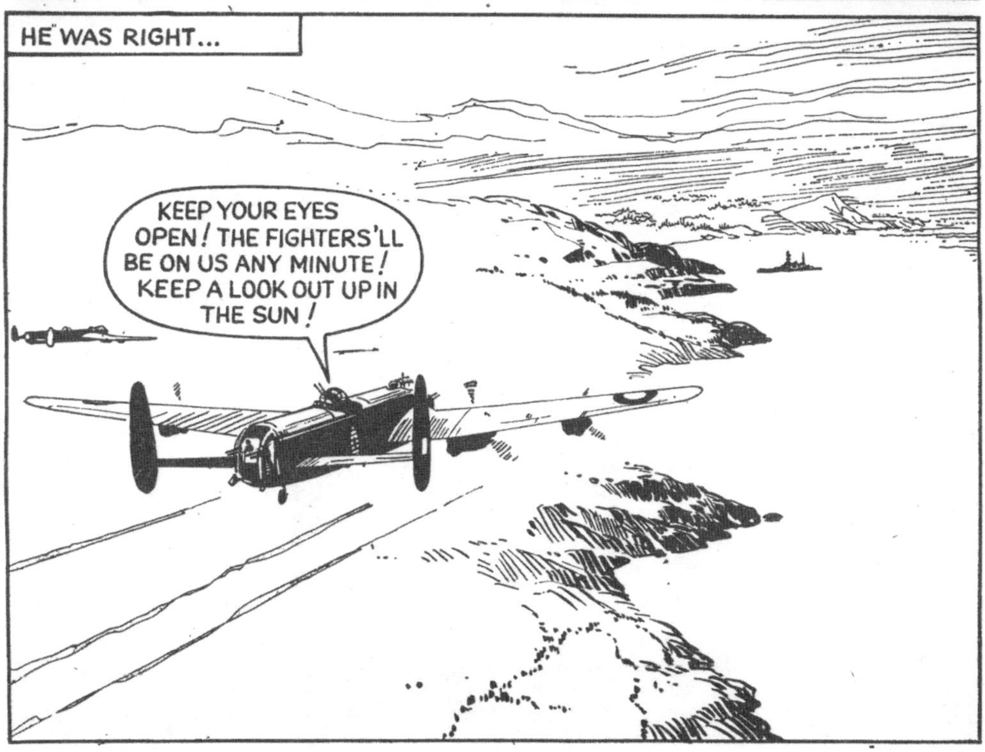
HE WAS RIGHT...
KEEP YOUR EYES OPEN! THE FIGHTERS'LL BE ON US ANY MINUTE! KEEP A LOOK OUT UP IN THE SUN!

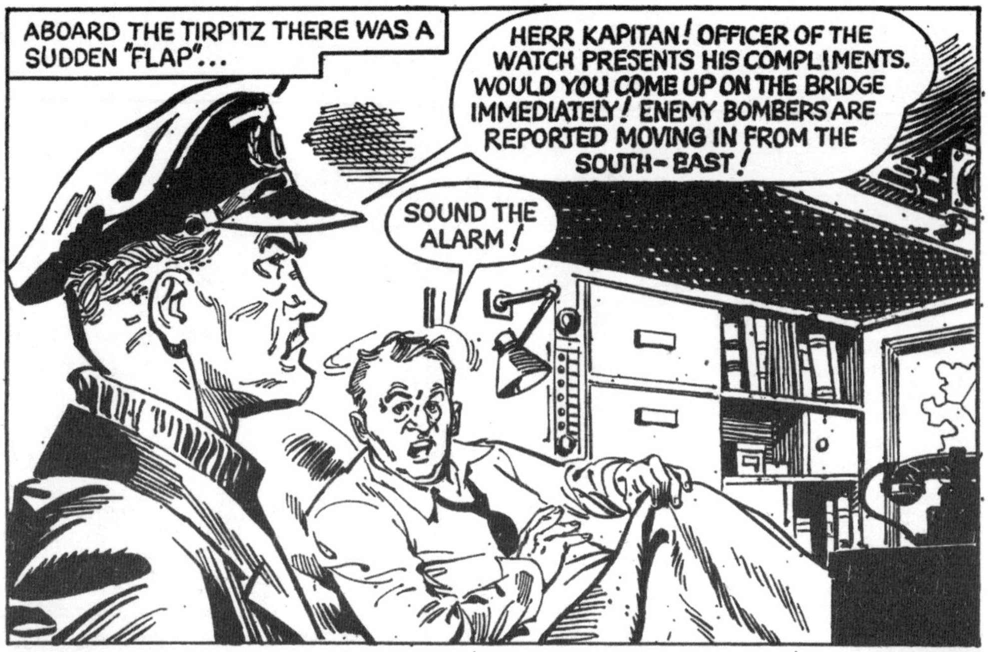
ABOARD THE TIRPITZ THERE WAS A SUDDEN "FLAP"...
HERR KAPITAN! OFFICER OF THE WATCH PRESENTS HIS COMPLIMENTS. WOULD YOU COME UP ON THE BRIDGE IMMEDIATELY! ENEMY BOMBERS ARE REPORTED MOVING IN FROM THE SOUTH-EAST!
SOUND THE ALARM!

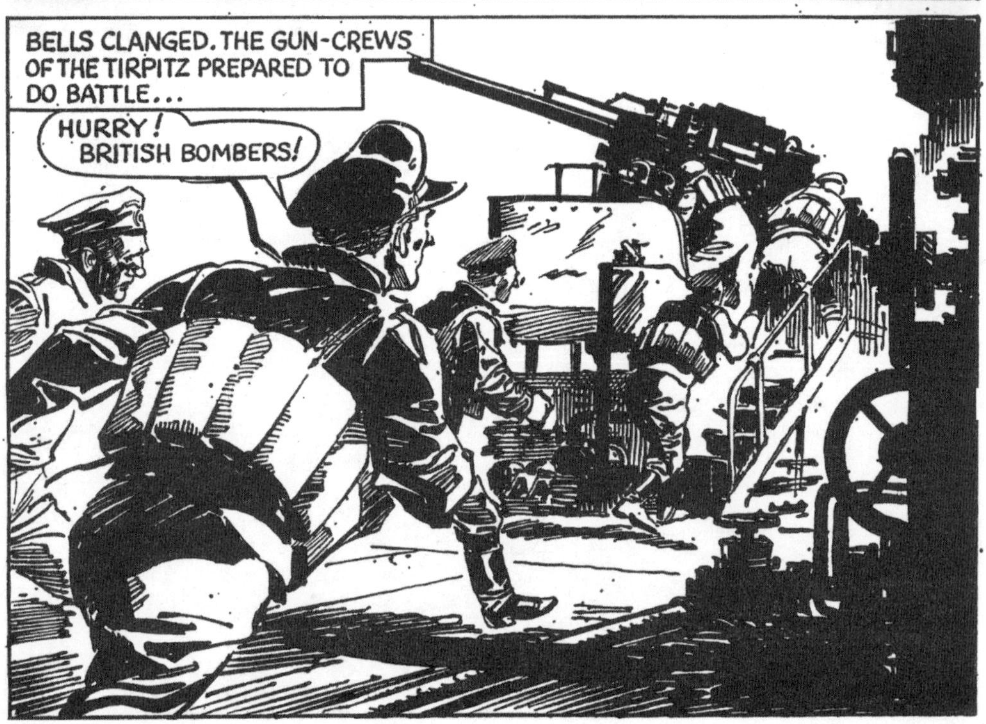
BELLS CLANGED. THE GUN-CREWS OF THE TIRPITZ PREPARED TO DO BATTLE...
HURRY! BRITISH BOMBERS!

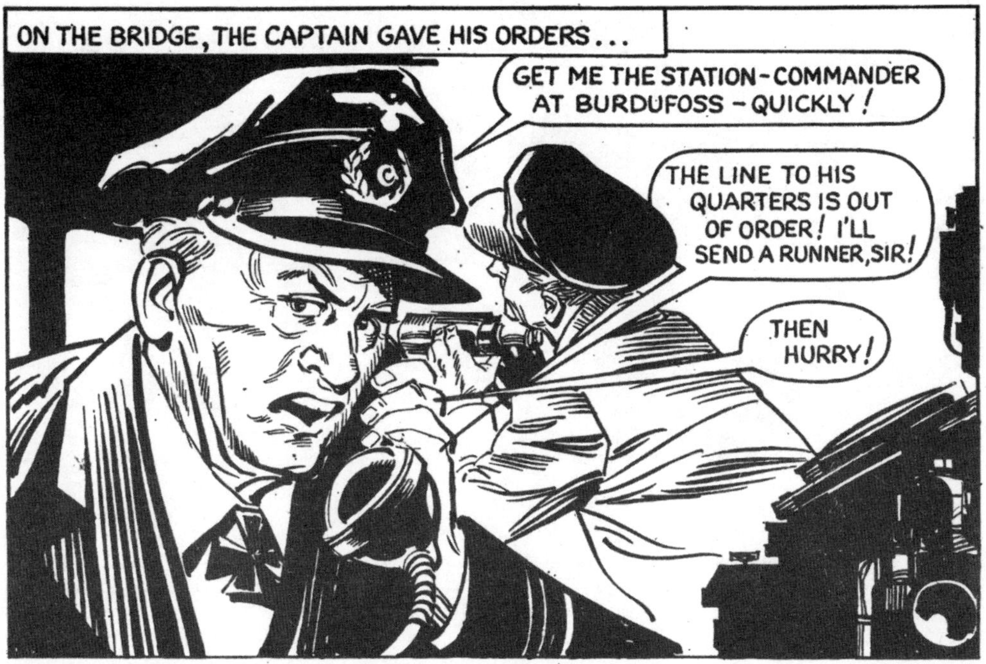
ON THE BRIDGE, THE CAPTAIN GAVE HIS ORDERS...
GET ME THE STATION-COMMANDER AT BURDUFOSS - QUICKLY!
THE LINE TO HIS QUARTERS IS OUT OF ORDER! I'LL SEND A RUNNER, SIR!
THEN HURRY!

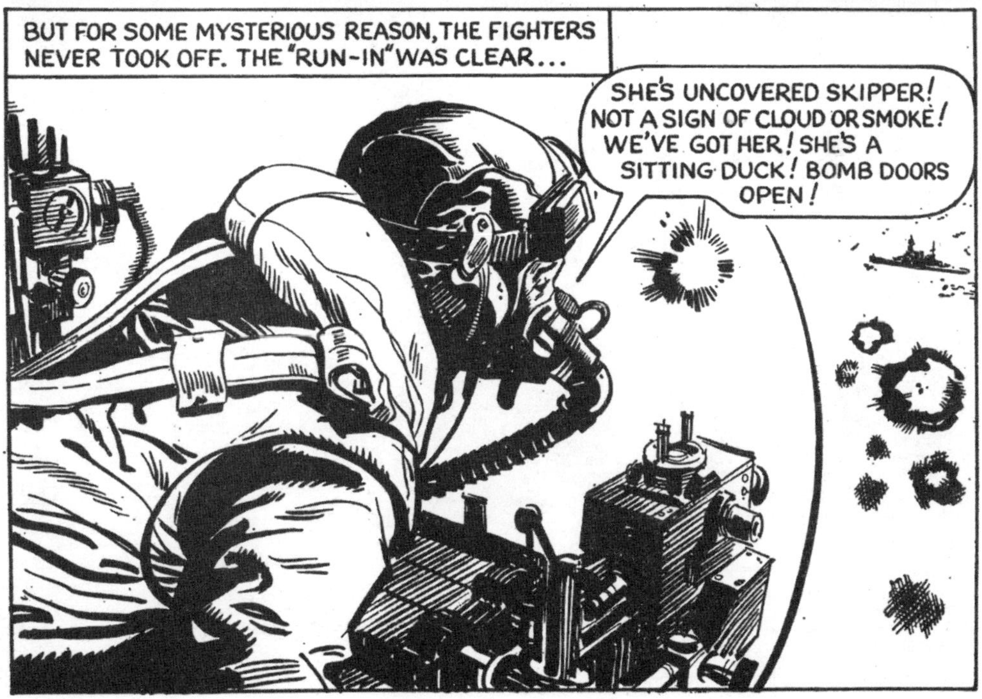
BUT FOR SOME MYSTERIOUS REASON, THE FIGHTERS NEVER TOOK OFF. THE "RUN-IN" WAS CLEAR...
SHE'S UNCOVERED SKIPPER! NOT A SIGN OF CLOUD OR SMOKE! WE'VE GOT HER! SHE'S A SITTING DUCK! BOMB DOORS OPEN!

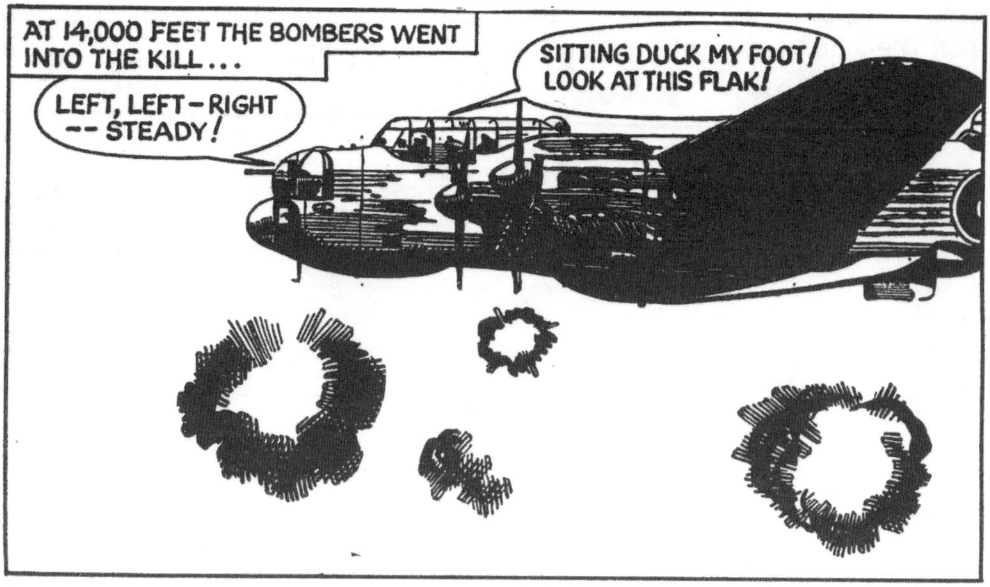
AT 14,000 FEET THE BOMBERS WENT INTO THE KILL...
LEFT, LEFT-RIGHT -- STEADY!
SITTING DUCK MY FOOT! LOOK AT THIS FLAK!

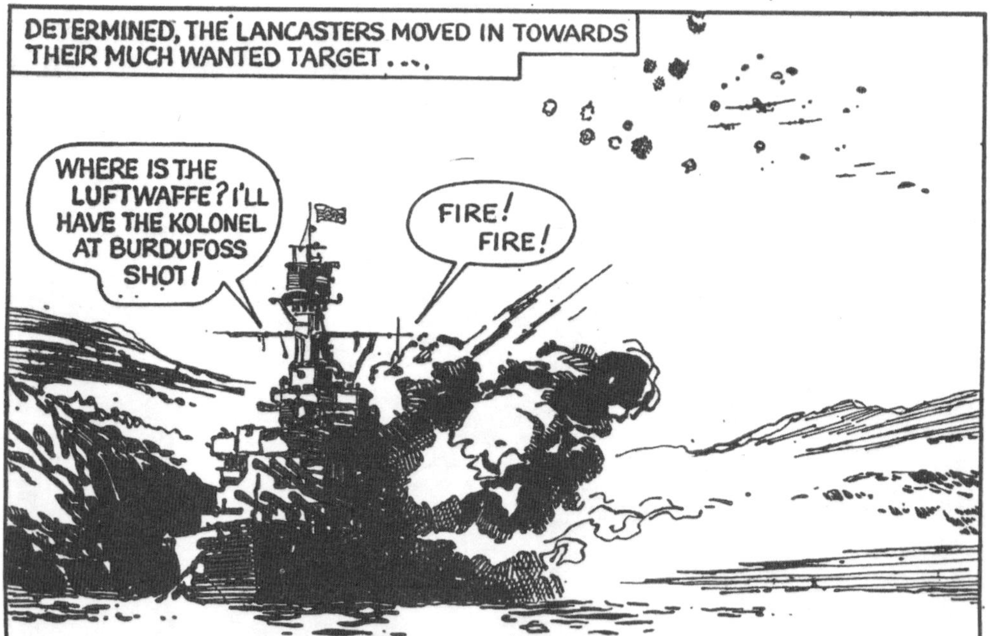
DETERMINED, THE LANCASTERS MOVED IN TOWARDS THEIR MUCH WANTED TARGET....
WHERE IS THE LUFTWAFFE? I'LL HAVE THE KOLONEL AT BURDUFOSS SHOT!
FIRE! FIRE!

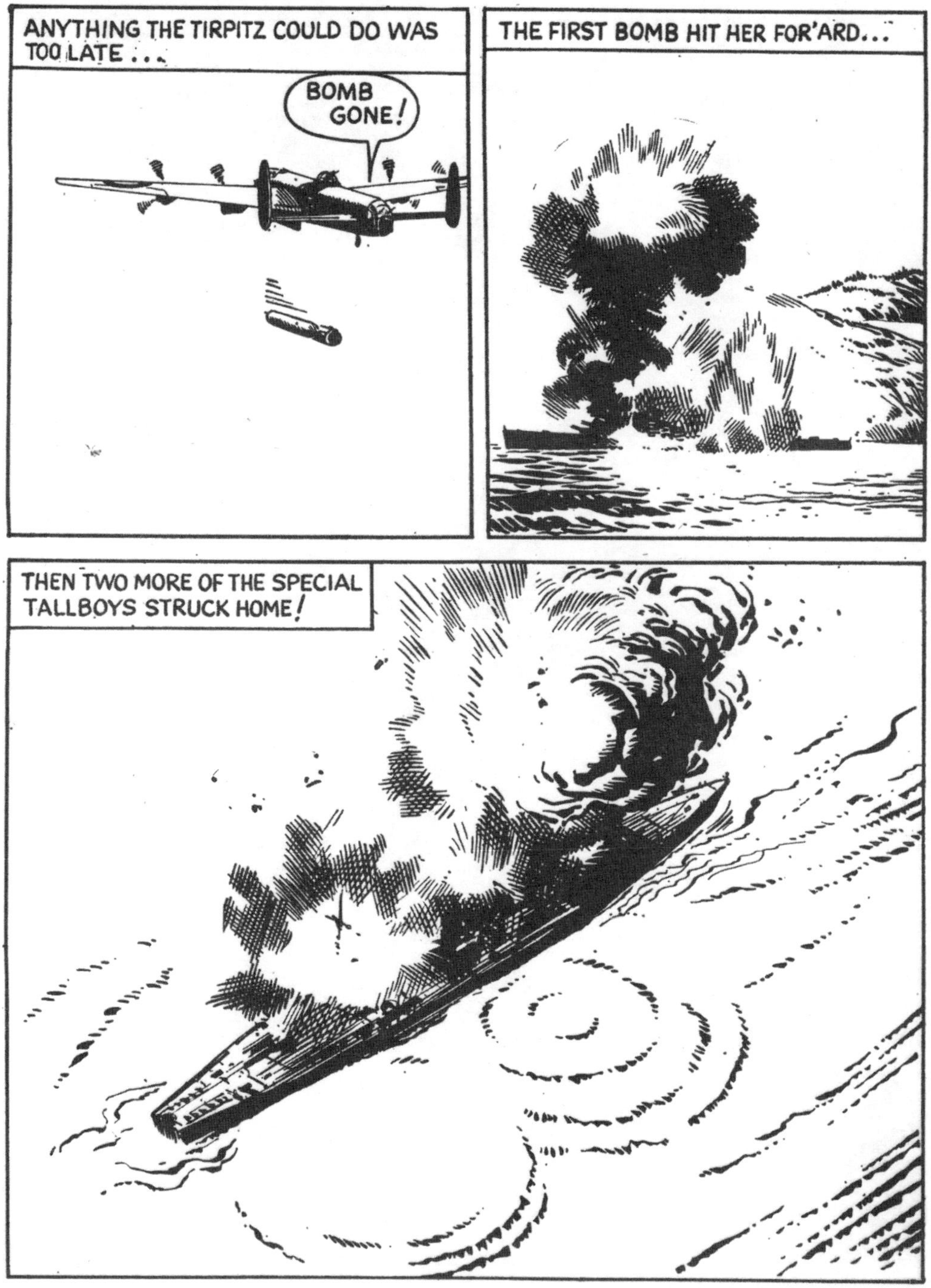
ANYTHING THE TIRPITZ COULD DO WAS TOO LATE . . .
BOMB GONE!
THE FIRST BOMB HIT HER FOR'ARD...
THEN TWO MORE OF THE SPECIAL TALLBOYS STRUCK HOME!

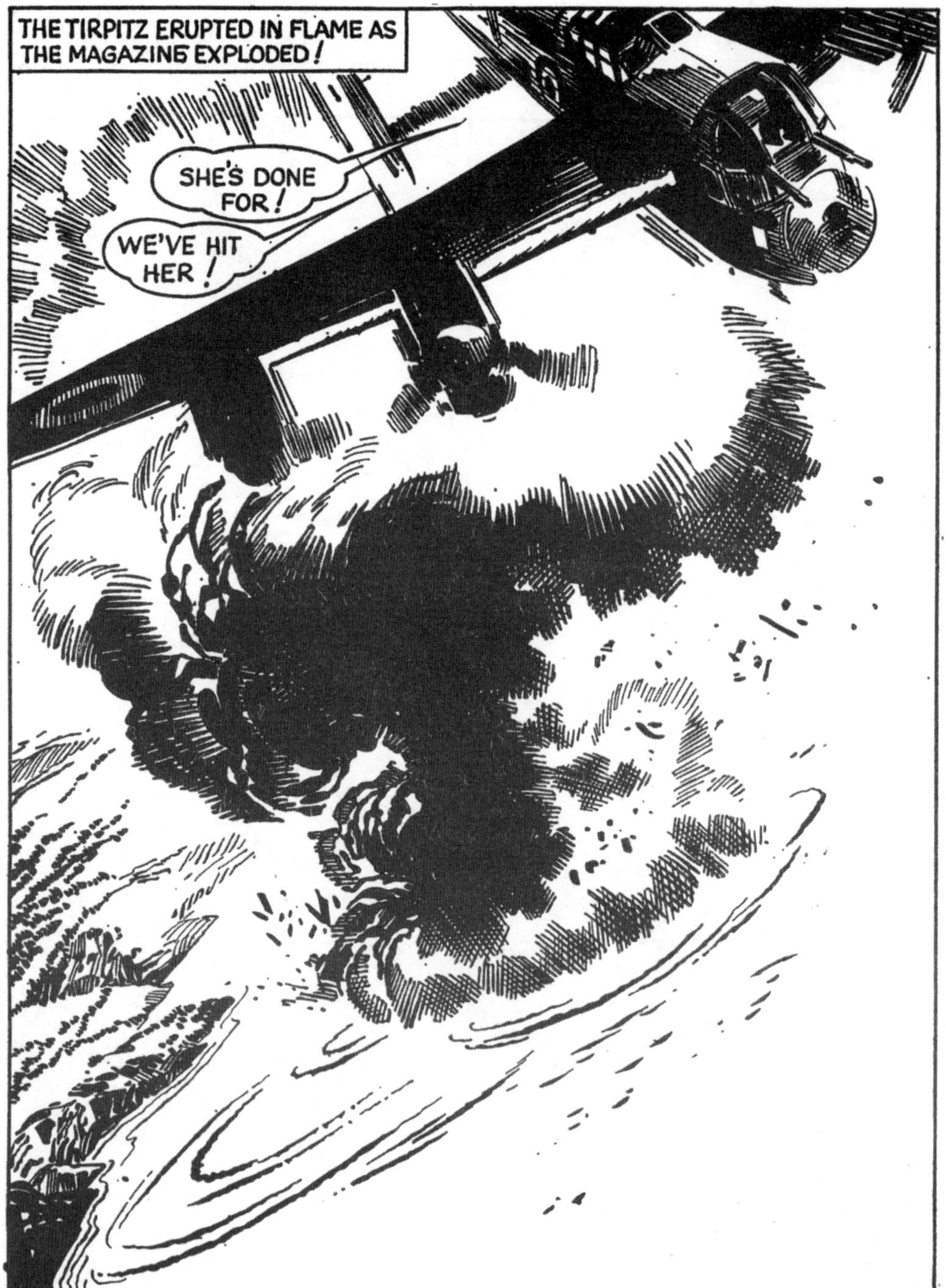
THE TIRPITZ ERUPTED IN FLAME AS THE MAGAZINE EXPLODED!
WE'VE HIT HER!
SHE'S DONE FOR!

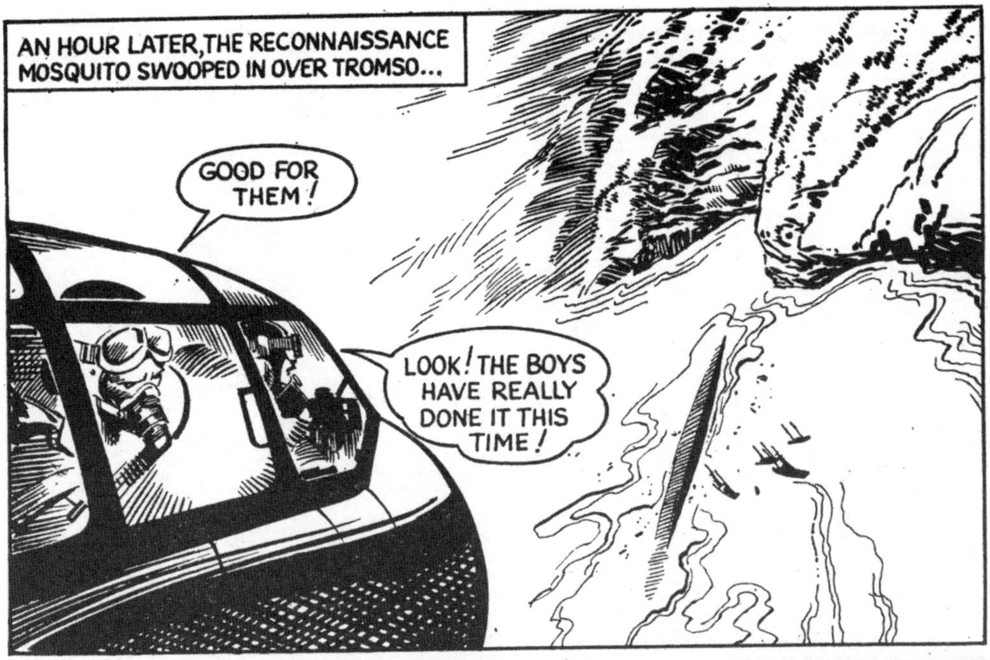
AN HOUR LATER, THE RECONNAISSANCE MOSQUITO SWOOPED IN OVER TROMSO...
GOOD FOR THEM!
LOOK! THE BOYS HAVE REALLY DONE IT THIS TIME!

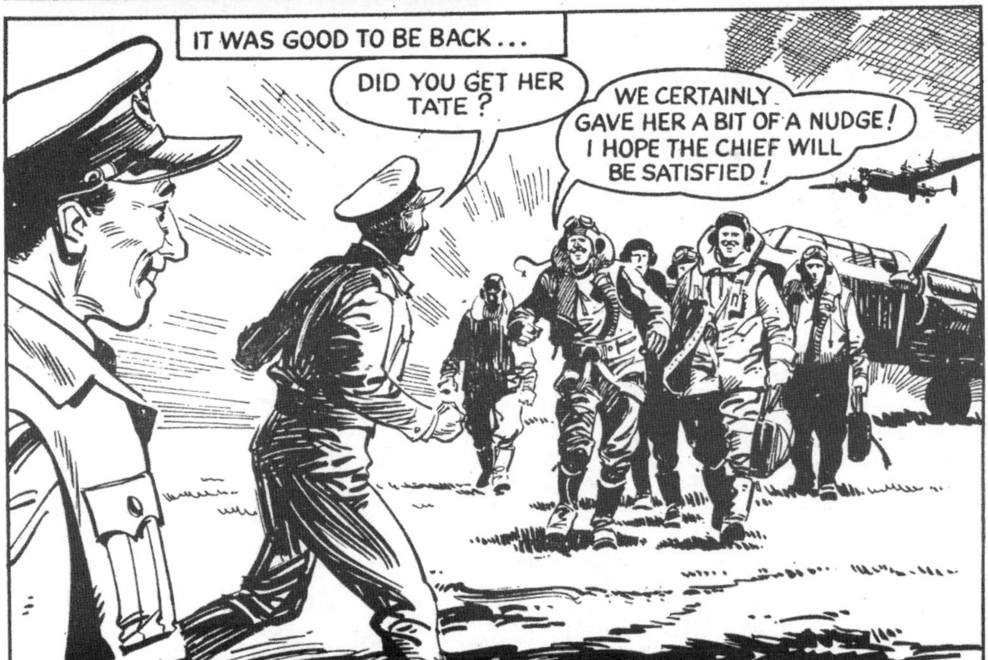
IT WAS GOOD TO BE BACK...
DID YOU GET HER TATE?
WE CERTAINLY GAVE HER A BIT OF A NUDGE! I HOPE THE CHIEF WILL BE SATISFIED!

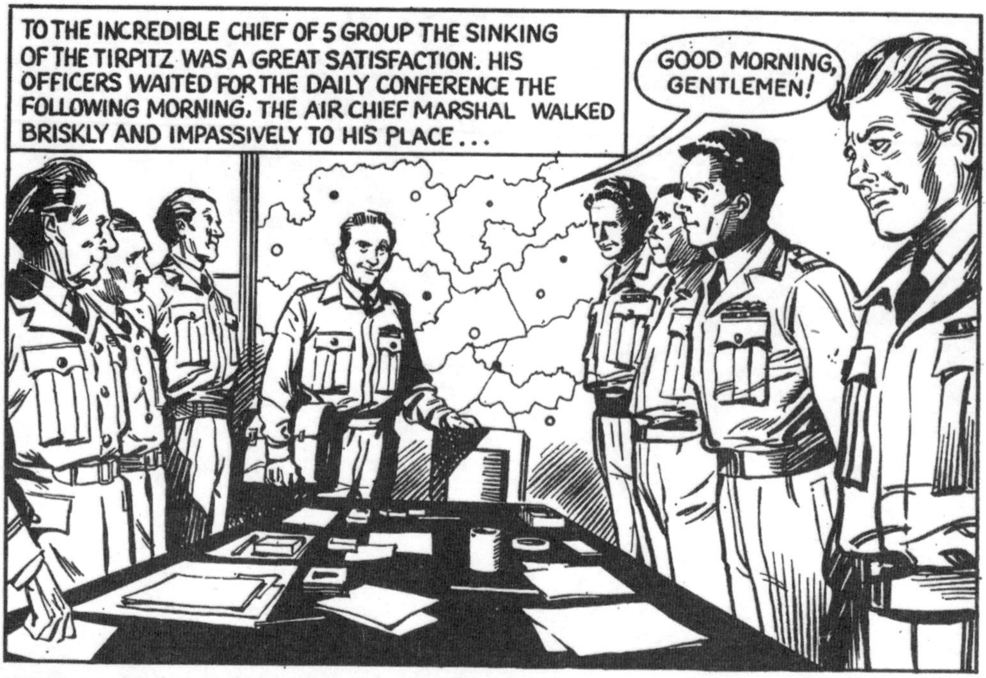
TO THE INCREDIBLE CHIEF OF 5 GROUP THE SINKING OF THE TIRPITZ WAS A GREAT SATISFACTION. HIS OFFICERS WAITED FOR THE DAILY CONFERENCE THE FOLLOWING MORNING. THE AIR CHIEF MARSHAL WALKED BRISKLY AND IMPASSIVELY TO HIS PLACE...
GOOD MORNING, GENTLEMEN!

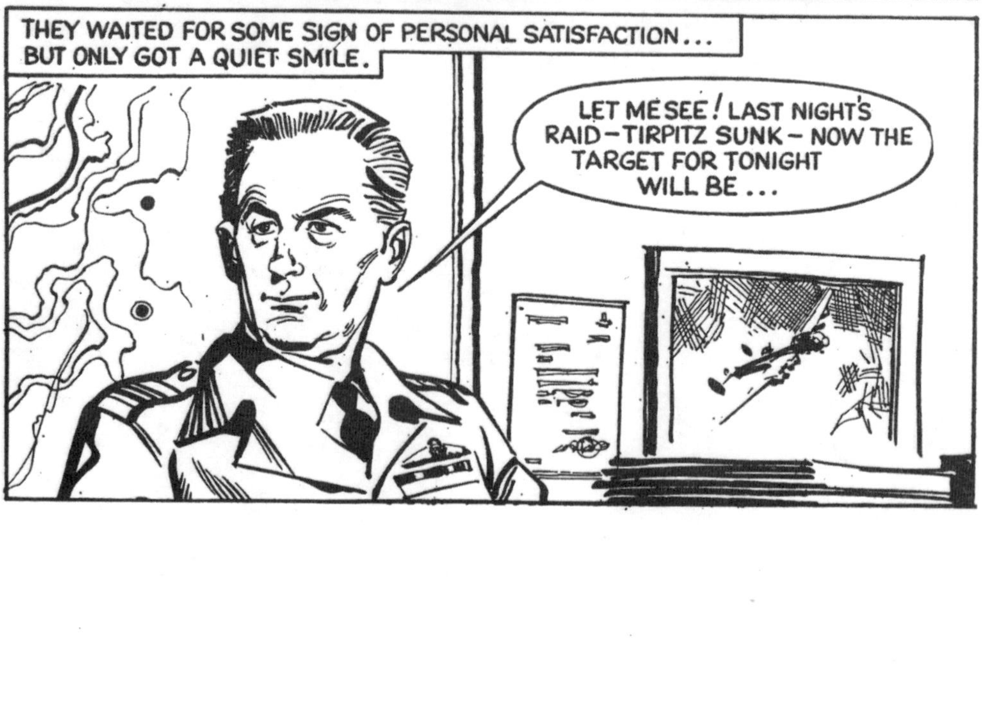
THEY WAITED FOR SOME SIGN OF PERSONAL SATISFACTION... BUT ONLY GOT A QUIET SMILE.
LET ME SEE! LAST NIGHT'S RAID – TIRPITZ SUNK – NOW THE TARGET FOR TONIGHT WILL BE...

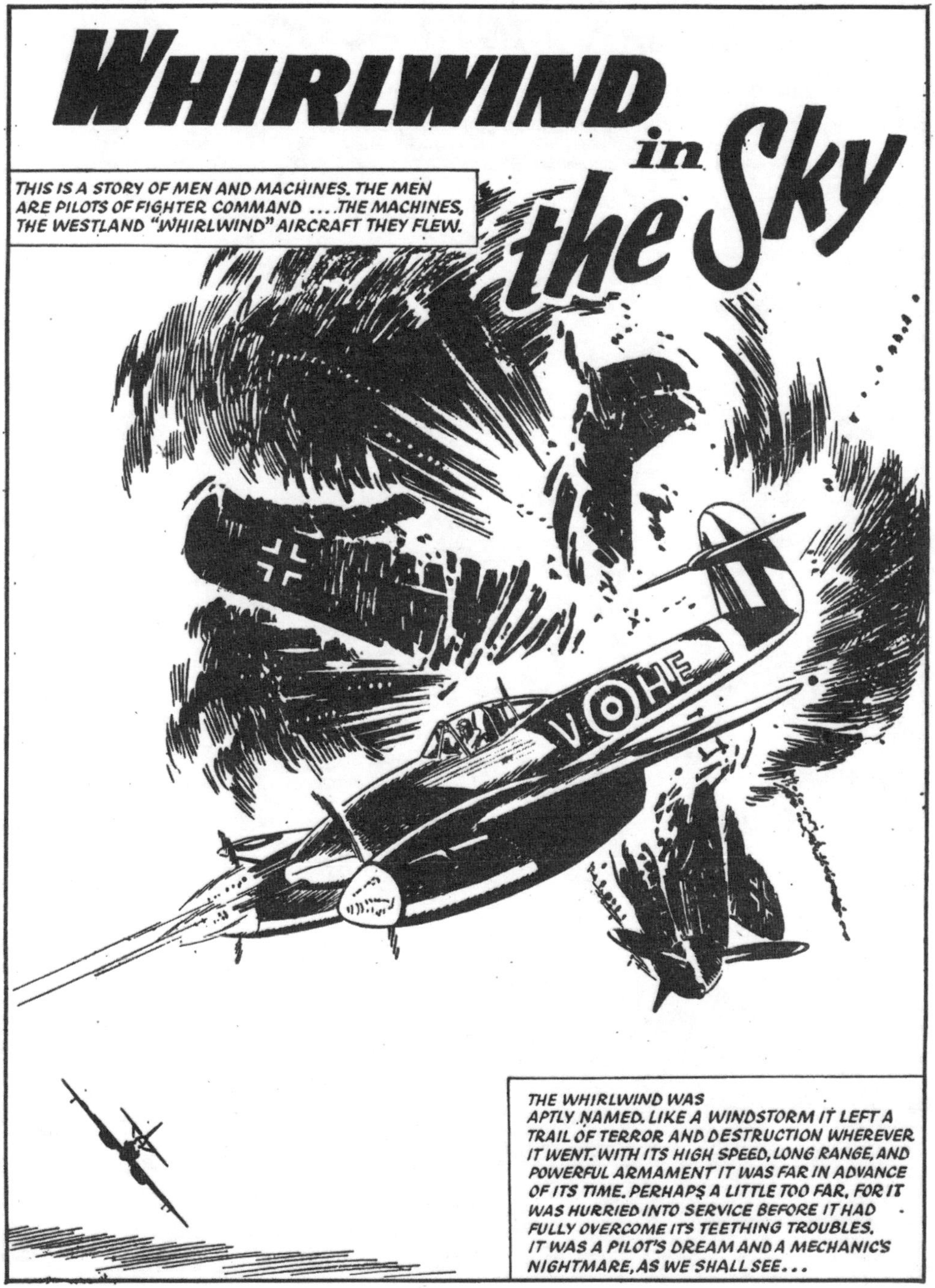
WHIRLWIND in the Sky
THIS IS A STORY OF MEN AND MACHINES. THE MEN ARE PILOTS OF FIGHTER COMMAND ....THE MACHINES, THE WESTLAND "WHIRLWIND" AIRCRAFT THEY FLEW.
THE WHIRLWIND WAS APTLY NAMED. LIKE A WINDSTORM IT LEFT A TRAIL OF TERROR AND DESTRUCTION WHEREVER IT WENT. WITH ITS HIGH SPEED, LONG RANGE, AND POWERFUL ARMAMENT IT WAS FAR IN ADVANCE OF ITS TIME. PERHAPS A LITTLE TOO FAR, FOR IT WAS HURRIED INTO SERVICE BEFORE IT HAD FULLY OVERCOME ITS TEETHING TROUBLES. IT WAS A PILOT'S DREAM AND A MECHANIC'S NIGHTMARE, AS WE SHALL SEE...

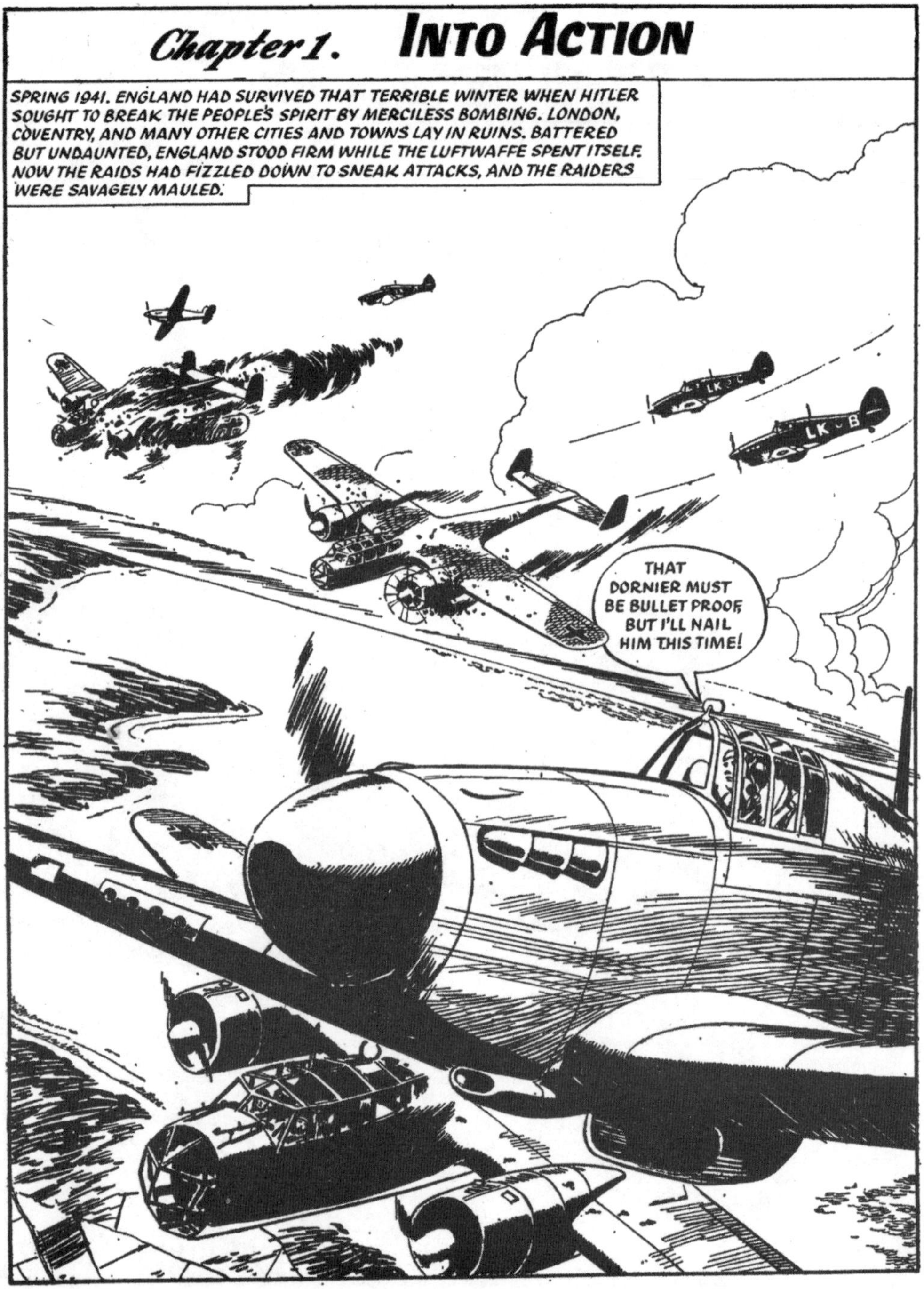
Chapter 1. INTO ACTION
SPRING 1941. ENGLAND HAD SURVIVED THAT TERRIBLE WINTER WHEN HITLER SOUGHT TO BREAK THE PEOPLE'S SPIRIT BY MERCILESS BOMBING. LONDON, COVENTRY, AND MANY OTHER CITIES AND TOWNS LAY IN RUINS. BATTERED BUT UNDAUNTED, ENGLAND STOOD FIRM WHILE THE LUFTWAFFE SPENT ITSELF. NOW THE RAIDS HAD FIZZLED DOWN TO SNEAK ATTACKS, AND THE RAIDERS WERE SAVAGELY MAULED.
LK C
LK B
THAT DORNIER MUST BE BULLET PROOF, BUT I'LL NAIL HIM THIS TIME!

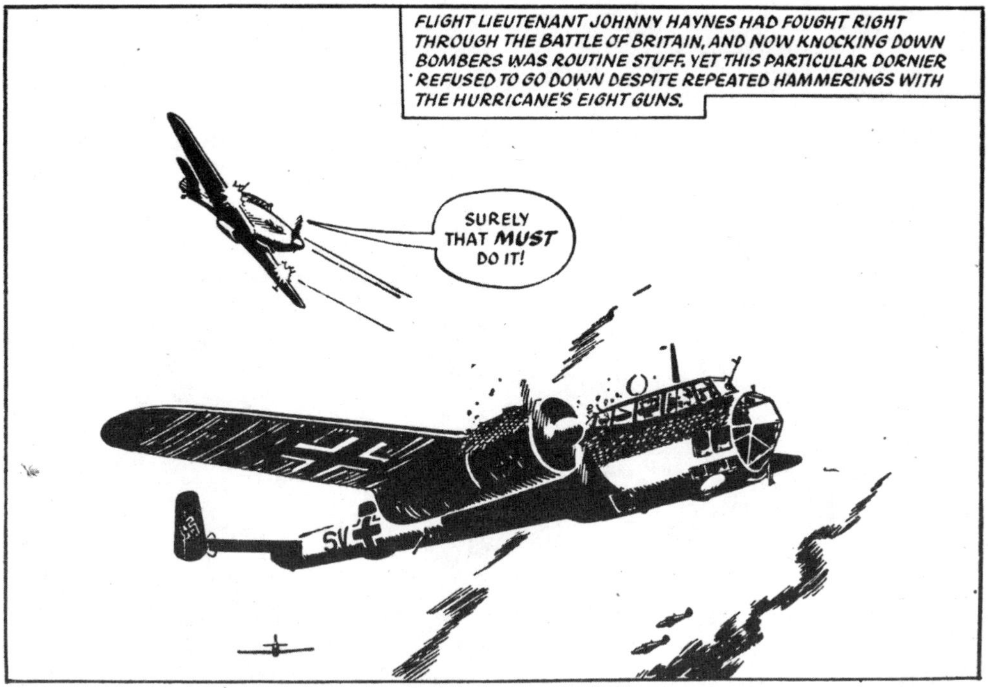
FLIGHT LIEUTENANT JOHNNY HAYNES HAD FOUGHT RIGHT THROUGH THE BATTLE OF BRITAIN, AND NOW KNOCKING DOWN BOMBERS WAS ROUTINE STUFF. YET THIS PARTICULAR DORNIER REFUSED TO GO DOWN DESPITE REPEATED HAMMERINGS WITH THE HURRICANE'S EIGHT GUNS.
SURELY THAT MUST DO IT!

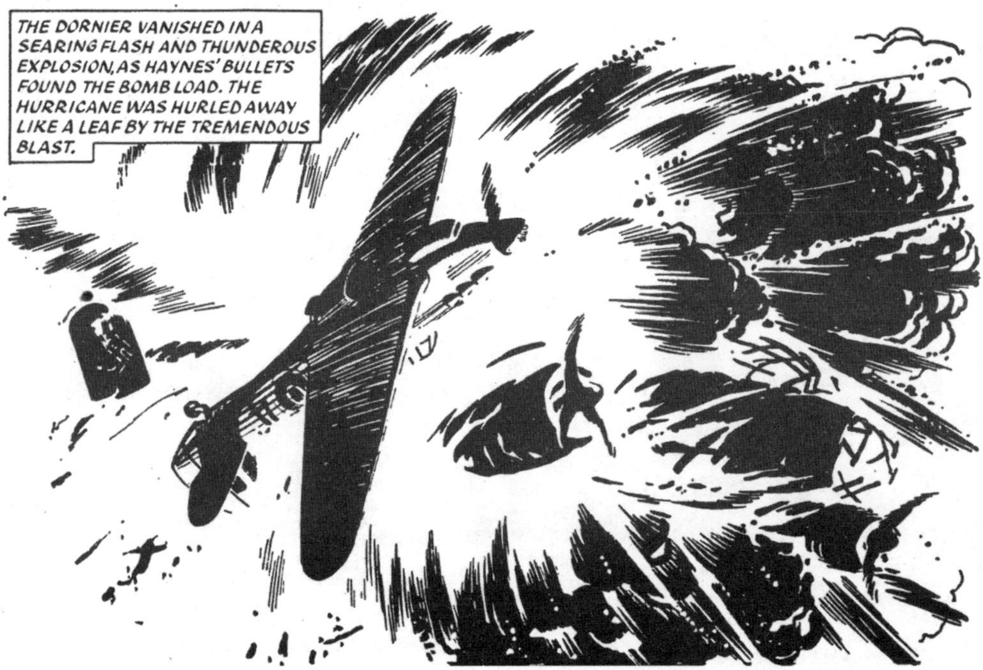
THE DORNIER VANISHED IN A SEARING FLASH AND THUNDEROUS EXPLOSION, AS HAYNES' BULLETS FOUND THE BOMB LOAD. THE HURRICANE WAS HURLED AWAY LIKE A LEAF BY THE TREMENDOUS BLAST.

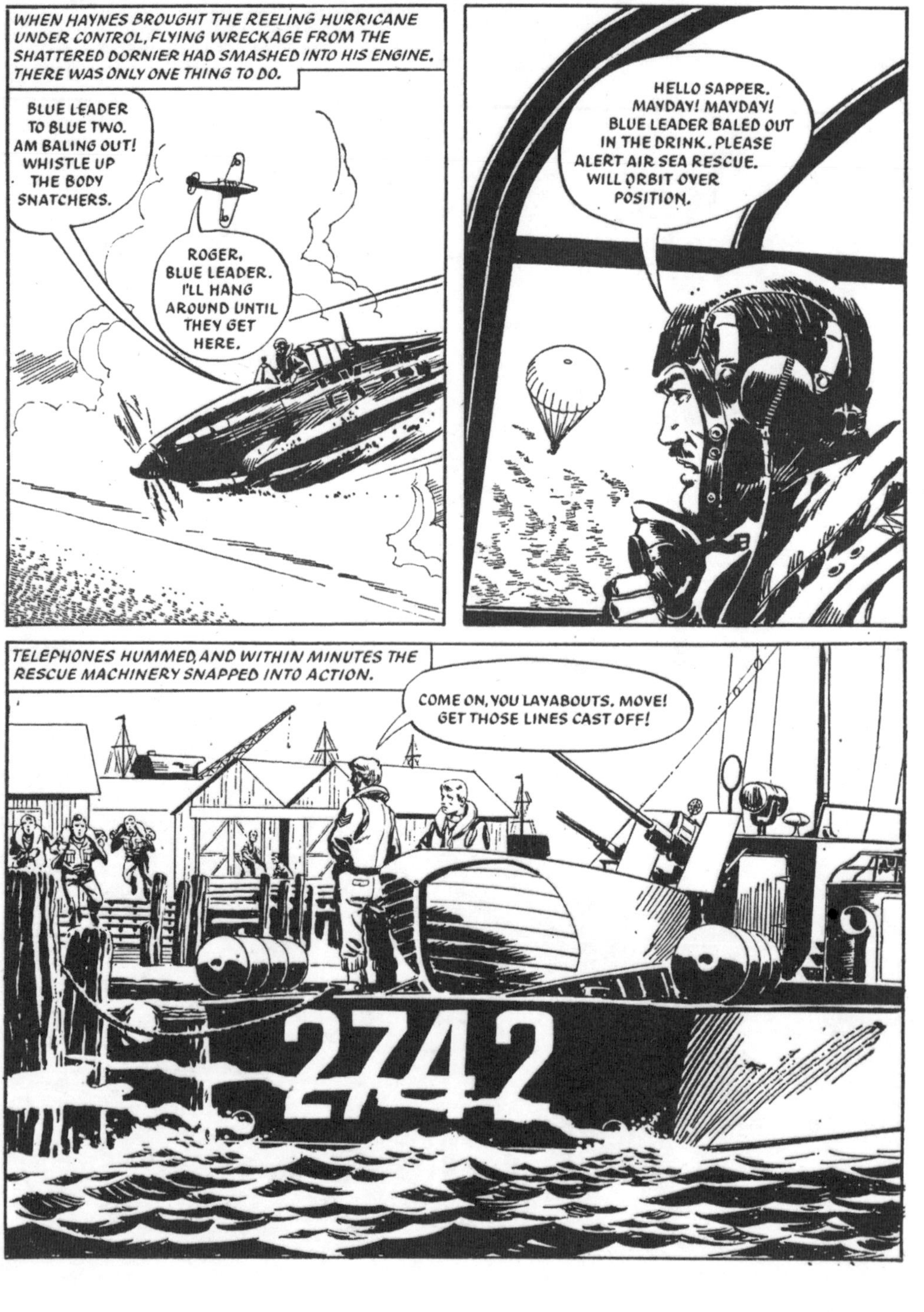
WHEN HAYNES BROUGHT THE REELING HURRICANE UNDER CONTROL, FLYING WRECKAGE FROM THE SHATTERED DORNIER HAD SMASHED INTO HIS ENGINE. THERE WAS ONLY ONE THING TO DO.
BLUE LEADER TO BLUE TWO. AM BALING OUT! WHISTLE UP THE BODY SNATCHERS.
ROGER, BLUE LEADER. I'LL HANG AROUND UNTIL THEY GET HERE.
HELLO SAPPER. MAYDAY! MAYDAY! BLUE LEADER BALED OUT IN THE DRINK. PLEASE ALERT AIR SEA RESCUE. WILL ORBIT OVER POSITION.
TELEPHONES HUMMED, AND WITHIN MINUTES THE RESCUE MACHINERY SNAPPED INTO ACTION.
COME ON, YOU LAYABOUTS. MOVE! GET THOSE LINES CAST OFF!
2742

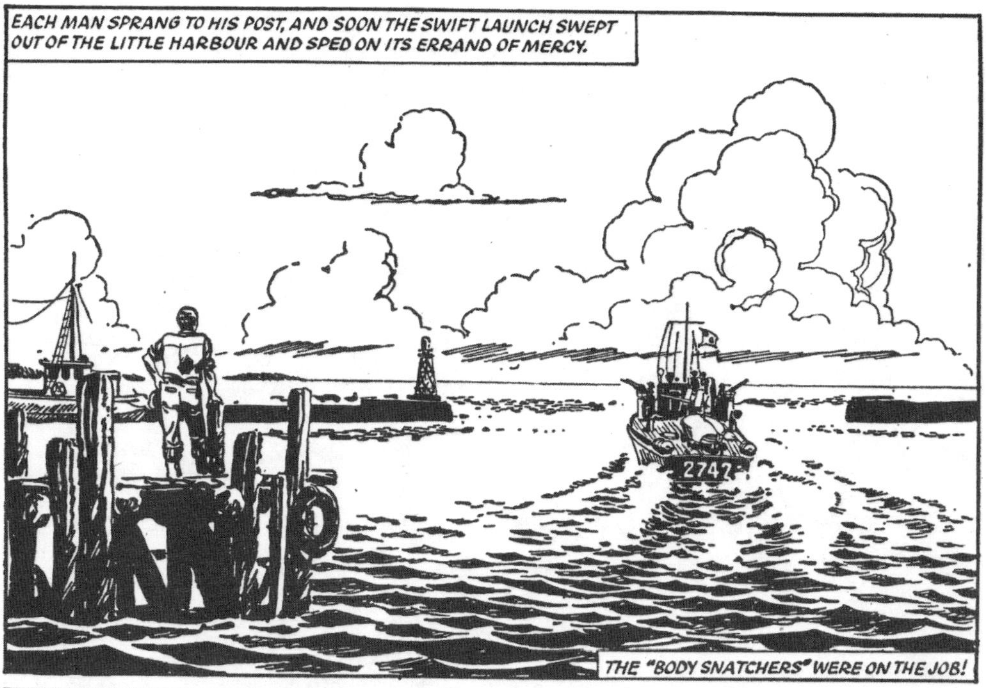
EACH MAN SPRANG TO HIS POST, AND SOON THE SWIFT LAUNCH SWEPT OUT OF THE LITTLE HARBOUR AND SPED ON ITS ERRAND OF MERCY.
2742
THE "BODY SNATCHERS" WERE ON THE JOB!

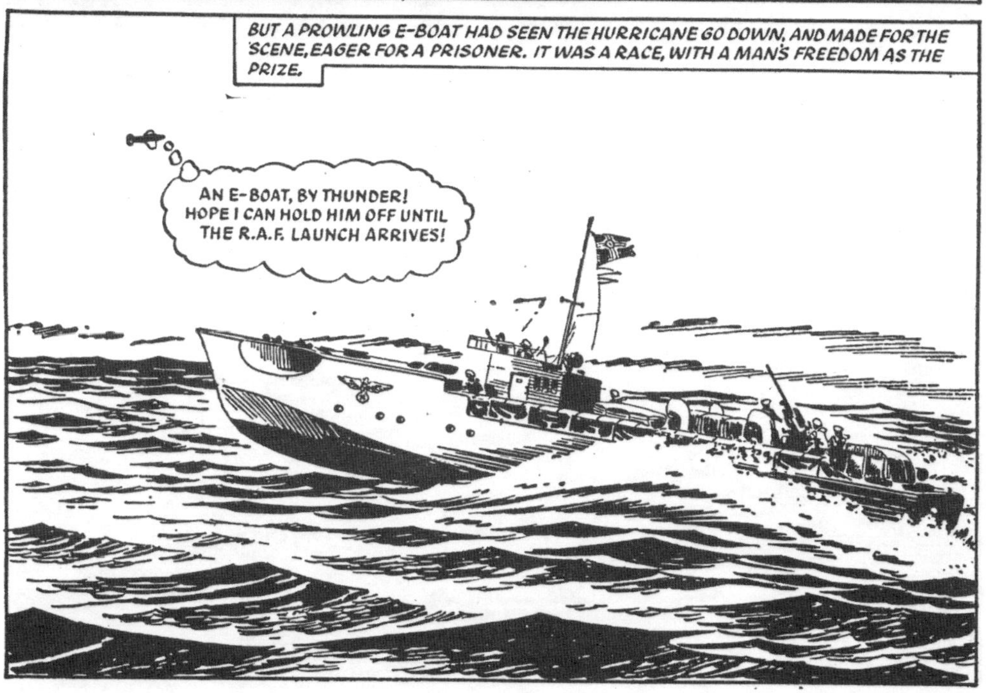
BUT A PROWLING E-BOAT HAD SEEN THE HURRICANE GO DOWN, AND MADE FOR THE SCENE, EAGER FOR A PRISONER. IT WAS A RACE, WITH A MAN'S FREEDOM AS THE PRIZE.
AN E-BOAT, BY THUNDER! HOPE I CAN HOLD HIM OFF UNTIL THE R.A.F. LAUNCH ARRIVES!

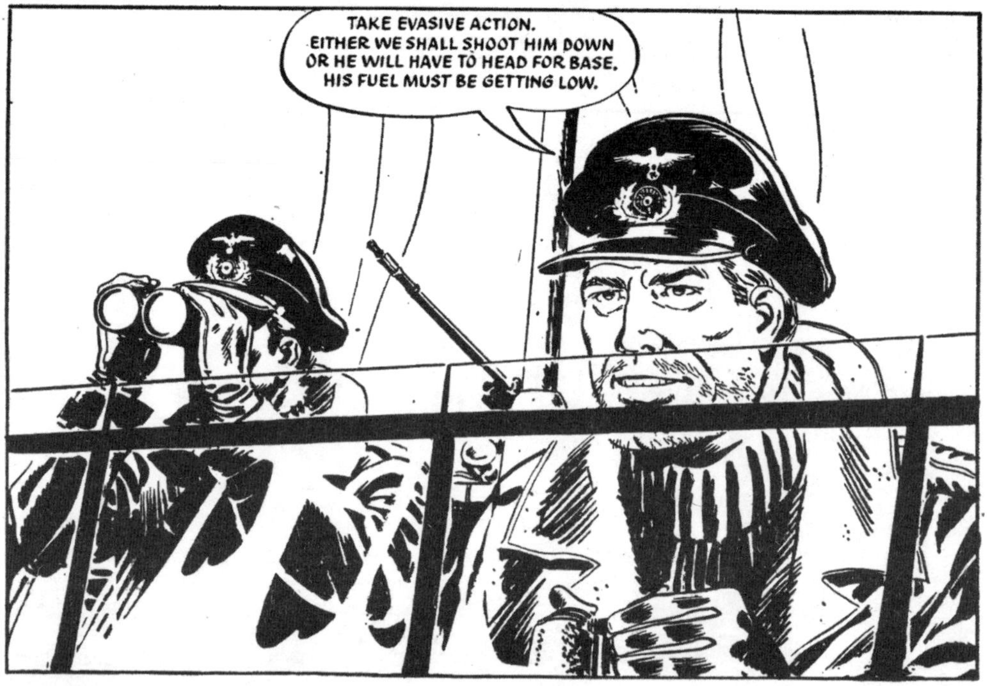
TAKE EVASIVE ACTION. EITHER WE SHALL SHOOT HIM DOWN OR HE WILL HAVE TO HEAD FOR BASE. HIS FUEL MUST BE GETTING LOW.

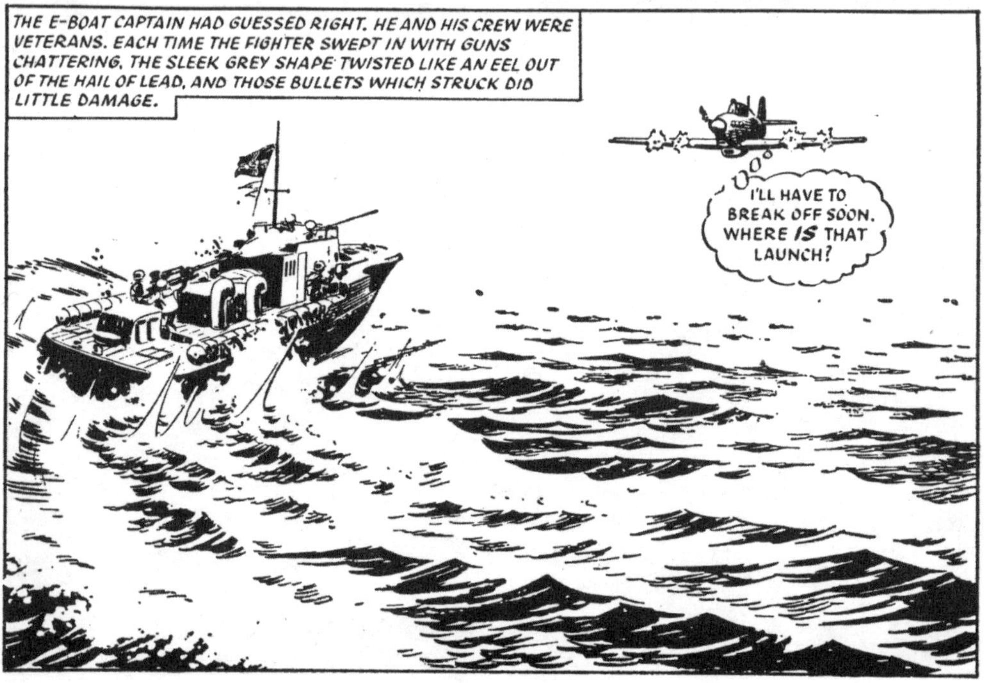
THE E-BOAT CAPTAIN HAD GUESSED RIGHT. HE AND HIS CREW WERE VETERANS. EACH TIME THE FIGHTER SWEPT IN WITH GUNS CHATTERING, THE SLEEK GREY SHAPE TWISTED LIKE AN EEL OUT OF THE HAIL OF LEAD, AND THOSE BULLETS WHICH STRUCK DID LITTLE DAMAGE.
I'LL HAVE TO BREAK OFF SOON. WHERE IS THAT LAUNCH?

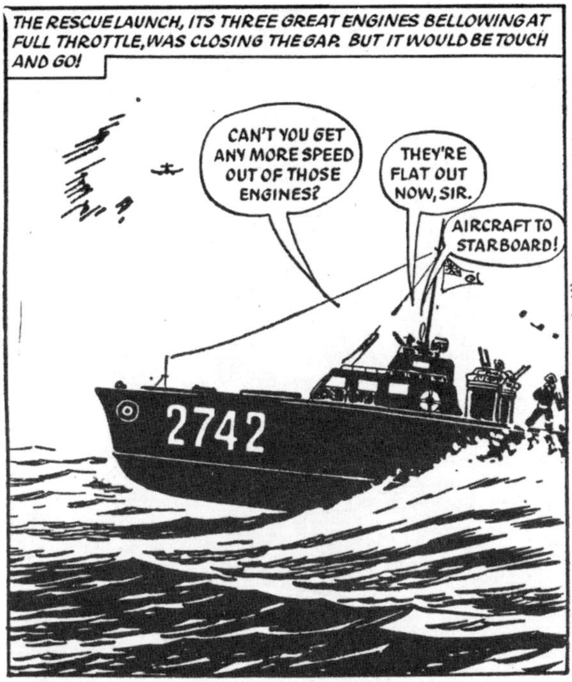
THE RESCUE LAUNCH, ITS THREE GREAT ENGINES BELLOWING AT FULL THROTTLE, WAS CLOSING THE GAP. BUT IT WOULD BE TOUCH AND GO!
CAN'T YOU GET ANY MORE SPEED OUT OF THOSE ENGINES?
THEY'RE FLAT OUT NOW, SIR.
AIRCRAFT TO STARBOARD!
2742

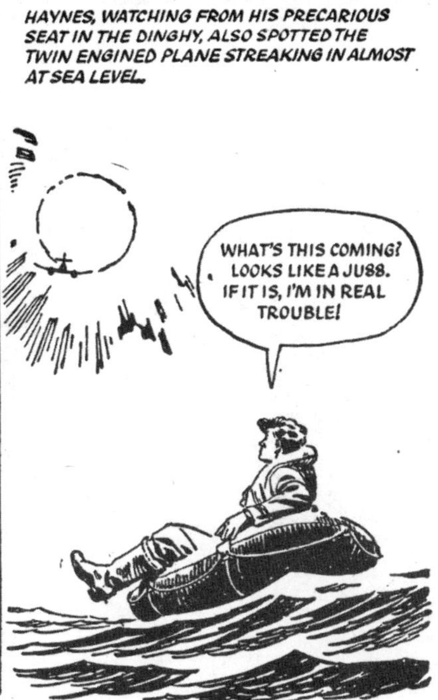
HAYNES, WATCHING FROM HIS PRECARIOUS SEAT IN THE DINGHY, ALSO SPOTTED THE TWIN ENGINED PLANE STREAKING IN ALMOST AT SEA LEVEL.
WHAT'S THIS COMING? LOOKS LIKE A JUSS. IF IT IS, I'M IN REAL TROUBLE!

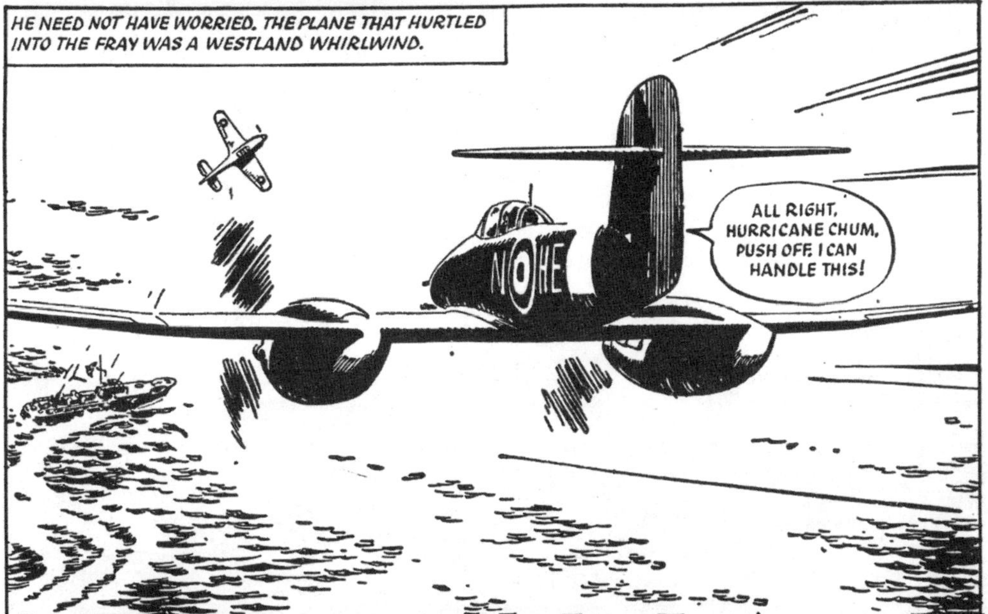
HE NEED NOT HAVE WORRIED. THE PLANE THAT HURTLED INTO THE FRAY WAS A WESTLAND WHIRLWIND.
ALL RIGHT, HURRICANE CHUM, PUSH OFF. I CAN HANDLE THIS!
HE

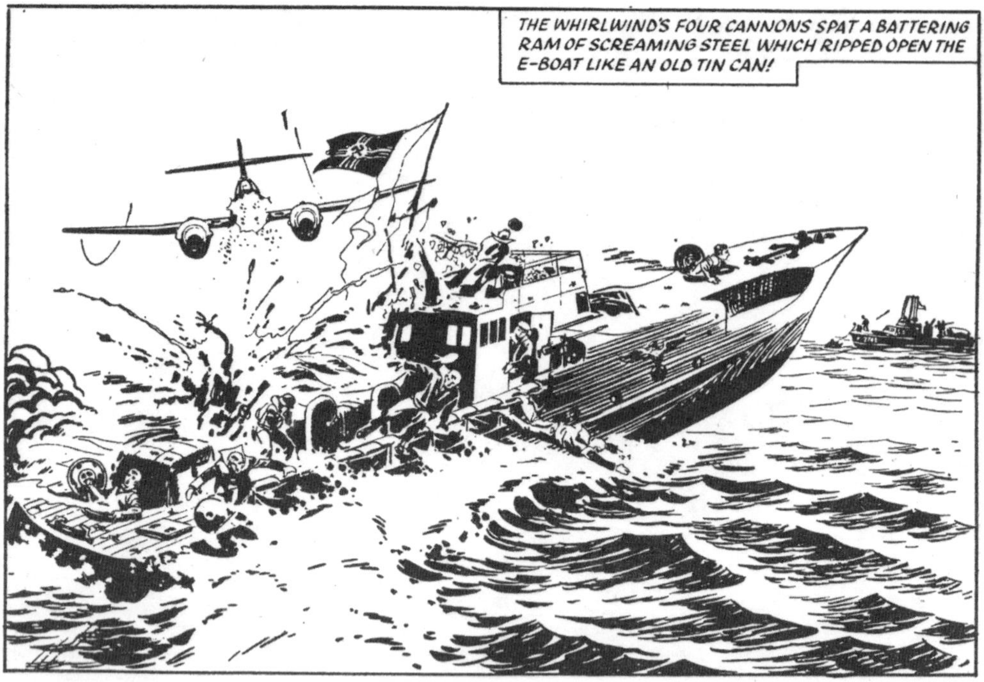
THE WHIRLWIND'S FOUR CANNONS SPAT A BATTERING RAM OF SCREAMING STEEL WHICH RIPPED OPEN THE E-BOAT LIKE AN OLD TIN CAN!

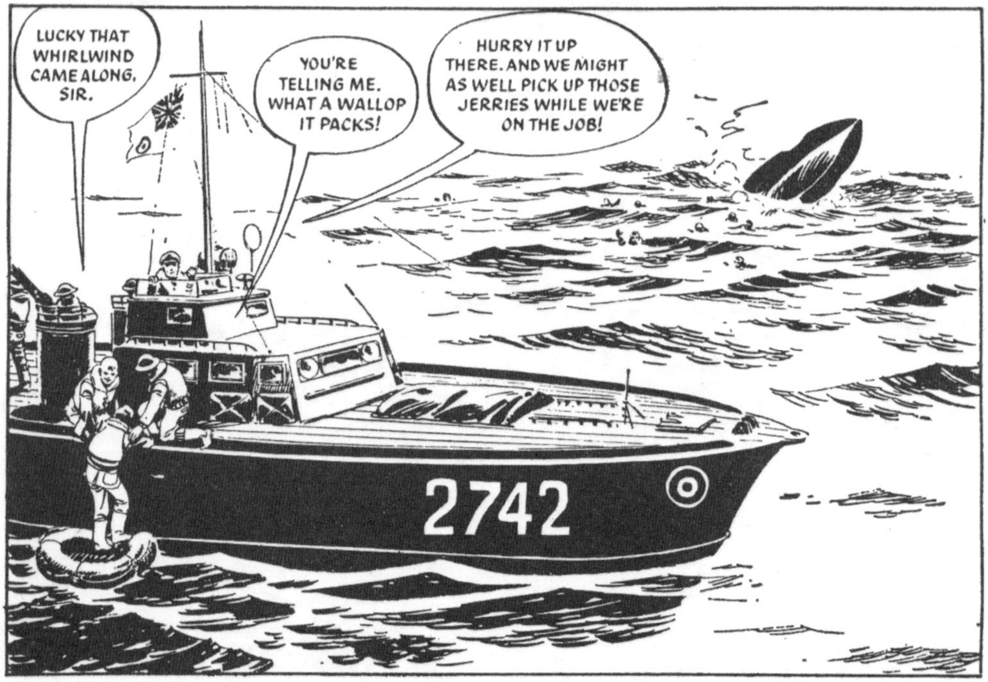
LUCKY THAT WHIRLWIND CAME ALONG, SIR.
YOU'RE TELLING ME. WHAT A WALLOP IT PACKS!
HURRY IT UP THERE. AND WE MIGHT AS WELL PICK UP THOSE JERRIES WHILE WE'RE ON THE JOB!
2742

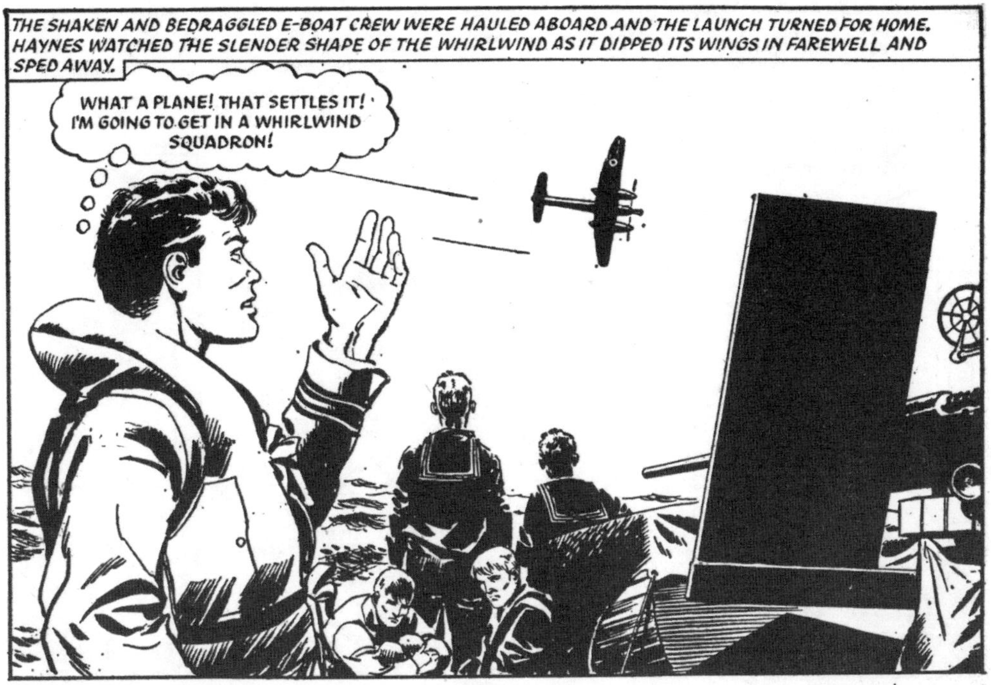
THE SHAKEN AND BEDRAGGLED E-BOAT CREW WERE HAULED ABOARD AND THE LAUNCH TURNED FOR HOME. HAYNES WATCHED THE SLENDER SHAPE OF THE WHIRLWIND AS IT DIPPED ITS WINGS IN FAREWELL AND SPED AWAY.
WHAT A PLANE! THAT SETTLES IT! I'M GOING TO GET IN A WHIRLWIND SQUADRON!

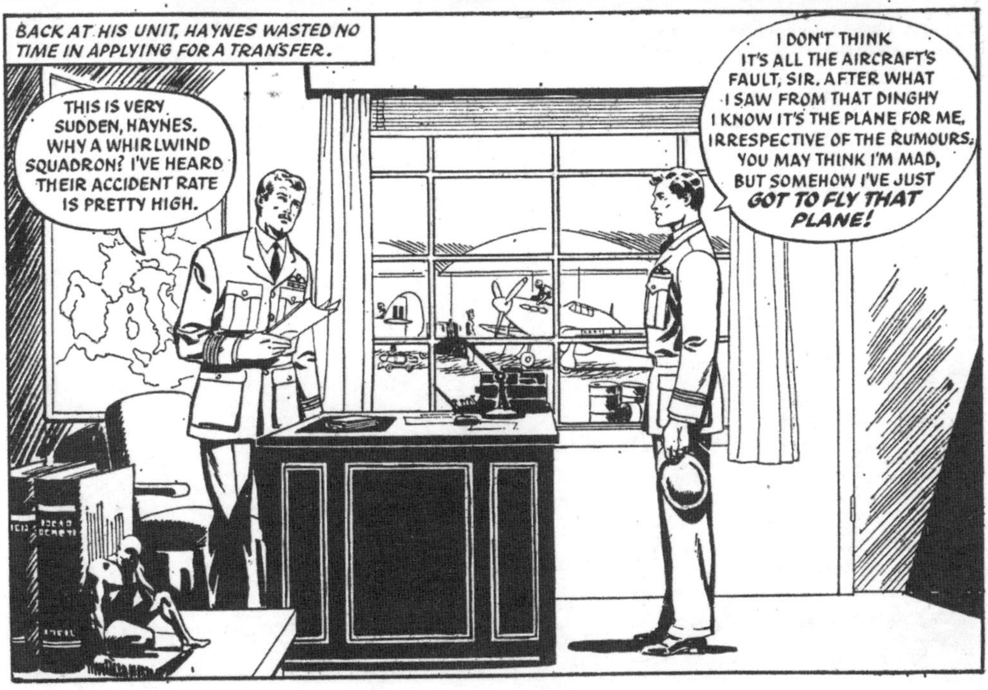
BACK AT HIS UNIT, HAYNES WASTED NO TIME IN APPLYING FOR A TRANSFER.
THIS IS VERY SUDDEN, HAYNES. WHY A WHIRLWIND SQUADRON? I'VE HEARD THEIR ACCIDENT RATE IS PRETTY HIGH.
I DON'T THINK IT'S ALL THE AIRCRAFT'S FAULT, SIR. AFTER WHAT I SAW FROM THAT DINGHY I KNOW IT'S THE PLANE FOR ME, IRRESPECTIVE OF THE RUMOURS. YOU MAY THINK I'M MAD, BUT SOMEHOW I'VE JUST GOT TO FLY THAT PLANE!

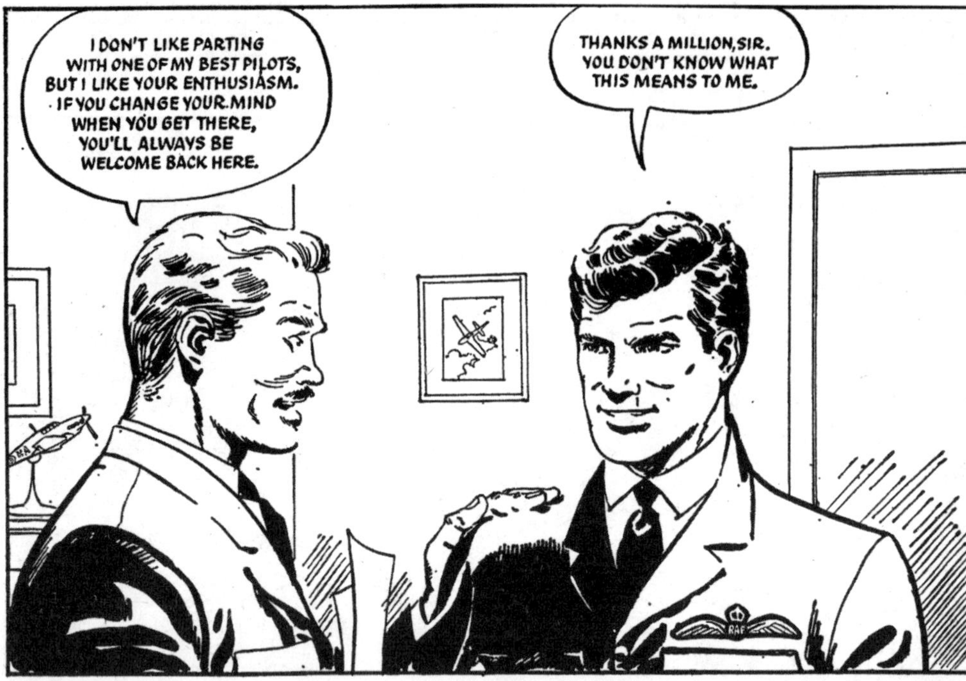
I DON'T LIKE PARTING WITH ONE OF MY BEST PILOTS, BUT I LIKE YOUR ENTHUSIASM. IF YOU CHANGE YOUR MIND WHEN YOU GET THERE, YOU'LL ALWAYS BE WELCOME BACK HERE.
THANKS A MILLION, SIR. YOU DON'T KNOW WHAT THIS MEANS TO ME.

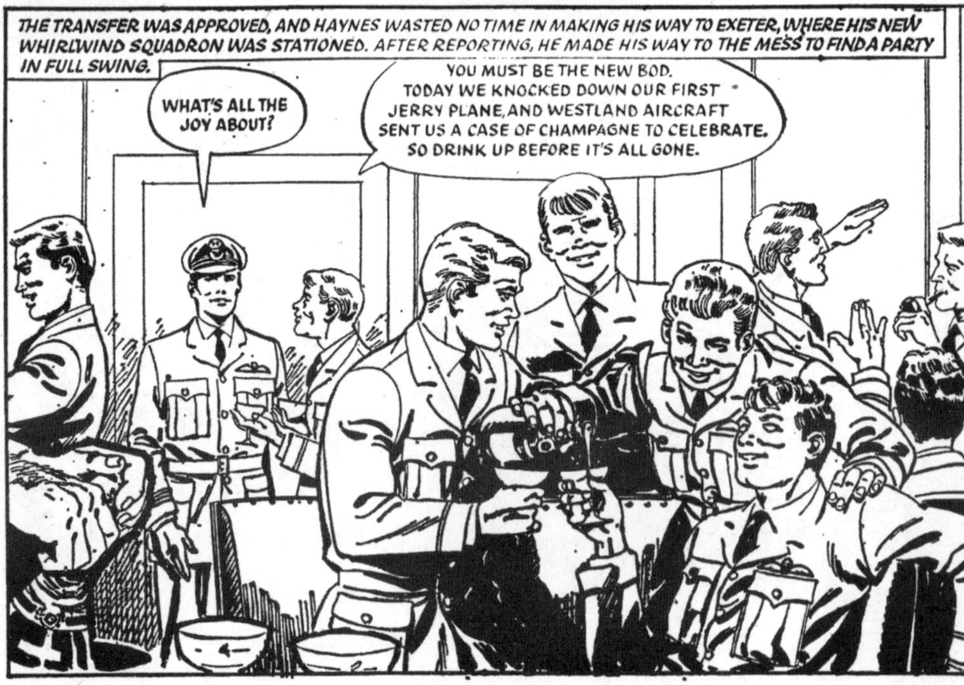
THE TRANSFER WAS APPROVED, AND HAYNES WASTED NO TIME IN MAKING HIS WAY TO EXETER, WHERE HIS NEW WHIRLWIND SQUADRON WAS STATIONED. AFTER REPORTING, HE MADE HIS WAY TO THE MESS TO FIND A PARTY IN FULL SWING.
WHAT'S ALL THE JOY ABOUT?
YOU MUST BE THE NEW BOD. TODAY WE KNOCKED DOWN OUR FIRST JERRY PLANE, AND WESTLAND AIRCRAFT SENT US A CASE OF CHAMPAGNE TO CELEBRATE. SO DRINK UP BEFORE IT'S ALL GONE.

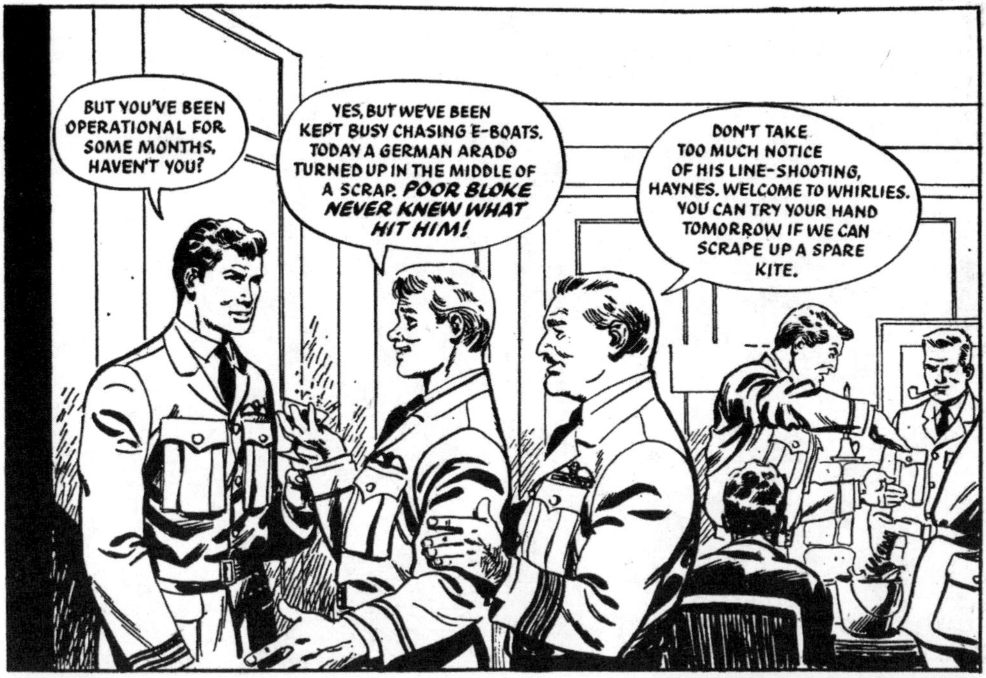
BUT YOU'VE BEEN OPERATIONAL FOR SOME MONTHS, HAVEN'T YOU?
YES, BUT WE'VE BEEN KEPT BUSY CHASING E-BOATS. TODAY A GERMAN ARADO TURNED UP IN THE MIDDLE OF A SCRAP. POOR BLOKE NEVER KNEW WHAT HIT HIM!
DON'T TAKE TOO MUCH NOTICE OF HIS LINE-SHOOTING, HAYNES. WELCOME TO WHIRLIES. YOU CAN TRY YOUR HAND TOMORROW IF WE CAN SCRAPE UP A SPARE KITE.

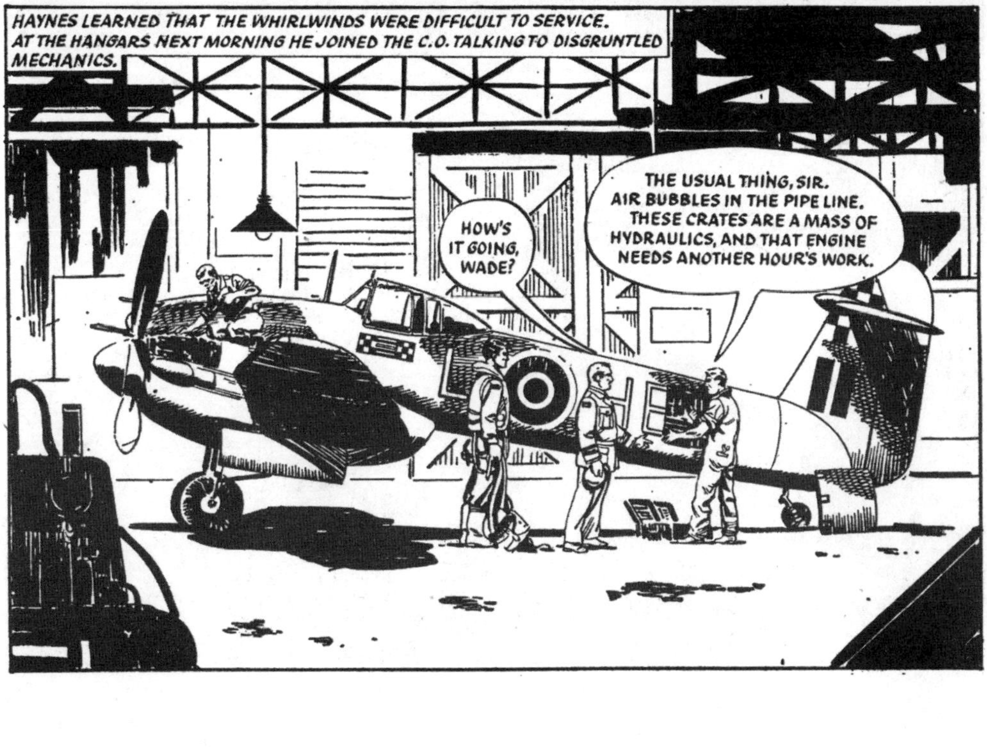
HAYNES LEARNED THAT THE WHIRLWINDS WERE DIFFICULT TO SERVICE. AT THE HANGARS NEXT MORNING HE JOINED THE C.O. TALKING TO DISGRUNTLED MECHANICS.
HOW'S IT GOING, WADE?
THE USUAL THING, SIR. AIR BUBBLES IN THE PIPE LINE. THESE CRATES ARE A MASS OF HYDRAULICS, AND THAT ENGINE NEEDS ANOTHER HOUR'S WORK.

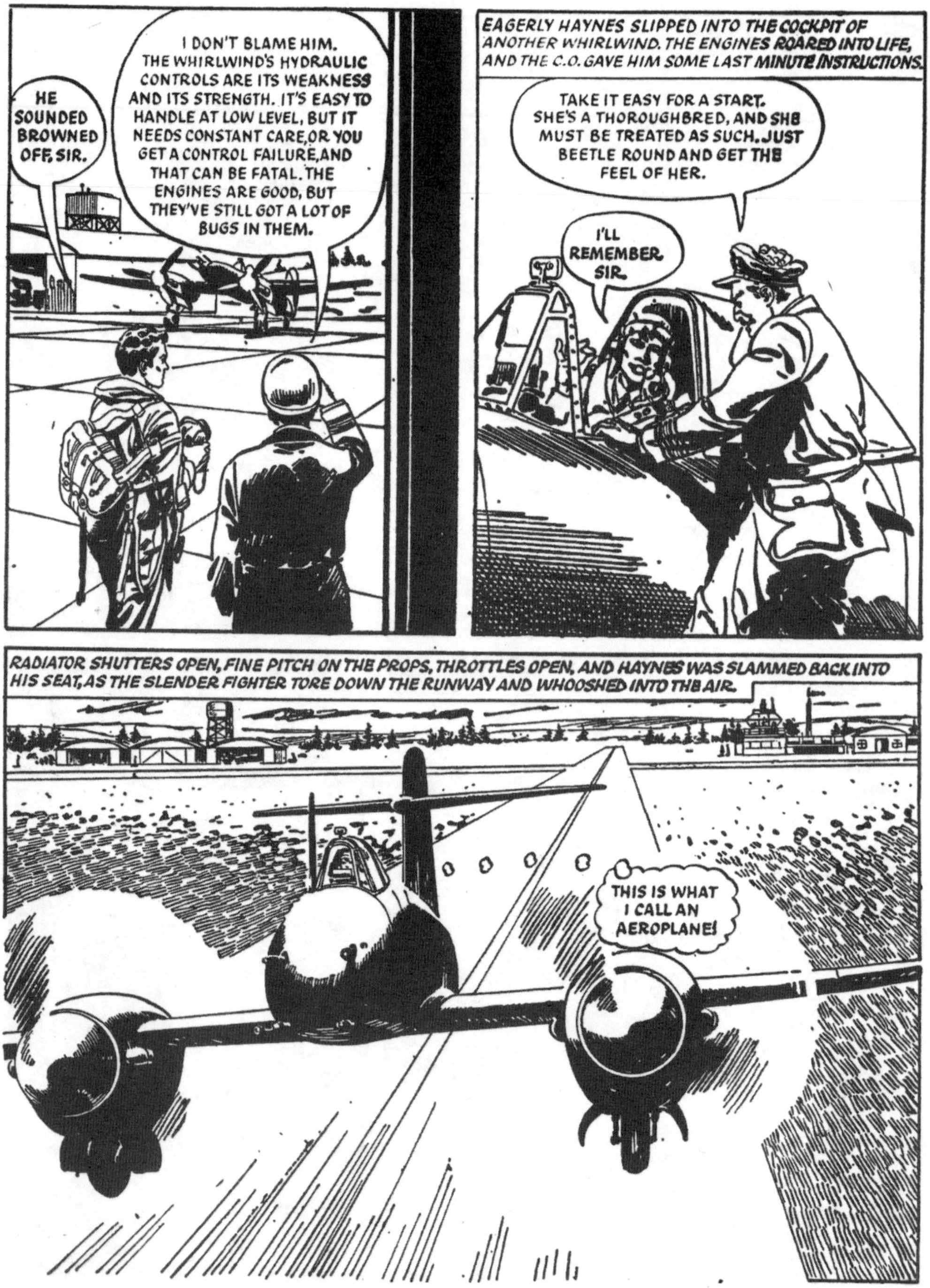
HE SOUNDED BROWNED OFF, SIR.
I DON'T BLAME HIM. THE WHIRLWIND'S HYDRAULIC CONTROLS ARE ITS WEAKNESS AND ITS STRENGTH. IT'S EASY TO HANDLE AT LOW LEVEL, BUT IT NEEDS CONSTANT CARE, OR YOU GET A CONTROL FAILURE, AND THAT CAN BE FATAL. THE ENGINES ARE GOOD, BUT THEY'VE STILL GOT A LOT OF BUGS IN THEM.
EAGERLY HAYNES SLIPPED INTO THE COCKPIT OF ANOTHER WHIRLWIND. THE ENGINES ROARED INTO LIFE, AND THE C.O. GAVE HIM SOME LAST MINUTE INSTRUCTIONS.
TAKE IT EASY FOR A START. SHE'S A THOROUGHBRED, AND SHE MUST BE TREATED AS SUCH. JUST BEETLE ROUND AND GET THE FEEL OF HER.
I'LL REMEMBER, SIR.
RADIATOR SHUTTERS OPEN, FINE PITCH ON THE PROPS, THROTTLES OPEN, AND HAYNES WAS SLAMMED BACK INTO HIS SEAT, AS THE SLENDER FIGHTER TORE DOWN THE RUNWAY AND WHOOSHED INTO THE AIR.
THIS IS WHAT I CALL AN AEROPLANE!

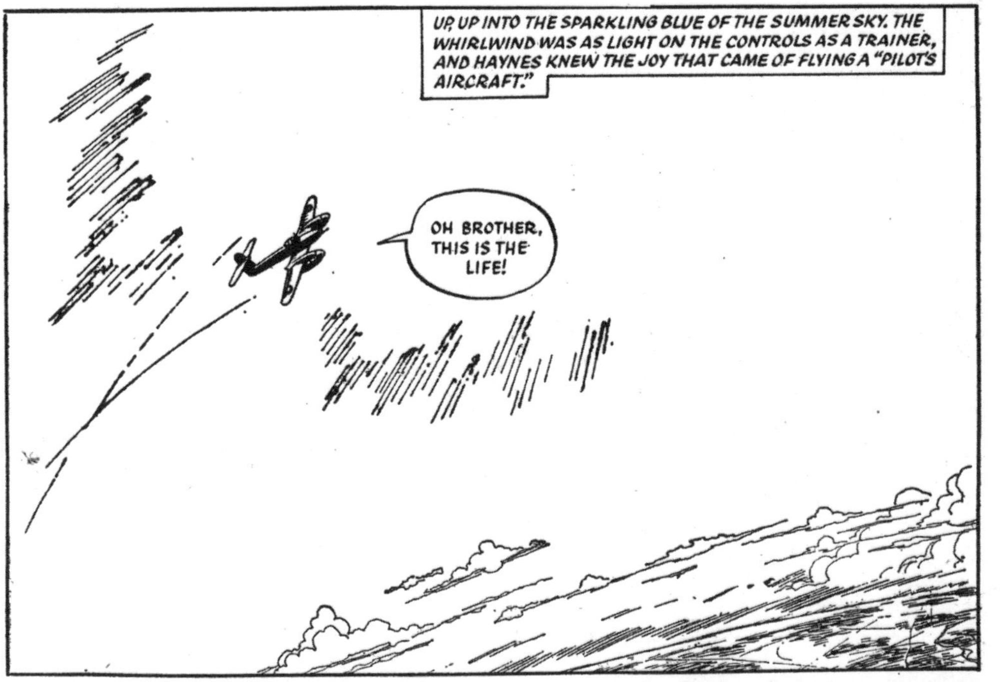
UP, UP INTO THE SPARKLING BLUE OF THE SUMMER SKY. THE WHIRLWIND WAS AS LIGHT ON THE CONTROLS AS A TRAINER, AND HAYNES KNEW THE JOY THAT CAME OF FLYING A "PILOT'S AIRCRAFT."
OH BROTHER, THIS IS THE LIFE!

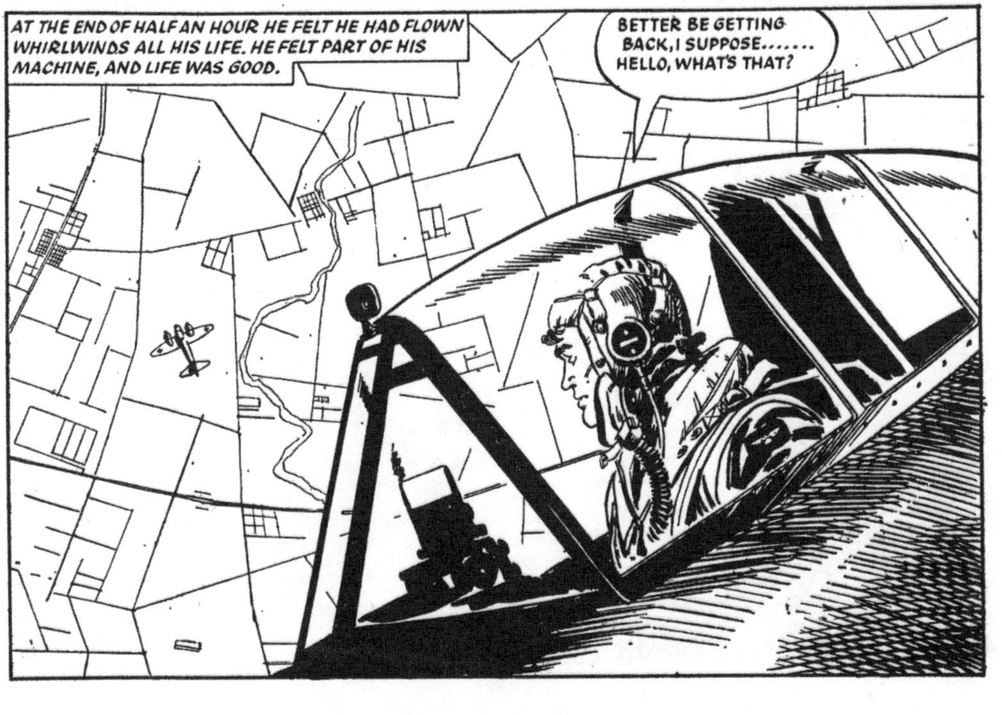
AT THE END OF HALF AN HOUR HE FELT HE HAD FLOWN WHIRLWINDS ALL HIS LIFE. HE FELT PART OF HIS MACHINE, AND LIFE WAS GOOD.
BETTER BE GETTING BACK, I SUPPOSE....... HELLO, WHAT'S THAT?

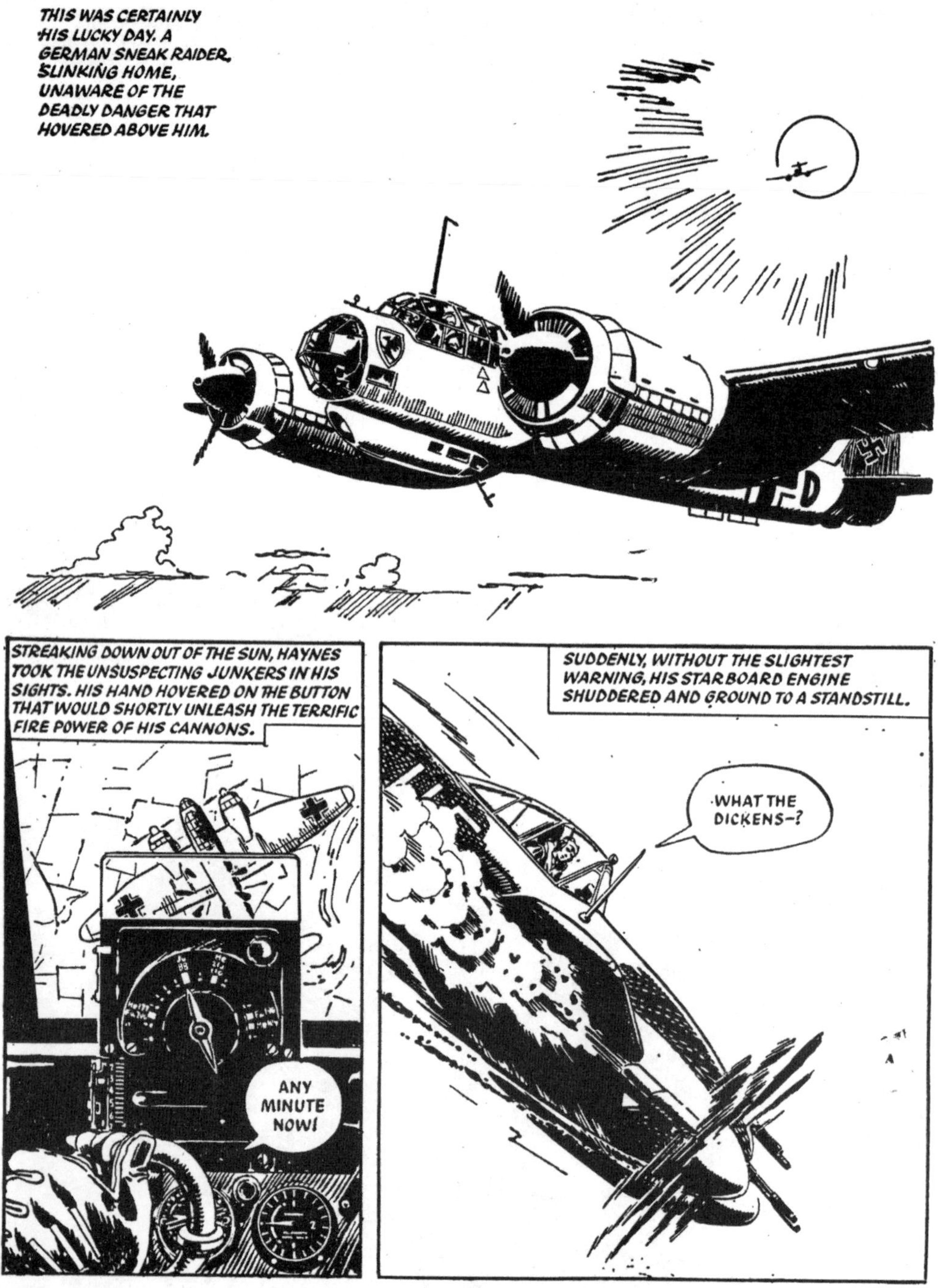
THIS WAS CERTAINLY HIS LUCKY DAY. A GERMAN SNEAK RAIDER, SLINKING HOME, UNAWARE OF THE DEADLY DANGER THAT HOVERED ABOVE HIM.
STREAKING DOWN OUT OF THE SUN, HAYNES TOOK THE UNSUSPECTING JUNKERS IN HIS SIGHTS. HIS HAND HOVERED ON THE BUTTON THAT WOULD SHORTLY UNLEASH THE TERRIFIC FIRE POWER OF HIS CANNONS.
ANY MINUTE NOW!
SUDDENLY, WITHOUT THE SLIGHTEST WARNING, HIS STARBOARD ENGINE SHUDDERED AND GROUND TO A STANDSTILL.
WHAT THE DICKENS–?

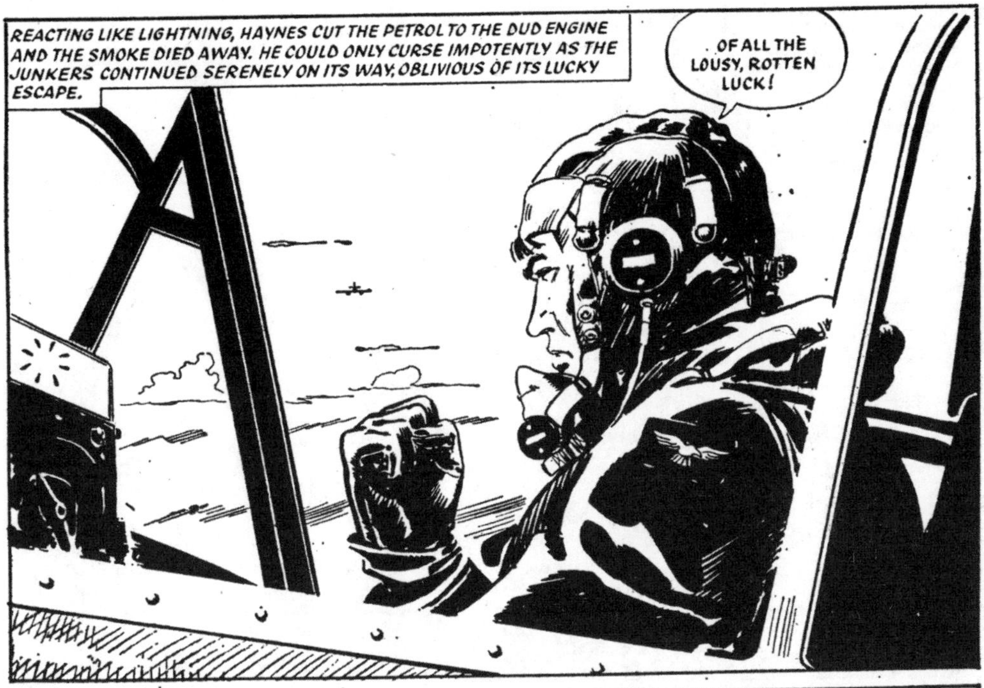
REACTING LIKE LIGHTNING, HAYNES CUT THE PETROL TO THE DUD ENGINE AND THE SMOKE DIED AWAY. HE COULD ONLY CURSE IMPOTENTLY AS THE JUNKERS CONTINUED SERENELY ON ITS WAY, OBLIVIOUS OF ITS LUCKY ESCAPE.
OF ALL THE LOUSY, ROTTEN LUCK!

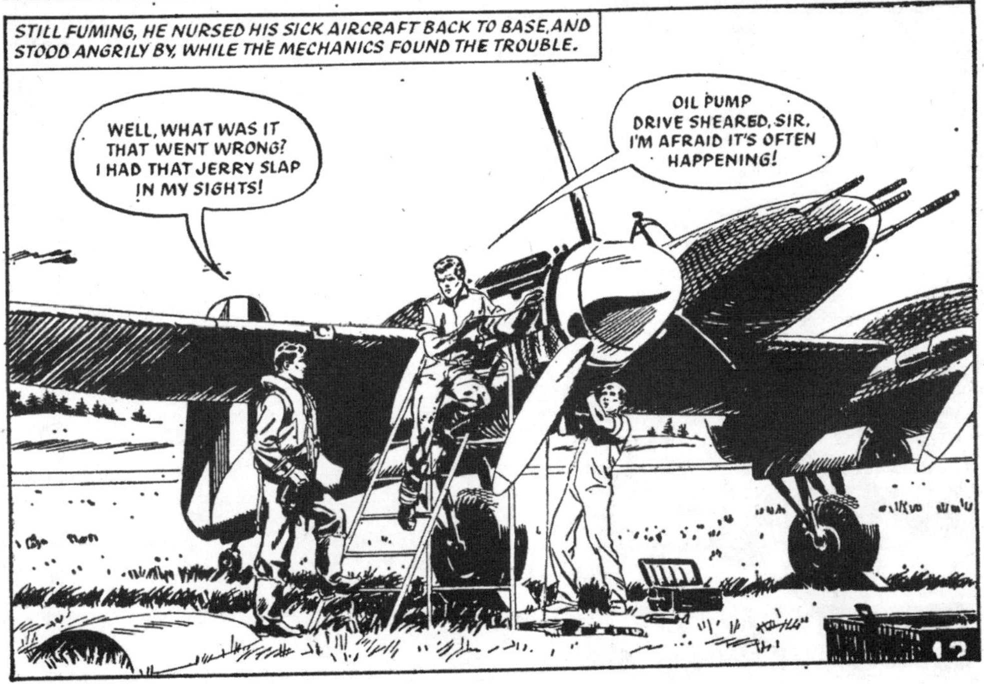
STILL FUMING, HE NURSED HIS SICK AIRCRAFT BACK TO BASE, AND STOOD ANGRILY BY, WHILE THE MECHANICS FOUND THE TROUBLE.
WELL, WHAT WAS IT THAT WENT WRONG? I HAD THAT JERRY SLAP IN MY SIGHTS!
OIL PUMP DRIVE SHEARED, SIR. I'M AFRAID IT'S OFTEN HAPPENING!
12

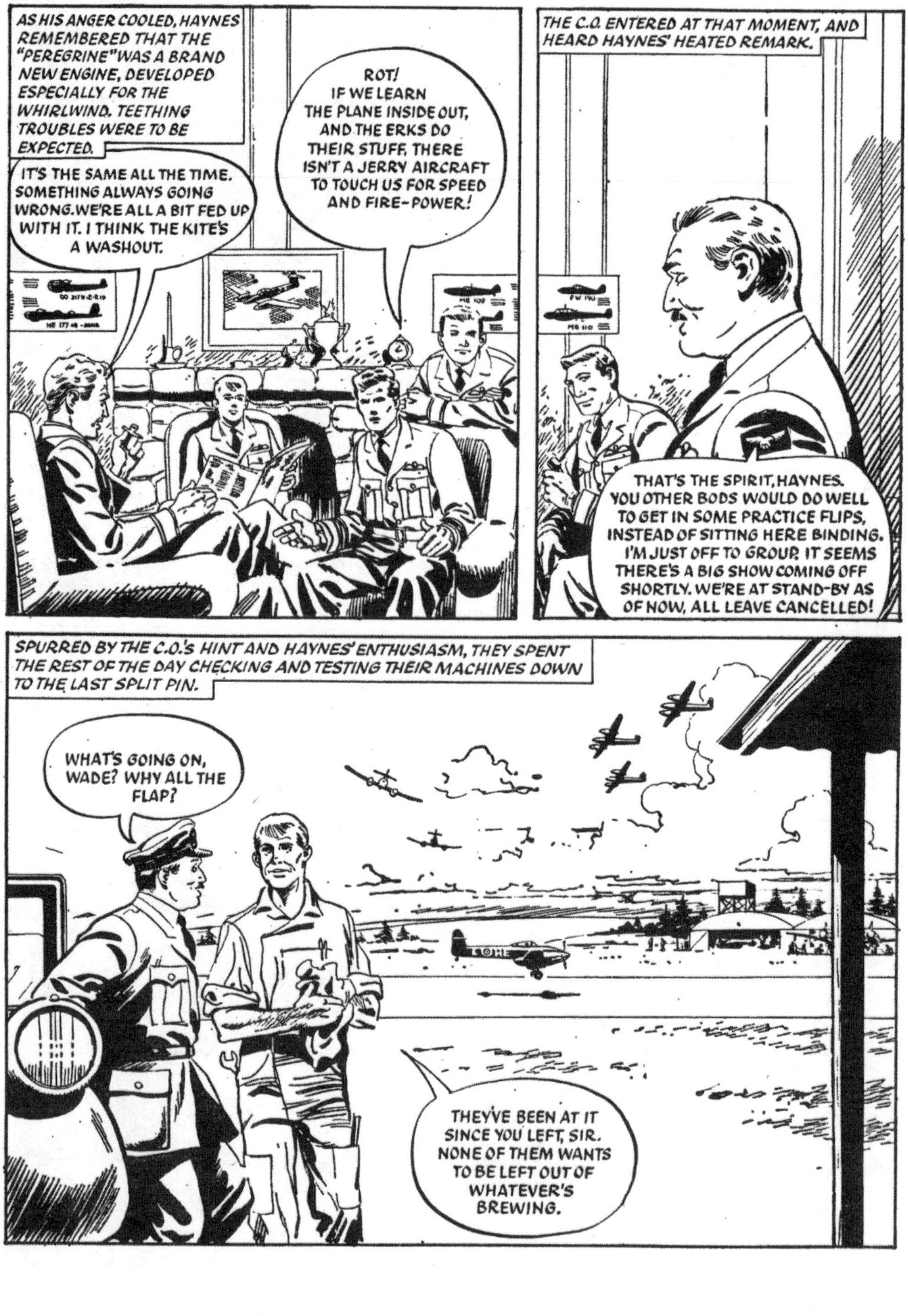
AS HIS ANGER COOLED, HAYNES REMEMBERED THAT THE "PEREGRINE" WAS A BRAND NEW ENGINE, DEVELOPED ESPECIALLY FOR THE WHIRLWIND. TEETHING TROUBLES WERE TO BE EXPECTED.
IT'S THE SAME ALL THE TIME. SOMETHING ALWAYS GOING WRONG. WE'RE ALL A BIT FED UP WITH IT. I THINK THE KITE'S A WASHOUT.
ROT! IF WE LEARN THE PLANE INSIDE OUT, AND THE ERKS DO THEIR STUFF, THERE ISN'T A JERRY AIRCRAFT TO TOUCH US FOR SPEED AND FIRE-POWER!
THE C.O. ENTERED AT THAT MOMENT, AND HEARD HAYNES' HEATED REMARK.
THAT'S THE SPIRIT, HAYNES. YOU OTHER BODS WOULD DO WELL TO GET IN SOME PRACTICE FLIPS, INSTEAD OF SITTING HERE BINDING. I'M JUST OFF TO GROUP. IT SEEMS THERE'S A BIG SHOW COMING OFF SHORTLY. WE'RE AT STAND-BY AS OF NOW, ALL LEAVE CANCELLED!
SPURRED BY THE C.O.'s HINT AND HAYNES' ENTHUSIASM, THEY SPENT THE REST OF THE DAY CHECKING AND TESTING THEIR MACHINES DOWN TO THE LAST SPLIT PIN.
WHAT'S GOING ON, WADE? WHY ALL THE FLAP?
THEY'VE BEEN AT IT SINCE YOU LEFT, SIR. NONE OF THEM WANTS TO BE LEFT OUT OF WHATEVER'S BREWING.

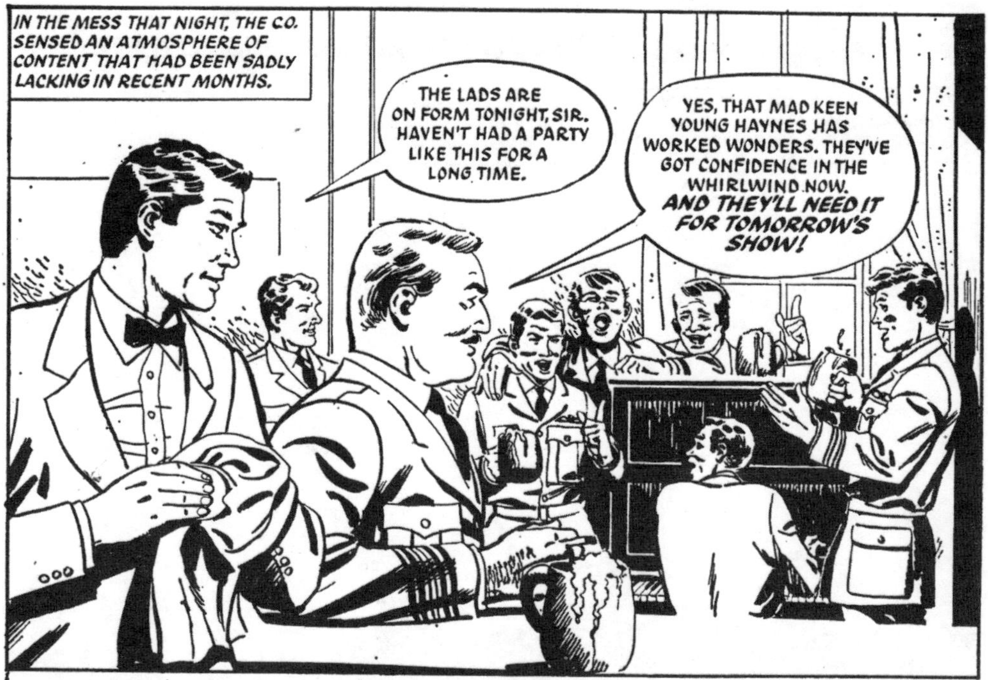
IN THE MESS THAT NIGHT, THE C.O. SENSED AN ATMOSPHERE OF CONTENT THAT HAD BEEN SADLY LACKING IN RECENT MONTHS.
THE LADS ARE ON FORM TONIGHT, SIR. HAVEN'T HAD A PARTY LIKE THIS FOR A LONG TIME.
YES, THAT MAD KEEN YOUNG HAYNES HAS WORKED WONDERS. THEY'VE GOT CONFIDENCE IN THE WHIRLWIND NOW. AND THEY'LL NEED IT FOR TOMORROW'S SHOW!

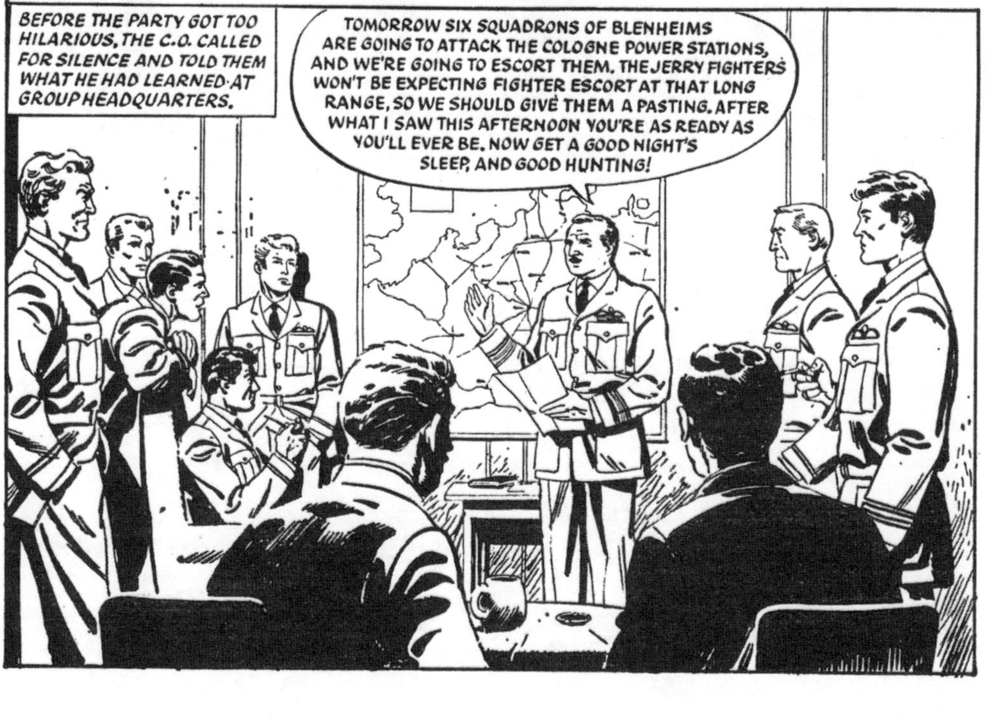
BEFORE THE PARTY GOT TOO HILARIOUS, THE C.O. CALLED FOR SILENCE AND TOLD THEM WHAT HE HAD LEARNED AT GROUP HEADQUARTERS.
TOMORROW SIX SQUADRONS OF BLENHEIMS ARE GOING TO ATTACK THE COLOGNE POWER STATIONS, AND WE'RE GOING TO ESCORT THEM. THE JERRY FIGHTERS WON'T BE EXPECTING FIGHTER ESCORT AT THAT LONG RANGE, SO WE SHOULD GIVE THEM A PASTING. AFTER WHAT I SAW THIS AFTERNOON YOU'RE AS READY AS YOU'LL EVER BE. NOW GET A GOOD NIGHT'S SLEEP, AND GOOD HUNTING!

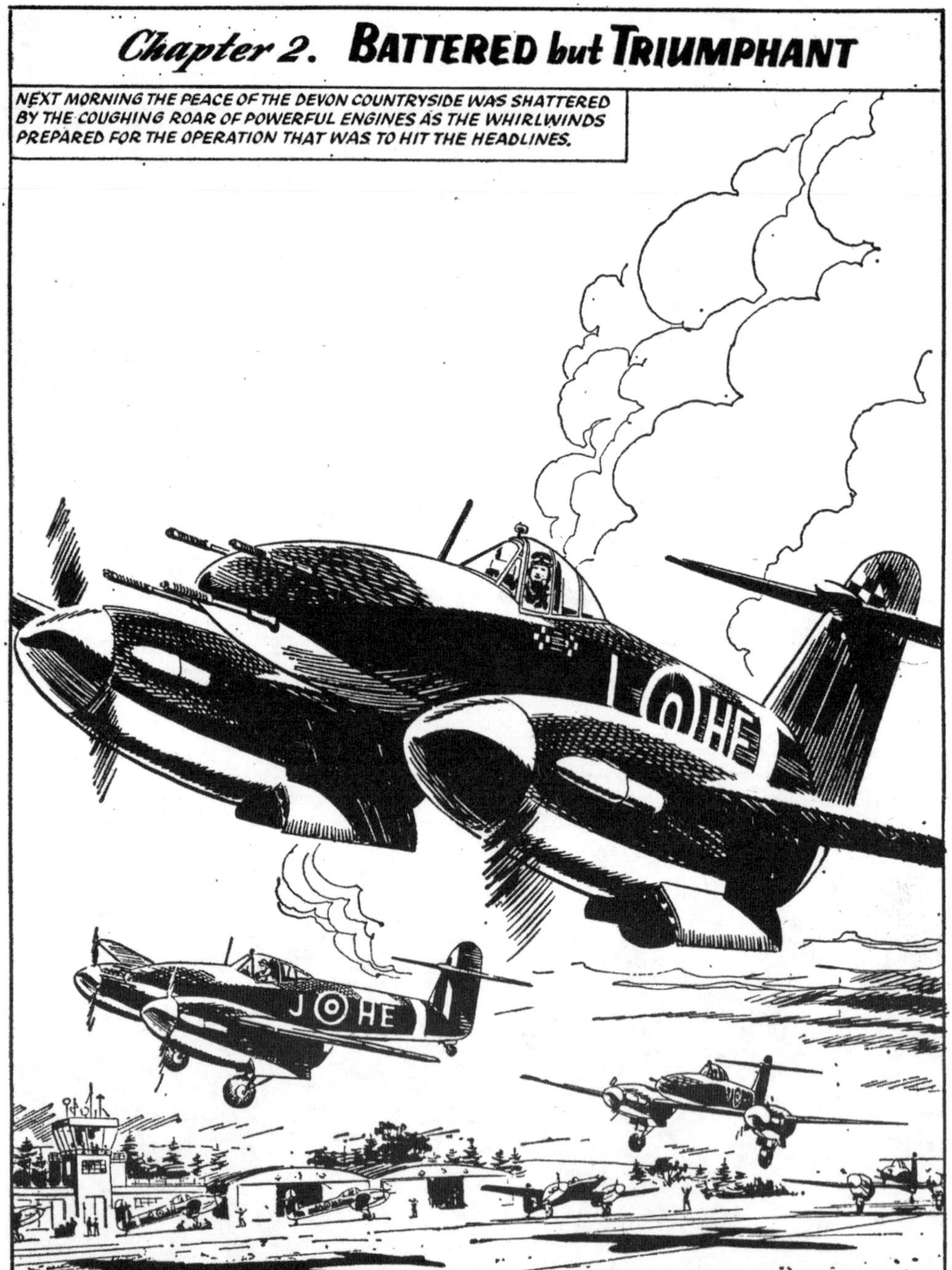
Chapter 2. BATTERED but TRIUMPHANT
NEXT MORNING THE PEACE OF THE DEVON COUNTRYSIDE WAS SHATTERED BY THE COUGHING ROAR OF POWERFUL ENGINES AS THE WHIRLWINDS PREPARED FOR THE OPERATION THAT WAS TO HIT THE HEADLINES.
J HE

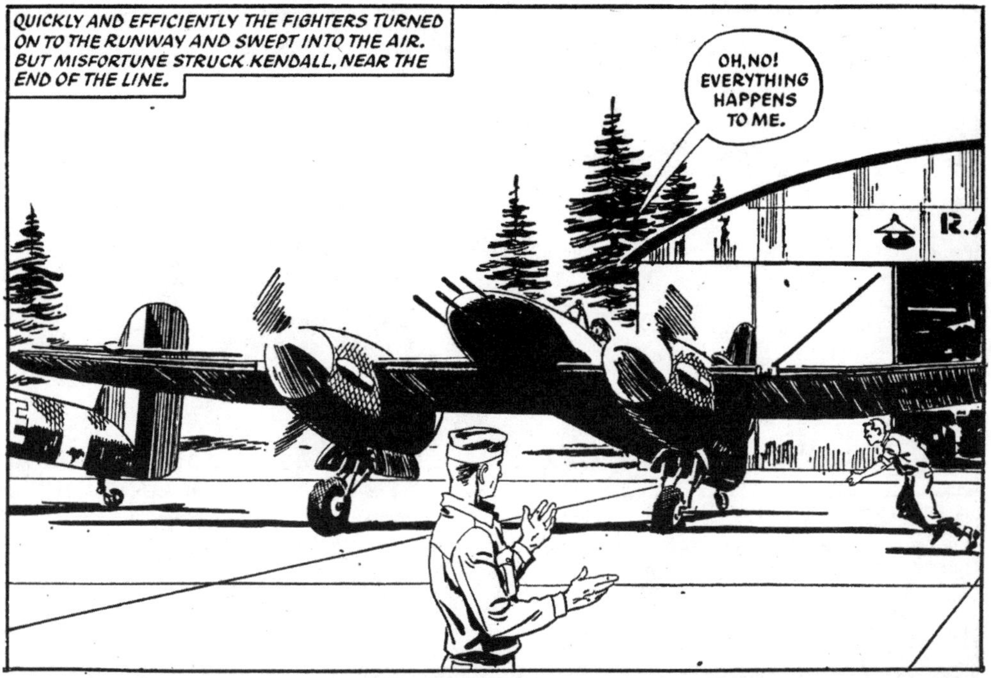
QUICKLY AND EFFICIENTLY THE FIGHTERS TURNED ON TO THE RUNWAY AND SWEPT INTO THE AIR. BUT MISFORTUNE STRUCK KENDALL, NEAR THE END OF THE LINE.
OH, NO! EVERYTHING HAPPENS TO ME.

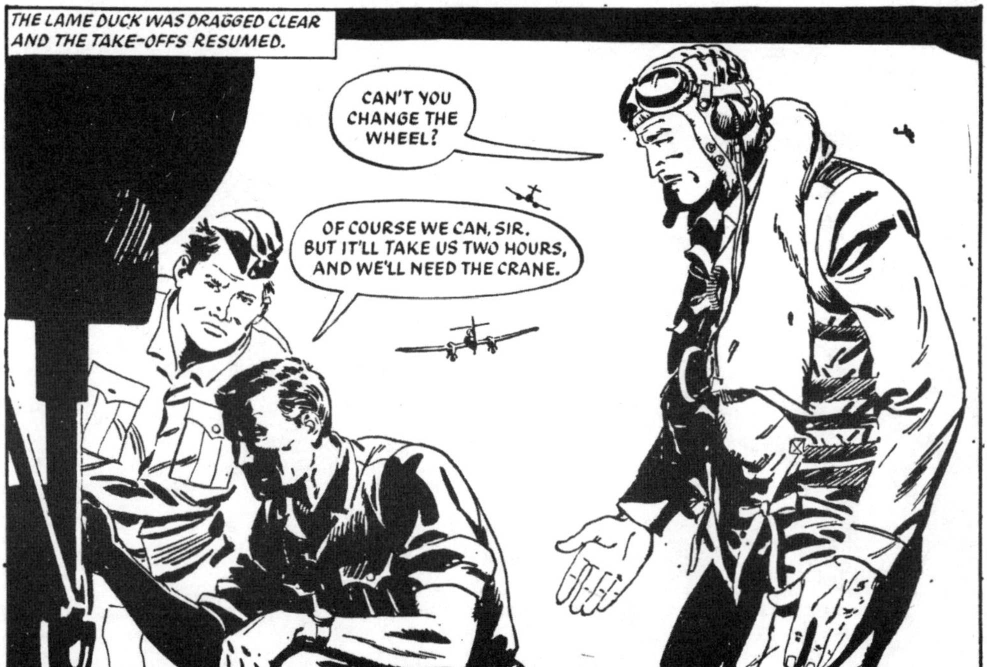
THE LAME DUCK WAS DRAGGED CLEAR AND THE TAKE-OFFS RESUMED.
CAN'T YOU CHANGE THE WHEEL?
OF COURSE WE CAN, SIR. BUT IT'LL TAKE US TWO HOURS, AND WE'LL NEED THE CRANE.

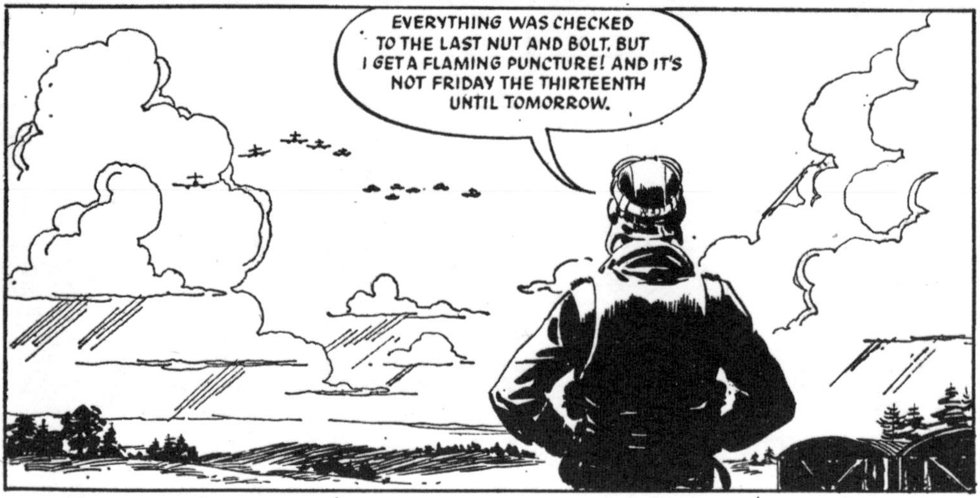
EVERYTHING WAS CHECKED TO THE LAST NUT AND BOLT, BUT I GET A FLAMING PUNCTURE! AND IT'S NOT FRIDAY THE THIRTEENTH UNTIL TOMORROW.

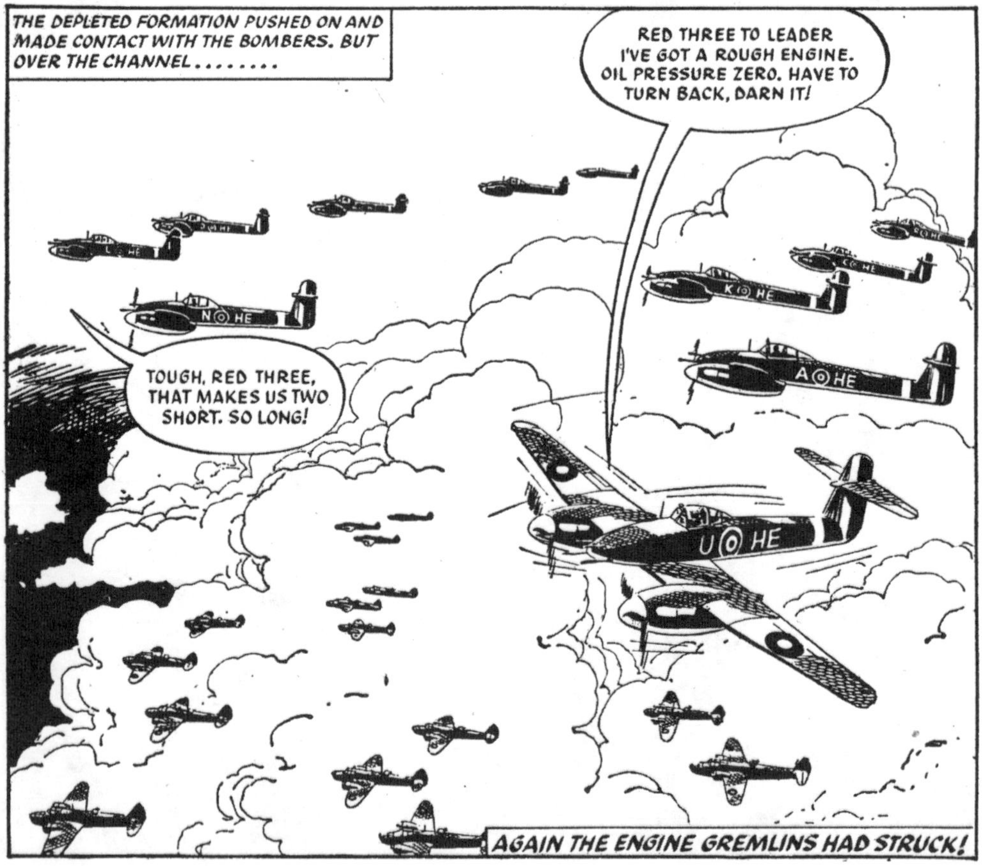
THE DEPLETED FORMATION PUSHED ON AND MADE CONTACT WITH THE BOMBERS. BUT OVER THE CHANNEL........
RED THREE TO LEADER I'VE GOT A ROUGH ENGINE. OIL PRESSURE ZERO. HAVE TO TURN BACK, DARN IT!
TOUGH, RED THREE, THAT MAKES US TWO SHORT. SO LONG!
AGAIN THE ENGINE GREMLINS HAD STRUCK!

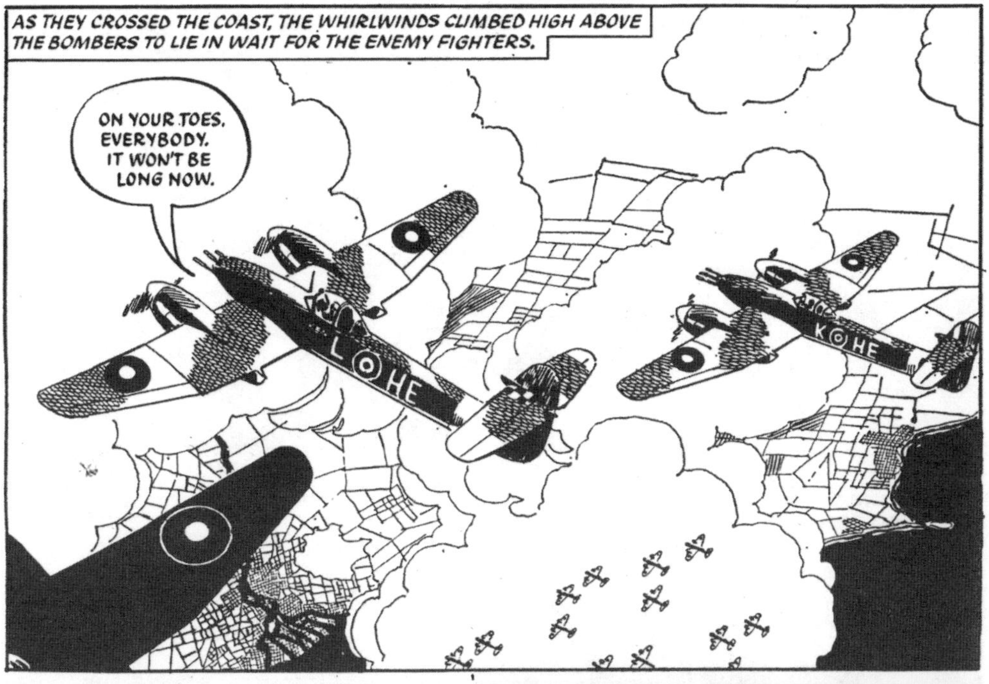
AS THEY CROSSED THE COAST, THE WHIRLWINDS CLIMBED HIGH ABOVE THE BOMBERS TO LIE IN WAIT FOR THE ENEMY FIGHTERS.
ON YOUR TOES, EVERYBODY. IT WON'T BE LONG NOW.
L HE
K HE

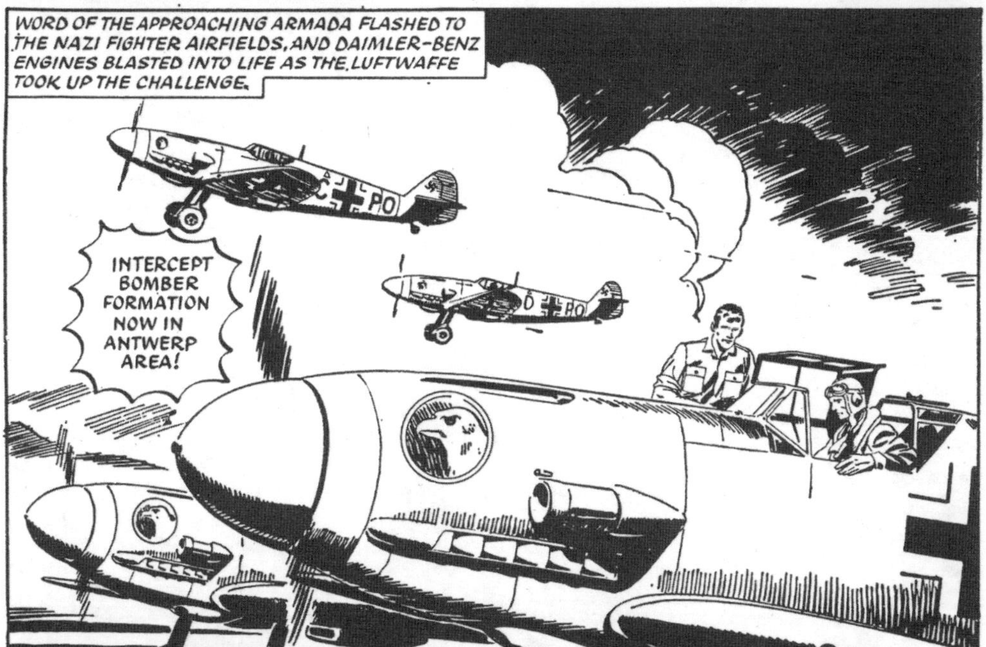
WORD OF THE APPROACHING ARMADA FLASHED TO THE NAZI FIGHTER AIRFIELDS, AND DAIMLER-BENZ ENGINES BLASTED INTO LIFE AS THE LUFTWAFFE TOOK UP THE CHALLENGE.
C PO
INTERCEPT BOMBER FORMATION NOW IN ANTWERP AREA!
D PO

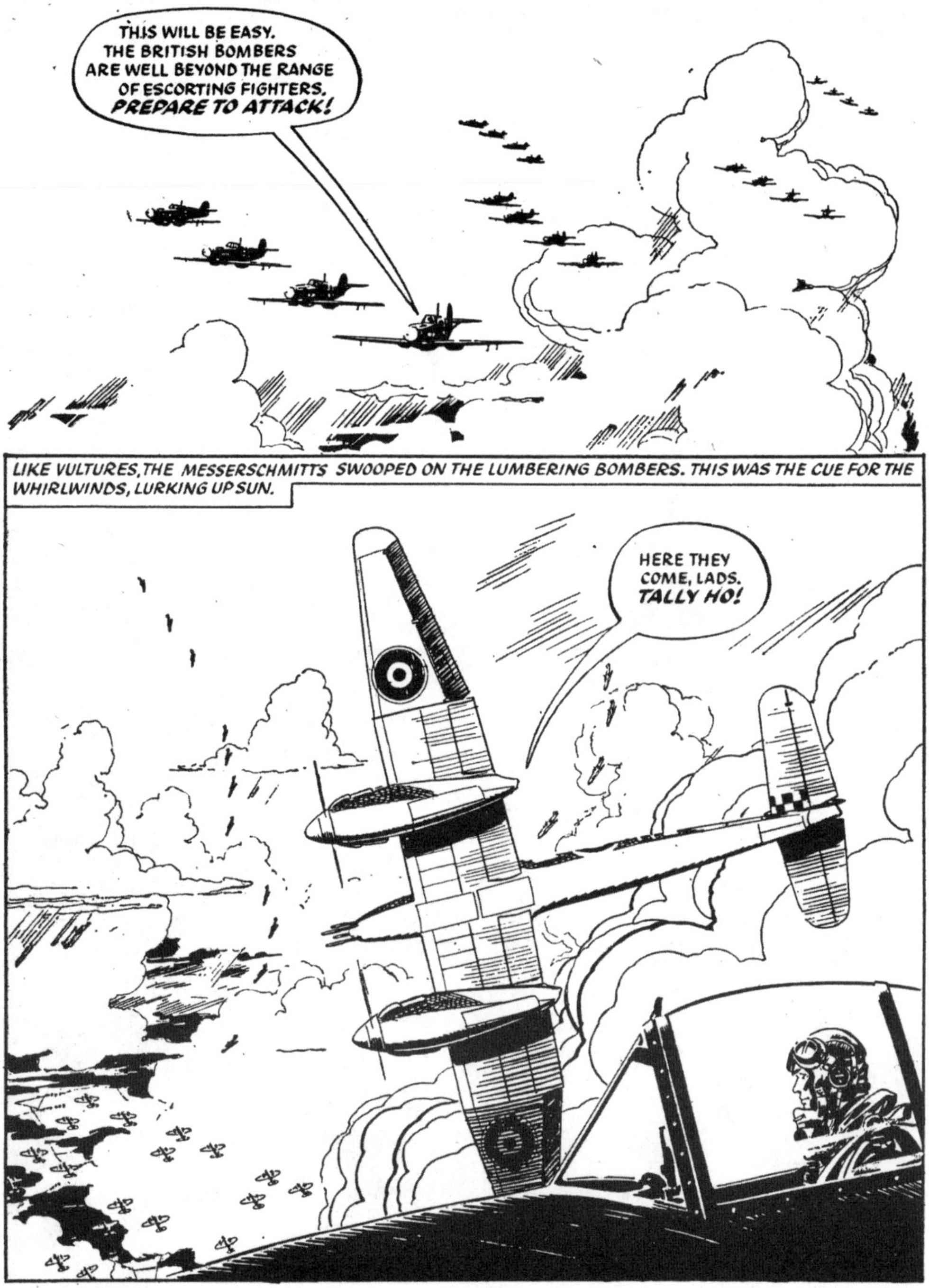
THIS WILL BE EASY. THE BRITISH BOMBERS ARE WELL BEYOND THE RANGE OF ESCORTING FIGHTERS. PREPARE TO ATTACK!
LIKE VULTURES, THE MESSERSCHMITTS SWOOPED ON THE LUMBERING BOMBERS. THIS WAS THE CUE FOR THE WHIRLWINDS, LURKING UP SUN.
HERE THEY COME, LADS. TALLY HO!

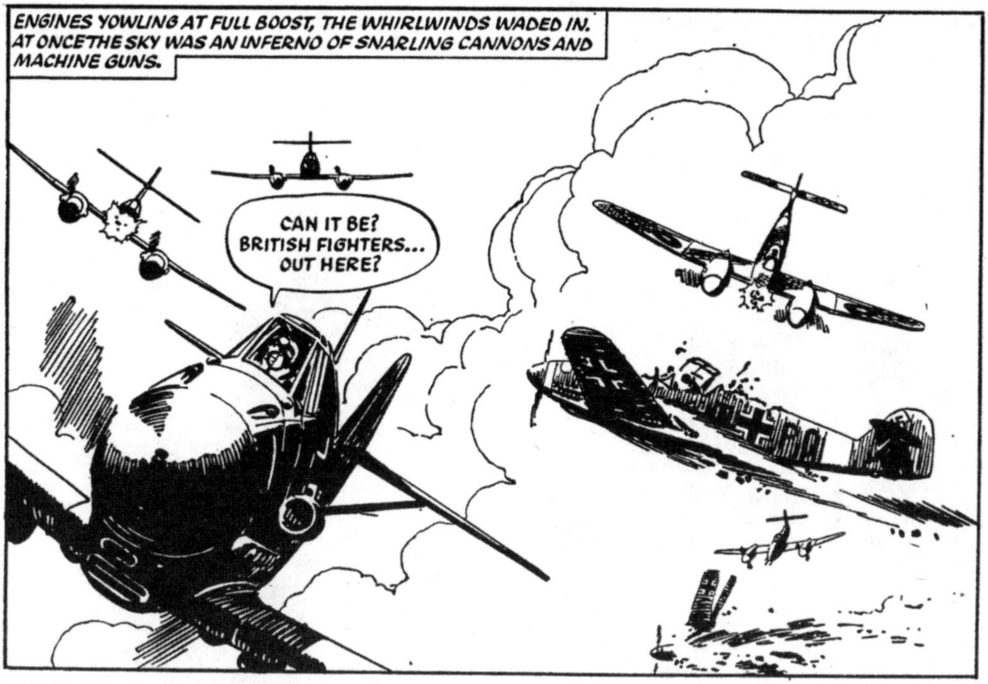
ENGINES YOWLING AT FULL BOOST, THE WHIRLWINDS WADED IN. AT ONCE THE SKY WAS AN INFERNO OF SNARLING CANNONS AND MACHINE GUNS.
CAN IT BE? BRITISH FIGHTERS... OUT HERE?

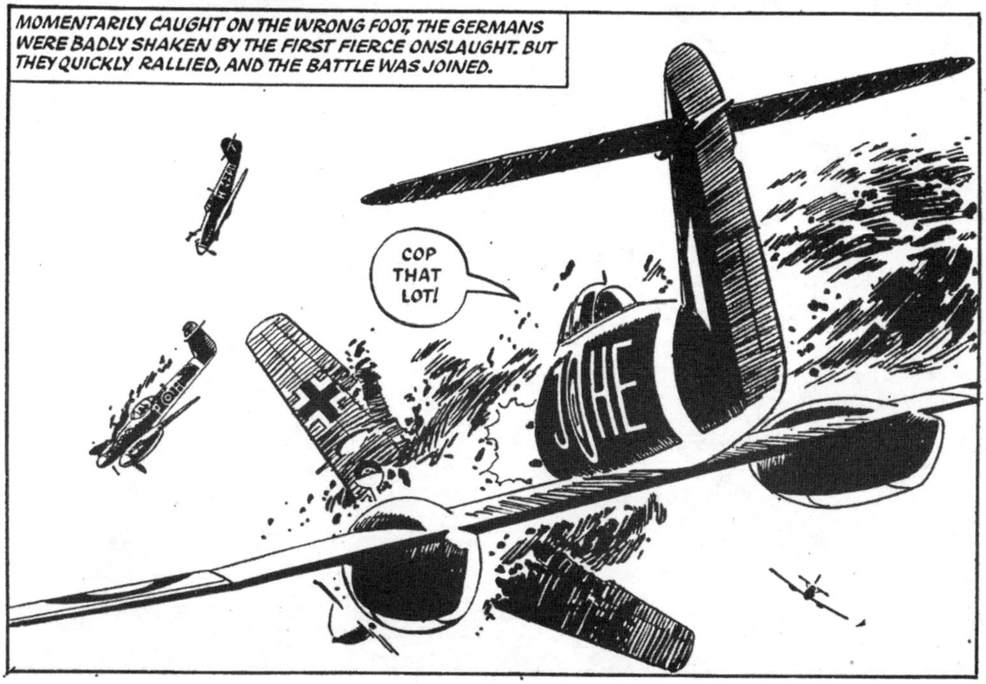
MOMENTARILY CAUGHT ON THE WRONG FOOT, THE GERMANS WERE BADLY SHAKEN BY THE FIRST FIERCE ONSLAUGHT. BUT THEY QUICKLY RALLIED, AND THE BATTLE WAS JOINED.
COP THAT LOT!

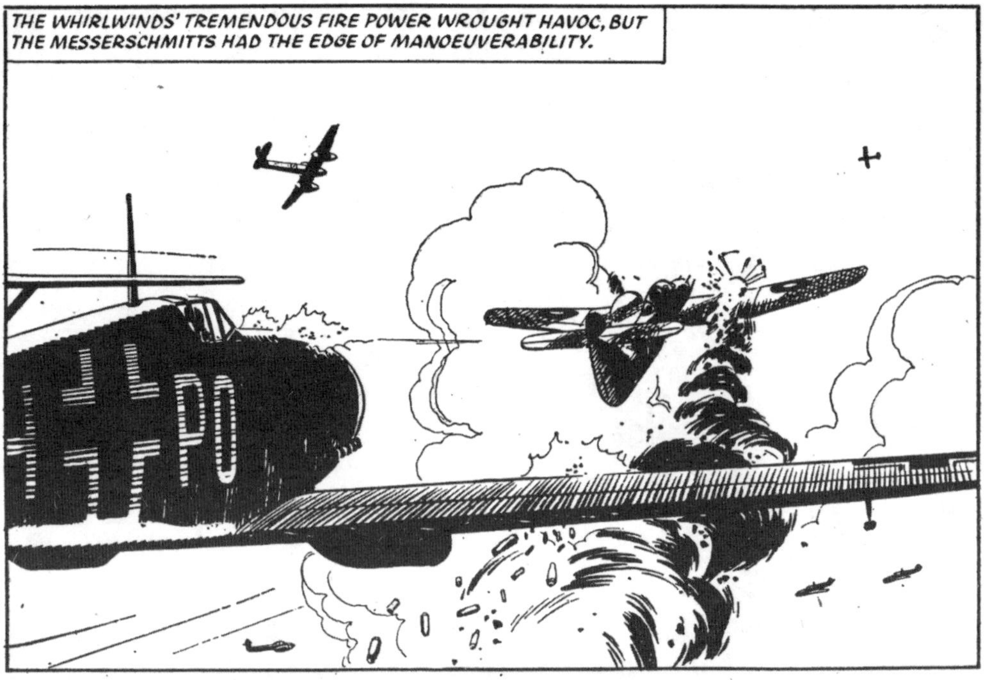
THE WHIRLWINDS' TREMENDOUS FIRE POWER WROUGHT HAVOC, BUT THE MESSERSCHMITTS HAD THE EDGE OF MANOEUVERABILITY.

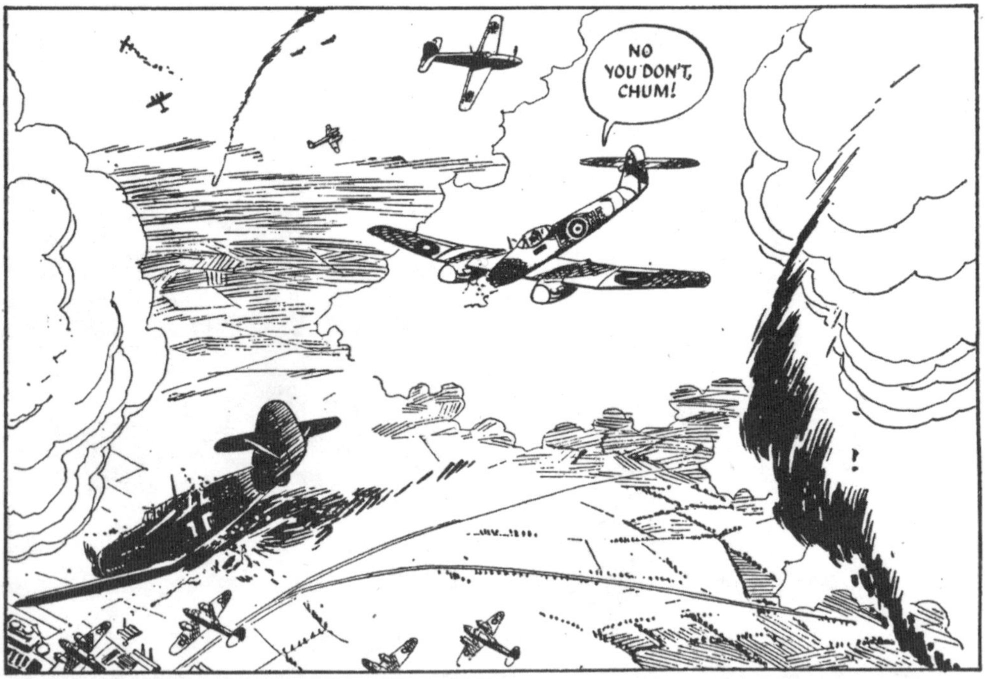
NO YOU DON'T, CHUM!

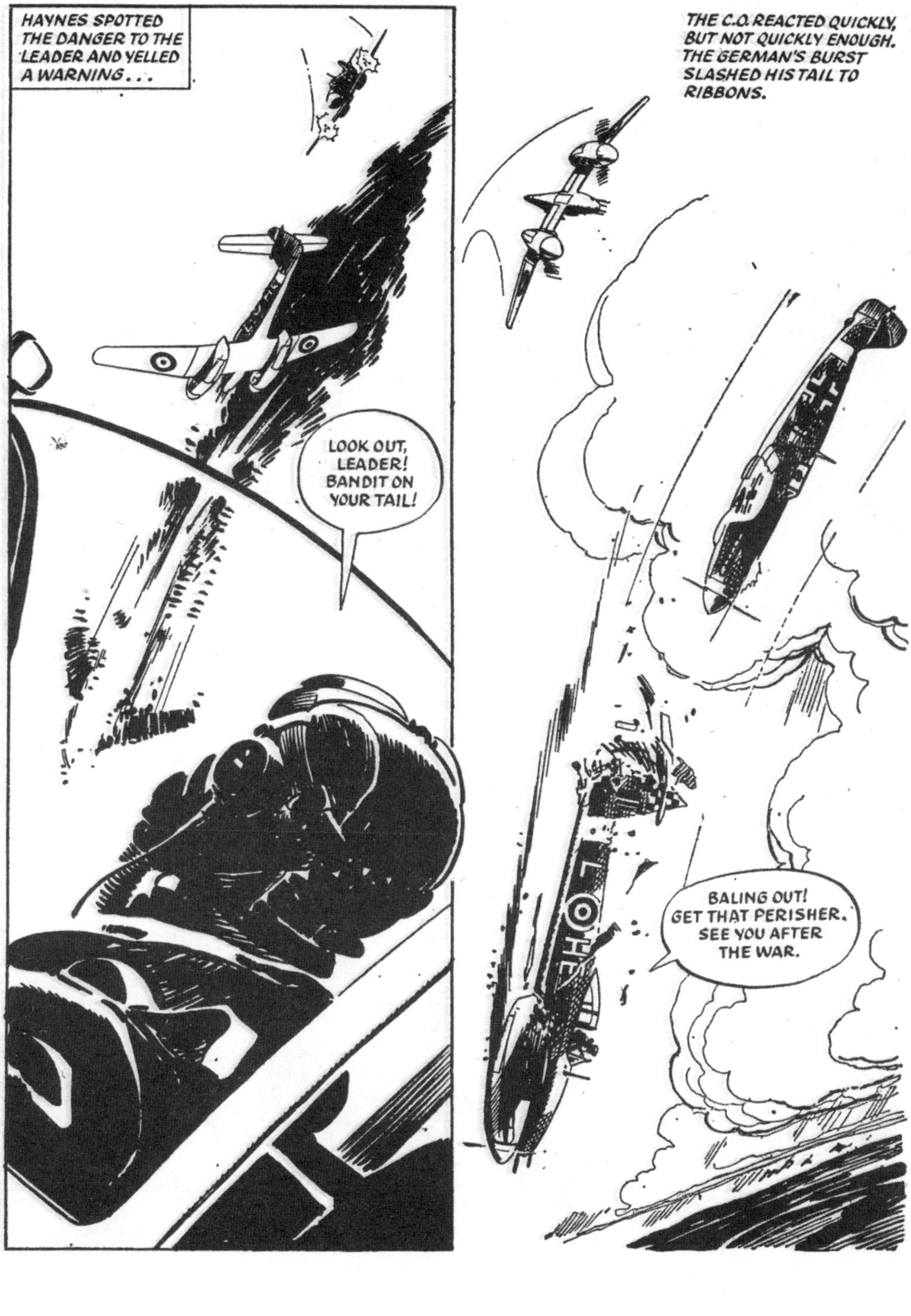
HAYNES SPOTTED THE DANGER TO THE LEADER AND YELLED A WARNING...
LOOK OUT, LEADER! BANDIT ON YOUR TAIL!
THE C.O. REACTED QUICKLY, BUT NOT QUICKLY ENOUGH. THE GERMAN'S BURST SLASHED HIS TAIL TO RIBBONS.
BALING OUT! GET THAT PERISHER. SEE YOU AFTER THE WAR.

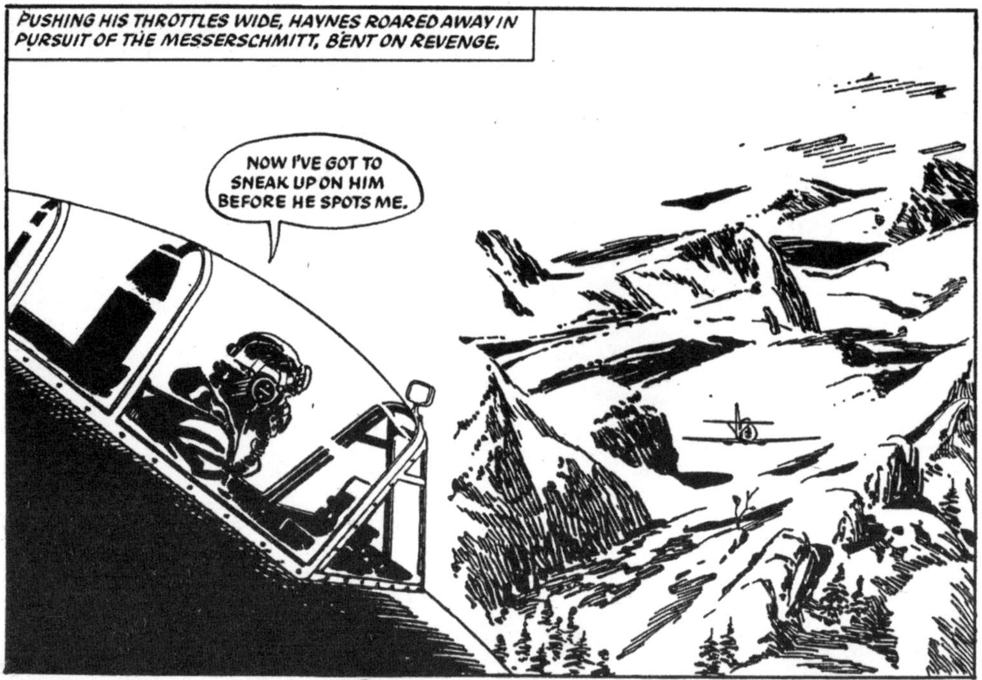
PUSHING HIS THROTTLES WIDE, HAYNES ROARED AWAY IN PURSUIT OF THE MESSERSCHMITT, BENT ON REVENGE.
NOW I'VE GOT TO SNEAK UP ON HIM BEFORE HE SPOTS ME.

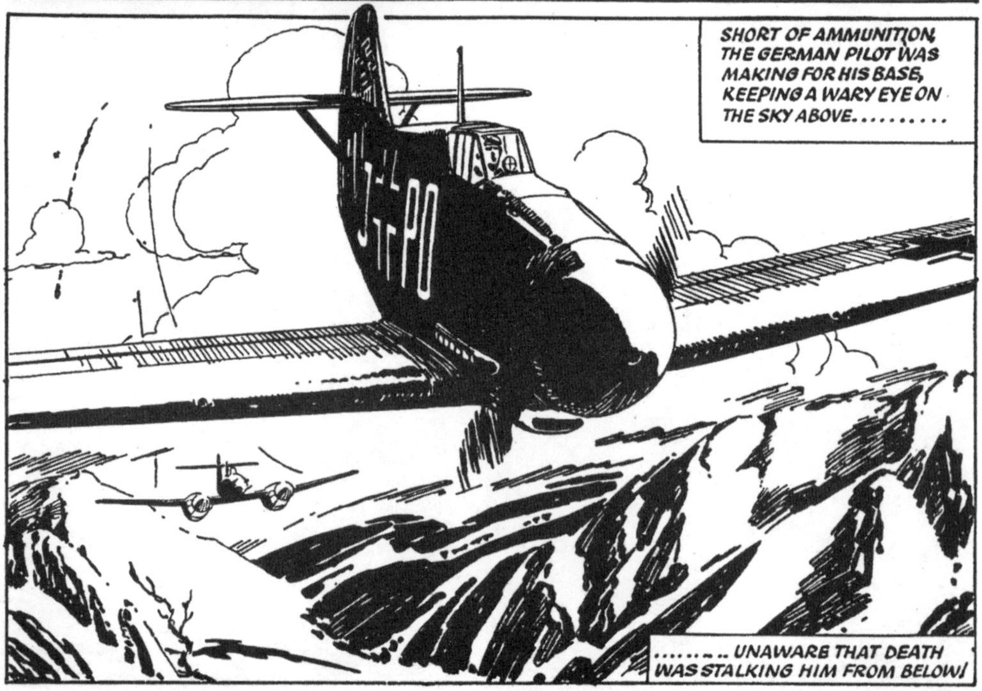
SHORT OF AMMUNITION, THE GERMAN PILOT WAS MAKING FOR HIS BASE, KEEPING A WARY EYE ON THE SKY ABOVE..........
.... UNAWARE THAT DEATH WAS STALKING HIM FROM BELOW!

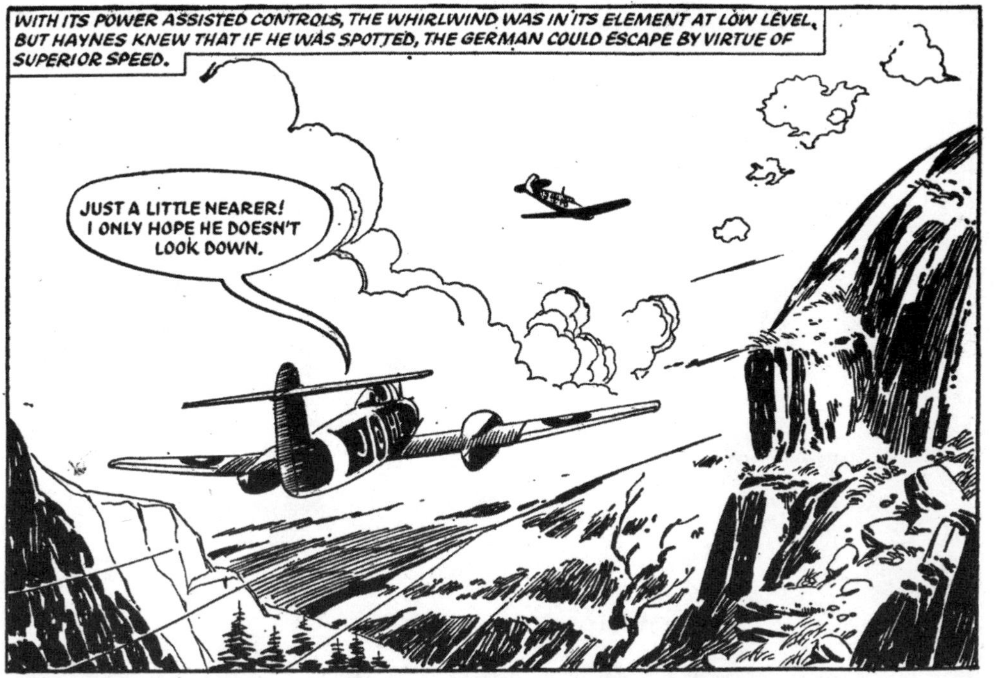
WITH ITS POWER ASSISTED CONTROLS, THE WHIRLWIND WAS IN ITS ELEMENT AT LOW LEVEL, BUT HAYNES KNEW THAT IF HE WAS SPOTTED, THE GERMAN COULD ESCAPE BY VIRTUE OF SUPERIOR SPEED.
JUST A LITTLE NEARER! I ONLY HOPE HE DOESN'T LOOK DOWN.

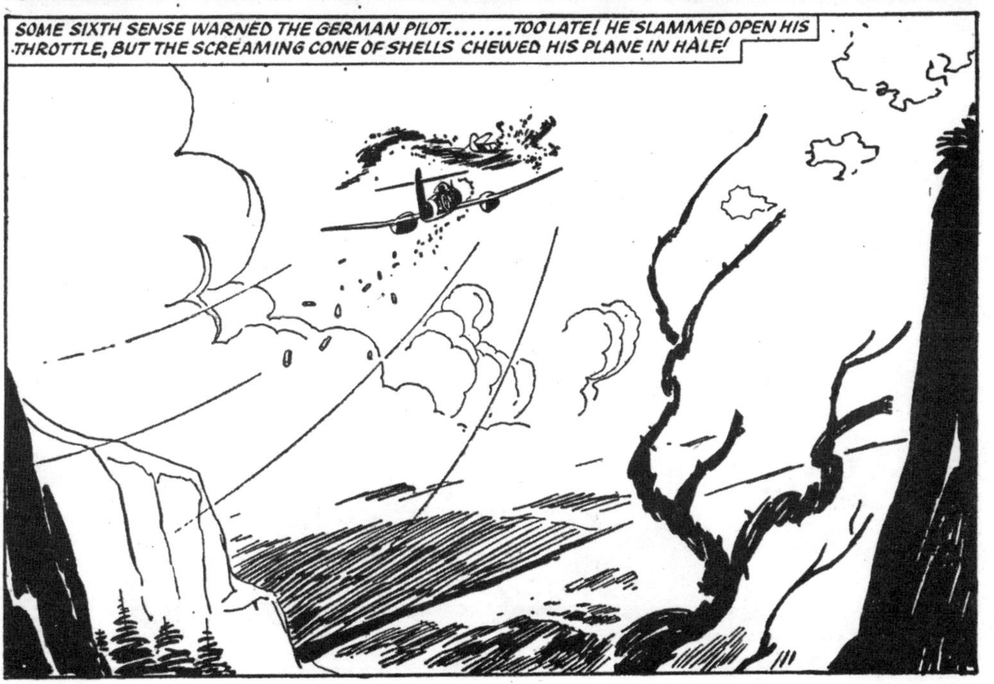
SOME SIXTH SENSE WARNED THE GERMAN PILOT........TOO LATE! HE SLAMMED OPEN HIS THROTTLE, BUT THE SCREAMING CONE OF SHELLS CHEWED HIS PLANE IN HALF!

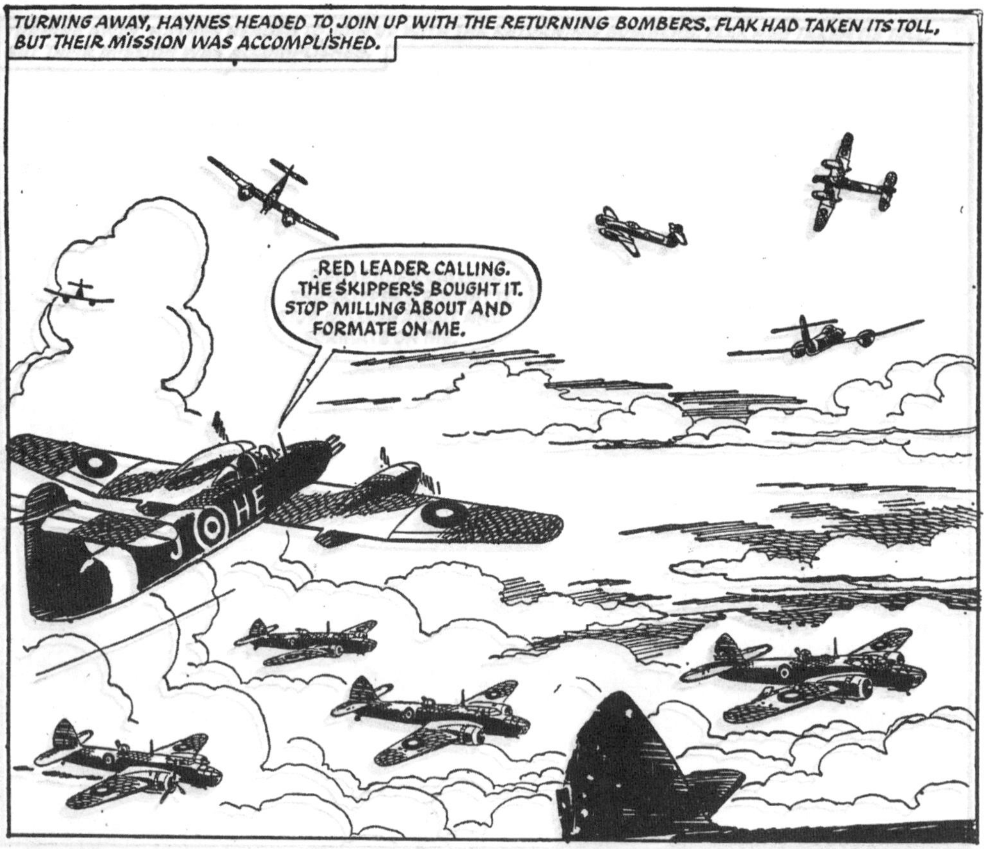
TURNING AWAY, HAYNES HEADED TO JOIN UP WITH THE RETURNING BOMBERS. FLAK HAD TAKEN ITS TOLL, BUT THEIR MISSION WAS ACCOMPLISHED.
RED LEADER CALLING. THE SKIPPER'S BOUGHT IT. STOP MILLING ABOUT AND FORMATE ON ME.
J HE

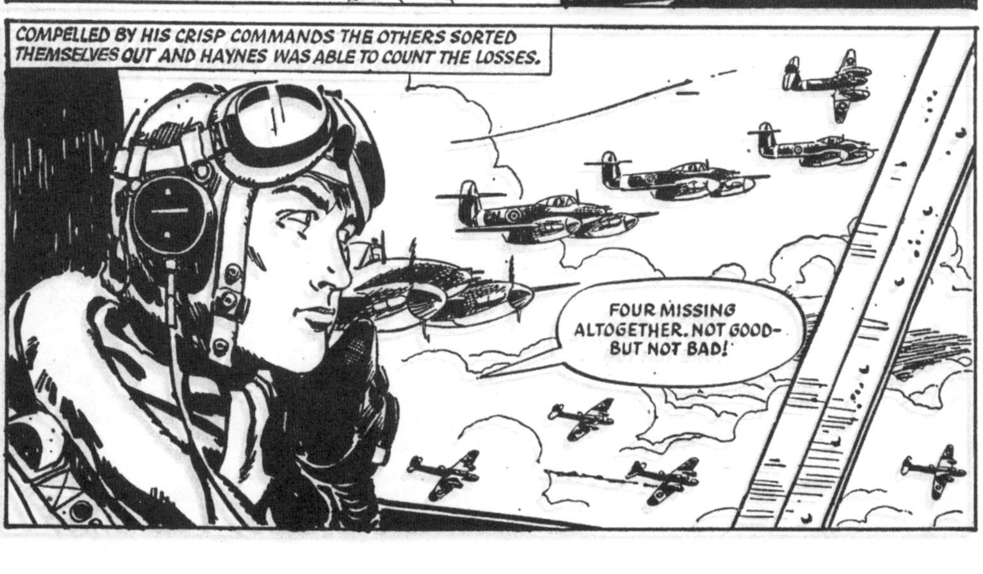
COMPELLED BY HIS CRISP COMMANDS THE OTHERS SORTED THEMSELVES OUT AND HAYNES WAS ABLE TO COUNT THE LOSSES.
FOUR MISSING ALTOGETHER. NOT GOOD- BUT NOT BAD!

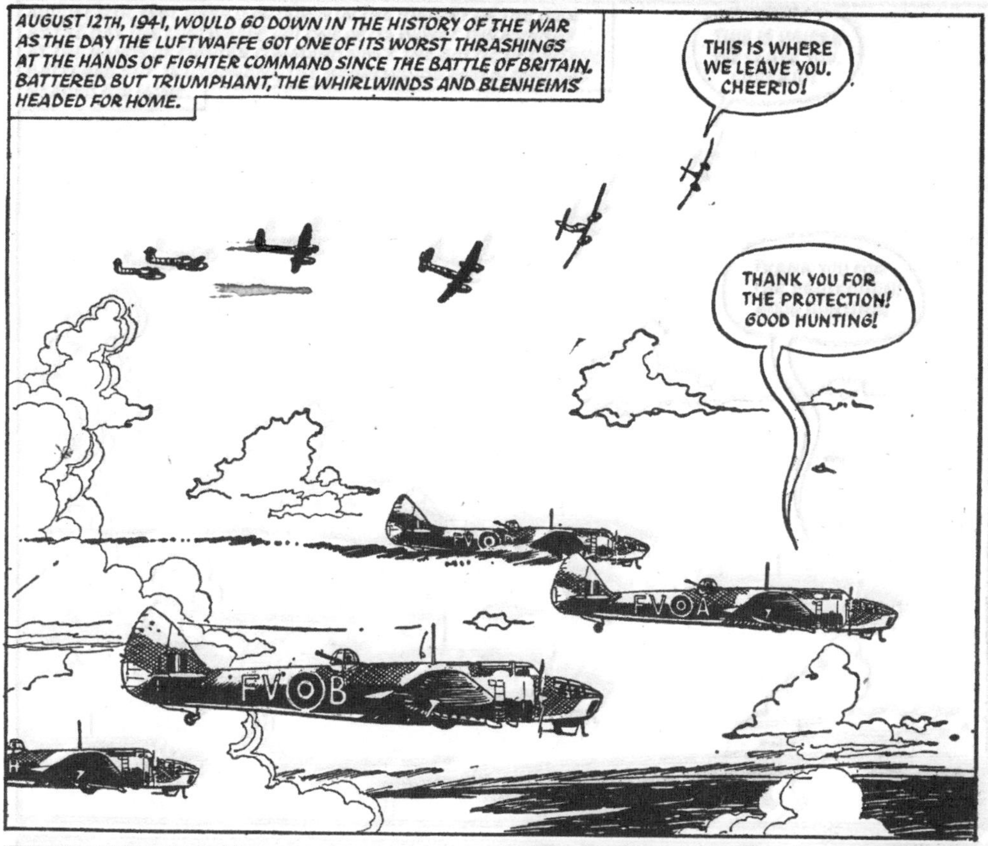
AUGUST 12TH, 1941, WOULD GO DOWN IN THE HISTORY OF THE WAR AS THE DAY THE LUFTWAFFE GOT ONE OF ITS WORST THRASHINGS AT THE HANDS OF FIGHTER COMMAND SINCE THE BATTLE OF BRITAIN. BATTERED BUT TRIUMPHANT, THE WHIRLWINDS AND BLENHEIMS HEADED FOR HOME.
THIS IS WHERE WE LEAVE YOU. CHEERIO!
THANK YOU FOR THE PROTECTION! GOOD HUNTING!
FV B
FV A
FV B

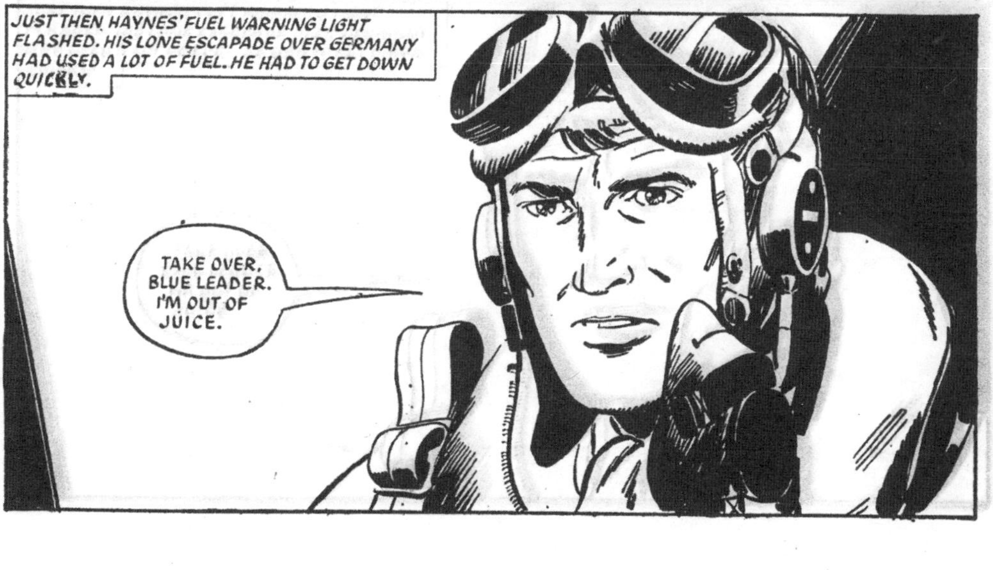
JUST THEN HAYNES' FUEL WARNING LIGHT FLASHED. HIS LONE ESCAPADE OVER GERMANY HAD USED A LOT OF FUEL. HE HAD TO GET DOWN QUICKLY.
TAKE OVER, BLUE LEADER. I'M OUT OF JUICE.

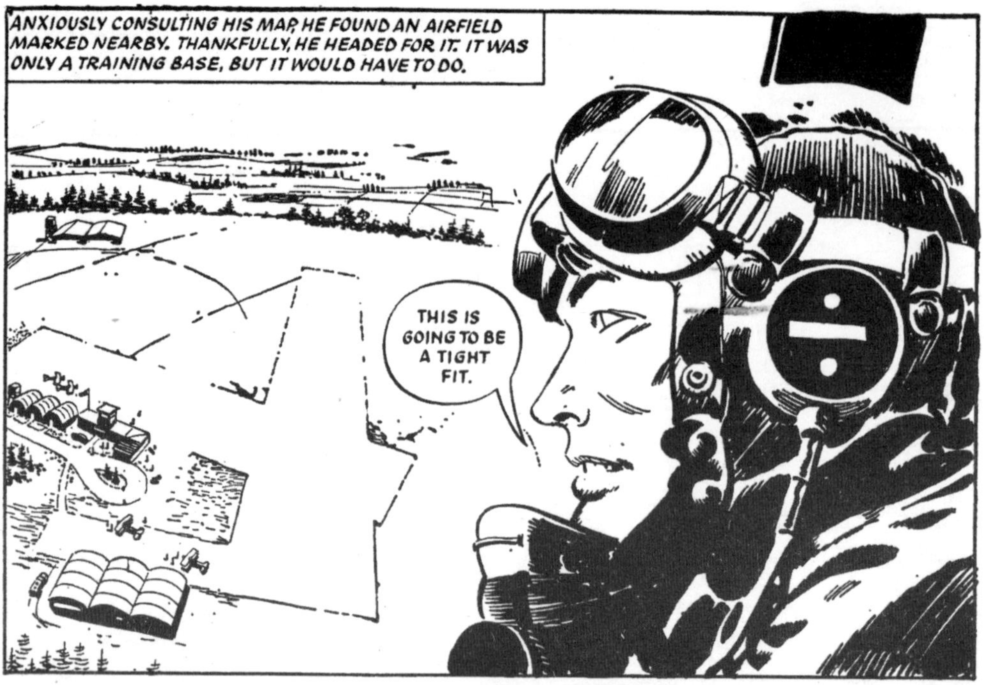
ANXIOUSLY CONSULTING HIS MAP, HE FOUND AN AIRFIELD MARKED NEARBY. THANKFULLY, HE HEADED FOR IT. IT WAS ONLY A TRAINING BASE, BUT IT WOULD HAVE TO DO.
THIS IS GOING TO BE A TIGHT FIT.

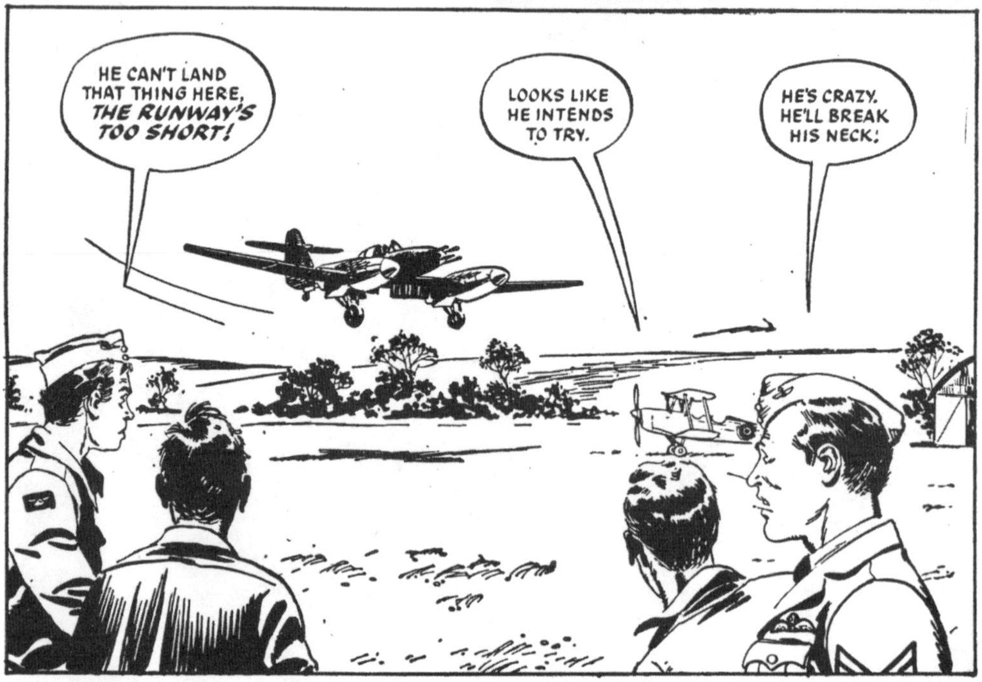
HE CAN'T LAND THAT THING HERE, *THE RUNWAY'S TOO SHORT!*
LOOKS LIKE HE INTENDS TO TRY.
HE'S CRAZY. HE'LL BREAK HIS NECK!

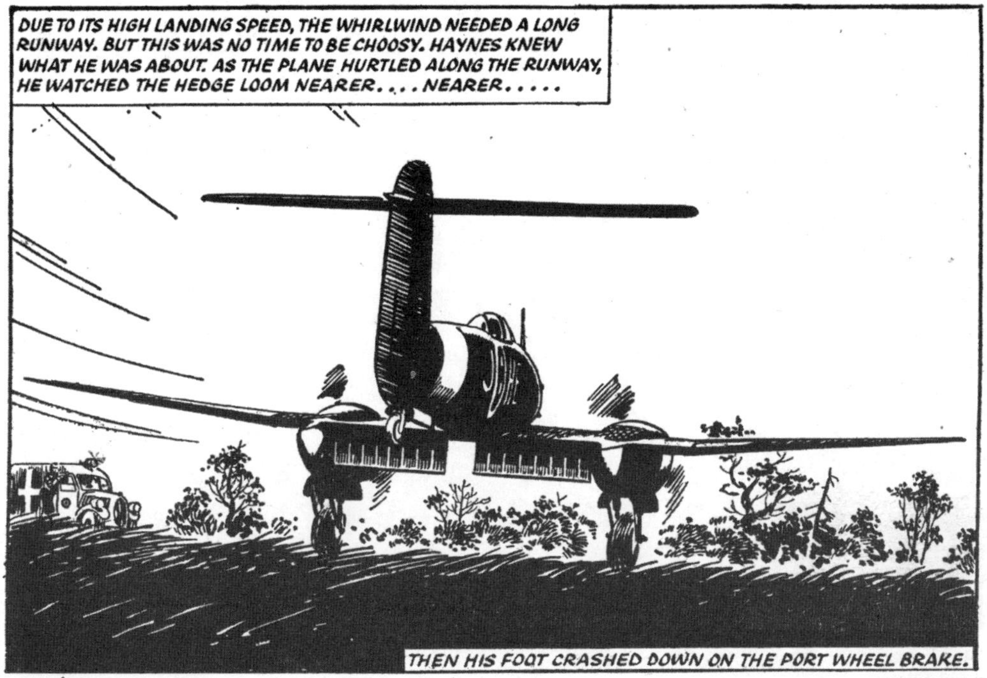
DUE TO ITS HIGH LANDING SPEED, THE WHIRLWIND NEEDED A LONG RUNWAY. BUT THIS WAS NO TIME TO BE CHOOSY. HAYNES KNEW WHAT HE WAS ABOUT. AS THE PLANE HURTLED ALONG THE RUNWAY, HE WATCHED THE HEDGE LOOM NEARER.... NEARER.....
THEN HIS FOOT CRASHED DOWN ON THE PORT WHEEL BRAKE.

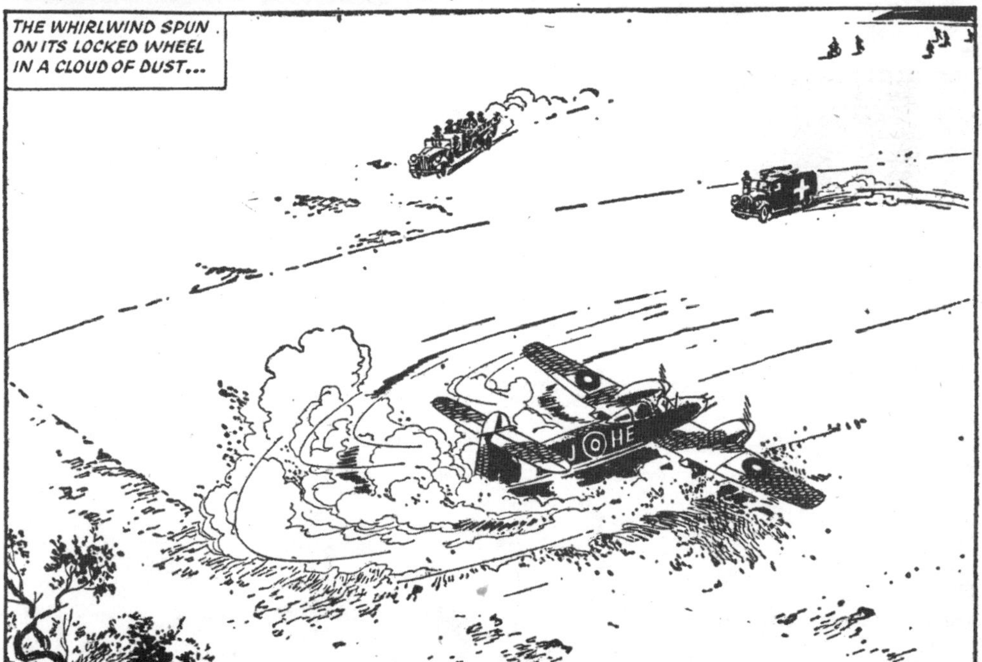
THE WHIRLWIND SPUN ON ITS LOCKED WHEEL IN A CLOUD OF DUST...

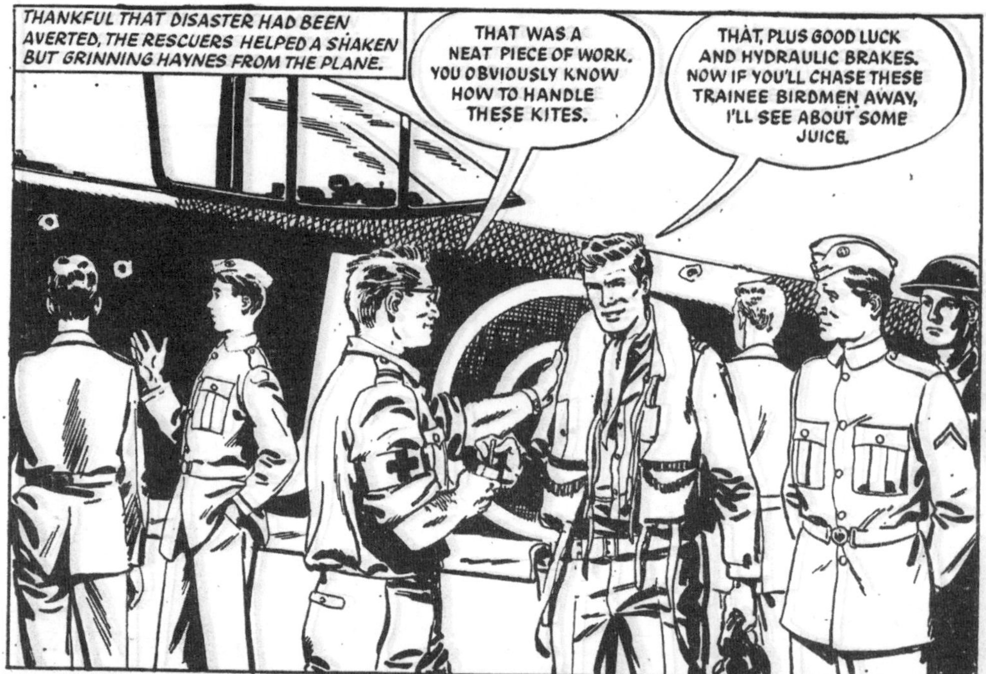
THANKFUL THAT DISASTER HAD BEEN AVERTED, THE RESCUERS HELPED A SHAKEN BUT GRINNING HAYNES FROM THE PLANE.
THAT WAS A NEAT PIECE OF WORK. YOU OBVIOUSLY KNOW HOW TO HANDLE THESE KITES.
THAT, PLUS GOOD LUCK AND HYDRAULIC BRAKES. NOW IF YOU'LL CHASE THESE TRAINEE BIRDMEN AWAY, I'LL SEE ABOUT SOME JUICE.

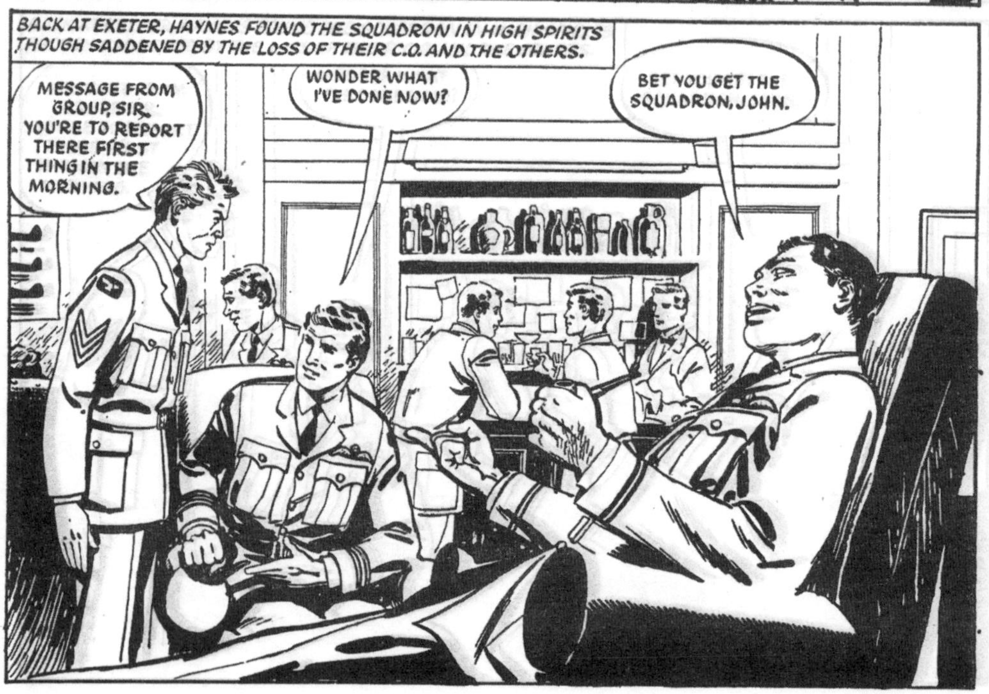
BACK AT EXETER, HAYNES FOUND THE SQUADRON IN HIGH SPIRITS THOUGH SADDENED BY THE LOSS OF THEIR C.O. AND THE OTHERS.
MESSAGE FROM GROUP, SIR. YOU'RE TO REPORT THERE FIRST THING IN THE MORNING.
WONDER WHAT I'VE DONE NOW?
BET YOU GET THE SQUADRON, JOHN.

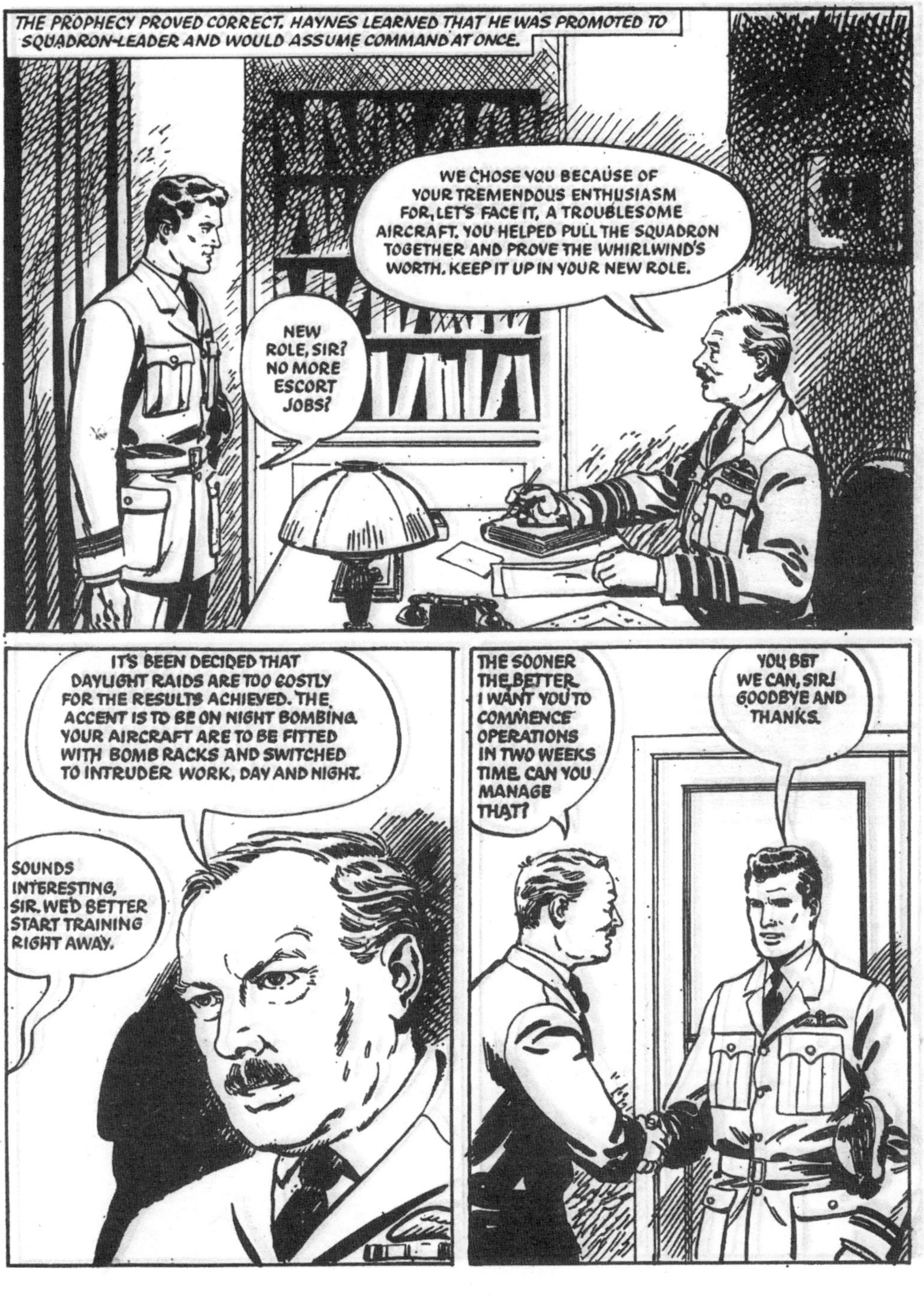
THE PROPHECY PROVED CORRECT. HAYNES LEARNED THAT HE WAS PROMOTED TO SQUADRON-LEADER AND WOULD ASSUME COMMAND AT ONCE.
WE CHOSE YOU BECAUSE OF YOUR TREMENDOUS ENTHUSIASM FOR, LET'S FACE IT, A TROUBLESOME AIRCRAFT. YOU HELPED PULL THE SQUADRON TOGETHER AND PROVE THE WHIRLWIND'S WORTH. KEEP IT UP IN YOUR NEW ROLE.
NEW ROLE, SIR? NO MORE ESCORT JOBS?
IT'S BEEN DECIDED THAT DAYLIGHT RAIDS ARE TOO COSTLY FOR THE RESULTS ACHIEVED. THE ACCENT IS TO BE ON NIGHT BOMBING. YOUR AIRCRAFT ARE TO BE FITTED WITH BOMB RACKS AND SWITCHED TO INTRUDER WORK, DAY AND NIGHT.
SOUNDS INTERESTING, SIR. WE'D BETTER START TRAINING RIGHT AWAY.
THE SOONER THE BETTER. I WANT YOU TO COMMENCE OPERATIONS IN TWO WEEKS TIME. CAN YOU MANAGE THAT?
YOU BET WE CAN, SIR! GOODBYE AND THANKS.

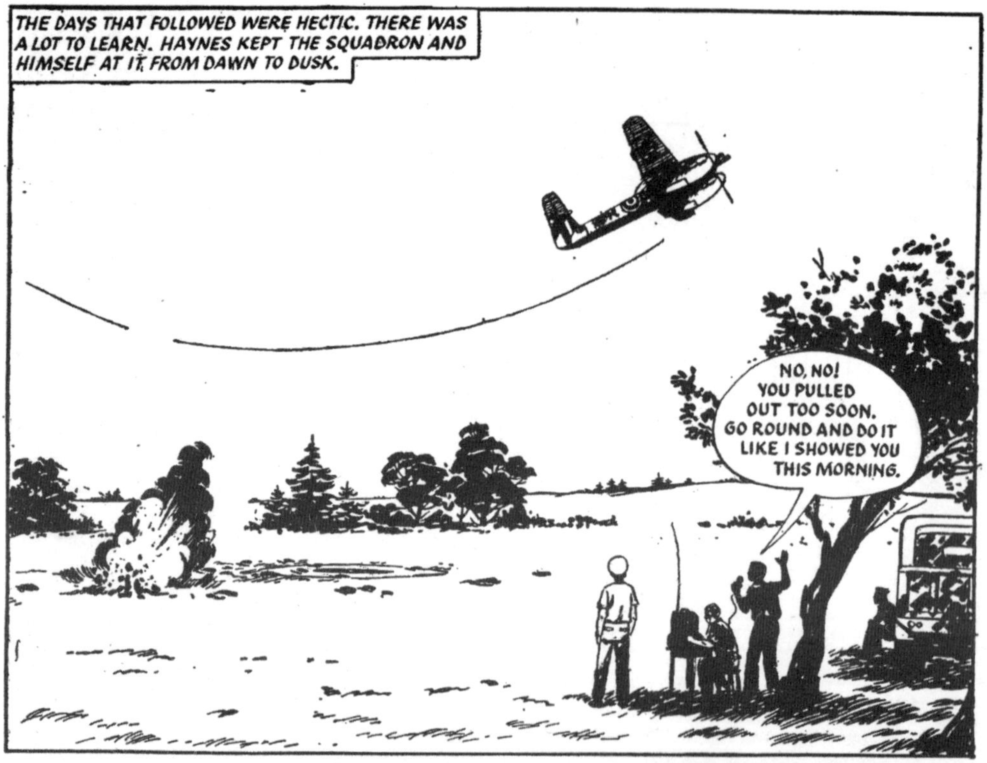
THE DAYS THAT FOLLOWED WERE HECTIC. THERE WAS A LOT TO LEARN. HAYNES KEPT THE SQUADRON AND HIMSELF AT IT FROM DAWN TO DUSK.
NO, NO! YOU PULLED OUT TOO SOON. GO ROUND AND DO IT LIKE I SHOWED YOU THIS MORNING.

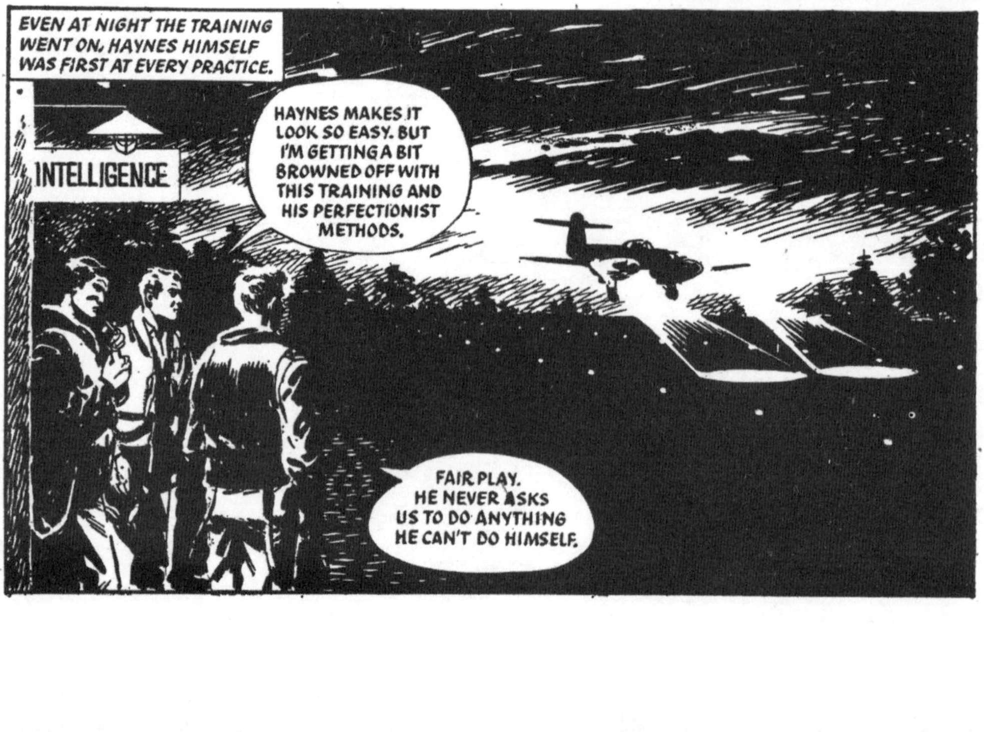
EVEN AT NIGHT THE TRAINING WENT ON. HAYNES HIMSELF WAS FIRST AT EVERY PRACTICE.
INTELLIGENCE
HAYNES MAKES IT LOOK SO EASY. BUT I'M GETTING A BIT BROWNED OFF WITH THIS TRAINING AND HIS PERFECTIONIST METHODS.
FAIR PLAY. HE NEVER ASKS US TO DO ANYTHING HE CAN'T DO HIMSELF.

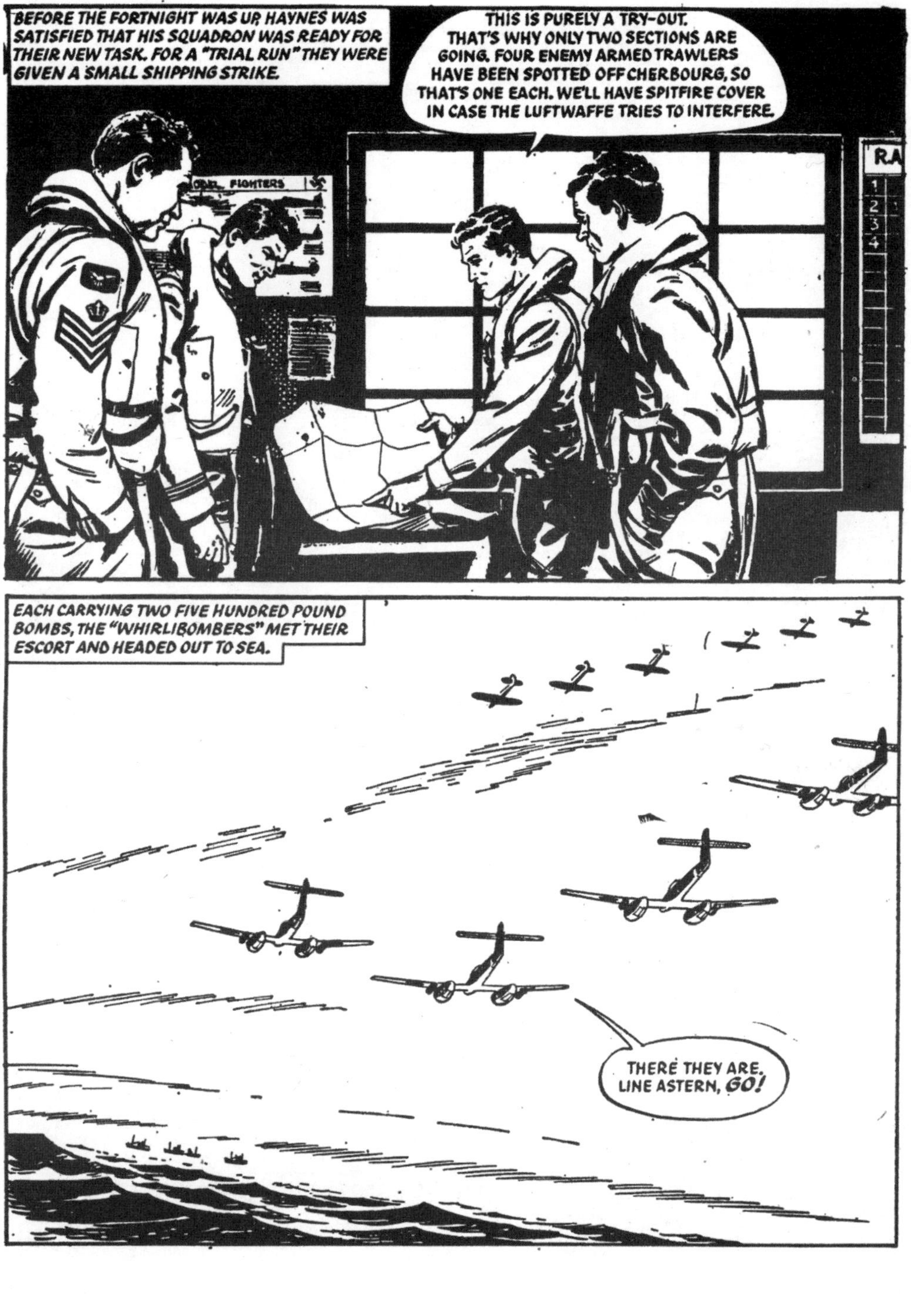
BEFORE THE FORTNIGHT WAS UP, HAYNES WAS SATISFIED THAT HIS SQUADRON WAS READY FOR THEIR NEW TASK. FOR A "TRIAL RUN" THEY WERE GIVEN A SMALL SHIPPING STRIKE.
THIS IS PURELY A TRY-OUT. THAT'S WHY ONLY TWO SECTIONS ARE GOING. FOUR ENEMY ARMED TRAWLERS HAVE BEEN SPOTTED OFF CHERBOURG, SO THAT'S ONE EACH. WE'LL HAVE SPITFIRE COVER IN CASE THE LUFTWAFFE TRIES TO INTERFERE.
FIGHTERS
EACH CARRYING TWO FIVE HUNDRED POUND BOMBS, THE "WHIRLIBOMBERS" MET THEIR ESCORT AND HEADED OUT TO SEA.
THERE THEY ARE. LINE ASTERN, GO!

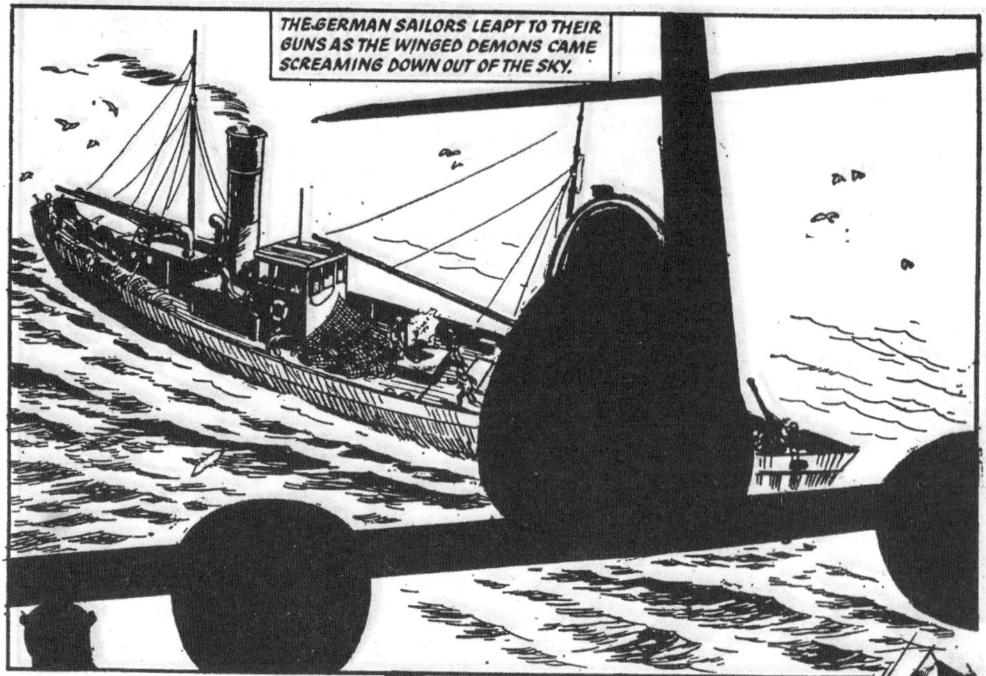
THE GERMAN SAILORS LEAPT TO THEIR GUNS AS THE WINGED DEMONS CAME SCREAMING DOWN OUT OF THE SKY.

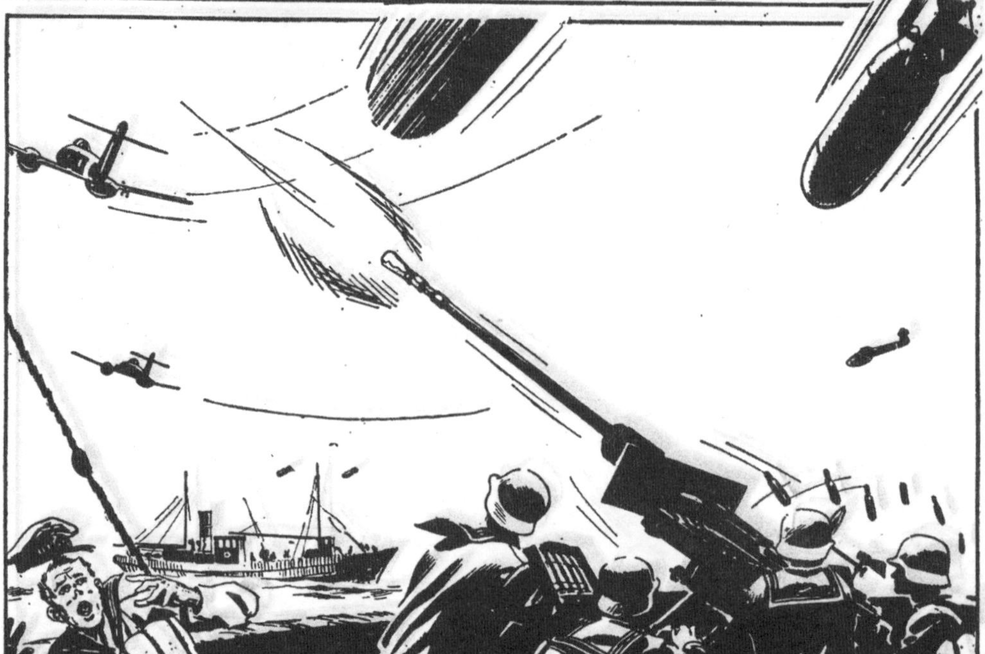

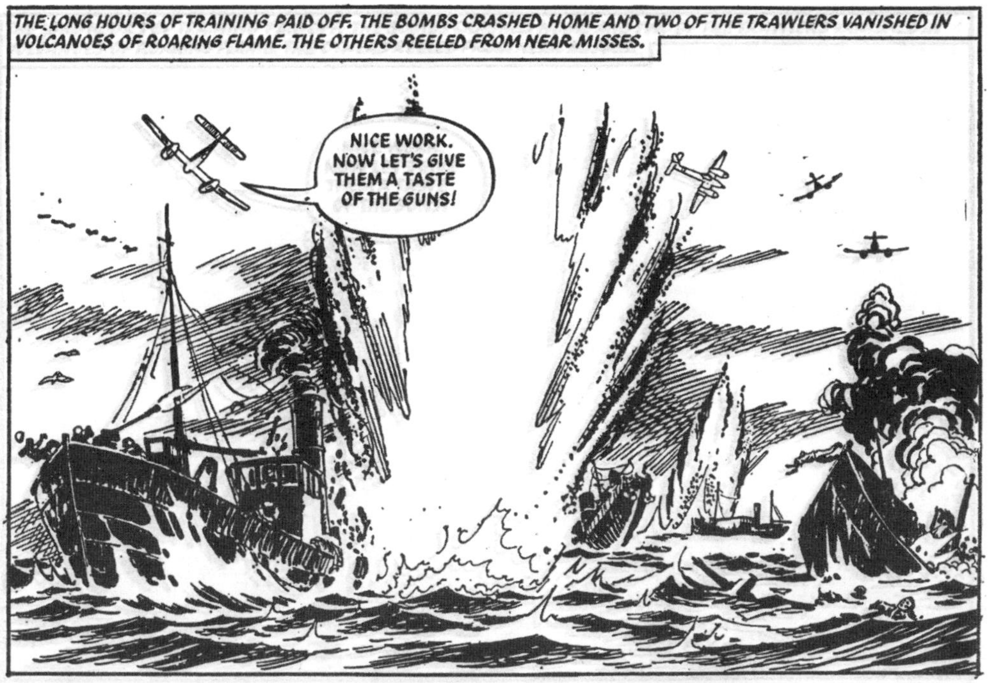
THE LONG HOURS OF TRAINING PAID OFF. THE BOMBS CRASHED HOME AND TWO OF THE TRAWLERS VANISHED IN VOLCANOES OF ROARING FLAME. THE OTHERS REELED FROM NEAR MISSES.
NICE WORK. NOW LET'S GIVE THEM A TASTE OF THE GUNS!

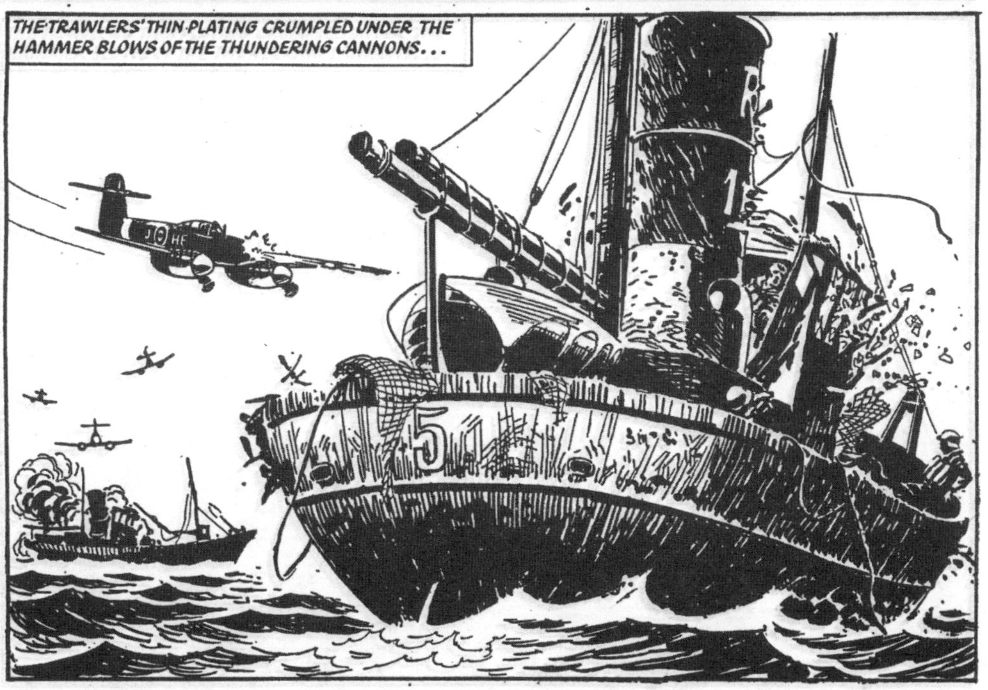
THE TRAWLERS' THIN PLATING CRUMPLED UNDER THE HAMMER BLOWS OF THE THUNDERING CANNONS...

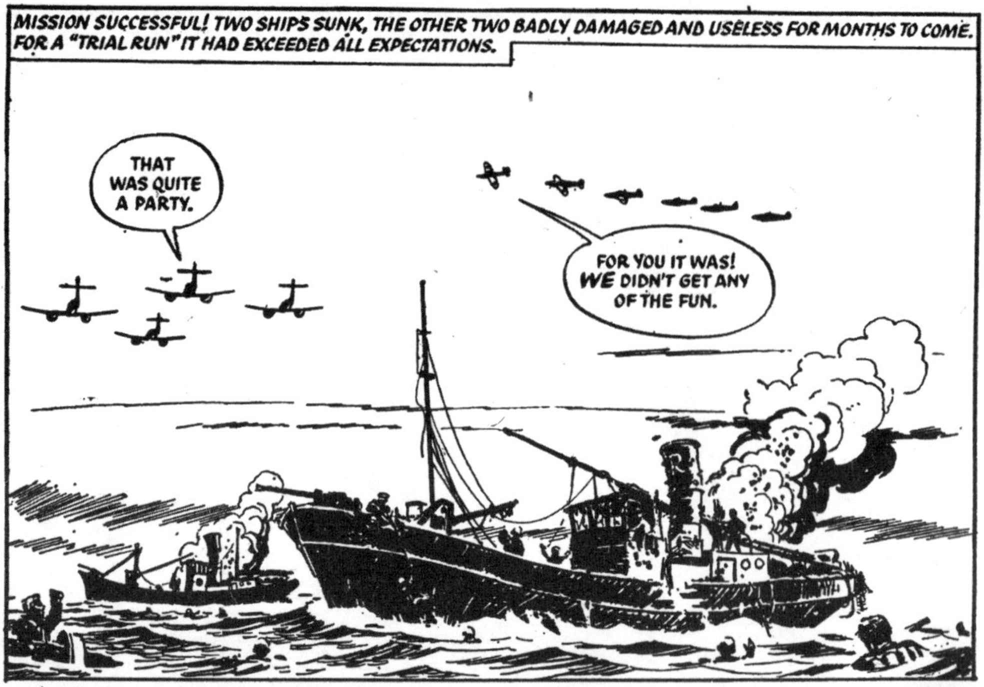
MISSION SUCCESSFUL! TWO SHIPS SUNK, THE OTHER TWO BADLY DAMAGED AND USELESS FOR MONTHS TO COME. FOR A "TRIAL RUN" IT HAD EXCEEDED ALL EXPECTATIONS.
THAT WAS QUITE A PARTY.
FOR YOU IT WAS! WE DIDN'T GET ANY OF THE FUN.

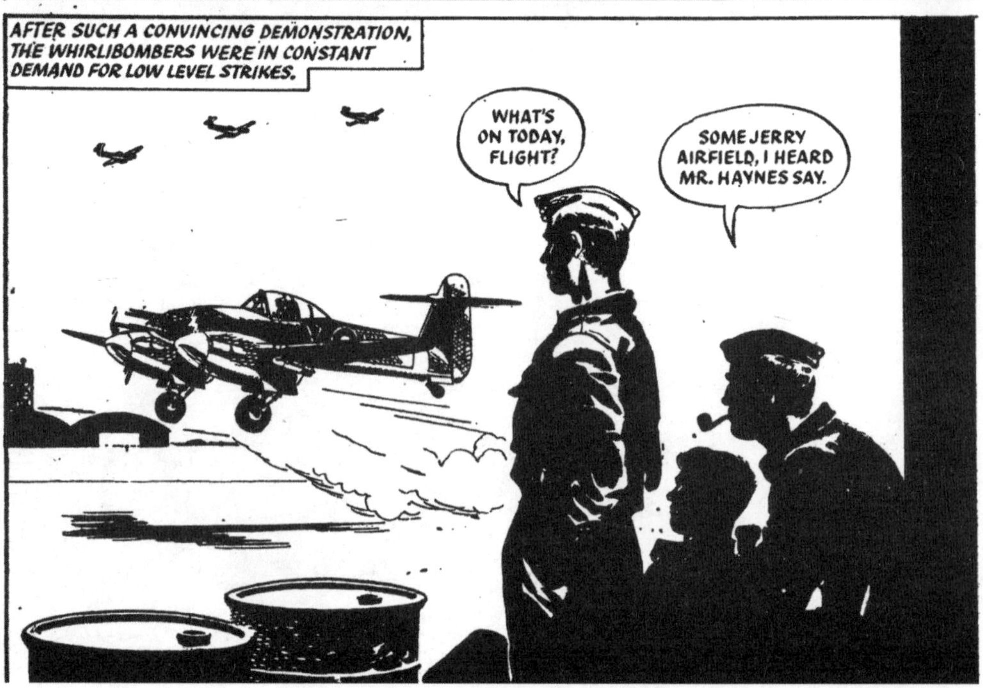
AFTER SUCH A CONVINCING DEMONSTRATION, THE WHIRLIBOMBERS WERE IN CONSTANT DEMAND FOR LOW LEVEL STRIKES.
WHAT'S ON TODAY, FLIGHT?
SOME JERRY AIRFIELD, I HEARD MR. HAYNES SAY.

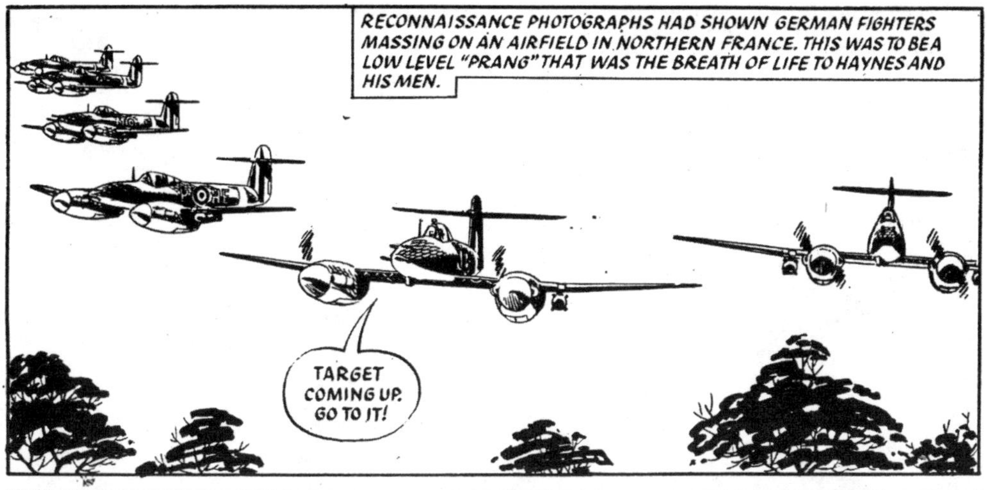
RECONNAISSANCE PHOTOGRAPHS HAD SHOWN GERMAN FIGHTERS MASSING ON AN AIRFIELD IN NORTHERN FRANCE. THIS WAS TO BE A LOW LEVEL "PRANG" THAT WAS THE BREATH OF LIFE TO HAYNES AND HIS MEN.
TARGET COMING UP. GO TO IT!

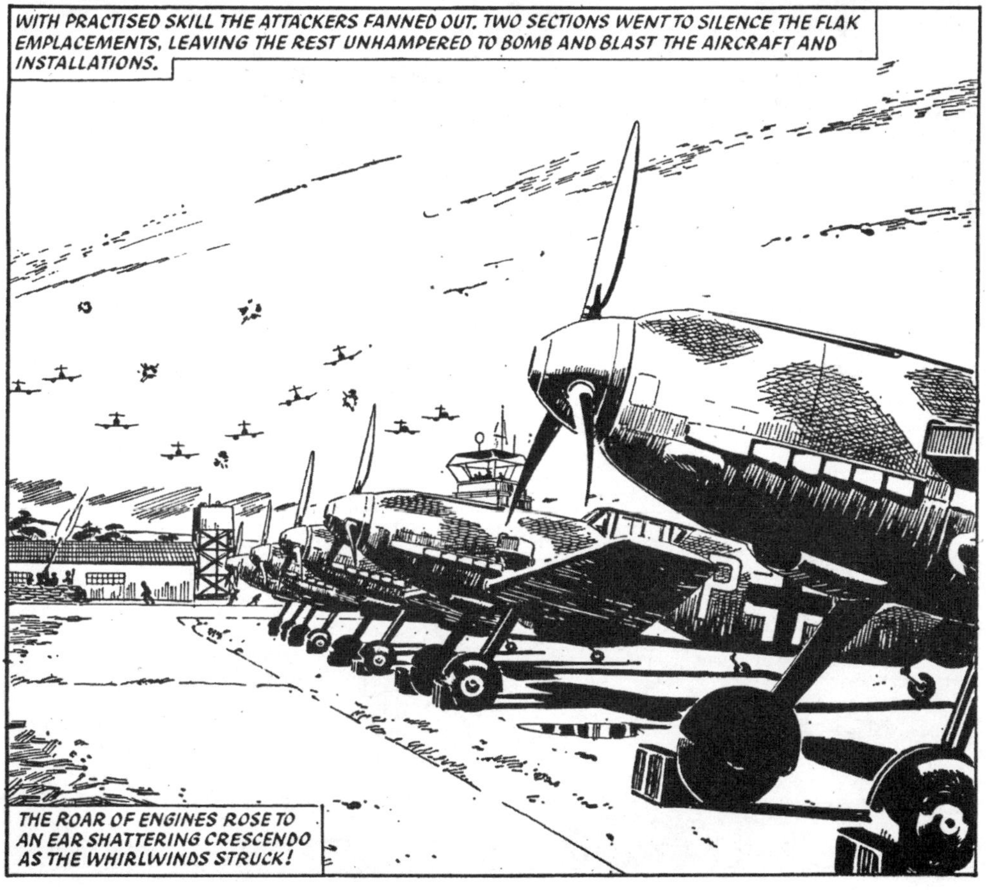
WITH PRACTISED SKILL THE ATTACKERS FANNED OUT. TWO SECTIONS WENT TO SILENCE THE FLAK EMPLACEMENTS, LEAVING THE REST UNHAMPERED TO BOMB AND BLAST THE AIRCRAFT AND INSTALLATIONS.
THE ROAR OF ENGINES ROSE TO AN EAR SHATTERING CRESCENDO AS THE WHIRLWINDS STRUCK!

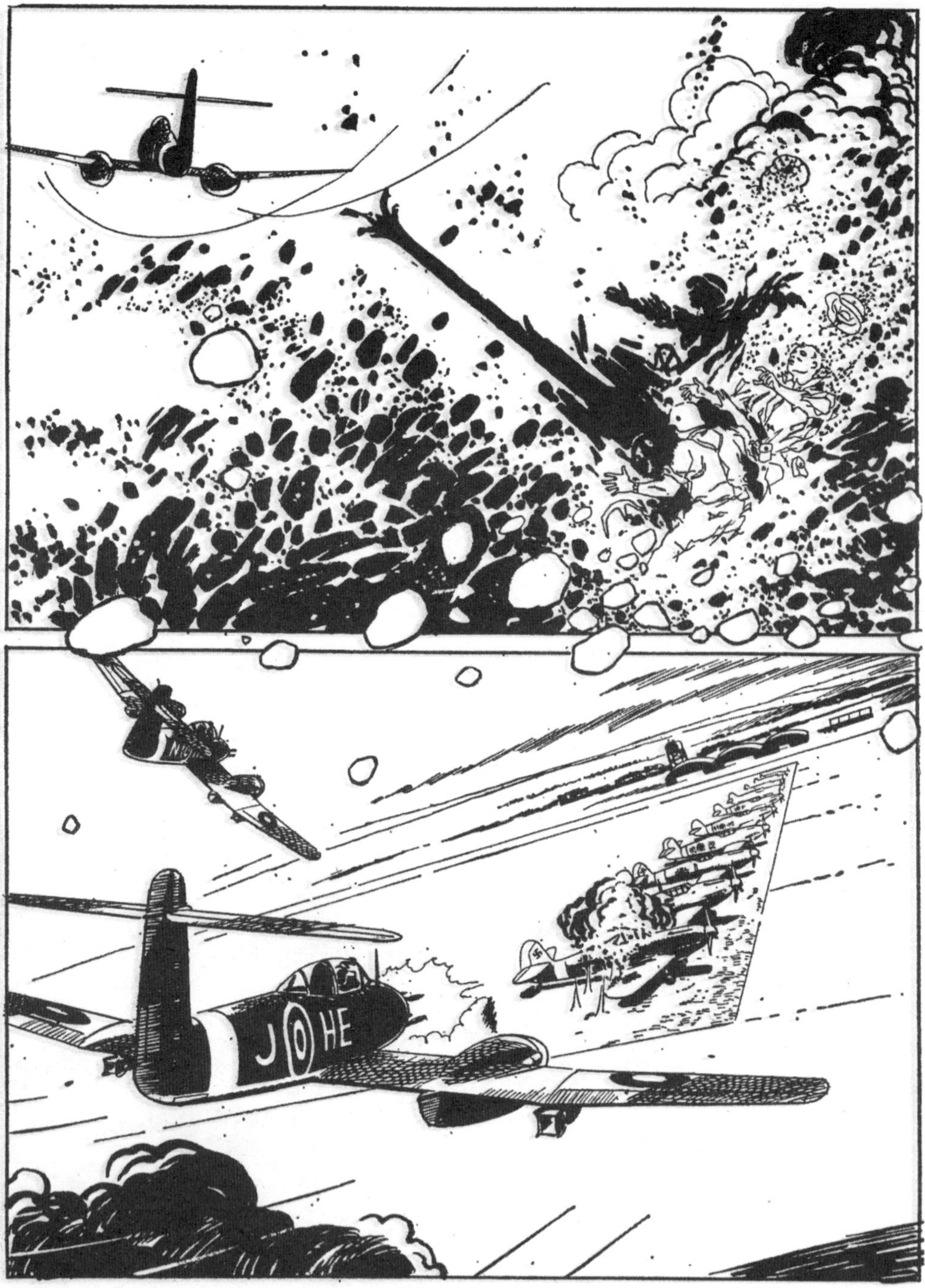
J HE

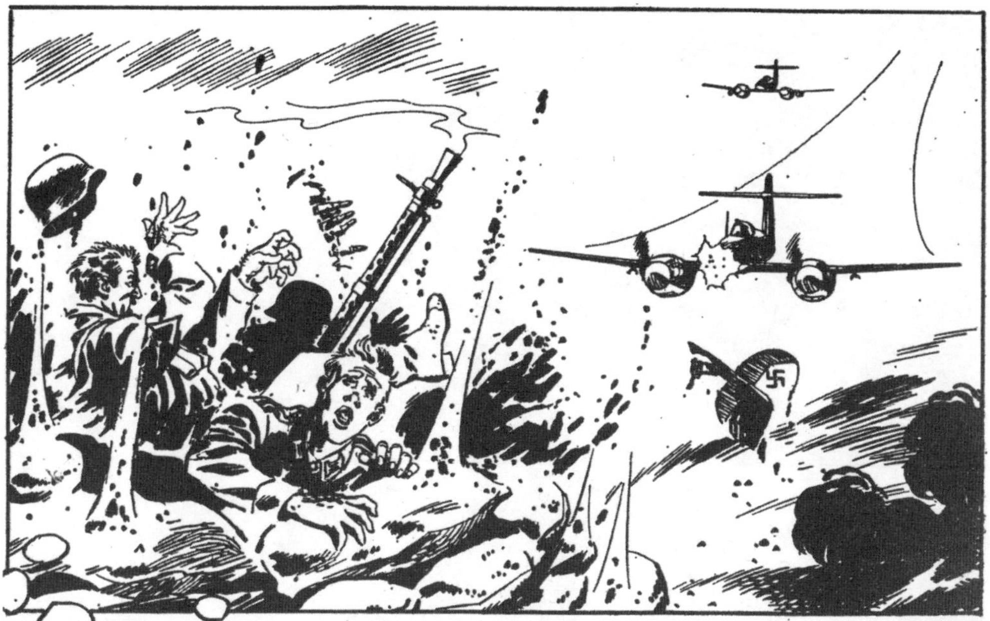

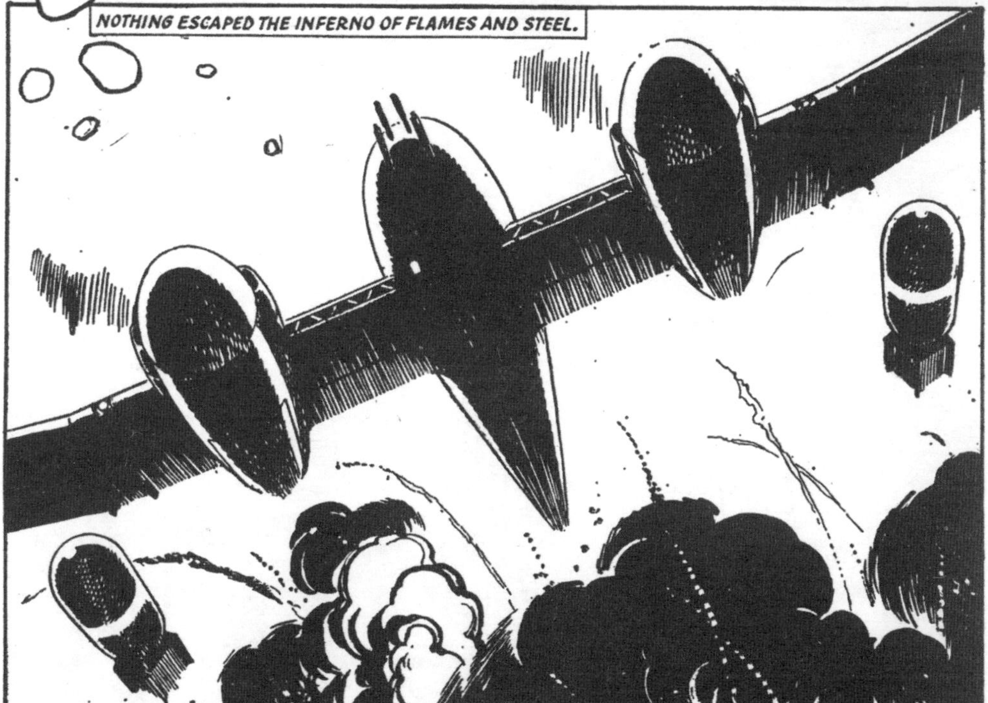
NOTHING ESCAPED THE INFERNO OF FLAMES AND STEEL.

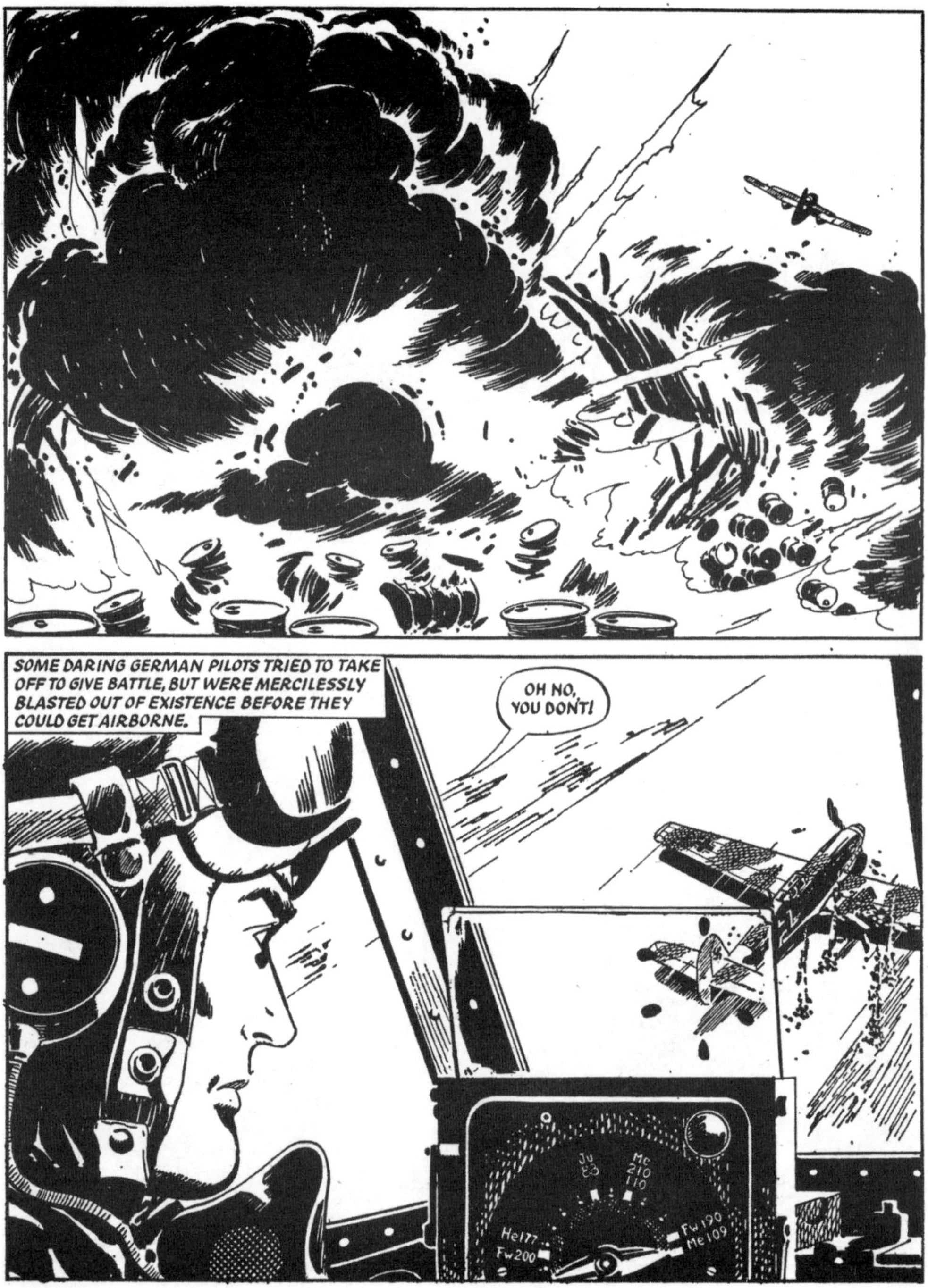
SOME DARING GERMAN PILOTS TRIED TO TAKE OFF TO GIVE BATTLE, BUT WERE MERCILESSLY BLASTED OUT OF EXISTENCE BEFORE THEY COULD GET AIRBORNE.
OH NO, YOU DON'T!
He177
Fw200
Fw190
Me109

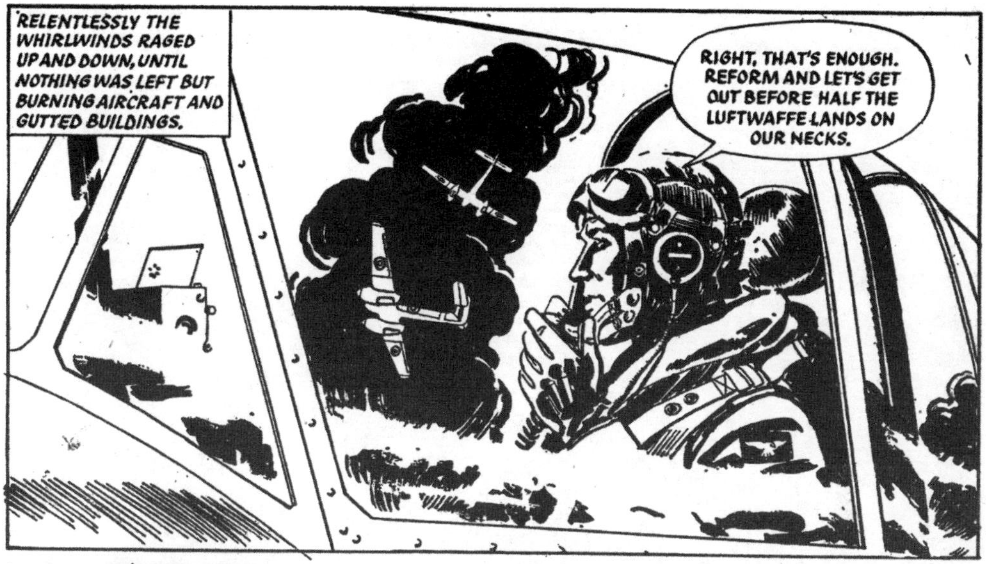
RELENTLESSLY THE WHIRLWINDS RAGED UP AND DOWN, UNTIL NOTHING WAS LEFT BUT BURNING AIRCRAFT AND GUTTED BUILDINGS.
RIGHT, THAT'S ENOUGH. REFORM AND LET'S GET OUT BEFORE HALF THE LUFTWAFFE LANDS ON OUR NECKS.

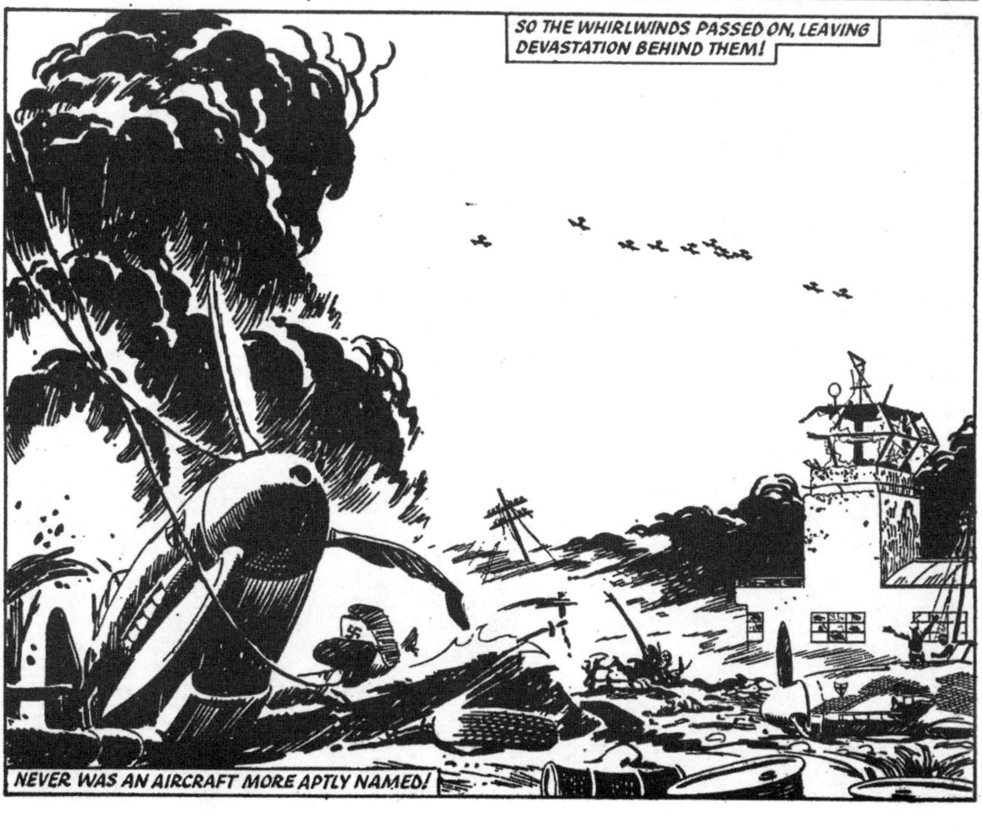
SO THE WHIRLWINDS PASSED ON, LEAVING DEVASTATION BEHIND THEM!
NEVER WAS AN AIRCRAFT MORE APTLY NAMED!

Chapter 3. Whirlibomber's Moon

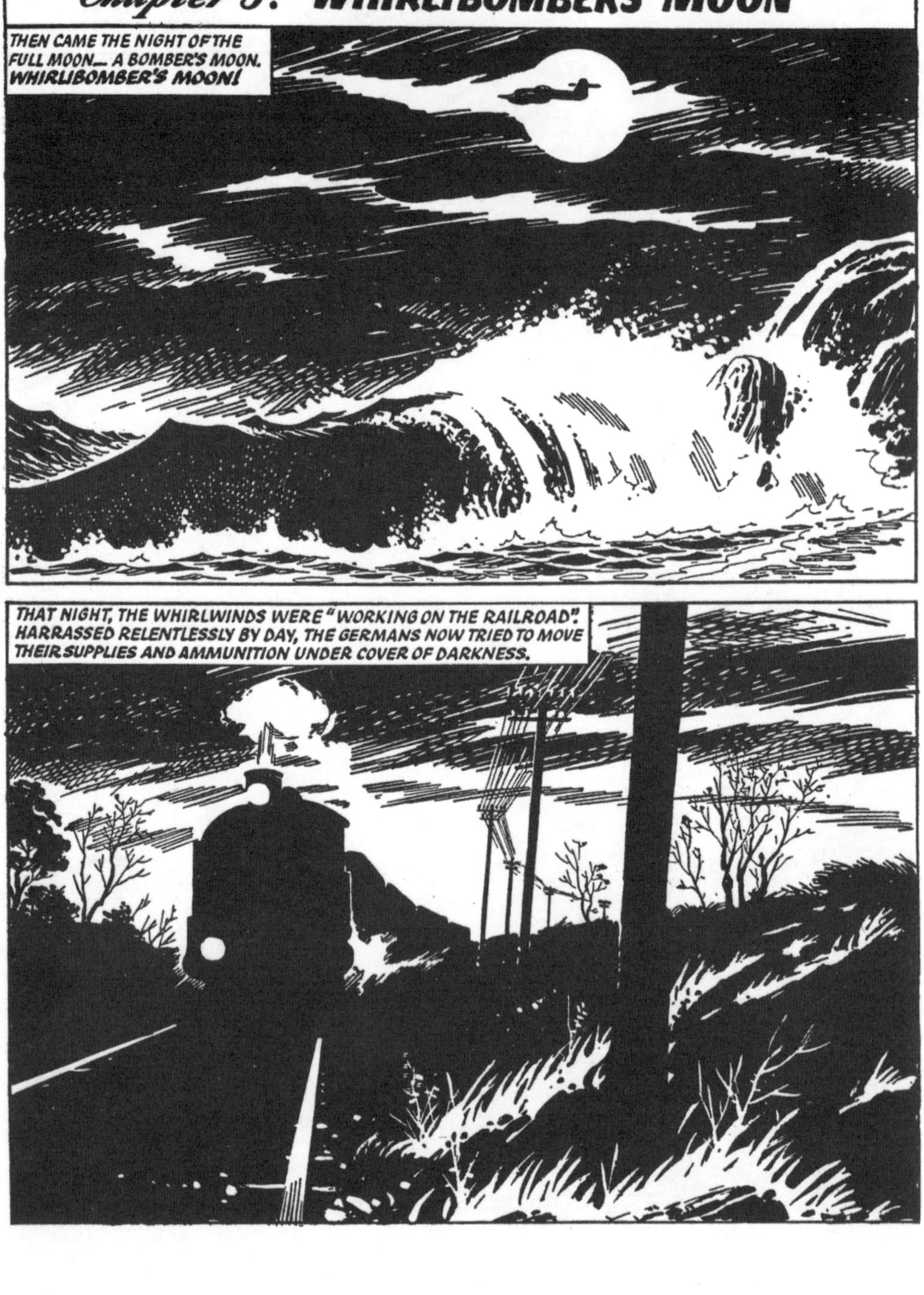
THEN CAME THE NIGHT OF THE FULL MOON... A BOMBER'S MOON. WHIRLIBOMBER'S MOON!
THAT NIGHT, THE WHIRLWINDS WERE "WORKING ON THE RAILROAD". HARRASSED RELENTLESSLY BY DAY, THE GERMANS NOW TRIED TO MOVE THEIR SUPPLIES AND AMMUNITION UNDER COVER OF DARKNESS.

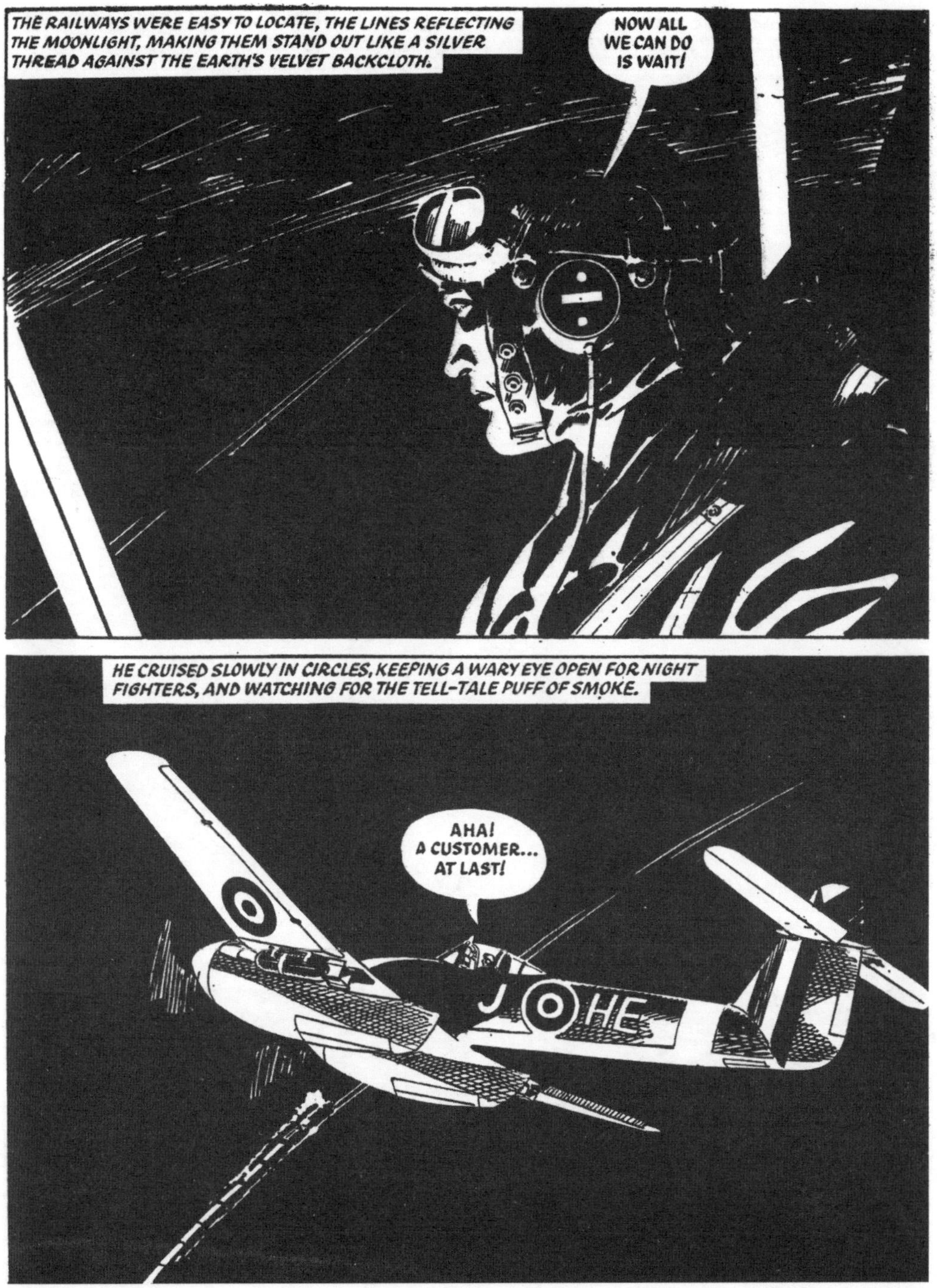
THE RAILWAYS WERE EASY TO LOCATE, THE LINES REFLECTING THE MOONLIGHT, MAKING THEM STAND OUT LIKE A SILVER THREAD AGAINST THE EARTH'S VELVET BACKCLOTH.
NOW ALL WE CAN DO IS WAIT!
HE CRUISED SLOWLY IN CIRCLES, KEEPING A WARY EYE OPEN FOR NIGHT FIGHTERS, AND WATCHING FOR THE TELL-TALE PUFF OF SMOKE.
AHA! A CUSTOMER... AT LAST!
J HE

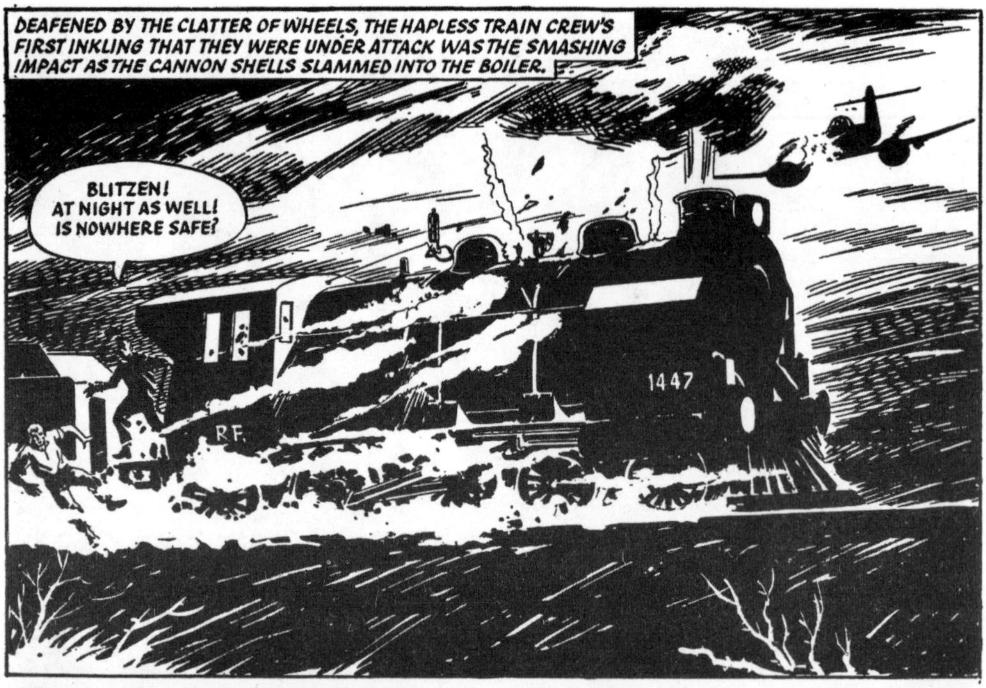
DEAFENED BY THE CLATTER OF WHEELS, THE HAPLESS TRAIN CREW'S FIRST INKLING THAT THEY WERE UNDER ATTACK WAS THE SMASHING IMPACT AS THE CANNON SHELLS SLAMMED INTO THE BOILER.
BLITZEN! AT NIGHT AS WELL! IS NOWHERE SAFE?
1447

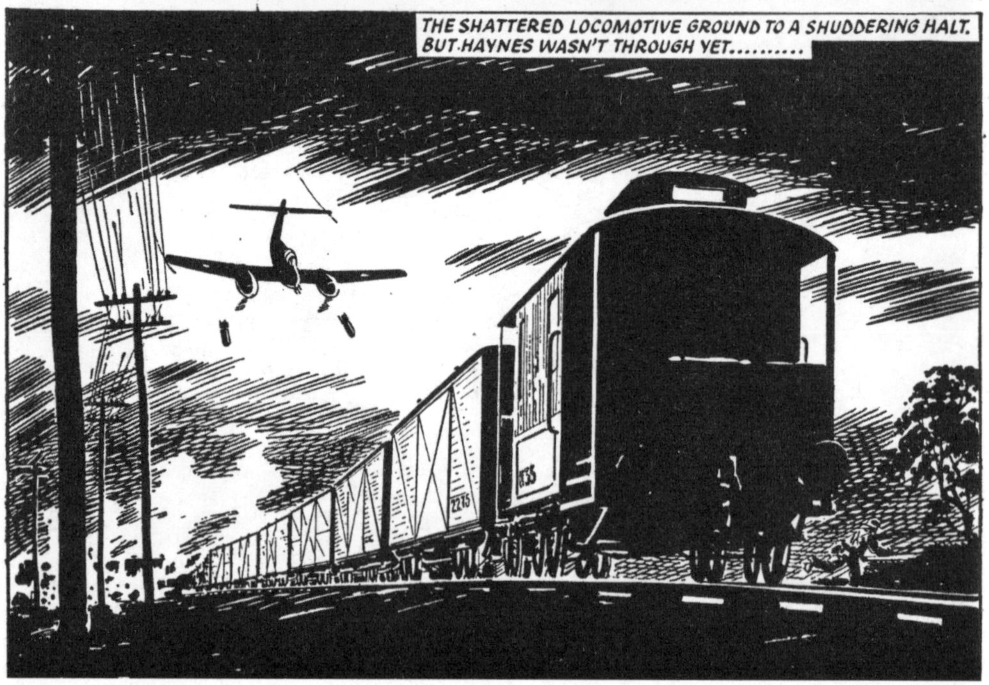
THE SHATTERED LOCOMOTIVE GROUND TO A SHUDDERING HALT. BUT HAYNES WASN'T THROUGH YET..........

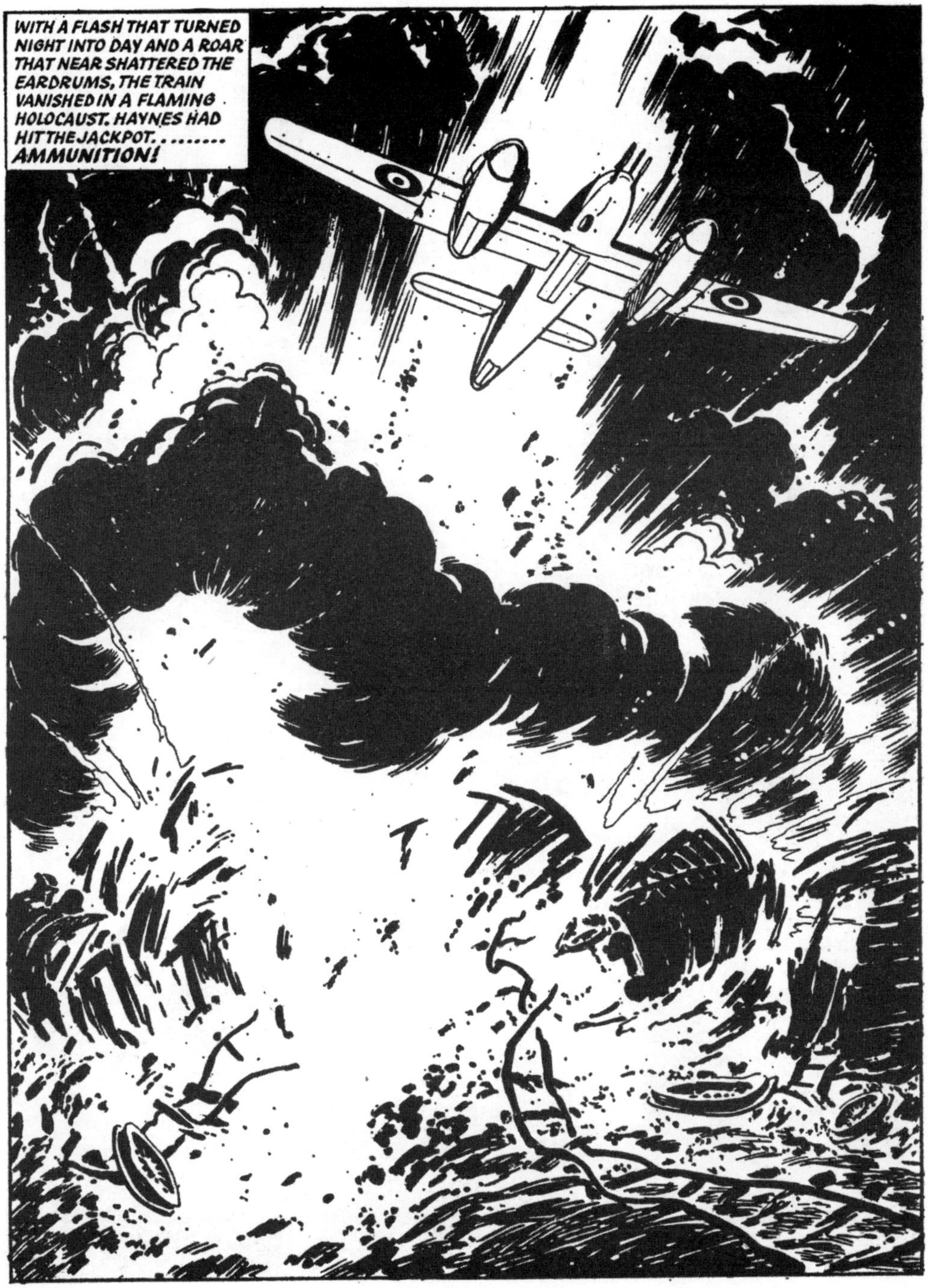
WITH A FLASH THAT TURNED NIGHT INTO DAY AND A ROAR THAT NEAR SHATTERED THE EARDRUMS, THE TRAIN VANISHED IN A FLAMING HOLOCAUST. HAYNES HAD HIT THE JACKPOT.........
AMMUNITION!

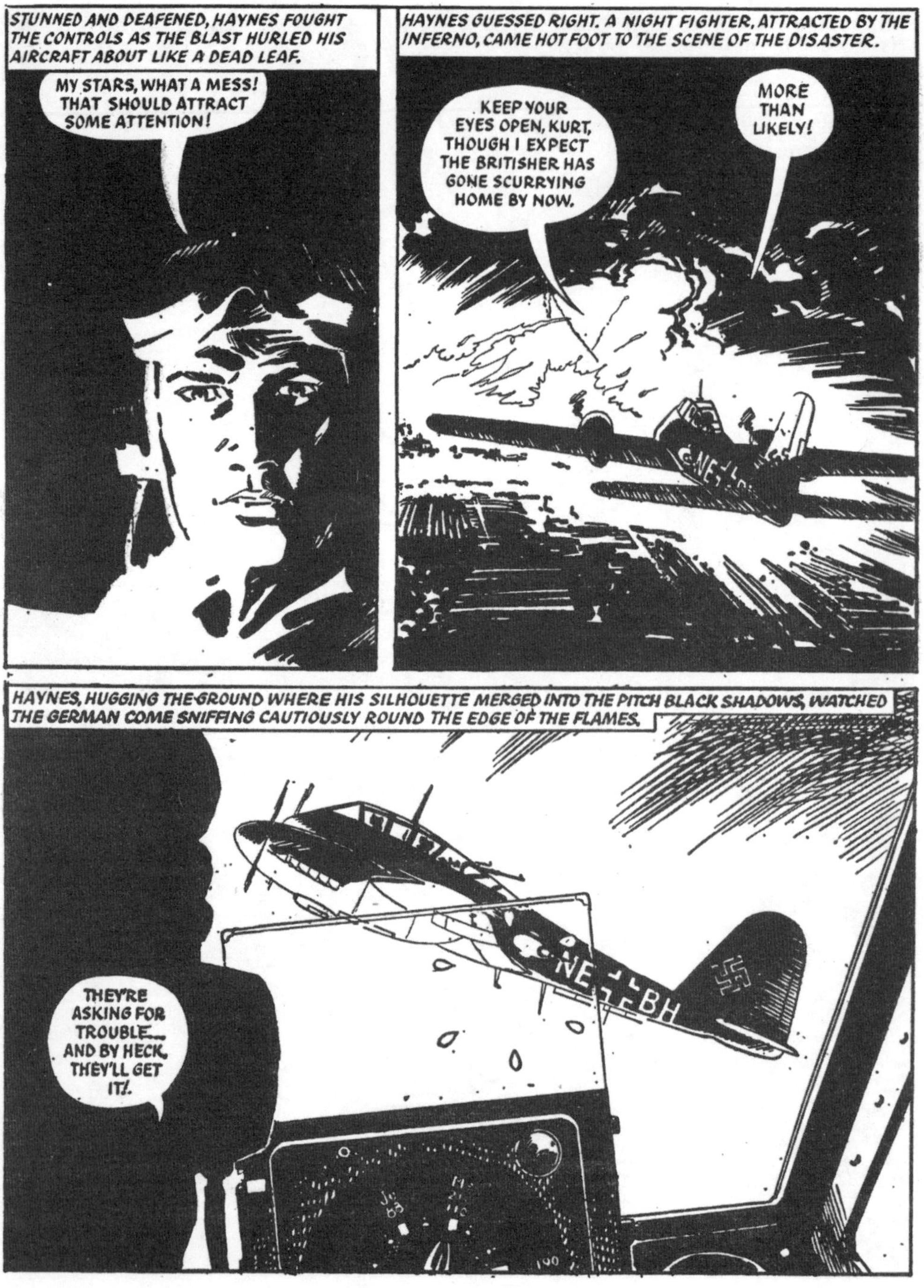
STUNNED AND DEAFENED, HAYNES FOUGHT THE CONTROLS AS THE BLAST HURLED HIS AIRCRAFT ABOUT LIKE A DEAD LEAF.
MY STARS, WHAT A MESS! THAT SHOULD ATTRACT SOME ATTENTION!
HAYNES GUESSED RIGHT. A NIGHT FIGHTER, ATTRACTED BY THE INFERNO, CAME HOT FOOT TO THE SCENE OF THE DISASTER.
KEEP YOUR EYES OPEN, KURT, THOUGH I EXPECT THE BRITISHER HAS GONE SCURRYING HOME BY NOW.
MORE THAN LIKELY!
HAYNES, HUGGING THE GROUND WHERE HIS SILHOUETTE MERGED INTO THE PITCH BLACK SHADOWS, WATCHED THE GERMAN COME SNIFFING CAUTIOUSLY ROUND THE EDGE OF THE FLAMES.
THEY'RE ASKING FOR TROUBLE... AND BY HECK, THEY'LL GET IT!

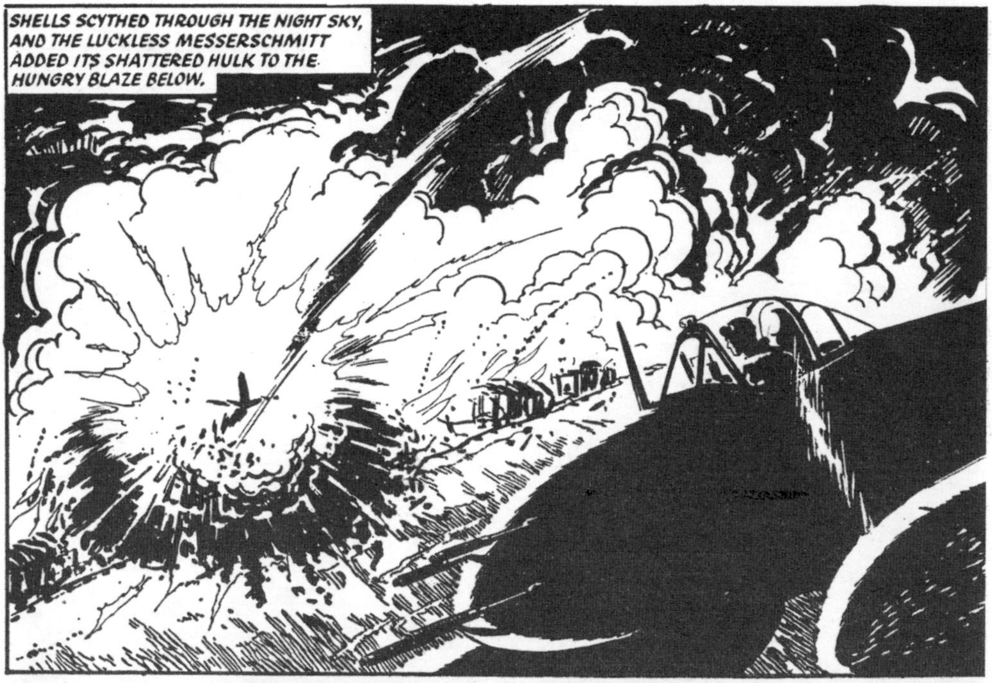
SHELLS SCYTHED THROUGH THE NIGHT SKY, AND THE LUCKLESS MESSERSCHMITT ADDED ITS SHATTERED HULK TO THE HUNGRY BLAZE BELOW.

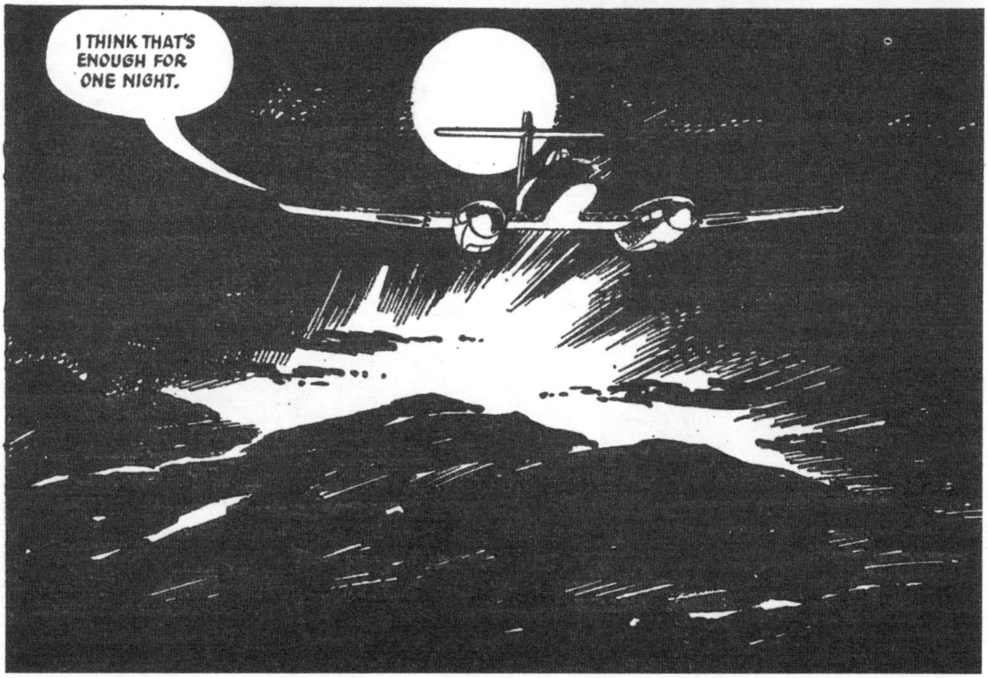
I THINK THAT'S ENOUGH FOR ONE NIGHT.

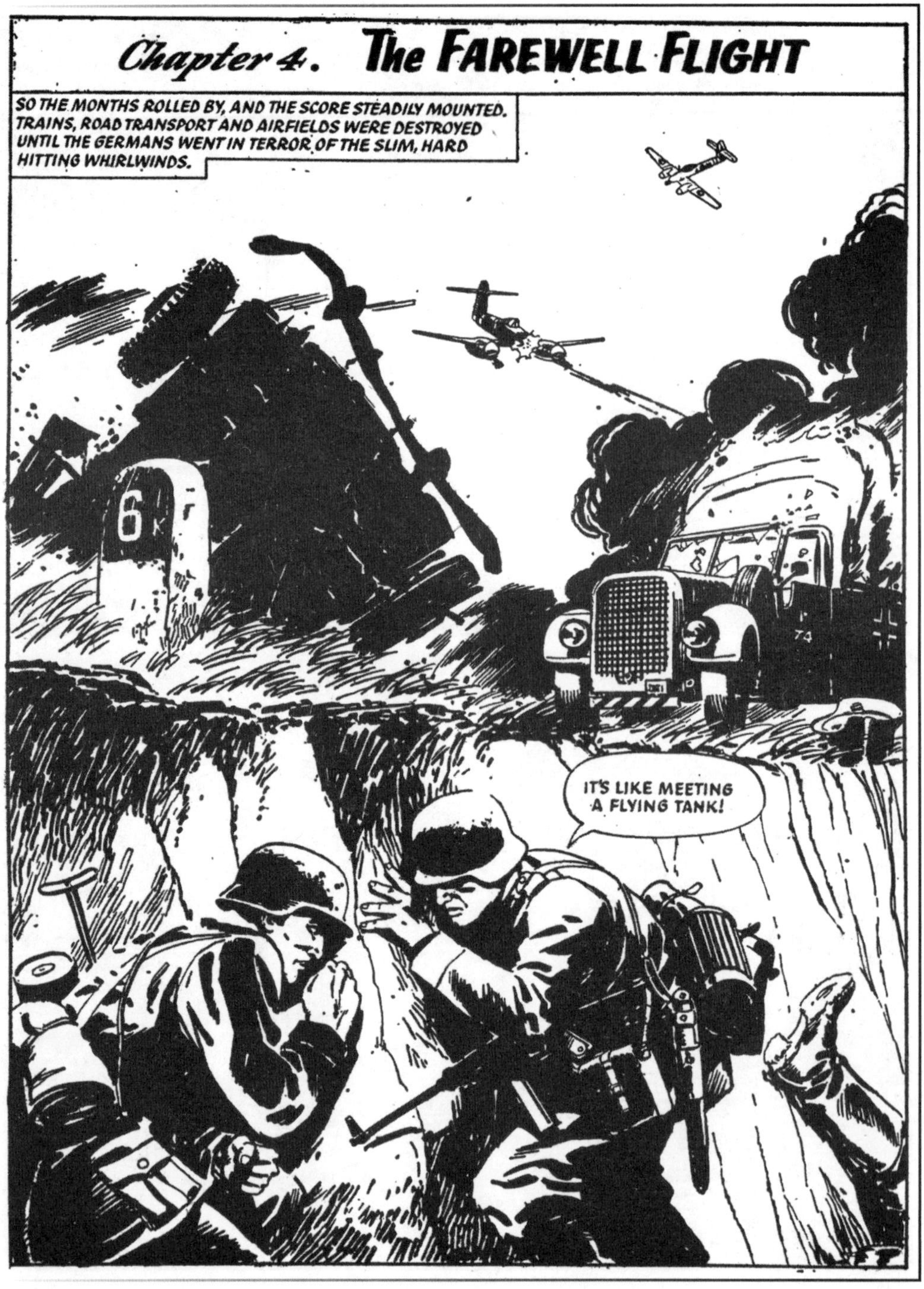
Chapter 4. The FAREWELL FLIGHT
SO THE MONTHS ROLLED BY, AND THE SCORE STEADILY MOUNTED. TRAINS, ROAD TRANSPORT AND AIRFIELDS WERE DESTROYED UNTIL THE GERMANS WENT IN TERROR OF THE SLIM, HARD HITTING WHIRLWINDS.
IT'S LIKE MEETING A FLYING TANK!

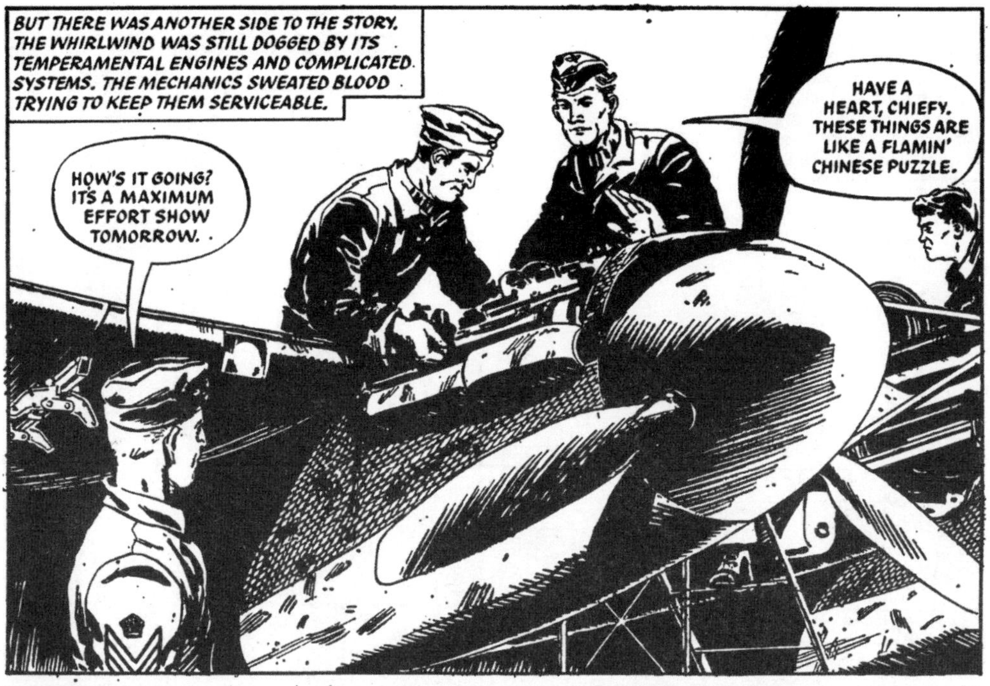
BUT THERE WAS ANOTHER SIDE TO THE STORY. THE WHIRLWIND WAS STILL DOGGED BY ITS TEMPERAMENTAL ENGINES AND COMPLICATED SYSTEMS. THE MECHANICS SWEATED BLOOD TRYING TO KEEP THEM SERVICEABLE.
HOW'S IT GOING? IT'S A MAXIMUM EFFORT SHOW TOMORROW.
HAVE A HEART, CHIEFY. THESE THINGS ARE LIKE A FLAMIN' CHINESE PUZZLE.

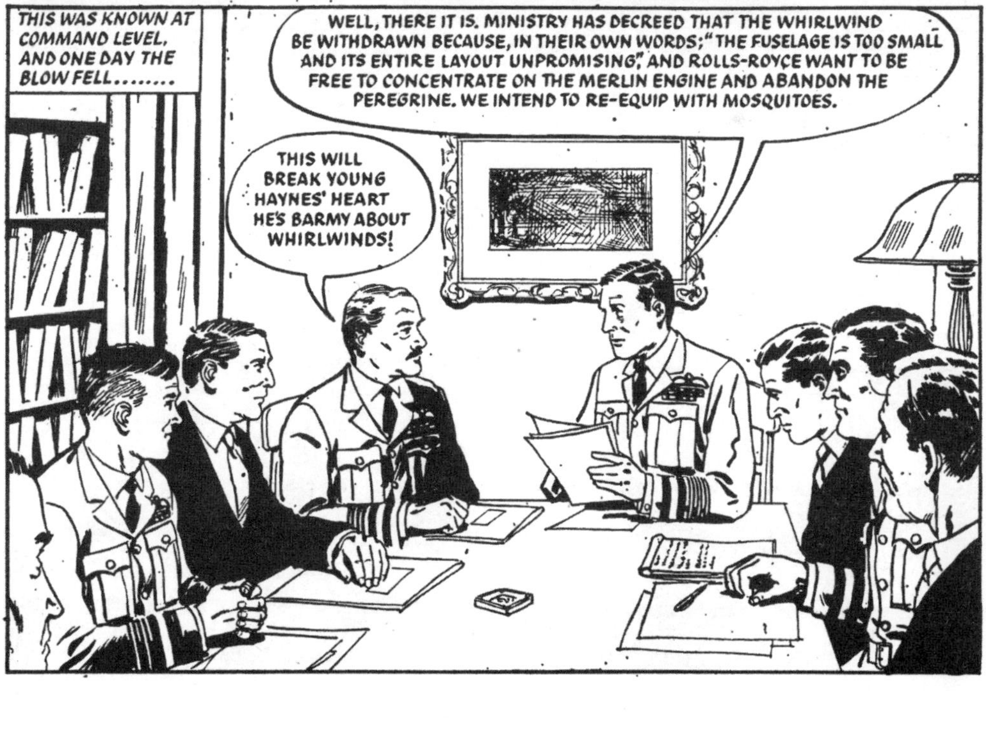
THIS WAS KNOWN AT COMMAND LEVEL, AND ONE DAY THE BLOW FELL........
WELL, THERE IT IS. MINISTRY HAS DECREED THAT THE WHIRLWIND BE WITHDRAWN BECAUSE, IN THEIR OWN WORDS; "THE FUSELAGE IS TOO SMALL AND ITS ENTIRE LAYOUT UNPROMISING," AND ROLLS-ROYCE WANT TO BE FREE TO CONCENTRATE ON THE MERLIN ENGINE AND ABANDON THE PEREGRINE. WE INTEND TO RE-EQUIP WITH MOSQUITOES.
THIS WILL BREAK YOUNG HAYNES' HEART HE'S BARMY ABOUT WHIRLWINDS!

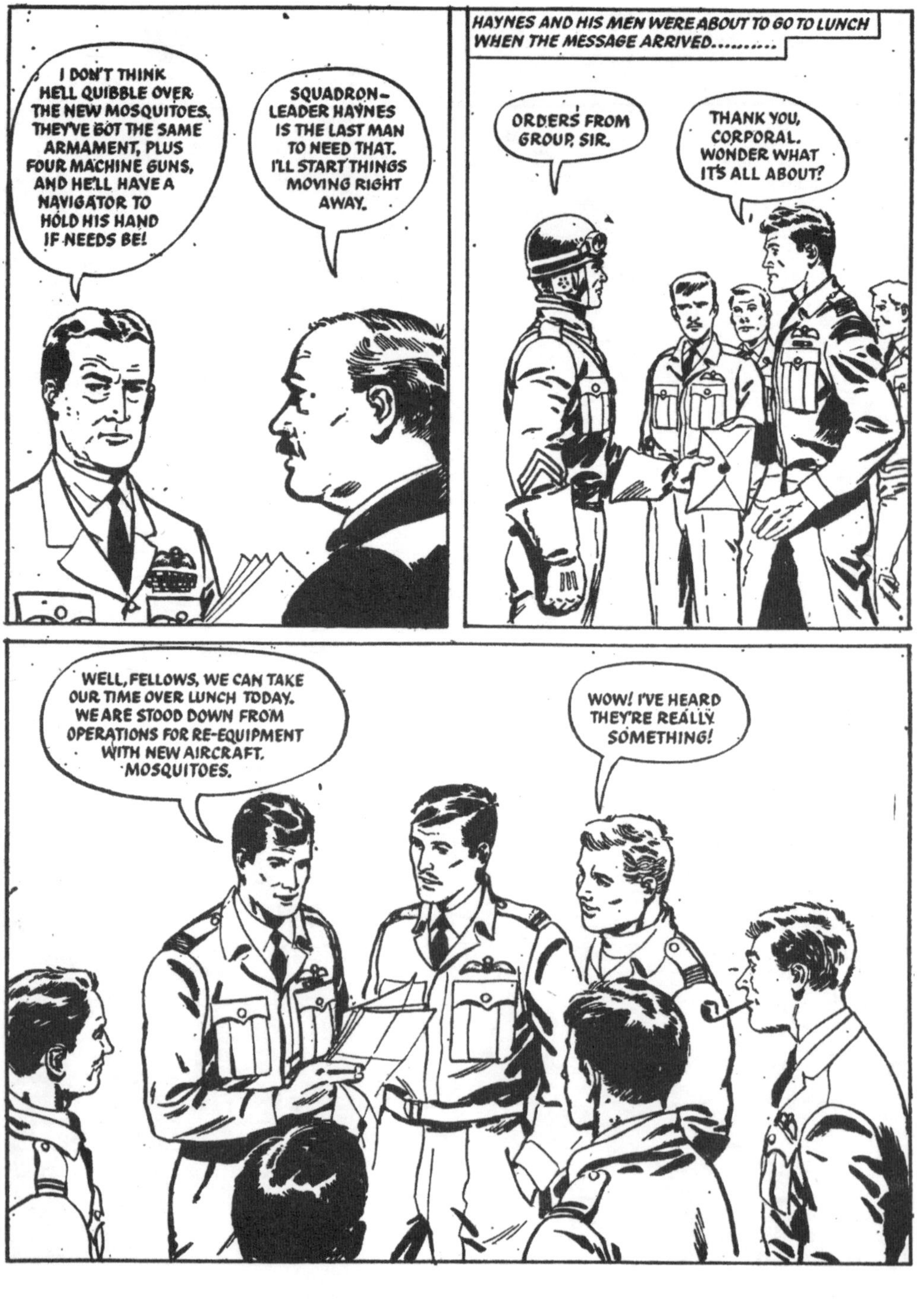
I DON'T THINK HE'LL QUIBBLE OVER THE NEW MOSQUITOES. THEY'VE GOT THE SAME ARMAMENT, PLUS FOUR MACHINE GUNS, AND HE'LL HAVE A NAVIGATOR TO HOLD HIS HAND IF NEEDS BE!
SQUADRON-LEADER HAYNES IS THE LAST MAN TO NEED THAT. I'LL START THINGS MOVING RIGHT AWAY.
HAYNES AND HIS MEN WERE ABOUT TO GO TO LUNCH WHEN THE MESSAGE ARRIVED..........
ORDERS FROM GROUP, SIR.
THANK YOU, CORPORAL. WONDER WHAT IT'S ALL ABOUT?
WELL, FELLOWS, WE CAN TAKE OUR TIME OVER LUNCH TODAY. WE ARE STOOD DOWN FROM OPERATIONS FOR RE-EQUIPMENT WITH NEW AIRCRAFT. MOSQUITOES.
WOW! I'VE HEARD THEY'RE REALLY SOMETHING!

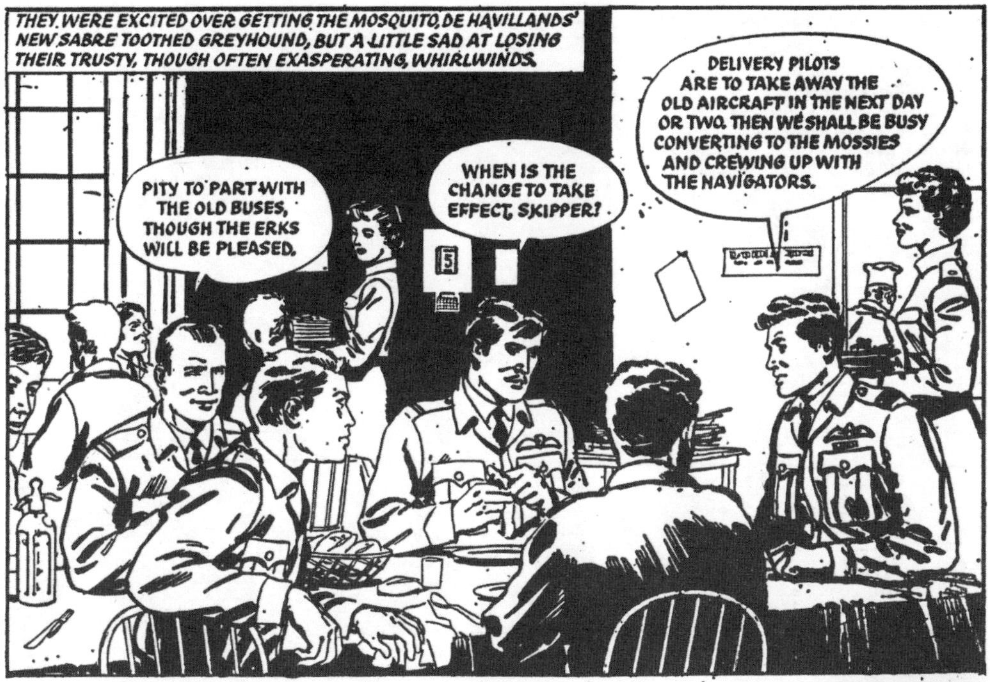
THEY WERE EXCITED OVER GETTING THE MOSQUITO, DE HAVILLANDS' NEW SABRE TOOTHED GREYHOUND, BUT A LITTLE SAD AT LOSING THEIR TRUSTY, THOUGH OFTEN EXASPERATING, WHIRLWINDS.
PITY TO PART WITH THE OLD BUSES, THOUGH THE ERKS WILL BE PLEASED.
WHEN IS THE CHANGE TO TAKE EFFECT, SKIPPER?
DELIVERY PILOTS ARE TO TAKE AWAY THE OLD AIRCRAFT IN THE NEXT DAY OR TWO. THEN WE SHALL BE BUSY CONVERTING TO THE MOSSIES AND CREWING UP WITH THE NAVIGATORS.
5

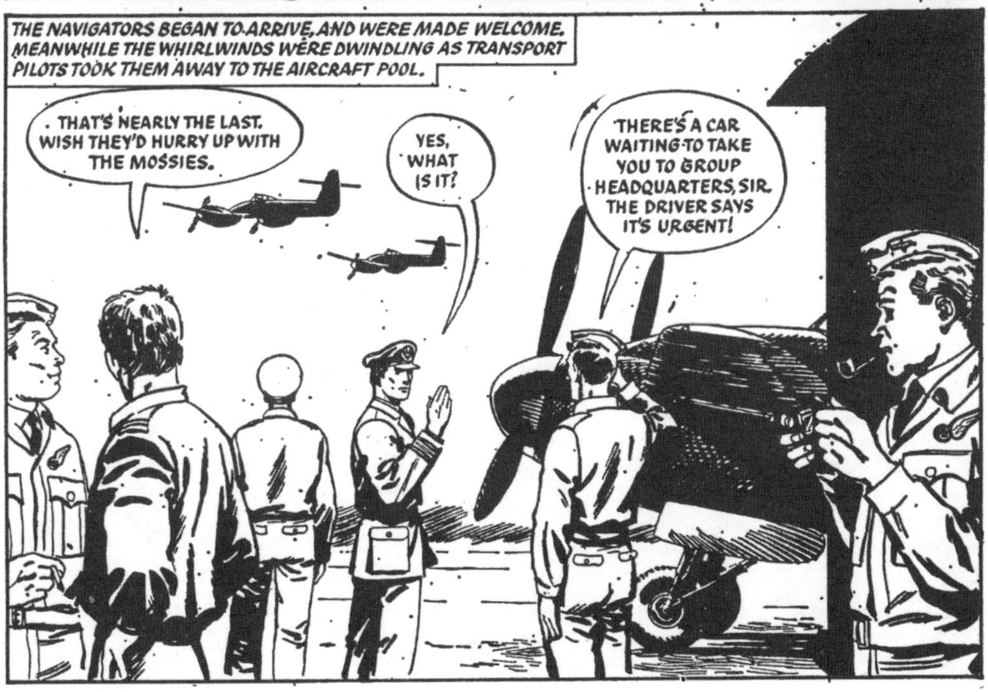
THE NAVIGATORS BEGAN TO ARRIVE, AND WERE MADE WELCOME. MEANWHILE THE WHIRLWINDS WERE DWINDLING AS TRANSPORT PILOTS TOOK THEM AWAY TO THE AIRCRAFT POOL.
THAT'S NEARLY THE LAST. WISH THEY'D HURRY UP WITH THE MOSSIES.
THERE'S A CAR WAITING TO TAKE YOU TO GROUP HEADQUARTERS, SIR. THE DRIVER SAYS IT'S URGENT!
YES, WHAT IS IT?

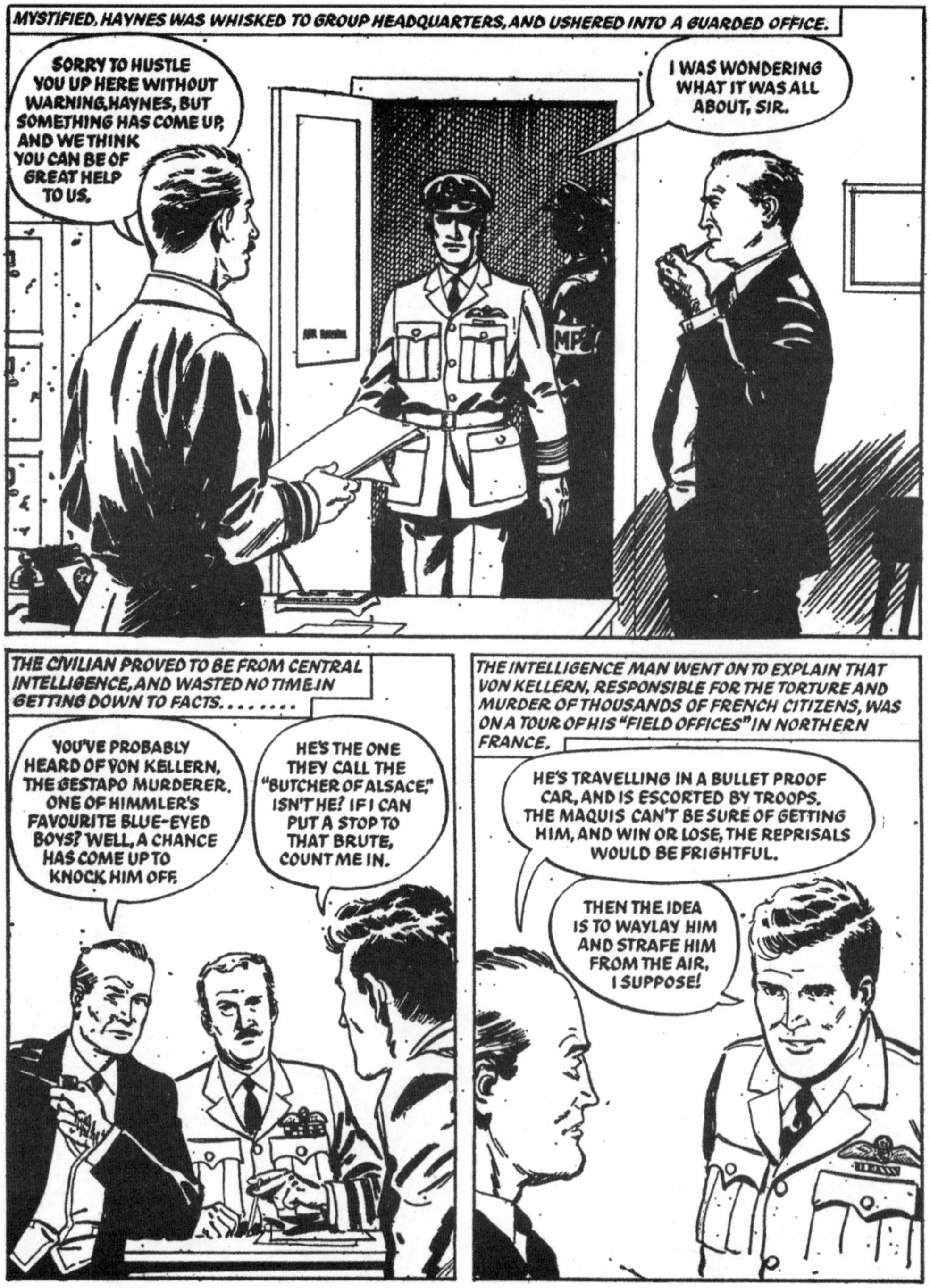
MYSTIFIED, HAYNES WAS WHISKED TO GROUP HEADQUARTERS, AND USHERED INTO A GUARDED OFFICE.
SORRY TO HUSTLE YOU UP HERE WITHOUT WARNING, HAYNES, BUT SOMETHING HAS COME UP, AND WE THINK YOU CAN BE OF GREAT HELP TO US.
I WAS WONDERING WHAT IT WAS ALL ABOUT, SIR.
THE CIVILIAN PROVED TO BE FROM CENTRAL INTELLIGENCE, AND WASTED NO TIME IN GETTING DOWN TO FACTS........
YOU'VE PROBABLY HEARD OF VON KELLERN, THE GESTAPO MURDERER. ONE OF HIMMLER'S FAVOURITE BLUE-EYED BOYS? WELL, A CHANCE HAS COME UP TO KNOCK HIM OFF.
HE'S THE ONE THEY CALL THE "BUTCHER OF ALSACE," ISN'T HE? IF I CAN PUT A STOP TO THAT BRUTE, COUNT ME IN.
THE INTELLIGENCE MAN WENT ON TO EXPLAIN THAT VON KELLERN, RESPONSIBLE FOR THE TORTURE AND MURDER OF THOUSANDS OF FRENCH CITIZENS, WAS ON A TOUR OF HIS "FIELD OFFICES" IN NORTHERN FRANCE.
HE'S TRAVELLING IN A BULLET PROOF CAR, AND IS ESCORTED BY TROOPS. THE MAQUIS CAN'T BE SURE OF GETTING HIM, AND WIN OR LOSE, THE REPRISALS WOULD BE FRIGHTFUL.
THEN THE IDEA IS TO WAYLAY HIM AND STRAFE HIM FROM THE AIR, I SUPPOSE!

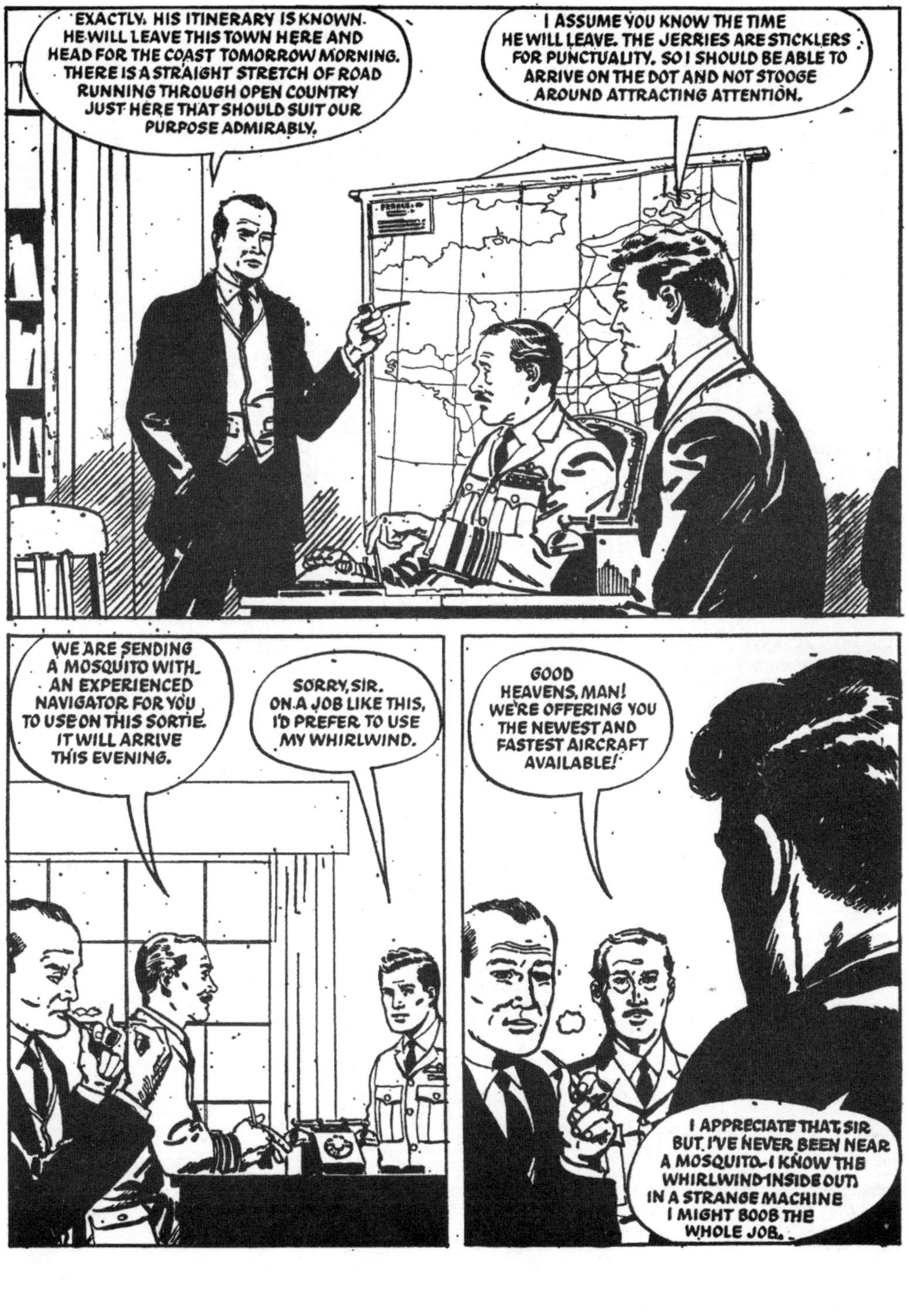
EXACTLY. HIS ITINERARY IS KNOWN. HE WILL LEAVE THIS TOWN HERE AND HEAD FOR THE COAST TOMORROW MORNING. THERE IS A STRAIGHT STRETCH OF ROAD RUNNING THROUGH OPEN COUNTRY JUST HERE THAT SHOULD SUIT OUR PURPOSE ADMIRABLY.
I ASSUME YOU KNOW THE TIME HE WILL LEAVE. THE JERRIES ARE STICKLERS FOR PUNCTUALITY. SO I SHOULD BE ABLE TO ARRIVE ON THE DOT AND NOT STOOGE AROUND ATTRACTING ATTENTION.
WE ARE SENDING A MOSQUITO WITH AN EXPERIENCED NAVIGATOR FOR YOU TO USE ON THIS SORTIE. IT WILL ARRIVE THIS EVENING.
SORRY, SIR. ON A JOB LIKE THIS, I'D PREFER TO USE MY WHIRLWIND.
GOOD HEAVENS, MAN! WE'RE OFFERING YOU THE NEWEST AND FASTEST AIRCRAFT AVAILABLE!
I APPRECIATE THAT, SIR BUT I'VE NEVER BEEN NEAR A MOSQUITO. I KNOW THE WHIRLWIND INSIDE OUT. IN A STRANGE MACHINE I MIGHT BOOB THE WHOLE JOB.

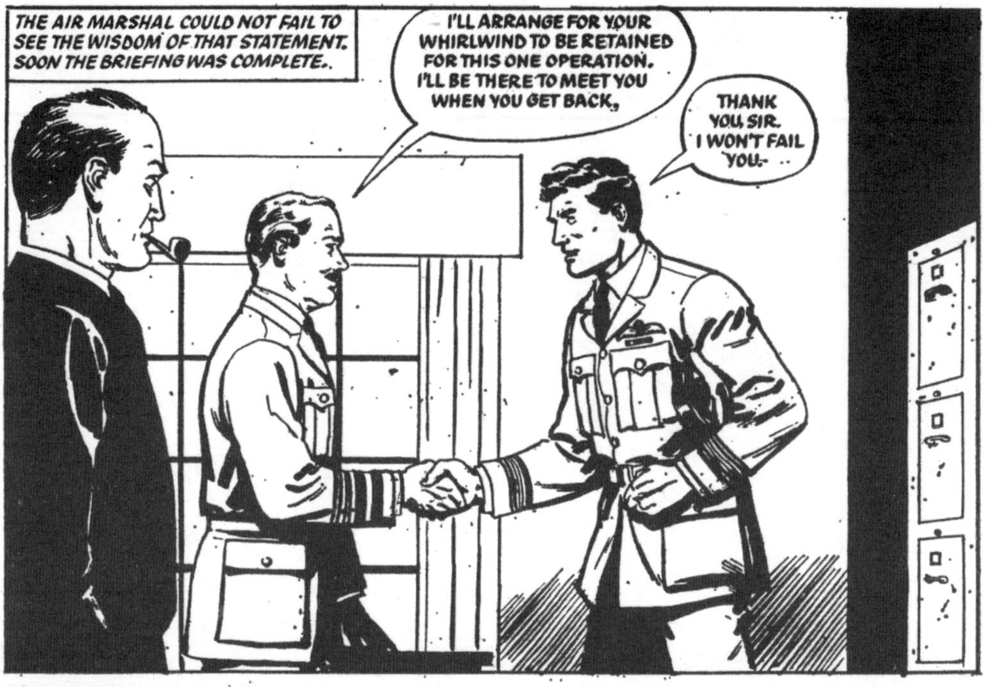
THE AIR MARSHAL COULD NOT FAIL TO SEE THE WISDOM OF THAT STATEMENT. SOON THE BRIEFING WAS COMPLETE..
I'LL ARRANGE FOR YOUR WHIRLWIND TO BE RETAINED FOR THIS ONE OPERATION. I'LL BE THERE TO MEET YOU WHEN YOU GET BACK.
THANK YOU, SIR. I WON'T FAIL YOU.

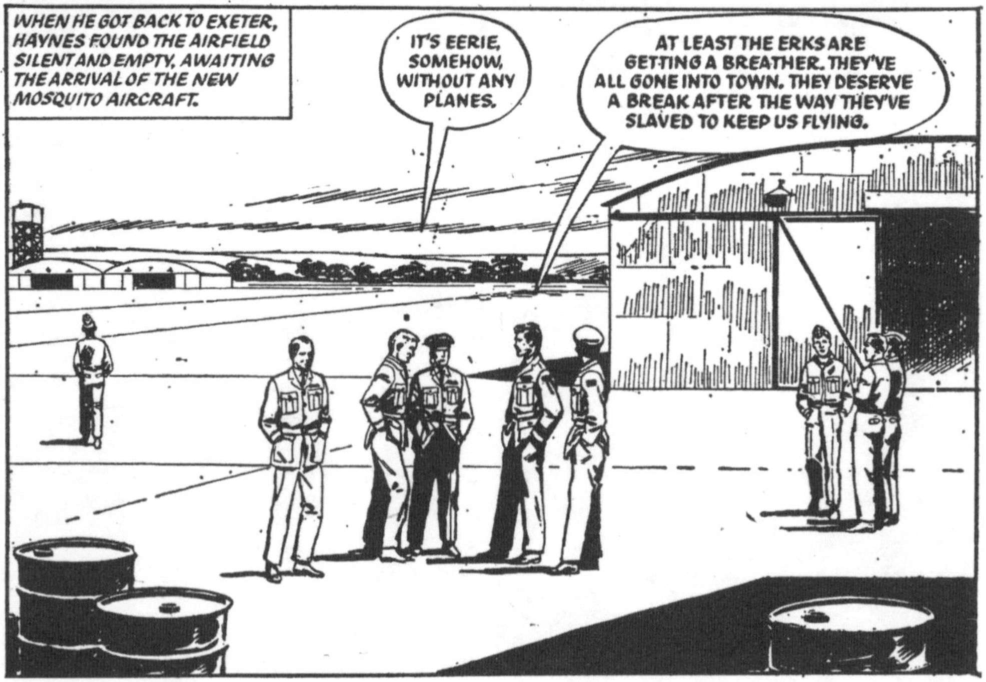
WHEN HE GOT BACK TO EXETER, HAYNES FOUND THE AIRFIELD SILENT AND EMPTY, AWAITING THE ARRIVAL OF THE NEW MOSQUITO AIRCRAFT.
IT'S EERIE, SOMEHOW, WITHOUT ANY PLANES.
AT LEAST THE ERKS ARE GETTING A BREATHER. THEY'VE ALL GONE INTO TOWN. THEY DESERVE A BREAK AFTER THE WAY THEY'VE SLAVED TO KEEP US FLYING.

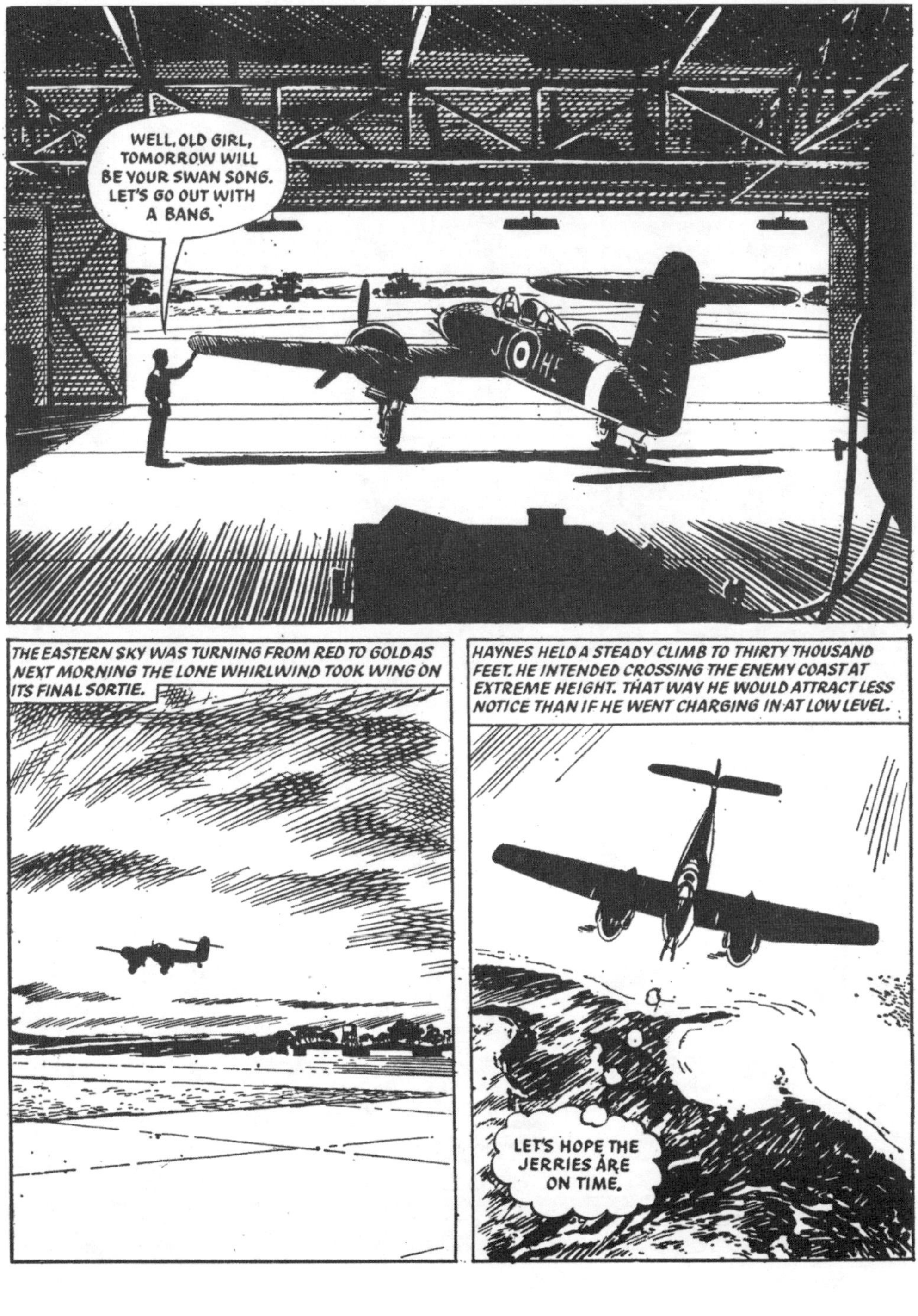
WELL, OLD GIRL, TOMORROW WILL BE YOUR SWAN SONG. LET'S GO OUT WITH A BANG.
THE EASTERN SKY WAS TURNING FROM RED TO GOLD AS NEXT MORNING THE LONE WHIRLWIND TOOK WING ON ITS FINAL SORTIE.
HAYNES HELD A STEADY CLIMB TO THIRTY THOUSAND FEET. HE INTENDED CROSSING THE ENEMY COAST AT EXTREME HEIGHT. THAT WAY HE WOULD ATTRACT LESS NOTICE THAN IF HE WENT CHARGING IN AT LOW LEVEL.
LET'S HOPE THE JERRIES ARE ON TIME.

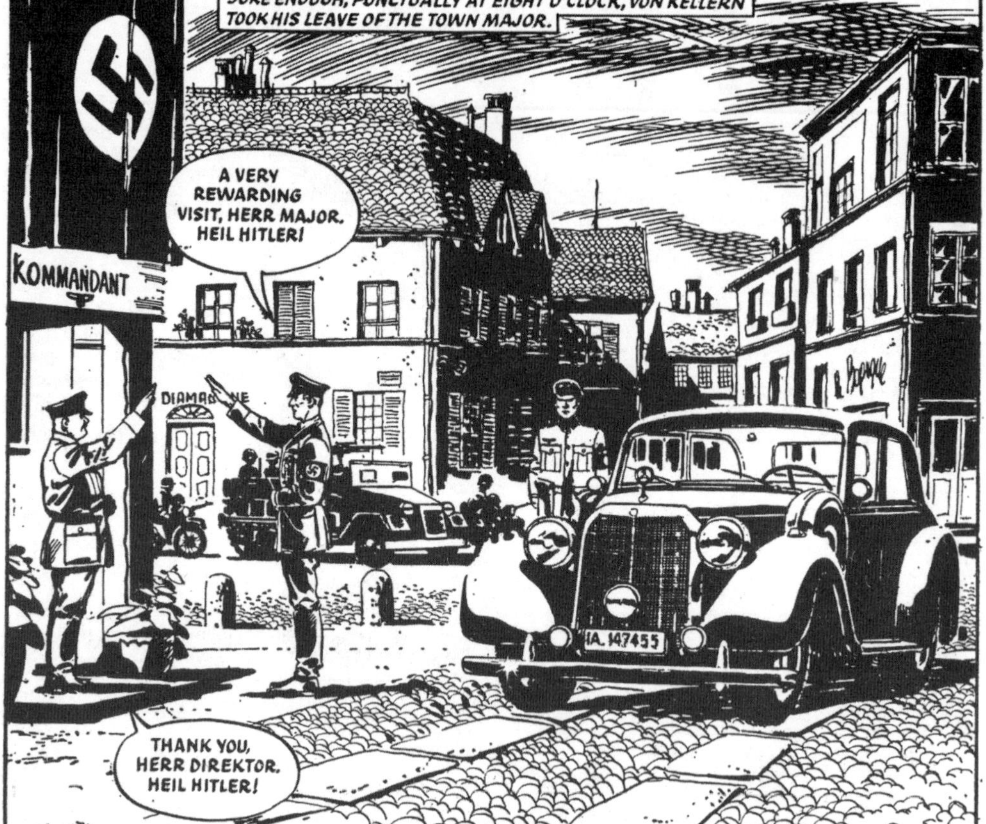
SURE ENOUGH, PUNCTUALLY AT EIGHT O'CLOCK, VON KELLERN TOOK HIS LEAVE OF THE TOWN MAJOR.
KOMMANDANT
A VERY REWARDING VISIT, HERR MAJOR. HEIL HITLER!
THANK YOU, HERR DIREKTOR. HEIL HITLER!
IA. 147455

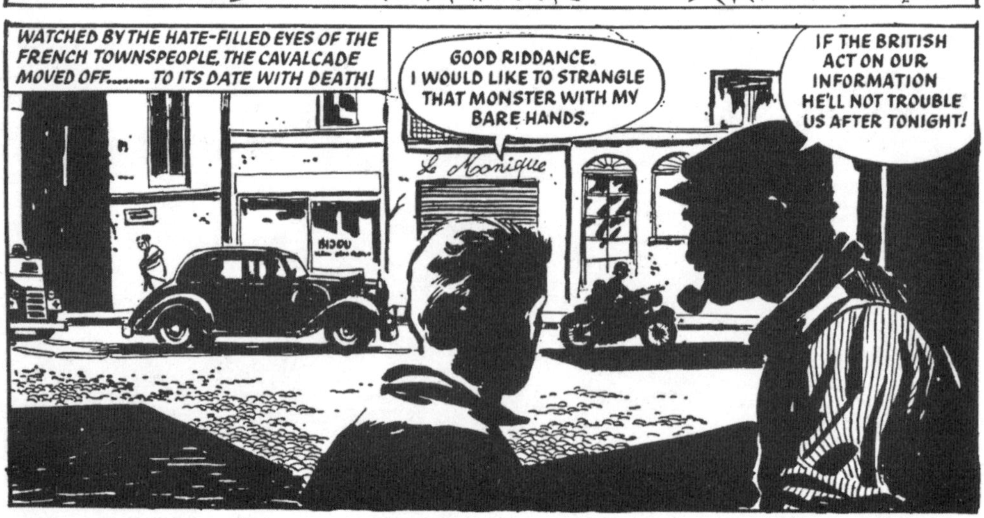
WATCHED BY THE HATE-FILLED EYES OF THE FRENCH TOWNSPEOPLE, THE CAVALCADE MOVED OFF........ TO ITS DATE WITH DEATH!
GOOD RIDDANCE. I WOULD LIKE TO STRANGLE THAT MONSTER WITH MY BARE HANDS.
IF THE BRITISH ACT ON OUR INFORMATION HE'LL NOT TROUBLE US AFTER TONIGHT!
Le Monique

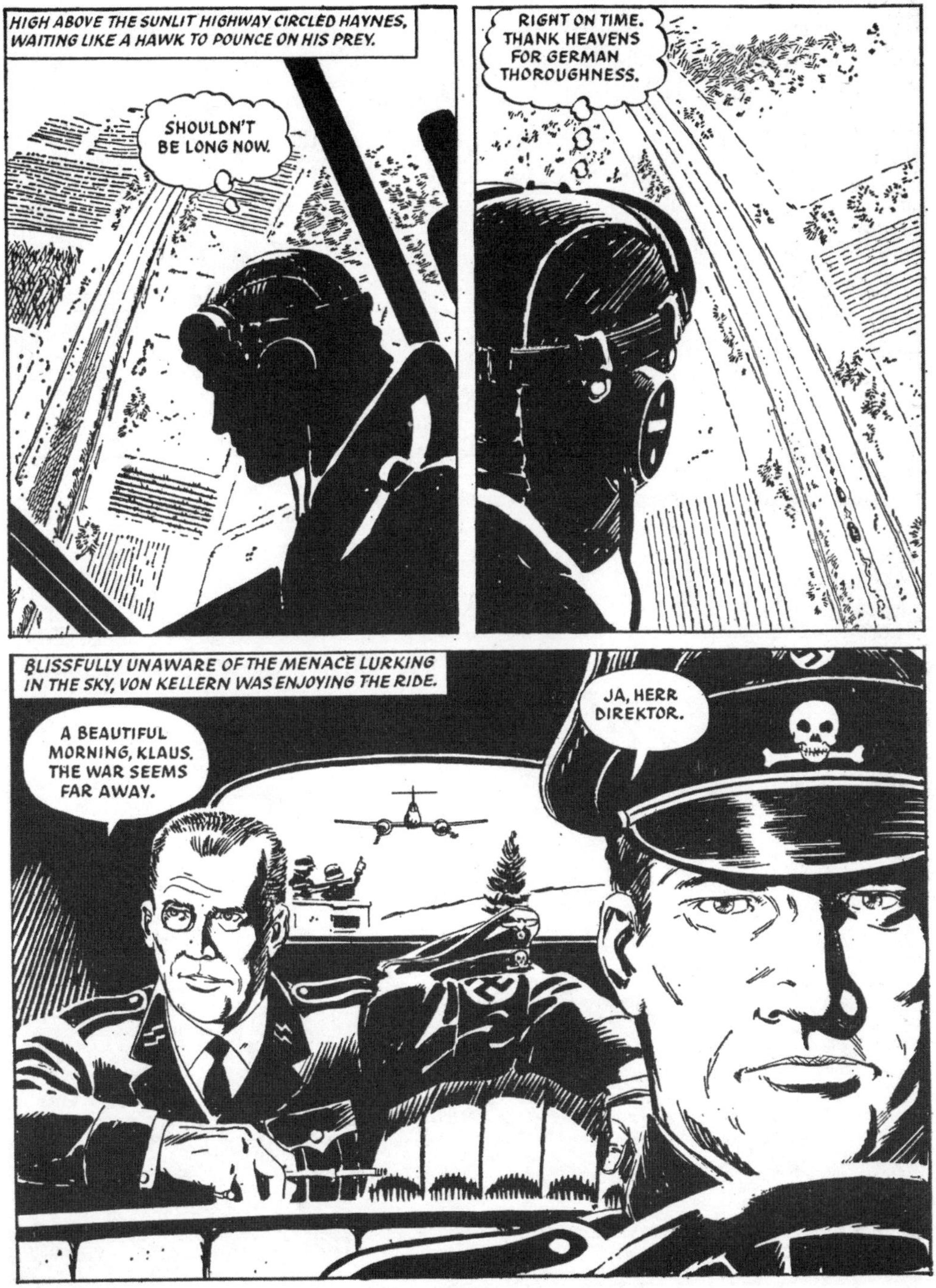
HIGH ABOVE THE SUNLIT HIGHWAY CIRCLED HAYNES, WAITING LIKE A HAWK TO POUNCE ON HIS PREY.
SHOULDN'T BE LONG NOW.
RIGHT ON TIME. THANK HEAVENS FOR GERMAN THOROUGHNESS.
BLISSFULLY UNAWARE OF THE MENACE LURKING IN THE SKY, VON KELLERN WAS ENJOYING THE RIDE.
A BEAUTIFUL MORNING, KLAUS. THE WAR SEEMS FAR AWAY.
JA, HERR DIREKTOR.

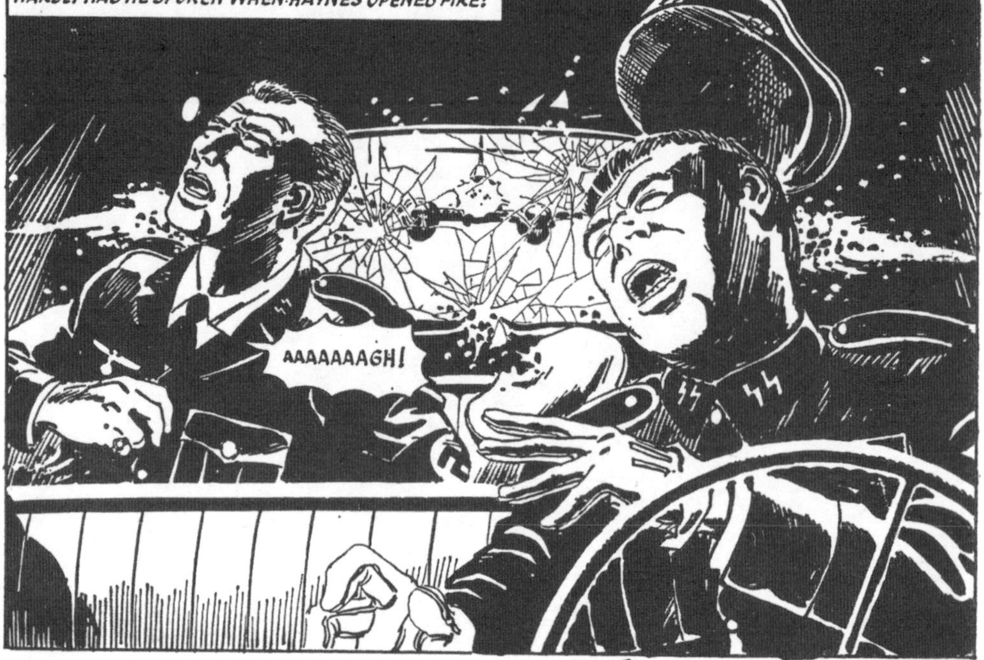
HARDLY HAD HE SPOKEN WHEN HAYNES OPENED FIRE!
AAAAAAAGH!

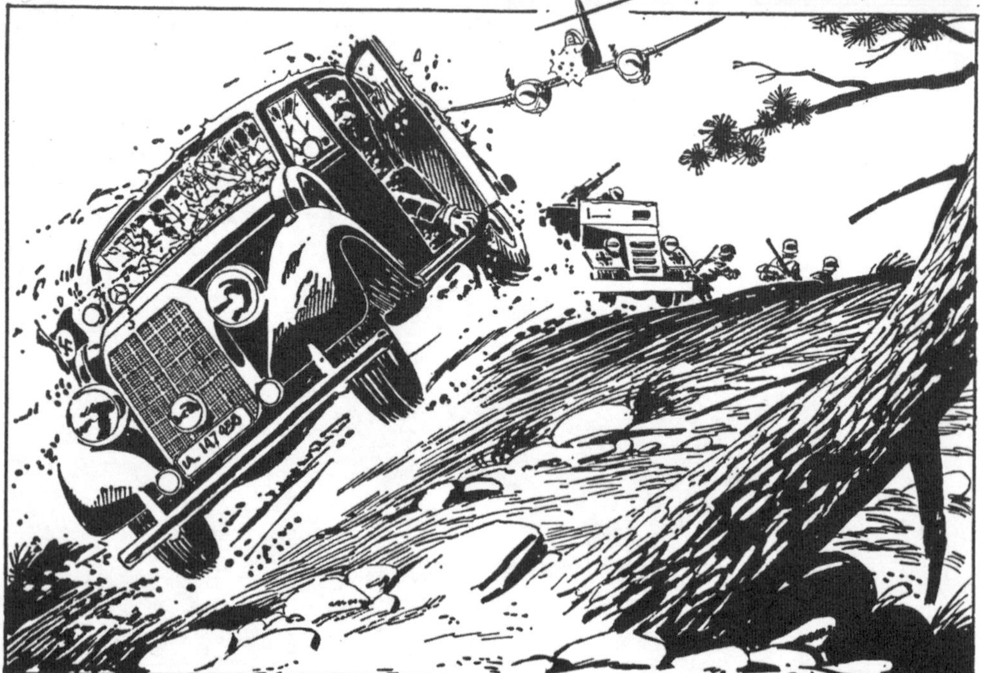

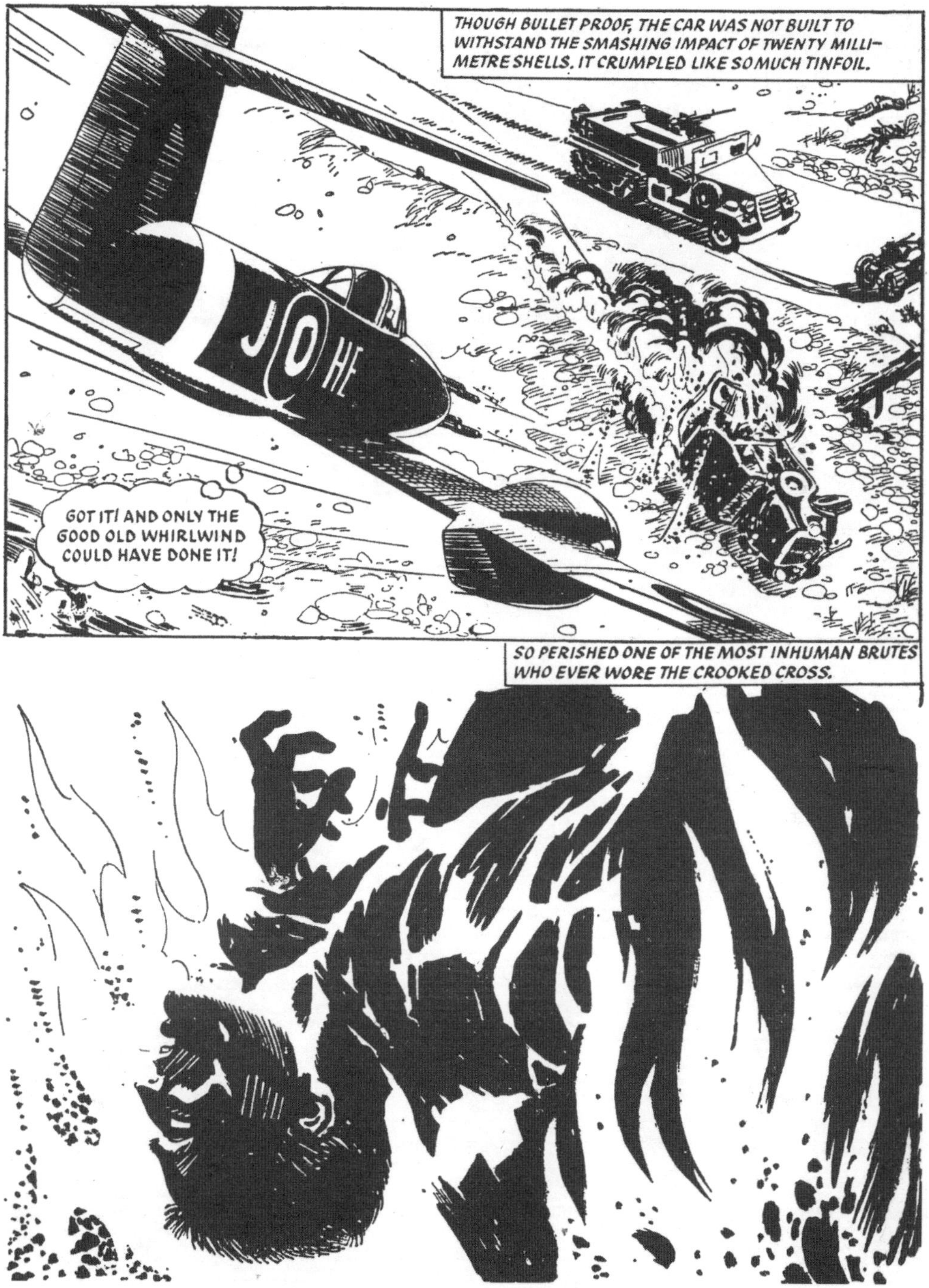
THOUGH BULLET PROOF, THE CAR WAS NOT BUILT TO WITHSTAND THE SMASHING IMPACT OF TWENTY MILLI-METRE SHELLS. IT CRUMPLED LIKE SO MUCH TINFOIL.
GOT IT! AND ONLY THE GOOD OLD WHIRLWIND COULD HAVE DONE IT!
SO PERISHED ONE OF THE MOST INHUMAN BRUTES WHO EVER WORE THE CROOKED CROSS.

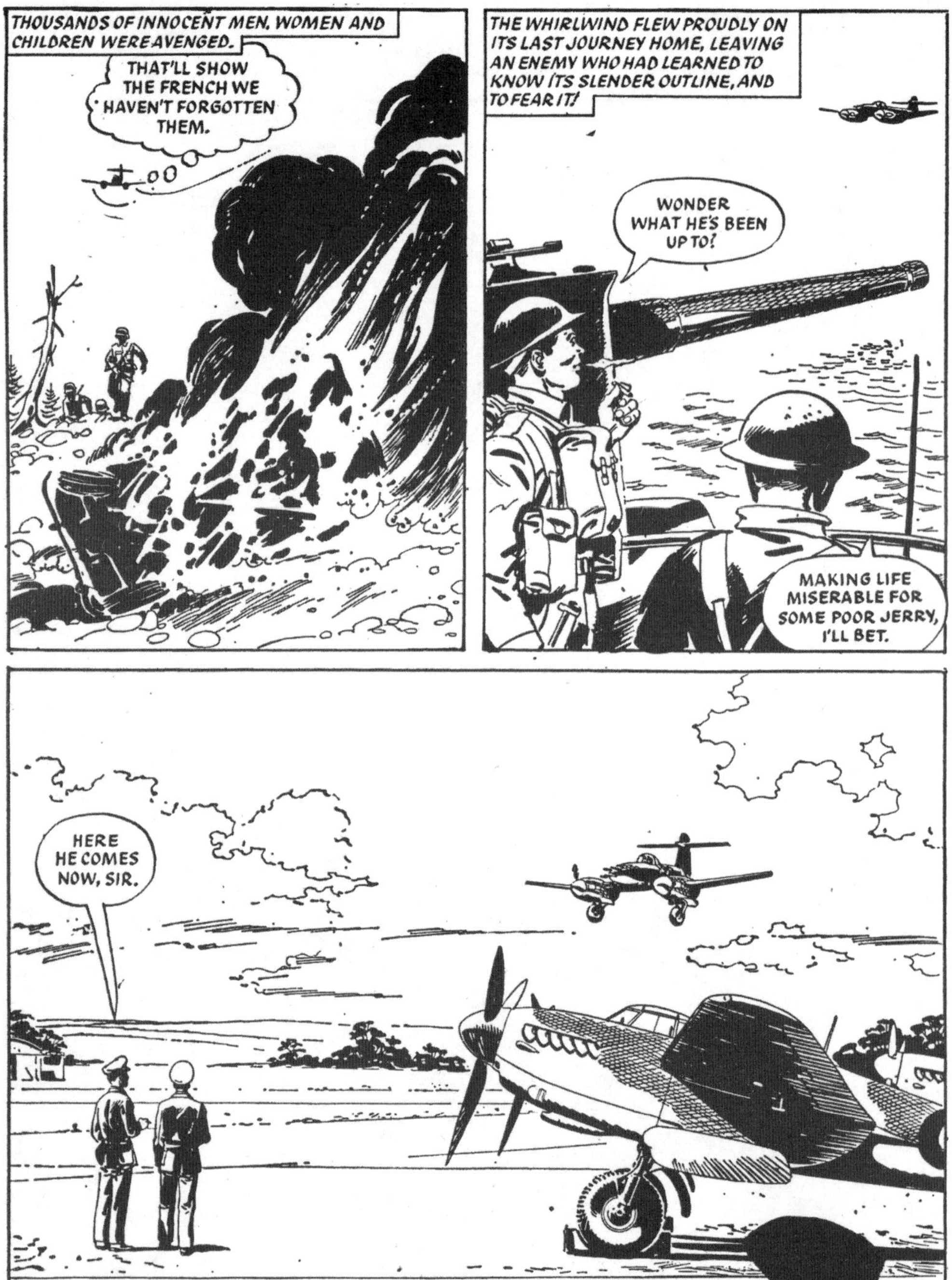
THOUSANDS OF INNOCENT MEN, WOMEN AND CHILDREN WERE AVENGED.
THAT'LL SHOW THE FRENCH WE HAVEN'T FORGOTTEN THEM.
THE WHIRLWIND FLEW PROUDLY ON ITS LAST JOURNEY HOME, LEAVING AN ENEMY WHO HAD LEARNED TO KNOW ITS SLENDER OUTLINE, AND TO FEAR IT!
WONDER WHAT HE'S BEEN UP TO?
MAKING LIFE MISERABLE FOR SOME POOR JERRY, I'LL BET.
HERE HE COMES NOW, SIR.

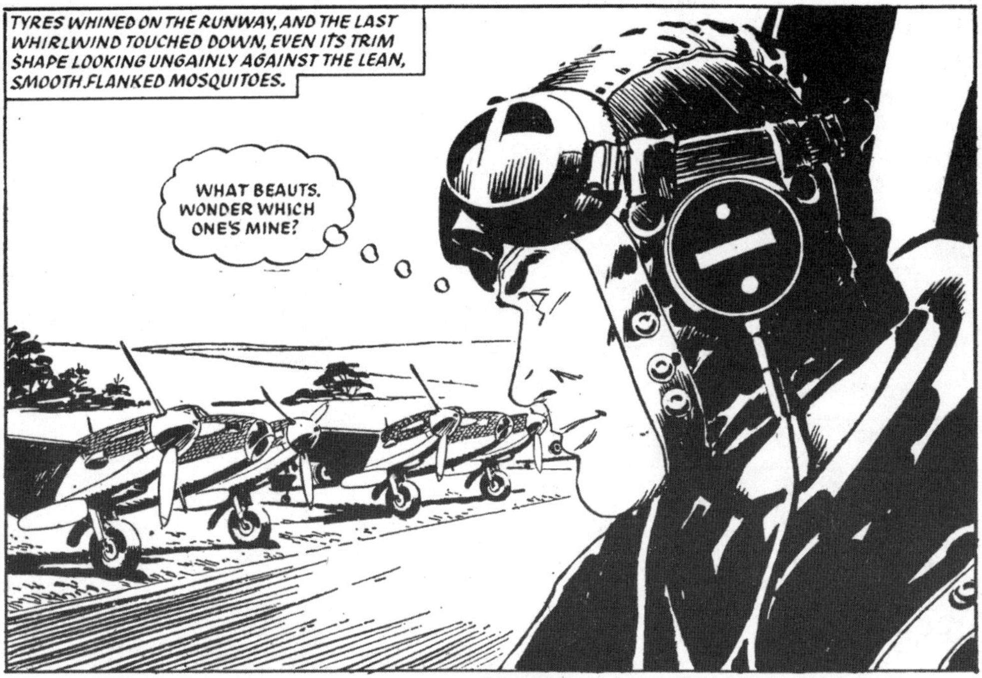
TYRES WHINED ON THE RUNWAY, AND THE LAST WHIRLWIND TOUCHED DOWN, EVEN ITS TRIM SHAPE LOOKING UNGAINLY AGAINST THE LEAN, SMOOTH-FLANKED MOSQUITOES.
WHAT BEAUTS. WONDER WHICH ONE'S MINE?

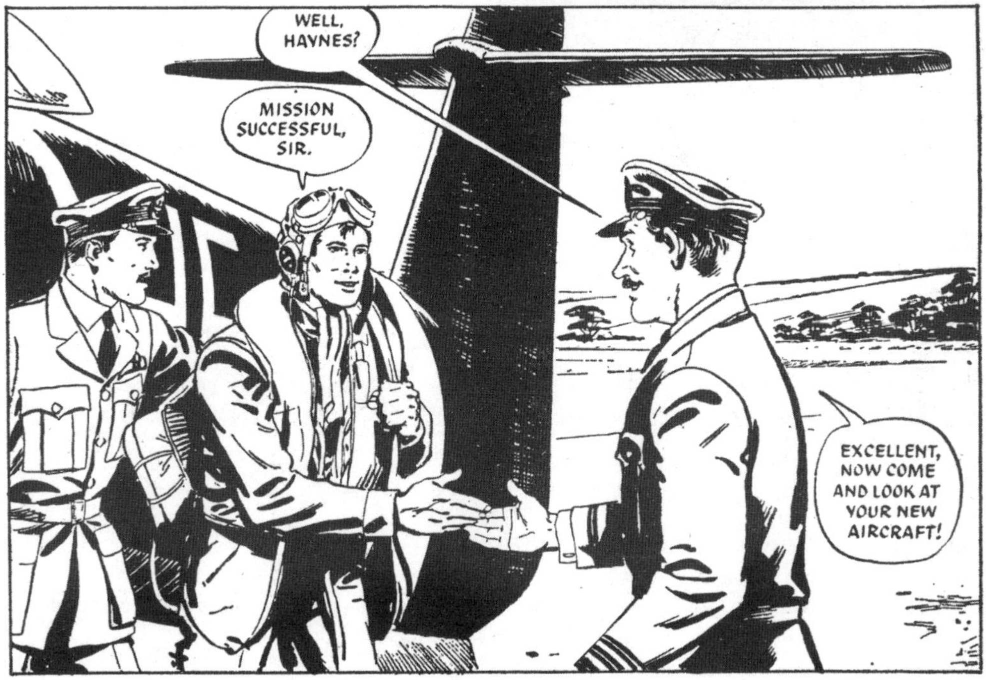
WELL, HAYNES?
MISSION SUCCESSFUL, SIR.
EXCELLENT, NOW COME AND LOOK AT YOUR NEW AIRCRAFT!

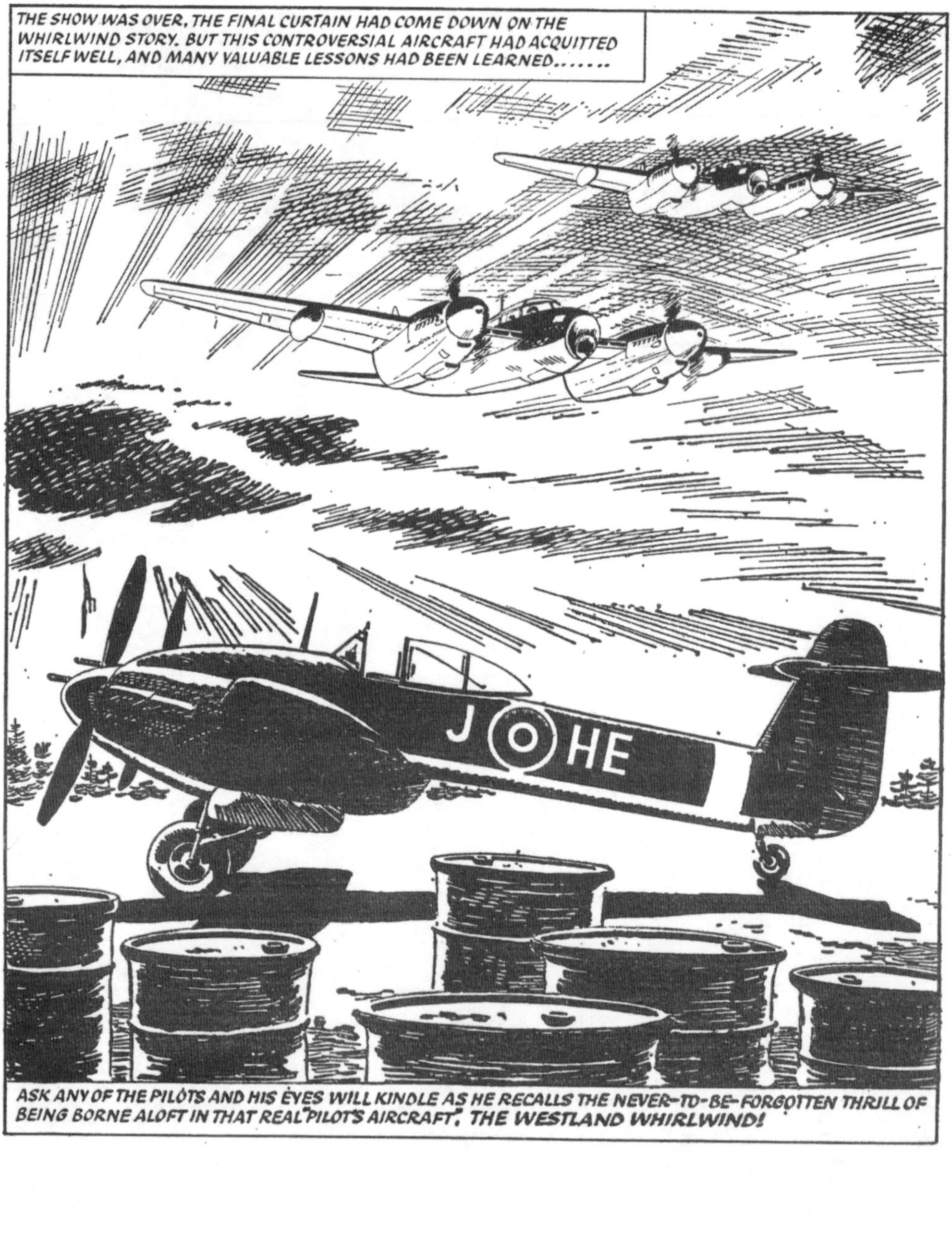
THE SHOW WAS OVER, THE FINAL CURTAIN HAD COME DOWN ON THE WHIRLWIND STORY. BUT THIS CONTROVERSIAL AIRCRAFT HAD ACQUITTED ITSELF WELL, AND MANY VALUABLE LESSONS HAD BEEN LEARNED.......
J HE
ASK ANY OF THE PILOTS AND HIS EYES WILL KINDLE AS HE RECALLS THE NEVER-TO-BE-FORGOTTEN THRILL OF BEING BORNE ALOFT IN THAT REAL "PILOT'S AIRCRAFT". THE WESTLAND WHIRLWIND!

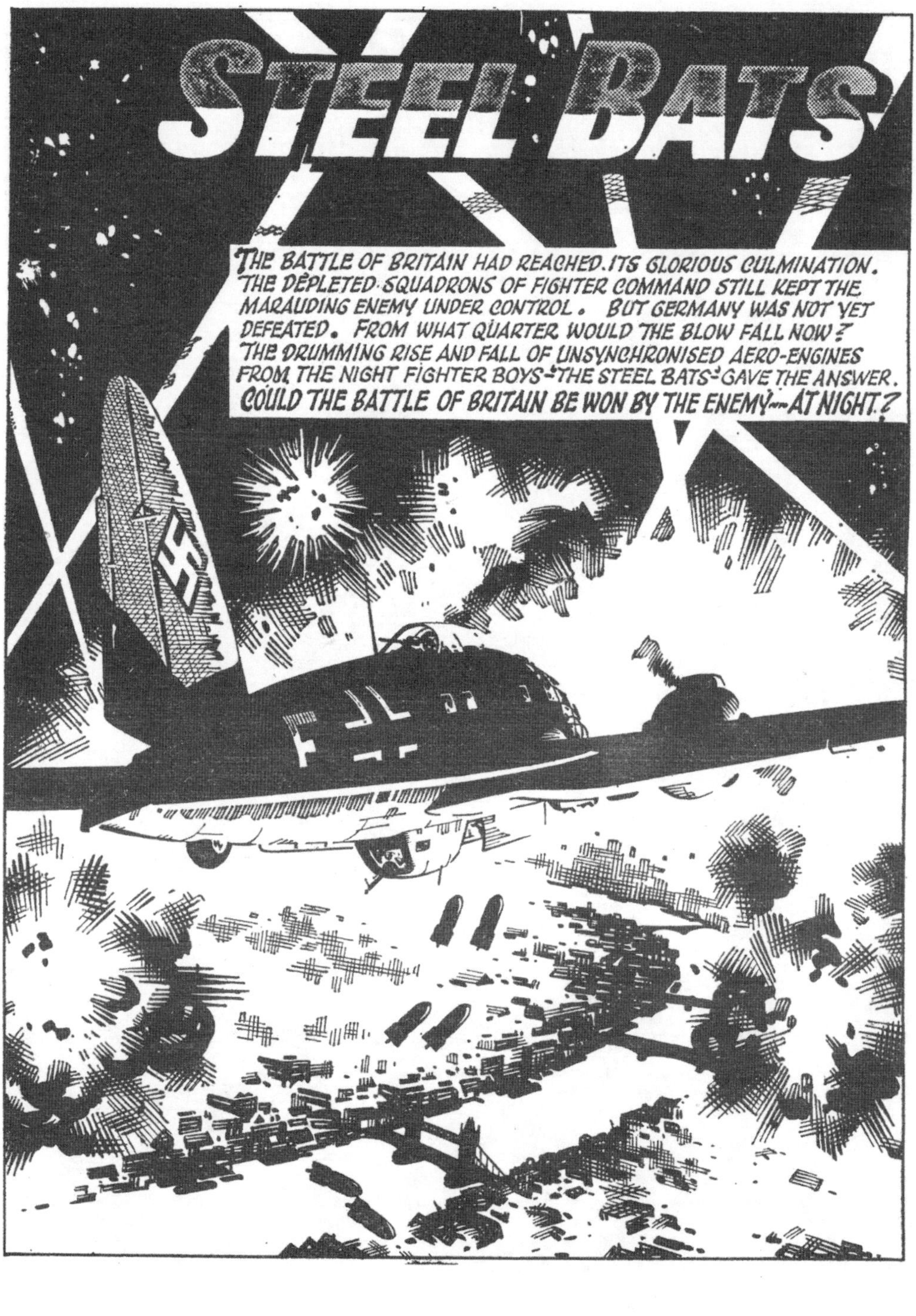
STEEL BATS
THE BATTLE OF BRITAIN HAD REACHED ITS GLORIOUS CULMINATION. THE DEPLETED SQUADRONS OF FIGHTER COMMAND STILL KEPT THE MARAUDING ENEMY UNDER CONTROL. BUT GERMANY WAS NOT YET DEFEATED. FROM WHAT QUARTER WOULD THE BLOW FALL NOW? THE DRUMMING RISE AND FALL OF UNSYNCHRONISED AERO-ENGINES FROM THE NIGHT FIGHTER BOYS—THE STEEL BATS—GAVE THE ANSWER. COULD THE BATTLE OF BRITAIN BE WON BY THE ENEMY—AT NIGHT?

Chapter 1. THE REBEL

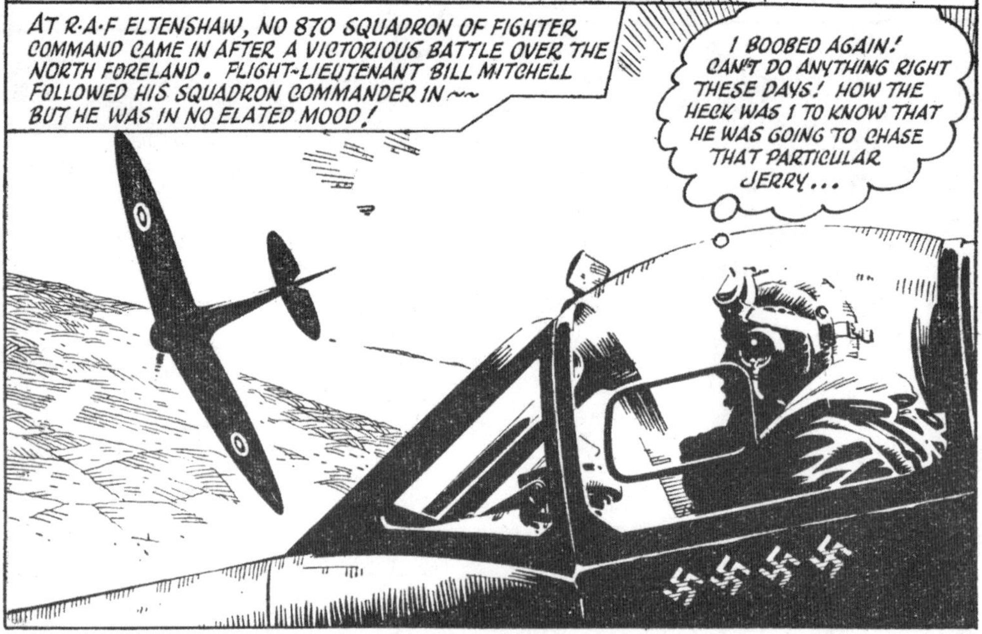
AT R.A.F ELTENSHAW, NO 870 SQUADRON OF FIGHTER COMMAND CAME IN AFTER A VICTORIOUS BATTLE OVER THE NORTH FORELAND. FLIGHT-LIEUTENANT BILL MITCHELL FOLLOWED HIS SQUADRON COMMANDER IN~~ BUT HE WAS IN NO ELATED MOOD!
I BOOBED AGAIN! CAN'T DO ANYTHING RIGHT THESE DAYS! HOW THE HECK WAS I TO KNOW THAT HE WAS GOING TO CHASE THAT PARTICULAR JERRY...

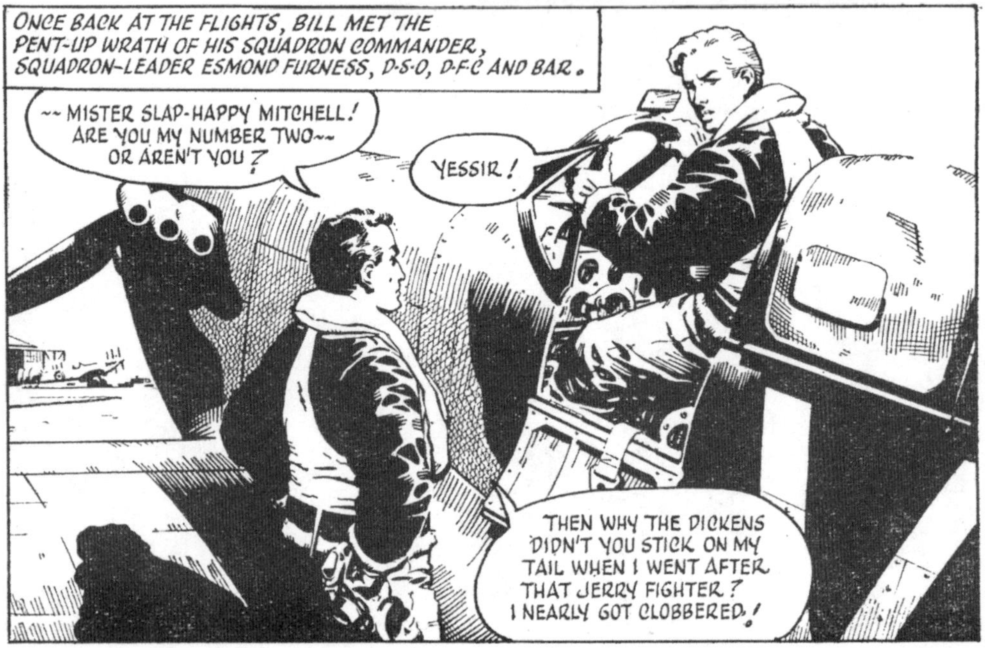
ONCE BACK AT THE FLIGHTS, BILL MET THE PENT-UP WRATH OF HIS SQUADRON COMMANDER, SQUADRON-LEADER ESMOND FURNESS, D.S.O, D.F.C AND BAR.
~~ MISTER SLAP-HAPPY MITCHELL! ARE YOU MY NUMBER TWO~~ OR AREN'T YOU?
YESSIR!
THEN WHY THE DICKENS DIDN'T YOU STICK ON MY TAIL WHEN I WENT AFTER THAT JERRY FIGHTER? I NEARLY GOT CLOBBERED!

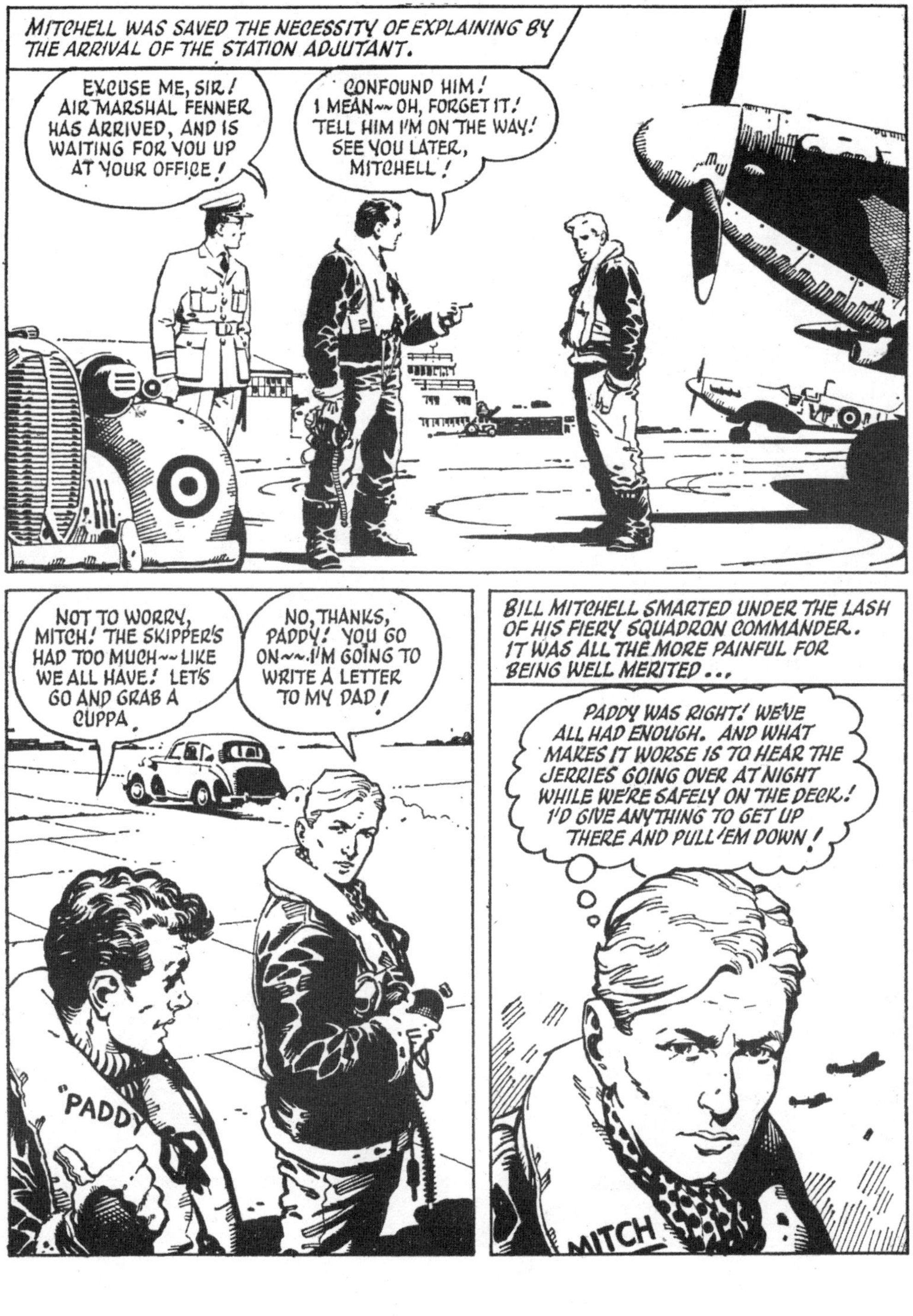
MITCHELL WAS SAVED THE NECESSITY OF EXPLAINING BY THE ARRIVAL OF THE STATION ADJUTANT.
EXCUSE ME, SIR! AIR MARSHAL FENNER HAS ARRIVED, AND IS WAITING FOR YOU UP AT YOUR OFFICE!
CONFOUND HIM! I MEAN~~ OH, FORGET IT! TELL HIM I'M ON THE WAY! SEE YOU LATER, MITCHELL!
NOT TO WORRY, MITCH! THE SKIPPER'S HAD TOO MUCH~~ LIKE WE ALL HAVE! LET'S GO AND GRAB A CUPPA.
NO, THANKS, PADDY! YOU GO ON~~. I'M GOING TO WRITE A LETTER TO MY DAD!
"PADDY
BILL MITCHELL SMARTED UNDER THE LASH OF HIS FIERY SQUADRON COMMANDER. IT WAS ALL THE MORE PAINFUL FOR BEING WELL MERITED...
PADDY WAS RIGHT! WE'VE ALL HAD ENOUGH. AND WHAT MAKES IT WORSE IS TO HEAR THE JERRIES GOING OVER AT NIGHT WHILE WE'RE SAFELY ON THE DECK! I'D GIVE ANYTHING TO GET UP THERE AND PULL 'EM DOWN!
MITCH

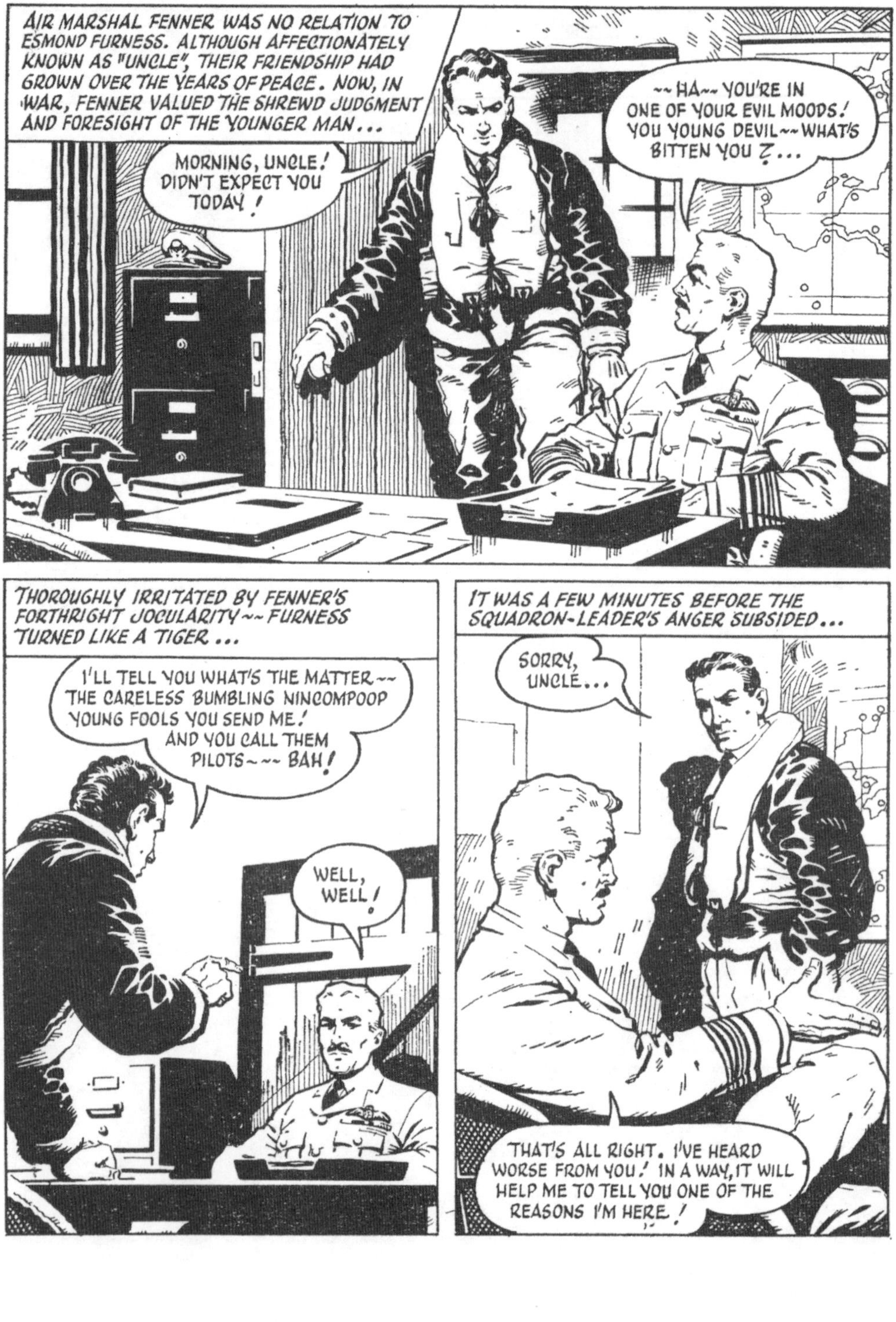
AIR MARSHAL FENNER WAS NO RELATION TO ESMOND FURNESS. ALTHOUGH AFFECTIONATELY KNOWN AS "UNCLE", THEIR FRIENDSHIP HAD GROWN OVER THE YEARS OF PEACE. NOW, IN WAR, FENNER VALUED THE SHREWD JUDGMENT AND FORESIGHT OF THE YOUNGER MAN...
MORNING, UNCLE! DIDN'T EXPECT YOU TODAY!
~~HA~~ YOU'RE IN ONE OF YOUR EVIL MOODS! YOU YOUNG DEVIL~~WHAT'S BITTEN YOU?...
THOROUGHLY IRRITATED BY FENNER'S FORTHRIGHT JOCULARITY~~FURNESS TURNED LIKE A TIGER...
I'LL TELL YOU WHAT'S THE MATTER~~ THE CARELESS BUMBLING NINCOMPOOP YOUNG FOOLS YOU SEND ME! AND YOU CALL THEM PILOTS~~~ BAH!
WELL, WELL!
IT WAS A FEW MINUTES BEFORE THE SQUADRON-LEADER'S ANGER SUBSIDED...
SORRY, UNCLE...
THAT'S ALL RIGHT. I'VE HEARD WORSE FROM YOU! IN A WAY, IT WILL HELP ME TO TELL YOU ONE OF THE REASONS I'M HERE!

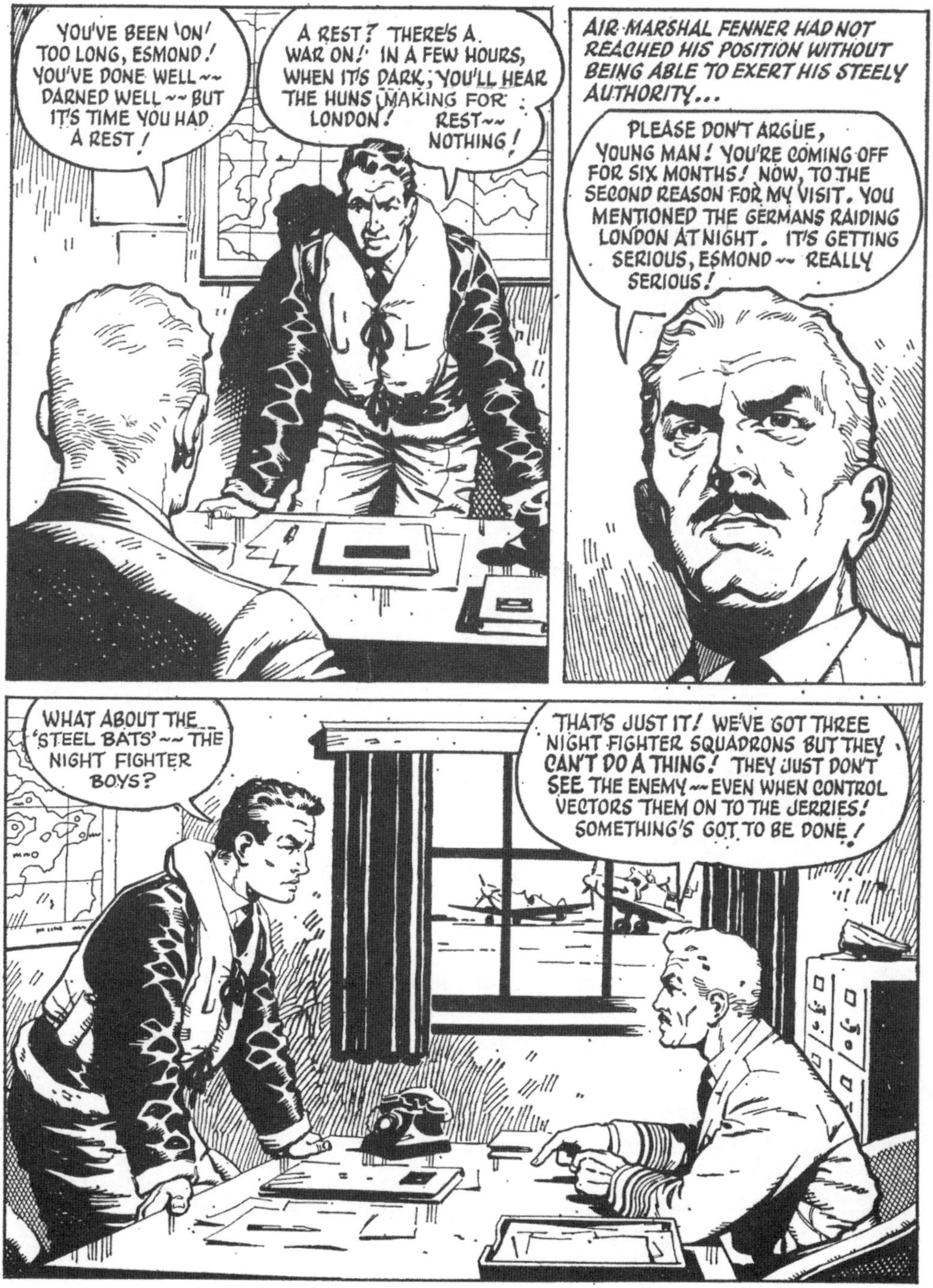
YOU'VE BEEN 'ON' TOO LONG, ESMOND! YOU'VE DONE WELL -- DARNED WELL -- BUT IT'S TIME YOU HAD A REST!
A REST? THERE'S A WAR ON! IN A FEW HOURS, WHEN IT'S DARK, YOU'LL HEAR THE HUNS MAKING FOR LONDON! REST -- NOTHING!
AIR MARSHAL FENNER HAD NOT REACHED HIS POSITION WITHOUT BEING ABLE TO EXERT HIS STEELY AUTHORITY...
PLEASE DON'T ARGUE, YOUNG MAN! YOU'RE COMING OFF FOR SIX MONTHS! NOW, TO THE SECOND REASON FOR MY VISIT. YOU MENTIONED THE GERMANS RAIDING LONDON AT NIGHT. IT'S GETTING SERIOUS, ESMOND -- REALLY SERIOUS!
WHAT ABOUT THE 'STEEL BATS' -- THE NIGHT FIGHTER BOYS?
THAT'S JUST IT! WE'VE GOT THREE NIGHT FIGHTER SQUADRONS BUT THEY CAN'T DO A THING! THEY JUST DON'T SEE THE ENEMY -- EVEN WHEN CONTROL VECTORS THEM ON TO THE JERRIES! SOMETHING'S GOT TO BE DONE!

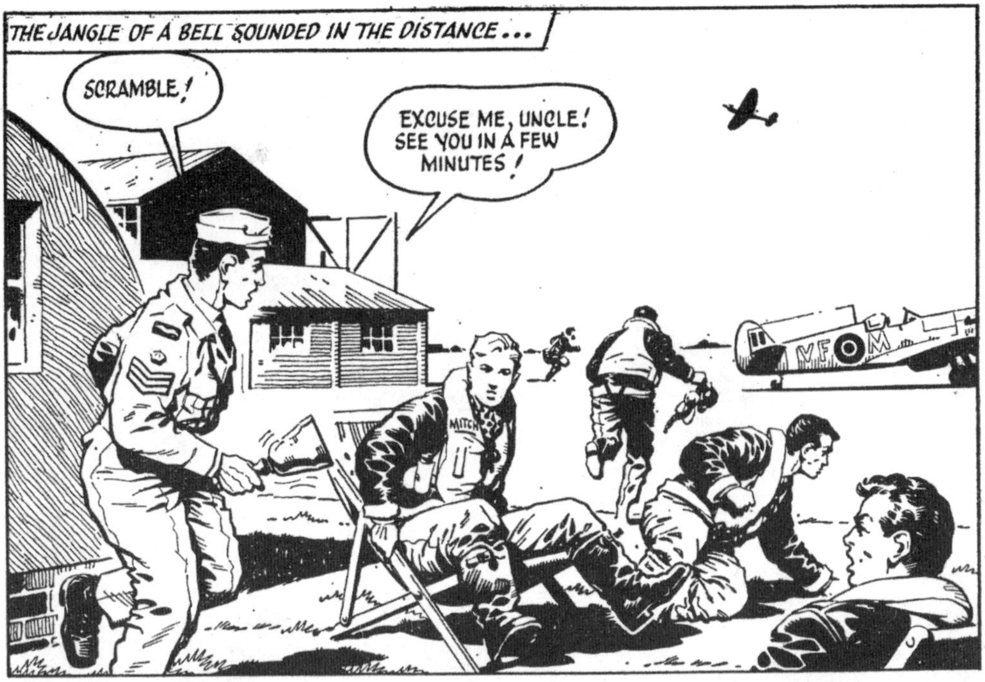
THE JANGLE OF A BELL SOUNDED IN THE DISTANCE ...
SCRAMBLE!
EXCUSE ME, UNCLE! SEE YOU IN A FEW MINUTES!
MITCH

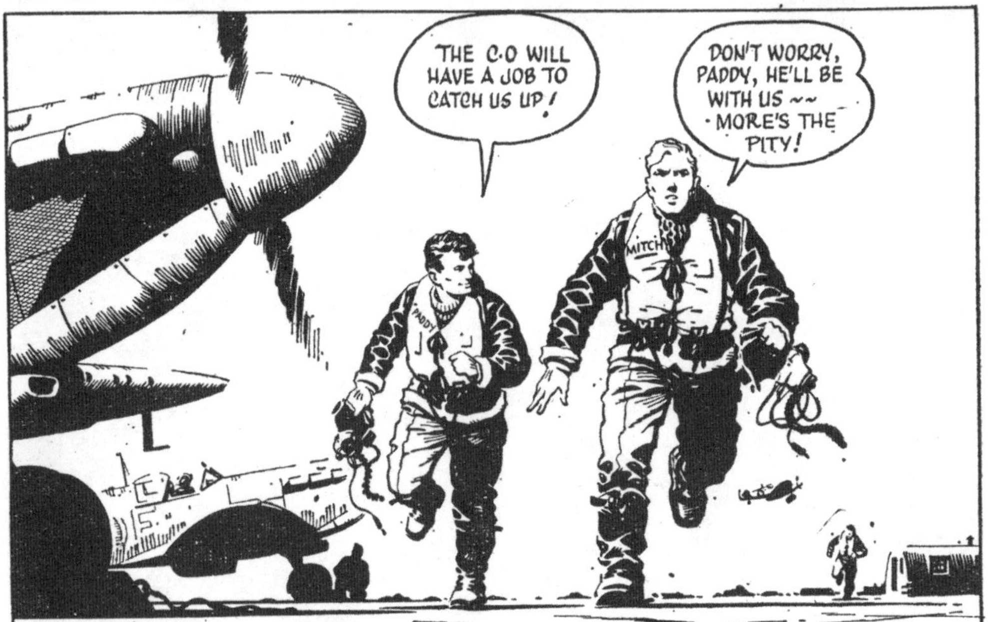
THE C·O WILL HAVE A JOB TO CATCH US UP!
DON'T WORRY, PADDY, HE'LL BE WITH US ~~ MORE'S THE PITY!
PADDY
MITCH

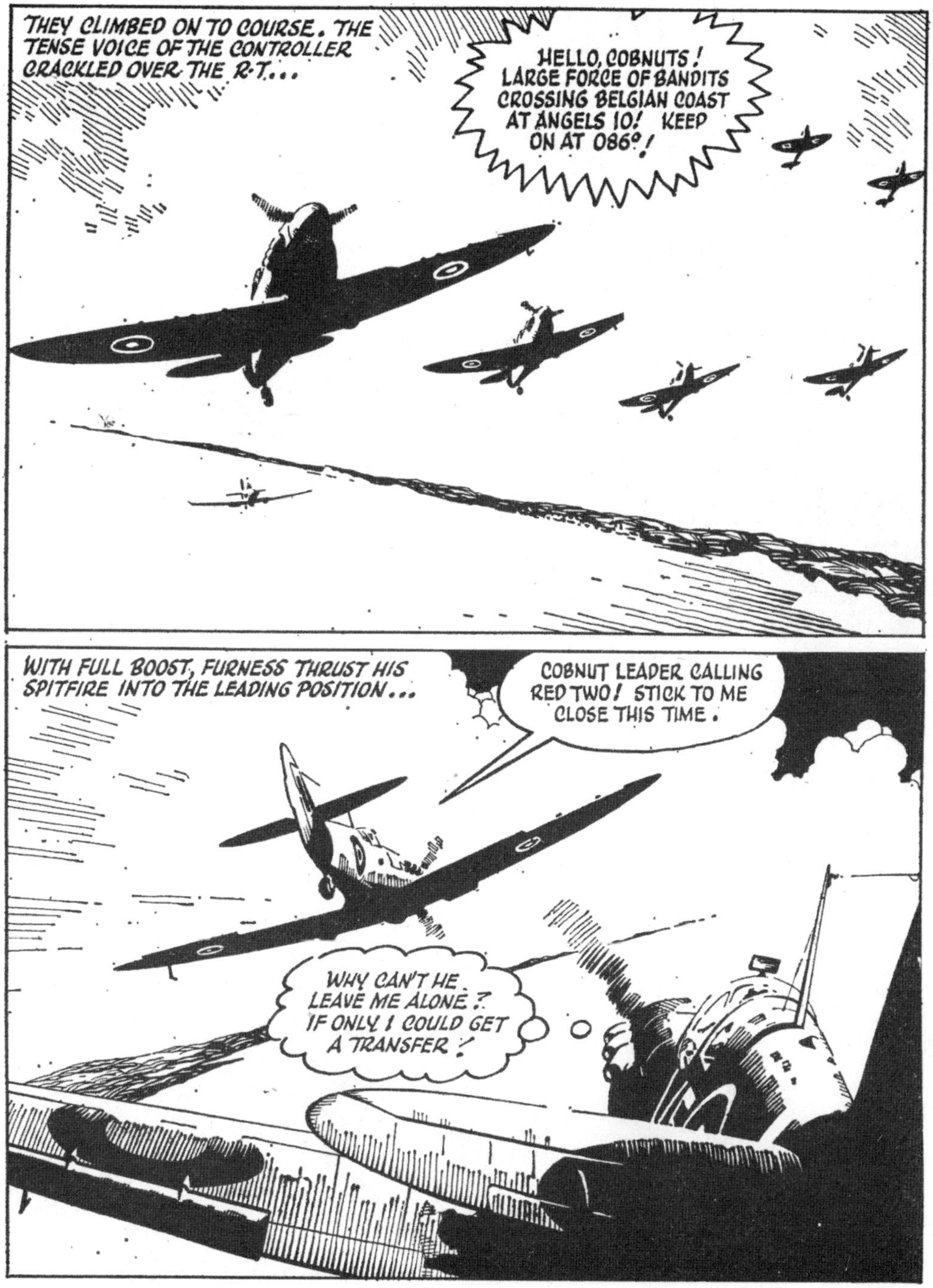
THEY CLIMBED ON TO COURSE. THE TENSE VOICE OF THE CONTROLLER CRACKLED OVER THE R-T...
HELLO, COBNUTS! LARGE FORCE OF BANDITS CROSSING BELGIAN COAST AT ANGELS 10! KEEP ON AT 086°!
WITH FULL BOOST, FURNESS THRUST HIS SPITFIRE INTO THE LEADING POSITION...
COBNUT LEADER CALLING RED TWO! STICK TO ME CLOSE THIS TIME.
WHY CAN'T HE LEAVE ME ALONE? IF ONLY I COULD GET A TRANSFER!

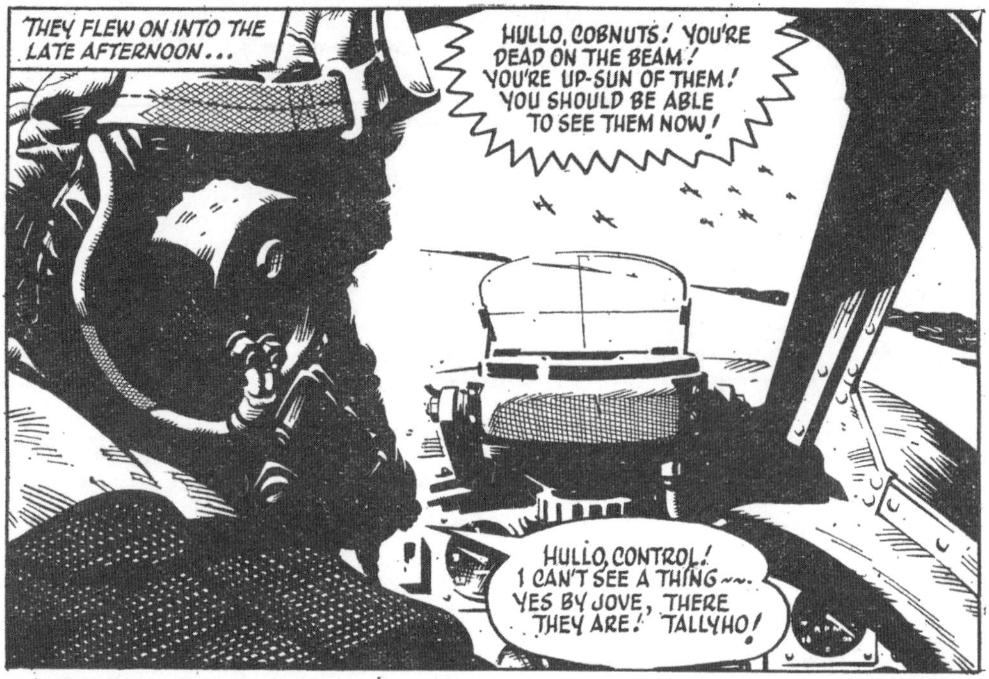
THEY FLEW ON INTO THE LATE AFTERNOON...
HULLO, COBNUTS! YOU'RE DEAD ON THE BEAM! YOU'RE UP-SUN OF THEM! YOU SHOULD BE ABLE TO SEE THEM NOW!
HULLO, CONTROL! I CAN'T SEE A THING~~. YES BY JOVE, THERE THEY ARE! TALLYHO!

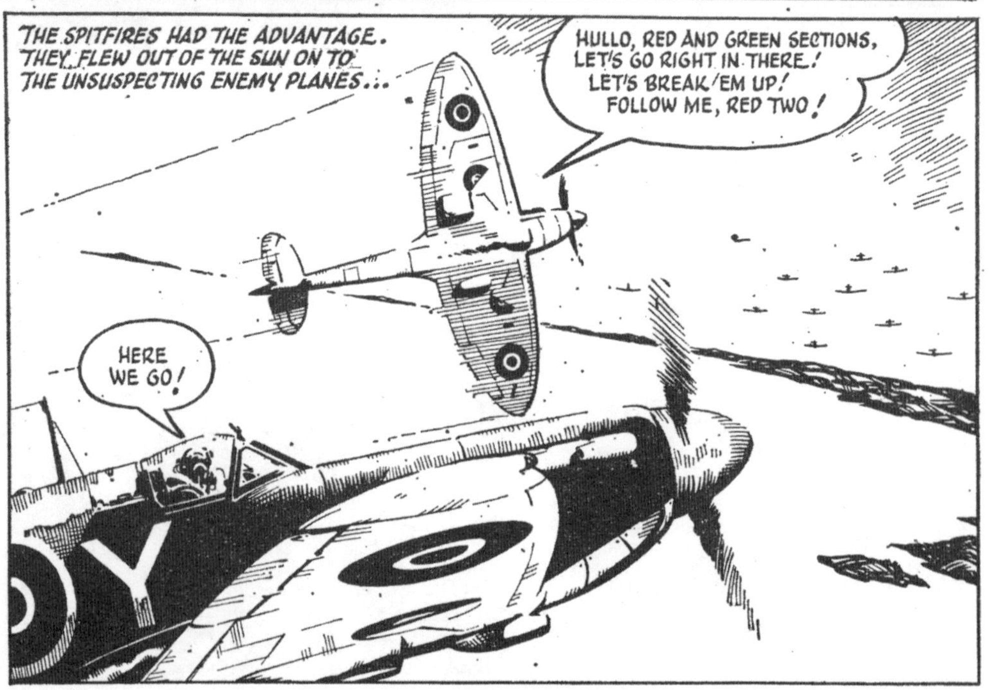
THE SPITFIRES HAD THE ADVANTAGE. THEY FLEW OUT OF THE SUN ON TO THE UNSUSPECTING ENEMY PLANES...
HULLO, RED AND GREEN SECTIONS, LET'S GO RIGHT IN THERE! LET'S BREAK 'EM UP! FOLLOW ME, RED TWO!
HERE WE GO!

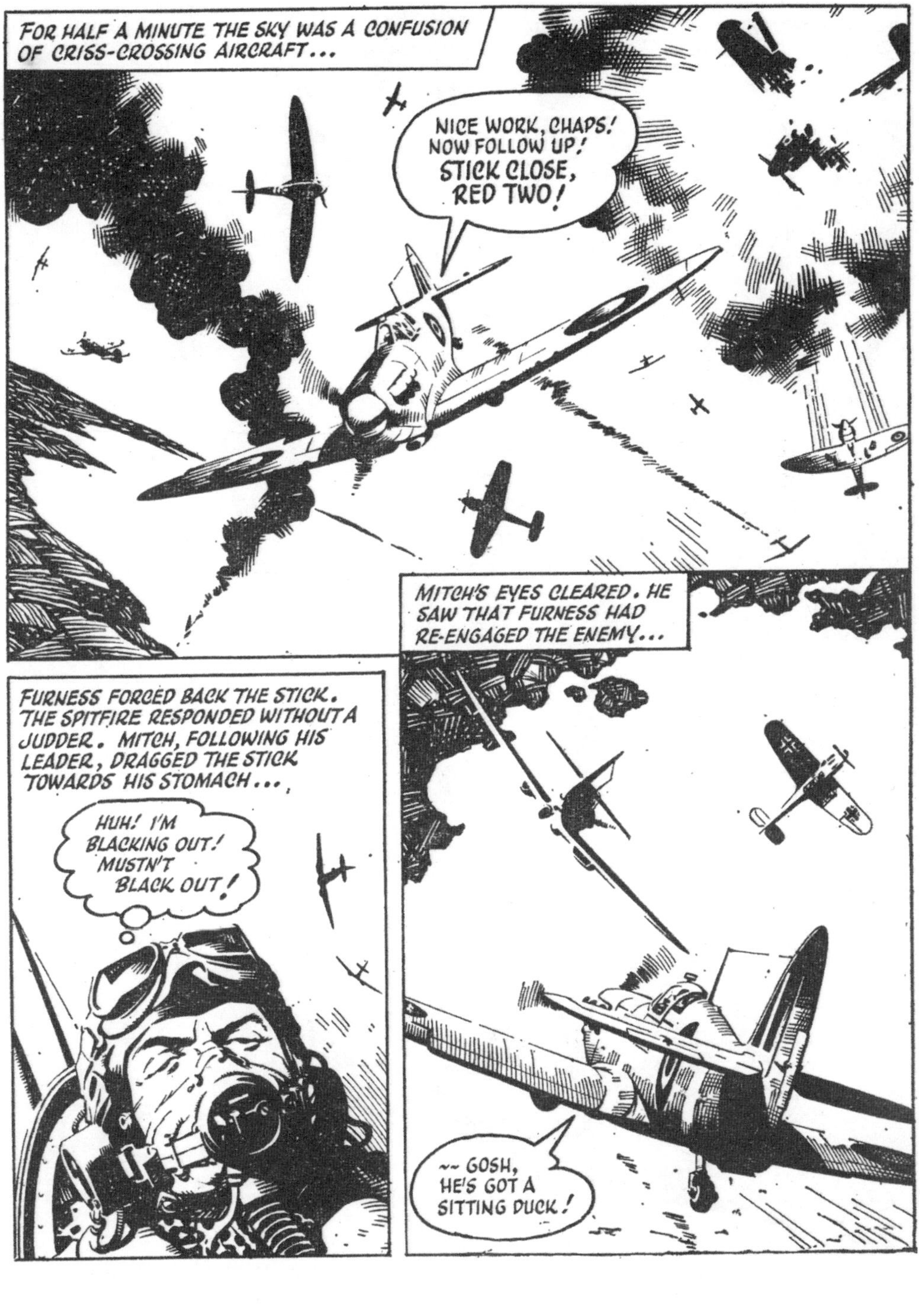
FOR HALF A MINUTE THE SKY WAS A CONFUSION OF CRISS-CROSSING AIRCRAFT...
NICE WORK, CHAPS! NOW FOLLOW UP! STICK CLOSE, RED TWO!
FURNESS FORCED BACK THE STICK. THE SPITFIRE RESPONDED WITHOUT A JUDDER. MITCH, FOLLOWING HIS LEADER, DRAGGED THE STICK TOWARDS HIS STOMACH...
HUH! I'M BLACKING OUT! MUSTN'T BLACK OUT!
MITCH'S EYES CLEARED. HE SAW THAT FURNESS HAD RE-ENGAGED THE ENEMY...
~~ GOSH, HE'S GOT A SITTING DUCK!

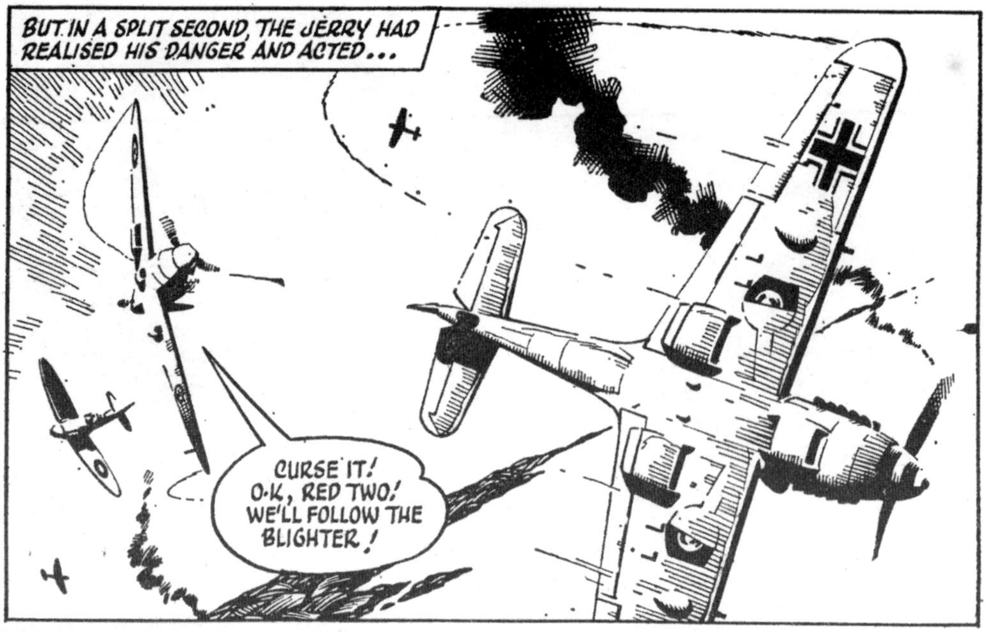
BUT IN A SPLIT SECOND, THE JERRY HAD REALISED HIS DANGER AND ACTED...
CURSE IT! O.K, RED TWO! WE'LL FOLLOW THE BLIGHTER!

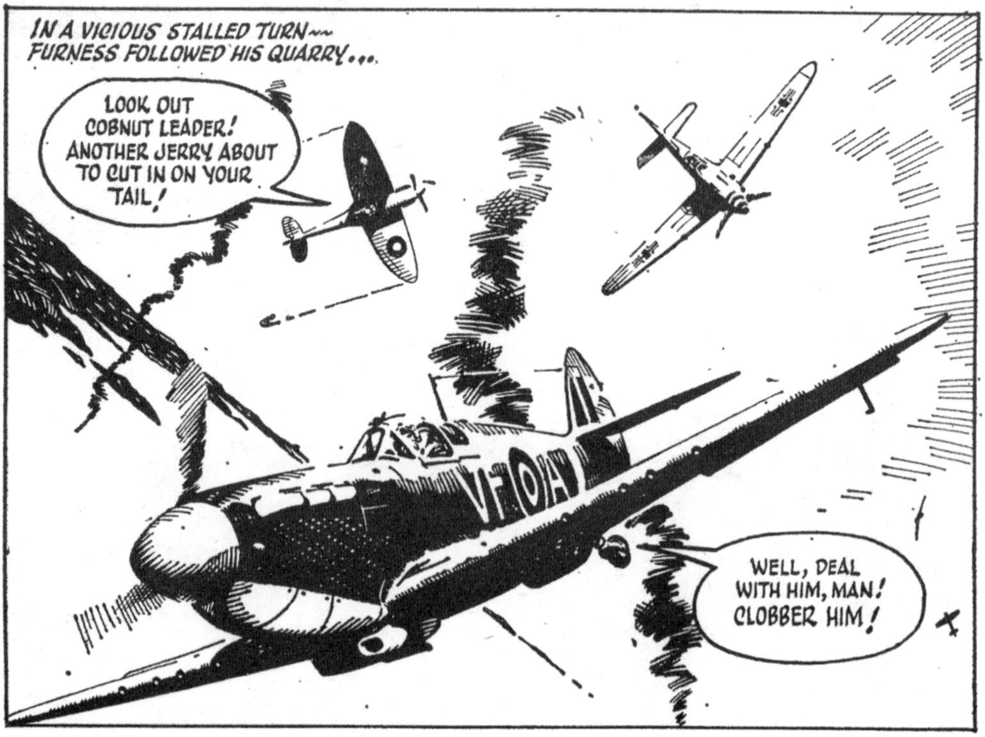
IN A VICIOUS STALLED TURN--- FURNESS FOLLOWED HIS QUARRY...
LOOK OUT COBNUT LEADER! ANOTHER JERRY ABOUT TO CUT IN ON YOUR TAIL!
WELL, DEAL WITH HIM, MAN! CLOBBER HIM!

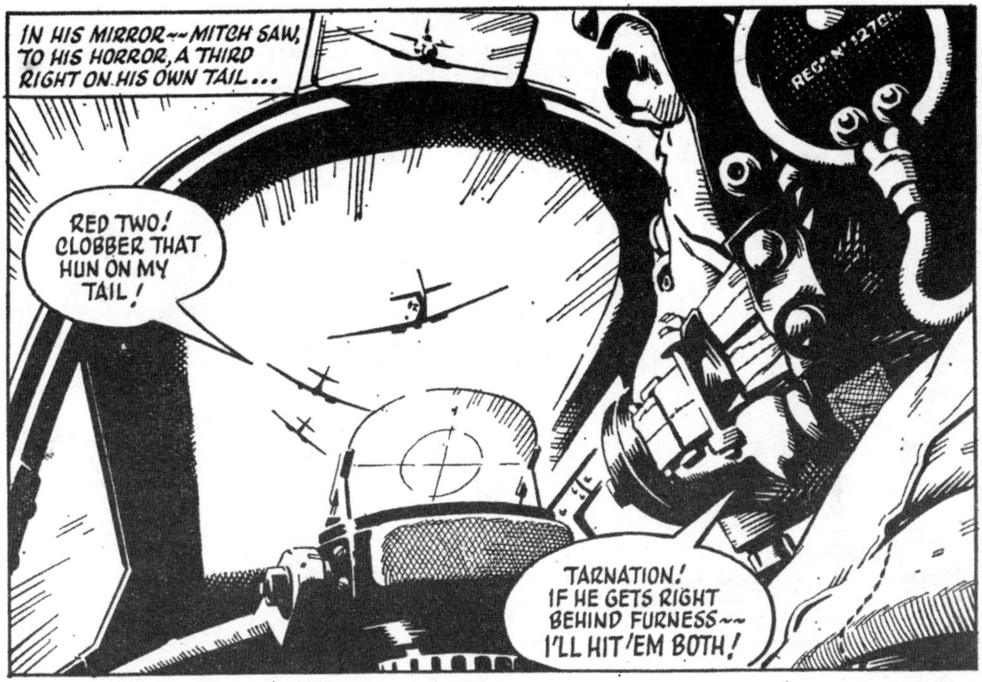
IN HIS MIRROR--MITCH SAW, TO HIS HORROR, A THIRD RIGHT ON HIS OWN TAIL...
RED TWO! CLOBBER THAT HUN ON MY TAIL!
TARNATION! IF HE GETS RIGHT BEHIND FURNESS-- I'LL HIT 'EM BOTH!

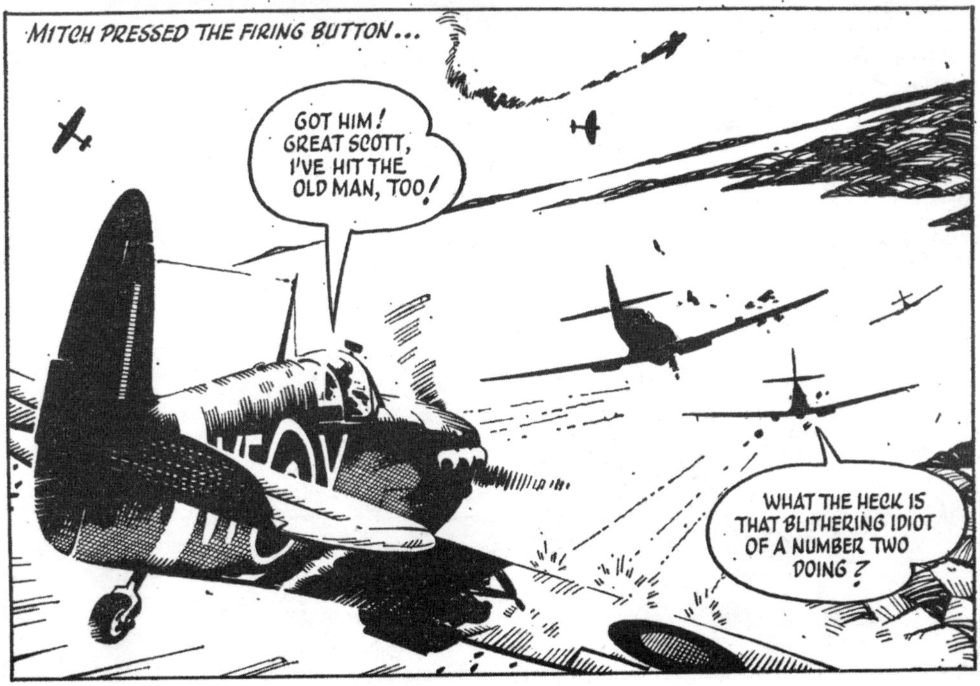
MITCH PRESSED THE FIRING BUTTON...
GOT HIM! GREAT SCOTT, I'VE HIT THE OLD MAN, TOO!
WHAT THE HECK IS THAT BLITHERING IDIOT OF A NUMBER TWO DOING?

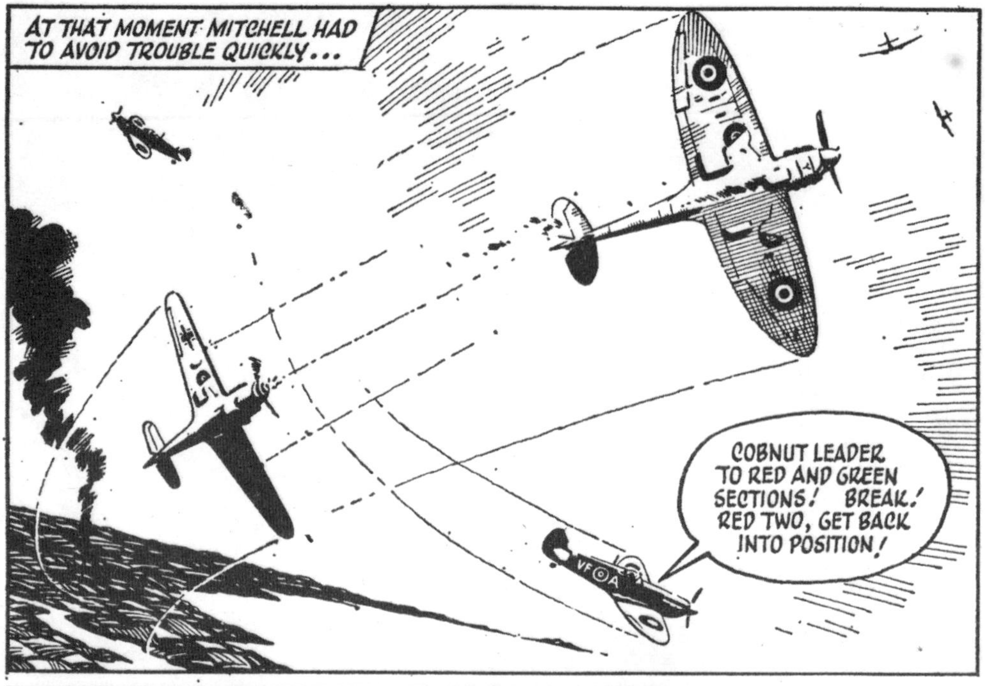
AT THAT MOMENT MITCHELL HAD TO AVOID TROUBLE QUICKLY...
COBNUT LEADER TO RED AND GREEN SECTIONS! BREAK! RED TWO, GET BACK INTO POSITION!

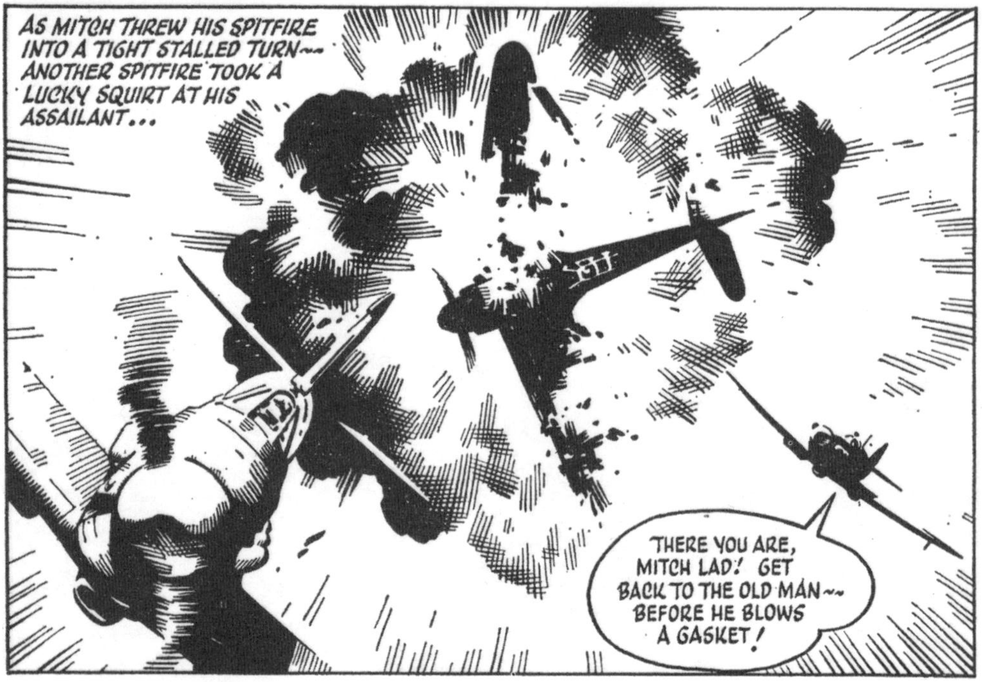
AS MITCH THREW HIS SPITFIRE INTO A TIGHT STALLED TURN-- ANOTHER SPITFIRE TOOK A LUCKY SQUIRT AT HIS ASSAILANT...
THERE YOU ARE, MITCH LAD! GET BACK TO THE OLD MAN-- BEFORE HE BLOWS A GASKET!

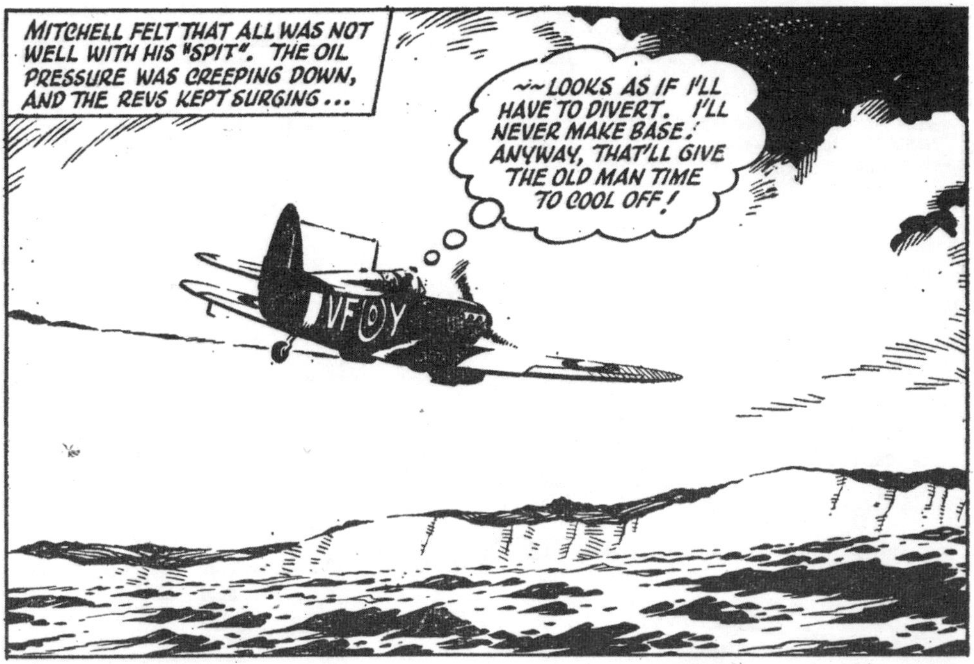
MITCHELL FELT THAT ALL WAS NOT WELL WITH HIS "SPIT". THE OIL PRESSURE WAS CREEPING DOWN, AND THE REVS KEPT SURGING...
~~LOOKS AS IF I'LL HAVE TO DIVERT. I'LL NEVER MAKE BASE! ANYWAY, THAT'LL GIVE THE OLD MAN TIME TO COOL OFF!
VF Y

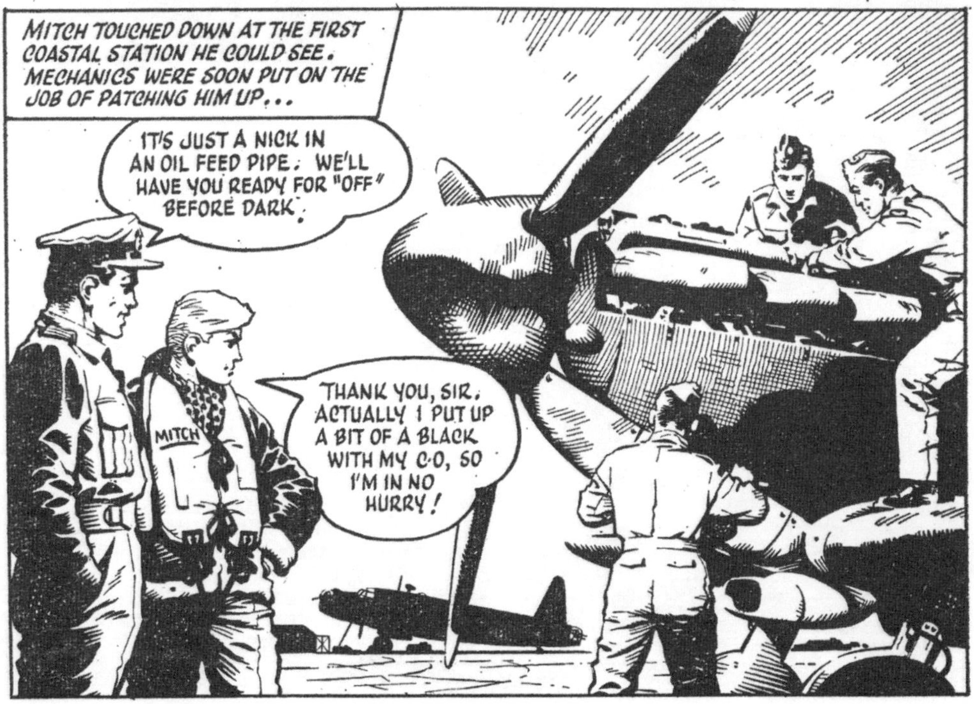
MITCH TOUCHED DOWN AT THE FIRST COASTAL STATION HE COULD SEE. MECHANICS WERE SOON PUT ON THE JOB OF PATCHING HIM UP...
IT'S JUST A NICK IN AN OIL FEED PIPE. WE'LL HAVE YOU READY FOR "OFF" BEFORE DARK.
THANK YOU, SIR. ACTUALLY I PUT UP A BIT OF A BLACK WITH MY C.O, SO I'M IN NO HURRY!
MITCH

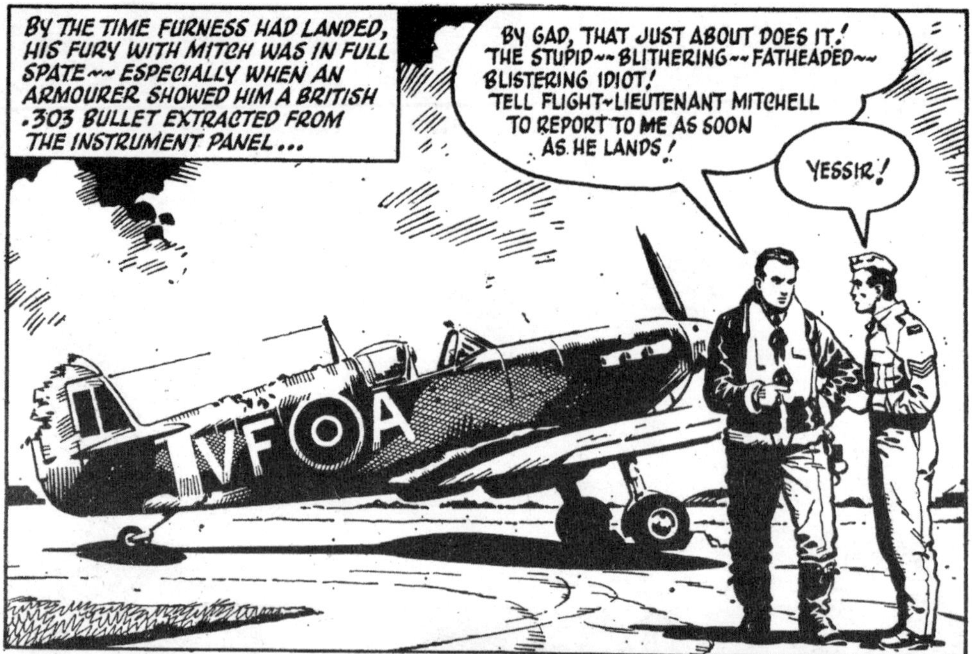
BY THE TIME FURNESS HAD LANDED, HIS FURY WITH MITCH WAS IN FULL SPATE~~ ESPECIALLY WHEN AN ARMOURER SHOWED HIM A BRITISH .303 BULLET EXTRACTED FROM THE INSTRUMENT PANEL...
BY GAD, THAT JUST ABOUT DOES IT! THE STUPID~~BLITHERING~~FATHEADED~~ BLISTERING IDIOT! TELL FLIGHT-LIEUTENANT MITCHELL TO REPORT TO ME AS SOON AS HE LANDS!
YESSIR!
TVFOA

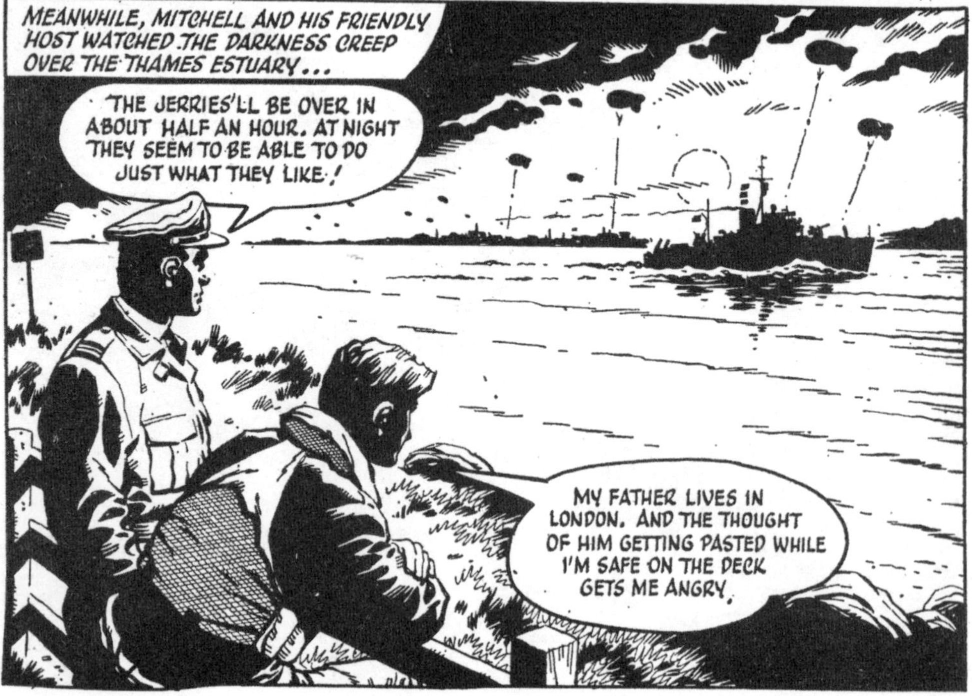
MEANWHILE, MITCHELL AND HIS FRIENDLY HOST WATCHED THE DARKNESS CREEP OVER THE THAMES ESTUARY...
THE JERRIES'LL BE OVER IN ABOUT HALF AN HOUR. AT NIGHT THEY SEEM TO BE ABLE TO DO JUST WHAT THEY LIKE!
MY FATHER LIVES IN LONDON. AND THE THOUGHT OF HIM GETTING PASTED WHILE I'M SAFE ON THE DECK GETS ME ANGRY.

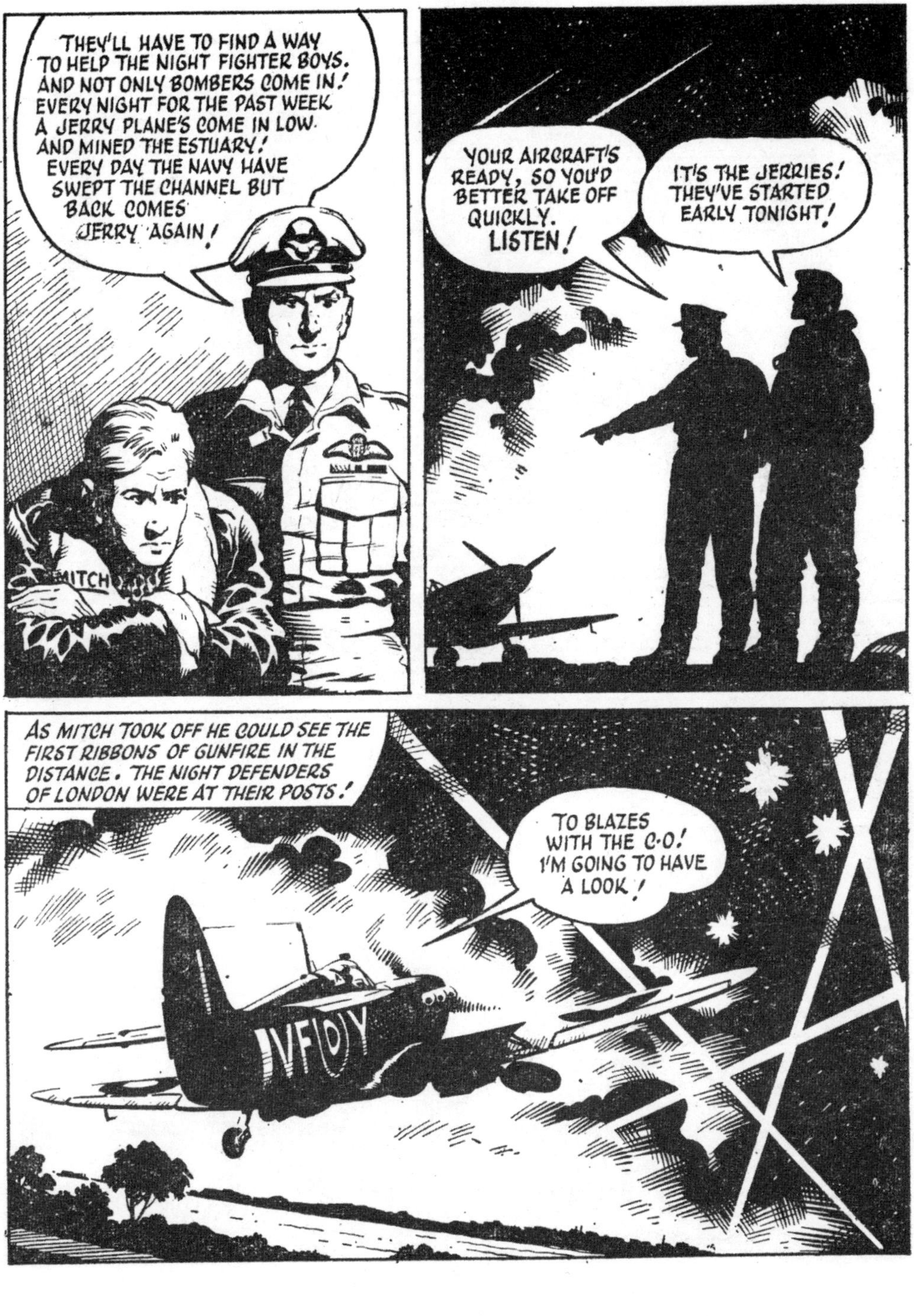
THEY'LL HAVE TO FIND A WAY TO HELP THE NIGHT FIGHTER BOYS. AND NOT ONLY BOMBERS COME IN! EVERY NIGHT FOR THE PAST WEEK A JERRY PLANE'S COME IN LOW AND MINED THE ESTUARY! EVERY DAY THE NAVY HAVE SWEPT THE CHANNEL BUT BACK COMES JERRY AGAIN!
MITCH
YOUR AIRCRAFT'S READY, SO YOU'D BETTER TAKE OFF QUICKLY. LISTEN!
IT'S THE JERRIES! THEY'VE STARTED EARLY TONIGHT!
AS MITCH TOOK OFF HE COULD SEE THE FIRST RIBBONS OF GUNFIRE IN THE DISTANCE. THE NIGHT DEFENDERS OF LONDON WERE AT THEIR POSTS!
TO BLAZES WITH THE C.O! I'M GOING TO HAVE A LOOK!
VF Y

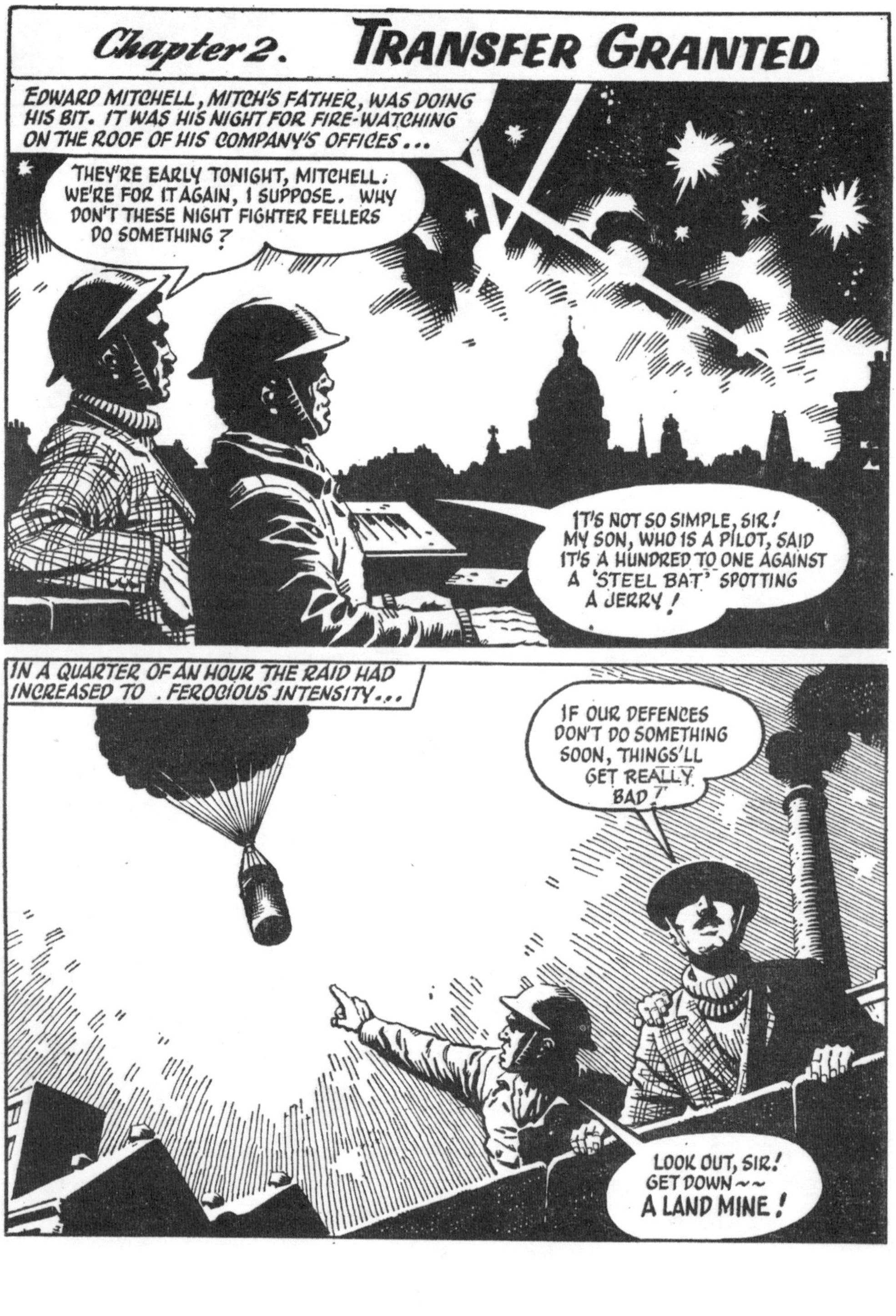
Chapter 2. TRANSFER GRANTED
EDWARD MITCHELL, MITCH'S FATHER, WAS DOING HIS BIT. IT WAS HIS NIGHT FOR FIRE-WATCHING ON THE ROOF OF HIS COMPANY'S OFFICES...
THEY'RE EARLY TONIGHT, MITCHELL. WE'RE FOR IT AGAIN, I SUPPOSE. WHY DON'T THESE NIGHT FIGHTER FELLERS DO SOMETHING?
IT'S NOT SO SIMPLE, SIR! MY SON, WHO IS A PILOT, SAID IT'S A HUNDRED TO ONE AGAINST A 'STEEL BAT' SPOTTING A JERRY!
IN A QUARTER OF AN HOUR THE RAID HAD INCREASED TO . FEROCIOUS INTENSITY...
IF OUR DEFENCES DON'T DO SOMETHING SOON, THINGS'LL GET REALLY BAD!
LOOK OUT, SIR! GET DOWN ~~ A LAND MINE!

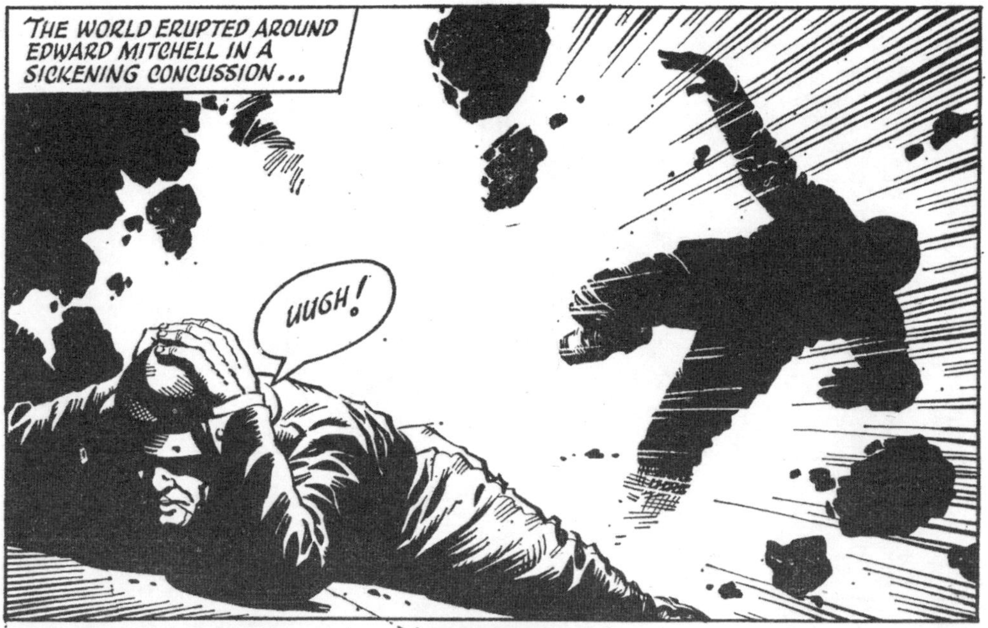
THE WORLD ERUPTED AROUND EDWARD MITCHELL IN A SICKENING CONCUSSION...
UUGH!

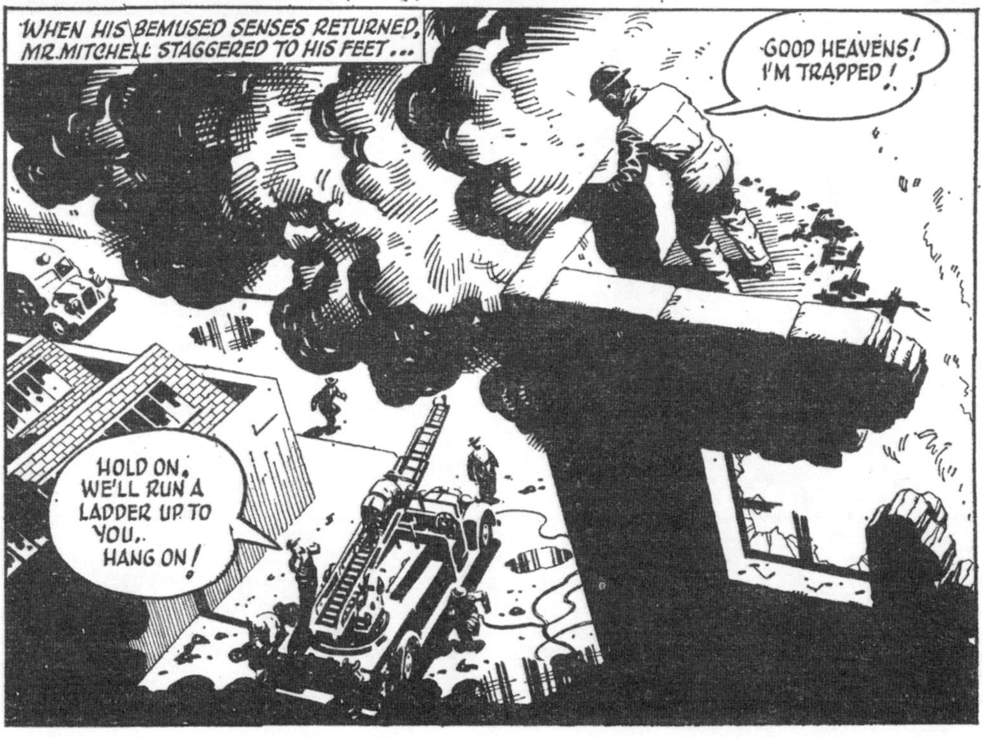
WHEN HIS BEMUSED SENSES RETURNED, MR.MITCHELL STAGGERED TO HIS FEET...
GOOD HEAVENS! I'M TRAPPED!
HOLD ON. WE'LL RUN A LADDER UP TO YOU.. HANG ON!

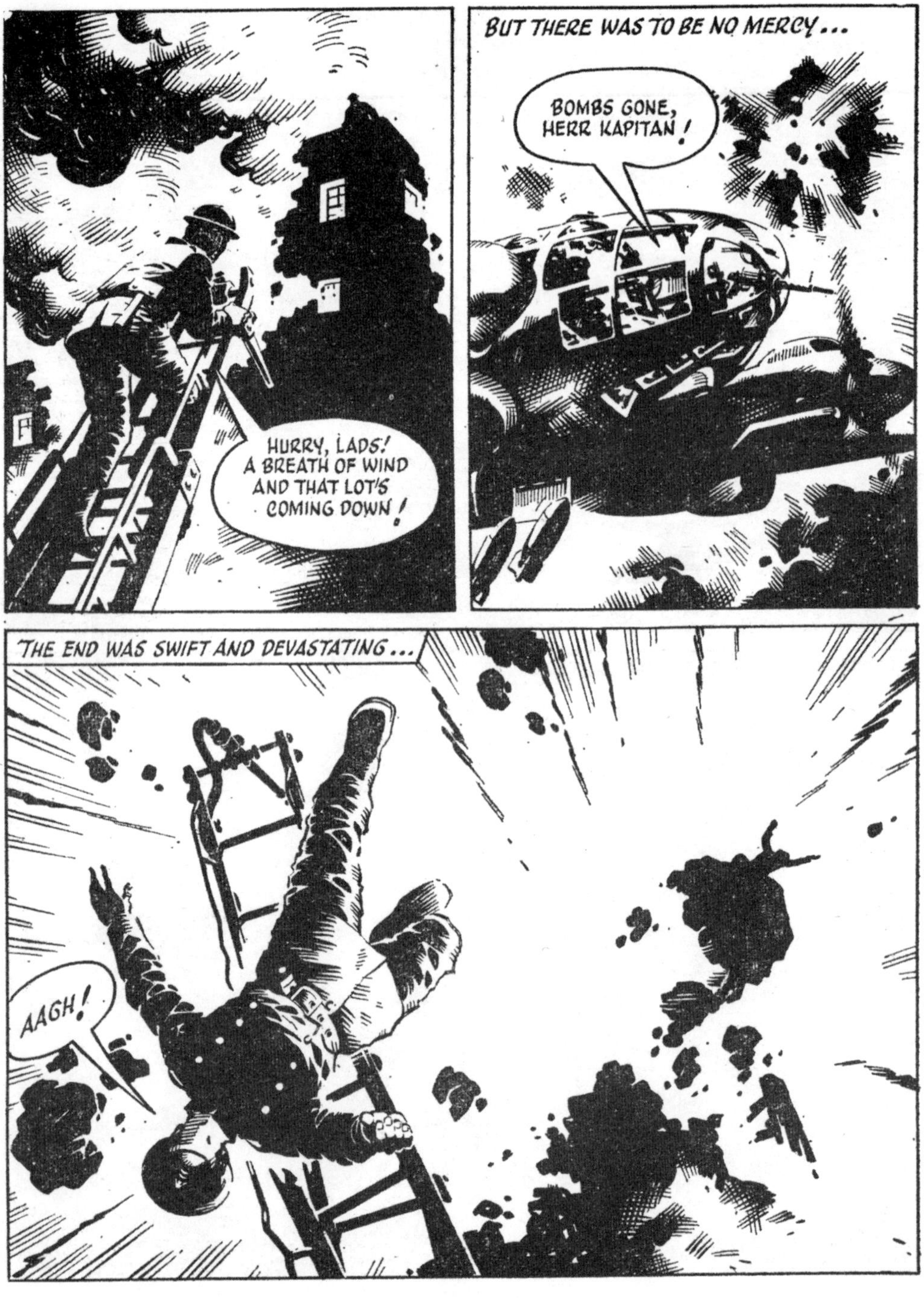
HURRY, LADS! A BREATH OF WIND AND THAT LOT'S COMING DOWN!
BUT THERE WAS TO BE NO MERCY...
BOMBS GONE, HERR KAPITAN!
THE END WAS SWIFT AND DEVASTATING...
AAGH!

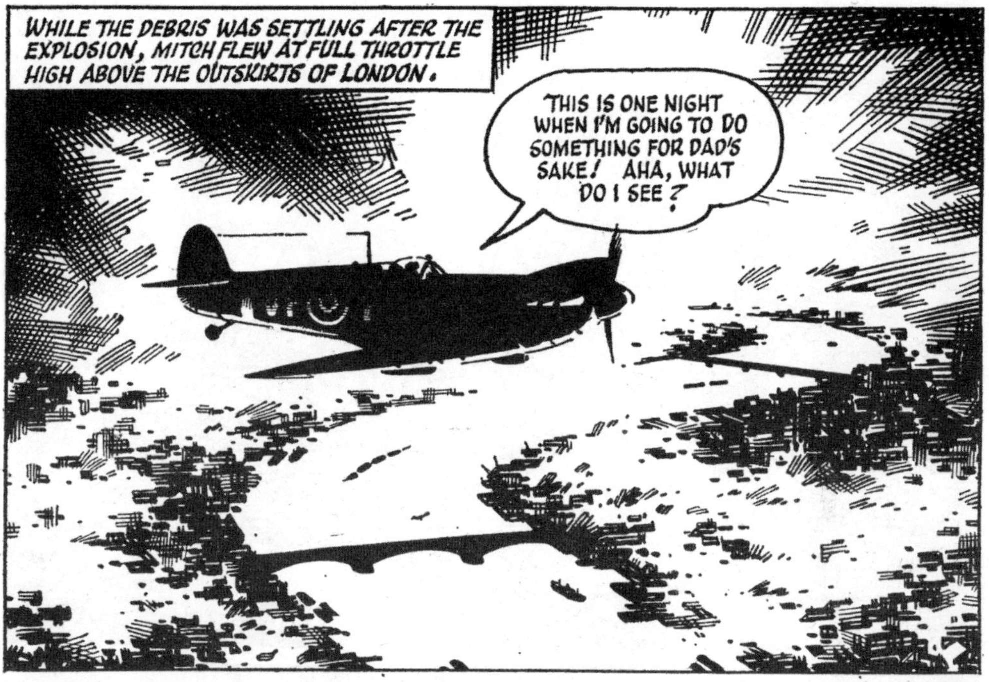
WHILE THE DEBRIS WAS SETTLING AFTER THE EXPLOSION, MITCH FLEW AT FULL THROTTLE HIGH ABOVE THE OUTSKIRTS OF LONDON.
THIS IS ONE NIGHT WHEN I'M GOING TO DO SOMETHING FOR DAD'S SAKE! AHA, WHAT DO I SEE?

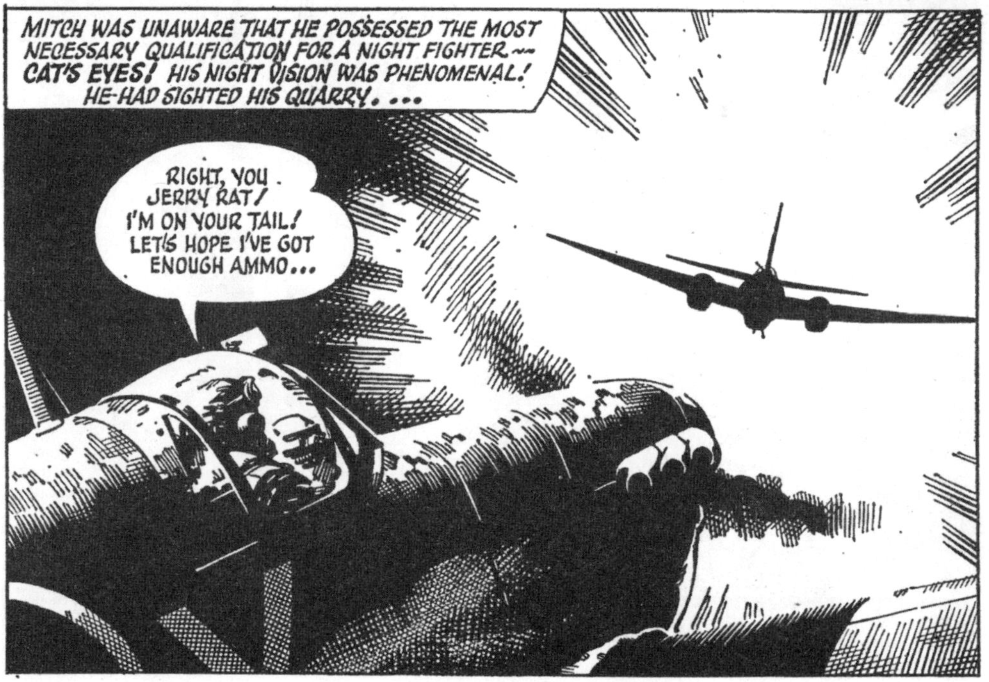
MITCH WAS UNAWARE THAT HE POSSESSED THE MOST NECESSARY QUALIFICATION FOR A NIGHT FIGHTER -- CAT'S EYES! HIS NIGHT VISION WAS PHENOMENAL! HE HAD SIGHTED HIS QUARRY....
RIGHT, YOU JERRY RAT! I'M ON YOUR TAIL! LET'S HOPE I'VE GOT ENOUGH AMMO...

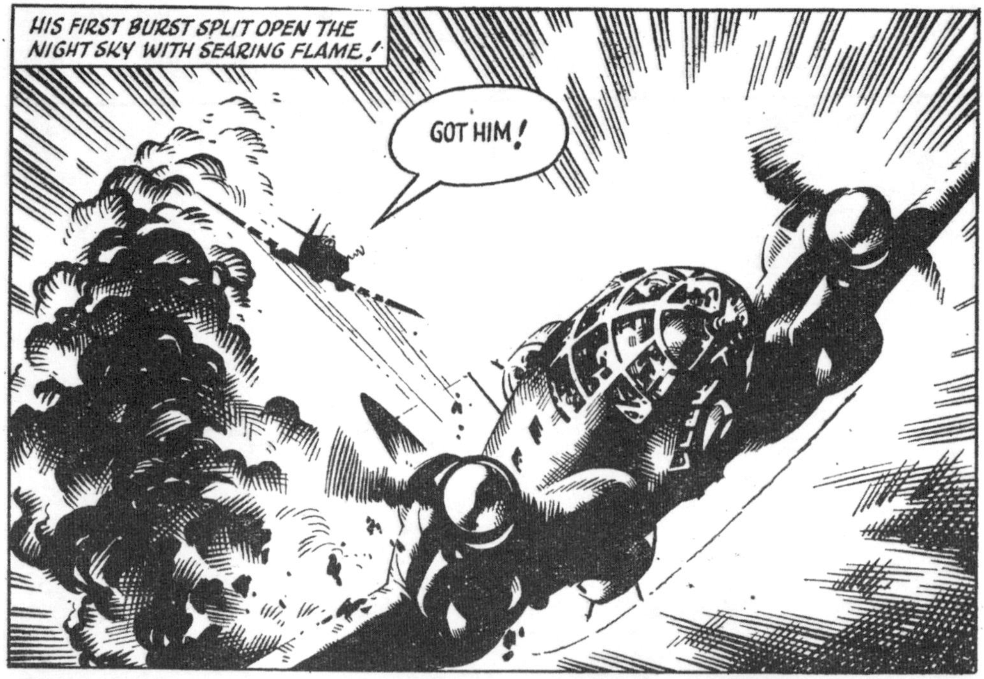
HIS FIRST BURST SPLIT OPEN THE NIGHT SKY WITH SEARING FLAME!
GOT HIM!

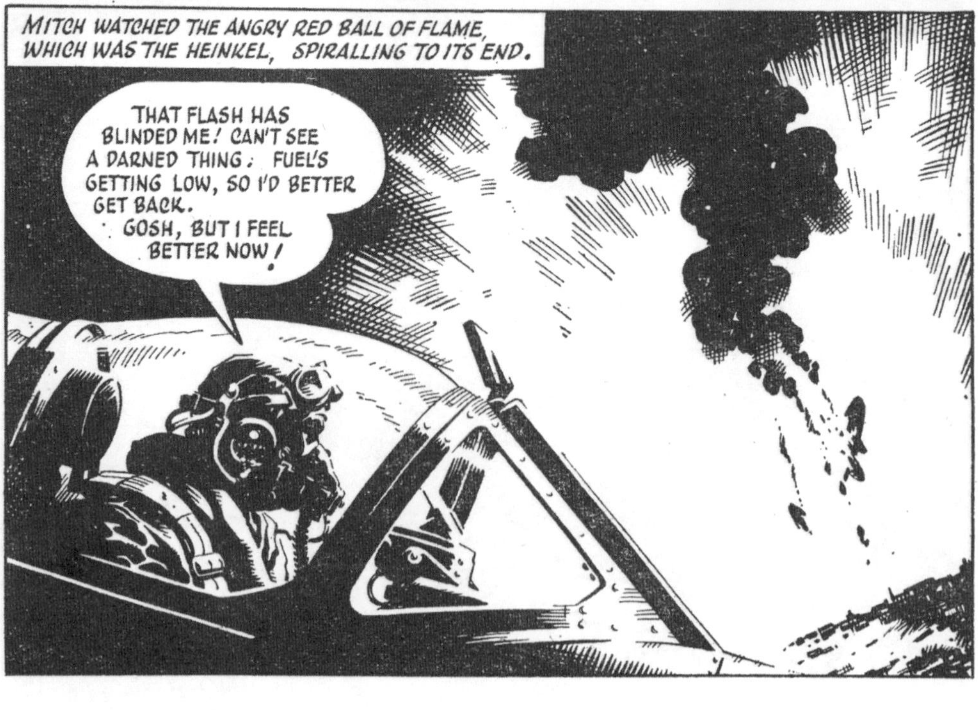
MITCH WATCHED THE ANGRY RED BALL OF FLAME, WHICH WAS THE HEINKEL, SPIRALLING TO ITS END.
THAT FLASH HAS BLINDED ME! CAN'T SEE A DARNED THING. FUEL'S GETTING LOW, SO I'D BETTER GET BACK. GOSH, BUT I FEEL BETTER NOW!

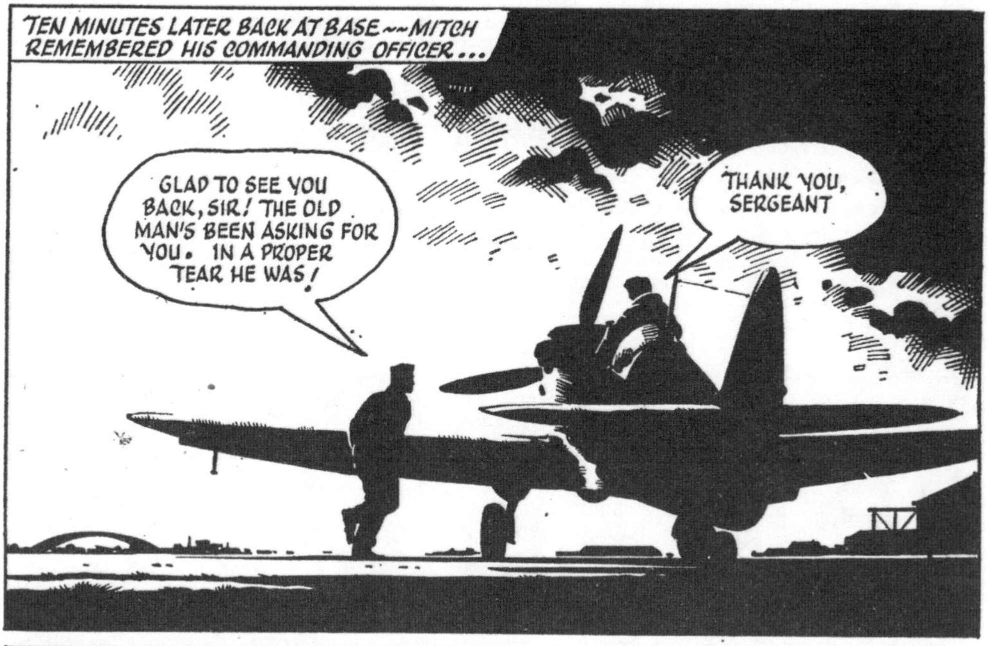
TEN MINUTES LATER BACK AT BASE -- MITCH REMEMBERED HIS COMMANDING OFFICER ...
GLAD TO SEE YOU BACK, SIR! THE OLD MAN'S BEEN ASKING FOR YOU. IN A PROPER TEAR HE WAS!
THANK YOU, SERGEANT

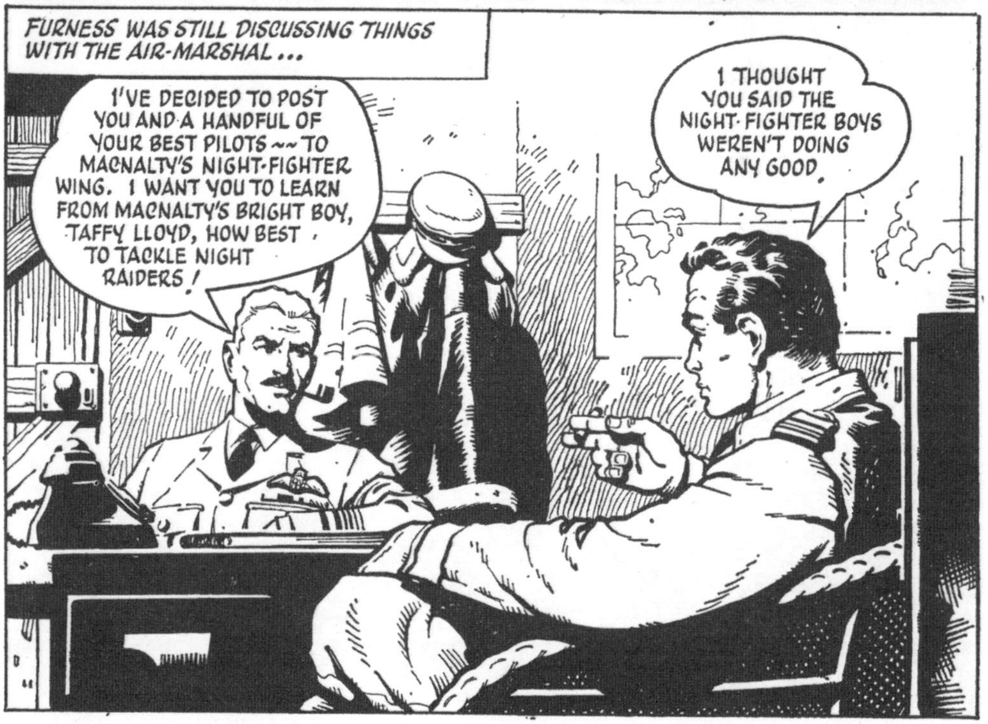
FURNESS WAS STILL DISCUSSING THINGS WITH THE AIR-MARSHAL ...
I'VE DECIDED TO POST YOU AND A HANDFUL OF YOUR BEST PILOTS -- TO MACNALTY'S NIGHT-FIGHTER WING. I WANT YOU TO LEARN FROM MACNALTY'S BRIGHT BOY, TAFFY LLOYD, HOW BEST TO TACKLE NIGHT RAIDERS!
I THOUGHT YOU SAID THE NIGHT-FIGHTER BOYS WEREN'T DOING ANY GOOD.

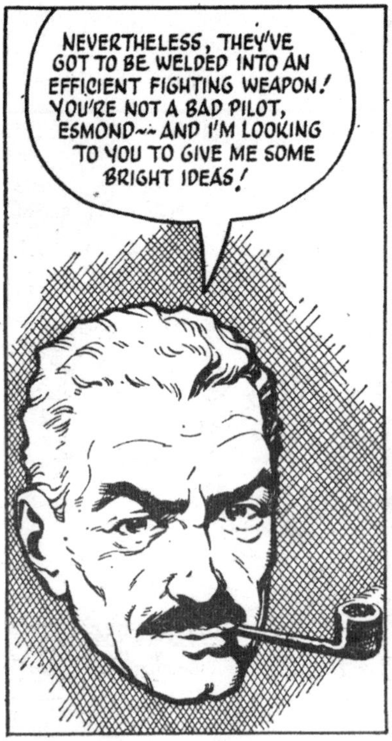
NEVERTHELESS, THEY'VE GOT TO BE WELDED INTO AN EFFICIENT FIGHTING WEAPON! YOU'RE NOT A BAD PILOT, ESMOND-- AND I'M LOOKING TO YOU TO GIVE ME SOME BRIGHT IDEAS!

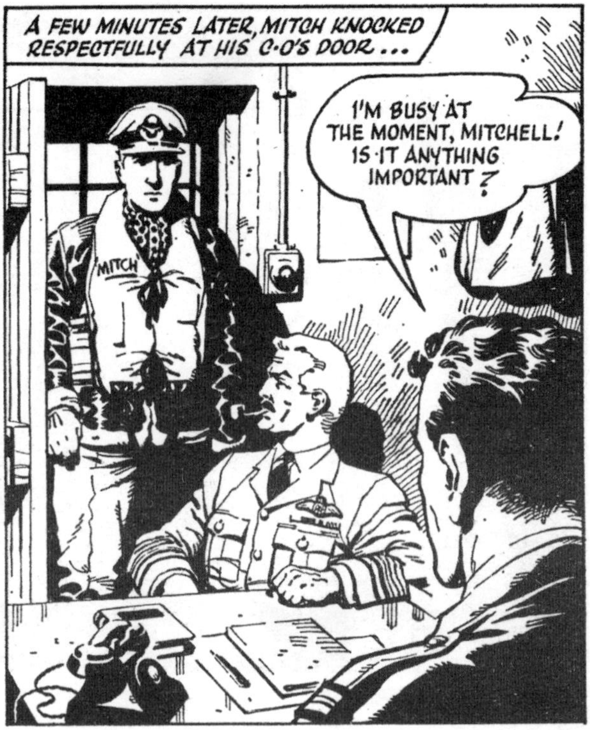
A FEW MINUTES LATER, MITCH KNOCKED RESPECTFULLY AT HIS C.O.'S DOOR...
I'M BUSY AT THE MOMENT, MITCHELL! IS IT ANYTHING IMPORTANT?
MITCH

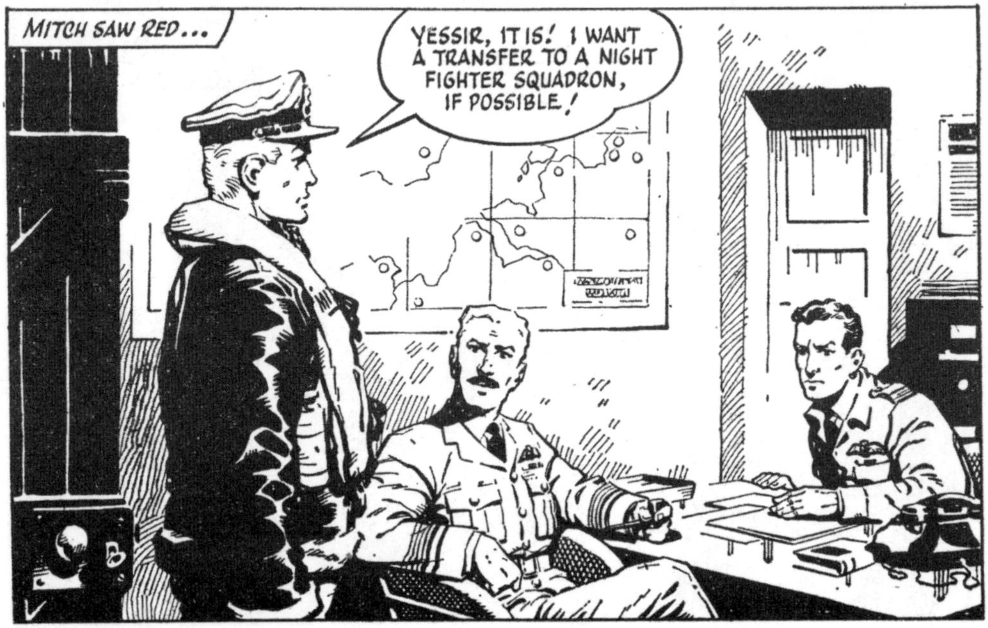
MITCH SAW RED...
YESSIR, IT IS! I WANT A TRANSFER TO A NIGHT FIGHTER SQUADRON, IF POSSIBLE!

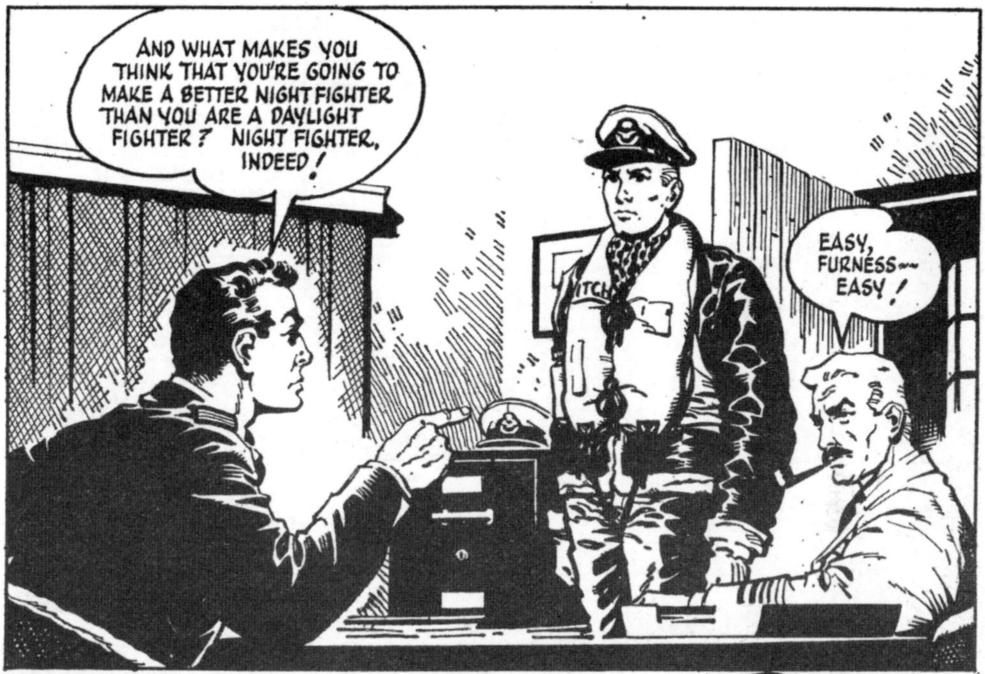
AND WHAT MAKES YOU THINK THAT YOU'RE GOING TO MAKE A BETTER NIGHT FIGHTER THAN YOU ARE A DAYLIGHT FIGHTER? NIGHT FIGHTER, INDEED!
EASY, FURNESS-- EASY!

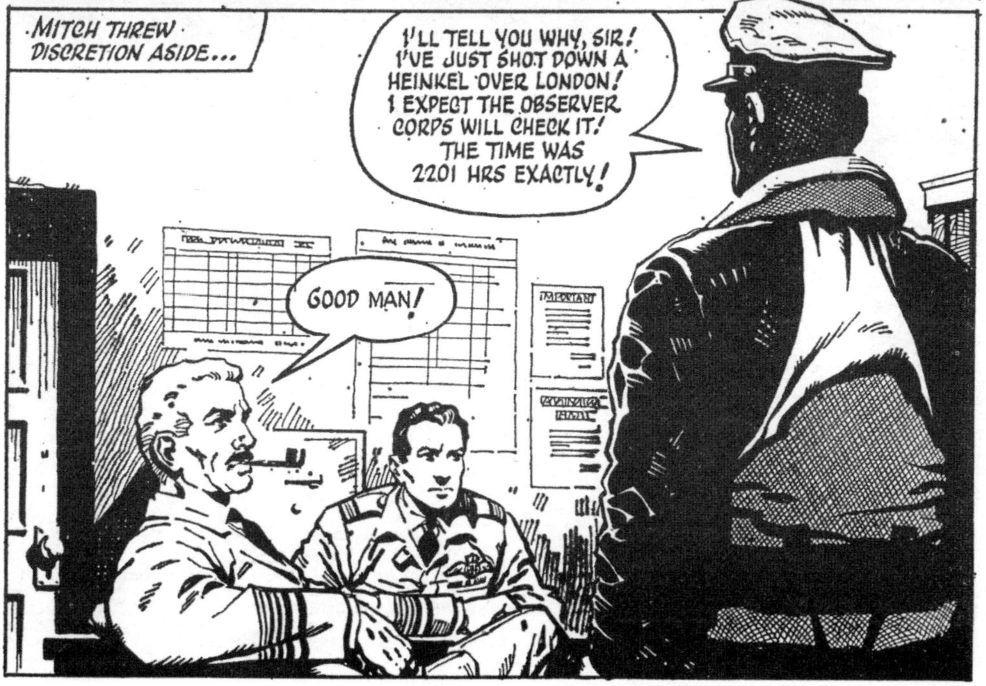
MITCH THREW DISCRETION ASIDE...
I'LL TELL YOU WHY, SIR! I'VE JUST SHOT DOWN A HEINKEL OVER LONDON! I EXPECT THE OBSERVER CORPS WILL CHECK IT! THE TIME WAS 2201 HRS EXACTLY!
GOOD MAN!

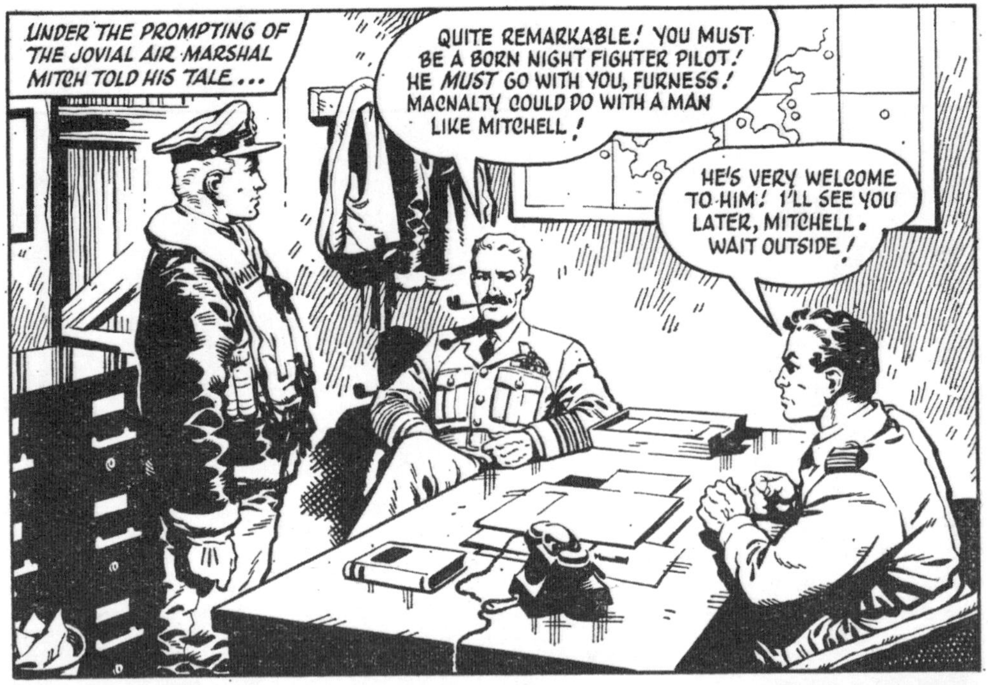
UNDER THE PROMPTING OF THE JOVIAL AIR MARSHAL MITCH TOLD HIS TALE ...
QUITE REMARKABLE! YOU MUST BE A BORN NIGHT FIGHTER PILOT! HE MUST GO WITH YOU, FURNESS! MACNALTY COULD DO WITH A MAN LIKE MITCHELL!
HE'S VERY WELCOME TO HIM! I'LL SEE YOU LATER, MITCHELL. WAIT OUTSIDE!

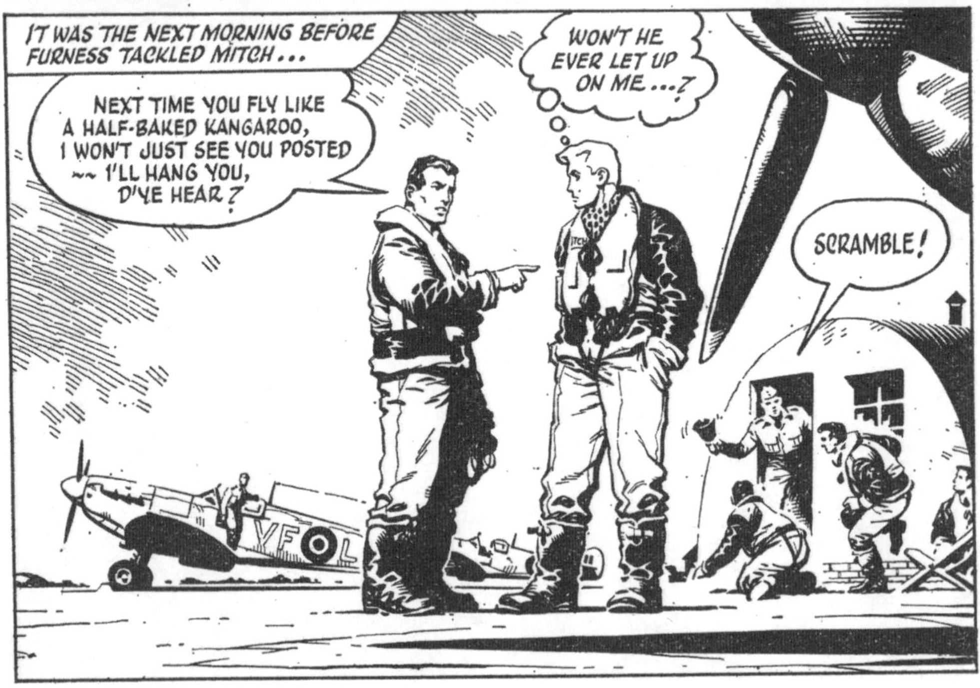
IT WAS THE NEXT MORNING BEFORE FURNESS TACKLED MITCH ...
NEXT TIME YOU FLY LIKE A HALF-BAKED KANGAROO, I WON'T JUST SEE YOU POSTED ~~ I'LL HANG YOU, D'YE HEAR?
WON'T HE EVER LET UP ON ME ...?
SCRAMBLE!

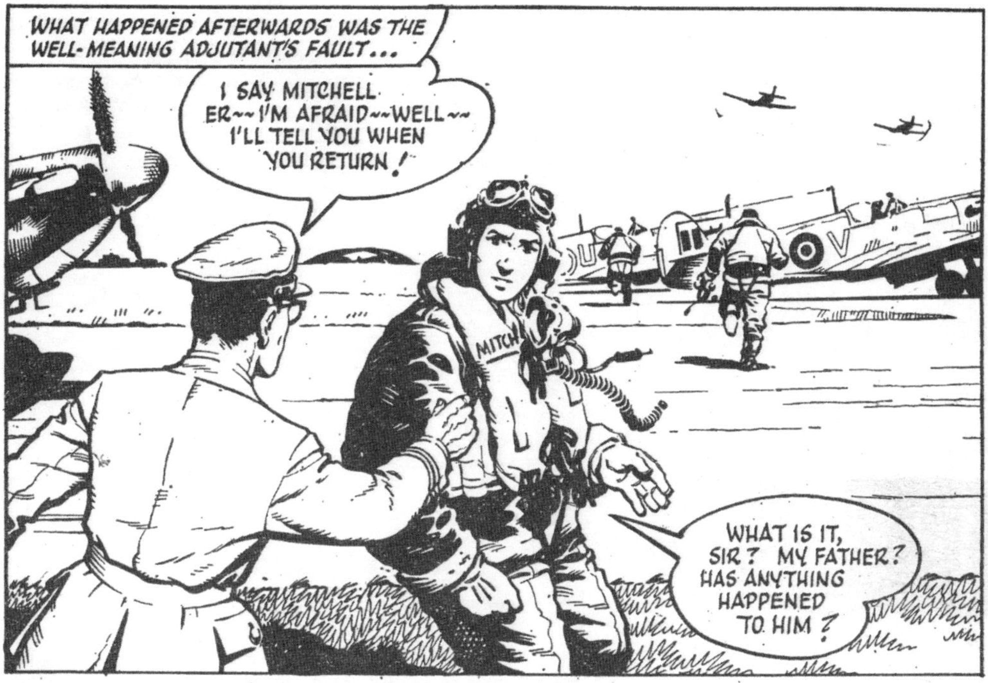
WHAT HAPPENED AFTERWARDS WAS THE WELL-MEANING ADJUTANT'S FAULT...
I SAY MITCHELL ER~~I'M AFRAID~~WELL~~ I'LL TELL YOU WHEN YOU RETURN!
WHAT IS IT, SIR? MY FATHER? HAS ANYTHING HAPPENED TO HIM?

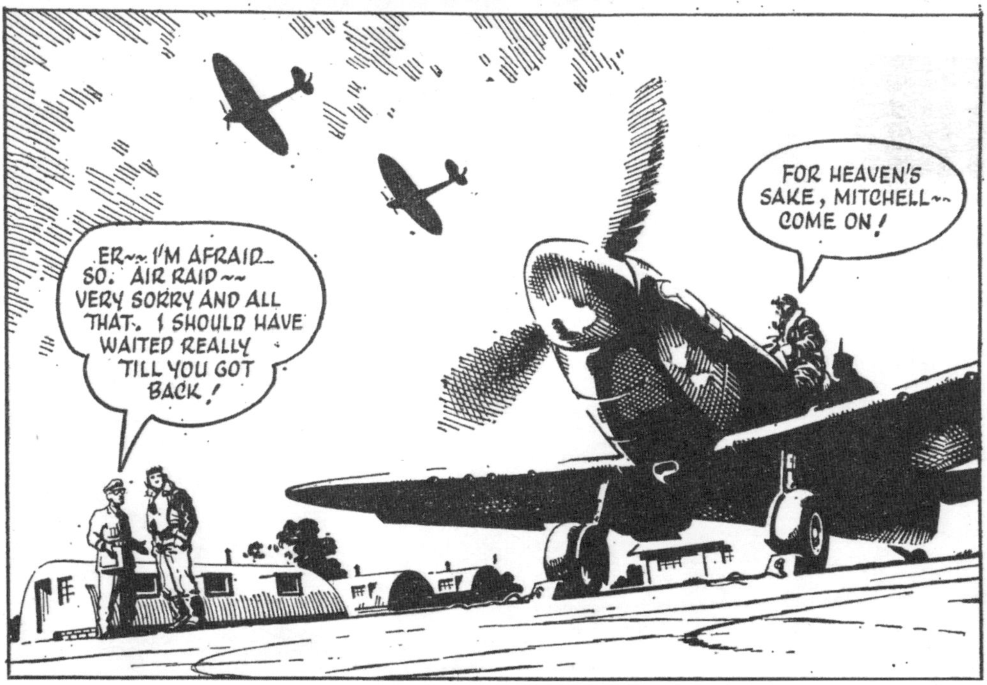
ER~~I'M AFRAID~ SO. AIR RAID~~ VERY SORRY AND ALL THAT. I SHOULD HAVE WAITED REALLY TILL YOU GOT BACK!
FOR HEAVEN'S SAKE, MITCHELL~~ COME ON!

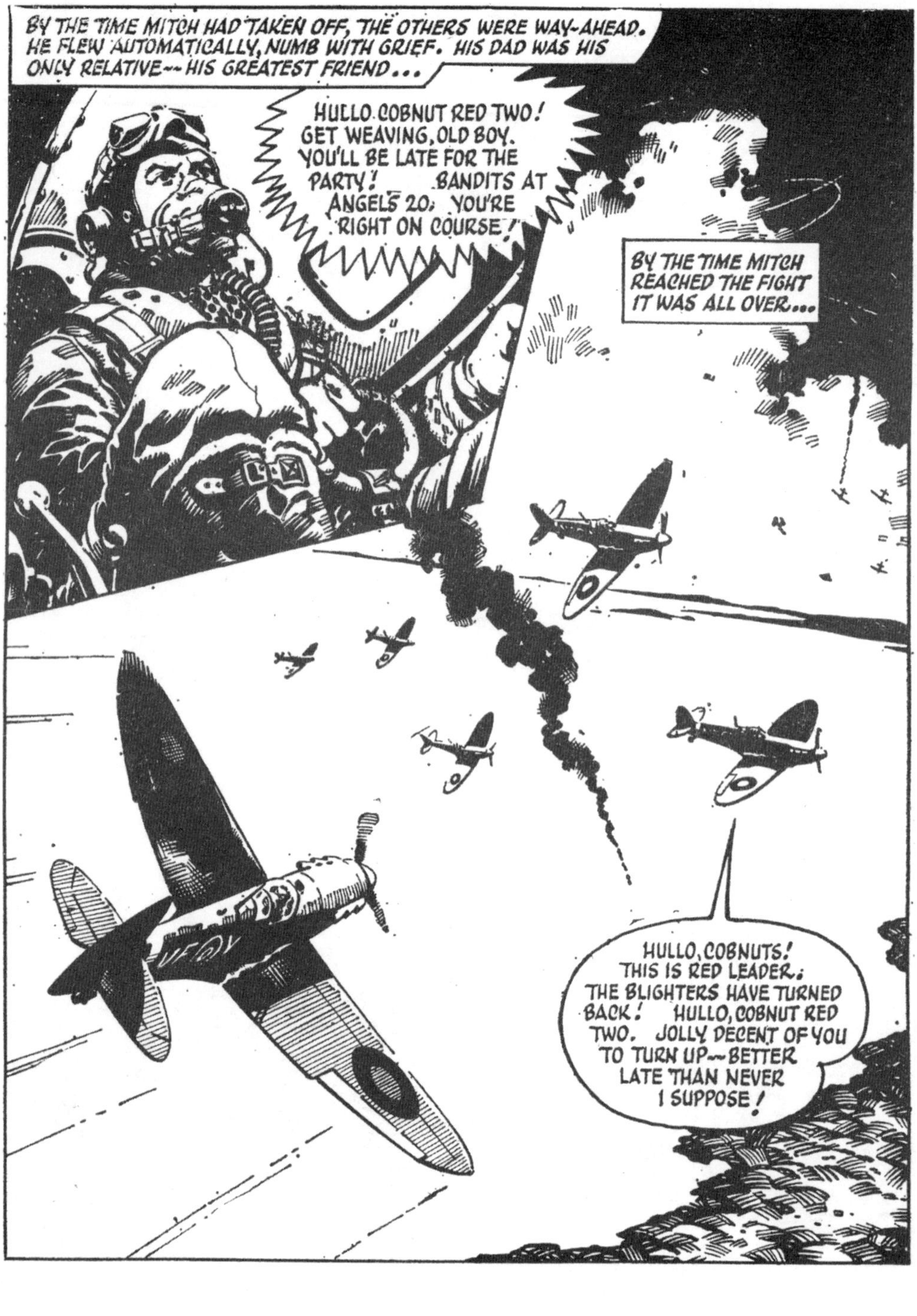
BY THE TIME MITCH HAD TAKEN OFF, THE OTHERS WERE WAY-AHEAD. HE FLEW AUTOMATICALLY, NUMB WITH GRIEF. HIS DAD WAS HIS ONLY RELATIVE-- HIS GREATEST FRIEND...
HULLO COBNUT RED TWO! GET WEAVING, OLD BOY. YOU'LL BE LATE FOR THE PARTY! BANDITS AT ANGELS 20; YOU'RE RIGHT ON COURSE!
BY THE TIME MITCH REACHED THE FIGHT IT WAS ALL OVER...
HULLO, COBNUTS! THIS IS RED LEADER; THE BLIGHTERS HAVE TURNED BACK! HULLO, COBNUT RED TWO. JOLLY DECENT OF YOU TO TURN UP--BETTER LATE THAN NEVER I SUPPOSE!

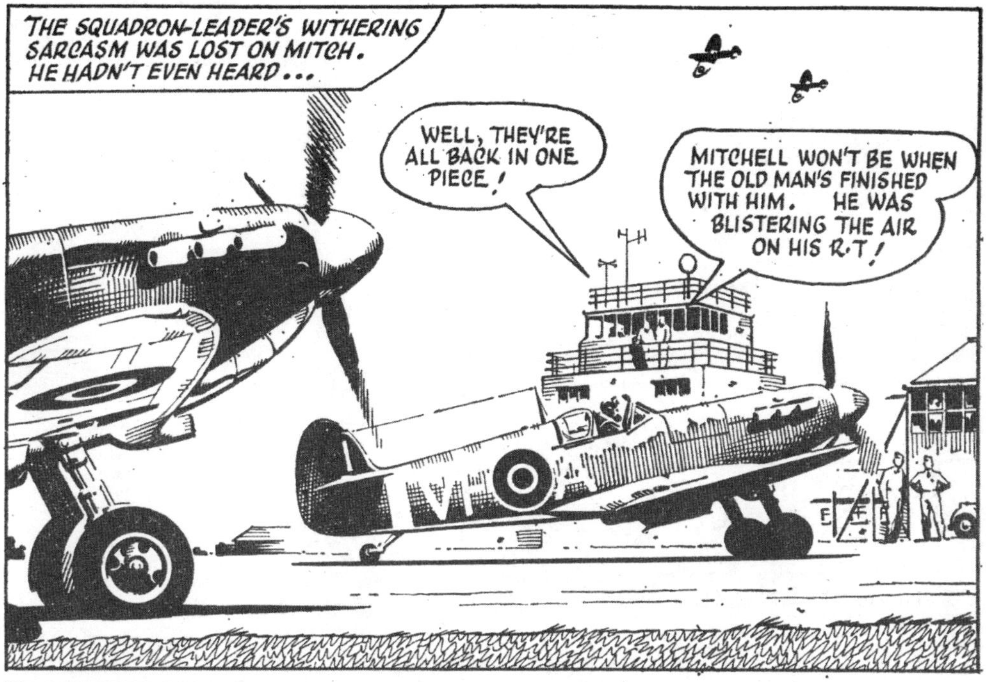
THE SQUADRON-LEADER'S WITHERING SARCASM WAS LOST ON MITCH. HE HADN'T EVEN HEARD...
WELL, THEY'RE ALL BACK IN ONE PIECE!
MITCHELL WON'T BE WHEN THE OLD MAN'S FINISHED WITH HIM. HE WAS BLISTERING THE AIR ON HIS R.T!

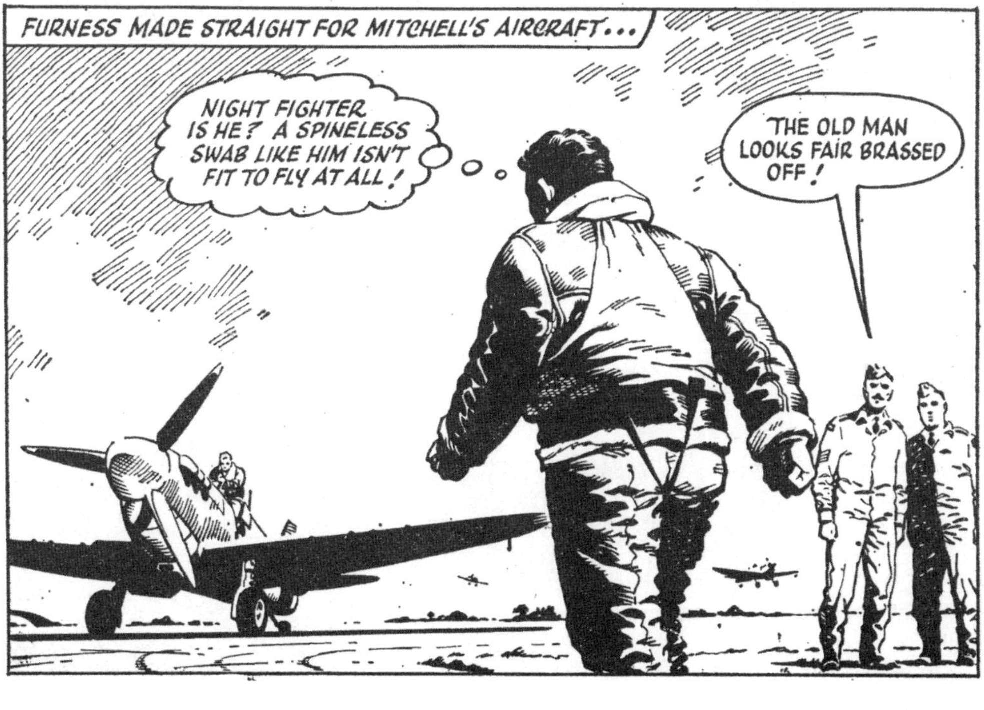
FURNESS MADE STRAIGHT FOR MITCHELL'S AIRCRAFT...
NIGHT FIGHTER IS HE? A SPINELESS SWAB LIKE HIM ISN'T FIT TO FLY AT ALL!
THE OLD MAN LOOKS FAIR BRASSED OFF!

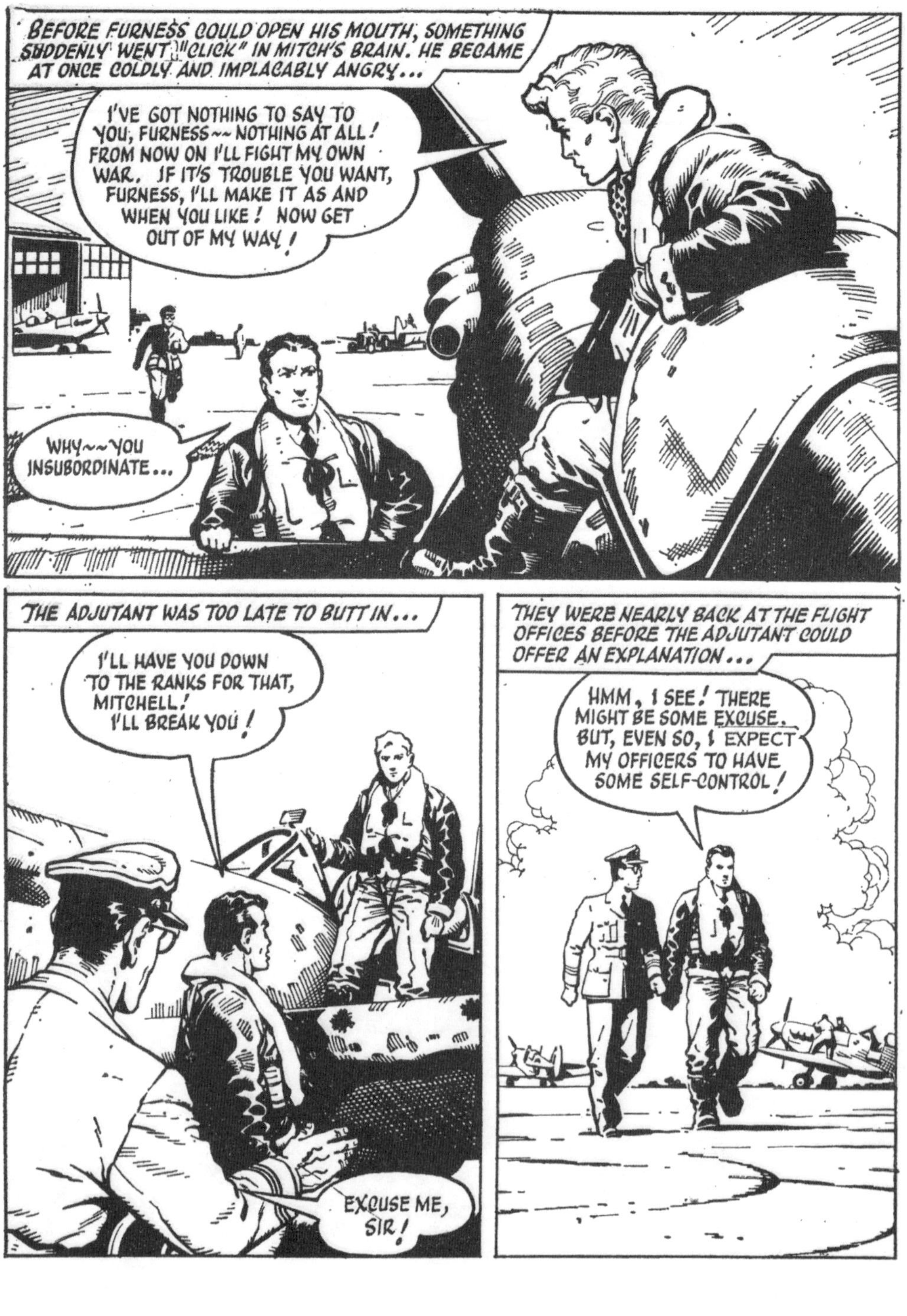
BEFORE FURNESS COULD OPEN HIS MOUTH, SOMETHING SUDDENLY WENT "CLICK" IN MITCH'S BRAIN. HE BECAME AT ONCE COLDLY AND IMPLACABLY ANGRY...
I'VE GOT NOTHING TO SAY TO YOU, FURNESS~~NOTHING AT ALL! FROM NOW ON I'LL FIGHT MY OWN WAR. IF IT'S TROUBLE YOU WANT, FURNESS, I'LL MAKE IT AS AND WHEN YOU LIKE! NOW GET OUT OF MY WAY!
WHY~~YOU INSUBORDINATE...
THE ADJUTANT WAS TOO LATE TO BUTT IN...
I'LL HAVE YOU DOWN TO THE RANKS FOR THAT, MITCHELL! I'LL BREAK YOU!
EXCUSE ME, SIR!
THEY WERE NEARLY BACK AT THE FLIGHT OFFICES BEFORE THE ADJUTANT COULD OFFER AN EXPLANATION...
HMM, I SEE! THERE MIGHT BE SOME EXCUSE. BUT, EVEN SO, I EXPECT MY OFFICERS TO HAVE SOME SELF-CONTROL!

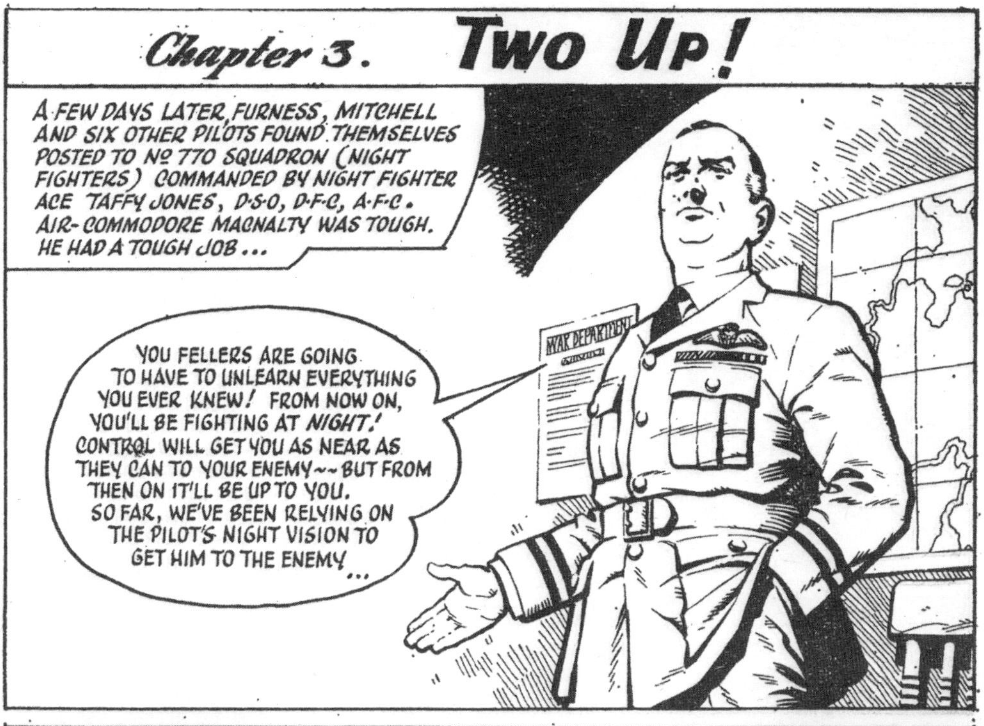
Chapter 3. TWO UP!
A FEW DAYS LATER, FURNESS, MITCHELL AND SIX OTHER PILOTS FOUND THEMSELVES POSTED TO Nº 770 SQUADRON (NIGHT FIGHTERS) COMMANDED BY NIGHT FIGHTER ACE TAFFY JONES, D.S.O, D.F.C, A.F.C. AIR-COMMODORE MACNALTY WAS TOUGH. HE HAD A TOUGH JOB...
WAR DEPARTMENT
YOU FELLERS ARE GOING TO HAVE TO UNLEARN EVERYTHING YOU EVER KNEW! FROM NOW ON, YOU'LL BE FIGHTING AT NIGHT! CONTROL WILL GET YOU AS NEAR AS THEY CAN TO YOUR ENEMY--BUT FROM THEN ON IT'LL BE UP TO YOU. SO FAR, WE'VE BEEN RELYING ON THE PILOT'S NIGHT VISION TO GET HIM TO THE ENEMY...

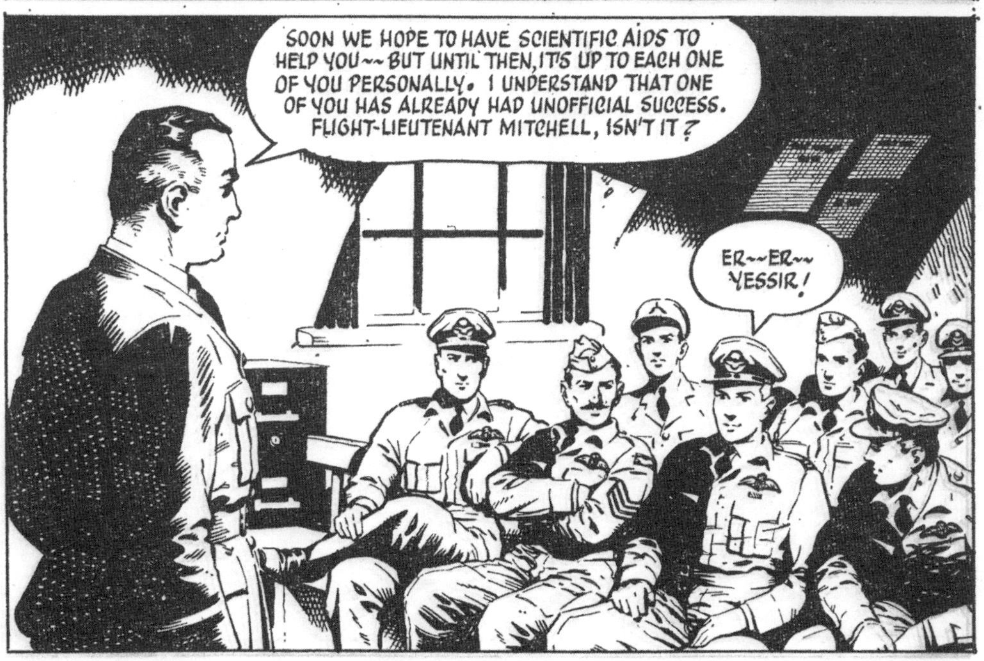
SOON WE HOPE TO HAVE SCIENTIFIC AIDS TO HELP YOU--BUT UNTIL THEN, IT'S UP TO EACH ONE OF YOU PERSONALLY. I UNDERSTAND THAT ONE OF YOU HAS ALREADY HAD UNOFFICIAL SUCCESS. FLIGHT-LIEUTENANT MITCHELL, ISN'T IT?
ER--ER-- YESSIR!

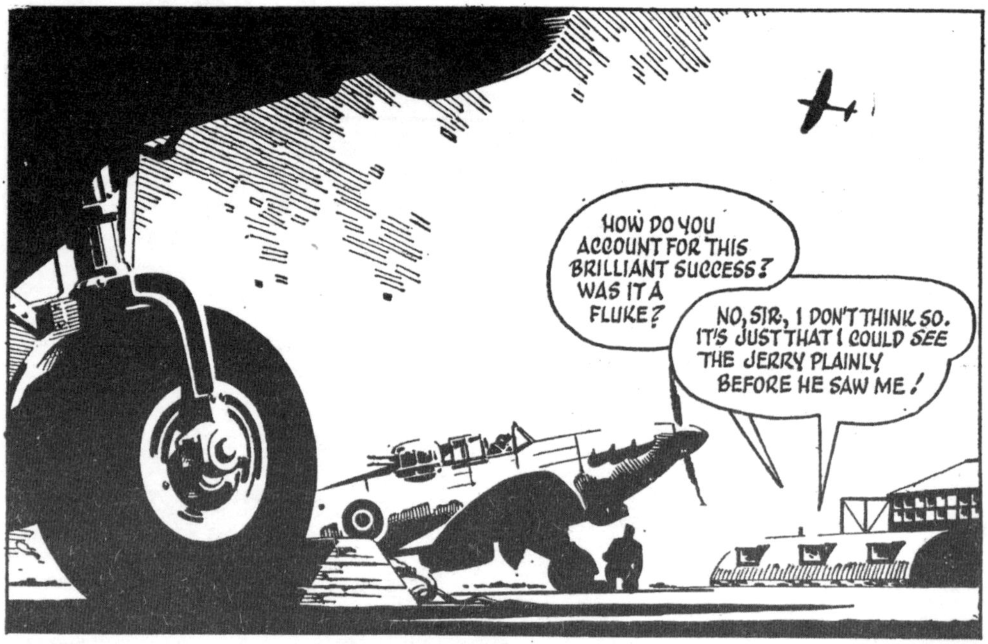
HOW DO YOU ACCOUNT FOR THIS BRILLIANT SUCCESS? WAS IT A FLUKE?
NO, SIR, I DON'T THINK SO. IT'S JUST THAT I COULD SEE THE JERRY PLAINLY BEFORE HE SAW ME!

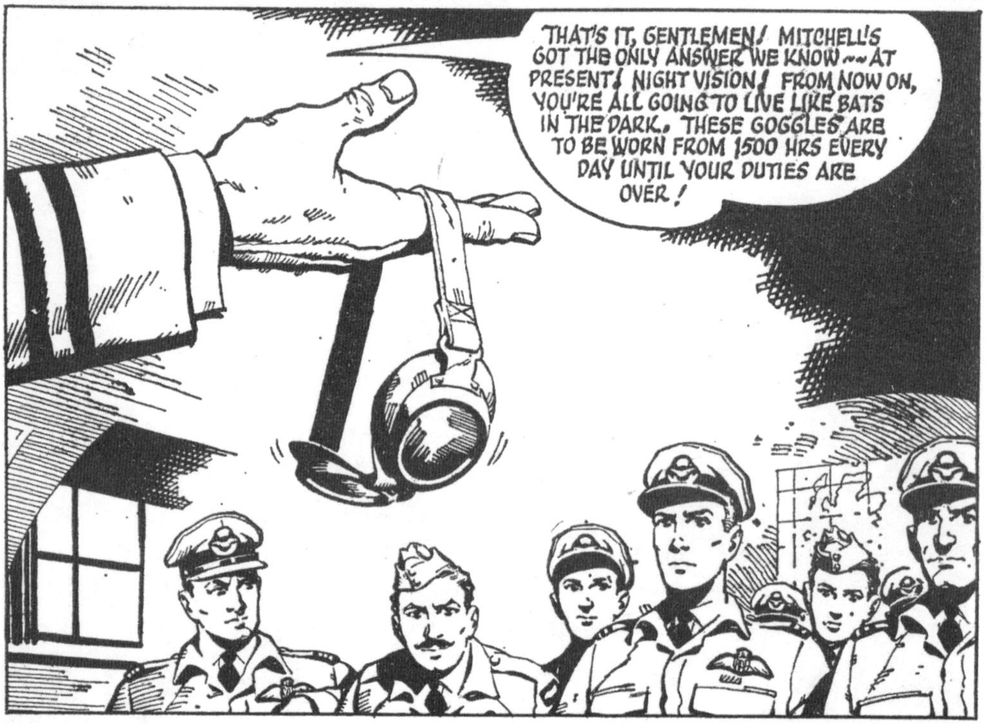
THAT'S IT, GENTLEMEN! MITCHELL'S GOT THE ONLY ANSWER WE KNOW -- AT PRESENT! NIGHT VISION! FROM NOW ON, YOU'RE ALL GOING TO LIVE LIKE BATS IN THE DARK. THESE GOGGLES ARE TO BE WORN FROM 1500 HRS EVERY DAY UNTIL YOUR DUTIES ARE OVER!

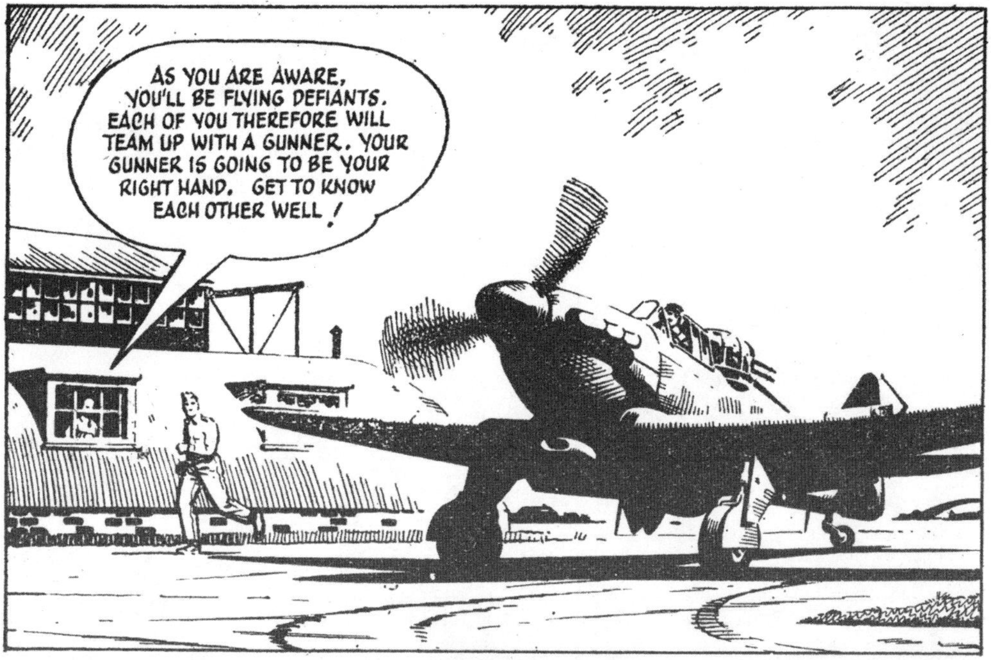
AS YOU ARE AWARE, YOU'LL BE FLYING DEFIANTS. EACH OF YOU THEREFORE WILL TEAM UP WITH A GUNNER. YOUR GUNNER IS GOING TO BE YOUR RIGHT HAND. GET TO KNOW EACH OTHER WELL !

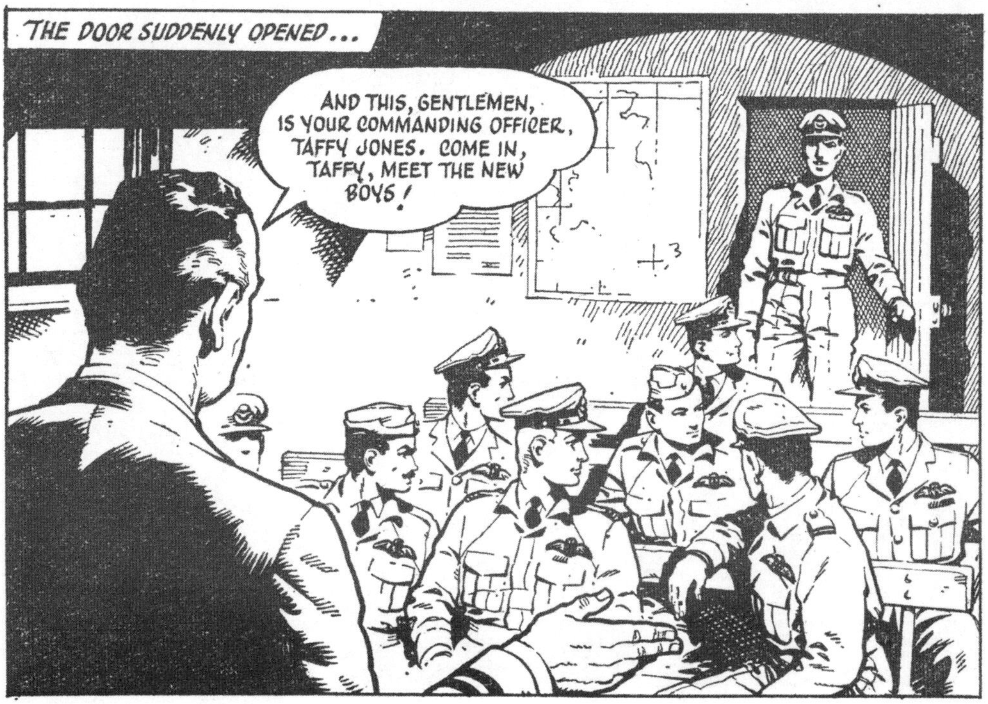
THE DOOR SUDDENLY OPENED...
AND THIS, GENTLEMEN, IS YOUR COMMANDING OFFICER, TAFFY JONES. COME IN, TAFFY, MEET THE NEW BOYS !

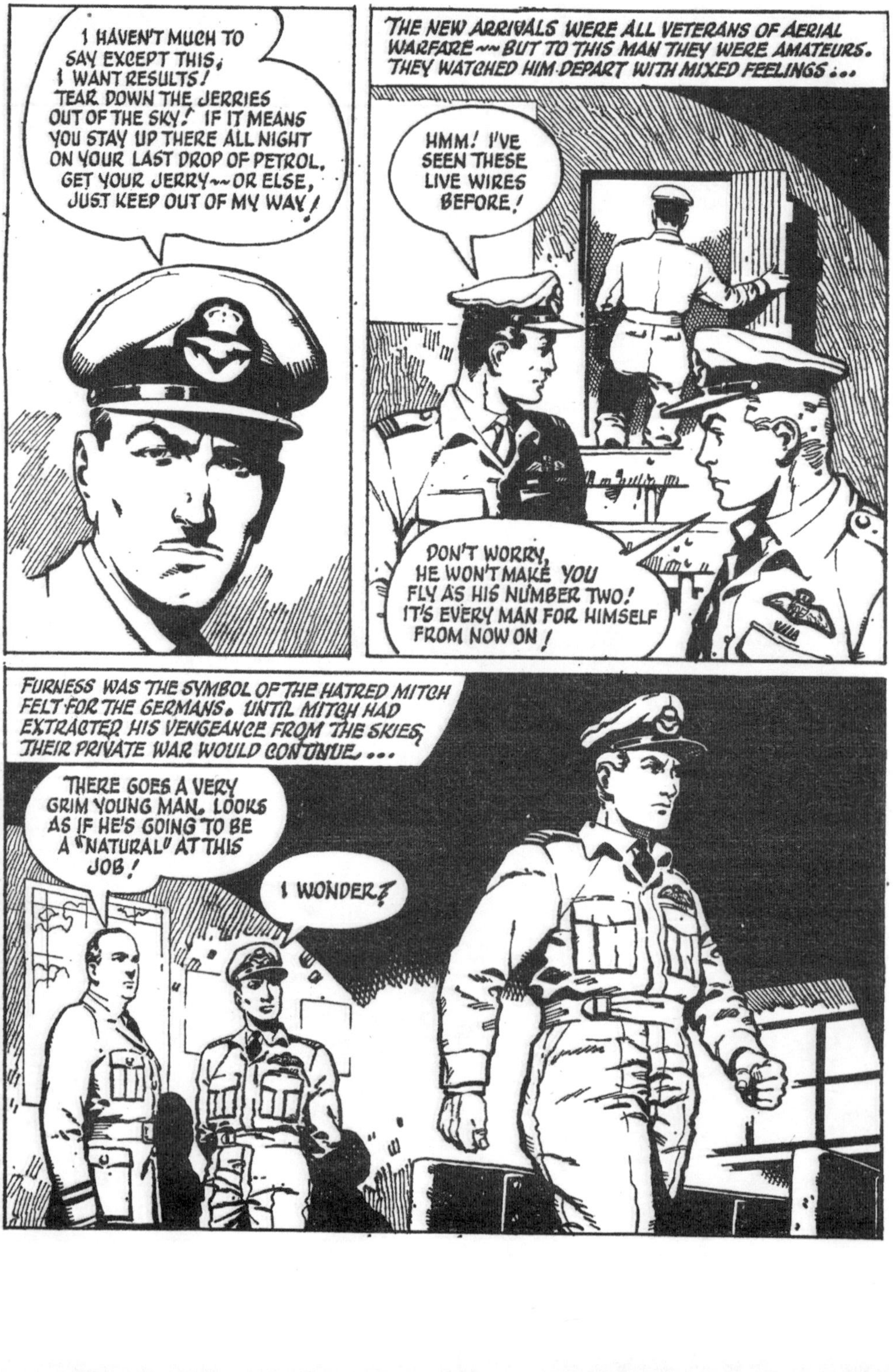
I HAVEN'T MUCH TO SAY EXCEPT THIS; I WANT RESULTS! TEAR DOWN THE JERRIES OUT OF THE SKY! IF IT MEANS YOU STAY UP THERE ALL NIGHT ON YOUR LAST DROP OF PETROL. GET YOUR JERRY—OR ELSE, JUST KEEP OUT OF MY WAY!
THE NEW ARRIVALS WERE ALL VETERANS OF AERIAL WARFARE—BUT TO THIS MAN THEY WERE AMATEURS. THEY WATCHED HIM DEPART WITH MIXED FEELINGS...
HMM! I'VE SEEN THESE LIVE WIRES BEFORE!
DON'T WORRY, HE WON'T MAKE YOU FLY AS HIS NUMBER TWO! IT'S EVERY MAN FOR HIMSELF FROM NOW ON!
FURNESS WAS THE SYMBOL OF THE HATRED MITCH FELT FOR THE GERMANS. UNTIL MITCH HAD EXTRACTED HIS VENGEANCE FROM THE SKIES, THEIR PRIVATE WAR WOULD CONTINUE...
THERE GOES A VERY GRIM YOUNG MAN. LOOKS AS IF HE'S GOING TO BE A "NATURAL" AT THIS JOB!
I WONDER?

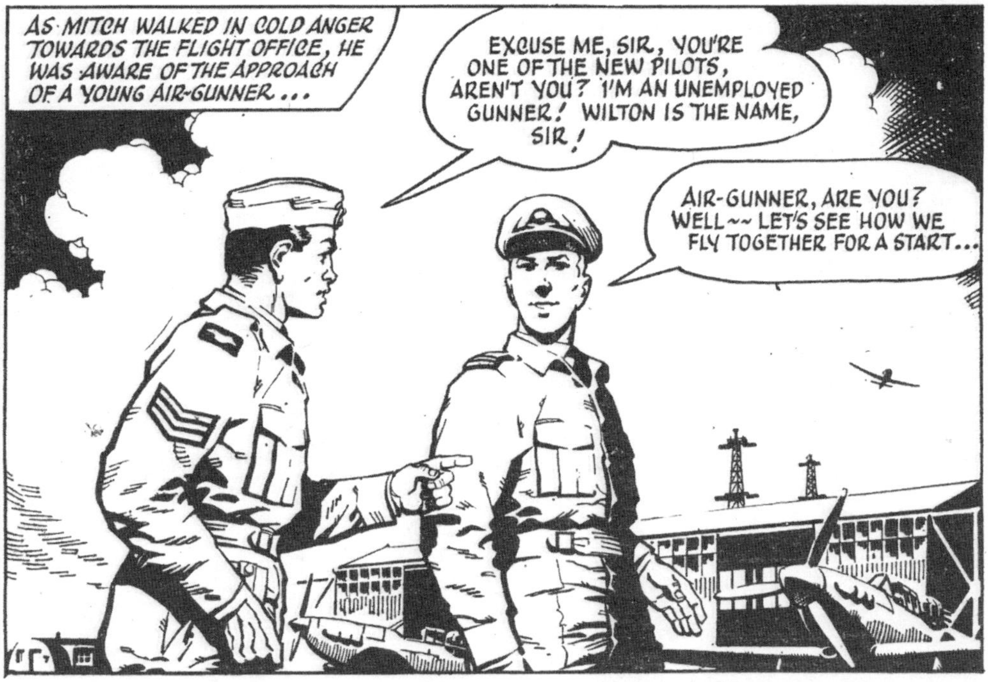
AS MITCH WALKED IN COLD ANGER TOWARDS THE FLIGHT OFFICE, HE WAS AWARE OF THE APPROACH OF A YOUNG AIR-GUNNER ...
EXCUSE ME, SIR, YOU'RE ONE OF THE NEW PILOTS, AREN'T YOU? I'M AN UNEMPLOYED GUNNER! WILTON IS THE NAME, SIR!
AIR-GUNNER, ARE YOU? WELL -- LET'S SEE HOW WE FLY TOGETHER FOR A START...

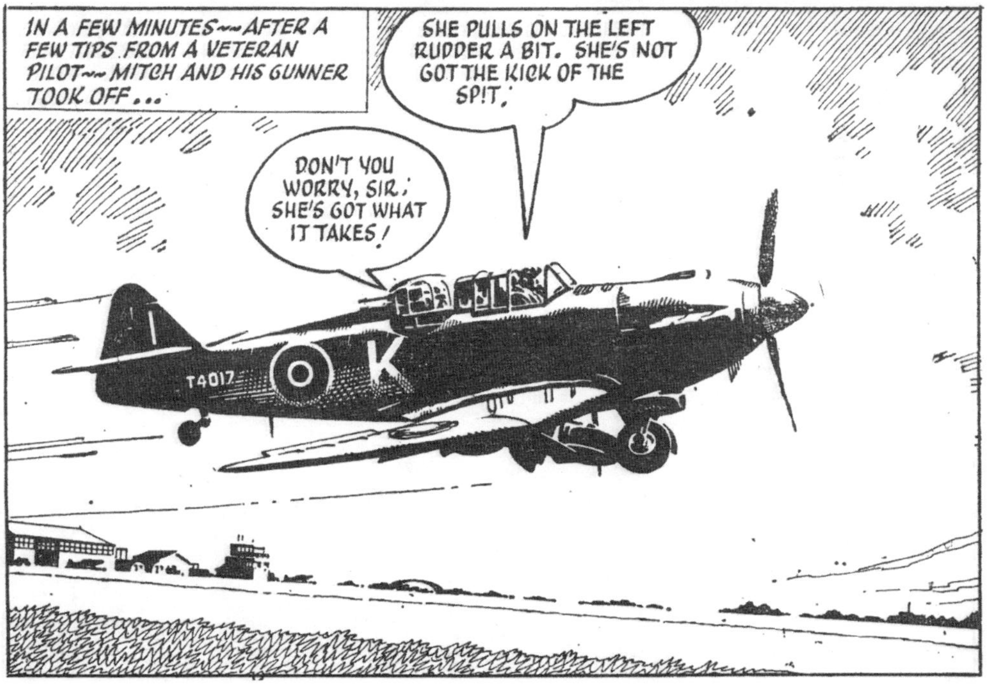
IN A FEW MINUTES -- AFTER A FEW TIPS FROM A VETERAN PILOT -- MITCH AND HIS GUNNER TOOK OFF ...
SHE PULLS ON THE LEFT RUDDER A BIT. SHE'S NOT GOT THE KICK OF THE SPIT.
DON'T YOU WORRY, SIR; SHE'S GOT WHAT IT TAKES!
T4017
K

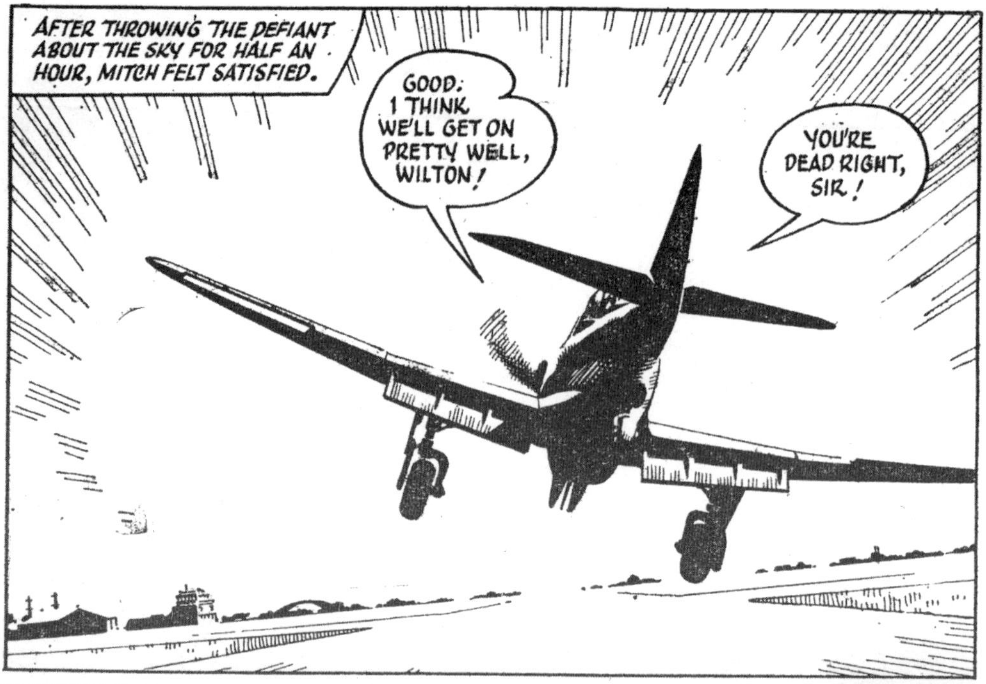
AFTER THROWING THE DEFIANT ABOUT THE SKY FOR HALF AN HOUR, MITCH FELT SATISFIED.
GOOD: I THINK WE'LL GET ON PRETTY WELL, WILTON!
YOU'RE DEAD RIGHT, SIR!

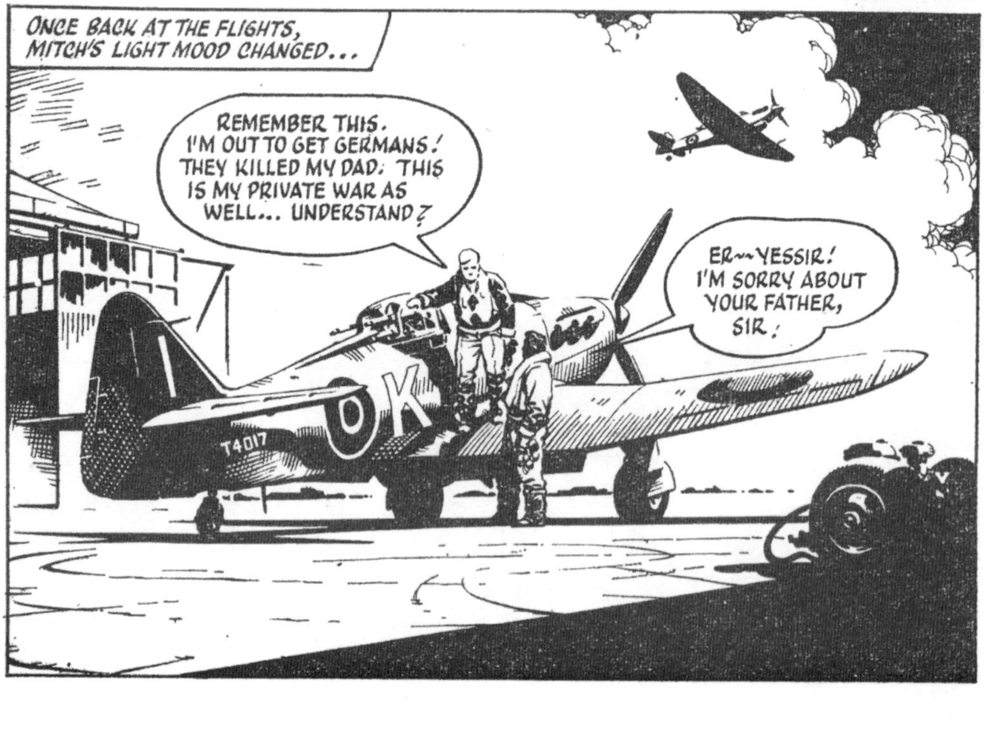
ONCE BACK AT THE FLIGHTS, MITCH'S LIGHT MOOD CHANGED...
REMEMBER THIS. I'M OUT TO GET GERMANS! THEY KILLED MY DAD: THIS IS MY PRIVATE WAR AS WELL... UNDERSTAND?
ER--YESSIR! I'M SORRY ABOUT YOUR FATHER, SIR!
T4017

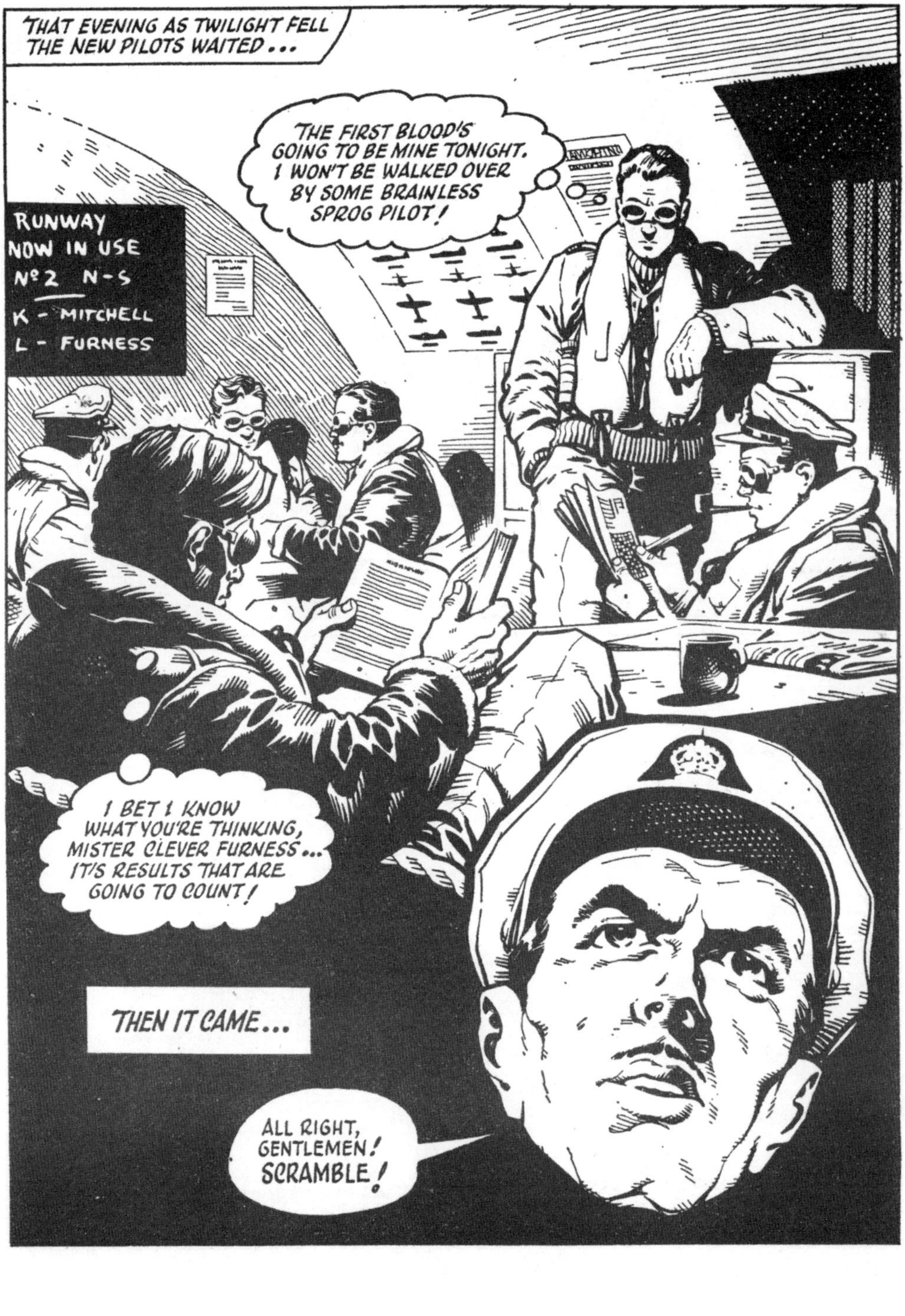
THAT EVENING AS TWILIGHT FELL THE NEW PILOTS WAITED...
THE FIRST BLOOD'S GOING TO BE MINE TONIGHT. I WON'T BE WALKED OVER BY SOME BRAINLESS SPROG PILOT!
RUNWAY NOW IN USE Nº2 N-S
K - MITCHELL
L - FURNESS
I BET I KNOW WHAT YOU'RE THINKING, MISTER CLEVER FURNESS... IT'S RESULTS THAT ARE GOING TO COUNT!
THEN IT CAME...
ALL RIGHT, GENTLEMEN! SCRAMBLE!

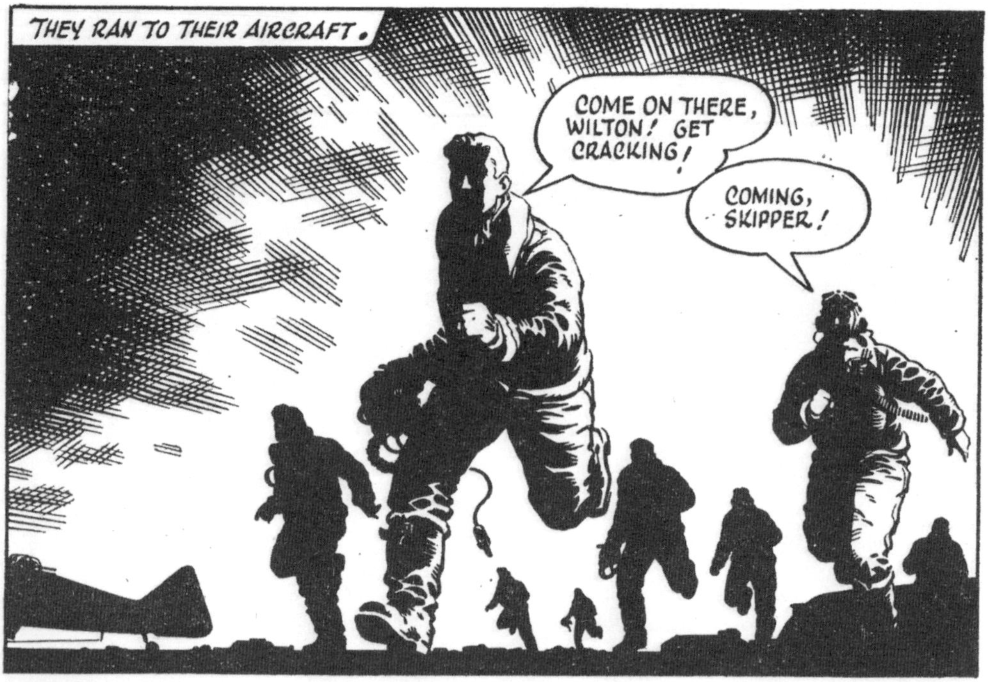
THEY RAN TO THEIR AIRCRAFT.
COME ON THERE, WILTON! GET CRACKING!
COMING, SKIPPER!

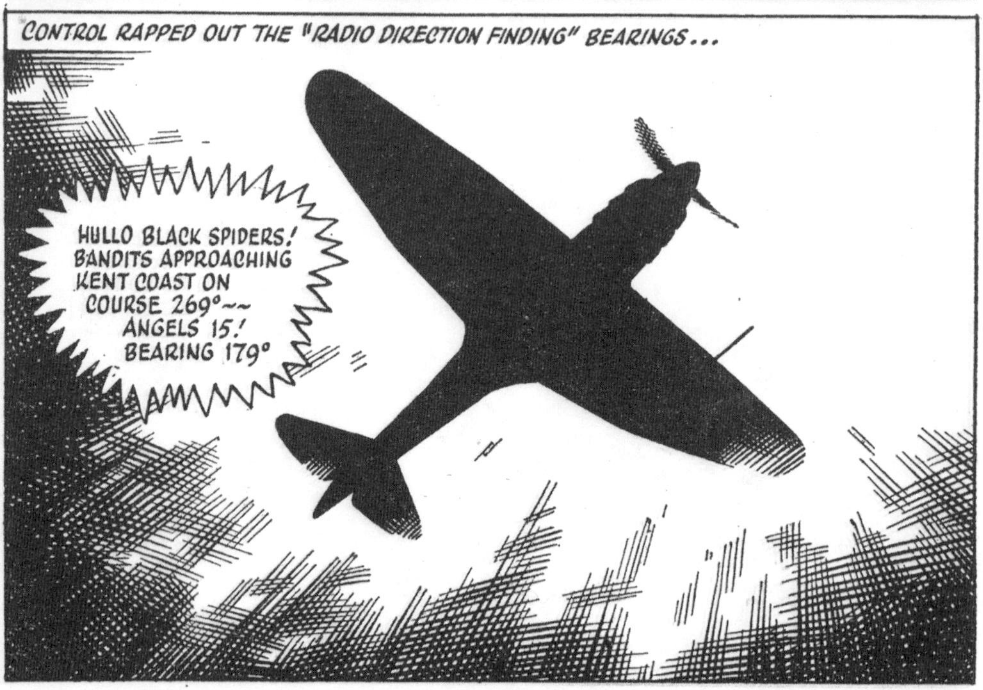
CONTROL RAPPED OUT THE "RADIO DIRECTION FINDING" BEARINGS...
HULLO BLACK SPIDERS! BANDITS APPROACHING KENT COAST ON COURSE 269°~~ ANGELS 15! BEARING 179°

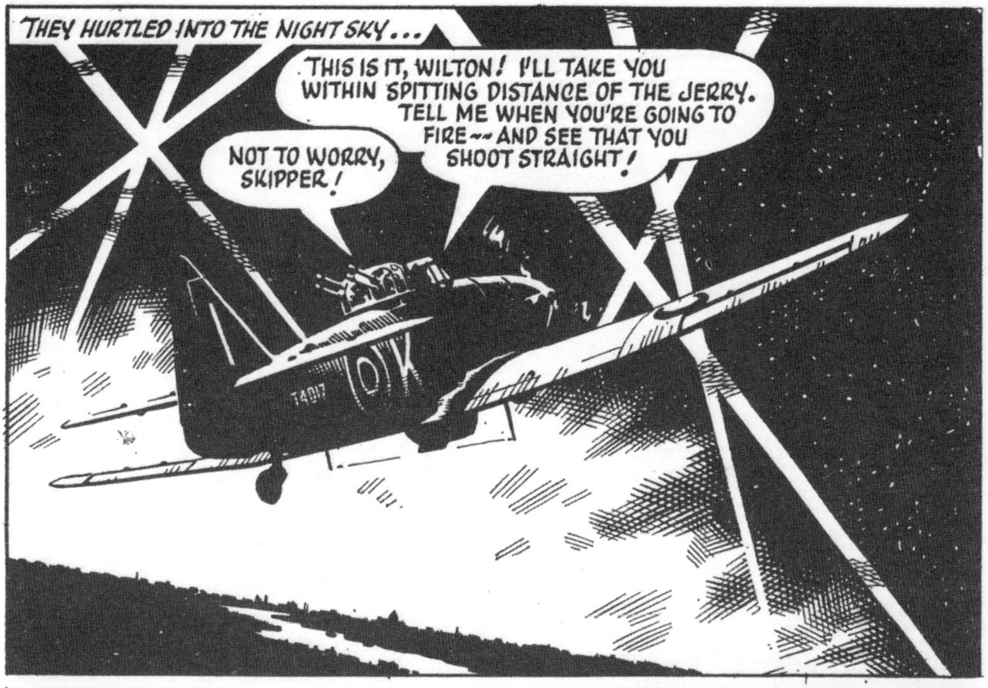
THEY HURTLED INTO THE NIGHT SKY...
THIS IS IT, WILTON! I'LL TAKE YOU WITHIN SPITTING DISTANCE OF THE JERRY. TELL ME WHEN YOU'RE GOING TO FIRE--AND SEE THAT YOU SHOOT STRAIGHT!
NOT TO WORRY, SKIPPER!

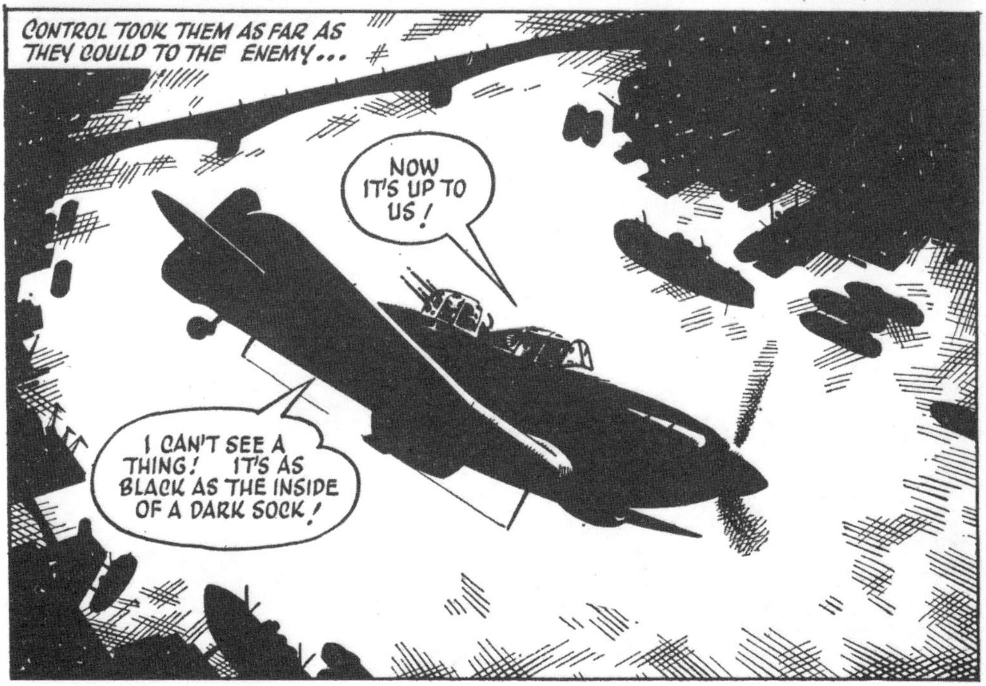
CONTROL TOOK THEM AS FAR AS THEY COULD TO THE ENEMY...
NOW IT'S UP TO US!
I CAN'T SEE A THING! IT'S AS BLACK AS THE INSIDE OF A DARK SOCK!

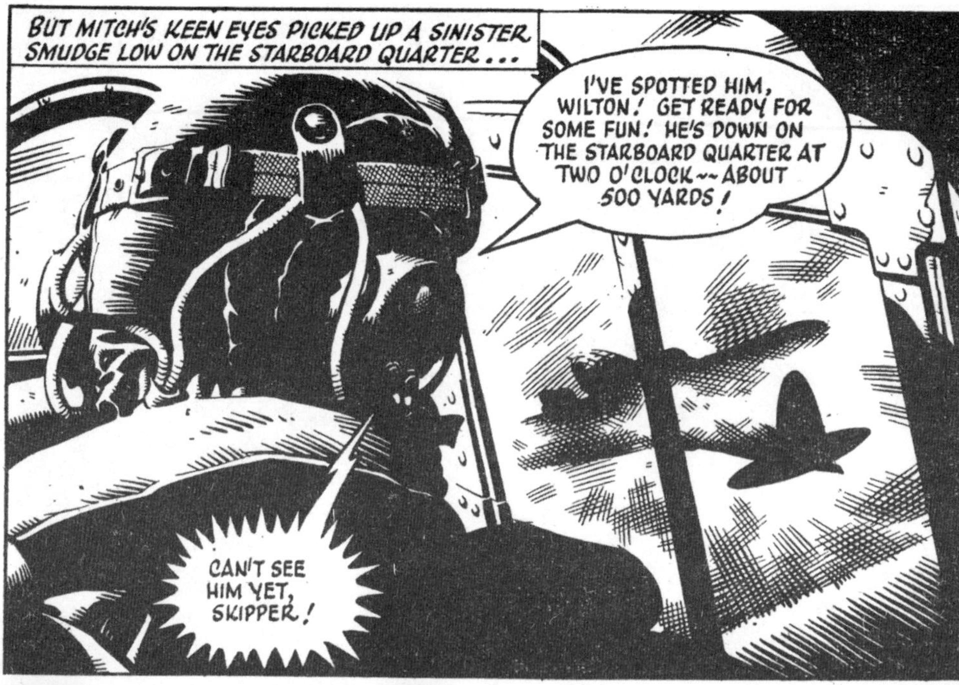
BUT MITCH'S KEEN EYES PICKED UP A SINISTER SMUDGE LOW ON THE STARBOARD QUARTER . . .
I'VE SPOTTED HIM, WILTON! GET READY FOR SOME FUN! HE'S DOWN ON THE STARBOARD QUARTER AT TWO O'CLOCK -- ABOUT 500 YARDS!
CAN'T SEE HIM YET, SKIPPER!

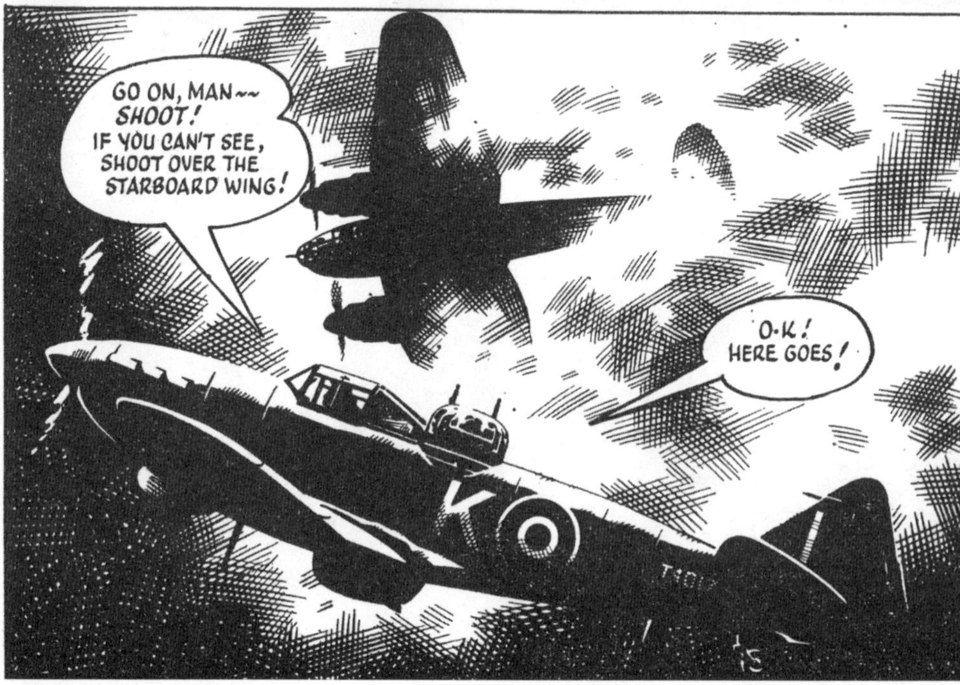
GO ON, MAN -- SHOOT! IF YOU CAN'T SEE, SHOOT OVER THE STARBOARD WING!
O.K.! HERE GOES!

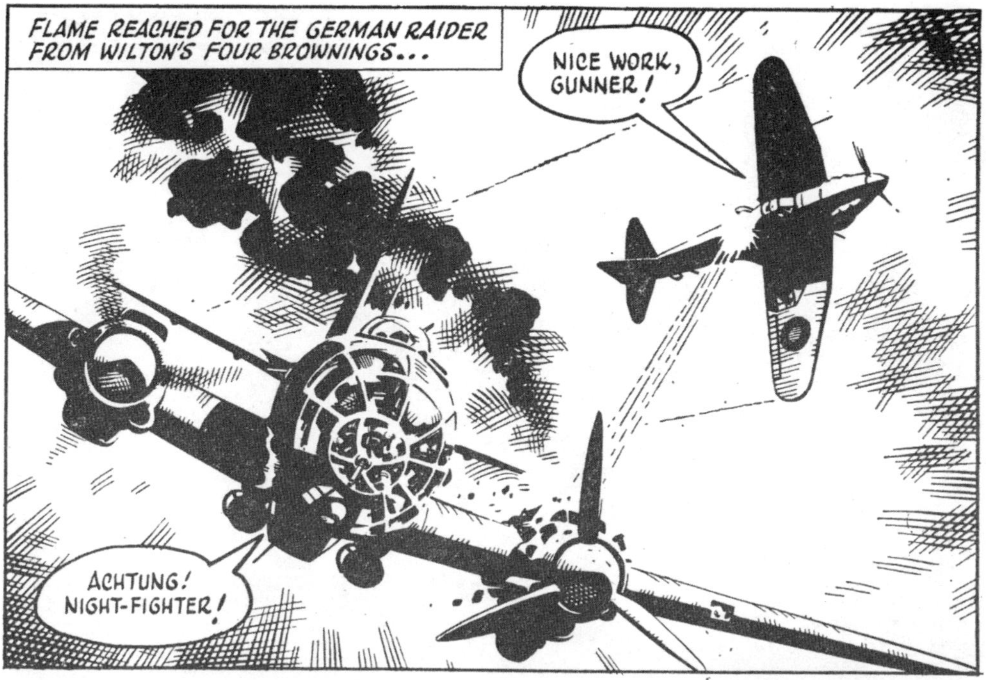
FLAME REACHED FOR THE GERMAN RAIDER FROM WILTON'S FOUR BROWNINGS...
NICE WORK, GUNNER!
ACHTUNG! NIGHT-FIGHTER!

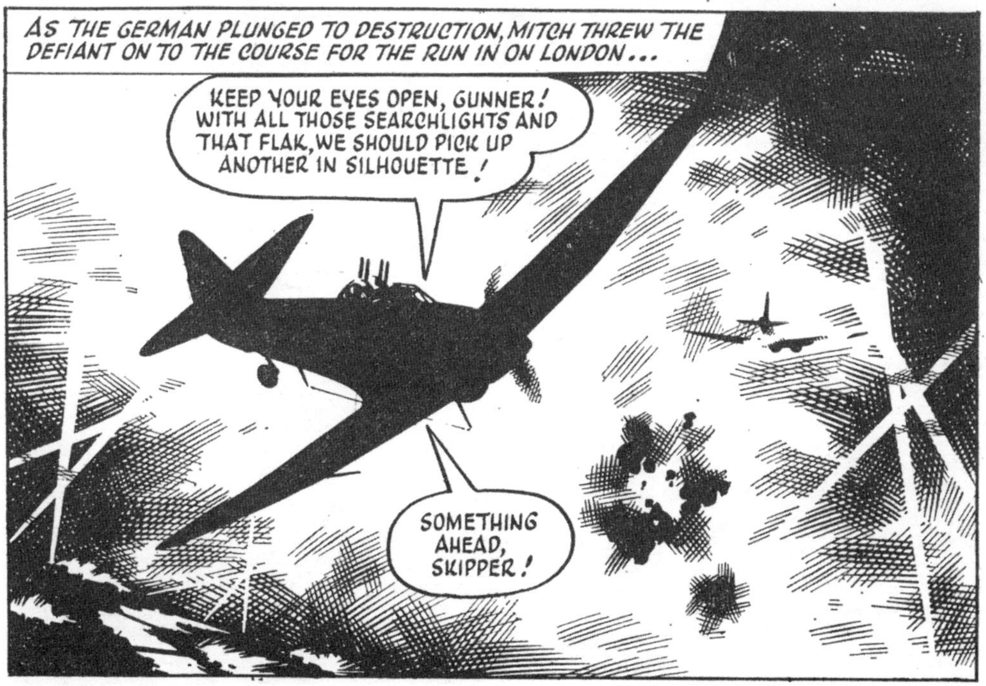
AS THE GERMAN PLUNGED TO DESTRUCTION, MITCH THREW THE DEFIANT ON TO THE COURSE FOR THE RUN IN ON LONDON...
KEEP YOUR EYES OPEN, GUNNER! WITH ALL THOSE SEARCHLIGHTS AND THAT FLAK, WE SHOULD PICK UP ANOTHER IN SILHOUETTE!
SOMETHING AHEAD, SKIPPER!

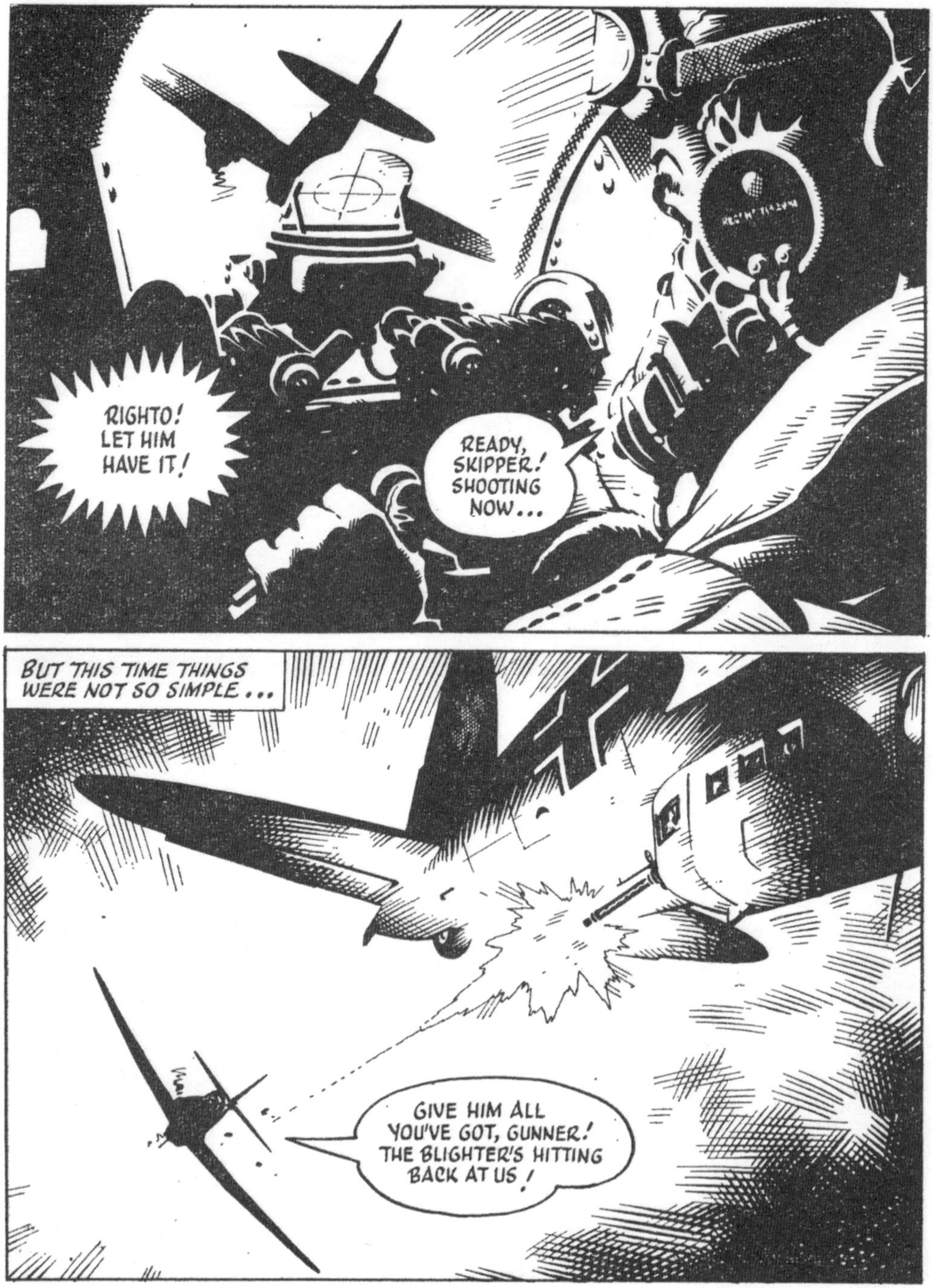
RIGHTO! LET HIM HAVE IT!
READY, SKIPPER! SHOOTING NOW...
BUT THIS TIME THINGS WERE NOT SO SIMPLE...
GIVE HIM ALL YOU'VE GOT, GUNNER! THE BLIGHTER'S HITTING BACK AT US!

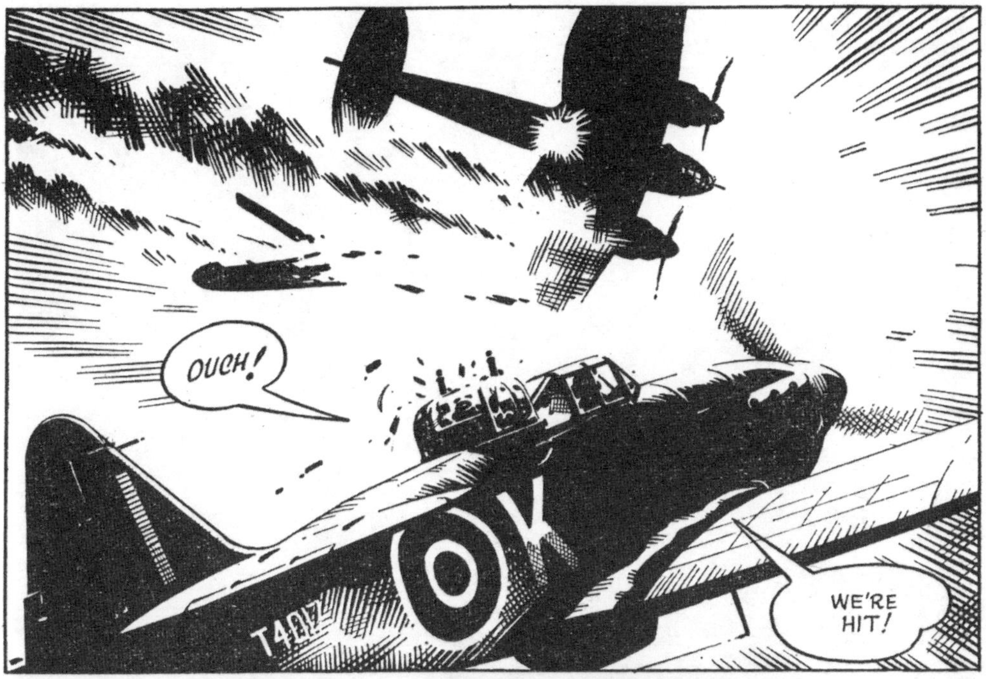
OUCH!
WE'RE HIT!

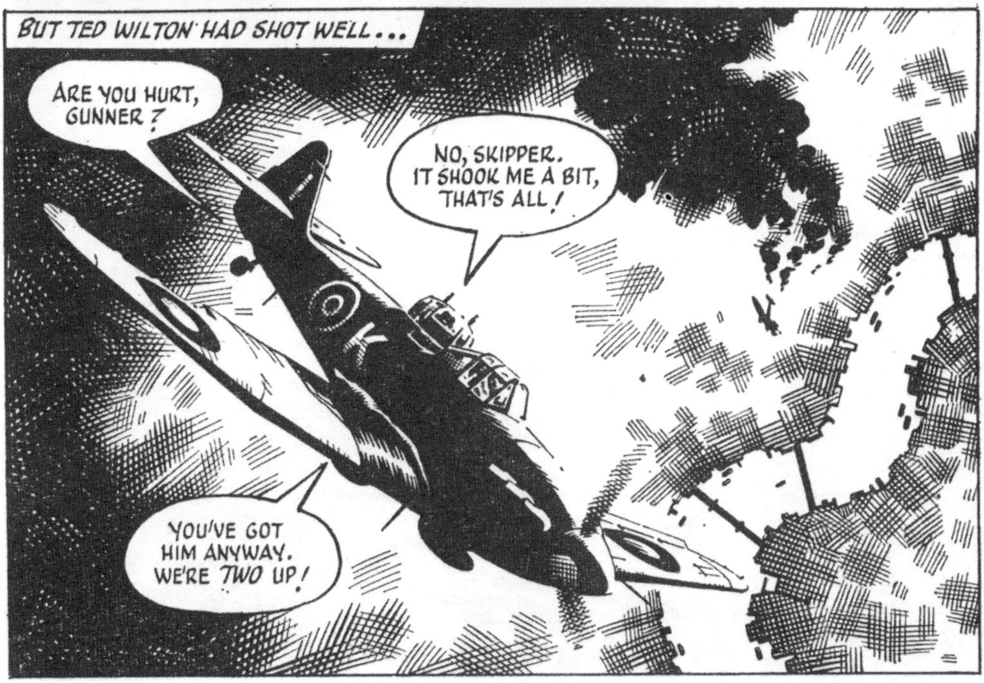
BUT TED WILTON HAD SHOT WELL...
ARE YOU HURT, GUNNER?
NO, SKIPPER. IT SHOOK ME A BIT, THAT'S ALL!
YOU'VE GOT HIM ANYWAY. WE'RE TWO UP!

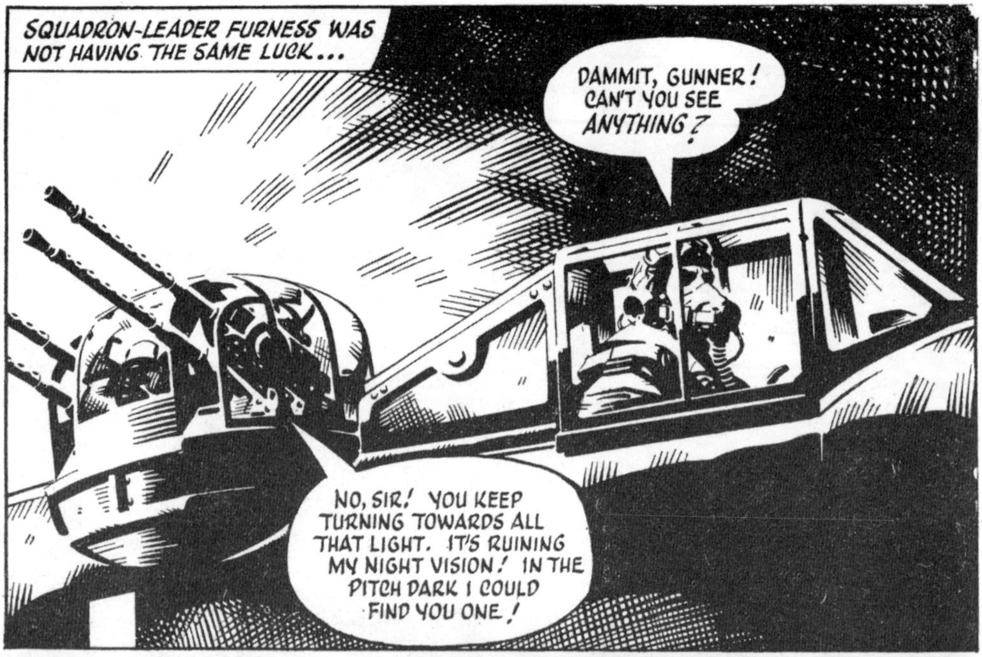
SQUADRON-LEADER FURNESS WAS NOT HAVING THE SAME LUCK...
DAMMIT, GUNNER! CAN'T YOU SEE ANYTHING?
NO, SIR! YOU KEEP TURNING TOWARDS ALL THAT LIGHT. IT'S RUINING MY NIGHT VISION! IN THE PITCH DARK I COULD FIND YOU ONE!

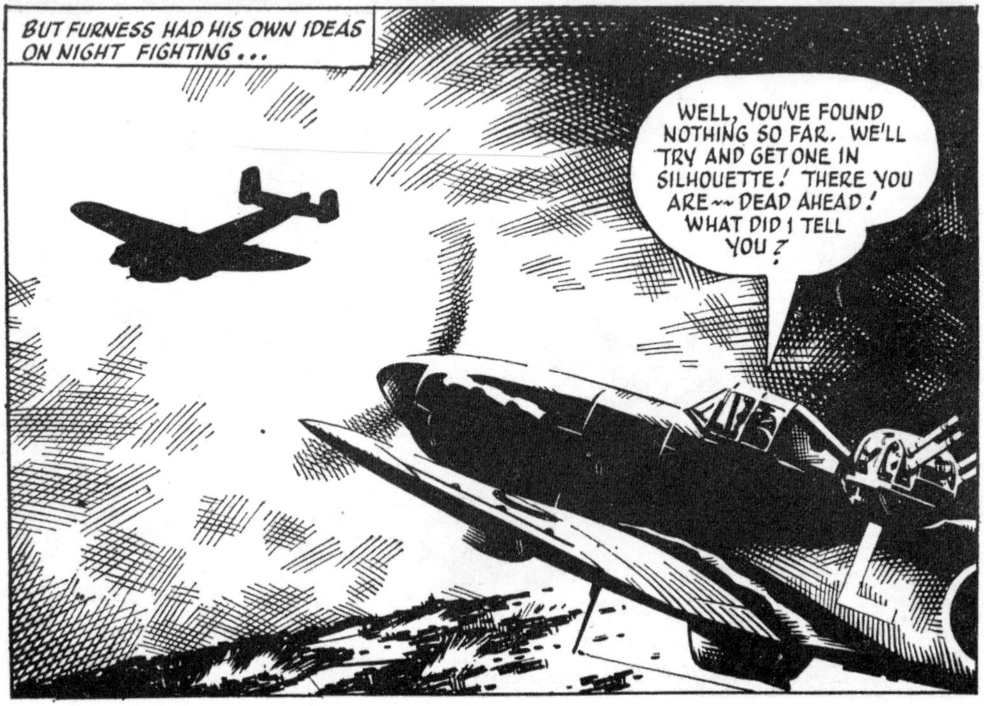
BUT FURNESS HAD HIS OWN IDEAS ON NIGHT FIGHTING...
WELL, YOU'VE FOUND NOTHING SO FAR. WE'LL TRY AND GET ONE IN SILHOUETTE! THERE YOU ARE -- DEAD AHEAD! WHAT DID I TELL YOU?

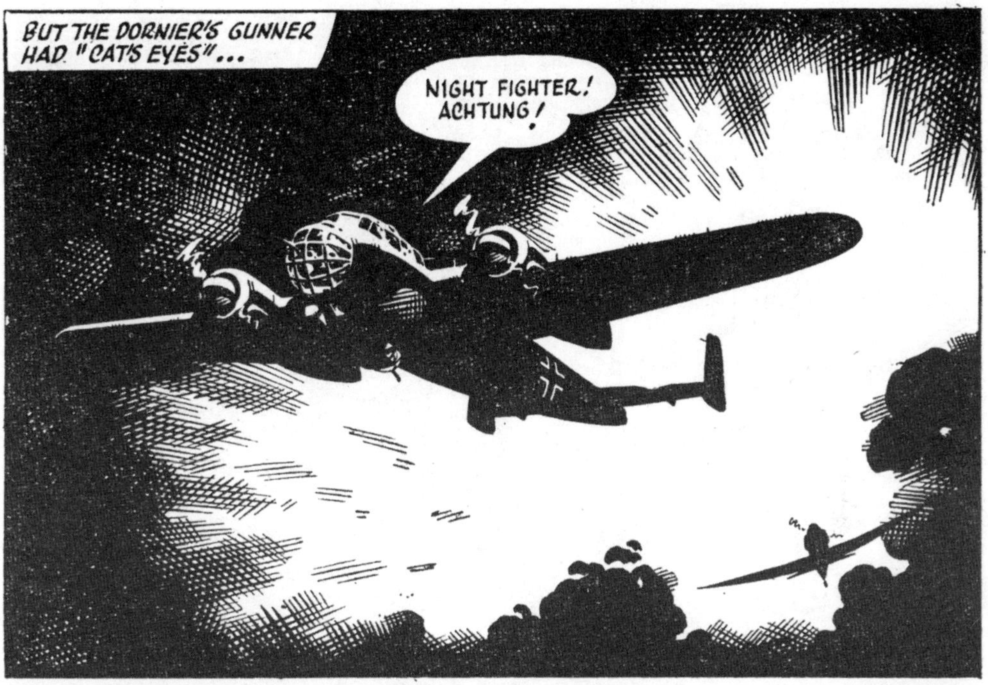
BUT THE DORNIER'S GUNNER HAD "CAT'S EYES"...
NIGHT FIGHTER! ACHTUNG!

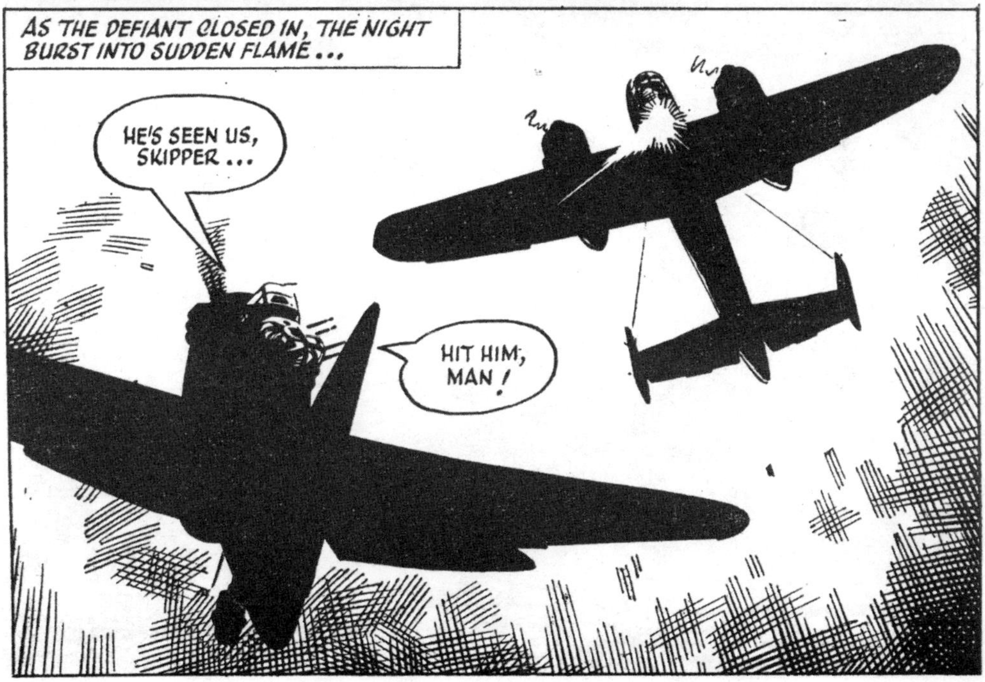
AS THE DEFIANT CLOSED IN, THE NIGHT BURST INTO SUDDEN FLAME...
HE'S SEEN US, SKIPPER...
HIT HIM, MAN!

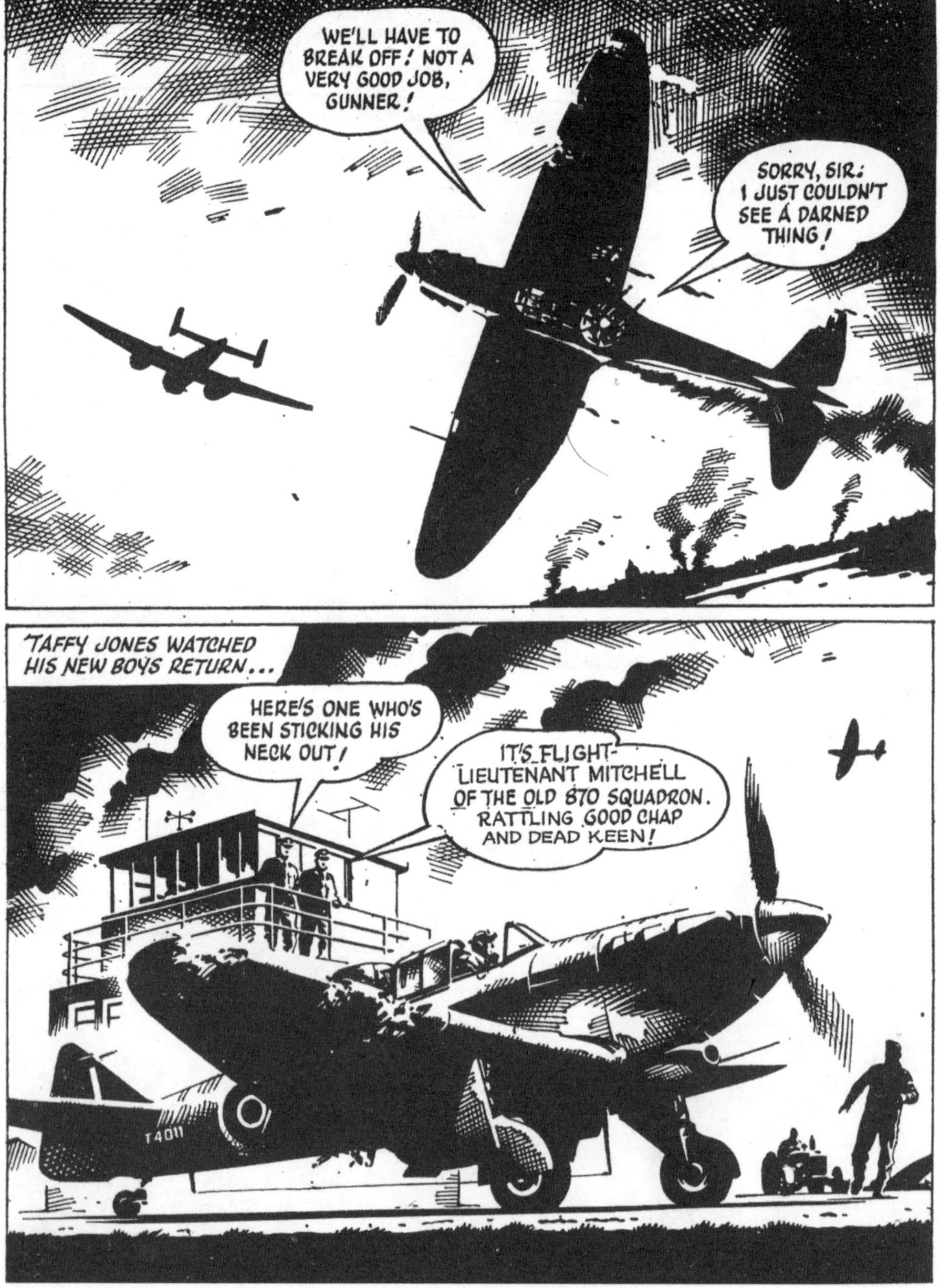
WE'LL HAVE TO BREAK OFF! NOT A VERY GOOD JOB, GUNNER!
SORRY, SIR: I JUST COULDN'T SEE A DARNED THING!
TAFFY JONES WATCHED HIS NEW BOYS RETURN...
HERE'S ONE WHO'S BEEN STICKING HIS NECK OUT!
IT'S FLIGHT-LIEUTENANT MITCHELL OF THE OLD 870 SQUADRON. RATTLING GOOD CHAP AND DEAD KEEN!
T4011

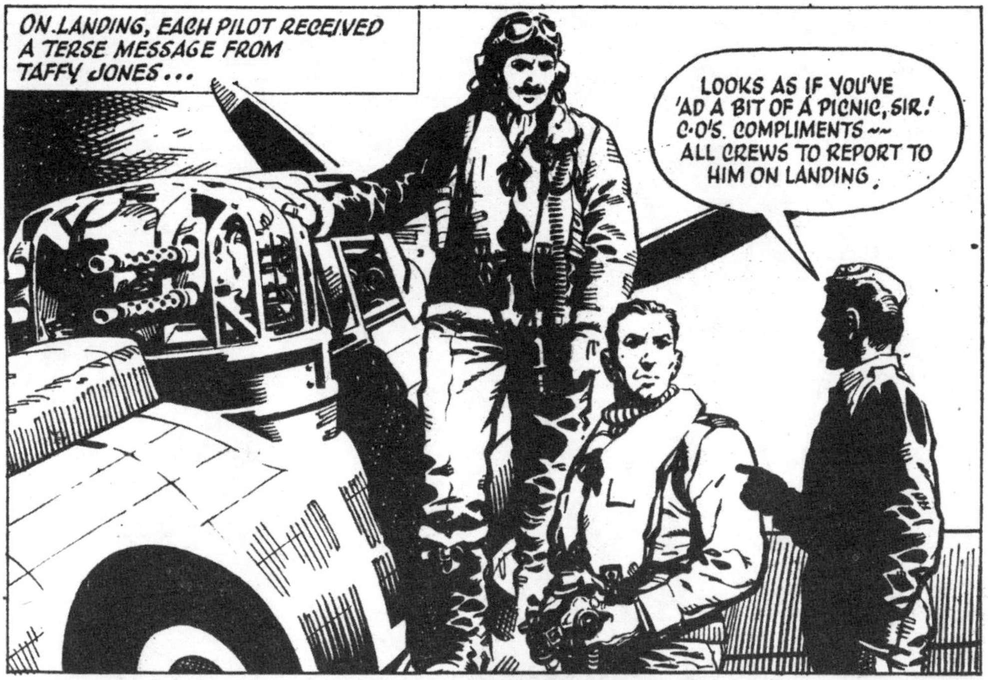
ON LANDING, EACH PILOT RECEIVED A TERSE MESSAGE FROM TAFFY JONES...
LOOKS AS IF YOU'VE 'AD A BIT OF A PICNIC, SIR! C.O'S. COMPLIMENTS -- ALL CREWS TO REPORT TO HIM ON LANDING.

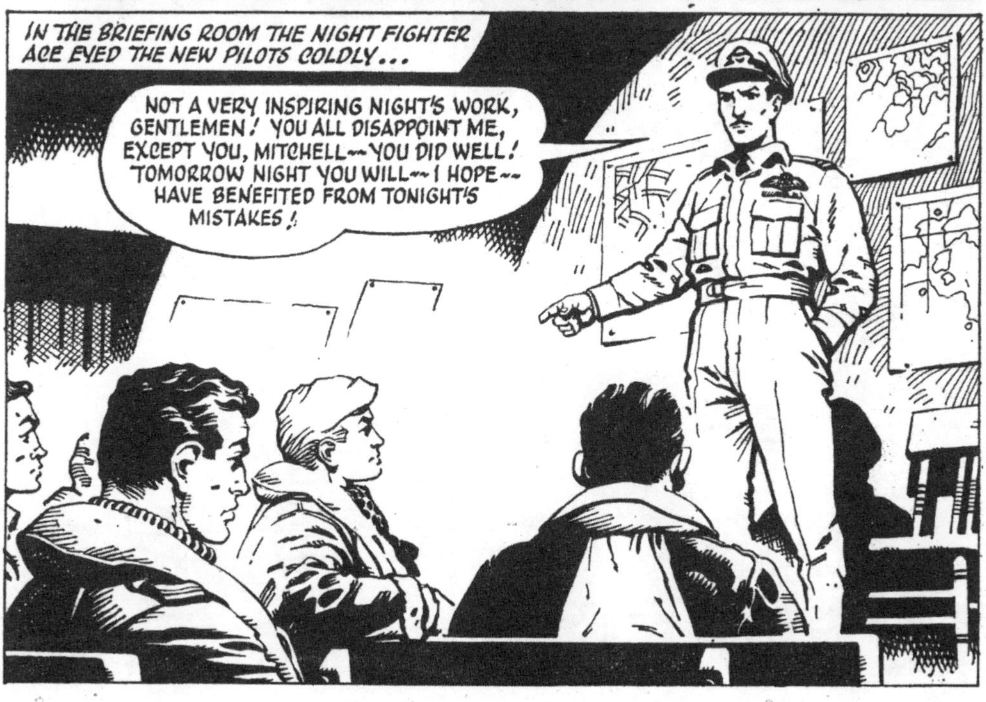
IN THE BRIEFING ROOM THE NIGHT FIGHTER ACE EYED THE NEW PILOTS COLDLY...
NOT A VERY INSPIRING NIGHT'S WORK, GENTLEMEN! YOU ALL DISAPPOINT ME, EXCEPT YOU, MITCHELL -- YOU DID WELL! TOMORROW NIGHT YOU WILL -- I HOPE -- HAVE BENEFITED FROM TONIGHT'S MISTAKES!

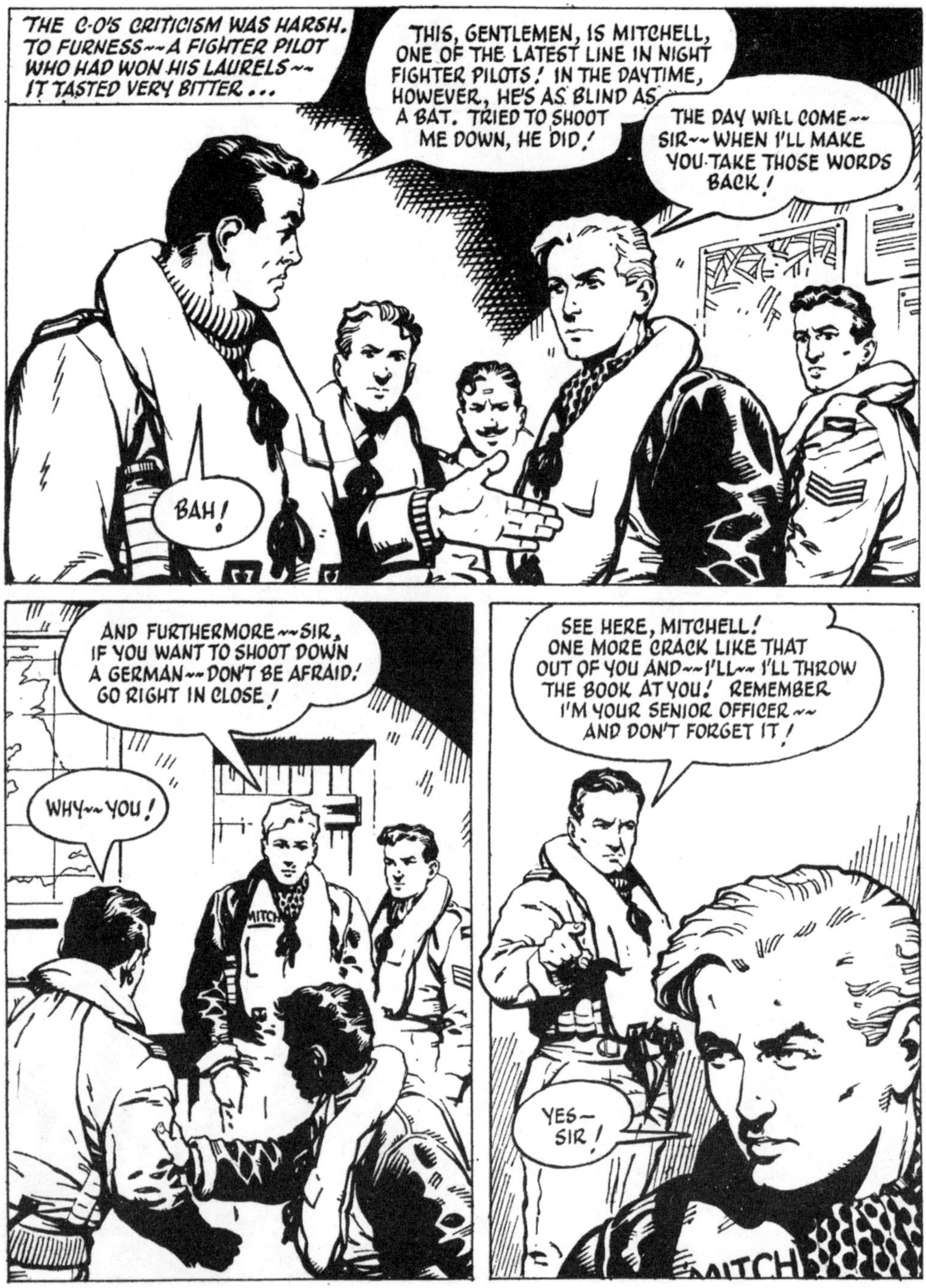
THE C-O'S CRITICISM WAS HARSH. TO FURNESS--A FIGHTER PILOT WHO HAD WON HIS LAURELS--IT TASTED VERY BITTER...
THIS, GENTLEMEN, IS MITCHELL, ONE OF THE LATEST LINE IN NIGHT FIGHTER PILOTS! IN THE DAYTIME, HOWEVER, HE'S AS BLIND AS A BAT. TRIED TO SHOOT ME DOWN, HE DID!
THE DAY WILL COME--SIR--WHEN I'LL MAKE YOU TAKE THOSE WORDS BACK!
BAH!
AND FURTHERMORE--SIR, IF YOU WANT TO SHOOT DOWN A GERMAN--DON'T BE AFRAID! GO RIGHT IN CLOSE!
WHY--YOU!
MITCH
SEE HERE, MITCHELL! ONE MORE CRACK LIKE THAT OUT OF YOU AND--I'LL--I'LL THROW THE BOOK AT YOU! REMEMBER I'M YOUR SENIOR OFFICER--AND DON'T FORGET IT!
YES-SIR!
MITCH

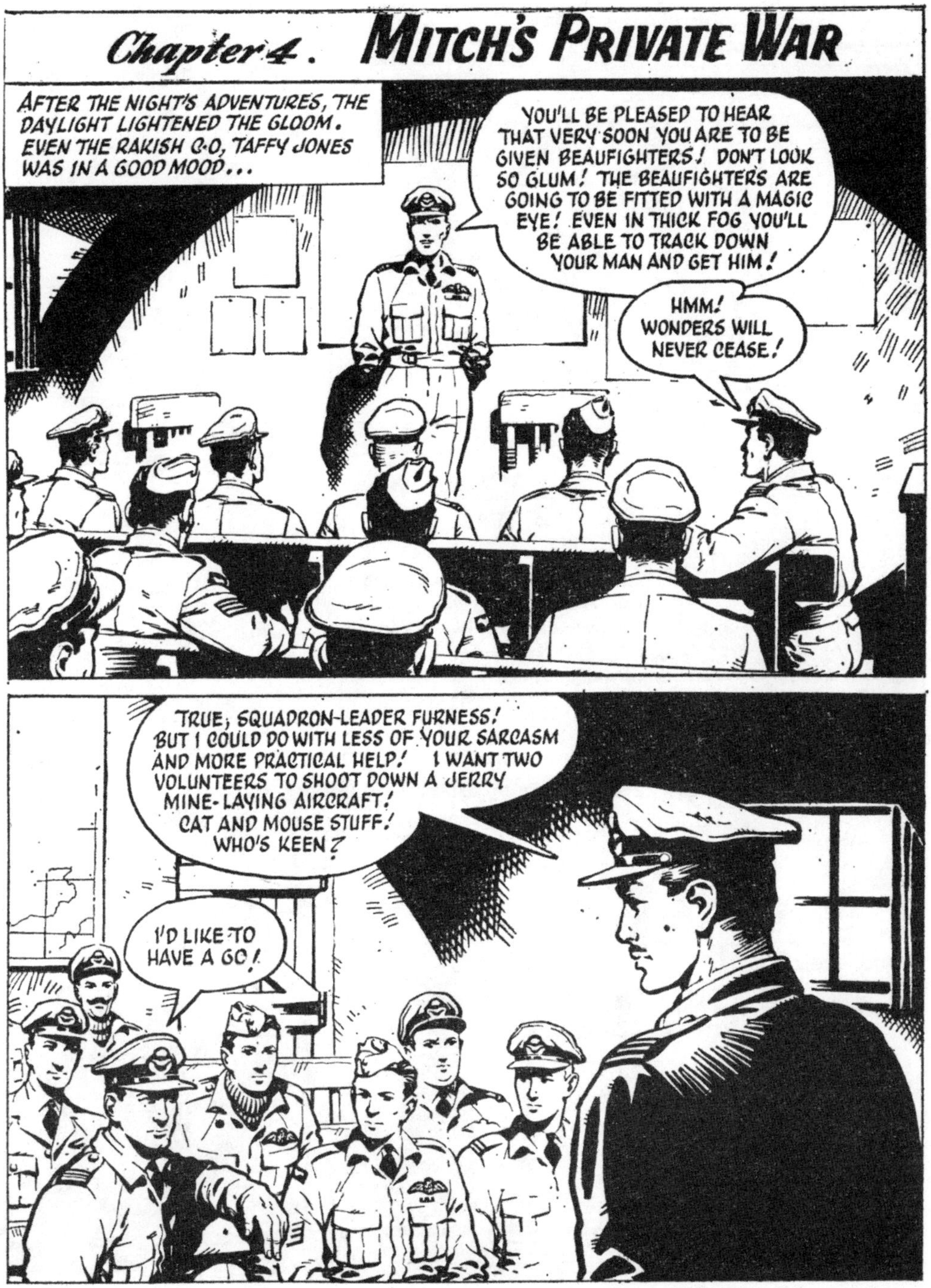
Chapter 4. MITCH'S PRIVATE WAR
AFTER THE NIGHT'S ADVENTURES, THE DAYLIGHT LIGHTENED THE GLOOM. EVEN THE RAKISH C.O, TAFFY JONES WAS IN A GOOD MOOD...
YOU'LL BE PLEASED TO HEAR THAT VERY SOON YOU ARE TO BE GIVEN BEAUFIGHTERS! DON'T LOOK SO GLUM! THE BEAUFIGHTERS ARE GOING TO BE FITTED WITH A MAGIC EYE! EVEN IN THICK FOG YOU'LL BE ABLE TO TRACK DOWN YOUR MAN AND GET HIM!
HMM! WONDERS WILL NEVER CEASE!
TRUE, SQUADRON-LEADER FURNESS! BUT I COULD DO WITH LESS OF YOUR SARCASM AND MORE PRACTICAL HELP! I WANT TWO VOLUNTEERS TO SHOOT DOWN A JERRY MINE-LAYING AIRCRAFT! CAT AND MOUSE STUFF! WHO'S KEEN?
I'D LIKE TO HAVE A GO!

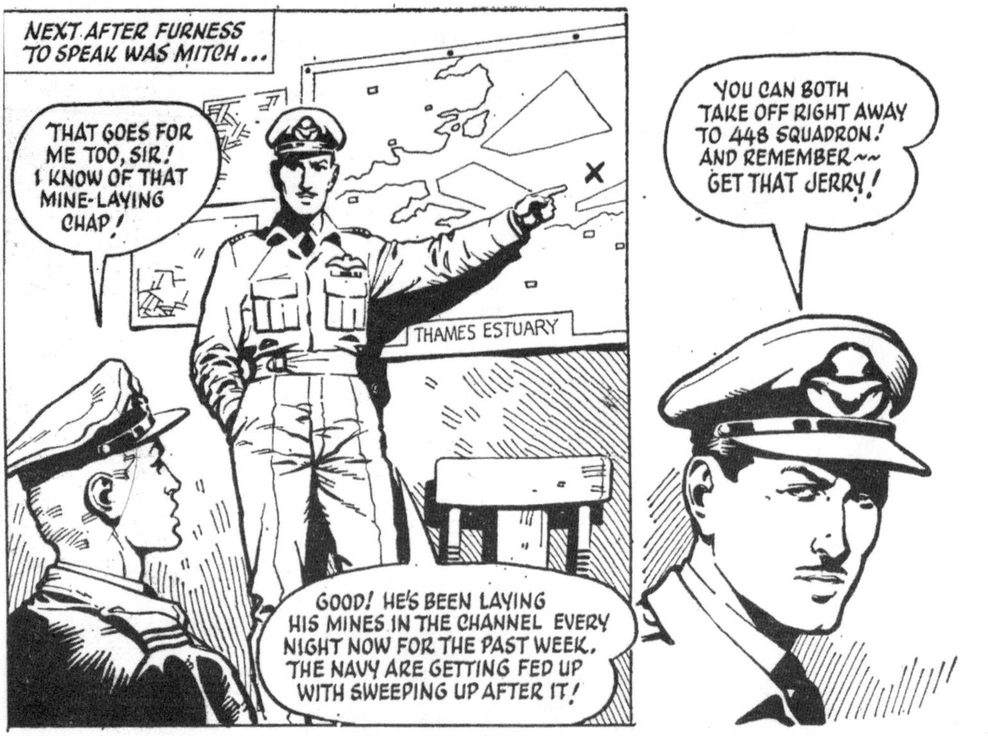
NEXT AFTER FURNESS TO SPEAK WAS MITCH...
THAT GOES FOR ME TOO, SIR! I KNOW OF THAT MINE-LAYING CHAP!
THAMES ESTUARY
GOOD! HE'S BEEN LAYING HIS MINES IN THE CHANNEL EVERY NIGHT NOW FOR THE PAST WEEK. THE NAVY ARE GETTING FED UP WITH SWEEPING UP AFTER IT!
YOU CAN BOTH TAKE OFF RIGHT AWAY TO 448 SQUADRON! AND REMEMBER~~ GET THAT JERRY!

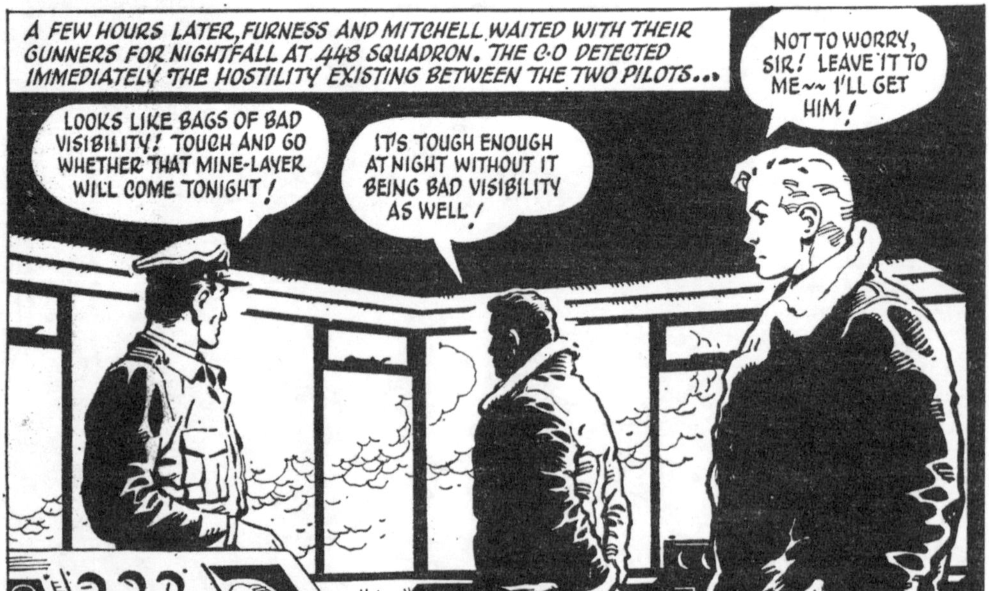
A FEW HOURS LATER, FURNESS AND MITCHELL WAITED WITH THEIR GUNNERS FOR NIGHTFALL AT 448 SQUADRON. THE C.O DETECTED IMMEDIATELY THE HOSTILITY EXISTING BETWEEN THE TWO PILOTS...
LOOKS LIKE BAGS OF BAD VISIBILITY! TOUCH AND GO WHETHER THAT MINE-LAYER WILL COME TONIGHT!
IT'S TOUGH ENOUGH AT NIGHT WITHOUT IT BEING BAD VISIBILITY AS WELL!
NOT TO WORRY, SIR! LEAVE IT TO ME~~ I'LL GET HIM!

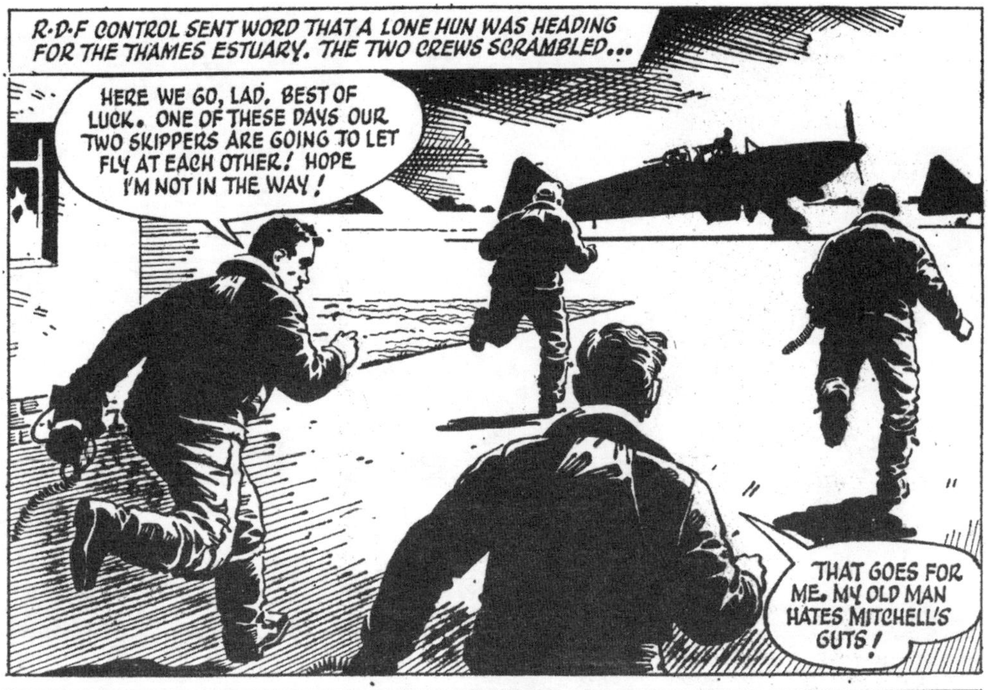
R·D·F CONTROL SENT WORD THAT A LONE HUN WAS HEADING FOR THE THAMES ESTUARY. THE TWO CREWS SCRAMBLED...
HERE WE GO, LAD. BEST OF LUCK. ONE OF THESE DAYS OUR TWO SKIPPERS ARE GOING TO LET FLY AT EACH OTHER! HOPE I'M NOT IN THE WAY!
THAT GOES FOR ME. MY OLD MAN HATES MITCHELL'S GUTS!

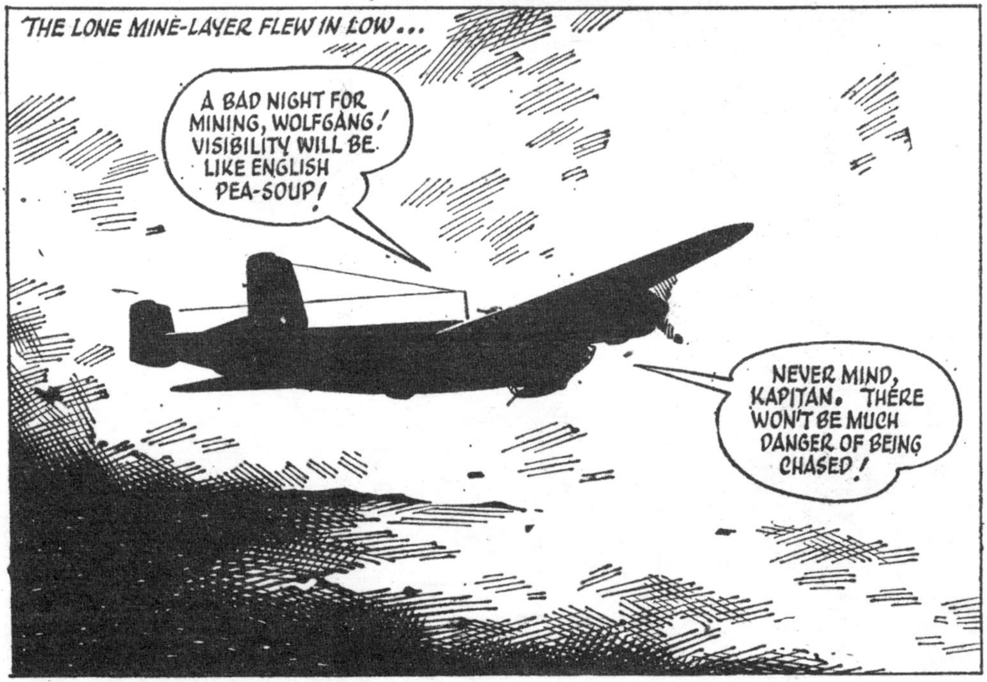
THE LONE MINE-LAYER FLEW IN LOW...
A BAD NIGHT FOR MINING, WOLFGANG! VISIBILITY WILL BE LIKE ENGLISH PEA-SOUP!
NEVER MIND, KAPITAN. THERE WON'T BE MUCH DANGER OF BEING CHASED!

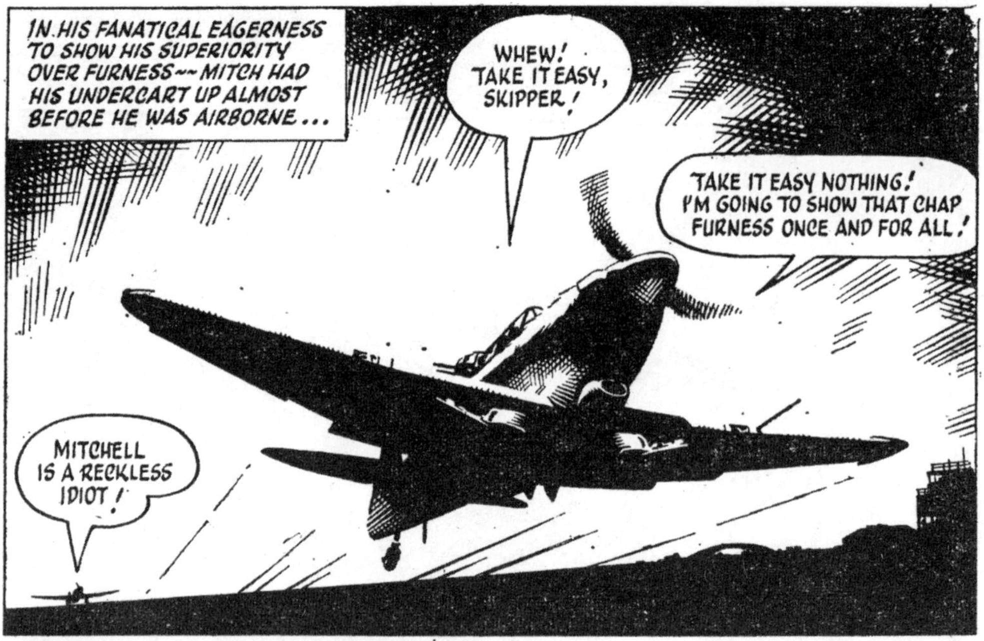
IN HIS FANATICAL EAGERNESS TO SHOW HIS SUPERIORITY OVER FURNESS~~MITCH HAD HIS UNDERCART UP ALMOST BEFORE HE WAS AIRBORNE...
WHEW! TAKE IT EASY, SKIPPER!
TAKE IT EASY NOTHING! I'M GOING TO SHOW THAT CHAP FURNESS ONCE AND FOR ALL!
MITCHELL IS A RECKLESS IDIOT!

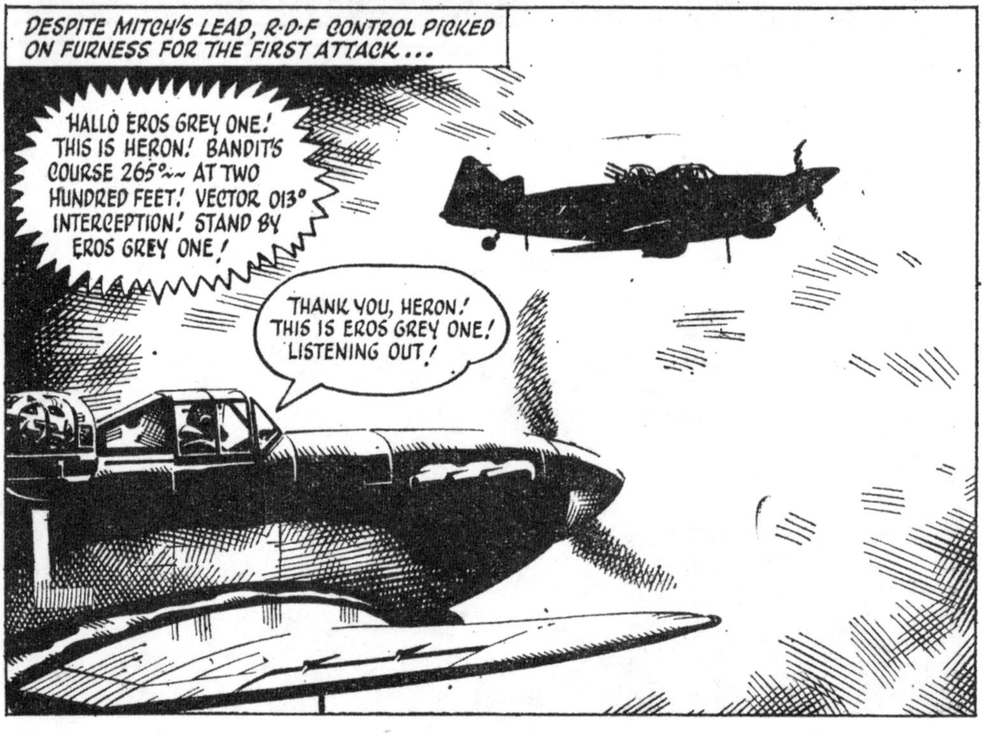
DESPITE MITCH'S LEAD, R·D·F CONTROL PICKED ON FURNESS FOR THE FIRST ATTACK...
HALLO EROS GREY ONE! THIS IS HERON! BANDIT'S COURSE 265°~~ AT TWO HUNDRED FEET! VECTOR 013° INTERCEPTION! STAND BY EROS GREY ONE!
THANK YOU, HERON! THIS IS EROS GREY ONE! LISTENING OUT!

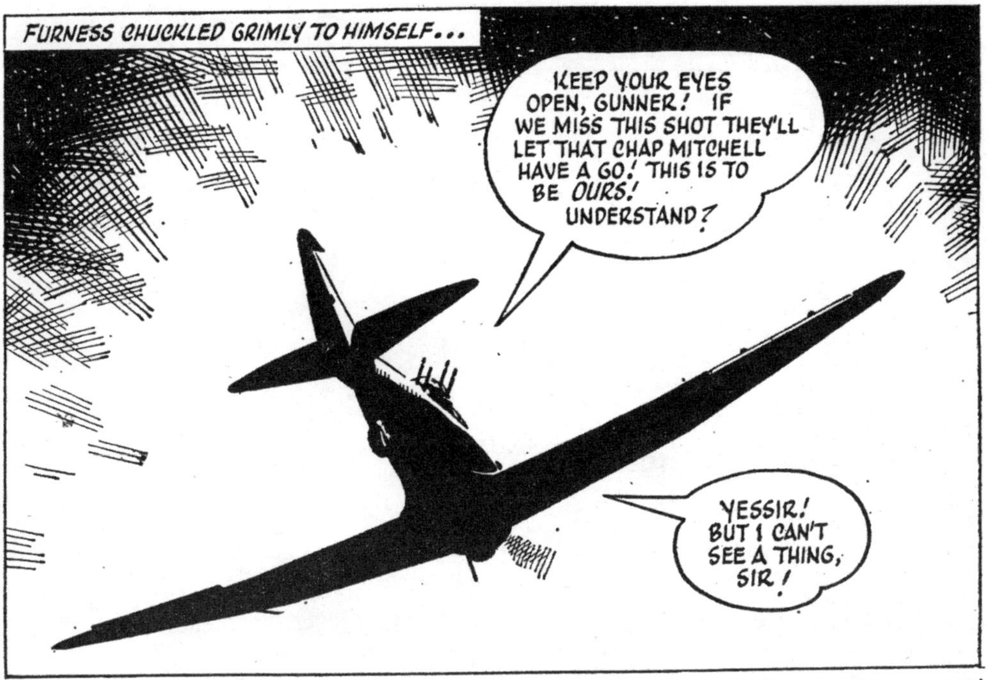
FURNESS CHUCKLED GRIMLY TO HIMSELF...
KEEP YOUR EYES OPEN, GUNNER! IF WE MISS THIS SHOT THEY'LL LET THAT CHAP MITCHELL HAVE A GO! THIS IS TO BE OURS! UNDERSTAND?
YESSIR! BUT I CAN'T SEE A THING, SIR!

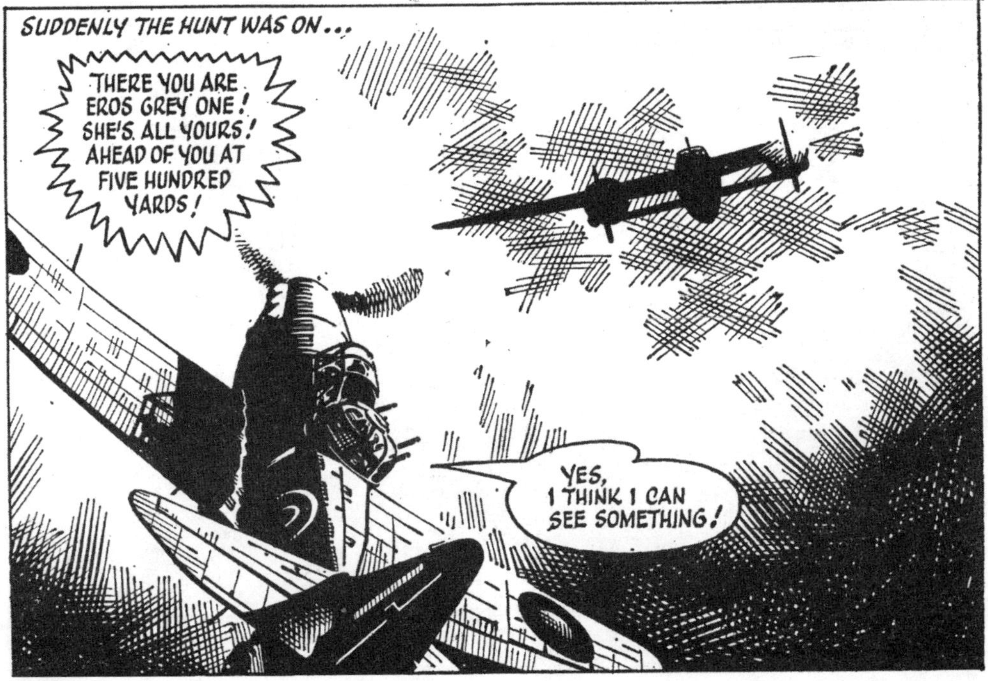
SUDDENLY THE HUNT WAS ON...
THERE YOU ARE EROS GREY ONE! SHE'S ALL YOURS! AHEAD OF YOU AT FIVE HUNDRED YARDS!
YES, I THINK I CAN SEE SOMETHING!

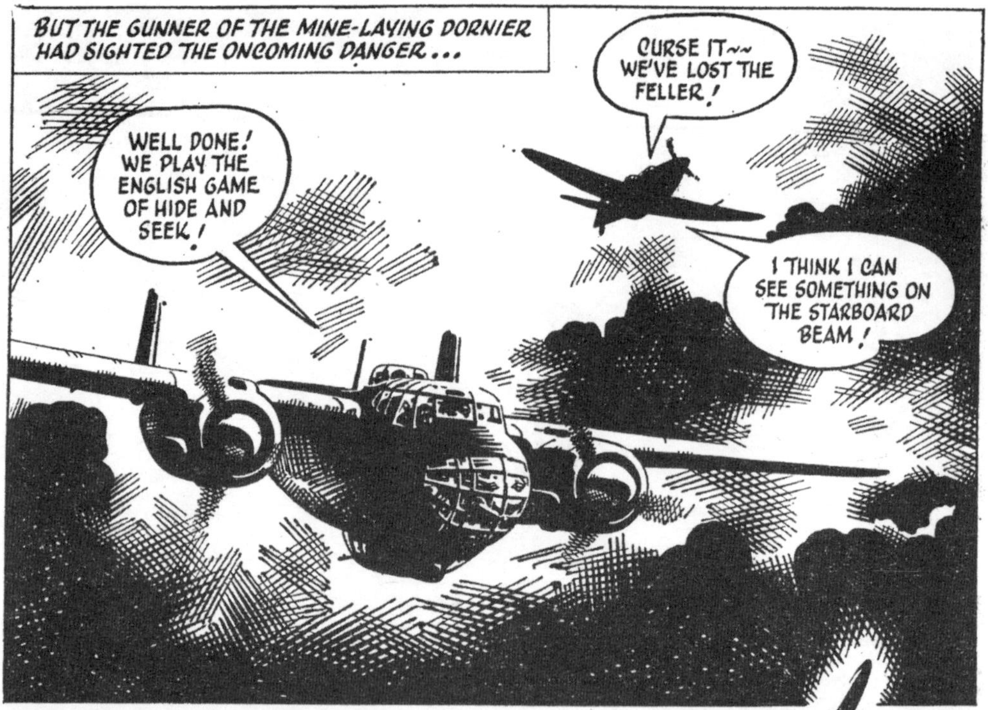
BUT THE GUNNER OF THE MINE-LAYING DORNIER HAD SIGHTED THE ONCOMING DANGER...
WELL DONE! WE PLAY THE ENGLISH GAME OF HIDE AND SEEK!
CURSE IT~~ WE'VE LOST THE FELLER!
I THINK I CAN SEE SOMETHING ON THE STARBOARD BEAM!

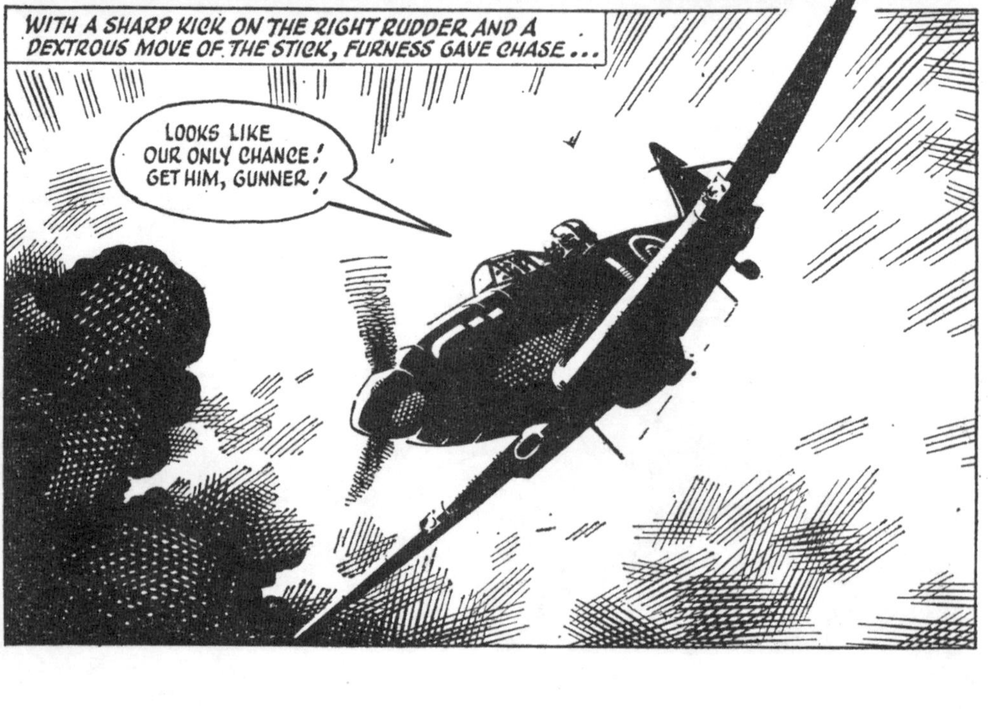
WITH A SHARP KICK ON THE RIGHT RUDDER AND A DEXTROUS MOVE OF THE STICK, FURNESS GAVE CHASE...
LOOKS LIKE OUR ONLY CHANCE! GET HIM, GUNNER!

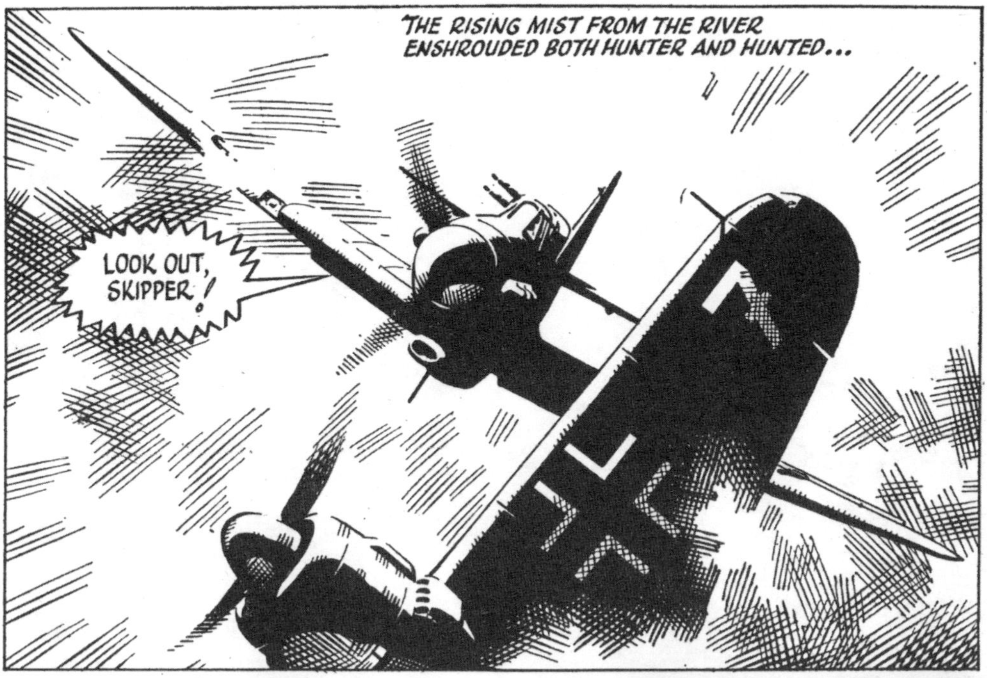
THE RISING MIST FROM THE RIVER ENSHROUDED BOTH HUNTER AND HUNTED...
LOOK OUT, SKIPPER!

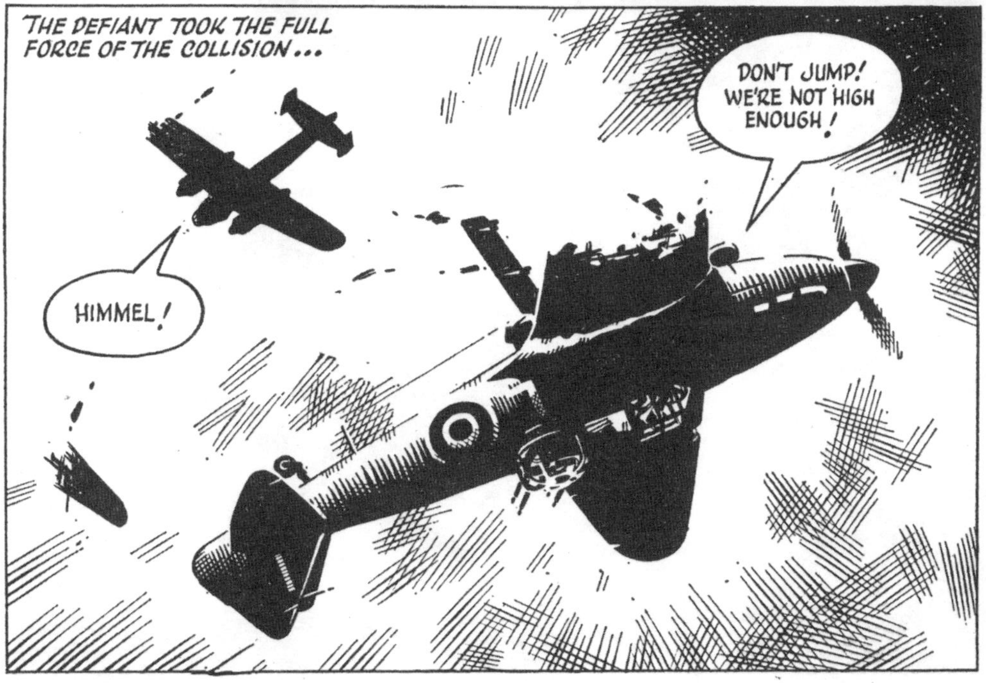
THE DEFIANT TOOK THE FULL FORCE OF THE COLLISION...
DON'T JUMP! WE'RE NOT HIGH ENOUGH!
HIMMEL!

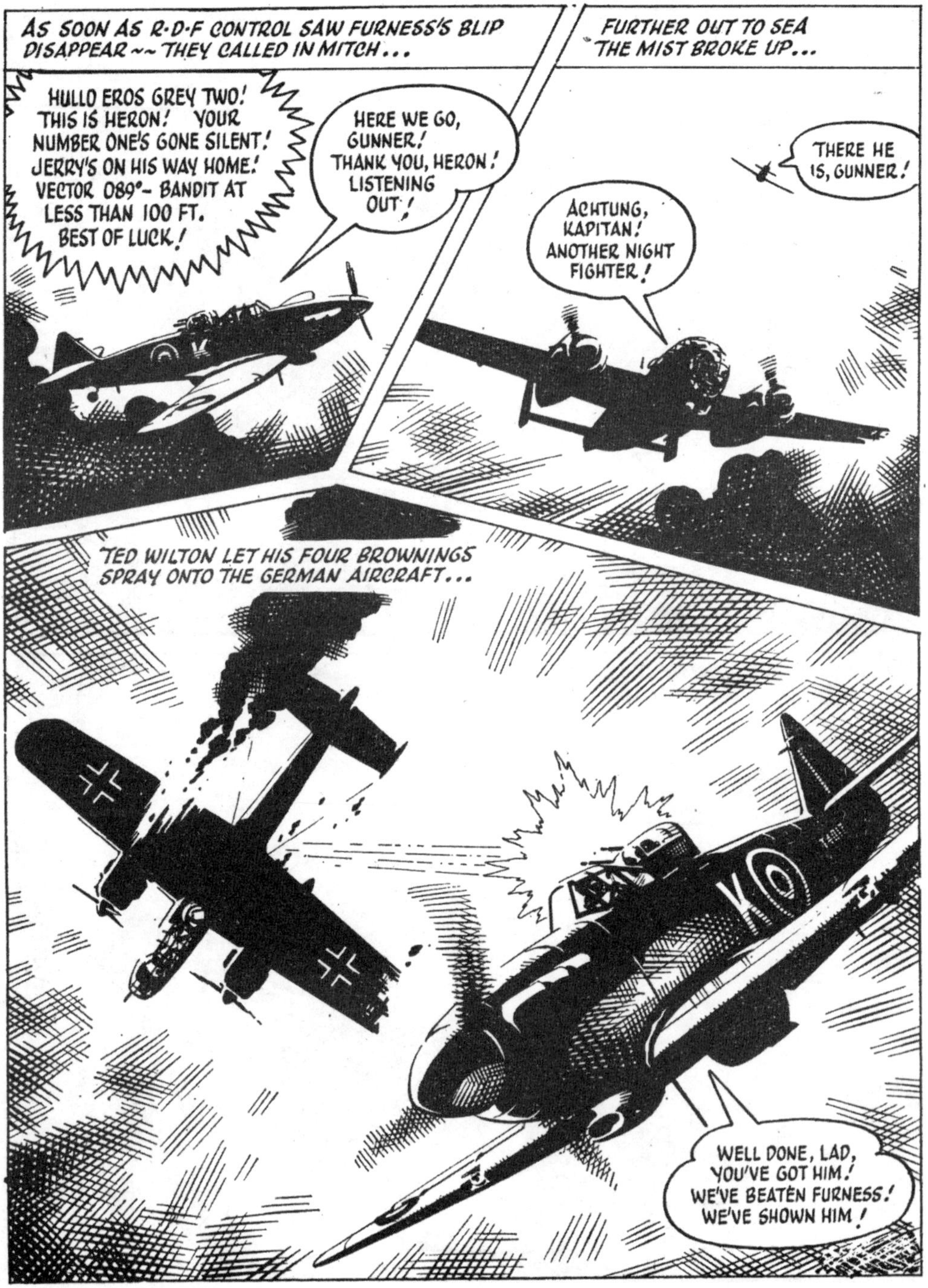
AS SOON AS R·D·F CONTROL SAW FURNESS'S BLIP DISAPPEAR ~~ THEY CALLED IN MITCH...
HULLO EROS GREY TWO! THIS IS HERON! YOUR NUMBER ONE'S GONE SILENT! JERRY'S ON HIS WAY HOME! VECTOR 089°- BANDIT AT LESS THAN 100 FT. BEST OF LUCK!
HERE WE GO, GUNNER! THANK YOU, HERON! LISTENING OUT!
FURTHER OUT TO SEA THE MIST BROKE UP...
THERE HE IS, GUNNER!
ACHTUNG, KAPITAN! ANOTHER NIGHT FIGHTER!
TED WILTON LET HIS FOUR BROWNINGS SPRAY ONTO THE GERMAN AIRCRAFT...
WELL DONE, LAD, YOU'VE GOT HIM! WE'VE BEATEN FURNESS! WE'VE SHOWN HIM!

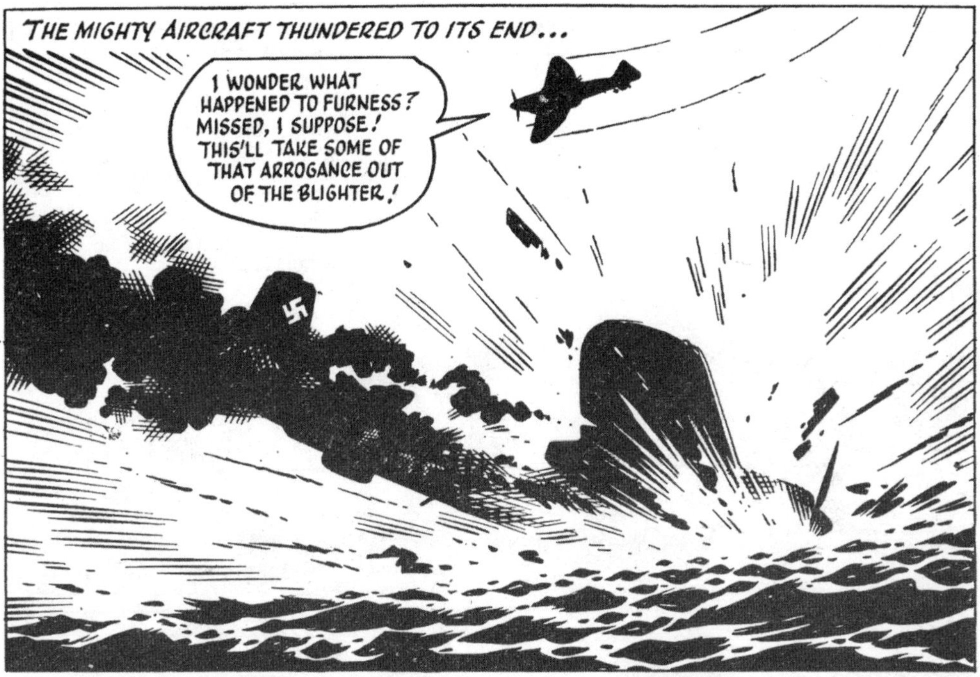
THE MIGHTY AIRCRAFT THUNDERED TO ITS END...
I WONDER WHAT HAPPENED TO FURNESS? MISSED, I SUPPOSE! THIS'LL TAKE SOME OF THAT ARROGANCE OUT OF THE BLIGHTER!

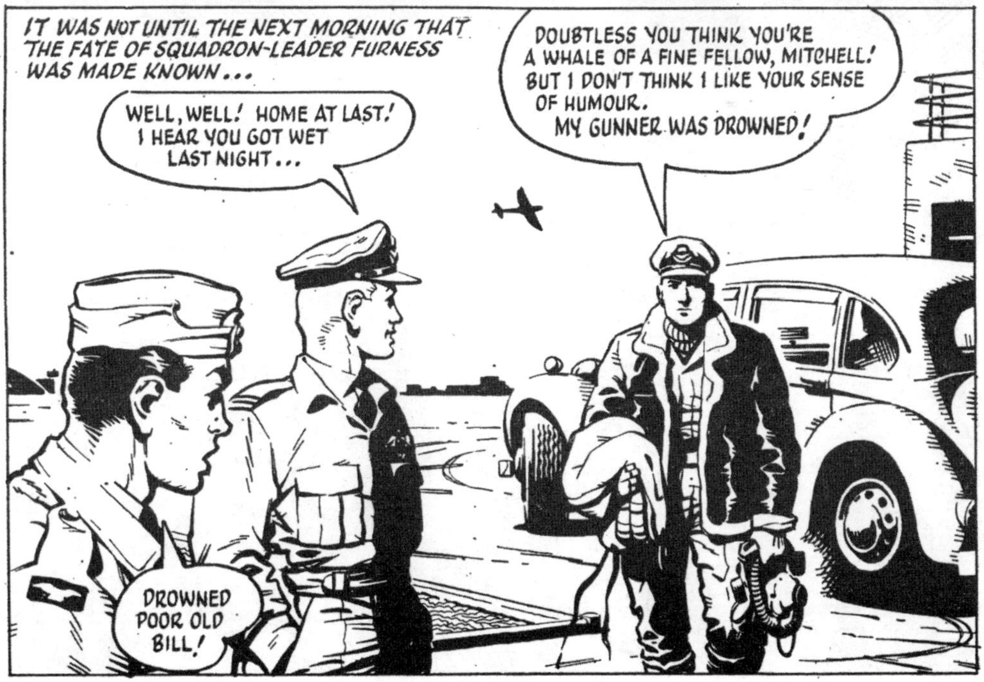
IT WAS NOT UNTIL THE NEXT MORNING THAT THE FATE OF SQUADRON-LEADER FURNESS WAS MADE KNOWN...
WELL, WELL! HOME AT LAST! I HEAR YOU GOT WET LAST NIGHT...
DOUBTLESS YOU THINK YOU'RE A WHALE OF A FINE FELLOW, MITCHELL! BUT I DON'T THINK I LIKE YOUR SENSE OF HUMOUR. MY GUNNER WAS DROWNED!
DROWNED POOR OLD BILL!

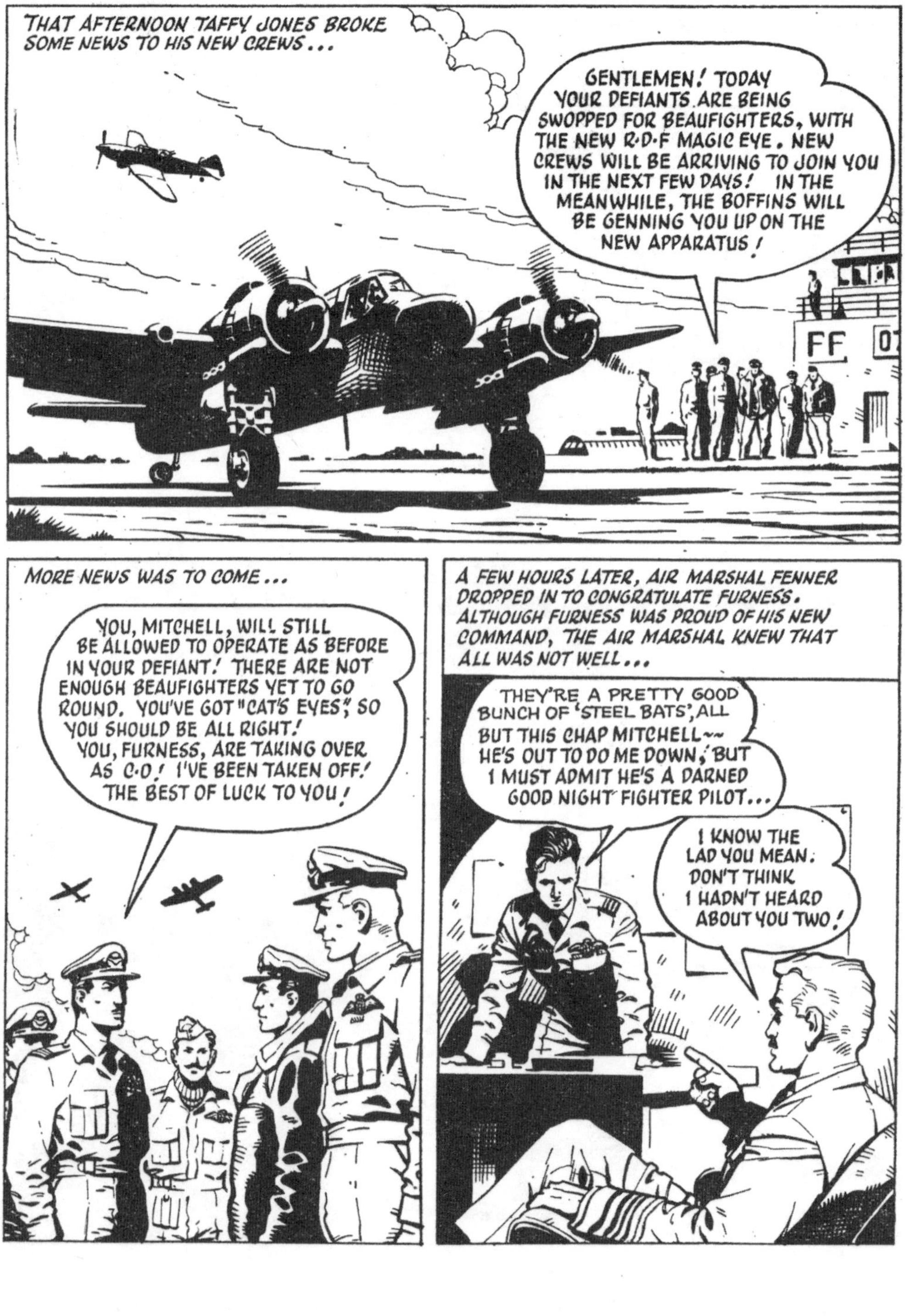
THAT AFTERNOON TAFFY JONES BROKE SOME NEWS TO HIS NEW CREWS...
GENTLEMEN! TODAY YOUR DEFIANTS ARE BEING SWOPPED FOR BEAUFIGHTERS, WITH THE NEW R.D.F MAGIC EYE. NEW CREWS WILL BE ARRIVING TO JOIN YOU IN THE NEXT FEW DAYS! IN THE MEANWHILE, THE BOFFINS WILL BE GENNING YOU UP ON THE NEW APPARATUS!
FF
MORE NEWS WAS TO COME...
YOU, MITCHELL, WILL STILL BE ALLOWED TO OPERATE AS BEFORE IN YOUR DEFIANT! THERE ARE NOT ENOUGH BEAUFIGHTERS YET TO GO ROUND. YOU'VE GOT "CAT'S EYES", SO YOU SHOULD BE ALL RIGHT! YOU, FURNESS, ARE TAKING OVER AS C.O! I'VE BEEN TAKEN OFF! THE BEST OF LUCK TO YOU!
A FEW HOURS LATER, AIR MARSHAL FENNER DROPPED IN TO CONGRATULATE FURNESS. ALTHOUGH FURNESS WAS PROUD OF HIS NEW COMMAND, THE AIR MARSHAL KNEW THAT ALL WAS NOT WELL...
THEY'RE A PRETTY GOOD BUNCH OF 'STEEL BATS', ALL BUT THIS CHAP MITCHELL-- HE'S OUT TO DO ME DOWN, BUT I MUST ADMIT HE'S A DARNED GOOD NIGHT FIGHTER PILOT...
I KNOW THE LAD YOU MEAN. DON'T THINK I HADN'T HEARD ABOUT YOU TWO!

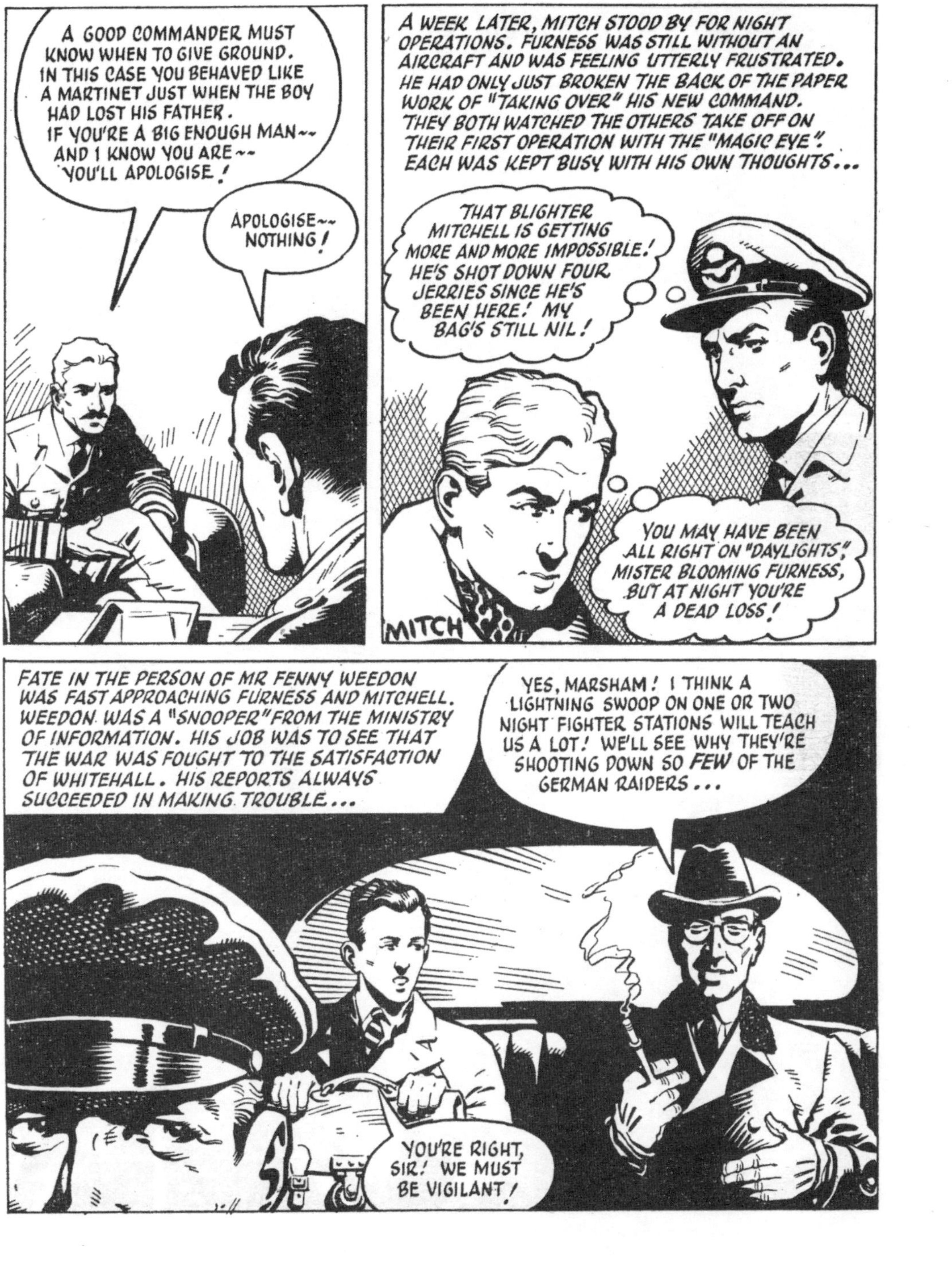
A GOOD COMMANDER MUST KNOW WHEN TO GIVE GROUND. IN THIS CASE YOU BEHAVED LIKE A MARTINET JUST WHEN THE BOY HAD LOST HIS FATHER. IF YOU'RE A BIG ENOUGH MAN-- AND I KNOW YOU ARE-- YOU'LL APOLOGISE!
APOLOGISE-- NOTHING!
A WEEK LATER, MITCH STOOD BY FOR NIGHT OPERATIONS. FURNESS WAS STILL WITHOUT AN AIRCRAFT AND WAS FEELING UTTERLY FRUSTRATED. HE HAD ONLY JUST BROKEN THE BACK OF THE PAPER WORK OF "TAKING OVER" HIS NEW COMMAND. THEY BOTH WATCHED THE OTHERS TAKE OFF ON THEIR FIRST OPERATION WITH THE "MAGIC EYE". EACH WAS KEPT BUSY WITH HIS OWN THOUGHTS...
THAT BLIGHTER MITCHELL IS GETTING MORE AND MORE IMPOSSIBLE! HE'S SHOT DOWN FOUR JERRIES SINCE HE'S BEEN HERE! MY BAG'S STILL NIL!
MITCH
YOU MAY HAVE BEEN ALL RIGHT ON "DAYLIGHTS", MISTER BLOOMING FURNESS, BUT AT NIGHT YOU'RE A DEAD LOSS!
FATE IN THE PERSON OF MR FENNY WEEDON WAS FAST APPROACHING FURNESS AND MITCHELL. WEEDON WAS A "SNOOPER" FROM THE MINISTRY OF INFORMATION. HIS JOB WAS TO SEE THAT THE WAR WAS FOUGHT TO THE SATISFACTION OF WHITEHALL. HIS REPORTS ALWAYS SUCCEEDED IN MAKING TROUBLE...
YES, MARSHAM! I THINK A LIGHTNING SWOOP ON ONE OR TWO NIGHT FIGHTER STATIONS WILL TEACH US A LOT! WE'LL SEE WHY THEY'RE SHOOTING DOWN SO FEW OF THE GERMAN RAIDERS...
YOU'RE RIGHT, SIR! WE MUST BE VIGILANT!

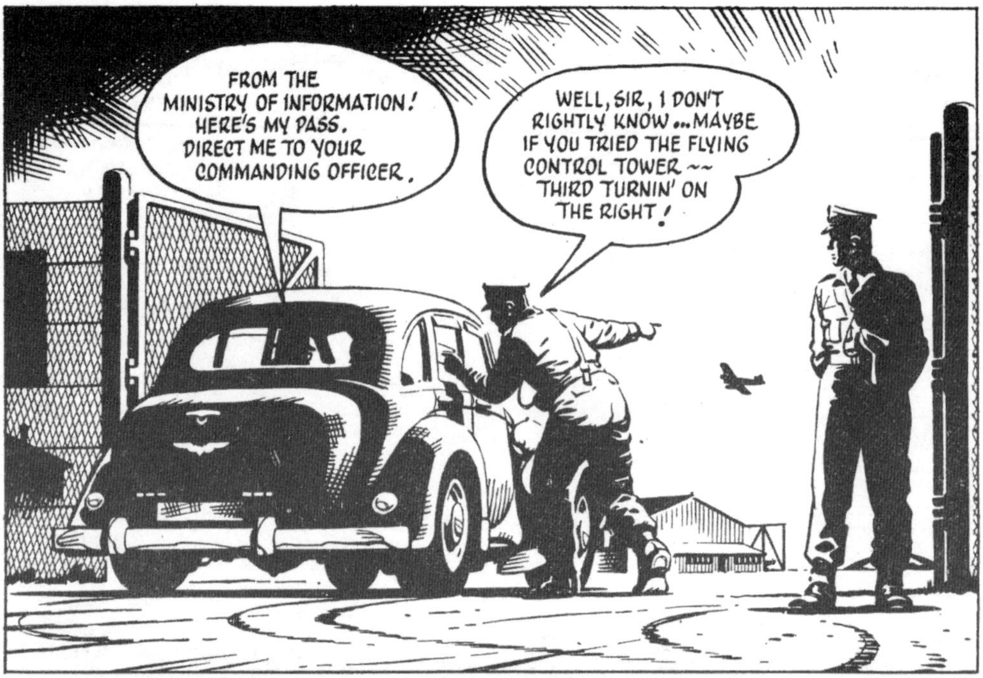
FROM THE MINISTRY OF INFORMATION! HERE'S MY PASS. DIRECT ME TO YOUR COMMANDING OFFICER.
WELL, SIR, I DON'T RIGHTLY KNOW ... MAYBE IF YOU TRIED THE FLYING CONTROL TOWER ~~ THIRD TURNIN' ON THE RIGHT!

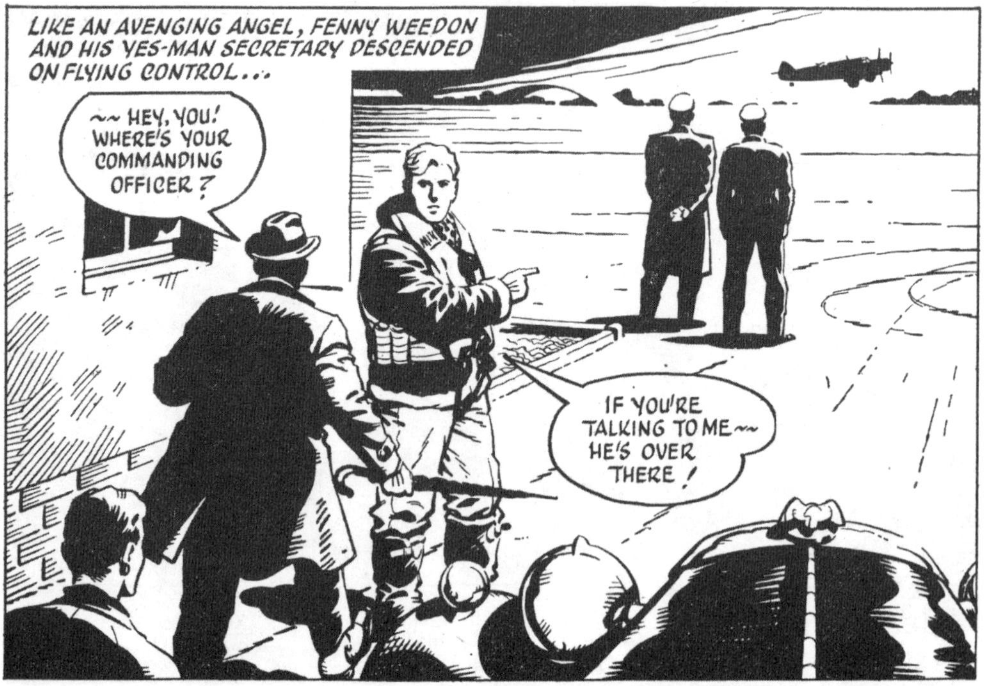
LIKE AN AVENGING ANGEL, FENNY WEEDON AND HIS YES-MAN SECRETARY DESCENDED ON FLYING CONTROL...
~~ HEY, YOU! WHERE'S YOUR COMMANDING OFFICER?
IF YOU'RE TALKING TO ME~~ HE'S OVER THERE!

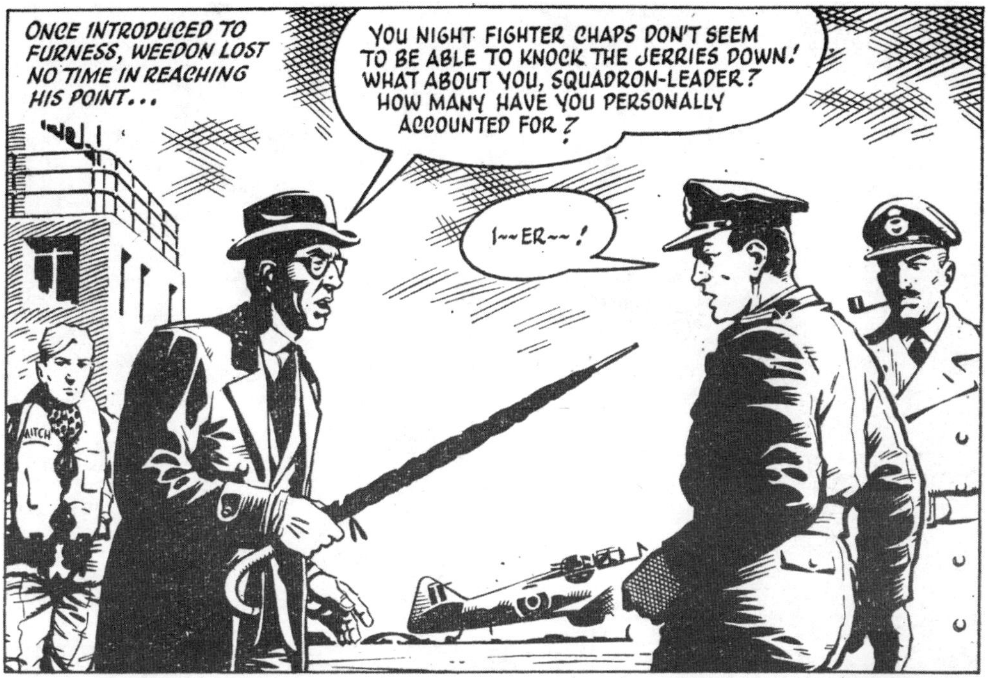
ONCE INTRODUCED TO FURNESS, WEEDON LOST NO TIME IN REACHING HIS POINT...
YOU NIGHT FIGHTER CHAPS DON'T SEEM TO BE ABLE TO KNOCK THE JERRIES DOWN! WHAT ABOUT YOU, SQUADRON-LEADER? HOW MANY HAVE YOU PERSONALLY ACCOUNTED FOR?
I--ER--!
MITCH

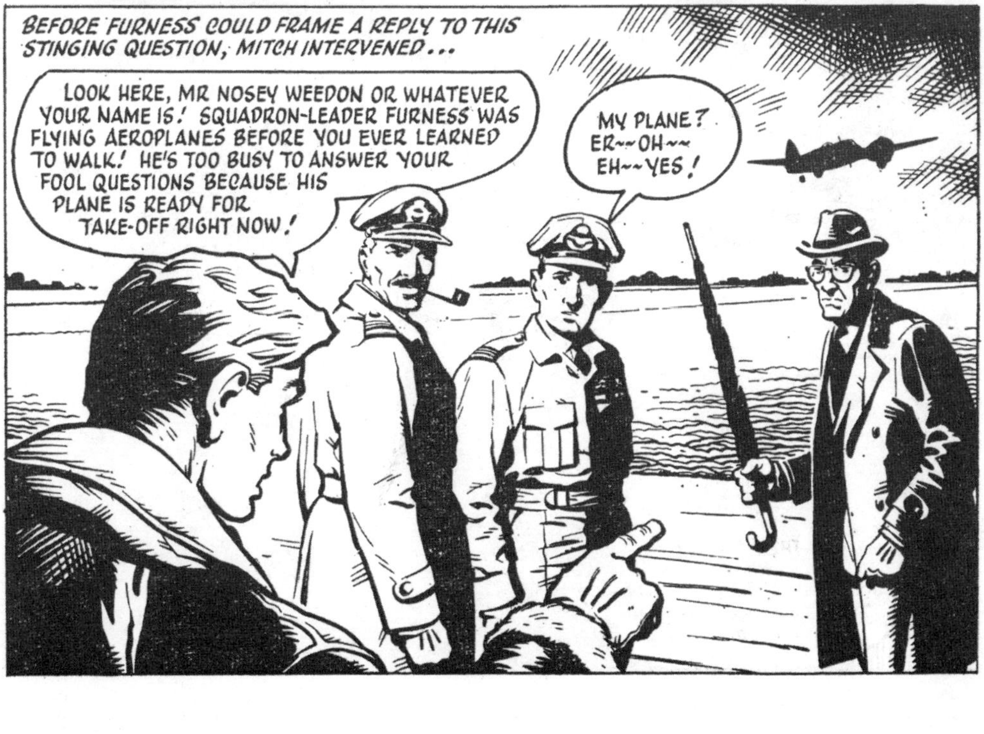
BEFORE FURNESS COULD FRAME A REPLY TO THIS STINGING QUESTION, MITCH INTERVENED...
LOOK HERE, MR NOSEY WEEDON OR WHATEVER YOUR NAME IS! SQUADRON-LEADER FURNESS WAS FLYING AEROPLANES BEFORE YOU EVER LEARNED TO WALK! HE'S TOO BUSY TO ANSWER YOUR FOOL QUESTIONS BECAUSE HIS PLANE IS READY FOR TAKE-OFF RIGHT NOW!
MY PLANE? ER--OH-- EH--YES!

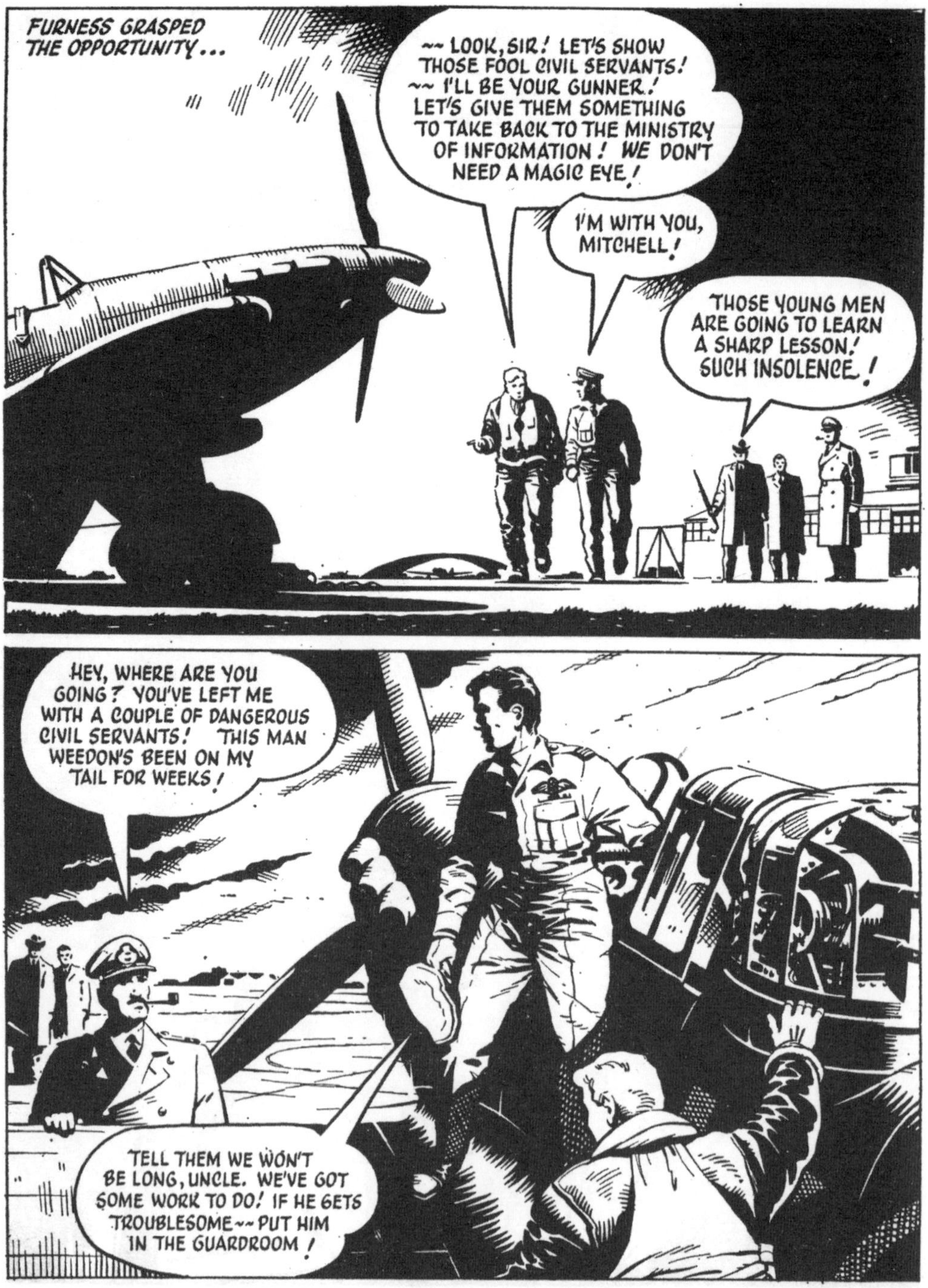
FURNESS GRASPED THE OPPORTUNITY...
~~ LOOK, SIR! LET'S SHOW THOSE FOOL CIVIL SERVANTS! ~~ I'LL BE YOUR GUNNER! LET'S GIVE THEM SOMETHING TO TAKE BACK TO THE MINISTRY OF INFORMATION! WE DON'T NEED A MAGIC EYE!
I'M WITH YOU, MITCHELL!
THOSE YOUNG MEN ARE GOING TO LEARN A SHARP LESSON! SUCH INSOLENCE!
HEY, WHERE ARE YOU GOING? YOU'VE LEFT ME WITH A COUPLE OF DANGEROUS CIVIL SERVANTS! THIS MAN WEEDON'S BEEN ON MY TAIL FOR WEEKS!
TELL THEM WE WON'T BE LONG, UNCLE. WE'VE GOT SOME WORK TO DO! IF HE GETS TROUBLESOME~~ PUT HIM IN THE GUARDROOM!

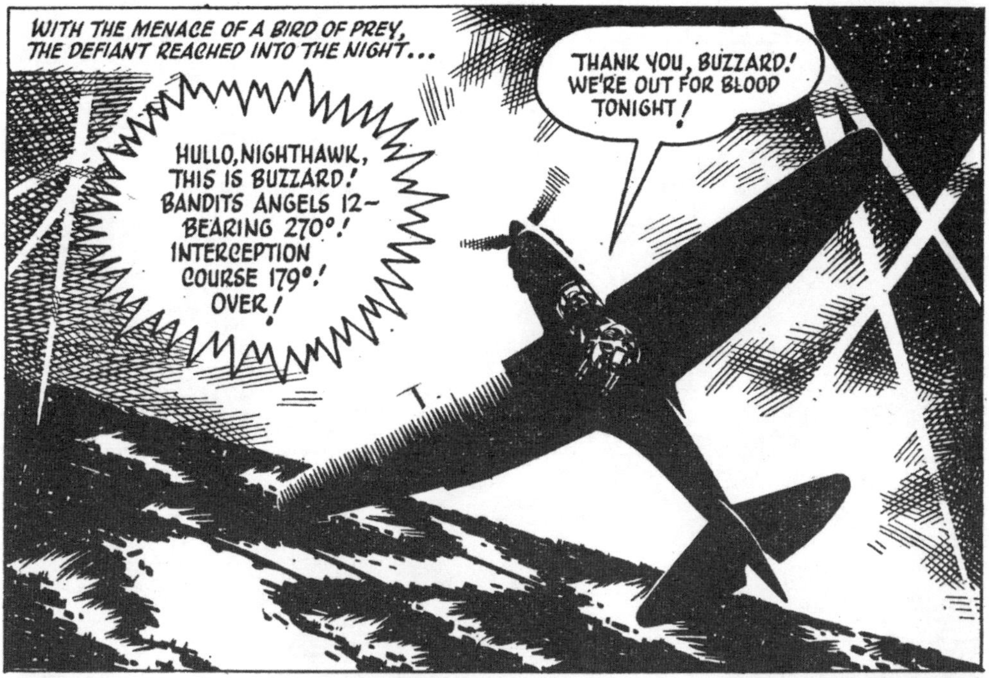
WITH THE MENACE OF A BIRD OF PREY, THE DEFIANT REACHED INTO THE NIGHT...
HULLO, NIGHTHAWK, THIS IS BUZZARD! BANDITS ANGELS 12–BEARING 270°! INTERCEPTION COURSE 179°! OVER!
THANK YOU, BUZZARD! WE'RE OUT FOR BLOOD TONIGHT!

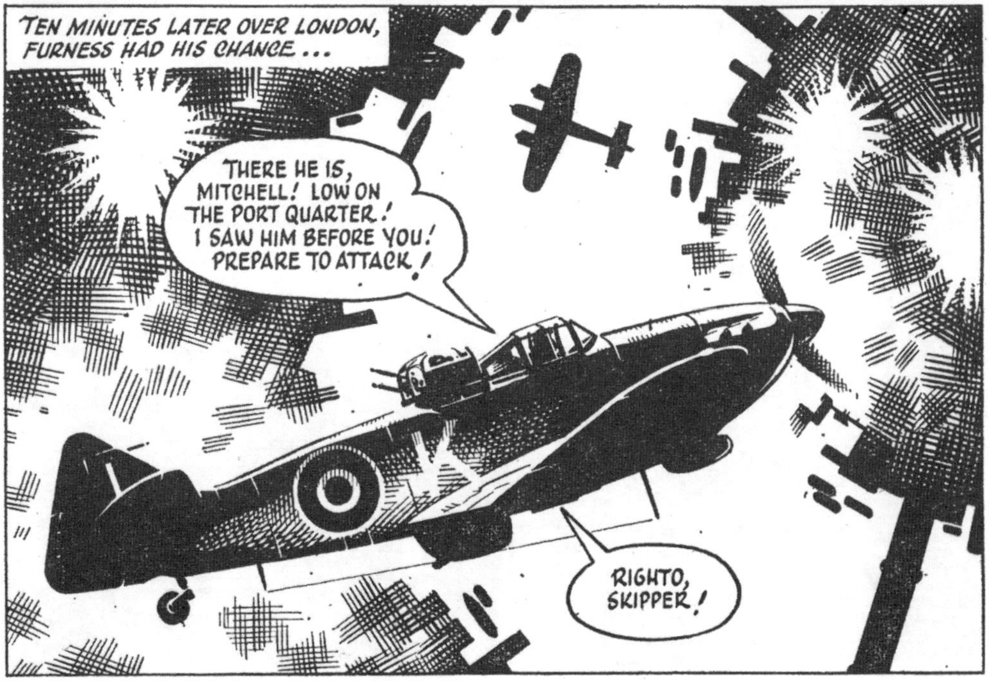
TEN MINUTES LATER OVER LONDON, FURNESS HAD HIS CHANCE ...
THERE HE IS, MITCHELL! LOW ON THE PORT QUARTER! I SAW HIM BEFORE YOU! PREPARE TO ATTACK!
RIGHTO, SKIPPER!

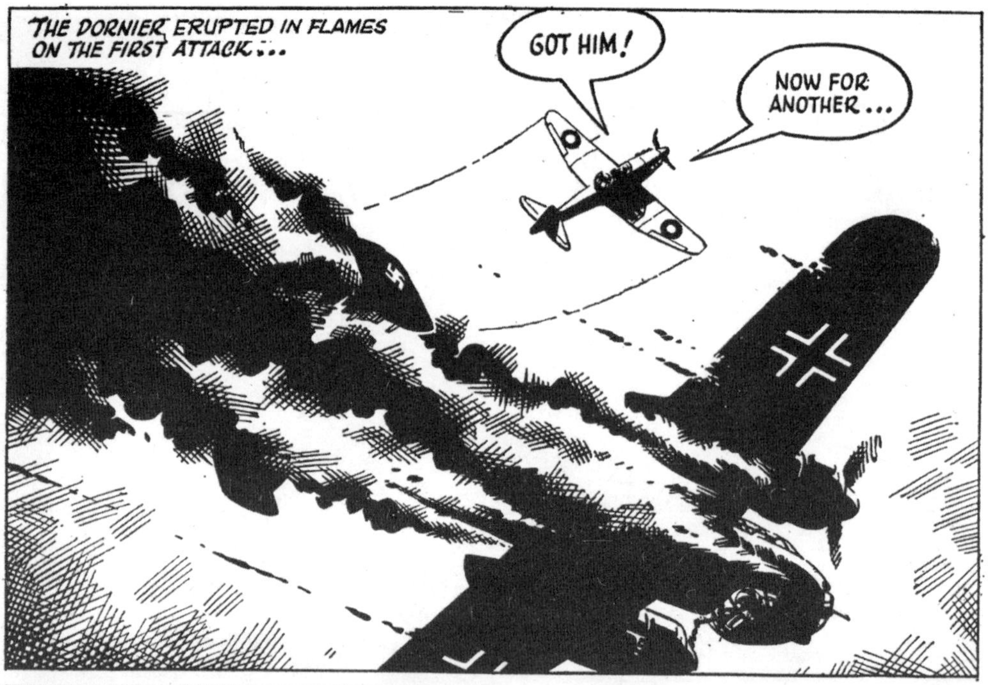
THE DORNIER ERUPTED IN FLAMES ON THE FIRST ATTACK...
GOT HIM!
NOW FOR ANOTHER...

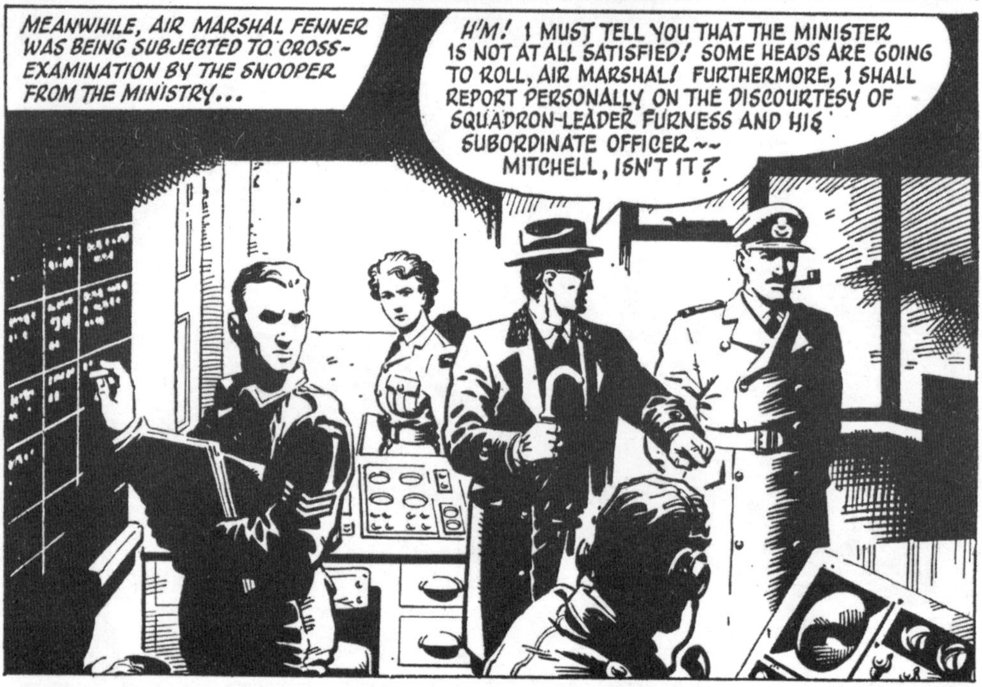
MEANWHILE, AIR MARSHAL FENNER WAS BEING SUBJECTED TO CROSS-EXAMINATION BY THE SNOOPER FROM THE MINISTRY...
H'M! I MUST TELL YOU THAT THE MINISTER IS NOT AT ALL SATISFIED! SOME HEADS ARE GOING TO ROLL, AIR MARSHAL! FURTHERMORE, I SHALL REPORT PERSONALLY ON THE DISCOURTESY OF SQUADRON-LEADER FURNESS AND HIS SUBORDINATE OFFICER-- MITCHELL, ISN'T IT?

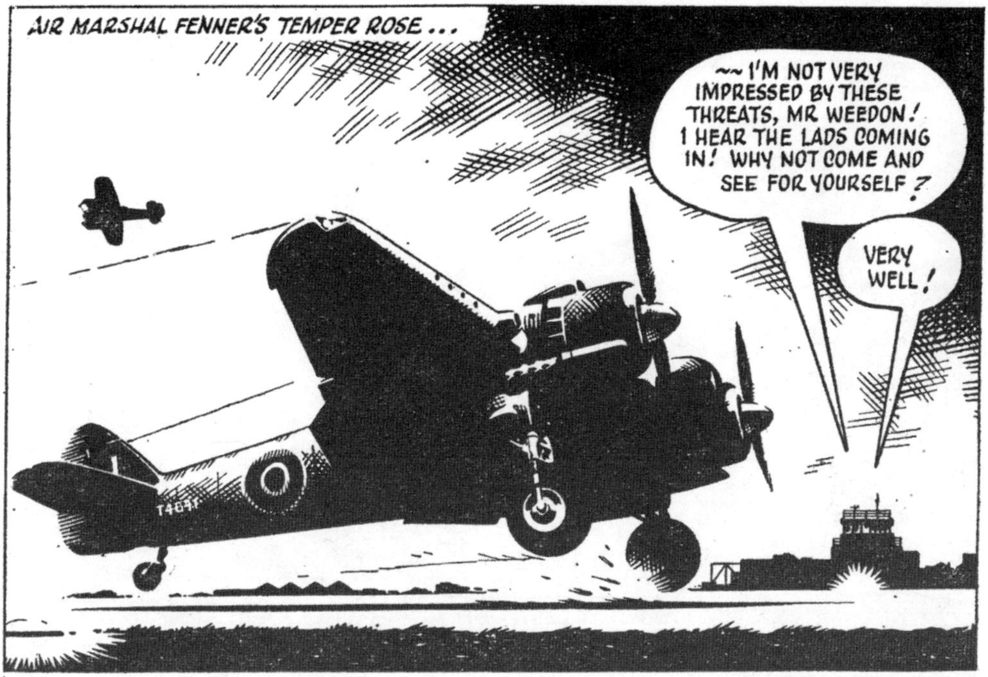
AIR MARSHAL FENNER'S TEMPER ROSE ...
~~ I'M NOT VERY IMPRESSED BY THESE THREATS, MR WEEDON! I HEAR THE LADS COMING IN! WHY NOT COME AND SEE FOR YOURSELF?
VERY WELL!
T4641

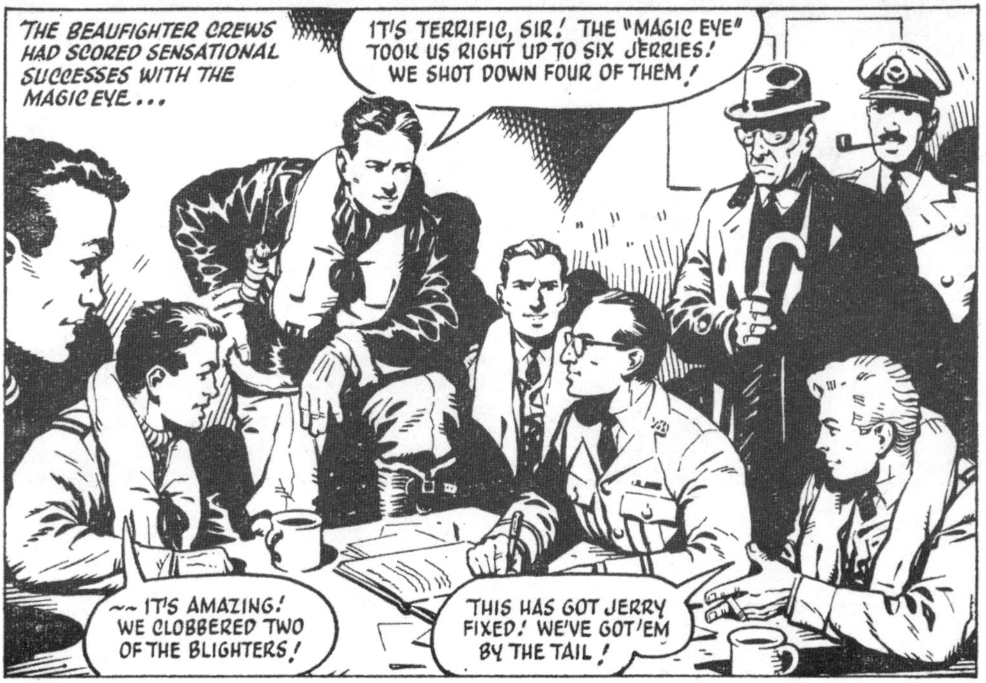
THE BEAUFIGHTER CREWS HAD SCORED SENSATIONAL SUCCESSES WITH THE MAGIC EYE ...
IT'S TERRIFIC, SIR! THE "MAGIC EYE" TOOK US RIGHT UP TO SIX JERRIES! WE SHOT DOWN FOUR OF THEM!
~~ IT'S AMAZING! WE CLOBBERED TWO OF THE BLIGHTERS!
THIS HAS GOT JERRY FIXED! WE'VE GOT 'EM BY THE TAIL!

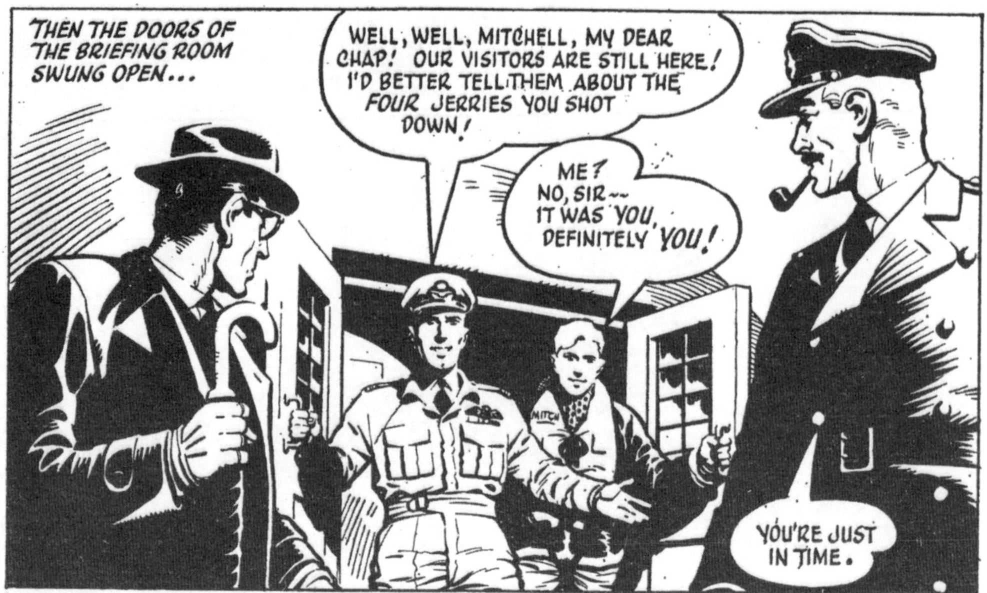
THEN THE DOORS OF THE BRIEFING ROOM SWUNG OPEN...
WELL, WELL, MITCHELL, MY DEAR CHAP! OUR VISITORS ARE STILL HERE! I'D BETTER TELL THEM ABOUT THE FOUR JERRIES YOU SHOT DOWN!
ME? NO, SIR-- IT WAS YOU, DEFINITELY YOU!
MITCH
YOU'RE JUST IN TIME.

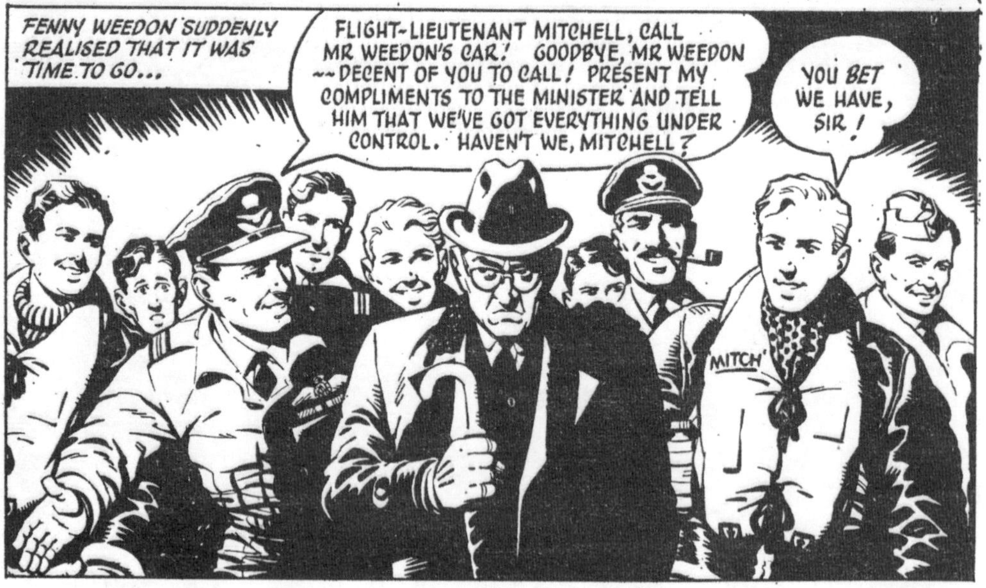
FENNY WEEDON SUDDENLY REALISED THAT IT WAS TIME TO GO...
FLIGHT-LIEUTENANT MITCHELL, CALL MR WEEDON'S CAR! GOODBYE, MR WEEDON -- DECENT OF YOU TO CALL! PRESENT MY COMPLIMENTS TO THE MINISTER AND TELL HIM THAT WE'VE GOT EVERYTHING UNDER CONTROL. HAVEN'T WE, MITCHELL?
YOU BET WE HAVE, SIR!
'MITCH'

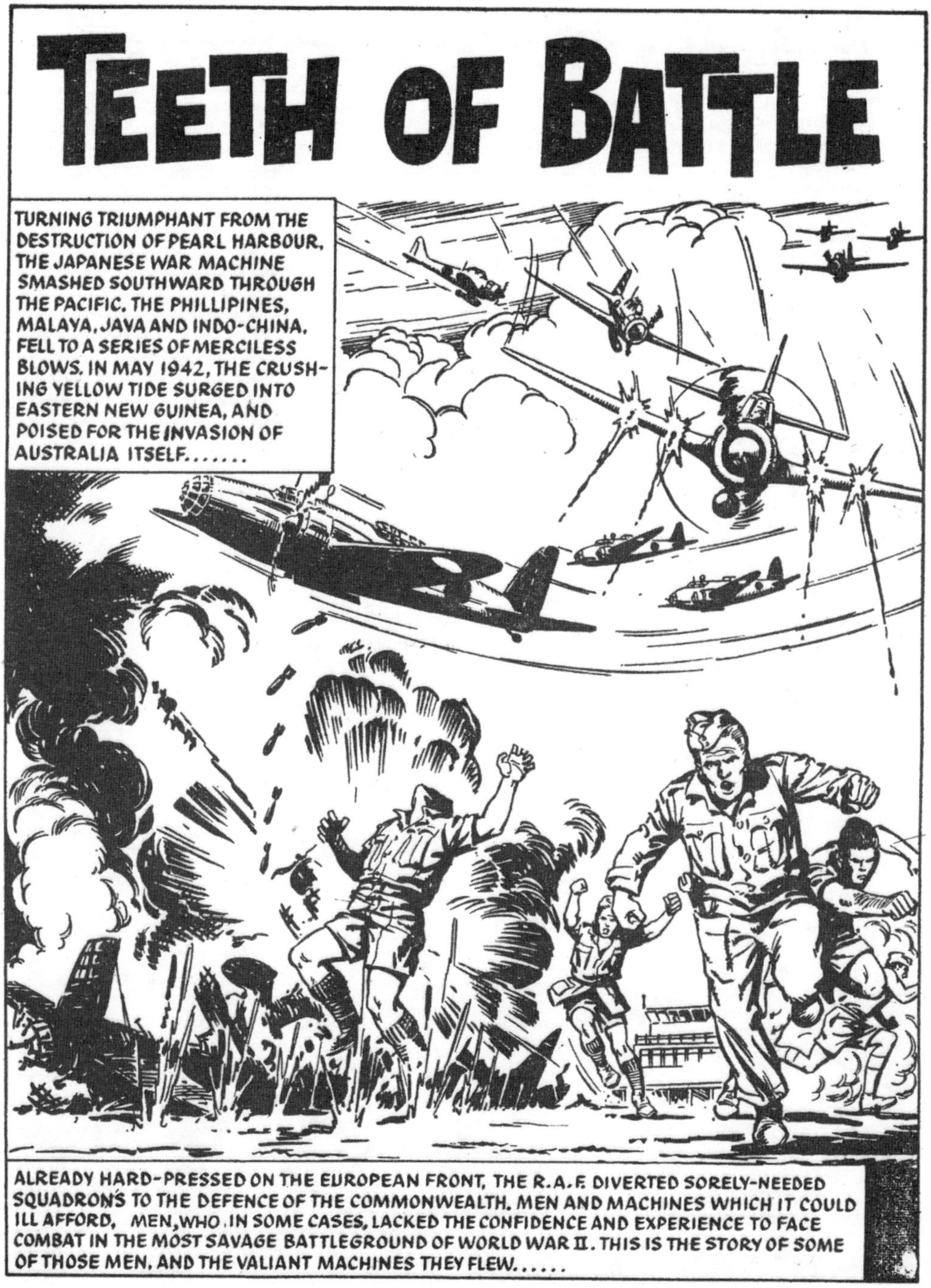
TEETH OF BATTLE
TURNING TRIUMPHANT FROM THE DESTRUCTION OF PEARL HARBOUR, THE JAPANESE WAR MACHINE SMASHED SOUTHWARD THROUGH THE PACIFIC. THE PHILLIPINES, MALAYA, JAVA AND INDO-CHINA, FELL TO A SERIES OF MERCILESS BLOWS. IN MAY 1942, THE CRUSHING YELLOW TIDE SURGED INTO EASTERN NEW GUINEA, AND POISED FOR THE INVASION OF AUSTRALIA ITSELF.......
ALREADY HARD-PRESSED ON THE EUROPEAN FRONT, THE R.A.F. DIVERTED SORELY-NEEDED SQUADRON'S TO THE DEFENCE OF THE COMMONWEALTH. MEN AND MACHINES WHICH IT COULD ILL AFFORD, MEN, WHO IN SOME CASES, LACKED THE CONFIDENCE AND EXPERIENCE TO FACE COMBAT IN THE MOST SAVAGE BATTLEGROUND OF WORLD WAR II. THIS IS THE STORY OF SOME OF THOSE MEN, AND THE VALIANT MACHINES THEY FLEW......

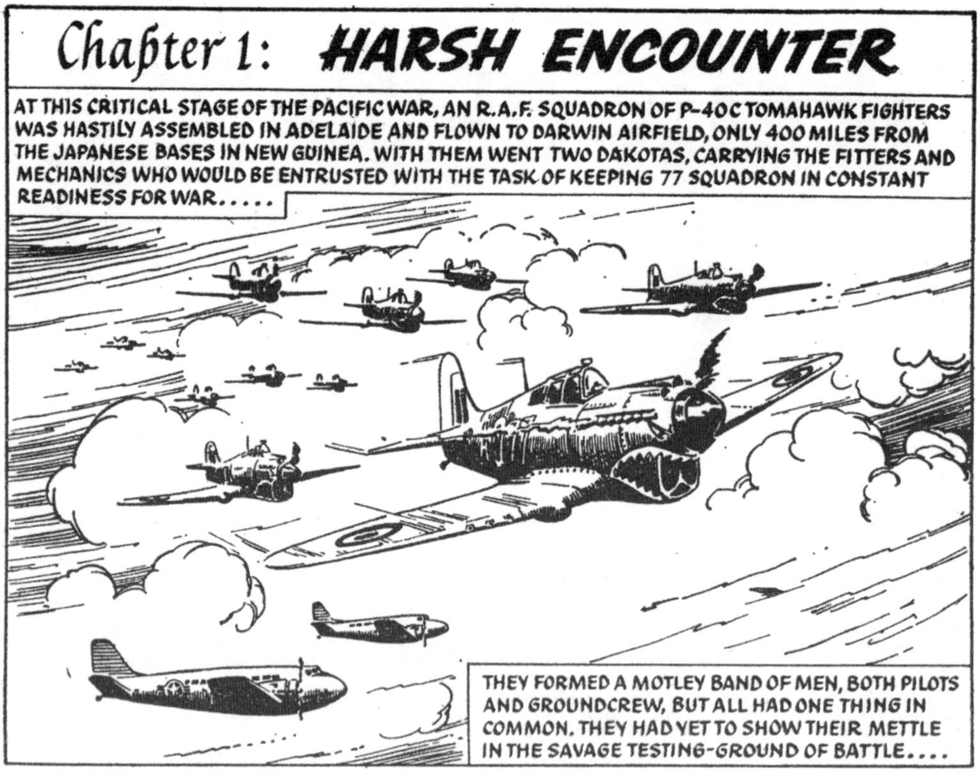
Chapter 1: HARSH ENCOUNTER
AT THIS CRITICAL STAGE OF THE PACIFIC WAR, AN R.A.F. SQUADRON OF P-40C TOMAHAWK FIGHTERS WAS HASTILY ASSEMBLED IN ADELAIDE AND FLOWN TO DARWIN AIRFIELD, ONLY 400 MILES FROM THE JAPANESE BASES IN NEW GUINEA. WITH THEM WENT TWO DAKOTAS, CARRYING THE FITTERS AND MECHANICS WHO WOULD BE ENTRUSTED WITH THE TASK OF KEEPING 77 SQUADRON IN CONSTANT READINESS FOR WAR.....
THEY FORMED A MOTLEY BAND OF MEN, BOTH PILOTS AND GROUNDCREW, BUT ALL HAD ONE THING IN COMMON. THEY HAD YET TO SHOW THEIR METTLE IN THE SAVAGE TESTING-GROUND OF BATTLE....

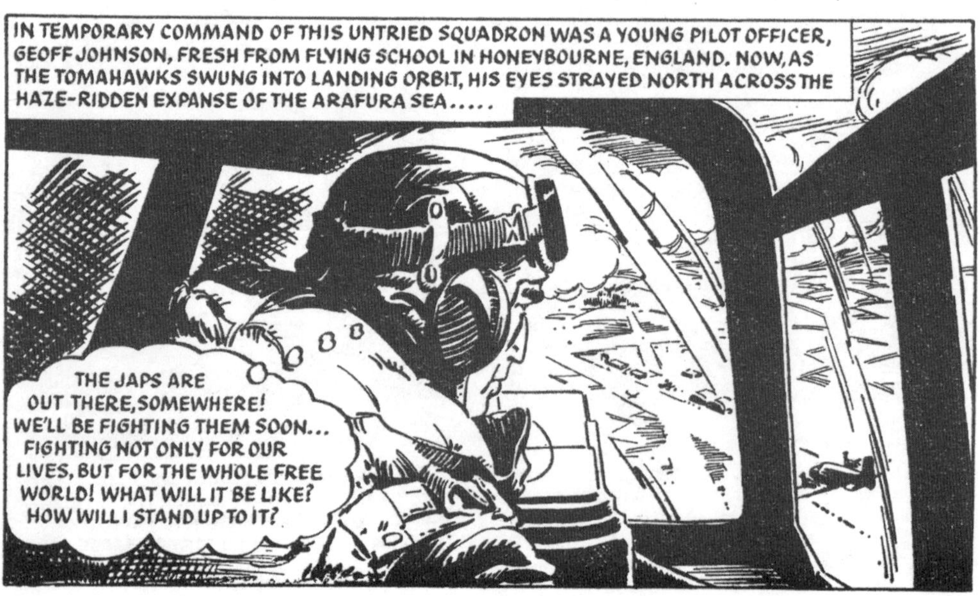
IN TEMPORARY COMMAND OF THIS UNTRIED SQUADRON WAS A YOUNG PILOT OFFICER, GEOFF JOHNSON, FRESH FROM FLYING SCHOOL IN HONEYBOURNE, ENGLAND. NOW, AS THE TOMAHAWKS SWUNG INTO LANDING ORBIT, HIS EYES STRAYED NORTH ACROSS THE HAZE-RIDDEN EXPANSE OF THE ARAFURA SEA.....
THE JAPS ARE OUT THERE, SOMEWHERE! WE'LL BE FIGHTING THEM SOON... FIGHTING NOT ONLY FOR OUR LIVES, BUT FOR THE WHOLE FREE WORLD! WHAT WILL IT BE LIKE? HOW WILL I STAND UP TO IT?

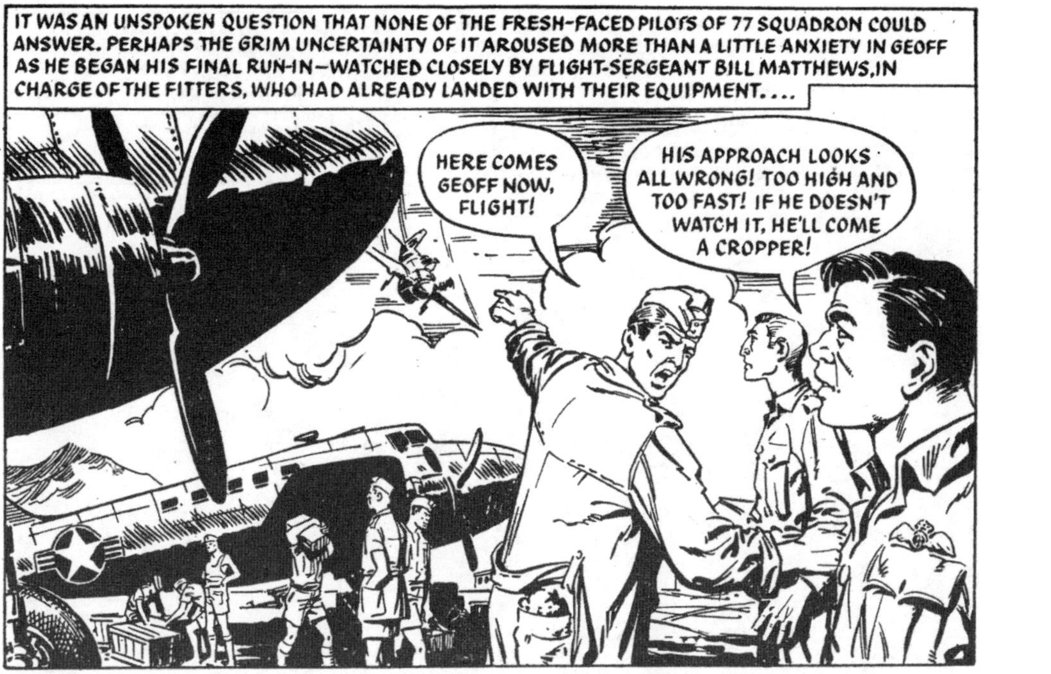
IT WAS AN UNSPOKEN QUESTION THAT NONE OF THE FRESH-FACED PILOTS OF 77 SQUADRON COULD ANSWER. PERHAPS THE GRIM UNCERTAINTY OF IT AROUSED MORE THAN A LITTLE ANXIETY IN GEOFF AS HE BEGAN HIS FINAL RUN-IN—WATCHED CLOSELY BY FLIGHT-SERGEANT BILL MATTHEWS, IN CHARGE OF THE FITTERS, WHO HAD ALREADY LANDED WITH THEIR EQUIPMENT....
HERE COMES GEOFF NOW, FLIGHT!
HIS APPROACH LOOKS ALL WRONG! TOO HIGH AND TOO FAST! IF HE DOESN'T WATCH IT, HE'LL COME A CROPPER!

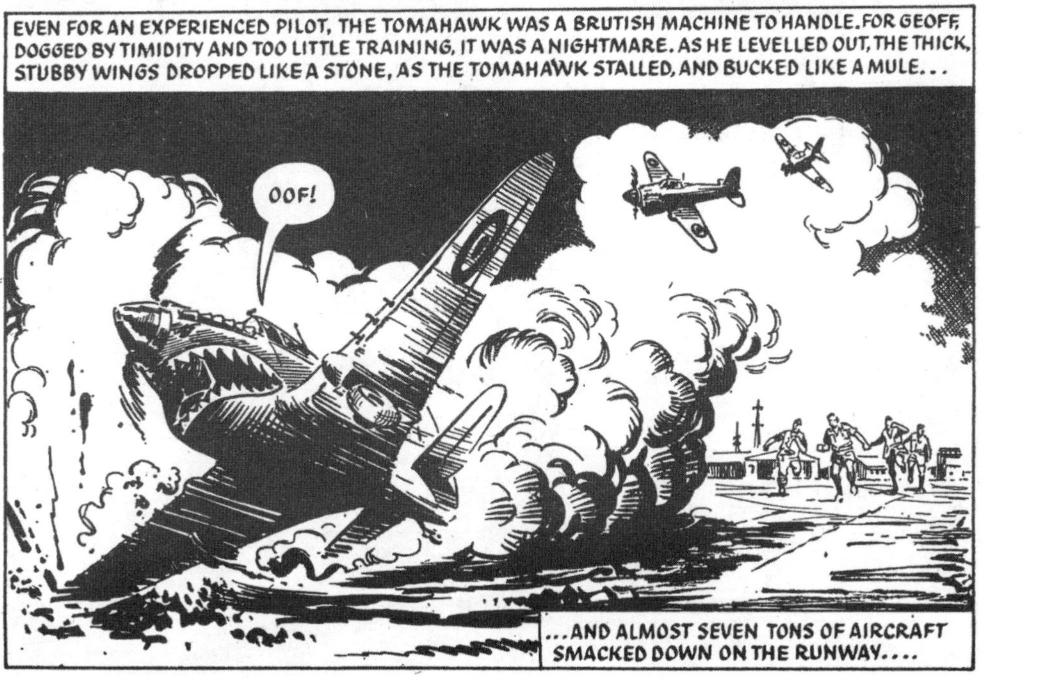
EVEN FOR AN EXPERIENCED PILOT, THE TOMAHAWK WAS A BRUTISH MACHINE TO HANDLE. FOR GEOFF, DOGGED BY TIMIDITY AND TOO LITTLE TRAINING, IT WAS A NIGHTMARE. AS HE LEVELLED OUT, THE THICK, STUBBY WINGS DROPPED LIKE A STONE, AS THE TOMAHAWK STALLED, AND BUCKED LIKE A MULE...
OOF!
...AND ALMOST SEVEN TONS OF AIRCRAFT SMACKED DOWN ON THE RUNWAY....

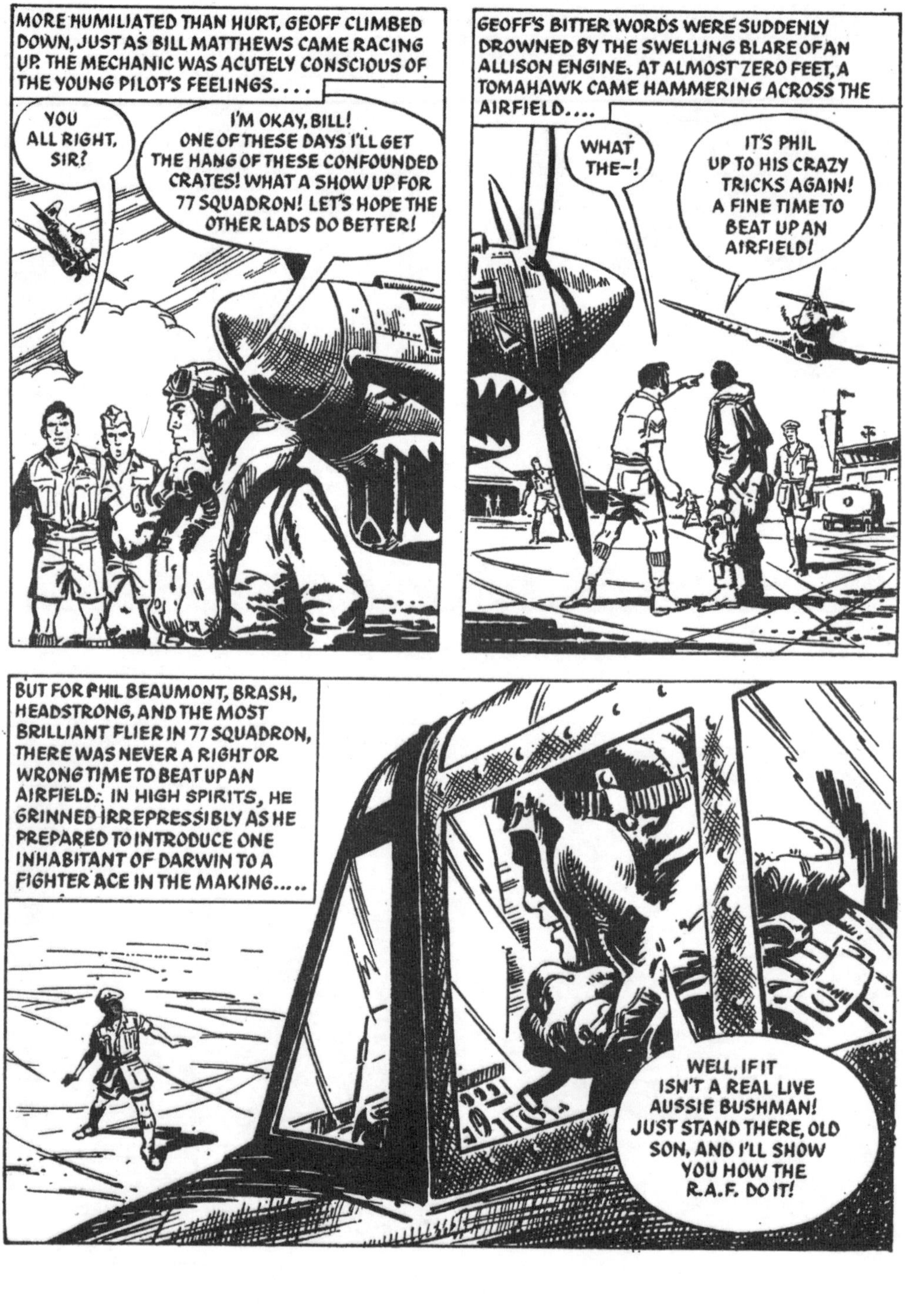
MORE HUMILIATED THAN HURT, GEOFF CLIMBED DOWN, JUST AS BILL MATTHEWS CAME RACING UP. THE MECHANIC WAS ACUTELY CONSCIOUS OF THE YOUNG PILOT'S FEELINGS....
YOU ALL RIGHT, SIR?
I'M OKAY, BILL! ONE OF THESE DAYS I'LL GET THE HANG OF THESE CONFOUNDED CRATES! WHAT A SHOW UP FOR 77 SQUADRON! LET'S HOPE THE OTHER LADS DO BETTER!
GEOFF'S BITTER WORDS WERE SUDDENLY DROWNED BY THE SWELLING BLARE OF AN ALLISON ENGINE. AT ALMOST ZERO FEET, A TOMAHAWK CAME HAMMERING ACROSS THE AIRFIELD....
WHAT THE–!
IT'S PHIL UP TO HIS CRAZY TRICKS AGAIN! A FINE TIME TO BEAT UP AN AIRFIELD!
BUT FOR PHIL BEAUMONT, BRASH, HEADSTRONG, AND THE MOST BRILLIANT FLIER IN 77 SQUADRON, THERE WAS NEVER A RIGHT OR WRONG TIME TO BEAT UP AN AIRFIELD. IN HIGH SPIRITS, HE GRINNED IRREPRESSIBLY AS HE PREPARED TO INTRODUCE ONE INHABITANT OF DARWIN TO A FIGHTER ACE IN THE MAKING.....
WELL, IF IT ISN'T A REAL LIVE AUSSIE BUSHMAN! JUST STAND THERE, OLD SON, AND I'LL SHOW YOU HOW THE R.A.F. DO IT!

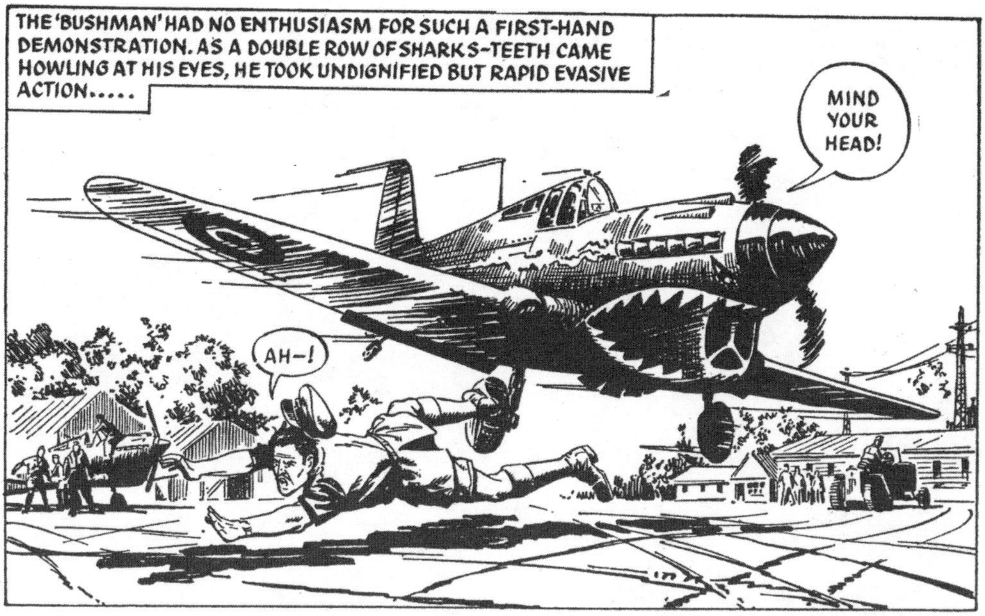
THE 'BUSHMAN' HAD NO ENTHUSIASM FOR SUCH A FIRST-HAND DEMONSTRATION. AS A DOUBLE ROW OF SHARKS-TEETH CAME HOWLING AT HIS EYES, HE TOOK UNDIGNIFIED BUT RAPID EVASIVE ACTION.....
MIND YOUR HEAD!
AH—!

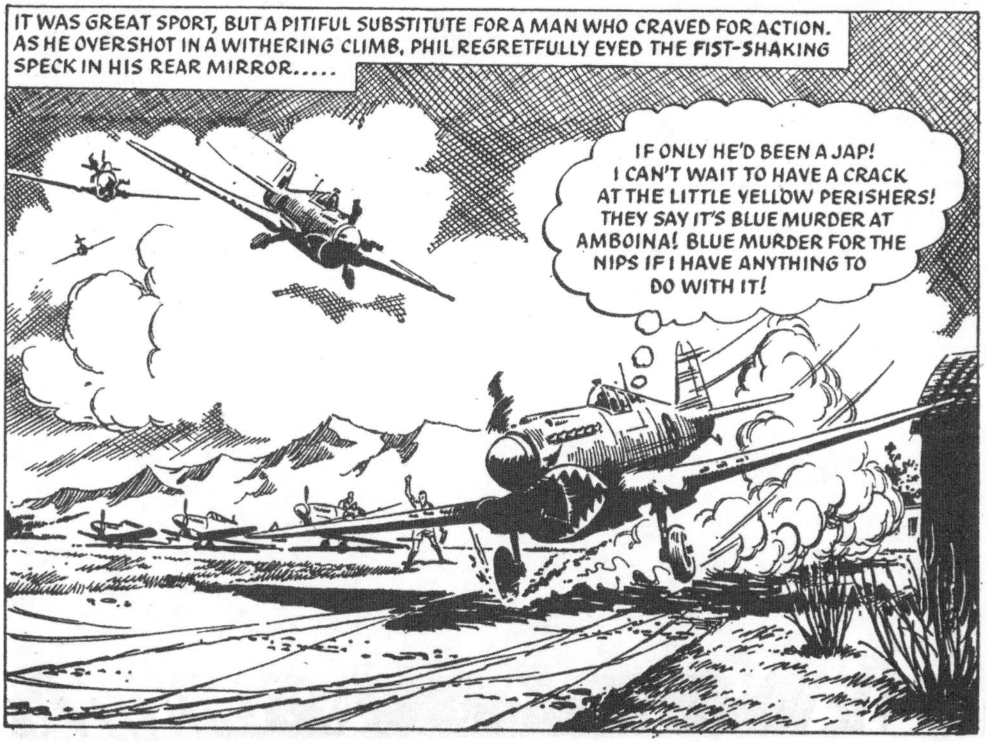
IT WAS GREAT SPORT, BUT A PITIFUL SUBSTITUTE FOR A MAN WHO CRAVED FOR ACTION. AS HE OVERSHOT IN A WITHERING CLIMB, PHIL REGRETFULLY EYED THE FIST-SHAKING SPECK IN HIS REAR MIRROR.....
IF ONLY HE'D BEEN A JAP! I CAN'T WAIT TO HAVE A CRACK AT THE LITTLE YELLOW PERISHERS! THEY SAY IT'S BLUE MURDER AT AMBOINA! BLUE MURDER FOR THE NIPS IF I HAVE ANYTHING TO DO WITH IT!

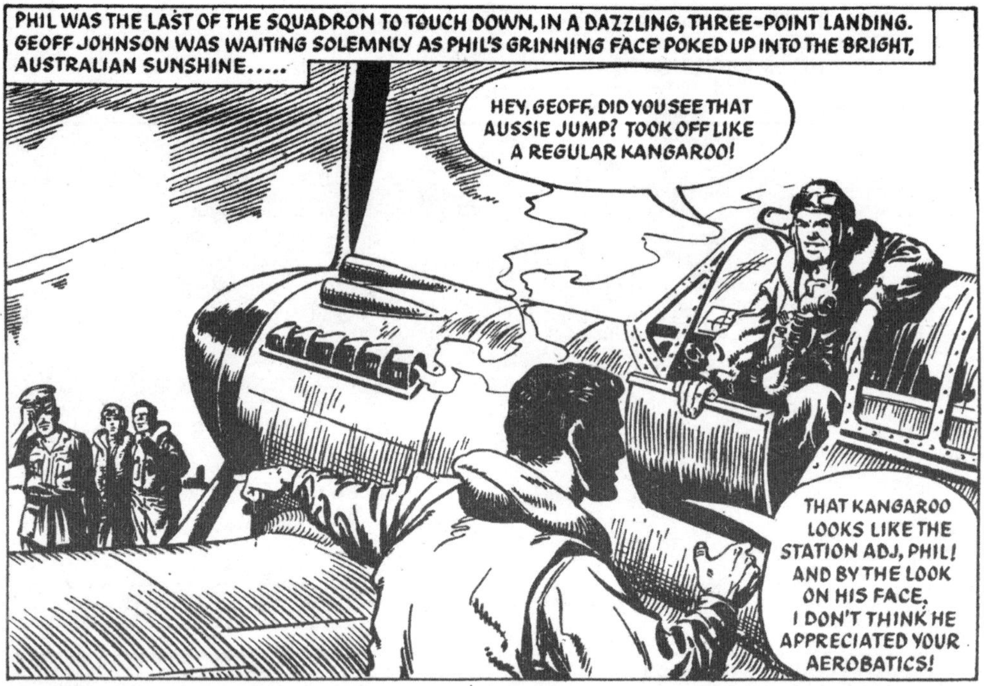
PHIL WAS THE LAST OF THE SQUADRON TO TOUCH DOWN, IN A DAZZLING, THREE-POINT LANDING. GEOFF JOHNSON WAS WAITING SOLEMNLY AS PHIL'S GRINNING FACE POKED UP INTO THE BRIGHT, AUSTRALIAN SUNSHINE.....
HEY, GEOFF, DID YOU SEE THAT AUSSIE JUMP? TOOK OFF LIKE A REGULAR KANGAROO!
THAT KANGAROO LOOKS LIKE THE STATION ADJ, PHIL! AND BY THE LOOK ON HIS FACE, I DON'T THINK HE APPRECIATED YOUR AEROBATICS!

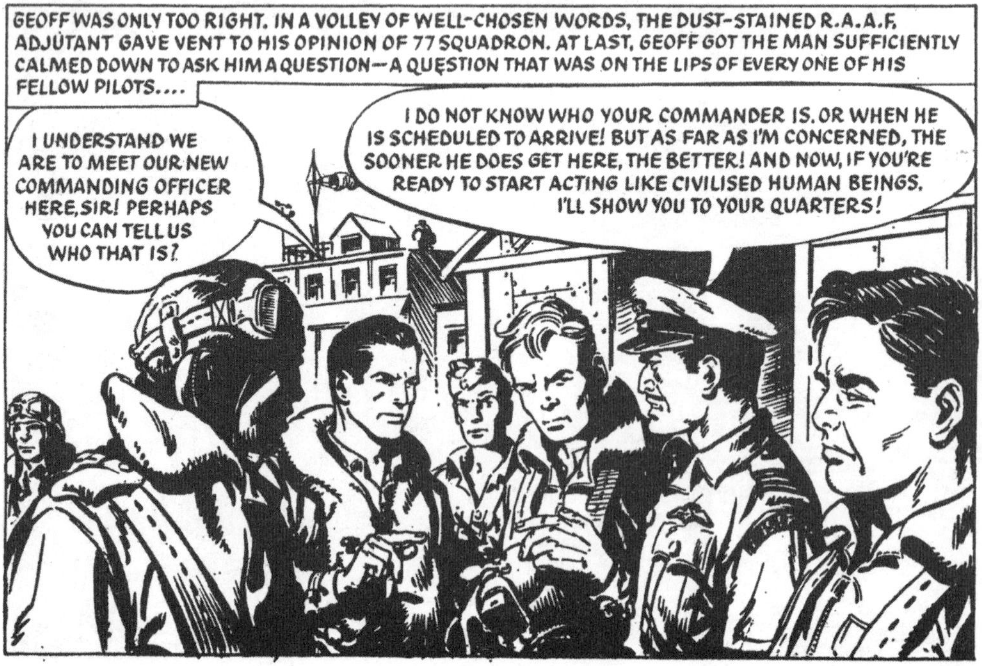
GEOFF WAS ONLY TOO RIGHT. IN A VOLLEY OF WELL-CHOSEN WORDS, THE DUST-STAINED R.A.A.F. ADJUTANT GAVE VENT TO HIS OPINION OF 77 SQUADRON. AT LAST, GEOFF GOT THE MAN SUFFICIENTLY CALMED DOWN TO ASK HIM A QUESTION—A QUESTION THAT WAS ON THE LIPS OF EVERY ONE OF HIS FELLOW PILOTS....
I UNDERSTAND WE ARE TO MEET OUR NEW COMMANDING OFFICER HERE, SIR! PERHAPS YOU CAN TELL US WHO THAT IS?
I DO NOT KNOW WHO YOUR COMMANDER IS, OR WHEN HE IS SCHEDULED TO ARRIVE! BUT AS FAR AS I'M CONCERNED, THE SOONER HE DOES GET HERE, THE BETTER! AND NOW, IF YOU'RE READY TO START ACTING LIKE CIVILISED HUMAN BEINGS, I'LL SHOW YOU TO YOUR QUARTERS!

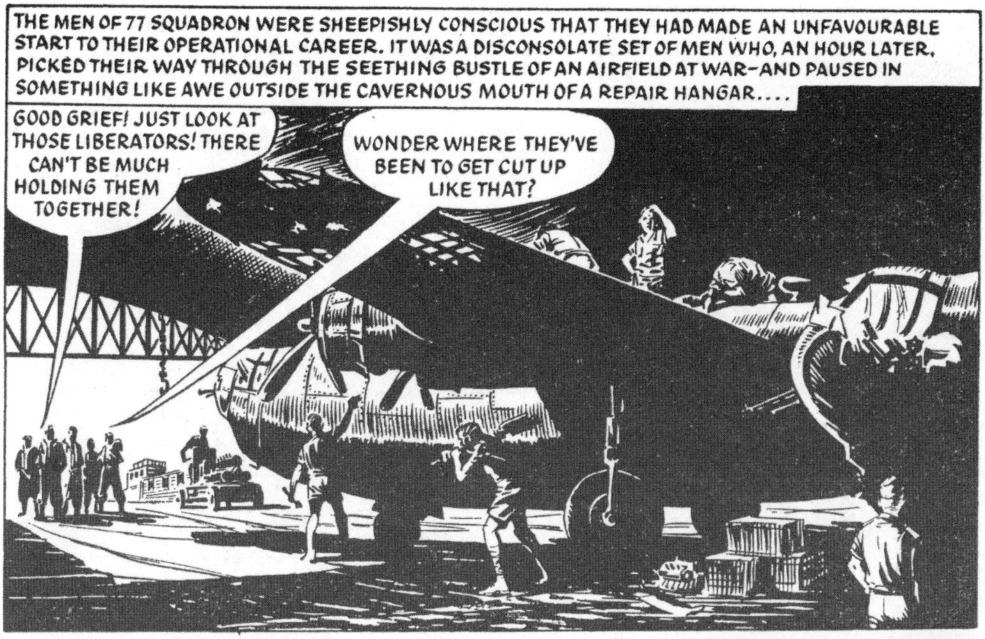
THE MEN OF 77 SQUADRON WERE SHEEPISHLY CONSCIOUS THAT THEY HAD MADE AN UNFAVOURABLE START TO THEIR OPERATIONAL CAREER. IT WAS A DISCONSOLATE SET OF MEN WHO, AN HOUR LATER, PICKED THEIR WAY THROUGH THE SEETHING BUSTLE OF AN AIRFIELD AT WAR–AND PAUSED IN SOMETHING LIKE AWE OUTSIDE THE CAVERNOUS MOUTH OF A REPAIR HANGAR....
GOOD GRIEF! JUST LOOK AT THOSE LIBERATORS! THERE CAN'T BE MUCH HOLDING THEM TOGETHER!
WONDER WHERE THEY'VE BEEN TO GET CUT UP LIKE THAT?

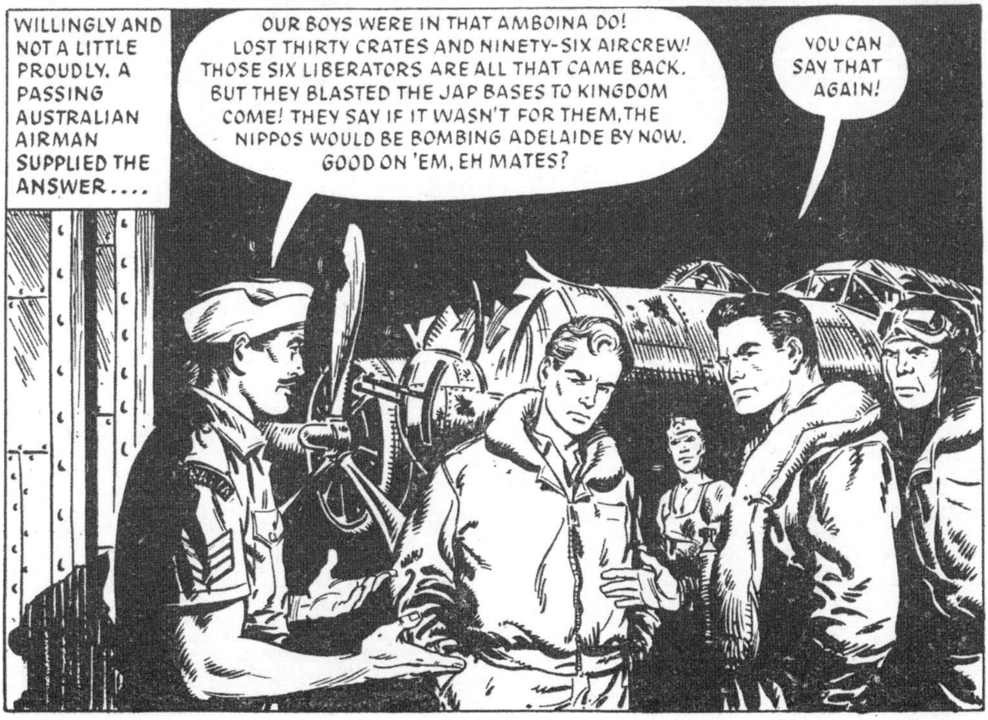
WILLINGLY AND NOT A LITTLE PROUDLY. A PASSING AUSTRALIAN AIRMAN SUPPLIED THE ANSWER....
OUR BOYS WERE IN THAT AMBOINA DO! LOST THIRTY CRATES AND NINETY-SIX AIRCREW! THOSE SIX LIBERATORS ARE ALL THAT CAME BACK. BUT THEY BLASTED THE JAP BASES TO KINGDOM COME! THEY SAY IF IT WASN'T FOR THEM, THE NIPPOS WOULD BE BOMBING ADELAIDE BY NOW. GOOD ON 'EM, EH MATES?
YOU CAN SAY THAT AGAIN!

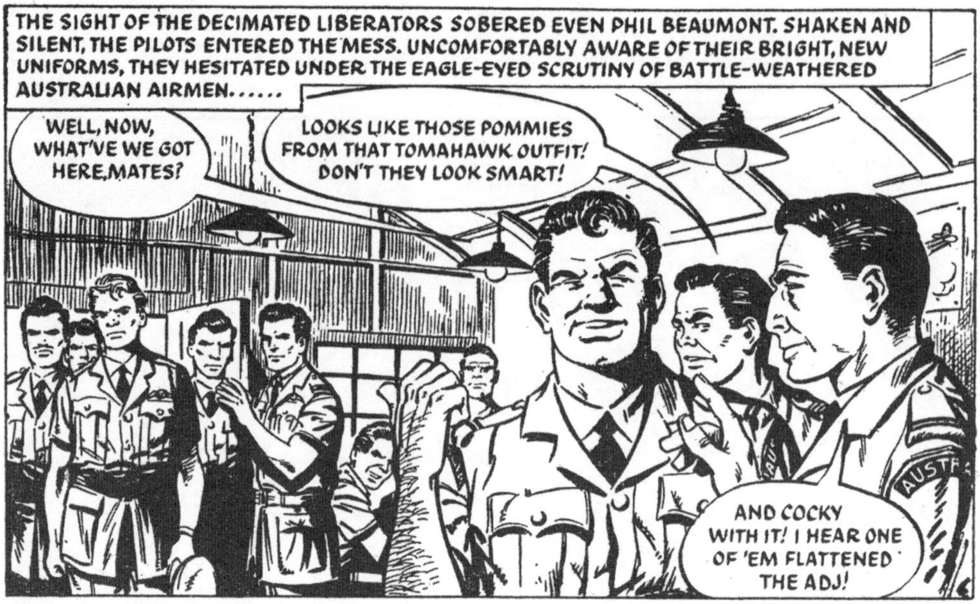
THE SIGHT OF THE DECIMATED LIBERATORS SOBERED EVEN PHIL BEAUMONT. SHAKEN AND SILENT, THE PILOTS ENTERED THE MESS. UNCOMFORTABLY AWARE OF THEIR BRIGHT, NEW UNIFORMS, THEY HESITATED UNDER THE EAGLE-EYED SCRUTINY OF BATTLE-WEATHERED AUSTRALIAN AIRMEN......
WELL, NOW, WHAT'VE WE GOT HERE, MATES?
LOOKS LIKE THOSE POMMIES FROM THAT TOMAHAWK OUTFIT! DON'T THEY LOOK SMART!
AND COCKY WITH IT! I HEAR ONE OF 'EM FLATTENED THE ADJ!

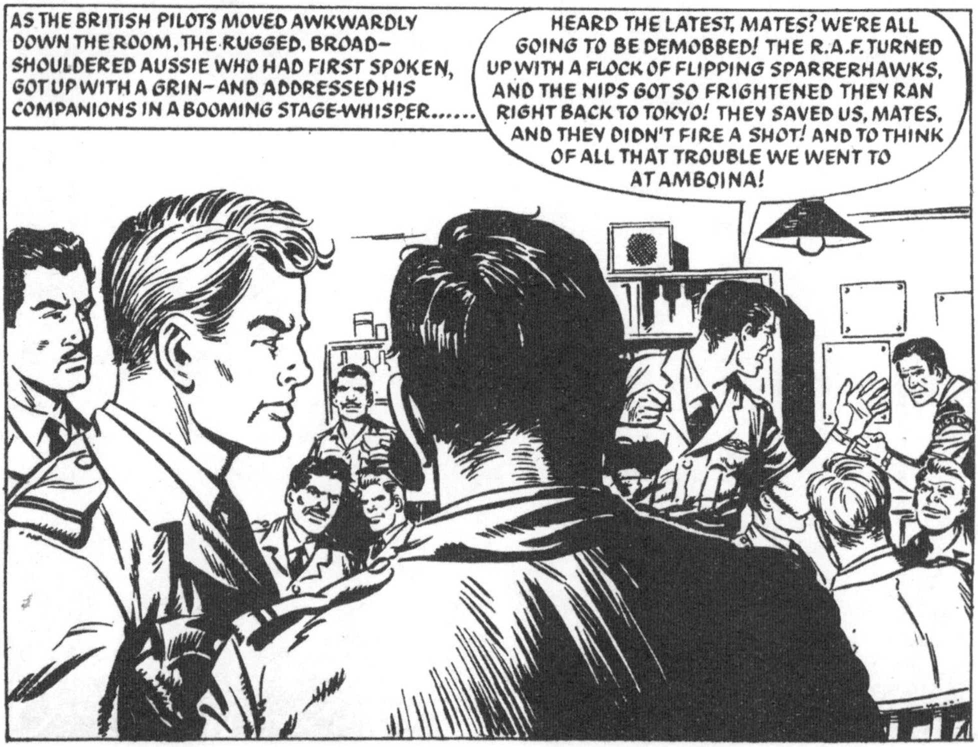
AS THE BRITISH PILOTS MOVED AWKWARDLY DOWN THE ROOM, THE RUGGED, BROAD-SHOULDERED AUSSIE WHO HAD FIRST SPOKEN, GOT UP WITH A GRIN-AND ADDRESSED HIS COMPANIONS IN A BOOMING STAGE-WHISPER......
HEARD THE LATEST, MATES? WE'RE ALL GOING TO BE DEMOBBED! THE R.A.F. TURNED UP WITH A FLOCK OF FLIPPING SPARRERHAWKS, AND THE NIPS GOT SO FRIGHTENED THEY RAN RIGHT BACK TO TOKYO! THEY SAVED US, MATES, AND THEY DIDN'T FIRE A SHOT! AND TO THINK OF ALL THAT TROUBLE WE WENT TO AT AMBOINA!

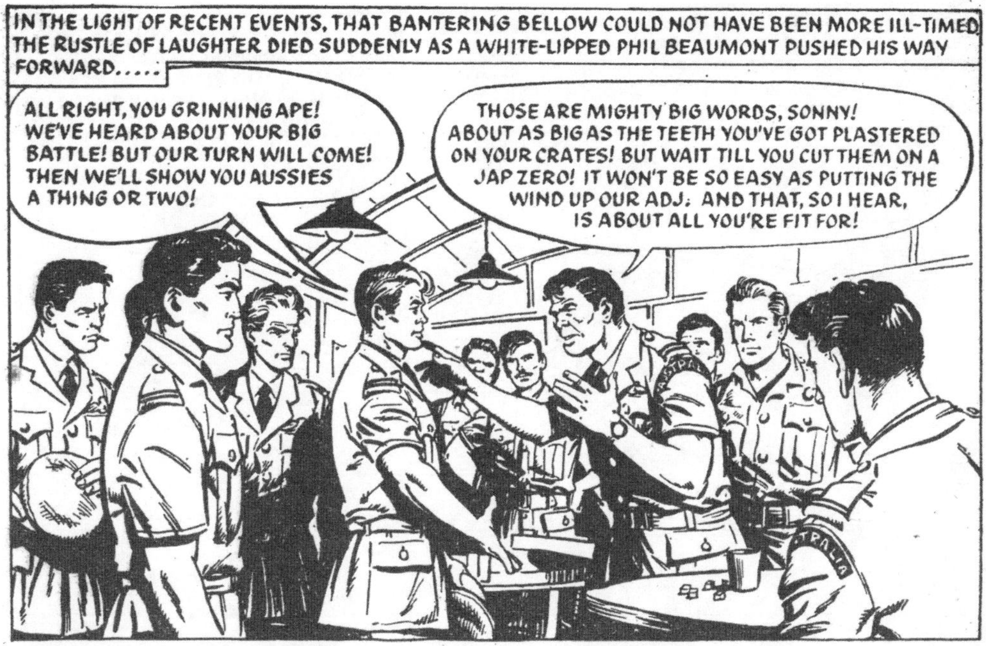
IN THE LIGHT OF RECENT EVENTS, THAT BANTERING BELLOW COULD NOT HAVE BEEN MORE ILL-TIMED. THE RUSTLE OF LAUGHTER DIED SUDDENLY AS A WHITE-LIPPED PHIL BEAUMONT PUSHED HIS WAY FORWARD.....
ALL RIGHT, YOU GRINNING APE! WE'VE HEARD ABOUT YOUR BIG BATTLE! BUT OUR TURN WILL COME! THEN WE'LL SHOW YOU AUSSIES A THING OR TWO!
THOSE ARE MIGHTY BIG WORDS, SONNY! ABOUT AS BIG AS THE TEETH YOU'VE GOT PLASTERED ON YOUR CRATES! BUT WAIT TILL YOU CUT THEM ON A JAP ZERO! IT WON'T BE SO EASY AS PUTTING THE WIND UP OUR ADJ. AND THAT, SO I HEAR, IS ABOUT ALL YOU'RE FIT FOR!

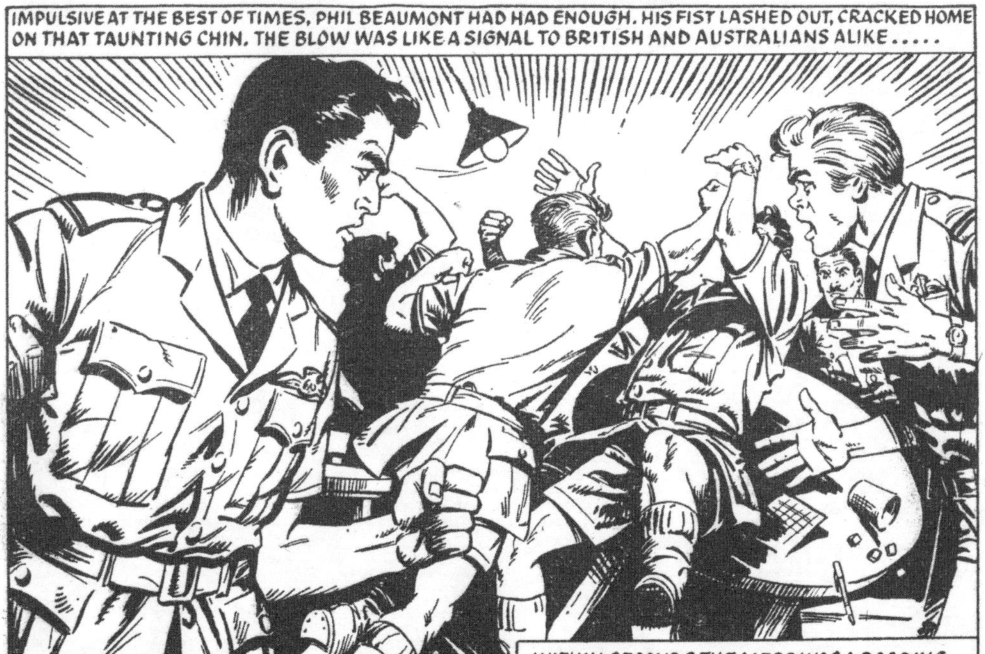
IMPULSIVE AT THE BEST OF TIMES, PHIL BEAUMONT HAD HAD ENOUGH. HIS FIST LASHED OUT, CRACKED HOME ON THAT TAUNTING CHIN. THE BLOW WAS LIKE A SIGNAL TO BRITISH AND AUSTRALIANS ALIKE.....
WITHIN SECONDS, THE MESS WAS A ROARING, FLAILING TANGLE OF FIGHTING MEN.....

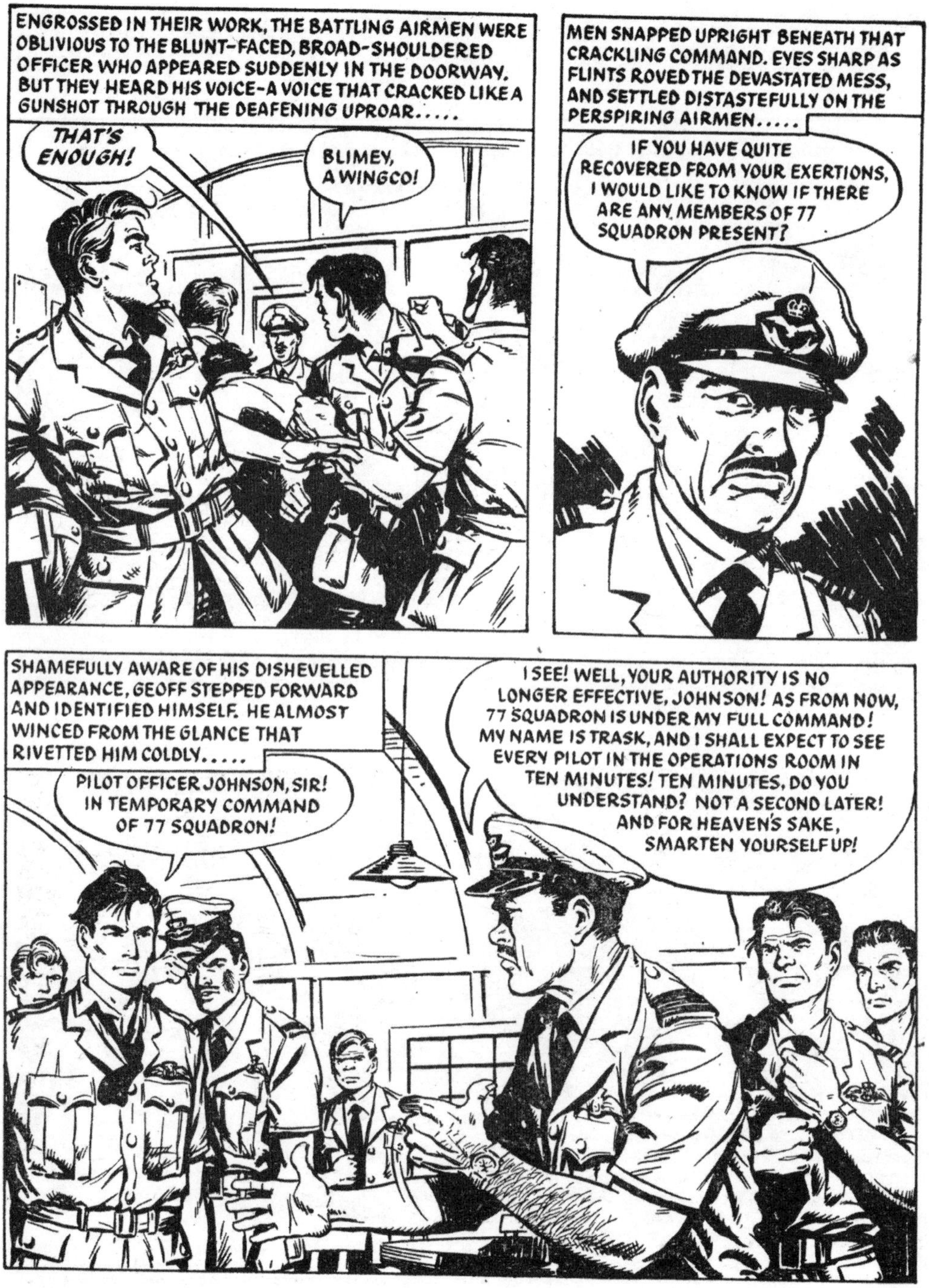
ENGROSSED IN THEIR WORK, THE BATTLING AIRMEN WERE OBLIVIOUS TO THE BLUNT-FACED, BROAD-SHOULDERED OFFICER WHO APPEARED SUDDENLY IN THE DOORWAY. BUT THEY HEARD HIS VOICE-A VOICE THAT CRACKED LIKE A GUNSHOT THROUGH THE DEAFENING UPROAR.....
THAT'S ENOUGH!
BLIMEY, A WINGCO!
MEN SNAPPED UPRIGHT BENEATH THAT CRACKLING COMMAND. EYES SHARP AS FLINTS ROVED THE DEVASTATED MESS, AND SETTLED DISTASTEFULLY ON THE PERSPIRING AIRMEN.....
IF YOU HAVE QUITE RECOVERED FROM YOUR EXERTIONS, I WOULD LIKE TO KNOW IF THERE ARE ANY MEMBERS OF 77 SQUADRON PRESENT?
SHAMEFULLY AWARE OF HIS DISHEVELLED APPEARANCE, GEOFF STEPPED FORWARD AND IDENTIFIED HIMSELF. HE ALMOST WINCED FROM THE GLANCE THAT RIVETTED HIM COLDLY.....
PILOT OFFICER JOHNSON, SIR! IN TEMPORARY COMMAND OF 77 SQUADRON!
I SEE! WELL, YOUR AUTHORITY IS NO LONGER EFFECTIVE, JOHNSON! AS FROM NOW, 77 SQUADRON IS UNDER MY FULL COMMAND! MY NAME IS TRASK, AND I SHALL EXPECT TO SEE EVERY PILOT IN THE OPERATIONS ROOM IN TEN MINUTES! TEN MINUTES, DO YOU UNDERSTAND? NOT A SECOND LATER! AND FOR HEAVEN'S SAKE, SMARTEN YOURSELF UP!

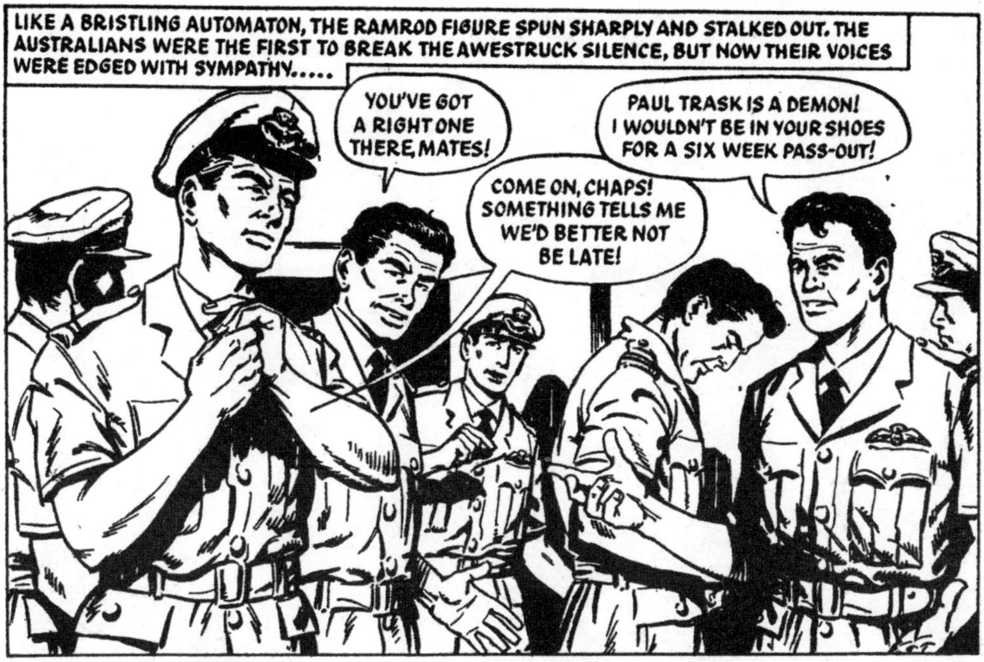
LIKE A BRISTLING AUTOMATON, THE RAMROD FIGURE SPUN SHARPLY AND STALKED OUT. THE AUSTRALIANS WERE THE FIRST TO BREAK THE AWESTRUCK SILENCE, BUT NOW THEIR VOICES WERE EDGED WITH SYMPATHY.....
YOU'VE GOT A RIGHT ONE THERE, MATES!
COME ON, CHAPS! SOMETHING TELLS ME WE'D BETTER NOT BE LATE!
PAUL TRASK IS A DEMON! I WOULDN'T BE IN YOUR SHOES FOR A SIX WEEK PASS-OUT!

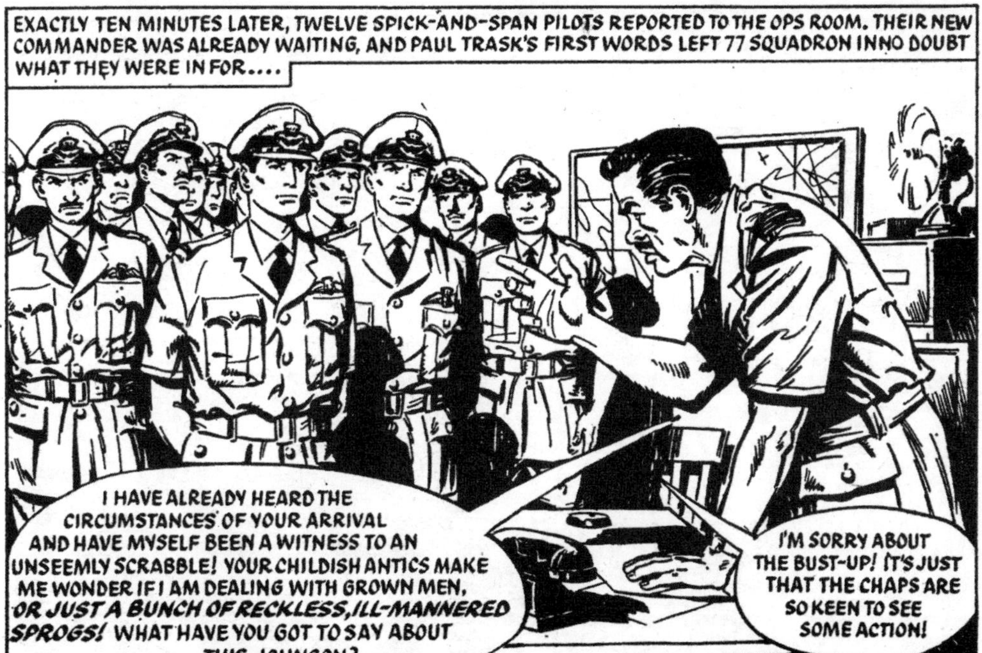
EXACTLY TEN MINUTES LATER, TWELVE SPICK-AND-SPAN PILOTS REPORTED TO THE OPS ROOM. THEIR NEW COMMANDER WAS ALREADY WAITING, AND PAUL TRASK'S FIRST WORDS LEFT 77 SQUADRON IN NO DOUBT WHAT THEY WERE IN FOR....
I HAVE ALREADY HEARD THE CIRCUMSTANCES OF YOUR ARRIVAL AND HAVE MYSELF BEEN A WITNESS TO AN UNSEEMLY SCRABBLE! YOUR CHILDISH ANTICS MAKE ME WONDER IF I AM DEALING WITH GROWN MEN, OR JUST A BUNCH OF RECKLESS, ILL-MANNERED SPROGS! WHAT HAVE YOU GOT TO SAY ABOUT THIS, JOHNSON?
I'M SORRY ABOUT THE BUST-UP! IT'S JUST THAT THE CHAPS ARE SO KEEN TO SEE SOME ACTION!

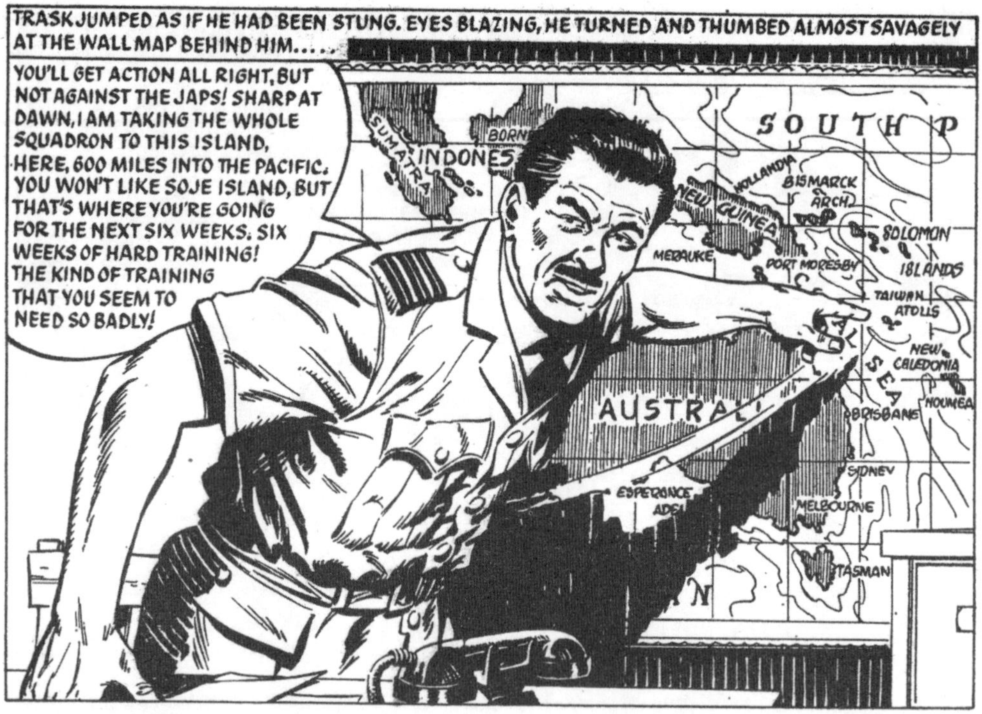
TRASK JUMPED AS IF HE HAD BEEN STUNG. EYES BLAZING, HE TURNED AND THUMBED ALMOST SAVAGELY AT THE WALL MAP BEHIND HIM....
YOU'LL GET ACTION ALL RIGHT, BUT NOT AGAINST THE JAPS! SHARP AT DAWN, I AM TAKING THE WHOLE SQUADRON TO THIS ISLAND, HERE, 600 MILES INTO THE PACIFIC. YOU WON'T LIKE SOJE ISLAND, BUT THAT'S WHERE YOU'RE GOING FOR THE NEXT SIX WEEKS. SIX WEEKS OF HARD TRAINING! THE KIND OF TRAINING THAT YOU SEEM TO NEED SO BADLY!
SOUTH P
SUMATRA
BORN
INDONES
HOLLANDIA
BISMARCK ARCH.
NEW GUINEA
SOLOMON ISLANDS
MERAUKE
PORT MORESBY
TAIWAN ATOLLS
NEW CALEDONIA
NOUMEA
AUSTRA
SEA
BRISBANE
SYDNEY
ESPERANCE
ADEL
MELBOURNE
TASMAN

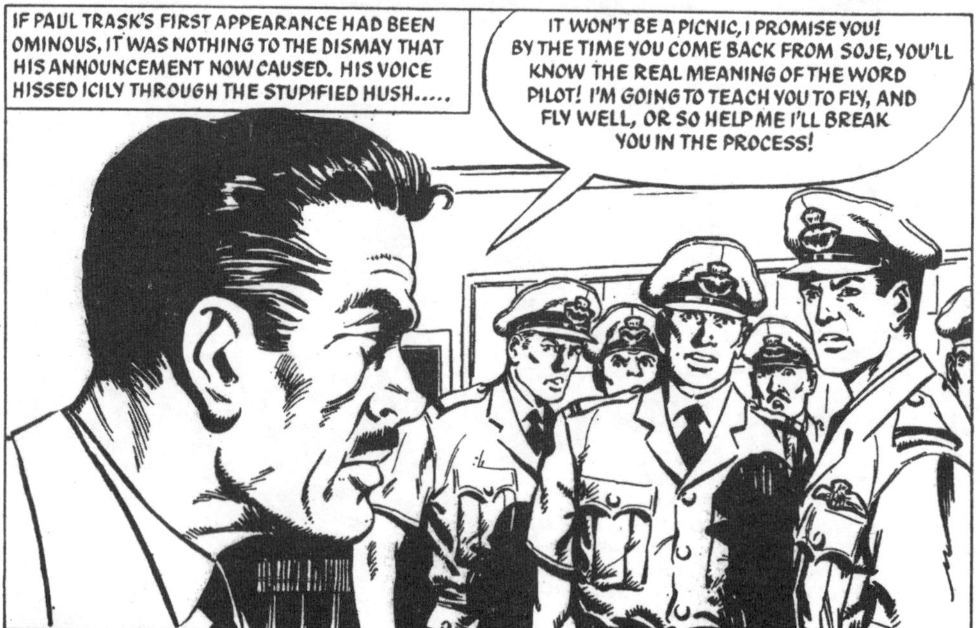
IF PAUL TRASK'S FIRST APPEARANCE HAD BEEN OMINOUS, IT WAS NOTHING TO THE DISMAY THAT HIS ANNOUNCEMENT NOW CAUSED. HIS VOICE HISSED ICILY THROUGH THE STUPIFIED HUSH.....
IT WON'T BE A PICNIC, I PROMISE YOU! BY THE TIME YOU COME BACK FROM SOJE, YOU'LL KNOW THE REAL MEANING OF THE WORD PILOT! I'M GOING TO TEACH YOU TO FLY, AND FLY WELL, OR SO HELP ME I'LL BREAK YOU IN THE PROCESS!

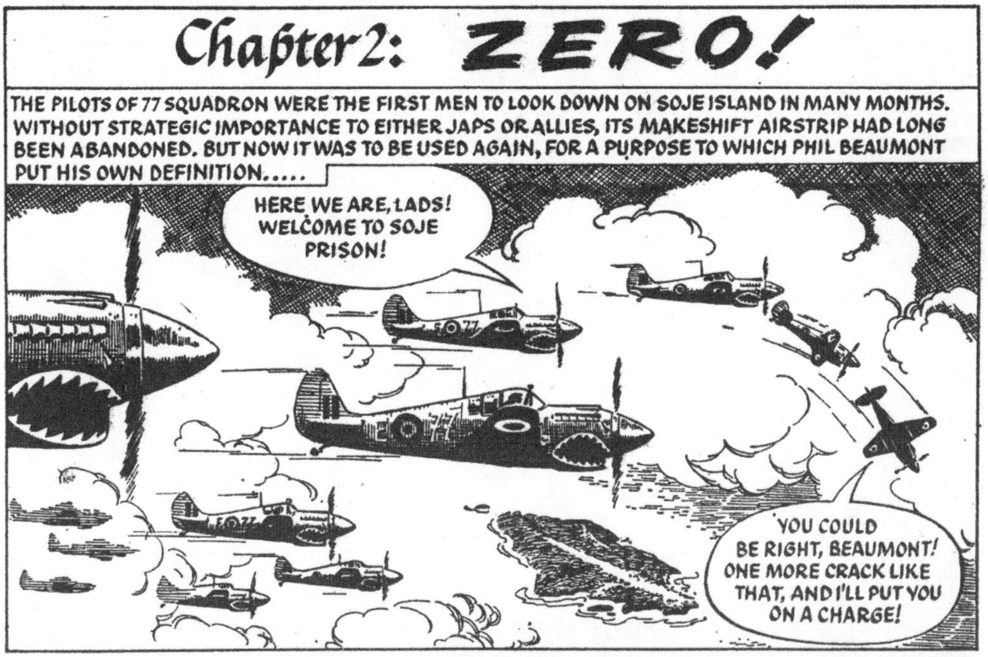
Chapter 2: ZERO!
THE PILOTS OF 77 SQUADRON WERE THE FIRST MEN TO LOOK DOWN ON SOJE ISLAND IN MANY MONTHS. WITHOUT STRATEGIC IMPORTANCE TO EITHER JAPS OR ALLIES, ITS MAKESHIFT AIRSTRIP HAD LONG BEEN ABANDONED. BUT NOW IT WAS TO BE USED AGAIN, FOR A PURPOSE TO WHICH PHIL BEAUMONT PUT HIS OWN DEFINITION.....
HERE WE ARE, LADS! WELCOME TO SOJE PRISON!
YOU COULD BE RIGHT, BEAUMONT! ONE MORE CRACK LIKE THAT, AND I'LL PUT YOU ON A CHARGE!

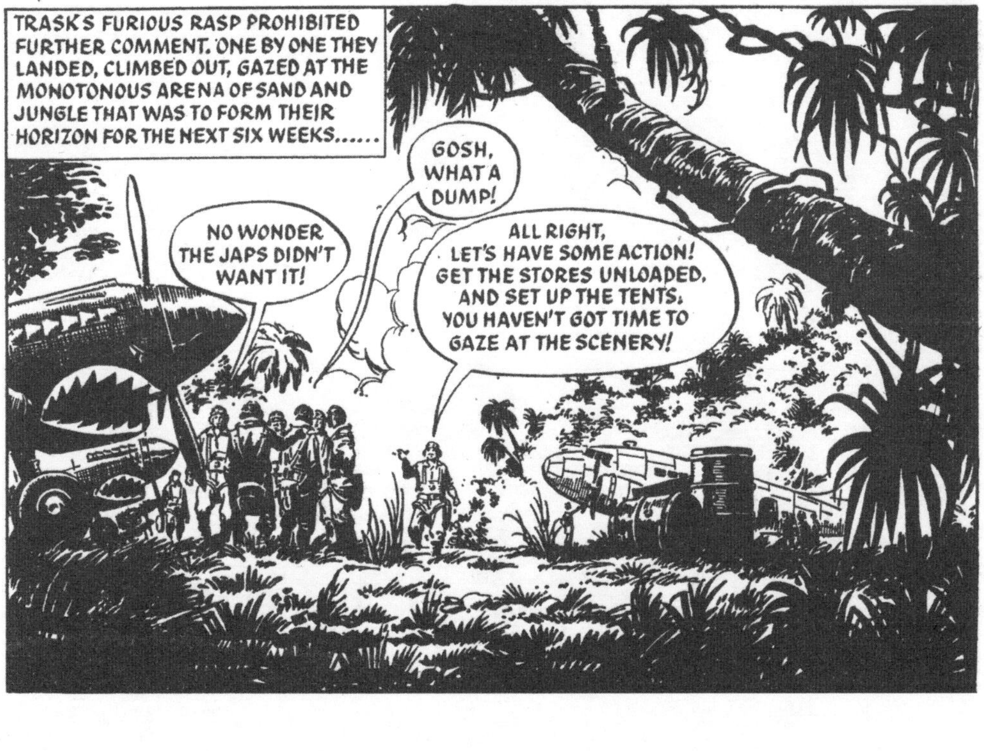
TRASK'S FURIOUS RASP PROHIBITED FURTHER COMMENT. ONE BY ONE THEY LANDED, CLIMBED OUT, GAZED AT THE MONOTONOUS ARENA OF SAND AND JUNGLE THAT WAS TO FORM THEIR HORIZON FOR THE NEXT SIX WEEKS......
NO WONDER THE JAPS DIDN'T WANT IT!
GOSH, WHAT A DUMP!
ALL RIGHT, LET'S HAVE SOME ACTION! GET THE STORES UNLOADED, AND SET UP THE TENTS. YOU HAVEN'T GOT TIME TO GAZE AT THE SCENERY!

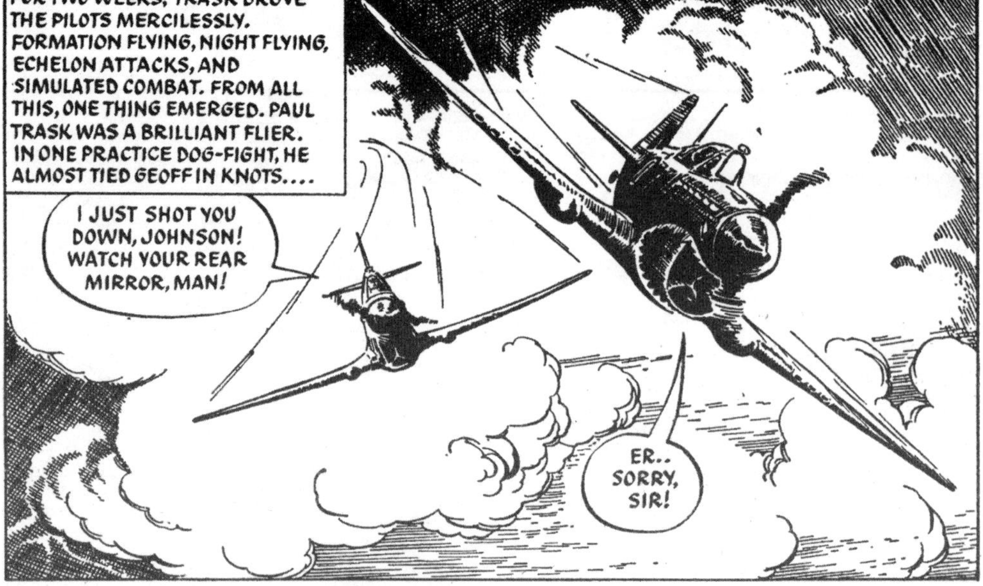
FOR TWO WEEKS, TRASK DROVE THE PILOTS MERCILESSLY. FORMATION FLYING, NIGHT FLYING, ECHELON ATTACKS, AND SIMULATED COMBAT. FROM ALL THIS, ONE THING EMERGED. PAUL TRASK WAS A BRILLIANT FLIER. IN ONE PRACTICE DOG-FIGHT, HE ALMOST TIED GEOFF IN KNOTS....
I JUST SHOT YOU DOWN, JOHNSON! WATCH YOUR REAR MIRROR, MAN!
ER.. SORRY, SIR!

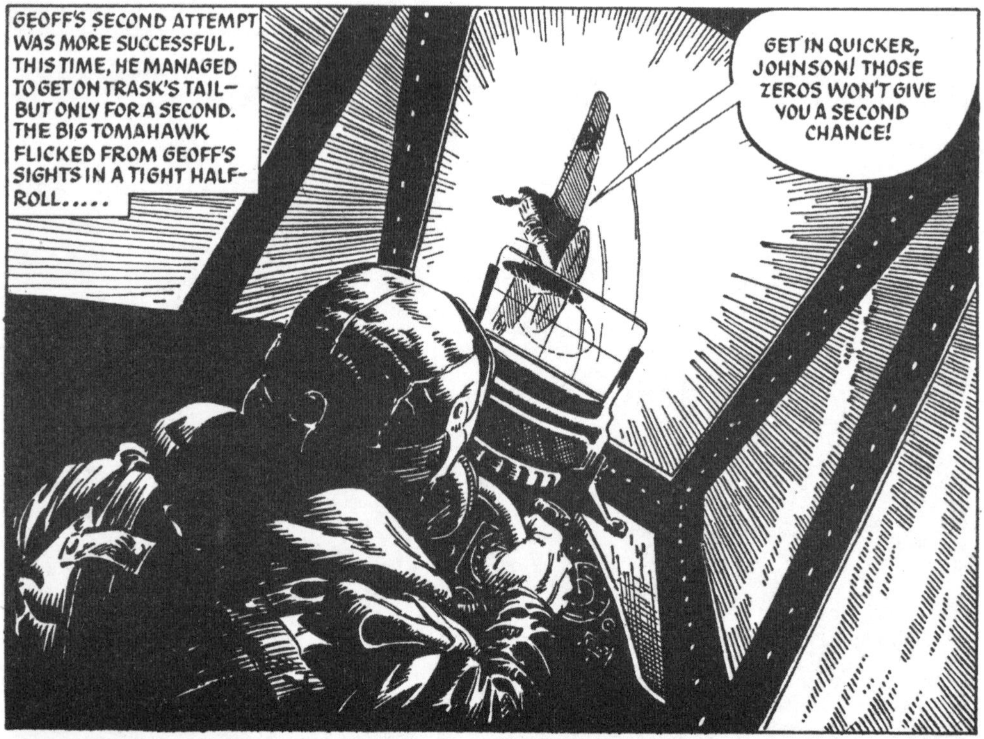
GEOFF'S SECOND ATTEMPT WAS MORE SUCCESSFUL. THIS TIME, HE MANAGED TO GET ON TRASK'S TAIL—BUT ONLY FOR A SECOND. THE BIG TOMAHAWK FLICKED FROM GEOFF'S SIGHTS IN A TIGHT HALF-ROLL.....
GET IN QUICKER, JOHNSON! THOSE ZEROS WON'T GIVE YOU A SECOND CHANCE!

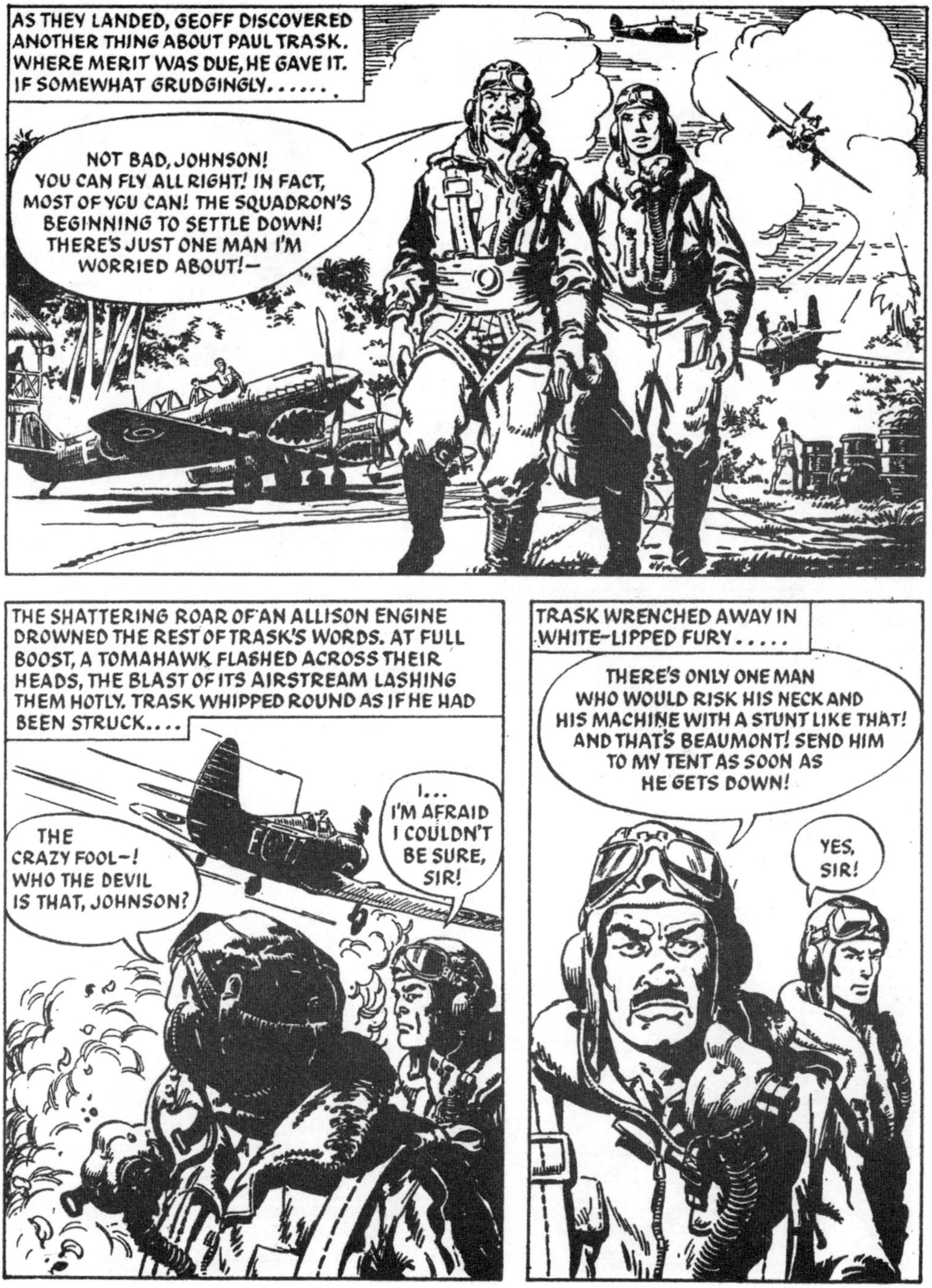
AS THEY LANDED, GEOFF DISCOVERED ANOTHER THING ABOUT PAUL TRASK. WHERE MERIT WAS DUE, HE GAVE IT. IF SOMEWHAT GRUDGINGLY......
NOT BAD, JOHNSON! YOU CAN FLY ALL RIGHT! IN FACT, MOST OF YOU CAN! THE SQUADRON'S BEGINNING TO SETTLE DOWN! THERE'S JUST ONE MAN I'M WORRIED ABOUT!–
THE SHATTERING ROAR OF AN ALLISON ENGINE DROWNED THE REST OF TRASK'S WORDS. AT FULL BOOST, A TOMAHAWK FLASHED ACROSS THEIR HEADS, THE BLAST OF ITS AIRSTREAM LASHING THEM HOTLY. TRASK WHIPPED ROUND AS IF HE HAD BEEN STRUCK....
THE CRAZY FOOL–! WHO THE DEVIL IS THAT, JOHNSON?
I... I'M AFRAID I COULDN'T BE SURE, SIR!
TRASK WRENCHED AWAY IN WHITE-LIPPED FURY.....
THERE'S ONLY ONE MAN WHO WOULD RISK HIS NECK AND HIS MACHINE WITH A STUNT LIKE THAT! AND THAT'S BEAUMONT! SEND HIM TO MY TENT AS SOON AS HE GETS DOWN!
YES, SIR!

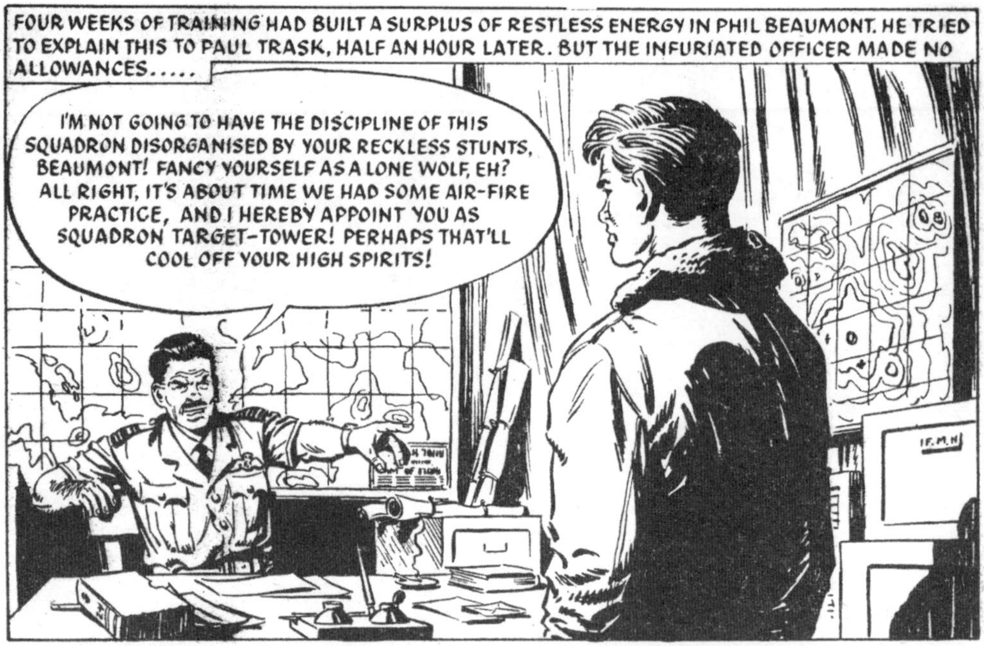
FOUR WEEKS OF TRAINING HAD BUILT A SURPLUS OF RESTLESS ENERGY IN PHIL BEAUMONT. HE TRIED TO EXPLAIN THIS TO PAUL TRASK, HALF AN HOUR LATER. BUT THE INFURIATED OFFICER MADE NO ALLOWANCES.....
I'M NOT GOING TO HAVE THE DISCIPLINE OF THIS SQUADRON DISORGANISED BY YOUR RECKLESS STUNTS, BEAUMONT! FANCY YOURSELF AS A LONE WOLF, EH? ALL RIGHT, IT'S ABOUT TIME WE HAD SOME AIR-FIRE PRACTICE, AND I HEREBY APPOINT YOU AS SQUADRON TARGET-TOWER! PERHAPS THAT'LL COOL OFF YOUR HIGH SPIRITS!

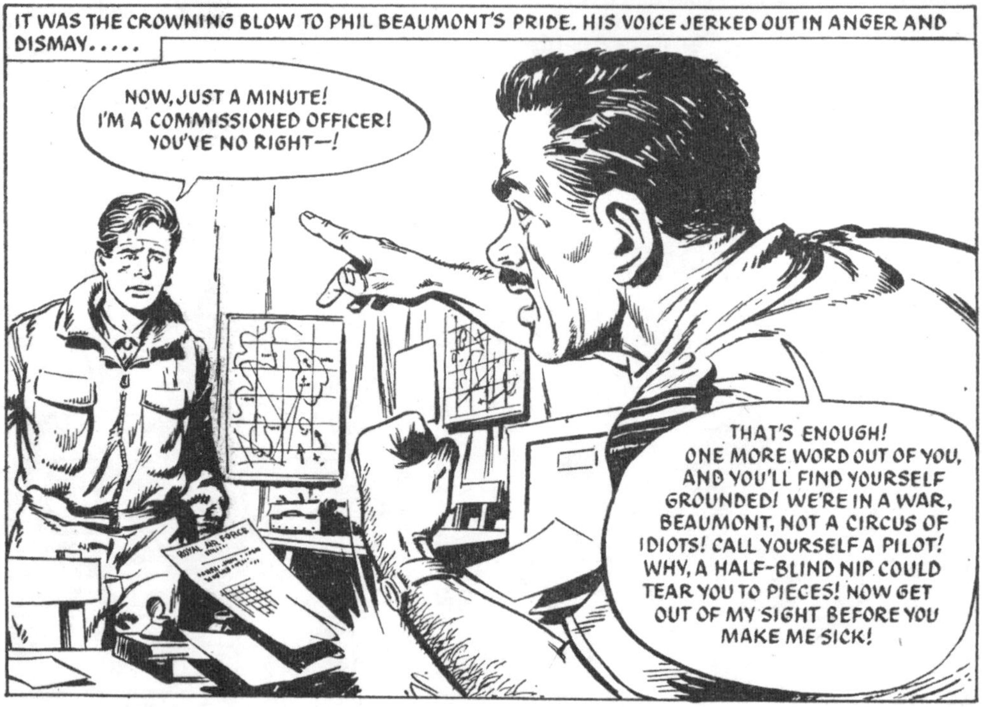
IT WAS THE CROWNING BLOW TO PHIL BEAUMONT'S PRIDE. HIS VOICE JERKED OUT IN ANGER AND DISMAY.....
NOW, JUST A MINUTE! I'M A COMMISSIONED OFFICER! YOU'VE NO RIGHT—!
THAT'S ENOUGH! ONE MORE WORD OUT OF YOU, AND YOU'LL FIND YOURSELF GROUNDED! WE'RE IN A WAR, BEAUMONT, NOT A CIRCUS OF IDIOTS! CALL YOURSELF A PILOT! WHY, A HALF-BLIND NIP COULD TEAR YOU TO PIECES! NOW GET OUT OF MY SIGHT BEFORE YOU MAKE ME SICK!

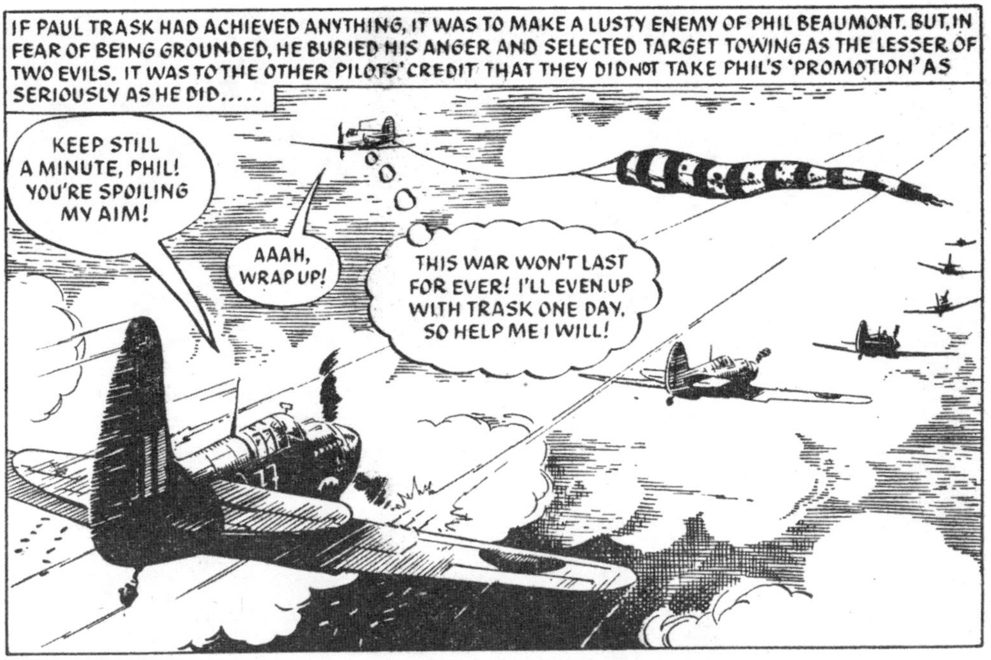
IF PAUL TRASK HAD ACHIEVED ANYTHING, IT WAS TO MAKE A LUSTY ENEMY OF PHIL BEAUMONT. BUT, IN FEAR OF BEING GROUNDED, HE BURIED HIS ANGER AND SELECTED TARGET TOWING AS THE LESSER OF TWO EVILS. IT WAS TO THE OTHER PILOTS' CREDIT THAT THEY DID NOT TAKE PHIL'S 'PROMOTION' AS SERIOUSLY AS HE DID.....
KEEP STILL A MINUTE, PHIL! YOU'RE SPOILING MY AIM!
AAAH, WRAP UP!
THIS WAR WON'T LAST FOR EVER! I'LL EVEN UP WITH TRASK ONE DAY. SO HELP ME I WILL!

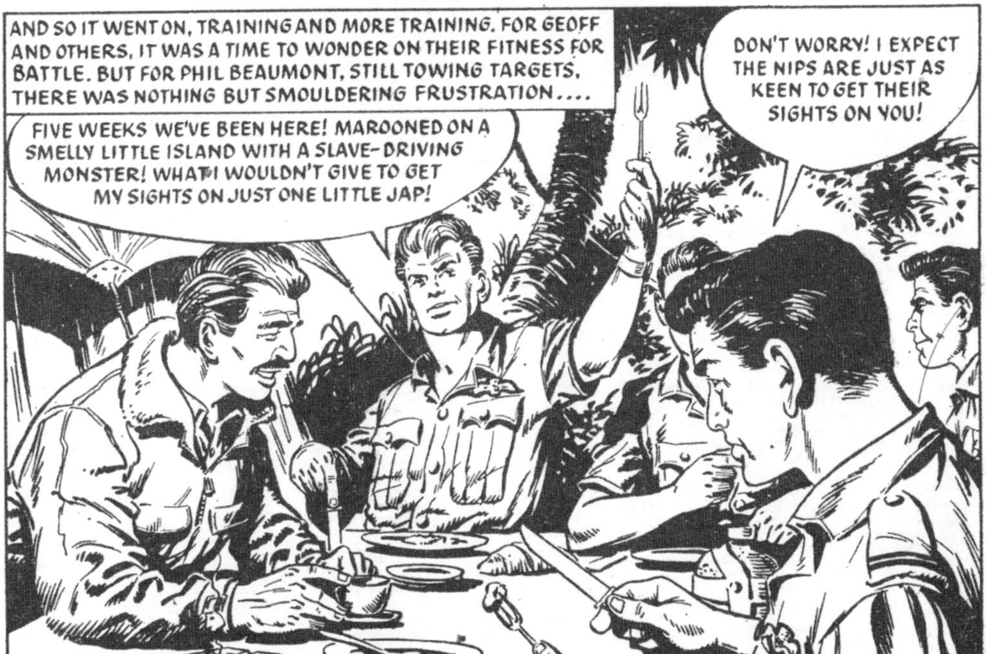
AND SO IT WENT ON, TRAINING AND MORE TRAINING. FOR GEOFF AND OTHERS, IT WAS A TIME TO WONDER ON THEIR FITNESS FOR BATTLE. BUT FOR PHIL BEAUMONT, STILL TOWING TARGETS, THERE WAS NOTHING BUT SMOULDERING FRUSTRATION....
FIVE WEEKS WE'VE BEEN HERE! MAROONED ON A SMELLY LITTLE ISLAND WITH A SLAVE-DRIVING MONSTER! WHAT I WOULDN'T GIVE TO GET MY SIGHTS ON JUST ONE LITTLE JAP!
DON'T WORRY! I EXPECT THE NIPS ARE JUST AS KEEN TO GET THEIR SIGHTS ON YOU!

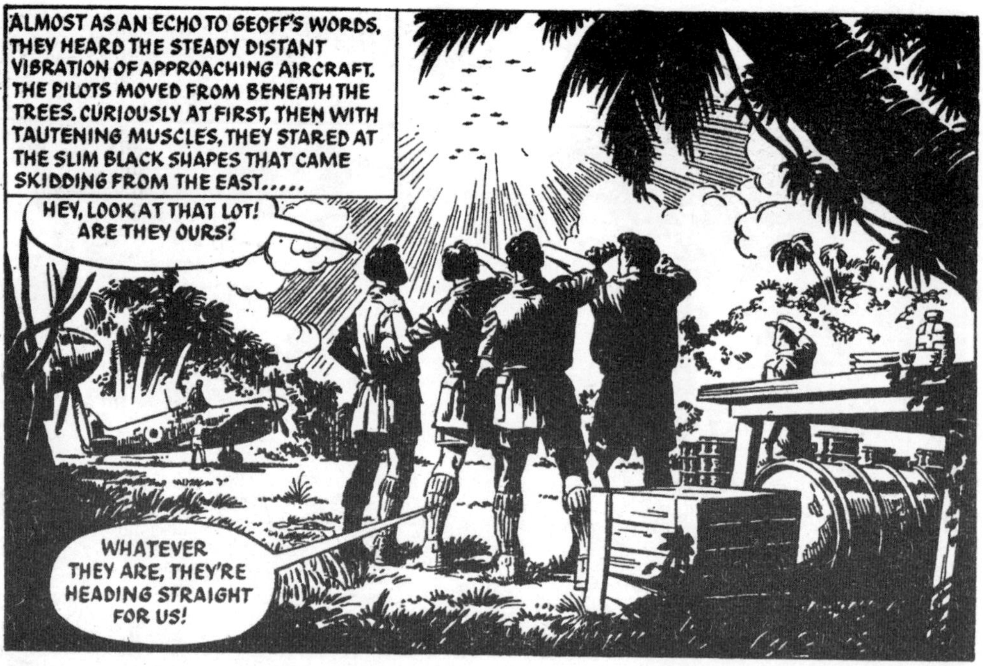
ALMOST AS AN ECHO TO GEOFF'S WORDS, THEY HEARD THE STEADY DISTANT VIBRATION OF APPROACHING AIRCRAFT. THE PILOTS MOVED FROM BENEATH THE TREES. CURIOUSLY AT FIRST, THEN WITH TAUTENING MUSCLES, THEY STARED AT THE SLIM BLACK SHAPES THAT CAME SKIDDING FROM THE EAST.....
HEY, LOOK AT THAT LOT! ARE THEY OURS?
WHATEVER THEY ARE, THEY'RE HEADING STRAIGHT FOR US!

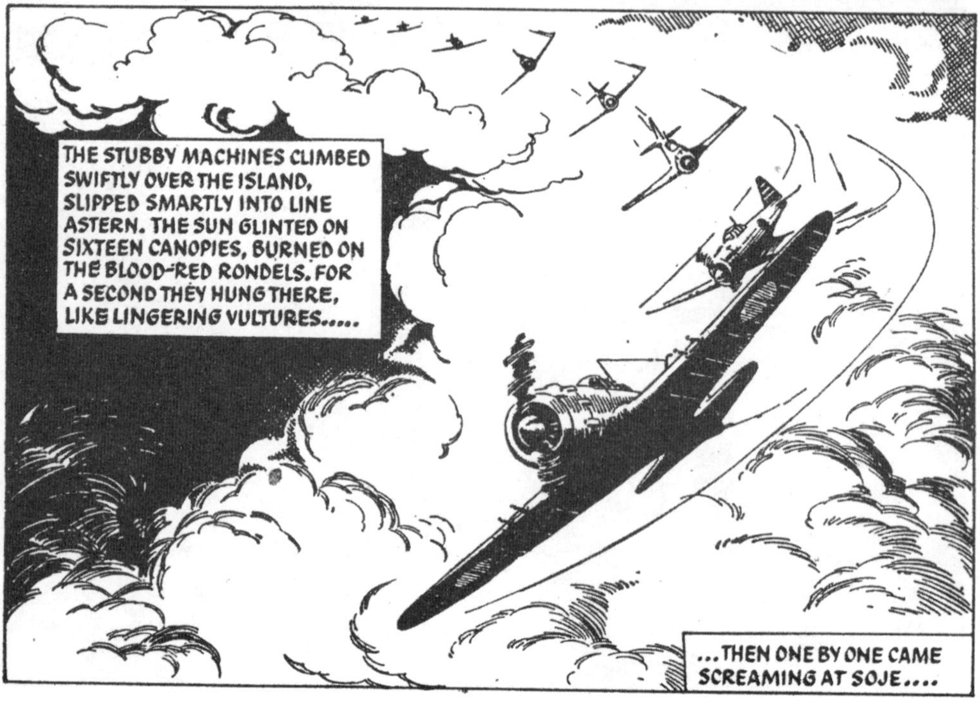
THE STUBBY MACHINES CLIMBED SWIFTLY OVER THE ISLAND, SLIPPED SMARTLY INTO LINE ASTERN. THE SUN GLINTED ON SIXTEEN CANOPIES, BURNED ON THE BLOOD-RED RONDELS. FOR A SECOND THEY HUNG THERE, LIKE LINGERING VULTURES.....
...THEN ONE BY ONE CAME SCREAMING AT SOJE....

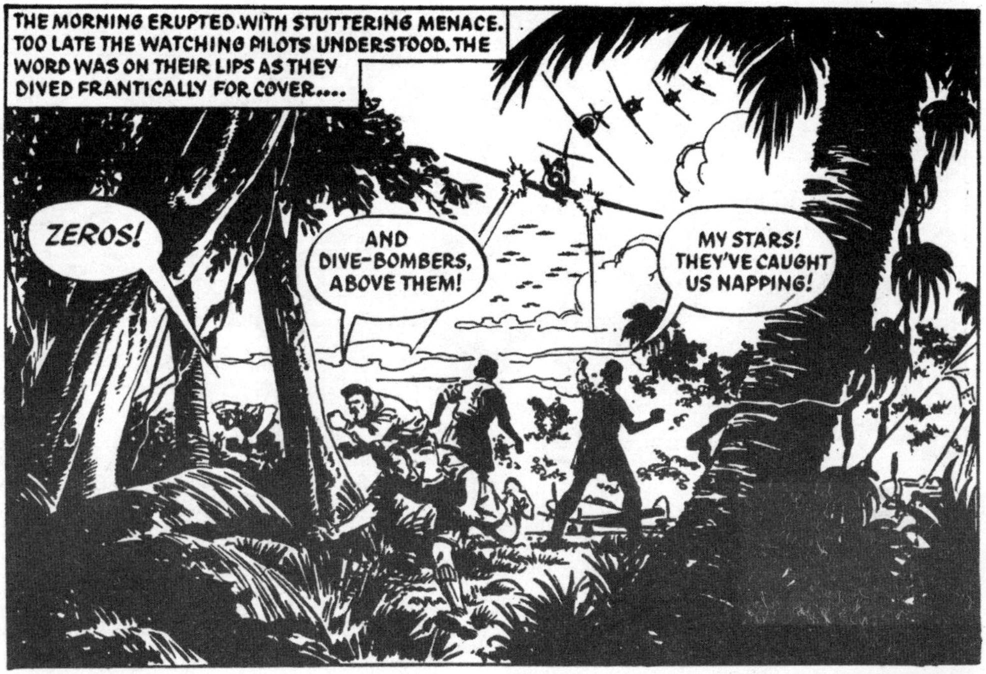
THE MORNING ERUPTED WITH STUTTERING MENACE. TOO LATE THE WATCHING PILOTS UNDERSTOOD. THE WORD WAS ON THEIR LIPS AS THEY DIVED FRANTICALLY FOR COVER....
ZEROS!
AND DIVE-BOMBERS, ABOVE THEM!
MY STARS! THEY'VE CAUGHT US NAPPING!

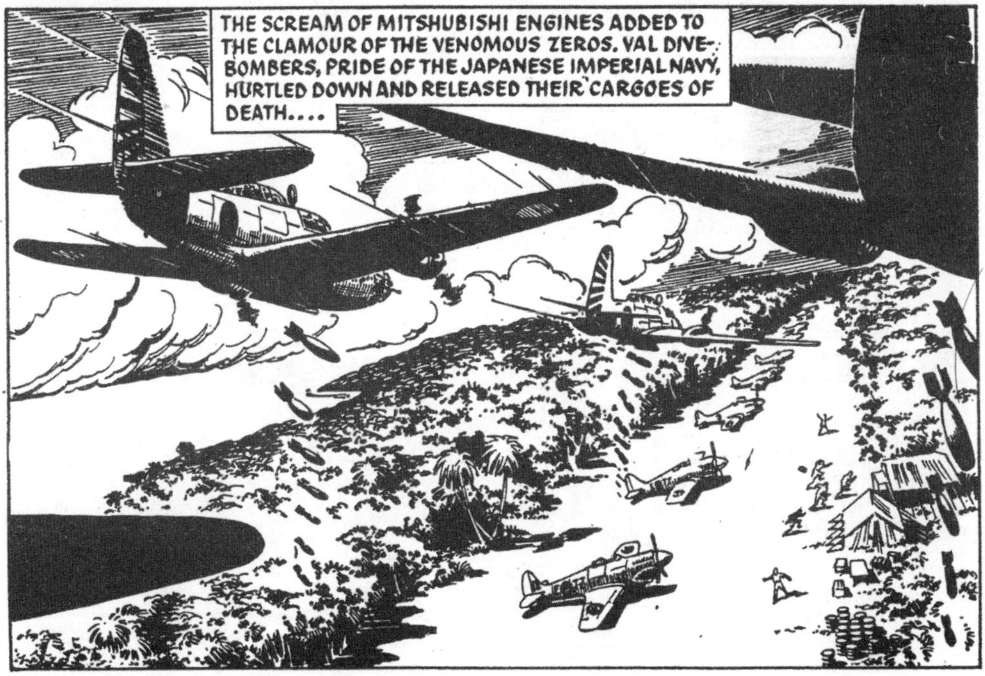
THE SCREAM OF MITSHUBISHI ENGINES ADDED TO THE CLAMOUR OF THE VENOMOUS ZEROS. VAL DIVE-BOMBERS, PRIDE OF THE JAPANESE IMPERIAL NAVY, HURTLED DOWN AND RELEASED THEIR CARGOES OF DEATH....

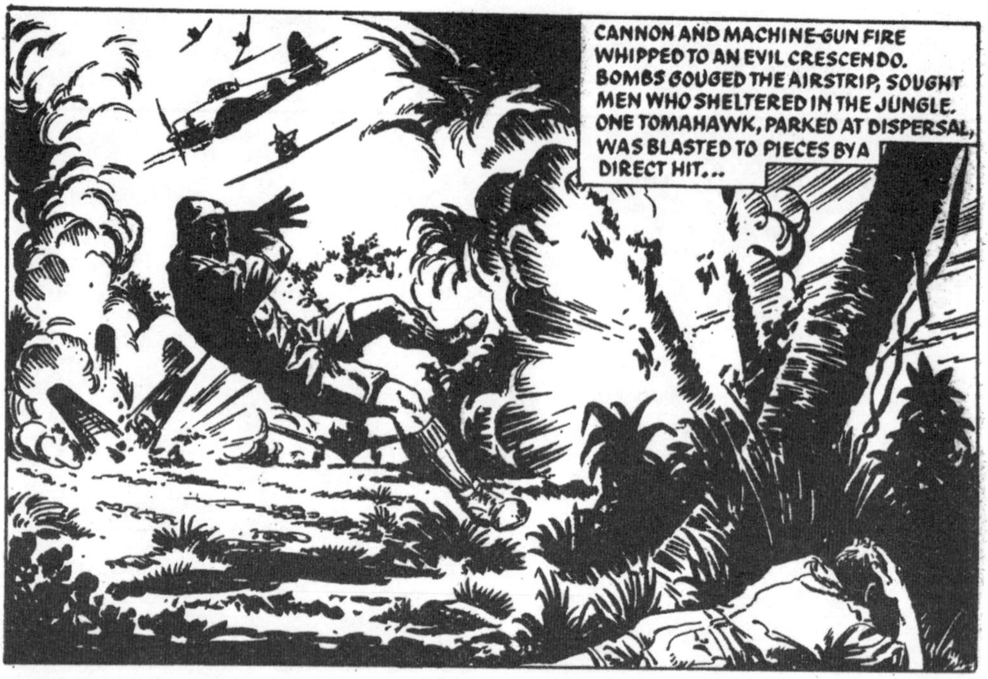
CANNON AND MACHINE-GUN FIRE WHIPPED TO AN EVIL CRESCENDO. BOMBS GOUGED THE AIRSTRIP, SOUGHT MEN WHO SHELTERED IN THE JUNGLE. ONE TOMAHAWK, PARKED AT DISPERSAL, WAS BLASTED TO PIECES BY A DIRECT HIT...

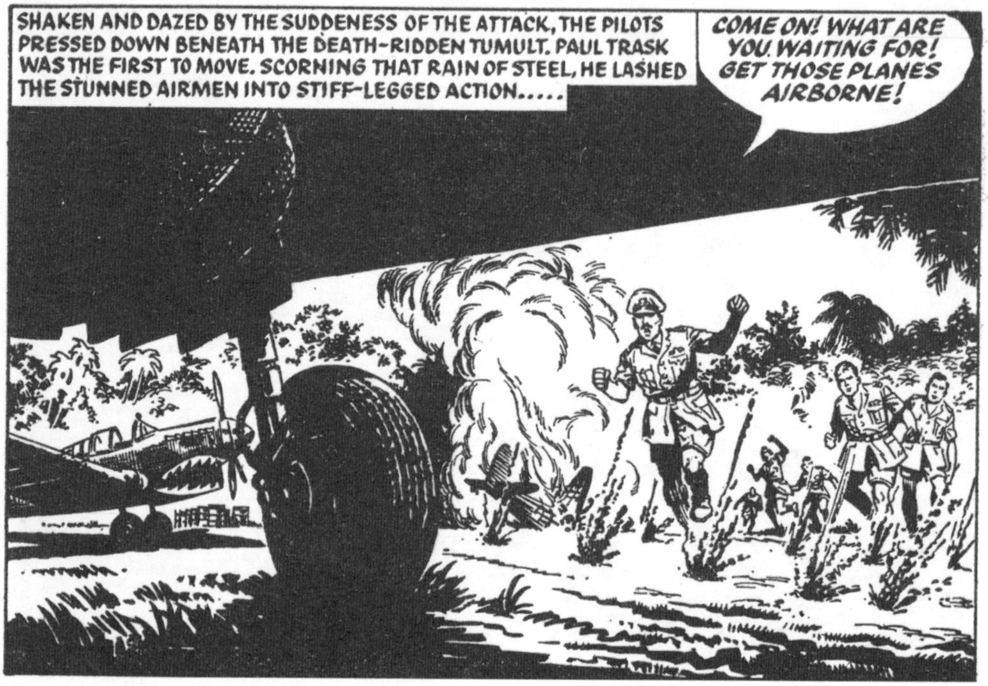
SHAKEN AND DAZED BY THE SUDDENESS OF THE ATTACK, THE PILOTS PRESSED DOWN BENEATH THE DEATH-RIDDEN TUMULT. PAUL TRASK WAS THE FIRST TO MOVE. SCORNING THAT RAIN OF STEEL, HE LASHED THE STUNNED AIRMEN INTO STIFF-LEGGED ACTION.....
COME ON! WHAT ARE YOU WAITING FOR! GET THOSE PLANES AIRBORNE!

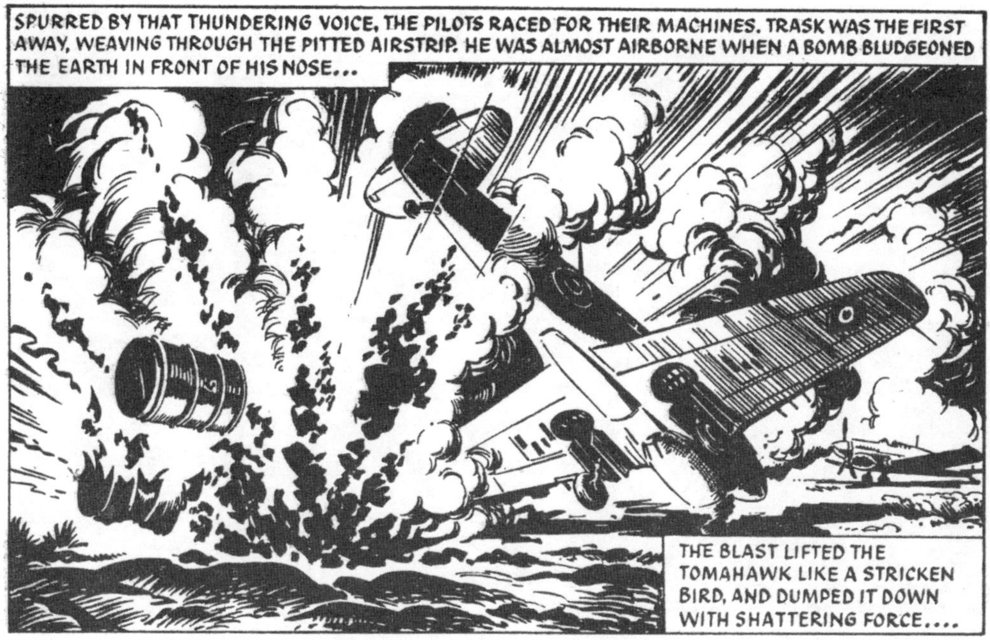
SPURRED BY THAT THUNDERING VOICE, THE PILOTS RACED FOR THEIR MACHINES. TRASK WAS THE FIRST AWAY, WEAVING THROUGH THE PITTED AIRSTRIP. HE WAS ALMOST AIRBORNE WHEN A BOMB BLUDGEONED THE EARTH IN FRONT OF HIS NOSE...
THE BLAST LIFTED THE TOMAHAWK LIKE A STRICKEN BIRD, AND DUMPED IT DOWN WITH SHATTERING FORCE....

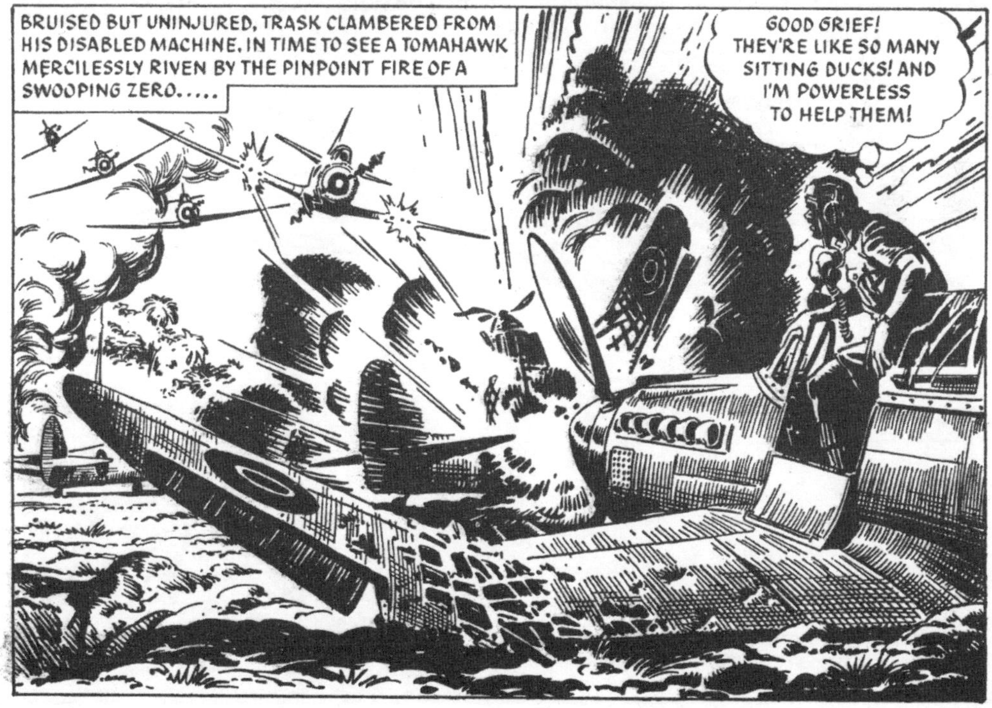
BRUISED BUT UNINJURED, TRASK CLAMBERED FROM HIS DISABLED MACHINE, IN TIME TO SEE A TOMAHAWK MERCILESSLY RIVEN BY THE PINPOINT FIRE OF A SWOOPING ZERO.....
GOOD GRIEF! THEY'RE LIKE SO MANY SITTING DUCKS! AND I'M POWERLESS TO HELP THEM!

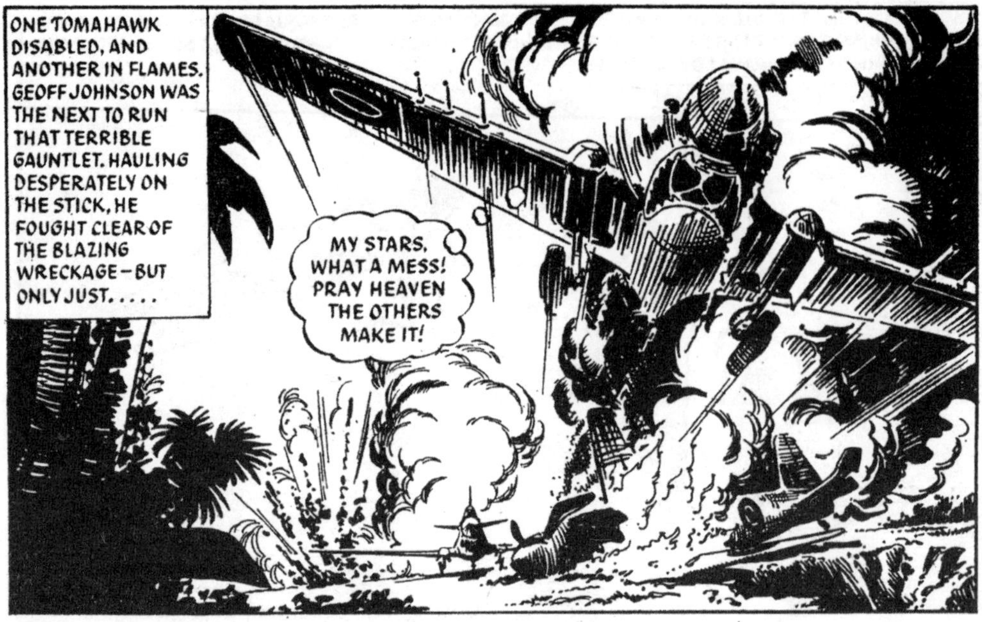
ONE TOMAHAWK DISABLED, AND ANOTHER IN FLAMES. GEOFF JOHNSON WAS THE NEXT TO RUN THAT TERRIBLE GAUNTLET. HAULING DESPERATELY ON THE STICK, HE FOUGHT CLEAR OF THE BLAZING WRECKAGE – BUT ONLY JUST.....
MY STARS, WHAT A MESS! PRAY HEAVEN THE OTHERS MAKE IT!

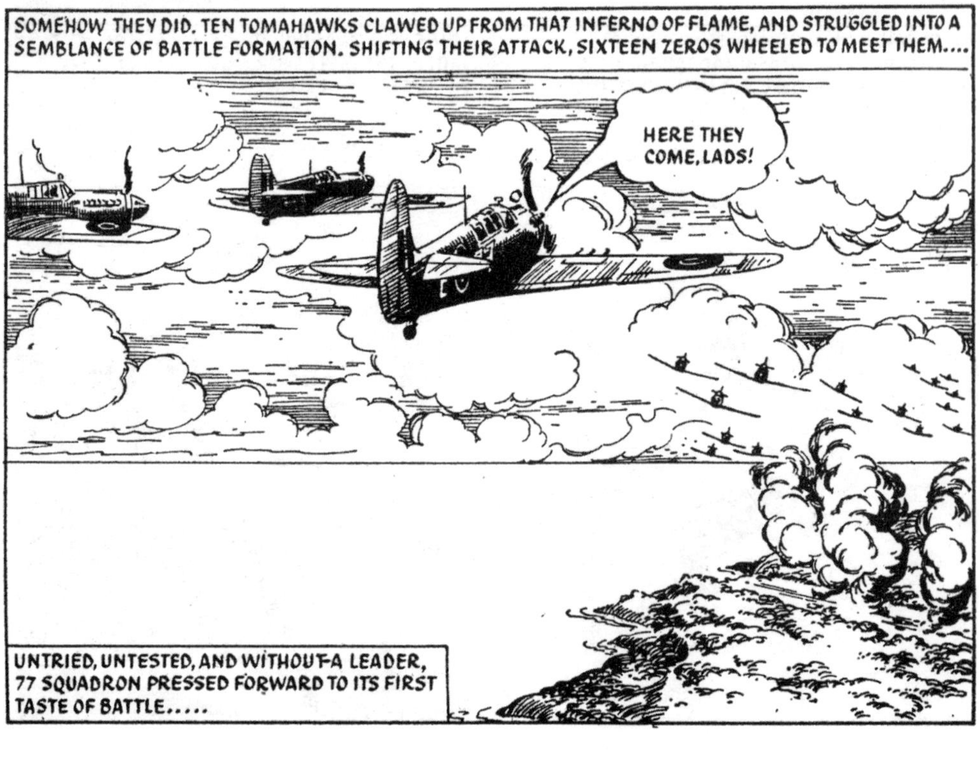
SOMEHOW THEY DID. TEN TOMAHAWKS CLAWED UP FROM THAT INFERNO OF FLAME, AND STRUGGLED INTO A SEMBLANCE OF BATTLE FORMATION. SHIFTING THEIR ATTACK, SIXTEEN ZEROS WHEELED TO MEET THEM....
HERE THEY COME, LADS!
UNTRIED, UNTESTED, AND WITHOUT A LEADER, 77 SQUADRON PRESSED FORWARD TO ITS FIRST TASTE OF BATTLE.....

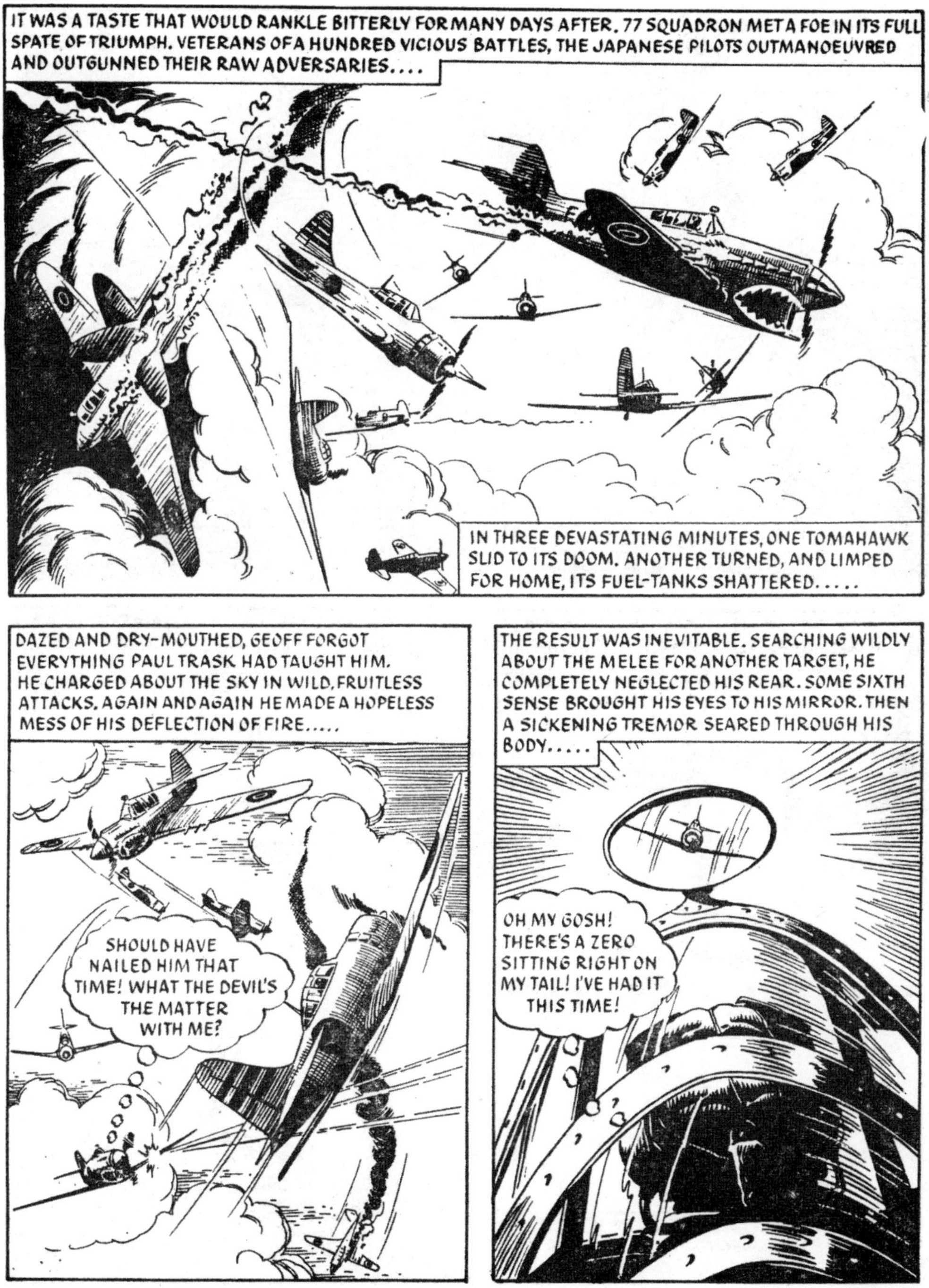
IT WAS A TASTE THAT WOULD RANKLE BITTERLY FOR MANY DAYS AFTER. 77 SQUADRON MET A FOE IN ITS FULL SPATE OF TRIUMPH. VETERANS OF A HUNDRED VICIOUS BATTLES, THE JAPANESE PILOTS OUTMANOEUVRED AND OUTGUNNED THEIR RAW ADVERSARIES....
IN THREE DEVASTATING MINUTES, ONE TOMAHAWK SLID TO ITS DOOM. ANOTHER TURNED, AND LIMPED FOR HOME, ITS FUEL-TANKS SHATTERED.....
DAZED AND DRY-MOUTHED, GEOFF FORGOT EVERYTHING PAUL TRASK HAD TAUGHT HIM. HE CHARGED ABOUT THE SKY IN WILD, FRUITLESS ATTACKS. AGAIN AND AGAIN HE MADE A HOPELESS MESS OF HIS DEFLECTION OF FIRE.....
SHOULD HAVE NAILED HIM THAT TIME! WHAT THE DEVIL'S THE MATTER WITH ME?
THE RESULT WAS INEVITABLE. SEARCHING WILDLY ABOUT THE MELEE FOR ANOTHER TARGET, HE COMPLETELY NEGLECTED HIS REAR. SOME SIXTH SENSE BROUGHT HIS EYES TO HIS MIRROR. THEN A SICKENING TREMOR SEARED THROUGH HIS BODY.....
OH MY GOSH! THERE'S A ZERO SITTING RIGHT ON MY TAIL! I'VE HAD IT THIS TIME!

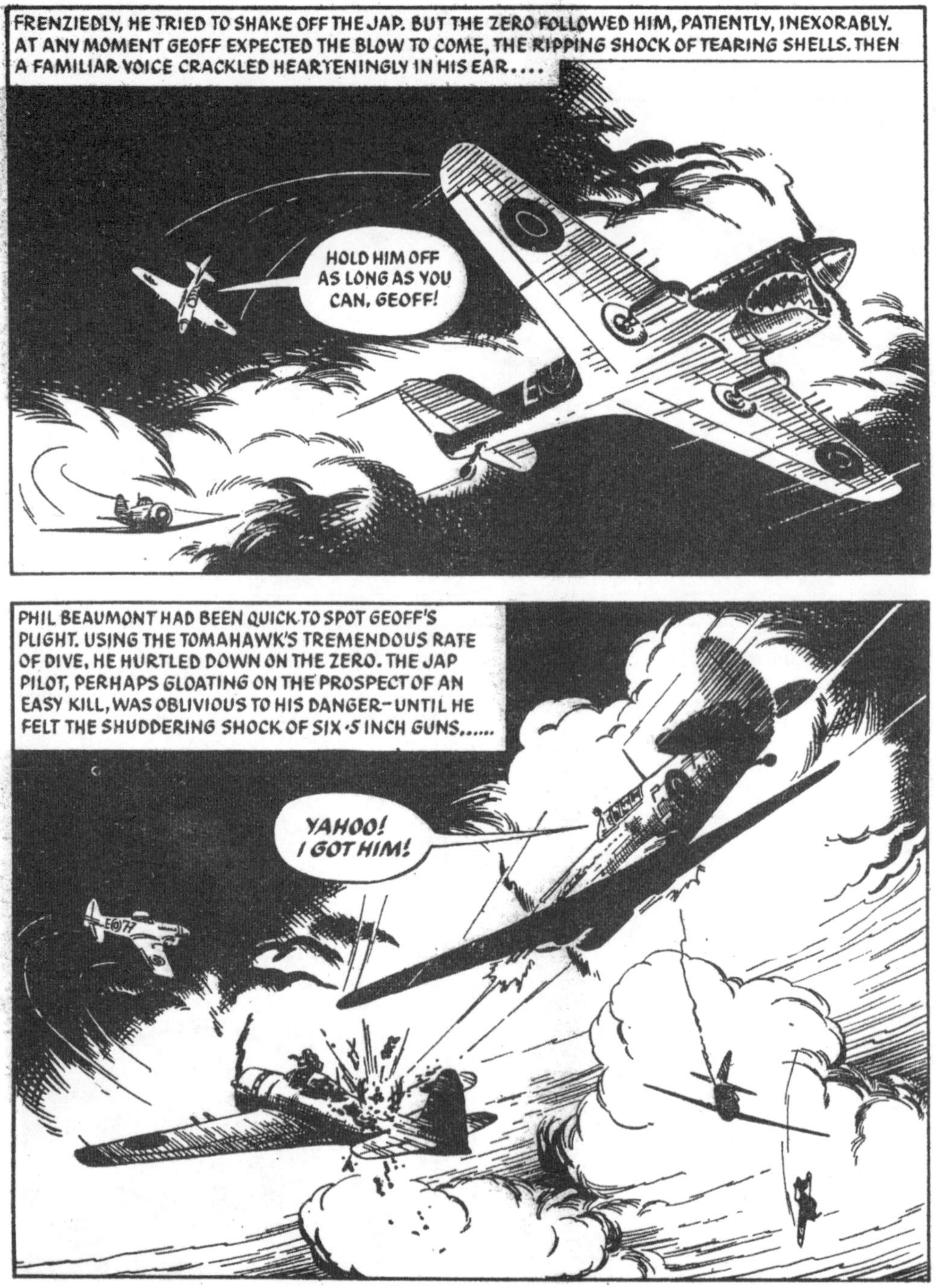
FRENZIEDLY, HE TRIED TO SHAKE OFF THE JAP. BUT THE ZERO FOLLOWED HIM, PATIENTLY, INEXORABLY. AT ANY MOMENT GEOFF EXPECTED THE BLOW TO COME, THE RIPPING SHOCK OF TEARING SHELLS. THEN A FAMILIAR VOICE CRACKLED HEARTENINGLY IN HIS EAR....
HOLD HIM OFF AS LONG AS YOU CAN, GEOFF!
PHIL BEAUMONT HAD BEEN QUICK TO SPOT GEOFF'S PLIGHT. USING THE TOMAHAWK'S TREMENDOUS RATE OF DIVE, HE HURTLED DOWN ON THE ZERO. THE JAP PILOT, PERHAPS GLOATING ON THE PROSPECT OF AN EASY KILL, WAS OBLIVIOUS TO HIS DANGER–UNTIL HE FELT THE SHUDDERING SHOCK OF SIX ·5 INCH GUNS......
YAHOO! I GOT HIM!

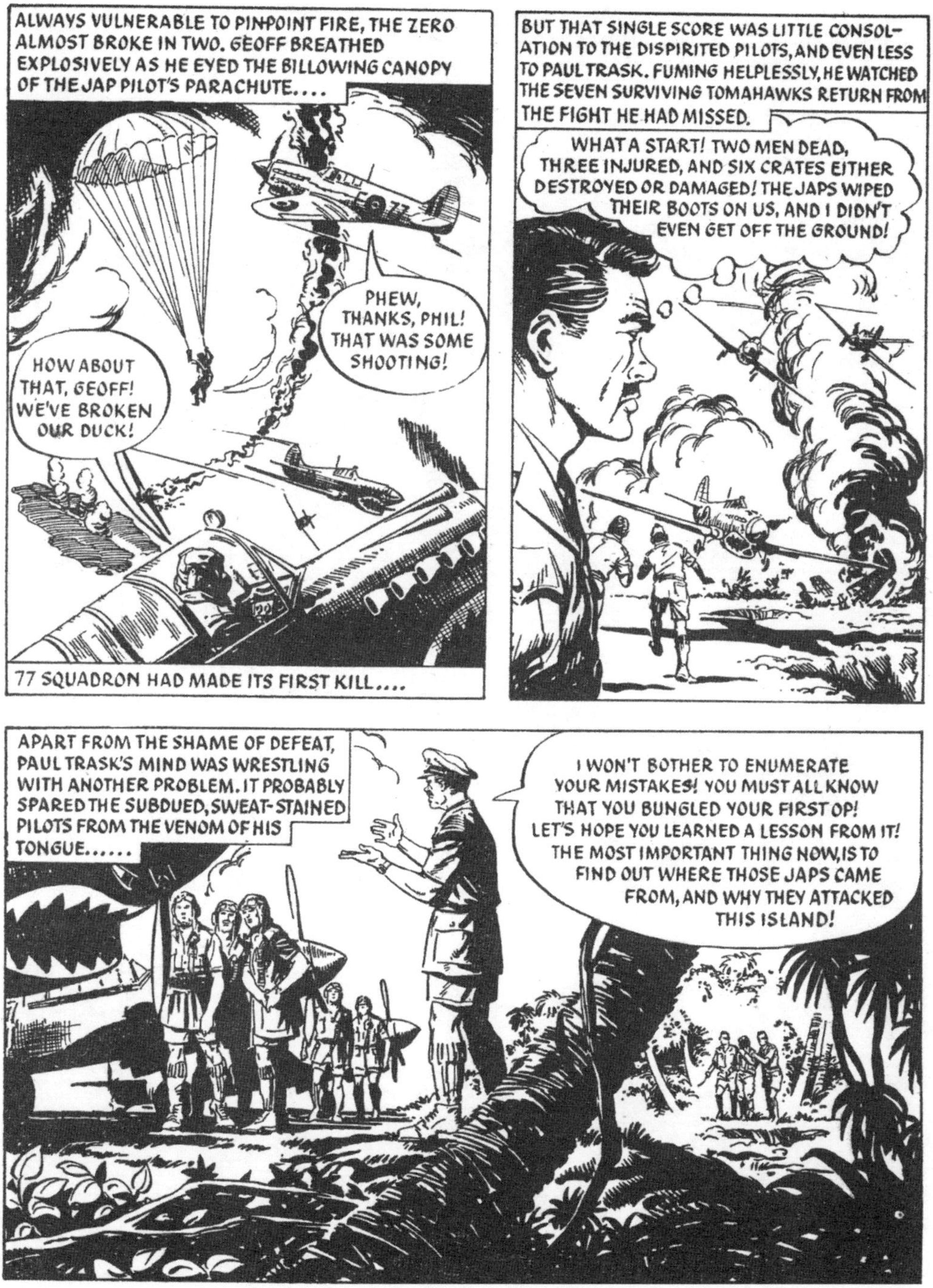
ALWAYS VULNERABLE TO PINPOINT FIRE, THE ZERO ALMOST BROKE IN TWO. GEOFF BREATHED EXPLOSIVELY AS HE EYED THE BILLOWING CANOPY OF THE JAP PILOT'S PARACHUTE....
PHEW, THANKS, PHIL! THAT WAS SOME SHOOTING!
HOW ABOUT THAT, GEOFF! WE'VE BROKEN OUR DUCK!
77 SQUADRON HAD MADE ITS FIRST KILL....
BUT THAT SINGLE SCORE WAS LITTLE CONSOL-ATION TO THE DISPIRITED PILOTS, AND EVEN LESS TO PAUL TRASK. FUMING HELPLESSLY, HE WATCHED THE SEVEN SURVIVING TOMAHAWKS RETURN FROM THE FIGHT HE HAD MISSED.
WHAT A START! TWO MEN DEAD, THREE INJURED, AND SIX CRATES EITHER DESTROYED OR DAMAGED! THE JAPS WIPED THEIR BOOTS ON US, AND I DIDN'T EVEN GET OFF THE GROUND!
APART FROM THE SHAME OF DEFEAT, PAUL TRASK'S MIND WAS WRESTLING WITH ANOTHER PROBLEM. IT PROBABLY SPARED THE SUBDUED, SWEAT-STAINED PILOTS FROM THE VENOM OF HIS TONGUE......
I WON'T BOTHER TO ENUMERATE YOUR MISTAKES! YOU MUST ALL KNOW THAT YOU BUNGLED YOUR FIRST OP! LET'S HOPE YOU LEARNED A LESSON FROM IT! THE MOST IMPORTANT THING NOW, IS TO FIND OUT WHERE THOSE JAPS CAME FROM, AND WHY THEY ATTACKED THIS ISLAND!

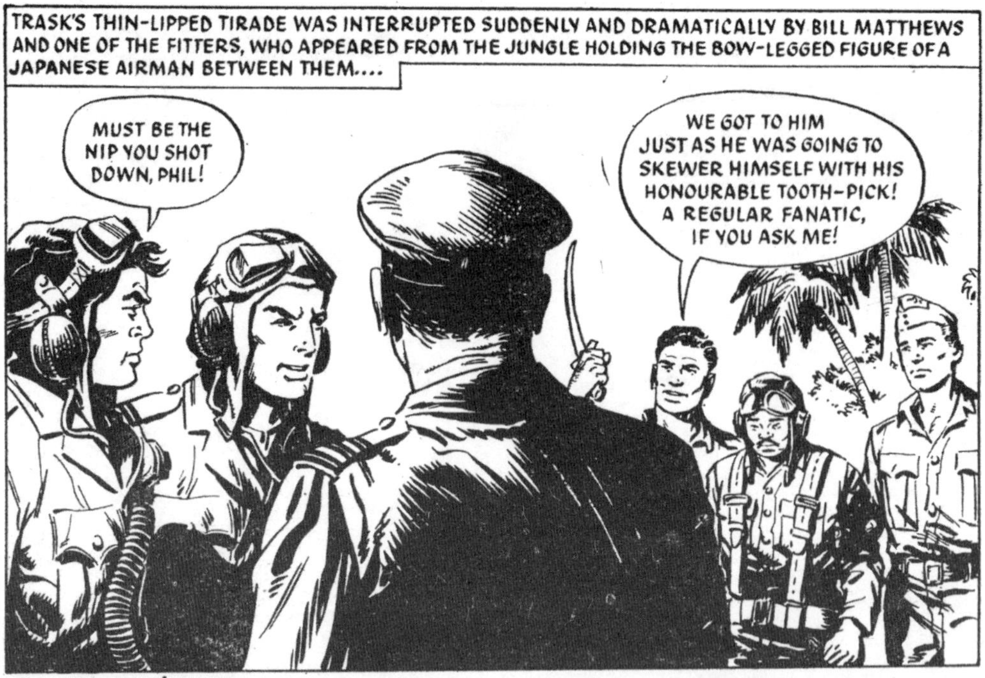
TRASK'S THIN-LIPPED TIRADE WAS INTERRUPTED SUDDENLY AND DRAMATICALLY BY BILL MATTHEWS AND ONE OF THE FITTERS, WHO APPEARED FROM THE JUNGLE HOLDING THE BOW-LEGGED FIGURE OF A JAPANESE AIRMAN BETWEEN THEM....
MUST BE THE NIP YOU SHOT DOWN, PHIL!
WE GOT TO HIM JUST AS HE WAS GOING TO SKEWER HIMSELF WITH HIS HONOURABLE TOOTH-PICK! A REGULAR FANATIC, IF YOU ASK ME!

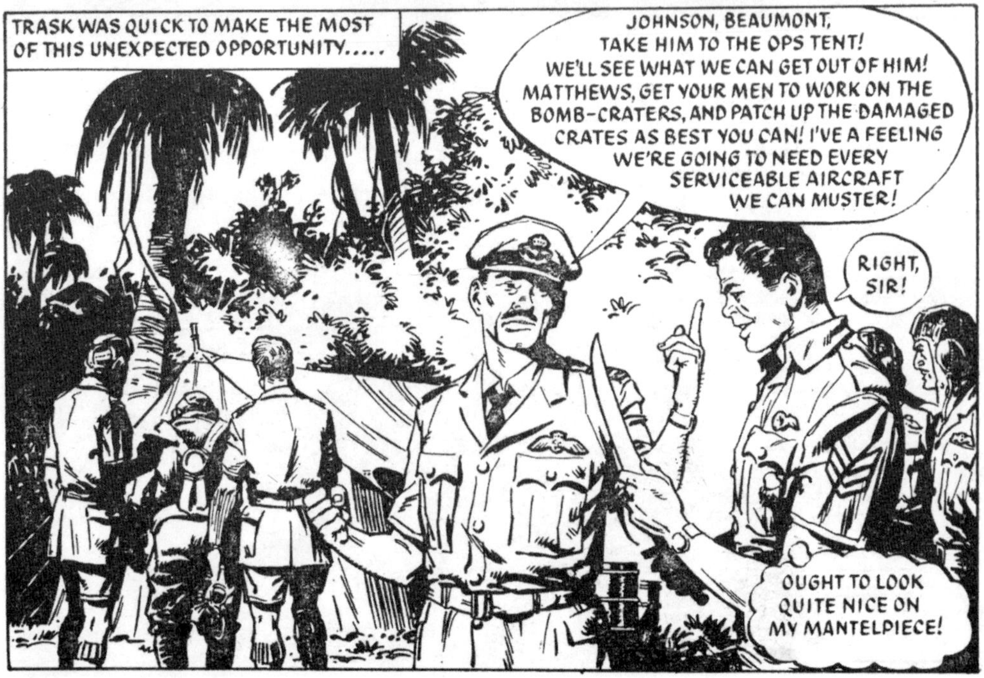
TRASK WAS QUICK TO MAKE THE MOST OF THIS UNEXPECTED OPPORTUNITY.....
JOHNSON, BEAUMONT, TAKE HIM TO THE OPS TENT! WE'LL SEE WHAT WE CAN GET OUT OF HIM! MATTHEWS, GET YOUR MEN TO WORK ON THE BOMB-CRATERS, AND PATCH UP THE DAMAGED CRATES AS BEST YOU CAN! I'VE A FEELING WE'RE GOING TO NEED EVERY SERVICEABLE AIRCRAFT WE CAN MUSTER!
RIGHT, SIR!
OUGHT TO LOOK QUITE NICE ON MY MANTELPIECE!

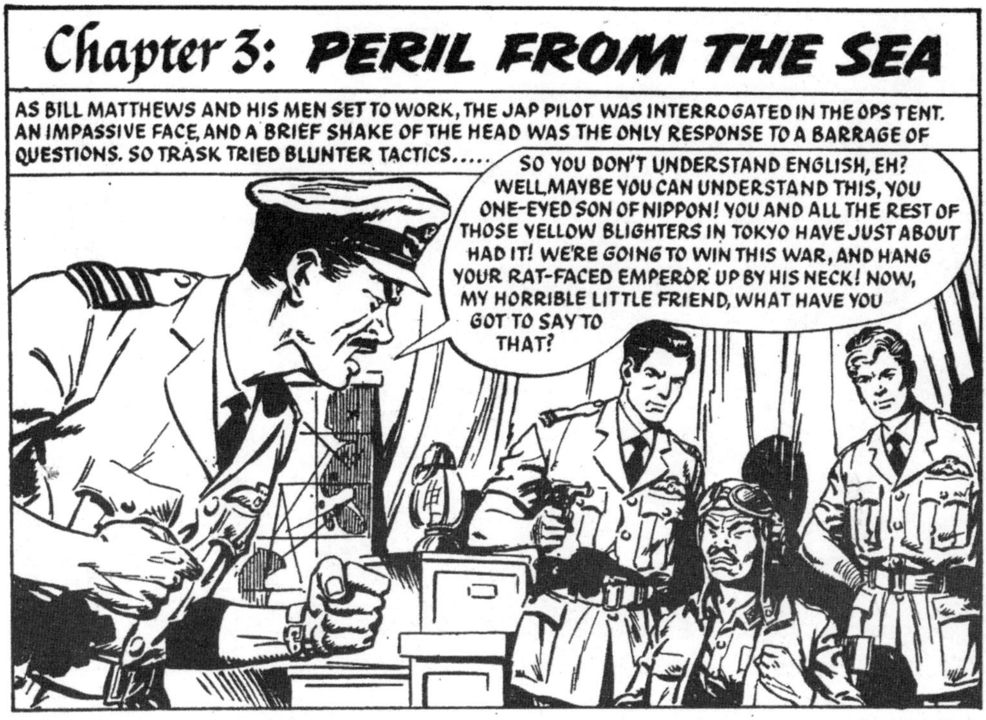
Chapter 3: PERIL FROM THE SEA
AS BILL MATTHEWS AND HIS MEN SET TO WORK, THE JAP PILOT WAS INTERROGATED IN THE OPS TENT. AN IMPASSIVE FACE, AND A BRIEF SHAKE OF THE HEAD WAS THE ONLY RESPONSE TO A BARRAGE OF QUESTIONS. SO TRASK TRIED BLUNTER TACTICS.....
SO YOU DON'T UNDERSTAND ENGLISH, EH? WELL, MAYBE YOU CAN UNDERSTAND THIS, YOU ONE-EYED SON OF NIPPON! YOU AND ALL THE REST OF THOSE YELLOW BLIGHTERS IN TOKYO HAVE JUST ABOUT HAD IT! WE'RE GOING TO WIN THIS WAR, AND HANG YOUR RAT-FACED EMPEROR UP BY HIS NECK! NOW, MY HORRIBLE LITTLE FRIEND, WHAT HAVE YOU GOT TO SAY TO THAT?

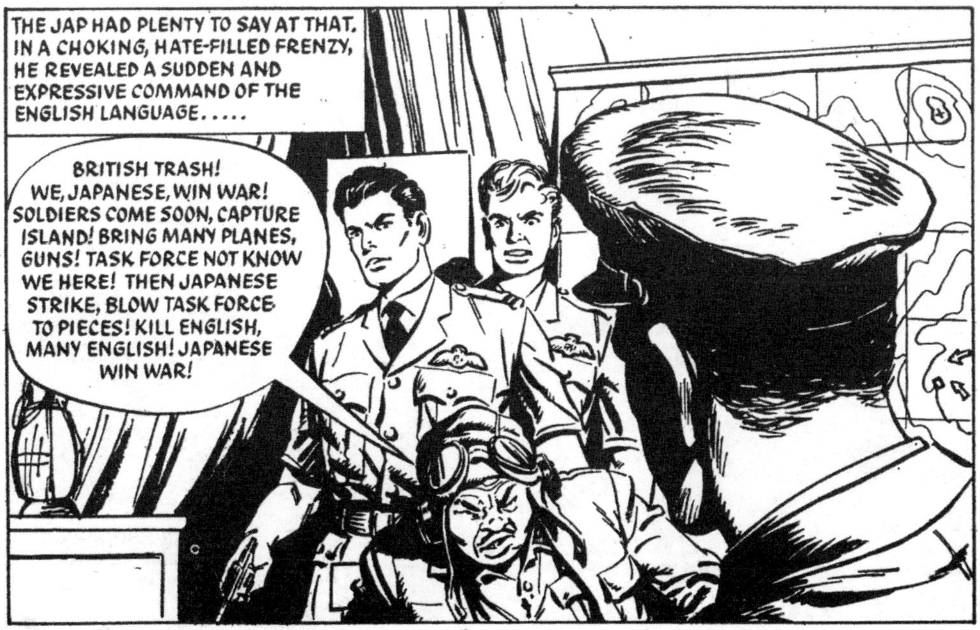
THE JAP HAD PLENTY TO SAY AT THAT. IN A CHOKING, HATE-FILLED FRENZY, HE REVEALED A SUDDEN AND EXPRESSIVE COMMAND OF THE ENGLISH LANGUAGE.....
BRITISH TRASH! WE, JAPANESE, WIN WAR! SOLDIERS COME SOON, CAPTURE ISLAND! BRING MANY PLANES, GUNS! TASK FORCE NOT KNOW WE HERE! THEN JAPANESE STRIKE, BLOW TASK FORCE TO PIECES! KILL ENGLISH, MANY ENGLISH! JAPANESE WIN WAR!

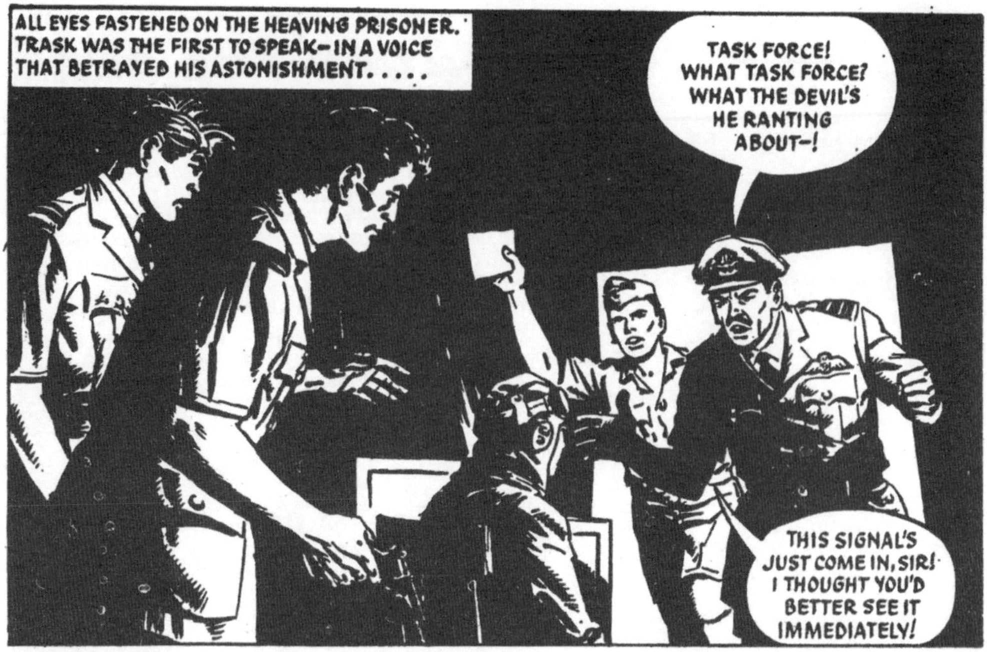
ALL EYES FASTENED ON THE HEAVING PRISONER. TRASK WAS THE FIRST TO SPEAK—IN A VOICE THAT BETRAYED HIS ASTONISHMENT. . . . .
TASK FORCE! WHAT TASK FORCE? WHAT THE DEVIL'S HE RANTING ABOUT—!
THIS SIGNAL'S JUST COME IN, SIR! I THOUGHT YOU'D BETTER SEE IT IMMEDIATELY!

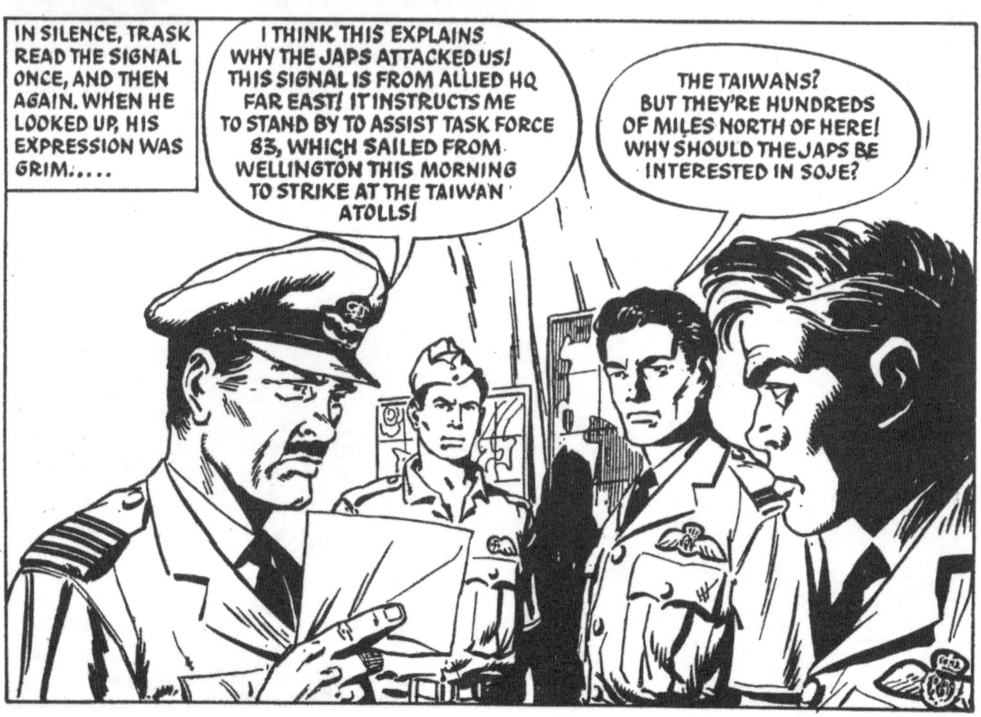
IN SILENCE, TRASK READ THE SIGNAL ONCE, AND THEN AGAIN. WHEN HE LOOKED UP, HIS EXPRESSION WAS GRIM. . . . .
I THINK THIS EXPLAINS WHY THE JAPS ATTACKED US! THIS SIGNAL IS FROM ALLIED HQ FAR EAST! IT INSTRUCTS ME TO STAND BY TO ASSIST TASK FORCE 83, WHICH SAILED FROM WELLINGTON THIS MORNING TO STRIKE AT THE TAIWAN ATOLLS!
THE TAIWANS? BUT THEY'RE HUNDREDS OF MILES NORTH OF HERE! WHY SHOULD THE JAPS BE INTERESTED IN SOJE?

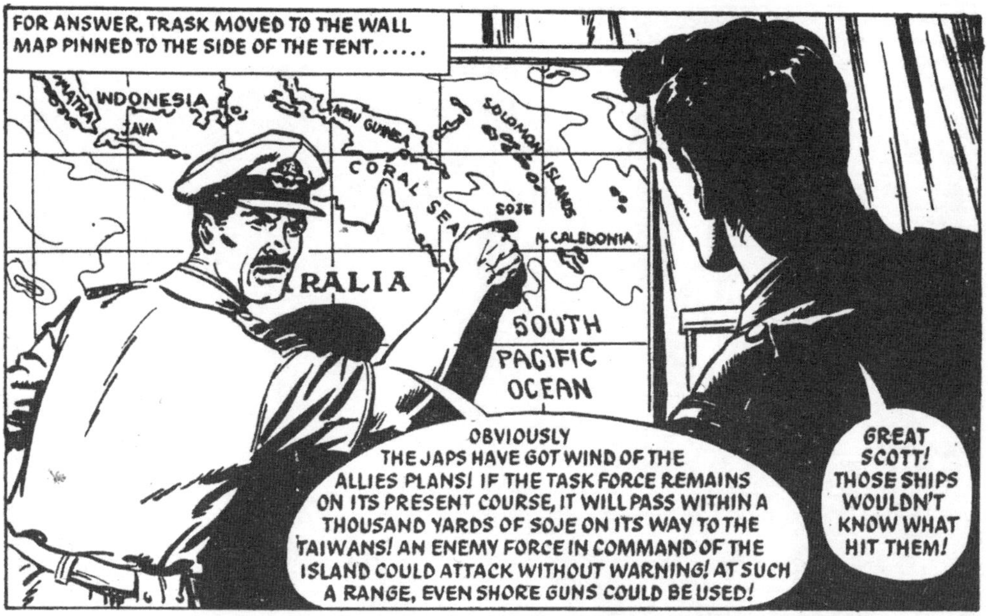
FOR ANSWER, TRASK MOVED TO THE WALL MAP PINNED TO THE SIDE OF THE TENT......
INDONESIA
JAVA
NEW GUINEA
SOLOMON ISLANDS
CORAL SEA
SOJE
N. CALEDONIA
RALIA
SOUTH PACIFIC OCEAN
OBVIOUSLY THE JAPS HAVE GOT WIND OF THE ALLIES PLANS! IF THE TASK FORCE REMAINS ON ITS PRESENT COURSE, IT WILL PASS WITHIN A THOUSAND YARDS OF SOJE ON ITS WAY TO THE TAIWANS! AN ENEMY FORCE IN COMMAND OF THE ISLAND COULD ATTACK WITHOUT WARNING! AT SUCH A RANGE, EVEN SHORE GUNS COULD BE USED!
GREAT SCOTT! THOSE SHIPS WOULDN'T KNOW WHAT HIT THEM!

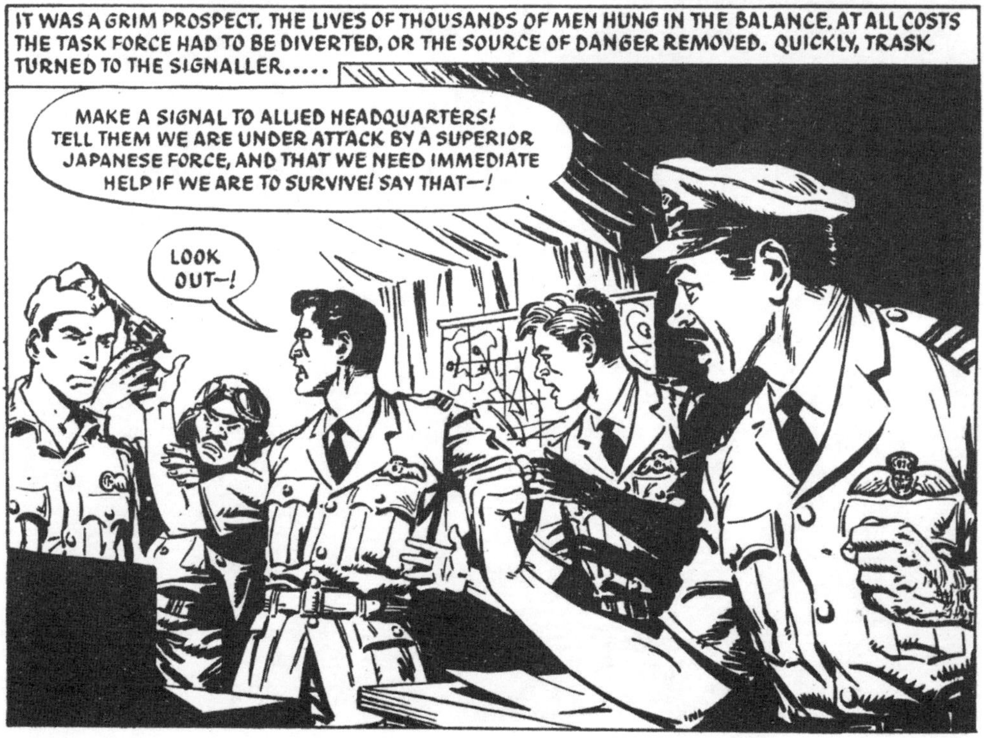
IT WAS A GRIM PROSPECT. THE LIVES OF THOUSANDS OF MEN HUNG IN THE BALANCE. AT ALL COSTS THE TASK FORCE HAD TO BE DIVERTED, OR THE SOURCE OF DANGER REMOVED. QUICKLY, TRASK TURNED TO THE SIGNALLER.....
MAKE A SIGNAL TO ALLIED HEADQUARTERS! TELL THEM WE ARE UNDER ATTACK BY A SUPERIOR JAPANESE FORCE, AND THAT WE NEED IMMEDIATE HELP IF WE ARE TO SURVIVE! SAY THAT—!
LOOK OUT—!

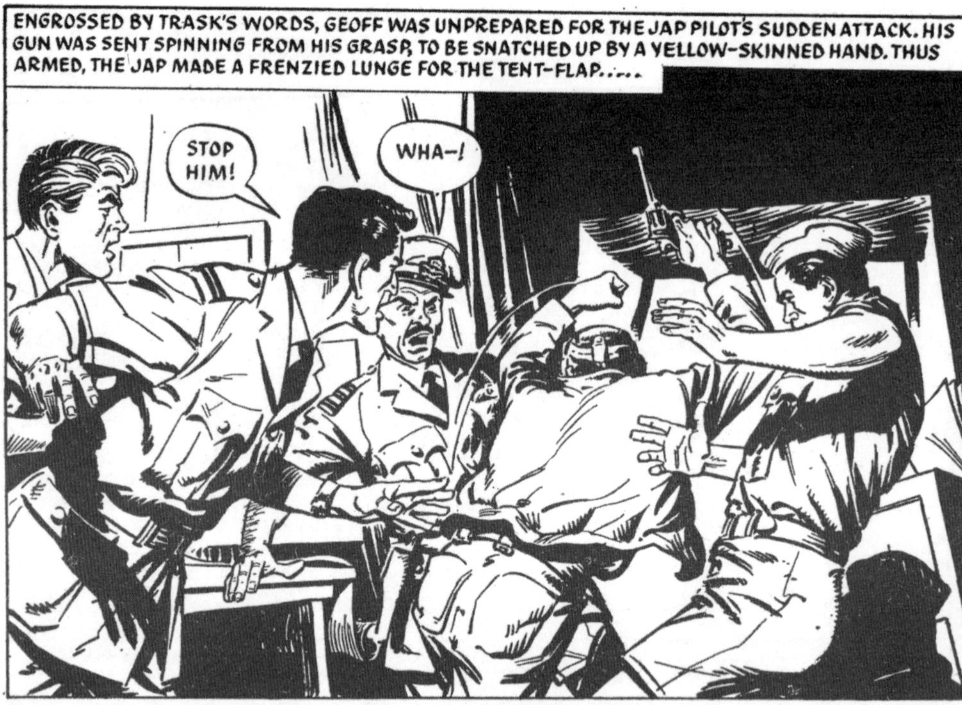
ENGROSSED BY TRASK'S WORDS, GEOFF WAS UNPREPARED FOR THE JAP PILOT'S SUDDEN ATTACK. HIS GUN WAS SENT SPINNING FROM HIS GRASP, TO BE SNATCHED UP BY A YELLOW-SKINNED HAND. THUS ARMED, THE JAP MADE A FRENZIED LUNGE FOR THE TENT-FLAP.....
STOP HIM!
WHA-!

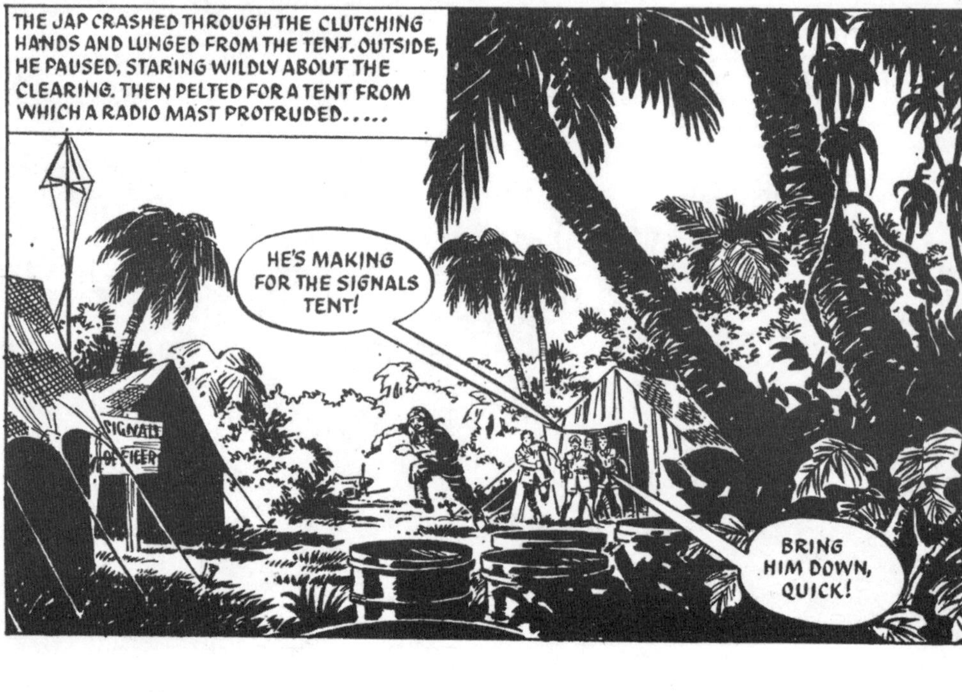
THE JAP CRASHED THROUGH THE CLUTCHING HANDS AND LUNGED FROM THE TENT. OUTSIDE, HE PAUSED, STARING WILDLY ABOUT THE CLEARING. THEN PELTED FOR A TENT FROM WHICH A RADIO MAST PROTRUDED.....
HE'S MAKING FOR THE SIGNALS TENT!
SIGNALS OFFICER
BRING HIM DOWN, QUICK!

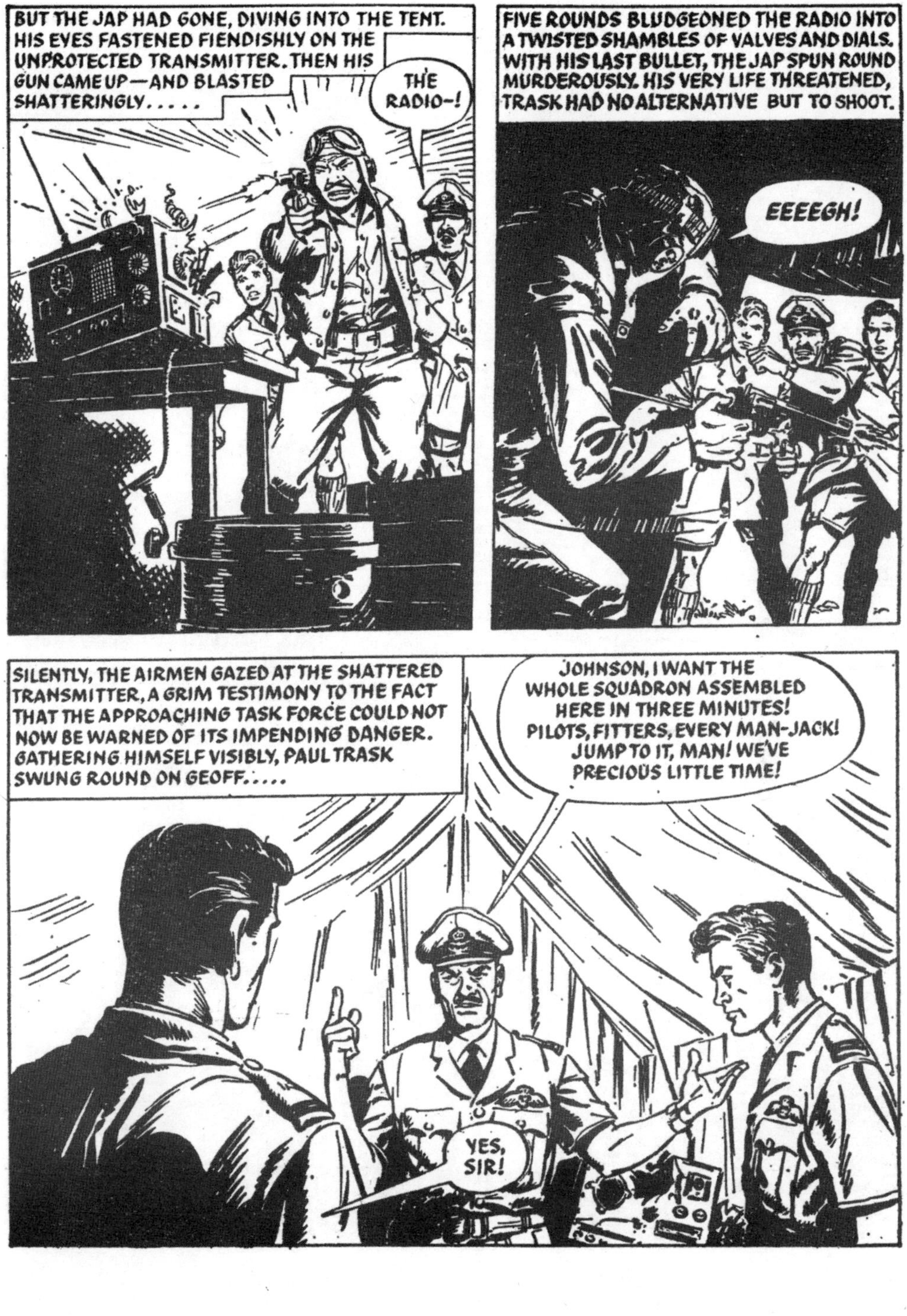
BUT THE JAP HAD GONE, DIVING INTO THE TENT. HIS EYES FASTENED FIENDISHLY ON THE UNPROTECTED TRANSMITTER. THEN HIS GUN CAME UP—AND BLASTED SHATTERINGLY.....
THE RADIO-!
FIVE ROUNDS BLUDGEONED THE RADIO INTO A TWISTED SHAMBLES OF VALVES AND DIALS. WITH HIS LAST BULLET, THE JAP SPUN ROUND MURDEROUSLY. HIS VERY LIFE THREATENED, TRASK HAD NO ALTERNATIVE BUT TO SHOOT.
EEEEGH!
SILENTLY, THE AIRMEN GAZED AT THE SHATTERED TRANSMITTER, A GRIM TESTIMONY TO THE FACT THAT THE APPROACHING TASK FORCE COULD NOT NOW BE WARNED OF ITS IMPENDING DANGER. GATHERING HIMSELF VISIBLY, PAUL TRASK SWUNG ROUND ON GEOFF.....
JOHNSON, I WANT THE WHOLE SQUADRON ASSEMBLED HERE IN THREE MINUTES! PILOTS, FITTERS, EVERY MAN-JACK! JUMP TO IT, MAN! WE'VE PRECIOUS LITTLE TIME!
YES, SIR!

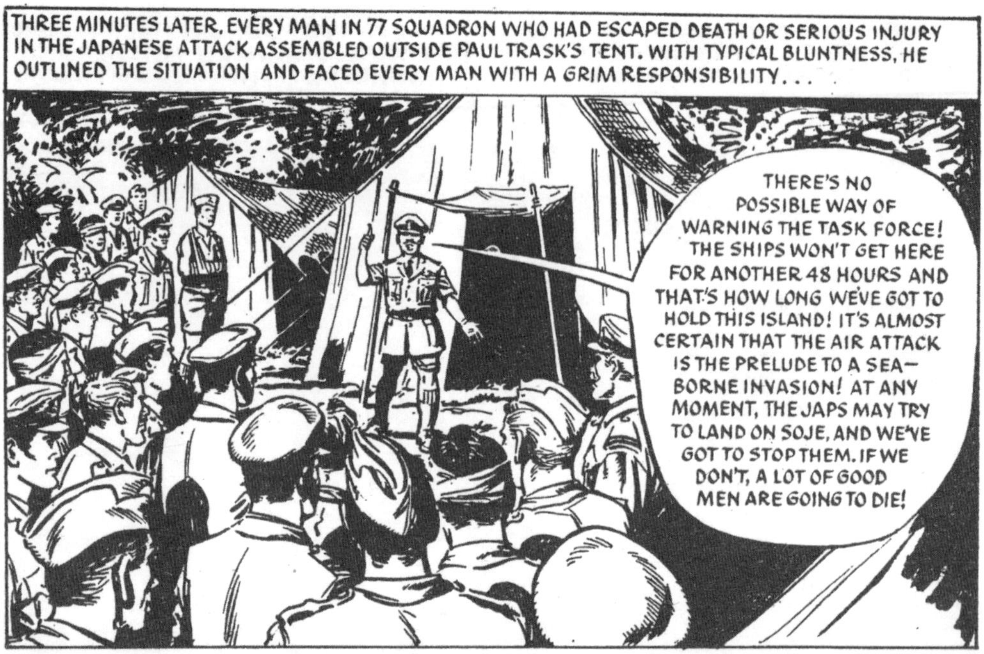
THREE MINUTES LATER, EVERY MAN IN 77 SQUADRON WHO HAD ESCAPED DEATH OR SERIOUS INJURY IN THE JAPANESE ATTACK ASSEMBLED OUTSIDE PAUL TRASK'S TENT. WITH TYPICAL BLUNTNESS, HE OUTLINED THE SITUATION AND FACED EVERY MAN WITH A GRIM RESPONSIBILITY . . .
THERE'S NO POSSIBLE WAY OF WARNING THE TASK FORCE! THE SHIPS WON'T GET HERE FOR ANOTHER 48 HOURS AND THAT'S HOW LONG WE'VE GOT TO HOLD THIS ISLAND! IT'S ALMOST CERTAIN THAT THE AIR ATTACK IS THE PRELUDE TO A SEA-BORNE INVASION! AT ANY MOMENT, THE JAPS MAY TRY TO LAND ON SOJE, AND WE'VE GOT TO STOP THEM. IF WE DON'T, A LOT OF GOOD MEN ARE GOING TO DIE!

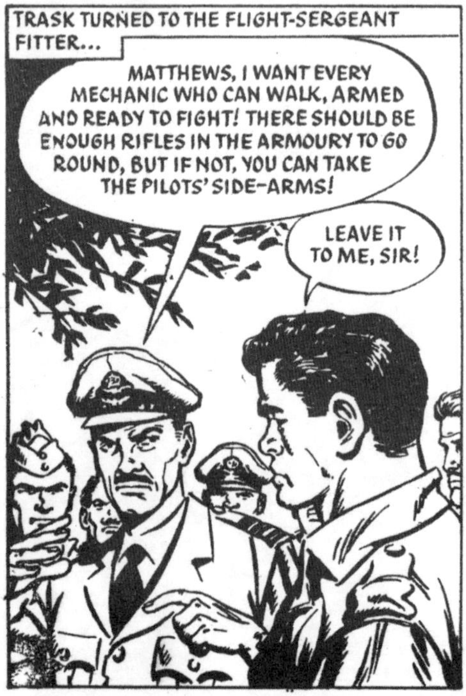
TRASK TURNED TO THE FLIGHT-SERGEANT FITTER...
MATTHEWS, I WANT EVERY MECHANIC WHO CAN WALK, ARMED AND READY TO FIGHT! THERE SHOULD BE ENOUGH RIFLES IN THE ARMOURY TO GO ROUND, BUT IF NOT, YOU CAN TAKE THE PILOTS' SIDE-ARMS!
LEAVE IT TO ME, SIR!

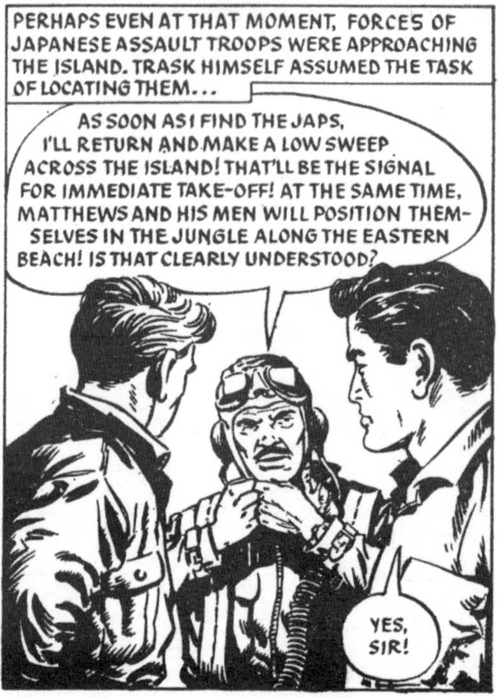
PERHAPS EVEN AT THAT MOMENT, FORCES OF JAPANESE ASSAULT TROOPS WERE APPROACHING THE ISLAND. TRASK HIMSELF ASSUMED THE TASK OF LOCATING THEM...
AS SOON AS I FIND THE JAPS, I'LL RETURN AND MAKE A LOW SWEEP ACROSS THE ISLAND! THAT'LL BE THE SIGNAL FOR IMMEDIATE TAKE-OFF! AT THE SAME TIME, MATTHEWS AND HIS MEN WILL POSITION THEMSELVES IN THE JUNGLE ALONG THE EASTERN BEACH! IS THAT CLEARLY UNDERSTOOD?
YES, SIR!

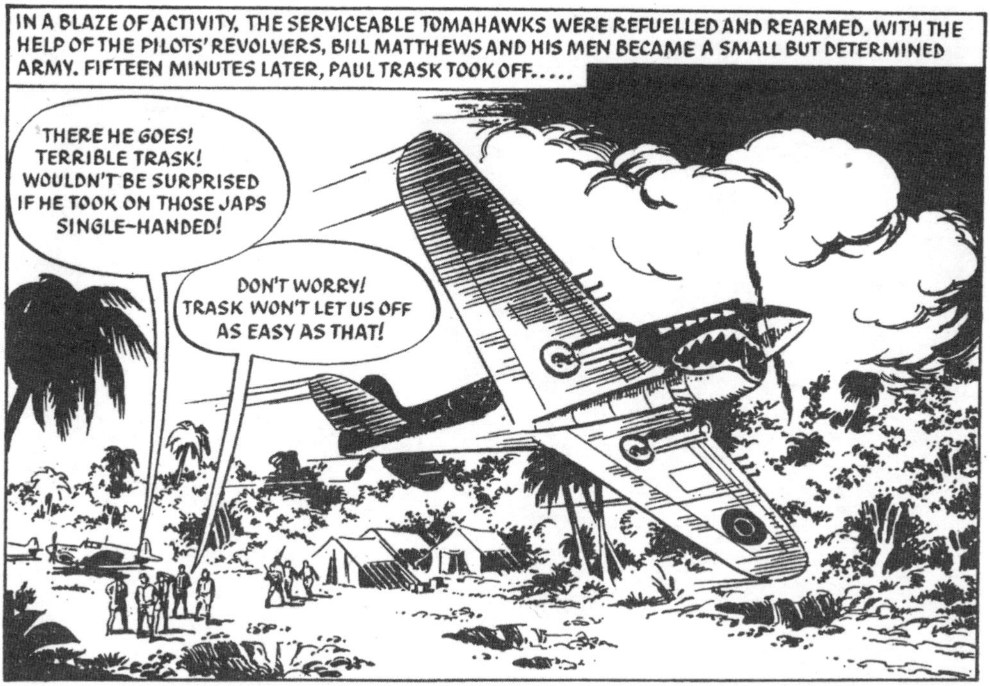
IN A BLAZE OF ACTIVITY, THE SERVICEABLE TOMAHAWKS WERE REFUELLED AND REARMED. WITH THE HELP OF THE PILOTS' REVOLVERS, BILL MATTHEWS AND HIS MEN BECAME A SMALL BUT DETERMINED ARMY. FIFTEEN MINUTES LATER, PAUL TRASK TOOK OFF.....
THERE HE GOES! TERRIBLE TRASK! WOULDN'T BE SURPRISED IF HE TOOK ON THOSE JAPS SINGLE-HANDED!
DON'T WORRY! TRASK WON'T LET US OFF AS EASY AS THAT!

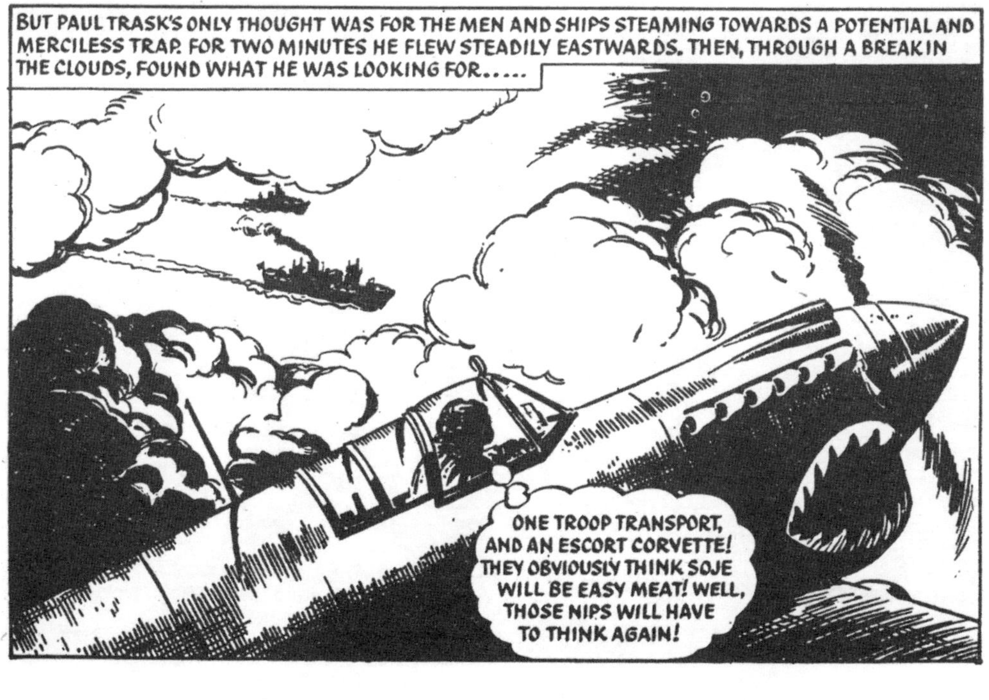
BUT PAUL TRASK'S ONLY THOUGHT WAS FOR THE MEN AND SHIPS STEAMING TOWARDS A POTENTIAL AND MERCILESS TRAP. FOR TWO MINUTES HE FLEW STEADILY EASTWARDS. THEN, THROUGH A BREAK IN THE CLOUDS, FOUND WHAT HE WAS LOOKING FOR.....
ONE TROOP TRANSPORT, AND AN ESCORT CORVETTE! THEY OBVIOUSLY THINK SOJE WILL BE EASY MEAT! WELL, THOSE NIPS WILL HAVE TO THINK AGAIN!

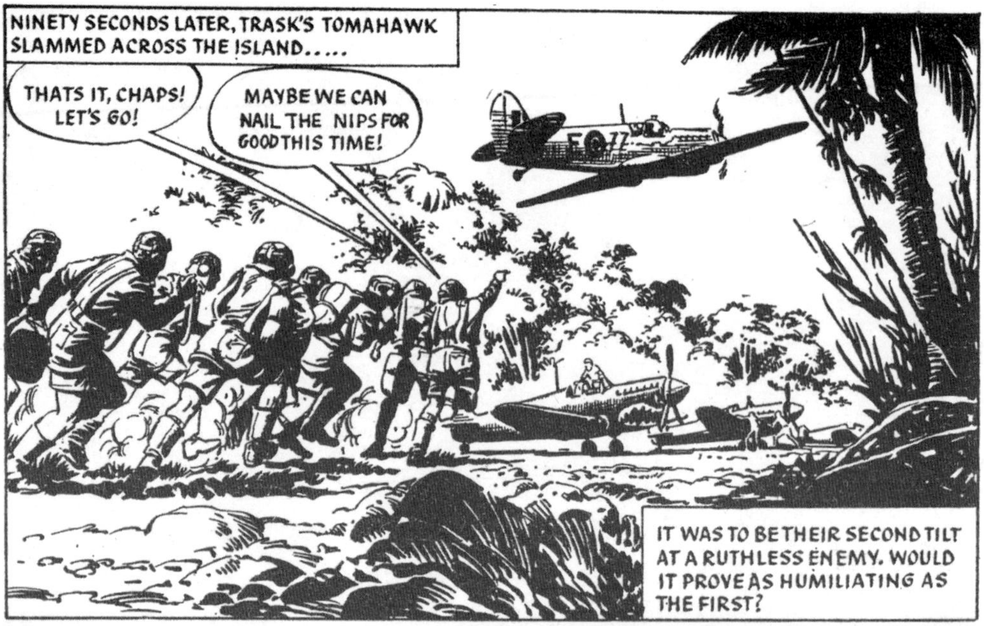
NINETY SECONDS LATER, TRASK'S TOMAHAWK SLAMMED ACROSS THE ISLAND.....
THATS IT, CHAPS! LET'S GO!
MAYBE WE CAN NAIL THE NIPS FOR GOOD THIS TIME!
IT WAS TO BE THEIR SECOND TILT AT A RUTHLESS ENEMY. WOULD IT PROVE AS HUMILIATING AS THE FIRST?

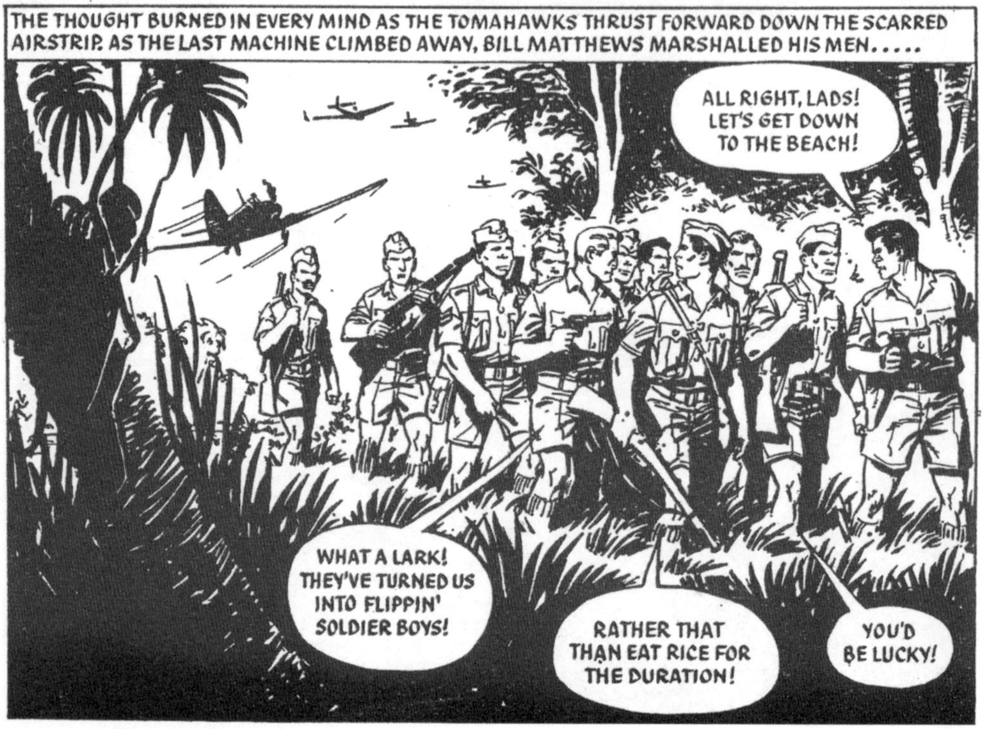
THE THOUGHT BURNED IN EVERY MIND AS THE TOMAHAWKS THRUST FORWARD DOWN THE SCARRED AIRSTRIP. AS THE LAST MACHINE CLIMBED AWAY, BILL MATTHEWS MARSHALLED HIS MEN.....
ALL RIGHT, LADS! LET'S GET DOWN TO THE BEACH!
WHAT A LARK! THEY'VE TURNED US INTO FLIPPIN' SOLDIER BOYS!
RATHER THAT THAN EAT RICE FOR THE DURATION!
YOU'D BE LUCKY!

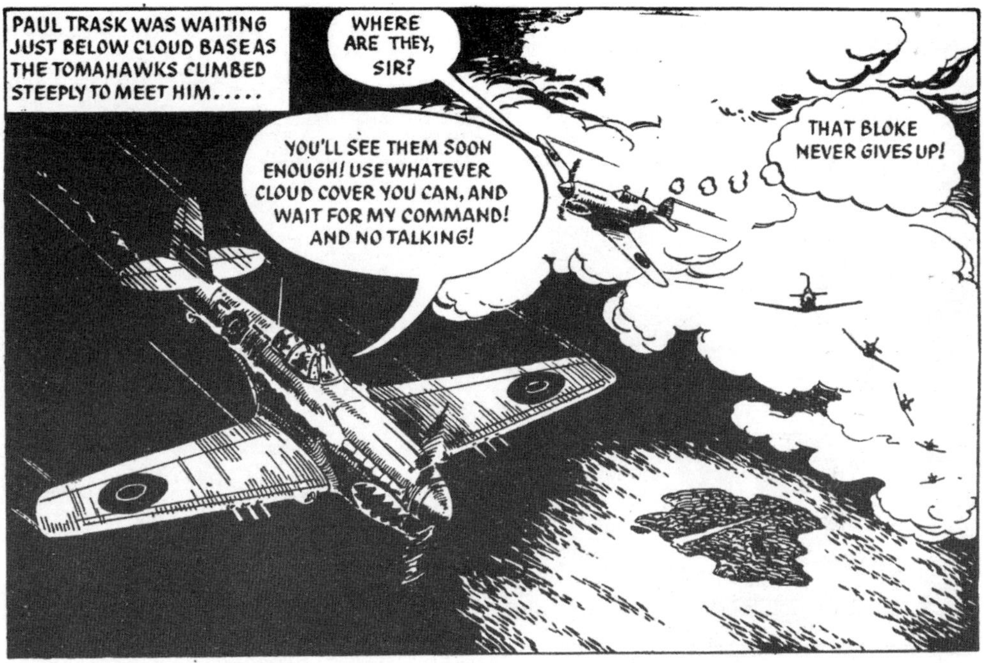
PAUL TRASK WAS WAITING JUST BELOW CLOUD BASE AS THE TOMAHAWKS CLIMBED STEEPLY TO MEET HIM.....
WHERE ARE THEY, SIR?
YOU'LL SEE THEM SOON ENOUGH! USE WHATEVER CLOUD COVER YOU CAN, AND WAIT FOR MY COMMAND! AND NO TALKING!
THAT BLOKE NEVER GIVES UP!

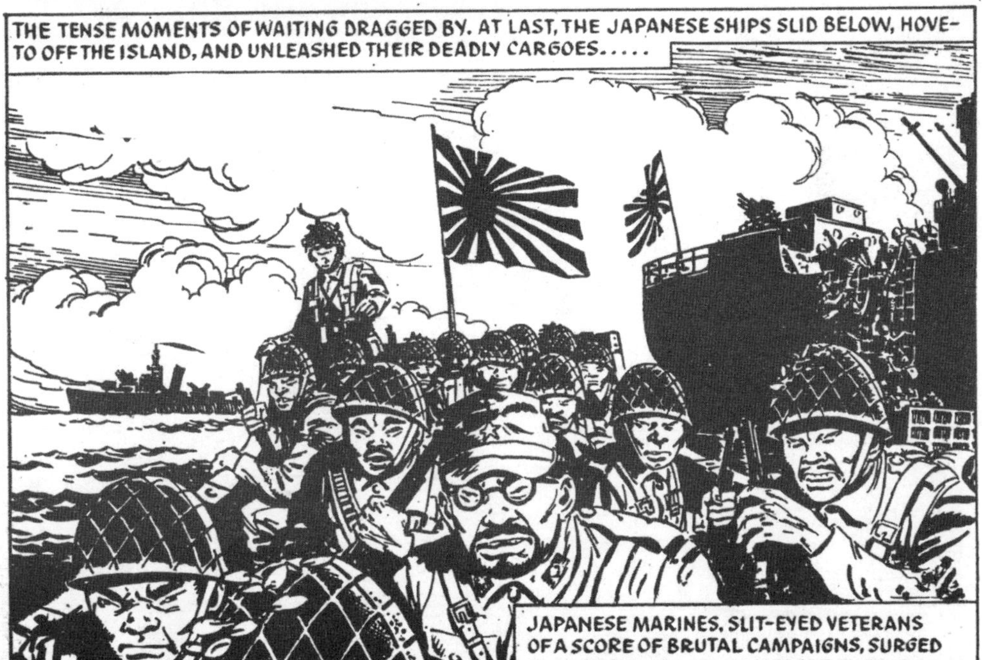
THE TENSE MOMENTS OF WAITING DRAGGED BY. AT LAST, THE JAPANESE SHIPS SLID BELOW, HOVE-TO OFF THE ISLAND, AND UNLEASHED THEIR DEADLY CARGOES.....
JAPANESE MARINES, SLIT-EYED VETERANS OF A SCORE OF BRUTAL CAMPAIGNS, SURGED TOWARDS SOJE, AND ITS MEAGRE GARRISON.....

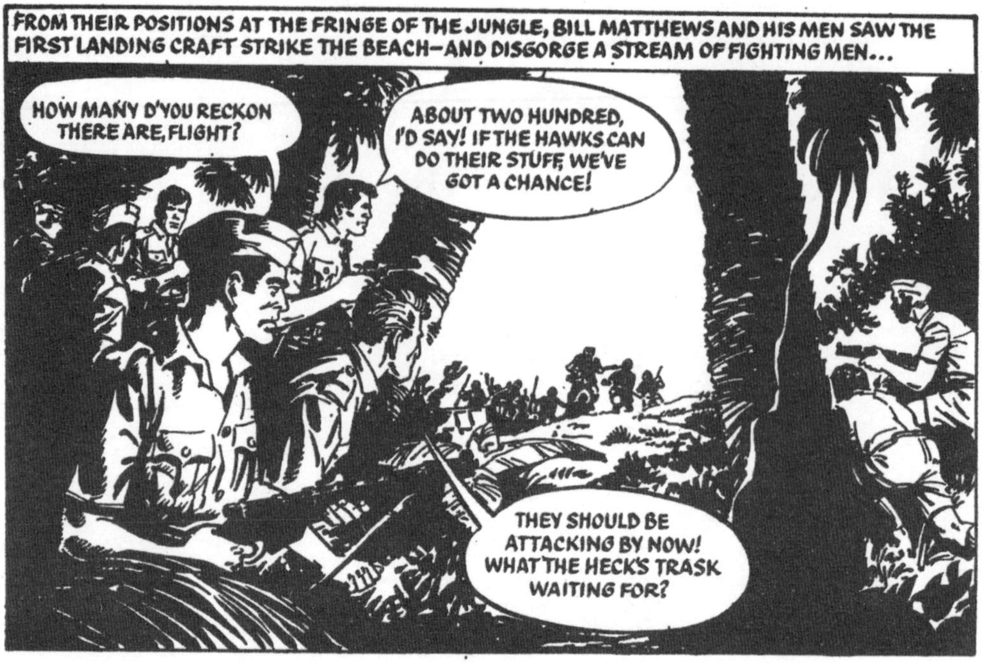
FROM THEIR POSITIONS AT THE FRINGE OF THE JUNGLE, BILL MATTHEWS AND HIS MEN SAW THE FIRST LANDING CRAFT STRIKE THE BEACH—AND DISGORGE A STREAM OF FIGHTING MEN...
HOW MANY D'YOU RECKON THERE ARE, FLIGHT?
ABOUT TWO HUNDRED, I'D SAY! IF THE HAWKS CAN DO THEIR STUFF, WE'VE GOT A CHANCE!
THEY SHOULD BE ATTACKING BY NOW! WHAT THE HECK'S TRASK WAITING FOR?

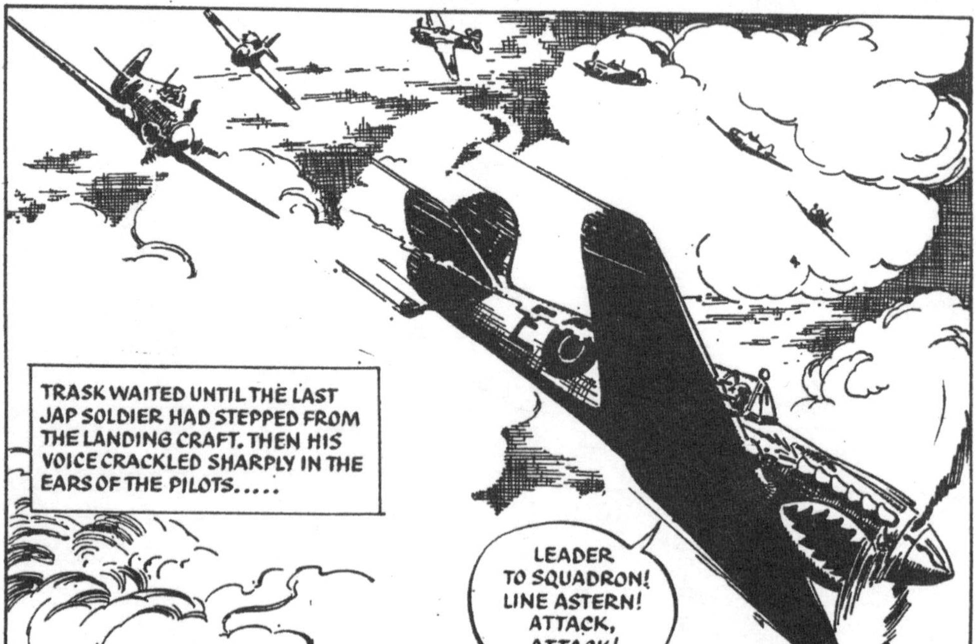
TRASK WAITED UNTIL THE LAST JAP SOLDIER HAD STEPPED FROM THE LANDING CRAFT. THEN HIS VOICE CRACKLED SHARPLY IN THE EARS OF THE PILOTS.....
LEADER TO SQUADRON! LINE ASTERN! ATTACK, ATTACK!

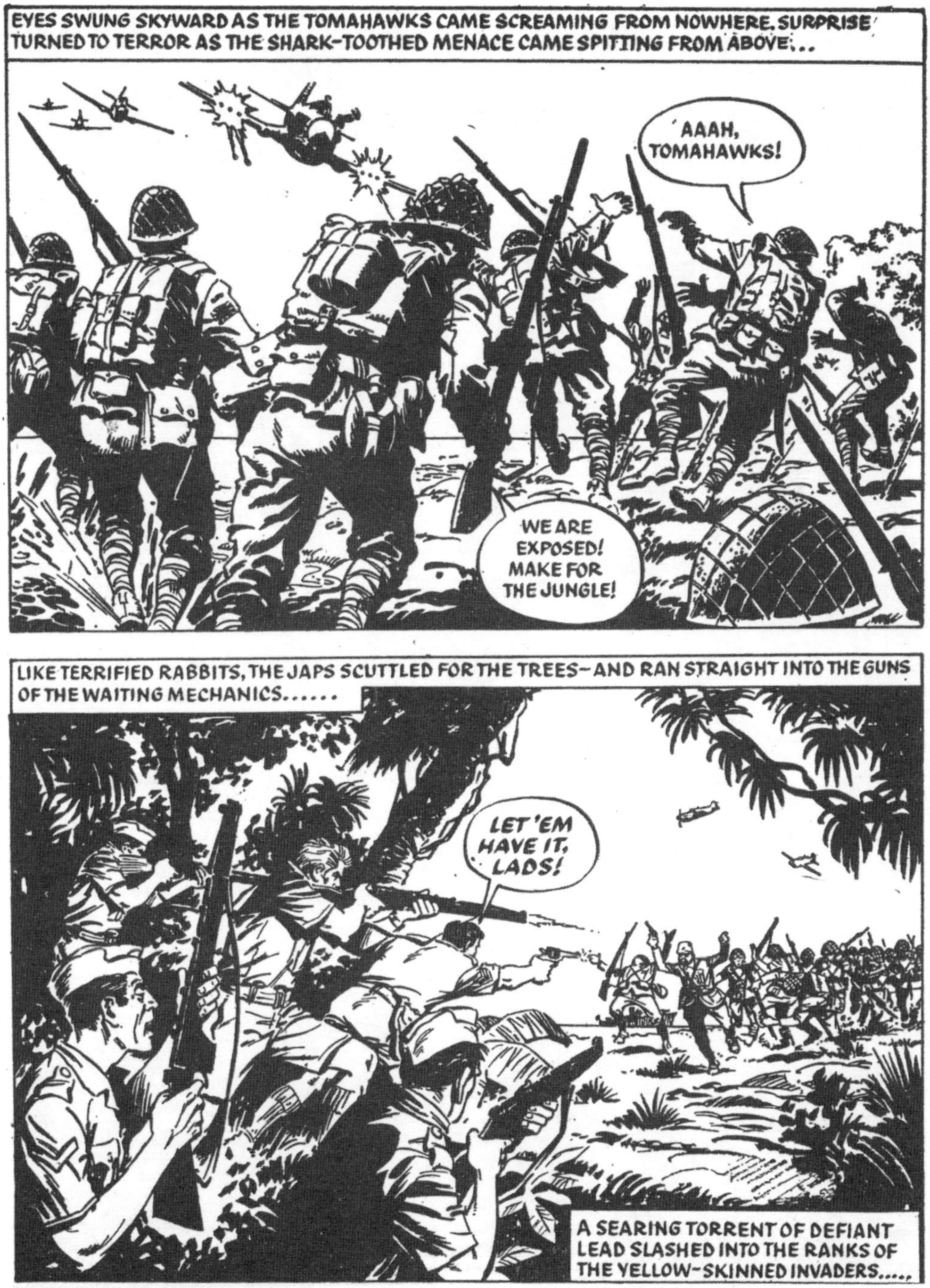
EYES SWUNG SKYWARD AS THE TOMAHAWKS CAME SCREAMING FROM NOWHERE. SURPRISE TURNED TO TERROR AS THE SHARK-TOOTHED MENACE CAME SPITTING FROM ABOVE...
AAAH, TOMAHAWKS!
WE ARE EXPOSED! MAKE FOR THE JUNGLE!
LIKE TERRIFIED RABBITS, THE JAPS SCUTTLED FOR THE TREES–AND RAN STRAIGHT INTO THE GUNS OF THE WAITING MECHANICS......
LET 'EM HAVE IT, LADS!
A SEARING TORRENT OF DEFIANT LEAD SLASHED INTO THE RANKS OF THE YELLOW-SKINNED INVADERS.....

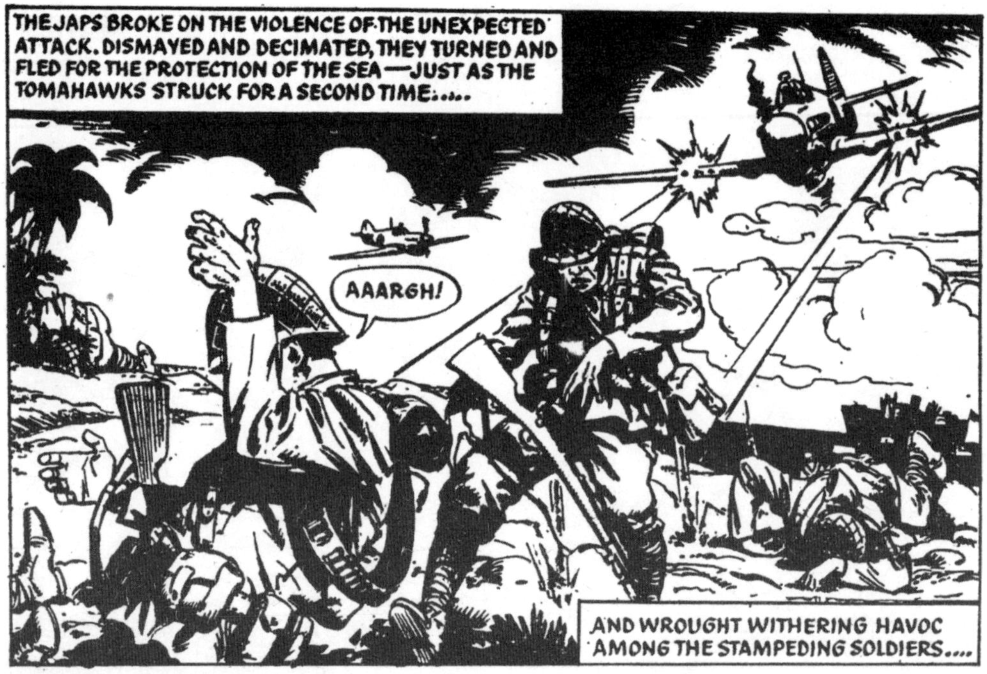
THE JAPS BROKE ON THE VIOLENCE OF THE UNEXPECTED ATTACK. DISMAYED AND DECIMATED, THEY TURNED AND FLED FOR THE PROTECTION OF THE SEA—JUST AS THE TOMAHAWKS STRUCK FOR A SECOND TIME.....
AAARGH!
AND WROUGHT WITHERING HAVOC AMONG THE STAMPEDING SOLDIERS....

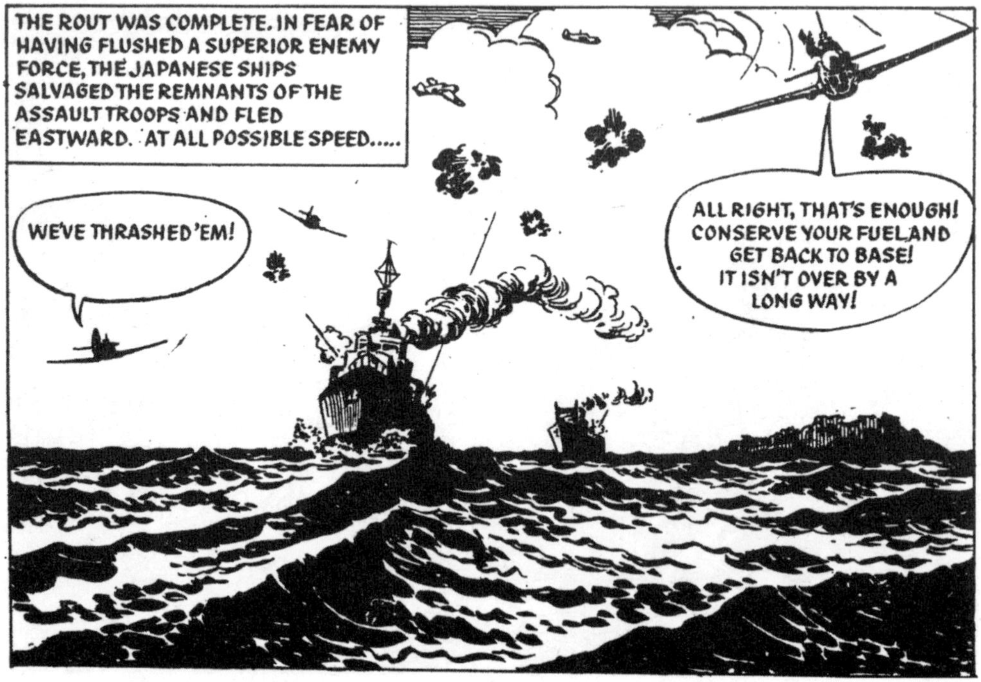
THE ROUT WAS COMPLETE. IN FEAR OF HAVING FLUSHED A SUPERIOR ENEMY FORCE, THE JAPANESE SHIPS SALVAGED THE REMNANTS OF THE ASSAULT TROOPS AND FLED EASTWARD. AT ALL POSSIBLE SPEED.....
WE'VE THRASHED 'EM!
ALL RIGHT, THAT'S ENOUGH! CONSERVE YOUR FUEL, AND GET BACK TO BASE! IT ISN'T OVER BY A LONG WAY!

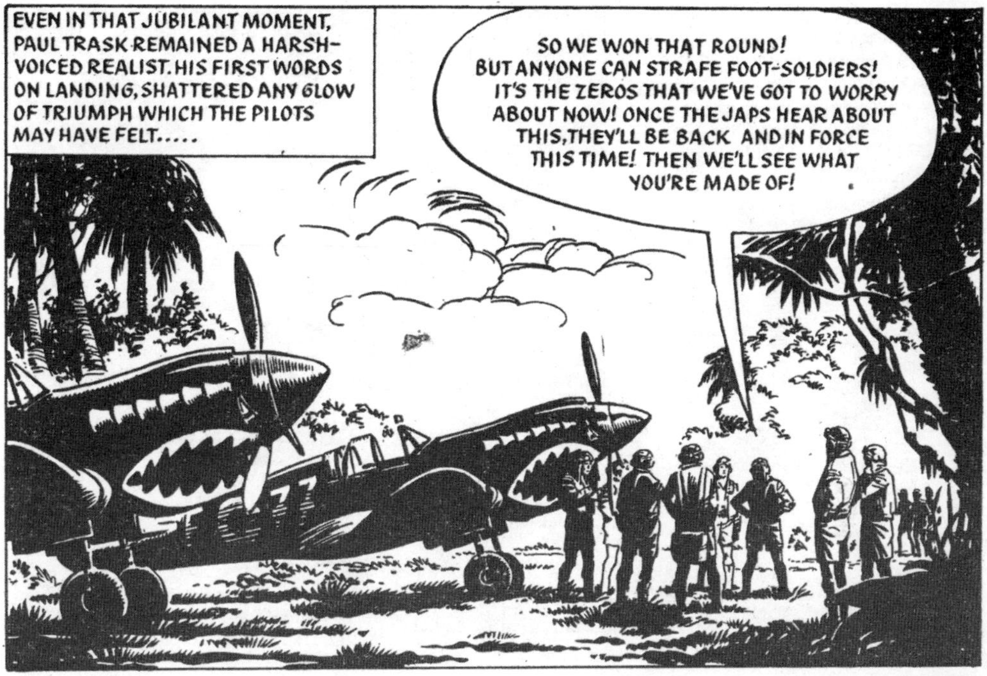
EVEN IN THAT JUBILANT MOMENT, PAUL TRASK REMAINED A HARSH-VOICED REALIST. HIS FIRST WORDS ON LANDING, SHATTERED ANY GLOW OF TRIUMPH WHICH THE PILOTS MAY HAVE FELT.....
SO WE WON THAT ROUND! BUT ANYONE CAN STRAFE FOOT-SOLDIERS! IT'S THE ZEROS THAT WE'VE GOT TO WORRY ABOUT NOW! ONCE THE JAPS HEAR ABOUT THIS, THEY'LL BE BACK AND IN FORCE THIS TIME! THEN WE'LL SEE WHAT YOU'RE MADE OF!

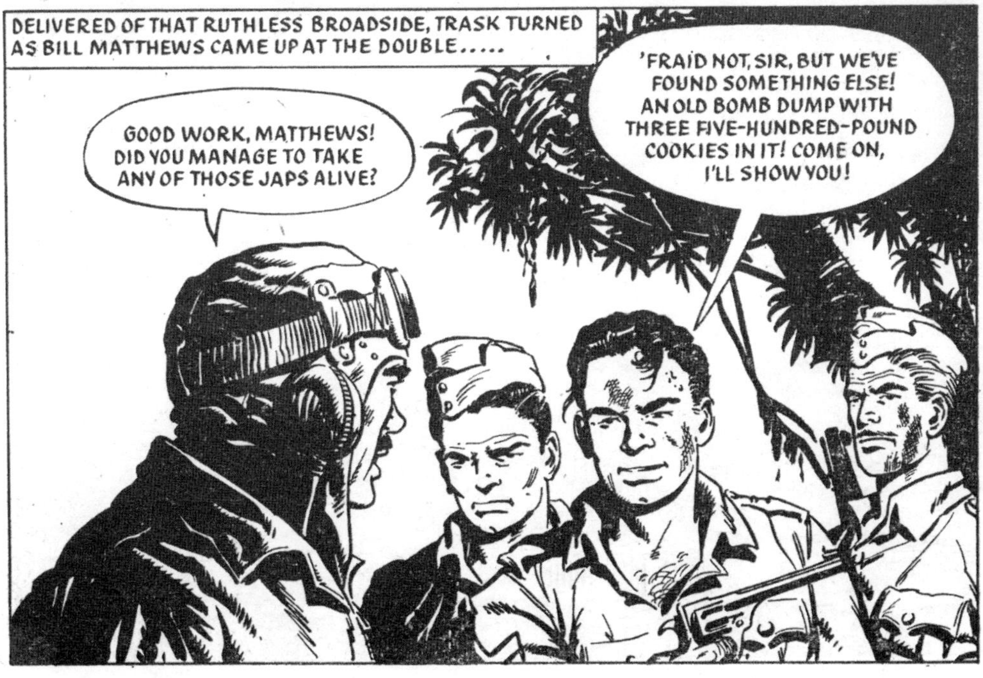
DELIVERED OF THAT RUTHLESS BROADSIDE, TRASK TURNED AS BILL MATTHEWS CAME UP AT THE DOUBLE.....
GOOD WORK, MATTHEWS! DID YOU MANAGE TO TAKE ANY OF THOSE JAPS ALIVE?
'FRAID NOT, SIR, BUT WE'VE FOUND SOMETHING ELSE! AN OLD BOMB DUMP WITH THREE FIVE-HUNDRED-POUND COOKIES IN IT! COME ON, I'LL SHOW YOU!

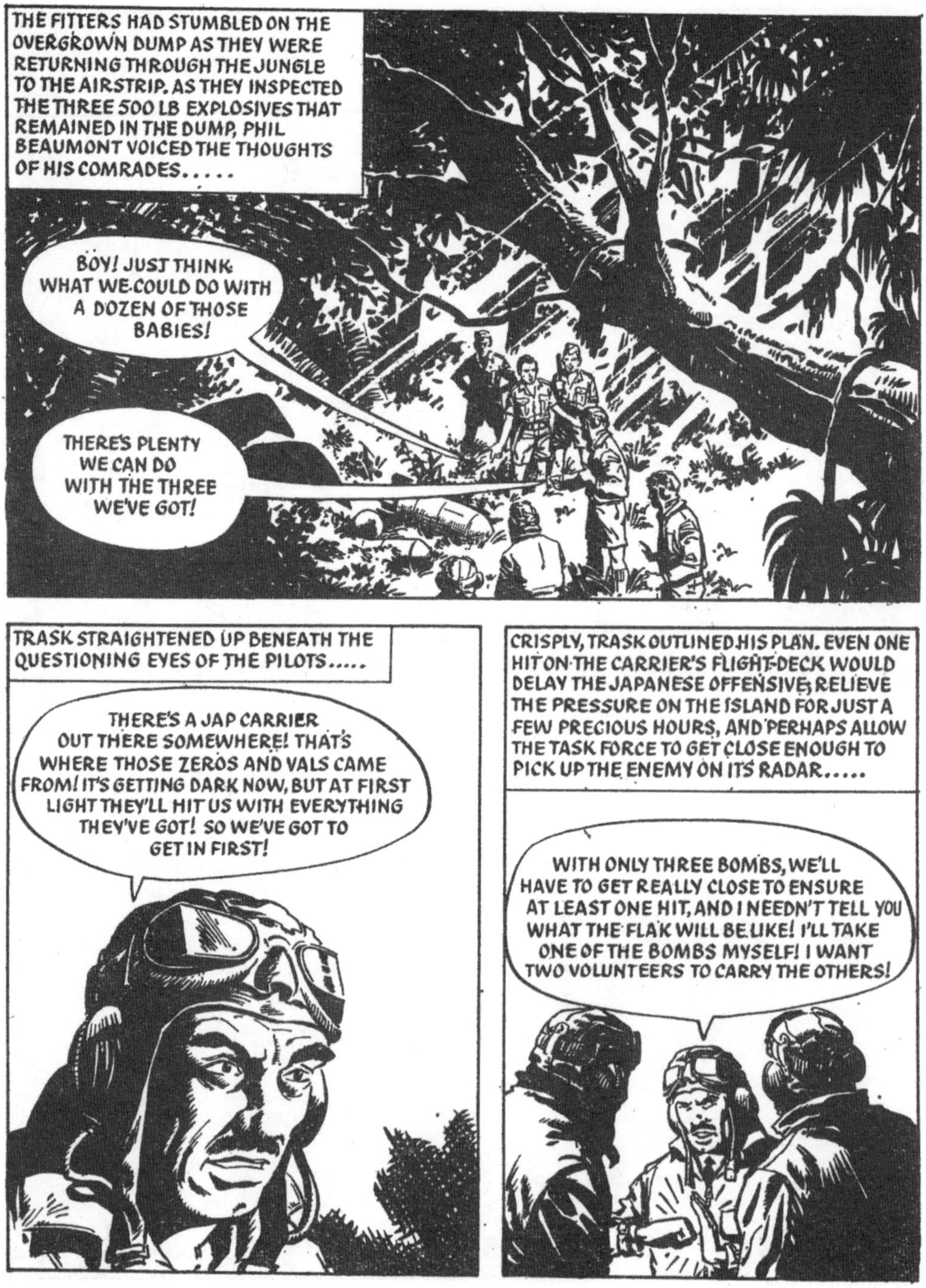
THE FITTERS HAD STUMBLED ON THE OVERGROWN DUMP AS THEY WERE RETURNING THROUGH THE JUNGLE TO THE AIRSTRIP. AS THEY INSPECTED THE THREE 500 LB EXPLOSIVES THAT REMAINED IN THE DUMP, PHIL BEAUMONT VOICED THE THOUGHTS OF HIS COMRADES.....
BOY! JUST THINK WHAT WE COULD DO WITH A DOZEN OF THOSE BABIES!
THERE'S PLENTY WE CAN DO WITH THE THREE WE'VE GOT!
TRASK STRAIGHTENED UP BENEATH THE QUESTIONING EYES OF THE PILOTS.....
THERE'S A JAP CARRIER OUT THERE SOMEWHERE! THAT'S WHERE THOSE ZEROS AND VALS CAME FROM! IT'S GETTING DARK NOW, BUT AT FIRST LIGHT THEY'LL HIT US WITH EVERYTHING THEY'VE GOT! SO WE'VE GOT TO GET IN FIRST!
CRISPLY, TRASK OUTLINED HIS PLAN. EVEN ONE HIT ON THE CARRIER'S FLIGHT-DECK WOULD DELAY THE JAPANESE OFFENSIVE, RELIEVE THE PRESSURE ON THE ISLAND FOR JUST A FEW PRECIOUS HOURS, AND PERHAPS ALLOW THE TASK FORCE TO GET CLOSE ENOUGH TO PICK UP THE ENEMY ON ITS RADAR.....
WITH ONLY THREE BOMBS, WE'LL HAVE TO GET REALLY CLOSE TO ENSURE AT LEAST ONE HIT, AND I NEEDN'T TELL YOU WHAT THE FLAK WILL BE LIKE! I'LL TAKE ONE OF THE BOMBS MYSELF! I WANT TWO VOLUNTEERS TO CARRY THE OTHERS!

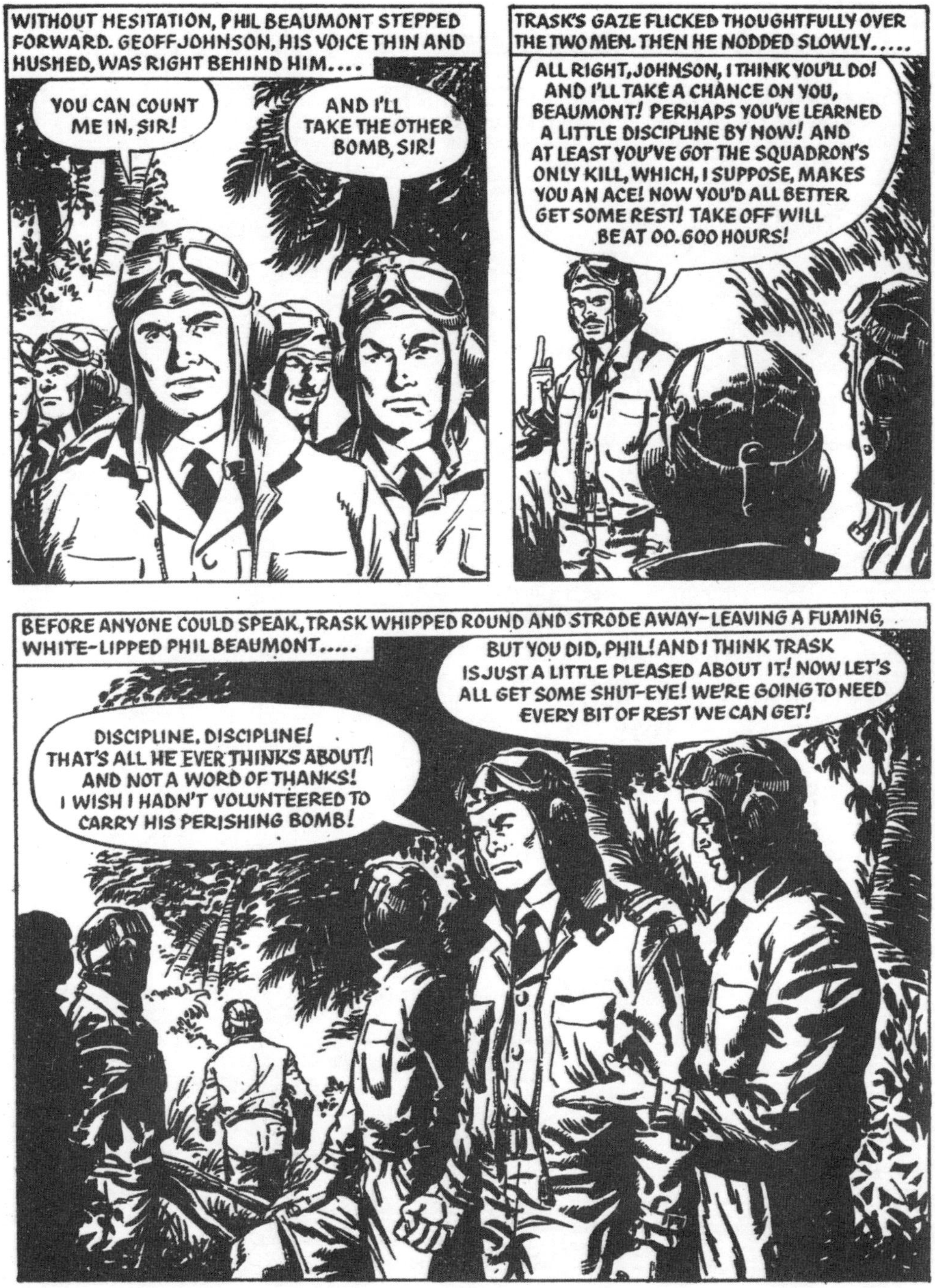
WITHOUT HESITATION, PHIL BEAUMONT STEPPED FORWARD. GEOFF JOHNSON, HIS VOICE THIN AND HUSHED, WAS RIGHT BEHIND HIM....
YOU CAN COUNT ME IN, SIR!
AND I'LL TAKE THE OTHER BOMB, SIR!
TRASK'S GAZE FLICKED THOUGHTFULLY OVER THE TWO MEN. THEN HE NODDED SLOWLY.....
ALL RIGHT, JOHNSON, I THINK YOU'LL DO! AND I'LL TAKE A CHANCE ON YOU, BEAUMONT! PERHAPS YOU'VE LEARNED A LITTLE DISCIPLINE BY NOW! AND AT LEAST YOU'VE GOT THE SQUADRON'S ONLY KILL, WHICH, I SUPPOSE, MAKES YOU AN ACE! NOW YOU'D ALL BETTER GET SOME REST! TAKE OFF WILL BE AT 00.600 HOURS!
BEFORE ANYONE COULD SPEAK, TRASK WHIPPED ROUND AND STRODE AWAY—LEAVING A FUMING, WHITE-LIPPED PHIL BEAUMONT.....
DISCIPLINE, DISCIPLINE! THAT'S ALL HE EVER THINKS ABOUT! AND NOT A WORD OF THANKS! I WISH I HADN'T VOLUNTEERED TO CARRY HIS PERISHING BOMB!
BUT YOU DID, PHIL! AND I THINK TRASK IS JUST A LITTLE PLEASED ABOUT IT! NOW LET'S ALL GET SOME SHUT-EYE! WE'RE GOING TO NEED EVERY BIT OF REST WE CAN GET!

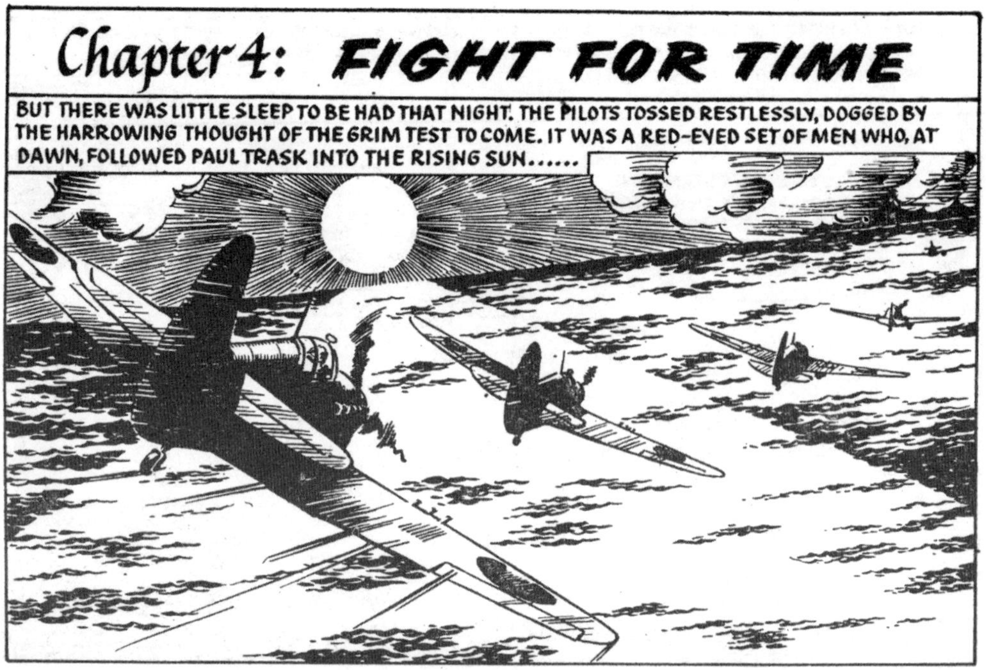
Chapter 4: FIGHT FOR TIME
BUT THERE WAS LITTLE SLEEP TO BE HAD THAT NIGHT. THE PILOTS TOSSED RESTLESSLY, DOGGED BY THE HARROWING THOUGHT OF THE GRIM TEST TO COME. IT WAS A RED-EYED SET OF MEN WHO, AT DAWN, FOLLOWED PAUL TRASK INTO THE RISING SUN......

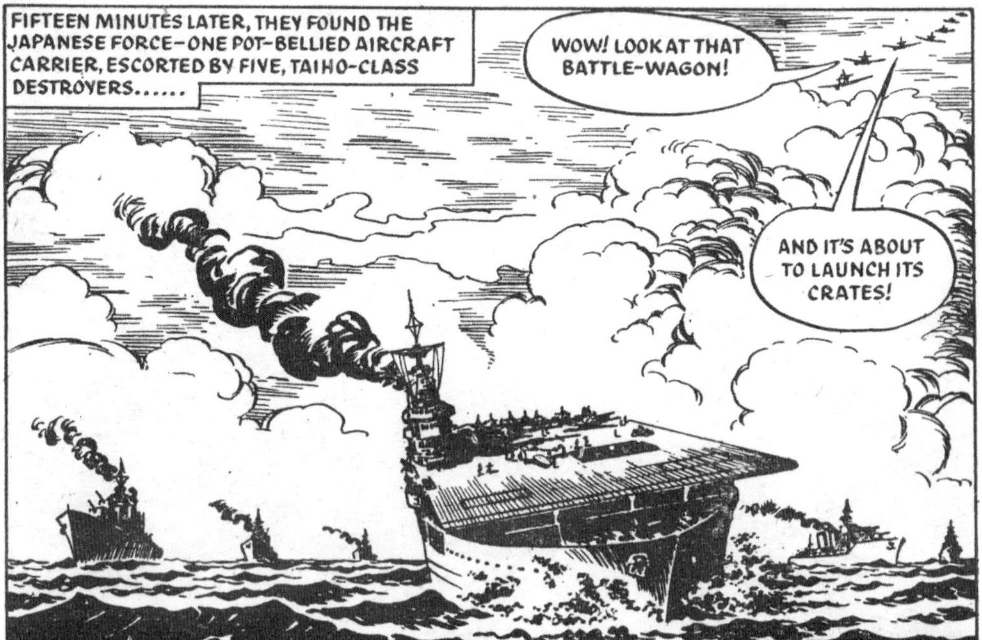
FIFTEEN MINUTES LATER, THEY FOUND THE JAPANESE FORCE—ONE POT-BELLIED AIRCRAFT CARRIER, ESCORTED BY FIVE, TAIHO-CLASS DESTROYERS......
WOW! LOOK AT THAT BATTLE-WAGON!
AND IT'S ABOUT TO LAUNCH ITS CRATES!

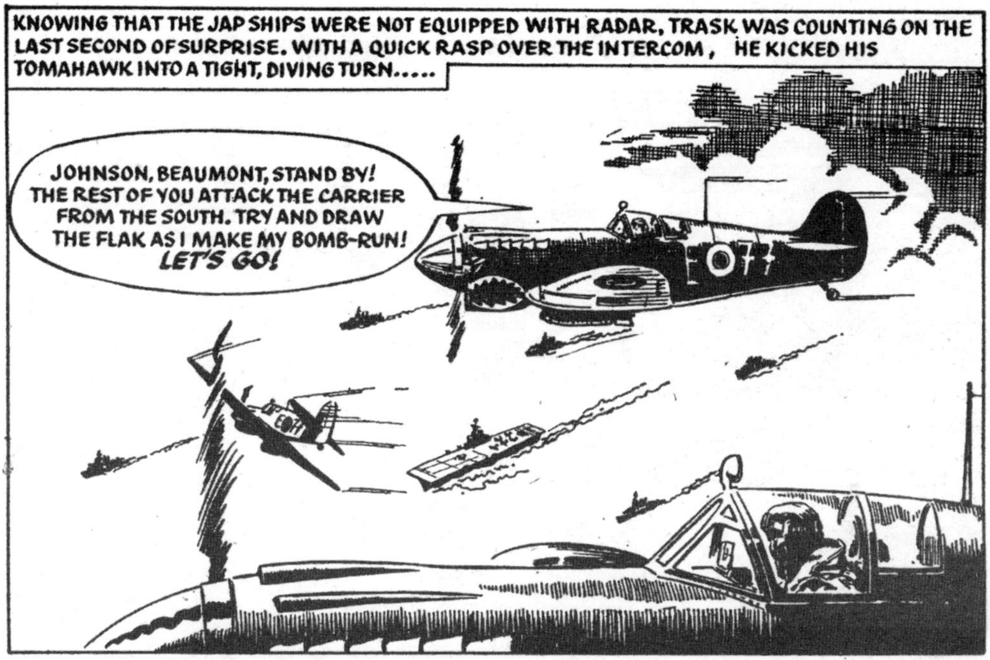
KNOWING THAT THE JAP SHIPS WERE NOT EQUIPPED WITH RADAR, TRASK WAS COUNTING ON THE LAST SECOND OF SURPRISE. WITH A QUICK RASP OVER THE INTERCOM, HE KICKED HIS TOMAHAWK INTO A TIGHT, DIVING TURN.....
JOHNSON, BEAUMONT, STAND BY! THE REST OF YOU ATTACK THE CARRIER FROM THE SOUTH. TRY AND DRAW THE FLAK AS I MAKE MY BOMB-RUN! LET'S GO!

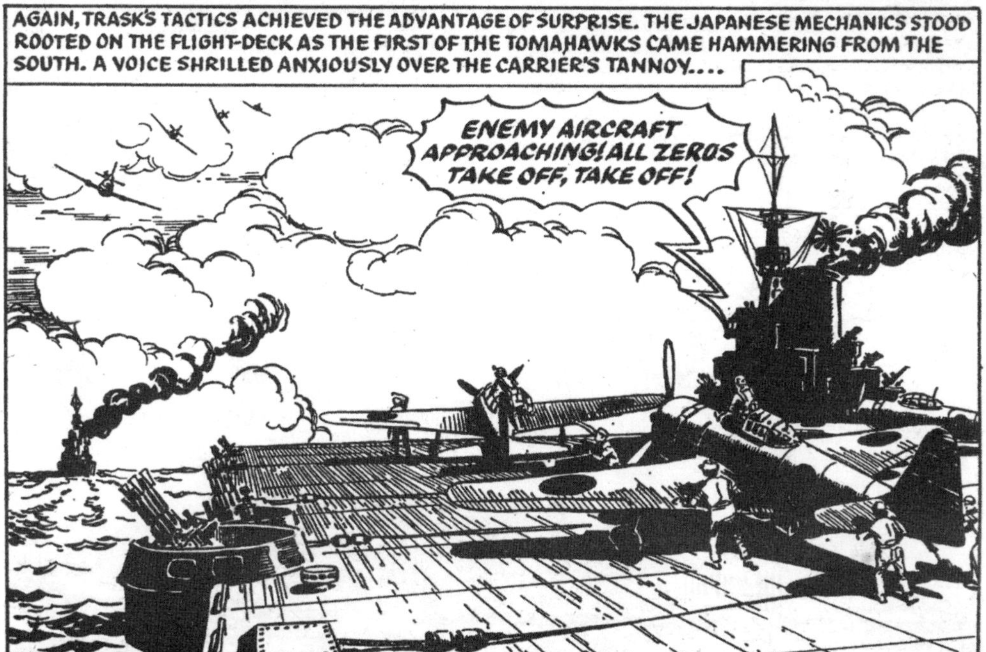
AGAIN, TRASK'S TACTICS ACHIEVED THE ADVANTAGE OF SURPRISE. THE JAPANESE MECHANICS STOOD ROOTED ON THE FLIGHT-DECK AS THE FIRST OF THE TOMAHAWKS CAME HAMMERING FROM THE SOUTH. A VOICE SHRILLED ANXIOUSLY OVER THE CARRIER'S TANNOY....
ENEMY AIRCRAFT APPROACHING! ALL ZEROS TAKE OFF, TAKE OFF!

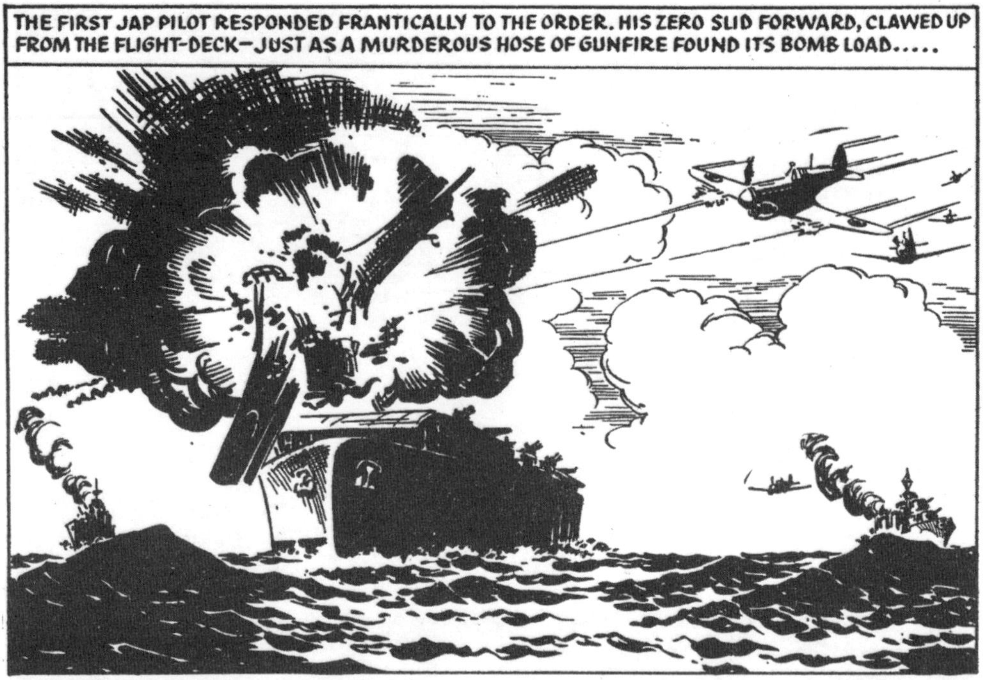
THE FIRST JAP PILOT RESPONDED FRANTICALLY TO THE ORDER. HIS ZERO SLID FORWARD, CLAWED UP FROM THE FLIGHT-DECK—JUST AS A MURDEROUS HOSE OF GUNFIRE FOUND ITS BOMB LOAD.....

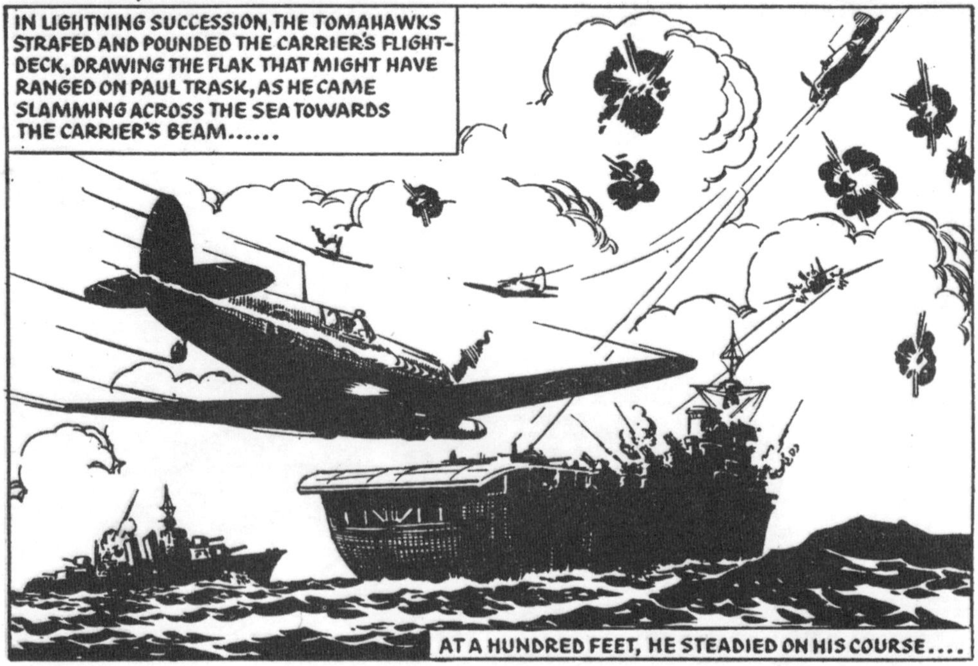
IN LIGHTNING SUCCESSION, THE TOMAHAWKS STRAFED AND POUNDED THE CARRIER'S FLIGHT-DECK, DRAWING THE FLAK THAT MIGHT HAVE RANGED ON PAUL TRASK, AS HE CAME SLAMMING ACROSS THE SEA TOWARDS THE CARRIER'S BEAM......
AT A HUNDRED FEET, HE STEADIED ON HIS COURSE....

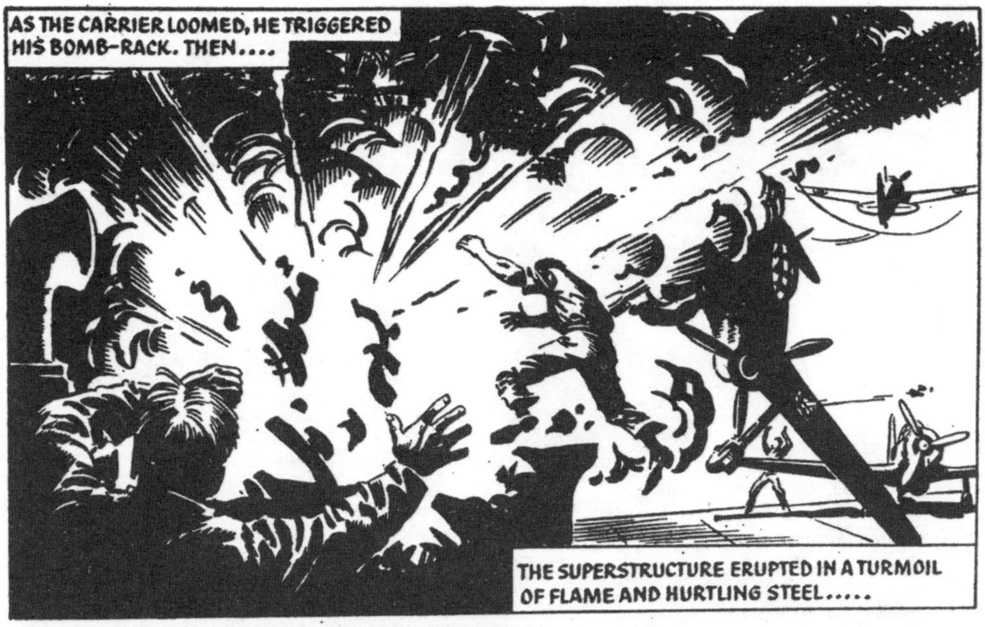
AS THE CARRIER LOOMED, HE TRIGGERED HIS BOMB-RACK. THEN....
THE SUPERSTRUCTURE ERUPTED IN A TURMOIL OF FLAME AND HURTLING STEEL.....

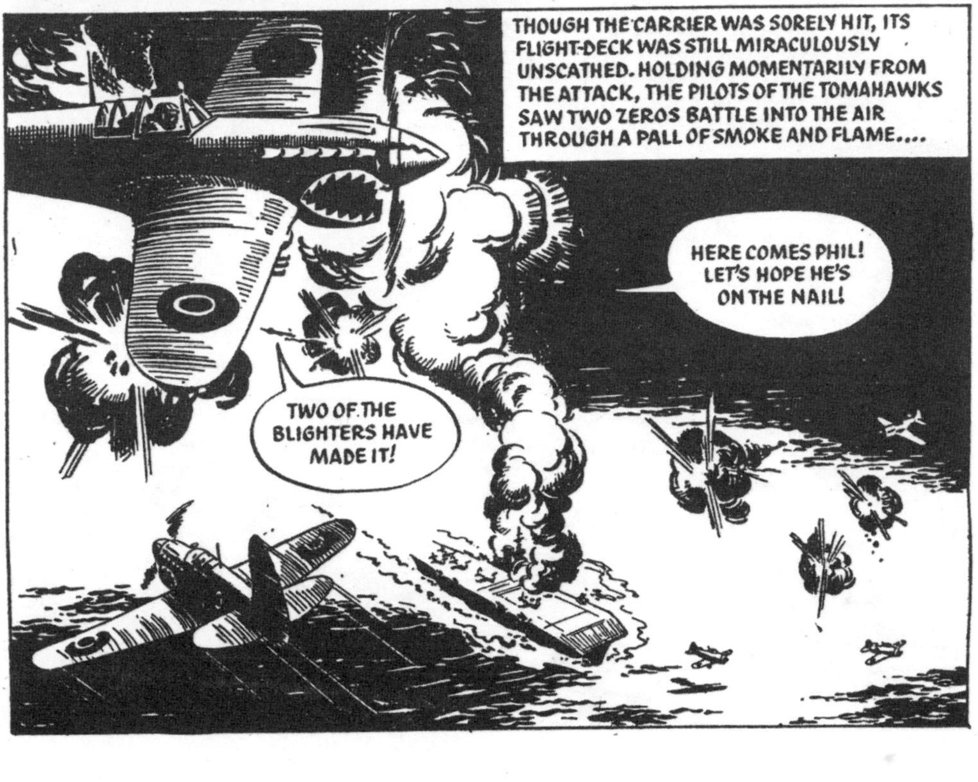
THOUGH THE CARRIER WAS SORELY HIT, ITS FLIGHT-DECK WAS STILL MIRACULOUSLY UNSCATHED. HOLDING MOMENTARILY FROM THE ATTACK, THE PILOTS OF THE TOMAHAWKS SAW TWO ZEROS BATTLE INTO THE AIR THROUGH A PALL OF SMOKE AND FLAME....
HERE COMES PHIL! LET'S HOPE HE'S ON THE NAIL!
TWO OF THE BLIGHTERS HAVE MADE IT!

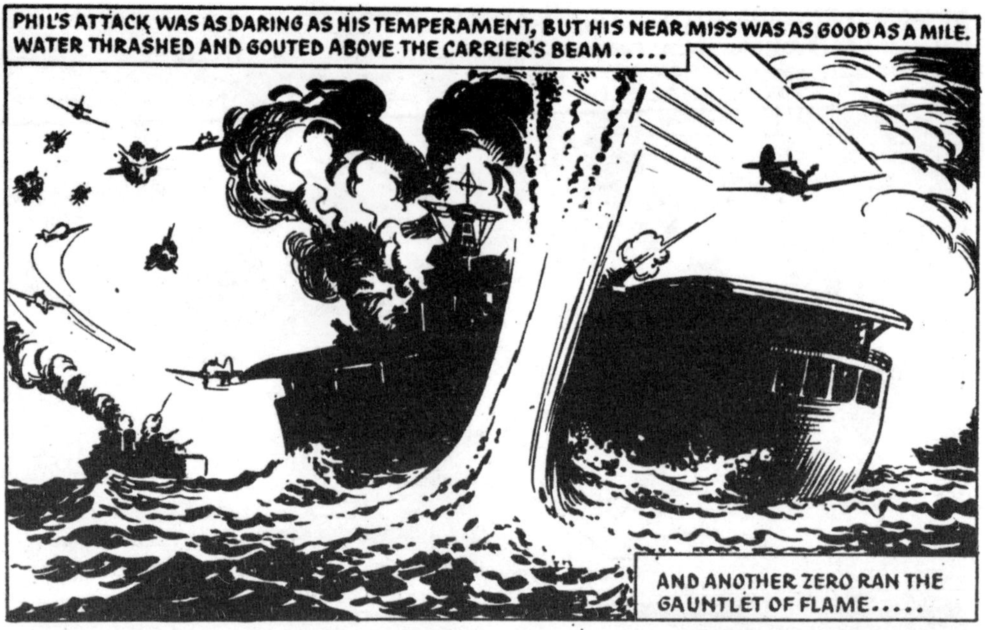
PHIL'S ATTACK WAS AS DARING AS HIS TEMPERAMENT, BUT HIS NEAR MISS WAS AS GOOD AS A MILE. WATER THRASHED AND GOUTED ABOVE THE CARRIER'S BEAM.....
AND ANOTHER ZERO RAN THE GAUNTLET OF FLAME.....

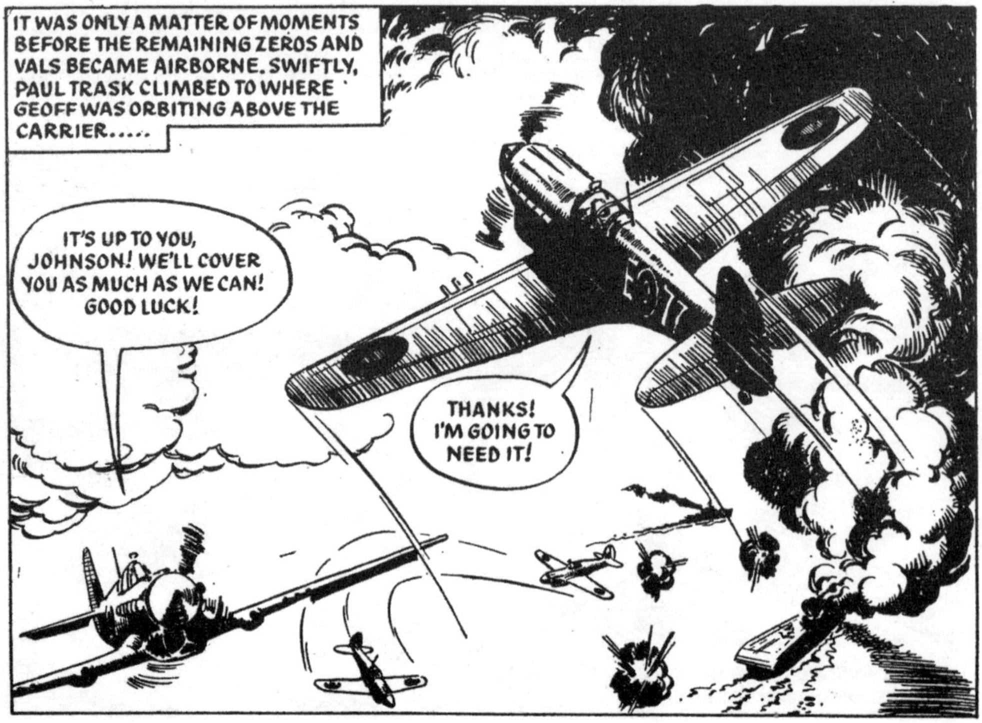
IT WAS ONLY A MATTER OF MOMENTS BEFORE THE REMAINING ZEROS AND VALS BECAME AIRBORNE. SWIFTLY, PAUL TRASK CLIMBED TO WHERE GEOFF WAS ORBITING ABOVE THE CARRIER.....
IT'S UP TO YOU, JOHNSON! WE'LL COVER YOU AS MUCH AS WE CAN! GOOD LUCK!
THANKS! I'M GOING TO NEED IT!

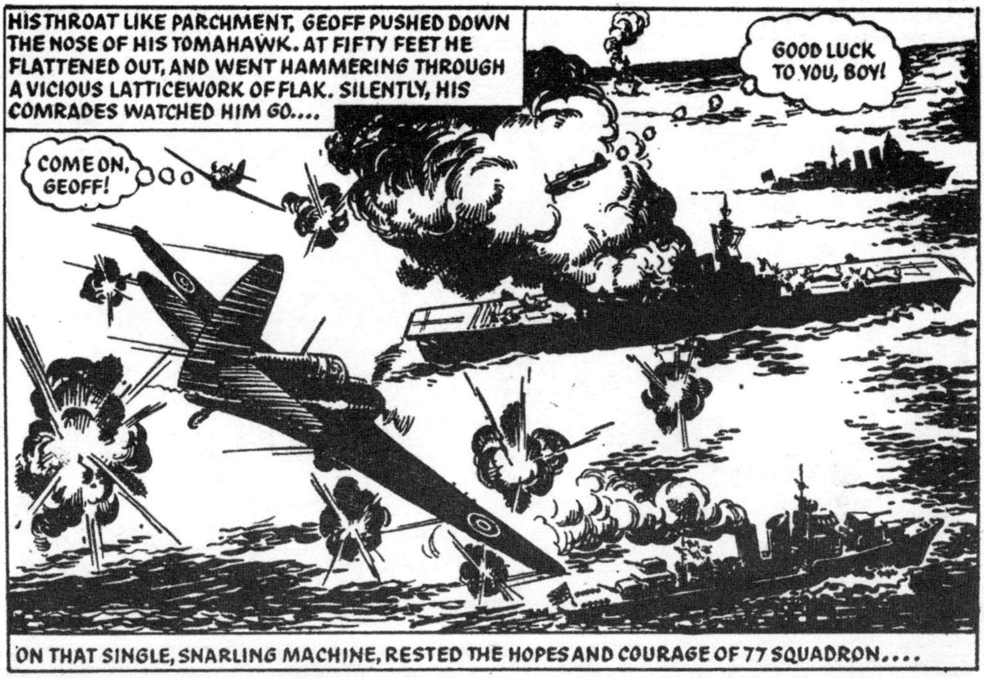
HIS THROAT LIKE PARCHMENT, GEOFF PUSHED DOWN THE NOSE OF HIS TOMAHAWK. AT FIFTY FEET HE FLATTENED OUT, AND WENT HAMMERING THROUGH A VICIOUS LATTICEWORK OF FLAK. SILENTLY, HIS COMRADES WATCHED HIM GO....
GOOD LUCK TO YOU, BOY!
COME ON, GEOFF!
ON THAT SINGLE, SNARLING MACHINE, RESTED THE HOPES AND COURAGE OF 77 SQUADRON....

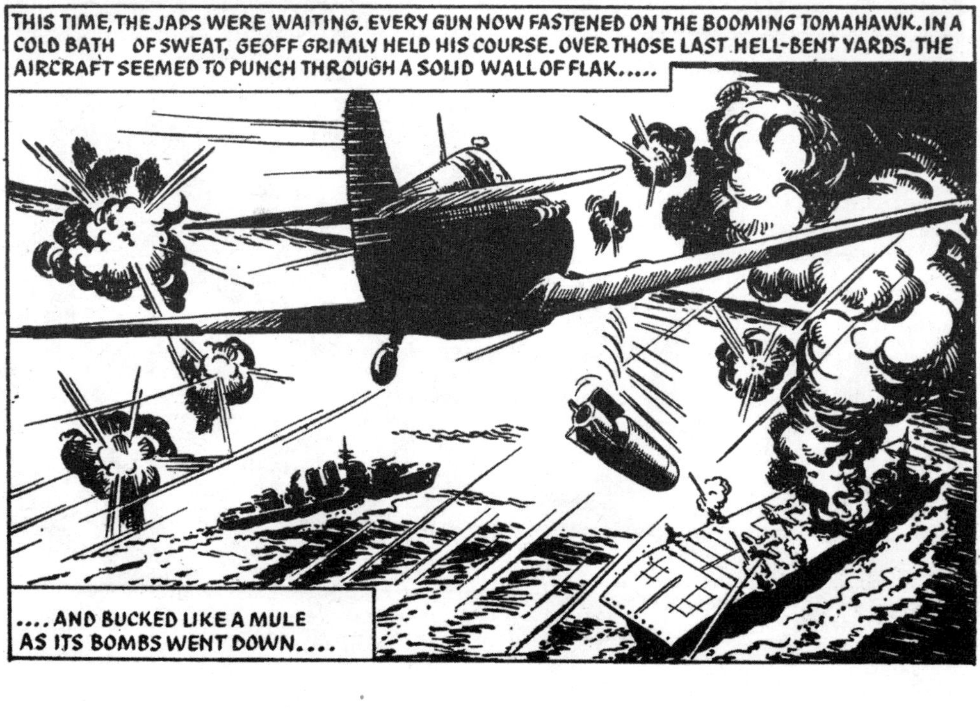
THIS TIME, THE JAPS WERE WAITING. EVERY GUN NOW FASTENED ON THE BOOMING TOMAHAWK. IN A COLD BATH OF SWEAT, GEOFF GRIMLY HELD HIS COURSE. OVER THOSE LAST HELL-BENT YARDS, THE AIRCRAFT SEEMED TO PUNCH THROUGH A SOLID WALL OF FLAK.....
.... AND BUCKED LIKE A MULE AS ITS BOMBS WENT DOWN....

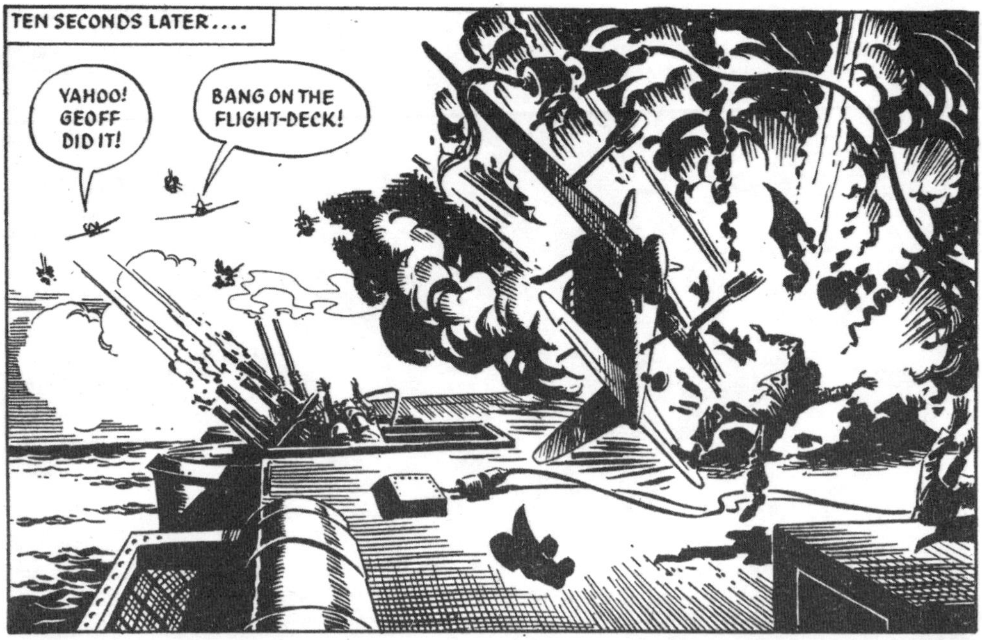
TEN SECONDS LATER....
YAHOO! GEOFF DID IT!
BANG ON THE FLIGHT-DECK!

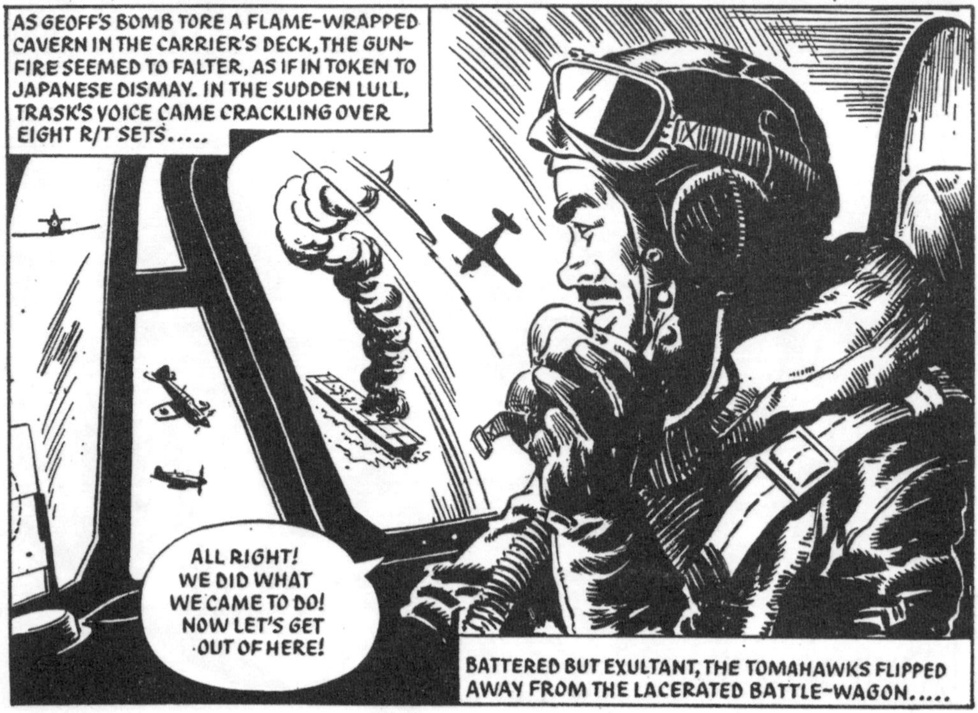
AS GEOFF'S BOMB TORE A FLAME-WRAPPED CAVERN IN THE CARRIER'S DECK, THE GUN-FIRE SEEMED TO FALTER, AS IF IN TOKEN TO JAPANESE DISMAY. IN THE SUDDEN LULL, TRASK'S VOICE CAME CRACKLING OVER EIGHT R/T SETS.....
ALL RIGHT! WE DID WHAT WE CAME TO DO! NOW LET'S GET OUT OF HERE!
BATTERED BUT EXULTANT, THE TOMAHAWKS FLIPPED AWAY FROM THE LACERATED BATTLE-WAGON.....

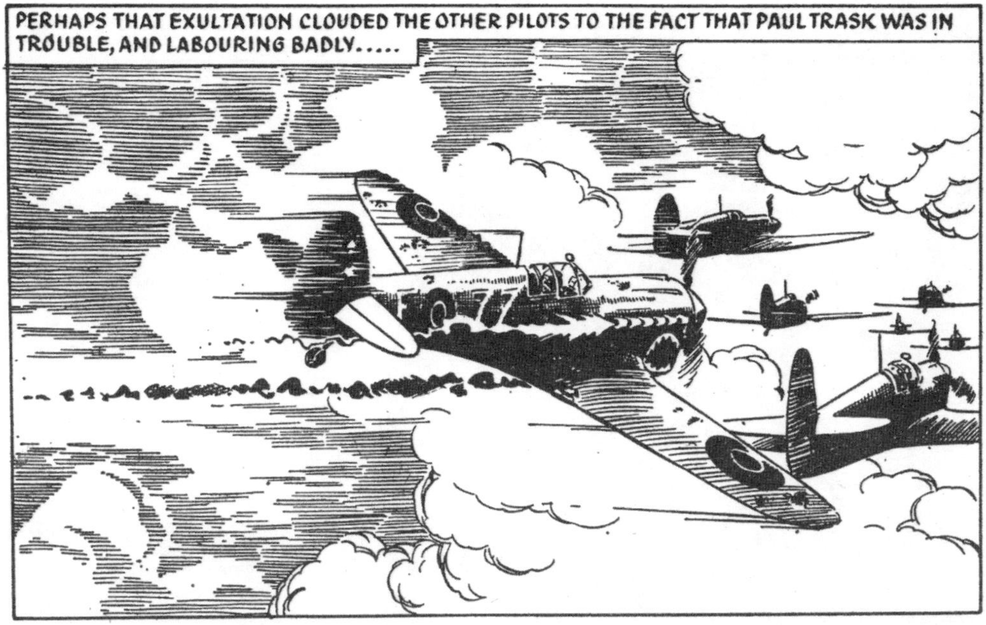
PERHAPS THAT EXULTATION CLOUDED THE OTHER PILOTS TO THE FACT THAT PAUL TRASK WAS IN TROUBLE, AND LABOURING BADLY.....

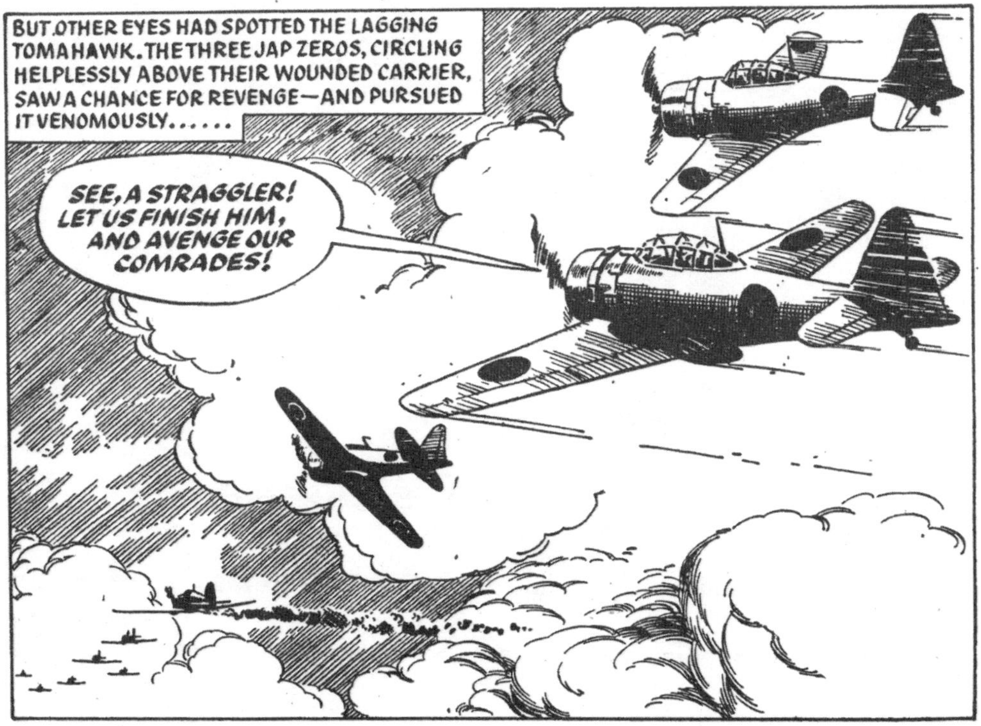
BUT OTHER EYES HAD SPOTTED THE LAGGING TOMAHAWK. THE THREE JAP ZEROS, CIRCLING HELPLESSLY ABOVE THEIR WOUNDED CARRIER, SAW A CHANCE FOR REVENGE—AND PURSUED IT VENOMOUSLY......
SEE, A STRAGGLER! LET US FINISH HIM, AND AVENGE OUR COMRADES!

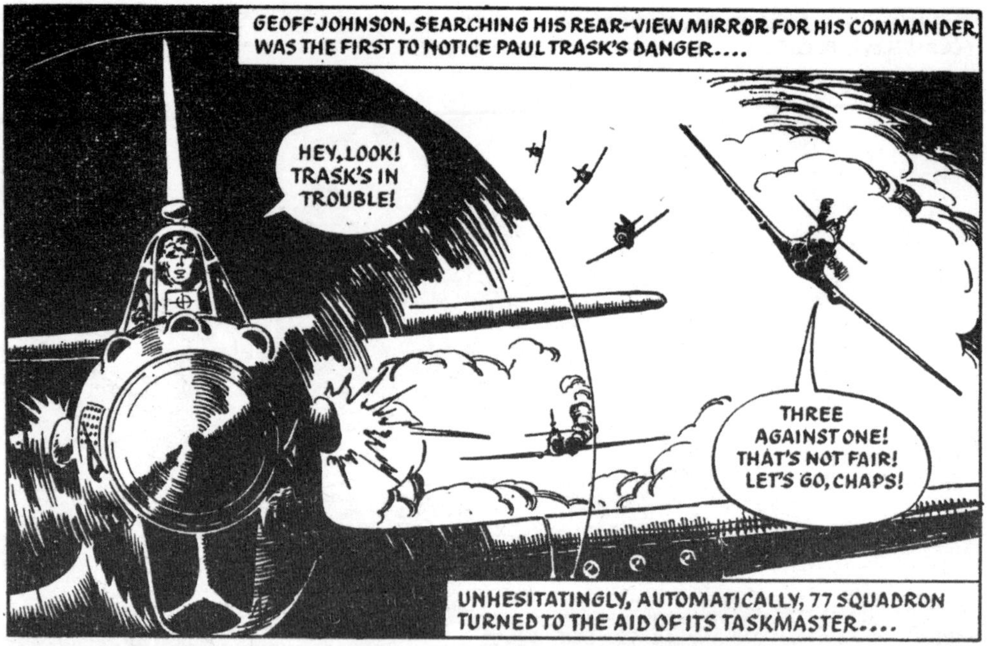
GEOFF JOHNSON, SEARCHING HIS REAR-VIEW MIRROR FOR HIS COMMANDER, WAS THE FIRST TO NOTICE PAUL TRASK'S DANGER....
HEY, LOOK! TRASK'S IN TROUBLE!
THREE AGAINST ONE! THAT'S NOT FAIR! LET'S GO, CHAPS!
UNHESITATINGLY, AUTOMATICALLY, 77 SQUADRON TURNED TO THE AID OF ITS TASKMASTER....

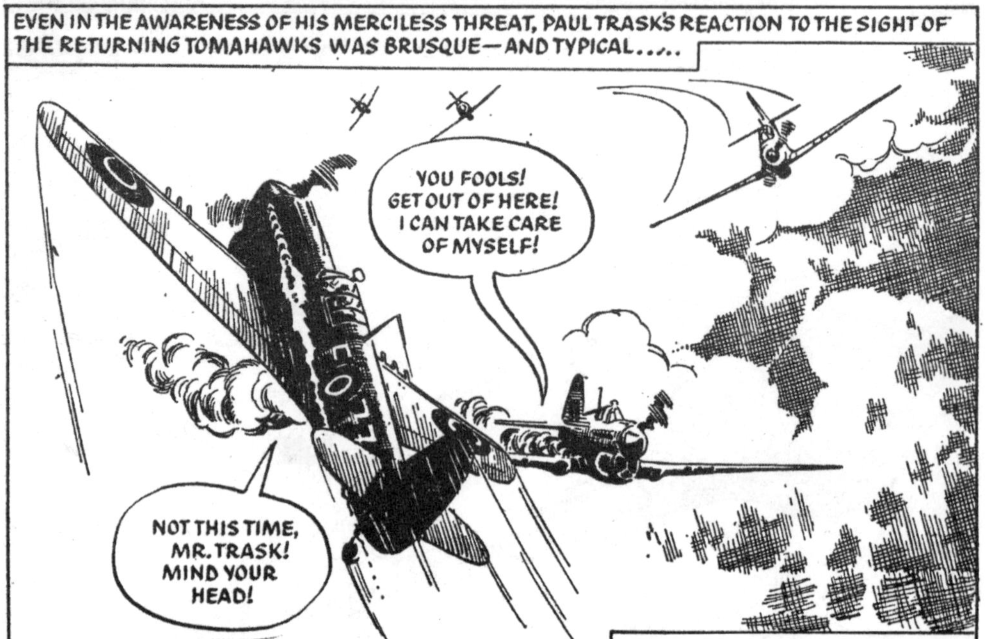
EVEN IN THE AWARENESS OF HIS MERCILESS THREAT, PAUL TRASK'S REACTION TO THE SIGHT OF THE RETURNING TOMAHAWKS WAS BRUSQUE—AND TYPICAL....
YOU FOOLS! GET OUT OF HERE! I CAN TAKE CARE OF MYSELF!
NOT THIS TIME, MR. TRASK! MIND YOUR HEAD!
CALMLY, PHIL BEAUMONT LINED UP ON THE FIRST SWOOPING ZERO....

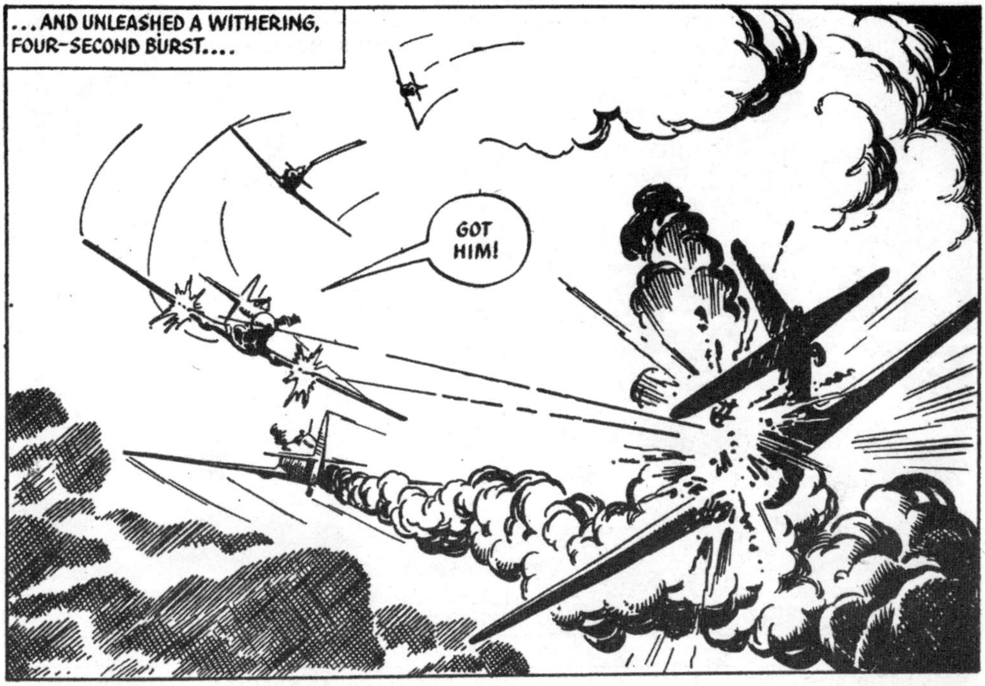
...AND UNLEASHED A WITHERING, FOUR-SECOND BURST....
GOT HIM!

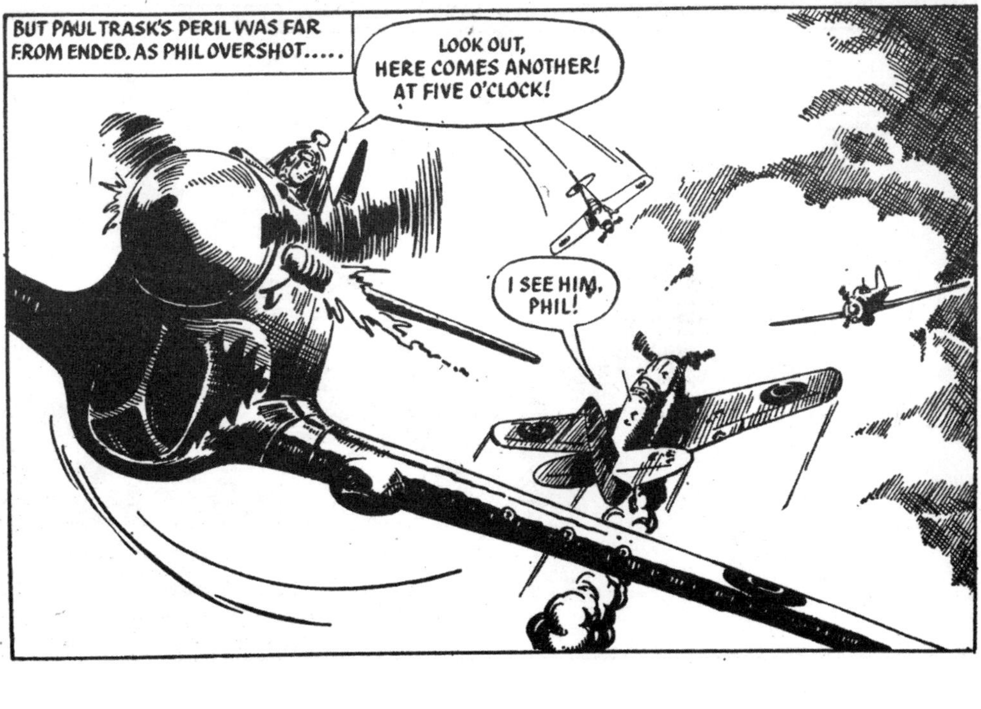
BUT PAUL TRASK'S PERIL WAS FAR FROM ENDED. AS PHIL OVERSHOT.....
LOOK OUT, HERE COMES ANOTHER! AT FIVE O'CLOCK!
I SEE HIM, PHIL!

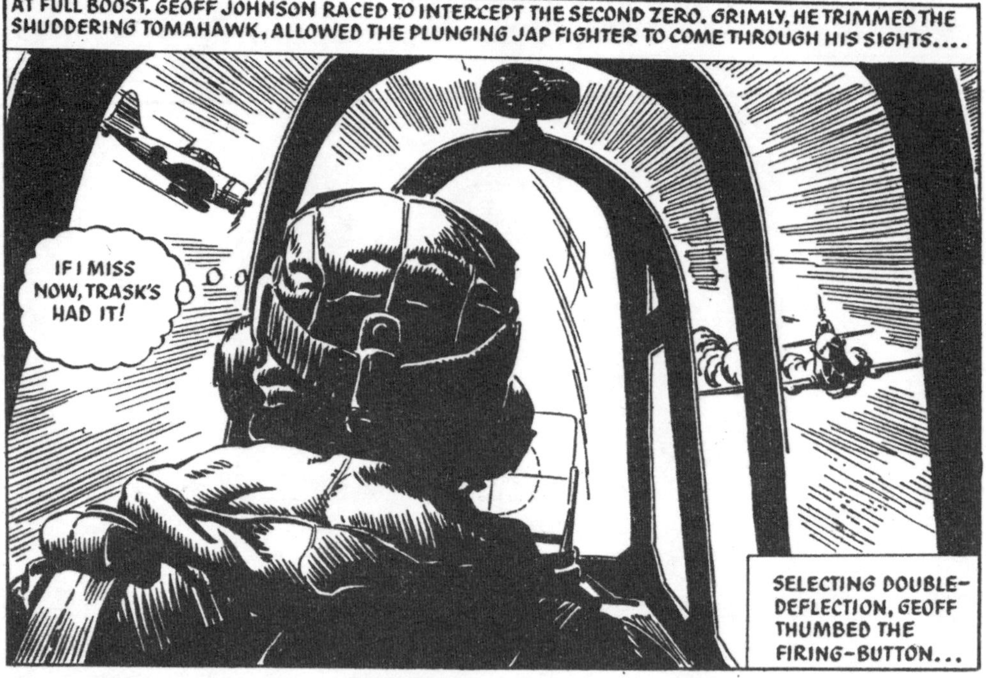
AT FULL BOOST, GEOFF JOHNSON RACED TO INTERCEPT THE SECOND ZERO. GRIMLY, HE TRIMMED THE SHUDDERING TOMAHAWK, ALLOWED THE PLUNGING JAP FIGHTER TO COME THROUGH HIS SIGHTS....
IF I MISS NOW, TRASK'S HAD IT!
SELECTING DOUBLE-DEFLECTION, GEOFF THUMBED THE FIRING-BUTTON...

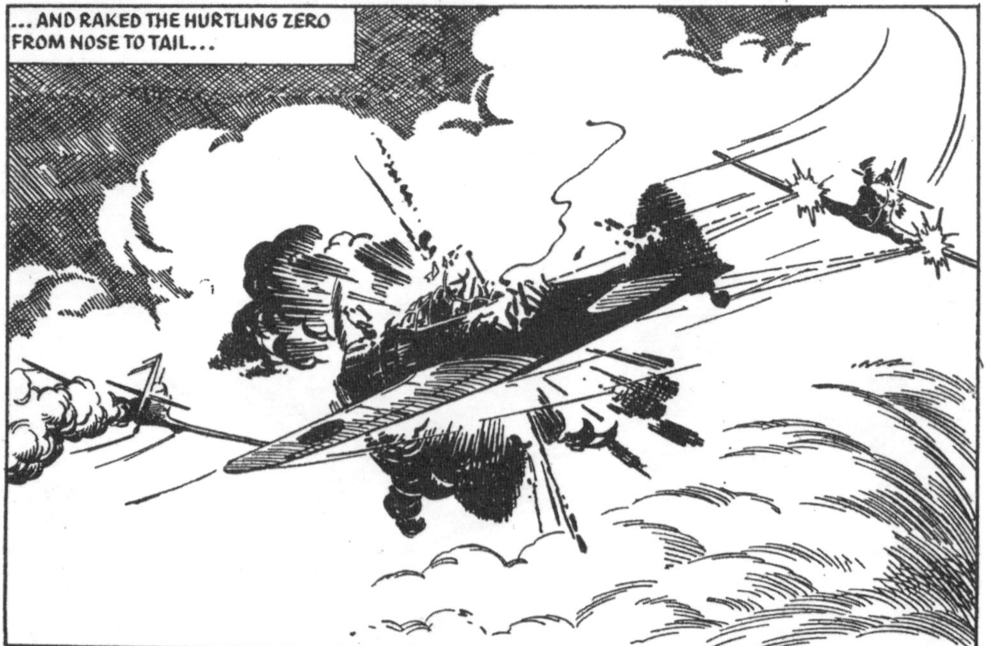
... AND RAKED THE HURTLING ZERO FROM NOSE TO TAIL...

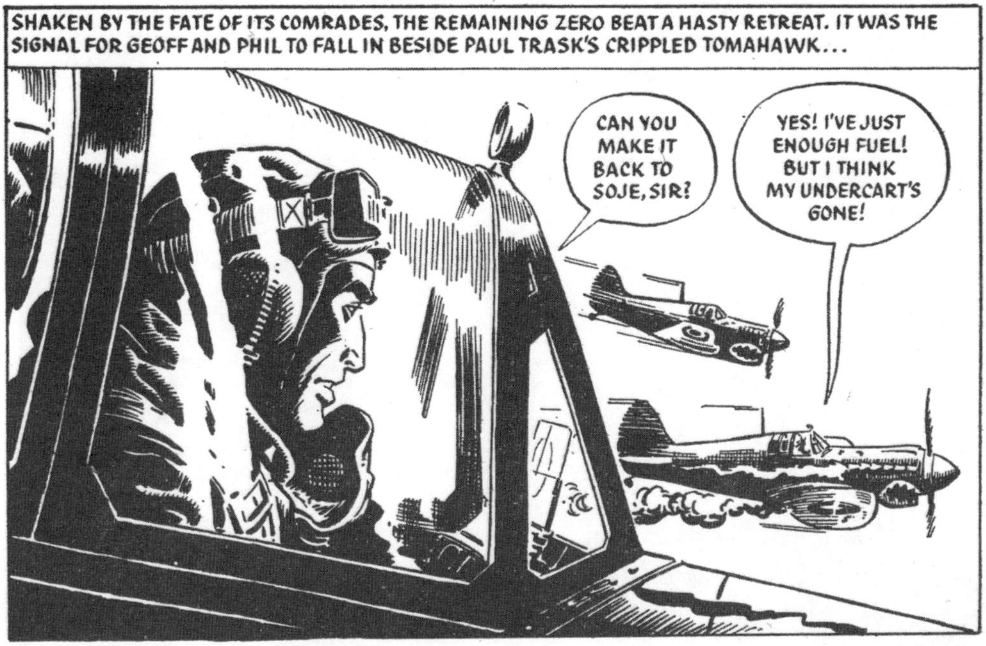
SHAKEN BY THE FATE OF ITS COMRADES, THE REMAINING ZERO BEAT A HASTY RETREAT. IT WAS THE SIGNAL FOR GEOFF AND PHIL TO FALL IN BESIDE PAUL TRASK'S CRIPPLED TOMAHAWK...
CAN YOU MAKE IT BACK TO SOJE, SIR?
YES! I'VE JUST ENOUGH FUEL! BUT I THINK MY UNDERCART'S GONE!

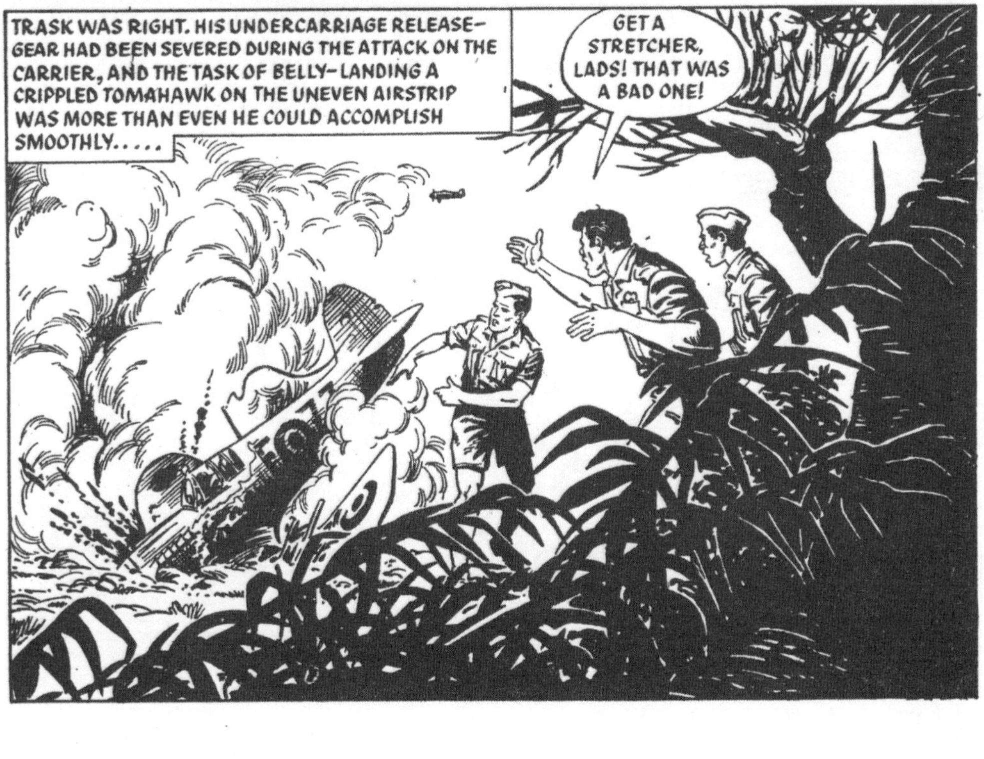
TRASK WAS RIGHT. HIS UNDERCARRIAGE RELEASE-GEAR HAD BEEN SEVERED DURING THE ATTACK ON THE CARRIER, AND THE TASK OF BELLY-LANDING A CRIPPLED TOMAHAWK ON THE UNEVEN AIRSTRIP WAS MORE THAN EVEN HE COULD ACCOMPLISH SMOOTHLY.....
GET A STRETCHER, LADS! THAT WAS A BAD ONE!

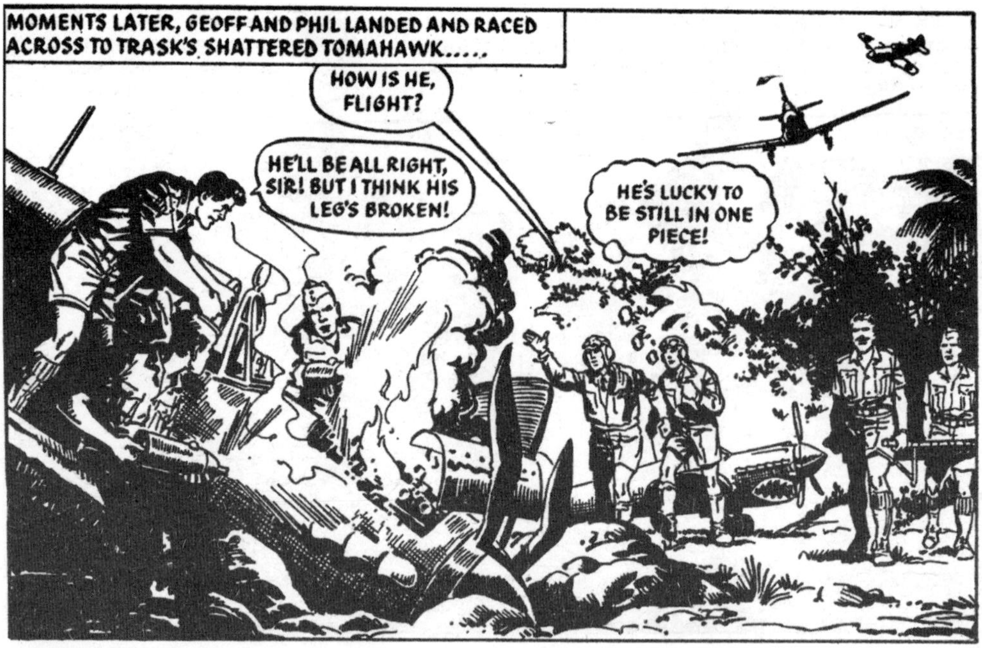
MOMENTS LATER, GEOFF AND PHIL LANDED AND RACED ACROSS TO TRASK'S SHATTERED TOMAHAWK.....
HOW IS HE, FLIGHT?
HE'LL BE ALL RIGHT, SIR! BUT I THINK HIS LEG'S BROKEN!
HE'S LUCKY TO BE STILL IN ONE PIECE!

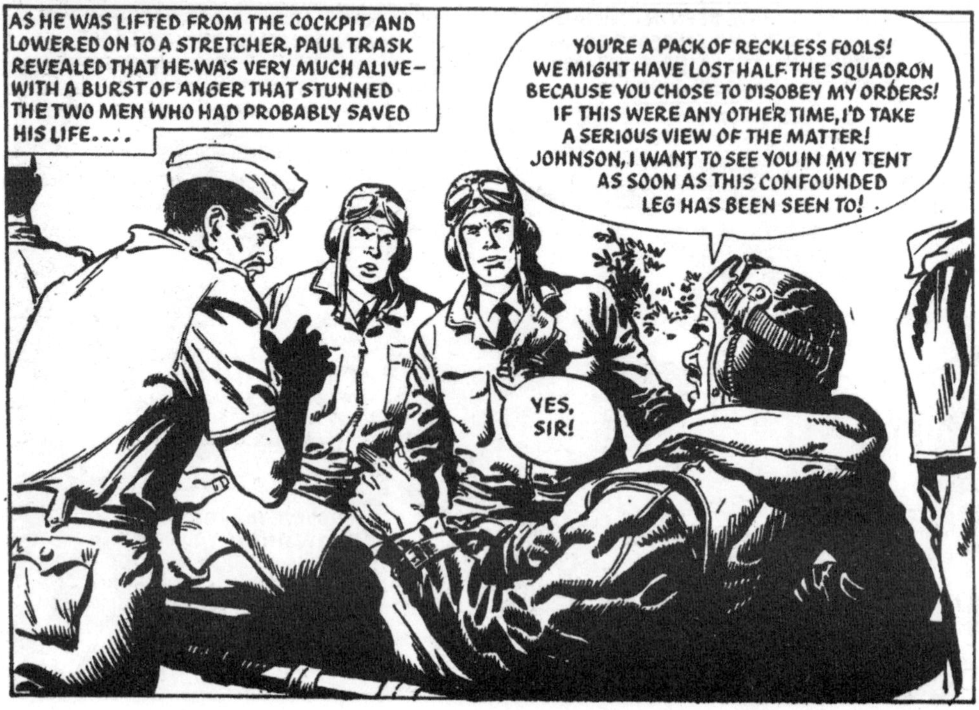
AS HE WAS LIFTED FROM THE COCKPIT AND LOWERED ON TO A STRETCHER, PAUL TRASK REVEALED THAT HE WAS VERY MUCH ALIVE—WITH A BURST OF ANGER THAT STUNNED THE TWO MEN WHO HAD PROBABLY SAVED HIS LIFE.....
YOU'RE A PACK OF RECKLESS FOOLS! WE MIGHT HAVE LOST HALF THE SQUADRON BECAUSE YOU CHOSE TO DISOBEY MY ORDERS! IF THIS WERE ANY OTHER TIME, I'D TAKE A SERIOUS VIEW OF THE MATTER! JOHNSON, I WANT TO SEE YOU IN MY TENT AS SOON AS THIS CONFOUNDED LEG HAS BEEN SEEN TO!
YES, SIR!

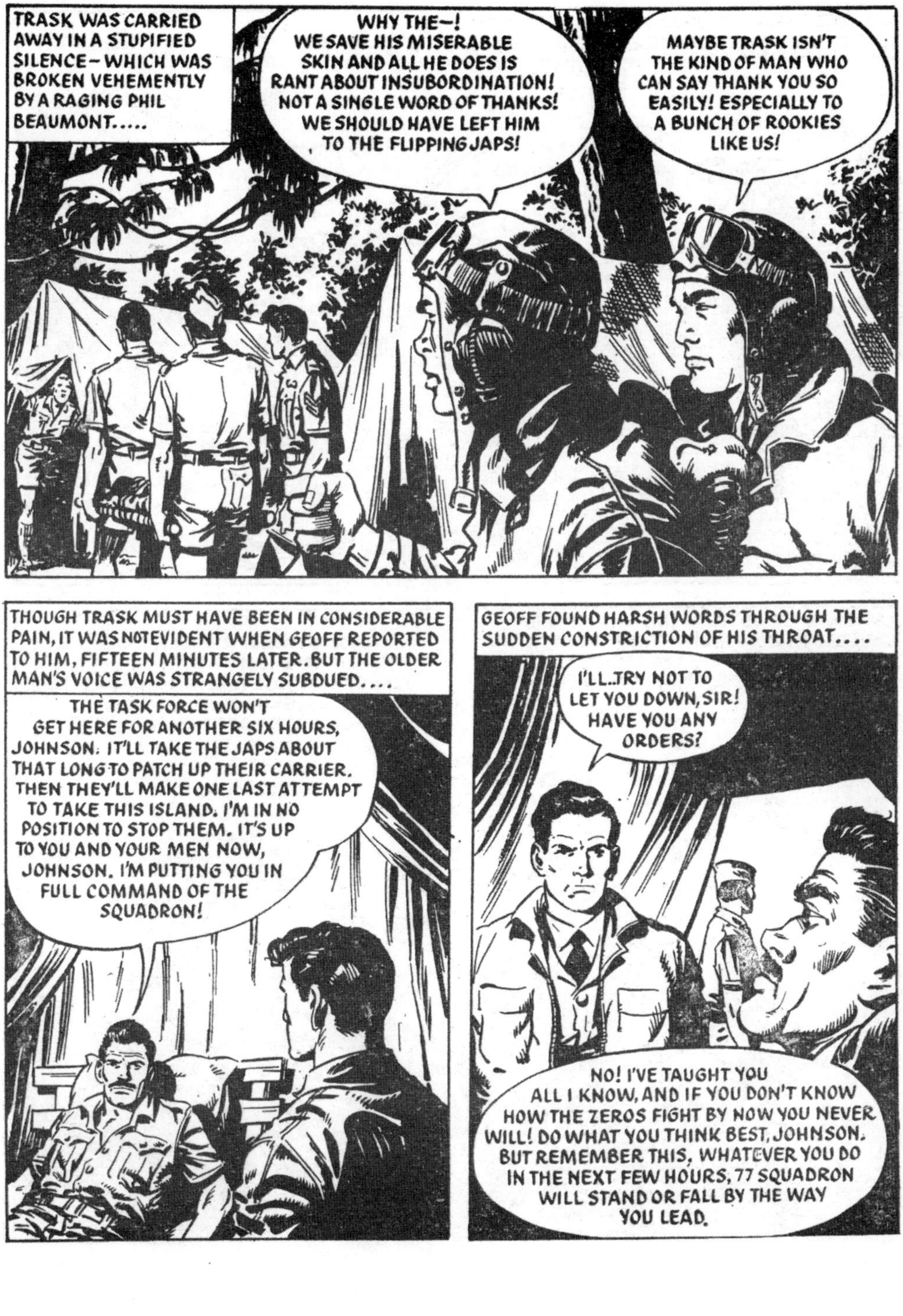
TRASK WAS CARRIED AWAY IN A STUPIFIED SILENCE – WHICH WAS BROKEN VEHEMENTLY BY A RAGING PHIL BEAUMONT.....
WHY THE–! WE SAVE HIS MISERABLE SKIN AND ALL HE DOES IS RANT ABOUT INSUBORDINATION! NOT A SINGLE WORD OF THANKS! WE SHOULD HAVE LEFT HIM TO THE FLIPPING JAPS!
MAYBE TRASK ISN'T THE KIND OF MAN WHO CAN SAY THANK YOU SO EASILY! ESPECIALLY TO A BUNCH OF ROOKIES LIKE US!
THOUGH TRASK MUST HAVE BEEN IN CONSIDERABLE PAIN, IT WAS NOT EVIDENT WHEN GEOFF REPORTED TO HIM, FIFTEEN MINUTES LATER. BUT THE OLDER MAN'S VOICE WAS STRANGELY SUBDUED....
THE TASK FORCE WON'T GET HERE FOR ANOTHER SIX HOURS, JOHNSON. IT'LL TAKE THE JAPS ABOUT THAT LONG TO PATCH UP THEIR CARRIER. THEN THEY'LL MAKE ONE LAST ATTEMPT TO TAKE THIS ISLAND. I'M IN NO POSITION TO STOP THEM. IT'S UP TO YOU AND YOUR MEN NOW, JOHNSON. I'M PUTTING YOU IN FULL COMMAND OF THE SQUADRON!
GEOFF FOUND HARSH WORDS THROUGH THE SUDDEN CONSTRICTION OF HIS THROAT....
I'LL..TRY NOT TO LET YOU DOWN, SIR! HAVE YOU ANY ORDERS?
NO! I'VE TAUGHT YOU ALL I KNOW, AND IF YOU DON'T KNOW HOW THE ZEROS FIGHT BY NOW YOU NEVER WILL! DO WHAT YOU THINK BEST, JOHNSON. BUT REMEMBER THIS, WHATEVER YOU DO IN THE NEXT FEW HOURS, 77 SQUADRON WILL STAND OR FALL BY THE WAY YOU LEAD.

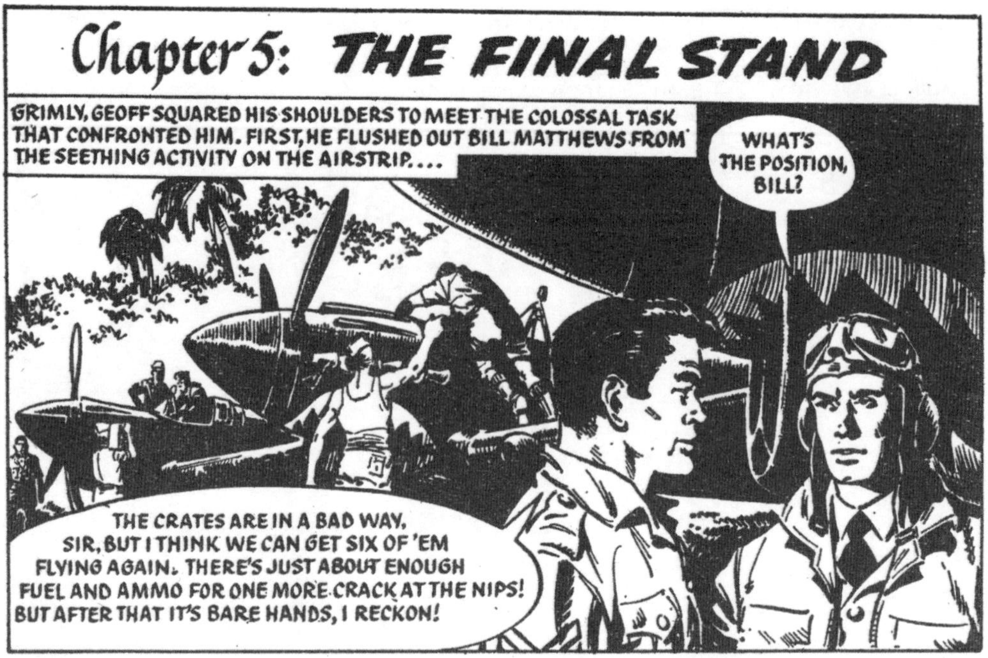
Chapter 5: THE FINAL STAND
GRIMLY, GEOFF SQUARED HIS SHOULDERS TO MEET THE COLOSSAL TASK THAT CONFRONTED HIM. FIRST, HE FLUSHED OUT BILL MATTHEWS FROM THE SEETHING ACTIVITY ON THE AIRSTRIP....
WHAT'S THE POSITION, BILL?
THE CRATES ARE IN A BAD WAY, SIR, BUT I THINK WE CAN GET SIX OF 'EM FLYING AGAIN. THERE'S JUST ABOUT ENOUGH FUEL AND AMMO FOR ONE MORE CRACK AT THE NIPS! BUT AFTER THAT IT'S BARE HANDS, I RECKON!

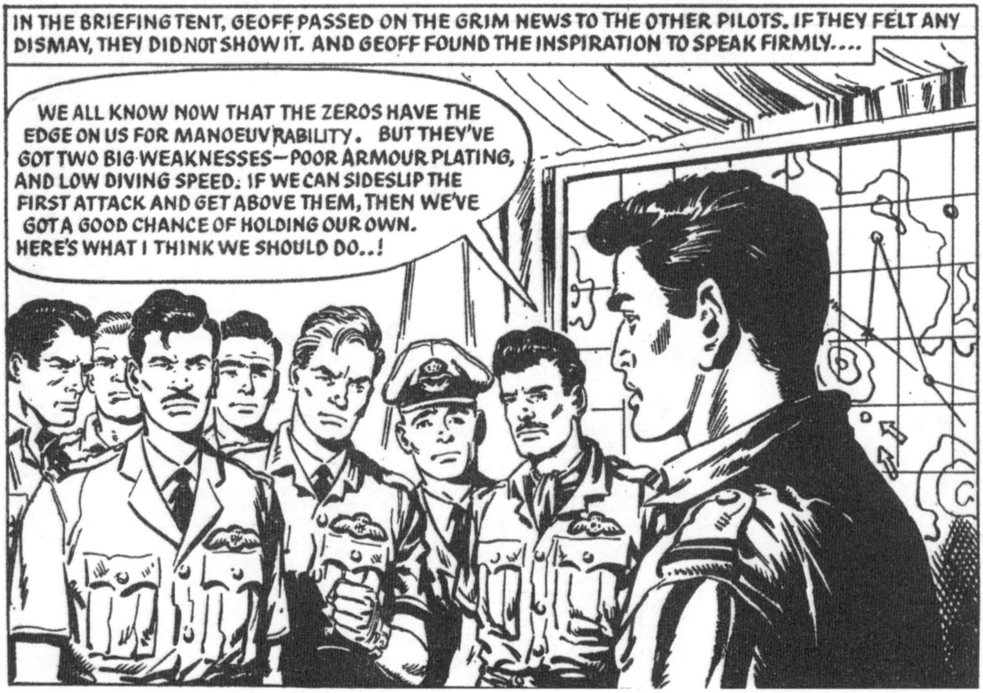
IN THE BRIEFING TENT, GEOFF PASSED ON THE GRIM NEWS TO THE OTHER PILOTS. IF THEY FELT ANY DISMAY, THEY DID NOT SHOW IT. AND GEOFF FOUND THE INSPIRATION TO SPEAK FIRMLY....
WE ALL KNOW NOW THAT THE ZEROS HAVE THE EDGE ON US FOR MANOEUV'RABILITY. BUT THEY'VE GOT TWO BIG WEAKNESSES—POOR ARMOUR PLATING, AND LOW DIVING SPEED. IF WE CAN SIDESLIP THE FIRST ATTACK AND GET ABOVE THEM, THEN WE'VE GOT A GOOD CHANCE OF HOLDING OUR OWN. HERE'S WHAT I THINK WE SHOULD DO..!

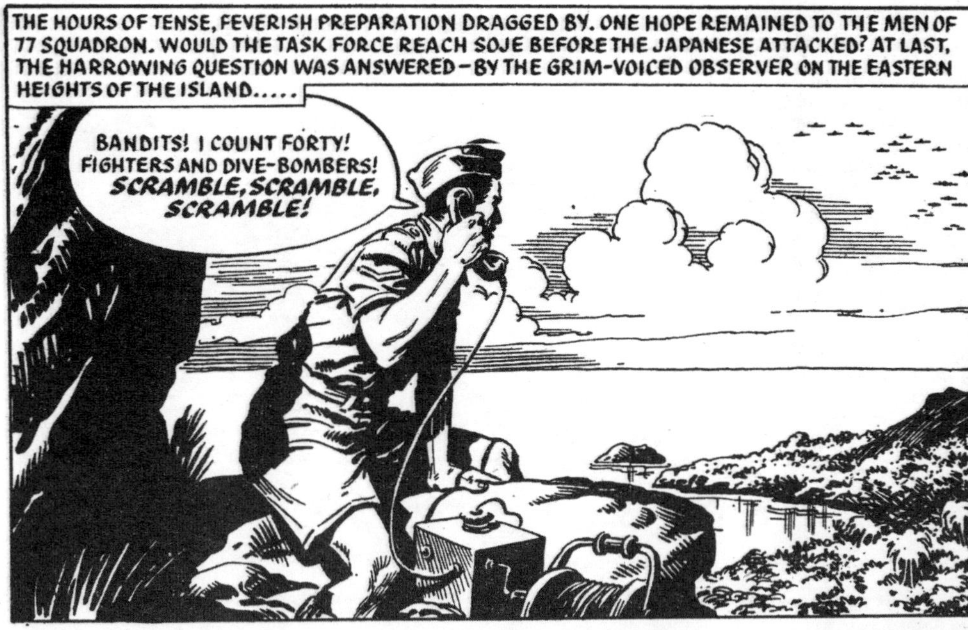
THE HOURS OF TENSE, FEVERISH PREPARATION DRAGGED BY. ONE HOPE REMAINED TO THE MEN OF 77 SQUADRON. WOULD THE TASK FORCE REACH SOJE BEFORE THE JAPANESE ATTACKED? AT LAST, THE HARROWING QUESTION WAS ANSWERED – BY THE GRIM-VOICED OBSERVER ON THE EASTERN HEIGHTS OF THE ISLAND.....
BANDITS! I COUNT FORTY! FIGHTERS AND DIVE-BOMBERS! SCRAMBLE, SCRAMBLE, SCRAMBLE!

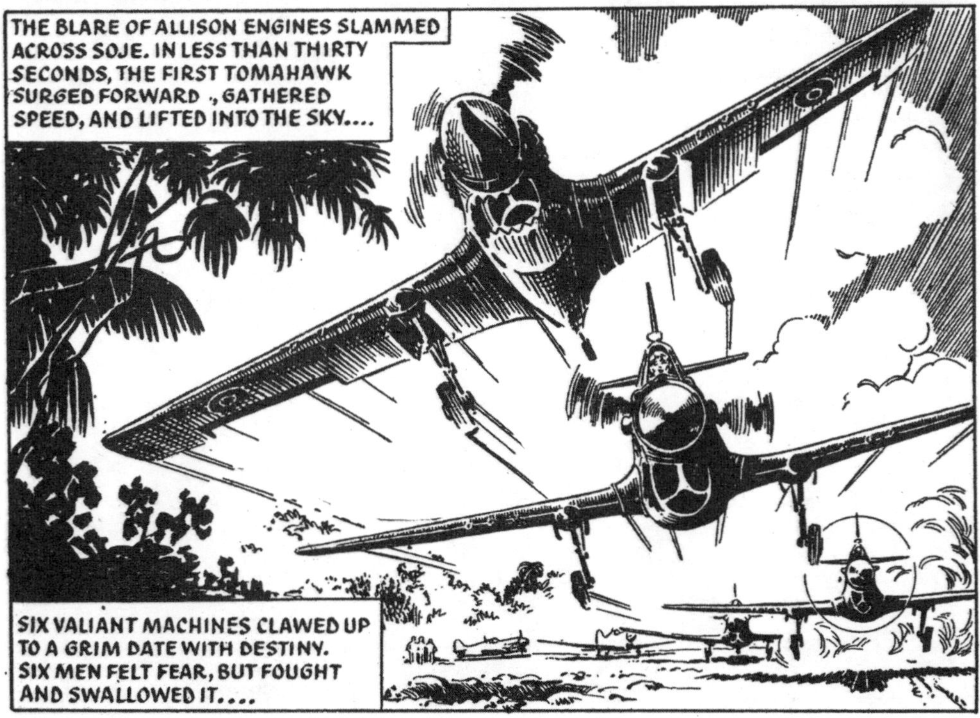
THE BLARE OF ALLISON ENGINES SLAMMED ACROSS SOJE. IN LESS THAN THIRTY SECONDS, THE FIRST TOMAHAWK SURGED FORWARD ., GATHERED SPEED, AND LIFTED INTO THE SKY....
SIX VALIANT MACHINES CLAWED UP TO A GRIM DATE WITH DESTINY. SIX MEN FELT FEAR, BUT FOUGHT AND SWALLOWED IT....

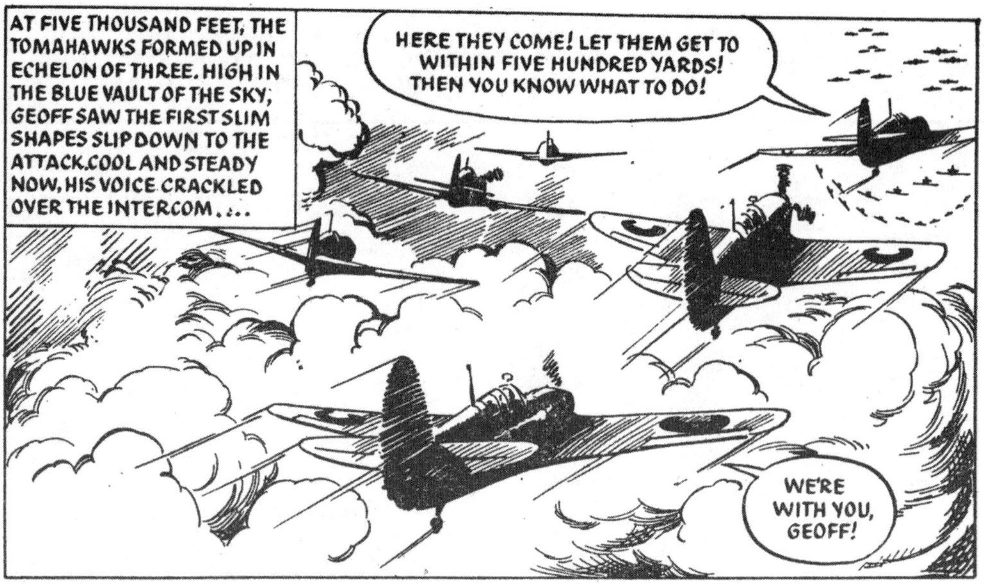
AT FIVE THOUSAND FEET, THE TOMAHAWKS FORMED UP IN ECHELON OF THREE. HIGH IN THE BLUE VAULT OF THE SKY, GEOFF SAW THE FIRST SLIM SHAPES SLIP DOWN TO THE ATTACK. COOL AND STEADY NOW, HIS VOICE CRACKLED OVER THE INTERCOM....
HERE THEY COME! LET THEM GET TO WITHIN FIVE HUNDRED YARDS! THEN YOU KNOW WHAT TO DO!
WE'RE WITH YOU, GEOFF!

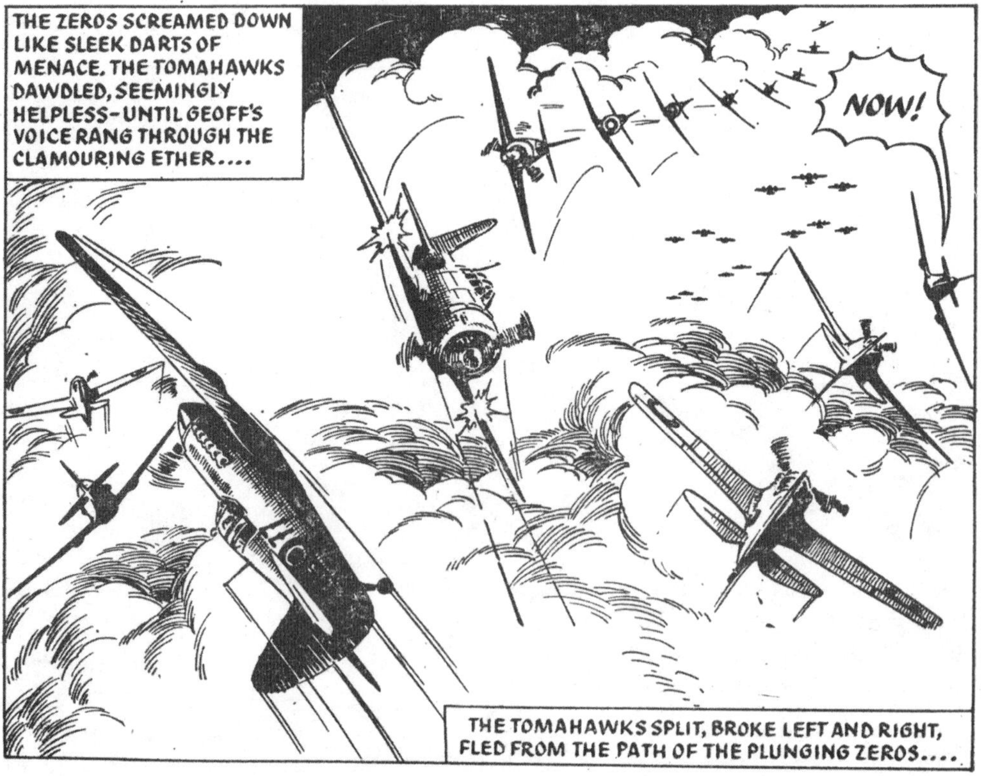
THE ZEROS SCREAMED DOWN LIKE SLEEK DARTS OF MENACE. THE TOMAHAWKS DAWDLED, SEEMINGLY HELPLESS–UNTIL GEOFF'S VOICE RANG THROUGH THE CLAMOURING ETHER....
NOW!
THE TOMAHAWKS SPLIT, BROKE LEFT AND RIGHT, FLED FROM THE PATH OF THE PLUNGING ZEROS....

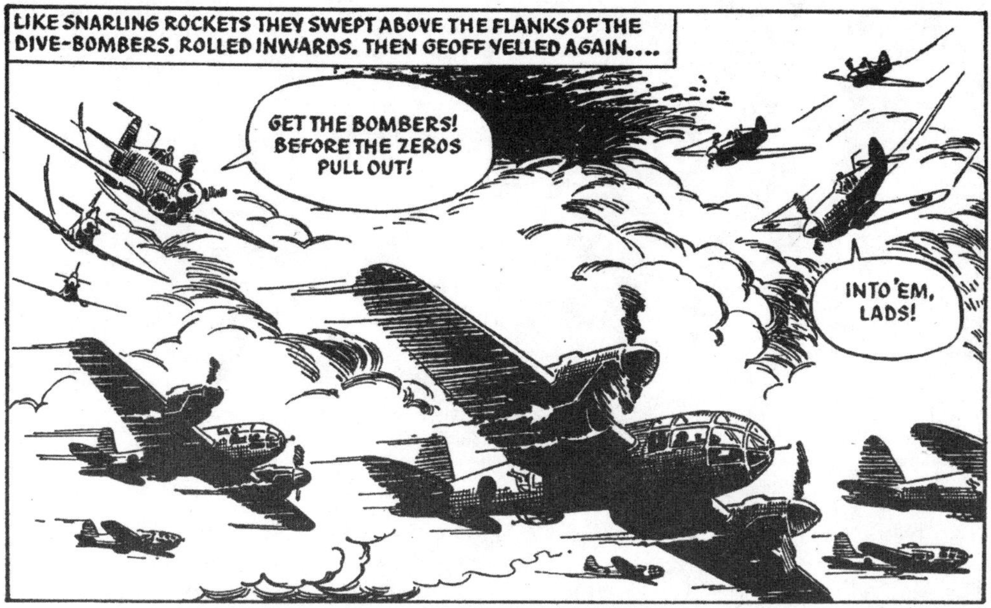
LIKE SNARLING ROCKETS THEY SWEPT ABOVE THE FLANKS OF THE DIVE-BOMBERS. ROLLED INWARDS. THEN GEOFF YELLED AGAIN....
GET THE BOMBERS! BEFORE THE ZEROS PULL OUT!
INTO 'EM, LADS!

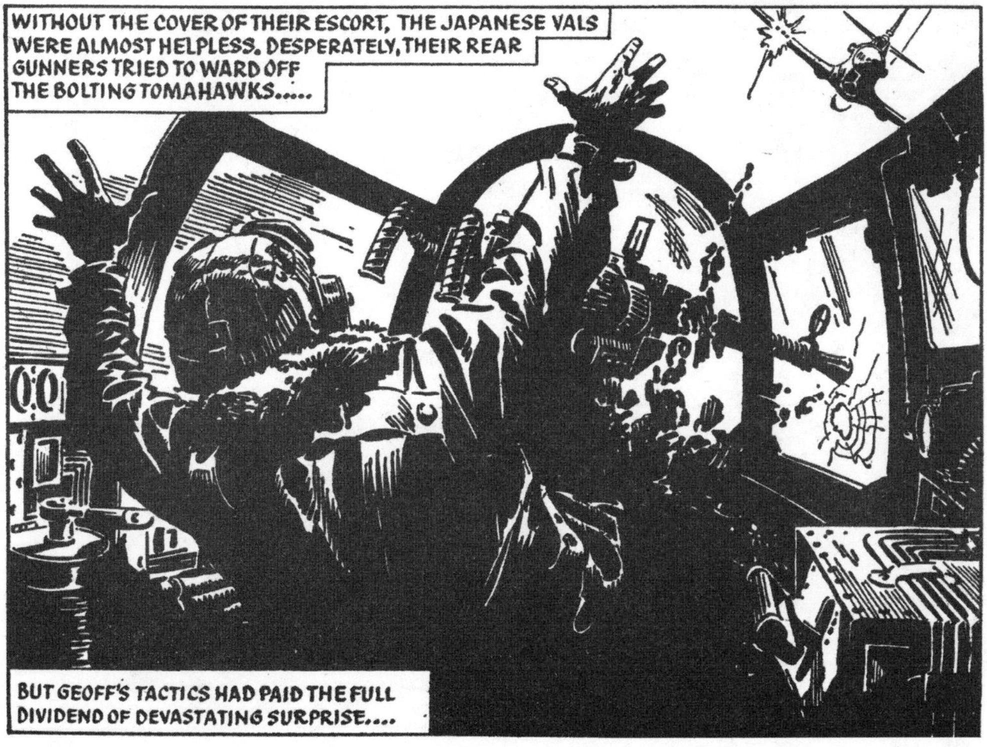
WITHOUT THE COVER OF THEIR ESCORT, THE JAPANESE VALS WERE ALMOST HELPLESS. DESPERATELY, THEIR REAR GUNNERS TRIED TO WARD OFF THE BOLTING TOMAHAWKS.....
BUT GEOFF'S TACTICS HAD PAID THE FULL DIVIDEND OF DEVASTATING SURPRISE....

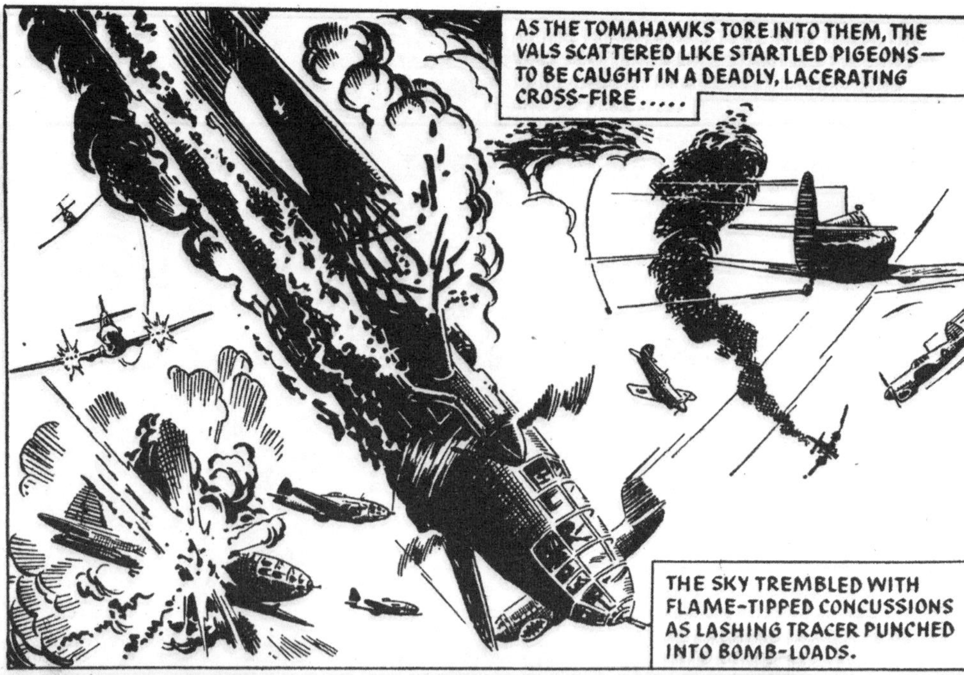
AS THE TOMAHAWKS TORE INTO THEM, THE VALS SCATTERED LIKE STARTLED PIGEONS— TO BE CAUGHT IN A DEADLY, LACERATING CROSS-FIRE.....
THE SKY TREMBLED WITH FLAME-TIPPED CONCUSSIONS AS LASHING TRACER PUNCHED INTO BOMB-LOADS.

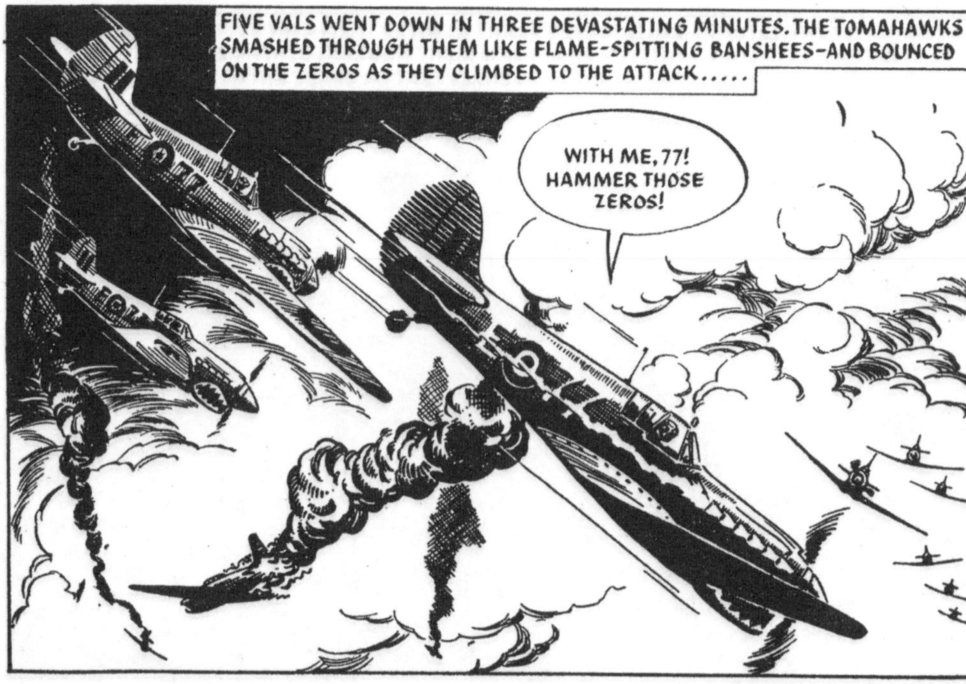
FIVE VALS WENT DOWN IN THREE DEVASTATING MINUTES. THE TOMAHAWKS SMASHED THROUGH THEM LIKE FLAME-SPITTING BANSHEES-AND BOUNCED ON THE ZEROS AS THEY CLIMBED TO THE ATTACK.....
WITH ME, 77! HAMMER THOSE ZEROS!

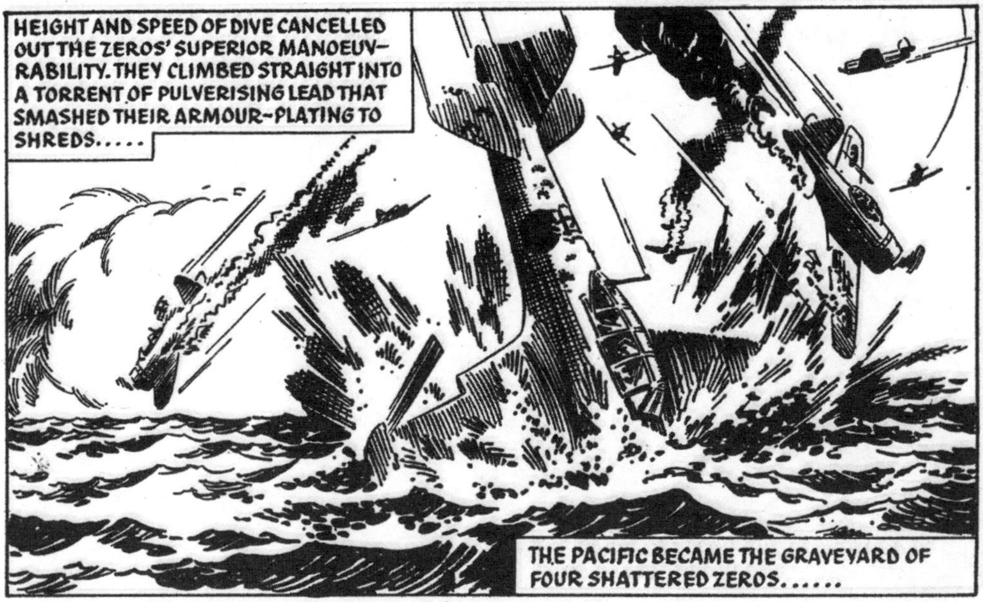
HEIGHT AND SPEED OF DIVE CANCELLED OUT THE ZEROS' SUPERIOR MANOEUV-RABILITY. THEY CLIMBED STRAIGHT INTO A TORRENT OF PULVERISING LEAD THAT SMASHED THEIR ARMOUR-PLATING TO SHREDS.....
THE PACIFIC BECAME THE GRAVEYARD OF FOUR SHATTERED ZEROS......

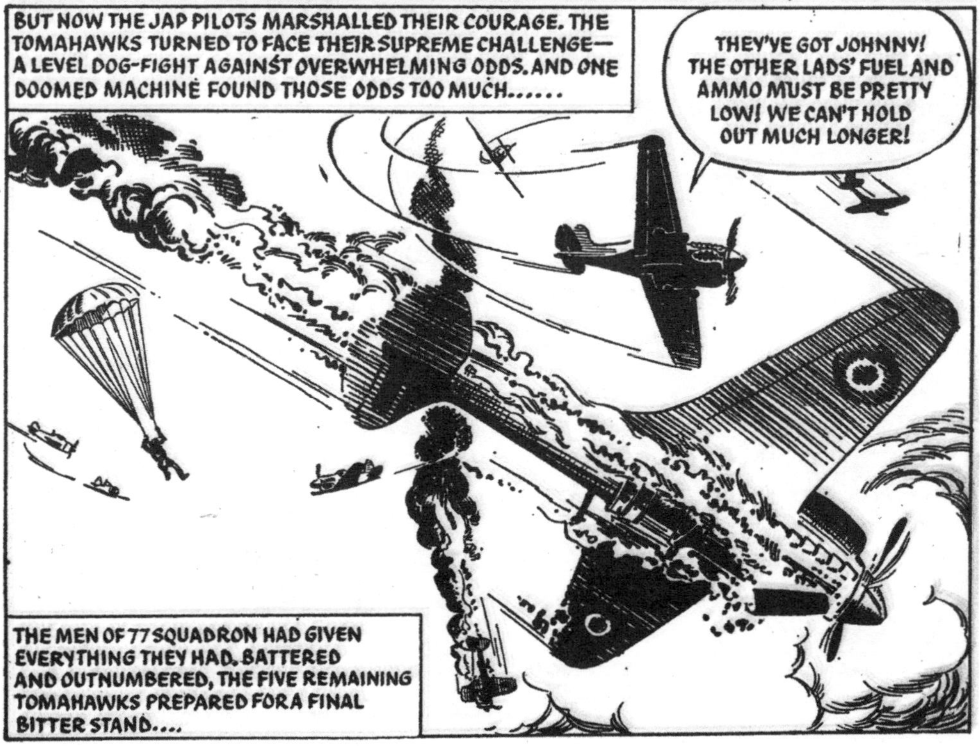
BUT NOW THE JAP PILOTS MARSHALLED THEIR COURAGE. THE TOMAHAWKS TURNED TO FACE THEIR SUPREME CHALLENGE—A LEVEL DOG-FIGHT AGAINST OVERWHELMING ODDS. AND ONE DOOMED MACHINE FOUND THOSE ODDS TOO MUCH......
THEY'VE GOT JOHNNY! THE OTHER LADS' FUEL AND AMMO MUST BE PRETTY LOW! WE CAN'T HOLD OUT MUCH LONGER!
THE MEN OF 77 SQUADRON HAD GIVEN EVERYTHING THEY HAD. BATTERED AND OUTNUMBERED, THE FIVE REMAINING TOMAHAWKS PREPARED FOR A FINAL BITTER STAND....

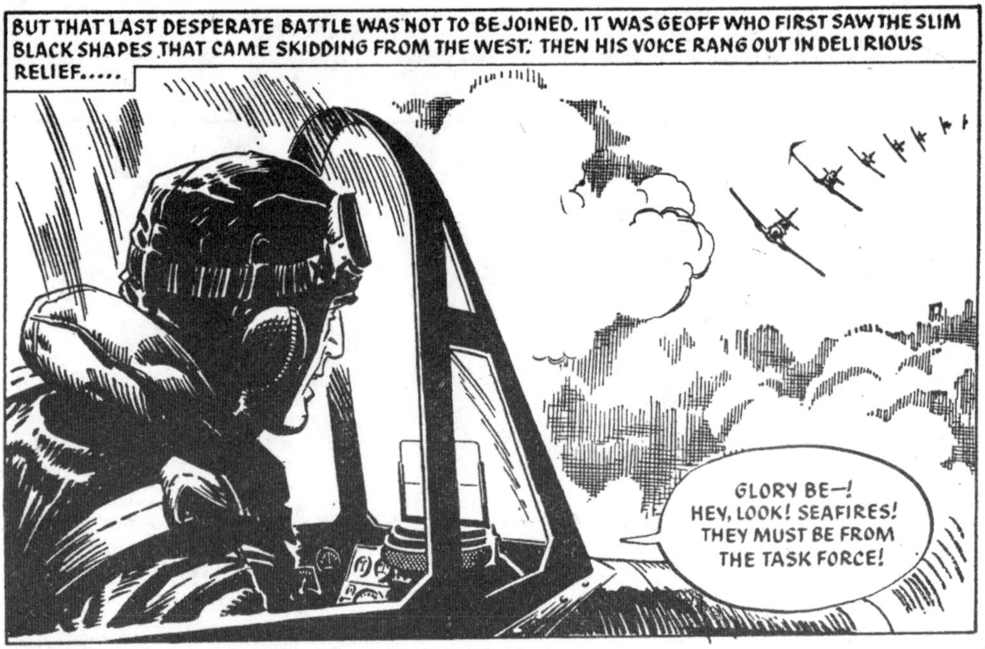
BUT THAT LAST DESPERATE BATTLE WAS NOT TO BE JOINED. IT WAS GEOFF WHO FIRST SAW THE SLIM BLACK SHAPES THAT CAME SKIDDING FROM THE WEST: THEN HIS VOICE RANG OUT IN DELIRIOUS RELIEF.....
GLORY BE—! HEY, LOOK! SEAFIRES! THEY MUST BE FROM THE TASK FORCE!

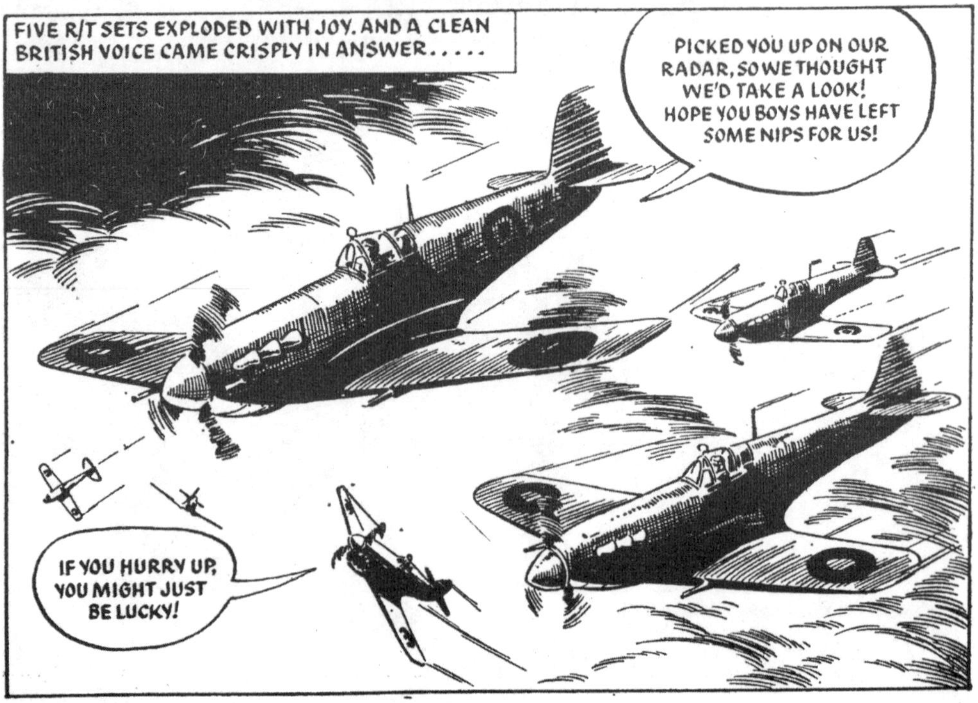
FIVE R/T SETS EXPLODED WITH JOY. AND A CLEAN BRITISH VOICE CAME CRISPLY IN ANSWER.....
PICKED YOU UP ON OUR RADAR, SO WE THOUGHT WE'D TAKE A LOOK! HOPE YOU BOYS HAVE LEFT SOME NIPS FOR US!
IF YOU HURRY UP, YOU MIGHT JUST BE LUCKY!

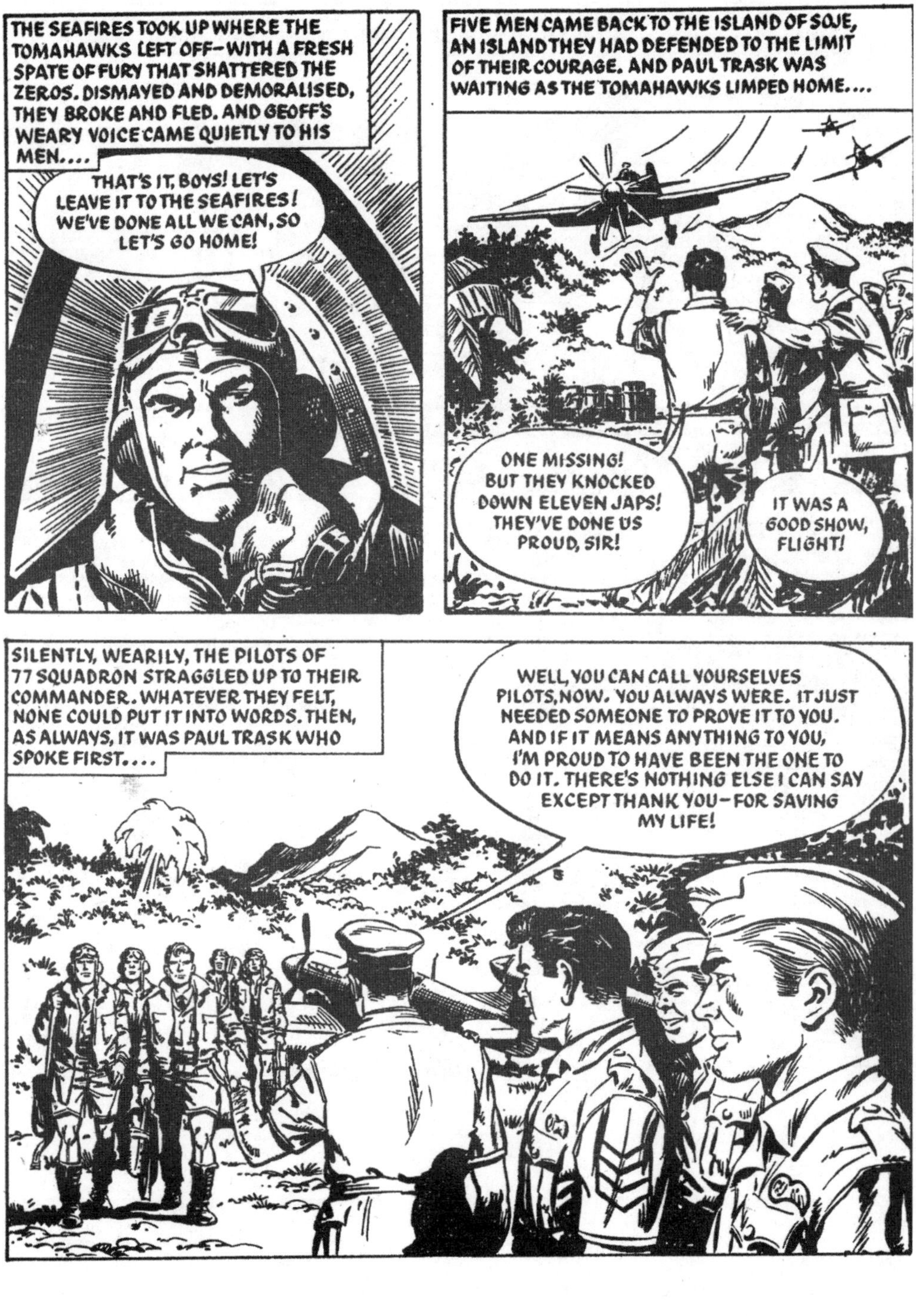
THE SEAFIRES TOOK UP WHERE THE TOMAHAWKS LEFT OFF—WITH A FRESH SPATE OF FURY THAT SHATTERED THE ZEROS. DISMAYED AND DEMORALISED, THEY BROKE AND FLED. AND GEOFF'S WEARY VOICE CAME QUIETLY TO HIS MEN....
THAT'S IT, BOYS! LET'S LEAVE IT TO THE SEAFIRES! WE'VE DONE ALL WE CAN, SO LET'S GO HOME!
FIVE MEN CAME BACK TO THE ISLAND OF SOJE, AN ISLAND THEY HAD DEFENDED TO THE LIMIT OF THEIR COURAGE. AND PAUL TRASK WAS WAITING AS THE TOMAHAWKS LIMPED HOME....
ONE MISSING! BUT THEY KNOCKED DOWN ELEVEN JAPS! THEY'VE DONE US PROUD, SIR!
IT WAS A GOOD SHOW, FLIGHT!
SILENTLY, WEARILY, THE PILOTS OF 77 SQUADRON STRAGGLED UP TO THEIR COMMANDER. WHATEVER THEY FELT, NONE COULD PUT IT INTO WORDS. THEN, AS ALWAYS, IT WAS PAUL TRASK WHO SPOKE FIRST....
WELL, YOU CAN CALL YOURSELVES PILOTS, NOW. YOU ALWAYS WERE. IT JUST NEEDED SOMEONE TO PROVE IT TO YOU. AND IF IT MEANS ANYTHING TO YOU, I'M PROUD TO HAVE BEEN THE ONE TO DO IT. THERE'S NOTHING ELSE I CAN SAY EXCEPT THANK YOU—FOR SAVING MY LIFE!

IT WAS AS IF THEY SAW PAUL TRASK FOR THE FIRST TIME. ALWAYS RUGGED, SOMETIMES CALLOUS, THERE WAS NO PLACE IN HIS MENTALITY FOR EMOTION OR SENTIMENT. IF SUCH A MAN GAVE PRAISE, THEN IT WAS RICHLY DESERVED. AND AS SUCH THEY CHERISHED IT—EVEN PHIL BEAUMONT....

I KNOW HOW HARD IT WAS FOR YOU TO SAY THAT, SIR! ABOUT AS HARD AS IT WAS FOR US TO GET USED TO YOU! BUT WHILE WE WERE HATING YOU, THERE WASN'T MUCH TIME TO WORRY ABOUT OURSELVES, OR THE JAPS. I SUPPOSE THAT WAS YOUR IDEA, ALL ALONG? YOU TAUGHT US WELL, SIR! EVEN IF IT WAS THE HARD WAY!

AN HOUR LATER, TASK FORCE 83 PASSED CLOSE TO THE SHORE OF SOJE ISLAND, ON ITS WAY TO STRIKE AT THE TAIWAN ATOLLS, THE SPRINGBOARD TO AN ALL-OUT ASSAULT ON THE SOLOMON ISLANDS. EVERY MAN IN 77 SQUADRON WHO COULD WALK OR HOBBLE WAS THERE TO WATCH AND WAVE. MEN LIKE PAUL TRASK AND GEOFF JOHNSON, WHO IN THEIR VARIOUS WAYS, HAD BROUGHT A HANDFUL OF MEN AND THE PLANES THAT THEY FLEW, TO THE HARD-WON SUMMIT OF COURAGE AND MANHOOD ...

THEY'RE SALUTING YOU, JOHNSON! YOU'VE GIVEN THEM A FIGHTING CHANCE OF SMASHING THE JAPS! AND THAT'S ALL WE NEED FROM NOW ON! A FIGHTING CHANCE!

HERE COME THE SEAFIRES! AND JUST LISTEN TO THOSE SHIPS' SIRENS!

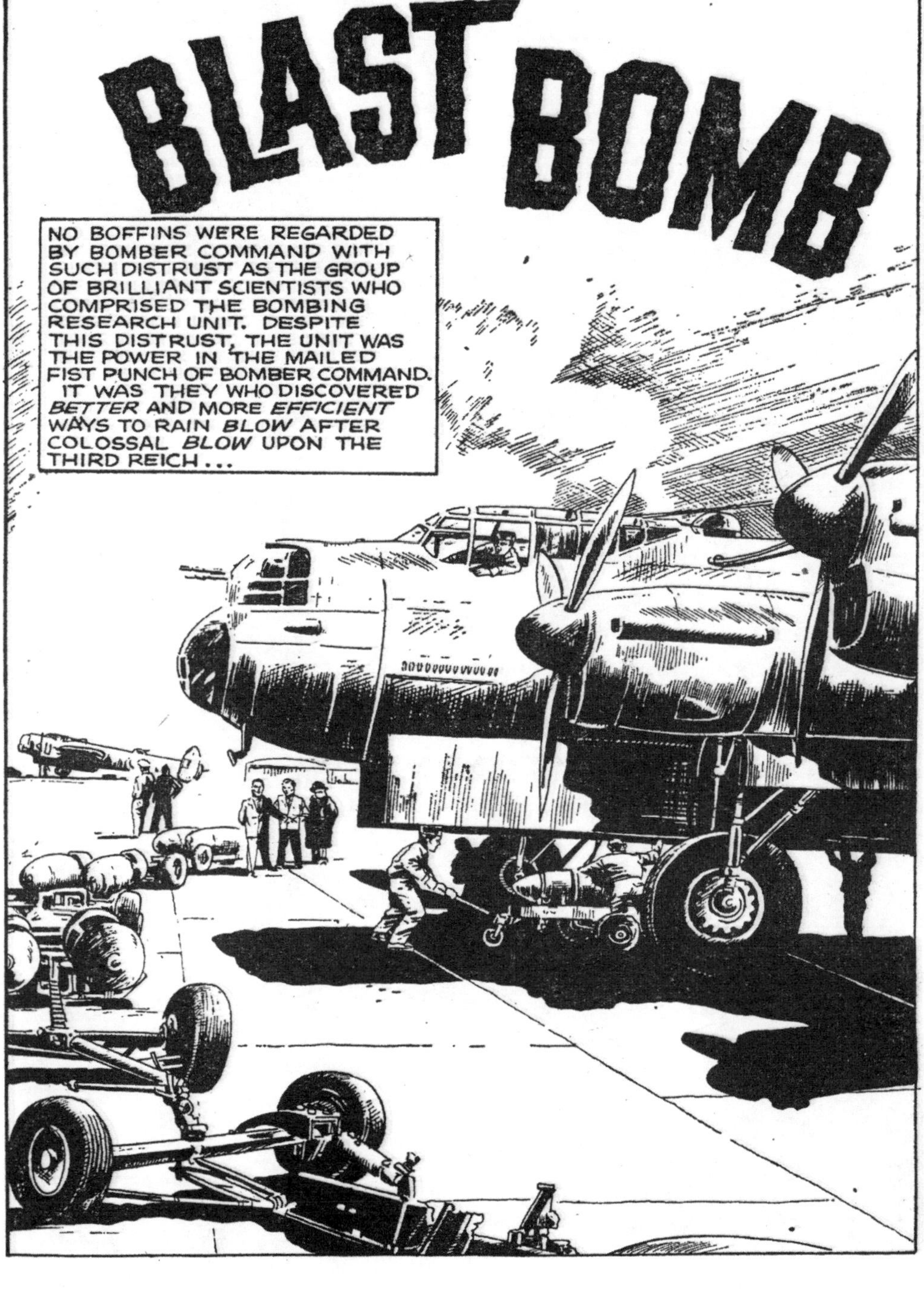
BLAST BOMB
NO BOFFINS WERE REGARDED BY BOMBER COMMAND WITH SUCH DISTRUST AS THE GROUP OF BRILLIANT SCIENTISTS WHO COMPRISED THE BOMBING RESEARCH UNIT. DESPITE THIS DISTRUST, THE UNIT WAS THE POWER IN THE MAILED FIST PUNCH OF BOMBER COMMAND. IT WAS THEY WHO DISCOVERED *BETTER* AND MORE *EFFICIENT* WAYS TO RAIN *BLOW* AFTER COLOSSAL *BLOW* UPON THE THIRD REICH...

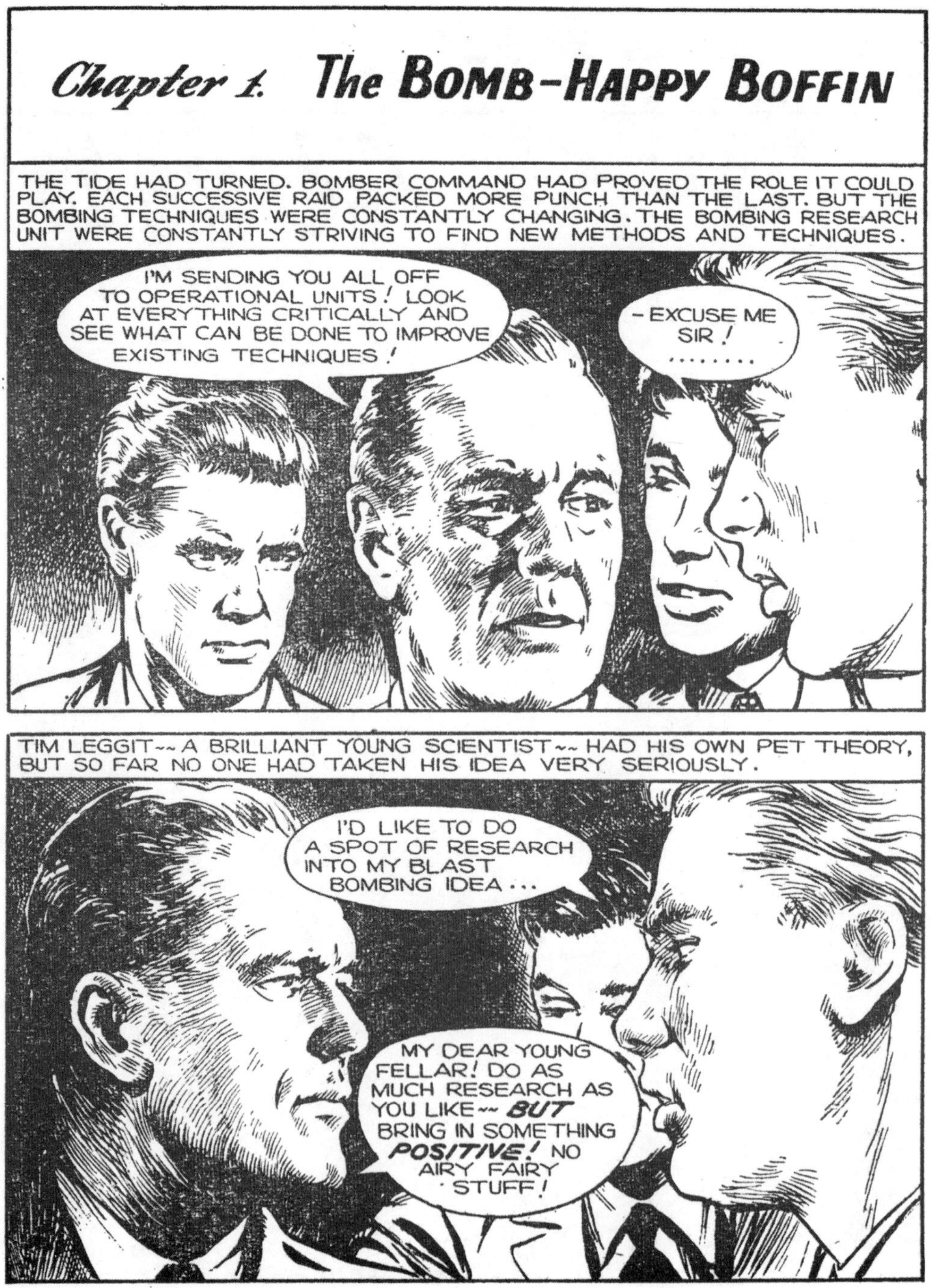
Chapter 1. The BOMB-HAPPY BOFFIN
THE TIDE HAD TURNED. BOMBER COMMAND HAD PROVED THE ROLE IT COULD PLAY. EACH SUCCESSIVE RAID PACKED MORE PUNCH THAN THE LAST. BUT THE BOMBING TECHNIQUES WERE CONSTANTLY CHANGING. THE BOMBING RESEARCH UNIT WERE CONSTANTLY STRIVING TO FIND NEW METHODS AND TECHNIQUES.
I'M SENDING YOU ALL OFF TO OPERATIONAL UNITS! LOOK AT EVERYTHING CRITICALLY AND SEE WHAT CAN BE DONE TO IMPROVE EXISTING TECHNIQUES!
-EXCUSE ME SIR! ....
TIM LEGGIT -- A BRILLIANT YOUNG SCIENTIST -- HAD HIS OWN PET THEORY, BUT SO FAR NO ONE HAD TAKEN HIS IDEA VERY SERIOUSLY.
I'D LIKE TO DO A SPOT OF RESEARCH INTO MY BLAST BOMBING IDEA...
MY DEAR YOUNG FELLAR! DO AS MUCH RESEARCH AS YOU LIKE -- BUT BRING IN SOMETHING POSITIVE! NO AIRY FAIRY STUFF!

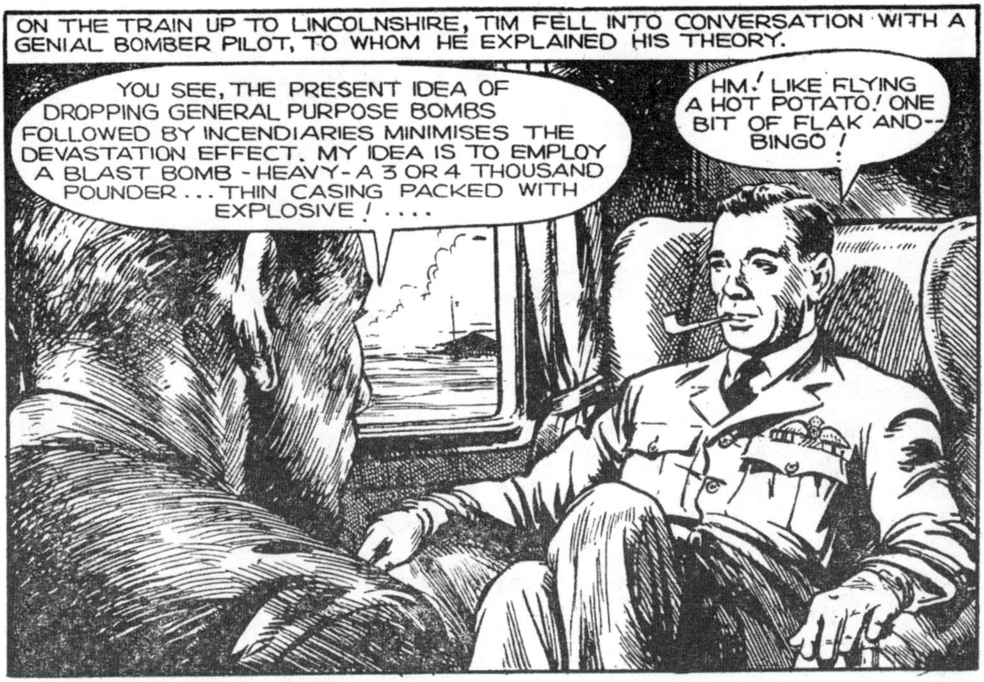
ON THE TRAIN UP TO LINCOLNSHIRE, TIM FELL INTO CONVERSATION WITH A GENIAL BOMBER PILOT, TO WHOM HE EXPLAINED HIS THEORY.
YOU SEE, THE PRESENT IDEA OF DROPPING GENERAL PURPOSE BOMBS FOLLOWED BY INCENDIARIES MINIMISES THE DEVASTATION EFFECT. MY IDEA IS TO EMPLOY A BLAST BOMB - HEAVY - A 3 OR 4 THOUSAND POUNDER ... THIN CASING PACKED WITH EXPLOSIVE! ....
HM! LIKE FLYING A HOT POTATO! ONE BIT OF FLAK AND-- BINGO!

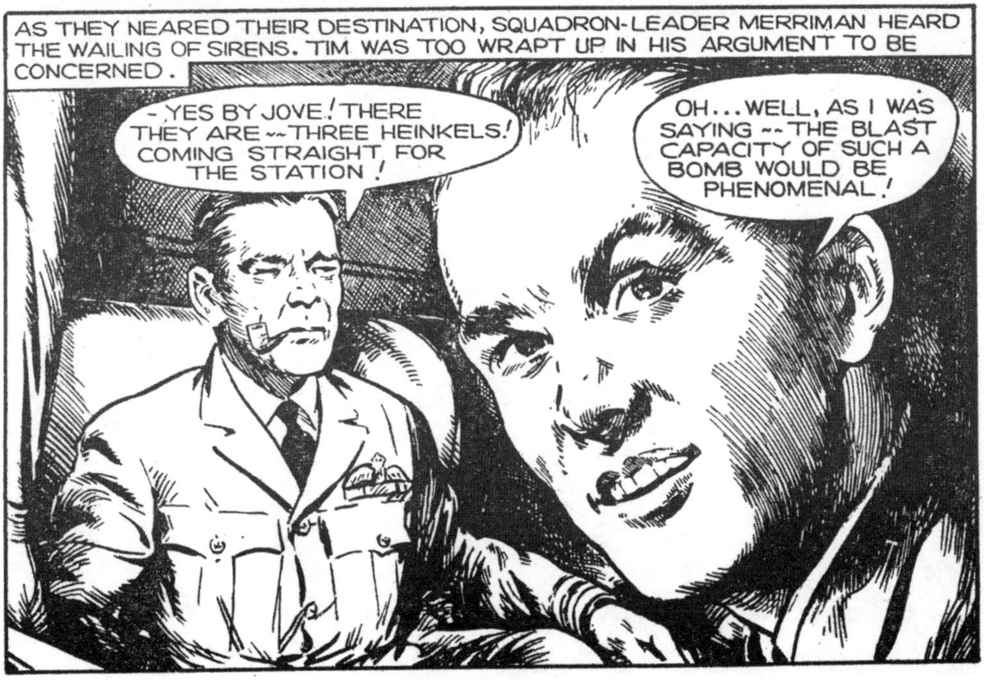
AS THEY NEARED THEIR DESTINATION, SQUADRON-LEADER MERRIMAN HEARD THE WAILING OF SIRENS. TIM WAS TOO WRAPT UP IN HIS ARGUMENT TO BE CONCERNED.
- YES BY JOVE! THERE THEY ARE -- THREE HEINKELS! COMING STRAIGHT FOR THE STATION!
OH ... WELL, AS I WAS SAYING -- THE BLAST CAPACITY OF SUCH A BOMB WOULD BE PHENOMENAL!

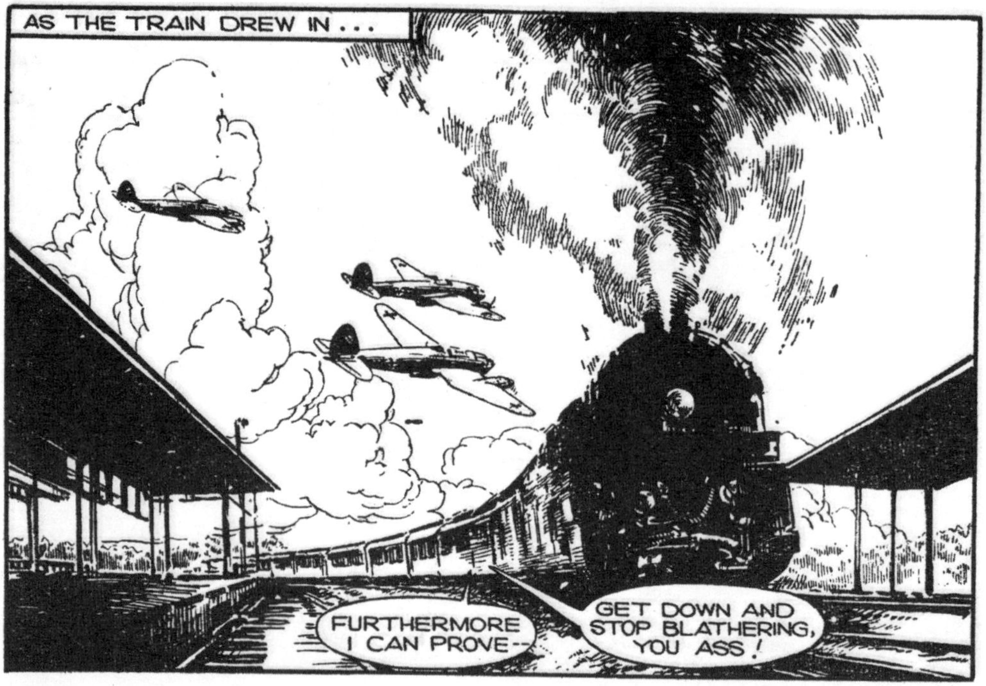
AS THE TRAIN DREW IN . . .
FURTHERMORE I CAN PROVE--
GET DOWN AND STOP BLATHERING, YOU ASS!

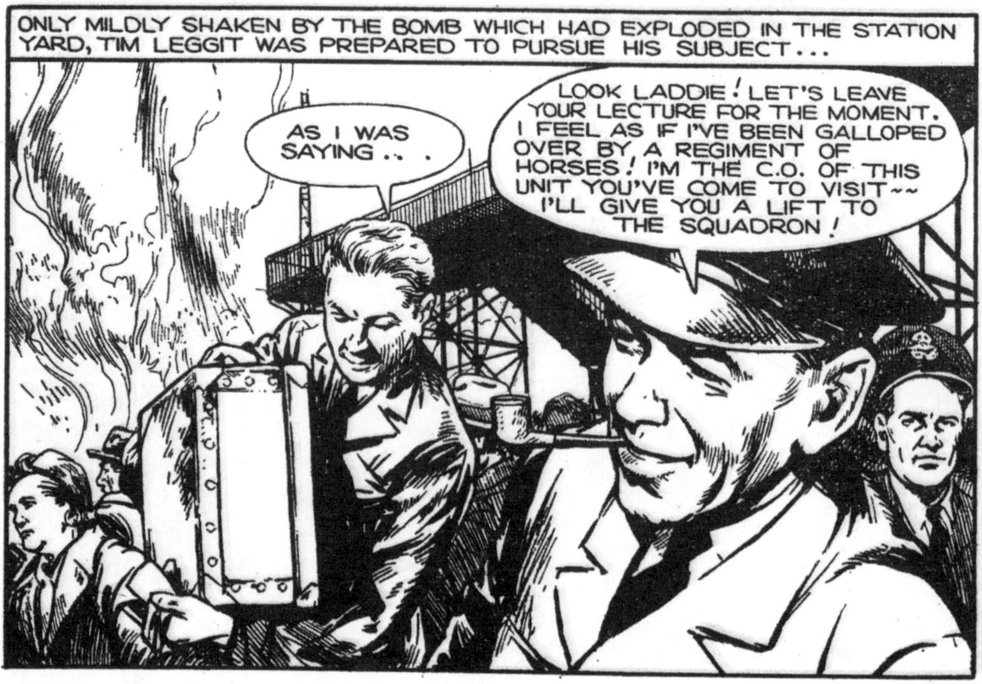
ONLY MILDLY SHAKEN BY THE BOMB WHICH HAD EXPLODED IN THE STATION YARD, TIM LEGGIT WAS PREPARED TO PURSUE HIS SUBJECT . . .
AS I WAS SAYING . . .
LOOK LADDIE! LET'S LEAVE YOUR LECTURE FOR THE MOMENT. I FEEL AS IF I'VE BEEN GALLOPED OVER BY A REGIMENT OF HORSES! I'M THE C.O. OF THIS UNIT YOU'VE COME TO VISIT-- I'LL GIVE YOU A LIFT TO THE SQUADRON!

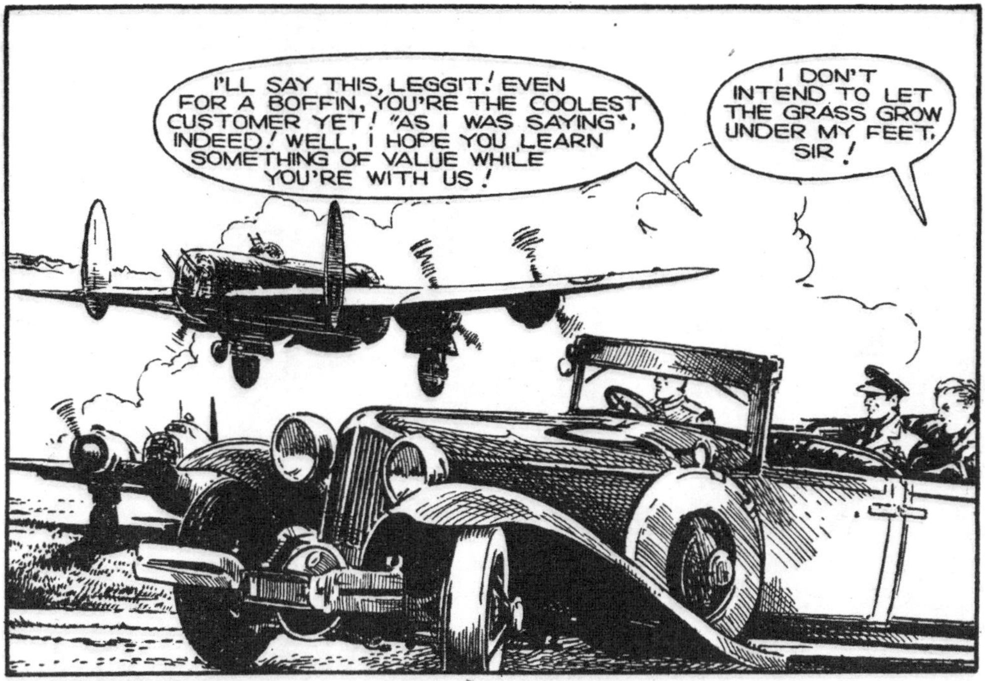
I'LL SAY THIS, LEGGIT! EVEN FOR A BOFFIN, YOU'RE THE COOLEST CUSTOMER YET! "AS I WAS SAYING", INDEED! WELL, I HOPE YOU LEARN SOMETHING OF VALUE WHILE YOU'RE WITH US!
I DON'T INTEND TO LET THE GRASS GROW UNDER MY FEET, SIR!

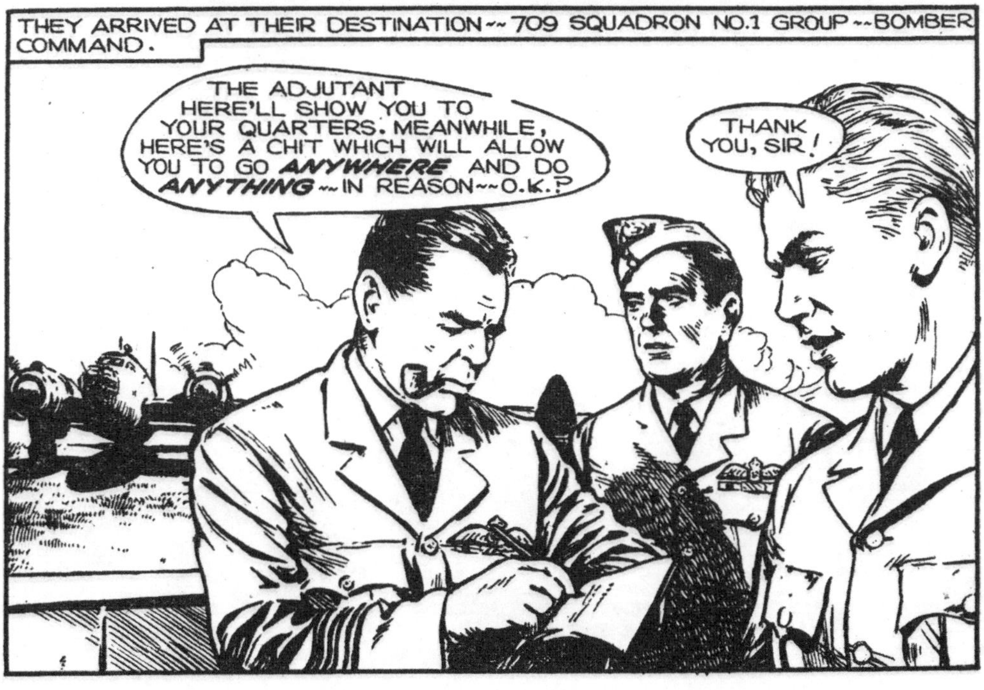
THEY ARRIVED AT THEIR DESTINATION--709 SQUADRON NO.1 GROUP--BOMBER COMMAND.
THE ADJUTANT HERE'LL SHOW YOU TO YOUR QUARTERS. MEANWHILE, HERE'S A CHIT WHICH WILL ALLOW YOU TO GO ANYWHERE AND DO ANYTHING--IN REASON--O.K.?
THANK YOU, SIR!

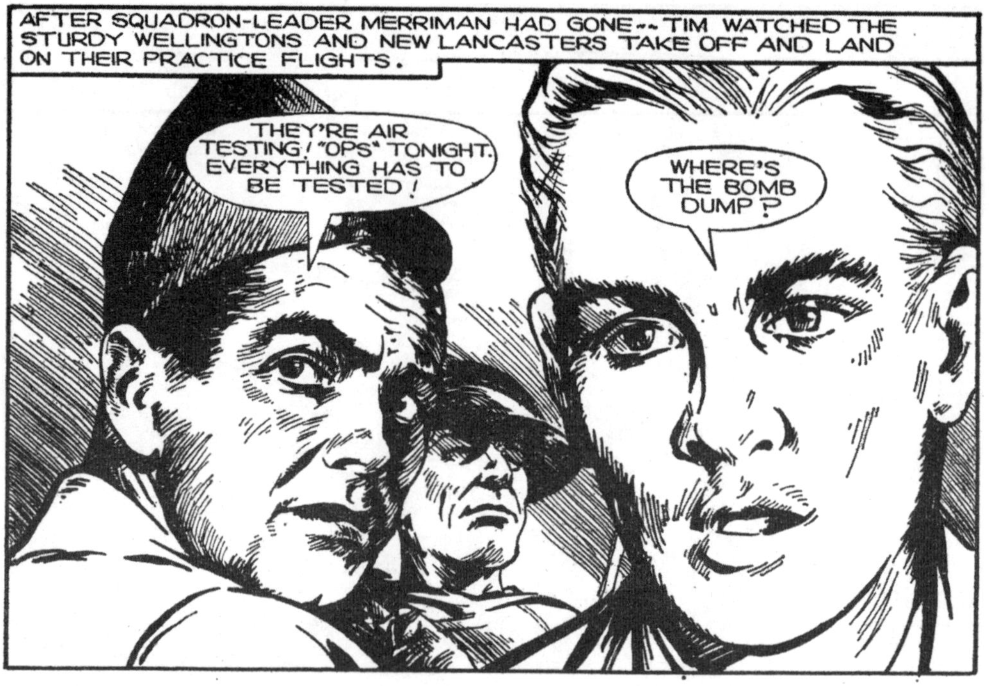
AFTER SQUADRON-LEADER MERRIMAN HAD GONE -- TIM WATCHED THE STURDY WELLINGTONS AND NEW LANCASTERS TAKE OFF AND LAND ON THEIR PRACTICE FLIGHTS.
THEY'RE AIR TESTING! "OPS" TONIGHT. EVERYTHING HAS TO BE TESTED!
WHERE'S THE BOMB DUMP?

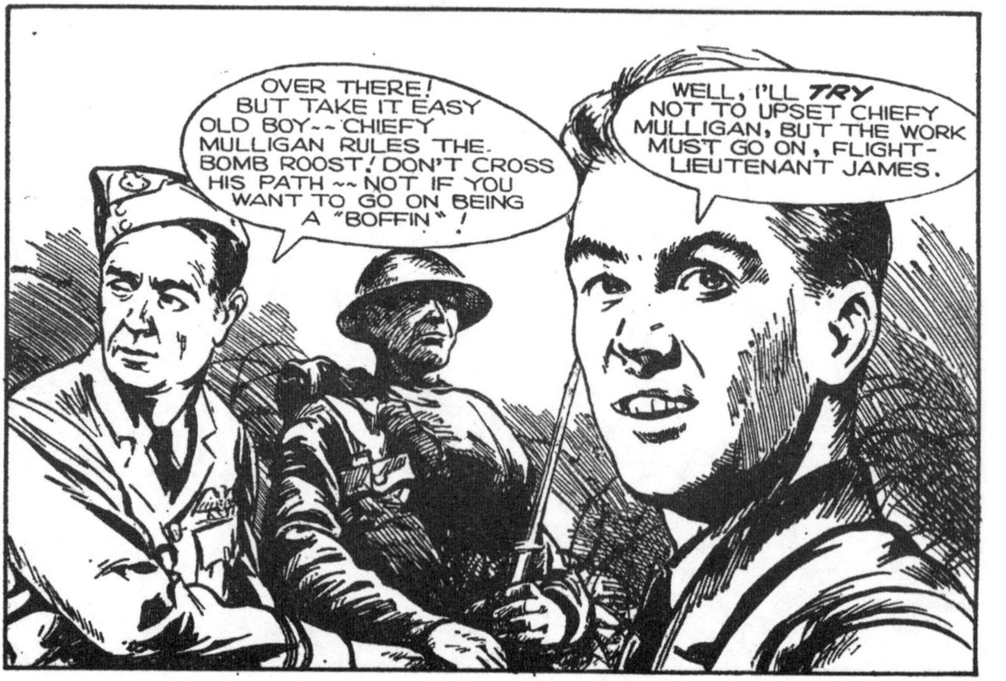
OVER THERE! BUT TAKE IT EASY OLD BOY -- CHIEFY MULLIGAN RULES THE BOMB ROOST! DON'T CROSS HIS PATH -- NOT IF YOU WANT TO GO ON BEING A "BOFFIN"!
WELL, I'LL TRY NOT TO UPSET CHIEFY MULLIGAN, BUT THE WORK MUST GO ON, FLIGHT-LIEUTENANT JAMES.

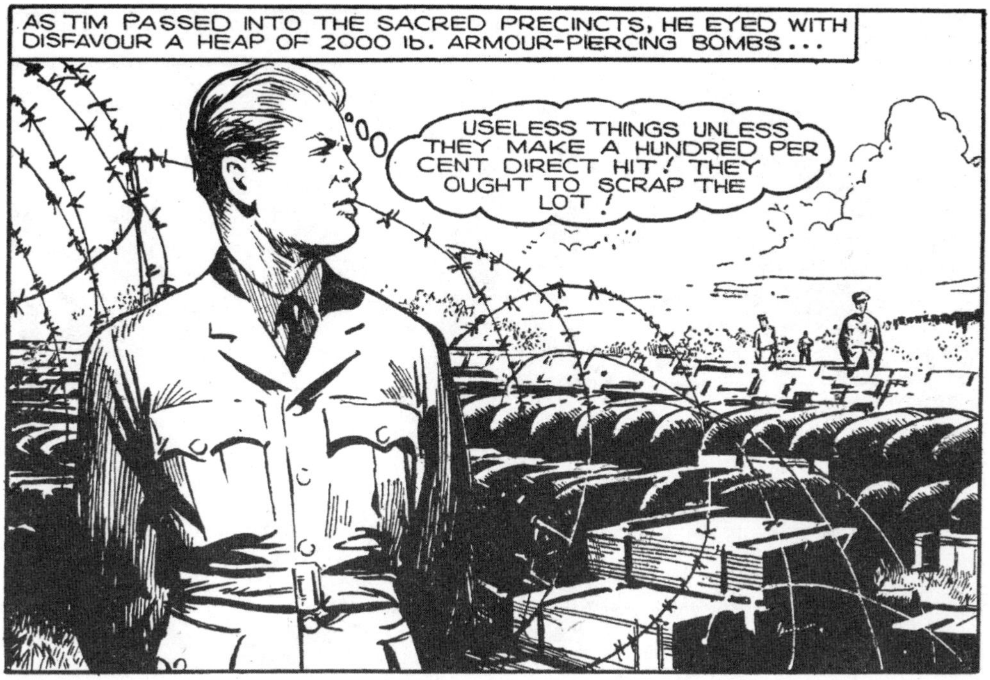
AS TIM PASSED INTO THE SACRED PRECINCTS, HE EYED WITH DISFAVOUR A HEAP OF 2000 lb. ARMOUR-PIERCING BOMBS . . .
USELESS THINGS UNLESS THEY MAKE A HUNDRED PER CENT DIRECT HIT! THEY OUGHT TO SCRAP THE LOT!

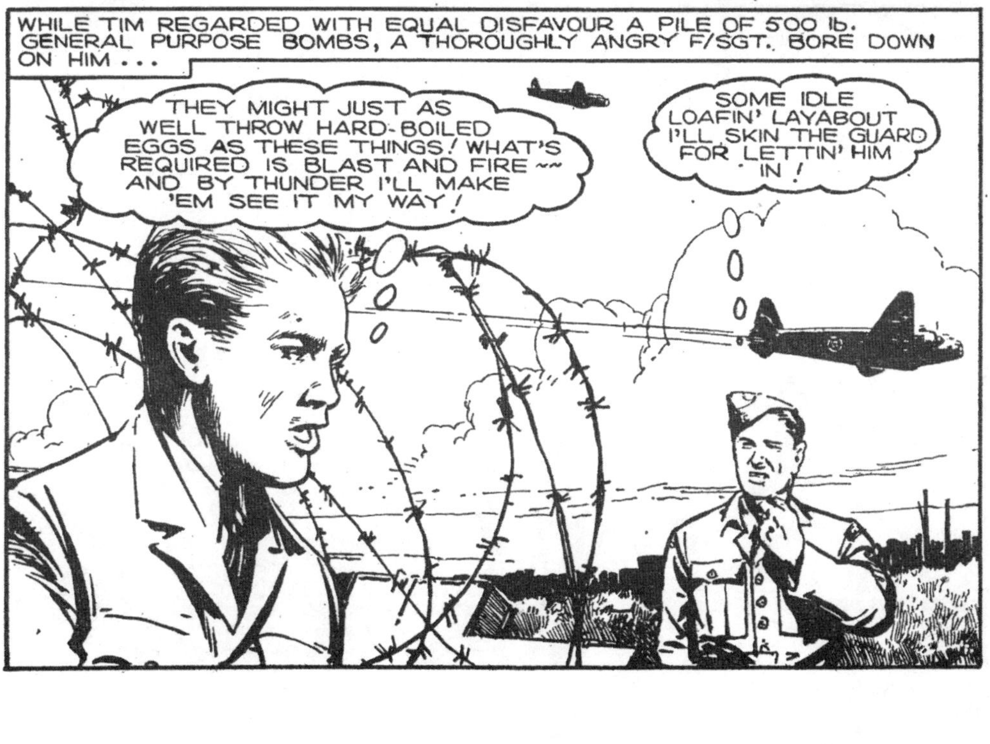
WHILE TIM REGARDED WITH EQUAL DISFAVOUR A PILE OF 500 lb. GENERAL PURPOSE BOMBS, A THOROUGHLY ANGRY F/SGT. BORE DOWN ON HIM . . .
THEY MIGHT JUST AS WELL THROW HARD-BOILED EGGS AS THESE THINGS! WHAT'S REQUIRED IS BLAST AND FIRE ~~ AND BY THUNDER I'LL MAKE 'EM SEE IT MY WAY!
SOME IDLE LOAFIN' LAYABOUT I'LL SKIN THE GUARD FOR LETTIN' HIM IN!

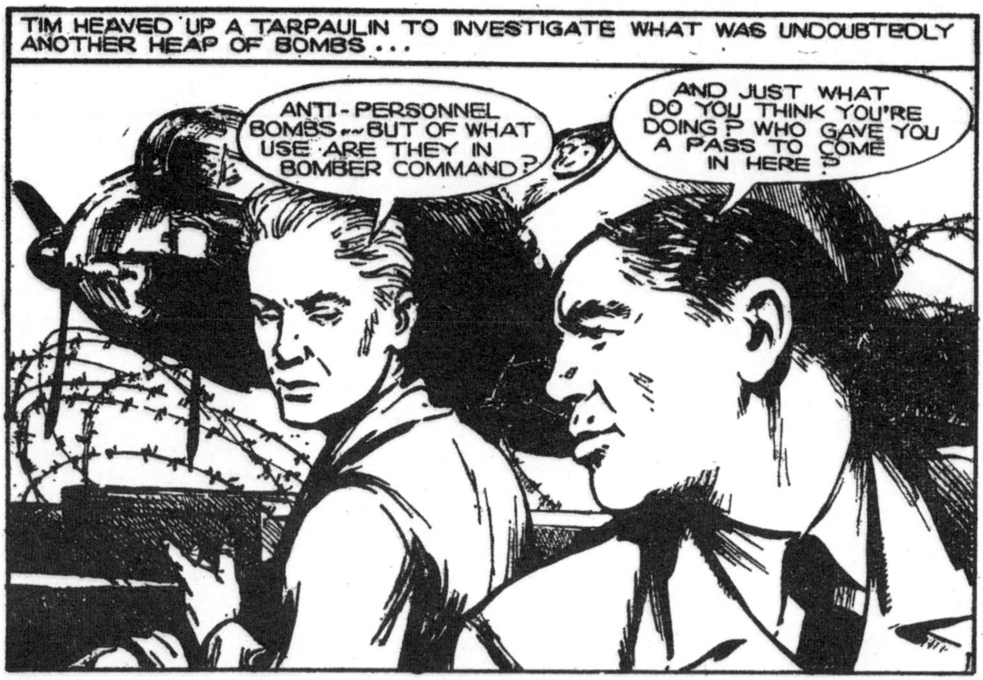
TIM HEAVED UP A TARPAULIN TO INVESTIGATE WHAT WAS UNDOUBTEDLY ANOTHER HEAP OF BOMBS . . .
ANTI-PERSONNEL BOMBS -- BUT OF WHAT USE ARE THEY IN BOMBER COMMAND?
AND JUST WHAT DO YOU THINK YOU'RE DOING? WHO GAVE YOU A PASS TO COME IN HERE?

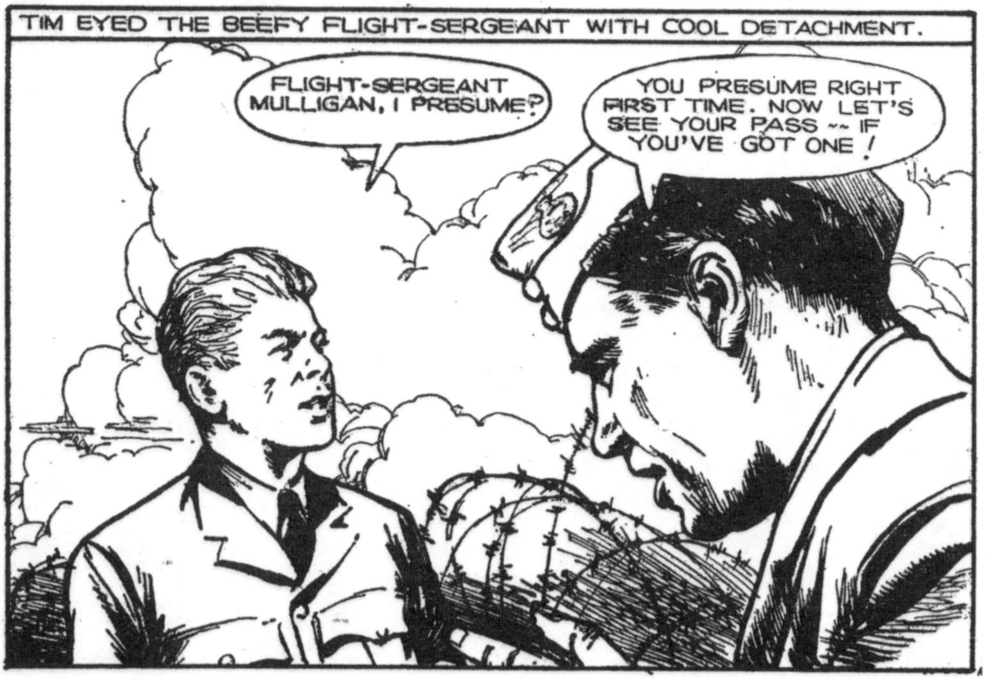
TIM EYED THE BEEFY FLIGHT-SERGEANT WITH COOL DETACHMENT.
FLIGHT-SERGEANT MULLIGAN, I PRESUME?
YOU PRESUME RIGHT FIRST TIME. NOW LET'S SEE YOUR PASS -- IF YOU'VE GOT ONE!

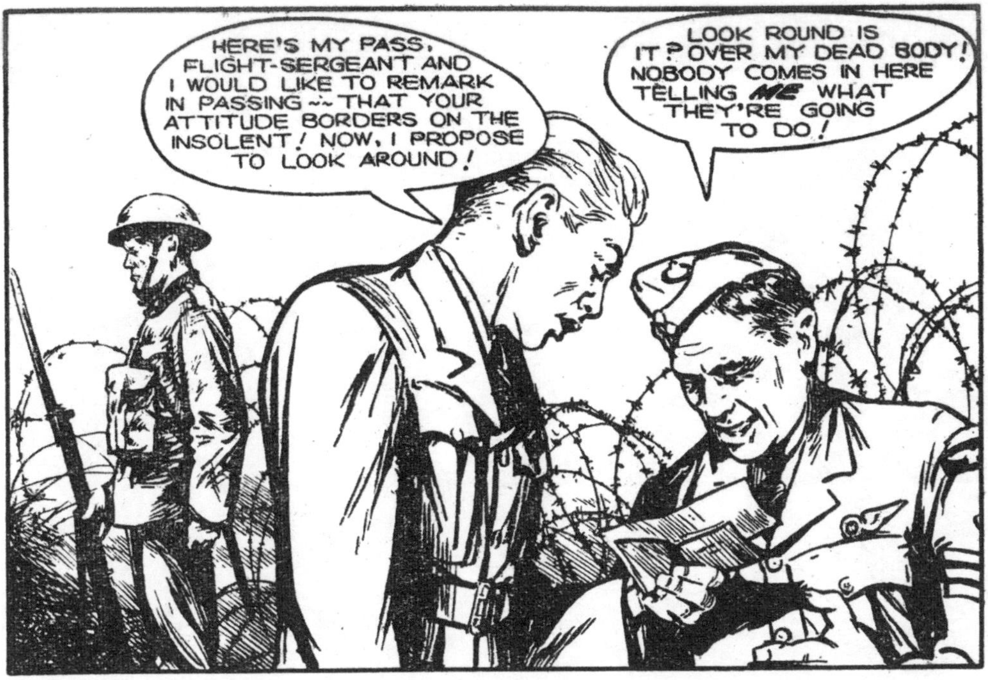
HERE'S MY PASS, FLIGHT-SERGEANT AND I WOULD LIKE TO REMARK IN PASSING -- THAT YOUR ATTITUDE BORDERS ON THE INSOLENT! NOW, I PROPOSE TO LOOK AROUND!
LOOK ROUND IS IT? OVER MY DEAD BODY! NOBODY COMES IN HERE TELLING ME WHAT THEY'RE GOING TO DO!

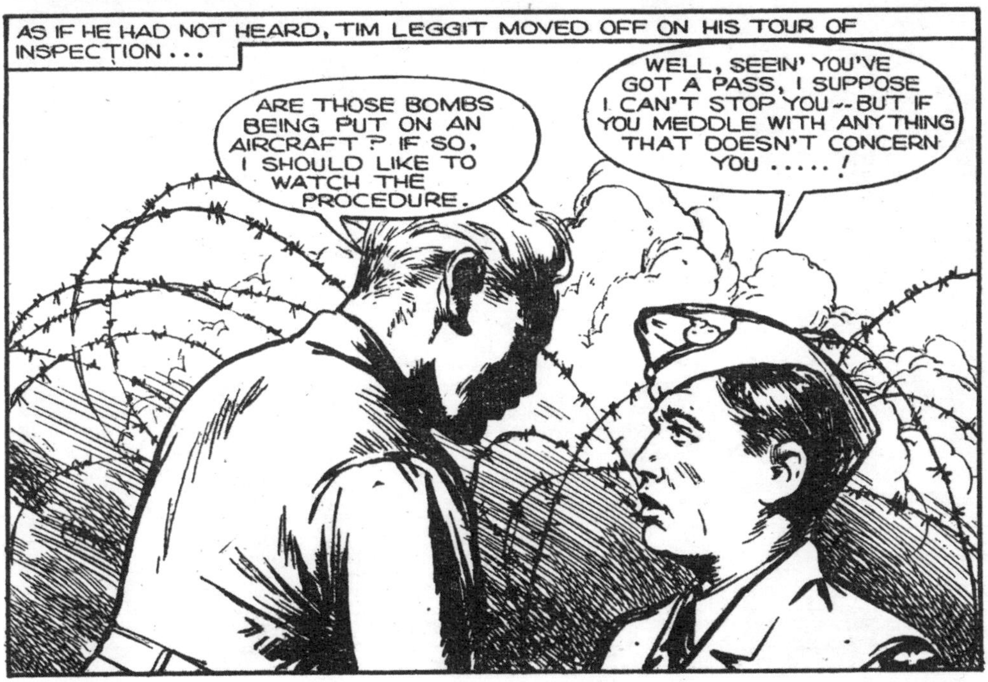
AS IF HE HAD NOT HEARD, TIM LEGGIT MOVED OFF ON HIS TOUR OF INSPECTION ...
ARE THOSE BOMBS BEING PUT ON AN AIRCRAFT? IF SO, I SHOULD LIKE TO WATCH THE PROCEDURE.
WELL, SEEIN' YOU'VE GOT A PASS, I SUPPOSE I CAN'T STOP YOU -- BUT IF YOU MEDDLE WITH ANYTHING THAT DOESN'T CONCERN YOU .....!

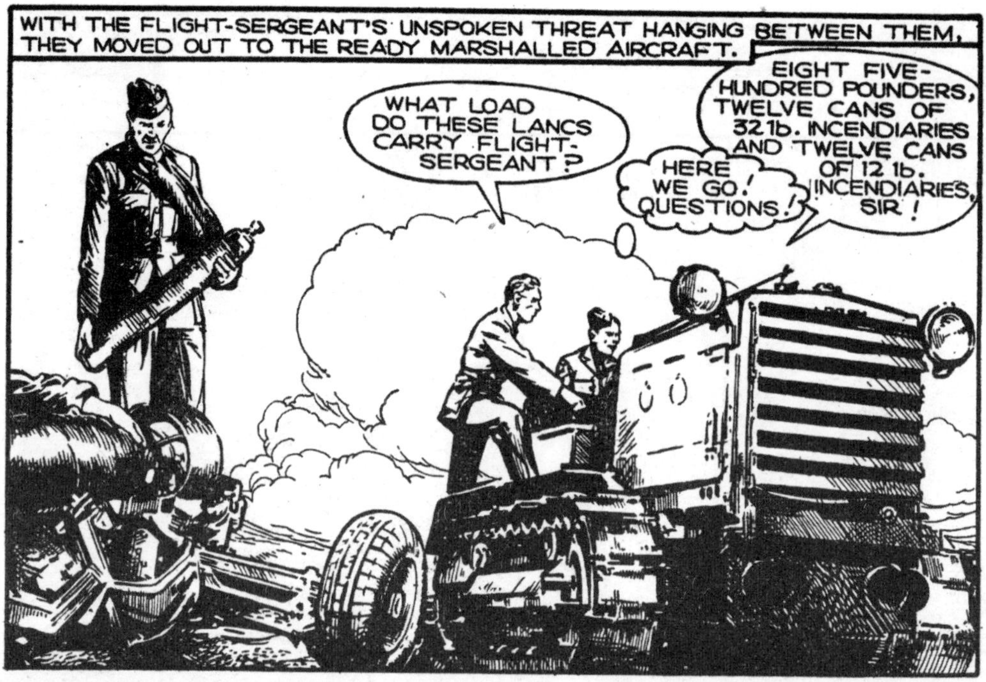
WITH THE FLIGHT-SERGEANT'S UNSPOKEN THREAT HANGING BETWEEN THEM, THEY MOVED OUT TO THE READY MARSHALLED AIRCRAFT.
WHAT LOAD DO THESE LANCS CARRY FLIGHT-SERGEANT?
HERE WE GO! QUESTIONS!
EIGHT FIVE-HUNDRED POUNDERS, TWELVE CANS OF 32 lb. INCENDIARIES AND TWELVE CANS OF 12 lb. INCENDIARIES, SIR!

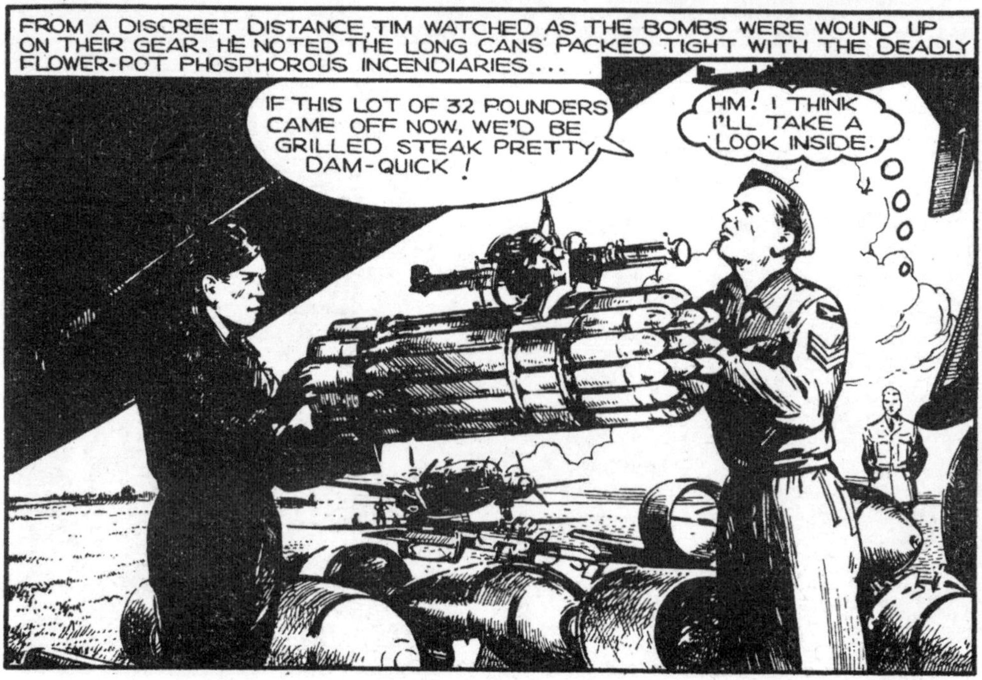
FROM A DISCREET DISTANCE, TIM WATCHED AS THE BOMBS WERE WOUND UP ON THEIR GEAR. HE NOTED THE LONG CANS PACKED TIGHT WITH THE DEADLY FLOWER-POT PHOSPHOROUS INCENDIARIES...
IF THIS LOT OF 32 POUNDERS CAME OFF NOW, WE'D BE GRILLED STEAK PRETTY DAM-QUICK!
HM! I THINK I'LL TAKE A LOOK INSIDE.

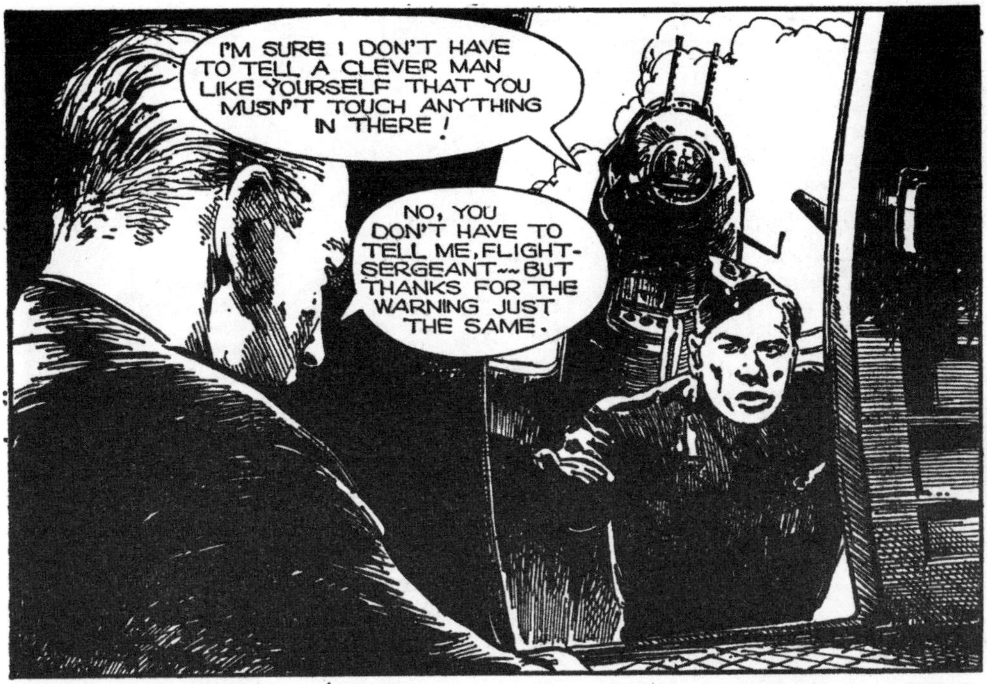
I'M SURE I DON'T HAVE TO TELL A CLEVER MAN LIKE YOURSELF THAT YOU MUSN'T TOUCH ANYTHING IN THERE!
NO, YOU DON'T HAVE TO TELL ME, FLIGHT-SERGEANT -- BUT THANKS FOR THE WARNING JUST THE SAME.

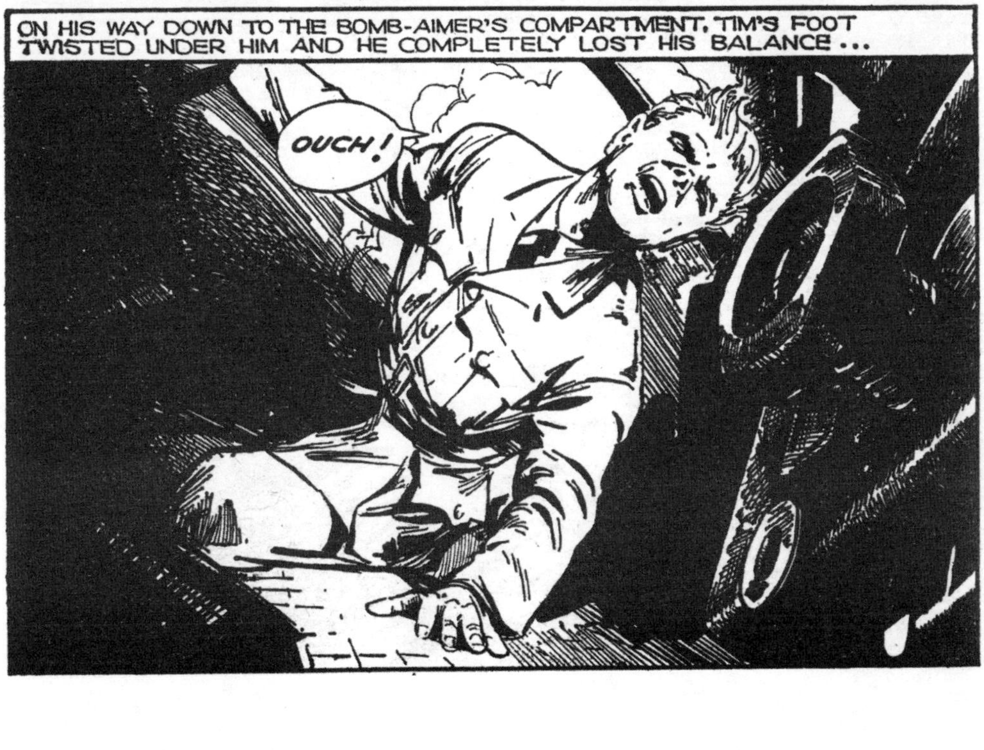
ON HIS WAY DOWN TO THE BOMB-AIMER'S COMPARTMENT, TIM'S FOOT TWISTED UNDER HIM AND HE COMPLETELY LOST HIS BALANCE...
OUCH!

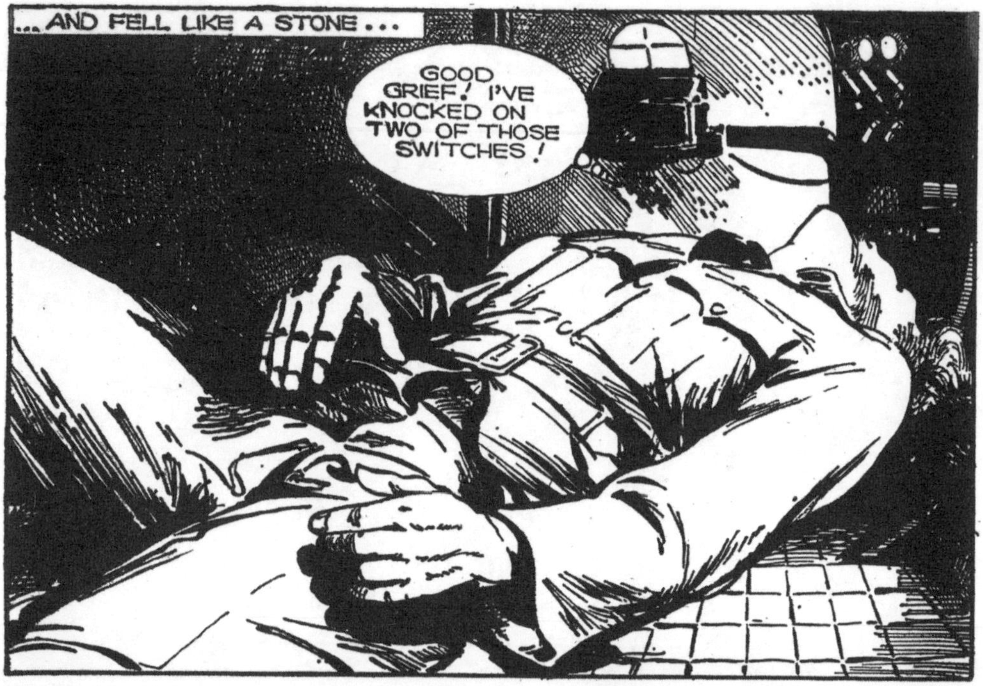
...AND FELL LIKE A STONE...
GOOD GRIEF! I'VE KNOCKED ON TWO OF THOSE SWITCHES!

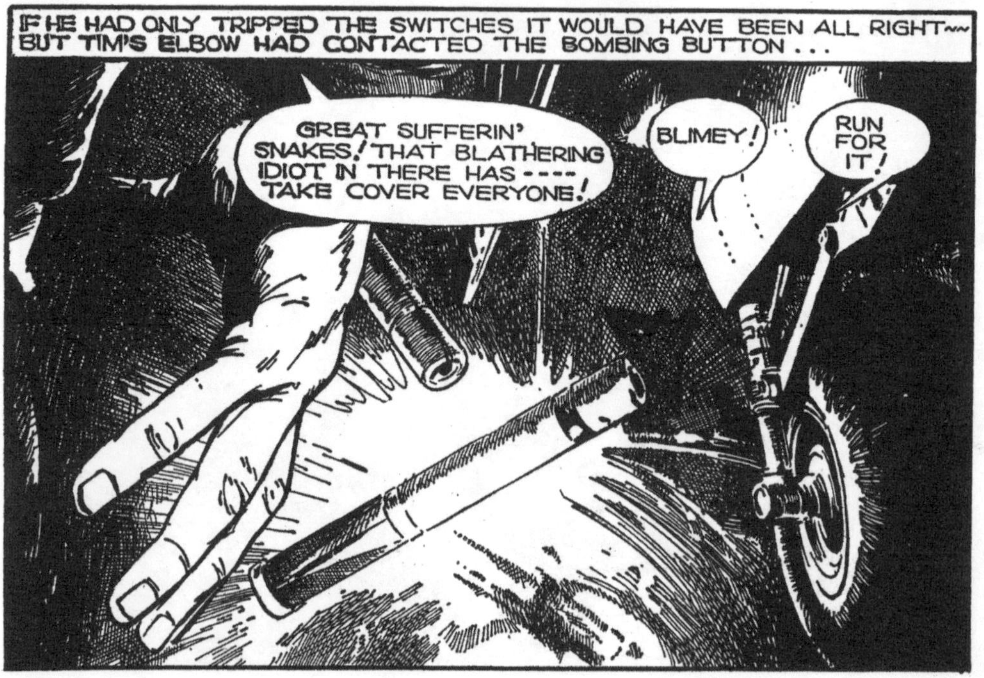
IF HE HAD ONLY TRIPPED THE SWITCHES IT WOULD HAVE BEEN ALL RIGHT~~ BUT TIM'S ELBOW HAD CONTACTED THE BOMBING BUTTON...
GREAT SUFFERIN' SNAKES! THAT BLATHERING IDIOT IN THERE HAS---- TAKE COVER EVERYONE!
BLIMEY!
RUN FOR IT!

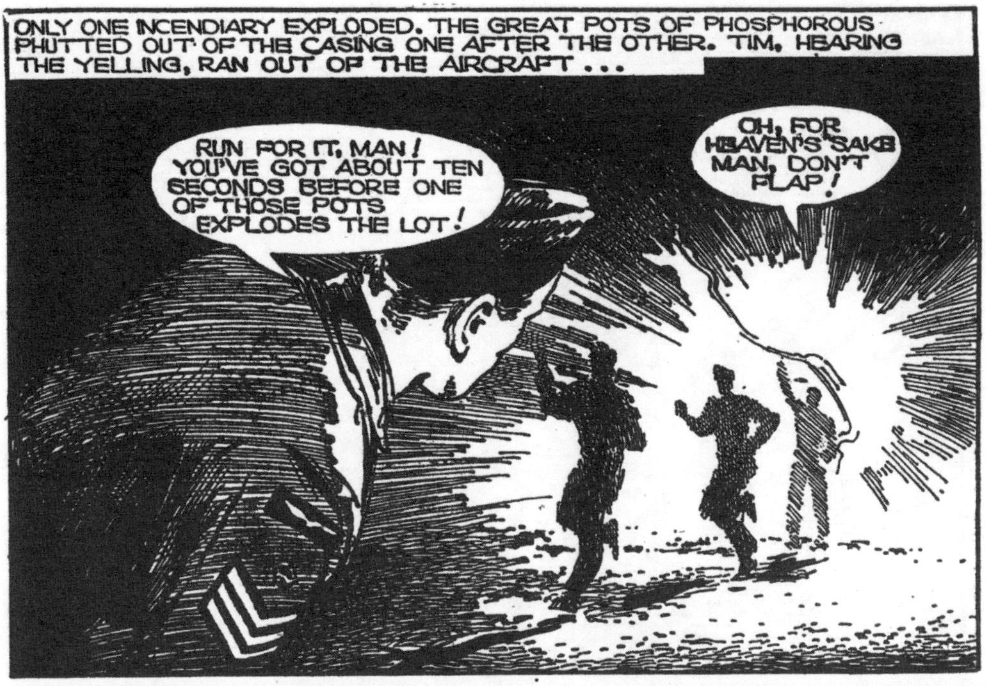
ONLY ONE INCENDIARY EXPLODED. THE GREAT POTS OF PHOSPHOROUS PHUTTED OUT OF THE CASING ONE AFTER THE OTHER. TIM, HEARING THE YELLING, RAN OUT OF THE AIRCRAFT ...
RUN FOR IT, MAN! YOU'VE GOT ABOUT TEN SECONDS BEFORE ONE OF THOSE POTS EXPLODES THE LOT!
OH, FOR HEAVEN'S SAKE MAN, DON'T FLAP!

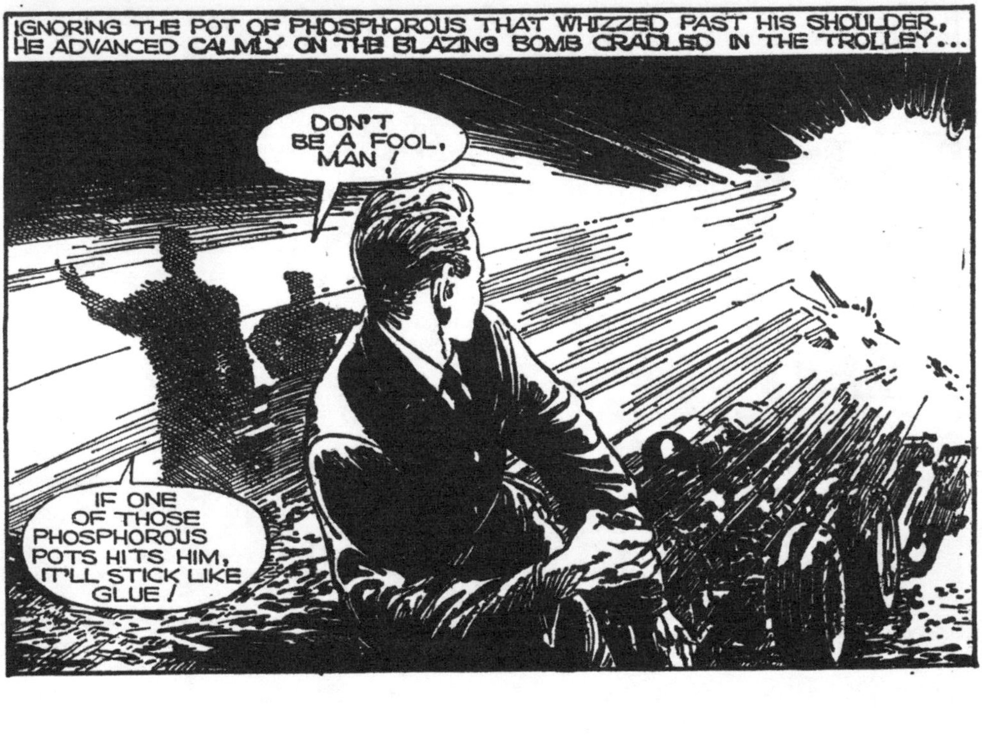
IGNORING THE POT OF PHOSPHOROUS THAT WHIZZED PAST HIS SHOULDER, HE ADVANCED CALMLY ON THE BLAZING BOMB CRADLED IN THE TROLLEY...
DON'T BE A FOOL, MAN!
IF ONE OF THOSE PHOSPHOROUS POTS HITS HIM, IT'LL STICK LIKE GLUE!

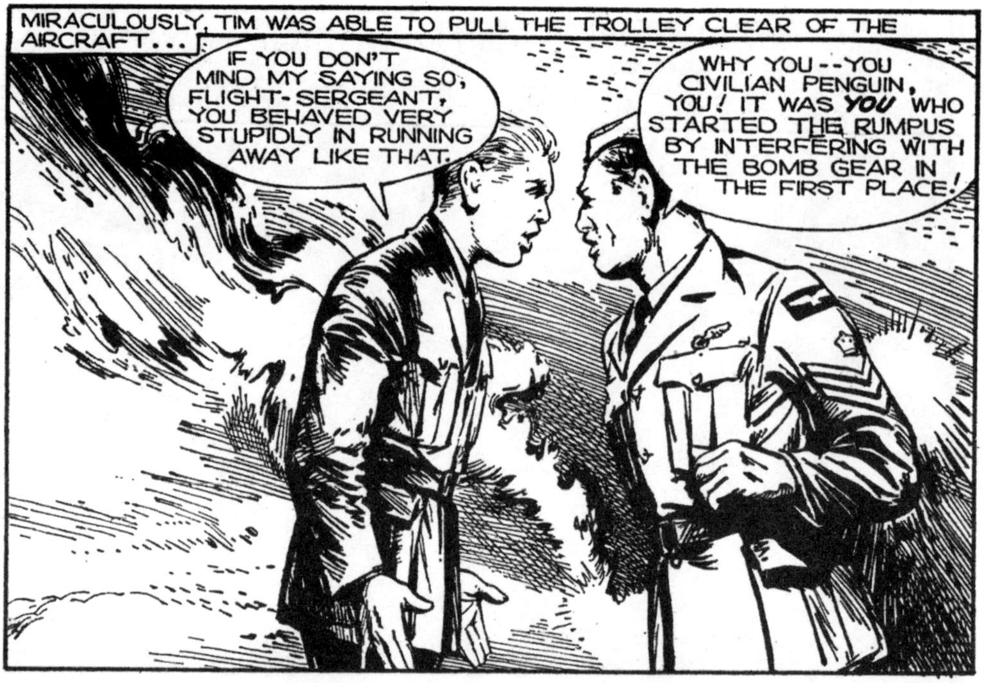
MIRACULOUSLY, TIM WAS ABLE TO PULL THE TROLLEY CLEAR OF THE AIRCRAFT...
IF YOU DON'T MIND MY SAYING SO, FLIGHT-SERGEANT, YOU BEHAVED VERY STUPIDLY IN RUNNING AWAY LIKE THAT.
WHY YOU--YOU CIVILIAN PENGUIN, YOU! IT WAS YOU WHO STARTED THE RUMPUS BY INTERFERING WITH THE BOMB GEAR IN THE FIRST PLACE!

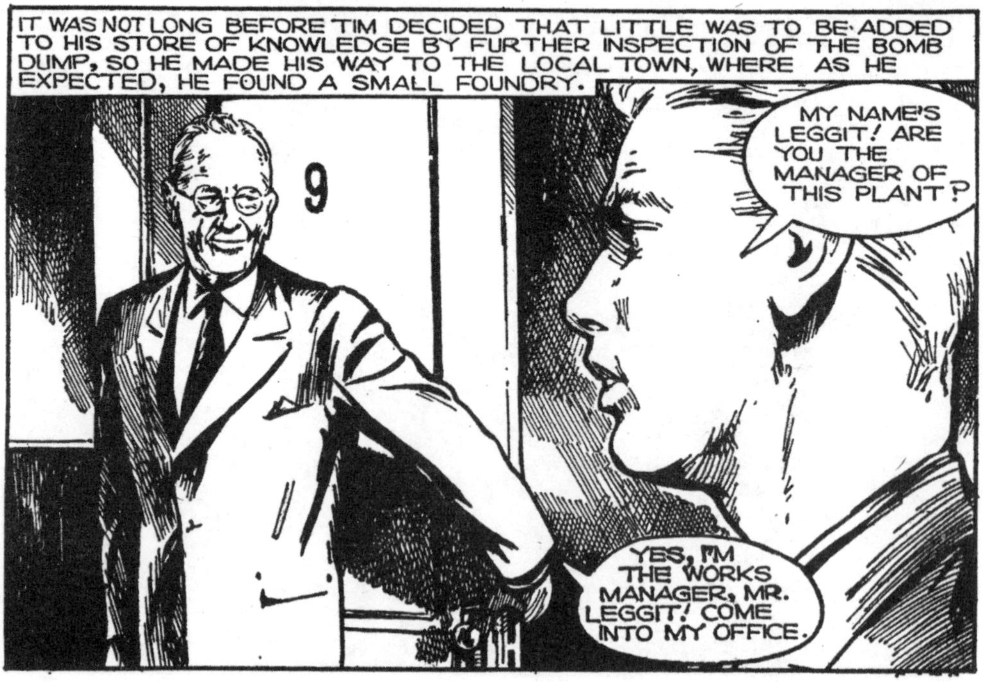
IT WAS NOT LONG BEFORE TIM DECIDED THAT LITTLE WAS TO BE ADDED TO HIS STORE OF KNOWLEDGE BY FURTHER INSPECTION OF THE BOMB DUMP, SO HE MADE HIS WAY TO THE LOCAL TOWN, WHERE AS HE EXPECTED, HE FOUND A SMALL FOUNDRY.
9
MY NAME'S LEGGIT! ARE YOU THE MANAGER OF THIS PLANT?
YES, I'M THE WORKS MANAGER, MR. LEGGIT! COME INTO MY OFFICE.

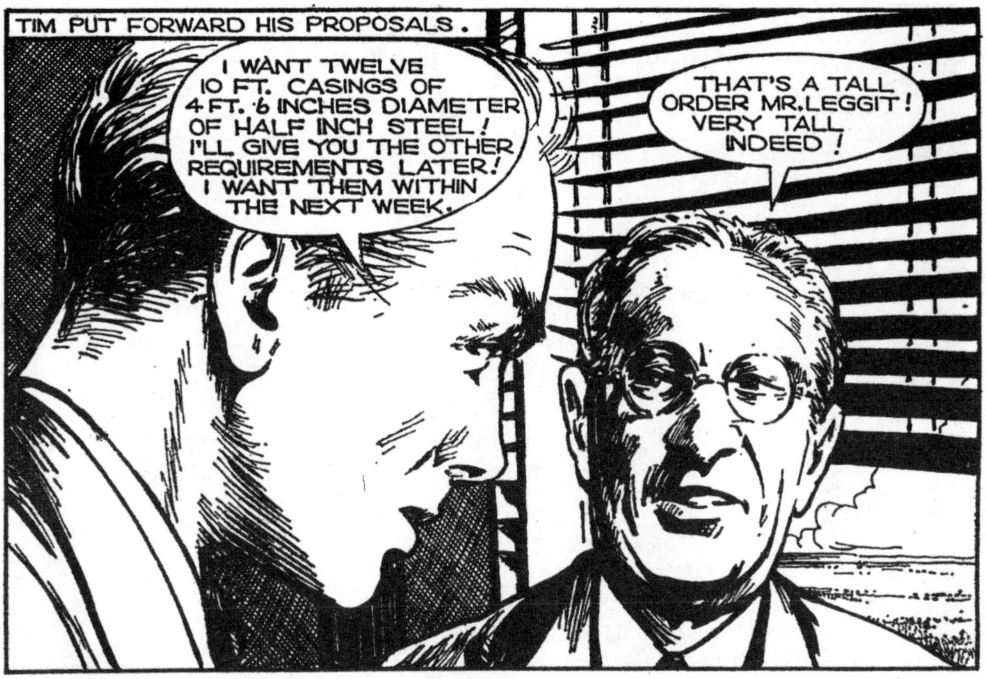
TIM PUT FORWARD HIS PROPOSALS.
I WANT TWELVE 10 FT. CASINGS OF 4 FT. 6 INCHES DIAMETER OF HALF INCH STEEL! I'LL GIVE YOU THE OTHER REQUIREMENTS LATER! I WANT THEM WITHIN THE NEXT WEEK.
THAT'S A TALL ORDER MR. LEGGIT! VERY TALL INDEED!

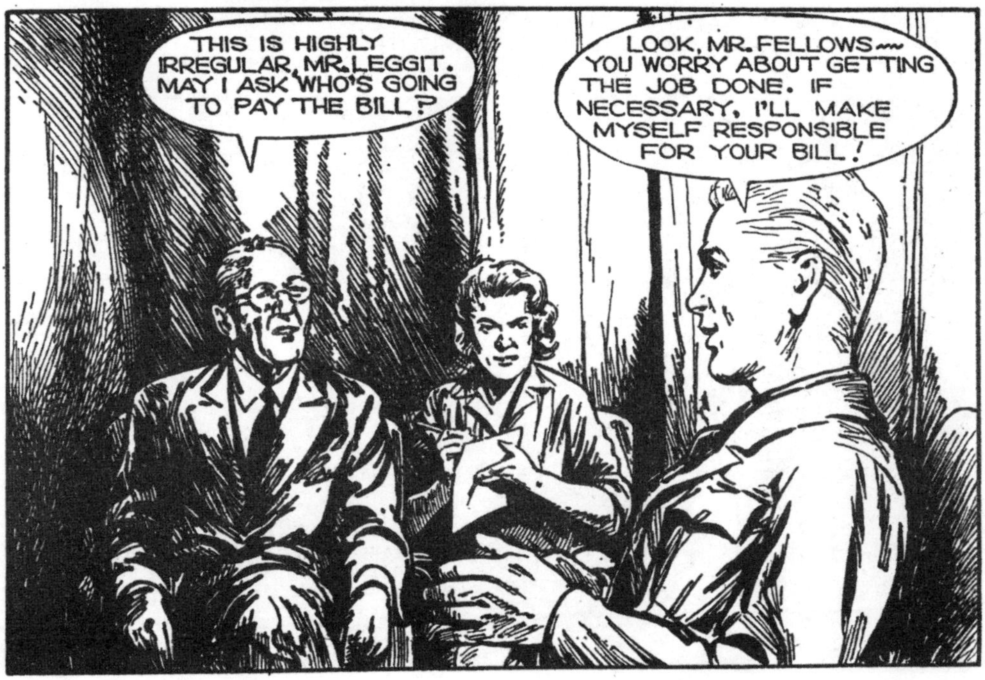
THIS IS HIGHLY IRREGULAR, MR. LEGGIT. MAY I ASK WHO'S GOING TO PAY THE BILL?
LOOK, MR. FELLOWS — YOU WORRY ABOUT GETTING THE JOB DONE. IF NECESSARY, I'LL MAKE MYSELF RESPONSIBLE FOR YOUR BILL!

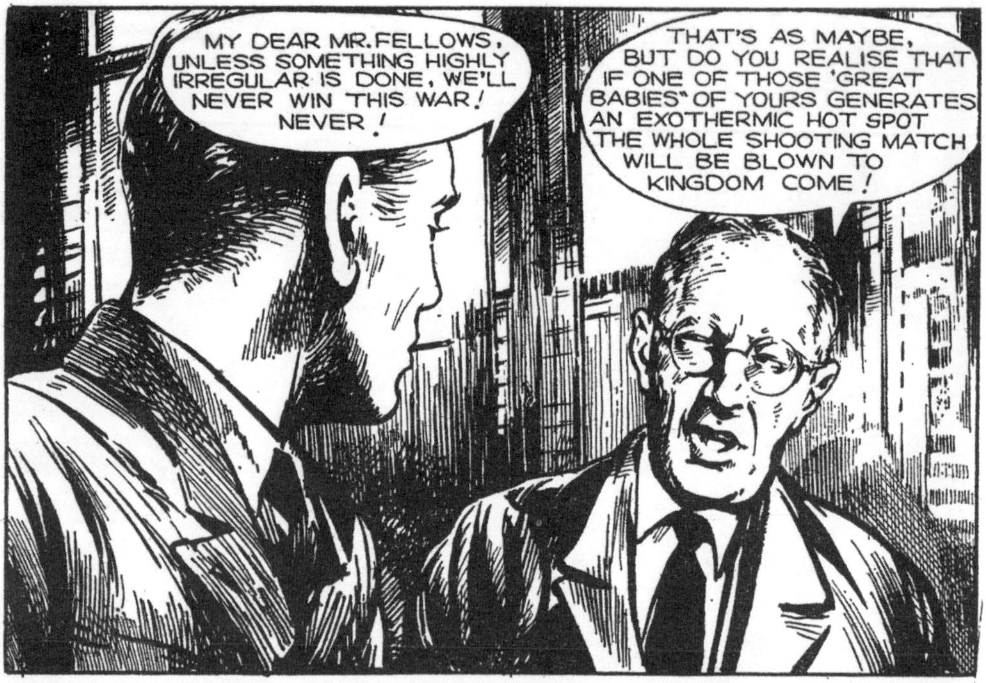
MY DEAR MR. FELLOWS, UNLESS SOMETHING HIGHLY IRREGULAR IS DONE, WE'LL NEVER WIN THIS WAR! NEVER!
THAT'S AS MAYBE, BUT DO YOU REALISE THAT IF ONE OF THOSE 'GREAT BABIES" OF YOURS GENERATES AN EXOTHERMIC HOT SPOT THE WHOLE SHOOTING MATCH WILL BE BLOWN TO KINGDOM COME!

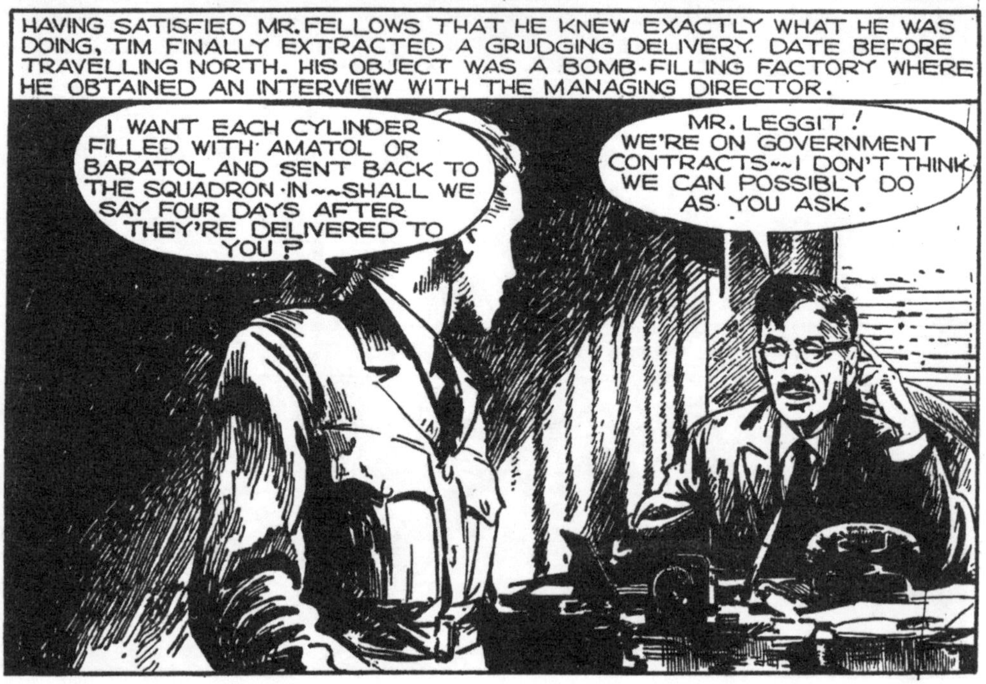
HAVING SATISFIED MR. FELLOWS THAT HE KNEW EXACTLY WHAT HE WAS DOING, TIM FINALLY EXTRACTED A GRUDGING DELIVERY DATE BEFORE TRAVELLING NORTH. HIS OBJECT WAS A BOMB-FILLING FACTORY WHERE HE OBTAINED AN INTERVIEW WITH THE MANAGING DIRECTOR.
I WANT EACH CYLINDER FILLED WITH AMATOL OR BARATOL AND SENT BACK TO THE SQUADRON IN~~SHALL WE SAY FOUR DAYS AFTER THEY'RE DELIVERED TO YOU?
MR. LEGGIT! WE'RE ON GOVERNMENT CONTRACTS~~I DON'T THINK WE CAN POSSIBLY DO AS YOU ASK.

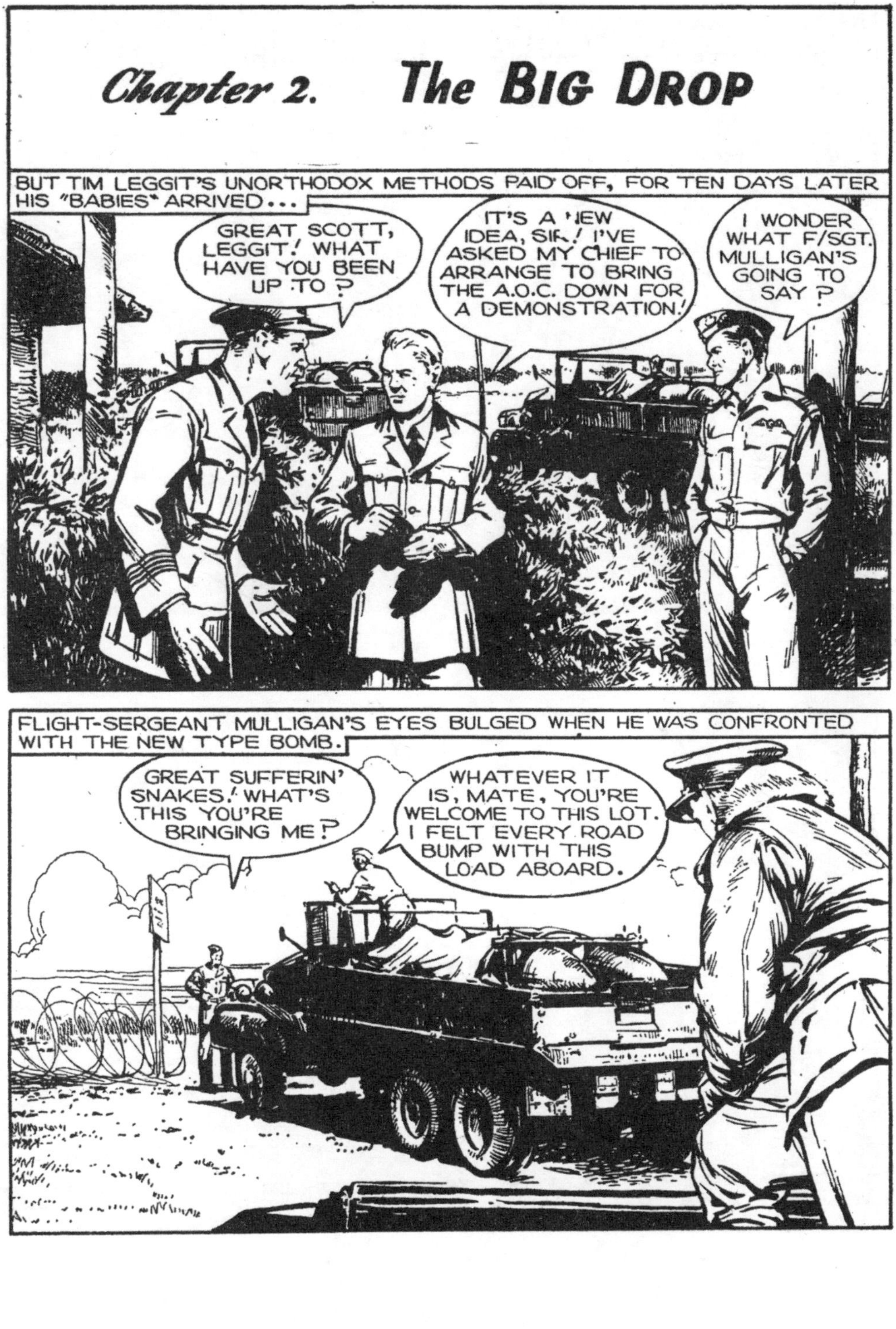
Chapter 2. The BIG DROP
BUT TIM LEGGIT'S UNORTHODOX METHODS PAID OFF, FOR TEN DAYS LATER HIS "BABIES" ARRIVED...
GREAT SCOTT, LEGGIT! WHAT HAVE YOU BEEN UP TO?
IT'S A NEW IDEA, SIR! I'VE ASKED MY CHIEF TO ARRANGE TO BRING THE A.O.C. DOWN FOR A DEMONSTRATION!
I WONDER WHAT F/SGT. MULLIGAN'S GOING TO SAY?
FLIGHT-SERGEANT MULLIGAN'S EYES BULGED WHEN HE WAS CONFRONTED WITH THE NEW TYPE BOMB.
GREAT SUFFERIN' SNAKES! WHAT'S THIS YOU'RE BRINGING ME?
WHATEVER IT IS, MATE, YOU'RE WELCOME TO THIS LOT. I FELT EVERY ROAD BUMP WITH THIS LOAD ABOARD.

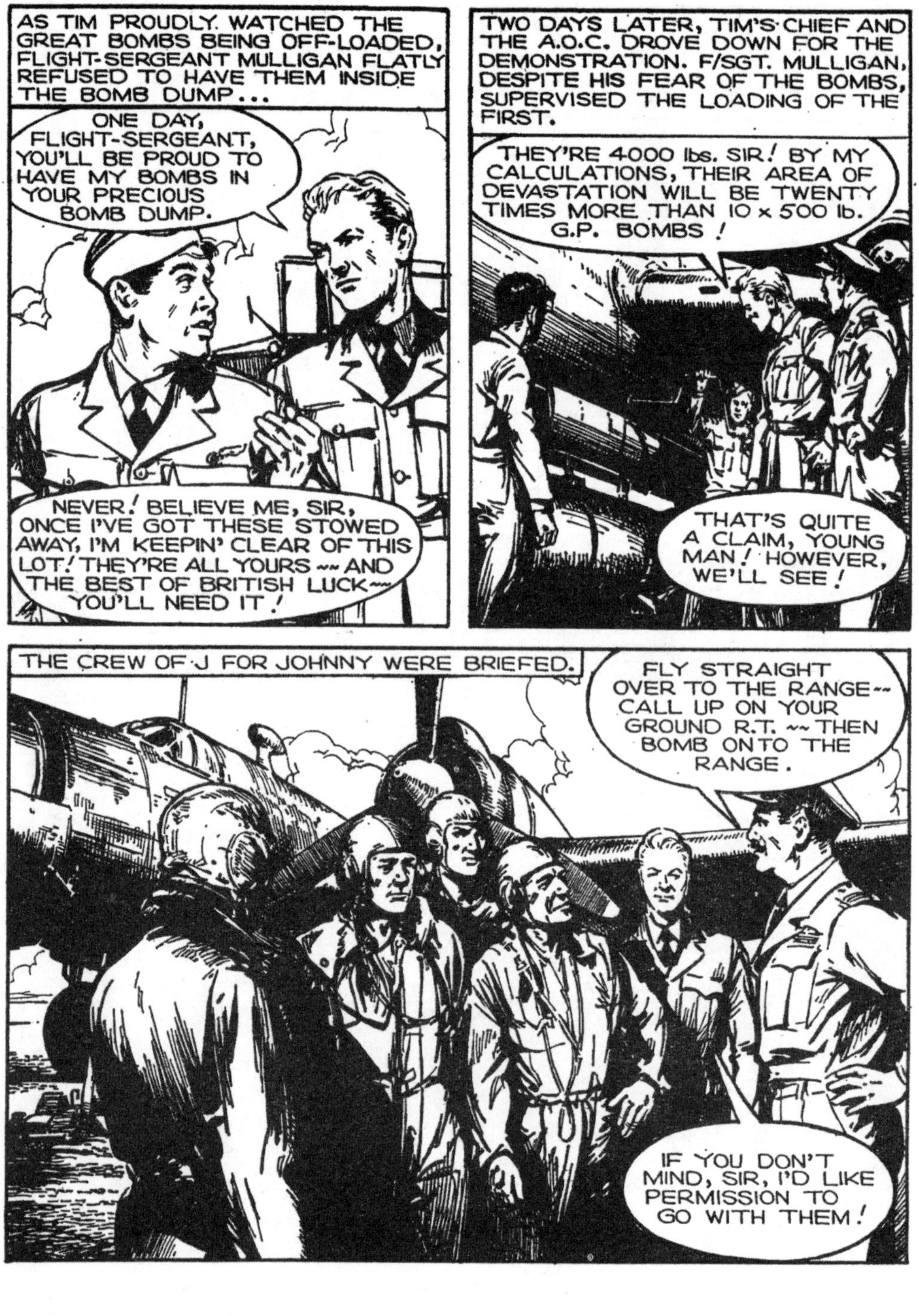
AS TIM PROUDLY WATCHED THE GREAT BOMBS BEING OFF-LOADED, FLIGHT-SERGEANT MULLIGAN FLATLY REFUSED TO HAVE THEM INSIDE THE BOMB DUMP...
ONE DAY, FLIGHT-SERGEANT, YOU'LL BE PROUD TO HAVE MY BOMBS IN YOUR PRECIOUS BOMB DUMP.
NEVER! BELIEVE ME, SIR, ONCE I'VE GOT THESE STOWED AWAY, I'M KEEPIN' CLEAR OF THIS LOT! THEY'RE ALL YOURS -- AND THE BEST OF BRITISH LUCK-- YOU'LL NEED IT!
TWO DAYS LATER, TIM'S CHIEF AND THE A.O.C. DROVE DOWN FOR THE DEMONSTRATION. F/SGT. MULLIGAN, DESPITE HIS FEAR OF THE BOMBS, SUPERVISED THE LOADING OF THE FIRST.
THEY'RE 4000 lbs. SIR! BY MY CALCULATIONS, THEIR AREA OF DEVASTATION WILL BE TWENTY TIMES MORE THAN 10 x 500 lb. G.P. BOMBS!
THAT'S QUITE A CLAIM, YOUNG MAN! HOWEVER, WE'LL SEE!
THE CREW OF J FOR JOHNNY WERE BRIEFED.
FLY STRAIGHT OVER TO THE RANGE-- CALL UP ON YOUR GROUND R.T. -- THEN BOMB ONTO THE RANGE.
IF YOU DON'T MIND, SIR, I'D LIKE PERMISSION TO GO WITH THEM!

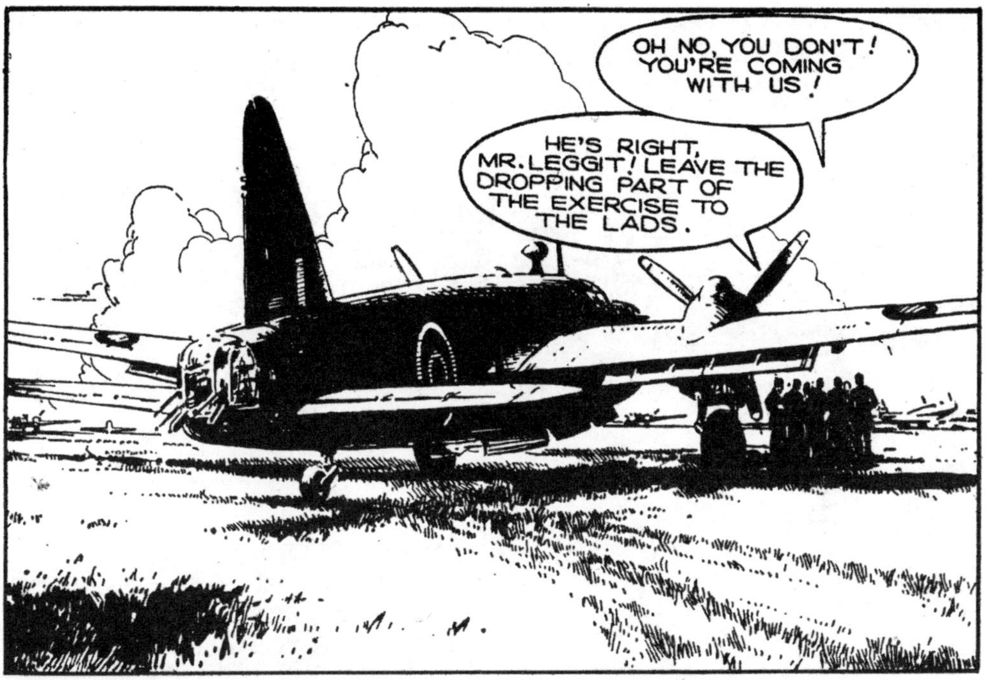
OH NO, YOU DON'T! YOU'RE COMING WITH US!
HE'S RIGHT, MR. LEGGIT! LEAVE THE DROPPING PART OF THE EXERCISE TO THE LADS.

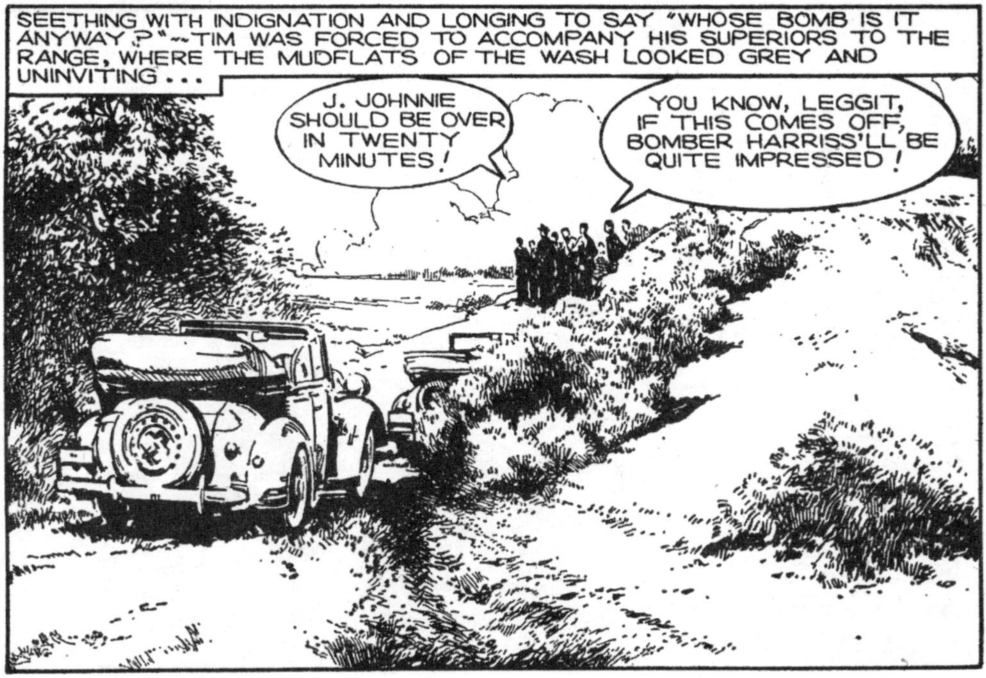
SEETHING WITH INDIGNATION AND LONGING TO SAY "WHOSE BOMB IS IT ANYWAY?" – TIM WAS FORCED TO ACCOMPANY HIS SUPERIORS TO THE RANGE, WHERE THE MUDFLATS OF THE WASH LOOKED GREY AND UNINVITING . . .
J. JOHNNIE SHOULD BE OVER IN TWENTY MINUTES!
YOU KNOW, LEGGIT, IF THIS COMES OFF, BOMBER HARRISS'LL BE QUITE IMPRESSED!

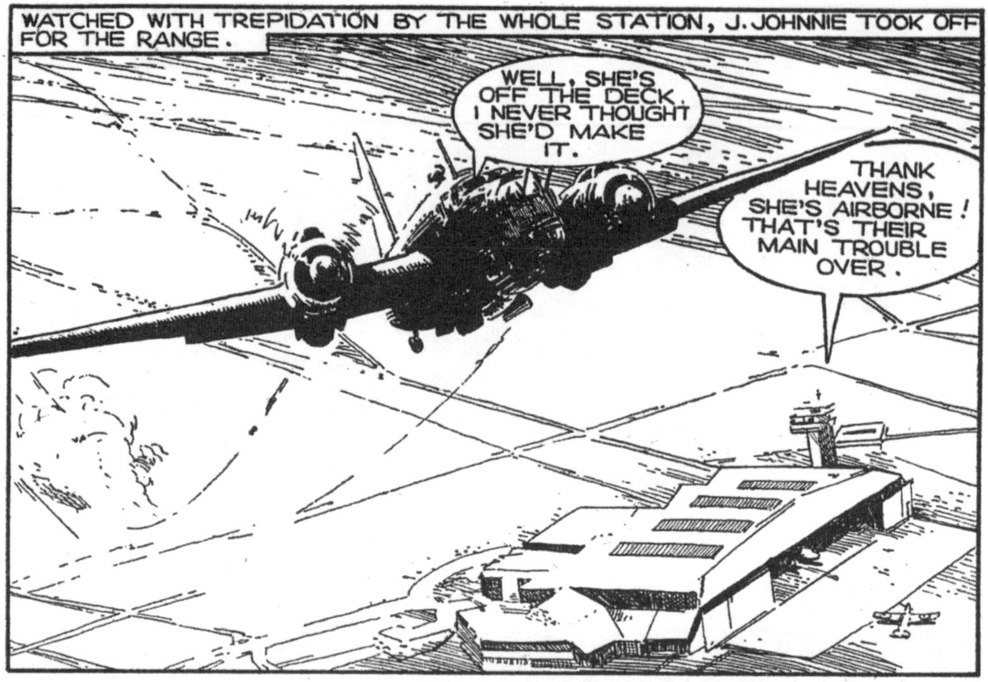
WATCHED WITH TREPIDATION BY THE WHOLE STATION, J. JOHNNIE TOOK OFF FOR THE RANGE.
WELL, SHE'S OFF THE DECK. I NEVER THOUGHT SHE'D MAKE IT.
THANK HEAVENS, SHE'S AIRBORNE! THAT'S THEIR MAIN TROUBLE OVER.

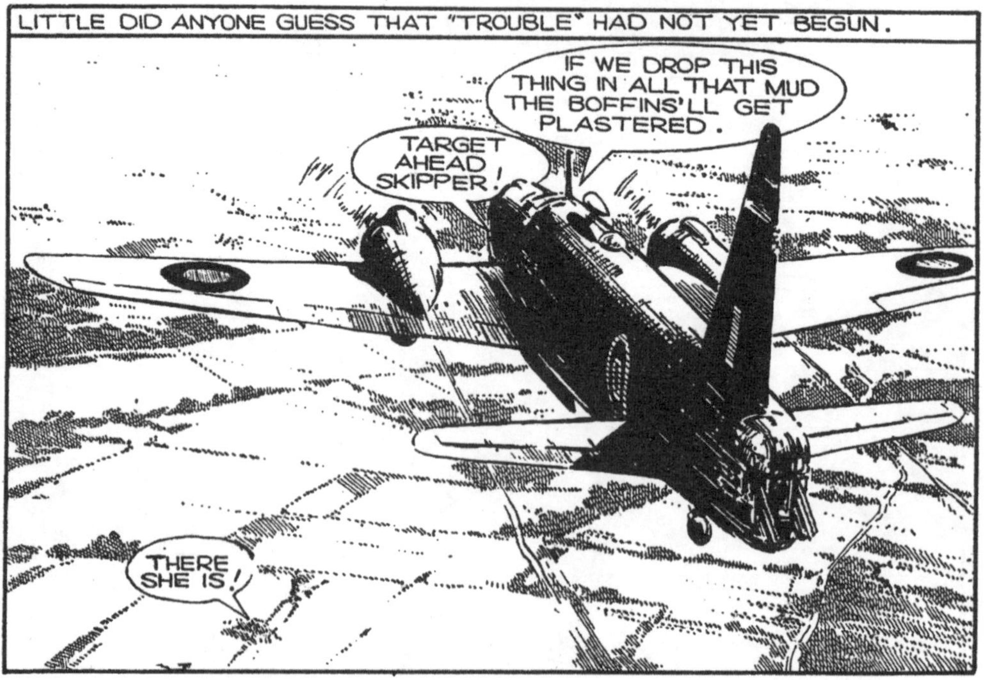
LITTLE DID ANYONE GUESS THAT "TROUBLE" HAD NOT YET BEGUN.
IF WE DROP THIS THING IN ALL THAT MUD THE BOFFINS'LL GET PLASTERED.
TARGET AHEAD SKIPPER!
THERE SHE IS!

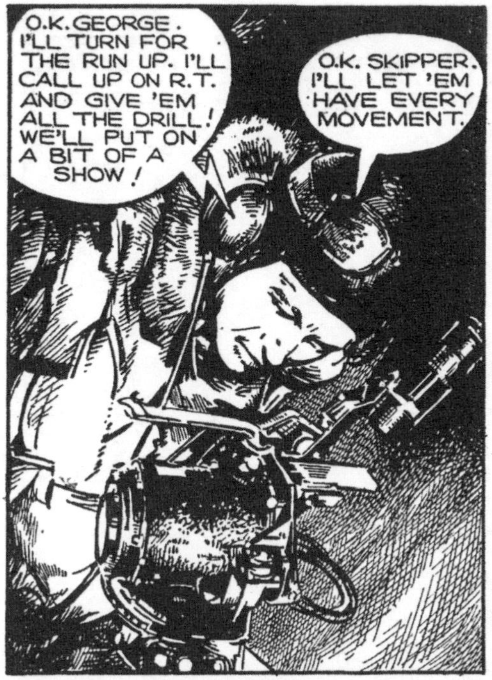
O.K. GEORGE. I'LL TURN FOR THE RUN UP. I'LL CALL UP ON R.T. AND GIVE 'EM ALL THE DRILL! WE'LL PUT ON A BIT OF A SHOW!
O.K. SKIPPER. I'LL LET 'EM HAVE EVERY MOVEMENT.

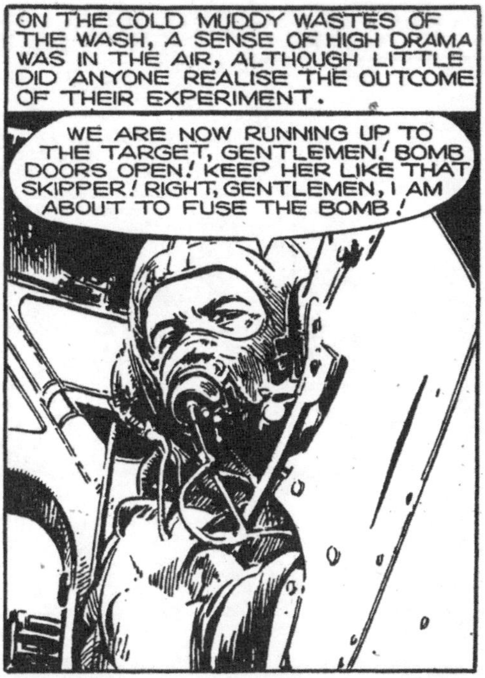
ON THE COLD MUDDY WASTES OF THE WASH, A SENSE OF HIGH DRAMA WAS IN THE AIR, ALTHOUGH LITTLE DID ANYONE REALISE THE OUTCOME OF THEIR EXPERIMENT.
WE ARE NOW RUNNING UP TO THE TARGET, GENTLEMEN! BOMB DOORS OPEN! KEEP HER LIKE THAT SKIPPER! RIGHT, GENTLEMEN, I AM ABOUT TO FUSE THE BOMB!

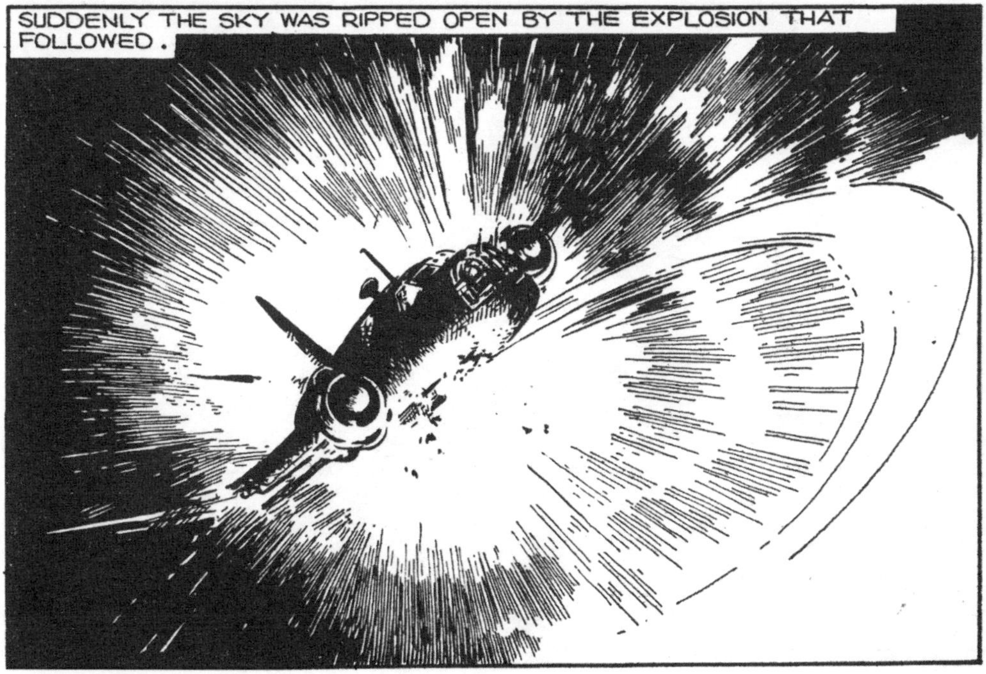
SUDDENLY THE SKY WAS RIPPED OPEN BY THE EXPLOSION THAT FOLLOWED.

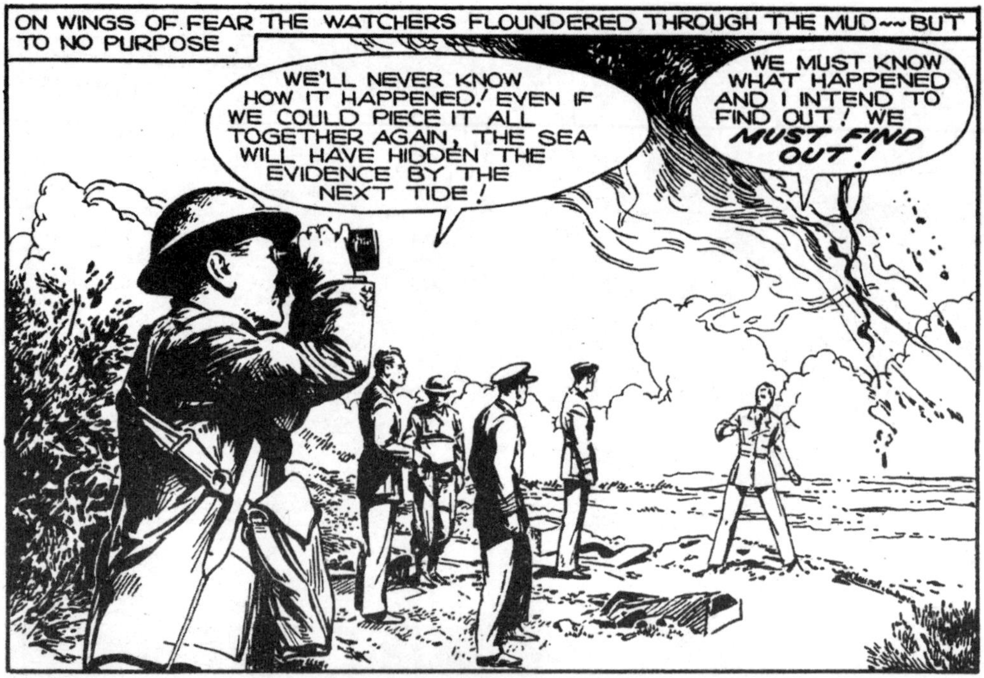
ON WINGS OF FEAR THE WATCHERS FLOUNDERED THROUGH THE MUD—BUT TO NO PURPOSE.
WE'LL NEVER KNOW HOW IT HAPPENED! EVEN IF WE COULD PIECE IT ALL TOGETHER AGAIN, THE SEA WILL HAVE HIDDEN THE EVIDENCE BY THE NEXT TIDE!
WE MUST KNOW WHAT HAPPENED AND I INTEND TO FIND OUT! WE MUST FIND OUT!

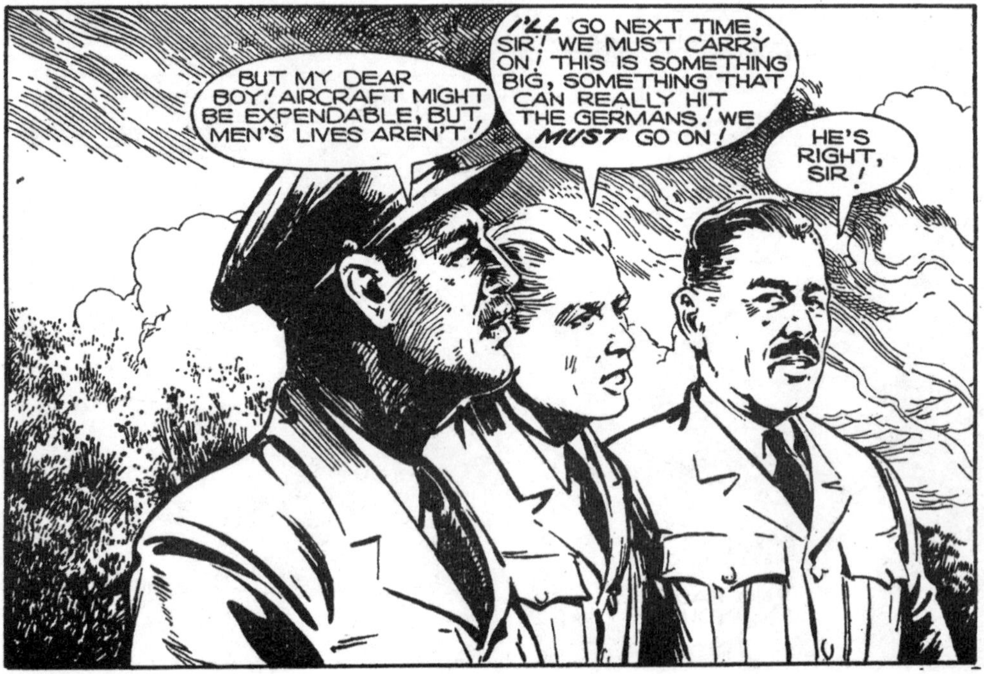
BUT MY DEAR BOY! AIRCRAFT MIGHT BE EXPENDABLE, BUT MEN'S LIVES AREN'T!
I'LL GO NEXT TIME, SIR! WE MUST CARRY ON! THIS IS SOMETHING BIG, SOMETHING THAT CAN REALLY HIT THE GERMANS! WE MUST GO ON!
HE'S RIGHT, SIR!

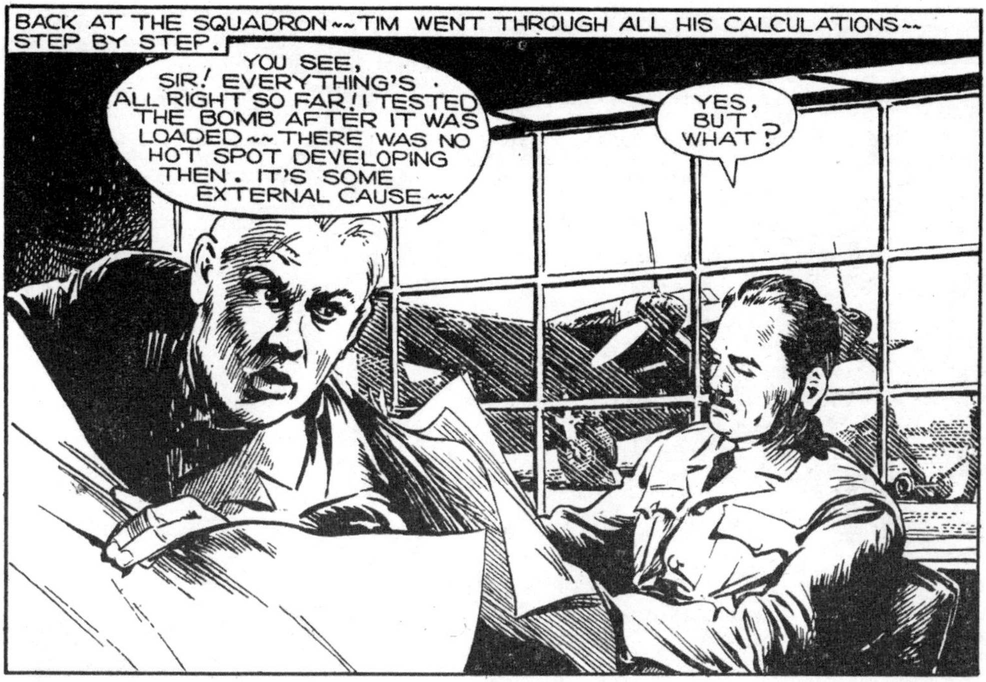
BACK AT THE SQUADRON ~~ TIM WENT THROUGH ALL HIS CALCULATIONS ~~ STEP BY STEP.
YOU SEE, SIR! EVERYTHING'S ALL RIGHT SO FAR! I TESTED THE BOMB AFTER IT WAS LOADED ~~ THERE WAS NO HOT SPOT DEVELOPING THEN. IT'S SOME EXTERNAL CAUSE ~~
YES, BUT WHAT?

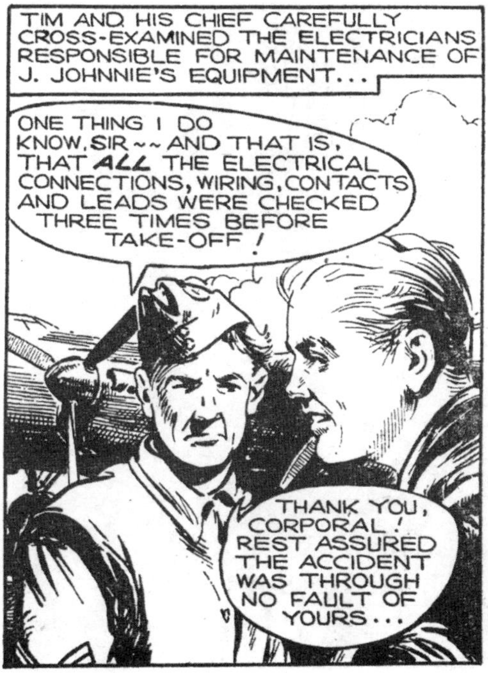
TIM AND HIS CHIEF CAREFULLY CROSS-EXAMINED THE ELECTRICIANS RESPONSIBLE FOR MAINTENANCE OF J. JOHNNIE'S EQUIPMENT...
ONE THING I DO KNOW, SIR ~~ AND THAT IS, THAT ALL THE ELECTRICAL CONNECTIONS, WIRING, CONTACTS AND LEADS WERE CHECKED THREE TIMES BEFORE TAKE-OFF!
THANK YOU, CORPORAL! REST ASSURED THE ACCIDENT WAS THROUGH NO FAULT OF YOURS...

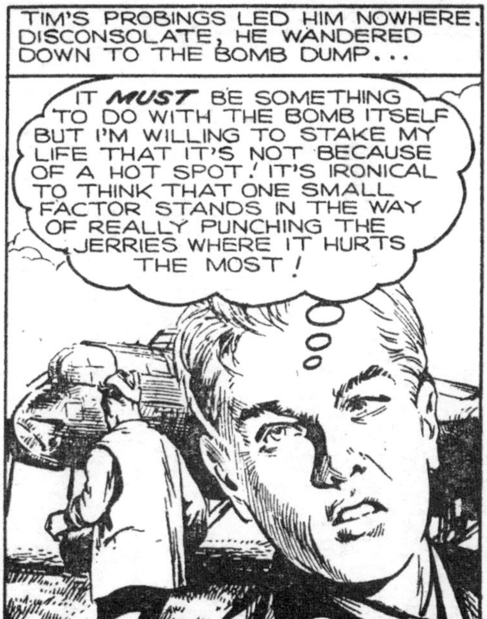
TIM'S PROBINGS LED HIM NOWHERE. DISCONSOLATE, HE WANDERED DOWN TO THE BOMB DUMP...
IT MUST BE SOMETHING TO DO WITH THE BOMB ITSELF BUT I'M WILLING TO STAKE MY LIFE THAT IT'S NOT BECAUSE OF A HOT SPOT! IT'S IRONICAL TO THINK THAT ONE SMALL FACTOR STANDS IN THE WAY OF REALLY PUNCHING THE JERRIES WHERE IT HURTS THE MOST!

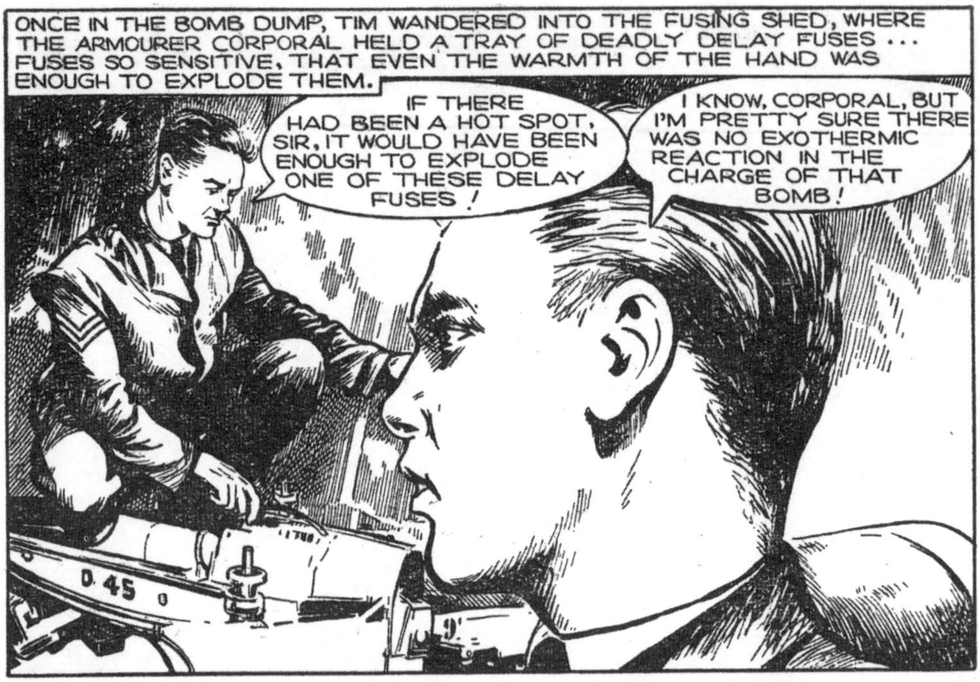
ONCE IN THE BOMB DUMP, TIM WANDERED INTO THE FUSING SHED, WHERE THE ARMOURER CORPORAL HELD A TRAY OF DEADLY DELAY FUSES ... FUSES SO SENSITIVE, THAT EVEN THE WARMTH OF THE HAND WAS ENOUGH TO EXPLODE THEM.
IF THERE HAD BEEN A HOT SPOT, SIR, IT WOULD HAVE BEEN ENOUGH TO EXPLODE ONE OF THESE DELAY FUSES!
I KNOW, CORPORAL, BUT I'M PRETTY SURE THERE WAS NO EXOTHERMIC REACTION IN THE CHARGE OF THAT BOMB!
D.45

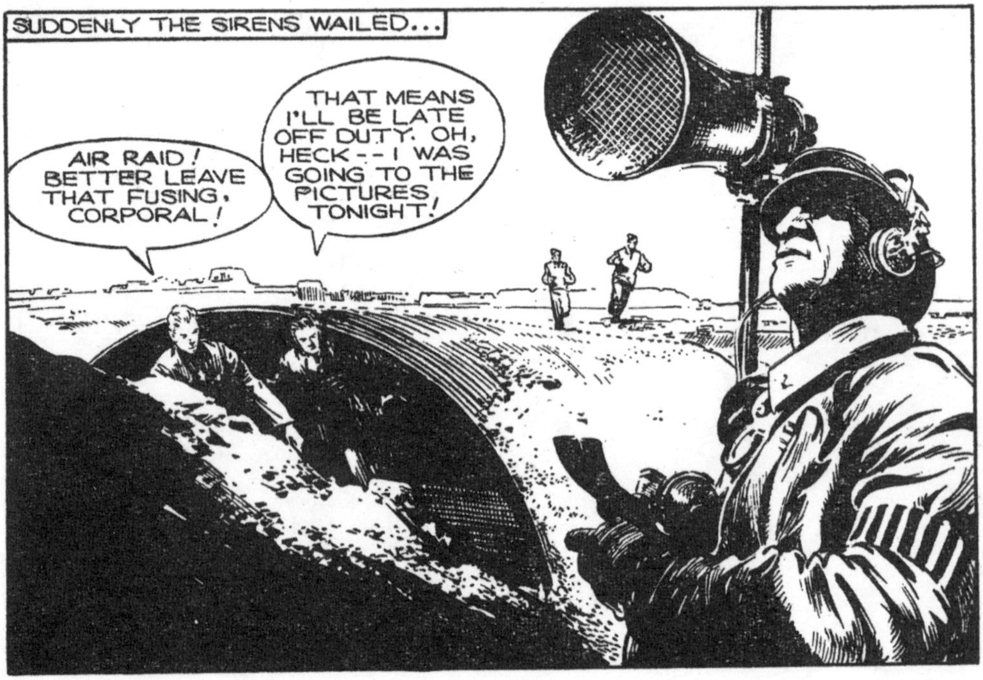
SUDDENLY THE SIRENS WAILED...
AIR RAID! BETTER LEAVE THAT FUSING, CORPORAL!
THAT MEANS I'LL BE LATE OFF DUTY. OH, HECK -- I WAS GOING TO THE PICTURES TONIGHT!

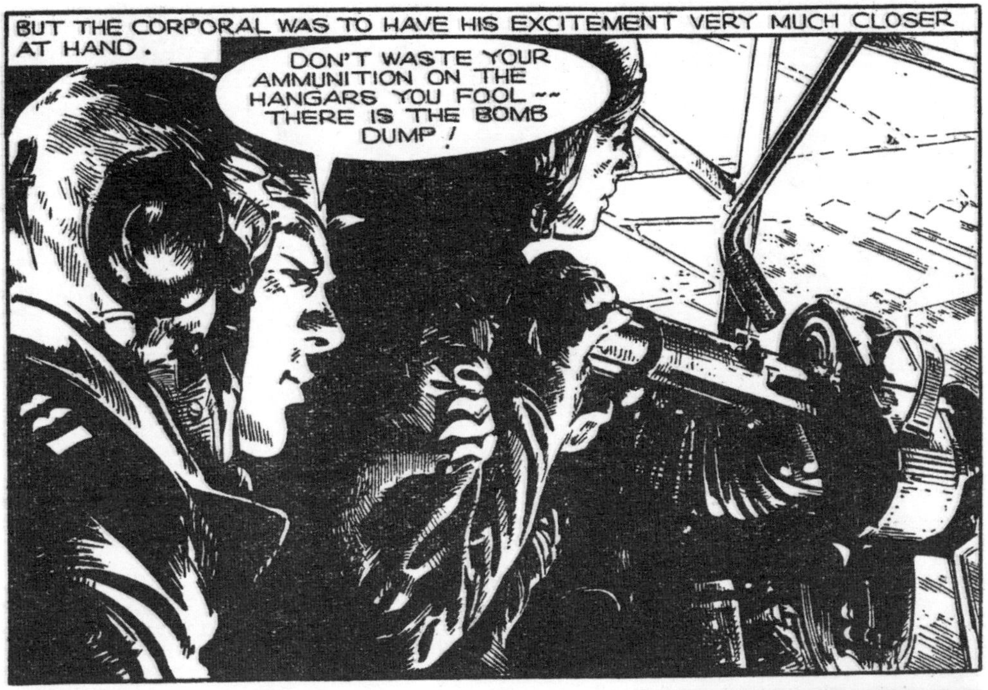
BUT THE CORPORAL WAS TO HAVE HIS EXCITEMENT VERY MUCH CLOSER AT HAND.
DON'T WASTE YOUR AMMUNITION ON THE HANGARS YOU FOOL -- THERE IS THE BOMB DUMP!

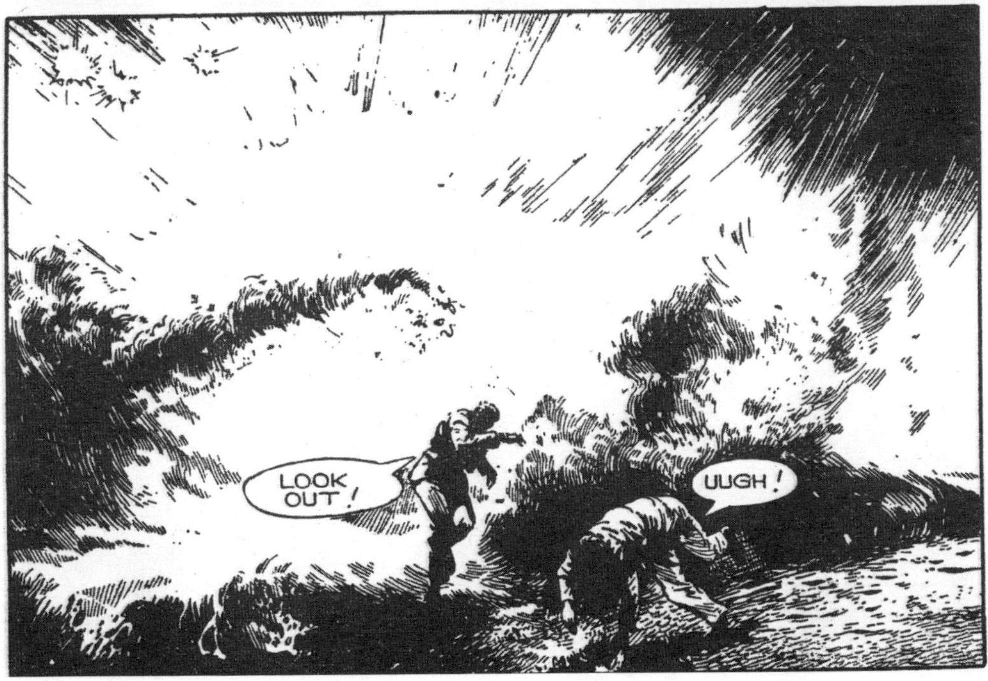
LOOK OUT!
UUGH!

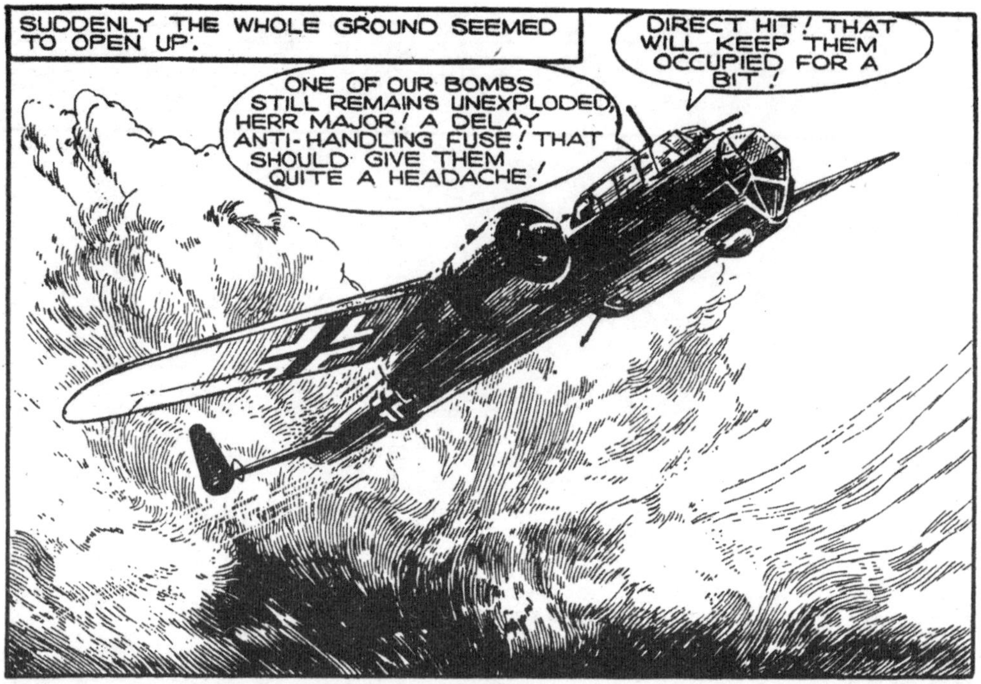
SUDDENLY THE WHOLE GROUND SEEMED TO OPEN UP.
ONE OF OUR BOMBS STILL REMAINS UNEXPLODED, HERR MAJOR! A DELAY ANTI-HANDLING FUSE! THAT SHOULD GIVE THEM QUITE A HEADACHE!
DIRECT HIT! THAT WILL KEEP THEM OCCUPIED FOR A BIT!

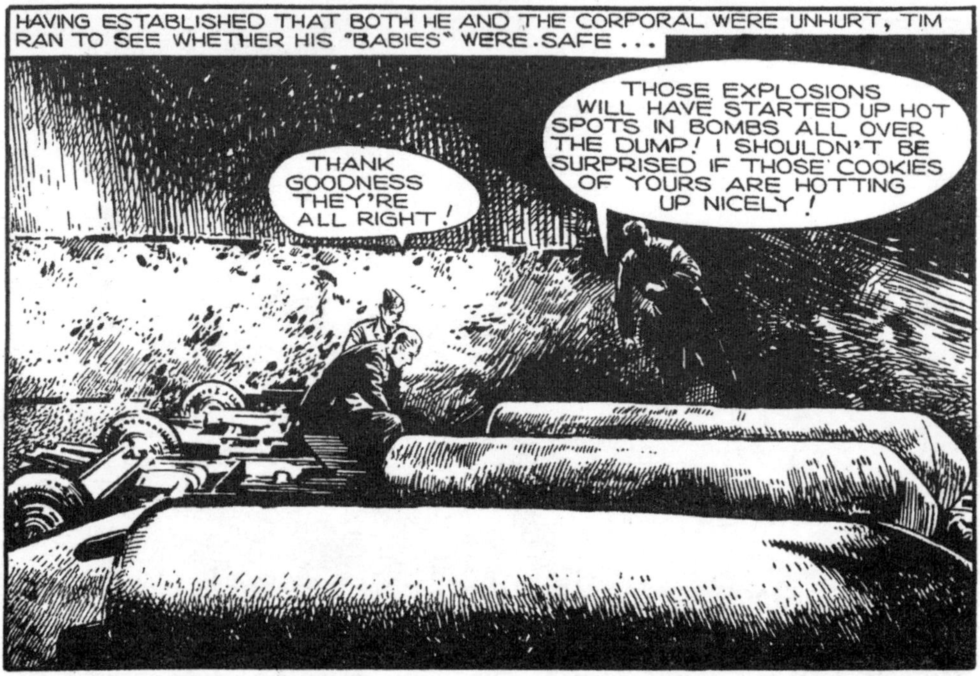
HAVING ESTABLISHED THAT BOTH HE AND THE CORPORAL WERE UNHURT, TIM RAN TO SEE WHETHER HIS "BABIES" WERE SAFE ...
THANK GOODNESS THEY'RE ALL RIGHT!
THOSE EXPLOSIONS WILL HAVE STARTED UP HOT SPOTS IN BOMBS ALL OVER THE DUMP! I SHOULDN'T BE SURPRISED IF THOSE COOKIES OF YOURS ARE HOTTING UP NICELY!

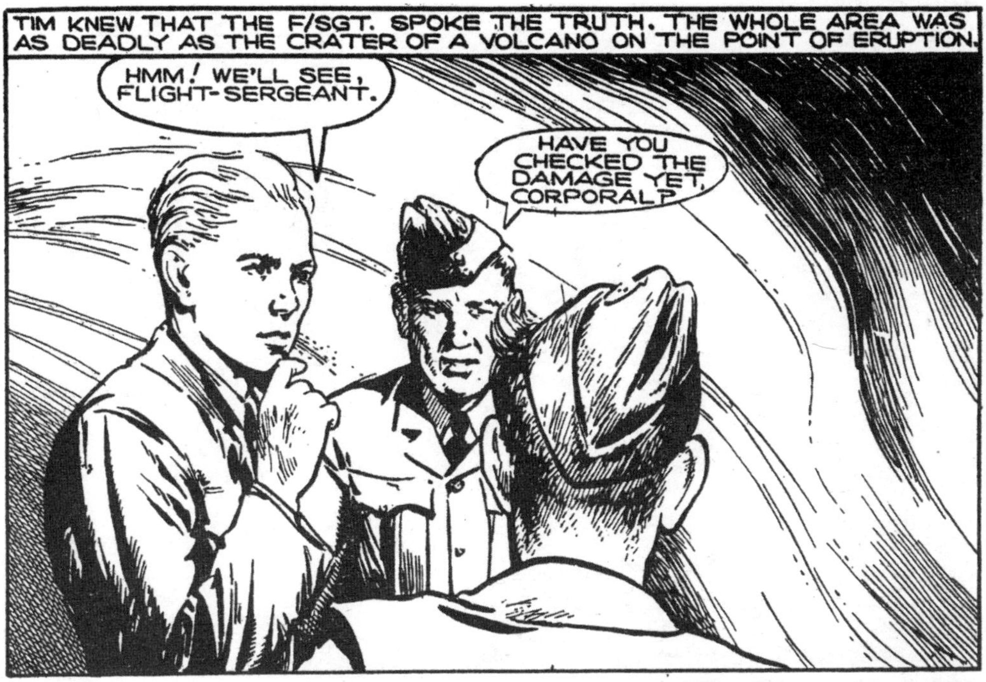
TIM KNEW THAT THE F/SGT. SPOKE THE TRUTH. THE WHOLE AREA WAS AS DEADLY AS THE CRATER OF A VOLCANO ON THE POINT OF ERUPTION.
HMM! WE'LL SEE, FLIGHT-SERGEANT.
HAVE YOU CHECKED THE DAMAGE YET, CORPORAL?

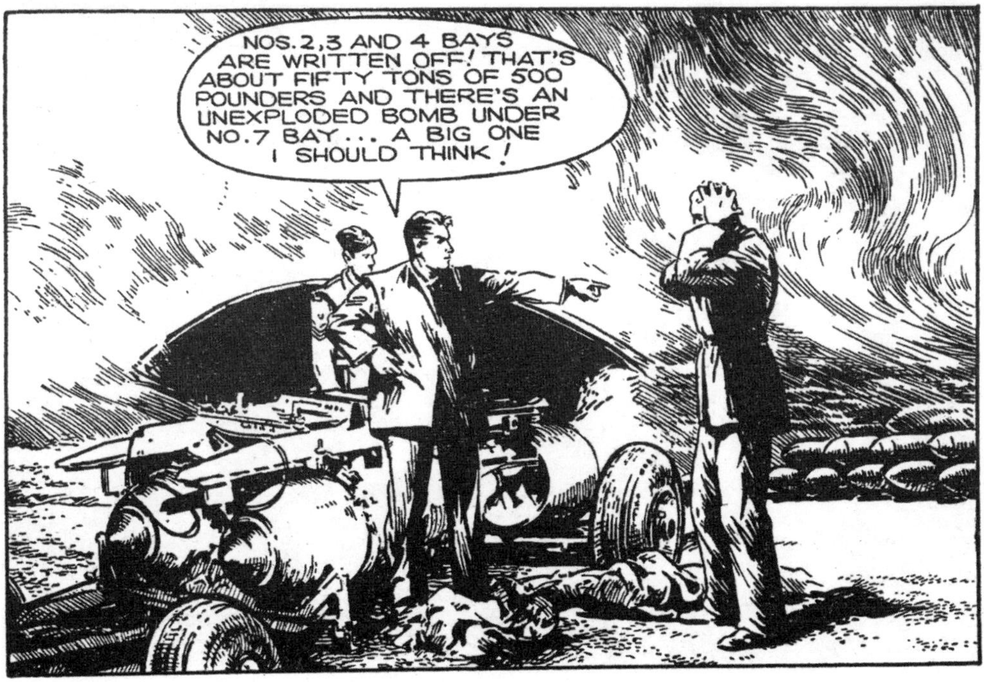
NOS. 2, 3 AND 4 BAYS ARE WRITTEN OFF! THAT'S ABOUT FIFTY TONS OF 500 POUNDERS AND THERE'S AN UNEXPLODED BOMB UNDER NO. 7 BAY ... A BIG ONE I SHOULD THINK!

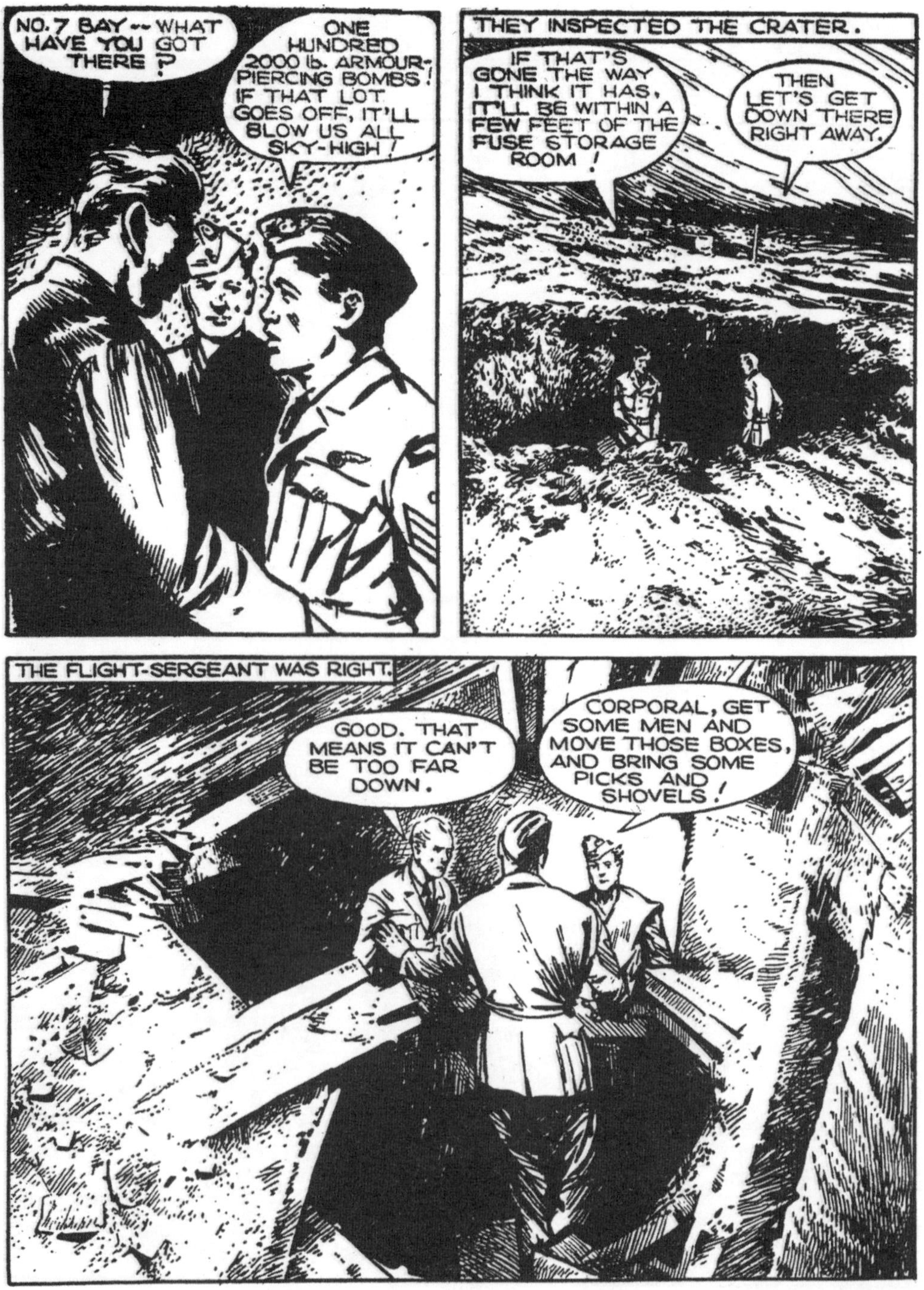
NO. 7 BAY -- WHAT HAVE YOU GOT THERE?
ONE HUNDRED 2000 lb. ARMOUR-PIERCING BOMBS! IF THAT LOT GOES OFF, IT'LL BLOW US ALL SKY-HIGH!
THEY INSPECTED THE CRATER.
IF THAT'S GONE THE WAY I THINK IT HAS, IT'LL BE WITHIN A FEW FEET OF THE FUSE STORAGE ROOM!
THEN LET'S GET DOWN THERE RIGHT AWAY.
THE FLIGHT-SERGEANT WAS RIGHT.
GOOD. THAT MEANS IT CAN'T BE TOO FAR DOWN.
CORPORAL, GET SOME MEN AND MOVE THOSE BOXES, AND BRING SOME PICKS AND SHOVELS!

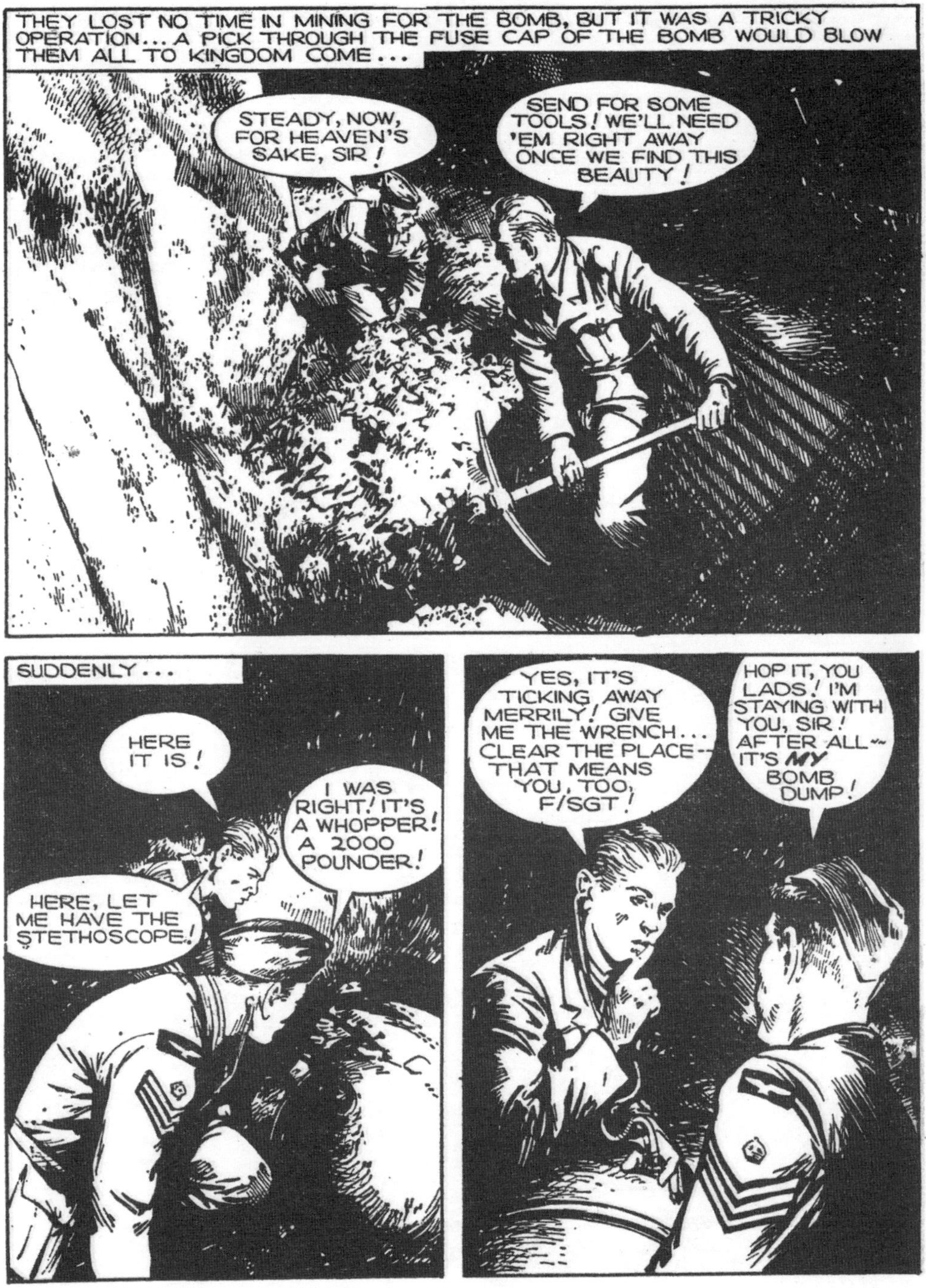
THEY LOST NO TIME IN MINING FOR THE BOMB, BUT IT WAS A TRICKY OPERATION... A PICK THROUGH THE FUSE CAP OF THE BOMB WOULD BLOW THEM ALL TO KINGDOM COME...
STEADY, NOW, FOR HEAVEN'S SAKE, SIR!
SEND FOR SOME TOOLS! WE'LL NEED 'EM RIGHT AWAY ONCE WE FIND THIS BEAUTY!
SUDDENLY...
HERE IT IS!
I WAS RIGHT! IT'S A WHOPPER! A 2000 POUNDER!
HERE, LET ME HAVE THE STETHOSCOPE!
YES, IT'S TICKING AWAY MERRILY! GIVE ME THE WRENCH... CLEAR THE PLACE-- THAT MEANS YOU, TOO, F/SGT!
HOP IT, YOU LADS! I'M STAYING WITH YOU, SIR! AFTER ALL-- IT'S MY BOMB DUMP!

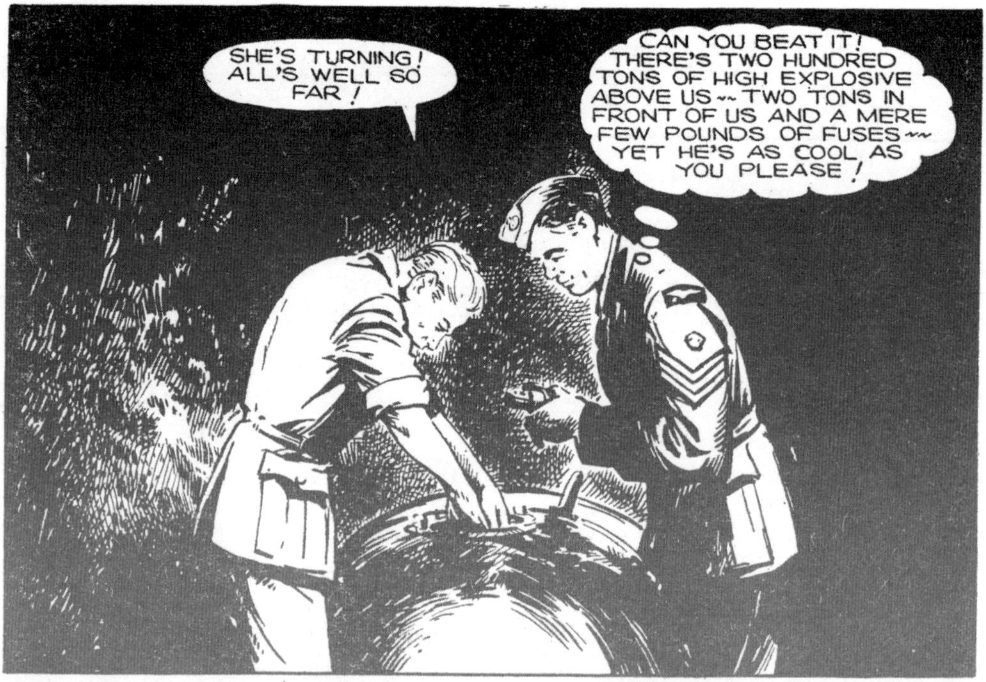
SHE'S TURNING! ALL'S WELL SO FAR!
CAN YOU BEAT IT! THERE'S TWO HUNDRED TONS OF HIGH EXPLOSIVE ABOVE US -- TWO TONS IN FRONT OF US AND A MERE FEW POUNDS OF FUSES -- YET HE'S AS COOL AS YOU PLEASE!

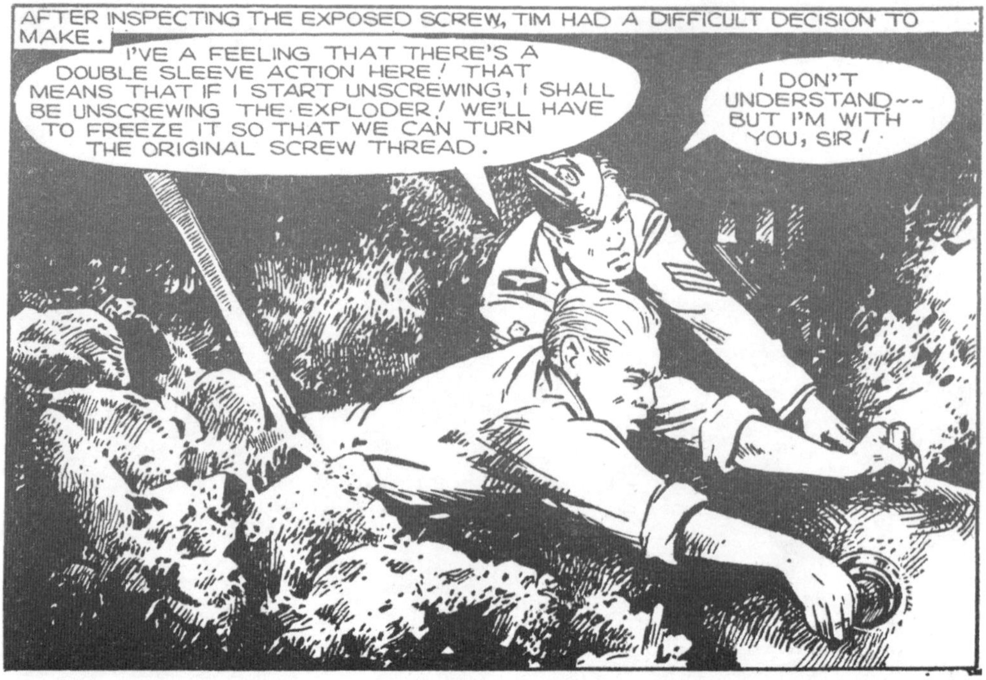
AFTER INSPECTING THE EXPOSED SCREW, TIM HAD A DIFFICULT DECISION TO MAKE.
I'VE A FEELING THAT THERE'S A DOUBLE SLEEVE ACTION HERE! THAT MEANS THAT IF I START UNSCREWING, I SHALL BE UNSCREWING THE EXPLODER! WE'LL HAVE TO FREEZE IT SO THAT WE CAN TURN THE ORIGINAL SCREW THREAD.
I DON'T UNDERSTAND -- BUT I'M WITH YOU, SIR!

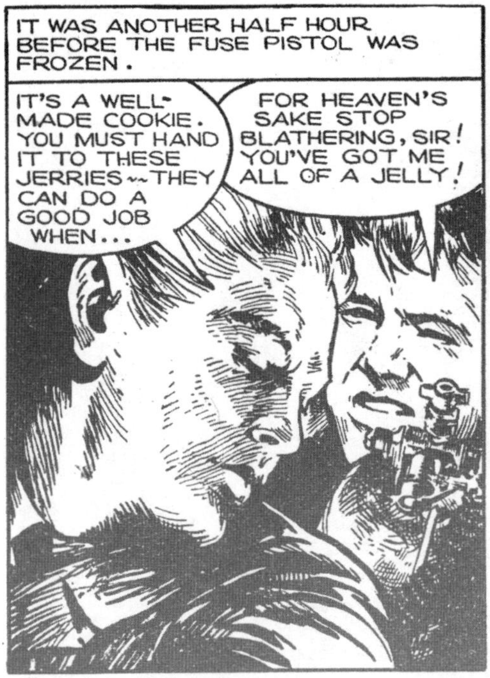
IT WAS ANOTHER HALF HOUR BEFORE THE FUSE PISTOL WAS FROZEN.
IT'S A WELL-MADE COOKIE. YOU MUST HAND IT TO THESE JERRIES -- THEY CAN DO A GOOD JOB WHEN...
FOR HEAVEN'S SAKE STOP BLATHERING, SIR! YOU'VE GOT ME ALL OF A JELLY!

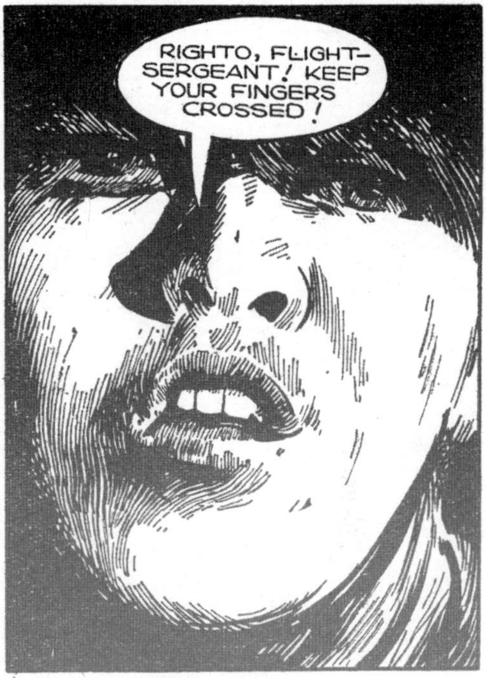
RIGHTO, FLIGHT-SERGEANT! KEEP YOUR FINGERS CROSSED!

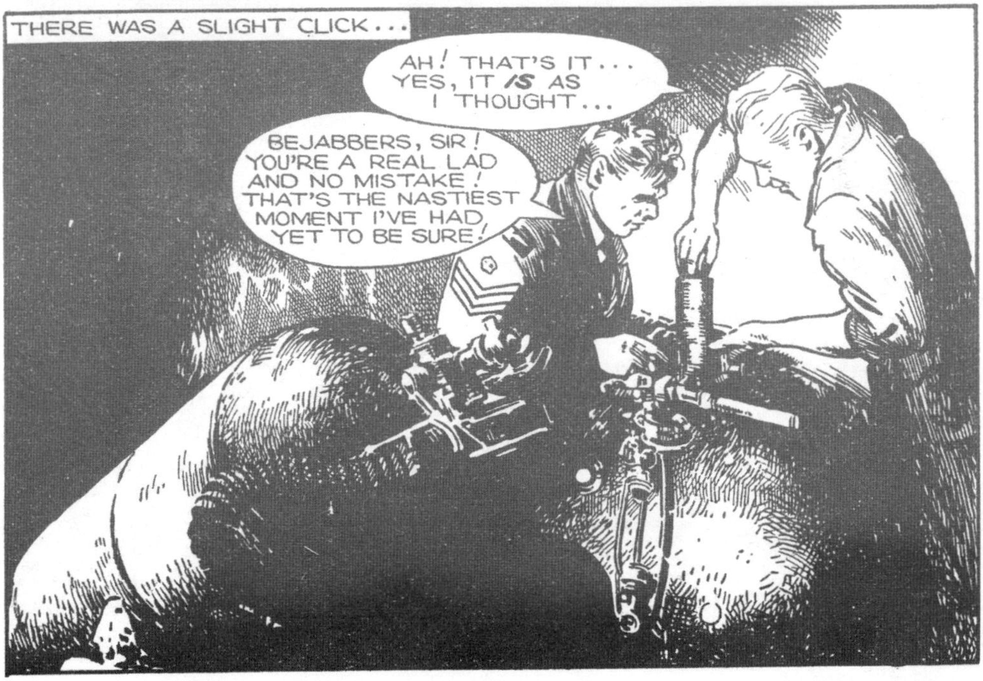
THERE WAS A SLIGHT CLICK...
AH! THAT'S IT... YES, IT IS AS I THOUGHT...
BEJABBERS, SIR! YOU'RE A REAL LAD AND NO MISTAKE! THAT'S THE NASTIEST MOMENT I'VE HAD YET TO BE SURE!

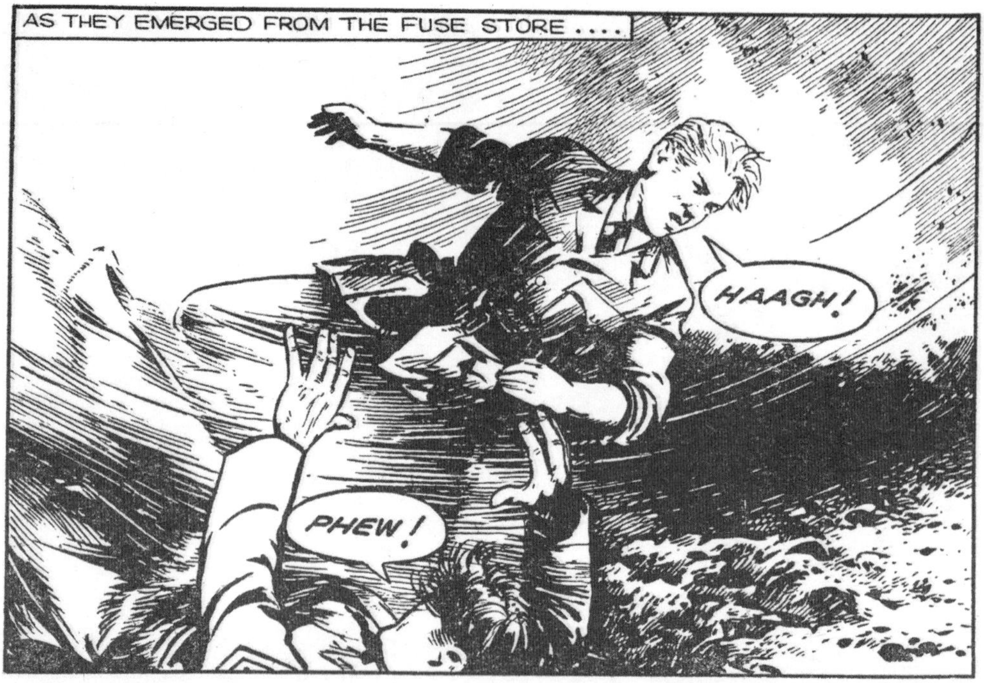
AS THEY EMERGED FROM THE FUSE STORE ....
HAAGH!
PHEW!

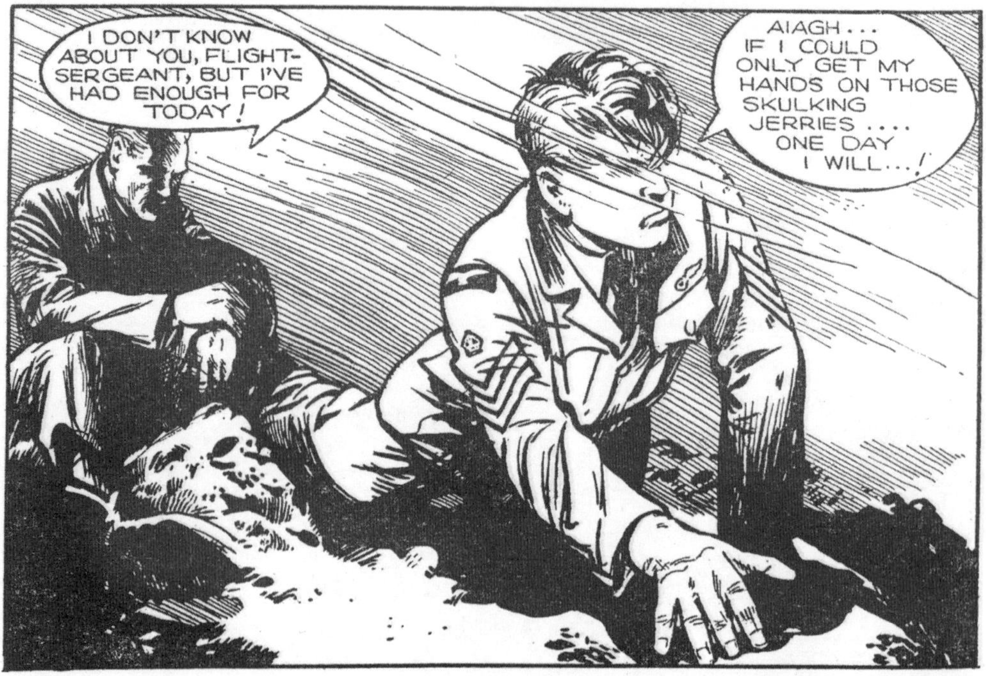
I DON'T KNOW ABOUT YOU, FLIGHT-SERGEANT, BUT I'VE HAD ENOUGH FOR TODAY!
AIAGH ... IF I COULD ONLY GET MY HANDS ON THOSE SKULKING JERRIES .... ONE DAY I WILL...!

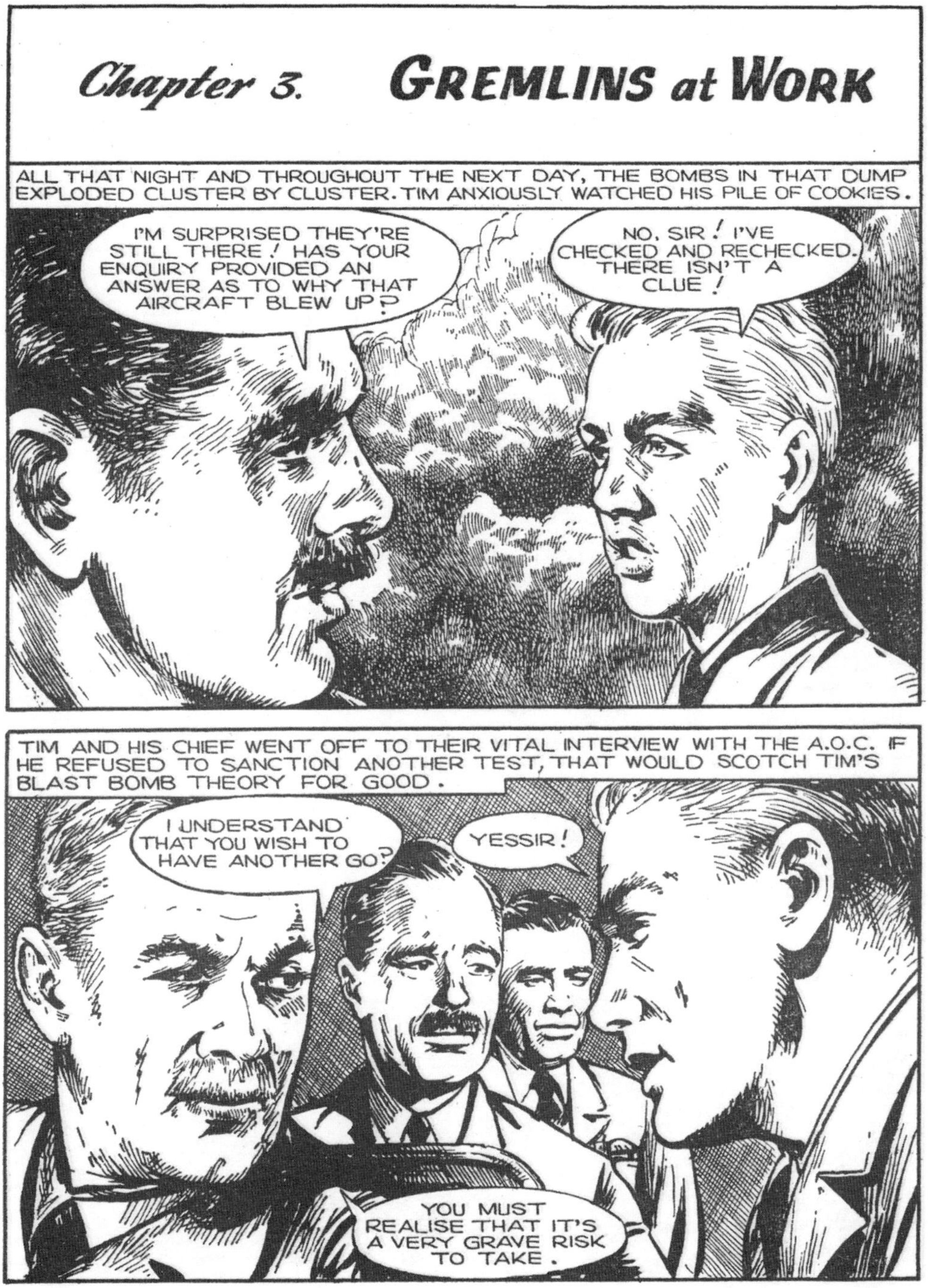
Chapter 3. GREMLINS at WORK
ALL THAT NIGHT AND THROUGHOUT THE NEXT DAY, THE BOMBS IN THAT DUMP EXPLODED CLUSTER BY CLUSTER. TIM ANXIOUSLY WATCHED HIS PILE OF COOKIES.
I'M SURPRISED THEY'RE STILL THERE! HAS YOUR ENQUIRY PROVIDED AN ANSWER AS TO WHY THAT AIRCRAFT BLEW UP?
NO, SIR! I'VE CHECKED AND RECHECKED. THERE ISN'T A CLUE!
TIM AND HIS CHIEF WENT OFF TO THEIR VITAL INTERVIEW WITH THE A.O.C. IF HE REFUSED TO SANCTION ANOTHER TEST, THAT WOULD SCOTCH TIM'S BLAST BOMB THEORY FOR GOOD.
I UNDERSTAND THAT YOU WISH TO HAVE ANOTHER GO?
YESSIR!
YOU MUST REALISE THAT IT'S A VERY GRAVE RISK TO TAKE.

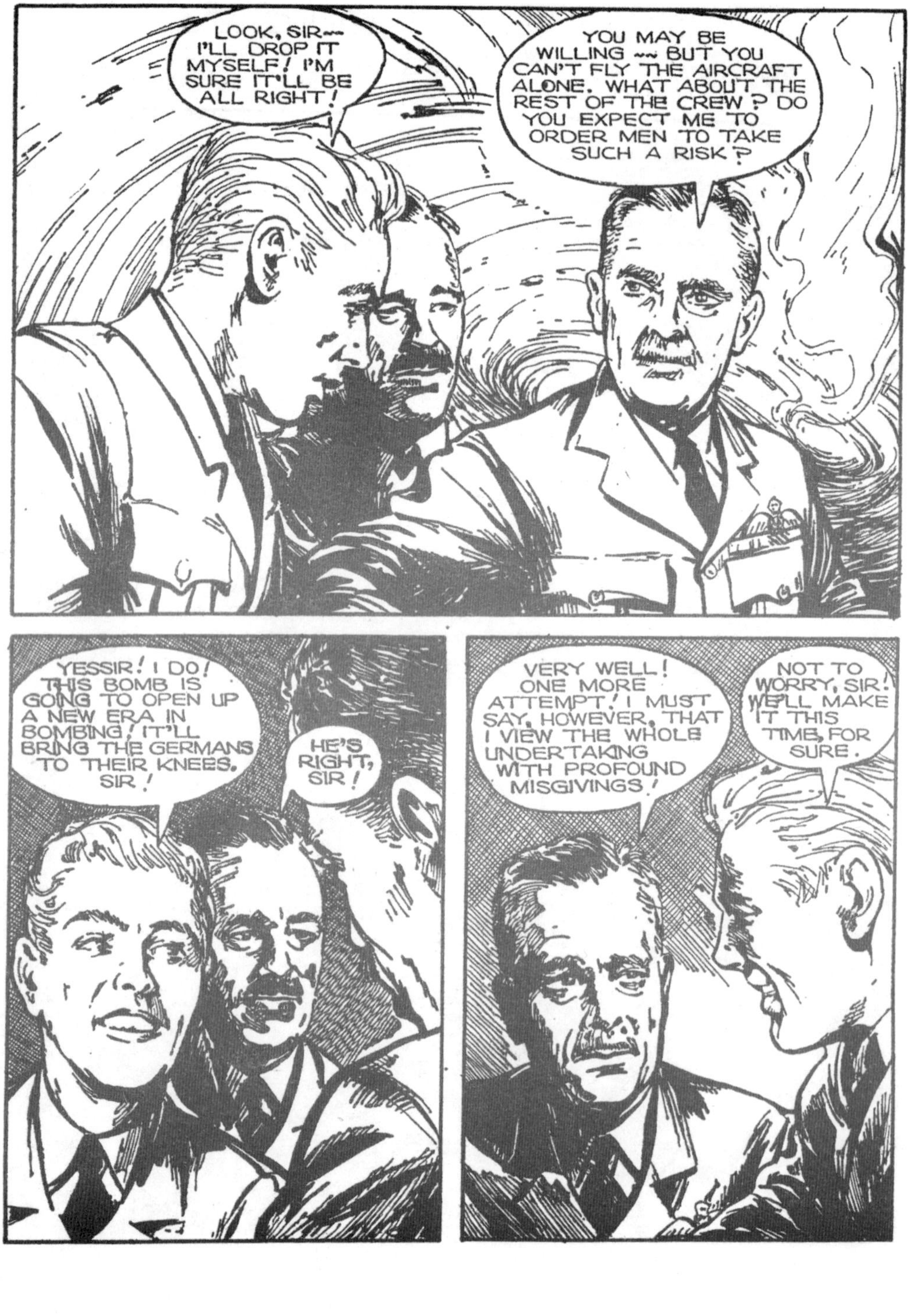
LOOK, SIR-- I'LL DROP IT MYSELF! I'M SURE IT'LL BE ALL RIGHT!
YOU MAY BE WILLING -- BUT YOU CAN'T FLY THE AIRCRAFT ALONE. WHAT ABOUT THE REST OF THE CREW? DO YOU EXPECT ME TO ORDER MEN TO TAKE SUCH A RISK?
YESSIR! I DO! THIS BOMB IS GOING TO OPEN UP A NEW ERA IN BOMBING! IT'LL BRING THE GERMANS TO THEIR KNEES, SIR!
HE'S RIGHT, SIR!
VERY WELL! ONE MORE ATTEMPT! I MUST SAY, HOWEVER, THAT I VIEW THE WHOLE UNDERTAKING WITH PROFOUND MISGIVINGS!
NOT TO WORRY, SIR! WE'LL MAKE IT THIS TIME, FOR SURE.

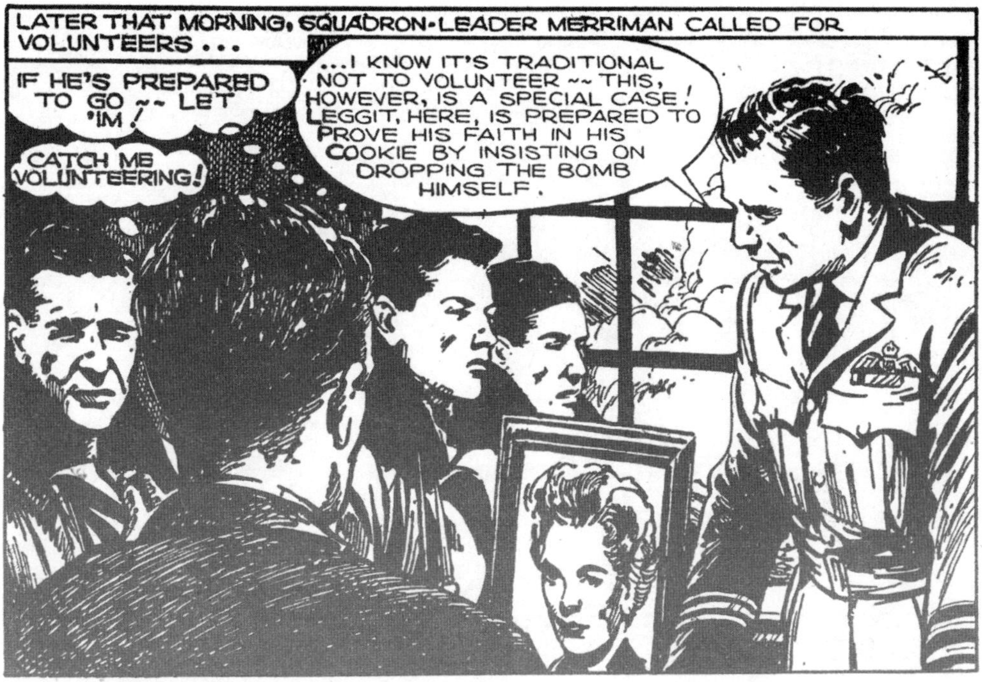
LATER THAT MORNING, SQUADRON-LEADER MERRIMAN CALLED FOR VOLUNTEERS . . .
IF HE'S PREPARED TO GO ~~ LET 'IM!
CATCH ME VOLUNTEERING!
. . . I KNOW IT'S TRADITIONAL NOT TO VOLUNTEER ~~ THIS, HOWEVER, IS A SPECIAL CASE! LEGGIT, HERE, IS PREPARED TO PROVE HIS FAITH IN HIS COOKIE BY INSISTING ON DROPPING THE BOMB HIMSELF.

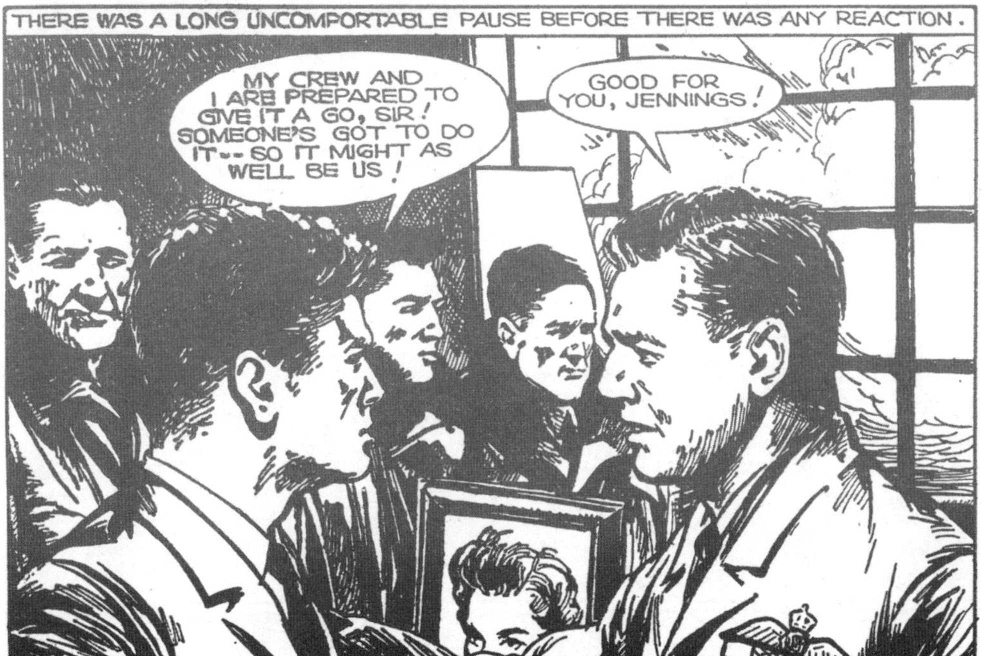
THERE WAS A LONG UNCOMPORTABLE PAUSE BEFORE THERE WAS ANY REACTION.
MY CREW AND I ARE PREPARED TO GIVE IT A GO, SIR! SOMEONE'S GOT TO DO IT -- SO IT MIGHT AS WELL BE US!
GOOD FOR YOU, JENNINGS!

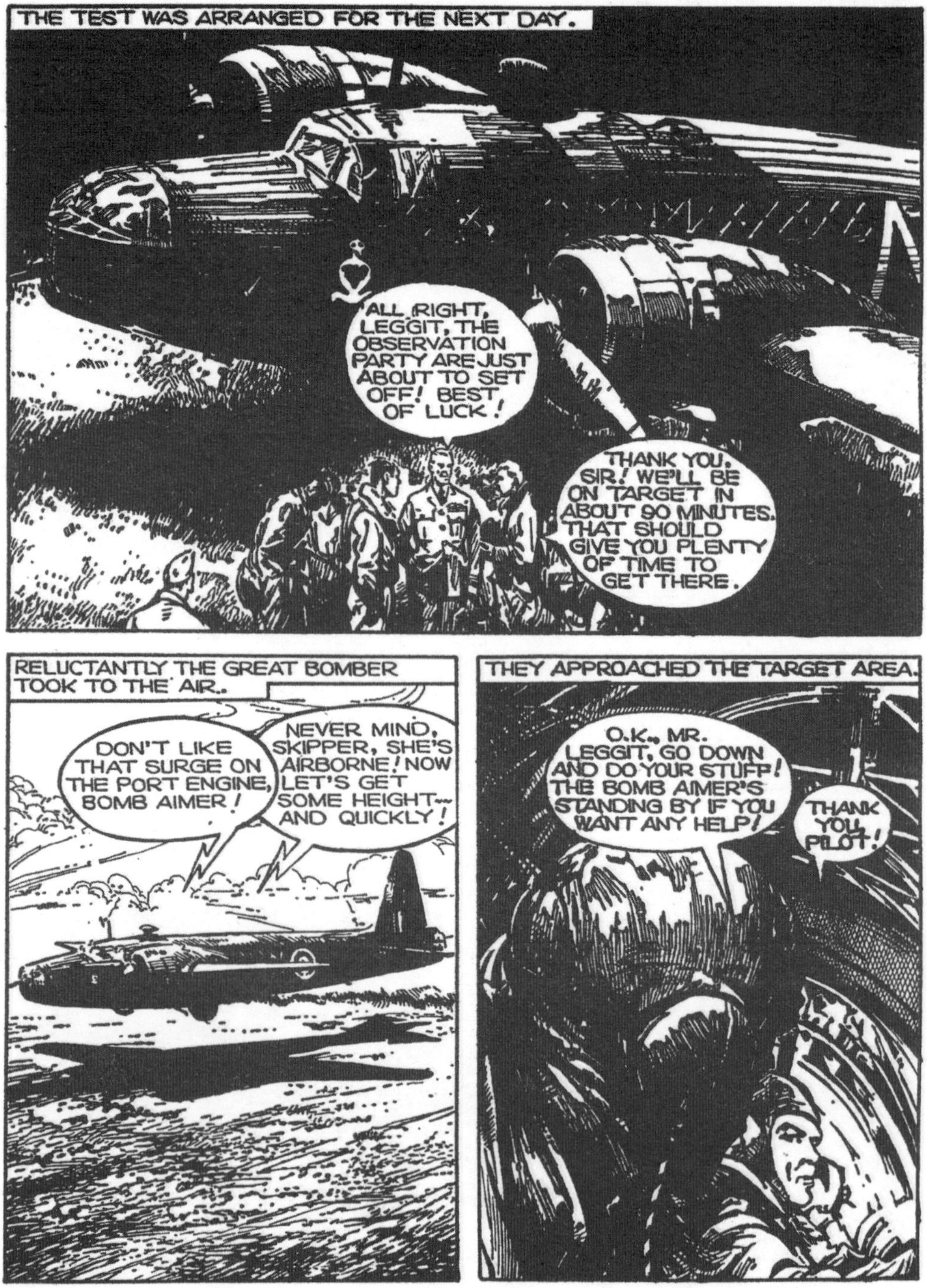
THE TEST WAS ARRANGED FOR THE NEXT DAY.
ALL RIGHT, LEGGIT, THE OBSERVATION PARTY ARE JUST ABOUT TO SET OFF! BEST OF LUCK!
THANK YOU, SIR! WE'LL BE ON TARGET IN ABOUT 90 MINUTES. THAT SHOULD GIVE YOU PLENTY OF TIME TO GET THERE.
RELUCTANTLY THE GREAT BOMBER TOOK TO THE AIR..
DON'T LIKE THAT SURGE ON THE PORT ENGINE, BOMB AIMER!
NEVER MIND, SKIPPER, SHE'S AIRBORNE! NOW LET'S GET SOME HEIGHT-- AND QUICKLY!
THEY APPROACHED THE TARGET AREA.
O.K., MR. LEGGIT, GO DOWN AND DO YOUR STUFF! THE BOMB AIMER'S STANDING BY IF YOU WANT ANY HELP!
THANK YOU, PILOT!

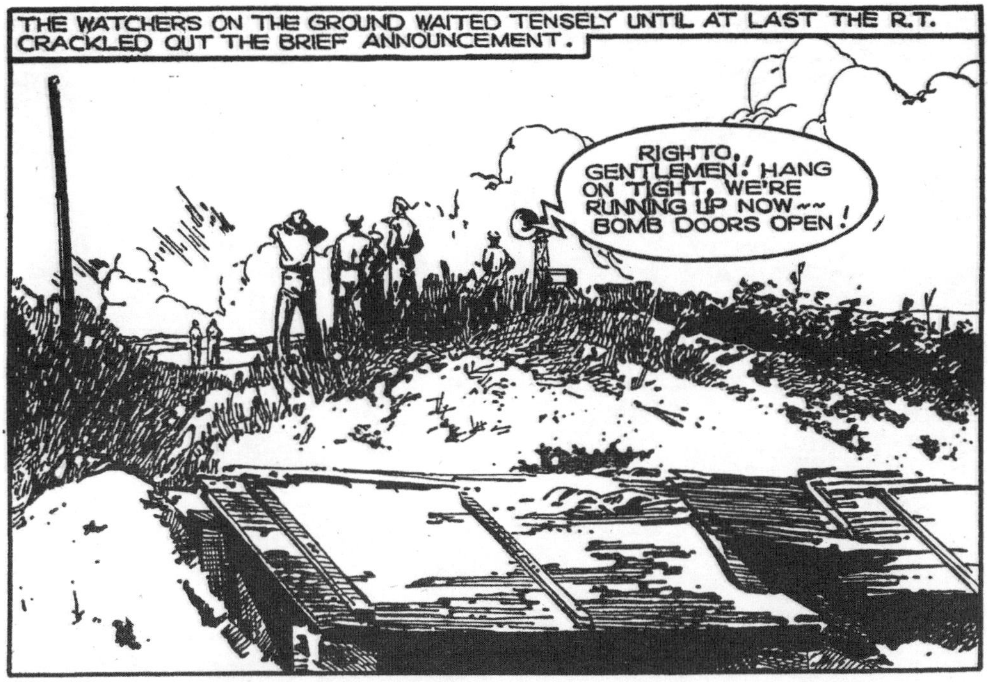
THE WATCHERS ON THE GROUND WAITED TENSELY UNTIL AT LAST THE R.T. CRACKLED OUT THE BRIEF ANNOUNCEMENT.
RIGHTO, GENTLEMEN! HANG ON TIGHT, WE'RE RUNNING UP NOW -- BOMB DOORS OPEN!

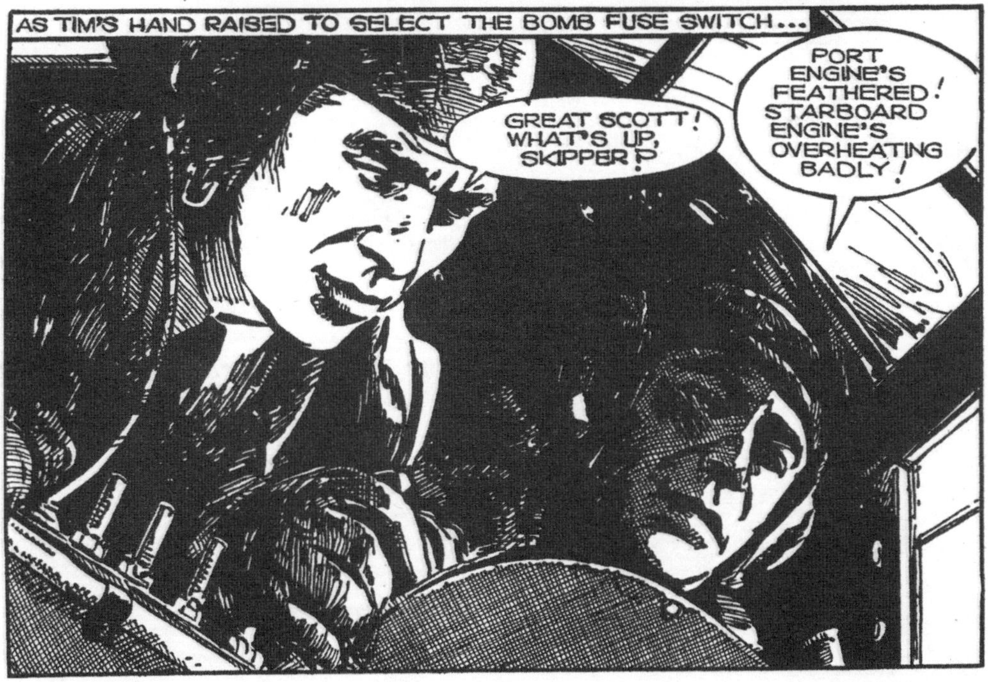
AS TIM'S HAND RAISED TO SELECT THE BOMB FUSE SWITCH...
GREAT SCOTT! WHAT'S UP, SKIPPER?
PORT ENGINE'S FEATHERED! STARBOARD ENGINE'S OVERHEATING BADLY!

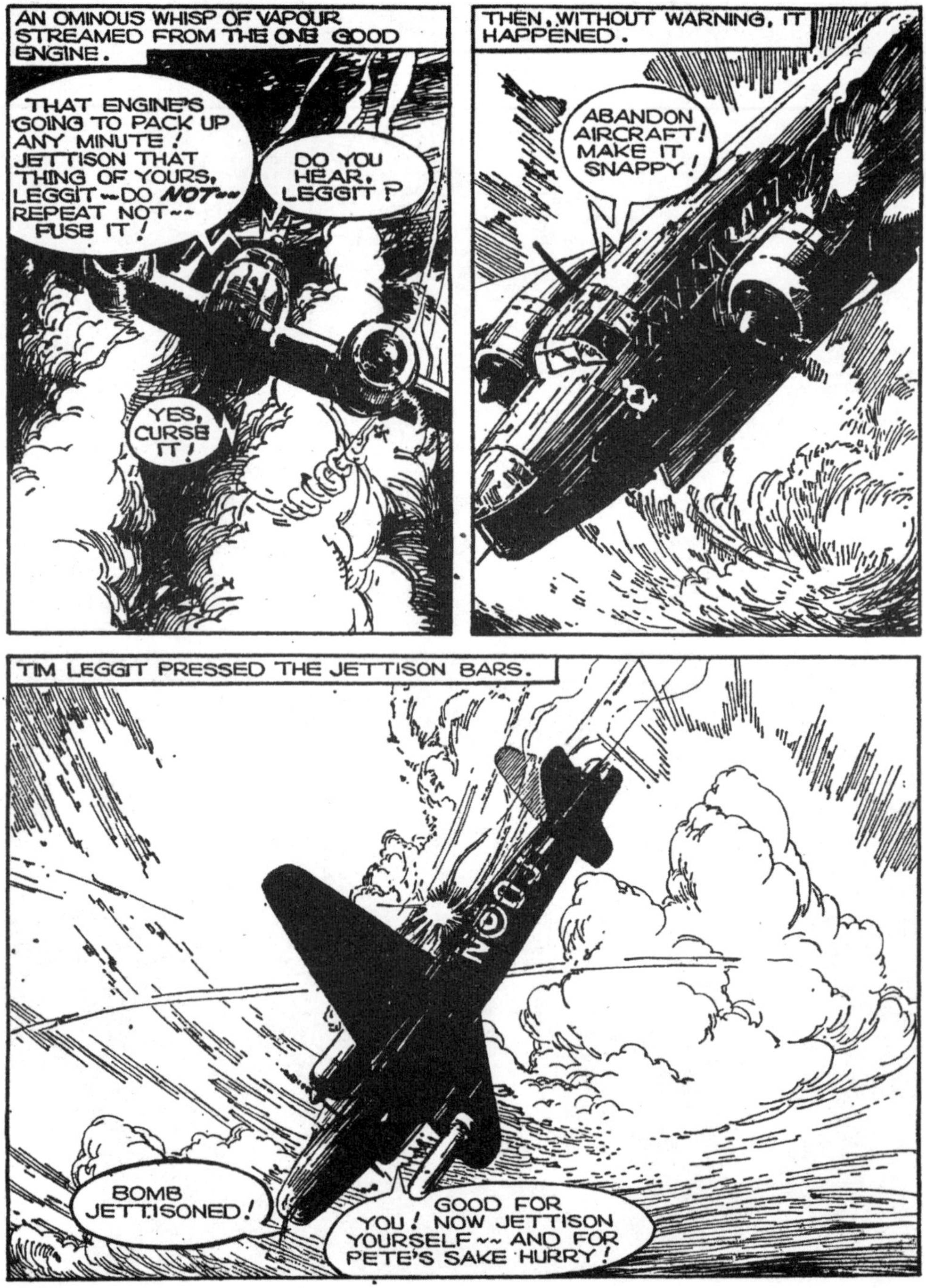
AN OMINOUS WHISP OF VAPOUR STREAMED FROM THE ONE GOOD ENGINE.
THAT ENGINE'S GOING TO PACK UP ANY MINUTE! JETTISON THAT THING OF YOURS, LEGGIT -- DO NOT -- REPEAT NOT -- FUSE IT!
DO YOU HEAR, LEGGIT?
YES, CURSE IT!
THEN, WITHOUT WARNING, IT HAPPENED.
ABANDON AIRCRAFT! MAKE IT SNAPPY!
TIM LEGGIT PRESSED THE JETTISON BARS.
BOMB JETTISONED!
GOOD FOR YOU! NOW JETTISON YOURSELF -- AND FOR PETE'S SAKE HURRY!

THE OBSERVERS ON THE GROUND WATCHED HELPLESSLY AS THE DRAMA SWIFTLY MOVED TO ITS CLIMAX.

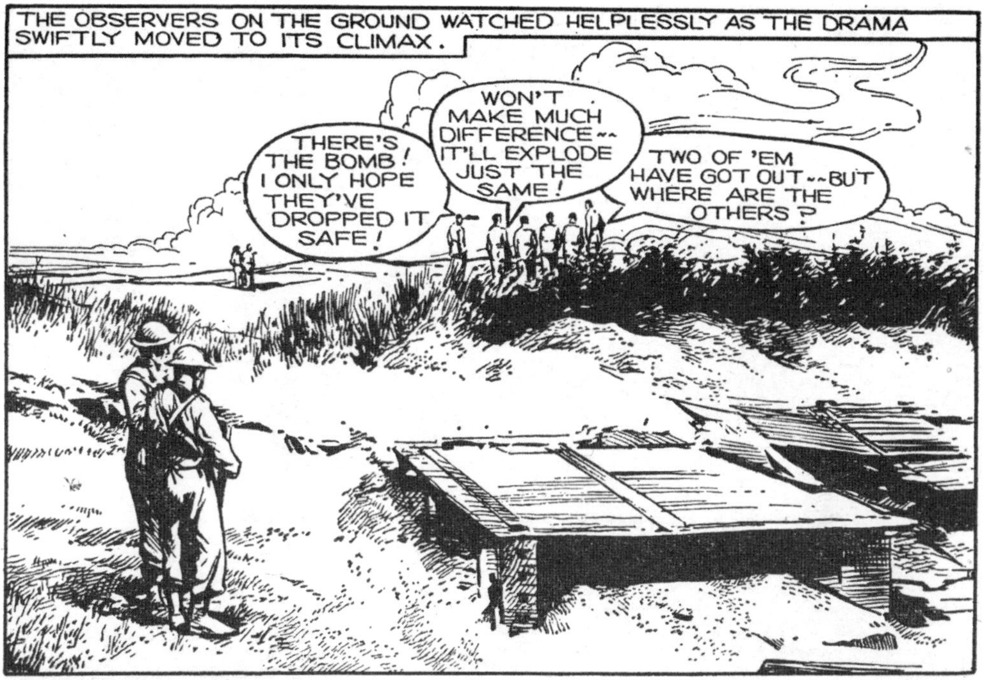
THERE'S THE BOMB! I ONLY HOPE THEY'VE DROPPED IT SAFE!
WON'T MAKE MUCH DIFFERENCE~~ IT'LL EXPLODE JUST THE SAME!
TWO OF 'EM HAVE GOT OUT~~BUT WHERE ARE THE OTHERS?

AS IF HYPNOTISED, TIM WATCHED THE BOMB FALLING.

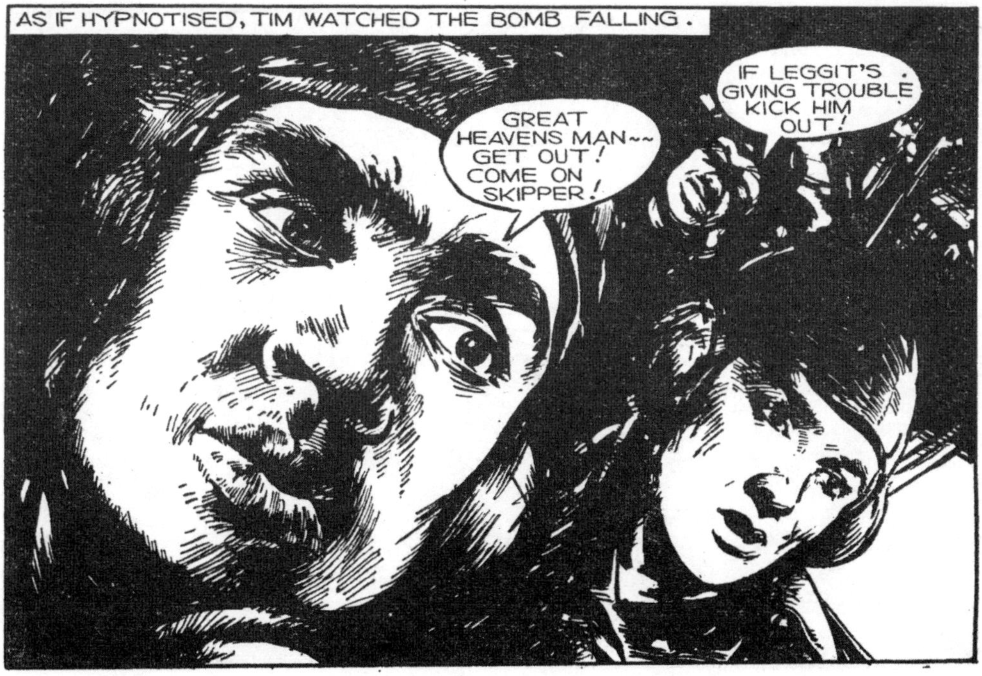
GREAT HEAVENS MAN~~ GET OUT! COME ON SKIPPER!
IF LEGGIT'S GIVING TROUBLE KICK HIM OUT!

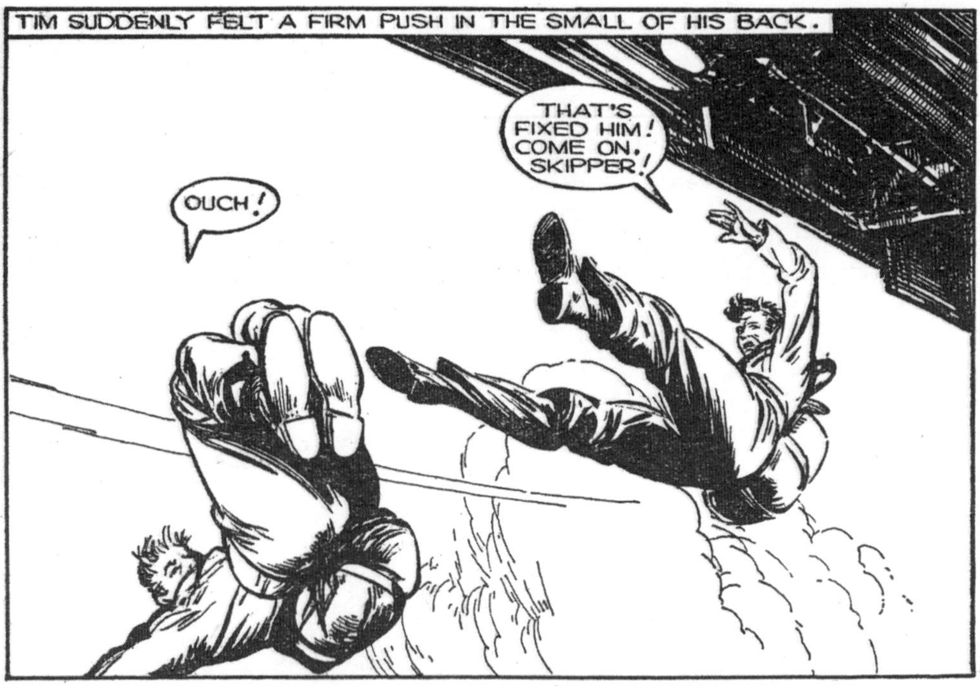
TIM SUDDENLY FELT A FIRM PUSH IN THE SMALL OF HIS BACK.
THAT'S FIXED HIM! COME ON, SKIPPER!
OUCH!

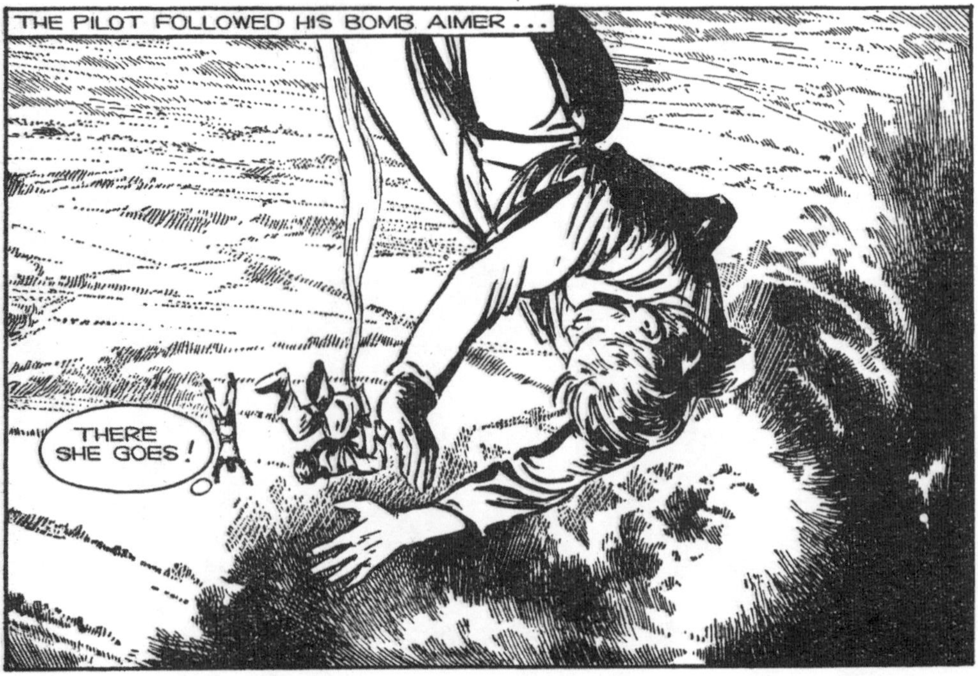
THE PILOT FOLLOWED HIS BOMB AIMER...
THERE SHE GOES!

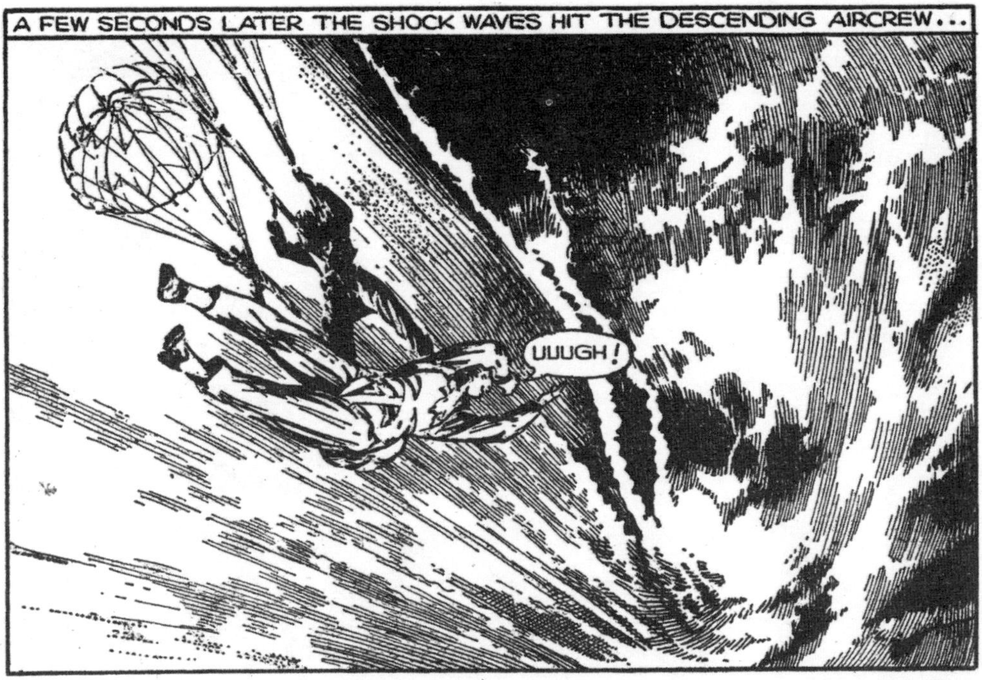
A FEW SECONDS LATER THE SHOCK WAVES HIT THE DESCENDING AIRCREW...
UUUGH!

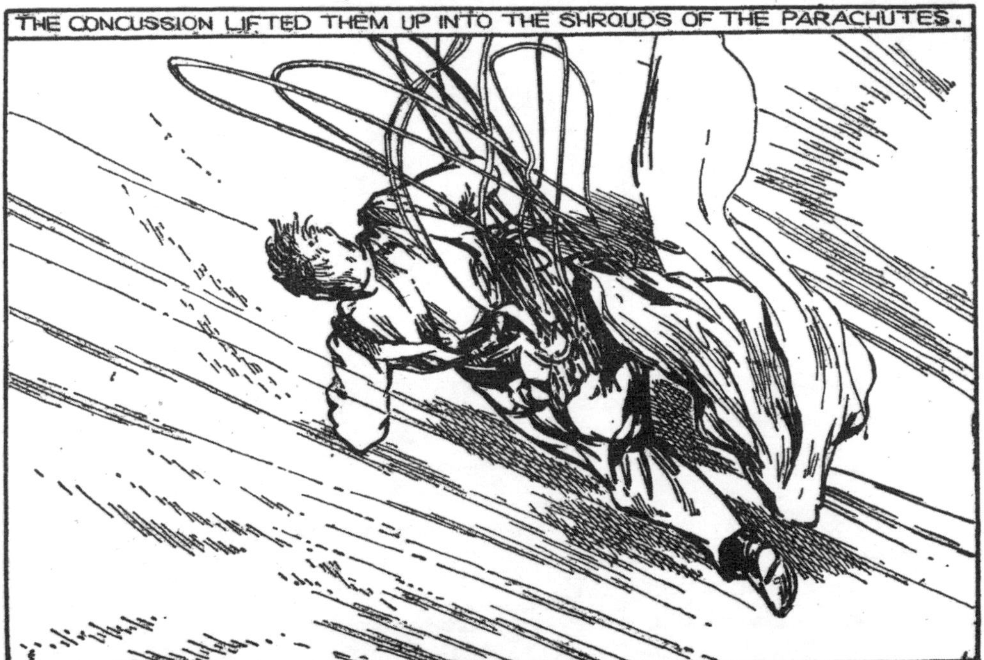
THE CONCUSSION LIFTED THEM UP INTO THE SHROUDS OF THE PARACHUTES.

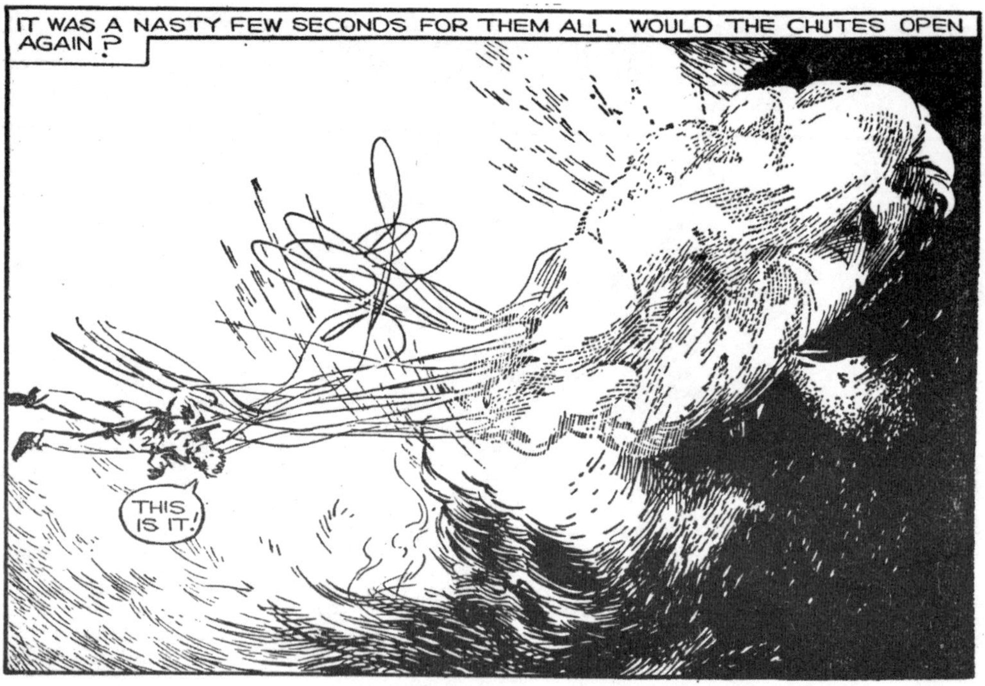
IT WAS A NASTY FEW SECONDS FOR THEM ALL. WOULD THE CHUTES OPEN AGAIN?
THIS IS IT!

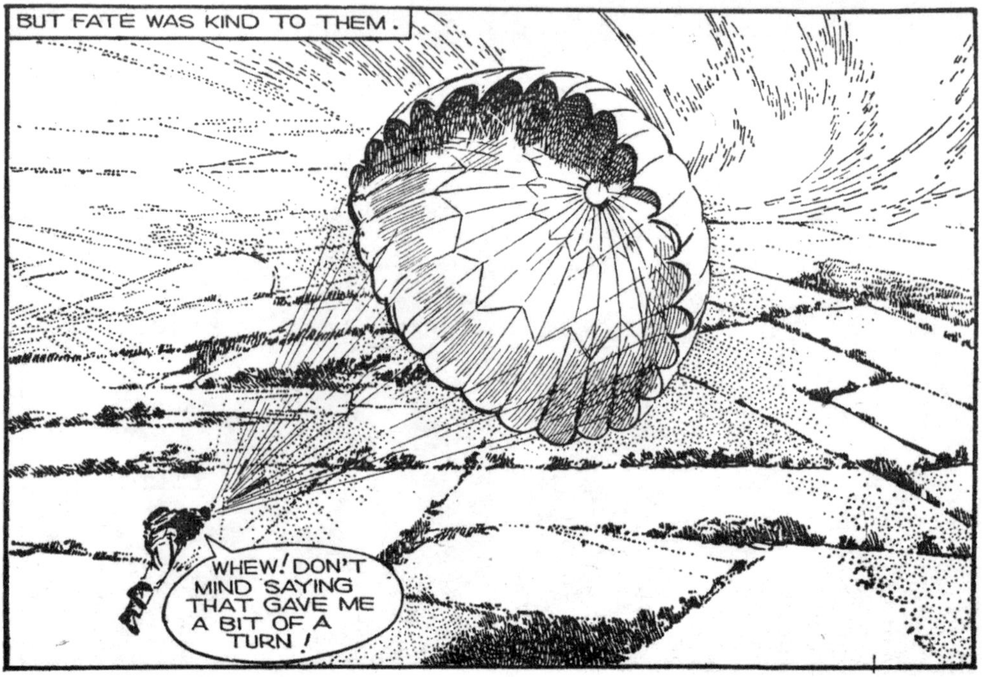
BUT FATE WAS KIND TO THEM.
WHEW! DON'T MIND SAYING THAT GAVE ME A BIT OF A TURN!

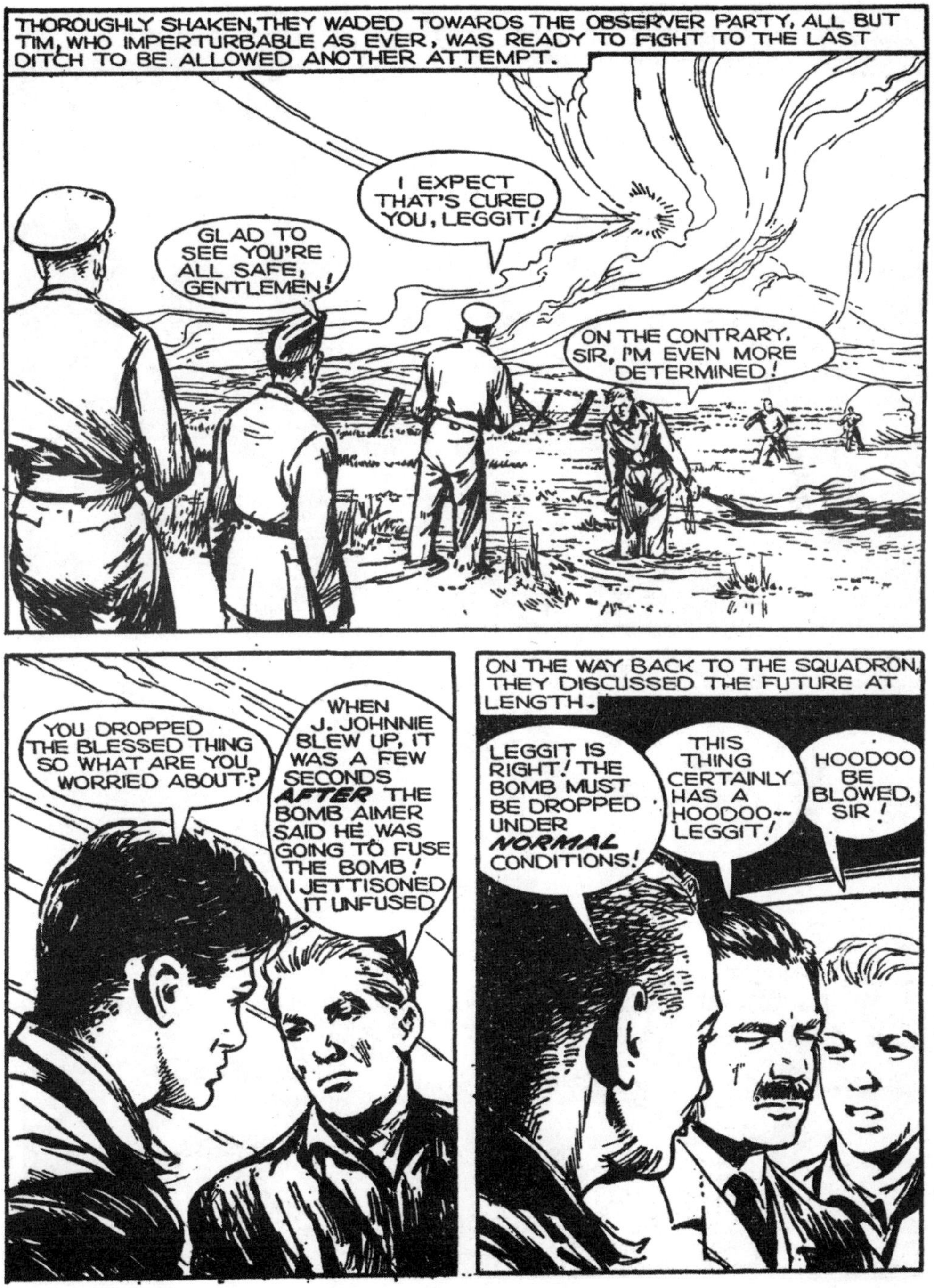
THOROUGHLY SHAKEN, THEY WADED TOWARDS THE OBSERVER PARTY, ALL BUT TIM, WHO IMPERTURBABLE AS EVER, WAS READY TO FIGHT TO THE LAST DITCH TO BE ALLOWED ANOTHER ATTEMPT.
GLAD TO SEE YOU'RE ALL SAFE, GENTLEMEN!
I EXPECT THAT'S CURED YOU, LEGGIT!
ON THE CONTRARY, SIR, I'M EVEN MORE DETERMINED!
YOU DROPPED THE BLESSED THING SO WHAT ARE YOU WORRIED ABOUT?
WHEN J. JOHNNIE BLEW UP, IT WAS A FEW SECONDS AFTER THE BOMB AIMER SAID HE WAS GOING TO FUSE THE BOMB! I JETTISONED IT UNFUSED
ON THE WAY BACK TO THE SQUADRON, THEY DISCUSSED THE FUTURE AT LENGTH.
LEGGIT IS RIGHT! THE BOMB MUST BE DROPPED UNDER NORMAL CONDITIONS!
THIS THING CERTAINLY HAS A HOODOO-- LEGGIT!
HOODOO BE BLOWED, SIR!

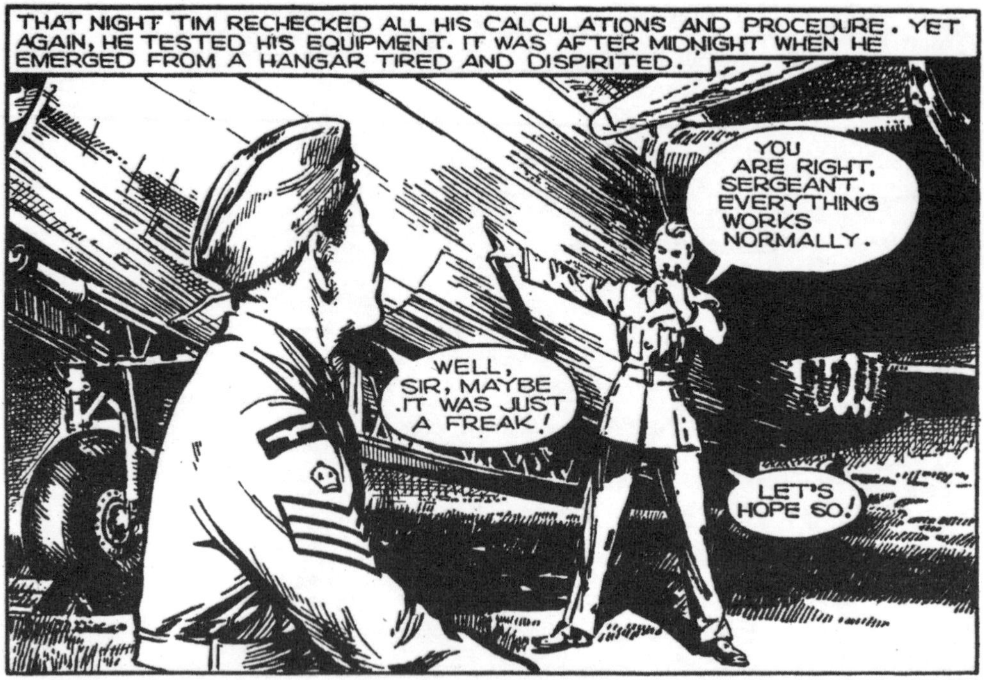
THAT NIGHT TIM RECHECKED ALL HIS CALCULATIONS AND PROCEDURE. YET AGAIN, HE TESTED HIS EQUIPMENT. IT WAS AFTER MIDNIGHT WHEN HE EMERGED FROM A HANGAR TIRED AND DISPIRITED.
YOU ARE RIGHT, SERGEANT. EVERYTHING WORKS NORMALLY.
WELL, SIR, MAYBE IT WAS JUST A FREAK!
LET'S HOPE SO!

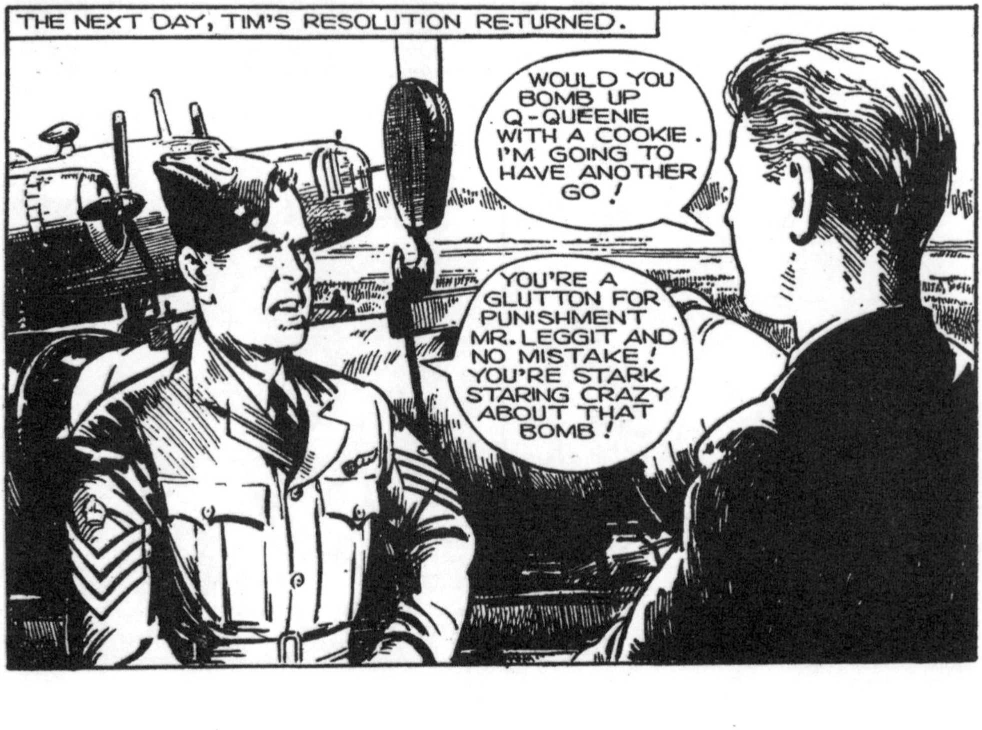
THE NEXT DAY, TIM'S RESOLUTION RETURNED.
WOULD YOU BOMB UP Q-QUEENIE WITH A COOKIE. I'M GOING TO HAVE ANOTHER GO!
YOU'RE A GLUTTON FOR PUNISHMENT MR. LEGGIT AND NO MISTAKE! YOU'RE STARK STARING CRAZY ABOUT THAT BOMB!

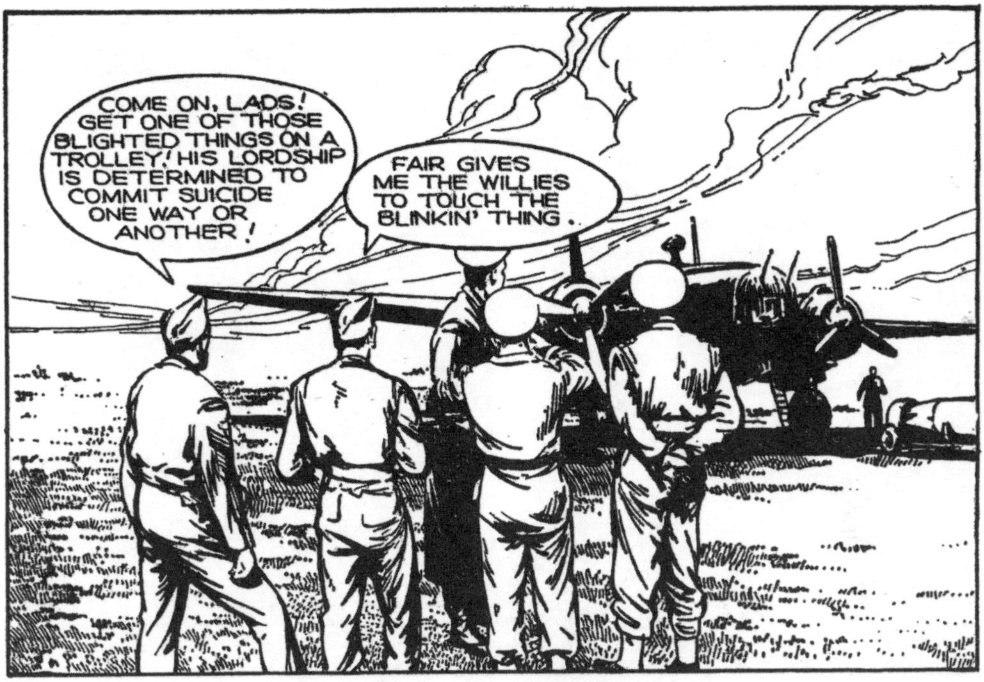
COME ON, LADS! GET ONE OF THOSE BLIGHTED THINGS ON A TROLLEY! HIS LORDSHIP IS DETERMINED TO COMMIT SUICIDE ONE WAY OR ANOTHER!
FAIR GIVES ME THE WILLIES TO TOUCH THE BLINKIN' THING.

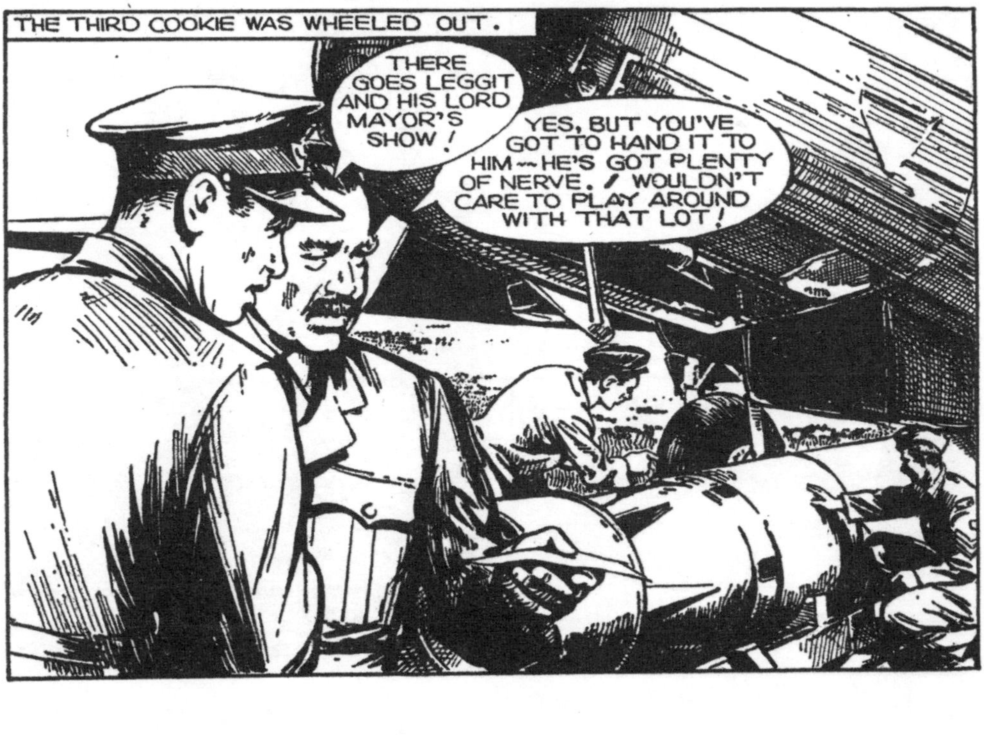
THE THIRD COOKIE WAS WHEELED OUT.
THERE GOES LEGGIT AND HIS LORD MAYOR'S SHOW!
YES, BUT YOU'VE GOT TO HAND IT TO HIM--HE'S GOT PLENTY OF NERVE. I WOULDN'T CARE TO PLAY AROUND WITH THAT LOT!

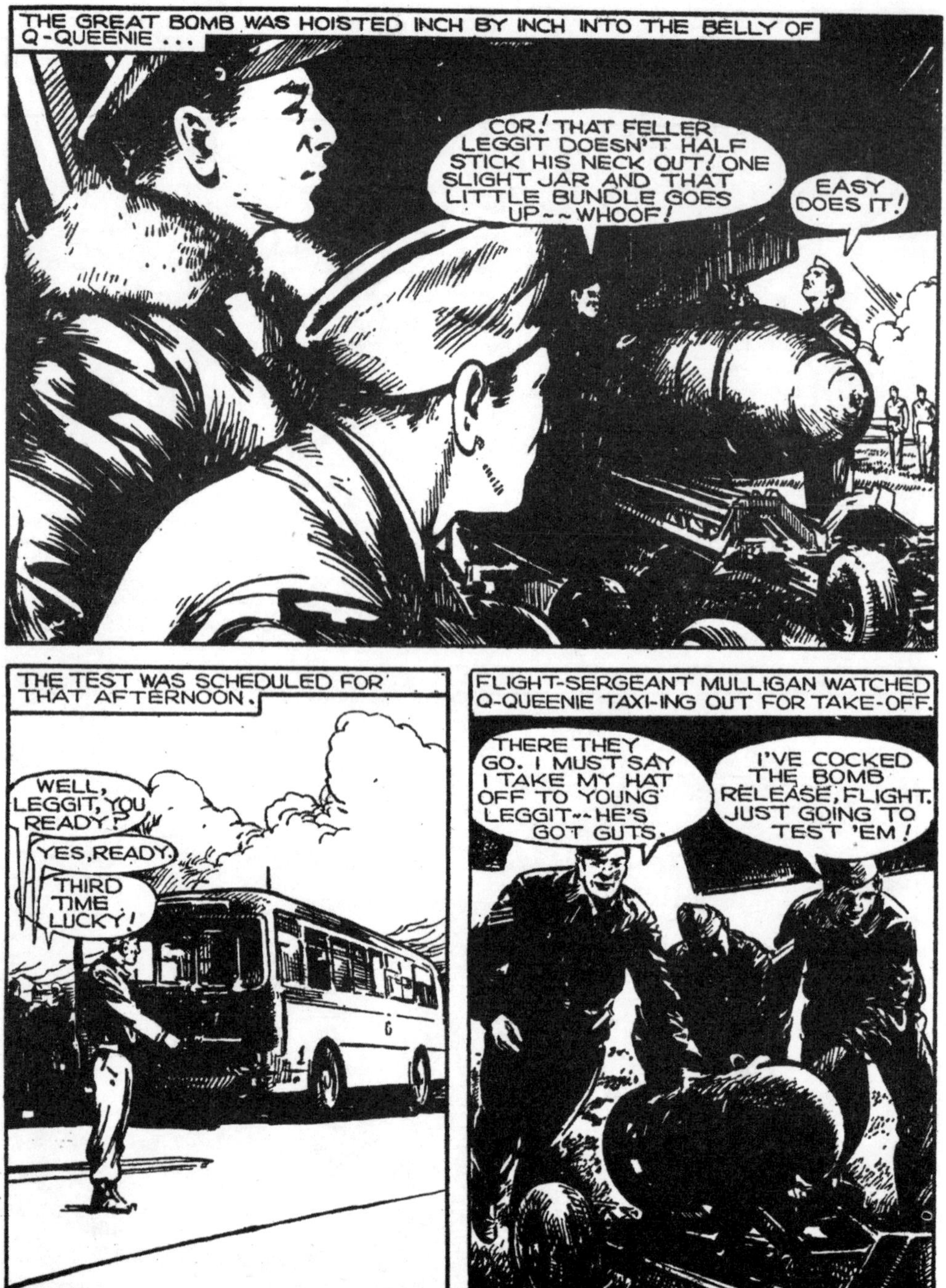
THE GREAT BOMB WAS HOISTED INCH BY INCH INTO THE BELLY OF Q-QUEENIE ...
COR! THAT FELLER LEGGIT DOESN'T HALF STICK HIS NECK OUT! ONE SLIGHT JAR AND THAT LITTLE BUNDLE GOES UP--WHOOF!
EASY DOES IT!
THE TEST WAS SCHEDULED FOR THAT AFTERNOON.
WELL, LEGGIT, YOU READY?
YES, READY.
THIRD TIME LUCKY!
FLIGHT-SERGEANT MULLIGAN WATCHED Q-QUEENIE TAXI-ING OUT FOR TAKE-OFF.
THERE THEY GO. I MUST SAY I TAKE MY HAT OFF TO YOUNG LEGGIT--HE'S GOT GUTS.
I'VE COCKED THE BOMB RELEASE, FLIGHT. JUST GOING TO TEST 'EM!

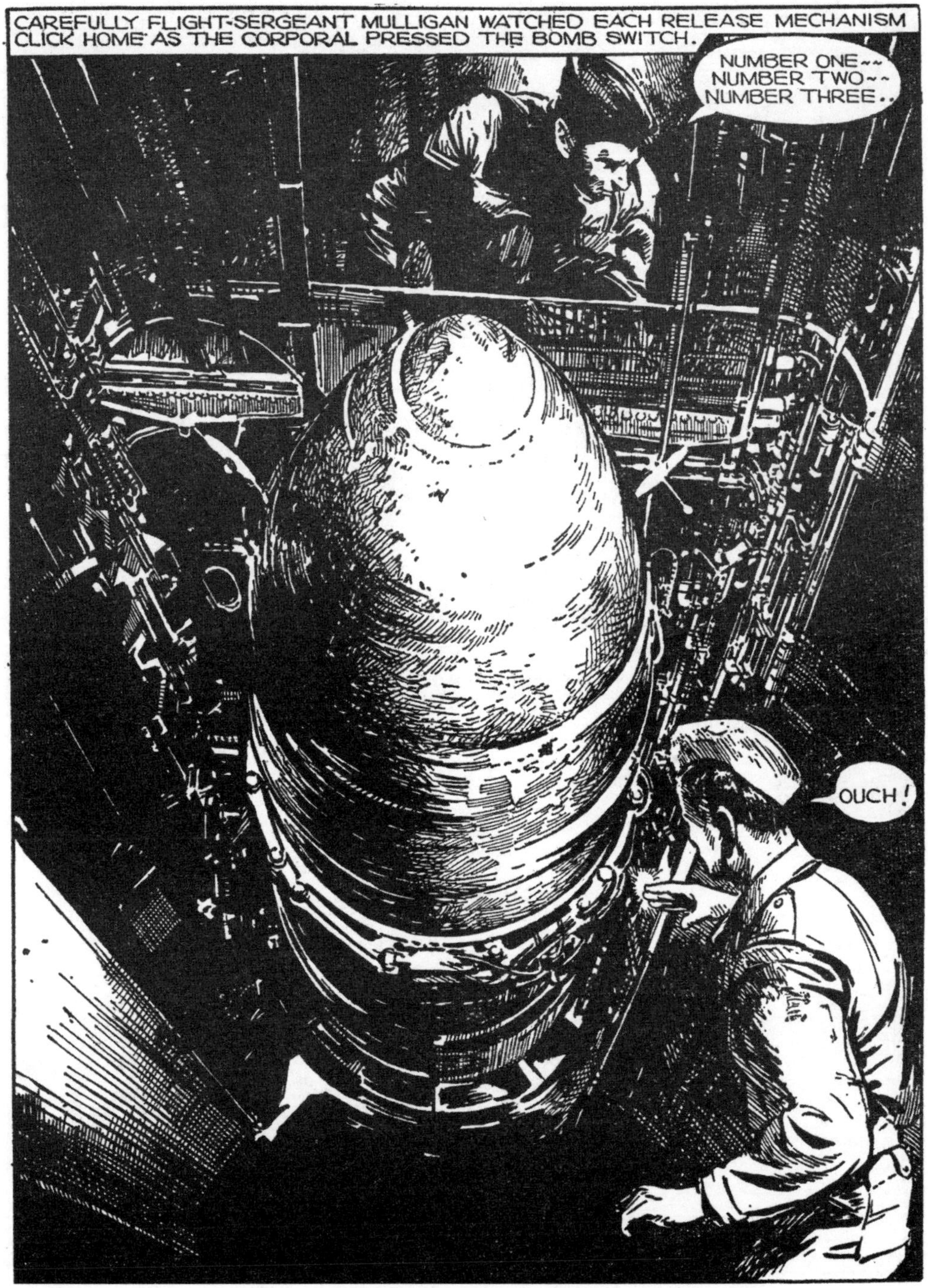
CAREFULLY FLIGHT-SERGEANT MULLIGAN WATCHED EACH RELEASE MECHANISM CLICK HOME AS THE CORPORAL PRESSED THE BOMB SWITCH.
NUMBER ONE-- NUMBER TWO-- NUMBER THREE..
OUCH!

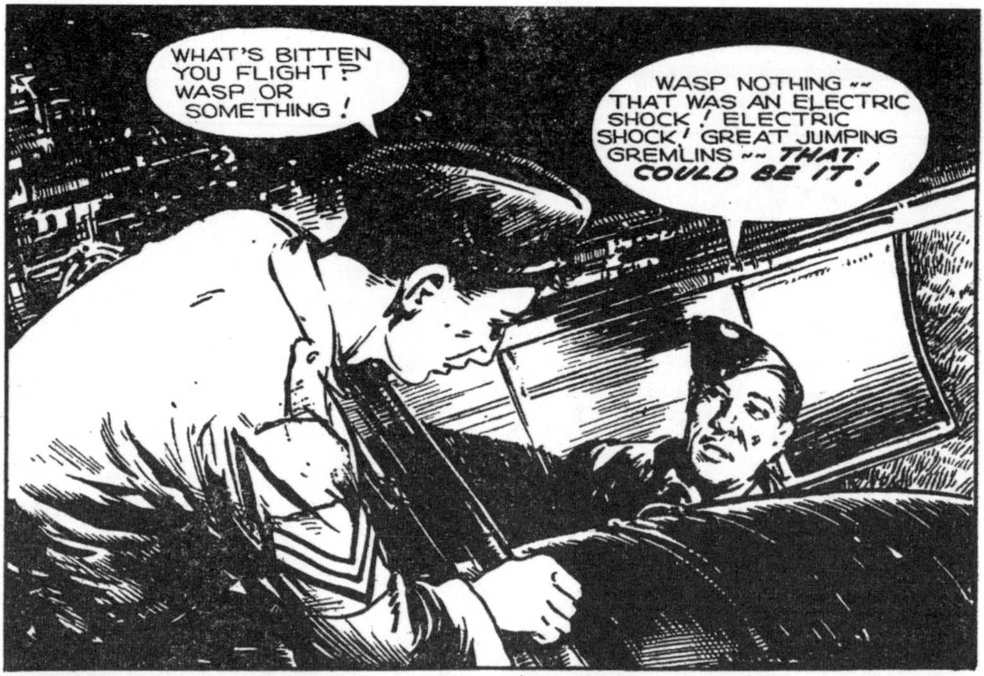
WHAT'S BITTEN YOU FLIGHT? WASP OR SOMETHING!
WASP NOTHING -- THAT WAS AN ELECTRIC SHOCK! ELECTRIC SHOCK! GREAT JUMPING GREMLINS -- THAT COULD BE IT!

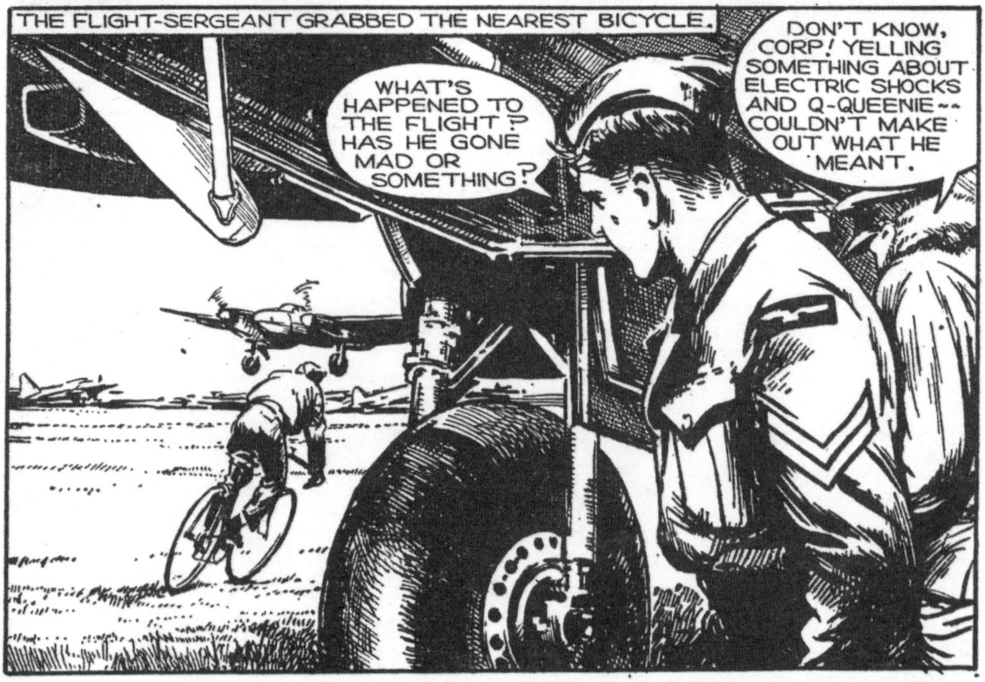
THE FLIGHT-SERGEANT GRABBED THE NEAREST BICYCLE.
WHAT'S HAPPENED TO THE FLIGHT? HAS HE GONE MAD OR SOMETHING?
DON'T KNOW, CORP! YELLING SOMETHING ABOUT ELECTRIC SHOCKS AND Q-QUEENIE -- COULDN'T MAKE OUT WHAT HE MEANT.

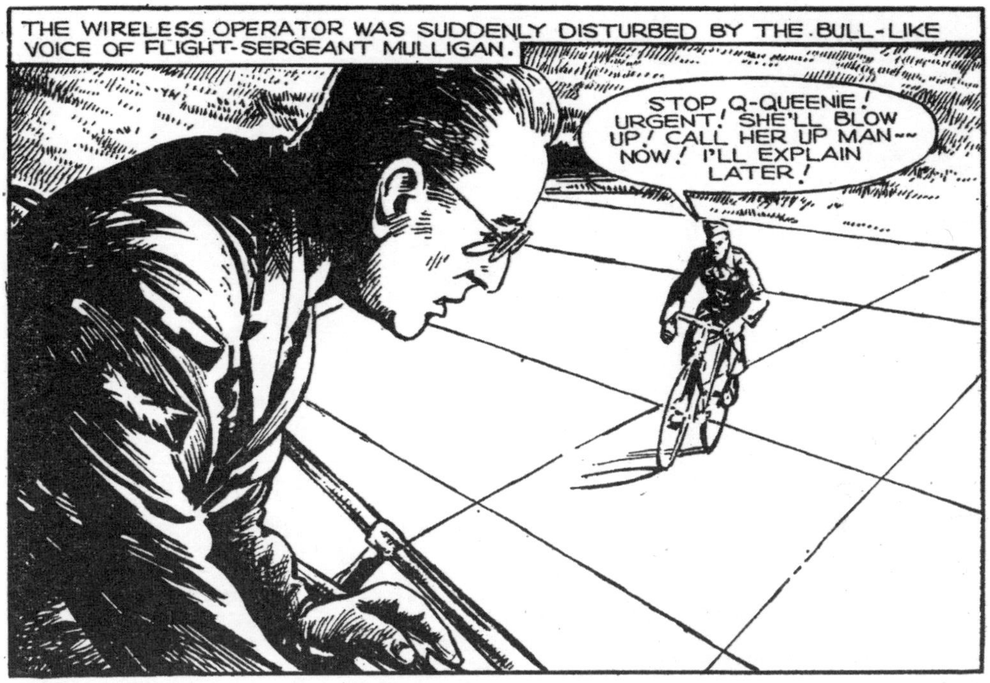
THE WIRELESS OPERATOR WAS SUDDENLY DISTURBED BY THE BULL-LIKE VOICE OF FLIGHT-SERGEANT MULLIGAN.
STOP Q-QUEENIE! URGENT! SHE'LL BLOW UP! CALL HER UP MAN-- NOW! I'LL EXPLAIN LATER!

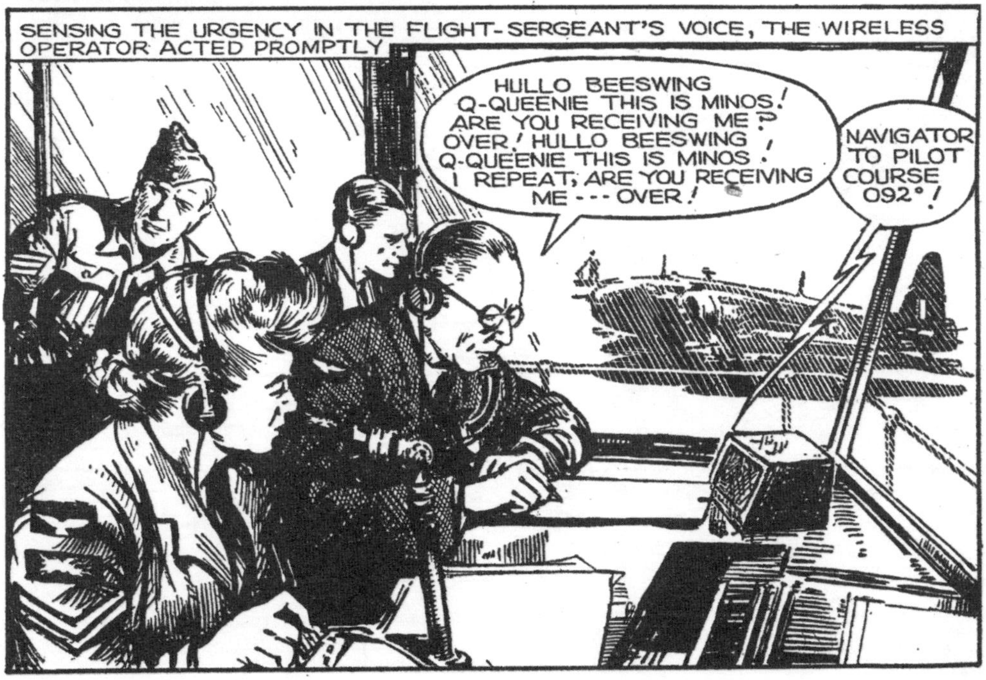
SENSING THE URGENCY IN THE FLIGHT-SERGEANT'S VOICE, THE WIRELESS OPERATOR ACTED PROMPTLY
HULLO BEESWING Q-QUEENIE THIS IS MINOS! ARE YOU RECEIVING ME? OVER! HULLO BEESWING, Q-QUEENIE THIS IS MINOS. I REPEAT, ARE YOU RECEIVING ME --- OVER!
NAVIGATOR TO PILOT COURSE 092°!

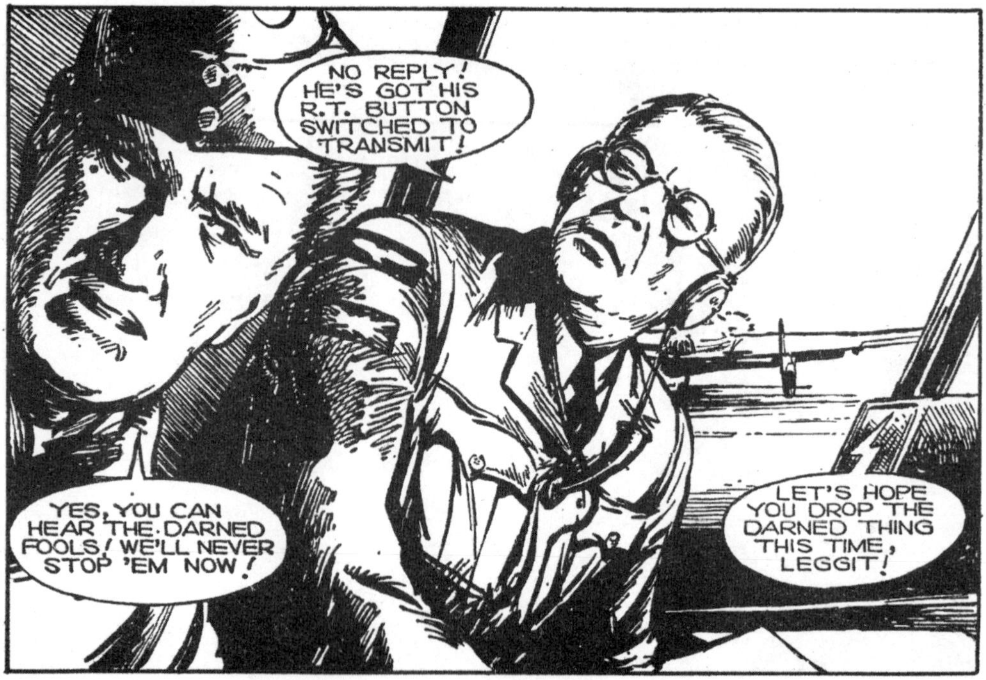
NO REPLY! HE'S GOT HIS R.T. BUTTON SWITCHED TO TRANSMIT!
YES, YOU CAN HEAR THE DARNED FOOLS! WE'LL NEVER STOP 'EM NOW!
LET'S HOPE YOU DROP THE DARNED THING THIS TIME, LEGGIT!

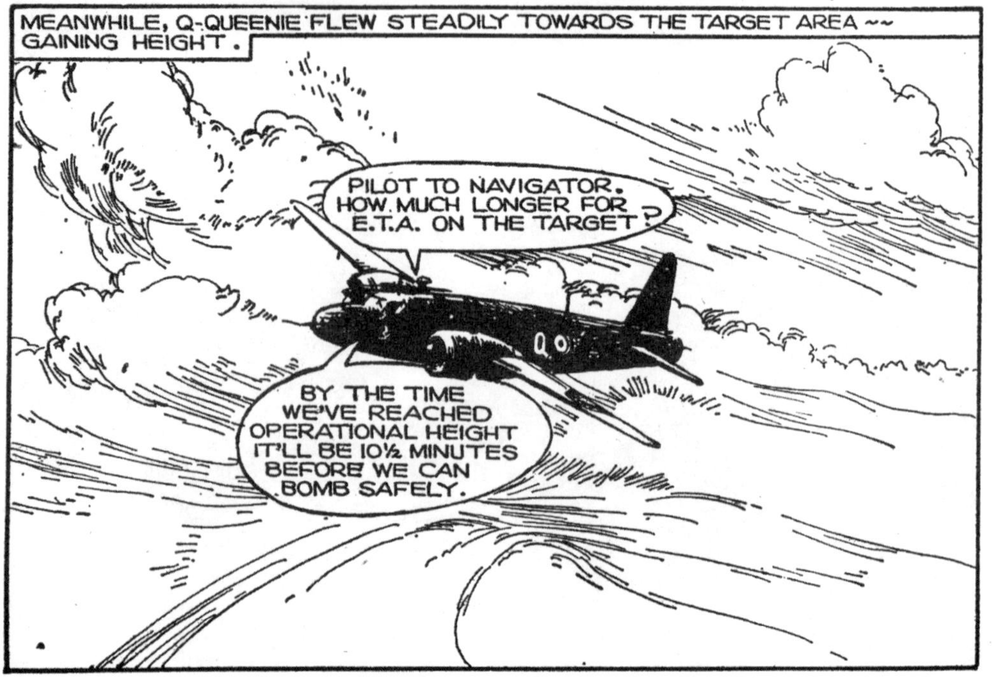
MEANWHILE, Q-QUEENIE FLEW STEADILY TOWARDS THE TARGET AREA ~~ GAINING HEIGHT.
PILOT TO NAVIGATOR. HOW MUCH LONGER FOR E.T.A. ON THE TARGET?
BY THE TIME WE'VE REACHED OPERATIONAL HEIGHT IT'LL BE 10½ MINUTES BEFORE WE CAN BOMB SAFELY.

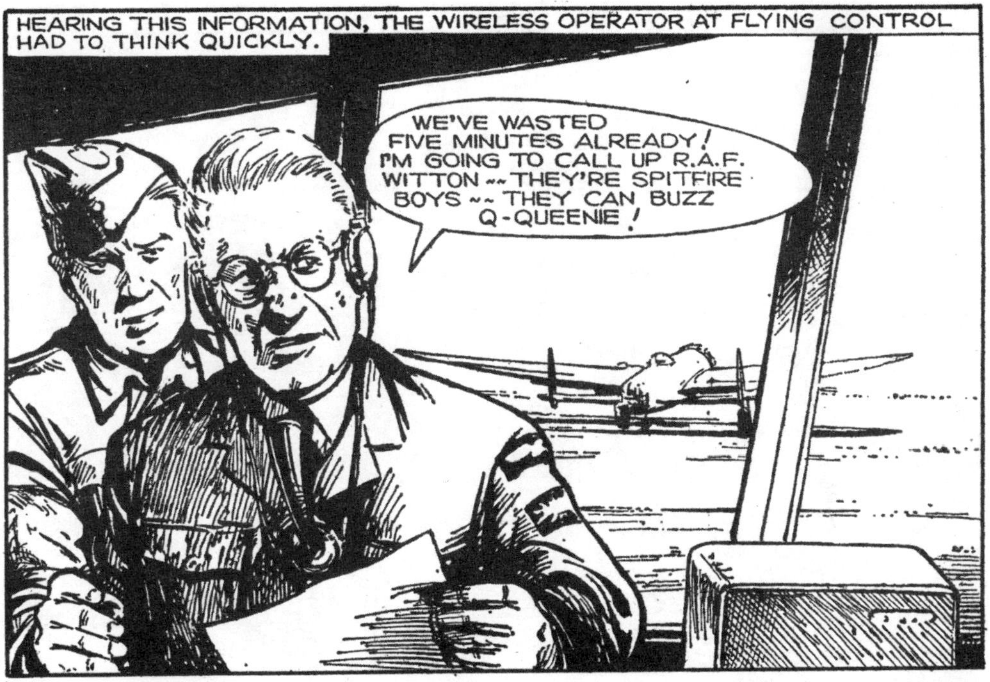
HEARING THIS INFORMATION, THE WIRELESS OPERATOR AT FLYING CONTROL HAD TO THINK QUICKLY.
WE'VE WASTED FIVE MINUTES ALREADY! I'M GOING TO CALL UP R.A.F. WITTON ~~ THEY'RE SPITFIRE BOYS ~~ THEY CAN BUZZ Q-QUEENIE!

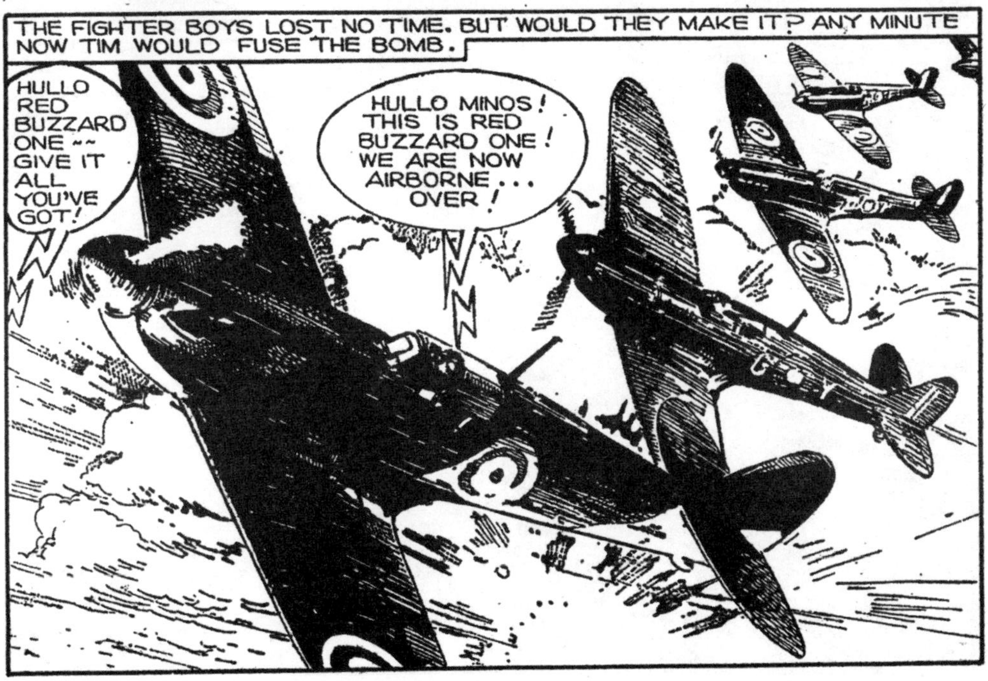
THE FIGHTER BOYS LOST NO TIME. BUT WOULD THEY MAKE IT? ANY MINUTE NOW TIM WOULD FUSE THE BOMB.
HULLO RED BUZZARD ONE ~~ GIVE IT ALL YOU'VE GOT!
HULLO MINOS! THIS IS RED BUZZARD ONE! WE ARE NOW AIRBORNE... OVER!

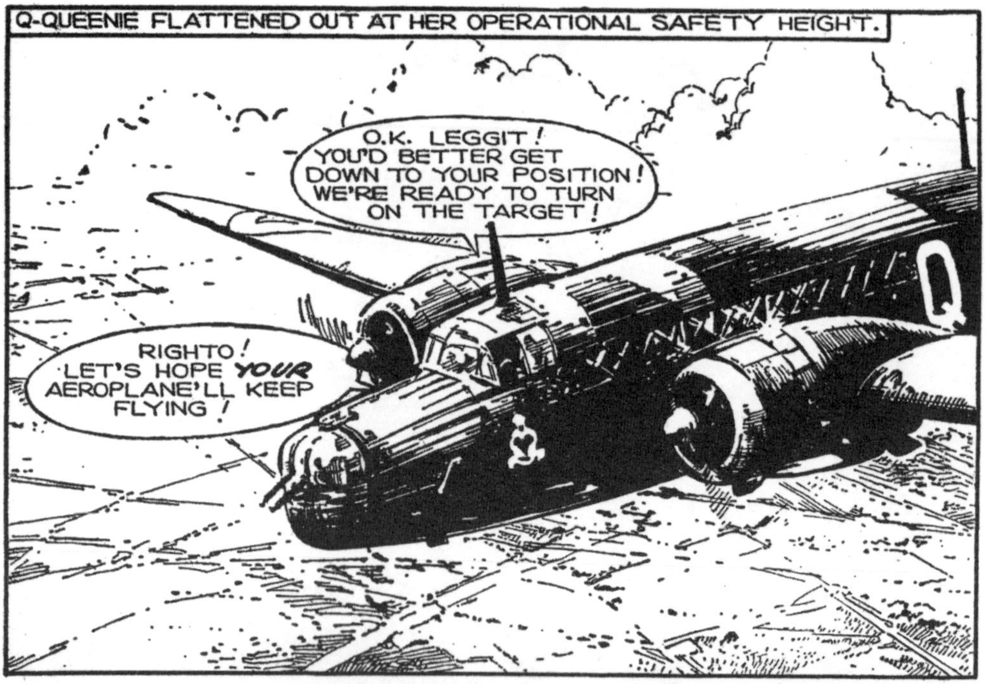
Q-QUEENIE FLATTENED OUT AT HER OPERATIONAL SAFETY HEIGHT.
O.K. LEGGIT! YOU'D BETTER GET DOWN TO YOUR POSITION! WE'RE READY TO TURN ON THE TARGET!
RIGHTO! LET'S HOPE YOUR AEROPLANE'LL KEEP FLYING!

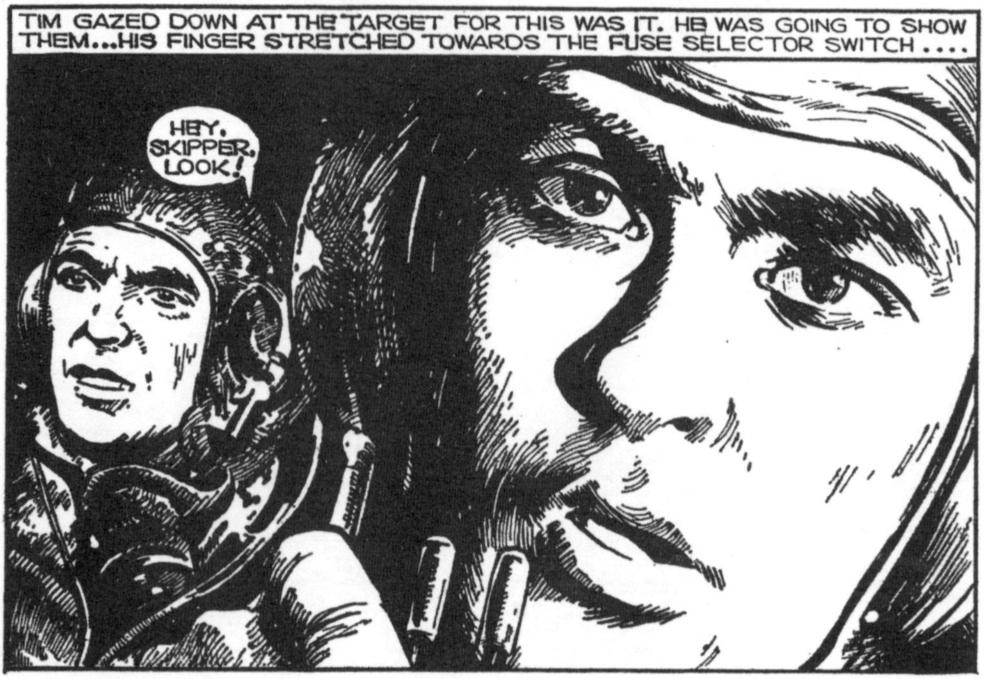
TIM GAZED DOWN AT THE TARGET FOR THIS WAS IT. HE WAS GOING TO SHOW THEM...HIS FINGER STRETCHED TOWARDS THE FUSE SELECTOR SWITCH....
HEY, SKIPPER, LOOK!

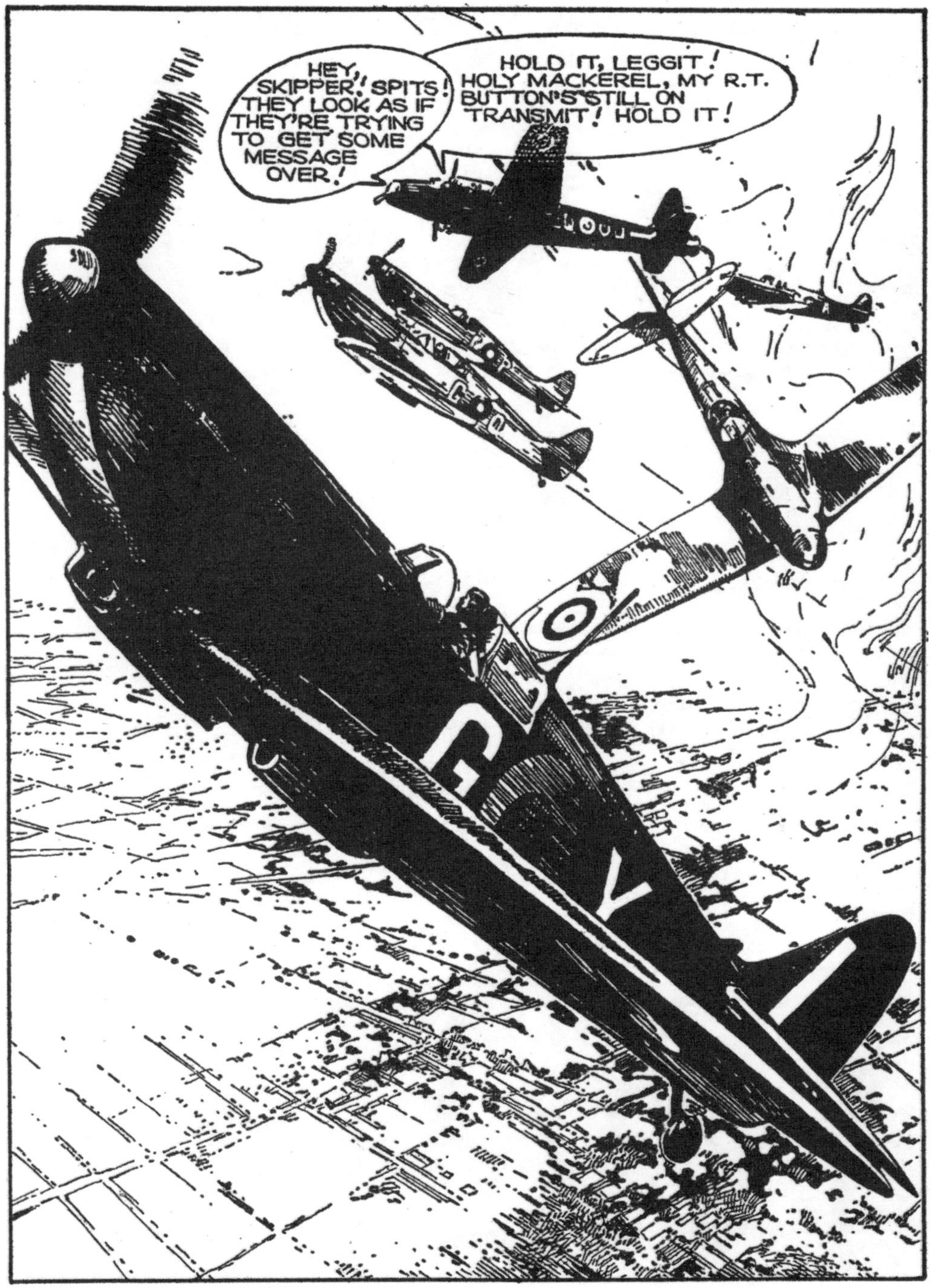
HEY, SKIPPER! SPITS! THEY LOOK AS IF THEY'RE TRYING TO GET SOME MESSAGE OVER!
HOLD IT, LEGGIT! HOLY MACKEREL, MY R.T. BUTTON'S STILL ON TRANSMIT! HOLD IT!

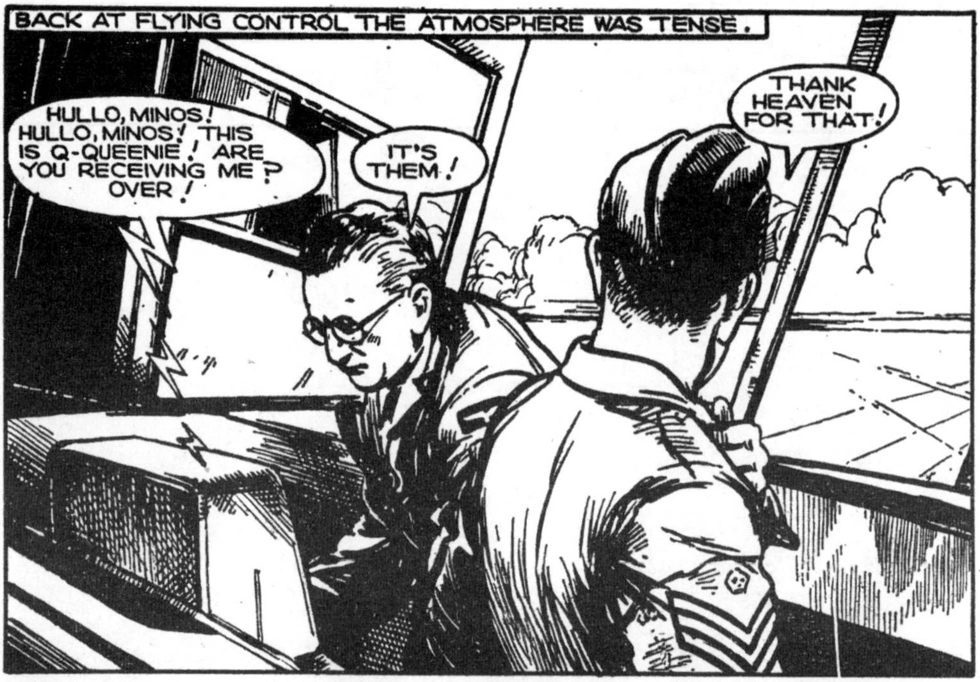
BACK AT FLYING CONTROL THE ATMOSPHERE WAS TENSE.
HULLO, MINOS! HULLO, MINOS! THIS IS Q-QUEENIE! ARE YOU RECEIVING ME? OVER!
IT'S THEM!
THANK HEAVEN FOR THAT!

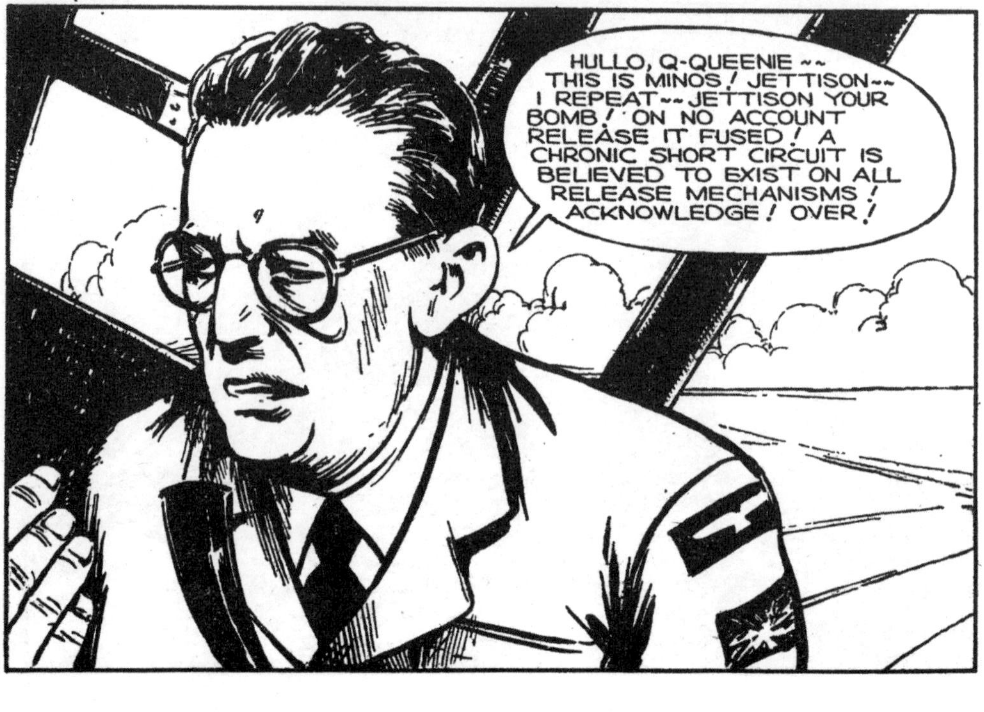
HULLO, Q-QUEENIE -- THIS IS MINOS! JETTISON -- I REPEAT -- JETTISON YOUR BOMB! ON NO ACCOUNT RELEASE IT FUSED! A CHRONIC SHORT CIRCUIT IS BELIEVED TO EXIST ON ALL RELEASE MECHANISMS! ACKNOWLEDGE! OVER!

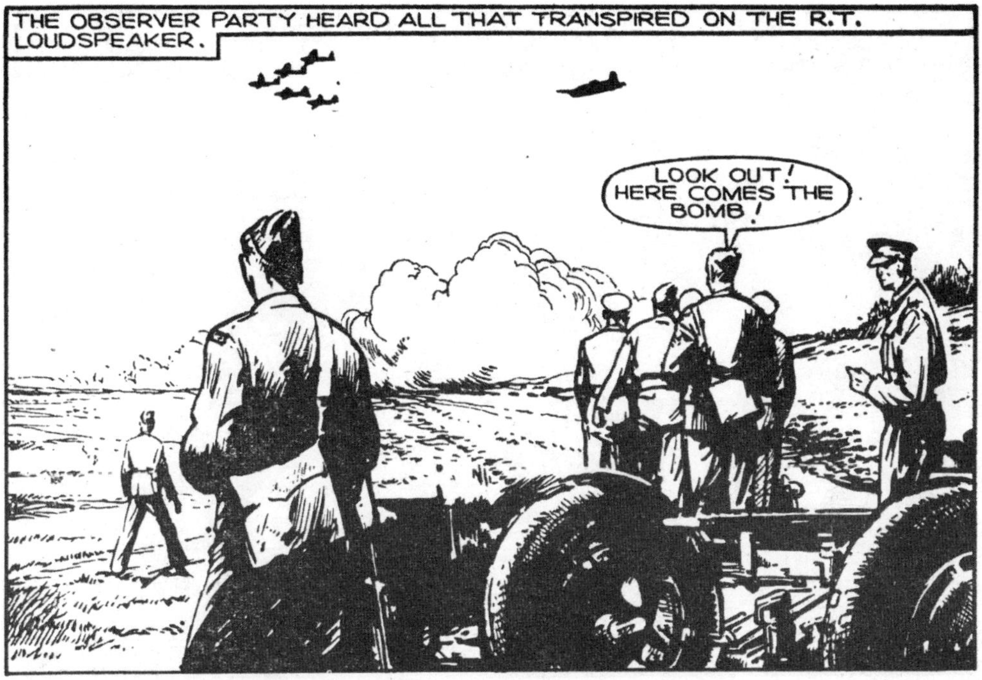
THE OBSERVER PARTY HEARD ALL THAT TRANSPIRED ON THE R.T. LOUDSPEAKER.
LOOK OUT! HERE COMES THE BOMB!

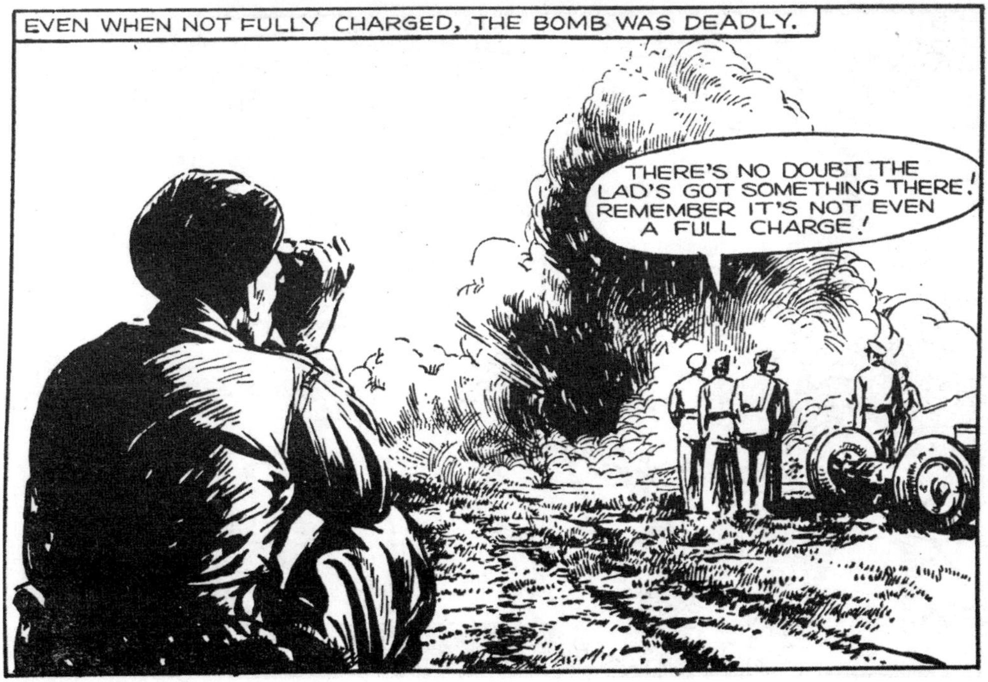
EVEN WHEN NOT FULLY CHARGED, THE BOMB WAS DEADLY.
THERE'S NO DOUBT THE LAD'S GOT SOMETHING THERE! REMEMBER IT'S NOT EVEN A FULL CHARGE!

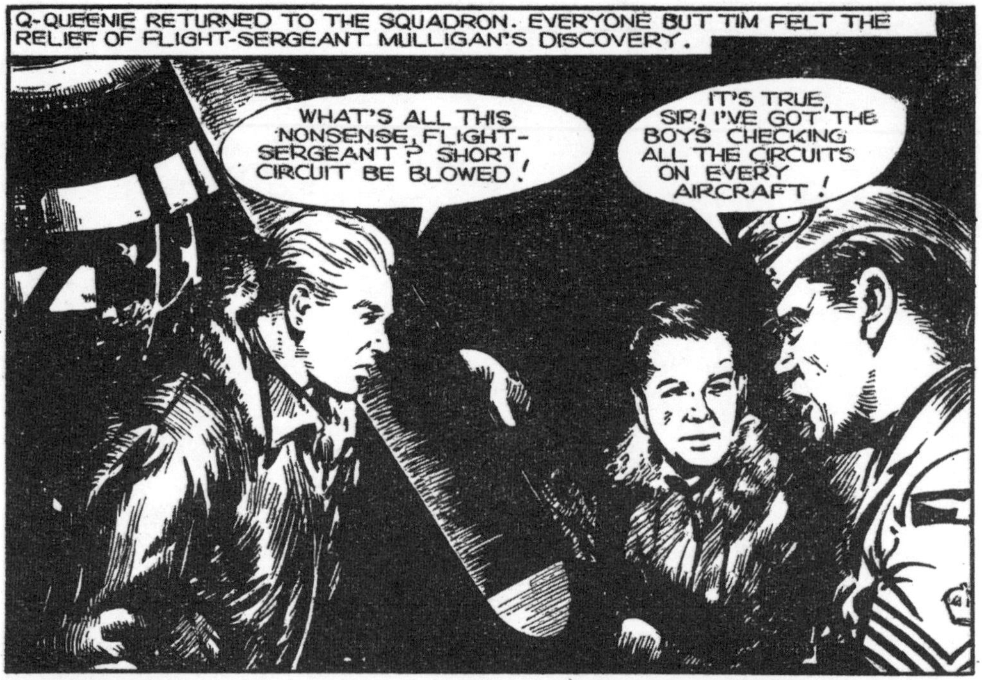
Q-QUEENIE RETURNED TO THE SQUADRON. EVERYONE BUT TIM FELT THE RELIEF OF FLIGHT-SERGEANT MULLIGAN'S DISCOVERY.
WHAT'S ALL THIS NONSENSE, FLIGHT-SERGEANT? SHORT CIRCUIT BE BLOWED!
IT'S TRUE, SIR! I'VE GOT THE BOYS CHECKING ALL THE CIRCUITS ON EVERY AIRCRAFT!

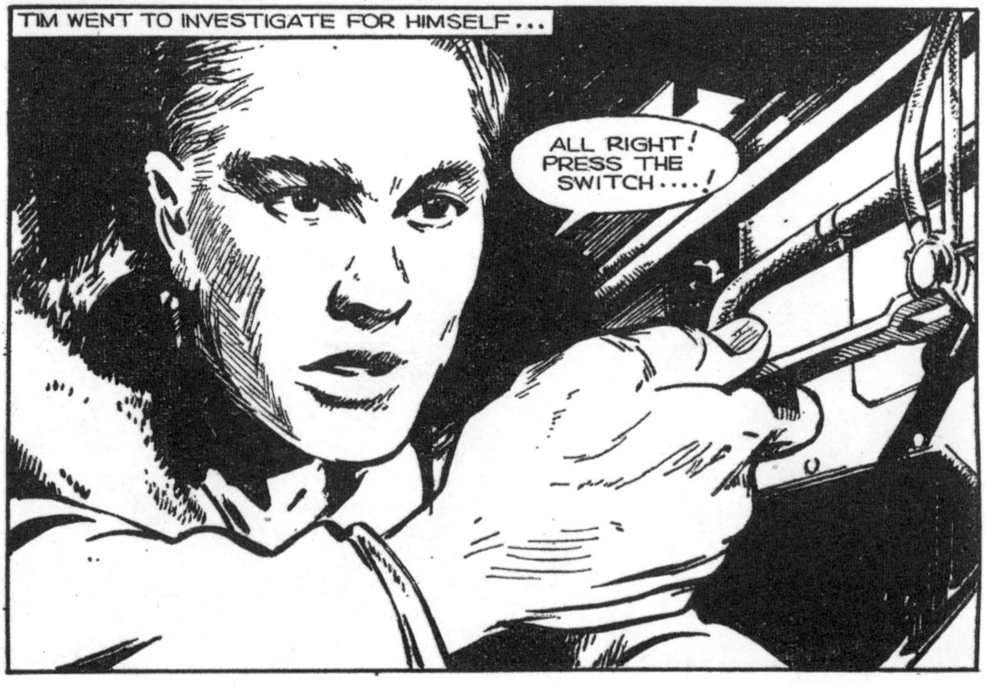
TIM WENT TO INVESTIGATE FOR HIMSELF...
ALL RIGHT! PRESS THE SWITCH....!

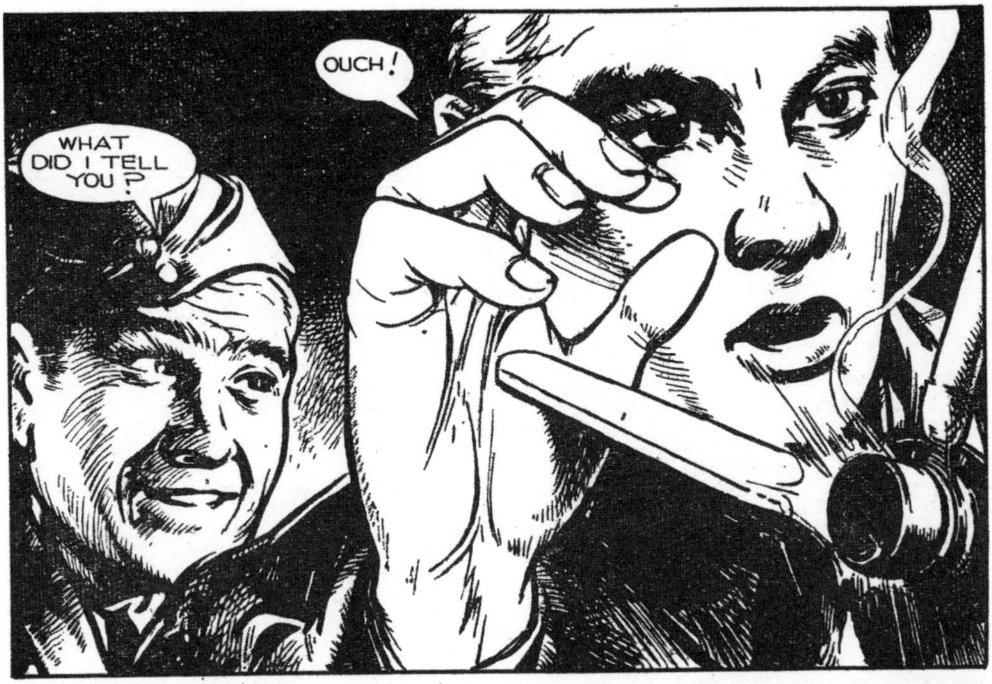
OUCH!
WHAT DID I TELL YOU?

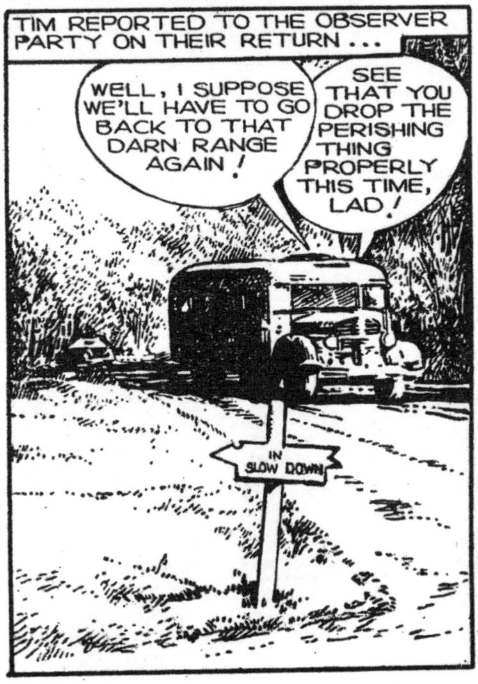
TIM REPORTED TO THE OBSERVER PARTY ON THEIR RETURN...
WELL, I SUPPOSE WE'LL HAVE TO GO BACK TO THAT DARN RANGE AGAIN!
SEE THAT YOU DROP THE PERISHING THING PROPERLY THIS TIME, LAD!
IN
SLOW DOWN

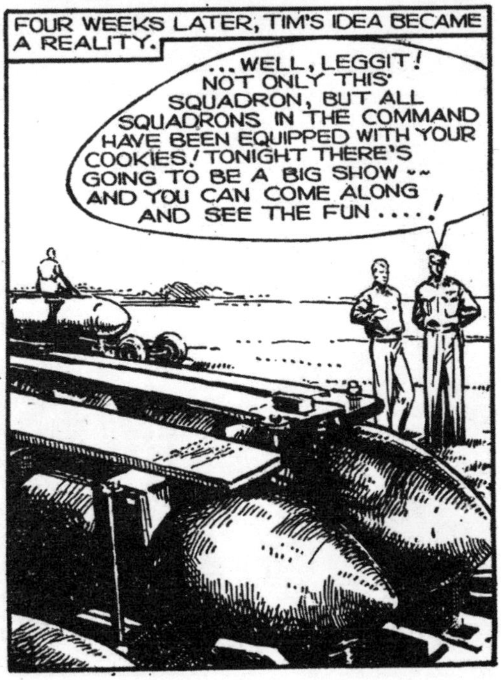
FOUR WEEKS LATER, TIM'S IDEA BECAME A REALITY.
...WELL, LEGGIT! NOT ONLY THIS SQUADRON, BUT ALL SQUADRONS IN THE COMMAND HAVE BEEN EQUIPPED WITH YOUR COOKIES! TONIGHT THERE'S GOING TO BE A BIG SHOW -- AND YOU CAN COME ALONG AND SEE THE FUN....!

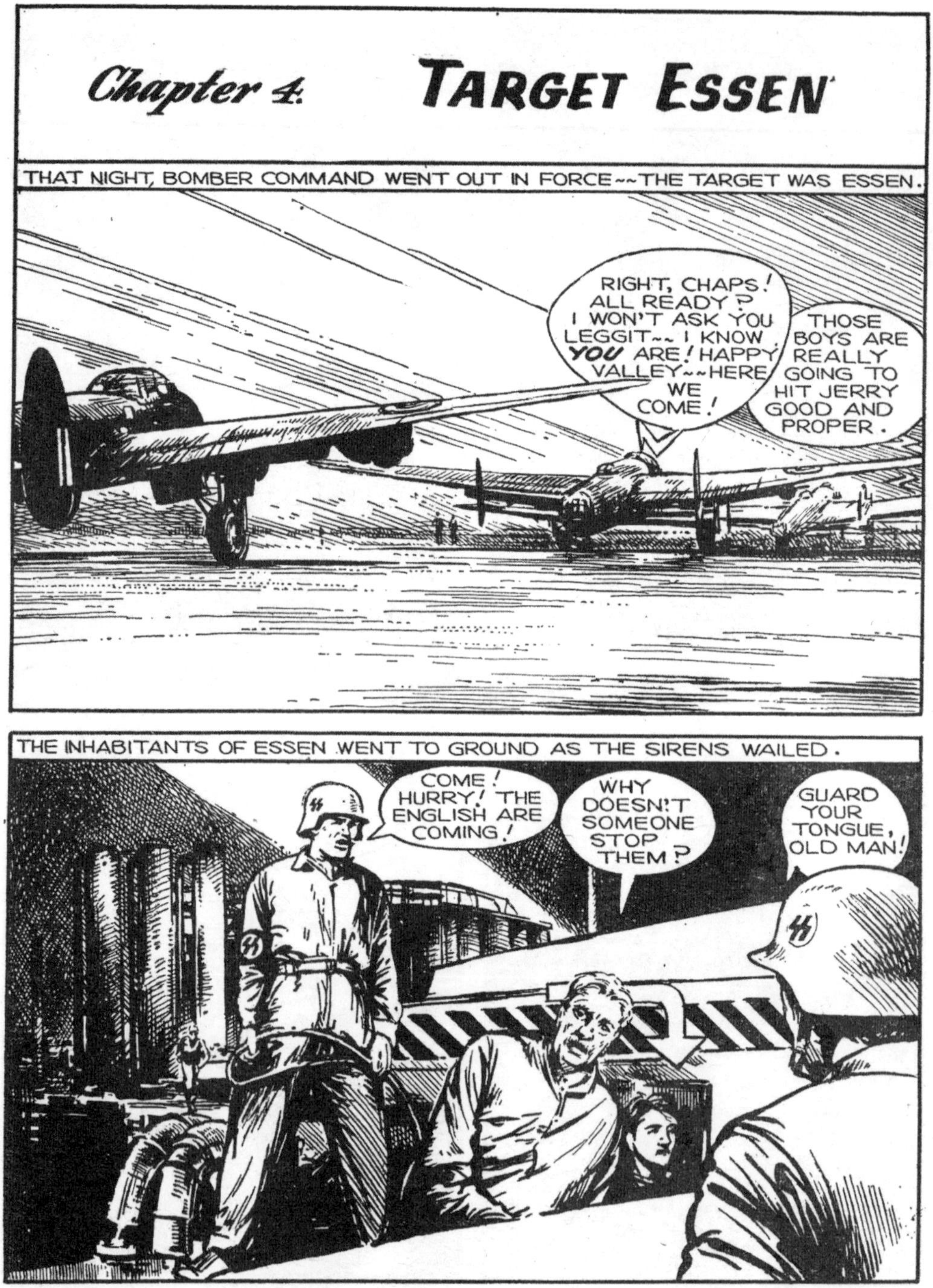
Chapter 4: TARGET ESSEN
THAT NIGHT, BOMBER COMMAND WENT OUT IN FORCE--THE TARGET WAS ESSEN.
RIGHT, CHAPS! ALL READY? I WON'T ASK YOU LEGGIT-- I KNOW YOU ARE! HAPPY VALLEY--HERE WE COME!
THOSE BOYS ARE REALLY GOING TO HIT JERRY GOOD AND PROPER.
THE INHABITANTS OF ESSEN WENT TO GROUND AS THE SIRENS WAILED.
COME! HURRY! THE ENGLISH ARE COMING!
WHY DOESN'T SOMEONE STOP THEM?
GUARD YOUR TONGUE, OLD MAN!

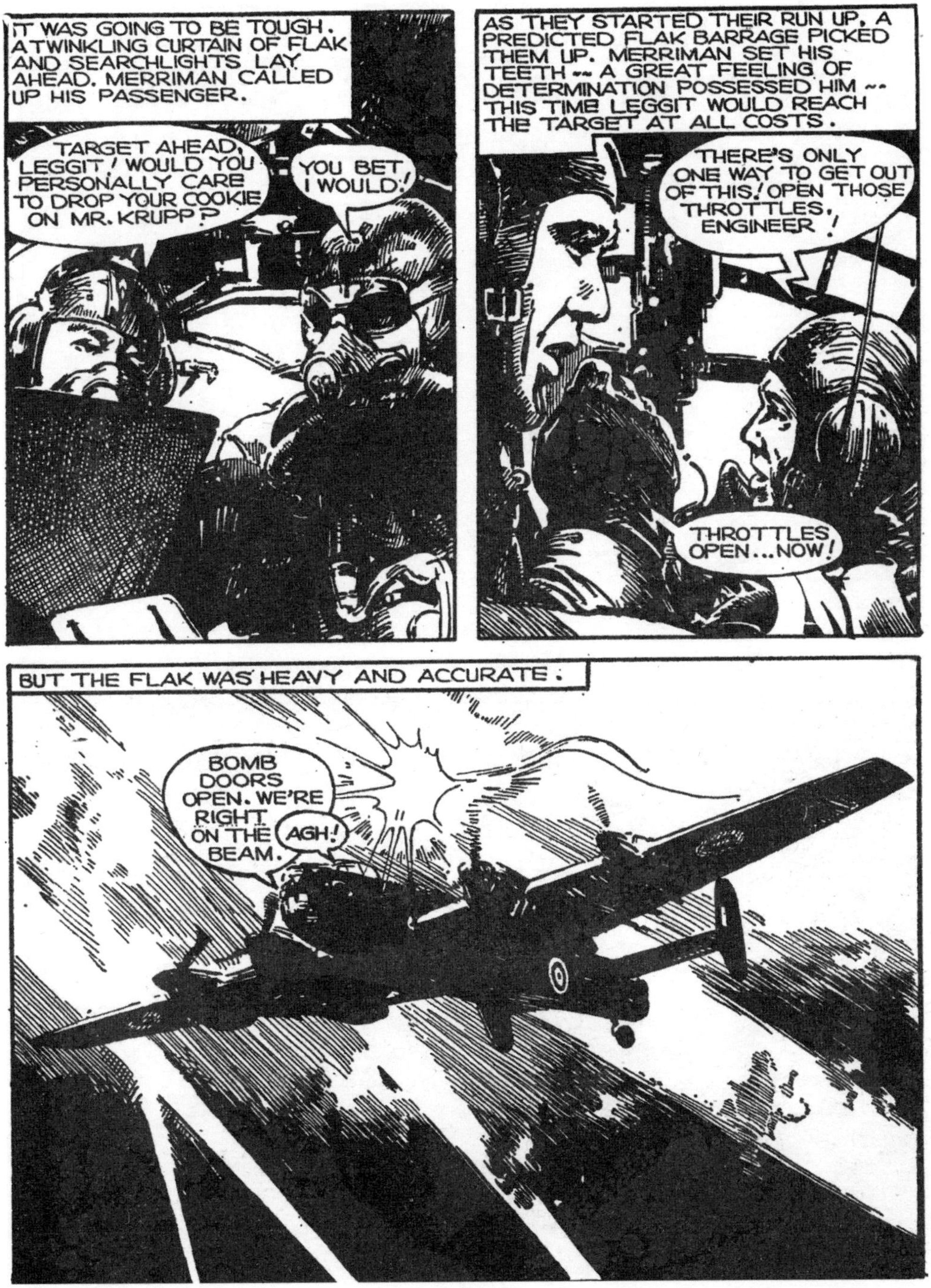
IT WAS GOING TO BE TOUGH. A TWINKLING CURTAIN OF FLAK AND SEARCHLIGHTS LAY AHEAD. MERRIMAN CALLED UP HIS PASSENGER.
TARGET AHEAD, LEGGIT! WOULD YOU PERSONALLY CARE TO DROP YOUR COOKIE ON MR. KRUPP?
YOU BET I WOULD!
AS THEY STARTED THEIR RUN UP, A PREDICTED FLAK BARRAGE PICKED THEM UP. MERRIMAN SET HIS TEETH -- A GREAT FEELING OF DETERMINATION POSSESSED HIM -- THIS TIME LEGGIT WOULD REACH THE TARGET AT ALL COSTS.
THERE'S ONLY ONE WAY TO GET OUT OF THIS! OPEN THOSE THROTTLES, ENGINEER!
THROTTLES OPEN...NOW!
BUT THE FLAK WAS HEAVY AND ACCURATE.
BOMB DOORS OPEN. WE'RE RIGHT ON THE BEAM.
AGH!

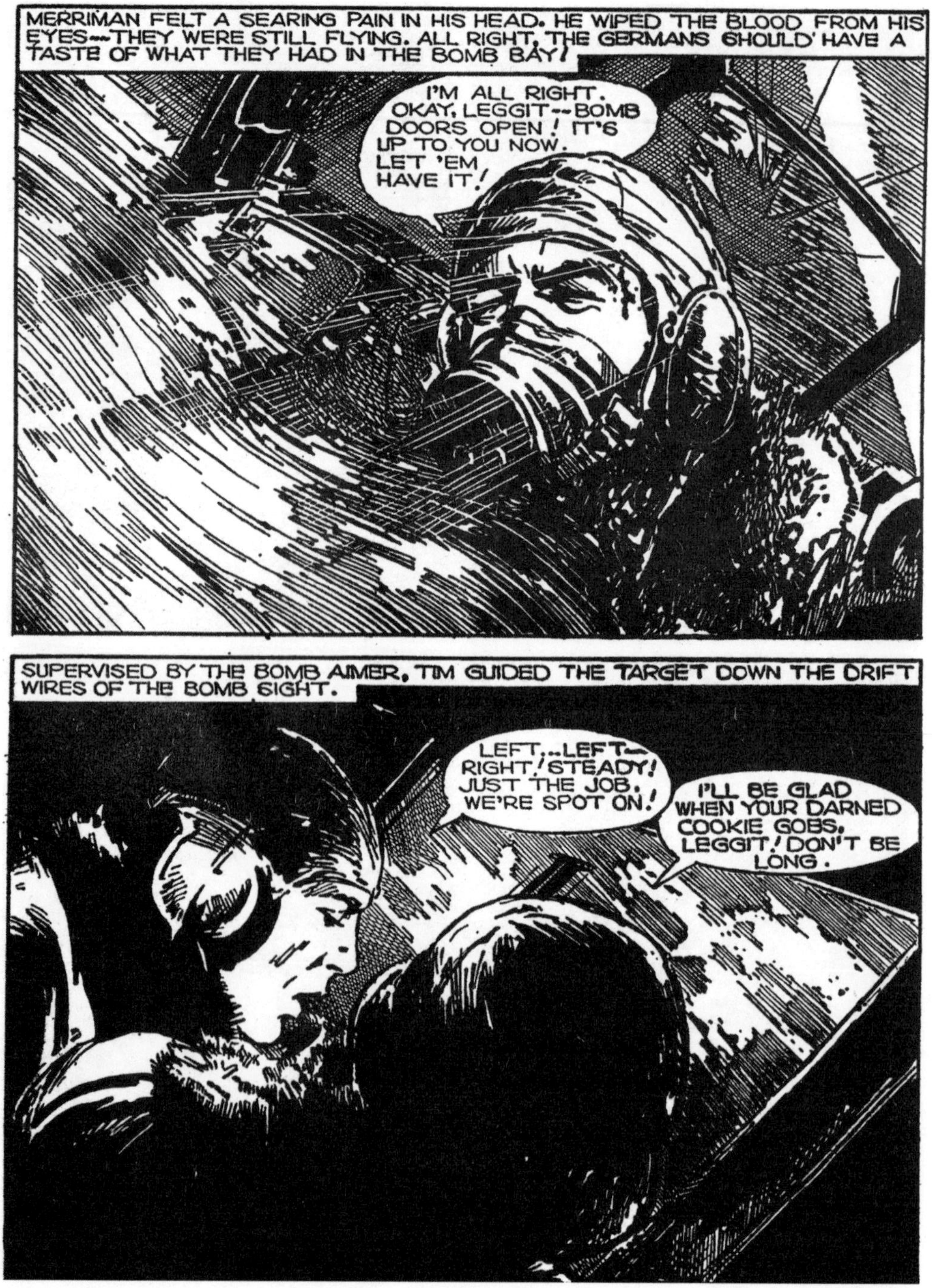
MERRIMAN FELT A SEARING PAIN IN HIS HEAD. HE WIPED THE BLOOD FROM HIS EYES--THEY WERE STILL FLYING. ALL RIGHT, THE GERMANS SHOULD HAVE A TASTE OF WHAT THEY HAD IN THE BOMB BAY!
I'M ALL RIGHT. OKAY, LEGGIT--BOMB DOORS OPEN! IT'S UP TO YOU NOW. LET 'EM HAVE IT!
SUPERVISED BY THE BOMB AIMER, TIM GUIDED THE TARGET DOWN THE DRIFT WIRES OF THE BOMB SIGHT.
LEFT...LEFT--RIGHT! STEADY! JUST THE JOB. WE'RE SPOT ON!
I'LL BE GLAD WHEN YOUR DARNED COOKIE GOBS, LEGGIT! DON'T BE LONG.

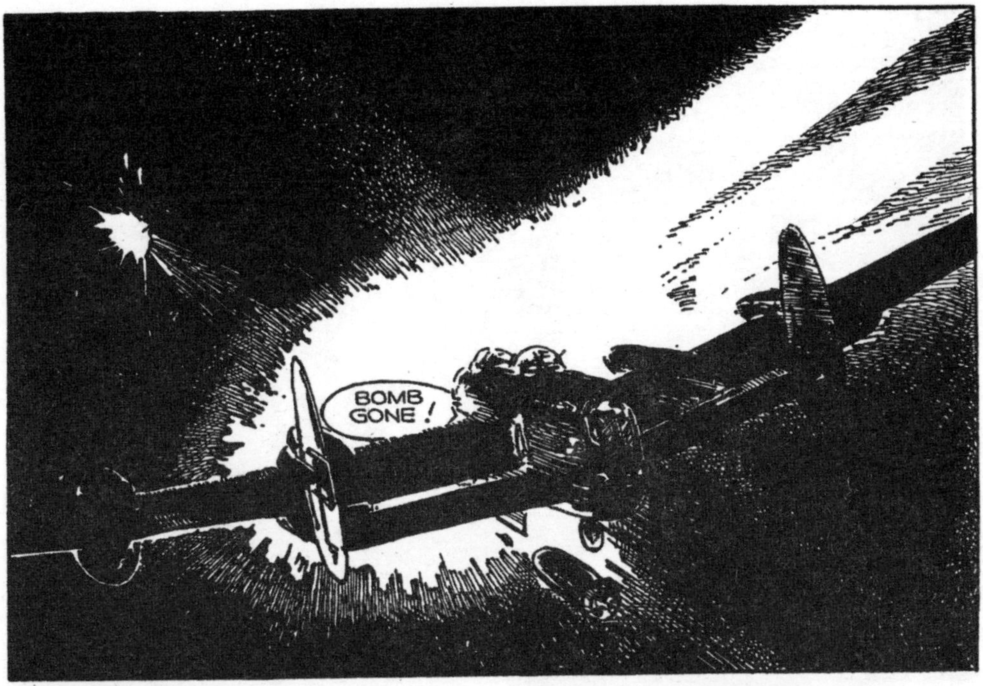
BOMB GONE!

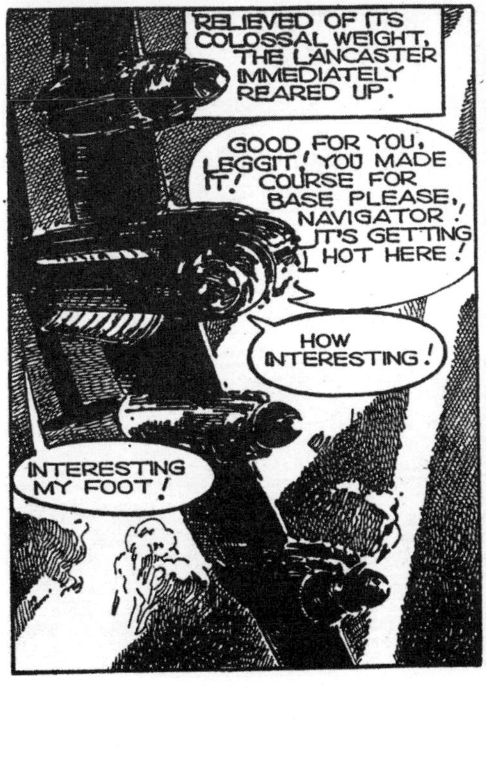
RELIEVED OF ITS COLOSSAL WEIGHT, THE LANCASTER IMMEDIATELY REARED UP.
GOOD FOR YOU, LEGGIT! YOU MADE IT! COURSE FOR BASE PLEASE, NAVIGATOR! IT'S GETTING HOT HERE!
HOW INTERESTING!
INTERESTING MY FOOT!

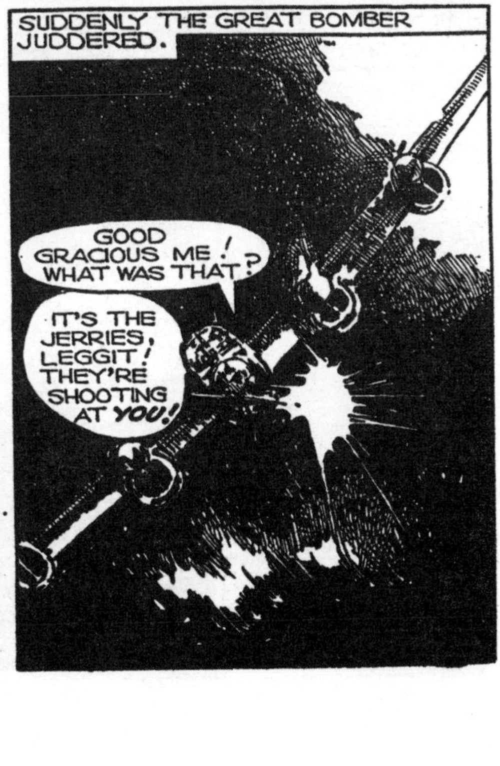
SUDDENLY THE GREAT BOMBER JUDDERED.
GOOD GRACIOUS ME! WHAT WAS THAT?
IT'S THE JERRIES, LEGGIT! THEY'RE SHOOTING AT YOU!

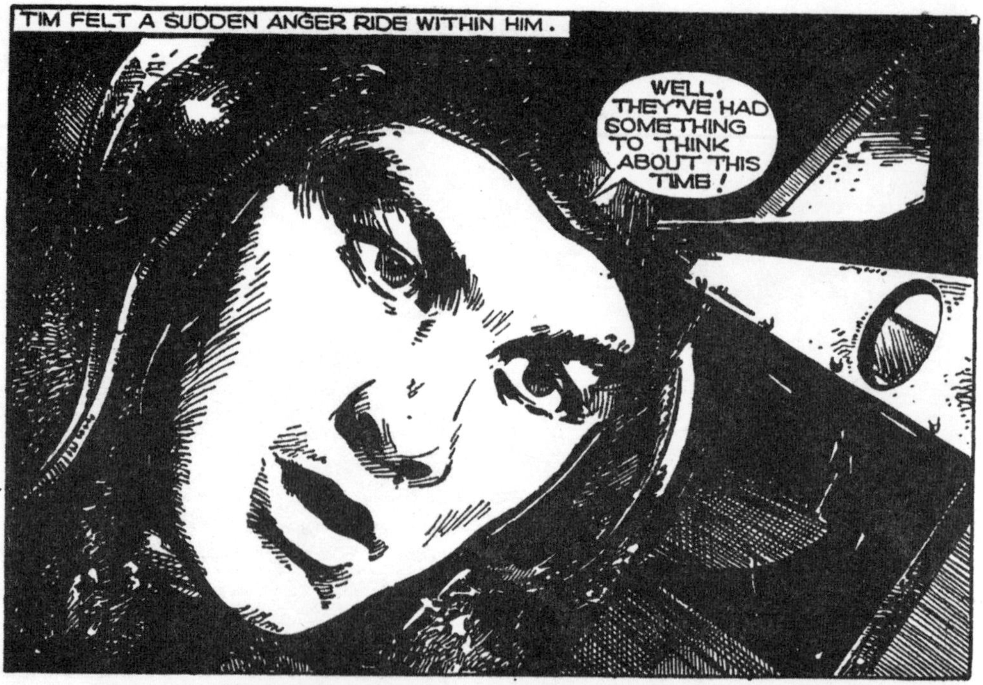
TIM FELT A SUDDEN ANGER RIDE WITHIN HIM.
WELL, THEY'VE HAD SOMETHING TO THINK ABOUT THIS TIMB!

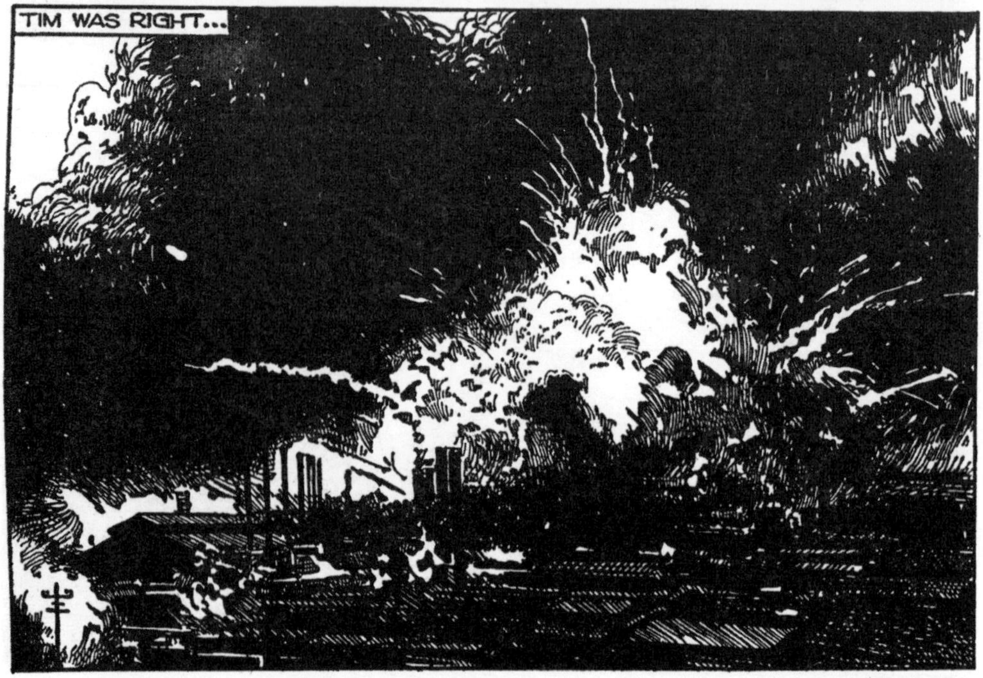
TIM WAS RIGHT...

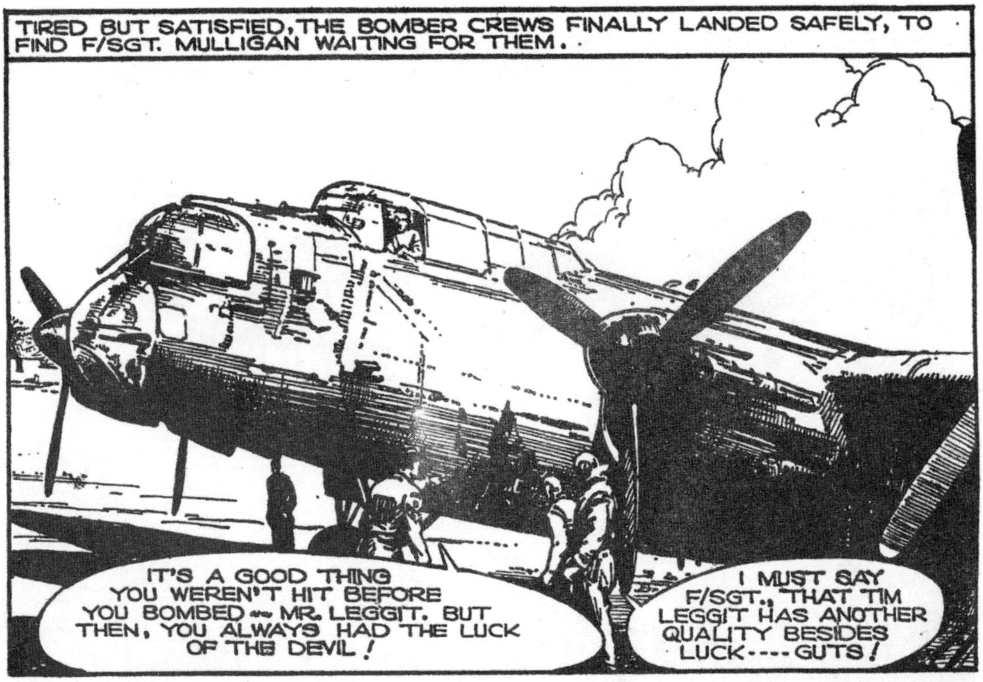
TIRED BUT SATISFIED, THE BOMBER CREWS FINALLY LANDED SAFELY, TO FIND F/SGT. MULLIGAN WAITING FOR THEM.
IT'S A GOOD THING YOU WEREN'T HIT BEFORE YOU BOMBED -- MR. LEGGIT. BUT THEN, YOU ALWAYS HAD THE LUCK OF THE DEVIL!
I MUST SAY F/SGT., THAT TIM LEGGIT HAS ANOTHER QUALITY BESIDES LUCK---- GUTS!

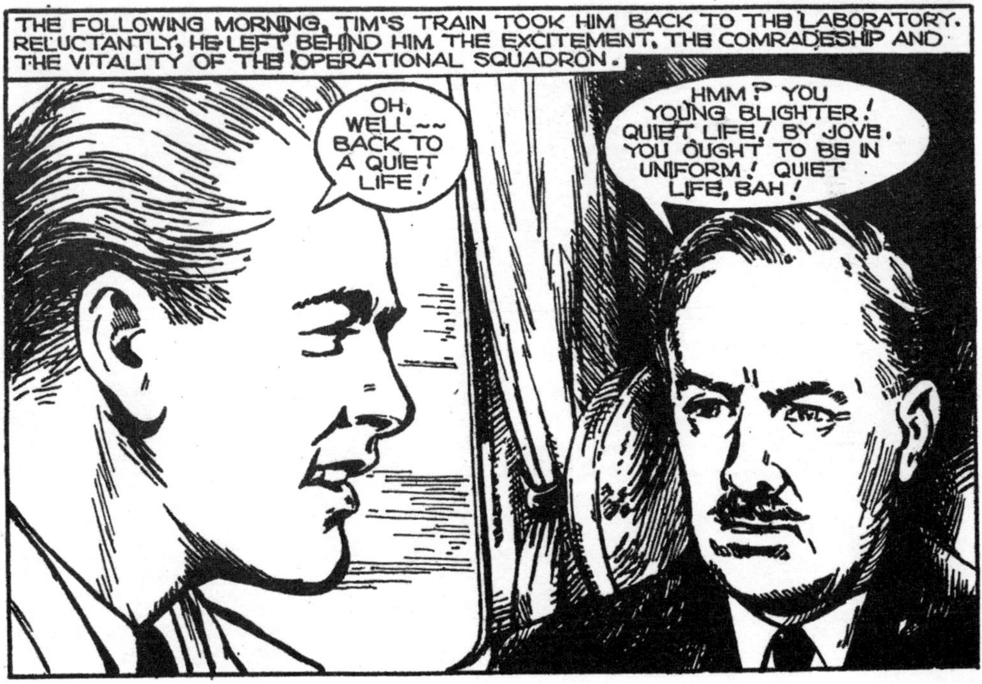
THE FOLLOWING MORNING, TIM'S TRAIN TOOK HIM BACK TO THE LABORATORY. RELUCTANTLY, HE LEFT BEHIND HIM THE EXCITEMENT, THE COMRADESHIP AND THE VITALITY OF THE OPERATIONAL SQUADRON.
OH, WELL -- BACK TO A QUIET LIFE!
HMM? YOU YOUNG BLIGHTER! QUIET LIFE! BY JOVE, YOU OUGHT TO BE IN UNIFORM! QUIET LIFE, BAH!

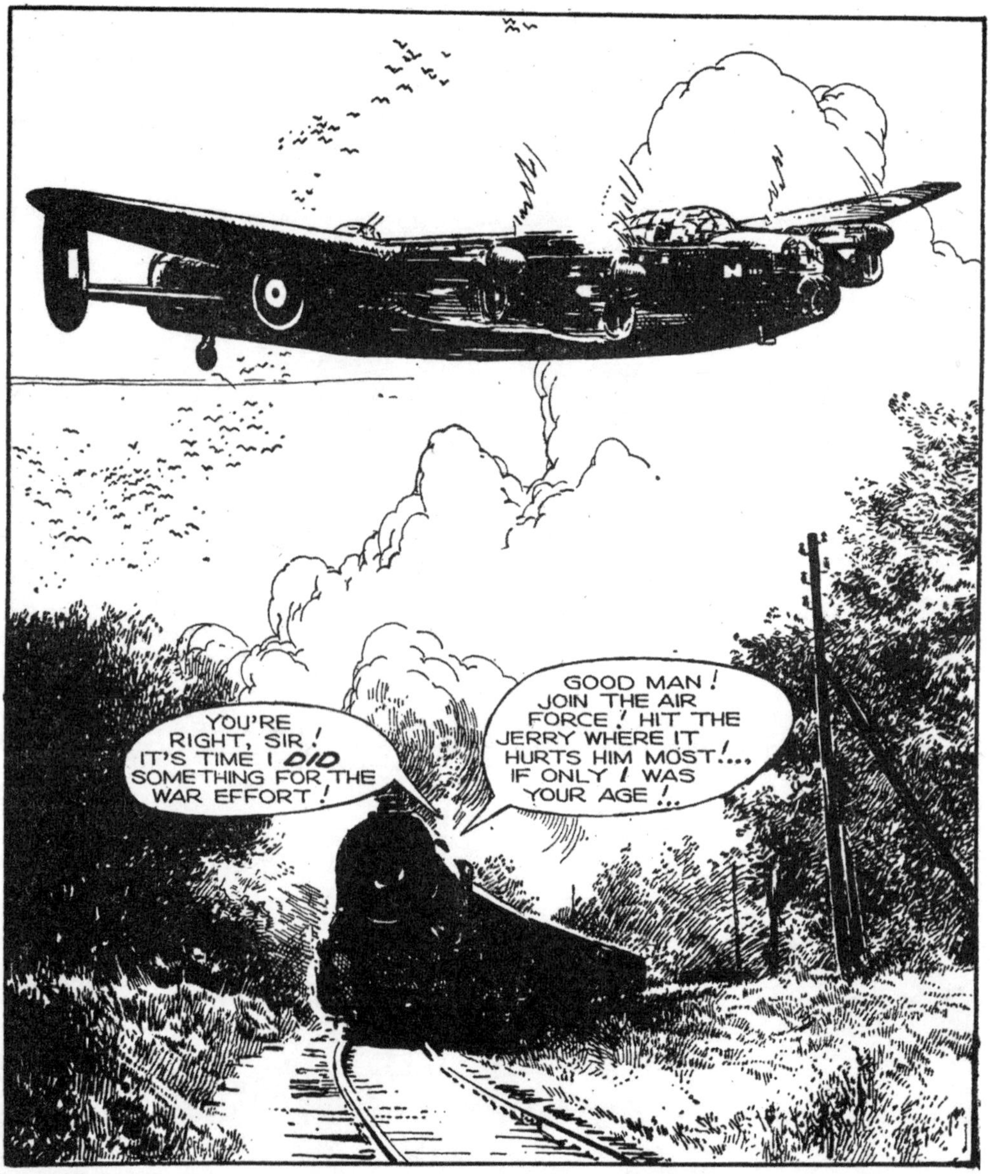
YOU'RE RIGHT, SIR! IT'S TIME I DID SOMETHING FOR THE WAR EFFORT!
GOOD MAN! JOIN THE AIR FORCE! HIT THE JERRY WHERE IT HURTS HIM MOST!... IF ONLY I WAS YOUR AGE!..

THE COVERS

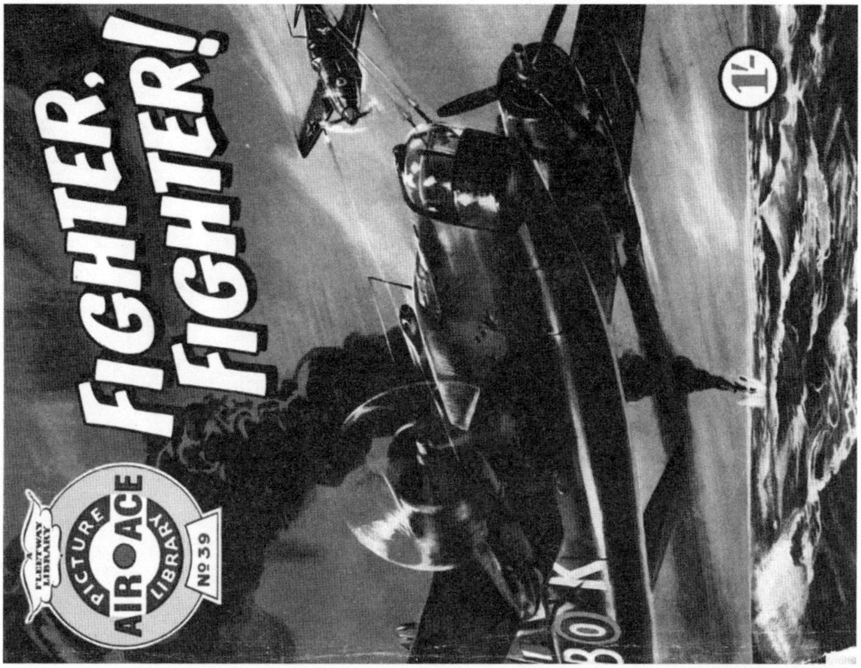
A FLEETWAY LIBRARY
PICTURE
AIR ACE
LIBRARY
№ 39
FIGHTER, FIGHTER!
1/-

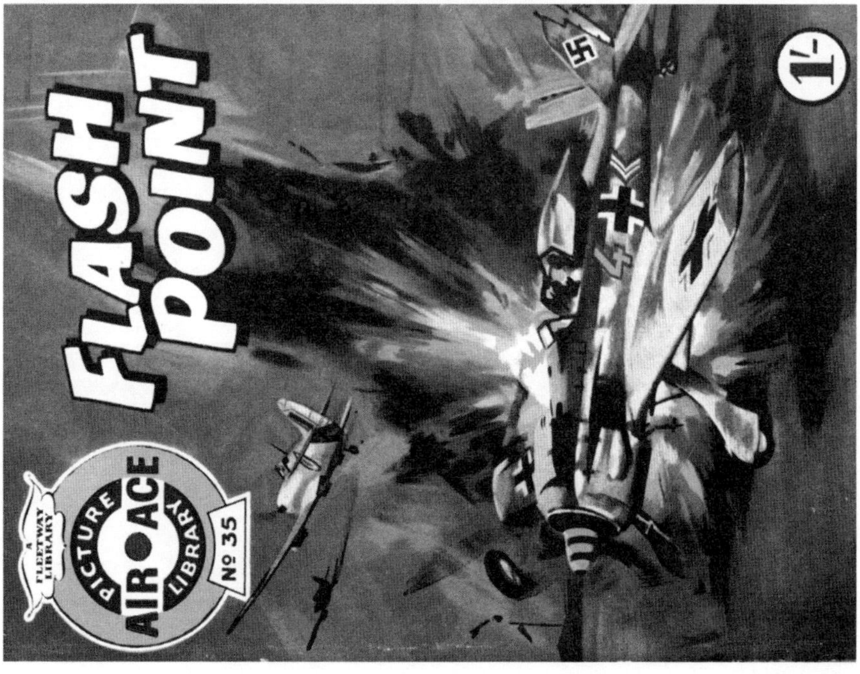
A FLEETWAY LIBRARY
PICTURE
AIR ACE
LIBRARY
№ 35
FLASH POINT
1/-

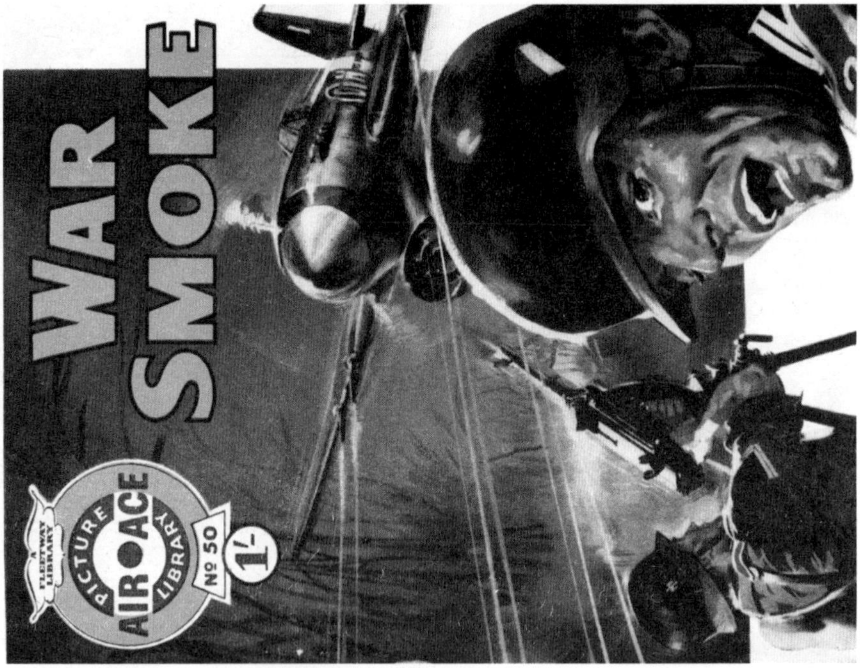
FLEETWAY LIBRARY
PICTURE
AIR ACE
LIBRARY
Nº 50
1/-
WAR SMOKE

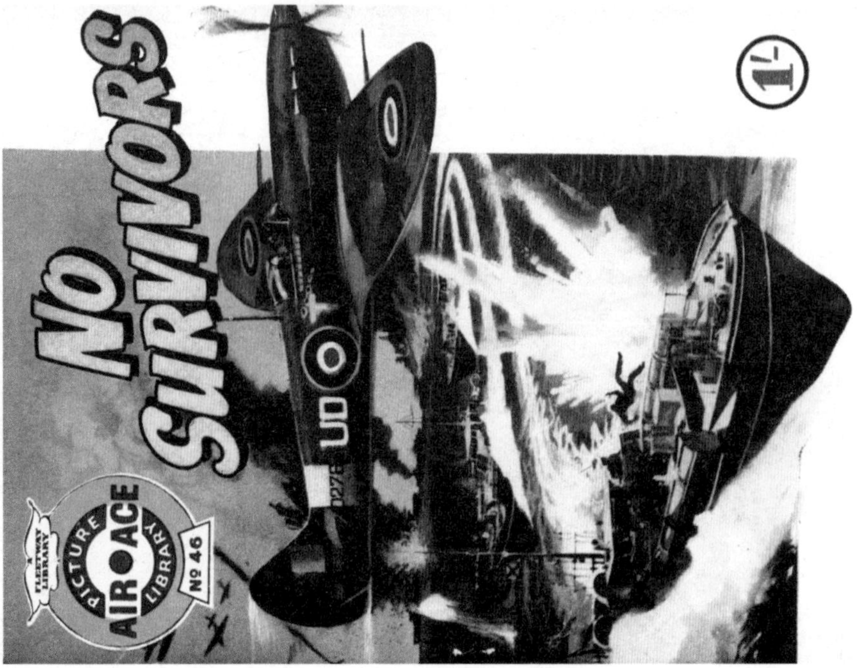
FLEETWAY LIBRARY
PICTURE
AIR ACE
LIBRARY
Nº 46
NO SURVIVORS
UD
1/-

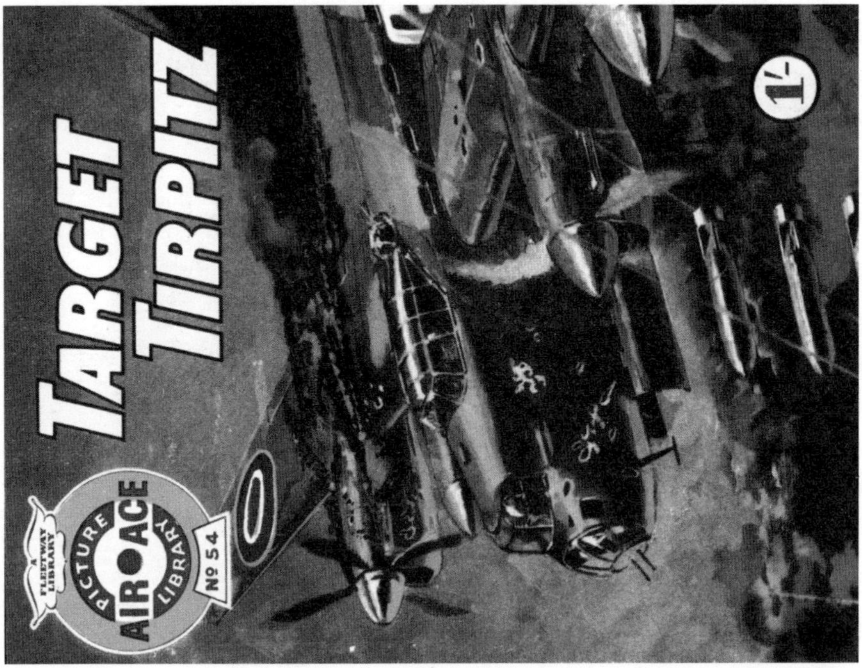
A FLEETWAY LIBRARY
PICTURE
AIR ACE
LIBRARY
Nº 54
TARGET TIRPITZ
1/-

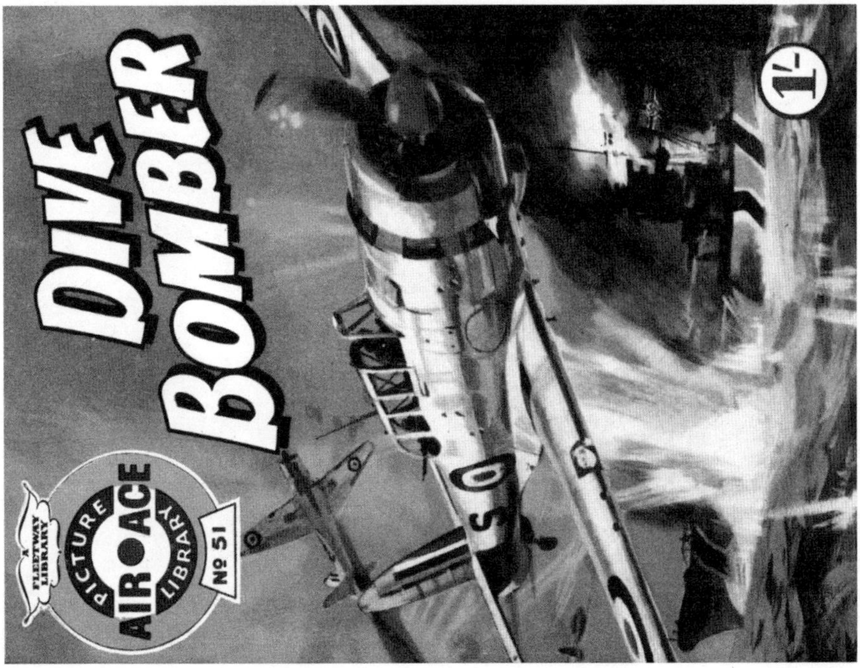
A FLEETWAY LIBRARY
PICTURE
AIR ACE
LIBRARY
Nº 51
DIVE BOMBER
1/-

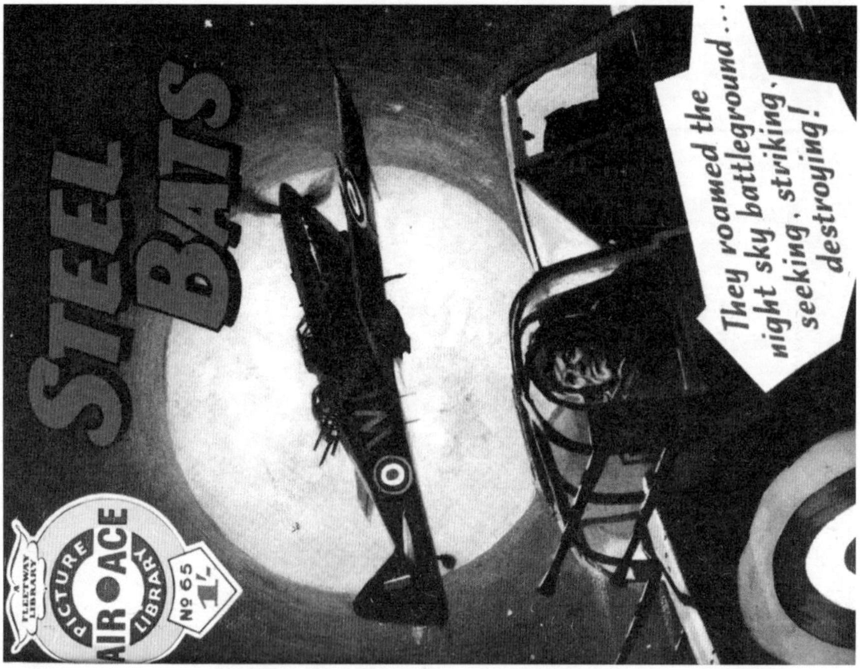
FLEETWAY LIBRARY
PICTURE
AIR ACE
LIBRARY
Nº 65
1/-
STEEL BATS
They roamed the night sky battleground ... seeking, striking, destroying!

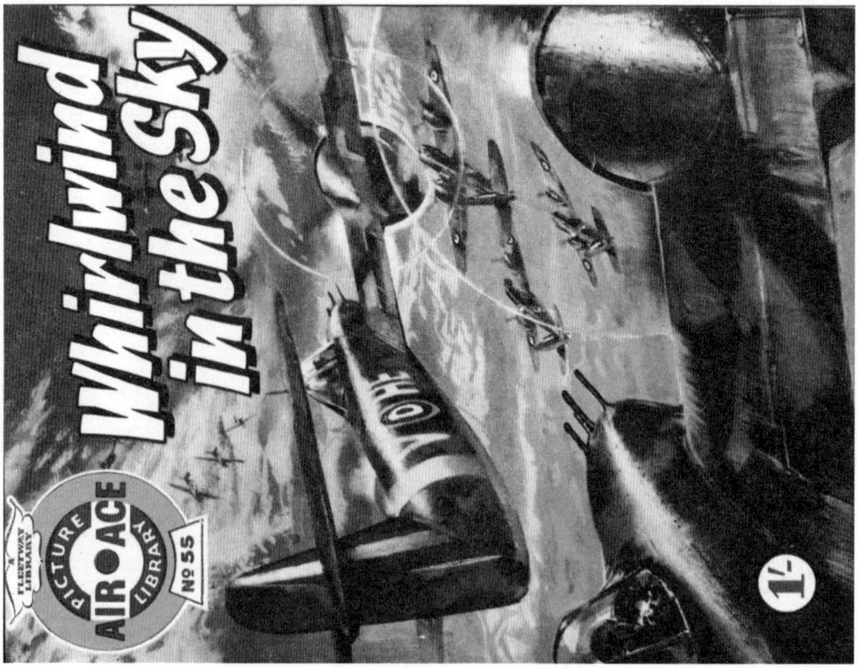
FLEETWAY LIBRARY
PICTURE
AIR ACE
LIBRARY
Nº 55
Whirlwind in the Sky
1/-

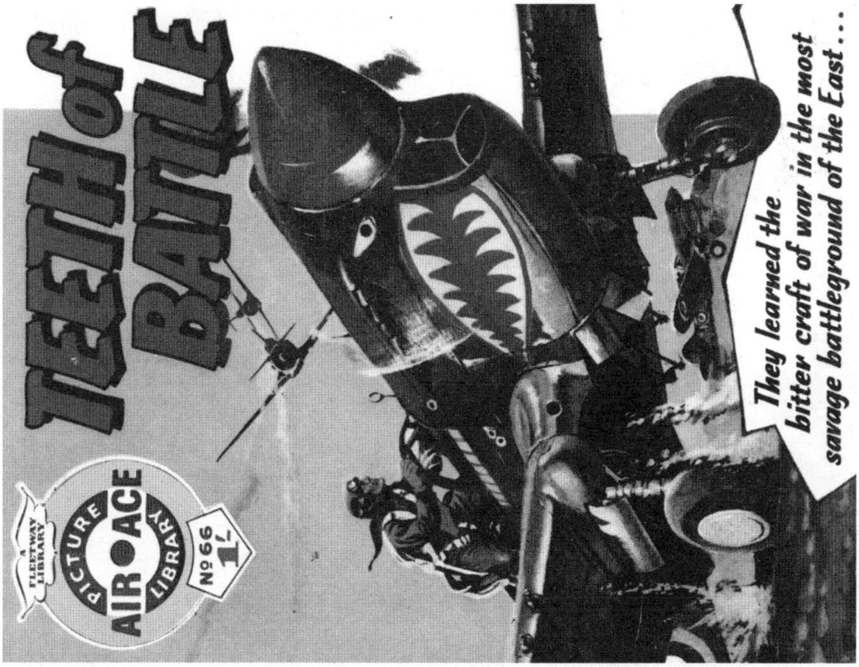
A FLEETWAY LIBRARY
PICTURE
AIR ACE
LIBRARY
No 66 1/-
TEETH of BATTLE
They learned the bitter craft of war in the most savage battleground of the East . . .

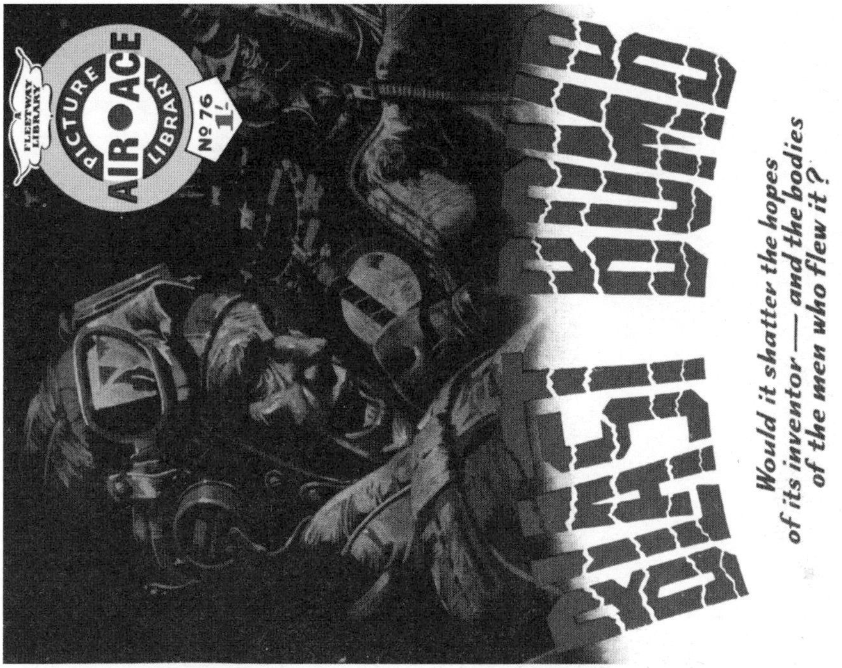
A FLEETWAY LIBRARY
PICTURE
AIR ACE
LIBRARY
No 76 1/-
BLAST BOMB
Would it shatter the hopes of its inventor — and the bodies of the men who flew it?

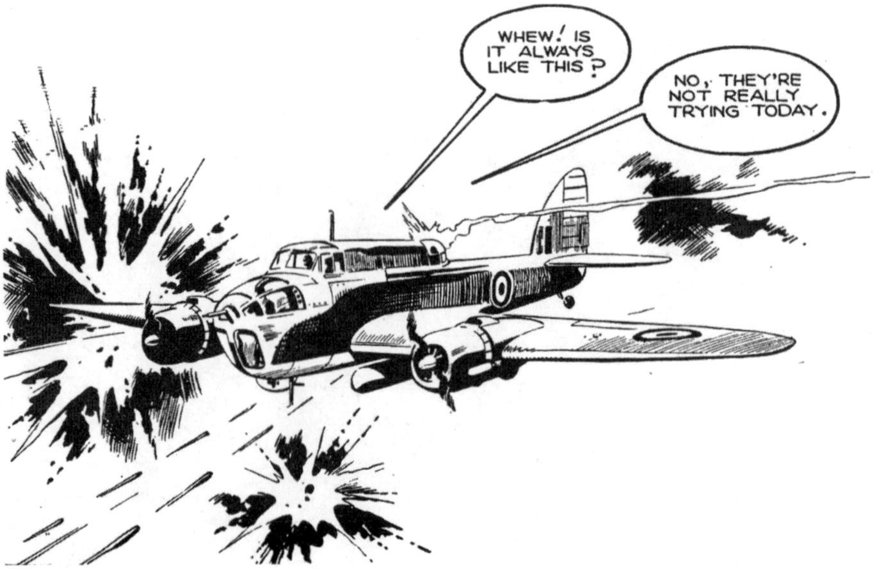
WHEW! IS IT ALWAYS LIKE THIS?
NO, THEY'RE NOT REALLY TRYING TODAY.

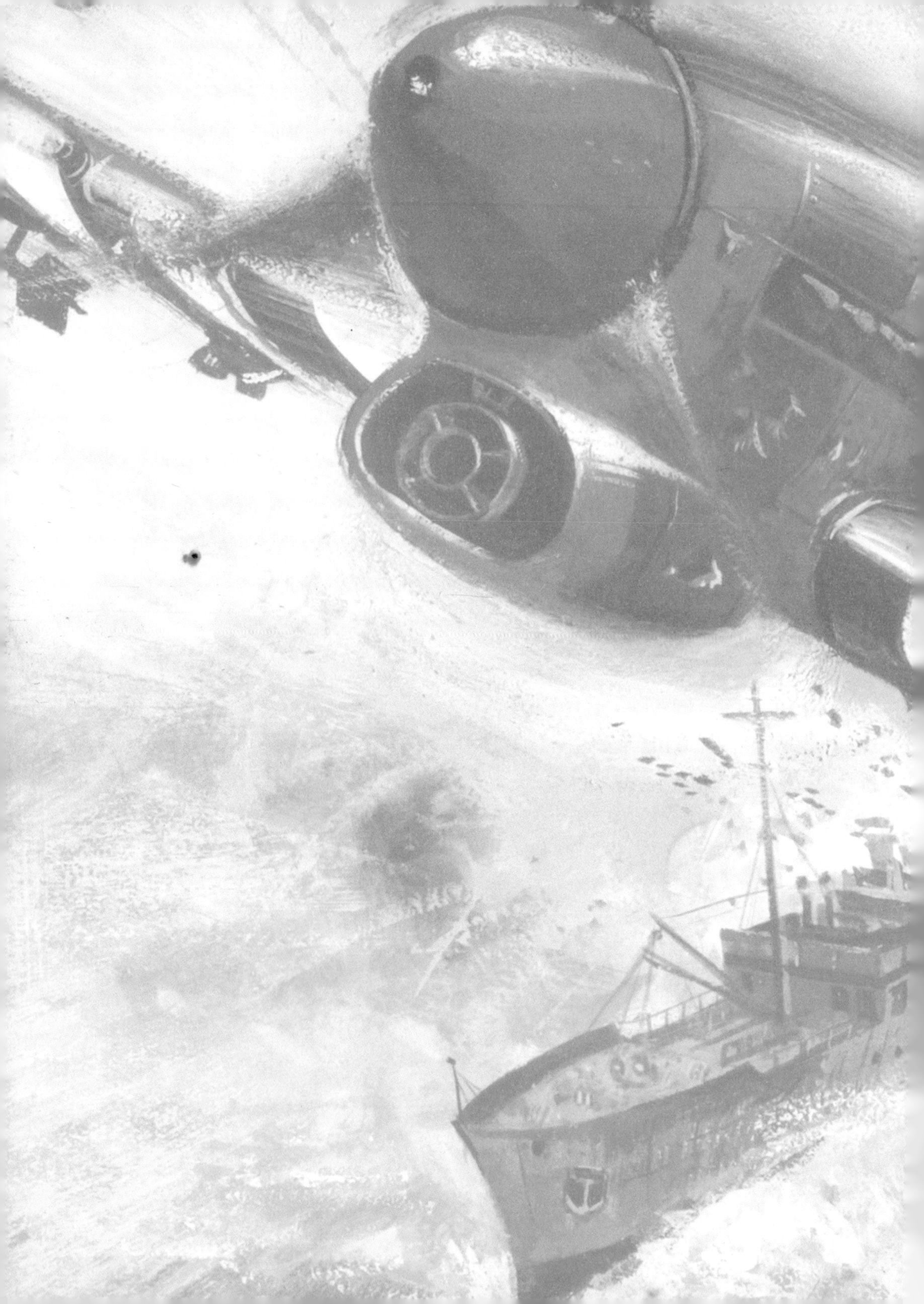